# BAEN BOOKS by DAVID WEBER

*Honor Harrington:*
On Basilisk Station
The Honor of the Queen
The Short Victorious War
Field of Dishonor
Flag in Exile
Honor Among Enemies
In Enemy Hands
Echoes of Honor
Ashes of Victory
War of Honor

*Honorverse:*
Crown of Slaves *(with Eric Flint)*
The Shadow of Saganami

*edited by David Weber:*
More than Honor
Worlds of Honor
Changer of Worlds
The Service of the Sword

Mutineers' Moon
The Armageddon Inheritance
Heirs of Empire
Empire from the Ashes

Path of the Fury

The Apocalypse Troll

The Excalibur Alternative

Bolo!
Old Soldiers

Oath of Swords
The War God's Own
Wind Rider's Oath

*with Steve White:*
The Stars At War
The Stars At War II

*with John Ringo:*
March Upcountry
March to the Sea
March to the Stars
We Few

*with Eric Flint:*
1633

# BAEN BOOKS by STEVE WHITE

Blood of the Heroes *(forthcoming)*

The Prometheus Project

Demon's Gate

Forge of the Titans

Eagle Against the Stars

Prince of Sunset

The Disinherited
Legacy
Debt of Ages

# THE
# STARS AT
# WAR II

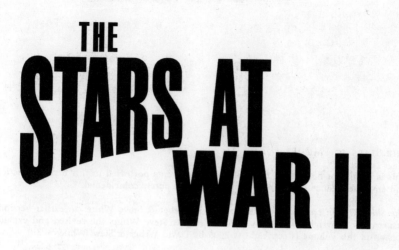

## DAVID WEBER

### &

## STEVE WHITE

THE STARS AT WAR II

This is a work of fiction. All the characters and events portrayed in this book are fictional, and any resemblance to real people or incidents is purely coincidental.

A Baen Books Original

Baen Publishing Enterprises
P.O. Box 1403
Riverdale, NY 10471
www.baen.com

ISBN: 0-7434-9912-3

Cover art by David Mattingly
Maps by Randy Asplund

First combined printing, July 2005

Library of Congress Cataloging-in-Publication Data

Weber, David, 1952-
    The stars at war II / David Weber & Steve White.
        p. cm.
    "A Baen Books Original"--T.p. verso.
    ISBN 0-7434-9912-3
    1. Life on other planets--Fiction. 2. Space warfare--Fiction. I. White, Steve, 1946- II. Title.

    PS3573.E217S73 2005
    813'.54--dc22

                                                                        2005011260

Distributed by Simon & Schuster
1230 Avenue of the Americas
New York, NY 10020

Production & design by Windhaven Press (www.windhaven.com)
Printed in the United States of America

10  9  8  7  6  5  4  3  2  1

# CONTENTS

# Operating Area for the 2nd CAW

Pajzomo   Bug-29   Bug-28   Bug-27

Jzotayar

SD05

Bug-26

Bug-25

To
Bug-23

Trahznagar

SD04   SD06

Bug-24

SD08   SD09

Rabahl

To
Bug-15

Kriiksa-28   SD11

Venn'ax   Stantars'ax

Retarra'ax

To The
Zarkolyan
Empire

## Special Notes

◆ This is a special warp point which is actually in a starless nexus 2 weeks travel at speed 3 from Jzotayar's "outer system border."

⊘ This closed warp point comes from somewhere in the Pitariad.

✗ To other Star Union "core sector" star systems.

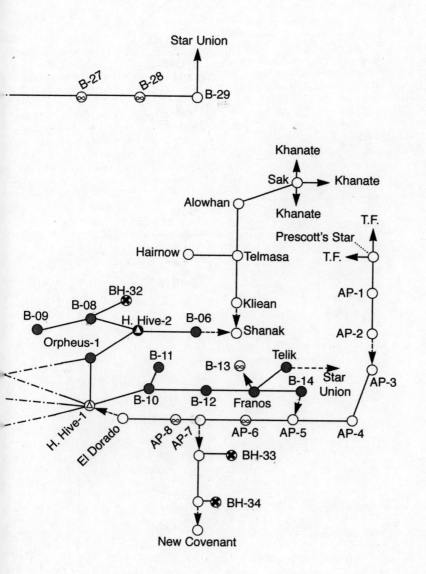

Star Union

B-27   B-28   B-29

Khanate

Sak   Khanate

Alowhan   Khanate

T.F.

Prescott's Star

Hairnow   Telmasa   T.F.

AP-1

BH-32

B-08   AP-2

B-09   H. Hive-2   B-06   Kliean

Orpheus-1   Shanak

AP-3

B-11   B-13   Telik

B-14   Star
Union

B-10   B-12   Franos

AP-4

H. Hive-1   AP-5

El Dorado   AP-8   AP-7   AP-6

BH-33

BH-34

New Covenant

# THE SHIVA OPTION

The authors would like to extend their sincere thanks to Fred Burton, war gamer and friend, who personally designed the entire Star Union of Crucis and not only made it live, but also gave us permission to steal . . . er, borrow it for our story.

Thanks, Fred.

# PROLOGUE

Their hands were still tightly clasped when the universe reappeared.

Feridoun had taken Aileen's hand in his just before TFNS *Jamaica* made warp transit. No one else on the flag bridge had noticed the thoroughly unmilitary gesture as he reached out to his admiral, for they'd been fleeing with the hounds of Hell baying at their heels. The rest of Survey Flotilla 19's battered survivors had already preceded the flagship into the unknown. Then it had been *Jamaica*'s turn, and Aileen had returned the pressure of his hand and smiled with the knowledge of a personal discovery that had come—as such things will—at the worst imaginable moment. That pressure, and that smile, had continued as the appropriately blood-red star had seemed to vanish down a well of infinity astern, and the two of them had gone through a hole in the continuum as one.

But then reality stabilized, and they were in a new stellar system, God knew how many light-years away in Einsteinian space, and reports of successful transit began to arrive from the ships ahead of them. As though with an electric shock of embarrassment, they each released the other's hand, and were once again simply Rear Admiral Aileen Sommers, Terran Federation Navy, commanding Survey Flotilla 19, and Captain Feridoun Hafezi, her chief of staff.

Not that the flotilla was much of a command anymore. It had escaped—barely, and with hideous losses—from the most horrifying enemy humankind had ever faced, or dreamed of facing. But the escape was only temporary. The Arachnids had witnessed their transit, and so should have little trouble locating the warp point

3

they'd used. No, she corrected herself: *would* have little trouble. After the events of the past three and a half standard Terran years, no human was apt to underestimate Arachnid capabilities.

So she took command of herself and ordered the flotilla onward into the system under cloaking ECM, getting lost in the immensity of space before the Bugs could follow them through the warp point. She also sent the *Hun*-class scout cruisers ahead to begin surveying. They reported almost immediately that the system wasn't one of those in the Terran Federation's databases, and there was no point in searching for a native high-tech civilization. This star was a red giant, and like some insane god of ancient myth it had long since devoured any planetary children it might once have possessed. So Sommers ordered the *Huns* to search for warp points other than the one they'd just transited—warp points through which they could continue their hegira.

She wanted to pause and appease a lack of sleep which had almost exceeded the human organism's capacity to function. But there was no time. Instead, she called a staff conference.

At some point, Hafezi had somehow managed to repair the haggardness of battle. Sommers, gazing across the conference table at him, saw that he'd even restored his beard to its neatly sculpted norm . . . but she detected a salting of gray hairs among the black. *Is it possible*, she wondered, *that what we've been through over the last few weeks could've done that already?*

*Or maybe it's been there all along and I've just never looked closely enough to notice.*

Since the escape from the last system, their behavior towards each other had been scrupulously correct. Not, she thought wryly, that they'd had much opportunity for incorrectness. And not that they'd actually avoided each other—their duties would've made that difficult. No, they'd just worn formality as armor against their own feelings. Feelings they couldn't openly express under the present circumstances, even if they'd known how.

*One crisis at a time*, Sommers told herself firmly. *And preferably not the personal one first.* She concentrated on listening to Feridoun's—no, her chief of staff's—report.

Concentrating was hard, though. She already knew most of the facts he was reciting, and they were too painful to bear thinking about.

First, her loss figures. Out of SF 19's original strength of seven battlecruisers, one fleet carrier, two light carriers (both from the space fleet of Terra's Ophiuchi allies), nine light cruisers, and two freighters, she'd lost two battlecruisers, three light cruisers, and a freighter—every one of which she felt like a stab wound. And it was worse than it sounded, for practically all the survivors—including and especially *Jamaica*—were damaged in varying degrees. And besides . . .

Hafezi voiced her own gloomy thoughts as he summed up.

"Both the battlecruisers we've lost were *Dunkerque-A*-class, out of the four we originally had. The impact on our firepower—"

"Yes, yes," Sommers interrupted. The *Dunkerque-A*'s were rated as BCRs: ships that combined a very respectable battery of capital missile launchers with a battlecruiser's speed and nimbleness at the expense of sacrificing almost everything else. They were formidable missile platforms, especially when knitted into datalinked firing groups by *Jamaica* and her other two *Thetis-A*-class command battlecruisers. All three of those had survived. But . . . her lips quirked into what could almost be mistaken for a smile. "Still just as many chiefs, but not as many Indians," she said aloud.

Hafezi looked puzzled for a moment—the joke belonged to her cultural background, not his. But then he caught the sense, and he responded with a smile as humorless as hers. It was a mistake, for their eyes met in a more direct contact than they'd known since the battle. Hafezi's shied away, and he hurried on.

"Furthermore, the carriers suffered heavy losses in their fighter squadrons." The figures appeared on the conference room's display screen. "And all our depletable munitions are in short supply after the loss of *Voyager*."

"That last loss worries me more than all the others. And not just—or even principally—because of the missiles she was carrying," Commander Arbella Maningo, the logistics officer, put in. In the earlier stages of their flight, she'd wavered on the ragged edge of panic. But she'd steadied as the situation had grown more desperate, as people sometimes did, and the freighter *Voyager* had been her special concern.

Sommers was inclined to agree with the logistics officer's observation. Still, she wished Maningo hadn't brought it up, for there was nothing they could do about it, and just thinking about it gave her the beginnings of a migraine.

With no other alternative but annihilation, Survey Flotilla 19 was fleeing outward into the unknown in the forlorn hope of eventually finding itself back in known space. The notion wasn't completely unrealistic—the warp connections sometimes formed clusters of interconnected nexi, and the Terran Federation and its allies encompassed a *lot* of warp points. But its chances of success were directly related to the length of time they could sustain the search. Under such circumstances, the loss of fifty percent of the flotilla's logistics support was a catastrophe so overwhelming that discussing it was pointless. Sommers had refrained from placing everyone on short rations; in the odd blend of shell shock and euphoria that had followed their escape, the morale impact of such a move would have been imponderable but almost certainly not good. She wouldn't be able to put it off much longer, though. . . .

"What *happened*?" Maningo was continuing, as much to herself as to the conference at large. "Where did they *come* from?" Sommers felt no inclination to slap the logistics officer down; she wasn't reverting to her former jitters, just voicing the question that had been in everyone's mind since the Arachnid ships had appeared behind them in the expanse of nothingness that was a starless warp nexus.

"That's clear enough," the electronic image of Captain Milos Kabilovic growled. Kabilovic, CO of the fleet carrier *Borsoi*, wasn't a member of the staff, but he was virtually present as commander of SF 19's "gunslingers"—the term for the explorers' Battle Fleet escorts that continued to be used even though the distinction between Battle Fleet and Survey Command had faded more than a little since the war began.

"It was a closed warp point," he went on, "either in that warp nexus or, more likely, one of those on the other side. The Bugs—" it had been years since anyone had called the Arachnids anything but that "—closed in on us as soon as they became aware of our presence."

At first, nobody showed any inclination to dispute the carrier commander's analysis. The anomalies in space and time known as warp points—usually, but not always, associated with stellar gravity wells—had been known to humans for over three centuries, ever since the day in 2053 when the exploration ship *Hermes*, *en route* to Neptune, had abruptly found itself in the system of Alpha Centauri, instead. They'd been known even longer to humanity's sometime enemies and current allies the Orions, the only known race to have theorized the phenomenon's existence rather than accidentally stumbling over it. Knowledge of the so-called *closed* warp points, invisible even to those who'd learned how to detect ordinary warp points by their associated grav surge, was of more recent vintage. But it was nonetheless common knowledge in this room, one of the fundamental background hazards of survey work, against which precautions were routinely taken. And SF 19's precautions had gone beyond routine. . . .

"But we were operating continuously in cloak!" Hafezi protested. "And we didn't even emplace any courier drone nav buoys at the warp points we passed through, just in case the Bugs had any cloaked pickets in those systems. How could they have found us?"

"None of that's foolproof. They could have detected us on any one of our warp transits, if they already had pickets in those systems." Kabilovic addressed the individual who had the most intimate knowledge of sensor systems. "Isn't that true, Lieutenant Murakuma?"

Fujiko Murakuma nodded slowly as everyone awaited her opinion, respectful of her expertise despite her junior rank. She was the flotilla's specialist in the new second-generation recon drones which had revolutionized survey work by marrying the technology of advanced sensors to that of the SBMHAWK missiles that allowed a bombardment of an unseen enemy at the other end of a warp line. Probing through unknown warp points in advance of the ships that launched them, the RD2 had removed some of the "shot-in-the-dark" quality from warp point exploration . . . and, with it, maybe some of the mystique, which was why certain old-timers affected to despise it. A generation which had grown up with the likelihood of Bugs on the far side of any unsurveyed warp point had little patience for such romanticism, on the other hand. It belonged to the days when survey ships had fared heedlessly into an illimitable frontier, seeking worlds to study and colonize rather than to incinerate.

Fujiko Murakuma belonged to the generation which had come to grips with the harsher, infinitely more terrifying present reality, and Sommers studied her. The fact that she put her individual name before her surname wasn't unusual; many Japanese-derived cultures had by now adopted that Western practice. Indeed, her name was more Japanese than her appearance, for she was tall and slender, her hair held a reddish glint in its midnight depths, and her eyes, despite a perceptible epicanthic fold, were hazel-green. But any ambivalence in her background was unimportant. What mattered was her professional competence, and as to that there was no uncertainty at all.

"That's true, Sir," she replied to Kabilovic. "I'm firmly convinced that the Bug force that attacked us entered one of the star systems through which we'd already passed—or, to be precise, one of the warp nexi, with or without a star system—rather than the one in which they attacked us. We weren't aware of their entry because of our lack of coverage of those nexi, even with nav buoys."

It could have been interpreted as a veiled criticism of Sommers' decision not to emplace such buoys, since their absence meant it was impossible for any courier drone to find its way home with word of the flotilla's fate. But emplacing them would also have been a tell-tale trail of bread crumbs for any Arachnid picket or survey force which had chanced upon them, and the lieutenant's odd eyes met the admiral's squarely. Looking into them, Sommers detected nothing behind the words except a junior officer gutsy enough to say what she thought even at the risk of misinterpretation. What she did detect was a desire on Murakuma's part to say *more*, to go beyond the expert opinion Kabilovic had solicited.

"Do you care to theorize any further, Lieutenant?" she inquired, clearing the way for Murakuma to speak up in the presence of her superiors.

"Well, Sir . . . May I?" Murakuma indicated the holographic display projector at the center of the conference table. Sommers nodded, and the lieutenant manipulated controls. A series of colored balls connected by sticks, rather like a very simplified representation of a molecule, appeared in midair: warp nexi and the warp lines that connected them. There were nine of the immaterial spheres, and everyone present recognized the display as SF 19's route. It had, of course, no relation whatsoever to those various stars' relative positions and distances in real-space. Nobody except astronomers thought in such terms when the warp points allowed interstellar transits without crossing the intervening light-years.

"We began here," Murakuma began, using a light-pencil to indicate the ball representing the Anderson One system. Then she flashed the immaterial pointer four balls further along the string. "And here's where they attacked us. When they appeared, they didn't give the impression of a force that had just piled into the system and was still in the process of getting itself organized. That's why I believe they entered a closed warp point in one of the intervening warp nexi." She created the broken strings that denoted warp lines leading to closed warp points, indicating hypothetical routes into the three nexi they'd transited before the Bugs had overtaken them.

"Precisely," Kabilovic said with a satisfied nod, but Murakuma wasn't finished.

"But the question then becomes," she went on, "why did they wait so long to attack us?"

"Well," Hafezi ruminated, running his fingers through his beard in a nervous gesture he'd only recently acquired, "we *were* operating in cloak. Even if they were aware of our presence in a general way, maybe they took a long time to locate us precisely."

"But, Sir," Murakuma persisted, "it wouldn't have taken them long to do that *if they'd come out of cloak themselves* to hunt aggressively for us. Maybe they were unwilling to do so."

"Why?" Sommers demanded.

"Well, Admiral, if we'd become aware that there were Bugs in this warp chain, wouldn't our first order of business have been to get at least one ship back with the warning? And with them out of cloak, we might have detected them soon enough to do just that. So it could make perfectly good sense to them to stay cloaked to keep us from doing that. But," Murakuma continued relentlessly into what had become a profound silence, *"why did they suddenly stop worrying about it?"*

She made further adjustments, expanding her display to include the warp line of the far side of Anderson One, leading to Alpha Centauri with its eight other warp points, one of which connected with . . . Sol.

She said nothing. Nothing was needed. They all sat, no longer a staff but rather a collection of individuals, each alone with his or her own horrified speculations.

Sommers knew she needed to bring them out of it. But she couldn't, at first. She, too, was face-to-face with a nightmare from which there was no awakening.

But because she was in command, and habituated to looking at the big picture, she ran her mind over the events that had led them, and the rest of the human race, to this point.

It wasn't that humankind's expansion into the galaxy had been a peaceful process.

Quite the contrary.

Oh, it had been at first. After *Hermes* had shown the gateway to the stars—or, more accurately, blundered through it—colonization of what were now called the Heart Worlds had proceeded without any difficulties other than those humans had created for themselves. No dangerously advanced aliens had been encountered, and after the dodged bullet called the China War, no human with the brain to organize an effective opposition had challenged the peaceful hegemony of the Terran Federation. Earth and its children had settled comfortably into the belief that the universe was a fundamentally benign place, holding no real enemies, only those to whom one had somehow given offense and with whom one should therefore make amends. That attitude had always been common enough, at least among peoples who'd enjoyed a vacation from history. (Sommers, whose ancestry was North American, winced mentally.) And experience had finally seemed to be confirming it.

Then, one fine day in 2205, humanity had met the Orions.

The First Interstellar War had been only the first movement of a symphony of carnage. One threat after another had materialized out of a galaxy which the conventional wisdom had never expected to hold so many species at essentially the same technological level in the same cosmological eyeblink of time. Next had come the three-cornered clash of Terran, Orion, and Ophiuchi known as the Second Interstellar War. Then all three erstwhile enemies had found themselves allies in the Third Interstellar War, for the Rigelians had offered none of them anything but equal opportunity genocide. But then had come a diminuendo of sorts, as the Terran Federation had dealt unaided with the truly weird Theban jihad for which humans were at least arguably responsible. That had been around the turn of the twenty-fourth century. Afterwards, there'd been no armed conflict to speak of for six decades. Even in this era of extended lifespans, that had been long enough to convince most humans that peace was the natural state of things.

The majority, as always, had been wrong. The orchestra of history hadn't come to a triumphant finale. It had barely paused before launching into the soul-shaking atonalities of what wasn't even like music composed by a madman ... for a madman is, after all, human.

Nothing in history had prepared the human race—even that minority capable of learning from history—for the horror that had begun when a survey mission had stumbled onto the Arachnids. Nothing ... not even the Rigelians, who'd been like a ghastly caricature—or, perhaps, surrealist painting—of the worst religious and ideological fanatics of Old Terra's past. (And presumably still were, on the few planets where they now existed, closely watched by orbital stations under standing orders to obliterate anything more advanced than a steam engine or a black powder muzzleloader.) The Bugs were something else altogether. And after three and a half years of war, no one was any closer to fathoming what that *something else* was than they'd been in 2360.

The Bugs were, of course, sentient . . . weren't they? Because they *had* to be . . . didn't they? Nonsentient lifeforms didn't build starships, or organize the kind of industrial base that had overwhelmed all initial resistance by sheer numbers, tonnage, and firepower. And yet . . . in all those three and a half years there had been *no communication* of any kind with them. Instead, mind-numbingly immense fleets had advanced in dead silence, indifferent to losses, grinding the defenses of one system after another to powder with a nonfeeling relentlessness even more horrible than Rigelian malevolence. Fantasies of runaway machine-life had soon been dispelled, however; the Bugs were organic. It would have been better if they hadn't been. The Frankenstein robots of popular fiction wouldn't have needed organic food. The Bugs did . . . and they regarded conquered sentients as a source of it. As they'd advanced along the Romulus Chain, whole human populations had vanished. So had Orion populations, after the Bugs broke into the Kliean Chain. Two races which had thought themselves inured to war had finally looked true horror full in the face.

Desperate fighting had eventually brought the war to a deadlock. And the Allies had finally gotten a break: the discovery of a system, Zephrain, which gave warp access to what was clearly an important system of the Bugs' unknowably large domain. Admiral Ivan Antonov—the victor of the Theban War, recalled from retirement as head of the Alliance's joint chiefs of staff—had begun to prepare an offensive, to be launched from that system. Not only would that offensive strike at a critically important Bug system, but it might well also open a fresh line of advance—a new point of contact which might allow Antonov to create a war of movement and put an end to the brutal, grinding, head-on war of attrition against an enemy who didn't seem to feel its losses.

But then the Bugs had appeared in the skies of Alpha Centauri, humanity's gateway to the galaxy, only one warp transit away from the home system itself. It was also the Grand Alliance's headquarters, and Antonov had abruptly changed his plans. Taking personal command of the forces being assembled for the Zephrain offensive, he'd led them through the previously unsuspected closed warp point that had admitted the Bugs into humanity's heartland.

Antonov's hastily organized Second Fleet had blasted its way into the system on the far side of that warp point, which he'd dubbed "Anderson One" in honor of his old friend and mentor Howard Anderson, hero of the first two interstellar wars. Then, judging the risks to be outweighed by the chance of putting a quick end to the war—and the Bugs—he'd pressed "Operation Pesthouse" onward towards the warp point into which the Bug defenders had fled.

But Anderson One had held a third warp point, and Antonov had been too canny an old campaigner to ignore the dangers that might lurk beyond it. Thus it was that Survey Flotilla 19 had departed through that third warp point, shortly after Second Fleet had fared deeper into the unknown.

They'd set out just after Antonov's first couriers had returned from his next conquest. Censorship had blanketed those couriers' tidings, but too late to prevent some disturbing rumors from circulating about what Antonov had found on Anderson Two's life-bearing world. Sommers had rejected those rumors out of hand as unthinkable. Yes, everyone knew the Bugs ate captured sentient beings. But *ranches* of such beings, raised as food animals that *knew* they were food animals . . . ? And there were human worlds that had been under Bug control for three years now—worlds on which there'd been children and adolescents. . . .

*No!* Once again, Sommers' mind dismissed the thought with a spasm of revulsion.

Anyway, there was nightmare enough without it.

Murakuma's voice resumed, bringing Sommers back to the present.

"The Bugs appeared from behind us, so they have precisely what we were dispatched to warn against: a way into Anderson One, enabling them to cut off Second Fleet."

The implications were lost on no one. Every pair of eyes was on the holo display, and every mind was following the arrangement of prettily colored lights to its logical conclusion.

Was there still a Second Fleet?

Even as Sommers watched, the horror on certain faces deepened visibly as those faces' owners allowed their eyes to follow the warp chains in the *other* direction from Anderson One, to Alpha Centauri . . . and Sol.

In their fight for survival, they'd had no time to contemplate their aloneness, cut off from the rest of the human race. But now people began to make hesitant eye contact, as they silently asked each other the question no one dared utter aloud: *Are we now really alone?*

Maningo's features began to tremble. Sommers opened her mouth, prepared to forestall whatever the logistics officer was about to release into the oppressive air of the conference room.

But Hafezi beat her to it, tossing his head like a tormented horse and speaking angrily—although who or what his anger was directed against was not immediately apparent.

"No! It's not possible! We've only been gone nine months. And the Bugs jumped us only about a month and a half ago. There hasn't been time for . . . well, anyway, remember all the other worlds we've settled! *They're* still there, even if . . . if . . ." He couldn't continue, nor was there any need for him to complete the thought. Everyone knew what he meant, and no one wanted to hear it. He rallied himself. "Whatever's happened, there's still a Federation for us to find our way back to. And there's still our duty!"

They all sat up a little straighter, and even Maningo's incipient quivering solidified into determination. *Thank you, Feridoun,* Sommers thought, and in that fierce hawklike face she thought to glimpse the Iranian mythic hero whose name he bore.

She didn't dare allow her gaze to linger on that face.

"Commodore Hafezi is correct," she rapped, reasserting control of the meeting. "We can't allow ourselves to dwell on speculative possibilities. All that can accomplish is to cripple our will. Our sole concern must be the accomplishment of our mission and the return to safety of the people entrusted to our command. To that end, we must locate another warp point as soon as possible." She felt no useful purpose would be served by mentioning the possibility that this might be one of the occasional "dead end" systems with only one warp point. Instead, she decided to attend to what she'd been putting off. "In the meantime, it's necessary for us to restrict our consumption of nonrenewable supplies, especially in light of the loss of *Voyager*. Therefore, effective immediately, we'll—"

The whoop of the general quarters klaxon shattered the air.

The voice of *Jamaica*'s captain came from Sommers' chair arm communicator, speaking to no one, for she was already off at a dead run for Flag Bridge. She needed no explanation of what that whooping meant.

*Well,* she thought as she ran, *at least I won't have to worry about breaking the news to people that we're going on short rations.*

She stood beside Hafezi and watched doom approach in the holo sphere.

"I'd hoped they wouldn't find us so soon," she said quietly. Not so long ago, she wouldn't have made a remark like that to her chief of staff. Now . . .

He didn't reply. His eyes, like hers, remained fixed on the display of the Bug pursuers, approaching on what wasn't quite a stern chase they could run directly away from and which would therefore intersect their course with the inevitability of death.

The wavefront of that oncoming force was composed of what humans termed gunboats—larger than fighters. In fact, they were larger even than the auxiliary small craft carried by starships, but they generated an intermediate form of reactionless drive field which conferred speed and maneuverability far greater than that of any conventional starship. Indeed, their speed approached that of the fighters the Bugs, for whatever reasons, couldn't or at least didn't use . . . and, unlike fighters, they could make unassisted warp transit. They were a Bug invention, and had come as a shocking surprise to the Allies, who hadn't thought the Bugs *could* invent. At least they had some countervailing disadvantages; they were energy hogs, and in consequence had emissions signatures that made them as readily detectable—and targetable—as full-sized starships.

Not that the Bug force would have been all that hard to detect in any case, for its second wave consisted of battlecruisers, advancing uncloaked in justifiable contempt of their quarry. Lots of battlecruisers . . . all the survivors from their fight in the last system, in fact. Some were simply gunboat tenders, but the majority were fighting vessels comparable to her own *Dunkerque-*A-class BCRs—the classes the Alliance's intelligence had dubbed *Antelope, Antler,* and *Appian.* Enough of them to smother SF 19's defenses with missiles.

"Commodore Hafezi," she said crisply. (Even at this time, there was no need to deny him the traditional courtesy "promotion" accorded to anyone aboard a ship other than its skipper whose normal rank-title was "captain." Indeed, Sommers was beginning to understand what she'd always read, that tradition became particularly important at times like this.) "We need to be able to launch the fighters at the precise moment when interception becomes unavoidable. Notify Captain Kabilovic." Milos, after all, wasn't aboard this ship. Tradition . . . again. "And order the *Huns* to stay well clear and continue their present survey pattern."

Hafezi's nod showed his understanding. The scout cruisers might, after all, find another warp point. And their combat value was almost negligible.

"Aye, aye, Admiral," he replied with a crispness matching hers. Then, as though by common consent, their eyes met in a way they hadn't been allowed to meet of late. And, a tremulous instant later, so did their hands.

*What does it matter, now that we're all dead?* She turned, with a look of what might have been called defiance, to face any of the flag bridge crew who might have seen them.

Some had. They were staring openly. But not with amazement. They were grinning.

The amazement was all Sommers'.

*They* knew? *But how long . . . ?*

Then, all at once, her sense of the ridiculous came bubbling up. Surprise, outrage, and even despair all drowned in it. She turned back to face Feridoun. A smile began to tremble on her lips. . . .

"Admiral!" Fujiko Murakuma—*not* one of those who'd been grinning—shattered the brittle moment, calling out in a puzzled voice from the sensor station where she'd been observing the Bugs. "We're picking up something *else*."

Wingmaster Demlafi Furra, commanding Sixth Strike Wing, felt a need to relieve her tension. So she spread her wings a little—not to their full two-meter span, of course, here in the confines of her flag bridge—and waved them gently back and forth. The mild enhancement of her blood's oxygen, though nothing like the full rush of flight, did its work, and she turned with renewed calmness and energy to the holo display.

The strike wing had been on full alert ever since the scout destroyer's courier drone had emerged from one of Pajzomo's three warp points, shattering the boredom of a routine patrol of vast emptiness lit by the sullen red glare of Pajzomo. But now they were closing to within eleven light-seconds of the hunters who didn't know yet that they were being hunted. And the need of everyone in the strike wing, from Furra on down, to open fire was becoming a sensual thing.

"Wingmaster," the flag captain, as humans would have called

him, interrupted Furra's thoughts, "what about the *other* group of aliens?"

"I haven't forgotten them, Nestmaster." The imprinted caution of generations had prevented Furra from trying to contact the unknowns when they first appeared. And after that, any electronic emissions that might have revealed the strike wing's presence to the Demons had been out of the question. Now she gazed at the icons representing those ships, whose unimaginable crews must be preparing themselves for their last battle. "What about them?"

"Well, Wingmaster," the flag captain spoke diffidently, "I mention this only as a possible option, but . . . we could wait and let the Demons overtake them. They don't stand a chance, of course. But they'd probably leave fewer Demons for us to deal with afterwards."

Furra didn't reprove him for a suggestion flagrantly contrary to the precepts of Kkrullott. She had her faults, but sanctimoniousness wasn't one of them. Neither was hypocrisy . . . and the same idea had crossed her own mind. Nevertheless, she gave her head the backward jerk that meant what shaking it would have to most humans. "No. Aside from the ethical issues involved. It occurs to me that we may be looking at an opportunity here."

"Wingmaster?"

"These beings are obviously enemies of the Demons." Which, she reflected, was merely to say they had *encountered* the Demons. "This makes them potential allies of ours."

"But how useful? They're in headlong flight!"

"These ships are, granted. But that doesn't mean the rest of their race isn't still holding out somewhere." Furra straightened up into a posture which put an end to discussion. "We'll proceed as planned. If the unknown ships initiate hostilities against us, we will of course defend ourselves. But if they try to communicate with us, we'll respond."

The flag captain gestured understanding and obedience and they resumed their waiting. It wasn't long before they closed to within the preplanned range of the unsuspecting Demons.

Furra leaned forward in a crouch and gazed at the icons of the Demon ships for another instant—a dreamy gaze, almost. Some might have thought it a *loving* gaze, completely misinterpreting the nature, but not the intensity, of the emotion it held.

But then she bared omnivore's teeth, and no one, of whatever species or whatever culture, could possibly have misunderstood any longer.

"Disengage cloaking," she ordered the flag captain. "And... *kill!*"

*The Fleet had run the Enemy to ground once more, and this time there would be no escape. This group of Enemy ships had proved as troublesome as any the Fleet had yet encountered, and there was no reason to suppose they would prove less troublesome once the Fleet managed to close with them. Still, it was obvious, despite their attempts to cloak themselves from the Fleet gunboats' sensors, that they'd taken serious losses and damage in their last clash with the Fleet. Indeed, had it not been for the fortuitous discovery of yet another warp point by the Enemy's scout ships, the Fleet would have finished them off the last time. It was a pity that the Fleet had never previously discovered that warp point for itself. Had it known that it existed, it might have been possible to place ships on this side of it to await the Enemy in ambush. In that case, none of the survey ships could possibly have survived. As it was, it was essential to overtake the Enemy and destroy him utterly lest he find yet another warp point somewhere in the depths of this unexplored star system and escape once more.*

*At least the infernally fast small attack craft which had done so much to fend off the Fleet's last attack had suffered heavy damage in the process, and it seemed apparent that there could not be many of them left. The Enemy was obviously aware of the Fleet's presence—the maneuvers of his surviving units was sufficient proof of that—yet the small attack craft had not yet been committed.*

*The battlecruisers held their courses, covered by the protective shield of the gunboats, waiting to pounce upon the Enemy small attack craft when they finally were committed, but the Fleet allowed itself to feel a cold anticipation of the upcoming victory. As the range dropped, the emissions signatures of the Enemy starships had become increasingly clear, and the evidence of severe damage to his long-range missile ships had been still further promise that the troublesome survey force and its escorts would soon be dealt with.*

*That would be good. Once the survey ships had been erased from existence, this component of the Fleet could retrace its steps and rejoin the remainder of the Fleet committed to the carefully prepared counterattack upon the Enemy core system from which the Enemy had emerged. And when that hap—*

❖          ❖          ❖

The first Bug starship blew up with no warning at all.

The *Antelope*-class battlecruiser on the flank of the Arachnid formation had never even realized its killer was there. All of its sensors had been locked upon the Allied survey flotilla fleeing before it, and it had never occurred to the beings which crewed that battlecruiser that there might be anyone else to worry about. And because it hadn't occurred to them, they were taken fatally by surprise as the missile salvo erupted out of the blind zone astern of it, created by the sensor interference of its own drive field. There were no point defense counter missiles, no fire from close-in laser clusters, and the lethal salvo smashed home like so many hammers of antimatter fury.

The battlecruiser's shields did their best, but the savagery of the attack was scarcely even blunted, and the entire ship vanished in a sun-bright bubble of fire.

The *Antelope* was the first to die; it wasn't the last. The other salvos which had accompanied the one that killed it began to arrive almost in the same instant, and ship-killing blasts of fury marched through the Arachnid formation like the hobnailed boots of some demented war god. A second battlecruiser, a third—and then the killing spasms of flame came for the gunboats, as well. They were smaller, easier and more fragile targets, without the shields that protected their larger consorts, and—like the battlecruisers—they'd never even guessed that any danger might lurk behind them. A single hit was sufficient to kill any one of them, and the hits came not in singletons, but in dozens. Shattered and vaporized hulls, clouds of plasma and blast fronts littered with the splintered fragments of battlecruisers . . .

The Arachnid fleet reeled under the devastating impact of the totally unanticipated carnage. For a handful of minutes, even the boulderlike discipline which had sent attack force after attack force of Bug superdreadnoughts unwaveringly into the teeth of the Alliance's most furious firepower wavered. The sheer surprise of their losses, far more than the scale of those losses—grievous though they were—stunned them, and separate squadrons reacted as separate squadrons, not the interchangeable units of the finely meshed machine their enemies were accustomed to facing. Some of them, in the absence of any order to the contrary, continued to close in on the fleeing remnants of Survey Flotilla 19, even as successive waves of missiles sliced into them from astern. Other squadrons of battlecruisers, and even more of the harrowed gunboats' survivors, turned abruptly to charge towards the source of that fire.

Even those who continued to close upon the Allied survey force were at least no longer taken completely unawares by the fire screaming down upon them. Their command datalink installations had taken charge of their point defense systems, concentrating counter missiles and laser clusters alike upon the incoming weapons which any unit of any battlegroup could see. Some of those missiles still got through, of course. Not all of them could be seen by any member of the battlegroups they targeted, and the uncaring laws of statistics said that even some of those which could be seen would evade all fire directed upon them. But the defensive systems managed to sharply reduce the number of warheads getting through to their targets, and whoever had suddenly attacked them found himself forced to concentrate his fire upon the hostile warships suddenly charging straight towards him.

*The Fleet staggered under the sudden, merciless fire ravaging its neat formation. It couldn't be coming from the Enemy survey force the Fleet had been pursuing, for there had never been a sufficient number of survey ships or escorts to generate the number of missiles sleeting in upon it.*

*Besides, the sensor sections reported as the Fleet quickly began to recover its balance, the Enemy had never used weapons similar to some of those blasting into its ships. No, these missiles carried warheads of types the Fleet had never seen before, and even if the Enemy had somehow developed them and put them into production without the Fleet realizing it, the survey ships would surely have used them in the previous battle had he possessed them.*

*Which meant that the Fleet had encountered yet another Enemy.*

On *Jamaica's* flag bridge, puzzlement at the strange ships that had suddenly emerged from cloak gave way to stunned incredulity as one Bug battlecruiser after another vanished in the hell-glare of antimatter annihilation.

Sommers was the first to recover.

"Commodore Hafezi! Order Captain Kabilovic to launch every fighter he's got, and take those gunboats. And have *Nomad* and the *Huns* proceed on course, but get the rest of the flotilla turned around. *Move!*"

The last word was yelled as much for the entire bridge crew's benefit as for Feridoun's. Everyone was staring, open mouthed, as two more Bug battlecruisers vanished from the threat board, and all but two of the others were rendered naked by some totally unknown weapon—some sort of missile warhead which evidently stripped away electromagnetic shields. It was too unexpected, too sudden a reversal of the inevitable course of whatever brief lives remained to them. Sommers was as whipsawed as the rest of them, but she couldn't let herself—or anyone else—remain paralyzed.

She rose from her command chair and strode towards the com console.

"Raise those unknown ships!" she commanded. As the com officer fumbled to obey, she watched data codes blossom beside the icons of the unknowns on her plot as the computers received more sensor data. She gulped as tight formations of superdreadnoughts appeared. But even those ships, she saw, were going to have to move in to closer range, now that the Bugs were aware of their presence and fighting back. One of the Bug squadrons had survived entirely intact, and now that it had turned to face its enemies, its datalinked point defense was proving impervious to the long-range missile bombardment that had been so devastating coming from the blind zones of surprised ships.

She spared a glance for the status of her own flotilla. Feridoun had passed her orders along, and the fighting ships were performing the kind of course reversal that was merely difficult nowadays, rather than impossible, as it would have been in the days of reaction drives. And either Kabilovic had set new records in responding to her command to launch his fighters, or else he'd already begun to do so on his own initiative.

Feridoun joined her.

"Are you sure this is wise?" he muttered.

"What do you mean? Joining the unknowns' battle with the Bugs? Or trying to communicate with them?"

"Both."

Sommers smiled in the way that transformed her appearance in a way she'd never suspected . . . any more than she'd ever realized how inaccurate her idea of that appearance as "mannish" was.

"There's an old saying: 'The enemy of my enemy is my friend.'"

"I've heard that saying. It doesn't necessarily follow."

"No, it doesn't, really." She drew a breath. "But what choice do we have, Feridoun? To continue fleeing in the hopeless way we have been?" Inasmuch as she was the one who'd been driving them so mercilessly in precisely that direction, she wouldn't have dared say such a thing to anyone else. Hafezi didn't respond, and she pressed on. "Besides, we *know* the Bugs are enemies. These new arrivals may turn on us and finish us off after they're done with the Bugs. But we don't know that. And maybe we can at least put them in our debt by helping them finish off this battle, first."

"Still . . ."

"Admiral!" The com officer cut Hafezi's skeptical voice off. "We're getting a response! They're—"

All conversation halted as the image appeared on the com screen.

Flying sentient races were one of those theoretical possibilities which had never panned out. It wasn't hard to understand why. If a species was going to specialize, it generally specialized in only one thing. Besides, it took a large body to support a large brain, and in any normal environment an avian couldn't afford a large body. At most, a *formerly* avian race like humanity's Ophiuchi allies might exchange flight for the ability to use tools in an evolutionary trade-off.

But Sommers, looking at the long arms of the being on the screen and the membranes they supported, had no doubts. Even in their present folded state, those wing-membranes were obviously too extensive to be vestigial. Despite the short, downy sand-colored fur and the red-trimmed black clothing, the overall impression was vaguely batlike—much as the Orions suggested bipedal cats to humans, who recognized the fallacy of the comparison but still couldn't avoid making it.

The being's mouth was working to produce sound: gibberish, of course. The com officer checked his readouts, nodded to himself, and turned to Sommers.

"The translator software is starting to kick in, Sir. Of course, it'll need some time to pull together enough vocabulary to start building on. The more he or she or whatever talks, the more it'll have to get its teeth into," he added, "and assuming that they've got similar capability, the more *you* talk, the faster they'll be able to translate what you're saying."

Sommers glanced at the plot again. Kabilovic's fighters were beginning to engage the surviving Bug gunboats. So were destroyer-sized vessels of the new arrivals.

"I don't think we've really got much in the way of options, Feridoun," she said quietly. And she began to speak, very distinctly, into the com pick up.

# CHAPTER ONE
## Gathering Stars

By the standard dating of Old Terra, it was the year 2364, and the month was May. But that had nothing to do with the revolution of the Nova Terra/Eden double-planet system around Alpha Centauri A, and wan winter light slanted through the lofty windows, making the air of the spacious conference room—well heated and crowded with human and other warm-blooded bodies though it was—seem chilly.

Which, thought Marcus LeBlanc, was altogether too damned appropriate. How could it be anything else, when every being sitting in that room was only too well aware of the catastrophic events which had swirled about them since Ivan Antonov had launched Operation Pesthouse?

They'd had such hopes. Even LeBlanc, whose job it was to remind them all of how little they truly knew—even now—about the Arachnids, had been unable to believe that any race could sacrifice so many ships, entire fleets of superdreadnoughts, even planets inhabited by its own kind, just to set a massive trap. Yet that was precisely what the Bugs had done, and Operation Pesthouse had turned into the most overwhelming disaster in the history of the Terran Federation Navy. The Arachnids had lured Antonov's Second Fleet on and on with sacrifice gambits beyond the bounds of sanity... then they'd closed in through undiscovered warp points in the systems through which he'd passed. They'd sprung a trap from which Antonov, with the help of a hastily organized relief force headed by Sky Marshal Hannah Avram herself, had only just managed to extricate less than half his force—not including himself, and not including Avram.

It was hard to say which had been the more paralyzing body blow to the TFN: the deaths of two living legends, or the loss of ships—more than a quarter of the fleet's total prewar ship count, and more than half its total prewar tonnage destroyed outright. And that didn't even count the crippling damage to many of the survivors. Nor did it count the two survey flotillas that had been probing beyond the warp points through which the Bugs had come . . . and which must have been like puppies under the wheels of a ground car against the massive armadas into whose paths they had strayed.

The losses were so horrifying that the survey flotillas scarcely constituted a material addition to the sum of destruction. But, the more LeBlanc thought about it, the loss that really couldn't be afforded was Antonov. His reputation had been that of a ruthless, unstoppable, unfeeling force of nature—in short, humankind's answer to the Bugs. If *he* could be overwhelmed, what hope had everyone else?

Ellen MacGregor and Raymond Prescott—whose brilliant execution of Antonov's escape plan had enabled some of Second Fleet to survive—had halted the tumble of Terran morale when they smashed the Bug counteroffensive that had followed the fleeing survivors of Operation Pesthouse into the Alpha Centauri System. The "Black Hole of Centauri," as it had come to be called after MacGregor's savage prediction of what the Bug invaders were going to fall into, had been only a defensive victory, but it had been one the Grand Alliance had needed badly. And it evidently had left the Bugs incapable of any further offensives for the time being, as there had been no such offensive since. So a lull had settled over the war as the TFN began to rebuild itself.

Yet even beginning that rebuilding had been an agonizingly painful process, and the dispersive demands of frightened politicians, terrified for the safety of other star systems whose population levels approached that of Alpha Centauri, hadn't helped. So, yes, he understood why a room which should have been warm felt anything but.

He was seated among the staffers who lined the room's periphery, well back from the oval table in its center. As a rear admiral, he had about as much chance of getting a seat at *that* table as did the young lieutenant beside him.

That worthy seemed to share his mood. Kevin Sanders looked

as foxlike as always, with his reddish sandy hair and sharp features. But the usual twinkle was absent from his blue eyes as he turned to LeBlanc, and his whisper was subdued, even though it held the customary informality that obtained between them.

"Quite a change since the last time I was here," he said.

After a moment's blankness, LeBlanc gave a nod of understanding. Sanders, then an ensign, had been in this very room three and a half years before, when the Grand Allied Joint Chiefs of Staff had first convened. That had been before he'd joined LeBlanc's intelligence shop of Bug specialists—before it had existed, even—and he'd been present as a subordinate of Captain Midori Kozlov. She hadn't been a captain then, when Ivan Antonov had been named the joint chiefs' chairman, and she'd served as his staff intelligence officer.

And now Kozlov, like Antonov himself and so many others—too many others, hundreds of thousands of others—existed only as cosmic detritus in the lonely, lonely depths of space where Second Fleet had gone to find its doom.

"Yes, quite a change," LeBlanc murmured in reply as he studied those positioned at the oval table.

Two members of the original joint chiefs that Sanders remembered were still there: Admiral Thaarzhaan of Terra's Ophiuchi allies, and Fleet Speaker Noraku of the Gorm, whose relationship with the Orions defied precise human definition. But Sky Marshal Ellen MacGregor now represented the Terran Federation, and there were others besides the joint chiefs, crowding the table's capacity. Admiral Raymond Prescott, who was to have commanded the Zephrain offensive, was seated beside Ninety-First Small Fang of the Khan Zhaarnak'telmasa, Lord Telmasa, who was to have been his carrier commander . . . and who, more importantly, was his *vilkshatha* brother, for Prescott was the second human in history to have held that very special warrior's relationship with an Orion. Across the table from them was another Orion, Tenth Great Fang of the Khan Koraaza'khiniak, Lord Khiniak, just in from Shanak, where he commanded Third Fleet on the stalemated second front of the Kliean Chain. Fleet Admiral Oscar Pederson of the Federation's Fortress Command was also there, in his capacity as the system CO of Alpha Centauri. And, at the end of the table . . .

There, LeBlanc's eyes lingered. Beside him, Sanders chuckled, once more his usual self.

"I wonder if there's ever been so much rank at one table?" the lieutenant mused. "You'd think it would reach critical mass!"

When he got no response from LeBlanc, he glanced sharply at his chief. Then he followed the rear admiral's gaze to the woman on whom it rested.

Admiral Vanessa Murakuma had the red hair, green eyes, and elvish slenderness of Irish genes molded by generations on a low-gravity planet. The initial impression, to eyes accustomed to the human norm, was one of ethereal fragility.

"Yeah, right," Sanders muttered to himself *sotto voce.*

Murakuma, thrust into command of the frantically improvised defenses of the Romulus Chain in the early days of the war, had fought the Bug juggernaut to a standstill in a nightmare thunder of death and shattered starships. She'd fallen back from star system to star system, always desperately outnumbered, always with her back to the wall . . . always aware of the civilians helpless beyond the fragile shield of her dying ships. Sanders knew that he would never—ever—be able to truly understand the desperation and horror which must have filled her as she faced that implacable avalanche of Bug warships, saw it grinding remorselessly and unstoppably onward towards all she was sworn to protect and defend. Yet somehow she'd met that avalanche and, finally, stopped it dead. She'd nearly died herself in the process, yet she'd done it, and in the doing earned the Lion of Terra, an award that entitled her to take a salute from anyone in the TFN, regardless of rank. And the intelligence analyst who'd been beside her throughout the entire hideous ordeal had been then-captain Marcus LeBlanc, the only intelligence officer the TFN had thought loose-screwed enough to have a prayer of understanding the Bugs.

And now, as Sanders watched, she made a brief eye contact with Rear Admiral LeBlanc, and smiled ever so slightly.

Once again, Sanders looked at LeBlanc, who was also smiling.

He wondered if the rumors were true.

But it seemed that his boss *had* heard him, after all.

"Yes," LeBlanc agreed, still smiling. "There are a hell of a lot of stars, and the various other things nonhumans use for flag-rank insignia, up there. But there's more to come."

"Attention on deck!" the master-at-arms at the main doorway announced, as if on cue.

Everyone rose as Kthaara'zarthan, Lord Talphon, Chairman of the Grand Allied Joint Chiefs of Staff, entered with the prowling stride of the *Zheeerlikou'valkhannaiee*—a name which humans, for reasons too obvious for discussion, preferred to render as *Orions,* after the constellation which held the heart of their interstellar domain.

Most Orions, including Zhaarnak and Koraaza, came in various shades of tawny and russet. But there was a genetic predisposition, which kept popping up in the Khanate's noblest families, toward fur of midnight-black. Kthaara epitomized that trait, and even though he was beginning to show the frosting of age, he still suggested some arcane feline death-god. It was an impression few humans, even those used to Orions in general, could avoid on first seeing him. And it had grown more pronounced since Operation Pesthouse.

Everyone had heard the stories of Kthaara's reaction on learning of the fate of Ivan Antonov . . . or Ivan'zarthan, as he was also entitled to be known, as the very first human to be admitted to *vilkshatha* brotherhood. It had been Kthaara who'd admitted him, at the height of the Theban War, when Antonov had allowed the Orion to serve under him because he'd understood the blood debt Kthaara had owed to the killers of his cousin, Khardanizh'zarthan. As he'd listened to the reports that Antonov's flagship had not been among the battered survivors that had limped back from Operation Pesthouse, the Orion hadn't emitted the howl a human, misled by the catlike countenance evolutionary coincidence had put atop a body not unlike that of a disproportionately long-legged man, might have expected. Nor had he made any sound of all. Nor any movement. Instead, like black lava freezing into adamantine hardness, he'd seemed to silently congeal into an ebon essence of death and vengeance.

Since then, his trademark cosmopolitan urbanity, the product of six decades of close association with humans, had returned somewhat. It was in evidence now as he sat down at the place at the head of the table he'd inherited from his *vilkshatha* brother and addressed the meeting.

"As you were, ladies and gentlemen," he said in the Tongue of Tongues. Orion vocal apparatus was incapable of pronouncing Standard English, and that of humans was almost as ill-adapted to the universal Orion language. No Orion had ever been able to speak Standard English, and only a tiny handful of gifted mimics—like Raymond Prescott—had ever been able to reproduce the sounds of the Tongue of Tongues. But the two races could learn to understand each other's speech, and many of the non-Orions present—including LeBlanc and Sanders—could follow the Tongue of Tongues. Those who couldn't (like Vanessa Murakuma, who was Orion-literate but whose tone deafness made it impossible for her to comprehend the spoken version of the language) had earplug mikes connected to translators who could.

Several new Orion-English translation software packages were in development, spurred by the absolute necessity the Grand Alliance had created for human-Orion communication across the incompatible vocal interface which separated them, but they still left a lot to be desired. Memory requirements were very large, which limited their use to systems—like those on planets, large space stations, and capital ships—which could spare the space from other requirements. Worse, however, was the fact that they tended to be very literal-minded, and Orion was *not* a language which lent itself well to literal translation into English. Which was one reason organic translators were employed at plenary meetings like this one, where clarity of understanding was essential. The steady improvement in the software, especially by the Orions (who were the known galaxy's best cyberneticists) was bound to solve all of those problems—probably fairly soon, to judge by current results—but in the meantime, the software was reserved for occasions when misunderstandings would be less critical.

"I wish to welcome Lord Khiniak, Lord Telmasa, Ahhdmiraaaal Murraaaakuuuuma, and their staffs," Kthaara continued. "You have been recalled because I consider it necessary to bring all our principal field commanders up to date on our current status and future intentions. This will occupy an extensive series of conferences and briefings, as you already know from the material you have received. The purpose of this initial session is twofold. First of all, I wish to inform you that the last six months' strategic lull is soon going to come to an end."

That got the undivided attention of everyone who'd been expecting to sit through lengthy platitudes. Kthaara smiled a tooth-hidden carnivore's smile.

"The course of events leading up to the lull," he added, "is, of course, well known to us all."

That, LeBlanc thought with a fresh inner twinge of pain as he recalled his own earlier thoughts, was one way to put it.

It still felt . . . odd to hear an Orion say it, though. Or, rather, to hear an Orion say it as the chairman of the Joint Chiefs. Not so long ago, that position would have gone as a matter of course to a representative of the Terran Federation, the Alliance's technological pacesetter and industrial powerhouse, as well as its premiere military power. But now the TFN lay prostrate, its proud tradition of victory tarnished and the sublime self-confidence born of that tradition badly shaken. True, the awesome shipbuilding capacity of the Federation's Corporate Worlds remained intact, and the reconstruction of the Navy had commenced. Yet for the time being, the Orions would have to take the lead in any initiatives the Alliance attempted. So the chairmanship had fallen to Kthaara—the logical choice anyway, in terms of seniority and prestige as well as his unique experience in dealing with humans.

And now his voice continued in the Tongue of Tongues ("Cats copulating to bagpipe music," as a human wit had once described the sound), bringing LeBlanc back to the matter at hand.

"It is therefore unnecessary to review those events at any great length. Instead, I would like to use this initial plenary session to bring everyone up to date on our intelligence specialists' evaluations of the wreckage retrieved from the force that attempted to penetrate this system. Ahhdmiraaaal LeBlaaanc, you have the floor."

LeBlanc stood, unconsciously smoothing back the sparse hairs on his scalp and then stroking the beard he'd grown to compensate. He manipulated a small remote unit, and a holo image appeared in midair above the table. An image of a warship of space.

A low rumbling arose from his audience, hushed with shock.

"That, ladies and gentlemen, is the new Arachnid ship type that BuShips has dubbed the 'monitor,'" he stated without preamble. "You've probably seen the computer-generated imagery based on the sensor data from Second Fleet." He saw Raymond Prescott, who'd brought that data back, wince. "But that was only inference. Accurate inference, as far as it went—this ship is approximately twice the tonnage of a superdreadnought, just as that initial data suggested." The room grew very quiet. "But now, on the basis of closer acquaintance, we're in position to show you what it really looks like. We've also identified three classes. This one, which seems to be the 'basic' monitor, we've assigned the reporting name of the *Awesome* class." A few grim chuckles at the appropriateness barely dented the silence, and they ceased abruptly when a holographically projected display screen showed the class's armament. "As you can see, it's primarily a missile platform. Given the time it must take to construct such a thing, they have to have laid the class down before they acquired command datalink—presumably in an effort to compensate for that very lack by packing the maximum possible firepower into a single ship. Now, of course, they *have* command datalink, and our analysis of the attack on this system indicates that they've retrofitted at least some of the *Awesome* class with it—we call the refitted version of it the *Awesome Beta* class. Their datalink seems to be as capable as ours, as well; it can coordinate the offensive and defensive fire of up to six of these ships."

LeBlanc noticed eyes flickering toward MacGregor and Prescott, who'd faced an invasion led by those leviathans . . . and stopped it cold. If any of the people in this room hadn't grasped what that meant before, they did now.

He manipulated his remote, and the image was replaced by another, about the same size but visibly different in detail.

"This is what we've designated the *Armageddon* class. It's primarily a gunboat tender. We've been aware for some time that the Bugs' gunboats are significantly larger than ordinary auxiliaries, so internal boat bays can't accommodate them. Rather, they're carried externally, using these racks." He used a light pencil to indicate the hull features. "The class has twenty-five of them. At the same time, as you can see from the armament specs, it also carries enough force beams to make it formidable at close range. And, like the *Awesome* class, it has a version refitted with command datalink."

LeBlanc could read his listeners' minds without difficulty. They were trying to imagine going up at close range against a battle-line with that many force beams—the deadly application of tractor/presser beam technology that overstressed the molecular bonds of matter at a distance—especially when the ships mounting those beams had the capacity these had to soak up punishment. And they were contemplating the fact that fighting that way was only this class's *secondary* function.

Without comment, he brought up a third image.

"Finally, this is the *Aegis* class. It also carries twenty-five gunboats. But it's primarily a command ship, with less ship-to-ship armament but—as you can see—*very* tough defenses."

He dismissed the holo imagery and faced his very subdued audience.

"In addition to information on these new ship classes, we've been able to glean something even more important: a new insight into the nature of the enemy we're fighting. As you all know, such knowledge has been in extremely short supply throughout the war. I'll now turn the briefing over to Lieutenant Sanders, who initially grasped the significance of the data we were seeing and subsequently developed the theory he'll be presenting."

As a lieutenant who'd only recently shed the chrysalis of j.g.-hood, Sanders was easily the most junior officer in the room. It didn't seem to bother him in the least as he got jauntily to his feet and accepted the remote from LeBlanc. What *did* bring a small frown to his face was that the audience had come unfocused, dissolving into little clusters from which rose the worried buzz of discussion concerning the Bug monitors. Quite simply, a lieutenant wasn't inherently important enough to be taken seriously, much less to command their attention.

Sanders smiled lazily, like a man who knew just the solution to a dilemma. He touched the remote, and where the images of the monitors had floated there appeared . . . something else.

The radially symmetrical being bore neither relation nor resemblance to any Terran lifeform. But the six upward-angled limbs surrounding and supporting the central pod, the whole covered with coarse black hair, made it easy to see why the term "arachnid" had been applied. Those limbs rose to pronounced "knuckles" well above the central pod before angling downward once more, and two other limbs ended in "hands" of four mutually opposable "fingers," while above the eight limbs were eight stalked eyes, evenly spaced around the pod's circumference. And if all that hadn't been sufficient to show that this thing had evolved from nothing that ever lived on Old Terra, there was the mouth—a wide gash low in the body-pod, filled with lampreylike rows of teeth and lined with wiggling tentacles. Everyone present knew what those tentacles were for: to hold living prey immobilized for ingestion.

The discordant buzzing of many unfocused conversations ceased. Instead, a single low sound, below the level of verbalization, arose from the room in general. That sound was like a single musical note sounded by a whole orchestra of instruments simultaneously, for while the mode of expression varied with species and temperament, the overall tone was uniform. A Terran dog, laying its ears back and growling low in its throat, couldn't have been any less ambiguous.

*All right, Kevin,* LeBlanc thought desperately in his young subordinate's direction. *That'll do. You've got their undivided attention.*

But Sanders knew what he was doing.

"The face of the enemy, ladies and gentlemen," he announced rather theatrically. Then he switched off the holographic Bug and continued in a more matter-of-fact tone. "Unfortunately, what his face—and the rest of him—looks like is just about *all* we've ever known about him. That, and the fact that I should be saying *it* rather than *him*, because contrary to an early misconception, the Bugs are either neuter workers and warriors, or hermaphroditic breeders. Every attempt to communicate with them has been an abject failure. It's not even clear that they *could* communicate with us if they wanted to. We assume, in the absence of any plausible alternative, that they're exclusively telepathic. We've captured mountains of electronically stored records—none of which has ever been made to yield an iota of intelligible output. We know nothing about their society, their government, their objectives—"

"Their objectives," Sky Marshal Ellen MacGregor cut in, "seem to be crystal clear." She was a Scot of the "old black breed" and her dark-brown eyes held none of the liquidity of similarly colored eyes from warmer climes. They were like chips of black ice, and Sanders had the grace to look abashed under their level, frigid weight.

"True, Sky Marshal, at least as viewed from our perspective," he agreed. "But we haven't had a clue as to how they're organized—until now."

That sent a rustle of interest through the audience, and he went on.

"I must emphasize that a 'clue' is *all* we've got even now. But our analysis of the Bug wreckage has led us to the conclusion that there are different . . . 'subsets' among the Bugs."

"What does that mean?" Pederson demanded.

"Simply this, Admiral: the ship classes we've long since identified, as well as the new monitors, can actually be subdivided into five groupings based on differences in construction."

"But," Fleet Speaker Noraku protested in his race's *basso profundissimo* but quite intelligible Standard English, "there are always *some* differences within a class. No two ships are truly identical." His face—unsettlingly humanlike despite its gray skin, broad nose, and double eyelids—looked perplexed, and he shifted his massive hexapedal form on the saddlelike couch that served the Gorm as a chair.

"Granted, Fleet Speaker. But we're not talking about slight variations or upgradings here. Rather, we're looking at different construction *techniques*, too pronounced to be accidents—especially since they're not random, but fall into five definite patterns. In other words, there are four or five sources of Bug warships, all of them working from the same blueprints, but each with its own idea as to how those blueprints should be translated into actual hardware.

"The details of the analysis that led us to this conclusion will be made available for your perusal. We can't say whether these sources of ship construction represent different systems or clusters of systems within a more or less decentralized Bug empire, or autonomous Bug star nations acting in alliance, or . . . something else. So, for the time being, we're assigning the convenience-label 'Home Hive' to each of them, with a number that was arbitrarily assigned as the distinctive construction technique was identified. Is assigned, I should say, given that the identification effort is an ongoing process, since we can't be certain there aren't still more of them out there."

Raymond Prescott sat up straighter, and spoke as much to himself as to Sanders. "So the system that the warp line from Zephrain leads to . . ."

"That's occurred to us, Admiral. The massive high-level energy emissions from that system's inhabited worlds, and the density of drive fields around them, clearly indicate a major industrial center. We would be very surprised if it wasn't one of the home hives. We're not in a position just yet to speculate as to which one it is. But, as you no doubt recall, the Bug system at the end of the Romulus Chain that Commodore Braun's survey flotilla discovered—and was ambushed in—at the very start of the war was also quite obviously a major center of population and industry. Presumably, it's supplied the bulk of the ships we've faced on that front. And, now that we know what to look for in the wreckage Admiral Murakuma retrieved after the Fourth Battle of Justin, we're prepared to go on record and identify it as Home Hive Five."

There was a thoughtful silence as they all assimilated what this whippersnapper had told them. It might not be much, but it was the first hint of detail or texture in what had been a featureless cliff-wall of menace and mystery. Kthaara allowed them to consider it for a moment, then spoke.

"Thank you, gentlemen," he said to the intelligence officers, then turned back to the gathering as a whole. "And now, we will adjourn, as we all have an early start ahead of us tomorrow." The word tomorrow was conventional usage. Actually, it would be nighttime. But none of the Allied races was accustomed to a day nearly as long as this double-planet system's sixty-one-hour rotation around its components' center of mass.

The meeting broke up, and the room began to empty. Sanders finished clearing the display from the holo system and stood up and spoke over his shoulder.

"Well, Sir, shall we—?"

Once again, he became aware that his boss wasn't listening to him. He turned around.

Among the scurrying figures still remaining, one was standing quite still. From across the room, Vanessa Murakuma held LeBlanc's eyes.

Sanders sighed, gathered up his things, and departed, whistling softly.

Murakuma and LeBlanc approached each other slowly, oblivious to anyone else. They paused within a few feet, but didn't touch—they still weren't entirely alone in the room.

"How are you?" she asked tentatively.

"Hanging in there . . . Sir." LeBlanc said, and gestured towards the row of French doors that lined one end of the room. Wordlessly, they went out onto the terrace. The nano-fabric of their black-and-silver uniforms adjusted its "weave" against the winter chill so automatically that neither of them even noticed.

The building, which the planetary government of Nova Terra had placed at the disposal of the Grand Allied Joint Staff, crowned a low cliff overlooking the Cerulean Ocean to the west. The ocean extended around the globe in that direction, covering the opposite hemisphere where the permanent tidal bulge created by the companion planet Eden submerged all but a few scattered chains of islands, including New Atlantis, where LeBlanc's intelligence outfit had its isolated digs.

He leaned on the balustrade and gazed westward. Alpha Centauri A hung at its protracted afternoon, but the clouds had rolled in to cover it, and there was a low rumble of distant thunder. Heavy weather coming, he thought with a small fraction of his mind, while the rest of it sought to organize his thoughts. Finally, he turned to meet Murakuma's gaze, which had never left him.

"Have you had a chance to see Nobiki?" he began lamely. Murakuma's older daughter was serving with Alpha Centauri Skywatch. LeBlanc hadn't actually spoken to her in over two months, however, and looking at the mother he felt a sudden pang of guilt over the neglect of his semiofficial uncle's duties to the daughter.

"No." Murakuma shook her head unsteadily. "I hope to manage

while I'm here. She and I have a lot of talking to do." Her eyes flickered for just a moment. "Especially about Fujiko."

LeBlanc savored the sensation of having put his foot in it up to mid-thigh.

There was no excuse. He'd just been thinking of the lost Survey Flotilla 19 earlier, and he'd allowed himself to forget that Vanessa's younger daughter had been one of those who'd vanished tracelessly into the darkness with it. He should have remembered. Should never have let himself forget the night Nobiki, despite the reserve of her upbringing, had wept for her sister on his shoulder. Perhaps it was the very pain of that memory which explained his failure to recall it now, but that was only the reason, not an excuse for it. No, there was no excuse—so he made none.

Instead, he started over. "I've missed you," he managed.

"And I you," she whispered. His heart leapt, but the accumulated hurt of many months would not be denied.

"You haven't answered my letters in a while," he got out in a very level voice, and she gestured vaguely.

"I've been . . . occupied."

"Occupied? With *what*, out there at Justin?"

The instant it was out of his mouth, he realized it had been precisely the wrong thing to say. Her eyes flared with green flame.

"Oh, nothing, of course! Just wait for the Bug offensive that never comes, and—"

"Vanessa, I'm sorry! I didn't mean that!" He shook his head, cursing himself for timing his maladroitnesses so close together. There were only three points of contact between the Alliance and the Bugs: the Romulus Chain, the Klean Chain, and Alpha Centauri. There would be a fourth once the Zephrain offensive finally began, but until then only those three existed . . . and LeBlanc knew most of the human race prayed nightly to God that it would stay that way.

"Look," he said after a very brief moment, "I know you're running a third of this war! Maybe you're bored, but it's thanks to *you* that it's been so quiet for so long out there. The very fact that you're covering the Justin System, and that you kicked the butts the Bugs haven't got out of it—"

"Yes. So I can still look down at that planet and all its ghosts, and wonder whether they'd still be alive if I'd done . . . something different."

All at once, LeBlanc understood. He remembered the day her Marine landing force had reported the hideous death toll on

Justin. The virtual annihilation—the *consumption*—of the millions of civilians the TFN—and, especially, its commander, Admiral Vanessa Murakuma—had been responsible for defending. The civilians they hadn't been able to defend, because if they'd stood to fight in their defense, they would have died and left the *billions* of civilians behind them unprotected.

It wasn't proper procedure for an intelligence officer of the TFN to hold his admiral in his arms while she sobbed her heartbroken grief and guilt, but "proper procedure" hadn't been very important to him just then.

"So you think you've been left in command of a stalemated front as a kind of exile?" he said quietly. "Because people blame you for the losses on Justin?" He took a deep breath. "Listen Vanessa: *nobody* blames you for that, except possibly yourself. You couldn't have prevented what happened there, and you know it. Hell, I've already told you all this in person! *No one* could have—and at least most of the people who died went down fighting because of the weapons and the advisors *you* left them. And, I might point out, if you hadn't retaken the system, the Bugs would still be occupying it. And we all know what *that* would mean!"

"Yes, yes," she muttered, and turned her back, turning away from both LeBlanc and that to which he was alluding. Ever since Ivan Antonov had entered the Anderson Two System and discovered the planet that had been named Harnah, the human race had lived with the knowledge that there were worse things than genocide.

The first grim lesson in that awareness had come over a communications link to an occupied planet from some forever unknown reporter's camera. The horrifying footage that anonymous witness to atrocity had recorded had been humanity's first hint that their utterly unknown, implacably advancing foes were, like the Orions, carnivores. But that same footage had also revealed that that was the Bugs' *only* point of similarity to the Orions, for they preferred their prey living . . . and human children were precisely the right size.

That had been horror enough for anyone. By itself, it had been enough to wrack Vanessa with guilt—indeed, to consume the entire human race with guilt and terror alike. Yet even that had paled beside what Second Fleet had discovered upon Harnah, where the local Bug population had fed upon vast herds of the domesticated animals who'd once built their own flourishing civilization ... and who clung still to the broken fragments of that culture even in the shadow of the hideous predators who battened upon them.

And that, too, Vanessa Murakuma's heroic stand had stopped short of the millions upon millions of human beings who lived in and beyond the Romulous Chain.

"Yes," she repeated dully, gazing westward at the Cerulean Ocean. "I know all that—at least with my forebrain. But even if the Navy doesn't blame me, maybe they think I'm ... burned out." She laughed harshly. "Sometimes *I* wonder if I am."

"Being bored isn't the same as being burned out."

"Maybe not. But still, I've made up my mind; I'm going to request a transfer, to take part in the Zephrain offensive."

"*What?* But Vanessa, that's already locked in. Raymond Prescott and Zhaarnak'telmasa are—"

"Oh, I'm not expecting to command it. I know I won't get another shot at command of a fleet. I just want to *do* something, in some capacity. You may be right that being burned out is one thing and being bored is another, but the fact remains that, at a minimum, I *am* bored."

"You're not going to get any sympathy from most combat veterans. They *like* being bored!" The corners of Murakuma's mouth quirked upward, and a ghost of the old jade twinkle arose in her eyes. LeBlanc pressed his advantage. "And as for being burned out ... do you really think they'd leave a burned-out admiral in command of forces that've been built up to the level yours have?"

Her head began to nod, as though acting on its own, but then her innate self-honesty stopped the gesture. Whatever else she might think, she had to admit that Fifth Fleet had been reinforced to a size that amply justified the presence of a full admiral as CO. And she'd been able to use the time to shake that massive force down into a smoothly functioning whole, its parts commanded by flag officers she understood and trusted.

"Yes, you're right of course. And you haven't told me anything I didn't already know. So ..." She turned to face him, smiling, and the old Vanessa Murakuma was back. "So why do I feel so much better?"

"Sometimes you can know something and still need to hear it from someone else. Especially from someone who ..." He didn't continue, nor was there any need for him to.

The raw ocean breeze had driven everyone else inside, leaving them alone on the terrace. As he took her hands in his, the weather finally fulfilled its promise with a gust of wind and a spatter of rain, and waves began to hiss and crash against the base of the cliff.

"I suppose we'd better get inside," Murakuma suggested.

"Yeah." LeBlanc nodded. "Uh, I've been assigned temporary quarters here. They're not far."

Moving as one, they turned away from the balustrade and, for a while, left the storm behind.

# CHAPTER TWO
## Forging the Sword

The VIP Navy shuttle drifted slowly through space. Although it was far larger than the cutters which normally played deep space taxi for the TFN's flag officers, it remained less than a minnow beside the looming bulk of the ship it had come here to see.

The trip wasn't really necessary, of course. Every one of the high-ranked officers aboard the shuttle, human, Orion, Ophiuchi, and Gorm alike, had seen the titanic hull time and again in holographic displays and on briefing room screens. By now, any one of them could have recited the design philosophy behind the vessel and even the major specifics of its armament. And yet, despite that, the trip *had* been necessary. These officers worked every day of their lives with electronically processed data, but there were still times when they had to see with their own eyes, touch with their own hands, to truly believe what the reports and briefings told them.

*And this*, Oscar Pederson told himself, *is one of those times.*

The shuttle was luxuriously equipped, as befitted the craft assigned to Pederson in his role as CO of Alpha Centauri Sky-watch, but the quality of its fittings wasn't the reason it was here today. No, like the four other shuttles keeping formation upon it, it had been chosen for its passenger capacity. Even with all five of them, it was going to take at least six trips to transport all of the rubbernecking admirals (or their other-species equivalents) who wanted to see the gleaming alloy reality.

*Horatio Spruance*, the first monitor ever commissioned by the Terran Federation Navy, was a mountain beyond the transparent viewport. Pederson was no stranger to huge artificial constructions.

The vast majority of the major space stations serving the Federation's inhabited planets were even larger. Of course, all but a tiny fraction of each of those space stations was devoted to commerce, freight, repairs, passenger transfers . . . anything and everything other than the deadly weapons of war. Still, the massive OWP from which he commanded the Centauri System's fixed defenses certainly was armed, and it was actually larger than *Spruance*. But there was a major difference even there, for that orbital weapons platform was designed to stay exactly where it was. It was, as its very name suggested, a fixed weapons platform, a fortress, armed and armored to fight to the death at need in *defense* of a specific planet or warp point.

*Horatio Spruance* wasn't. This menacing mountain of missile launchers and beam projectors was designed for mobility. It wasn't designed to defend, but rather to project power. It floated there, looming like a titan over the construction ships and the suited yard workers clustered about it like microbes as they worked around the clock to put the finishing touches upon it. And a titan was precisely what it was . . . or perhaps that hopelessly overused cliche 'juggernaut' truly applied in this case. Slow and cumbersome compared to any other warship ever built, even a superdreadnought, it was also twice as large and powerful as that same superdreadnought.

*And she's also a more conservative design than I really would have liked,* Pederson admitted to himself. *Balancing long-range and short-range weaponry has saved the Navy's ass more than once. And there's definitely something to be said for having something to shoot at an enemy who manages to get to any range of your ship, instead of limiting yourself to one ideal "design" engagement range. But it may just be that this time the Bugs had a better idea what they were about than we do. A six-ship battlegroup of ships this size could throw down one hell of a weight of fire if they were all pure missile designs.*

Of course, he could hardly complain that no one had asked his opinion, because BuShips had done just that. In fact, they'd solicited design suggestions from every Fortress Command system CO in the entire Federation, as well as the Battle Fleet flag officers who would actually take those designs into combat. And, to be perfectly fair, they'd incorporated quite a few of the Fortress Command suggestions. And, again, to be perfectly fair, even without a pure missile design, a battlegroup of *Horatio Spruances* would still be able to pump out an awesome quantity of missile fire.

*It's just that, good as they are, they could have been so much better . . . if we'd only had time,* he told himself.

He sighed quietly as the shuttle drifted around one flank of the behemoth he and his fellows had come to see. Lord Khiniak stood just to Pederson's left, and the Terran admiral smothered a smile as he heard a soft, rustling purr from the Tabby fleet commander. It wasn't easy to strangle that smile, either, because Pederson had become enough of a "Tabby expert" to recognize the Orion equivalent of his own sigh, and he knew exactly what had produced it.

Lord Khiniak, too, regretted the desperate haste with which the *Spruance* design—and that of her Orion counterparts—had been finalized. But not, of course, for quite the same reasons. It wasn't the missiles which could have been crammed into the design that *he* missed; it was the fighter bays.

Vanessa Murakuma had also heard Lord Khiniak's sigh, and she was actually forced to turn away to hide her own expression as she recognized Pederson's struggle not to smile. It would never do to give in to the most unprofessional giggle threatening her own self-control, but she knew precisely what the Fortress Command admiral was thinking. She hadn't personally discussed design concepts with Third Fleet's commander, but she didn't really need to, for Lord Khiniak was a regular contributor to the *Heearnow Salkiarno Naushaanii.*

Although her tone deafness had always prevented her from understanding spoken Orion, she was completely fluent in the written forms of both High and Middle Orion—a fluency she'd acquired in no small part to follow the Khanate's military journals in their original forms. As a result, she knew that Lord Khiniak was a highly respected (despite a certain iconoclastic streak) commentator in the *Heearnow Salkiarno Naushaanii*'s pages. Yet even though the functional equivalent of the *Federation Naval Institute Journal* could wax just as contentious on matters of strategy and force projection concepts as its Terran counterpart, the *Heearnow*'s articles and editorials were far less fractious on an operational or tactical level, for the Orion Navy had no doubts at all about the proper tactical mix for its fleet units.

The arguments in favor of that tactical mix were impeccably logical and occasionally downright brilliant, yet in the end, all that rationality was the handmaid of cultural imperatives so deep-seated that they might as well be instinctual. That was as true for Terrans as for Tabbies, of course, but the Orion honor code of *Farshalah'kiah*—"the Warrior's Way"—required the individual warrior to risk his pelt in personal combat and had come over the centuries to enshrine an unhesitating commitment to the attack. Even when forced to assume the strategic defense, an Orion automatically looked for a way to seize the *tactical* offense. *Cover your six* was a Terran idiom that did not translate well into the Tongue of Tongues. When humans had first met them, the Tabbies had fought in swarms of dinky ships, although even then there'd been no technological barrier to constructing a smaller number of more capable and better protected ones—like the ships with which the unpleasantly hairless, severely outnumbered aliens from Terra had defeated them. In the end, they'd been forced to accept a similar design theory, even if they'd done so kicking and screaming the entire way. If they'd wanted a fleet which stood a chance in combat, they'd had no option but to match the combat capability of their opponents, because the disparity in effectiveness had meant that there'd simply been no other choice.

Until, that was, the Rigelians had introduced the single-seat strikefighter and restored individualism to space war. It might be going a bit far to argue, as some TFN officers occasionally did, that the Tabbies were actually *grateful* to the Rigelians (who, after all, had cherished their own genocidal notions where Orions and humans alike were concerned). Yet there was no denying that the KON had never been truly happy until the fighter gave its warriors back their souls. Ever since ISW 3, all their capital ships had featured integral fighter squadrons, despite the inefficiency involved in designing launch bays and all of their associated support hardware into ships that weren't purpose-built carriers. Show them a ship even bigger than the superdreadnoughts they'd never really liked anyway, and their reaction was totally predictable: *By Valkha, imagine how many* fighters *something that size could carry!* And they were disposed to see the bright side of whatever tactical models rationalized that predisposition.

Pederson, on the other hand, had never belonged to the TFN's strikefighter enthusiasts. *His* idea of a proper warp point assault ship leaned much more heavily towards missile launchers and beam weapons protected by the heaviest possible shields and armor, and he couldn't quite conceal his skepticism over the Tabby ideal, although the crusty old fire-eater was obviously doing his manful best.

"A most impressive vessel," Lord Khiniak said now, and despite her tone deafness, Murakuma thought she detected a certain sly amusement in the angle of the fang's ears and the tilt of his head as he glanced sidelong at Pederson. It was hard to be sure without the body language cues, especially since her earbug was tied into the translating software of the shipyard building *Spruance*, and this particular package had a particularly irritating, nasal atonality. "Of course, it will not be possible to realize the full potential of a military hull of this size until the carrier version reaches production. As a fighter platform capable of surviving long enough in a warp point assault to carry its fighters through and then launch them, it will make it possible for us to—"

"Yes," Pederson interrupted just a tad briskly. "We've all seen the specifications for your *Shernaku* class, Great Fang. Ninety-six fighters . . . very impressive. But it will be a while before it can be put into production." At least the Fortress Command admiral was too tactful to add, *In Terran yards*, although Murakuma suspected it had been a near thing. "And to be honest, there are some modifications *I'd* like to see in the *Spruance* design, myself. But we don't really have the latitude to experiment with the initial classes. You must admit that given the pressure to get our own monitors into production as quickly as possible, more conservative designs must have priority. In fact, you *have* admitted it, with the other two classes you've shown us. Those are balanced designs, and—"

"We don't need to go into that at the moment," Ellen MacGregor cut in.

As Sky Marshal she was completely familiar with the design features of all of the Allied monitor designs. Like Pederson, she would really have preferred a somewhat greater degree of specialization in the Terran designs, but the Fortress Command admiral was quite correct about the time pressure. BuShips had decided—with her own not entirely enthusiastic support—that it was more important to go with tried and proven hardware and weapons mixes which could be put into production in the shortest possible time rather than to waste months the Grand Alliance might well not have in trying to come up with the perfect design before they even laid the first ship down. In fact, the *Spruance* design had been frozen within three months of Pesthouse's disastrous conclusion, with construction commencing exactly fifty-nine days after the design was sealed.

*Which let us set a new all-time record for the speed with which any TFN ship has ever moved from concept to construction . . . much less something like* this *one*, she reminded herself. And at least the designers had been given two additional months to work on the *Howard Anderson* class which was the command ship equivalent of the *Horatio Spruances*. That had paid substantial dividends in the final design, and without setting it back *too* badly.

*And then there's the "escort" design*, she thought in something very like a gloating mental tone. BuShips was still arguing internally over what class name to assign to the MTE design, but that was perfectly all right with MacGregor. The bookmakers were putting their money on the *Hannah Avram* class, but what mattered to the Sky Marshal was what the ships would be capable of, not what they would be named. She'd argued for years that it was a waste of fire control capacity to fill one or more of the datalink slots in a battlegroup with some little dipshit light cruiser. Using up that much command and control capacity on a dedicated anti-fighter/anti-missile platform that small (and lightly armed) had made absolutely no sense with battleship and superdreadnought battlegroups . . . and it made even less with these things. Stripping out the *Spruance*-class's capital missile launchers and heavy beam projectors had allowed the new design to cram in a huge number of standard missile launchers and point defense clusters. The clouds of counter missiles it could put out ought to put a crimp into any Bug missile salvo—even one from one of their own monitor battlegroups! And the first mob of Bug kamikazes which tried to swarm one of them was going to get a most unpleasant surprise, as well. Not to mention the fact that it would be a monster in ship-to-ship combat once the engagement range dropped into the standard missile envelope.

Satisfying as that thought was, however, MacGregor wasn't about to dwell on it at the moment. The MTE design, in particular, represented a triumph for BuShips and the Corporate World shipyards, which had not only produced it in record time, but had actually found ways to bring it to the construction stage without dislocating the building plans for the *Spruance* or *Anderson* class ships. No one else in the explored Galaxy could have pulled that off . . . and she wasn't about to trust Oscar's uncharacteristic attack of diplomacy to keep him from mentioning that the Orion "generalist" monitor designs were lower-tech than their Terran counterparts, or that their keels hadn't even been laid yet.

"The diversity of our design philosophies," she went on, with a carefully tight-lipped, tooth-hiding smile at Lord Khiniak, "is one of the Alliance's strengths. With our various races bringing their unique viewpoints and insights to bear on the problem, our chances of arriving at the optimal weapons mix are maximized."

Murakuma was impressed. *Damn, but she's gotten good at that sort of thing since becoming Sky Marshal! Bet she's even learned how to deal with those* svolochy *in the Legislative Assembly.* She smiled to herself, realizing she'd thought the Russian word for "scum"—one of Ivan Antonov's milder epithets for politicians. But then the smile quickly died. It was too painful, recalling the living legend who'd accompanied her as she'd blasted her way back into the Justin System. Hannah Avram, then Sky Marshal, had torn a strip off her for letting the Chairman of the Grand Allied Joint Chiefs of Staff put his superannuated ass at risk like that, and . . . But, no. That memory also hurt too much.

"Are there any other specific features of the design which any of you would like to observe more closely before we return to Nova Terra?" MacGregor asked, bringing her back to the present. No one replied, although one or two of the oh-so-senior flag officers aboard the shuttle gazed through the viewports with the wistful expressions of children hovering on the brink of playing hookey for just a *little* longer. If MacGregor noticed, she gave no sign, and the shuttle turned away from the drifting ship it had come to observe.

A quiet murmur of conversation filled the passenger compartment, but Murakuma leaned back in her comfortable seat and closed her eyes, projecting an unmistakable image of deep thoughtfulness. It wasn't really that she wanted to avoid the Ophiuchi vice admiral who was her seat mate. It was only that she had something else entirely on her mind, and—

A soft, musical chime sounded in her earbug, and she stiffened in her seat as she recognized the priority of the attention signal.

"Admiral Murakuma," a respectful voice from the shipyard com center told her over the private channel, "the Chairman of the Joint Chiefs of Staff extends his compliments and asks to see you in his office as soon as convenient upon your return to Nova Terra."

Murakuma's heart began to race a little faster as she pulled out her personal communicator and tapped in an acknowledgment of the politely phrased order. Then she leaned back once more, turning her head to gaze out the viewport at the glittering jewel box of the stars while her mind raced.

*Already? I hadn't expected any action on it so soon. Is that a good sign, or a bad one?*

It was a question she couldn't answer . . . not that she didn't keep trying to all the way back to the planet.

As the receptionist ushered her into Kthaara'zarthan's office, she saw that he had a human-style desk and chairs, although the piled cushions of ordinary Orion domestic furnishings were in evidence elsewhere. Behind that desk was a large eastward-facing window, and this was a sunny morning. Silhouetted against the glare, she could see that the Chairman already had two visitors, and as she advanced across the expanse of carpet, one of them—human, male, rather on the short side—rose from his chair.

"Ah, welcome, Ahhdmiraaaal Muhrakhuuuuma," Ktharaa greeted her via her earbug. "I assume you have met Fang Zhaarnak' and Fang Pressssssscottt."

"Only briefly, Sir." She examined the two, especially the human, to whom Kthaara, like every other Tabby, always referred by the Orion form of his rank title.

She'd heard stories about how much of Raymond Prescott was prosthetics by now, but he'd adjusted to it so well that no one would ever notice. And although his hair was iron-gray, with white streaks radiating back from the temples, he didn't look prematurely aged, as one might have expected. Not, that was, until one looked closely at his hazel eyes.

He had, presumably, risen in deference to her as a wearer of the Lion of Terra. But there was really little to choose between them in that regard, she thought, gazing at a certain blue-and-gold ribbon nestled among the rest of the fruit salad on his chest. The TFN had had to design that one hastily, for the Orions didn't use ribbons to represent decorations, and no one had ever expected a human to be awarded the *Ithyrra'doi'khanhaku*. Both of the only two non-Orions in history who'd won it had been Gorm, and the assumption had been that no TFN officer would ever find himself in a position where even the possibility of his receiving it might arise.

Until, that was, Raymond Prescott and a xenophobic, human-hating bigot named Zhaarnak'diaano had been thrown together in the defense of the inhabited twin planets of the Orion system of Alowan and the multibillion Orions civilians beyond it. Their combined forces had been, if anything, even more brutally outnumbered than her own had been in the Romulus Chain, but somehow—by dint of what sacrifices she doubted anyone who hadn't been there would ever truly understand—they'd held. Not only that, but they'd actually *counterattacked*, against vastly superior forces, and retaken the Telmasa System . . . which had saved yet another billion and a half Orions. In the process, Prescott had left one arm behind him forever; Zhaarnak'diaano had become Zhaarnak'telmasa, the first *Khanhaku* Telmasa and the ultimate first father of the proud warrior clan whose name would forever preserve the honor of the battle he'd fought; and both of them had received the *Ithyrra'doi'khanhaku*. Among other things.

"I've been hoping to talk to you at greater length, Admiral Prescott," she said extending her hand. "I wanted to tell you personally how instrumental your brother's scouting mission in the Justin System was. It was also one of the most amazing displays of nerve I've ever seen."

Prescott smiled at her.

"Andrew's always been the daredevil of the family. I'm the more cautious type—"

"So we have all noticed," Zhaarnak interjected dryly.

"But I must admit, he excelled himself with *that* stunt," Prescott continued with a brief smile at his *vilkshatha* brother. "Volunteering to stay behind in Justin when you'd withdrawn to Sarasota was nervy enough. But lying with his engines shut down so he would have been dead meat if the Bugs had happened onto him. . . !"

Prescott shook his head and chuckled, but Murakuma nodded back much more seriously.

"True, he would have been unable to maneuver if he'd been caught. But his ship's lack of emissions was probably the very thing that prevented him *from* being caught. We'd given him up for lost when we didn't hear from *Daikyou* for a month. But when he finally risked sending a courier drone through, the information he sent back was absolutely crucial."

"Yes," Prescott agreed in a more sober tone. "As I understand, that information made your attack back into the system possible. So it was fortunate for several thousand of Justin's citizens that . . ."

The look on Murakuma's face brought Prescott to a puzzled halt. What could have bothered her about an allusion to the Justin Raid and the thousands of refugees she'd managed to pluck from the jaws—literally—of death in one of her most renowned exploits? After all, it wasn't as if anyone blamed her for the civilians who *hadn't* been retrieved. God and Howard Anderson together couldn't have gotten them *all* out.

After a moment, Murakuma's expression smoothed out, and she spoke quietly.

"Indeed. I couldn't have been happier when he received the accelerated promotion to commodore I'd recommended. I was only sorry to lose him."

"Let me take this opportunity to thank you for that recommendation," Prescott said, relieved to be moving on past whatever ghost he'd unwittingly awakened to flit across Murakuma's path. "Since then, he's really found his niche as a 'gunslinger' over in Survey Command."

"Confidentially," Kthaara put in, "Sky Maaarshaaal Maaac-Gregggorr has informed me that he is on the short list for yet another promotion. Which reminds me of the reason I asked the three of you here."

Even Murakuma recognized Kthaara's getting-down-to-business tone, and she and Prescott both took their seats.

"This concerns the projected Zephrain offensive," Kthaara began. He actually pronounced it as *Zaaia'pharaan*, the name assigned by the system's Orion discoverers. But Murakuma's mind automatically rendered it into the form used by the humans to whom the Khanate had ceded it. And her heart leapt.

If she showed any outward sign, Kthaara gave no indication of having noticed.

"First of all," he continued, "I want to reaffirm my commitment to commencing the operation as soon as possible, despite the risks involved in resuming the offensive before our monitors are ready. There is no real need for me to recapitulate those risks, of course, as they have been aired quite thoroughly by Human politicians." Tufted ears flicked briefly in Orion amusement, and Murakuma knew the sable-furred Tabby was hearing a rumbling string of Russian obscenities as clearly as though Ivan Antonov had been in the room. "And, to be fair, many of my own race also shrink from the prospect of exposing the population of the Rehfrak System, only one warp transit from Zephrain, to the possibility of a monitor-led counterattack. However, I and the rest of the Joint Chiefs are convinced that these risks are outweighed by the need for us to regain the initiative as quickly as possible. And—" a significant pause "—I am authorized to tell you that the *Khana'khanaaeee* has accepted our view of the matter, and commanded full participation by his fleets."

All three of his listeners abruptly sat up straighter.

Humans, on first hearing the title of the Orion ruler, had

immediately shortened it to *Khan*, and dubbed his domain *Khan-ate*. Orions like Kthaara who knew their human history weren't quite sure how to take this. But they had to admit that the associations weren't altogether unfair when applied to a polity which, in its expansionist period before the First Interstellar War, had been given to practices such as "demonstration" nuclear strikes on inhabited planets. And the nomenclature was appropriate in another way as well: the Khan was an absolute monarch, his power restrained only by the ultimate and almost-never-invoked sanction of removal by the *Khanhath'vilkshathaaeee*, the "Caste of Assassins." To Orions, democracy was just one more manifestation of human eccentricity—or silliness, as most of them had better manners than to say. If Kthaara had sold the plan to his imperial relative, then that settled that as far as the Khanate was concerned.

Zhaarnak gave a low, humming growl.

"Personally, I hope they do counterattack with monitors!" He turned hastily to his human *vilkshatha* brother. "Oh, yes, Raaymmonnd, I know. The building projects in Zephrain have required the establishment of a substantial Human population on the habitable planet, I forget the name they have given it—"

"Xanadu," Prescott supplied.

"—and I do not ignore the potential danger to them. But consider: since we ceded it to you Humans, you have fortified Zephrain with orbital fortresses and minefields until it is almost as strongly held as this system. If you and First Fang MaaacGregggorr could butcher them here, then we can butcher them there! And their losses in monitors here have forced them to relinquish the initiative ever since."

"That's just inference," Murakuma put in. "We can't be sure that's why they haven't mounted any new offensive operations."

"But it makes sense," Zhaarnak insisted. "We ourselves are confirming how expensive monitors are, and how long it takes to construct them. We still have no idea of the size of the enemy's industrial base—not even your Cub of the Khan Saaanderzzz claims to know that. But surely *no one* can continue to lose monitors in wholesale lots indefinitely without feeling the loss!"

Kthaara smiled at the fiery younger Orion.

"There is much in what you say, Zhaarnak'telmasa. And these very considerations were among those which led the Strategy Board to conclude that the risk of a counteroffensive was an acceptable one. As for actually seeking to *lure* the Bugs into a counteroffensive . . ." For the second time that morning, Murakuma heard the rustling Orion sigh. "Such a suggestion is a political impossibility, whatever you—or *anyone*—may think of its merits. So I suggest that you put it from your mind."

"Of course, Lord Talphon," Zhaarnak said in a perceptibly smaller voice.

"And now," Kthaara resumed briskly, "I have certain announcements to make." He looked from Prescott to Zhaarnak and back again. "When the Zephrain offensive was initially discussed, it was assumed that Eeevaahn'zarthan—Ahhdmiraaaal Antaanaaav, I meant to say—would command Sixth Fleet personally, with you, Fang Presssssscottt, as his second in command, and you, Lord Telmasa, as the carrier commander. More recently, the assumption has been that each of you two would simply move up one rung, with Fang Presssssscottt in command." His gaze remained on Prescott and intensified, though his voice remained expressionless. "I have now decided, with Sky Marshaaal MaaacGregggorr's concurrence, that you, Zhaarnak'telmasa, will command Sixth Fleet, with you as deputy . . . Raaymmonnd'presssssscott-telmasa."

In the ensuing silence, Murakuma reflected that Kthaara's use of the Orion form of Prescott's name carried a large and complex freight of meaning.

In the first place, by calling attention to a human's membership in a *vilkshatha* bonding, he was reminding everyone present that he himself had initiated the first such bond. If there was one sin of which any court under Heaven would have to acquit Kthaara'zarthan, it was Orion chauvinism. On another level, he was reminding these two of their own brotherhood, and the relative insignificance of which rectangle within an organization chart each of them occupied.

Despite that, Zhaarnak's discomfort would have been obvious even to a human less familiar with Orions than Murakuma.

"Ah, Lord Talphon, this . . . unexpected announcement places me in a most awkward position. I cannot in good conscience—"

Prescott turned to him with a lazy smile which was pure Orion and spoke in the Tongue of Tongues.

"Say nothing more, brother. It is of no consequence. And besides, Lord Talphon is right." He turned back to Kthaara. "I understand entirely. For the present, we humans are a *zeget* recovering from a deep wound. If the offensive is to commence without delay, as we all agree it should, then the *Zheeerlikou'valkhannaiee* must bear the brunt of it. Under the circumstances, it is appropriate that—"

"No member of my race would object to serving under *you*," Zhaarnak protested hotly. "And if one did, he would hear from me! Besides," he looked away ever so briefly, then met his *vilk-shatha* brother's eyes levelly once more, and his voice was quieter, yet even more intense, "you have already served under me once when the command should have been yours."

If Prescott appreciated the irony of this outburst from an Orion who, a scant two years before, had been noted for his anti-human bigotry, he gave no sign. His smile remained that of a drowsy carnivore.

"Still, Zhaarnak, it is better this way. Does it truly matter, when brother serves with brother, which of them holds the *official* command? And as for what passed between us in Alowan—" He gave a completely human-style shrug. "The circumstances were very different, and had things worked out other than as they did, neither you nor I would be here to have this argument!"

Murakuma sat very still, almost as if by doing so she could avoid drawing attention to herself. So, there'd been a kernel of truth in the rumors after all. She'd wondered at the time . . . even as she'd wondered if in Prescott's position she could have willingly served under an officer junior to her when she also knew that that officer hated her species. But it seemed that the stories which insisted Prescott had done just that—more, had done it without ever even allowing Zhaarnak to suspect that he was senior to the Orion—had been true after all.

Now that same Orion sat gazing at that same human with troubled eyes and ears half-flattened in dismay. Prescott gave him a few more seconds, then chuckled.

"Do not be so concerned, Zhaarnak. We humans will not always have to rely on our allies to take the lead. Maybe our roles will reverse again before the war is over. But either way . . . may our claws strike deep, brother!"

Kthaara let a silence heavy with unspoken meaning continue for a human heartbeat, then spoke in a quiet voice.

"Thank you, Raaymmonnd'presssssscott-telmasa. You react as I thought you would." That said, he turned to Murakuma, his briskness back. "Also on the subject of the command structure for the Zephrain offensive, Ahhdmiraaaal Muhrakhuuuuma . . ."

"Yes, Sir?" Despite her resolve to maintain tight self-control, she leaned forward expectantly.

"Each of the Alliance's constituent navies retains full control of its own personnel assignments. However, postings of high-level flag officers to crucial positions are a matter of concern to the entire Alliance. So Sky Marshaaal MaaacGregggorr and I have taken counsel regarding your request to be relieved of Fifth Fleet's command and reassigned." He held her green eyes with his amber ones and spoke with a surgeon's merciful swiftness. "Your request is denied."

It was as if the trapdoor of a gallows dropped open under Murakuma's feet, leaving her hanging in a limitless, empty darkness which held only one thought: *So they do blame me for all those civilian dead in Justin. It will never end. . . .*

"With all due respect, Sir," she heard her own voice, from what seemed a great distance, "I'd like to hear that from Sky Marshal MacGregor."

"That is your right. But before you exercise it, I ask that you hear me out. You see, I would like nothing better than to have you take an active role in the Zephrain operation."

In Murakuma's current mental state, it took a moment for the seeming paradox to register. "Uh . . . Sir?"

"Unfortunately, I need you precisely where you are, for at least three reasons. First, the Strategy Board considers it a very real possibility that our attack from Zephrain will provoke the Bahgs into launching an attack of their own elsewhere, in an effort to regain the strategic initiative. If they should do so, their options will be limited to those points at which we have contact with them. One of those is here, and they are aware of how strongly held this system is." Kthaara showed a flash of teeth. "*Very* well aware. So we think them more likely to attempt one of the other two: Justin or Shanak. And to show their hand in Shanak would be to give up one of their most priceless strategic assets, the location of their closed warp point in that system."

"You mean—?"

"Precisely. We believe Justin is the more likely target. And, on the basis of your past record, we want *you* there in case this does happen."

"But, with all due respect, Sir, no counterattack may ever be launched. We've been wrong about their intentions before—inevitably, given the alienness of their mentality."

"Truth. And we hope we *are* wrong in this case. Because, you see, my second reason is that we hope to use Fifth Fleet as a kind of training command, cycling officers through it before sending them to fronts where we are on the offensive." Kthaara held up a clawed hand in a forestalling gesture which, like so many others, he'd picked up in the course of decades among humans. "Do not think of this as a negative reflection on your capabilities as a combat commander. Quite the contrary. The very reason we intend to 'raid' Fifth Fleet for command personnel is that we have been deeply impressed by the way you have molded your subordinates into a superbly organized command team. We want to expose as many officers as possible to that same seasoning experience.

"Third—and I believe you will find this reason more congenial than the others—we are already thinking ahead to possible uses of Fifth Fleet in offensive operations."

"But, Sir, the Bug defenses at the other end of the Justin/K-45 warp line—"

"Do not misunderstand me. We have no intention of throwing away your command in a useless, headlong attack into such concentrated firepower. Rather, I refer to offensive operations *elsewhere*." Kthaara steepled his fingers in yet another human gesture, although the clicking together of his claws somewhat spoiled the effect. "When the static warp point defenses in Justin—the minefields, the orbital fortresses and fighter platforms, and all the rest—have been built up to a level which allows us to be confident of their ability to stop any attack unaided, we intend to deploy Fifth Fleet elsewhere, to exploit the opportunities for future offensives that we hope the Zephrain operation will open up."

"I hope not to be within earshot of Lord Khiniak when he hears that Fifth Fleet, and not Third Fleet, is earmarked to go on the offensive," Zhaarnak remarked. "Permanent hearing loss could result."

"But," Prescott argued, this time in Standard English, "after he's given vent to his feelings, surely he'll see why it has to be that way. We can't pull our mobile forces out of Shanak, because they're all we've got there. In that system, the threat is an invasion through a closed warp point. A fixed defense is workable in Justin only because we know where its warp points are."

"Not that he would really enjoy conducting such a fixed defense even if it were possible," Kthaara opined. "The prospect of a war of movement should reconcile him to continuing to mount guard against a possible Bahg attack on Shanak. But at any rate," he continued, turning back to Murakuma, "Fifth Fleet's destiny is otherwise. And when it assumes the offensive, I cannot imagine anyone but yourself in command of it. Fifth Fleet is your *farshatok*." The Orion word had no precise Standard English translation;

it encased the term "command," but like so many other Orion words, it implied considerably more. "So, to repeat, I need you where you are. The Alliance needs you there."

*What an old smoothie,* Murakuma thought. But she was smiling as she thought it.

For a split second, Murakuma wondered who the no-longer-really-young commander was who stood up as she entered the room. *Where's Nobiki? She was supposed to meet me here, and she knows we've only got a few minutes.*

But then the commander turned to face her, and it crashed into her.

*My God! It can't be! But,* came the small, hurt thought, *it's been so long. . . .*

"Hello . . . Sir." Nobiki Murakuma gave a smile that was too much like Tadeoshi's.

"Hello, Nobiki." *Yes, she's always looked more like Tadeoshi than . . .* The thought broke off, flinching away in familiar pain from a name she dared not let herself think of overmuch. Once again, she felt the ambiguity that shouldn't have been there, not when setting eyes on her older daughter for the first time in years. *But how are we going to get through this conversation? How do we dance around the subject of Fujiko?*

They hugged—this was a small private meeting room Murakuma had managed to reserve, and formality could be discarded.

"I can't stay," she began, a shade too chattily. "The final conference has been moved up, and afterwards I have to leave at once. I'm just glad you were able to get in from Skywatch without any delays."

"Yes, I was lucky." The smile grew tremulous. "This is always the way it seems to be, isn't it?"

"Well, at least this time we're able to . . ." Murakuma's voice trailed off. She began to feel a little desperate, but Nobiki drew a deep breath and faced her squarely.

"I don't suppose you've heard anything new? I mean, anything you can tell me."

*She's braver than I am,* Murakuma thought. She felt ashamed because her daughter had been the one to broach the subject, and even more ashamed for being relieved by it.

"No, Nobiki. You know I'd tell you anything I knew. But no, there's absolutely nothing. And there won't be, either. We can't let ourselves cherish any false hopes in that regard, and I think we both know it. It's been well over a year now—and SF 19 departed through a warp point that was almost certainly one the Bugs came through to trap Second Fleet. It must have been like running into an avalanche. And even if they'd somehow survived that, or evaded the attack force by hiding in cloak, the Bugs still hold that warp point." She shook her head, and her nostrils flared as it was her turn to inhale deeply. "No," she repeated very, very quietly. "Even if they'd survived, there's no road home."

"They could have pressed on, and tried to find another way back to Alliance space," Nobiki said, as though fulfilling a duty to say it.

"The odds against that are incalculable." Murakuma drew another breath and closed her eyes briefly, fiercely against the pain. "And even if that was what they tried, they must have run out of supplies by now. No. If that's the alternative, I hope they ... I hope Fujiko found a clean death instead." *There, I've spoken the name. And it doesn't help.* "We have to go on with our lives."

"Whatever that means, nowadays." Nobiki wasn't going to cry—Murakuma was certain of that. But, looking at her daughter's face, she was certain the tears would come later. "What kind of lives are we—are any humans—looking at?"

"No lives at all—if the Bugs win!" Murakuma stopped and reined herself in. "I'm sorry. I didn't mean to snap at you. But we've got to carry on as if this war *is* going to have an end. Otherwise, Fujiko's—" She caught herself. "Otherwise, what happened to Fujiko will have no meaning."

"Meaning? I'm not even sure what that is anymore."

For an instant, the barrier of years wavered and Murakuma glimpsed the girl Nobiki had been. And, with renewed sadness, she knew she was having trouble calling to mind all the details of that girl's face, because she'd never seen enough of it at any one given age.

"I wasn't much of a mother to you, Nobiki," she said softly. "And it's too late now."

As though with one will, they embraced, and held each other tightly for a long time. And still neither mother nor daughter could let herself weep.

The weather was a little better, but otherwise the terrace overlooking the Cerulean Ocean was unchanged since the other time they'd stood at the balustrade, as though the intervening weeks had never happened.

"Where did all the time go?" Vanessa Murakuma wondered aloud.

The round of conferences and briefings was over, the concluding session had just broken up in the same hall where the opening one had taken place, and a line of skimmers waited outside to take the various commanders to the spacefield. Murakuma really had no business pausing to step through the French doors. But she'd known who would be there.

"It wasn't long enough, was it?" Marcus LeBlanc's question was as rhetorical as hers had been, and he interposed his body between her and any prying eyes that might still be lingering inside the doors as he took her hands in his.

"How many years will it be this time?" he asked.

"I don't know." She drew a deep, unsteady breath. "I've got to go."

"Yes, I suppose you do." But he made no move to release her hands, even though they'd said the real goodbyes the previous night, in his quarters. "Vanessa, someday this will all be over. And then—"

"No, Marcus." Her headshake sent her red hair swirling, and she withdrew her hands. "We can't talk about it now. The war's going to last for a long time, and a lot more people are going to be killed, and neither of us is immune, any more than—" She jarred to a halt.

"Any more than Tadeoshi was," LeBlanc finished for her quietly, and she dropped her eyes.

"I've been through it once, Marcus," she said in a voice the wind almost carried away into inaudibility. "Twice now, with Fujiko, and this time there's not even the closure of a confirmed death. And Nobiki. All the years, all the wasted, empty years when she—and Fujiko—were little girls, growing into wonderful young women my career never gave me time to know."

She gazed out over the wind-whipped ocean, and more than the wind alone put tears in the corners of her eyes.

"I've lost too much, failed too many people," she told the man who knew she loved him. "I can't risk it again. Oh, I suppose you're risking it any time you let yourself care about someone. But now, with what's coming in this war . . . No, I can't take *that* kind of risk again. And I won't let you take it, either."

She took his hands once more, with a grip stronger than she looked capable of, then released them and was gone.

# CHAPTER THREE
## "I am become Death . . ."

There was a long moment of brittle tension on the flag bridge after TFNS *Dnepr* emerged from the indescribable grav surge of warp transit. But then surrounding space began to crackle with tight-beam communications, and Commander Amos Chung, the staff intelligence officer, turned eagerly to Raymond Prescott. His face, despite its Eurasian features, was light-complexioned—his homeworld of Ragnarok had a dim sun—and now it was flushed with excitement.

"It worked, Admiral! We're in, and there's no indication that they've detected our emergence!"

"Thank you, Commander," Prescott acknowledged quietly. He didn't really want to deflate the spook's enthusiasm, but at times like this the most useful thing an admiral could do was project an air of imperturbable calm and confidence.

And, after all, it wasn't so surprising that Sixth Fleet had succeeded in entering the Bug system undetected. This was a closed warp point of which the Bugs knew nothing, little more than a light-hour out from the primary. The "vastness of space" was a hideously overused cliche, and like most cliches it tended to be acknowledged and then promptly forgotten. People looked at charts that showed the warp network as lines connecting dots, and they tended to lose sight of the fact that each of those dots was a whole planetary system—hundreds of thousands of cubic light-minutes of nothingness in which to hide.

Besides, Sixth Fleet had spent over a year stealthily probing this system with second-generation recon drones from Zephrain. They knew all about the scanner buoys that formed a shell around the system's primary at a radius of ten light-minutes. Armed with a careful analysis of the sensor emissions of those buoys, Commander Jacques Bichet, Raymond Prescott's operations officer, and his assistants had been able to rig a "white-noise" jammer to cripple their effectiveness. Coupled with the Allies' shipboard ECM, that ought to enable them to emerge unnoticed from this closed warp point and vanish back into cloak before anyone noticed them.

It was the kind of trick that could only work once. But evidently it had worked this time. So far, the long-awaited Zephrain offensive had succeeded in defying the great god Murphy.

Prescott stood up from his command chair and stepped to the system-scale holo display, already alight with downloaded sensor data. As per convention, the system primary was a yellow dot at the center of the plot. Just as conventionally, Prescott's mind superimposed the traditional clock face on the display. Warp points generally, though not always, occurred in the same plane as a system's planetary orbits, which was convenient from any number of standpoints. The closed warp point through which they'd emerged was on a bearing of about five o'clock from the primary. No other warp points were shown—they hadn't exactly been able to do any surveying here—but planets were. The innermost orbited at a six-light-minute radius, but at a current bearing of two o'clock. The second planet's ten-light-minute-radius orbit had brought it to four o'clock. An asteroid belt ringed the primary at fourteen light-minutes, and other planets orbited still further out, but Prescott ignored them. Planets I and II were the ones Sixth Fleet had come to kill.

A display on this scale wasn't set up to show individual ships or other astronomical minutiae. In a detailed display, those two planets would have glowed white hot from the neutrino emissions of high-energy technology and nestled in cocoons of encircling drive fields. This system was almost certainly one of the nodes of Bug population and industry that Marcus LeBlanc's smartass protégé Sanders had dubbed "home hives." It would have been a primary target even in a normal war—and this war had ceased to be normal when the nature of the enemy had become apparent. The Alliance had reissued General Directive Eighteen, which had lain dormant since the war with the Rigelians. For the second time in history, the Federation and its allies had sentenced an intelligent species to death.

*If, in fact, an "intelligent species" is what we're dealing with here.*

Prescott dismissed the fruitless speculation from his mind. The question of whether the Bugs were truly sentient, or merely possessed something that masqueraded as sentience well enough to produce interstellar-level technology, was one which had long exercised minds that he freely admitted were more capable than his own. It wasn't something he needed to concern himself with at the moment, anyway, and he turned to the tactical display.

One ship after another was materializing at the warp point, their icons blinking into existence on the plot, and as Sixth Fleet arrived, it shook down into its component parts. Prescott smiled as he watched. He and Zhaarnak had had four months since they'd returned from Alpha Centauri to Zephrain. They'd used the time for exhaustive training exercises, and it showed as the swarming lights on the display arranged themselves with a smoothness that had to be understood to be appreciated.

Sixth Fleet comprised two task forces. Prescott commanded TF 61, which held the bulk of the Fleet's heavy battle-line muscle: forty-two superdreadnoughts, including both *Dnepr* and *Celmithyr'theaarnouw*, from which Zhaarnak was flying his lights, accompanied by six battleships, ten fleet carriers, and twenty-four battlecruisers. Force Leader Shaaldaar led TF 62, and the stolidly competent Gorm's command was further divided into two task groups. TG 62.1, under 106th Least Fang of the Khan Meearnow'raaalphaa, had twelve fast superdreadnoughts and three battlecruisers, but those were mainly to escort its formidable array of fighter platforms: twenty-seven attack carriers and twelve fleet carriers. In support was Vice Admiral Janet Parkway, with the forty-eight battlecruisers that made up TG 62.2.

It was strictly a fighting fleet. There was no fleet train of supply ships, no repair or hospital ships, no assault transports full of Marines. None were needed, for the objective was not conquest and occupation, but pure destruction.

As he watched, Shaaldaar implemented the plan that had been contingent on an undetected emergence from warp. He detached ten of Meearnow's fleet carriers and temporarily assigned them to Parkway, with orders to stand ready to take out all the buoys within scanner range of the warp point the instant the main force was detected. Prescott gazed closely at TG 62.2's icons as they maneuvered away from the warp point and headed in-system to reach attack range of the buoys. And to be sure Parkway was far enough from the warp point when her carriers eventually launched that their fighters, whose drive field emissions couldn't be cloaked, didn't give away its location. They were Terran carriers—*Borsoi-B*-class ships—and they were more dangerous than they looked. Prescott had lobbied and fought and finally achieved his goal of putting two squadrons of Ophiuchi fighters aboard every TFN carrier in Sixth Fleet. The two species were sufficiently similar biologically that putting both aboard the same ship didn't complicate the supply picture *too* much . . . and those fighter squadrons were well worth whatever inconvenience they did cause. The ancestral proto-Ophiuchi might have traded the ability to fly for the ability to use tools, but renunciation of the innate sense of relative motion in three dimensions that went with natural flight hadn't been included in the evolutionary deal. Even the Orions grudgingly admitted that they were the best fighter pilots in the known galaxy.

As Parkway's reinforced command peeled off, a call from the com station interrupted Prescott's thoughts.

"Signal from the flagship, Admiral."

"Acknowledge."

Zhaarnak looked sternly out from the com screen. This, Prescott knew, wasn't a personal message—Shaaldaar and Meearnow were also in the hookup. It was the Fleet commander, not the *vilkshatha* brother, who spoke.

"As our arrival has gone undetected, Sixth Fleet will execute Contingency Plan Alpha."

Having delivered an order that his chief of staff could have passed along, Zhaarnak drew a breath and continued.

"In the past, the Alliance's offensive operations have only been in the nature of counterattacks, usually to liberate systems of our own. Even Operation Pessthouse, our first venture into enemy space, was in response to the enemy's appearance in the Alpha Centauri System. But now, for the first time, we are striking at one of the enemy's home systems, from a quarter he has no reason to suspect poses any threat whatever to him. We possess complete strategic and tactical surprise. If we fail to capitalize upon those advantages, the fault will be ours alone, and we will have no excuse. However, I am confident that everyone in Sixth Fleet will live up to the unique opportunity that is ours."

Zhaarnak's eyes flashed yellow hell, and his speech grew more idiomatic.

"This is the beginning of the *vilknarma*, the blood-balance. The ghosts of Kliean, and of the Human systems which have fallen to these *chofaki*, fly with us, shrieking for vengeance!" He let a heartbeat of silence reverberate while the lethal fire of Orion retribution blazed in his eyes, and then he repeated the prosaic command, "Execute Contingency Plan Alpha," and signed off.

Prescott passed the command formally to his chief of staff. Captain Anthea Mandagalla nodded in reply, her eyes gleaming in her night-black face, and began firing off the long prepared orders—in space warfare, a flag officer's chief of staff performed many of the functions that the wet navies of old had assigned to his flag captain.

TF 61 shaped a course for its objective of Planet I, a flat hyperbola with the local sun to port. TF 62—meaning, in practical terms, TG 62.1—moved outward toward Planet II.

"It's Fleet Flag again, Sir," the com officer called out.

"Put him on." Prescott smiled. He had a feeling this one *was* going to be a personal message.

"Did I overdo it, Raaymmonnd?" Zhaarnak asked, looking unwontedly abashed. For all the sincerity of his emotions, his last speech had been most un-Orion, for the Tabby ideal eschewed volubility, and the more important the occasion, the fewer words they were likely to use. But Sixth Fleet's personnel—and flag officers—were drawn from every one of the Alliance's races, and Zhaarnak had tried to adjust his words accordingly. Which, unfortunately, had carried him into unknown territory.

"Not at all," Prescott assured him. "Although some might take exception to your use of the word *chofaki*." The Orion term, delicately translated into Standard English as "dirt-eaters," meant beings so lost to any sense of honor as to be inherently incapable of ever being amenable to the code of *Farshalah'kiah*. It was also one of the two or three deadliest insults in the Tongue of Tongues. "Lord Talphon, for example, claims that using it for the Bugs is like debasing currency, as it pays them too much honor."

"I lack his way with words. I must use the insults I know, even at the risk of diluting them." Zhaarnak straightened. "At any rate, the time for words is past. We will speak to the Bahgs in another language when we arrive at Planet I."

Prescott nodded, and his eyes strayed to the view-forward display. A tiny bluish dot was slightly less tiny than it had been when they'd begun accelerating.

✧          ✧          ✧

All expanses of deep space are essentially alike, even when they possess a sun for a reference point. It takes the curved solidity of a nearby planet to create a sensation of *place*. Depending on the planet, it can also create a psychological atmosphere.

The planet ahead did that, in spades.

Prescott told himself that there were perfectly good practical reasons to view that waxing sphere with apprehension. Planet I was the primary population center of this system, and its defenses were commensurate with its importance: twenty-six orbital fortresses, each a quarter again as massive as a monitor and able to fill all the hull capacity a monitor had to devote to its engines with weaponry and defenses. But the space station that was the centerpiece of the orbital installations dwarfed even those fortresses to insignificance. They were like nondescript items of scrap metal left over when that titanic junk sculpture had been welded together.

But none of that accounted for the psychic aura that affected even the most insensitive. Planet I was a blue-and-white swirled marble, glowing with the colors of life against the silent ebon immensity of the endless vacuum. Prescott had seen that gorgeous affirmation of life more times in his career than he could possibly have counted, yet this time its very beauty only added to the surreal hideous reality his mind perceived beneath the reports of his eyes.

Space itself seemed to stink with the presence of billions upon billions of Bugs. Despite its familiar loveliness, it was all too easy to imagine that the planet itself was nothing more than an obscenely pullulating spherical mass of them. For this was one of the central tumors of the cancer that was eating the life out of the galaxy.

Prescott was bringing TF 61 as close to it as he dared. Shaaldaar, with faster ships and less distance to cover, had already placed TF 62 within easy fighter range of Planet II—a relatively cold, bleak place by human standards and less heavily populated than Planet I, but just as well defended. And now he, like Parkway, waited. There was no indication that the Bugs suspected the presence of any of them.

Zhaarnak checked in again.

"Is it time, Raaymmonnd?"

He was neither ordering nor nagging. But, as Fleet commander, he had a legitimate interest, for Shaaldaar and Parkway were to commence their attacks as soon as they detected Prescott's. In effect, the human would give the go-ahead signal for all of Sixth Fleet.

"Almost," Prescott replied. He was glad Zhaarnak's flagship was in TF 61's formation. They could carry on a conversation—which, as the sage Clarke had foretold, was impossible across even the least of interplanetary distances, whatever the capabilities of one's com equipment. If Prescott had been talking to Shaaldaar or Parkway, minutes would have elapsed between each question and answer.

The same time lag would apply to the energy signatures by which they would know he'd launched his assault. It was another factor that had to be taken into account. . . .

"Excuse me, Sir," Jacques Bichet interrupted his thoughts. "We're coming up on Point *Vilknarma.*"

"Yes, I see we are. In fact, I believe we're in a position to commence a countdown."

"Will do, Sir." The ops officer turned away and began giving orders, and Prescott looked back into the com screen.

"I'll have the countdown transmitted directly to *Celmithyr'theaarnouw*'s CIC," he told Zhaarnak. "I'll be giving the order to launch immediately after it reaches zero."

Zhaarnak gave a human nod and added the emphasis of his own race's affirmative ear flick. He spared a smile for the name Prescott had given to the point at which they would be too close to the planet ahead to have any realistic hope of remaining undetected. Then he signed off.

They reached Point *Vilknarma* and slid past it, and Prescott spoke one quiet word to Bichet.

"Execute," he said.

Long-prepared orders began to go out, and TF 61 responded with drilled-in smoothness.

Prescott's ten fleet carriers were Orion ships of the *Manihai* class. In accordance with Orion design philosophies, they were pure fighter platforms, with forty-two launching bays and little else. Now they flung half their fighters—two hundred ten new Terran-built F-4's, to which the Orion pilots had taken with predatory enthusiasm—toward the Bug orbital fortresses. The deadly, fleet little vessels streaked away, homing on their prey like so many barracuda flashing in to rend and tear at a school of sleeping killer whales, and the capital ships, all thought of concealment forgotten, roared along in their wakes.

Prescott watched the plot anxiously as the fighters neared their targets. The F-4's carried full loads of close-attack antimatter missiles, whose suicidally over-powered little drives built up such tremendous velocities in the course of their brief lives as to render them virtually immune to interception by point defense . . . but which also made them very short ranged on the standards of space warfare. The fragile fighters would have to get very close. Whether or not they could survive to do so all depended on how complete the surprise was.

As he watched, he saw that it was very complete indeed. He saw it even before Bichet turned from his and Chung's analysis of the incoming data.

"Admiral, those forts don't even have their shields up!" the ops officer exulted.

"So I see, Jacques."

Even as Prescott spoke, carefully keeping his matching exultation out of his voice, the fighters began to launch, and the fortresses began to die. Those warheads held only specks of antimatter, but they were striking naked metal, and their targets vanished in fireballs like short-lived suns. The intolerably brilliant flashes of fury in the visual display gouged at his optic nerve, even at this range and even through the display's filters, but he didn't look away. There was a hideous beauty to those lightning bolts of destruction, and something deep within him treasured the knowledge that thousands of Arachnids were dying at their hearts, like spiders trapped in so many candle flames.

Then the battle-line entered missile range of the space station, and Prescott made himself look away from the dying fortresses as he faced his second worry. How well would that station coordinate its fire with the as yet unknown defensive installations of the planet below? He had a bad moment as the computer traced a luminous dotted line around the schematic of the station, indicating that its shields had just come on-line. But as his capital ships' missiles went in, there was no point defense from the planet . . . nor even from the station. And, as detailed sensor readings began to come in and scroll up the plot's sidebar, he could see that the shields weren't state-of-the-art ones, either.

Chung didn't state the obvious, Prescott noted with approval—he was getting better. Instead, he merely offered a diffident observation.

"They must not have thought it was worthwhile to refit this station, Sir, since this is obviously one of their core systems—and therefore, by definition, not on the front lines."

"No doubt, Commander. Also . . ."

Prescott closed his mouth and didn't allow Chung's look of frank curiosity to tempt him into completing his thoughts aloud. *The losses they've suffered, between Operation Pesthouse and the Black Hole of Centauri, may have forced them to concentrate on starship construction, to the exclusion of upgrading their orbital installations.* No, this wasn't the time to float that concept.

Nor was it the time to be thinking of anything at all except the reports that poured in as the missiles reached the space station. With no point defense to thin out that onrushing wave front of death, the shields' level of sophistication hardly mattered. They flashed through a pyrotechnic display of energy absorption that a living eye—had it remained living and unblinded in such an environment—could barely have registered. Then they went down, and devastating explosions began to rock that titanic orbital construct with brimstone sledgehammers as antimatter met matter.

Each of TF 61's ships had flushed its external ordnance racks, and the tidal wave of massive capital ship missiles slammed lances of searing flame deep into the now unprotected alloy. But the station *was* titanic—so huge that its mass seemed to belie its obvious artificiality, for surely nothing so colossal could be an artifact. So huge that it could absorb a great deal of damage—even the kind of damage dealt out by antimatter warheads. A major portion of it lasted long enough to get its point defense on-line, and Prescott needed no specialist's analysis to see that his missile fire had suddenly become markedly less effective as fewer warheads evaded the active defenses long enough to strike their targets.

Well, there was a solution for that. A little unprecedented, but . . .

He turned to the intraship communicator in his command chair's armrest and spoke to *Dnepr*'s commanding officer. Certain things still lay in the province of the flag captain, especially where the leadership of the battle-line was concerned.

"Captain Turanoglu, you will proceed at maximum speed to beam-weapon range of the space station and . . . engage the enemy more closely."

Prescott couldn't be sure Turanoglu recognized the quote, which lay outside his cultural background. But the banditlike Turkish face showed no lack of understanding.

"Aye, aye, Sir!" he barked, and he'd barely cut the circuit before *Dnepr*, with the rest of TF 61's capital ships behind her, surged forward.

Mandagalla, Bichet, Chung, and everyone else near enough to have overheard the exchange stared at Prescott. He could understand why. Missiles, unlike directed-energy weapons, were equally destructive regardless of the range from which they were launched. And at missile range, the Allies' generally superior fire control and point defense had always given them the advantage. No Terran admiral had ever closed to within energy-weapon range of the Bugs if he could help it, and Prescott braced himself for a call from Zhaarnak.

None came. His *vilkshatha* brother was being as good as the word he'd given on Xanadu before they'd departed: TF 61 was Prescott's, and as fleet commander Zhaarnak would support to the hilt whatever decisions the human made. So the task force's capital ships swept onward in formation with *Dnepr*—including *Celmithyr'theaarnouw*, for Zhaarnak's body, as well as his honor, stood behind his promises.

They drew still closer, the space station swelled to gargantuan dimensions upon the visual display . . . and the stares of his staffers turned into looks of comprehension. The key words in Prescott's orders to Turanoglu had been *maximum speed*. It stood to reason that the Bugs, taken by surprise by the missile-storm and struggling to bring their systems on-line, would have given priority to their point defense. So, Prescott had reasoned, their anti-ship energy weapons might well still be silent. And so it proved, as his battle-line closed to point-blank range, pouring unanswered fire into the disintegrating mass of the flame-wracked station. The holocaust blazing against the serene blue and white backdrop of the planet TF 61 had come to kill doubled and redoubled as force beams, hetlasers, and the unstoppable focused stilettos of primary beams ripped and tore.

Yet even that unimaginable torrent of energy and the dreadful waves of antimatter warheads seemed insufficient to the task. The space station bucked and quivered as the carnage streaming from the capital ship gnats stinging and biting at it hammered home, yet *still* it survived. And as Prescott watched the plot's sidebars, he realized that his ships' sensors were detecting the first Ehrlicher emissions as somewhere inside that glaring ball of fury Bug warriors fought to bring their own surviving force beams and primaries into action.

"Admiral," Mandagalla reported in an awed voice, "our projected course will bring us within ninety *kilometers* of the station."

Prescott's mouth opened, then closed. *That can't be right*, had been his initial reaction. It simply didn't *sound* right. In space warfare, ranges weren't measured in kilometers!

But even at minimal magnification, the space station now filled much of the big viewscreen with its death agony. It was a spectacle none of them would ever forget. The Brobdingnagian structure burned, crumpled, collapsed in on itself, shed streamers of debris. Rippling waves of stroboscopic explosions ran across its shattered surface as a new volley of missiles, in uninterceptable sprint mode now that the range had dropped so low, struck home.

Then *Dnepr* was past, and the dying wreck was receding in the screen. Another superdreadnought followed in her wake, adding to the conflagration with force beams, lasers, and everything else that could be brought to bear.

And then, all at once, the uncaring computer calmly and automatically darkened the screen to spare its organic masters' vulnerable eyes. The space station had entered its final cataclysm, with a series of secondary explosions that blew the ruined hulk apart. When the view returned to normal, all that was left of Planet I's orbital defenses were drifting, glowing chunks of wreckage.

Prescott ignored the cheers and glanced at the chronometer. Less than twelve minutes had elapsed since he'd given the order to commence the attack. Shaaldaar at Planet II, and Parkway back in the vicinity of the warp point, would have detected his attack and commenced their own about two minutes ago. It was, of course, far too soon for any reports from them.

"Fleet Flag, Sir."

The com officer had barely spoken before Zhaarnak's face appeared, a mask of fierce exultation held grimly in check.

"Congratulations, Raaymmonnd! But let us not delude ourselves that this walkover will continue indefinitely."

"No. We achieved total surprise, beyond our wildest hopes. But it's wearing off. Have you looked at the sensor readouts from the planet in the last few seconds?"

Zhaarnak's eyes flicked to something outside the pickup's range, and a low growl escaped him.

The electronic indications of active point defense installations were winking into life all over the planet. And, like a fountain of tiny icons, two hundred and fifty ground-based gunboats were rising to the attack.

Prescott fired off a fresh series of orders. TF 61's battle-line had swung past the space station on a hyperbolic course which was now curving away from the planet, and he commanded it to continue on that heading, opening the range to the planet and forcing the gunboats to follow. With no other option, they accepted the stern chase he'd forced upon them. Even with their superior speed and maneuverability, the need to overtake from directly astern would slow their rate of closure considerably . . . and expose them to what he'd held in reserve for them.

The Orion fighters that had swept Planet I's skies clean of orbital fortresses were now back aboard their carriers, rearming. Even as they did so, the other half of those carriers' fighter complements roared out into the void. Once in free space, they jettisoned the external ordnance that they hadn't taken time to have offloaded in their launching bays. The close-range FRAMs with which they had been armed in preparation for attacks on the orbital defenses were too short-ranged to be truly effective against these new, smaller foes. Perhaps even worse, they lacked the reach to permit them to be fired from beyond the range of the fighter-killing AFHAWK missiles the gunboats could carry on their own external racks. If the Bug vessels had been properly configured to engage fighters, FRAMs would only degrade the maneuverability which might allow the strikefighters to survive within the Bugs' weapons envelope. And at least the F-4's integral heterodyned lasers would enable them to kill gunboats with lethal efficiency once they managed to close.

The Orion pilots screamed in to meet the gunboats head-on, and a hungry snarl of anticipation sounded over the com links as they realized that the Bug ground crews had been too surprised, too rushed, to arm them against fighters. The unexpectedness of the sudden, savage attack—and the need to get the gunboats launched before the Allies got around to taking out the ground bases from which they came—had left too little time to adjust what must have been standby armament loads. The gunboats had gotten off the ground with whatever ordnance they'd had on their racks when the attack came in . . . and none of that ordnance included AFHAWKs.

But as the onrushing gunboats and defending fighters interpenetrated and the killing began, it became apparent that what the Bugs were carrying was quite as bad as any AFHAWK might have been. Not for the fighter jocks, perhaps, but then the fighters weren't the gunboats' true targets anyway.

Prescott watched the suspicious ease with which his fighters clawed gunboats out of existence, and his jaw tightened. The

Bugs weren't really fighting back—they were just trying to break through. But breaking through sometimes required combat, and those observing the combat had an unpleasant surprise when a few fighters came in close and died in the blue-white novae of antimatter warheads.

"So the Bahgs have developed the close-attack antimatter missile." Zhaarnak was now in continuous com linkage with Prescott, and his voice was ashen.

"So they have," Prescott acknowledged. "But why should we be surprised? It was bound to come eventually."

"Truth. But perhaps a matter of greater immediate concern is the fact that they seem uninterested in using their new weapon against our fighters, except as a means to the end of breaking through to reach our battle-line."

Prescott instantly grasped the point. Zhaarnak had put two and two together: the Bugs' long-established indifference to individual survival, and their new possession of antimatter gunboat ordnance. Now the human admiral did the same sum and swung toward his ops officer and chief of staff.

"Anna! Warn all ships to stand by for suicide attacks!" he barked, and had it been possible, Anthea Mandagalla would have blanched.

"Aye, aye, Sir!"

Prescott turned back to the plot, and his anxiety eased somewhat. The Orion fighter pilots were slaughtering the gunboats too fast for the computer to keep the kill total up to date. The incandescent, strobing fireflies of gunboats, consumed by their own ordnance as hits from fighter lasers disrupted the warheads' magnetic containment fields, speckled the visual display like the dust of ground dragon's teeth. Only a handful of the Bugs survived at the heart of that furnace, but the few gunboats that got through proceeded to prove Zhaarnak a prophet. They made no attempt to fire at the capital ships. They merely screamed in to ram.

Of those few, fewer still reached their targets. The humans and Orions who crewed those targets' defensive weapons were, to say the least, highly motivated. But whenever a gunboat with a heavy load of antimatter-armed external ordnance did succeed in ramming a capital ship . . .

Prescott winced as the violence of those explosions registered on the sensors. A ship so ravaged, even if not destroyed outright, would almost certainly have to be abandoned and scuttled.

But as the last of those gunboats died, Prescott met Zhaarnak's eyes in the com screen, and neither needed to voice what they both knew. Planet I had no defenders left in space.

"And now," Zhaarnak said quietly, "we will carry out our orders and implement General Directive Eighteen."

*The gunboats raced ahead of the monitors and superdreadnoughts as the Fleet's units moved away from their station at the only warp point from which, it had been believed, this system need fear any threat. They had commenced the maneuver the moment their own sensors had detected the Enemy forces' announcement of their inexplicable presence with salvos of antimatter missiles.*

*Yet it had taken many minutes for the signatures of those missiles' detonation to cross the light-minutes to the Fleet, and it would take far longer than that for the Fleet to respond. By the time even the gunboats, at top speed, could hope to reach the system's two Worlds Which Must Be Defended—both of which were presently on the far side of the primary—those worlds would long since have come under direct attack. Clearly, losses were inevitable, despite all that the planetary defense centers might hope to achieve. Losses which must be considered very serious.*

*Unacceptable losses, in fact. For these were Worlds Which Must Be Defended.*

*The Fleet's ships' interiors were labyrinthine corridors and passages, forever dimly lit, filled only with the muffled scuttering of their eternally mute crews' feet and claws as they went about their tasks in silent efficiency. But now those interiors were filled with grinding, rasping noise and harshly acrid smoke of drive systems straining desperately against their safety envelopes to crowd on more speed.*

The Bugs, it seemed, didn't favor massively hardened one-to-a-continent dirtside installations like the TFN's Planetary Defense Centers. Instead, the planet's whole land surface was dotted with open-air point defense installations. But even though they might be unarmored, there were scores of them, and each of them was capable of putting up a massive umbrella of defensive fire against incoming missiles or fighters.

And they'd gotten that point defense on-line. That became clear when the first missile salvos went in.

Zhaarnak and Prescott looked at the readouts showing the tiny percentage of the initial salvo which had gotten through. Then they looked at each other in their respective com screens.

"The task force doesn't have enough expendable munitions to wear down anti-missile defenses of that density," Prescott said flatly.

"No," Zhaarnak agreed. "We would run out of missiles before making any impression. But . . . our fighter strength is almost intact."

At first, Prescott said nothing. He hated the thought of sending fighter pilots against that kind of point-defense fire. And, given the fact that TF 61's fighter pilots were Orions, it was possible that Zhaarnak hated it even more.

"I did not want to be the one to broach the suggestion," the human finally said in the Tongue of Tongues.

"I know. And I know why. But it has to be done." Steel entered Zhaarnak's voice, and it was the Commander of Sixth Fleet who spoke. "Rearm all the fighters with FRAMs—and with ECM pods, to maximize their survivability. And launch *all* of them. This is not the time to hold back reserves."

"Aye, aye, Sir," Prescott responded formally, and nodded to Commander Bichet. The ops officer had recognized what would be needed sooner than his admiral had made himself accept the necessity, and he'd worked up the required orders on his own initiative. Now they were transmitted, and more than four hundred fighters shot away toward the doomed planet's nightside.

It helped that the Bugs initially made the miscalculation of reserving their point defense fire for missiles. Perhaps they expected the fighters to be armed with standard, longer-ranged fighter missiles. Or perhaps they even believed that the fighter pilots were acting as decoys, trailing their coats to deceive the defenders into configuring their point defense to engage *them* instead of the battle-line's shipboard missiles in hopes of helping those missiles to sneak through. But then the defenders realized they were up against FRAMs, against which no tracking system could produce a targeting solution during their brief flight, and they began concentrating on the fighters that were launching those FRAMs.

A wave of flame washed through the Orion formation, pounding down upon it in a fiery surf of point defense lasers and AFHAWK missiles. It glared like a solar corona, high above the night-struck planetary surface, and forty-one fighters died in the first pass.

But despite that ten percent loss ratio, the remaining fighters put over two thousand antimatter warheads into the quadrant of Planet I which was their target on that pass.

The darkened surface erupted in a myriad pinpricks of dazzling brightness. From those that were ocean strikes, complex overlapping patterns of tsunami began to radiate, blasting across the planetary oceans at hundreds of kilometers per hour like the outriders of Armageddon. More explosions flashed and glared, leaping up in waves and clusters of brilliant devastation, and as he watched, a quotation rose to the surface of Raymond Prescott's mind. Not in its original form—classical Indian literature wasn't exactly his subject. No, he recalled it at second hand. Four centuries earlier, one of the fathers of the first primitive fission bomb, on seeing his brain child awake to apocalyptic life in the deserts of south-western North America, had whispered it aghast.

And now Raymond Prescott whispered it, as well.

"*I am become Death, the destroyer of worlds.*"

Amos Chung was close enough to hear.

"Uh . . . Sir?"

"Oh, nothing, Amos," Prescott said, without looking up from the display on which he was watching a quarter of a planet die. "Just a literary quote—a reference to Shiva, the Hindu god of death."

Chung was about to inquire further, but something in the computer readouts caught his eye and he bent closer to his own display. After a moment, he spoke.

"Admiral, something very odd is going on."

"Eh?" Prescott finally looked up from the visual display and frowned. The intelligence officer was visibly puzzled. "What are you talking about?"

"Sir, the computer analysis shows that, all of a sudden, there's been a dramatic degradation of the defensive fire from the *rest* of the planet. The percentage of our stuff that's getting through confirms it."

"What?" Prescott blinked, then glanced across at Bichet. "Jacques?"

"Strike reports from the follow-up squadrons confirm the same thing, Sir," the ops officer said. "And Amos is right—it does look like it's a planet-wide phenomenon . . . whatever 'it' is!"

"Put the material on my screen, Amos," Prescott said. Chung did so, and the admiral's eyebrows went up. "Hmm . . . maybe the planetary command center was in the quadrant we just hit, and we put a FRAM right on top of it."

"But, Sir, this seems to be more than just a case of losing the top-level brass. The fire from their individual installations has become wild and erratic. And besides," Chung went on, military formality falling by the wayside, as it often did when an intelligence specialist warmed to his subject, "it generally takes *time* for the effects of a loss of central command-and-control to percolate downward through a large organization. This was *abrupt!*"

Prescott studied the data. Everything Chung had said was true. And yet, something below the level of consciousness told him he shouldn't be as surprised as he was. Was there some connection he wasn't making . . . ?

Then it burst in his brain like a secondary explosion.

"Commodore Mandagalla! Order all capital ships to resume missile bombardment of the planet. And," he continued without a break, turning to the com station, "raise Fleet Flag."

"Actually, Sir," the com officer reported, "he's already calling us."

"Raaymmonnd," Zhaarnak began without preamble, "have you been observing—?"

"Yes! And I think I know what's happening." Prescott paused to organize his thoughts. "We've been assuming the Bugs are telepathic merely because that was the only way to account for their apparent lack of any *other* kind of communication. It's just been a working hypothesis. Now I think we've just proved it."

"I do not follow—" Zhaarnak began, and Prescott recognized Orion puzzlement in the unequal angles of his ears.

"Our fighter strike just killed God knows how many of them in the space of a few minutes," the human said urgently. "Every Bug on the planet—maybe in the entire system—must all be in some form of continuous telepathic linkage. The sudden deaths of that many of them disoriented the rest—sent them into a kind of psychic shock."

"But, on other occasions, we have inflicted high casualty rates on Bahg forces, and never observed anything like this among the survivors."

"It may be a matter of absolute numbers, not percentages. We've never killed this *many* of them before. And, to repeat, we killed them all *at once.*" Prescott drew a deep breath, protocol forgotten as completely as Chung had forgotten it. "Look, Zhaarnak, I'm just theorizing as I go along—blowing hot air out my rear end. But it's a theory that accounts for the observed facts!"

"Yes," the Orion said slowly, as he watched his own tactical display. TF 61's missiles were arrowing in through ineffectual point defense fire. "So it does. We can turn those data over to the specialists for analysis later. For now, continue to employ your task force in accordance with your instincts." Zhaarnak sat back with the calm that comes of irrevocable commitment to a course of action. "I only hope Force Leader Shaaldaar and Least Fang Meearnow are finding that this . . . phenomenon is system-wide in scale, not just planetary."

"Oh, yes." Prescott felt unaccustomedly sheepish. By now, Sixth Fleet's other elements would have reported to Zhaarnak. "What's the word from them and Janet?"

"Ahhdmiraaaal Paaarkwaaay has swept her assigned sector clean of sensor buoys. All of them which might have been able to track us to the warp point have definitely been destroyed. Indeed, she believes her fighters destroyed as many as a quarter of the total number of such buoys in this system, without encountering a single hostile unit."

"Good." The fleet's egress was clear . . . unless, of course, some cloaked picket ship managed to get close enough to shadow its withdrawal.

"As for Shaaldaar," Zhaarnak went on, "he faced orbital defenses around Planet II which had rather more warning than the ones here—their shields and point defense alike were functional when he struck. But he was also able to launch far heavier fighter strikes against them."

"That's one way to put it." TG 62.1, while it lacked Prescott's heavy battle-line, had three times as many fighters as TF 61.

"Least Fang Meearnow lost three percent of his fighter strength, but obliterated the orbital works. At last report, Force Leader Shaaldaar was ordering him to rearm his fighters and send them in against the planet. In fact, that assault should have commenced only shortly after your attack on this planet did in real-time."

Prescott said nothing. Instead, he thought of all those Terran and Ophiuchi and Orion fighter pilots in TG 62.1 and hoped his theory was right.

"All right, people," Lieutenant Commander Bruno Togliatti, CO of Strikefighter Squadron 94, operating off of the *Scylla*-class assault carrier TFNS *Wyvern*, said. "Don't get cocky! Whatever is going on, I'll have the ass of anybody I see relying on it. Until the last frigging Bug on that dirt ball is dead, we assume their defenses are at one hundred percent. So I want a tight formation maintained, and all standard tactical doctrines observed. Acknowledge!"

"Aye, aye, Sir," the pilots chorused, each from the cockpit of his or her F-4. Lieutenant (j.g.) Irma Sanchez answered up with the rest, but most of her attention was elsewhere. Some of it was on the planet looming ahead, with its white expanses of desert, its less extensive blue oceans, and its gleaming polar caps. But mostly she was seeing a night of horror, more than four years earlier.

She and Armand had been climate-engineering techs on a new colonization project at the far end of the Romulus Chain. The "colony" had been a drab five-thousand-person outpost, and Golan A II had been an oversized dingleberry misnamed a planet—and the two of them had never noticed, because they'd been together, and she'd been carrying their child.

Then the warships had appeared, the rumors of some horrific threat had begun to spread, and martial law had been imposed . . . along with an order to evacuate all pregnant women and all children under twelve to the warships of the scratch defense force, whose life systems could not support everyone.

She and Armand had said their goodbyes on the edge of the spacefield amid the chaos of that night—the sirens, the floodlights, the masses of bewildered human misery, and the Marines looming like death-gods in their powered combat armor. Then she'd gotten in line behind the Borisovs, a pleasant, harmless couple in Agronomics. Ludmilla had been on the verge of hysterics when her two-year-old had been taken from her, and Irma had yielded to a sudden impulse and promised to look after the child. She'd also pretended to believe the narcotic line the Marines were pushing—it was all only temporary, those left behind would be picked up later, more transports were on their way—while hating them for making her an accomplice in their lies.

After that, it had been a succession of overcrowded warships, almost equally overcrowded transports, and bleak refugee camps, always with Lydia Sergeyevna in tow. She'd been about to give birth in one of those camps when the word had spread, despite all ham-fisted efforts at censorship, of what had happened to the populations of the Bug-occupied worlds. That was when she'd finally broken down, which was doubtless why she'd lost the child who would have preserved something of her lover who now existed only as Bug digestive byproducts.

The therapists had finally put her mind back together. Afterwards, she'd done three things. She had legally adopted Lydochka. She had returned to her parents' home on Orphicon and left her daughter in their care. And then she'd gone to the nearest recruiting station.

She'd never thought much of the military, and she'd thought even less of it since that night on Golan A II. But if putting on a uniform was the only way she could assuage her need to do something—*anything*—then so be it.

She'd been prepared to push papers, or direct traffic, or shovel shit, if she could thereby free someone else to go kill Bugs. But for once, BuPers had gotten it right. Their tests had recognized in her the qualities of a natural strikefighter pilot—including, and most especially, motivation. She'd gone directly to the new combined OCS/fighter school at Brisbane, on Old Terra.

Wartime losses plus rapid Navy expansion had created a voracious need for fighter pilots. The result had been a radical de-emphasis of what the old-school types called "military polish" and certain others called "Mickey Mouse" without knowing the term's origin. An incandescently eager Irma had never appreciated that fact. But it still took time to train a fighter jock; and she did come to appreciate—later—that the seemingly eternal program had kept her at Brisbane too long to be shipped out for Operation Pesthouse.

"Attention Angel-Romeo-Seven!" The sharp voice in her earphones that snapped her back to the present belonged to Captain Dianne Hsiao, the task force *farshathkhanaak*. Unlike some of the older, broom-up-the-ass regulars she'd been forced to put up with, Irma didn't find it at all strange that the TFN had contaminated the pristine purity of its own operational doctrines by adopting a Tabby innovation. The title translated roughly as "lord of the war fist" (which Irma considered entirely too artsy-fartsy), but what it actually meant was that Hsiao was *the* senior fighter jock of the entire task force. She represented all of them at the task force staff level, she was in charge of their operational training and planning, and she chewed their asses when they screwed the pooch. But she also fought their battles against their own brass when that was necessary, too, and from what Irma had heard, she had a hell of a temper when it cut loose. No doubt all of that was important, but all that really mattered to Irma Sanchez, was that Hsiao was talking to *her* carrier's strikegroup now . . . and that the *farshathkhanaak* was the voice of command which would free her to kill.

"Angel-Romeo-Seven, execute Omega!" Hsiao's voice snapped now. "I say again, Execute Omega!"

"Follow me in!" Lieutenant Commander Bruno Togliatti, VF 94's CO, barked like a basso echo of Hsiao's soprano voice of doom, and the entire squadron rolled up behind him, put their noses down, and hit their drives. No detailed instructions were needed. They all knew the area of the planet they'd been assigned, and they all knew the standing orders to hit "targets of opportunity," meaning the dense concentrations of sensor returns that indicated Bug population centers.

The squadron followed Togliatti in, and presently Irma heard a thin whistle as her F-4 bit into the uppermost reaches of Planet II's atmosphere. The defensive fire was as sporadic and ineffectual as they'd heard. She didn't try to understand why—she merely dismissed it from her mind and concentrated on her heads-up display where her small tactical plot superimposed downloaded sensor readings on a scrolling map.

VF-94's target area rolled onto the HUD while missiles which should have torn bleeding holes in its ranks went wide or staggered and wove like drunkards and energy fire stabbed almost randomly into the heavens. Irma locked in her targeting solutions—or rather, instructed the F-4's narrowly specialized but highly effective computer to do so. In turn, it signaled her as she swept into launch range.

Her FRAMs flashed away, and as they screamed downward, she pulled up, vision graying as she went to full power and sought the reuniting formation. Ahead there were only the clean, uncaring stars . . . and Armand's face against them, smiling as she remembered him while her weapons shrieked downward at the same monsters who'd murdered him. She stared upward at the memory of the man she'd loved, and the memory of that love only made the anguish and loss—and hatred—burn even hotter at her core.

Behind and below her, bits of antimatter were released from their nonmaterial restraints and the planet rocked to energy releases beyond the dreams of any gods human minds had ever imagined. For an instant, an entire planetary quadrant was one vast, undifferentiated glare. Then as it faded, enormous fireballs were seen to swell, often touching each other and merging, growing until their tops flattened because they'd reached altitudes where there was insufficient air to superheat.

Irma became aware that the sound she was hearing as she stared down at that Valkyrie's-eye view of Hell was that of her own teeth, grinding together in a grimace of fulfilled hate.

"Out-fucking-standing, people!" Togliatti yelled. "If everybody did that well, we may not *need* a second strike!"

Irma felt like a kid who'd been told it might not be necessary to miss another day of school because of snow.

As it turned out, they *did* go back. Nevertheless, and despite having started their attack later, they finished it before TF 61 was done with Planet I.

Zhaarnak and Prescott didn't know that at first, of course, given the communications lag. What they did know, as they drew away from Planet I an hour and ten minutes after launching their first missile at it, was that they had killed at least ninety-five percent of its population outright, and that the few survivors were too irradiated to live long enough to experience nuclear winter on that dust-darkened surface.

They knew something else, as well. They knew that the Bug mobile forces they'd known must be somewhere in the system were sweeping down upon them.

The wavefront of gunboats had arrived in the vicinity of Planet I just as TF 61 departed. Far behind, but coming into sensor range, was a battle-line from Hell: thirty monitors, seventy super-dreadnoughts, and twenty-two battlecruisers, including gunboat tenders.

But whatever had rendered Planet I's groundside defenders so ineffectual was also infecting those ships. That had been obvious from the moment the gunboats were detected; Prescott hadn't needed Chung's prompting to recognize signs of confusion and disorder in that array. Zhaarnak had seen it, too, whatever doubts he might still have harbored about the "psychic shock" theory.

Now it was uppermost in their minds as they gazed into their respective plots at identical displays in which their task force and Shaaldaar's moved from Planets I and II respectively, on courses that converged to join TG 62.2 at the closed warp point whose location, Parkway firmly assured them, no Bug knew. They turned to their com screens and met each other's eyes.

"It has never been part of our plan to fight a fleet action here," Zhaarnak said. But his eyes kept flickering away from the pickup, and Prescott knew he was looking at the red icon of the disordered force pursuing them.

"No, it hasn't. And that plan was formulated even before we knew the Bugs had developed the FRAM."

"Truth," Zhaarnak admitted dutifully.

"Furthermore," Prescott continued, warming to his role as devil's advocate, "Admiral Parkway assures us she's eliminated all scanner buoys that could track us through the warp point, and her fighters can deal with any gunboats likely to get close enough to shadow us. And, of course, their battle-line can't possibly catch us, especially with those monitors to slow it down. In short, we can withdraw without compromising the warp point's location."

"As was our original plan," Zhaarnak finished for him. "And which will leave Zephrain completely secure."

"Lord Talphon *did* indicate that that was a high-priority consideration."

"So he did." Zhaarnak gave his *vilkshatha* brother a vaguely disappointed look. "I suppose it is, arguably, our duty to follow the course you are advocating," he said, but then his ears flew straight up in surprise as Prescott gave the human laugh he had learned not to misinterpret.

"Zhaarnak, the only thing I advocate is that we *take* them!"

Zhaarnak hadn't had Kthaara'zarthan's decades of familiarity with human mannerisms. Nevertheless, his lower jaw fell in a most human way and his ears flattened.

"But . . . after all that you have been saying—"

"I only wanted to get all the objections out on the table now. Look, Zhaarnak, we can wait for the intelligence experts' verdict on what's caused the Bugs to be so shaken up ever since our attack began. But for now, we know that, whatever the reason, the ships chasing us *are*. How often are we going to get a chance like this?"

"But, Raaymmonnd, there are thirty *monitors* out there!"

"Thirty monitors we can kill! Haven't we been arguing for months now that a lighter, faster battle-line with adequate fighter support can beat monitors if it's handled aggressively? Well this is our chance to prove it!"

"But we will give them a chance to pinpoint the location of the Zephrain warp point!"

"Granted. But we both know how strongly held Zephrain is. Those defenses can deal with anything that might get past us—not that I expect anything to."

Zhaarnak stared at him for a moment, then spoke with an obvious effort.

"Lord Talphon *did* say we were not to try to lure the Bahgs into a counterattack on Zephrain."

"Yes, he did, didn't he? I believe he called it a 'political impossibility.'" Prescott looked morose for a moment, then brightened. "But, strictly speaking, we're not actually 'luring' them, are we?" he asked, and Zhaarnak's amber eyes gleamed.

"No. Of course not. We are merely taking a calculated risk of revealing the warp point's location in order to seize a priceless strategic advantage and destroy a major enemy fleet. No reasonable person could adopt any other interpretation."

"Of course not." Prescott and Zhaarnak exchanged solemn nods, having talked each other into the conclusion they'd both wanted to reach from the first.

Fresh orders went out. The three elements of Sixth Fleet proceeded to their rendezvous, heavily cloaked and screened by a cloud of fighters. Then they completed their rendezvous . . . and Zhaarnak'telmasa, using fine-honed military skills to effectuate the instincts of a thousand generations of ancestors, turned on his pursuers.

And then something completely unexpected happened.

For only the second time in the war, a powerful Bug battle fleet—not a decoy like those in Operation Pesthouse—tried to refuse battle.

*It was hard—so hard—in their stunned disorientation. But the intelligences that controlled the Fleet knew they must avoid battle until they could function at something like their normal level.*

*Nothing like it had ever happened before. Never had a World Which Must Be Defended been seared clean in such a manner. So there had been no way to foresee its effects.*

*The Fleet had continued on its course towards the first stricken planet by sheer inertia, after that first stunning psychic impact, and the others that had followed in rapid succession. By the time it had arrived, the attackers had been departing. The obvious course of action—therefore the only course the Fleet was capable of adopting in its present state—had been to follow them across the system, seeking to determine the location of the closed warp point by which they had entered it.*

*But now the Enemy had reunited his various elements and was seeking battle. And the controlling minds had recovered sufficiently to realize they were in no condition to fight such a battle. They must avoid one until they could function at something like their normal capabilities.*

*Sluggishly, the Fleet gathered itself and began to turn away.*

✧   ✧   ✧

Sixth Fleet had the speed advantage, its command and control functions were unimpaired, and Zhaarnak'telmasa had no intention of letting the Bugs decline battle. They did their best to evade him, but in four days of relentless maneuvering, he'd finally brought them to bay.

Now he sat on *Celmithyr'theaarnouw*'s flag bridge and watched his plot as a tidal wave of fighter icons streaked towards the enemy. The diamond dust of the icons was a densely packed mass, belying the wide separations that even such small vessels required when traveling at such velocities in precise formations. Yet there was a greater truth to the illusion of density than to the reality of dispersion, for those light codes represented a maximum-effort strike from every carrier in his force. It was a solid mailed fist, driving straight down the throat of the Bug fleet.

Ophiuchi pilots from the TFN carriers went in first, blasting a way through the Bugs' gunboat screen with missiles, and the familiar eye-tearing fireballs of deep-space death began to flash and glare as the gunboats sought clumsily to intercept. Had it been possible for a warrior of the Khan to feel pity for such soulless *chofaki*, Zhaarnak would have felt it as he sensed the desperate, drunken effort with which the gunboats fought to protect the larger starships.

For all its desperation, that effort was the most ineffectual one Zhaarnak had seen since the war began. The gunboats stumbled this way and that, some of them actually *colliding* in midspace, as helpless as *hercheqha* under the claws of *zegets*. All their frantic efforts accomplished was the destruction of fewer than twenty Allied fighters—most of them killed by nothing more than blind luck—even as the antimatter pyres of their own deaths lit a path to the starships they had striven to protect for the main attack wave of strikefighters.

The Terrans and Orions who'd followed the Ophiuchi in ignored the tattered handful of surviving gunboats. They left the Ophiuchi to pursue the remainder of their prey; *they* had targets of their own, and they slashed inward, seeking out the monitors.

The leviathans within the Bug formation were easy sensor targets, and the fighters streaking vengefully down upon them carried a new weapon: external pods with primary beam projectors. The primary, with its very intense but very narrow and short-duration beam of gravitic distortion, did little damage per shot compared to its wide-aperture cousin, the force beam. But its tight-focused fury burned straight through shields and armor, like a white-hot knitting needle through butter, to rend at a ship's vitals.

The nimble little F-4s could have maneuvered into the lumbering monitors' blind zones even if the minds controlling those monitors hadn't been reeling from psychic trauma. And armed with the recognition data Marcus LeBlanc had provided, they sought out the command ships.

That, too, was easier by far than it ought to have been. The emissions signatures of the ships were distinctive enough to have been picked out with ease, but one of the functions of ECM was to disguise those signatures. Only the Bugs' ECM was as disorganized and confused as any other aspect of the Arachnid fleet's operations. The primary-armed fighters picked them out of their battlegroups with ease.

Disoriented or not, the Bugs had their wits—or whatever—about them sufficiently to follow standard tactical doctrine. Indeed, it almost seemed that standard doctrine was *all* they were capable of, for they executed it with a sort of rote, mechanical fatalism, like poorly designed robots executing a program which had been written equally poorly.

Yet however clumsy they might have been, they remained deadly dangerous foes for such fragile attackers. The monitors were positioned to cover each others' blind zones, and whatever might have happened to the organic intelligences aboard them, the cybernetic ones remained unaffected. The monitor battlegroups threw up solid walls of missiles and laser clusters, force beams, and even primaries. Space blazed as the close-in defenses vomited defiance, and yet . . .

The Bugs' cybernetic servants did their best, and many fighters died. But there were limits in all things, including the effectiveness of computers and their software when the organic beings behind those computers were too befuddled and confused to recognize that their efforts to direct the defensive effort actually undermined it. Even as Zhaarnak watched, entire broadsides of missiles and force beams flailed away at single squadrons of attackers. Whenever that happened, the squadron under attack ceased to exist, for nothing could survive under such a massive weight of fire—certainly not something as fragile as a strikefighter. But those concentrations of defensive fire came at a terrible price for the defenders. It was obvious that the Bugs responsible for repelling the attack were pouring the fire of every weapon they had at the first squadron which attracted their attention. And as they compelled their computers to concentrate exclusively upon the single threat their shocked organic senses were capable of singling out, dozens—scores—of threats they *hadn't* engaged streaked through the chinks they'd opened in the wall of their defensive fire.

The vast bulk of the attacking fighters swept past the fireballs and expanding vapor where less fortunate strike craft had died. Their pilots knew what had happened—how dearly such an opening had been purchased for them—and they pressed in grimly. They swarmed about the Bug command ships, stabbing deeper and deeper with their needlelike primaries until the unstoppable stilettos of energy reached the command datalink installations.

Those systems' intricate sophistication, and the interdependency of their components, made them vulnerable to any damage—even the five-centimeter-wide cylinder of destruction drilled by a primary beam. It was like lancing a boil.

Command ship after command ship bled atmosphere as the primary beams chewed deep into their hearts. And the defensive fire of battlegroup after battlegroup became even more ineffectual as the command ships' central direction was stripped away. As they looked at their readouts, Zhaarnak and Raymond Prescott watched the Bug battle-line devolve into a collection of individual ships as its datalink unraveled and its corporate identity lost its integrity.

And against the finely meshed, coordinated *offensive* fire of a fleet whose datalink was unimpaired, individual ships stood no chance at all.

Zhaarnak turned to his com screen, now split into two segments.

"I believe, Force Leader Shaaldaar, that it is time to bring the fighters back. They can interdict the remaining gunboats while TF 61 deals with the battle-line."

Prescott cleared his throat.

"As Fleet commander, I presume you'll want to assume direct command of TF 61 for the attack."

"By no means. Our original understanding holds. The task force is yours."

Prescott's eyes met Zhaarnak's in the com screen, and when he spoke, it was in the Tongue of Tongues.

"You give me honor, brother, by allowing me the kill. It will not be forgotten."

And then, with the fighters warding its flanks against despairing gunboat attacks, TF 61 advanced grimly.

It was almost twenty-four standard Terran hours later when, again in split-screen conference, they received the report that the last fugitive Bug ship had been run down and destroyed. But however long the mopping up had required, the actual battle had lasted only two of those hours.

With their command datalink gone, the point defense of individual Bug ships—even monitors—had been unable to abate the missile-storm which had broken over them. In silent desperation, they had been reduced to trying to ram as many Allied ships as possible, but they were slower and less maneuverable than their opponents, even at the best of times . . . which this most certainly was not.

The outcome had never really been in doubt.

Yet the magnitude and completeness of that outcome had still been awe inspiring. If anyone had still been able to doubt Raymond Prescott's abilities after the Kliean Chain campaign, Operation Pesthouse, and the defense of Centauri, no one could now. He had wielded his battle-line as a *kendo* master wields a *katana*, and that superbly tempered blade had responded with the readiness he had trained into it over the months of preparation in Zephrain. For the Bugs, the result had been not defeat, but annihilation.

But now their wide-ranging recon fighters had brought word that they were still not alone in the system.

"It stands to reason," Shaaldaar said in his deliberate way. "We are all agreed that this is—or was—one of their important systems. So it must be linked to other Bug systems by various warp points. As soon as they became aware of our presence here, they must have summoned reinforcements from those systems by courier drone. The five standard days it took us to bring their mobile forces to bay and then fight the battle must have given those reinforcements time to arrive."

"Yes," Zhaarnak muttered. Prescott had no difficulty recognizing the emotions raging behind that alien face. It was a characteristic of Orions—and Zhaarnak, more than most—that a successful kill only whetted their appetite for more.

"They have no idea of our strength, or even of exactly where we are. We could go back into cloak, ambush them. . . ."

Zhaarnak let his voice trail off as he met Prescott's eyes. He could read his *vilkshatha* brother as readily as the human could read him.

"We must face facts," Prescott said into the silence. "We've taken losses ourselves—nine superdreadnoughts, seven battlecruisers, over seven hundred fighters. . . . And our stores of missiles of all kinds have been depleted. More importantly, the recon fighters' reports make it pretty clear that *these* Bugs are behaving normally. Whatever affected the Bugs in this system evidently doesn't have interstellar range. We had an opportunity, and we were justified in seizing it. But boldness is one thing, and recklessness is another."

Shaaldaar gave a smile that was as disconcertingly humanlike as everything else about his face.

"I believe it was your Human philosopher Clausewitz who observed that a plan which succeeds is bold and that one which fails is reckless."

Prescott smiled back at him.

"That's precisely the distinction. And to take on unshaken monitor battlegroups, even if we did manage to obtain tactical surprise, would be to risk a judgment of recklessness when history got around to considering us."

Zhaarnak's features reflected his inner conflict so well as to remind Prescott that the Orion face, like that of humans but unlike that of Terran cats, had evolved as an instrument of communication. Finally, his ears tilted forward and he gave the fluttering purr that was his race's sigh.

"You are correct. We have accomplished our objectives, and more. We will return to Zephrain in accordance with our original plan."

Sixth Fleet fell back toward the warp point, covered by its weary fighter pilots as the strikegroups fought a series of bickering actions at extreme range against the fresh Bug gunboats.

*The last Enemy units were gone, escaped from this system that they had rendered uninhabitable.*

*The Fleet had failed to protect the Worlds Which Must Be Defended, or to arrive in time to prevent the destruction of the Fleet component which had been assigned originally to that task. The repercussions of the destruction of the Worlds Which Must Be Defended would have grave consequences for the war effort, and the loss of so many ships in such futile combat was . . . annoying.*

*Yet the affair hadn't been a total loss. The gunboats had been ordered to track the withdrawing Enemy starships to their warp point of exit, regardless of casualties—and they'd succeeded.*

*A handful of them had even survived long enough to report that warp point's location.*

TFNS *Dnepr* transited before KONS *Celmithyr'theaarnouw*. So Raymond Prescott had a few moments to appreciate the sight of Zephrain A's yellow glow, and the distant orange spark of Zephrain B, before turning to his com screen and speaking formally.

"Fang Zhaarnak, I relieve you."

"I stand relieved, Fang Presssssscott."

The little ceremony had been agreed to in advance. Now they were back in the Zephrain system, which was part of the Terran Federation, duly ceded by the Khan, and where the massive Terran orbital fortresses made the TFN the predominant service in terms of both tonnage and personnel. So Prescott was now in command of Sixth Fleet, and they exchanged closed-lipped grins at the formality.

Those grins faded for a moment as they looked into one another's eyes and recalled those who would not be returning to Zephrain. The count was in now: 22,605 personnel of all races. There were also 5,017 wounded aboard the remaining ships.

But then the grins were back.

"Did your staff intelligence officer ever complete that estimate of the system's total population, Raaymmonnd?"

"Yes. Commander Chung did an extensive analysis of the sensor returns from Planets I and II. Based on the Bug population density the energy outputs imply, he estimates a total of—"

"—at least *twenty billion* Bugs!" Lieutenant Commander Togliatti looked around the ready room, where VF-94's surviving pilots sprawled, exhausted. "The spooks figure that there were eight to ten billion of them on the planet we waxed, and another twelve to fourteen billion on the other one."

They stared at him, punch-drunk. They'd gone sleepless for days, sustained by drugs, and completed their recovery aboard *Wyvern* just before warp transit. They no longer had any response in them.

But then Irma Sanchez gave him a look of disappointment.

"Twenty billion? Come on, Skipper! Is that *all* we killed?"

# CHAPTER FOUR

## "Surely that can't be right!"

Zephrain was a distant binary system. The orange K8v secondary component, with its small retinue of what were by courtesy referred to as planets, followed an orbit of over fifty percent eccentricity. Even at periastron, it barely swung within three light-hours of Component A. Currently, it was headed out to the Stygian regions where it spent most of its year and was barely visible from Xanadu, the second of that privileged coterie of inner planets that basked in Zephrain A's warm yellow G5v light. Gazing out the window of his office, Raymond Prescott could almost imagine himself on Old Terra.

Not quite, of course. It was always "not quite." The tree whose branches almost brushed against the window was a featherleaf, product of a well-developed local ecosystem which showed little sign of yielding to Terran imports. And practiced senses told him that the gravity was a shade on the low side—0.93 G, to be exact. Still, Zephrain A II was a singularly hospitable world for the humans who'd dubbed it Xanadu.

It was equally comfortable for Orions—and *they* had discovered it first. Reactionaries like Zhaarnak's father, and even relatively enlightened old-timers like Kthaara'zarthan, had never recovered from the Khan's precedent-shattering act of ceding the system to the Terran Federation.

The move had made sense, though. Indeed, it had become unavoidable the moment the teeming Bug system was found on the far side of one of Zephrain's four warp points. On the far side of another of those warp points lay Rehfrak, a sector capital of the Orions, with billions of the Khan's subjects, squarely in the path of any Bug counterattack an offensive might provoke. Only the Terran Federation, with its prodigious industrial capacity, could fortify Zephrain so heavily as to make any offensive use of the system thinkable.

A project on that scale had required a workforce of millions, and millions more to service the workforce. They'd come from every corner of the Federation. In the streets of Xanadu's instant prefab "cities" could be seen every variety of human being that Old Terra had spawned, and quite a few it hadn't. That was unusual in today's Federation. The Heart Worlds' once-polyglot populations had long since blended into "planetary ethnicities," while the young Fringe Worlds had been settled by people seeking to preserve various traditional ethnicities from disappearance by giving each its own planet.

Nevertheless, this motley crew had sunk tendrils of root into the soil of Xanadu with surprising rapidity. The population had already outgrown government by a Navy administrator, and a provisional government had been organized under the duly appointed Federal governor preparatory to seeking full Federation membership. Watching the constitutional convention, Prescott had occasionally found himself wondering if someone had formed a club for disbarred lawyers. And yet, oddly enough, some genuine political creativity had come out of it. Architectural creativity, too; looking to the future, they'd approved plans for a stately Government House on a hill above the river—named the Alph, naturally—that Prescott could see in the distance, beyond the spacefield. Of course, actual construction was being deferred until things became a little less unsettled here . . . meaning, no Bugs a single warp transit away.

*Which,* Prescott reminded himself briskly, *is why we're here.* He turned away from the window. Zhaarnak was waiting with the patience that was one facet of his seemingly contradictory character.

"Have they arrived yet?" the human asked.

"Yes. In fact, they are waiting in the outer office."

Prescott nodded, sat down at his desk, and touched a button.

"Send Small Claw Uaaria and Captain Chung in."

Uaaria'salath-ahn, Zhaarnak's staff intelligence officer, was the senior of the two spooks. By the generally recognized rank equivalencies, a "small claw of the khan" was somewhere between a captain and a commodore. So she led the way into the room, and Prescott reflected on how unusual it was to see an Orion female wearing the jeweled harness that was their navy's uniform. Not so very long ago, it would have been unheard of, and that, too, was a change which owed more than a little to the Terran example. The patriarchal Khanate had been headed in that direction even before it discovered just how capable *human* females could be as warriors in the first two interstellar wars. Since then—and especially since ISW 3—the move towards full female integration into the military had gone on with what (for the extremely tradition-bound Orions) was enormous rapidity.

On the other hand, female Orions still had to "prove" their worthiness for their ranks by being even better at the same job than the vast majority of males could have been. In some ways, Uaaria's position was a bit easier than most, for Prescott knew that her father was an old friend and war comrade of Zhaarnak's. He also knew his *vilkshatha* brother well enough to realize that he retained enough of his race's old sexism to find his intelligence officer extremely pleasant to look upon, although he would no more consider taking liberties with her than he would have considered it with one of his own daughters. But in one respect, at least, Uaaria was a perfect exemplar of what it took for a female to succeed in the Khanate's military: she was very good at her job. In fact, she was very, *very* good. Despite her youth, Prescott considered her to be one of the half dozen finest intelligence officers, human or Orion, he'd ever met, and he knew Zhaarnak relied upon her analyses implicitly.

As did Prescott himself.

"Sit down," he invited.

"Thank you for seeing us on such short notice Fang Presssss-cottt, Small Fang," Uaaria murmured, lowering herself into one of the chairs in front of Prescott's desk as naturally as if she hadn't been raised to sit on piles of floor cushions.

"No problem. When the two of you requested this meeting, we were eager to hear the results of your analysis of what we observed during the offensive."

"Particularly," Zhaarnak added, "your interpretation of the unprecedented confusion that overtook the Bahgs after our first major surface strike on Planet I."

"We still cannot be certain as to the cause," Uaaria replied cautiously. "Our working hypothesis is still the same one Fang Presssssscottt advanced at the time: that all the Bahgs in a given system are in some kind of telepathic rapport, and that destroying that many of them at once had an effect on the rest similar to . . . to . . ."

"To hitting them over the head with a hammer," Chung offered.

"Something of the sort," Uaaria allowed. "But whatever the precise mechanism of the phenomenon, its effects were clearly system-wide."

"A pity they are not universal," Zhaarnak muttered.

"That wouldn't do us much good, considering that the disorientation is only temporary and no one's ever figured out how to coordinate attacks in different systems," Prescott observed. One human head nodded and two sets of Orion ears flicked in agreement. Simultaneity was a meaningless concept in interstellar space. "But even so," the admiral continued, turning back to Uaaria, "this seems to offer an advantage we can exploit when attacking heavily populated Bug systems."

"Indeed, Fang. In order to throw such a system's defenders off balance, the inhabited planets should be bombarded as early and as heavily as possible."

"Hmmm. . . ." Prescott considered that for a moment. The ethical issues such a policy would have raised in a war with any other race never even entered his mind—these were Bugs. But that didn't mean there weren't practical problems.

"An ideal combination of circumstances let us land the punch we did," he mused aloud. "Possibly an unrepeatable combination. Still, it's something to bear in mind. For now, though, please continue with your other conclusions."

"A few conclusions and a great deal of speculation," Uaaria demurred. "I will let my colleague here state our first conclusion, as it was he who arrived at it."

"Before we left Alpha Centauri last May," Amos Chung began, "I got Admiral LeBlanc to copy me the data by which his Lieutenant Sanders had inferred the existence of five Bug 'home hives.' Based on the observations and sensor information we recorded during the engagement, I'm prepared to state that the system we attacked was Home Hive Three."

Prescott and Zhaarnak exchanged glances. Chung's announcement had the same kind of resonance as Sanders' briefing at Alpha Centauri: it imposed at least the beginnings of *form* on the threat they faced.

"We are not," Chung went on, "in a position as yet to place

Home Hive Three in any larger context, as we have no idea where it lies in relation to any other Bug system—"

"Naturally," Zhaarnak said, and it was Prescott's turn to nod agreement. Not a single scrap of Bug navigational data had been captured in the entire war. Or, more accurately, tonnes of it *might* have been captured, but no one had any way to know.

"—but I've run a cost analysis of the defenses we encountered there. You may find the results informative."

"A 'cost analysis'?" Even someone far less familiar with the Tongue of Tongues than Prescott could have read the incredulity in Zhaarnak's voice. "How was this possible?"

"The energy-emission readings allowed us to estimate the system's total economic output. And by analogizing to our own defensive installations, we can estimate how much of such output is required to maintain them. Admittedly, this is a case of estimate piled atop estimate. But if our figures are at all valid—and we believe they are—the defenses were strangely light for the system they were protecting."

Both admirals sat up straight.

"*Light?*" Prescott echoed. He recalled that mastodonic space station. "Surely that can't be right!"

Chung read the admiral's thoughts.

"Yes, Sir, I know. That space station at Planet I was *huge*, and they had another one like it at Planet II. And I don't like to think about the firepower those orbital fortresses could have put out if we hadn't caught them flat footed." The spook visibly braced himself against an anticipated blast of high-ranking skepticism. "Nevertheless, if our assumptions are correct, the maintenance costs of those defenses amounted to only about forty-eight percent of the gross system product."

"That sounds like quite a lot," Prescott observed mildly, understating the case by several orders of magnitude. He tried to imagine the reaction of certain human politicians to a proposal to spend that much on orbital defenses. *The perfect crime*, an inner imp whispered. *Give 'em all heart failure and then laugh like Hell....*

"On the face of it, Sir, perhaps. But the corresponding percentages for Sol, Alpha Centauri, Valkha'zeeranda, and Gormus are much higher. The figures are available for your perusal."

"Well, of *course*," Zhaarnak interjected. "After all, those systems are—"

The Orion stopped abruptly as understanding dawned, some

fraction of a second after it had dawned on Prescott, and Chung nodded, recognizing that they'd grasped the point.

"Yes. Those systems can't be considered in isolation. They draw on other systems—many other systems. They're the capitals of interstellar polities, except for Alpha Centauri, whose unique strategic importance lifts it into the same class: systems which must be protected at any cost, including the diversion of resources from elsewhere. But . . . if our assumptions are even close to right, that's precisely the status the 'home hive' systems ought to hold among the Bugs! They shouldn't have to rely solely on *their* own resources, either."

"All right, Commander," Prescott acknowledged. "You've made your point. Home Hive Three wasn't as heavily defended as it should have been. Do you have a theory to account for this?"

"The majority view among the intelligence community here," Chung answered obliquely, "is that it's a matter of resource allocation. The Bugs skimp on static defenses in order to build the biggest mobile fleet possible."

"There is historical precedent for that," Zhaarnak remarked to Prescott. "The Rigelians had similar priorities."

"And," Prescott ruminated, "it would help account for the size of the mobile fleets they've kept throwing at us. And for the fact that those fleets have taken terrific losses without batting an eyelash—or whatever their equivalent is." He nodded to Chung. "Yes, Amos, your theory seems to make sense."

"Excuse me, Sir." Chung was all diffidence. "I didn't say it's *my* theory."

"But didn't I understand you to say that it's the consensus of the sp—of the intelligence community?"

"It is, Sir. But I don't happen to agree with it."

"So," Zhaarnak inquired, "only *you* are right, then?"

Uaaria's eyes met those of the Ninety-first Small Fang of the Khan unflinchingly.

"Not only him, Sir. I share his view," she said, and Prescott's lips gave a quirk too brief to be called a smile.

"I begin to understand why you two asked for a private meeting. All right, talk to us," he ordered, and Uaaria leaned forward earnestly.

"It is our considered judgment that the Bahgs did not draw on more outside resources for the defense of Home Hive Three—and, presumably, the other home hive systems, as well—because they do not *have* such resources."

Zhaarnak recovered first.

"In light of the resources we have watched the Bahgs expend without apparently so much as flinching over the past few years, Small Claw, I suggest that you have a bit of explaining to do."

"Certainly, Sir." Uaaria seemed to gather her thoughts. "To begin, let me cite two facts we observed in Home Hive Three. First, the incredible population densities on the two habitable planets. Second, the total absence of energy emissions or other indications of any Bahg presence elsewhere in the system. There were no orbital habitats, no hostile environment colonies on any moons or asteroids."

She paused expectantly.

"Well, yes," Prescott said. "That's undeniable enough. Although . . ."

"Although the precise relevance is not yet apparent," Zhaarnak finished for him, just a bit more tartly, and Uaaria gave an ear flick of acknowledgment.

"I believe that the relevance will become apparent, Small Fang. Taken together, these two facts indicate that the Bahgs are interested only in life-bearing planets of the same kind favored by both our species, and that they are willing to accept what we *Zheeerlikou'valkhannaiee*, or even Humans, would consider obscene overcrowding of such planets. Admittedly, we cannot begin to estimate how many such planets they have thus packed with their species. But as Ahhdmiraaaal LeBlaaanc and his subordinate Saaanderzzz have deduced, the existence of five subtypes within their ship classes, distinguished by differences in construction technique as marked as those between two closely associated races—Humans and Ophiuchi, let us say—implies the existence of five distinct subgroups among the Bahgs, each with its own identity."

"I think I see where this is leading," Prescott interjected. "But please continue."

"It seems to us, given the Bahgs' apparent propensity for overcrowding any available life-bearing planet to the limits of its capacity before considering expansion, that each of these five subgroups occupies no more than a few densely populated systems like Home Hive Three."

Chung could restrain himself no longer.

"Which means that, contrary to what we've been assuming all along, the Bugs don't have a far-flung interstellar imperium like the Federation or the Khanate. If Home Hive Three, say, was the nodal system of a sub-empire with anything like the number of sparsely settled colonial systems *we* have for each nodal system, they'd've drawn on the resources of those colonies and built *really* scary defenses for it."

"And so," Uaaria concluded as Chung stopped for breath, "Home Hive Three had to rely on its own resources, and those of no more than a very few other systems. By extension, that should be the case with the other four home hive systems, as well."

"I see." Prescott thought for a moment, in a silence which, he noted, Zhaarnak didn't break. Then he looked from Uaaria to Chung and back again. "Very cogently argued. But I wonder if you've thought out the full implications of what you're saying."

"Sir?" Chung sounded puzzled.

"Your theory is that the Bugs have put all their eggs in a small number of baskets. *Not* fragile baskets, unfortunately; I don't like to think about the battle those 'light' defenses could have given us if we hadn't caught them with their metaphorical pants down. But if you're right, the number of similar battles we're going to have to fight is *much* lower than anyone has dared to believe or even hope."

"Do not forget, we must first find those 'baskets.'" Zhaarnak's expressive face was a battleground for excitement and caution, and his tone reflected that struggle. "Of the remaining four home hive systems, we have only identified one so far. And five occupied systems—meaning up to five warp point assaults—stand between that one and Ahhdmiraaaal Muhrakhuuuuma's fleet."

"Granted. Still . . ."

Prescott turned to the spooks.

"All right. Set your conclusions down as a formal report and tell Anna I want it dispatched by special courier to Alpha Centauri. I want to bounce your theory off Admiral LeBlanc ASAP. Maybe he can poke a few holes that haven't occurred to any of us in it. But if you're right, you've just given us the first piece of good news the Alliance has had since the war began. *If* you're right," he repeated sternly.

He understood, and shared, Zhaarnak's inner conflict. He wanted to believe Uaaria and Chung were right, as he instinctually felt they were. But he also understood *why* he wanted to believe it. And because he did, he was reluctant to trust his instincts, influenced as they were by a hope bordering on desperation.

"And there is another aspect to the matter," Zhaarnak said heavily. "If this theory is correct, Home Hive Three's defenses were maintained by that system alone, with the help of a few others—for it goes without saying that a mere five industrialized systems, be they ever so heavily developed, could not possibly produce the forces we have already encountered in combat."

"Of course not, Small Fang," Uaaria agreed quickly enough to beat Prescott to it.

"So therefore," Zhaarnak resumed, "your initial cost estimate for maintaining Home Hive Three's defenses is somewhat high as a percentage of that one system's economic output, for it had *some* outside help. But still, the figure is probably correct to well within one order of magnitude. Say, *ten* percent of the gross system product. Not, be it noted, ten percent of the government's budget, whatever that may mean for Bahgs. No—ten percent of the *gross system product*. And that is just what they are prepared to spend for their *static* defenses, and completely exclusive of their mobile forces! Can you imagine what that would mean in terms of . . . well, of the standard of living of the population?"

"No," Prescott admitted flatly. In fact, he'd thought of it before Zhaarnak brought it up, but only to reject it as unthinkable. It suggested a society, if that was the word, which existed only to expand, and expanded only to secure the means for further expansion. A true cancer. They'd be eating each other simply to stave off famine . . . temporarily.

*Dear God*, Prescott, not normally a religious man, thought with full appreciation of what he was thinking. *What are we really dealing with?*

# CHAPTER FIVE
## "We know it's coming."

By the standard dating of Old Terra, December 2364 passed into January 2365. Prescott and Zhaarnak were out with Sixth Fleet in the cold reaches of the Zephrain system, five light-hours from the glowing yellow hearth of Zephrain A, as the year changed, holding station on the warp point leading to what they now knew to be Home Hive Three.

January became February, and they were still there.

"We can't go back yet," Prescott said patiently, looking into Zhaarnak's grumpy visage on the com screen. He was back aboard TFNS *Dnepr*, and the Orion was back aboard *Celmithyr'theaarnouw*, and they were both in Task Force 61's formation again. Of course, here in Zephrain space, *Dnepr* was Sixth Fleet's flagship, while Zhaarnak commanded TF 61 from *Celmithyr'theaarnouw*. There'd been examples in Terran history of rotating command structures which had actually worked in practice. Not a lot of them, of course, but Amos Chung, who was something of a historian, was fond of bringing up the ancient pre-space admirals Halsey and Spruance. Prescott, who'd done a little research of his own, harbored some fairly strong suspicions that even those two semi-mythical commanders had experienced their fair share of bumps and bruises along the way. Not to mention a not-so-minor pothole at a place called Leyte Gulf. And even if they hadn't, no inter-species alliance in history had ever attempted a similar arrangement.

Not successfully, at any rate.

Yet this time, it actually did work. In point of fact, Prescott was more than a little surprised by how well the entire Alliance managed to function in partnership. There was still the occasional spat, and there'd even been one or two knock-down, drag-out fights. The worst of them had been between so-called political leaders, and Prescott was forced to admit that more often than not those quarrels had been provoked by human politicos. There seemed to be something about human nature which promoted a more bare-knuckles approach to political interaction. The Khanate of Orion had its own political factionalism, and even the Ophiuchi had experienced the odd generation or so of feuding political combinations. As far as anyone knew, the Gorm never had, but, then, the Gorm were strange in a lot of ways.

On the other hand, when Orion disagreements and character assassination reached the level which appeared to be the normal state of affairs for the Terran Federation, the bodies were usually already stacked two or three deep and another round of civil war couldn't be too far away. The steadily increasing tension between the Corporate Worlds and the Fringe Worlds made that even worse, normally, but at least Samuel Johnson's famous formulation still held: the prospect of hanging *did* concentrate one's mind wonderfully. It even helped Fringer and Corporate Worlder find sufficient common ground to concentrate on fighting the Bugs instead of one another. Sort of.

Well, on fighting the Bugs *as well as* one another. Humans being humans, they seemed quite capable of waging both battles simultaneously.

Because of that, the sometimes prickly Orions had been unwontedly tactful and forbearing where human political processes—and even individual politicians—were concerned. The fact that for all of their differences over how to go about manipulating their fellow politicians Tabby and human politicos were very much alike under the skin probably also helped. Many of them might cherish boundless contempt for the other side's tactics, but all of them understood precisely what the object of the game was.

Differences of opinion on the military side tended to be more concrete and immediate and less about personalities and ideology. Oh, there were chauvinistic bigots (like Zhaarnak's father, for example) on both sides of almost any interspecies line, and fundamental differences in outlook and honor codes could contribute mightily to the ... energy with which questions of strategy, tactics, and logistics were debated. But by and large, the people on the opposing sides of those debates found themselves forced to confront hard and fast limitations on physical resources and strategic opportunities. And, of course, all of them knew that if they let themselves get distracted by infighting over pet projects or priorities and lost *this* war, there wouldn't be another in which they could restore their position. If all else failed, the Joint Chiefs and the chiefs of naval operations of the Alliance's member navies had all demonstrated a ruthless willingness to summarily sack any officer who habitually created unnecessary problems between species. There'd been quite a few such "reliefs for cause" during the first year or so of the war; there had been exactly none of them since.

Of course, even without any chauvinism at all, there would have been plenty of other factors to kick sand into the gears. Language differences, for one. The recent advances in translation software were a great help . . . when the software was available. Unfortunately, the demands that software made on the computers on which it ran meant that it wasn't really practical on anything much smaller than a capital ship. That left the crews of lesser starships and strikefighter squadrons to labor under all of the inherent limitations of an organic translating interface.

The worst potential problems of all lay between human and Orion. Standard English had emerged as the *lingua franca* of the non-Orion members of the Alliance, because both the Gorm and the Ophiuchi were at least capable of reproducing the sounds English used. *None* of the other Allies, however, could do the same thing for the Tongue of Tongues, whatever the occasional highly atypical individual—like Prescott himself—might be able to manage. And in what was clearly a special dispensation of the great Demon Murphy, the Orions whose language no one else could speak were not only the touchiest and most prone to take offense of the lot but far and away the second most powerful member of the Alliance.

After so many years of brutal warfare against a common foe with whom *any* sort of accommodation was clearly impossible, however, most of the rough edges had been ground away . . . on the military side, at least. There simply wasn't any other choice when the only alternative to close cooperation was annihilation. The worst of the bigots on both sides had been retired or shifted into less sensitive positions, although a significant but thankfully small number of them continued to crop up—always at extremely inopportune moments, of course. And the occasional officer who created problems for everyone out of stupidity or ambition continued to survive . . . usually because they enjoyed the protection of powerful political patrons.

Yet there remained an enormous difference between the ability of allies to fight in cooperation, however close, and the ability to switch the ultimate command authority of a fleet back and forth across species lines without any friction at all. In fact, Prescott had come to the conclusion that Sixth Fleet's rotating command structure probably wouldn't have worked at all if it hadn't been headed by Zhaarnak'telmasa and himself—or, at least, by two beings who shared their relationship or something equivalent to it.

"I was not speaking of *us* so much as of *you.*" Zhaarnak's response to his original observation pulled Prescott back up out of his thoughts. "I can stay out here with this task force, and Force Leader Shaaldaar with his. But you are needed back on Xanadu. There are too many details which require the Fleet commander's personal attention, and you could exercise overall supervision of these exercises from there as well as from here."

Prescott shook his head.

"At the moment, Xanadu is five light-hours away. I couldn't exercise on-scene command from there."

"Do you really need to?"

"Yes. And I'm not talking about the exercises."

"You mean—?"

"We *know* it's coming, Zhaarnak."

They both knew what "it" was.

Not long after their meeting with Uaaria and Chung, reports from second generation recon drones sent through the Home Hive Three warp point had laid to rest any doubts they might have cherished about whether Sixth Fleet's departure had been tracked. It was now clear, beyond any possibility of self-deception, that the Bugs knew the location of the closed warp point through which death had come to Home Hive Three's worlds. For now they were tractoring their orbital weapons platforms there from Home Hive Three's other warp points, and positioning clouds of mines and armed deep space buoys to support them. The next incursion through that warp point would be far less pleasant than the last.

Prescott and Zhaarnak had taken a calculated risk when they'd lingered in Home Hive Three to annihilate the disoriented Bug mobile forces even at the possible cost of giving away the warp point's location, but that kind of choice was what admirals were paid to make. The *vilkshatha* brothers had earned their salaries.

And afterwards, they'd viewed the recon drones' reports with equanimity. Having made their decision, they were prepared to accept its consequences. To have been spared the need to face those consequences would have been sheer luck. And, as a wise man had noted centuries before, luck is like government. We can't get along without it, but only a fool relies on it.

Neither Prescott nor Zhaarnak was a fool, and so neither was unduly disturbed by the Bugs' fortification of their end of the Home Hive Three warp connection. What *was* disturbing was the large, fresh mobile fleet the Bugs were steadily amassing behind those static defenses.

"All right," Zhaarnak conceded, "we both know that an attack on this system is inevitable. But not necessarily during the course of these exercises! You cannot stay out here permanently, you know."

"I know. But all indications from the RD2s are that it's coming soon."

"If so, what of it? We have allowed for this possibility all along. And you cannot say we have not prepared for it."

Zhaarnak gestured at something outside the range of his com pickup—probably, Prescott guessed, an auxiliary plot like his own, displaying TF 63 as a cloud of color-coded lights swarming in stately procession around the violet circle of the warp point.

Sixth Fleet's third task force hadn't joined the other two in the scorching of Home Hive three for the excellent reason that it didn't include a single vessel that could move under its own power. Instead, Vice Admiral Alex Mordechai commanded orbital fortresses—fifty-seven of them, the smallest as big as a super-dreadnought and the largest even bigger than the Bug monitors. Untrained eyes might have looked at the arrangement of those icons in the sphere and seen chaos. But Prescott recognized the product of careful planning rooted in well-developed tactical doctrine.

Interstellar travel was possible only via warp transit, and only one ship at a time could safely perform such transit, lest multiple ones irritate the gods of physics by trying to materialize in overlapping volumes of space. So it had always been a truism of interstellar war that the defender of a known warp point knew exactly where attacking ships had to appear . . . one at a time. In the face of such an advantage, many people—disproportionately represented, it often seemed, in the fields of politics and journalism—were at a loss to understand how *any* warp point assault could possibly succeed except through the defenders' incompetence. To be fair, a similar attitude hadn't been unknown among military officers in the early days—especially given the momentary disorientation that overtook both minds and instruments after the profoundly unnatural experience of warp transit. With beam-weapon-armed ships or fortresses stationed right on top of the warp point, the befuddled attackers would emerge one by one into a ravening hell of directed-energy fire. If missile-armed vessels were available for supporting bombardment from longer ranges, so much the better. The pre-space expression "make the rubble bounce" wasn't apropos to the environment, but it nevertheless came to mind.

Things hadn't quite worked out that way, for the lovely picture had run aground on certain hard realities. One was that, while the defender knew *where* the attack would come, he had no way of knowing *when* it would come. Another was that no military organization could keep all its units permanently at the highest state of alert. Taken together, those facts meant that attackers might appear at any time, without warning and in unanticipated strength, to pour their own point-blank energy fire into surprised defenders. Nor had it proven possible to clog the mouth of a warp point with mines; the grav surge and tidal forces associated with the warp phenomenon made it impossible to keep the things on station directly atop it. The space *around* a point could be—and was—covered with lethal concentrations of the things, backed up by independently deployed energy weapon platforms, but any mine or platform left directly on top of an open warp point was inevitably sucked into it and destroyed. So although it was possible to severely constrain an attacker's freedom of maneuver, the defender was seldom able to deny him at least *some* space in which to deploy his fleet as its units arrived.

And then, with the passage of time, had come what the TFN designated the SBMHAWK: the Strategic Bombardment Homing All the Way Killer—a carrier pod that was a small robotic spacecraft, capable of transiting a warp point only to belch forth three to five strategic bombardment missiles programmed to home in on defending ship types. Because they were throwaway craft, the carrier pods could and did make mass simultaneous transits, accepting a certain percentage of losses as the price of smothering a warp point's defenders with sheer numbers of missiles. With such a bombardment to precede it, the prospect of a warp point assault had become as nerve racking for the defender as for the attacker—arguably more so, because the attacker at least knew in advance when he was going in, and could prepare himself for the probability of death.

But eventually the march of technology had provided the defense with what it had most conspicuously lacked: warning of the attack. The second-generation recon drone had been designed to allow covert warp point survey work by robotic proxy—an excellent idea in a universe that held Bugs. But it also had a more directly military use. With its advanced stealth features, it could probe through a known warp point undetected and report back on any mobilization that portended an attack . . . just as Sixth Fleet's RD2s had been doing.

One thing, however, hadn't changed. The name of the game was to position your assets so that every unit was at its own principal weapons' optimum range from the warp point, and Alex Mordechai had done just that. His beam and missile-armed fortresses clustered around the warp point in concentric shells, prepared to pour fire into that immaterial volume of space. His six BS6Vs, each one the base for a hundred and sixty-two fighters, maintained station further out, outside direct weapons' range of the warp point. All the bases were on rotating general-quarters status, and had been ever since the RD2s first reported the Bug force building up like a thunderhead at the other end of the warp line. And in addition to the fortresses, the plot showed the lesser lights of unmanned munitions in multicolored profusion: twelve hundred patterns of antimatter mines, seven hundred and fifty laser-armed deep space buoys, twelve hundred independently deployed energy weapons (less powerful than the buoys' detonation-lasers, but reusable), and eight hundred SBMHAWK carrier pods tied into the fortresses' fire control.

Nothing, surely, could come through that warp point and live.

"Maybe you're right," Prescott conceded. "And I have got desk work waiting on Xanadu." *Lots of it*, he thought bleakly. *Lots and lots of it.* "I tell you what. Admiral Mordechai has an RD2 that's due to return from Home Hive Three in about four hours. I'll just wait until he's had a chance to study its data. If nothing's changed dramatically, then I'll go back."

"You are procrastinating, Raaymmonnd," Zhaarnak said sternly.

"I am not! It just can't hurt to—"

"Excuse me, Admiral."

Surprised by the interruption, Prescott turned to face his chief of staff.

"What is it, Anna?"

"Sir," Captain Mandagalla's black face was very controlled, "Jacques has just received a message from Admiral Mordechai. The RD2's just returned. Its data hasn't been downloaded yet, but—"

Prescott spared a quick glance for Zhaarnak, who'd heard it too—Mandagalla was within the pickup's range—before breaking in on her.

"Have Captain Turanoglu sound General Quarters, Commodore."

"Aye, aye, Sir." Mandagalla hurried off towards the com section, waving urgently for Jacques Bichet to join her, and Prescott heard Zhaarnak giving similar orders in the Tongue of Tongues.

They didn't need to wait for the RD2's report. The drones were dispatched through the warp point for twenty-four-hour deployments. That represented their maximum endurance, and they returned before that time limit only if their electronic and neutrino-based senses told them one thing.

The attack was under way.

The general quarters call whooped through *Dnepr's* echoing corridors, and the other elements of Sixth Fleet were uncoiling themselves to lunge towards the warp point to support Mordechai's command. Prescott ignored it all and kept his eyes riveted on the plot and— Yes, there was the tiny light of the fleeing RD2. He watched, unblinking, for what he knew would follow it.

He knew . . . but even so, he sucked in his breath when it happened.

It wasn't something anyone grew accustomed to—not even someone like Raymond Prescott or Zhaarnak'telmasa, who'd seen it before.

The Bugs had introduced the tactic, unthinkable for any other race, of mass simultaneous warp transits. Prescott knew he had no business being shocked by the phalanx of red "hostile" icons that suddenly appeared—and, in fact, he wasn't. What he felt was flesh-crawling, stomach-quivering horror at the mindset behind it: absolute indifference to personal survival.

As if to emphasize the point, the usual percentage of those scarlet lights began going out.

Prescott had seen actual visual imagery, not just CIC's dispassionate icons—recorded robotically from long range, of course—of a similar assault when he and Zhaarnak stood with their backs against the wall in defense of Alowan. That had been bad enough, yet he'd seen worse—and from a much closer perspective—in the final desperate stages of the Bugs' assault on Centauri. So he wasn't deceived by the peaceful way those lights flickered and then vanished, leaving a fleeting afterimage on the retina. When two solid objects tried to resume existence in the same volume, the result was of an intensity to stress the very fabric of space/time. Indeed, no one really knew precisely what happened—the phenomenon had never been studied closely enough, and doubtless never would be.

Every TFN officer had seen imagery *like* that . . . in a way. The Federation had learned the hard way that there was only so much simulators, however good, could teach its personnel. And so regular deep-space drills, with real hardware, were part of the day-to-day existence of the Fleet. As part of those drills, SBMHAWKs were fired through warp points, where—as always—a certain percentage of them disappeared in those intolerably brilliant spasms of madly released energy.

Yet there was a difference between those exercises and this. SBMHAWKs were, after all, just expendable machinery.

But, then, so were the Bugs . . . by their own definition. And as Prescott watched those icons vanish, he realized anew that humankind and the Bugs were too alien to share the same universe.

The deaths of Bug ships from interpenetration ceased immediately after transit. But those ships kept dying without letup, for Mordechai was clearly resolved to burn Zephrain space clean of them before they could deploy away from the warp point. Swathes of deep space buoys vanished from the sphere, committing thermonuclear suicide to focus the gathered energies of their deaths into lances of coherent X-rays that impaled the Bug ships almost too fast for their types to be identified. Almost too fast, but not quite . . . and Prescott frowned. These were all light cruisers.

That wasn't like the Bugs. True, in the first years of the war, they'd used light cruisers for their initial assault waves. But that had changed with their introduction of the gunboat. Smaller and far cheaper than even an austere light cruiser design, gunboats were even better suited for this self-immolating form of attack, and that was precisely how the Bugs had come to use them. But today they weren't, and Prescott began to worry.

"Raise Admiral Mordechai," he ordered his com officer. The command was barely out of his mouth when a second mass simultaneous transit appeared. These *were* gunboats—and Prescott's worry hardened into certainty.

Mordechai must have seen it too. He'd let himself be drawn into expending practically all of his bomb-pumped lasers on the light cruisers of the first wave. He still had his reusable independently deployed energy weapons—but the IDEWs' puny powerplants took half an hour to power them up between shots, which meant effectively that they were good for only one shot per engagement each. He was faced with the choice of using them against the gunboats, or holding them in reserve against the big ships he knew were coming.

Fortunately, he had another card to play: the defensively deployed SBMHAWKs. By the time the communications lag allowed Prescott to speak with him, he'd already decided to use those, rather than the IDEWs, to counter the gunboats.

An SBMHAWK pod's fire control was normally extremely effective, but only within limited parameters. Designed to survive the addling effect of warp transit and then find and attack its designated target type, its fire control suite was extremely powerful but limited to a single target for every bird in the pod. The entire idea, after all, was for the pods' combined fire to swamp and overwhelm the defenses of their targets, so dispersing the individual pod's missiles between multiple targets was contraindicated.

Bug gunboats were far more fragile targets than even the smallest starships. Although they did mount point defense, unlike strikefighters, they didn't have very much of it, and a single hit from any weapon was sufficient to destroy them. Which meant that just as dispersing fire against starships was an exercise in futility, concentrating the entire load of an SBMHAWK on such a vulnerable target would have been a wasteful misuse of critically valuable weapons.

But there was a way to avoid doing that. The pods Mordechai committed were linked directly to the *extremely* capable fire control systems of TF 63's fortresses. The *pods* didn't have to find their targets; the fortresses did that for them, and the clouds of missiles they expelled were more than sufficient to compensate for the targeting problem posed by the gunboats' numbers. The space between the warp point and the nearest fortress shell began to blaze as the energies of antimatter annihilation expended themselves on the relatively insignificant masses of mere gunboats, leaving no debris. But the little craft pressed the attack with the insensate persistence humans had come to know over the last few years, and the fortress crews braced themselves for the worst:

kamikaze attacks by gunboats whose crews knew they'd have no
chance at a second pass.

As it happened, they were mistaken about what constituted
the worst.

After the attack on Home Hive Three, it was no news that
the Bugs had developed the close-attack antimatter missile. But
no one had fully reasoned out the implications of that fact, as
applied to mass assaults by gunboats which could externally
mount *sixteen* of the things and ripple-fire twelve of them in the
course of a single firing pass. They should have, but the Allies
were accustomed to thinking of FRAMs as *fighter* munitions,
and even the TFN's F-4, the most capable strikefighter anyone
had yet deployed, could mount only four of them. There was
an enormous difference between that weight of fire and what a
gunboat was capable of putting out . . . as the Bugs proceeded to
make horrifyingly evident.

The gunboats drove in through the defensive fire of the forts.
Scores of them perished in the attempt, but there were simply
too many of them for the fortresses to destroy them all, and as
each individual that broke through reached knife range, it salvoed
twelve FRAMs. No point defense system in the galaxy could stop
a FRAM once it launched, and even the mightiest fortress staggered like a galleon in a hurricane as that concentrated flail of
super heated plasma and radiation smashed home.

Prescott was as horrified as anyone by the sheer carnage a
single gunboat could wreak with a full ripple-salvo, and even
as he watched, the surviving Bugs departed from their standard
practice by breaking off after that devastating pass rather than
seeking self-immolation. Instead, they broke back towards the
warp point, firing their remaining FRAM on the way out.

Jacques Bichet, studying the readouts intently, offered an explanation.

"It makes sense, Sir. Four FRAM hits can inflict almost two
and a half times as much damage as a ramming attack by a 'clean'
gunboat could."

"So of course they're not ramming." Prescott's voice sounded far
too calm to his own ears, but he nodded. "It would be better if
they were," he went on, and Bichet gave him a puzzled look. But
he was speaking more to himself than to the ops officer. "Their
willingness to make suicide attacks has always caused us to unconsciously picture them in the mold of human religious fanatics,
eagerly seeking self destruction. But they're not. The Bugs don't

want to die. It's just that they also don't want *not* to die. They simply *don't care*. We'll never understand that—never understand *them*. And I don't think we *want* to understand them."

Bichet shivered and turned away, seeking the concrete world of facts and figures. He studied the readouts of the subsequent waves of mass simultaneous emergences from warp, and his eyes narrowed as he realized that something else was happening that was new. He started to call it to Prescott's attention, but Amos Chung was studying the same data, and he beat the ops officer to it.

"Admiral, there are some gunboats in these latest waves, but fewer in each. Most of what's coming through now seem to be pinnaces."

Prescott looked at him sharply. The pinnace was the largest type of small craft which could be carried internally in a starship's boatbay, and the only small craft type (other than a gunboat) that was independently warp-capable. Now that he knew what to look for, he recognized the signs in the readouts himself: the lesser mass combined with inferior speed and maneuverability, relative to gunboats. The Bugs had used them in the kamikaze role before, especially against Fifth Fleet in the original Romulus fighting, but the Allies hadn't seen much of them in the past year or two. The assumption had been that the Bugs had finally decided that pinnaces did too little damage, even as kamikazes, to make practical weapons—particularly because they were much easier to kill than gunboats were.

"What can they be thinking?" Chung jittered as he watched the pinnaces take murderous losses from Mordechai's AFHAWKs. "Granted, they're too small for the mines to lock them up as targets, and we can't use standard anti-ship weapons against them, but still . . ."

"We'll soon find out," Prescott muttered as the first of the pinnaces closed to attack range of the inner fortress shell.

Part of the answer emerged instantly. The Bugs had loaded the pinnaces' external ordnance racks with FRAMs. They couldn't mount anywhere near the load a gunboat could manage, but what they could mount was devastating enough in its own right, and more shields went flat under antimatter fists, more armor vaporized and splintered, more atmosphere streamed through broken plating, and more human beings died.

*Nasty stingers when they get close enough to fire*, Prescott conceded grimly to himself as he watched them attack . . . and watched the fortresses' defensive fire thresh their splintered formations with death. *But not many of them will.*

He was right. Very few of them got close enough to fire, but then he watched as one of the pinnaces continued straight onward in the wake of its FRAMs, closing in on the fortress it had targeted. Unlike the gunboats, it *was* making a suicide run, and the range was too short and its closing velocity too high for it to be stopped. Its icon converged with the fortress's, blended . . .

The readouts went wild, and the icon of the fortress vanished as completely as that of the pinnace.

"Admiral!" Chung yelled. "We getting downloaded data from the nearby fortresses—we can assess the force of that explosion."

He paused momentarily while the computers did just that, and his pale-complexioned face went bone-white as the uncaring cybernetic brains presented the numbers.

"Sir, that pinnace must've had its cargo bay loaded with at least *six hundred FRAMs!* That's the equivalent of sixty times an SBMHAWK's entire missile load!"

Prescott blanched. No fortress could take that!

*Maybe not many of them will have to take it,* he thought a moment later, as he watched whole flights of pinnaces vanish like moths in the flame of defensive fire. Small craft, like fighters, could be engaged by point defense, and the fortresses' point defense crews had suddenly become very highly motivated.

"Jacques!" the admiral snapped. "Order all standby carriers to launch their ready fighters. They can get into range faster than we can."

Mordechai's fighter bases, further from the warp point than his innermost fortress shell and thus far unscathed, were already launching.

But even as they did, the tactical picture became still more complicated. Bug monitors began to emerge from warp, and as they did, they began to deploy small craft of their own. These were assault shuttles . . . and they, too, had been crammed full of antimatter munitions to enhance their deadliness as kamikazes. As they came streaking in to ram, the fortresses were forced to divert still more fire from the retreating gunboats to concentrate on the incoming threat—which, of course, improved the latter's chances of completing their own firing runs and then breaking off.

On the main plot, the spherical area of space around the warp point, inside the innermost shell, now resembled a stroboscopic ball of swarming, flashing lights. And through that maelstrom, the first monitors were advancing ponderously towards the fortresses—fewer fortresses than anyone had expected to be there at this stage of the battle.

"My fighters are fully engaged," Mordechai reported, as *Dnepr* and her consorts drew into position to reinforce the decimated fortresses and a conversation without time lags became possible. "But the ready squadrons were configured to engage ships and gunboats. None of them are armed with gun packs. Most of the BS6Vs don't even have the packs in stores!"

Prescott's face tightened in understanding. Against targets as small, fragile, and nimble as small craft, "guns" were far and away the most efficient close-in weapon. They weren't actually anything a pre-space human would have considered a "gun," of course, but they were the closest thing twenty-fourth-century humanity had, and their clusters of individually powered flechettelike projectiles covered a far greater volume than the focused pulse of any energy weapon.

"They'll just have to use their internal lasers, Alex," Prescott told the fortress commander grimly. "And at least my fighters are joining in, as well."

"Thank God for that!" Mordechai's face was smoke-blackened, and behind him Prescott glimpsed a scene of desperate damage-control activity. "Are you arming the next wave with gun packs?"

Prescott hesitated some fraction of a heartbeat.

"Negative, Alex. Their battle-line's main body is bound to come through any time. I'm going to need them in the anti-ship role. They'll launch with FRAMs, not guns."

"But, Admiral—"

"*Incoming!*" The scream from somewhere behind Mordechai interrupted the task force commander. His head snapped around towards the shout, and . . .

. . . Prescott's com screen dissolved into a blizzard of snow, then went dark.

"Code—"

Prescott closed his eyes and waved the young com rating silent.

"I know, son," he said. "I know."

He didn't need to hear the "Code Omega" from Mordechai's command fortress. He'd seen its icon blink out of existence on the plot.

Yet he had no time to grieve, for the Bugs' final surprise appeared on the plot with soul-shaking suddenness.

By now, everyone was inured to mass simultaneous warp transits of Bug gunboats and even light cruisers, however incomprehensible the mentality behind them might be. But suddenly Raymond Prescott was back at the "Black Hole of Centauri," face-to-face with something no human being, no Orion, could ever become inured to. Not gunboats, not cruisers—*superdreadnoughts.*

Twenty-four of them appeared as one, lunging through the invisible hole in space between Zephrain and Home Hive Three. He watched them come, watched them pay the inevitable toll to the ferryman as five of them interpenetrated and died, and a part of him wanted to flatly deny that any living creature could embrace such a tactic.

But these living creatures could do just that, and they had. It was a smaller wave than they'd thrown through at Centauri, yet "smaller" was a purely relative term which meant nothing. Not when any navy was prepared to sacrifice so many personnel, so many megatonnes of warships, so casually.

*People wonder why the Bugs have never developed the SBM-HAWK. There's no technological reason for them not to have it. But the problem isn't technological. It's . . . philosophical, if the word means anything as applied to Bugs. They probably can't imagine why anyone would want to use technology to minimize casualties.*

The surviving superdreadnoughts began to fire. They were using second-generation anti-mine ballistic missiles, sweeping away the minefields and the independently deployed energy weapons—and as seconds turned to minutes, the latter didn't fire back.

"Why are the IDEWs just sitting there?" Prescott demanded.

"Admiral Mordechai's fortress was the one tasked to control them," Mandagalla replied. "Admiral Traynor is shifting control now, but it takes time for the standby to gear up to order them to fire."

*Something that will have to be rectified in the future,* Prescott thought behind his mask of enforced calm.

"Are Force Leader Shaaldaar's second-wave fighters ready to launch?" he asked aloud.

"Yes, Sir," Bichet said. "In fact—"

"Good. Tell him to launch them."

Three minutes had ticked by before the seriously reduced volley of energy-weapon buoy fire lashed out at the Bug capital ships. But now Prescott's battle-line was moving inward, pouring in long-range missile fire to support the fighters that were already beginning to engage, and there was something odd about the fire coming to meet it.

"What's the matter with the Bugs' fire control?" the admiral asked, and Bichet looked up from his console.

"We've been able to identify the classes of those superdreadnoughts, Sir. And they don't have as many *Arbalest* command ships as they should for that many *Archers*. Their interpenetration losses must've included a couple of *Arbalests*."

"Thank God for that," Prescott said with feeling. *About time we got a break*, he added silently as he watched Shaaldaar's fighters slash in.

Irma Sanchez functioned as emotionlessly as any other component of the F-4 as she maneuvered the fighter around the flying steel mountain of death that was a Bug superdreadnought. It was only after she'd commenced her attack run in the big ship's blind zone and launched her FRAM load that she allowed herself to visualize Armand's face, and the imagined face of a certain unborn child.

Segments of the superdreadnought bulged outward in a shroud of blinding flame as the matter/antimatter explosions tore out the ship's insides. To Irma, it was as though she had thrust a knife into a Bug's guts, forearm-deep, and dug and dug. . . .

*Can you feel* pain, *you motherfuckers? I know you can't scream, but can you hurt? I want* you *to hurt, and go on hurting. . . .*

"Sanchez!" Lieutenant Commander Togliatti's yell ripped from her earphones. "Pull up!"

But she raked the flanks of the wounded monster with hetlaser fire before she wrenched the F-4 into a hard turn and flashed away.

The battle was stunning in its intensity, but not as long in duration as it seemed at the time. Afterwards, Prescott and Zhaarnak would freely admit that the Bugs might have broken through if they'd used *all* their superdreadnoughts in mass waves. But the remaining SDs and monitors began coming through the warp point in a more conventional fashion. There wasn't a single undamaged fortress in the inner shell left to receive them, but Prescott's battle-line was there. And the second wave of fighters from the BS6Vs arrived, armed with primary packs and eager to hunt monitors. After six of those titanic ships had died, the Bugs broke off the attack.

Prescott was left staring at a plot that was far less colorful than it had been. Few of the fortresses of the inner shell remained, and virtually all of those were critically damaged. The stardustlike lights of mine patterns and weapon buoys were largely gone. And Sixth Fleet had lost six superdreadnoughts, three assault carriers, two battleships, nine battlecruisers and over six hundred fighters.

*But,* he thought wearily, *we held.*

*All things considered, the Fleet had had the better of the exchange. True, in addition to six monitors, forty-one superdreadnoughts had been lost. So had all ninety-three light cruisers, and over ninety-five percent of the gunboats—but they didn't count. Admittedly, the failure to penetrate to the system's inhabited planet was disappointing. Still, the probe of the defenses had yielded valuable information, which could be put to good use when the new technology currently nearing the end of its development process was operationally deployed.*

Prescott put down the sheet of hardcopy he'd been studying as Zhaarnak entered the office.

"You should not let yourself dwell upon it, Raaymmonnd," the Orion said with the reproving concern a warrior's *vilkshatha* brother was permitted.

"I know." But Prescott's eyes kept straying toward the flimsy paper, then shying away from it towards the window with its swaying featherleaf limbs and the panorama of Xanadu beyond them.

Sixth Fleet's final casualty figures were in: 24,302 dead. Fortress Command was still tracking down some unaccounted-for escape pods, but the fortresses' confirmed dead were around 23,000. It was worse than the losses in ships and orbital fortresses. And it had been inflicted despite months of preparation aimed at preventing it.

Zhaarnak studied his *vilkshatha* brother as unobtrusively as possible. His caution wasn't really required, for Prescott carried too heavy a load of grief and guilt to notice.

It was odd, really. Until this Human had come like some *chegnatyu* warrior from the ancient myths to succor his own bleeding command and save the lives of billions of his people, Zhaarnak'diaano had never thought about how Humans might deal with the aftermath of battle. What true warrior would have cared how *chofaki* felt? And even if he'd ever felt the slightest curiosity, how could he have understood how such an alien being, sprung from such an alien culture, felt about such things?

But Raymond Prescott had overturned that comfortable, bigoted chauvinism. He had stunned Zhaarnak with his courage, shamed him with the gallantry with which Human ships stood and died to defend an entire twin-planet system of people not their own. He had astonished Zhaarnak with his command of the Tongue of Tongues, his grasp of the precepts of *Farshalah'kiah* . . . and his understanding of a warrior's grief for his *farshatok* and his pride in all they'd died to accomplish.

And because Raymond Prescott had done and understood those things, Zhaarnak'telmasa knew what a *chofak* felt when those under his command fell. And he knew that as well as Prescott understood and honored the ways of the *Zheeerlikou'valkhannaiee*, he was also the product of his Human code, his Human sense of honor . . . and responsibility. It was difficult for Zhaarnak to wrap his mind around some aspects of that part of his *vilkshatha* brother, yet he'd made great strides in the years since Prescott had shown him there was another truth, another Warriors' Way that was just as valid, just as true, as the *Farshalah'kiah* itself. And so he knew it would take time for his brother to heal. Time for him to accept what any Orion commander would already have seen—that no one could have anticipated what the Bugs would do. Alex Mordechai's death wasn't Raymond Prescott's fault, yet that death was one more burden Prescott would bear, and it would weigh all the heavier upon him because he would tell himself that Mordechai had died believing his Fleet commander had refused to commit the fighters which might have saved so many of his people from the Bugs' kamikazes.

There was little Zhaarnak could do to speed that healing process. What he could do, he would. But for the moment, all that consisted of was distracting his brother from his grief.

"At least," he said briskly, "we have a definite set of recommendations to submit to the Joint Chiefs of Staff."

"Right!" Prescott swung around to face him, ghosts put behind him . . . for the moment, at least. "If necessary, I'll go to Alpha Centauri and argue it to Lord Talphon and the Sky Marshal personally. We need more BS6Vs and more fighters for them. The day of the close-in warp point defense is over. Energy weapon-armed fortresses are nothing but death traps." He ordered himself not to recall his last glimpse of Alex Mordechai's face. "We need to smother the approaches to that warp point in mines and IDEWs, supported by distant missile-armed fortresses and even more distant fighter platforms."

"In particular," Zhaarnak added, eyes gleaming as his *vilk-shatha* brother roused himself from his melancholy, "we want enough fighters to maintain a constant patrol of the warp point in strength."

"Precisely!"

Zhaarnak let his own eyes stray to the window. The featherleaf had grown.

"We will be able to report something else, as well. Something that should be of interest to your Ahhdmiraaaal LeBlaaanc."

"You mean the new tactics the Bugs employed? Their small craft's heavier antimatter loads and the gunboats' new effectiveness?"

"No. Those were implicit in our initial report of the action. I mean the inference we have drawn from the Bahgs' uncharacteristic withdrawal after sustaining heavy but not annihilating losses."

"Ummm . . ." Prescott frowned thoughtfully. "It *is* just inference, you know," he cautioned after a moment.

"Truth. Nevertheless, they seem to be displaying a new sensitivity to losses, at least by their own previous standards. You and I both saw them recoil in Alowan, but that was a special case. That time, they were obviously exploiting an unexpected opening with whatever forces were locally available, and they could not afford to see those forces destroyed until they were able to reinforce behind them. But *this* time, they had months to prepare their assault. No doubt that explains much about the sheer weight of their attack, but surely it must also mean that they were given sufficient time to assemble all available forces to support the operation. Yet despite the time they were given to concentrate, they broke off rather than accept annihilation. Can it be that they are finally beginning to feel a need to conserve their major combatants? That it was not possible for them to assemble sufficient reserves to feel confident of their ability to resist *our* attacks if they persisted in their own as they always have before?"

He cocked his ears at Prescott, his expression eager, and watched the line of speculation he had sparked working behind his brother's eyes.

"It is not unreasonable, Raaymmonnd," he continued, "considering the number of such ships we have destroyed in the course of the war." He leaned forward with a predator's controlled eagerness. "And if it is true, perhaps it is time for a riposte into Home Hive Three."

Prescott considered. He couldn't let himself believe that the Bugs were at last beginning to scrape the bottom of their barrel of major combatants—not without stronger evidence.

"Remember how many fortresses the RD2s have detected covering their end of the warp line," he cautioned Zhaarnak. "Even if they're running short of starships, they've got plenty of firepower waiting for us."

"Granted. But that very drone data provides us with excellent SBMHAWK targeting information on those fortresses. And their supporting mobile forces have just received a serious battering, including the loss of practically all of their gunboats."

"We took losses, too." For a moment, Prescott's eyes flickered back toward the sheet of hardcopy, then shied away once more.

"But we have reinforcements on the way—heavy carrier and battle-line units to more than make up our losses."

"Until those reinforcements get here, we can't afford to risk heavy losses to our own mobile forces. For now, those forces are essential to the defense of the system."

Prescott recognized the signs of sobering in his *vilkshatha* brother. Zhaarnak knew that the warp point lay practically denuded of its inner defenses, but the Orion stuck to his guns.

"Agreed. But we have the shipyard facilities here to repair our units' battle damage and replenish our expendable munitions—unlike the Bahgs in what was once Home Hive Three." Very briefly, carnivore's teeth flashed in russet fur.

Prescott considered only a moment. Characteristically, he'd been attempting to moderate Zhaarnak's aggressive instincts because he understood them only too well.

"All right. I agree. Our strikegroups should be back up to strength by the first of standard April. We'll tell the staff to plan on that date, and factor in those of our damaged ships we can get back into action by then—which should be all but the really heavily damaged ones."

"Good. Let us set up a staff conference to discuss the details." Zhaarnak stood, and as he did, something outside the window caught his eye. "Raaymmonnd, what is *that*?"

Prescott stood up and followed Zhaarnak's pointing hand. In the distance, beyond the spacefield, the land rose in a curve of the Alph River. Atop that hill, a building of monumental proportions was in the early stages of construction.

"Oh, that. The provisional government of Xanadu has decided to go ahead with the plans for Government House. It's going to be quite an establishment for such a young colony. A lot bigger than they need or can afford, really."

"But it was my impression that they were postponing actual construction until such time as the system is secure from attack."

"That's what they *were* planning. But after the battle, they voted to go ahead with it."

Zhaarnak reminded himself that his *vilkshatha* brother was, after all, an alien—and, as such, was bound to occasionally say things that made no apparent sense.

"Ah . . . Raaymmonnd, do they not understand that—?"

"Oh, yes. We haven't tried to censor the news of the battle. They know that even though the Bugs were stopped, it was a near thing. They also know the Bugs are still only one transit away, and that, barring a miracle, they'll be back to try again."

"Then. . . ?" Zhaarnak's voice trailed to an uncomprehending halt, and Prescott smiled.

"I believe it's their way of saying that Xanadu is theirs, and that they mean to stay here permanently."

"But, Raaymmonnd, we have never even considered evacuating this planet!"

"Oh, no. They're not making the statement to us. They're making it to the Bugs."

"To the *Bahgs*?!"

"Yes. What they're telling the Bugs is . . ." Prescott sought for a way to explain it. "Zhaarnak, are you familiar with this human gesture?" He held up his right hand, loosely formed into a fist but with the middle finger vertically upraised.

"I know of it. Like so much else that pertains to Humans, I have never really understood what it means. But I believe I am beginning to."

# CHAPTER SIX
## April Fool!

KONS *Celmithyr'theaarnouw* hovered motionless in space while the units of Sixth Fleet gathered about her in ponderous ranks of destruction. The superdreadnought was once again the fleet flagship, for Sixth Fleet was going back to Home Hive Three, and that meant Zhaarnak'telmasa was once again its commander.

Zhaarnak sat in his command chair, watching the quiet, efficient bustle of his staff, and allowed himself once more to feel that pride in his warriors which only an Orion—and, he reminded himself, one or two very special Humans—could truly understand. Since Raymond Prescott had changed his perception of all things Human, Zhaarnak had attempted to make up for the many years he'd lost in understanding the virtually hairless, naked-skinned, flat-faced aliens who once had humbled almost a thousand of their own years of the *Zheeerlikou'valkhannaiee's* pride and were now their allies. The demands of the war had left him precious little time for his studies, but his *vilkshatha* relationship with Prescott had compensated by giving him a priceless and unique perspective. And because he'd gained that perspective, he was aware of the difficulty inherent in correctly translating the term *farshatok* into Standard English. The best the Humans had been able to do was a mere literal rendering: "warriors of the fist." So far as it went, that was a fair enough translation, but the full concept—the concept of a group of warriors so finely and completely integrated as to represent the individual fingers which combined into a lethal weapon as their commander's fist was closed—carried connotations and implications few Human analysts had ever truly grasped. There were levels of mutual commitment, strands of trust and courage, a willingness to sacrifice everything for victory—or for one another—and a fine fusion of efficiency in it which seemed to have eluded even some of the best Humans who had considered the concept.

Perhaps that was because so few Humans truly understood the full implications of the *Farshalah'kiah*. Raymond did, of course, but, then, Raymond was an extraordinary individual, whatever his birth race. Most Humans, though, Zhaarnak knew, viewed his own species' concept of honor through a veil woven of obstacles that ranged from the same sort of stereotypical contempt he himself had once had for the ill-understood concepts of *Human* honor, to simple incomprehension which strove with genuine open-mindedness to cross the gap between two very different races... and failed. He knew that many—perhaps most—Humans found his own people unreasonably touchy in matters of personal honor. That they found the notion that the only truly honorable form of combat required a warrior to risk his own life bizarre and vainglorious, and that many of them believed the *Zheeerlikou'valkhannaiee* never truly bothered to *think* at all, because it was so much simpler to react as an honor-bound automaton.

Perhaps that was chauvinistic of them, but he'd been more than sufficiently chauvinistic himself in his time. And, although he might not particularly care to admit it, there were those among the Khan's warriors who fit that stereotype depressingly well. But what those Humans missed was the absolute centrality of an Orion warrior's sense of honor to the way in which he defined himself. It was that sense of honor which told him who he was, which linked him to all of the generations of his fathers and mothers in honor and charged him never to disgrace them. It gave him the ability to know what his Khan and his people expected of him, and—even more importantly—what he expected of himself as his Khan's representative in the defense of his people. And so, in a way he sometimes wondered if even Raymond fully recognized, it was that sense of honor which tied a species of fiery individuals, with all of the natural independence the Humans associated with the Terran species called "cats," into the unified cohesion of the *Zheeerlikou'valkhannaiee* and had launched them into the creation of the first interstellar imperium in recorded history.

It was what made all of his people, warriors and civilians alike, *farshatok* in a greater sense, and he wished he could find the way to explain that side of them to their Human allies.

*But perhaps it is not something which* can *be "explained,"* he thought, watching the icons of Sixth Fleet settle into their final formation in his plot. *Perhaps it is something which may only be demonstrated. Yet whether it can be explained or analyzed or not, it can certainly be shared, for surely each and every one of the warriors of this Fleet, whatever their races, have become* farshatok.

It was almost time, and he made himself lean back in his command chair. He felt the tips of his claws gently kneading in and out of its padded armrests, and his mind went back to that moment when the awareness of the many strands of honor which bound this force together had suddenly flowed through him.

"I don't like it," Raymond Prescott said unhappily, looking back and forth between Zhaarnak and Force Leader Shaaldaar.

"I am not especially delighted with it myself, Raaymmonnd," Zhaarnak replied mildly. "Unfortunately, I do not see an alternative."

"Truth," Least Fang Meearnow'raalphaa agreed glumly, and the Tabby carrier commander and Rear Admiral Janet Parkway, his human counterpart, exchanged grim looks.

Unhappy as Prescott might be, Meearnow was even less happy, although for somewhat different reasons. Like every Orion carrier commander, he disapproved in principle of the gunboat. He was far too canny a tactician to reject the innovation, even if it had come from the Bugs, but he regarded it as no more than a clumsy substitute, fit to be adopted only by those species so handicapped by nature as to be incapable of true fighter operations.

But however little he might care for the weapon system, he wasn't about to underestimate the effectiveness of massed gunboat attacks, especially upon starships during the first moments after a warp transit. Not only was the effectiveness of shipboard weapons degraded by the addling effect of transit, but so were the electromagnetic catapults of Meearnow's beloved carriers. In those brief instants of vulnerability when no weapon could fire and no fighter could launch, the shoals of gunboats with which the Bugs routinely smothered warp points could be lethal.

"The SRHAWKs should blunt of the worst of the threat without this sort of desperation tactic," Prescott argued, yet he heard a note of obstinacy in his own voice, a stubborn resistance to accepting Shaaldaar's proposal based less on logic than on acute discomfort with the entire notion.

"Yes, they will blunt the worst of the threat . . . if they perform as their developers hope and if the Bahgs react to them as *we* hope," Zhaarnak agreed, and his *vilkshatha* brother nodded in unhappy acknowledgment of his point. "We dare not rely upon those hopes, however. Certainly not before we have had the opportunity to test them in actual battle. And we do know that we cannot task the SBMHAWKs with the anti-gunboat role this time."

Prescott nodded once more. The sheer scale of the fixed fortifications the Bugs had thrown up on the far side of the warp point to Home Hive Three had stunned even the most pessimistic Allied analyst. As of the last RD2 report, they had emplaced no less than two hundred and seventeen OWPs, supported by just over sixty of their specially designed warp point defense heavy cruisers. The cruisers were extremely slow, but that was because they'd been designed as little more than slightly mobile weapons barges whose sole function was to back up more conventional fortifications. That made each of them considerably more dangerous than any normal starship design of the same displacement would have been.

Nor were the fortresses and cruisers alone. No Allied analyst was prepared to explain why the Bugs failed to make the same heavy use of laser buoys and IDEW that the Alliance did. Prescott certainly wasn't, but that didn't mean he couldn't be grateful for that particular Buggish blindspot. Unfortunately, they compensated to some degree for the oversight by the sheer density of the minefields they routinely employed.

Those inevitable clouds of mines had been duly laid to cover the approaches to this warp point, and the fact that it was a closed warp point made it even worse. Still, there were ways to deal with mines, even on closed warp points. Besides, *that* much had been anticipated. The numbers of fortresses being picked up by the RD2s had not, and they were the true reason for Sixth Fleet's disquiet. Even now, it was less the sheer number of OWPs the Fleet must confront than the speed with which they'd been assembled which had taken Sixth Fleet's intelligence types by surprise. Everyone had seen ample previous examples of the resources the Bugs were prepared to commit to defensive works, but in the past, they'd always been slower to emplace fortifications in forward star systems. Certainly, they'd never been able to equal the speed with which the Terran Federation's Fortress Command could do the same thing.

*This* time was different. They'd obviously assembled the core of their new fortress shell by simply towing the OWPs which had guarded the star system's other warp points into position to cover this one. But that accounted only for a relatively small percentage of the total number of forts now placed within weapons range of it. Obviously, they'd taken a page from the Terran playbook and shipped the individual fortresses forward as component parts, to be assembled on site. It was something they'd done before, but this time they'd set records for construction speed that not even the Federation's technicians could have equaled.

And that was the crux of the problem which had brought the senior flag officers of Sixth Fleet to this conversation. The numbers of fortresses waiting to resist them left them no choice but to commit the full fury of their SBMHAWKs against the OWPs. Which, in turn, meant that few or none of those SBMHAWKs could be used for the task of suppressing the combat space patrol of gunboats the Bugs routinely maintained to cover the warp point.

The SRHAWKs *might* provide at least partial compensation, although as Zhaarnak had just pointed out, they remained an unproven concept. Personally, Prescott expected the new system to prove much more effective than its detractors predicted, and much *less* effective than its proponents hoped. Not that he didn't approve of the somewhat devious thinking behind it. Or of the notion of hoisting the Bugs by their own petard . . . literally.

The Arachnids had introduced what the Allies had code-named the "suicide-rider" at the Battle of Alpha Centauri. As usual, it was a tactical concept which emphasized their alienness: a sizeable antimatter containment field and the equipment necessary to manufacture the large quantity of antimatter intended to go into it just before battle. It required relatively little internal hull volume, yet if a ship mounting it managed to perform a successful ramming attack, the ensuing explosion was invariably lethal to the attack's target. While not very effective at catching targets which were capable of evasive maneuvers, it had demonstrated its effectiveness against immobile OWPs and cripples only too convincingly.

It had a secondary effect, as well, for the sheer power of the explosion was sufficient to damage starships and forts even without striking them directly if they were in sufficiently close proximity to the blast. And as a sort of tertiary side effect, it was capable of completely destroying any fighter, gunboat, mine, buoy, or small craft which found itself within the blast zone when it went up.

The Gorm were widely and correctly noted for a methodical, logical approach to problem solving, and not for leaps of the imagination or sudden flashes of inspiration. Yet it was the Gorm who'd come up with the notion of applying the same principle—with a few modifications—to the Bugs. The initial suggestion had languished for several months without attracting much support, until the Ophiuchi, who'd lost more than a few strikefighter pilots to suicide-riders and the blast effect of small craft kamikazes overloaded with antimatter, heard about it. They thought it was a marvelous idea, and after some strenuous lobbying, the OADC had convinced the TFN's BuWeaps to devise what looked exactly like a standard SBMHAWK carrier pod, right down to ECM which duplicated its active sensor emissions, but was, in fact, stuffed to the gills with an antimatter charge almost twenty percent the size of that carried by a suicide-rider. The idea was that since the Bugs used their gunboat CSPs to attack and destroy SBMHAWKs before the pods could stabilize their systems, find their targets, and launch their missiles, those gunboats would also swoop down on the SRHAWKs, attack them . . . and be destroyed in the resultant explosion.

Given that the Bugs regarded themselves as completely expendable, the new weapon was almost certain to inflict heavy losses on them, and those losses would continue even after the Bugs figured out what the SRHAWK was. After all, it should be effectively impossible to distinguish between the two even if one knew they existed. That meant that any SRHAWK could be a standard SBMHAWK, and from the Bugs' viewpoint it would undoubtedly make perfectly good sense to sacrifice a gunboat and its crew in exchange for the destruction of a weapon which *might* threaten to damage a larger vessel.

But Sixth Fleet didn't have enough SRHAWKs to destroy all of the gunboats in the combat space patrol waiting in Home Hive Three, even assuming that they worked perfectly and that the gunboats attacked every one of them.

*Unfortunately, we also don't have time to do anything about it,* Prescott thought, feeling as glum as Meearnow looked. *That's another consequence of how quickly the Bugs got their defenses organized this time around. It would take months—weeks, at the very least—to ship in enough additional SBMHAWKs to take out the fortresses and the CSP, and we don't have months. In fact,*

*we've had to move Heaven and Earth just to make our April first
schedule. And if we let it slip past, who knows how many more
OWPs the bastards will have dredged up in the meantime?*

"I still don't like it," he sighed, "but I don't see any alternative,
either." He looked at Shaaldaar. "Please don't take my resistance
to the idea wrongly, Shaaldaar. Believe me, I fully appreciate your
crews' willingness to run such risks. And the cold blooded part of
me can accept the logic behind it. I suppose it's just . . . too similar
to too many things we've seen Bugs do. I know the reasons for it
are completely different, but the thought of *anything* that makes
us even remotely like them in any way . . . bothers me."

"I appreciate that, Admiral," the massive Gorm replied. "But,
as you say, our reasons for making the suggestion are quite different. And all of the crews have volunteered."

"And we shall accept their offer," Zhaarnak said firmly, speaking as the commander responsible for the operation and meeting
his *vilkshatha* brother's eye levelly. Unlike their Human allies, the
*Zheeerlikou'valkhannaiee* had amassed a vast store of experience
in fighting and training shoulder to shoulder with their Gorm
partners. They were not Gorm themselves, and Zhaarnak knew
there were nuances of the Gorm philosophical concept of *synklomus* they had not completely grasped even now. Yet they'd seen
what that concept meant to the Gorm, and they fully accepted
that however different the Gorm might be, they understood the
essence of the *Farshalah'kiah*.

He deeply respected his *vilkshatha* brother's Human determination to safeguard his Gorm allies' personnel as fiercely
as he would his own. It was, he knew, a fundamental part of
Raymond's own unyielding code of honor. But Zhaarnak'telmasa
also understood the Gorm who had made this offer, and he
would not diminish *their* honor by rejecting it.

*The Fleet had anticipated the moment when the Enemy would
return to the System Which Must Be Defended which had died.
Nothing of importance remained here, whether for the Fleet to
defend or for the Enemy to destroy, and yet the ruined system was
still a point of contact between them. Eventually, the Enemy must
attempt to expand that point of contact.*

*Once, the Fleet would not have concerned itself with the Enemy's
plans to exploit an avenue of attack, for it would have been the
Fleet which sought to use that same avenue to attack the Enemy.
But that doctrine had come to require . . . modification as the result*

*of recent unfortunate events. Fortunately, although the concept of passive defense had never been an acceptable strategic stance for the Fleet, the tactical need to occasionally stand upon the defensive had been recognized. The wherewithal with which to do so existed, if not in the quantities or with the degree of sophistication which the Enemy appeared to bring to the same task, and so did a doctrine to employ that wherewithal.*

*The Enemy's development of his stealthy reconnaissance drones complicated things, of course, just as the destruction of the industrial node within this System Which Must Be Defended had reduced the resources available. It had taken the Fleet some time to realize that the new drones even existed, far less to hypothesize their capabilities, and to date there was no immediate prospect of similar devices for the Fleet. Or, rather, the Fleet had more pressing concerns than the need to develop a robotic survey device when they could use swarms of expendable gunboats or pinnaces for the same sorts of missions. The Enemy's new reconnaissance capability did pose its own problems, however, particularly the fact that, as yet, the Fleet could neither reliably intercept and destroy the drones nor even know for certain when one might have spied upon its own defensive deployments. Still, there might actually be a way to make the Fleet's reconnaissance disadvantage compensate for its material weakness.*

Craft Commander Laalthaa crouched on the saddlelike construction which served his people as an acceleration couch and watched his small tactical repeater plot as the rest of the squadron settled into place about his gunboat.

Unlike the Orions, the Gorm thought the gunboat was a marvelous idea. Part of that difference in viewpoints could have resulted from the psychological differences between the two species, but the vast majority of it stemmed from the *physical* differences. Quite simply, the three-meter-long, centauroid, massively-thewed Gorm made extremely poor fighter pilots. Just cramming someone their size into something as small as a fighter cockpit was hard enough in the first place. Add the fact that the reactionless drive used by strikefighters had a much shallower inertial sump and so imposed brutal g-forces on their flight crews—and that Gorm physiology was poorly adapted to handle such forces—and the reasons Laalthaa's species preferred the gunboat became evident. The fact that gunboats, unlike fighters, could make independent warp transits was another major factor, but Laalthaa, like most Gorm, was honest enough to admit that in some ways that was almost an afterthought.

Yet it was that "afterthought" which had brought Laalthaa and his squadron to this moment, and he felt his own tension and anticipation reaching out to and returning from his crewmates.

Laalthaa knew that none of the other races allied to the Gorm shared their sense of *minisorchi*, but he was devoutly glad that *he* did—especially at a moment like this one.

On an emotional level, it was difficult for him to understand how anyone could function without that ability to sense the emotions and the innermost essence of his fellows. On an intellectual level, it was obvious to him it was not only possible but that in very many ways it appeared to be the norm. But that intellectual acceptance that beings could live and love and even attain greatness without *minisorchi* did nothing to abate his pity for them. What must it be like for them, at a moment like this, when each found himself trapped within the unbreachable boundaries of his own mind and heart? When he faced the crucible of combat all alone?

He shivered inwardly at the very thought and made himself concentrate once more upon his instruments even while the other members of his crew stood at the back of his thoughts and feelings.

"Stand by for transit!" Force Leader Shaaldaar's order sounded over his helmet communicator, stripped of its *minisorchi* by the impersonality of electronics, and Laalthaa settled his double-thumbed hands more firmly upon his controls.

"Begin the attack," Zhaarnak'telmasa commanded, and the waiting shoals of SBMHAWKs, SRHAWKs, and AMBAMPs flashed into the invisible flaw in space Sixth Fleet had come to invade. They flicked out of existence in Zephrain and rematerialized in Home Hive Three, and the boiling light and fury as dozens of them interpenetrated and destroyed one another announced their coming to the Bugs.

*The Fleet was as ready as it could have been.*

*Of course, not even the Fleet could be completely ready at all times, and so, as had been anticipated, the actual moment of the Enemy's attack came as a surprise. But the Fleet had allowed for that in its own planning, and the gunboat combat space patrol responded almost instantly to the fiery wall of explosions as the robotic missile pods erupted from the warp point. They turned directly into the attack, accepting that at least some of those pods would be targeted on them, not the sensor images of the orbital weapons platforms awaiting the attackers. Turning into them would simplify their targeting solutions and make them marginally more accurate, but it would also permit the gunboats' point defense to most effectively engage any missiles which were fired . . . and it was necessary if the gunboats were to lock up and destroy the pods before they attacked more important units.*

*Of course, some of the pods managed to stabilize their internal systems, lock on to the targets they'd been programmed to seek out, and fire before the gunboats could range upon them. Still others—the ones which carried the minesweeping missiles—fired even more quickly, since they were area attack weapons which were not required to pick out individual targets. That was inevitable. But the vast majority were still stabilizing when the gunboats opened fire upon them.*

*As important as it was to destroy the pods, it was almost equally important for the gunboats to retain the ability to engage the starships which must follow them into the system. The Fleet had considered the two responsibilities, which were at least partly mutually exclusive, and devised an approach to reconcile them. All external ordnance—missiles and FRAMs alike—would be reserved to engage the starships. Only the gunboats' internal weapons systems would be released for employment against the pods. That might make them somewhat less efficient as pod-killers, and it would inevitably require them to close to shorter attack ranges, but it would also preserve their ability to engage larger targets when the time came.*

*And so the Fleet's combat space patrol swooped into the clouds of stabilizing missile pods, selected its targets, and fired.*

*The result was . . . unanticipated.*

"Transit now!"

Laalthaa heard Force Leader Shaaldaar's order, and he obeyed.

*The Fleet's CSP staggered in surprise as the gunboat-trap pods hidden among their missile-carrying counterparts blew up in its face. The resultant explosions were less violent—marginally—than the fiery holocaust of a proper suicide-rider or the blast when two missile pods interpenetrated upon transit. But they were quite violent enough for their designed function, and over thirty gunboats vanished almost simultaneously in the firebulls of their own creation.*

*The remainder of the combat space patrol hesitated briefly. Not in fear or out of self-preservation, for those concepts had no meaning for the Fleet. Rather, the surviving gunboats paused long enough for the intelligences which commanded the Fleet to decide whether or not to continue expending them. The decision was made quickly, dispassionately, with none of the need to balance crew survivability against military expediency which might have afflicted another species.*

*The gunboats swerved back to the attack, closing in on their targets and engaging at minimum range, and the devastating explosions of the SRHAWKs resumed.*

*As always, the CSP's efforts were insufficient to destroy more than a relatively small percentage of the total number of missile pods the Enemy had committed to the attack, and the cost in destroyed gunboats was relatively high. Certainly it was much higher than the Fleet had experienced in any similar operation in previous engagements, and the gunboat squadrons suffered a higher than anticipated level of disorganization as a result.*

*The Fleet wasn't particularly disturbed by that outcome, however. By the very nature of things, gunboats were designed to be lost, and the degradation of the Enemy's pre-attack bombardment was well worth the price. Besides, the losses they'd taken, numerous though they might have been, remained considerably lower than would have been the case under normal circumstances. As the Fleet had anticipated, the Enemy had programmed few or none of the standard robotic missile pods to target gunboats in this attack. The Fleet took note of how well the new technology had performed its intended function and prepared for the next stage of the engagement, confident that any confusion from which the surviving CSP units might suffer would be more than offset by the inevitable disorganization any fleet suffered in any warp point assault.*

*The minesweeping missiles were a matter for somewhat greater concern. As this was a closed warp point, it had been possible to place mines directly atop it, and the Fleet had done just that. Unfortunately, the Enemy's mine-clearance missiles had proven even more effective than usual at blowing lanes through the minefields. If the Enemy's starships succeeded in breaking through the CSP, they would find numerous chinks in the mine barrier to exploit.*

*But, of course, first he had to get past the CSP.*

*The surviving gunboats prepared themselves to maneuver into the blind zones of the Enemy starships as they emerged one by one, in the Enemy's usual, inefficient manner, from the warp point. The greater than normal number of surviving gunboats should wreak havoc upon an opponent too persistently stupid to recognize how he handicapped himself by inserting his units into combat piecemeal rather than simultaneously. When the first starships appeared, they would—*

*And then, abruptly, the Fleet's calculations went awry.*

It was called "*synklomus.*" The Gorm word translated into Standard English as "House Honor," and it was a very simple concept. But, like many simple concepts, its implications were profound.

The Gorm homeworld was a place of massive gravity, deadly background radiation, and the dangerous flora and fauna of an ecosystem evolved to survive in such an . . . extreme environment. That homeworld had bestowed upon the Gorm a physical strength and toughness, and a radiation resistance, which gave them many advantages over other species who had evolved in kinder, gentler environments. And it also explained what fueled the Gormish soul.

Virtually every aspect of Gorm society, religion, and honor focused on the *lomus*, or household. The *lomus* was central to everything any Gorm was or might become. It was not a limitation—rather, it was a liberation. A support structure which encouraged each individual to explore his or her own capabilities, talents, and desires. But even more importantly, membership within the *lomus* carried with it *synklomchuk*, the duty owed to the house-kin under *synklomus*.

In the final analysis, every aspect of *synklomchuk* came down to a single obligation, a response to the harshness and danger of their homeworld which was programmed into the Gorm on an almost genetic level. And that obligation was to die before they allowed any other member of the *lomus* to come to preventable harm. *Any* harm.

For all their dispassion, all of their justly renowned logic, there was no fiercer protector in the known galaxy than a Gorm. Nor was there a more implacable avenger. Perhaps they lacked the fire of the Orion, or the flexibility of the Terran, or the instinctive cosmopolitanism of the Ophiuchi, but the Gorm compensated with a determination and a remorseless, driving purpose which Juggernaut might have envied.

It was *synklomus* and *synklomchuk* which had once brought the

Orions and the Gorm to war, for the Gorm had been determined to protect the *lomus* of their species from conquest by the militant Khanate. But in the course of fighting one another, Gorm and Orion had also learned to respect one another, and at the end of their war, the Orions had offered the Gorm the unique associated status with the Khanate they continued to enjoy to this very day. It had been a mark of the Orions' respect for the smaller and less powerful opponent who had fought superbly, with a gallantry and a determination any adherent of *Farshalah'kiah* could not but appreciate, and who had come within centimeters of victory before they were defeated. And as the Gorm came to understand the Orions better, they had extended the concept of their *lomus* to include their one-time enemies and newfound allies.

Just as they had now extended it to the entire Grand Alliance.

That was what the Bugs in Home Hive Three faced on April 1, 2365. An enemy they would never be able to comprehend or understand, but one whose determination and refusal to yield fully equaled their own.

There were only sixty Gorm gunboats in all of Sixth Fleet. Every one of them made simultaneous transit into Home Hive Three on the heels of the SBMHAWK bombardment.

Nine of them interpenetrated and destroyed one another, and ninety-nine Gorm died with them. But fifty-one of them survived, and the Bugs had never expected to see them. The defenders had anticipated the normal Allied assault pattern—a stream of tightly focused but individual transits, designed to get the maximum number of starships through the warp point in the minimum amount of time without interpenetrations. That was what they'd always seen before, and it was what their doctrine had been adjusted to confront.

And because it was, the surviving gunboats of the warp point combat space patrol were taken totally by surprise. With their squadron organizations and datanets already badly damaged by the SRHAWK surprise, they were still maneuvering to swing into the blind spots of the anticipated starships when the Gorm gunboats emerged instead and began to fire into their *own* blind spots.

Craft Commander Laalthaa and his fellows were still hideously outnumbered, but they rode the advantage of that surprise with ruthless efficiency. Of the sixty gunboats which made transit into Home Hive Three, only twelve survived to return to Zephrain, but their attack shattered what remained of the Bug combat space patrol.

Laalthaa was not among those who returned.

✧    ✧    ✧

Raymond Prescott's face was like a stone as Jacques Bichet and Anthea Mandagalla tallied the surviving Gorm gunboats.

The losses weren't quite as severe as Prescott had anticipated. But that, he told himself as Bichet completed the list of the dead, was only because he'd never expected *any* of them to return alive.

Bichet finished his report, and Prescott inhaled deeply. Zhaarnak had delegated tactical command of the initial assault to his *vilkshatha* brother, since Prescott's TF 61 contained virtually all of the heavy battle-line units suitable for a warp point assault operation. That responsibility left no time to let himself truly feel the weight of the sacrificial price Shaaldaar's gunboats had just paid.

"Enemy losses?" he asked in a dreadfully expressionless tone.

"The SRHAWKs must've taken a real bite out of them even before the Gorm ever made transit," the ops officer replied. "CIC estimates that between them and the gunboats, they destroyed virtually the entire combat space patrol."

"And the fortresses?"

"Concentrating all of the SBMHAWKs on them and the warp point cruisers paid off in a big way, Sir!" Mandagalla replied exultantly before the ops officer could answer. The chief of staff was bent over her console, studying the raw numbers from CIC. "My God, Admiral! According to the Gorm's sensor data, the SBMHAWKs killed *all* of the cruisers—all sixty of them! And they blew hell out of the fortresses, too! There's no more than seventy of them left!"

Prescott's eyebrows flew up in surprise. Only seventy? There'd been over two hundred of them before the attack!

"Do the RD2 results confirm those numbers, Jacques?" he demanded.

"As far as I can tell, yes, Sir," the operations officer said. "It's hard to be certain. There were so many explosions going on during the actual shooting that the on-site drones' sensor records leave a lot to be desired, and we're only just beginning to get the follow-on flight back through the point. CIC is setting up the analysis now, but the preliminary take tracks right with the Gorm's estimates."

"There is one odd aspect to it, though, Sir," Amos Chung offered from where he'd been studying the same data.

"Odd?"

"Yes, Sir. There doesn't seem to be enough wreckage."

"What do you mean?"

"Just that, Sir. There doesn't seem to be enough wreckage for the leftovers from the better part of two hundred OWPs."

"Come on, Amos," Bichet said. "We took the damned things out with antimatter warheads! Enough of those don't leave very much in the way of wreckage."

"I understand that," Chung replied. "But we didn't *have* that many warheads, Jacques. That was the entire reason we couldn't spare any of them to go after the gunboats."

"We can worry about the amount of wreckage later," Prescott decided. "What matters right now is whether or not we killed enough of them to continue to the next phase of the assault. Jacques? Anna?"

"We're within parameters, Sir . . . barely," Mandagalla said after a moment. She and Bichet exchanged glances. "We've done much better against the fortresses than we anticipated, and there are open assault lanes in the minefields. On the other hand, there seem to have been substantially stronger reserve forces in the system than we expected. Before they pulled back out, Shaaldaar's people picked up two more waves of incoming gunboats, each of them considerably more powerful than the CSP was. They also detected the approach of a Bug fleet built around at least twenty-five monitors. And although Jacques is right about the numbers of fortresses we've already taken out, the seventy or so survivors appear to be pretty much intact. They were putting out plenty of fire when Shaaldaar's gunboats pulled out, anyway."

"And we don't have enough reserve SBMHAWKs to take them out with a second wave," Prescott thought aloud.

"Doesn't look that way, Sir," Bichet agreed.

"On the other hand, Raaymmonnd," Zhaarnak put in from the com screen at Prescott's elbow, "we seem to have earned a high return on the investment we made with the first wave."

"Agreed." Prescott nodded firmly. "I'm just not certain that the return was high enough for our purposes."

"Sir," Bichet said diffidently, "if we move quickly, we'll have more than enough time to get the entire fleet through the minefield lanes before the main Bug force can get into shipboard weapons range of the warp point. We'll take some heavy fire from the surviving fortresses, and at least one gunboat strike will reach us before we get completely clear of the mines, but we can do it."

"And in deep space, we can match our speed and maneuverability and our advantage in fighters against their numbers," Zhaarnak observed.

"We could," Prescott agreed. "But would we be justified in doing that?" He held up one hand before Zhaarnak could reply. "I don't doubt that we can get through the mines before they hit us, Zhaarnak. I'm just questioning whether or not we can justify risking heavy losses—or even, conceivably, the complete loss of Sixth Fleet? I'd be more than willing to fight the mobile units, if it weren't for the fortresses—or the fortresses, if it weren't for the mobile units. But I don't think we have the reserve strength to justify taking both of them on when we don't have to."

"I dislike the thought of allowing any of them to escape," Zhaarnak grumbled. "Especially when the SBMHAWKs and Shaaldaar's *farshatok* have already achieved such an enormous success! Such opportunities should not be wasted."

"I hate not following up on an opportunity the Gorm paid such a price to buy for us," Prescott agreed. "And I'd prefer to finish them off, myself. The only problem I have is that I'm not sure they'd be the ones who got finished!"

"There *is* that," Zhaarnak admitted with the ghost of a purring chuckle. Then he inhaled deeply. "I am always impressed by your ability to maintain your strategic equilibrium, Raaymmonnd. And, as always, you are correct once more. This is not Telmasa or Shanak. Desperate chances may be justified under desperate circumstances, but even the Bahg forces which the gunboats detected are insufficient to threaten our grip on Zephrain . . . unless we advance too rashly and allow them to whittle down our own strength before they counterattack."

"My own thought, exactly." Prescott nodded. "What we've already accomplished represents a major victory, and I feel confident that we've forestalled any thoughts the Bugs might have entertained of launching another offensive against Zephrain." He shrugged. "We structured this entire operation from the beginning so that we could shut it down at any moment of our choice, right up to the instant we actually made transit into Home Hive Three and committed to action with their main forces. I'd say this is a time to count our winnings and walk away from the table."

"My heart may not be fully in it," Zhaarnak sighed, "but my brain agrees with you. Very well. We shall satisfy ourselves with the 'mere' destruction of a hundred and fifty fortresses, their entire CSP, sixty heavy cruisers, and several hundred patterns of mines."

He bared his fangs in a lazy carnivore's smile and chuckled once again, this time more loudly.

"A modest little victory," he observed, "but our own."

Three standard weeks later, they were in Prescott's office on Xanadu, staring at each other. Prescott let the sheet of hardcopy flutter down onto the desktop.

"I dislike being had," he finally said through lips that were an immobile straight line of anger.

"That is a trifle strong, Raaymmonnd."

"The hell it is! You've read this report. One of our RD2s actually caught them in the act of emplacing the buoy and observed what happened when they activated it! Presto! A new fortress!"

"I suppose," Zhaarnak philosophized, "that it was inevitable that they would develop third-generation ECM buoys. We ourselves have had them for some time."

"And never deployed them because there was no percentage in revealing the system's existence to them," Prescott agreed. "After all, it isn't nearly as useful to us as it is to them. The great advantage of something that can spoof sensors into thinking it's any class of ship—or fortress—is that it can dilute the effect of mass SBMHAWK attacks. And *they* don't have SBMHAWKs!"

"Truth," Zhaarnak agreed with a dry humor and an outward control that would have fooled most humans. "On the other hand, we now possess empirical proof that our own ECM3 buoys should function just as well as their developers predicted if the Bahgs ever *do* develop the SBMHAWK."

Prescott gave a furious snort and scowled ferociously down at the hardcopy report, and Zhaarnak joined his own scowl to his *vilkshatha* brother's. Uaaria and Amos Chung had delivered the latest bad news less than an hour before this meeting. Now that the analysts knew what to look for in their probe data, they'd been able to amass a more complete statistical picture, and the current estimates were that no more than ninety of the fortresses Sixth Fleet had attacked—and *none* of their supporting heavy cruisers—had been real. All of the others had been artificially generated sensor ghosts.

"Remember how puzzled we were by the shortage of wreckage?" Prescott said after a long, fulminating moment. His voice was less harsh than it had been, for he'd reached the stage where he was once again capable of wryness.

"Indeed . . . even though we did destroy a full third of the *real* fortresses."

The Orion spent a moment in silent, brooding contemplation of the number of SBMHAWKs that had been wasted. Thanks to the enormous productivity of the heavily industrialized Human Corporate Worlds, the expenditure was only an inconvenience, not a disaster. Still, it would require months to ship replacement missile pods to Zephrain, and while Sixth Fleet waited for them, any fresh offensive would be out of the question. He found that he . . . disliked the notion of having been so thoroughly taken in by something like the Arachnids, and he felt his claws creep ever so slightly out of their sheaths. Then he shook himself out of the mood.

"If anyone was *had*, in your human idiom, Raaymmonnd," he said, "it was me. I was in command for the operation."

"I was sucked in just as far as you were," Prescott reminded him. "If you'll recall, you took the course of action you did on my advice."

"Nevertheless, the responsibility is mine. So is the embarrassment."

Prescott groaned.

"There's going to be plenty of that to go around," he observed. "By now, our initial report of the action—complete with our original estimate of Bug losses—has reached GFGHQ. Which means it's probably reached the media—"

An indescribable low moaning sound escaped Zhaarnak, and Prescott cocked an eyebrow at him.

"It is even worse than that, Raaymmonnd," Zhaarnak admitted. "I have been putting off telling you this, but. . . . Well, the news has also reached Rehfrak."

"Yes?" Prescott prompted, puzzled by the reference to the Orion sector capital that lay one warp transit away from Zephrain, and Zhaarnak looked out the window to avoid his eyes.

"The governor there has decreed a celebration, complete with a spectacular parade, in honor of our 'victory.' He has invited you and me to participate. I am afraid I took the liberty of accepting for both of us, before . . ."

He indicated the sheet of hardcopy with a vague wave, like an object to which there was no well-bred way to refer by name.

Prescott buried his face his hands, muffling his groan.

Presently, he looked up and sought Zhaarnak's eyes. The Orion was already looking at him levelly.

"You're thinking what I'm thinking," Prescott stated, rather than asked.

"Yes, I suspect I am."

There was no need to verbalize what it was they were both thinking: that the new findings, unlike the preliminary report, had not yet been dispatched to Alpha Centauri. Instead, they considered each other in speculative silence. Then Prescott gave his head an emphatic shake.

"No, of course not—"

"Out of the question," Zhaarnak declared simultaneously.

"GFGHQ needs to know that the Bugs have the DSB-ECM3."

"Most certainly."

Thus they briskly put temptation behind them. Afterwards, the human sigh and the Orion rustling purr were almost inaudible.

*Well*, Prescott reflected with a small, crooked grin as he considered the date of the battle, *Zhaarnak has been after me to explain some of our human holidays to him. At least now I have an* excellent *example of how April Fool's Day works!*

Kthaara'zarthan looked across his desk at his two human visitors and nodded reassuringly in the manner of their race.

"Yes, Sky Marshaaal, I have sent personal messages to both Lord Telmasa and Fang Presssssscottt, assuring them of my unabated confidence in them. I have also sent a personal message to the *Khana'khanaaeee* stating the same thing—although that was really little more than a formality, for Small Fang Zhaarnak was never in any real danger. I imagine your own similar message was of more urgency."

Ellen MacGregor winced. The media-induced hysteria was dying down by now. But it had created such an uproar in the Legislative Assembly that she'd thought it was worth explaining the facts of life to Federation President Alicia DeVries directly. Admittedly, the Presidency wasn't what it once had been. The Corporate Worlds had amended the Federation's Constitution into a parliamentary cabinet system, with the actual levers of government in the hands of the Legislative Assembly that they and their Heart World allies controlled. But the popularly elected president still commanded a kind of prestige unequaled by the prime minister . . . and was still commander-in-chief of the armed forces.

"I think we're past the point where there's any danger of anything stupid being actually done, as opposed to merely *said*," she said cautiously. "It wouldn't have been so bad at any other time."

Kthaara knew his human politics well enough by now to understand what she meant. The second message from Sixth Fleet headquarters had reached Alpha Centauri while a special select subcommittee of the Assembly's Naval Oversight Committee—including Chairman Waldeck—had been on a junket to Nova Terra. Naturally, they'd seized the opportunity to extend their stay and hold endless hearings, basking in the media limelight and artificially prolonging the furor.

"You are due to appear before them later this afternoon, are you not?" the Orion asked with a twinkle of mischievous malice.

"Don't remind me!" MacGregor kneaded her forehead, behind which she felt the beginnings of a migraine.

The other human present didn't quite dare to emulate Kthaara's smile, although the temptation was undeniable.

"There's a good side to this," he ventured cautiously instead, and MacGregor turned her brooding, dark-brown eyes on him.

"Whatever would that be, Admiral LeBlanc?"

"Well, Sky Marshal, if you think about it, the public's reaction has been one of disappointment that not as *many* Bugs were killed as they'd been led to believe. It may be petulance, but at least it isn't panic."

"Hmmm . . . Something to be said for that, I suppose."

"Also," LeBlanc continued, stroking his beard thoughtfully, "there's the analysis by Sixth Fleet's two top intelligence types, Uaaria and Chung."

"The—?" MacGregor furrowed her brow, then nodded. "You're talking about the addendum to the second report?"

"Yes, Sir. Admiral Prescott and Lord Telmasa both endorsed it."

"I remember seeing it, but I haven't had time to read it, what with the hearings," MacGregor admitted, looking back over the vistas of wasted time much as Zhaarnak and Prescott had contemplated their wasted SBMHAWKs.

"What do they say?" Kthaara asked.

"They were struck by the way the Bugs' behavior in seeking to exaggerate the strength of their warp point defenses seemed to dovetail with their behavior at the time of their attack on Zephrain. As you'll recall, they broke off the assault while they still had forces left."

"So they did," Kthaara acknowledged. "Very out of character. They have always pressed on without regard to losses when an outcome was still in the balance."

"Well, Uaaria and Chung put all this together with their theory of the Bugs' socioeconomic structure, which Admiral Prescott forwarded to us after the initial incursion into Home Hive Three—"

"Yes, I remember," MacGregor put in impatiently. "You briefed us on it. I found myself wondering if we dared to let ourselves believe a bit of it."

"Then you'll be even more hesitant to believe what they're theorizing now, Sky Marshal. They think the Bugs' new sensitivity to losses, and their attempt to defend the warp point as cheaply as possible, argue that they're finally getting overextended. If they are, then the loss of Home Hive Three's industrial base would have made them even more so—which would help explain why it's only just now becoming apparent."

"The very fact that they have nothing left to defend in Home Hive Three might have influenced their decision not to commit as much actual—as opposed to illusory—force to its defense as they could have," Kthaara observed.

"Still and all," LeBlanc rejoined, sticking to his guns, "they've never passed up an opportunity to bleed an attacking force before, regardless of losses to themselves." He met his superiors' eyes unflinchingly. "I don't know for certain that Uaaria and Chung have the right answer. But *something* has changed in the Bugs' behavior."

"Hmmm . . ." MacGregor frowned. "Interesting. Possibly even relevant." She stood up slowly. "But at the moment, I'm due for another hearing before the select subcommittee—where, you can be assured, interest and relevance will both be in short supply."

Legislative Assemblywoman Bettina Wister's irritatingly nasal voice had never been an insufferable political handicap, because sound mixers directed by a sophisticated computer program edited it out of her broadcast campaign speeches. But Ellen MacGregor, sitting across the table from her, had to endure it, for this was a closed session of the subcommittee . . . and an opportunity for Wister to vent her raging contempt for all things military without risk of voter fallout.

"I am *appalled*, Sky Marshal, by your *blatant* bypassing of properly constituted civilian authority! Your *improper* and *illegal* action in communicating directly with President DeVries, attempting to shield your Prescott from the consequences of his *criminal* incompetence, is a slap in the face to the Legislative Assembly—and to the people of the Federation, whom it represents!"

MacGregor didn't need to consult the legal officer seated behind her to answer that one.

"I remind the honorable assemblywoman that as Sky Marshal, I report directly to the President, in her capacity as Commander in Chief. The Naval Oversight Committee is not in my chain of command, for all the profound respect in which I hold it." Since becoming Sky Marshal, she'd learned to say things like that without gagging, and a lifetime's habit of self-discipline had held her alcohol intake steady.

"How typical! I warn you, Sky Marshal, the time will come when the human race, under the enlightened guidance of the Liberal-Progressive Party, will have evolved to a state of consciousness far above the mindless aggressiveness you and your kind represent! We will no longer need hired thugs like you and Prescott to fight the wars that you yourselves provoke, creating imaginary enemies in order to justify your own existence!"

"Point of personal privilege, Mr. Chairman," MacGregor said with a mildness which deceived absolutely no one—except, perhaps, Bettina Wister—as she turned to the corpulent figure at the head of the table. "Do I gather that the honorable assemblywoman from Nova Terra is accusing the Navy of 'provoking' the war with the Bugs? A war in which a large number of 'hired thugs' have forfeited their own existence by dying in defense of the Federation against this 'imaginary enemy'?"

Agamemnon Waldeck sighed inwardly. Wister represented Nova Terra, so there'd been no way to keep her off the select subcommittee visiting her own bailiwick. And there were times when it was useful to let her rant on unchecked. But this wasn't one of those times.

The problem was that she actually believed the slogans she spouted. Which, Waldeck thought, explained her long-term political success, although it might be a tactical liability at just this moment. She was mush-minded enough to reflect her constituency perfectly. Wealth and security had insulated Heart Worlders like those of Nova Terra from the real universe for so long that they could ignore it and float blissfully about in a rarefied atmosphere of ideological abstraction, and, under normal circumstances, Wister had to periodically reassure them that she floated with them, lest they worry that she might be letting her feet come into contaminating contact with reality.

Otherwise, they could fly off on a hysterical tangent, like the arrested adolescents they were.

At the moment, of course, Nova Terran public opinion had suffered something of a sea change where the military was concerned. Playing host to the most powerful warp point assault in the history of the galaxy, conducted by creatures which intended—literally—to eat you and your children alive if they broke through, was enough to make even Heart Worlders as militant as any Fringer could have desired. That had required a certain ... modification of Wister's public attitude towards the Navy, and she *hated* it. She (or her staff organization and handlers, at least) was canny enough to know she had no choice but to embrace her voters' current pro-war enthusiasm, and she'd done it, but that in turn only strengthened the virulence of her true contempt and hatred for the military.

Eventually, Waldeck knew, when the war had been won, Nova Terra's present militancy would fade back into its usual mush-mindedness. It might take a while, but it would happen as surely as the sun would rise, and when it did, the original, unmodified Wister would once again become a political asset rather than a liability.

Waldeck himself had no such worries. Corporate Worlds like his own New Detroit were quite democratic; the voters simply voted as they were told, just as they did everything else as they were told, by those who dispensed their livelihood. Waldeck was a great believer in democracy. No other system was so perfectly controllable.

And, he reminded himself, it was by manipulating the Heart Worlds into supporting them that the Corporate Worlds had gotten a choke hold on the Legislative Assembly. So it ill behooved him to complain about the necessary elements of that manipulation—such as indulging cretins like Wister. Putting up with her tirades in closed sessions like this one was probably the only way to keep the bile she felt over what she was forced to say in public from killing her off before the war could be won, after all. But she could be *so* boring! After a while, there came a time when the grownups simply had to cut her off—as he proceeded to do.

"I am certain, Sky Marshal," he rumbled from deep inside his enormous bulk, silencing Wister in mid-sentence, "that you won't read unintended meanings into what was perhaps an unfortunate choice of words on the part of the honorable assemblywoman." He gave Wister a side-glance that killed a renewed bleat aborning.

"Indeed," he continued, "this entire course of events has placed all of us under a great deal of stress. It all points up the need for better coordination between the military and civilian authorities, to prevent future misunderstandings. Don't you agree?"

MacGregor's eyes narrowed with suspicion at Waldeck's conciliatory tone.

"Misunderstandings are certainly to be deplored, Mr. Chairman," she observed cautiously.

"Excellent! We're in agreement." Waldeck leaned back and folded his hands over his ample paunch. "I believe the current unpleasantness could have been avoided if Sixth Fleet's command structure had included a high-ranking human officer who was more . . . Well, let us say, more sensitive to the political nuances than Admiral Prescott. His battle record speaks for itself." Another quelling side-glance at Wister. "But he tends to lose sight of the need for the Federation's high-ranking military officers to cultivate political awareness."

MacGregor's eyes narrowed still further, becoming dark slits of apprehension.

"What, precisely, are you proposing, Mr. Chairman?" she asked, and Waldeck settled his bulk into an even more comfortable position.

"There is an officer whose services have, in my view, been sadly under-utilized since Operation Pesthouse, owing to certain . . . unresolved questions concerning his conduct in the campaign. I suggest that he be assigned to Sixth Fleet in some appropriate capacity. There, he could advise Admiral Prescott on the political realities, a subject on which he's demonstrated admirable sensitivity in the past." Waldeck heaved himself up and leaned forward. "I refer to Vice Admiral Terence Mukerji."

At first, only shocked speechlessness saved MacGregor from saying the unsayable. Then, as that faded, cold calculation took its place. Waldeck had been about as clear as his compulsive deviousness ever allowed him to be: *Rehabilitate Mukerji and send him to Sixth Fleet, and this committee will make no further trouble about Prescott.*

"Yes!" Wister exclaimed, no longer able to restrain herself. "Admiral Mukerji understands the proper role of the military in a constitutional democracy—unlike a fascistic beast like Prescott! He's always shown the proper deference to the elected representatives of the people! He—"

MacGregor ignored the noise and looked steadily into the eyes that peered out from between Waldeck's rolls of fat. She knew she would have to accept this. So it wasn't worth the political price to say what she wanted to say: *"Unresolved questions" my ass, you tub of rancid lard! There was never any question about Mukerji's cowardice in Operation Pesthouse. He should have been shot—and* would *have been, if he hadn't spent years assiduously sucking up to you and other maggots like you.*

*No, the most we could do was relieve him. And it was Raymond Prescott's report that enabled us to do even that much. And now even that is going to have to be undone, as the price of keeping Prescott where he is and able to function effectively.*

She waited until Wister had run out of breath or rhetoric or, perhaps, both. Then, ignoring the assemblywoman totally, she addressed Waldeck.

"I'll certainly take your suggestion under advisement, Mr. Chairman. Perhaps something of the sort can be arranged." She told herself that her self-imposed limits in the matter of Scotch could go to hell, just for tonight. But even that thought couldn't keep her from adding one thing, in a carefully diffident voice. "One point, Mr. Chairman. In light of the . . . history of Admiral Mukerji's relationship with Admiral Prescott, have you considered the possible impact of this move on the efficiency of Sixth Fleet's command structure?" Waldeck looked blank. She tried again. "I mean, the effectiveness of Admiral Prescott—and, by extension, of Sixth Fleet—in doing its job, which is protecting all of us from the Bugs."

Waldeck continued to wear an uncomprehending look, as though MacGregor had spoken in a foreign language—as, in fact, she had. Then he brushed it aside.

"Well, I'm sure any difficulties can be worked out. And now, the Chair will entertain a motion to adjourn."

# CHAPTER SEVEN
## To Hold Back Hell

Another wave of fighters swept outward, glinting in the light of the blue giant star called Reymiirnagar—dazzling even across 3.6 light-hours—and arrowed away towards a warp point which, from the standpoint of the Bugs, justified this system's nickname: "Hell's Gate."

Actually, Reymiirnagar was called that because one of its eight warp points led to the system of Telik, which the Bugs had turned into a fair approximation of Hell after their first war with the Star Union of Crucis. Still, the mammoth asteroid fortresses which now guarded the system had given the name a whole new meaning. There were only six of those monstrous constructs, squatting sullenly within the minefields that protected them from ramming attacks. But they had expelled waves of missiles, over and over, each armed with the warhead equivalent of a deep-space laser buoy, to sear the warp point's circumambient space with bomb-pumped x-ray lasers.

*And that warp point is about to get even more hellish*, thought a shaken Aileen Sommers.

She stood before the great curving observation screen on the flag deck of *Glohriiss*. The flagship was a converted *Niijzahr*-class fast superdreadnought, but she thought of it as an assault carrier—which, functionally speaking, it now was. The deck vibrated under her feet as another squadron of fighters began to launch—the first fighters the Crucians had ever built.

*No*, she reminded herself firmly. *Not "Crucians." The correct term is* ghornaku, *or "sharers of union." The Zarkolyans and Telikans and Br'stoll'ee and so forth like being called "Crucians" almost as much as the Scots and Welsh like being called "Englishmen."*

*But,* she amended the thought as she watched the fighters streak outward, *it's appropriate for those pilots.* They really *were* Crucians, members of the batlike (to Terran eyes) race which had founded and still dominated the Star Union.

Wingmaster Demalfii Furra had also been a racial Crucian. Sommers would take to her grave the memory of her first sight of Survey Flotilla 19's mysterious rescuer in the com screen—the first time the two races had ever set eyes on each other. How long ago had it been ... ? She did the mental arithmetic with practiced ease. Fourteen standard months. It was now April, 2365, on the world she didn't let herself spend too much time remembering.

She felt another launch through the soles of her feet, and watched as the fighters flashed outward into the starfields. "Green" was too weak a word for these pilots, going into action for the first time after crash training in their race's first fighters. But Sommers had watched that training, and understood the implications of what she was watching. The Crucians were unique: toolmakers who were also functional flyers. A species that possessed two such extreme specializations at once was like a custard pie in the pompous face of scientific dogma. Sommers couldn't bring herself to worry about the headache the news would give human xenologists. What mattered was that the Grand Alliance now had an ally—without knowing about it just yet—with the potential to produce even better fighter pilots than the Ophiuchi.

*Now that they have fighters,* came the inevitable, guilt-inducing afterthought.

As if to underline it, Feridoun Hafezi appeared beside her, looking his most disapproving.

"Don't say it!"

"Don't say what?" Hafezi's black eyebrows were arches of uncomprehending innocence.

"You know perfectly well what! You're going to tell me I had no authorization to give the Crucians strikefighter technology."

"I wasn't going to say that. Besides, I don't have to. Your own guilty conscience obviously already did it for me."

"I do *not* have a guilty conscience! How could I have kept it from them, short of blowing up all of SF 19's fighters and carriers, as well as wiping all our databases? Should I have done that just to keep a vital technological edge away from a race that's fighting for its existence against the Bugs? A race, I might add, that saved our personal bacon! And furthermore—"

"All right, I admit it! You don't have a guilty conscience." Hafezi held up a hand to ward off renewed expostulations. "Besides, that really wasn't what I was thinking of."

"Oh?" Sommers cocked her head. "Then how come you're looking like the righteous wrath of Allah?"

"You know perfectly well why," he grumped, echoing her in a way of which neither of them was aware, and she sighed.

"I thought we'd been over that. It's vital that I accompany this fleet personally, as an earnest of our commitment to—"

"You could have sent me to represent you. Or Milos." He waved vaguely outward, indicating the part of the formation where Kabilovic was launching his human and Ophiuchi-piloted fighters—the few that weren't scattered around the Star Union to serve as training cadre—in support of the Crucians. "Or . . . somebody. But you've got no business anywhere near this battle, Aileen!"

It had been some time since they'd called each other by anything but first names in private. She gazed at him appraisingly.

"There wouldn't, by any chance, be any personal feelings behind this line of argument, would there?"

"Of course not! I'm merely pointing out that you're too valuable to be risked."

"As is obvious to any dispassionate, objective person," she deadpanned.

"Precisely! You're the ambassador, damn it! The Crucians trust you. You're irreplaceable."

Sommers could no longer sustain a straight face.

"What a crock! You know as well as I do that my ambassadorial status is, to put it very politely, unofficial. I don't exactly carry credentials from the Federal Foreign Secretary, you know. How could I? In case you haven't noticed, we're completely out of contact with home."

"That's just the point. Survey commanders have always had broad latitude in dealing with newly contacted races. As senior officer, you represent the Federation. Your status may be a little irregular, but it's still real." His sudden smile was like the sun through a rift in dark clouds. "Don't be such a damned hypocrite! You didn't let questions about your authority prevent you from going ahead and handing the Crucians every bit of technology in our databases, and offering them full membership in the Grand Alliance."

"No, I didn't, did I?" Sommers looked thoughtful. "All things considered, maybe it's just as well that we're out of touch with the Federation!"

After their combined commands had finished off the last Bugs in the red-giant system Sommers had come to know as Pajzomo, she and Wingmaster Furra had managed to establish communication of a rudimentary sort. It hadn't been up to deep philosophical discourse, but it had sufficed for Furra to suggest that SF 19 proceed, escorted by the Scout Wing she'd been supporting, to the great base at Reymiirnagar, four systems away. The suggestion had made excellent sense to Sommers, who'd been only too willing to put as much distance as possible between SF 19 and the Bugs.

Reymiirnagar's blue giant primary had a red dwarf companion, one of whose barren moons held a hostile-environment settlement of Telikans. Their koala-bear-like forms (albeit with arms of gorilla length) had brought home to Sommers that she was dealing with a multispecies polity. The tales they'd told had brought home even more.

A little over a standard century before, the Crucians had encountered an enemy beyond their most diseased minds' imaginings of horror—an enemy who committed acts inconceivable to any save the demons of Iierschtga, the anti-god of their theology. Hence, in the absence of any responses to communication, the Crucians had named their enemy the Demonic Realm (it might sound a little old-fashioned, but Sommers' specialists had assured her that no other translation captured the flavor of the Crucian term) and its denizens the Demons. The Star Union had survived only through a fortunate dispensation of astrographics ... which hadn't been so fortunate for the Telikans.

The Demon onslaught—the kind of grinding, crushing, unfeeling advance Sommers found all too familiar—had never been halted by the outmatched Crucians. Rather, it had finally reached a system where its sole avenue of further advance had been a closed warp point through which the Crucians retired ... without revealing its location. That closed warp point had been in the Telik system. Heroic efforts by the forces of Warmaster Nokajii Rikka—now the most revered, almost deified, figure in Telikan history, Crucian though he'd been—had won time for the evacuation of part of the Telikan population. But at length the last ship had departed through the cosmic anomaly which the Demons could not find unless shown the way. The Telikan refugees had received two things from the Star Union whose location their race's tragic sacrifice had preserved inviolate: resettlement on the world of Mysch-Telik ("New Telik"), and confirmation of Nokajii Rikka's dying pledge that their homeworld would eventually be liberated.

Sommers had learned all of this as she and her experts labored to establish in-depth communications with the Star Union's representatives. Given both sides' experience in such things, it hadn't taken long. Less than two standard months had passed before she offered the Star Union co-equal status in the Grand Alliance—including full access to technology the Crucians found dauntingly advanced—in exchange for assistance to her command and a promise of future cooperation in taking the war to the Bugs. Little more time than that had passed before the *Niistka Glorkhus*, the "Speaking Chamber," or all-Union legislature, had ratified the treaty produced by Sommers' legal officer—a mere lieutenant, who was surely the most junior individual ever to draw up such a document.

It was well that matters had proceeded so swiftly. Barely was the figurative ink metaphorically dry on the treaty when the word had arrived: the Demons had returned to Pajzomo.

The Crucians had held, but only at the cost of heavy casualties—including Warmaster Tuuralii Kerra, who'd arrived to take over from Wingmaster Furra during the four months that had passed since the latter's first contact with Sommers. Less than three standard weeks later, when the Bugs had come again in greater force, Furra—once again in command, following the warmaster's death—had been unable to do much more than beat a fighting retreat through a warp point other than the one Sommers had traversed to reach Reymiirnagar, seeking to draw the Bugs away from the most direct routes into the Star Union's heart.

However, in doing so Furra had led them *toward* the worlds of the Star Union member race known as the Br'stoll'ee. First in the Bugs' path, three systems away from Pajzomo, had been the infant Br'stoll'ee colony of Rabahl—a fabulously rich system with no less than three habitable planets.

Over the long generations of watchful waiting, the Star Union had built up a massive Reserve Fleet of mothballed warships, ready for instant activation, and the Reserve's mobilization had begun the moment Wingmaster Furra's first courier drones from

Pajzomo had spread the tidings that the War of Vengeance had begun. The first of the Reserve formations to reach the front had, by a suicidal self-sacrifice against a technologically superior enemy that Sommers wondered if humans could have matched, won time to evacuate Rabahl's colonists. The Bugs had taken possession of an empty system, which they'd proceeded to convert into an impregnable bastion.

By then, the Bugs had completed their survey of Pajzomo, and located the system's third warp point—the one leading eventually to Reymiirnagar.

The heroes of Rabahl had inflicted losses sufficient to bring Bug offensive operations to a few months' halt. But it couldn't last, and at length the remorseless machine had begun clanking forward again, smashing its way through system after system in a series of battles almost unimaginable in their destructiveness and intensity.

But by then, desperate improvisation had borne fruit. Despite all the difficulties—language barriers, technological incompatibilities, building up a Crucian infrastructure that could make the machines that made other machines—fighter production had commenced earlier than anyone had a right to expect. Those first fighters and their half-trained pilots had been rushed to Reymiirnagar. They'd arrived there by the time the remnants of the defending force had straggled in from the neighboring system of Tevreelan, convoying that system's evacuated Telikan colonists and bearing the news that Reymiirnagar was next.

Warmaster Robalii Rikka, great-great-grandson of the famous Nokajii Rikka, commanding First Grand Wing, joined the two humans at the observation screen, bringing Sommers back to the present.

"Ambassador," the Crucian addressed her gravely, "the fighters are all away. Would you like to observe at my holo display?"

"Thank you, Warmaster." Sommers knew it was a little irregular for the ambassador of an allied power to be allowed on the flagship of a war fleet engaged in battle, but this whole situation was irregular. The Crucians, vastly experienced in interspecies diplomatic relations, had possessed a pretty good idea of how spurious the title "ambassador" was even as they granted it to her. But they'd also learned how far behind the Federation they were in technological terms—and she hadn't tried to hold back the fact that this meant they were very nearly as far behind the

Demons. She might not be an officially accredited diplomatic representative, but to them she'd represented something far more important than that: hope.

Something else she hadn't held back was her total ignorance of how her own race and its friends were faring. It mattered scarcely more than the legalities of her status. Even the *possibility* of powerful aid against the Demons was enough to win a wholehearted commitment from the Crucians to join the Grand Alliance at such time as it could be contacted.

*Too bad the Grand Alliance doesn't know it has a new member,* Sommers reflected. *A member which, while maybe not in the same league as the Federation or the Khanate, is considerably larger than either the Ophiuchi Association or the Empire of Gormus. And one with some offsetting tech advantages of its own, like those anti-shield missiles and their laser warheads. Or those box launchers of theirs. And one whose peoples are just as motivated as any human or Orion to hate the Bugs.*

She thought of that motivation as she looked into Rikka's holo display and recalled the earlier stages of this battle. The Crucians had displayed once again their capacity for countering Bug technological superiority with sheer guts, and she'd watched, speechless, as swarms of corvettes had gone unflinchingly in against the mammoth ships emerging from the warp point. Those corvettes, smaller than any starships the TFN had used since the Second Interstellar War, almost a century and a half ago, were little more than second-generation ECM installations with engines strapped on, and their crews had spent themselves like wastrels to get in among the invaders and use their ECM2 to jam the Bugs' command datalink. By their suicide—there was no other word—they'd momentarily stripped away the Bug battlegroups' ability to coordinate their offensive fire . . . or point defense.

The Crucians had prepared for this moment by towing their asteroid fortresses and orbital weapon platforms across the Reymi-irnagar system from the Telik warp point to this one, which they'd never expected to have to defend. Now that awesome array of fixed defenses had taken ruthless advantage of the Bugs' fleeting vulnerability and poured missile fire into the maw of the warp point, turning it into a searing hell of x-ray detonation lasers. Bug ships had died at a rate that, Sommers had told herself, must surely be more than even Bugs could endure.

Robalii Rikka had evidently been thinking the same thing.

"I hadn't wanted to commit the fighters in this action," he said.

"I'd hoped to hold them in reserve for a time when they're truly ready and can be employed with decisive effect."

Sommers nodded. It seemed a shame to tip their hand now, revealing the Star Union's new fighter capability rather than waiting until it could be sprung as an overwhelming surprise. She knew exactly how Rikka felt.

But, like Rikka, she'd watched in the holo display as the Bugs, characteristically, kept coming without any apparent consciousness of the terrific losses they'd sustained. And as the deaths of the last of the gallant little corvettes had given the invaders back their command datalink and the rate of those losses had dropped, Rikka had seen that every remaining card had to be played.

He'd given the order to launch the fighters.

Now they were sweeping outward from *Glohriiss* and her sisters, a curving wall of tiny lights in the holo display that converged on the warp point and the spreading infection of "hostile" icons. No words were spoken as Rikka and his two human companions watched. They knew that, but for the few fighters piloted by Kabilovic's veterans, every one of those lights represented a young being about to pit an untried vehicle and all-too-brief training against enemies that summoned up nightmares from the depths of his culture's most terrible mythology.

But, Sommers reminded herself, those pilots had more than their inadequate training and nonexistent experience standing behind them. They had countless generations of ancestors who'd sought prey in the skies of the Crucian homeworld, swooping and soaring through a three-dimensional environment. Humans had to be taught the kind of spatial sense the Crucians got gratis from their upbringing and from their chromosomes.

The light-points swept in, and swatches of them were blotted out by the tremendous wealth of defensive fire from the Bug ships. But the missile-storm from the fortresses was unabated, and the damage it inflicted inched back up as the fighters distracted the Bugs' point defense. And as the Bugs sought to apportion their resources in response to multiple threats, more and more of the fighters got through, as well.

Sommers wasn't a specialist in fighter operations, but she was sure Kabilovic would confirm the impression that grew on her as she watched the display with occasional side-glances at the statistical readouts. The Crucian pilots displayed the raggedness one might expect of newbies, but little of the awkwardness and none of the hesitancy. What they performed was an inexpert dance, but it was a dance. And they remembered the fundamental rule of fighter warfare, and used their superior maneuverability to work their way into the blind zones created by enemy starships' drive fields. It was what made the tiny craft so deadly, despite their limited ordnance loads, that Federation and Khanate had once been forced to forget their own enmity, however temporarily, out of sheer self-preservation in the face of the fighter's genocidal Rigelian inventors.

Sommers maintained her ambassadorial *gravitas* when the fighters claimed their first Bug ship. Hafezi, under no such constraints, whooped something in Iranian.

There weren't enough fighters to be decisive by themselves. But they complicated the tactical problem faced by Bug ships already dealing with the massive bombardment from the fortresses, rather like a swarm of mosquitos around the head of a man trying to fend off a bear. And Rikka's battle-line was closing in to missile range.

And yet the Bugs kept emerging from the warp point, in their patented nightmare way.

*Will that nightmare ever stop coming back for me?* Sommers wondered.

But then there came a kind of crack, almost audible. Rikka, Sommers and Hafezi looked at each other wordlessly, recognizing it a heartbeat before the readouts confirmed it. The Bug ships already in Reymiirnagar space turned away, and new ones ceased to appear. The cacophony of death began to give way to a diminuendo.

Sommers became aware that she was drenched with sweat. Barely able to make the effort of turning her head, she looked around the flag spaces. The Crucians were physically and psychologically able to at least partly suppress their need for room, which otherwise would have made space vehicles out of the question for them. But this area was still more open and spacious than any human ship's interior, and she was able to see many of the crew.

Their reaction was interesting. It wasn't the demonstrative jubilation that humans might have evinced. It wasn't her own drained weariness. It was a kind of dawning awe. The Demons had been stopped.

"They'll be back," Rikka was saying. "And in greater strength. But reinforcements are on the way ... including *many* more fighters. We will be ready for them."

Sommers nodded. They would. Reymiirnagar would hold. Humanity, without knowing it, had an ally that would live.

*Assuming,* said the voice she could never dismiss, *that it's not too late for humanity.* And once again her nightmare returned—her *real* nightmare, the one that battle and sex and a few other things could momentarily banish but which always came crowding back to fill her waking consciousness with unthinkable dread.

*So it was confirmed. The elusive survey flotilla had survived after all. There was no other explanation for the fact that these other Enemies—rediscovered after their seeming vanishment so long ago—now had the small attack craft that had given the Fleet so much trouble, and which their own technological base could not have produced unaided. Worse, much of the huge stockpile of mothballed warships the Fleet had built up since the Old Enemies' disappearance, steadily assembling the mammoth reserve forces its doctrine called for, had been seriously depleted by the war against the New Enemies. Those ships had been intended as the spiked mace which would demolish any fleet the Old Enemies might have managed to build up by the time the Fleet found them once more. Now, at the very moment for whose inevitable coming all of those years of industrial effort had been committed, virtually all of the reserve had already been destroyed.*

*It was most inconvenient.*

*Of course, the strength of the warp point defenses—especially those asteroid fortresses—had also been unexpected. Such fortresses, unlike ordinary orbital weapons platforms, could hardly have been brought in piecemeal from elsewhere. To justify such extraordinary protection, there must be something special about the system from which the Fleet had just been repulsed. Perhaps it was these Enemies' equivalent of one of the Systems Which Must Be Defended.*

*But the attack craft had been the worst surprise. Now the Old Enemies had access to the technology of the new ones. That made it even more imperative that the two threats be kept from communicating with each other. Which, in turn, necessitated diverting more resources to this front. One of the Systems Which Must Be Defended had been assigned the responsibility for dealing with the Old Enemies while the others continued to concentrate upon the new, but that decision had been made in large part because the Old Enemies' technology had appeared substantially inferior to that of the New Enemies. Now, it seemed, that might no longer be the case . . . and that the resources of a single System Which Must Be Defended might not be enough.*

*But it would have to be. For one of the other four was now radioactive cinders, leaving only three to deal with the far greater threat posed by the New Enemies.*

*It was, indeed, inconvenient.*

# CHAPTER EIGHT
## Ride Boldly

Rear Admiral Andrew Prescott had discovered that he hated survey missions. This was only the third he'd commanded, but that was enough to know that he *hated* survey missions.

Someone had to command them, he admitted, and the ships assigned to them these days certainly made them big enough to be a rear admiral's responsibility. And the rise to flag rank which had made him a candidate for the job, while less meteoric than his brother Raymond's explosive elevation, was both professionally satisfying and a mark of his superiors' confidence in him. For that matter, his assignment to Survey Command at this particular point in the war was an enormous compliment . . . looked at in the proper light, of course.

He sighed and tipped back in his command chair on TFNS *Concorde*'s quiet, efficiently functioning flag bridge while he contemplated the peaceful imagery of the main plot. They were nine months out of System L-169, floating near yet another anonymous, uncharted flaw in space, and he'd spent a lot of time on Flag Bridge over that long, weary voyage. The flotilla had charted sixteen new warp points during that time, including the present object of its attention, which wouldn't have been all that many for a peacetime cruise of that length but was quite an accomplishment under wartime conditions of stealth and caution. Yet despite their achievements, the peculiar amalgam of tension, concentration, and utter boredom of their mission so far would have been impossible to beat. It was far harder than a civilian might have believed for people to remain alert and watchful—even deep in unexplored, potentially hostile space for weeks on end—when absolutely nothing happened.

*Of course, boredom is a lot better than what we'd be feeling if something did happen,* he reminded himself, and let his eyes linger on the icons representing his command. Every unit was cloaked, and *Concorde*'s sensors couldn't actually have found them all, even knowing where to look, but CIC managed to keep track of all their positions anyway.

Survey Flotilla 62 boasted twenty-three ships, from *Concorde* and the *Borsoi-B*-class fleet carrier *Foxhound* all the way down to four *Wayfarer*-class freighters and the escort cruisers *Dido* and *Yura*. They were all fast ships, too, and the flotilla's nine battlecruisers and three carriers represented a powerful striking force. But they weren't supposed to do any striking. If they were forced to, then their mission would have failed in at least one respect, for all this effort and tonnage truly focused on insuring that the five *Hun*-class survey cruisers and their crews of highly trained specialists were allowed to do their jobs unmolested and undetected, and everyone knew it. Especially the aforementioned specialists, who somehow managed (solely out of deeply ingrained professionalism and courtesy, no doubt) not to look too obviously down their noses at the ignorant louts from Battle Fleet assigned to do unimportant things like keeping the Bugs off their backs.

Prescott's lips twitched in a faint smile. It was possible, he supposed, that he was being just a bit overly sensitive. Under more normal circumstances, he suspected he would actually have enjoyed Survey Command. Even under those which presently applied, he wasn't completely immune to the wonder and delight of going places and seeing things no human could possibly have seen ever before. Unfortunately, circumstances weren't normal. Worse, he was one of those ignorant louts the specialists deprecated (although *very* respectfully in his case), for he'd never served aboard a single Survey Command vessel before he was assigned to ramrod an entire flotilla.

If it hadn't been for the war—and the Bugs—he probably would have repaired that omission in his resumé by now. The Prescott family had a long, distinguished tradition of service to the Federation's navy. Indeed, there'd been Prescotts in the TFN for as long as there'd *been* a TFN, and before that they'd served in the pre-Navy survey ships of the Federation, and before *that* they'd served in wet-navy ships clear back to the days of sail and muzzle-loading cannon. In many ways, the Prescotts and the handful of families like them were anachronisms in a service whose officer corps took self-conscious pride in its tradition as a meritocracy. Ability was supposed to matter more than family connections, and by and large, it did. Yet everyone knew there were also dynasties within the Navy, families whose members were just a bit more equal than anyone else.

Andrew Prescott had always known it, at least. There were times he'd felt guilty over the inside track an accident of birth had bestowed upon him, yet in an odd way, that advantage had actually conspired to make him a better officer than he might otherwise have been. Family tradition was a powerful force, and generation after generation of Prescotts had simply taken it for granted that their sons and daughters would carry on their own tradition and excel in the process. Andrew's parents had been no exception to that rule, and there'd never been any question in anyone's mind, Raymond's and his own included, what the two of them would do with their lives. Yet the knowledge that the name he bore might give him an unfair advantage or let him get by with less than the maximum performance of which he was capable (and, worse, that some among his fellow officers would think it might, whether it did or not) had given Andrew a special incentive to prove it hadn't. He'd entered the Academy determined that no one would ever have the slightest reason to believe he hadn't earned whatever rank he might attain, and that determination had stayed with him ever since.

At the same time, he'd been aware for years that he was being groomed for eventual flag rank, and in the peacetime TFN, that had meant at least a brief stint attached to Survey Command. An admiral was supposed to have well-rounded experience in all phases of the Navy's operations, which meant that on his way to his exalted status he had to have his ticket punched in battle-line and carrier ops, survey missions, dirtside duty with BuShips and BuWeaps, War College duty, JCS staff duty, and probably some diplomatic service, as well. As both a Prescott and an officer who'd demonstrated high ability (and ambition), Andrew had been in line for the appropriate ticket punching when the Bugs appeared. He'd commanded the battlecruiser *Daikyu*, and he'd already known his next command would be the *Borsoi*-class fleet carrier *Airedale*, after which he'd been almost certain to move over to Survey for at least one tour with one of the smaller prewar flotillas. Not as its CO, of course. That was a job for the specialists who spent virtually their entire careers in Survey. But he would have commanded one of the survey cruisers, which would have given him some hands-on experience with the job. From there, he would probably have moved up to take over a destroyer squadron or a cruiser division and might well have finished up with a second Survey tour as a flotilla's tactical coordinator, in command of its attached escort of "gunslingers."

But all nonessential personnel reassignments, including his transfer to *Airedale*, had been frozen when the sudden explosion of combat rocked the Navy back on its heels. That had been fortunate in many ways, given *Airedale*'s destruction with all hands at Third Justin, but it also meant that, as the war's enormous casualty toll shattered the Bureau of Personnel's neat, peacetime training and promotion plans, Prescott never had gotten a carrier command. On the other hand, he'd been kicked up to commodore, despite his lack of carrier experience, at least eight years sooner than could possibly have happened in time of peace, and he'd made rear admiral by forty, barely two years after that. He could wish his indecently rapid promotions owed less to the old tradition of stepping into dead men's shoes, but he was scarcely alone in that. And by prewar standards, virtually all of his new-minted flag officer colleagues and he were drastically inexperienced for their ranks. Ticket punching had been placed on indefinite hold, because the holders of those tickets had suddenly found themselves faced with doing something no Navy officer had done in sixty years: fighting an actual war.

But it also meant he'd never gotten that assignment to Survey, either, and more than a few Survey officers (including, unfortunately, Captain George Snyder, who commanded SF 62's *Huns* from TFNS *Sarmatian*) deeply resented being placed under the command of someone who had no exploration experience of his own. Snyder was at least professional enough to keep his resentment under control and accept Prescott's authority gracefully, but he was Survey to his toenails. He might be forced to admit the force of the logic which put experienced Battle Fleet officers in command of flotillas which might run into Bugs at any moment, yet that didn't mean he had to like it. And, truth to tell, Prescott had to admit that there was at least a little reason on Snyder's side. Survey work *was* a specialist's vocation, and it was painfully obvious to Prescott that Snyder, two ranks his junior or not, knew far more about the art and science of their current mission than *he* did.

The rear admiral rummaged in a tunic pocket and dragged out his pipe, and a throat cleared itself pointedly behind him.

He glanced over his shoulder with a grin as he extracted a tobacco pouch as well, then stuffed the pipe slowly under the disapproving frown of Dr. Melanie Soo. He met her gaze squarely, noting the twinkle lurking in her dark eyes, and replaced the pouch and reached for his lighter.

Dr. Soo—Surgeon Captain Melanie Soo, formally speaking—was the flotilla's chief medical officer. But her commission was a "hostilities only" one, and she would always remain a civilian at heart, with little of the veneration career Navy types extended to the lordly persons of flag officers. And for all that she was technically his subordinate, he always felt just a little uncomfortable giving her orders, since the white-haired surgeon captain was almost thirty years his senior. But all that was fine with Prescott. Soo had more medical experience than any three regular Fleet surgeons, and although she was the only officer of the flotilla who could legally remove him from command, he found her enormously likable. Which was one reason he enjoyed provoking her with his pipe.

Smoking wasn't—quite—officially banned on TFN ships, but that was solely a concession to the Fleet's increasing percentage of Fringe Worlders. Modern medicine had been able to handle the physical consequences of abusing one's lungs with tobacco smoke for centuries, and the lingering Heart World and Corporate World laws banning the vice in public places had less to do with health concerns than with core world standards of courtesy. Or that was they way *they* saw it, anyway. Fringers were more inclined to see it as an *enforced* courtesy, one more example of the intrusion of the Federal government into matters of personal choice which were none of its business, and the result had been an amazing resurgence of a habit which had been almost entirely wiped out over three hundred years earlier. And an insistence that they be permitted to indulge in that habit publically, as per the personal liberty provisions of the Constitution.

As a Heart Worlder himself, Prescott felt no need to make his pipe into a political statement. It was simply something he enjoyed, although he'd found lately that he took a sort of gloomy pleasure in knowing his vice was bad for him. And in indulging a habit he knew at least half his staff—and especially Dr. Soo—disapproved of strongly.

*Does them good,* he thought. *Hell, think how miserable they'd be if I didn't give them* something *to disapprove of!*

He chuckled mentally as he applied the lighter and sucked in the first fragrant smoke. As always, the ritual was soothing and comforting, and the fond resignation of his staffers only made it more so, in an odd sort of way.

*Probably a sign of senility on my part,* he told himself with another mental laugh, studying his unlined face in an inactive com screen. *Or maybe it's just the beginning of lunacy brought on by terminal boredom.*

Or tension, perhaps.

"That is a truly disgusting habit . . . Sir," Soo's soprano voice observed. It was, perhaps, a sign of her essentially civilian background that a mere surgeon captain would make such a remark to a rear admiral, and Prescott smiled around the pipe stem.

"Oh, yes? Well, at least it's not as disgusting as something like chewing gum!" he retorted. "And given all the other things that could happen to me—or any of us—out here, I fear that even your disapproval, much though it pains me, is endurable. Besides," he jabbed a thumb upward at the mesh covered opening directly above his command chair, "I had that air intake relocated specifically to prevent my smoke from offending your effete, over-civilized nostrils."

"And sinuses. And lungs," she agreed.

"*All* those persnickety internal components," he said with a lordly dismissive gesture.

"Just wait until *your* next physical, boy-o."

"Ha!" He grinned at her again, then looked over his other shoulder. Commander Joshua Leopold, his chief of staff, was bent over a console with Lieutenant Commander Chau Ba Hai, his operations officer, conversing in lowered voices rather like those of students who hoped the professor wasn't going to call on them until they got their class notes straightened out.

"Problems, Josh?" Prescott asked mildly, and Leopold looked up quickly.

"We don't have a complete report yet, Sir," he said.

"What's the delay, Commander?"

Leopold was not misled by the admiral's amiable tone. Andrew Prescott was a fair man and a considerate boss, but God help the man or woman he decided was incompetent or (far worse, in his book) a slacker.

"We're having problems with interference and disorientation

again, Sir," Lieutenant Commander Chau said before Leopold could respond. The dark-haired, slightly built ops officer was the staff officer technically responsible for the use of the new RD2 recon probes, and he met the admiral's gaze squarely. "I know the probes are officially cleared for field use, but they still don't reorient well after emergence—especially from an uncharted point. The guidance and memory systems just aren't tough enough to handle the grav surge yet."

"You're saying the data have been delayed."

"Yes, Sir. I'm afraid I am. We lost seven out of eight from our flight, and the docking program on the only one we got back aborted. I had to bring it in on a tractor, and it's pretty well scrambled. In fact, the computer rejected our first two data runs. I've got two yeomen decoding now, but I'm afraid these things can still stand some improvement."

"Understood," Prescott said after a moment. "Inform me as soon as you have something positive; don't bother with preliminary reports. And check with *Sarmatian*, too, Josh. Captain Snyder and his people seem to have some sort of mystical understanding with those drones of yours."

"Aye, aye, Sir," Leopold said just a tad stiffly, and Prescott nodded and turned back to his own plot.

"That was nasty, Andy," Soo chided too quietly for other ears to hear, and he quirked an eyebrow at her.

"Nasty? Whatever do you mean, Melly?" he asked equally softly.

"Commander Leopold is a nice young man, and that crack about Captain Snyder was a low blow. We all know he's some kind of electronic genius. Is it really fair to underline his superior performance for Commander Leopold and Commander Chau?"

"It keeps them on their toes, Melly. Besides, why do you think Snyder *is* an 'electronic genius'—aside, of course, from his extensive Survey Command experience? I'll tell you why. Some senior SOB like me dumped all over him when he was just a little feller, and he got good just to spite the bastard. That's known as proficiency enhancement."

"I don't believe I've ever had the mysteries of command explained to me quite so clearly, Admiral." Dr. Soo grinned. "But, then, I'm only an old country doctor who got drafted. As soon as this unpleasantness with the Bugs is over, I'll hie me back to my cottage and retire for good."

Prescott snorted derisively. Dr. Soo had been number two in

the neurosurgery department at Johns Hopkins-Bethesda back on Old Terra before she *volunteered* for naval service. And she'd volunteered only because she knew about the grim, genocidal reality behind the "unpleasantness" with the Bugs and couldn't not try to do something about it. She knew he knew it, too, and that he was damned glad to have her. It had always been TFN policy to assign only the best medical talent to survey flotillas, for there was always the chance of running into some new and nasty microorganism or disease, and there was no time to reach base med facilities if something went wrong in the Long Dark. The longer (and much more risky) survey missions which had become the norm over the last five years had only reinforced the logic behind that policy, but Dr. Soo was heavy metal even for survey duty.

"Watch me," she assured him. "But as a pseudo-civilian, I've been wanting to ask you something. It's driving me crazy, in fact."

"What? Asking for free professional advice? For shame, Doctor!" Prescott chuckled, but he also swung his chair to face her fully and cocked it back. "Okay, Melly. What's on your mind?"

"These probes keep breaking down. Everybody knows that, and Josh and Ba Hai just lost seven out of eight, and the one they got back at all is obviously pretty addled. So how come you professional military types carry on like they're the greatest thing since sliced bread if they're so temperamental and unreliable?"

"Because those probes are what's going to win the war—if anything will—once we get the kinks out," Prescott said flatly. Soo's eyebrows rose at his suddenly dead serious tone, and he reminded himself that she really was the pseudo-civilian she'd called herself. It was easy to forget, most of the time, given how thoroughly and well she'd gained command of the areas of responsibility which were her own. But questions about things like the probes drove home the fact that she truly wasn't a Navy surgeon. Not the way men and women who'd spent their entire careers attached to the Fleet were, at any rate. She simply didn't have the background to understand why the new probes were like a gift from the gods themselves in the eyes of professional naval officers.

"I mean it," he told her, and then puffed on his pipe again while he considered how to continue. "This war isn't like any of the others we've fought," he went on after a moment. "We knew a hell of a lot more about the opposition from the outset when we went up against the Tabbies and the Rigelians—even the Thebans—than we do about the Bugs. Aside from the fact that this time the galaxy really *isn't* big enough for the two of us, of course."

He smiled around his pipe stem, totally without humor.

"Even the best failsafe system can't guarantee total destruction of a ship's astrogation database, Melly. And even when the main system's scrubbed exactly as intended, there are so many backup data files, or even hard copy records, that after most really big battles one side or the other usually captures at least part of the other side's nav data. We catch some of theirs; they catch some of ours; and we both churn it through computers to translate and correlate it. And what do we get for our trouble?"

"Information, I suppose," Dr. Soo said.

"Exactly. We get pictures of how their systems look, possibly an idea of how many inhabited systems and worlds they have, and maybe we can even figure out how some of their internal warp lines run. Even in best case situations, it's information we can't use without a starting point, a break-in on one of their warp lines we can recognize . . . and one where there's not a damned fleet or fortifications from Hell to keep us out. But at least it gives us *some* notion of what we're up against.

"But not this time. I suppose it's possible some egghead back at Centauri will eventually figure out how to read what—if anything—we've actually captured from the Bugs, but it's not going to happen soon. Which means that everything we know, or think we know, about the enemy in *this* war is pure speculation. We like to think it's informed, intelligent speculation, but the hard evidence we have to work from is mighty sparse, and that's particularly true where their astrogation data is concerned.

"Oh, we know more than we did before the war began." He tamped the tobacco in his pipe and sucked in more smoke. "We know how the Anderson Chain lays out, for example. As far as Pesthouse, at least," he added grimly, and Soo nodded soberly. "And we know that Zephrain links directly to one of their central systems—one of the 'home hive' systems, to use Admiral LeBlanc's terminology. But we don't know *anything* about any point in their territory beyond Pesthouse or Home Hive Three, and every time we poke our heads through from Zephrain, they chop us off at the ankles. And we do the same for them, of course."

He smiled again, this time much less grimly, with pride in his older brother.

"But even if we were able to break through from Zephrain, take Home Hive Three completely away from them, and keep it, they'd only fall back fighting and fort up in the next systems down the warp lines, because by now they know about that connection. We managed to do to them more or less what they wanted to do to Centauri . . . and did do to Kliean. However big they are, we know we must have hurt them badly in the process, but we need to do it again. We need to break into their internal warp lines again somewhere else—preferably somewhere important enough that they have to commit to defending it—and rip them up. Cut loose in their rear areas and hit their battle fleet from as many directions as we can. Doing as much damage as possible before they can redeploy to stop us would be worthwhile in its own right, but a big part of our objective is to *force* them to redeploy. We want to avoid easily predicted frontal attacks and their casualty tolls as much as possible, but we also want to stretch them out, force them to defend as many points as we can. Given the nature of warp points, it's virtually certain that there are more points of contact waiting to be found, too—ones that would *let* us into their rear areas . . . or them into ours. But we don't know where they are."

"Well, the same thing's true for them, isn't it?" Dr. Soo pointed out. "I mean, we're no worse off than they are in that respect."

"'No worse off' doesn't win wars, Melly. Besides, how can we be sure that's true? The Tabbies thought Kliean was a safe rear area, and we thought the same thing about Centauri, but we were both wrong, and the Bugs found both connections before we did. Remember the Centauri Raid? We were lucky as hell we spotted their survey force and that they didn't have one of their damned assault forces handy. *And* that they probably don't have any more of a clue about how our warp lines lay out, or how close to Sol they were, than we have about theirs. By the time they were ready to try a real assault, Ray and Sky Marshal MacGregor were ready to slap them down, but it was all a matter of timing, and it could have broken in their favor just as easily as in ours.

"But what if the same thing happens again? What if they find a closed warp point in Galloway's Star? Or what if they find *the* warp point—in Sol or New Valkha—this time *without our noticing* before they bring in the heavy attack force? I'm sure you've heard what everyone's calling what Ray and Zhaarnak did to Home Hive Three. How would you like the Bugs to apply 'the Shiva Option' to Old Terra?"

"But they haven't found anything like that," Dr. Soo pointed out with a shiver. "Damn you, Andy! You shouldn't give old lady doctors the shakes!"

"No, they haven't found it . . . yet," Prescott agreed. "But they still can if we don't find them first. And find them *quietly*, without an engagement that tells them we've done it. Which is why we're sweating bullets to make these probes work. We've already proved at Home Hive Three that they're our best chance to sneak into the Bugs' backyard without their knowing we've done it, and sending them through does two things. It *doesn't* risk lives sending ships into God knows what, and, more important, we may get a glimpse of another El Dorado without alerting the local Bugs. If we get a look-see at another of their home hives, say, and they'd don't know it . . . Well, let's just say Battle Fleet would drop in one afternoon without calling ahead for reservations."

"I see." Dr. Soo rubbed her chin thoughtfully. "But if the probes are so good—or will be, once the bugs (you should pardon the expression) are out of them—wouldn't that also let us send out smaller survey forces?"

She gestured at the tactical display, whose three-dimensional sphere showed the glittering light codes of everything within thirty light-seconds, by way of illustration. *Concorde* herself showed gold, denoting her flag status. The other battlecruisers, the carriers, and the destroyers and freighters burned the color-codes of their types, all ringed in the green which identified them as friendly Battle Fleet ships. Only the *Huns* gleamed the blue-banded white of Survey Command.

"Surely that would let us use our strength more economically! And wouldn't smaller forces be less likely to be detected in the first place?"

"What? Leave the gunslingers behind?" Prescott's grin was just a trifle sour as he used Survey's derisive nickname. "Melly, you're a hell of a doctor, but you'd make a lousy fleet commander. Space is pretty big, you know, and an entire flotilla isn't measurably easier to spot than a single unit, assuming the flotilla in question exercises proper caution. So sending out a smaller force wouldn't appreciably lessen the risk of detection but *would* lessen the flotilla's ability to stand up to anything that did detect it. Hence the gunslingers. Only five of those ships really matter—*Sarmatian* and her bunch." He jabbed his pipe stem at the white dots. "The rest of us are just along to make sure their information gets home.

That's why a mere light cruiser like *Sarmatian* has a full captain for a CO. And why Snyder is my second in command."

"Redundancy?"

"Partly. Any good com net has built-in redundancy, of course. We could lose every ship but one and still do the job, which is why all our databases copy *all* astro data. In fact, though, the rest of us are here to protect those cruisers. They've got better instrumentation and specialist crews, thus our Captain Snyder, who's so good at his job. If only one ship gets home, GHQ hopes she'll be one of those five, though they'd never be so tactless as to tell the rest of us so."

"They don't have to with *you* along," Dr. Soo told him.

"Upset to find out you're expendable?" he teased.

"At my age, you're always expendable. But is there any chance of transferring to *Sarmatian*? I'd feel better knowing you were protecting me along with the crown jewels over there."

"Shame on you, Melly!"

"Cowardice is a survival trait," Dr. Soo said tartly.

"Well, there *is* always the chance of running into—or over—a cloaked Bug picket," Prescott conceded. "They don't seem to survey on anywhere near the scale we do, but intelligence's estimate is that they probably station picket ships in permanent cloak in every system they know about. Which is another reason for the probes, of course. We send them through to sanitize the area within scanner range of any warp point before we send any manned units through, then go back into cloak ourselves immediately. But the chance of our actually running into one of those pickets—and being spotted—is pretty slim, so the odds are a thousand to one that you'll get home safe and sound. Even aboard the flotilla flagship."

"Oh? And if we do run into Bugs?" She was suddenly serious.

"If they're electronic, we sic Captain Snyder on them. And if they're eight-legged, warm-blooded pseudo-insects," he turned serious himself, "why, then, Melly, we gunslingers do our job."

Soo was about to reply when Prescott's console beeped the tone of an outside com connection. He raised an eyebrow and touched a stud, and the com screen lit with Captain Snyder's boyish face.

"Captain," the admiral said with the courtesy he and Snyder were always careful to show one another. "A welcome surprise."

"I've got a bigger one for you, Admiral," Snyder said, and

his taut, barely suppressed excitement pulled Prescott up in his command chair. Snyder had spent over twelve years in Survey command. He wouldn't be this excited just because his probes had worked.

"Perhaps you'd better tell me about it, Captain," the admiral said quietly.

"The point's a type fourteen, Sir," Snyder said, and Prescott's intent gaze sharpened. A type fourteen was rare—a closed warp point, with extreme tidal stresses, which probably helped explain the high RD2 loss rate Chau and Leopold had reported.

"A type fourteen, eh? How close in is it?"

"About six light-hours, Sir," Snyder replied. "That's our best guess, anyway. The probe data are pretty badly scrambled, and we could be off by as much as ten or fifteen light-minutes. The tidal stress is more wicked than usual, even for a type fourteen, but we can use it all right."

"And you think we'll *want* to use it?" the admiral asked softly.

"I think we'll have to, Sir," Snyder said soberly, but still with that undertone of excitement.

"Why?"

"As I said, the data are badly scrambled, but I've got my best people working on it, and their consensus is that there's a high-tech presence in the system. A *big* one. And even if our astro data are less than perfect, we've been able to establish that this *isn't* any system we've ever seen before." His eyes blazed on the com screen, and he showed his teeth in a hungry grin. "Admiral, I may be wrong, but it looks to me like there's a damned good chance we just hit an El Dorado!"

" . . . so all we can really say," Commander Leopold concluded in his most tactful tones, "is that this *may* be an El Dorado." He looked around the table in Prescott's flag briefing room and met Snyder's eyes squarely. "The data absolutely confirm a high-tech presence, but from this far out, and with such poor resolution, there's no way to positively identify it as belonging to the Bugs. And while the system clearly doesn't belong to any member of the Alliance, that's no proof that it belongs to the Bugs, either."

"With all due respect, Admiral," Snyder said through what the uncharitable might have described as clenched teeth, "in my professional judgment," he stressed the adjective ever so slightly, "and despite all qualifications, I say this *is* an El Dorado. Exactly the thing we were sent out here to find."

He held Leopold's gaze with his own without quite glaring, and Prescott hid a sigh behind a calm, thoughtful expression as the tension between Survey and gunslingers reared its head once more. He knew Snyder was working very hard at keeping that tension in check, but he also knew Leopold's cautionary remarks held a sting of personal criticism for Snyder. Not that they were intended to, as Prescott was positive Snyder also knew, but because they had the unmistakable sound of disagreement. The fact that everyone knew it was Leopold's job to be the voice of caution on his admiral's staff wasn't quite enough to defuse Snyder's resentment at being forced to submit to the critique of someone with less than a tenth of his own survey expertise. Especially since that someone was junior to him and on the staff of an admiral who had even less survey experience than that . . . and who nonetheless was in command.

It wasn't easy for a Survey Command professional to accept the complete reversal of the prewar authority between the exploration specialists and the gunslingers at the best of times. Being figuratively rapped on the knuckles in his own undeniable area of competence at a time like this could only make that worse.

"You may very well be right, George," the admiral said after a moment, deliberately using the captain's first name. Snyder turned to meet his eyes, and Prescott took his pipe from his mouth and waved it gently, trailing a thin strand of smoke from the mouthpiece. "In fact, I think you are. And I certainly *want* you to be, just as I'm sure Commander Leopold does. But he does have a point, you know. Whether you're right or not, we can't prove anything one way or the other with the limited data we currently possess, and we can't whistle up an assault fleet until we *can* prove something. Besides," he allowed himself a grin, "if these aren't Bugs but someone entirely new instead and we drop an entire fleet in on some poor, inoffensive third party, the diplomatic corps will have our guts for garters!"

Several people around the table chuckled, and even Snyder's mouth twitched with an unwilling ghost of a smile. Then he drew a deep breath and nodded.

"You're right, of course, Sir," he admitted, and gave Leopold a brief, half-apologetic look. "But that only means we have to get our hands on the data that does prove something."

"Agreed. But from your own reports, as well as Commander

Chau's, it doesn't sound to me like the probes are going to do that for us."

His tone made the statement a half-question, and he raised an eyebrow.

"No, Sir. They aren't," Snyder agreed. He rubbed the tip of his nose for a moment, frowning down at the display of the memo pad in front of him, then shook his head. "A type fourteen's just too tough for them, Sir. That might not be true in a couple of years, given the rate of improvement in the technology, but it is for now. Half the ones we get back at all are so addled they're useless, and there's no way we'll get a probe through the point, far enough in-system to positively tell us if what we're seeing are Bug emissions, *and* back to the warp point and through it to us. Not from this far out. It's always possible we might get lucky and have one pass close enough to a local ship for a hard read on its drive frequencies, but the odds against that are enormous this far from the primary. And even if we did, that would mean the probe might come close enough to a Bug ship for *it* to be spotted and identified, given that we know they know about the capability now." He shook his head again. "No, if we want positive confirmation either way, we're going to have to put a ship through."

A flicker of tension flashed around the table as the words were finally said, and Prescott smiled faintly. He was quite certain that Snyder had recognized the necessity as quickly as he himself had, but The Book had required the consideration of all other possible actions first, because putting a manned ship through that warp point would up the stakes tremendously. Not just for the crew of the ship in question, but for the entire Alliance. A ship was a far more capable survey platform than a recon probe, and had much better electronic warfare capability. But if it was seen at all, it would almost certainly be identified for what it was, not dismissed as a minor sensor glitch, and that would warn the Bugs (if Bugs they were, he reminded himself conscientiously) that there was a closed warp point somewhere in their system. Without knowing where the point in question was, they could do very little to ambush an attack force as it made transit, but they could certainly reinforce the system massively and bring all of their fixed defenses on-line and keep them there. If that happened, the casualties involved in any attack on the system would rise catastrophically, and no one who survived the operation would be sending any thanks to the fumble-fingered survey flotilla who'd screwed up by being seen.

"You're right, of course," he said aloud, leaning back in his chair to gaze at Snyder. The captain nodded and leaned back in his own chair, and despite his relaxed body language there was a fresh but different edge of tension in his eyes.

"In that case, Sir," he said in an almost painfully neutral tone, "I would submit that *Sarmatian* is the logical ship to be used."

"You would, would you?" Prescott murmured, a slight smile taking the potential sting from the rhetorical question.

"Yes, Sir. She has the best sensors and, with all due modesty, the best and most experienced Survey staff of any ship in the flotilla. She's also just as fast as any other unit of the flotilla, and her ECM is just as good as anyone else's. And under the circumstances, it would be appropriate for the flotilla's second in command to take personal responsibility for the operation."

"I see." Prescott swung his chair very gently from side to side in small, precise arcs. "Those are cogent points, Captain," he acknowledged, "but there are a few others to consider as well, I believe. For example, *Concorde*. She doesn't have your own excellent Survey staff, but let's face it, this is essentially a tactical situation, not a regular exploration mission. Commander Chau and his people are probably even better in a *tactical* sense than your own people, and Captain Kolontai is a very experienced combat officer. *Concorde's* also bigger, tougher, and much better armed than your *Sarmatian*, so if the crap does hit the fan, she'd have a better chance of fighting her way clear. And the same circumstances which might make this an appropriate mission for the flotilla's *second* in command also make it an appropriate one for the flotilla's CO, don't you think?"

"With all due respect, no, Sir," Snyder said. "Your responsibility is to the flotilla as a whole. To be blunt, a second in command is more expendable than a commanding officer, and a light cruiser is more expendable than a battlecruiser."

"In most ways, perhaps," Prescott acknowledged. "But as we all know, this is primarily a *survey* mission, and that means that our survey ships—and their specialists—are less expendable than their escorts. And if something should go wrong on the other side of that warp point, I would prefer to have the very best person available on this side of it to evaluate any courier drones which might come back through it. But even if both those things weren't true—which they are, of course—there are still two other points you haven't addressed."

"There are, Sir?" Snyder regarded him suspiciously when he paused, and Prescott's smile grew.

"Indeed there are, George. First, this sort of operation is sort of a specialty of mine, unfortunately." Snyder's eyes flickered as he, like everyone else around the table, recalled Prescott's nerve-wracking, brilliantly executed mission as Vanessa Murakuma's spy, left behind with *Daikyu* in Justin when the Bugs forced Fifth Fleet out of the system. "And second," Prescott went on, "there's the fact that I outrank you. So if I decide to poach this little operation for myself, there isn't much you can do about it except say 'Aye, aye, Sir.'"

Snyder's mouth twitched again at the twinkle in Prescott's eyes, but he shook his head once more.

"Even if both of those things are true, Sir, I strongly recommend that you let *Sarmatian* fly the mission. *Concorde*'s not just the flagship, but a command datalink unit. Her loss would seriously weaken the flotilla's tactical posture if we should encounter any opposition on the way home."

"Now that," Prescott admitted, "is a valid point. But not enough to change my mind. Captain Kolontai and *Concorde* will make the transit and check things out."

"But, Sir—" Snyder began, respectfully but stubbornly, only to be cut off.

"The decision is made, George," Prescott said firmly. "If this really is an El Dorado, then it's time someone rode boldly looking for it, and those someones are me and my flagship. Understood?"

"Understood, Sir," Snyder sighed.

It had, Andrew Prescott reflected, seemed far more reasonable to claim this particular mission for himself before he actually set out on it.

He sat calm-faced in his command chair, feeling the jagged tension all about him, and watched his displays as Captain Kadya Kolontai conned her ship ever so slowly in-system. *Concorde* was at general quarters, with every weapon, sensor, and defensive system manned, but all active sensors were on inactive standby as she crept silently through space. With her cloaking ECM engaged, she was doing her very best to imitate a hole in space, with no active emissions to betray her presence, while the exquisitely sensitive cat's whiskers of her passive sensors probed and pried.

The transit into the system had been just as rough as the partial probe data had suggested it would be. They'd had too little information to adjust for the tidal stresses, and *Concorde* had emerged from transit headed almost directly away from the system primary, which had aimed her stern—always the aspect of a ship most liable to detection under cloak—straight at any sensors which might have been looking her way.

Captain Kolontai had allowed for that, however, and *Concorde* had come through at dead slow, under minimum power to reduce any betraying drive signature to the lowest possible level. Everyone had breathed an internal sigh of relief as the ship swung her stern away from the inner system, but then she'd begun her alley-cat prowl inward, and the tension had begun to ratchet up once more.

"I have a report from Tracking, Sir." Lieutenant Commander Chau's voice wasn't particularly loud, but it seemed almost shocking in the quiet tension, and Prescott swivelled his command chair to face him and nodded for him to continue.

"Lieutenant Morgenthau says we have enough data now, Sir. It's definitely a Bug system, and a major one at that. The primary's a G3, and it looks as if all three of the innermost planets are habitable. And . . . fully developed."

Prescott suppressed an urge to purse his lips in a silent whistle. If Chau was right, then this system might well be even more heavily populated—and dangerous—than Home Hive Three, and the best estimate was that Ray and his *vilkshatha* brother had killed over twenty billion Bugs in that system. But it had possessed only two habitable planets. Which meant this one might easily hold as many as thirty or even forty billion Bugs . . . and all the war-making infrastructure that massive population implied. Elation at the size of the prize SF 62 had discovered warred with cold horror at the thought of the defenses any attack might face, and he ordered his face to remain calm.

"What else can you tell me, Ba Hai?" he asked levelly.

"Not a great deal at this range, Sir," the ops officer admitted. "All three of the inner planets are on our side of the primary right now, but we're still an awful long way out. We've got massive energy signatures and neutrinos all over the place, but at this range there's no way to isolate individual sources or targets. We'd have to get a lot closer for anything like that."

"I see." Prescott reached into his pocket and caressed the smooth, well worn bowl of his pipe with a thumb while he thought. He hadn't really needed Chau to tell him they were too far out for details . . . or that they'd have to go closer to learn any more than they already had. But the rules of the game had required him to ask, just as they now required him to make a decision. And that, though he hadn't raised the point with Snyder, was the real reason he'd been determined to take this assignment for himself. The flotilla was his command. Any decisions which had to be made, and the responsibility for the consequences of those decisions, had to be his, and the potential consequences of getting too close to the Bugs loomed before him like a gas giant.

On the one hand, he'd already accomplished everything SF 62 had set out to do, and far more than anyone could reasonably have asked or predicted. If he turned back now, the information he already possessed would hit the Grand Alliance's strategists like a lightning bolt, for the opportunity it presented was literally priceless. But those same strategists would have to plan their response to that opportunity with only the vaguest of operational information. Certainly they wouldn't have anything like the mountains of data they'd been able to assemble for the attack on Home Hive Three, and the consequence would probably be higher casualties. Possibly even total disaster, if they underestimated the opposition too greatly or were unable to get in close and apply Ray's "Shiva Option" before the defenders detected them and swarmed over them.

Andrew Prescott was in a position to do something about that. As far as he knew, no Bug was aware of *Concorde*'s presence, and she had the finest ECM in known space. He'd been able to avoid detection in Justin even after it became obvious the Bugs knew there were human ships about, and *these* Bugs didn't even know there was anyone around to hunt for. He wasn't about to underestimate the sensitivity of their sensors—not after what had happened to Commodore Braun in the very first human-Bug contact—but the odds against his being picked up coming in down the bearing from an unknown closed warp point were great. And if he did manage to avoid detection and get in close enough for detailed reads on the inner system, and any mobile units or orbital defenses those planets might have...

*"Ride boldly." That's what you told Snyder was needed,* he told himself. *And you were right. But how much of this is hubris? You fooled a whole fleet of Bugs once ... now you want to take on an entire star system? And if you blow it, if you go in close and get picked up ...*

He sat motionless, no sign of his inner debate showing in his expression as he weighed opportunity against risk, the value of better information against the danger of losing strategic surprise. Time seemed to crawl for him as he pondered the options, but less than one minute actually passed before he nodded to himself and looked down at the armrest com screen tied into *Concorde's* command deck. Captain Kolontai looked back at him from it, and he smiled at the sharp question in her dark blue eyes.

"Send a drone back to Captain Snyder, Kadya," he told her. "Append all our current data, and inform him that I intend to head further in-system for a closer look at the defenses. He's to give us one standard week. If we aren't back by then, he's to assume command and return to L-169 at his best speed."

"Yes, Sir," Kolontai said, and Andrew suppressed a chuckle, born as much of tension as of amusement, for her tone told him she'd anticipated exactly those orders from the outset.

*Am I really* that *predictable?* he wondered, then decided he didn't really want to know.

# CHAPTER NINE
## We Do Our Job

"The last probe flight is back, Sir. Or part of it, anyway."

Captain George Snyder paused in his restless prowl of TFNS *Sarmatian*'s command deck and looked at his exec. Lieutenant Commander Harris didn't notice the sharpness of her captain's gaze. Her attention was on her display, and Snyder saw her mouth tighten.

"No changes according to the preliminary run, Sir," she said, looking up at last. "We may turn up something when we fine-tooth it, but until then—"

She shrugged apologetically, and Snyder nodded. It was hard to keep the gesture courteous and not simply curt, but Sonja Harris had been his XO for over a year. Before that, she'd been his astrogator for almost twenty months, and she deserved better than to have her head bitten off just because her CO was feeling antsy.

And he *was* feeling antsy, Snyder admitted as he turned back to the visual display and resumed his pacing. He really shouldn't be doing that, either, since it advertised his impatience and concern to all eyes, but he couldn't help it, and he glared at the cool, barren class M star burning at the heart of the lifeless system they'd dubbed El Dorado.

Five days. Prescott had been gone for five full days, and the tension was getting to the entire flotilla, not just George Snyder. In theory, the continued probe flights might give them some clue of what was happening, but the odds of that were infinitesimal.

172

Unless something had happened to cause a truly massive Bug redeployment in this direction (like the pursuit of a retreating TFN battlecruiser), or unless *Concorde's* cloaking systems hiccuped at exactly the right point in her return, no probe was going to see anything from this far out. Which meant that, for all anyone knew, *Concorde* had been destroyed with all hands days ago. Or she could be minutes away from returning to El Dorado, coasting towards them under cloak, invisible to their transit-addled probes. Or she could be fighting a desperate running battle against hopeless odds even as he paced *Sarmatian's* bridge. Or—

He chopped the useless speculation off . . . again, and his mouth twitched with something far too biting to be called humor.

*You always told yourself you could do as well as Prescott in the worry seat,* he told himself. *At least you've shown you can worry as well as he can!*

He chuckled, then made himself settle into the captain's chair at the center of the bridge and look around with approving eyes. Survey Command skippers always got to hang on to their ships longer than officers in other branches. It only made sense, given the megacredits it cost to train a Survey captain and the lengthy deployments such ships regularly undertook. It would hardly be worthwhile to spend all that time and effort training a man for his job just to snatch it away from him when he'd carried out no more than two or three missions, after all. But Snyder knew he was lucky, even so, for he'd commanded *Sarmatian* for over five years. He'd been her XO before the war, and he'd moved up to the captain's chair when she emerged from refit to the *Hun-B* standard, with military engines and fourth generation ECM.

That meant he'd had plenty of time to fine-tune his personnel . . . and that he'd operated under the new, wartime guidelines from the moment he took command. Which ought, he conceded, to have given him plenty of time to accustom himself to the new realities. Yet it still seemed . . . unnatural to have a gunslinger telling the senior Survey officer what to do. Unnatural and wrong. Gunslingers didn't have the exhaustively trained instincts a Survey officer could acquire only by actually doing the job. No matter how good they were at their own jobs, they simply didn't *understand* Snyder's, and exploration work was far too important to have someone screw up out of something as avoidable as inexperience.

But there was nothing he could do about it, and truth to tell, however much he might resent the situation, just now he wished Prescott would hurry up and get himself and his flagship back

from the far side of the warp point. It was past time for them
to be headed home with their data, and he seriously questioned
Prescott's decision to remain in the Bug system for so long. They'd
confirmed who owned it, and that they had an unsuspected point
of access, and that information was too important for them to
risk compromising it—or even, in a worst-case scenario, getting
themselves detected, caught, and destroyed and never getting
their data home at all. But however George Snyder might feel
about it, Andrew Prescott was the one sitting in the admiral's
chair . . . assuming he and his command chair still existed. And no
matter how questionable Snyder found Prescott's current actions,
he had to admit that in most respects, the admiral had been a
pleasant surprise.

The captain hadn't been at all certain that would be the case
when he learned who his new flotilla CO was to be. The entire
Navy had heard about the Prescott brothers, and Snyder had
wondered whether someone with a reputation for derring-do
was the right man to command a mission designed completely
around stealth and sneakiness. The older Prescott had certainly
demonstrated guts, determination, and tactical savvy, but he
wasn't exactly noted for constructive timidity. And the younger
Prescott's Justin exploit had constituted a very mixed review for
any Survey officer. He'd shown an impressive flair for operating
covert, but according to the rumor mill, he'd also actually *shut
down his drive* at one point rather than let himself be pushed
away from the warp point he was keeping under observation. In
Snyder's book, that sort of "gutsy move" verged on lunacy. Prescott
wouldn't have done Admiral Murakuma any good if he'd gotten
his entire ship and crew blown out of space, after all! Surely the
proper move would have been to pull back, evade in deep space,
well away from the warp point, and then creep back into position
once the coast was a bit closer to clear.

*You weren't there, George,* he reminded himself once more.
*And aside from this latest escapade of his, he hasn't exactly been a
loose warhead since he took command of the flotilla. And be honest
with yourself. How much of your resentment is really a matter
of principled disagreement with Fleet policy or questions about
his competence and how much of it stems from the fact that if he
weren't here,* you'd *be the one in command?*

That was the aspect of the entire situation which bothered him
most, if he was going to be candid. He didn't want to suspect
his own motivation, yet he was too self-honest not to admit the

possibility. Especially since it was beginning to look like *no* Survey officer was going to be allowed to command his own branch of the Navy's missions for the duration of the war.

He sighed and tipped his chair a bit further back and stared into the depths of the visual display while he wondered what the hell was keeping *Concorde*.

"That's it, Sir. Or as close as we're going to be able to get to complete info, anyway," Captain Kolontai said quietly, and Andrew Prescott nodded. The captain was right, he thought, studying the chilling information displayed on his display. They'd never gotten a really good look at the innermost planet, but he saw no reason not to assume that it, too, was orbited by its own titanic, massively armed space station and twenty-six of the largest orbital forts anyone aboard *Concorde* had ever seen. And that didn't even mention the shoals of starships, headed by the massive monitors, whirling in silent orbit around those same planets. It was even worse than Home Hive Three, he thought numbly . . . but at least the weapons aboard every one of the forts and both of the space stations they'd seen seemed to be at powered-down standby.

*Now if we can just* keep *them that way. . . .*

"You're right, Kadya," he said after a moment. "Even a gambler has to know when to fold and run, and we can't justify risking getting ourselves detected in the hopes of squeezing just a little more info out of them. Turn us around and get us out of here."

"Yes, Sir." Kolontai didn't—quite—allow herself to sigh in relief.

The sharp buzz of a com cut the darkness, and George Snyder rolled up on his elbow with the instant spinal reflex of five years of command. One hand rubbed sleep-gritty eyes, and the other stabbed the acceptance button.

"Captain," he rasped, then stopped and cleared his throat. "Talk to me," he said more intelligibly.

"Officer of the watch, Sir," the crisp voice of Lieutenant Laurence Giancomo, *Sarmatian*'s astrogator replied. "Sir, *Concorde* has just transited the warp point!"

Snyder jerked upright in his bunk and swung his feet to the floor, the last rags of sleep vanishing.

"Very good, Larry. I'll be on the bridge in five minutes," he said, and reached for the uniform he'd taken off when he turned in.

✧    ✧    ✧

"My God, Admiral."

Snyder's voice was little more than a whisper in *Concorde's* briefing room as he stared at the steadily scrolling data the flagship had brought back from the enemy star system. The Survey Command officer's eyes were shocked, more than half stunned while he tried to absorb the deadly import of the massive fortifications, the serried ranks of orbiting warships. He'd heard about the Home Hive Three defenses Raymond Prescott and Zhaarnak'telmasa had smashed, but only the unclassified details, and that had been hopelessly inadequate to prepare him for the reality of *this* system. George Snyder was face to face with the reality of a home hive's horrific firepower at last, and for the first time since Andrew Prescott had assumed command of Survey Flotilla 62, Snyder felt acutely out of his depth. He was a *Survey* officer, for God's sake, not a—

He strangled the thought stillborn, understanding—*really* understanding—at last why GFGHQ had decreed the primacy of Battle Fleet for the duration. And why Andrew Prescott had run the "unwarranted risk" of getting close enough for a detailed evaluation of the Bugs' defenses.

"I never imagined anything like this—certainly not on this scale," he said in a more normal voice, then shook his head irritably. "Oh, I know Old Terra is almost this strongly defended, but that's only a single planet, for God's sake! They've got *three* of the things, and you have to be right: all of them must be fortified to this extent."

"I wish I *weren't* right, George," Prescott said quietly, feeling his own initial reaction afresh as he watched Snyder's shocked expression. He glanced across the briefing room table to smile briefly at an ashen-faced Melanie Soo, returned—along with the rest of *Concorde's* nonessential personnel—from the other ships of the flotilla now that the flagship had rejoined. "And we got a look at a couple of their warp points, too," he added, and nodded to Leopold. The chief of staff touched his own console's controls, and a fresh schematic showed the icon of a warp point surrounded by no less than sixty of those massive OWPs. Snyder swallowed audibly, and the rear admiral gave him a wintry smile. "Both the ones we were able to get into scanner range of had identical fortifications. We were too far out for detail resolution, but I'll lay whatever odds you like that they're mined to a fare-thee-well, too."

"They'd have to be," Snyder agreed almost absently. "It wouldn't make sense even to Bugs to fort up on this scale and not stuff the warp point approaches with mines and energy platforms." He shook his head again, less stunned than before. "Do we actually have anything strong enough to take this place on even with the element of surprise, Admiral?"

It was the Survey specialist asking Battle Fleet for an answer, and Prescott pursed his lips and leaned back in his chair.

"If we don't now, we soon will, I think," he said after a moment. "But only if they *do* have the element of surprise when they go in. And only if they know there's someplace for them to be going in the first place. But think about this side of it, too, George. The defenses may be tough, but that's because of what they're protecting. I don't care who or what the Bugs are, losing a system like this one—especially after what already happened to Home Hive Three—has *got* to knock the stuffing out of them!"

"You've got that right, Sir," Snyder murmured, eyes narrow as he came back on stride. "And with all due respect, I suggest we get started taking this news home. Now."

"Or even a little sooner," Prescott agreed, and looked at Leopold. "Josh, please ask Captain Kolontai to have Commander Isakovic put the flotilla on a course for home immediately."

Survey Flotilla 62 was underway within twenty minutes, but the drive's fusion-backed snarl was muted compared to the chatter on the ships' mess decks. The grapevine functioned with its wonted speed, and jubilation was the order of the day.

It was understandable enough, Prescott thought. The full details of what *Concorde* had found on the far side of the El Dorado warp point were restricted to the flotilla's senior officers. All the rest of their personnel knew was that they'd found what every survey mission had dreamed of finding since the Bugs massacred Commodore Floyd Braun's Twenty-Seventh Survey Flotilla in the opening shot of the war. They spent their off-duty time thinking long and homicidal thoughts about what the assault carriers and the monitors about to enter service would do with the information they'd won, and who could blame them? *They* hadn't seen the raw ranks of orbital destruction awaiting those monitors and assault carriers.

"Whatever's the matter with you, Andy?" Melanie Soo demanded as she gathered the pinochle cards and began to shuffle.

"What? Oh, nothing. Nothing." He waved a dismissive hand.

"'Nothing' my caduceus! You missed three easy tricks, and you *knew* I had the ace of trump, but you sure didn't play it that way!"

"And about time," Kadya Kolontai said with a huge grin. "Josh and I may even break even with you two yet!"

Kolontai's partner, Commander Leopold, grinned back at her. Their ill luck against the team of Soo and Prescott was proverbial.

"Sorry, Melly," Prescott said with a smile. "Just thinking, is all."

"About all the nice medals for El Dorado?" she teased.

"No," the admiral said quietly. "Or, yes, in a way. I'm just hoping we get home to collect them."

"Admiral," Kolontai said with the respectful familiarity of almost two years service as his flag captain, "the Terran Cross is as good as on your chest."

"I'd like to think so, but right now I'd settle for the Plazatoro Award," Prescott replied, and his companions laughed. The Plazatoro Award was the fictitious medal awarded to the officer who ran away the fastest.

"Then ask for it, Sir," Kolontai advised. "After this, the Navy will give you anything you want."

"Wait a minute, Andy," Dr. Soo said, her voice as much that of his chief surgeon as of his friend. "Why the gloom? We've got the data. We're headed home, using only warp points we scouted on the way out, so we won't get lost. Come on, confess. What's eating you badly enough to distract *you* from a pinochle game?"

"It's an admiral's job to worry, Doctor," Kolontai answered for him. "And at the moment, he's worried we may stub our toe on a Bug battle force at the last minute."

"Isn't that sort of unlikely?"

"Unlikely? Of course." Prescott shook his head. "But it was 'unlikely' that Captain Vargas and Small Claw Maariaah would run into a Bug home hive only two transits from Rehfrak. Or that the Bugs would stumble onto two closed warp points in a row and hit Kliean. Just the fact that these warp lines are new to *us* and there weren't any Bugs—that we know of—around on the way out doesn't mean there won't be any on the way back. And remember what I told you about their cloaked picket ships. It's remotely possible one of them spotted us on our way through in the first place, you know. Or that one could spot us now if we happen to run through a system they know about."

"But if they knew about any of the systems we've explored, then surely they would have explored them themselves," Soo protested. "And if they'd done that, they'd know about the closed warp point from El Dorado. But they don't, because if they did, they would have fortified it just as heavily as they did everything else in that system!"

"You're undoubtedly correct that they don't know about the closed point," Prescott conceded. "I can't conceive of anyone, even a Bug admiral—if there *are* Bug admirals—leaving an opening like that for any reason at all. But as I also mentioned to you, Admiral LeBlanc's people have concluded, partly on the basis of information not available to me, that the Bugs simply don't explore as extensively as we do. As I understand the logic, LeBlanc thinks it's a conscious security decision on their part. The further they expand in peacetime, the more risk there is of running into another sentient race—like us. And the more they explore in wartime, the greater the risk that they'll contact the enemy somewhere they don't want to, which seems to be what happened initially at Centauri."

Soo snorted, and Prescott cocked an eyebrow at her.

"I suppose it's inevitable that anything that looks like a Bug would prefer to sit like a spider at the heart of its web until the opposition comes to it," she said sourly, and he gave a brief, mirthless chuckle.

"You could put it that way, I guess. But the point is that their explored space could intersect the warp lines we've scouted at any point without their necessarily having fanned out down them the way we would."

"Which is why we're at Condition Two," Kolontai told her. "And why we're expending almost as many RD2s probing warp points on our way home as we did on the way out, and why we go to General Quarters whenever we make transit. Mind you, the odds are with us, but the Admiral—" the Novaya Rodinian nodded at Prescott "—is paid to sweat bullets over things like that so mere captains like me don't have to. All *we* have to worry about is being killed, which is a much more minor concern."

"I see." And Dr. Soo did see. She'd known, intellectually, that the flotilla was moving homeward with all the caution it had shown on the way out, but somehow euphoria had blinded her to the fact that they might just as easily be intercepted on the way home.

"Don't worry, Melly," Prescott said. "Like Kadya says, the odds are with us. It's just part of my job to worry about the things that won't happen as well as the ones that will."

The flotilla drove onward, moving at the highest economical speed consonant with the maximum efficiency of its cloaking systems and slowing only to probe each warp point with exquisite care before making transit. They weren't surveying now, and after four weeks they were close to halfway home. Of course, "close" was a more than usually relative term in the topsy-turvy geometry of warp transit, and there was no telling which warp point might suddenly disclose a Bug task force, no matter how "close" to L-169 they were. But optimism rose steadily, however subjective its justification, as they raced along without incident.

Yet one man resisted that optimism: the man in the worry seat. Andrew Prescott began losing weight, and Dr. Soo chided him and prescribed a high caloric diet. But behind her teasing, she began to worry secretly about his stability. Yet he passed every response analysis with flying colors, and she concluded that it was only an acute case of fully understandable tension. So her log indicated, but in the silence of her own thoughts, she wondered if it was something more. It was as if he had some private information channel and actually *expected* to meet the Bugs, and his attitude worried her.

It worried her most because she was afraid he might just be right.

Andrew Prescott sat quietly, watching his display. There was no logical reason for the tension curdling his spine. The RD2s had functioned flawlessly as they scouted the warp point before them, for it was a type three, with relatively mild stresses which had been thoroughly charted on their outward journey months before. The probes had searched the space on the far side of the warp point to the full range of their prodigiously sensitive scanners and found absolutely nothing. And yet he couldn't shake his sense of apprehension, of the universe holding its breath. Perhaps it was because the upcoming transit would mark the exact halfway point of their voyage home, he told himself, but deep inside he knew it was more than that.

Damn it, what was *wrong* with him? He sensed his staff watching his back, felt their curiosity, not yet strong enough to be called concern, as they wondered why he hesitated over the order to make transit, and there was nothing at all he could have explained to them. He leaned back and once more found himself wishing he could confide in Soo. Melly was levelheaded, if not a trained tactician. Maybe she could shake him out of this. But she was also his chief surgeon, and he'd recognized the concern under her teasing. If she thought he was coming unglued, she'd do her duty and yank him out of the line of command in a minute, and how could he expect her *not* to decide he was losing it when all he had was a "hunch" he couldn't describe even to himself.

He reached for his pipe and looked at his link to *Concorde's* command deck.

"All right, Kadya," he told his flag captain calmly. "Start sending them through."

SF 62 forged steadily across the nameless system towards the next warp point on its list, just under five light-hours from its warp point of entry, and Prescott felt himself begin to relax ever so slightly as nothing happened.

*Nerves,* he told himself. *Just nerves. And I need to get a grip on myself if I expect to make it back to base* without *Melly relieving me!*

He chuckled sourly at the thought and reached for his lighter. He'd just puffed the fresh tobacco alight when the sudden, shocking wail of a priority alarm sliced through Flag Deck's calm quiet.

"We have bogies!" Lieutenant Commander Chau's voice was flat, almost sing-song with the half-chant of long training while his emotions raced to catch up with the shocking realization of his intellect. "Multiple hostile contacts bearing two-eight-one by zero-one-one, range three light-minutes! CIC calls them gunboats, coming in across a broad front. Minimum of forty-plus confirmed inbound, Admiral!"

Andrew Prescott stared down into his repeater plot, watching the venomous red icons spring into existence off *Concorde's* port bow and come sweeping to meet his flotilla, and a fist of ice closed about his heart. Gunboats couldn't cloak. There were very few things in the universe easier to detect than a gunboat under power, even at extreme range, and their sudden appearance at such relatively close quarters could only mean they'd launched from cloaked mother ships.

*They must have launched on a time estimate,* he thought with a queer, detached sense of calm. *Can't have been a hard sensor contact, or they'd have closed up before launch, sent them at us in a tighter stream. But if it's a time estimate, it's a damned good one. So they must've had something sitting there in cloak the whole time, something the probes missed. But that didn't miss us coming through before we could go back into cloak. And even if whoever launched them doesn't see us directly when we launch our own birds, that many gunboats are bound to spot us pretty damned quick.*

"I see them, Ba Hai," he said, and the calm of his own voice amazed him. He felt that calm reaching out, meeting and overcoming his staffers' ripples of panic, and made himself sit back in his command chair before he began issuing orders.

"Bring the flotilla to one-one-zero, same plane," he said then. "I want those gunboats held directly astern of us to slow their overtake. Then contact Captain Shaarnaathy." Shaarnaathy was the skipper of *Zirk-Ciliwaan*, one of the two Ophiuchi light carriers attached to SF 62. Although they were much smaller than the *Foxhound*, the larger Terran fleet carrier, each carried twenty-four fighters, over half as many as the *Foxhound*, and Shaarnaathy was senior to *Foxhound*'s skipper. "Tell him I want a full deck launch from all three carriers. And get the *Cormorants*' gunboats out there, too. If the Bugs think forty or fifty gunboats are enough to deal with us, I think it's time we taught them the error of their ways!"

That actually won a small chuckle from someone, and Prescott smiled and shoved his pipe back into his mouth. But he himself felt no temptation to laughter. Forty or fifty gunboats *was* too small a force to stop SF 62. Between them, *Condor* and *Corby*, his two *Cormorant*-class battlecruisers, alone, carried twenty gunboats of their own, and *Foxhound* and her two attached CVLs could put almost ninety fighters into space, forty-eight of them with Ophiuchi pilots. Against that sort of firepower, the gunboats sweeping towards them didn't stand a chance.

But if he was right about how the Bugs had known when to launch, then presumably they also had a good notion of what they faced, and while Bugs were capable of suicidal attritional attacks no human admiral would contemplate for a moment, they were also capable of a much higher degree of subtlety than he could have wished. And by now they'd had ample opportunity to analyze standard Allied doctrine for using fighters to blunt gunboat attacks . . . and to come up with a response of their own.

*The Enemy's small craft swept towards the gunboats, and there were rather more of them than had been anticipated. Of course, there were also more Enemy starships than expected, as well. Clearly the picket which had detected them when they passed through this system months before had missed almost half of them. That was most unfortunate. With more accurate initial information, a larger force could have been dispatched to absolutely insure these intruders' destruction. As it was, reinforcements had been called for, but it was unlikely they could arrive in time to affect the issue.*

*On the other hand, the Fleet should have sufficient strength on hand to deal with the situation, despite the numbers of Enemy small craft so far detected. A matter for somewhat greater concern than the absolute numbers was the presence of gunboats among the more usual attack craft. Their presence had been completely unexpected, and no provision had been made for their ability to mount standard shipboard anti-attack craft missiles on their ordnance racks. There was neither time nor means to adjust for their presence, however, and the second wave of the fleet's own gunboats separated from their racks.*

"We have a second gunboat wave coming in from zero-zero-two zero-six-three, at least as strong as the first, Admiral!" Chau reported tersely. "Range is only two light-minutes. Tracking is picking up some of the launch platforms now. They look like battlecruisers. CIC designates this Force Beta, Sir."

Prescott grunted, but it wasn't really a surprise. Either the Bugs had gotten an excellent passive sensor lock on them as they made transit and managed to hold them long enough to project their course, or else they already knew which warp point the flotilla was bound for. It didn't really matter which at the moment. What *did* matter was that, armed with their knowledge, they'd managed to position their units so as to catch SF 62 between two forces . . . and one of them was between Prescott and the only way home. Worse, the second one was in *front* of him on his present course, positioned so that he had to close with it if he meant to keep running away from the first gunboat wave. And worse yet, with that many starships, plus the gunboats' onboard scanners, the Bugs must know precisely where Prescott's forces were. The fighter and gunboat launch would have defined a general locus for them, just as the second wave's launch had pinpointed Force Beta for *Concorde*'s sensors, for not even the best ECM could defeat that horde of passive and active sensors when it knew where to look. And once they'd been located the first time, dropping back into cloak and evading would be enormously more difficult.

Yet one aspect of the Bugs' tactics did puzzle him. The new gunboat wave was headed to join the first in a clear bid to engage Shaarnaathy's fighters and gunboats rather than trying to pounce on SF 62's starships while its fighter cover was away. The flotilla's shipboard weapons would undoubtedly have inflicted heavy casualties on the gunboats if they'd come in on the ships, but Bugs had never shied away from losses before, and it would probably have been their best shot at getting in among the datagroups. So why—?

Of course. The Bugs knew his carriers' strikegroups were both his primary defense against kamikaze small craft *and* his best offensive weapon, and they wanted to destroy that weapon before they sought a decisive engagement. Or they might be present in sufficient strength to feel confident of crushing the flotilla in a standard ship-to-ship engagement if Prescott's fighters could simply be whittled down. Yet either way, he had no choice but to meet the gunboats head-on and try to whittle *them* down, and at least his own strikegroups were positioned to engage the two Bug forces sequentially and in isolation. It would probably be his best opportunity to defeat the gunboats in detail. It might also be the only one he got, and so he said nothing as his pilots' icons began to merge in the plot with the angry red hash of the Bug gunboats' first wave.

The *Cormorants'* human-crewed gunboats struck first, and they hit the Bugs hard. The enemy clearly hadn't expected to face such units, for they'd opted to equip their own craft with standard fighter missiles. Against pure fighter opposition, that made sense, since they could fit far more of the smaller fighter-sized missiles onto their racks. But the human gunboats were armed with all-up AFHAWKs, and they salvoed their less numerous but heavier weapons from outside even FM2 range.

Brief, vicious fireballs spalled the Bug formation as the big missiles tore home, and almost half the first wave was destroyed before it could get a shot off in reply. But the remainder kept coming, and now it was their turn, for unlike the fighters which opposed them, they had point defense. They had to enter the fighters' range to engage them, but they stood an excellent chance of picking off return missile fire, and they arrowed straight at the Terran and Ophiuchi strikegroups behind a cloud of missiles of their own.

They ignored the human gunboats completely, electing not to

waste missiles against the bigger vessels' matching point defense, and now explosions glared among SF 62's defenders. The tornado of fighter-launched missiles was sufficient to wipe out virtually all the Bugs, despite their point defense, without ever entering energy weapon range, but Prescott felt a cold sense of foreboding as he watched his plot. The two or three first-wave gunboats to evade destruction were no longer headed for the flotilla. They were breaking off, turning to run from the fighters rather than trying to get through to his starships, and that was very unlike standard Bug tactics.

The fugitives' courses back towards their launch platforms took them directly away from their own second wave. Perhaps they hoped the Allied fighters, feeling the pressure of the second wave bearing down upon them, would turn to face it and let the survivors make good their escape. If so, they were wrong, and Prescott clenched his teeth on his pipe as his faster fighters went in pursuit. They ran down the escapees and nailed them, not without losses of their own, then wheeled once more and turned back as the second Bug wave drew into extreme missile range. Again clouds of missiles erupted into his fighters' formations, and this time the long-range losses were completely one-sided, for there were no answering Allied missiles. But they were only one-sided for the time it took the vengeful human and Ophiuchi pilots to overtake the slower gunboats, despite their efforts to evade, and rip them apart with energy fire.

A sidebar in his plot gave his losses, and he felt a spasm of pain as he absorbed them. Only two of his gunboats had been destroyed, but twenty-one of his eighty-plus fighters were dead. The Bugs had lost well over twice that many units, and each of theirs carried much larger crews than his fighters, but they were *Bugs*. There was no such thing as an "acceptable rate of exchange" against Bugs . . . and he'd lost almost a quarter of his own fighter strength in killing them.

He watched a small cluster of icons speeding even further outward as the rest of the strike wheeled to return to their motherships to rearm and reorganize. Those were *Foxhound*'s recon fighters, splitting up to sweep down reciprocals of both gunboat waves' tracks to seek out the ships from which they'd come. If SF 62 was lucky, those ships would be the old, original Bug designs, with commercial grade engines Prescott's own starships could easily outrun.

*If* SF 62 was lucky.

❖     ❖     ◆

"It's confirmed, Admiral," Chau said unhappily. "We probably don't have a complete count on them—*Foxhound* only carries six recon birds, and the Bugs are still cloaked—but we've positively IDed a minimum of five *Antelopes* and two *Antlers* in Force Alpha." Prescott nodded. Force Alpha was the one which lay between them and their escape warp point. "We have military grade drives on all but five of the other Alpha units our pilots saw, as well," Chau went on. "The commercial-drive ships look like *Adder*-class BCs, which makes sense, given the weight of gunboats we saw coming at us. Our IDs on Beta Force are more tentative, but it *looks* like there may be a higher percentage of *Adders* out there."

"I see." Prescott rubbed his jaw thoughtfully while he glanced around at the com images of his ship commanders and Commander Hiithylwaaan, his Ophiuchi *farshathkhanaak*. A matching awareness of what that meant looked back at him from every face, and he hid a mental sigh.

The *Adders* were gunboat carriers, with only standard missile launchers to back up their attack groups, and they were from the old, slow philosophy of Bug warship design. *Antlers* and *Antelopes* were very different propositions, however, for they were capital missile ships, at least as heavily armed as his own *Concorde* and the flotilla's five *Dunkerque-C*-class ships. They had not only the speed to match SF 62 stride for stride, but also the weapons fit to engage it from well beyond the range of most of its starships, and if his recon pilots had seen seven of them, there were probably more with the forces already engaged against him. Even if there weren't, it was highly likely that still more Bug ships were headed towards him, either already in-system or *en route* for it.

Much of the Bugs' shipboard gunboat strength must have been killed, but that, unfortunately, didn't necessarily mean as much as it might have, given gunboats' ability to make transit on their own. There could be hordes of the things lurking just beyond his sensor range, waiting to pounce, although he tended to doubt it. If they were present in that kind of overwhelming strength, the Bugs wouldn't have bothered with fancy attritional tactics. They would simply have bored straight in to overwhelm the flotilla and be done with it.

But their data on his strength was almost certainly at least as good as his estimate of theirs. And whether they knew it or not, they were between him and his exit warp point. Worse, their speed meant they could *stay* between him and his warp point unless he could somehow drop back into cloak. Which he couldn't do as long as they had any gunboats with which to shadow him. And since said shadowers were too spread out for him to get all of them, that meant the only way to prevent the Bug starships from intercepting him was to destroy or at least lame those ships so that they could no longer catch his own vessels.

Which meant fighter and gunboat strikes at extreme range, he admitted unhappily to himself. He didn't like it, and he hated the thought of the casualties his strikegroups would suffer. But he had no choice, for only six of his own battlecruisers were armed with capital missiles. He would be outnumbered and outgunned in any duel with the similarly armed *Antelopes*, and his ships would be just as vulnerable to drive damage as they would . . . except that any of *his* ships slowed by damage would be doomed, for the rest of the flotilla could not slow its own pace to cover them.

"We'll have to take them out—or at least slow them down—with fighter strikes," he said finally, unable to keep the heaviness from his tone. "And we're going to have to do it in a way that leaves us enough reserve fighter strength to catch and finish off their shadowers once the starships are dealt with. Can your people hack that, Commander Hiithylwaaan?"

"I believe so, Sir," the fierce-beaked Ophiuchi replied after a moment. "It will not be easy, but we should have the strength for it, especially with the gunboats to assist." It was a mark of the direness of their straits that not a trace of the habitual Ophiuchi disdain for the slow, heavy-footed gunboats colored his manner. "I suggest that we engage the *Antelopes* and *Antlers* first, then go back and kill the *Adders* later if we must. We are unlikely to catch them with gunboats actually on their racks, but they will probably commit their surviving gunboat strength to the combat space patrol role against our strikes on their faster units, which will give us the opportunity to engage and destroy them in passing."

"I agree," Prescott said, nodding sharply. "But I don't want to expose your pilots to high attrition with repeated strikes, so let's try to do this in a single wave if we can. I want two-thirds of the fighters fitted with primary packs. The remaining third can fly escort with missiles, but a primary-armed squadron or two should be able to take out enough of an *Antelope*'s engines to cut its speed in half in a single pass."

"It will mean more exposure to their close-in defenses," Hiithylwaaan pointed out, then made the small gesture his people used for a shrug. "But you are correct, Admiral. We will have to enter their defensive envelope anyway; best to engage with our most effective crippling weapon so that we need not enter it a second time."

"Very well, then." Prescott turned to Leopold and Chau. "At the same time, the flotilla will alter course to follow the strike towards Alpha Force. I want to be close enough to take them out completely if the strike results warrant it, and I *don't* want to get any closer to any of Beta's surviving gunboats than we have to. I don't want us in missile range of Alpha yet, either, but there's no point pretending they don't have a damned good idea of where we are already."

"No, Sir, there isn't," Leopold agreed. "On the other hand, closing the range on them will make it even easier for them to track us . . . and harder for us to drop back into cloak if the opportunity presents itself."

"Josh, every time we launch or recover—or engage one of *their* strikes—they'll find us all over again, anyway, and as Ba Hai just pointed out, we have a much poorer idea of what Beta has. On top of that, Alpha is the one between us and our warp point, and until we can cripple at least one group badly enough to give us a chance of outrunning it—and deal with their damned gunboats once and for all—we're not going to shake them. That being so, I'd rather keep our combat strength concentrated and give our pilots as short a recovery flight time as possible."

"Yes, Sir," Leopold said, and Prescott nodded.

"All right, then, people. Let's do it," he said briskly.

*Sensors detected the sudden resurgence of drive sources as the Enemy launched his attack craft once more. It was unfortunate, though scarcely unexpected. Clearly the Fleet units between him and escape must be destroyed or disabled if the Enemy were to have any hope of disengaging and evading successfully. And it was quite possible he would succeed, for rather more of his attack craft survived than the plan had allowed for at this point. But there were ways that situation might be redressed, and orders went out to the special units to prepare to initiate the new anti-attack craft tactics.*

Commander Hiithylwaaan, OADC, led the massed pilots of SF 62 towards their foes. The *Cormorants'* gunboats came with them, but they were too big and slow, relatively speaking, for the close-in attack role. Instead, they carried AFHAWKs once again, and the plan was for them to lie well back and provide long-range supporting fire against any Bug gunboats which might attempt to intercept the main strike.

Unfortunately, the Bugs seemed disinclined to commit their gunboats . . . and their ECM was more effective than usual, making exact unit identification difficult. It couldn't successfully disguise a military-grade drive as a commercial one, yet there was more uncertainty than Hiithylwaaan could have desired, and a few additional military-drive ships had turned up. Some of them clearly weren't *Antelopes* or *Antlers*, but that was about all he could say for certain. It was even possible they represented a new class no Allied force had previously encountered. In any case, they wouldn't have had military drives unless the Bugs thought it was important for them to be able to keep pace with Allied designs, and that made them worthwhile targets.

Four or five of the unknowns lay between his strikegroups and the *Antelopes*, and he began to tap commands into his onboard computer, designating them as the first targets. The Bugs had allowed a gap to open between them and the rest of their fast starships, he noted, putting them beyond the range at which the *Antelopes'* point defense could assist their own close-in defenses, and he clicked his beak in the Ophiuchi equivalent of a smile. He would hit each of them simultaneously with a two or three-squadron attack, he decided. That would swamp their own point defense and let him kill them quickly, with minimal losses, before he turned on their more distant consorts.

*The special units watched the Enemy strike bear down upon them, noting the distribution of drive sources. It would appear that the deception measures had succeeded. The removal of certain weapons and systems and the reconfiguration of the special units' shields had significantly altered their emissions signatures. The Fleet had hoped that the alteration would prevent the Enemy from guessing what the special units truly were—rather as the Enemy had done to the Fleet by disguising his antimatter laden gunboat lures as standard missile pods. There was, of course, no way to be certain that the deception had succeeded in this instance, yet the developing pattern of the attack appeared hopeful. Certainly the Enemy seemed to have decided to sweep the special units aside before they could fall back within the defensive perimeter of the remainder of the Fleet.*

*Fortunately, the special units had no intention of doing anything of the sort.*

Hiithylwaaan's eyes narrowed as his five-pronged strike's components reached their IPs and turned in to the attack. At this range, his fighters' scanners should have been able to see through the Bug EW and recognize their targets, and they couldn't. Or, at least, what they were seeing didn't match any Bug ship types in his onboard computer's threat recognition files.

He didn't like that. The first people to attack any new class of warship were likely to encounter unpleasant surprises, especially if the infernal Bugs had come up with another nasty innovation like the plasma gun or the suicide-rider. On the other hand, someone always had to be the first . . . although he could have wished for a more convenient time.

He considered the readouts carefully. There wasn't a great deal of time to make up his mind, and he wished he had even a little more information. The Bugs' ECM might be being more effective than usual, but some details were leaking through. He didn't see any sign of new and fiendish weapons—as nearly as he could tell, this was simply a new fast-battlecruiser design with standard weapons, albeit in a slightly different configuration.

He considered aborting the attack, but it was too late to do it without engendering mass confusion in his squadrons. Better to carry through and hope that these things were important enough to justify the effort he was going to expend killing them. And even if they weren't, he had to start the killing *somewhere*.

Whatever these ships were, they'd just have to do.

*The Enemy strike craft screamed down on the special units, and a ripple of surprise ran through the Fleet as they opened fire not simply with the anticipated lasers, but with primary beams, as well. That had not been expected, and the special units staggered as unstoppable stilettos of energy stabbed through them again and again. The implications of the Enemy's choice of armament was not lost upon the Fleet, however. Clearly the Enemy had been as badly deceived as the Fleet could have hoped, or he would not have elected to employ a weapon which brought him so close to his targets.*

*It was true that the primary beams could knock out internal systems—possibly even the critical internal systems—without having to first smash their way through shields and armor. Yet in the long run, it would not matter greatly. The crews of the special units engaged the attacking small craft with missiles as they closed, and then opened fire with their point defense. The attack craft took only moderate losses, and their crews continued to bore in, closing to minimum range to make every shot count.*

*Exactly as the Fleet had anticipated.*

Commander Hiithylwaaan led the strike on the center unidentified battlecruiser himself, and he felt a deep, abiding sense of pride as his Human and Ophiuchi pilots followed him in. They drove through the weak, poorly coordinated point defense of their targets, closing in multisquadron strikes that were precisely sequenced to put the greatest number of fighters—and hence the heaviest possible weight of fire—onto their victims simultaneously from the closest possible range.

SF 62's pilots executed their attacks perfectly. And at the precise moment of their closest approach, each target's crew calmly threw a switch.

Andrew Prescott felt as if someone had kicked him in the belly.

He sensed the same shocked horror rippling through all the officers and ratings on Flag Bridge, and there was nothing he could do about it at all. He was as much a spectator as they were, staring at the plot. The information on it was minutes old, the events it showed already over and done, but it didn't feel that way, and his face clenched with pain as he watched two-thirds of his remaining fighter strength be wiped away in mere seconds.

*Etnas. Those had to be* Etnas, he thought numbly. *But why didn't Hiithylwaaan recognize them? He was right on top of them, for God's sake! And he thought they were a brand new class, so—*

His thought chopped off abruptly. Hiithylwaaan had thought they were a new class because the Bugs had *wanted* him to think that. The *farshathkhanaak* had been far too close for simple ECM to have deceived him, which meant that the ships *had* been a new design—or, at least, an older design which had been altered to make it appear to be something else entirely.

*The SRHAWK. It's the Bugs' answer to the SRHAWK,* he thought. *We disguised those to look like SBMHAWK pods, so they returned the compliment. Our fighter pilots have gotten too smart to close in tight on suicide-riders unless they have to to intercept them short of an OWP or capital ship. So the bastards disguised an Etna as something else in the hope that our strikes would come into "fighter-trap" range of it, anyway.*

The numbness of the moment of disaster began to pass, taking the anesthesia of shock with it, and he sucked in a deep breath. From the power of the explosions, he suspected the antimatter loads on these particular ships had been even heavier than the ones aboard the suicide-riders at Centauri had been. No doubt that had been part of the redesign which had fooled his pilots.

*Wait a minute, Andrew,* he told himself. *Don't make the mistake of giving of the Bugs too much credit. It may have been a deliberate deception attempt that succeeded, but it could also just be that they have more classes of suicide-riders than we knew about, and this was simply one we hadn't seen yet.*

He shook himself. Whether the Bugs had done it on purpose or not, didn't really matter. Once Hiithylwaaan had committed to attack the suicide-riders, the result had been all but inevitable. All the Bugs had needed to do was wait until the maximum number of fighters were within sufficiently close proximity and then blow themselves up . . . and in the process trap a horrific percentage of SF 62's precious fighters within the blast effect and destroy them.

He watched the remainder of the strike falling back and silently blessed whoever was in command over there now. He doubted very much that it was Hiithylwaaan, given the Ophiuchi strikefighter tradition of leading from the front. Not that Prescott blamed the *farshathkhanaak* for what had just happened. *He* hadn't seen it coming either, after all. No one had. But at least whoever had taken over had sufficient good sense and initiative to abort the rest of the attack on his own authority rather than throw away what remained of the tattered strikegroups against the unshaken defenses of the main Bug formation.

He made himself sit very still while the damage sidebar tallied the returning icons, and his jaws ached as his teeth clenched on his pipe. Only twenty-six of them were coming home again—barely four full strength squadrons from all three carriers—and he had only eighteen surviving gunboats to support them. That wasn't enough for long-range strikes to do what had to be done, and—

His thoughts broke off as a fresh wave of gunboats suddenly accelerated away from the Bugs.

"Sir—" Chau began hoarsely, but Prescott cut him off.

"I see them, Ba Hai. Contact Captain Shaarnaathy. Tell him we can't afford to send the fighters and gunboats back out for long-range interceptions. They're to engage only from within the rest of the flotilla's missile envelope so that we can support them with shipboard missile fire."

"Sir," Leopold pointed out very carefully, "if we let them in that close, we're likely to have leakers."

"I know that," Prescott replied, more harshly than he'd intended. "But we don't have a lot of choice. We need to—"

"Admiral, Tracking reports additional Bug small craft, probably assault shuttle and pinnace kamikazes, following the gunboats in!" Chau interrupted.

*The small craft swept off on the heels of the remaining gunboats. The special units had performed well, crippling the Enemy attack craft. Now it was time to finish him off, and the Fleet's faster battlecruisers went to full power.*

Andrew Prescott watched with a face of stone as the Arachnid attack came in. The Bugs were doing a better job than usual of keeping their pure kamikazes and gunboats together as a single coordinated force, and his own shaken squadrons had been given only minimal time to rearm and reorganize. His gunboats, in particular, reached the flotilla bare minutes before their Bug pursuers, although the fleeter fighters had been given at least a little more precious time.

But it wasn't going to be enough, and he heard his own voice giving orders as the Bug attack roared down on his command.

*The gunboats and small craft swooped down upon their targets, and their motherships seized the opportunity to close. The Enemy had no option but to go to evasive maneuvering as the deadly little vessels streaked toward his starships, and that reduced his formation's forward speed drastically. The Fleet's long-range missile ships, unhampered by any similar need to bob and weave, closed the range quickly, and by now their sensors had hard locks on most of the Enemy ships. When battle damage began to slow their targets, the missile ships would be ready.*

Space was ugly with butchery as the Bug gunboats led the attack into the heart of SF 62. Yet another wave of gunboats—much smaller, and with fewer accompanying kamikazes—raced towards the flotilla from Beta Force, but in that instance, at least, the Bug coordination had been thankfully poor. Whatever damage Alpha

Force might do, its attack would be over and done before the Beta gunboats entered engagement range.

Andrew Prescott had little time to feel grateful for small favors, however, as the ships of his command and the men and women, human and Ophiuchi alike, who crewed them fought desperately against a tide of destruction. The gunboats were far less numerous than the kamikazes, but they were also faster and far harder to kill, and so he was forced to commit his fighters against them. He hated it. He would far rather have sent the fighters against the relatively defenseless small craft, but those gunboats *had* to be stopped, and his already riven and harrowed fighter squadrons stopped them.

At a cost. Half his remaining fighters died in the dogfight, and four gunboats broke through despite all the exhausted fighter jocks could do. They charged down on *Foxhound*, the battlecruiser *Courageous*, and the freighter *Vagabond*, and all four of the gunboats ripple-salvoed their external ordnance loads of FRAMS . . . then streaked in to ram.

*Foxhound* and *Vagabond* vanished with all hands in hideous blossoms of light and fury, and *Courageous* staggered. She managed to pick off her single assailant just before the gunboat could follow its FRAMs in, but she was brutally wounded and fell out of formation. The flotilla's small craft swarmed out of their boat bays, ignoring the carnage raging around them, and dashed towards her to take off her survivors before the charging Bug battlecruisers came into range to finish her off, but she was obviously a total loss . . . and a sixth of Prescott's capital missile launchers went with her.

The small craft kamikazes accomplished much less, despite their greater numbers. Captain Shaarnaathy had vectored his own gunboats to meet them, and, intercepted far short of the flotilla's perimeter, they were mowed down without ever reaching attack range. But then the strike from Beta Force arrived, and Shaarnaathy's fighters were too spent and disorganized to stop them. It was up to the gunboats and the batteries of the flotilla's ships, and the Bugs came streaking in through the savage defensive fire.

Six gunboats got through this time, and all six charged squarely down on the battlecruiser *Frolic*, the command ship for the flotilla's battlegroup of *Huns*. The *Guerriere-C*-class battlecruiser was heavily armed with standard missile launchers, not the capital missile launchers of the *Dunkerque*-class BCRs, and they went to maximum rate sprint-mode fire as the Bugs entered her envelope. One of them survived to get off its FRAMs, and the big ship staggered as her shields vanished and explosions ripped at her armor. But that armor held, and she raced on, holding her place in formation and maintaining the Survey Command ships' datanet intact.

Then it was over, and an ashen-faced Andrew Prescott counted his losses. His flotilla was still essentially intact, but the Bugs had succeeded in their primary goal, for *Zirk-Ciliwaan* and *Zirk-Likwyn*, his only remaining carriers, had only eleven fighters, less than two full strength squadrons, between them, and only nine of *Condor*'s and *Corby*'s twenty-three gunboats survived. The Bugs had stripped away his long-range striking power . . . and their *Antelopes* had closed the range sharply while his own ships maneuvered to avoid attack. His sensor crews had their positions clearly plotted now, and that meant that *they* had *his* ships plotted just as clearly.

And that he wasn't going to shake them.

The faces on the com screens were grim as Prescott took his place before them. They understood the situation just as well as he did, but he was their commander, and the lack of condemnation in their expressions as they listened to Leopold's summary cut him like a sword. Intellectually, he knew they were right. It *wasn't* his fault, and even if he'd somehow managed to realize at the last minute what the *Etnas* were and what would happen if Commander Hiithylwaaan closed with them, there would have been nothing he could have done. The choice of exactly which units to attack, and in what order, had been Hiithylwaaan's; that was what a *farshathkhanaak* did. And even if Prescott had known all those things, the light-speed communications lag would have prevented him from overriding Hiithylwaaan's decision in time to matter.

But even though his intellect knew that, it didn't matter. Not deep down inside where an officer's responsibility to the men and women under his command lived.

"I believe," he said quietly, when Leopold had finished, "that we have to assume additional Bug units are *en route* to this system. They may even already have arrived, although they obviously have not yet reached a position from which they can engage us, or they would have done so in support of Alpha and Beta. Further, the fact that Beta hasn't closed the range on us as Alpha has suggests that Beta probably *is*, as Commander Chau suggests, composed primarily of *Adders,* which lack the speed to overhaul us.

"But Alpha has us firmly on its sensors, just as we have it, and it has almost three times our long-range missile capability now that *Courageous* is gone. Worse, it remains between us and our exit warp point, and while we can't be positive that the Bugs know where that warp point lies, it's certainly possible that they do. In either case, the Flotilla's only hope is to somehow break contact with—or cripple or destroy—Alpha and make a break for that warp point. At least," he smiled bitterly, "we appear to have finished off all of their available gunboats, so if we *can* get beyond Alpha's sensor range, we should be able to go back into cloak and, with a little luck, stay there.

"The problem, of course, is how we deal with Alpha."

Silence hovered for a moment, and in its depths he heard their understanding. They had no idea how deep into Bug territory they were at this moment, how soon or in what strength other enemy forces might sweep down upon them. But they knew what painful losses they'd already taken and that their enemy had them on his sensors.

And they also knew that the information they possessed might mean victory or defeat in the war against the Bugs . . . and that in this war, defeat and extinction were identical.

"With your permission, Admiral?"

Prescott blinked as the unfamiliar voice cut the silence of awareness. He had to sweep his eyes across the com screens before he found the speaker, and then his eyebrows rose. Lieutenant Eleanor Ivashkin was the most junior officer present for the electronic conference. With Hiithylwaaan's death, SF 62 no longer had a *farshathkhanaak,* but Ivashkin was the senior of TFNS *Corby*'s surviving gunboat skippers. That made her as close to a *farshathkhanaak* as they were likely to come, and he nodded for her to continue.

"Admiral," she said, dark eyes intent in a thin, severely attractive face, "everyone in this flotilla knows how important an El Dorado is. And everyone in it knows how deep the shit is. But if we're going to break free of Alpha Force long enough to get back into cloak and get anyone home with our data, we have to take out *all* their fast ships. Or that's the way it looks to me. Would you agree?"

"I would," he said, sitting very still as he met her eyes on the screen. There was something about the young woman's voice, the set of her shoulders. Something frightening, and he felt his jaw tighten as she nodded slowly.

"In that case, Sir, I think it's time to take a page from the Bugs' book." She drew a deep breath. "Admiral, I request permission to load a full load of FRAMs and show the Bugs what it feels like when someone rams *them* for a change."

Someone started an instant, instinctive protest, but Prescott's raised hand stilled it just as quickly, and he held Ivashkin's eyes steadily.

"Do you realize what you're saying, Lieutenant?" he asked quietly.

"I do, Sir," she replied in a very level tone. "What's more, I believe I speak for the rest of the gunboat skippers and their crews." She smiled ever so slightly. "We're not going home from this one whatever happens to the rest of the Flotilla, Sir. Whether it's fresh Bug gunboats coming after us, or whether we get picked off trying to make conventional attacks on *them*, every one of us is going to be destroyed." She shrugged, and her smile grew a bit wider, a bit more crooked. "They warned us when we volunteered that gunboats are 'expendable assets,' Admiral, and I guess our luck just crapped out. But if I'm going to be expended against these monsters, then I *damned* well want to take as many of them to Hell with me as I can!"

Prescott gazed at her for a seeming eternity, and behind his eyes, his brain raced.

She was right, of course. In another war, against another enemy, perhaps she wouldn't have been, but there were no surrenders, no prisoner of war camps, in this one. And her gunboats weren't the flotilla's only "expendable assets," either.

"Very well, Lieutenant," he heard himself say. "I accept your offer. But you know as well as I do how vulnerable to battle-group missile fire gunboats are, and the Bugs are undamaged and unshaken, while there are only nine of you, even assuming that you're correct and all the gunboat crews volunteer."

In an odd sort of way, he and Ivashkin were completely alone at that moment. He could feel the shock, the stillness of the other conference attendees, but there was no real surprise. Not in this war.

"I think it's unlikely that you or your fellows can break through those defenses and get close enough to ram. Unless, of course," he smiled very thinly, "we arrange to distract the enemy some-how."

✧       ✧       ✧

"Andy, are you sure you're doing this for the right reasons?" Melanie Soo's eyes searched Prescott's face intently, her expression tight with concern and waiting grief, as they stood in *Concorde's* boat bay, and he met her gaze squarely.

"Yes," he said simply, and raised one hand, squeezing her shoulder when she tried to speak again. "I know what you're asking, Melly. And, no, I'm not 'throwing my life away' out of any sense of guilt."

"But—" she began, and he gave her a little shake.

"Ivashkin's gunboats would never get through the Bugs' missile fire alive on their own," he said almost patiently. "They need someone to break trail for them. And what Ivashkin said about expendable assets is true for more than just gunboats under these circumstances."

She started to speak again, then stopped, staring into his face, and tears welled in her eyes. All around her, nonessential personnel filed silently, somberly—almost ashamedly—into the flotilla's small craft as *Concorde* stripped down to the minimum crew needed to fight her weapons and run her systems effectively, and a crushing sense of guilt afflicted her. She was a doctor, not a warrior, yet her place was here, on the flotilla flagship with the staff officers and crewmen who had become her friends.

"At least let me stay, then," she said very softly, almost pleadingly. "Please, Andy. I . . . belong here."

"No, you don't," he said gently. "You belong with Snyder, looking after my people for me. And after the war ends, you belong in that cottage you're always teasing me about." Her mouth trembled, and she drew a deep breath, but he shook his head. "No, Melly." He drew her close and gave her a brief, unprofessional hug, then stepped back.

"Take care, Melly," he said, and turned away without another word.

George Snyder sat on his bridge once more, watching *Sarmatian's* plot, and his belly was a lump of lead as the flotilla's formation shifted. He looked up briefly as the hatch opened, and nodded with curt courtesy to Dr. Soo. The surgeon had no business on the command deck at a time like this, but he never even considered ordering her off it.

The formation shift completed itself, and the face of Andrew Prescott appeared on his com screen. The admiral looked calm, almost relaxed, and Snyder bit his lip as the other man nodded to him.

"You have your orders, George. Captain Shaarnaathy's remaining fighters should be able to give you some cover, but it's going to be up to you to evade the enemy."

"Understood, Sir." Snyder made it come out almost naturally.

"Just get the data home, George," Prescott said quietly. "I'm counting on you. Get the data and my people home."

"I will, Sir. You have my word."

"I never doubted it." Prescott drew a deep breath and nodded again, crisply, with an air of finality. "Very well, George. Stand by to execute."

"Aye, aye, Sir. And, Sir?" Prescott raised an eyebrow and Snyder cleared his throat. "It's been an honor, Sir," he said then. "God bless."

"And you, George. And you. Prescott out."

The com screen went blank, and the "gunslingers" of Survey Flotilla 62 began to alter course.

*The Enemy was up to something.*

*Seven of his starships altered course suddenly, swinging around to head directly for the Fleet's missile ships, and a tentacle cluster of gunboats came with them. It was . . . unexpected. The sort of thing the Fleet might have done, but not the sort of thing the Enemy did. Yet his purpose became quickly evident as the rest of his formation altered to a course headed directly away from the missile ships.*

*But expected or not, the Fleet wasn't unduly concerned. There was no option but to meet the attack head-on; to do anything else would allow the fleeing ships to open the range sufficiently to drop back into cloak and disappear once more. But the sensor readings were clear. The Enemy possessed no more than five capital missile ships of his own, no match for the firepower awaiting him. He would be smashed to wreckage as he attempted to close, and while he would undoubtedly succeed in crippling or destroying some of the Fleet's units, he couldn't possibly cripple enough of them.*

*Had the crews of the Fleet's ships been capable of such a thing, they might have smiled in anticipation, for the attack craft and the gunboats and the kamikazes on both sides had been expended or rendered impotent. This would be a battle in the old style, from the days before the Enemy had introduced his infernal attack craft. One that came down to tonnages and missile launchers and*

*determination, with no subtle manoeuvers or technological tricks,
and the Enemy was too weak to win that sort of fight.*

*I wonder if I should have recorded some final message for Ray?*
Prescott wondered as he watched his plot. Then he shook his
head. There simply hadn't been time to record messages from
everyone aboard *Concorde* and her consorts, and it would have
been a gross abuse of his rank to have sent one when the rest
of his personnel could not. *Besides, he'll understand. If anyone
in the galaxy will, Ray will understand.*

"Entering SBM range in twenty seconds, Sir," Chau Ba Hai said,
and the admiral nodded.

"Engage as previously instructed, Commander," he said formally.

George Snyder's eyes burned as he watched the plot.

Seven battlecruisers and nine gunboats charged straight down
the throats of their pursuers, and as he watched, *Concorde* and
the surviving *Dunkerques* launched their first strategic bombardment missiles. Matching Bug missiles sped outward in answer to
the Allied SBMs, and there were three times as many of them.
ECM and point defense defeated the first few salvos, but there
were more behind them. And more. And still more.

*Delaware* took the first hit. The *Dunkerque*-class ship staggered as an antimatter warhead scored a direct hit on her
shields, but she shook the blow off and continued to charge,
and her short-ranged consorts—the *Cormorants* and their command ship, *Vestal*—followed on her heels, still far out of the
range of their own weapons as they surged straight into the
Bugs' fire. Eleanor Ivashkin's frailer gunboats rode the battlecruisers' flanks, sheltering behind them, hiding in their sensor
shadow, but the Bugs were ignoring them . . . just as Andrew
Prescott had planned. Battlecruisers were a far greater threat
than gunboats, and Bug missiles sleeted in upon them as the
range spun downwards.

He heard someone breathing harshly beside him and looked
up to see Soo's face streaked with tears as she watched the same
icons. He wanted to reach out to her, to say something, but there
was nothing he *could* say, and he returned his eyes to the plot.

*The Enemy missile ships began to take hits. Shields flared and
died, armor vaporized, atmosphere trailed behind them like tangled*

*skeins of blood, but they charged onward, ignoring their damage, and the Fleet lunged to meet them.*

*Australia* was the first to die.

Snyder knew no one would ever know how many hits she'd taken, but she was still driving forward, still riding the thunder of her remaining launchers, when her magazines let go and she vanished in the horrific glare of matter meeting antimatter.

A Bug *Antelope* blew up a moment later, but then it was *Vestal's* turn, and *Corby* and *Condor* were suddenly without a datanet. But only for a moment. There were openings in *Concorde's* now, and they slotted into them, swelling the flagship's defensive fire once more, as they and their sisters charged to their dooms.

"Gunslingers," the Survey Command crews called them, and so had Snyder, with the tolerant contempt of specialists for men and women whose only duty was to fight and die. And die they did. Shields blazed and flared like forest fires, and the plot seemed to waver before Snyder's burning eyes, but they never slowed, never hesitated. Never turned aside.

*Delaware* blew up, then *Condor.* Code Omega transmissions sang their death songs, but they were all in range now, and more Bug ships died or staggered out of formation, drives faltering. A handful of hoarded Bug kamikazes streaked in, launched at the last moment to hurl themselves upon the bleeding gunslingers. Point defense and Ivashkin's gunboats killed most of them, but TFNS *Corby* and *Musashi* were blasted apart, and then there was only *Concorde.*

Melanie Soo wept openly as the savagely wounded flagship charged single-handed into the tempest of missile fire which had killed all of her consorts. Half a dozen Bug starships had been destroyed or crippled, as well, but eight remained, pouring their fire into her broken, staggering hull, and *still* she came on, with nine human-crewed gunboats trailing in her wake. Nine gunboats the Bug gunners had completely ignored to concentrate upon the battlecruisers because they *knew* Allied gunboats didn't suicide.

But this time they were wrong. Lieutenant Ivashkin's gunboats went suddenly to full power, screaming past *Concorde,* hurling themselves bodily upon their targets. Eight of them broke through the last-second defensive fire of their targets, smashing squarely into their foes and taking the Bug battlecruisers with them in dreadful, antimatter pyres.

And as the other, fleeing units of Survey Flotilla 62 watched,

TFNS *Concorde* followed them. Half her engine rooms were already gone, only two of her launchers remained in action. God alone knew how anyone could live or fight aboard that broken, dying ship, but somehow they did, and George Snyder closed his eyes in anguish as the flagship's icon met the last undamaged *Antelope* head-on and her exploding magazines wiped them both from the universe.

# CHAPTER TEN

## The Vengeance of
## Clan Prescott

"Attention on deck!"

The officers who filled TFNS *Irena Riva y Silva*'s flag briefing room rose as Raymond Prescott—now Fleet Admiral Prescott, commanding Seventh Fleet—entered. The humans among them may have risen even faster than the others.

Not that the Gorm and Ophiuchi were tardy, by any means. And the Orions were even less so. They'd been vehement in their rejection of the idea that anyone else might command the fleet that would avenge his brother. They understood.

Indeed, they understood better than Prescott's own species . . . which was why the humans, including his own staffers who'd known him for years, came to attention like cadets in the presence of something that was changed, and cold, and more than a little frightening.

It wasn't that Prescott was outwardly different—at least not much. His hair was uniformly iron-gray now, and close inspection of his face revealed lines and creases that were more deeply graven, as though his features had settled under the weight of a grief he'd never vented aloud. He and Andrew had been very close, for all the age difference between them—twenty years was exceptional spacing, even for parents who'd both had access to the antigerone treatments—and many had expected the news from what was now being called the Prescott Chain to break him.

It hadn't.

A standard year and a half had passed since he and Zhaarnak had launched their abortive "April Fool" attack on Home Hive Three in 2365. After that, they'd settled into a routine of cautious probing, varied by occasional Bug gunboat raids. Zephrain was no different from Justin in that regard, and just as Fifth Fleet in Justin, Sixth Fleet's massive fighter patrols in Zephrain had burned any intruding gunboat instantly out of the continuum. Prescott and Zhaarnak had replied to the raids with SBMHAWK bombardments of the orbital fortresses on the Bugs' end of the warp connection, aware even as they did so that some of their firepower was almost certainly being wasted on electronic mirages. They would have been aware of that even if Vice Admiral Terence Mukerji, for whom Prescott had been forced to create a staff position ("governmental liaison," which at least sounded better than "commissar") hadn't repeatedly pointed it out from behind the shelter of his unassailable political protection.

Then, after more than a year of stalemate, had come the news that had electrified the Grand Alliance: a second El Dorado had been found! No one even claimed to have been present when Raymond Prescott received that news—or the other, personal, news which had accompanied it. Zhaarnak had arranged matters so that he would read that portion of the report in private. After he'd emerged from that enforced seclusion, the respect, admiration, and, yes, love that his human subordinates had always felt for him had been joined by something else: fear.

Not that his customary affable courtesy and sensitive consideration were gone. Not at all. But behind them was something new. Or maybe something was missing. It was hard to tell which . . . and that may have been the most frightening thing all.

The new monitors were finally coming into service, and SF 62's tidings had caused a radical rethinking of their deployment. Instead of being sent to Zephrain, or to Murakuma's fleet, they would form the core of a new offensive formation, to be designated Seventh Fleet. Rather than battering their way through long-established and well-prepared Bug defenses at known points of contact, they would carry the war to the Bugs through the doorway Andrew Prescott had died to open. And Kthaara'zarthan had surprised some humans by refusing to even consider the notion that one of his own race might command that Fleet.

Or perhaps it wasn't so surprising. By swearing the *vilkshatha* oath, Raymond Prescott had become one with the *Zheeerlikou'va lkhannaiee*, and they understood the imperatives of vengeance.

Now Prescott took his place at the head of the table, facing officers who wondered anew at the change that everyone recognized, but no one could really define. A few of the older ones—those who could see beyond a total lack of physical resemblance—came closer than the rest. For their short, compact commander had acquired something they remembered in the bearlike Ivan Antonov. He had become embodied, ruthless Purpose. Like the Furies of ancient myth, he now existed only to be the agent of doom. Every aspect of his nature that might stand between him and the extirpation of the Bug species had been burned out of his soul, leaving him both more and less than human.

"As you were," he said quietly, and feet shuffled softly as the officers obeyed. As they took their seats, the holo sphere between them and the head table came to life, displaying the system designated Andrew Prescott-4 with its two warp points: the one through which they'd entered, and the one leading to AP-5. After a moment, the view zoomed in on the latter, and the icons of their own units became visible, deployed not far from the violet circle of the warp point.

On this scale, the icons represented task groups. Seventh Fleet would (eventually) consist of two task forces, and Prescott had led TF 71 here in his dual capacity as its commanding officer and overall fleet commander. Its backbone was Task Group 71.1, headed by Force Leader Shaaldaar. The imperturbable Gorm commanded an awesome battle-line of thirty monitors (including *Riva y Silva*) and thirty superdreadnoughts. Four of his monitors were fighter-carrying MT(V)s of the new *Minerva Waldeck* class, and six assault carriers provided additional fighter support. But the bulk of the fighter strength was concentrated in Task Group 71.2, whose Ophiuchi commander, Vice Admiral Raathaarn, led ten assault carriers and twelve fleet carriers, escorted by thirty-three battlecruisers. Either could call on Vice Admiral Janos Kolchak's Task Group 71.3, with its twelve fast superdreadnoughts and thirty-four battlecruisers, for assistance. Finally, Vice Admiral Alexandra Cole commanded Task Group 71.4, a support group whose thirteen transports and supply ships were protected by twelve battleships, nineteen battlecruisers, and twelve light cruisers.

The cluster of four innocuous-looking icons in the holo sphere represented the greatest concentration of tonnage and firepower the Grand Alliance had yet fielded. And it didn't include Seventh Fleet's *other* task force. Zhaarnak'telmasa was still organizing TF 72, and was to bring it up to rendezvous with TF 71 in the AP-5 system after Prescott's command had returned from . . . what it was about to embark on.

"As you know," Prescott resumed in that same quiet voice, "this will be our last staff meeting before we commence Operation Retribution by entering AP-5." *The system in which my brother died*, he didn't add, nor did he need to. "I will now ask Commodore Chung to brief us on what we can expect in that system."

The intelligence officer stood up. His recent promotion to captain helped compensate—somewhat—for the separation from Uaaria'salath-ahn. He'd come to rely on the Orion spook as a supporter and a sounding board, and they'd both asked Prescott not to break up a good team. But it had been decided to keep each of the two staffs intact, so Uaaria had remained with Zhaarnak.

"With your permission, Admiral, before going into what we can expect in the AP-5 System, I would like to share with everyone the information I reported to you personally after we received our most recent courier drone from Alpha Centauri."

Prescott nodded, and Chung turned to the assembly.

"The usual security restrictions apply to this information, ladies and gentlemen," he began using the form of address which, as a matter of sheer practicality, had become acceptable usage for females and males of all the Grand Alliance's member races. A war to the death had done much to erase cross-cultural diplomatic misunderstandings. "But with that caveat, I'm authorized to tell you that detailed analysis of the data brought back by TF 62's survivors has confirmed the conclusion reached by the survey flotilla's own specialists. Admiral LeBlanc's team agrees that the Bug system they discovered is Home Hive One."

A stir ran through the compartment. There'd never been any real doubt that what lay on the other side of the closed warp point from the system Andrew Prescott had dubbed "El Dorado" was one of the home hives. Still, there was something to be said for being able to give their target a name.

"And now," Chung resumed, "turning to the system we're about to attack, we've been going on the assumption that the Bugs aren't aware of the El Dorado/Home Hive One connection that SF 62 discovered. If they were so aware, we can be sure they would have mobilized everything capable of reaching AP-5 and made the system impregnable. But our assumption, it turns out, was correct. The Bugs have only the minimal forces we would expect in AP-5, to discourage further visits by stronger survey expeditions."

Chung's audience responded with nods and various nonhuman equivalents thereof. Prescott had assumed from the outset that the Bugs, not knowing what SF 62 might have discovered, would take precautionary measures. So he'd done no less, advancing slowly down the Prescott Chain and probing with RD2s through all the warp points his brother had discovered. He'd continued to do so after arriving here in AP-4, and the drone reports from that system were the basis for Chung's current briefing.

"Turning to the defenses of AP-5, we've detected eight hundred patterns of mines around the warp point, covered by an estimated four hundred laser-armed deep space buoys." The audience reacted with steadiness. That was no more than what they would have expected from Bugs who knew that part of SF 62 had gotten away. "In addition, our RD2s have detected several emissions signatures suggesting the presence of Bug superdreadnoughts sitting virtually on top of the warp point, within energy weapons range." That got an uneasy mutter out of Chung's listeners. "However, we're proceeding on the assumption that these are, in fact, third-generation ECM buoys masquerading as superdreadnoughts—"

"A thoroughly unjustified and highly dangerous assumption," Terence Mukerji blustered from his seat at the far end of the head table, with the sneer he customarily bestowed on those he outranked. "And, I might add, only to be expected from an intelligence analyst who's previously suffered the embarrassment of being taken in by the same type of subterfuge. 'Once burned, twice shy,' eh, Commodore Chung?"

Raymond Prescott leaned forward, turned to his left, and stared down the table at Mukerji, and his voice was even quieter than before.

"In point of fact, Admiral Mukerji, it was *I* who made the decision to regard these sensor returns as spurious." The compartment grew very still, and Mukerji visibly wilted. "The reasoning behind the assumption is unrelated to our experience at Second Home Hive Three. Rather, it's based on the fact—established by SF 62's thorough survey—that there are no other open warp points to any Bug system along the Prescott Chain. That means the Bug force which ambushed SF 62 must have entered the AP-5 system through a closed warp point. That closed warp point might conceivably be in any of the systems of the chain, but the fact that SF 62 was ambushed *here*, strongly suggests that it lies in this system. Whether it's in this system or another one, however, is less significant than the fact that it must be a closed one. And since it is, it's my considered judgment that they're unlikely to have diverted any units as heavy as superdreadnoughts—especially given their new sensitivity to losses in such units—to cover the system when a dispensation of astrographics causes them to believe they have no security concerns here in the first place. I trust, Admiral, that this makes my reasoning clear."

Prescott's voice remained quiet and even throughout, but the last sentence's tone said he was unaccustomed to explaining himself . . . and was unlikely to make a habit of it.

Mukerji managed a jerky nod. Everyone else kept very quiet. Prescott's elaborate public explanation of what a member of his staff ought to have already known would have been a staggering insult, had it not been inherently impossible to insult Mukerji.

"And now," Prescott resumed, "if there are no further questions or comments, we'll proceed with the operational portion of the briefing. Commodore Bichet, if you please."

Jacques Bichet was another relatively new-minted captain. He went back even further on Prescott's staff than Chung, however, and by now the fighter types had gotten over their original misgivings at having an ops officer whose background was line-of-battle . . . as, for that matter, was Prescott's.

"Thank you, Admiral," he began, and adjusted the holo sphere to strategic scale, showing the entire Prescott Chain.

"We believe that the AP-5 System represents the only real barrier we face between here and El Dorado, and Home Hive One beyond it." He indicated the El Dorado System, and the broken string-light beyond it that denoted a warp line leading to a closed warp point. "The Bugs have no reason to suppose that there's anything in the rest of the chain that needs defending."

He switched to tactical scale.

"In accordance with our analysis of the RD2 returns, we'll concentrate on the minefields and laser buoys, conserving our SBMHAWKs for tactical deployment within the AP-5 System." He didn't even glance at Mukerji. "We'll clear a path through the mines with an initial AMBAMP bombardment, after which TG 71.1 will lead the way through the warp point, in this order."

A readout appeared on a flat screen behind the head table. The initial waves consisted of Terran assault carriers and Gorm superdreadnoughts of the gunboat-carrying *Gormus-C* and *Zakar-B* classes. Bichet allowed a few moments for his audience to study the display, then answered the unspoken question in the minds of many.

"Our new monitors are still unknown to the Bugs. The longer we can postpone revealing their existence, the better. Nor should they be required to deal with AP-5's defenses."

There was some muttering, but no discussion. The briefing moved on into the comfortable realms of detail.

*The presence of superdreadnoughts among the opening waves of this assault was even more disturbing than the unexpectedly heavy AMBAMP bombardment which had preceded them. A reinforced survey mission was only to be expected, since the attack on the Enemy survey flotilla had established that this chain of systems must contain some point of contact with the Fleet. A further probe to attempt to determine where that contact lay had been inevitable, and had been planned for. But this level of force was beyond any mere survey operation.*

*Clearly, the first survey flotilla had found something.*

*But* what?

*The question was unimportant from the standpoint of this system's defenders—sixty battlecruisers, thirty-three of them configured to carry ten gunboats each. Their role had suddenly narrowed to inflicting as many casualties as possible before their own unavoidable cessation of existence.*

TG 71.1's leading elements hadn't yet detected the Bug ships—doubtless cloaked, and hanging back from the warp point—when a wave of more than a hundred and sixty gunboats came sweeping down on them. In the gunboats' wake came assault shuttles that everyone knew to be antimatter-laden kamikazes.

But that response had been anticipated. Even as the Terran and Ophiuchi-piloted fighters and Gorm gunboats launched, courier drones sped back through the warp point into AP-4.

On *Riva y Silva's* flag bridge, Raymond Prescott read the report and nodded grimly. He turned to his com screen and met the eyes of Force Leader Shaaldaar, where the latter waited on his own flag bridge aboard Task Group 71.1's flagship, the Gorm monitor *Jhujj.*

"It appears you are correct," Shaaldaar rumbled. "If there really were Bug superdreadnoughts here, they would be actively involved in the warp point defense, seeking to take as many of our major combatants with them as possible."

Prescott gave only a grunt of acknowledgment, then turned and nodded to Anthea Mandagalla. The chief of staff nodded in return, and she and Bichet began to transmit already prepared orders.

Serried ranks of SBMHAWK carrier pods powered up and streaked through the warp point. They transited in massed formations, ignoring their interpenetration losses with cybernetic fatalism, and rushed on, past the capital ships of the first waves, past even the fighters and gunboats those capital ships had launched. Then they seemed—or would have seemed, in extreme slow motion—to disintegrate in the process of releasing clouds of high-tech spores . . . but spores that carried death, not life. Those missiles sped outward, seeking out the approaching Bug gunboats, homing in with a persistence that defeated any but the most rigorous maneuvers. And such maneuvers left the Bugs in less-than-optimum formation to meet the fighters and Gorm gunboats that followed.

Not a single defending gunboat got through. The assault shuttles did . . . to fly into a blizzard of second generation anti-fighter missiles from the capital ships. Four of them worked their way through a momentary lull in that death storm of AFHAWK2s and converged on GSNS *Chekanahama*. The Gorm point defense gunners exploded three of them at point-blank range. But the fourth smashed head-on into the superdreadnought with a cargo of antimatter that no mobile construct could absorb. There were no survivors.

The sanitized medium of a courier drone reported the cataclysm to Prescott, and he stole a glance at the com screen. Shaaldaar's broad nose—the most alien feature of the disturbingly human face—flared in a Gorm expression the Terran had learned to read only too well. But that indication of grief was the only one the force leader allowed to show through the stoicism of one paying the price *synklomus* demanded. Still, a moment passed before he turned to face Prescott from his own screen and spoke evenly.

"Well, now we know the approximate location of their ships."

"Yes." It had been the other part of the message. The gunboat attack on the leading formations of ships had been anticipated, so those ships' sensors had been prepared to trace its origin. Now a vague, pink-stippled area appeared in Prescott's plot, denoting the area where the gunboats had appeared. The cloaked bug ships which had launched them must be lurking somewhere in its midst, and he nodded at it. "Now we know where to send our fighter sweep."

"Remember, they must surely have held back gunboat reserves," Shaaldaar cautioned, with the matter-of-fact informality, even to a fleet commander, which was so much a part of the Gorm personality.

"No doubt. But we're agreed that they don't have anything bigger than battlecruisers, and I doubt if they have many of those. They must appreciate the hopelessness of their position in the system, so I imagine they committed almost all their gunboats to that first strike. Our fighters should be able to deal with whatever's left."

Shaaldaar didn't look entirely happy, but he made no protest.

As a general rule, the TFN preferred to keep the same group of fighter squadrons associated with a given carrier. But the formation of Seventh Fleet had involved a certain amount of reshuffling. Strikefighter Squadron 94 had been temporarily transferred from *Wyvern* to *Basilisk*, a new ship with a new strikegroup, which, it was felt, needed the leavening of some veterans of the Zephrain/ Home Hive Three campaign.

Thus it was that Irma Sanchez found herself a participant in Operation Retribution, after one of her infrequent furloughs home.

She spared a thought for the all too brief time she'd had with Lydochka, almost unrecognizable at age eight. She was a big girl now, and it had been almost too hard to say goodbye. Then she brought herself back to the present, and looked around at the vast emptiness, lit only by the tiny white flame of AP-5's primary, shining across 5.2 light-hours. She was part of the vast screen of fighters that swept ahead of Admiral Prescott's advancing battle-line, curving in to wrap around targets that appeared only fitfully on Irma's scope, flickering in out of existence as the sensors of the recon fighters whose downloaded readings she was seeing struggled to overcome the Bugs' cloaking ECM.

"Heads up, people." Bruno Togliatti was a full commander now—as Irma was a full lieutenant, for fighter pilots who survived got promoted fast—but he was still in a lieutenant commander's billet as CO of VF-94. After this tour, he was due to move up to command of a carrier strikegroup. Irma wasn't particularly looking forward to that.

"We're not getting much on our displays yet," Togliatti went on, "but there's enough for the computers to have allocated targets. Stand by." Irma's scope went to tactical schematic as Captain Quincy, Seventh Fleet's *farshathkhanaak* assigned each of the ghostly battlecruisers ahead to one or more of his strikegroups while Togliatti's voice continued in her earphones. "We should be picking up visuals soon."

But before they could see the targets—the cloaking ECM operated on various wavelengths, but not that of visible light— they saw something else: the flashes up ahead that marked the graves of dying decoy missiles. Other squadrons, coming behind them, had launched those decoys, each of which simulated an F-4 to draw and disperse the Bug defensive fire. VF-94 and the other front line squadrons were fitted with ship-gutting primary packs.

Then there were flashes to port and starboard. Fighters were starting to die as well.

But then Irma began to glimpse the targets, glinting in the bright F-class starshine, growing in a way that gave a sense of breathtaking motion that hadn't existed against the backdrop of the distant stars as the fighters raced towards them.

"All right, people," Togliatti's voice rasped in her headset. "We're going in."

Raymond Prescott looked up from the last report, and his face wore a look of cold satisfaction.

"Fighter trap" suicide-riders had claimed thirty of the fighters, but few others had been lost. Indeed, Seventh Fleet's total losses so far, aside from *Chekanahama*, amounted to only sixty-three fighters and seven Gorm gunboats. In exchange, the fighters had savaged the Bug battlecruisers with their primary packs and hetlasers. With engine rooms reduced to twisted wreckage by the primary beams, those battlecruisers had been unable to outrun the Gorm superdreadnoughts—as fast as any other race's *undamaged* battlecruisers—which had pulled into standoff missile range and blown them apart.

Prescott turned to his staff and gestured at the report he'd been reading, which detailed the Gorm gunboats' hunting down of the last enemy battlecruisers with fully functional drives.

"Very well. I think we can declare AP-5 secured and bring the rest of the task forces through. . . . Yes, Amos?"

"Well, Sir," Captain Chung looked uncomfortable, "I can't help wondering about the rest of their gunboats."

"The *rest* of their gunboats?"

"Yes, Sir. Battlecruisers can carry ten gunboats each, which means that the battlecruisers confirmed as destroyed were just about sufficient to carry the gunboats in the attack wave we wiped out. But it's not like the Bugs to send in *all* of their available gunboats in one wave. Which suggests that they have other assets in the system."

Prescott frowned at the spook's unconscious echo of Shaaldaar. And a stubborn honesty forced him to wonder if he had reasons, unrelated to military rationality, for his haste to declare himself the conqueror of the system . . . and, almost certainly, the killer of the particular Bugs who'd wiped out the last elements of SF 62's gunslingers.

"Thank you, Amos," he acknowledged quietly. "You've raised a point we can't ignore. Nor have I forgotten the possibility of cloaked Bug pickets still in the vicinity of the warp point. We'll advance cautiously. As our monitors enter AP-5, they'll engage deception-mode ECM to appear as superdreadnoughts, and proceed in tight formation, with fighters deployed to secure the flanks." He turned to the com screen and addressed Shaaldaar, who hadn't commented. "Your *real* superdreadnoughts will lead the advance across the system, along with the CVAs, which will maintain a screen using the fighters that aren't detached to cover the monitors."

Task Force 71 completed its transit into AP-5, shook itself down into the formation Prescott had outlined, and proceeded to cross the two hundred and ninety-light-minute gulf to the warp point leading to the AP-6 System, the next way station on the road to El Dorado.

VF-94 had done its time in the forward fighter screen and would soon be relieved by another of *Basilisk*'s squadrons. Irma Sanchez was starting to feel the "home free" sensation of one nearing the end of a watch.

That may have slowed her reaction a trifle when her HUD's tactical display suddenly blossomed with scarlet "hostile" icons. But not by much.

"What the—?!"

Togliatti cut her automatic exclamation short.

"Heads up, people!" He fired off a series of orders, which boiled down to "Ignore the gunboats and concentrate on the kamikaze assault shuttles." But few orders were necessary for veterans like these. Then he was off under emergency power, with the rest of the squadron in his wake.

*Yeah,* Irma had time to think. *We didn't get all their battlecruisers after all, and the ones they held in reserve were really cagy. They maneuvered into position to launch their gunboats and kamikazes as close as possible to our fighter screen, so we'd have the least possible reaction time after detecting them.*

*Damned lucky we were about to be relieved. Our relief is already coming up behind us, and we can sure as hell use the support.*

*On the other hand, it means* we've *got minimal life support left. . . .*

She chopped the thought brutally off, and focused her entire being on the task of zeroing in on one of the antimatter-laden assault shuttles that spelled potential death for *Basilisk*.

Raymond Prescott looked up and faced his staff, then turned to the com screen and faced Shaaldaar.

The understrength fighter screen had killed every one of the kamikaze shuttles that had erupted into their faces. But to do so, they had to pretty much leave the gunboats for the defenses of the superdreadnoughts and assault carriers of the vanguard. Only six gunboats had survived long enough to launch ripple salvos of FRAMs, and of those, only three had gone on to successfully ram their targets. But four Gorm superdreadnoughts (including *Sakar*, a datalink command ship) and the Terran CVAs *Mermaid* and *Basilisk* had suffered damage. The last two had come through despite devastating hits—which, Prescott reflected, argued in favor of the Terran design philosophy of treating an *assault* carrier as just that, and not as a fragile platform for as many fighters as could be crammed into it. *Sakar* and one of the other Gorm ships had been just as fortunate . . . but the third was almost destroyed, and the fourth totally so.

The aftermath of this second Bug strike had been even more definitive than the first. The Bug battlecruisers' close-range launch, whatever its short-term tactical advantages, had rendered escape impossible, and TF 71's full massive fighter strength had remorselessly hunted them down. The advance to the AP-6 warp point continued.

"Are our cripples on their way back to AP-4, Anna?" Prescott asked, breaking into everyone's mental rehashing of the engagement.

"Yes, Sir," Captain Mandagalla replied. *Mermaid* and *Basilisk*, and the Gorm superdreadnought *Chekanos*, were withdrawing, escorted by Task Group 71.4's light cruisers. "As per your orders, the damaged carriers' remaining fighters are being redistributed among the undamaged ones. How that's going to affect the squadrons' continuity is still being worked out. To a great extent, it will depend on which of them have the highest percentage of survivors."

"Survival of the fittest, eh?"

"Yes, Sir . . . although the seniority of the surviving squadron commanders is, inevitably, going to play a part."

Prescott grunted, dismissed the matter from his mind, and looked at his plot, with its system-scale display. It showed the warp point through which they'd entered, and the one toward which they were advancing. It did not show the one which must have admitted the Bug ambush force into the system.

The tale of SF 62's survivors made it clear that there must be such a third warp point—probably a closed one, and if not closed, certainly hidden somewhere in the cold vastness of the outer system beyond the region of anything but the kind of extended survey he didn't have time for. And he didn't doubt for a second that there were still cloaked pickets in the system, reporting the battle that had just ended to whatever Bug command echelons lay beyond that warp point. Leaving such pickets here was precisely what he himself would have done—in fact, what he intended to do before departing.

No question about it. He'd have to fight his way back through AP-5 on his return from Home Hive One.

*But Zhaarnak will be here by then with Task Force 72,* he told himself. *Won't he?*

The ready room deep inside TFNS *Banshee* had belonged to one of that assault carrier's squadrons. Now, what little remained of that squadron had been merged with VF-94, off the crippled *Basilisk*.

One of VF-94's newly acquired pilots, his j.g.'s insignia still shinily new, was holding forth to his equally junior fellows.

"The Skipper and the XO had just bought it, and the rest of us were maneuvering to let that shuttle have it up the ass, when two gunboats came at us out of the—"

Commander Bruno Togliatti stretched out his weary form in one of the comfortable chairs and muttered to his senior surviving pilot. "Christ, will you listen to this kid? Maybe four months out of Brisbane. Five max."

"And now he thinks he's King Shit on Turd Island," Irma Sanchez remarked from the depths of the chair to his right, and Togliatti chuckled. Then he sobered.

"Hey, listen, Irma. We're still getting the organizational details straightened out. But you're in line for ops officer of this bastard outfit. Tradition says that the former ops officer of what used to be the squadron here becomes XO . . . and besides, he's got the seniority on you. You haven't been a full lieutenant long. If I had my way—"

"Aw, don't worry about it, Skipper. You know me. I'm not hung up on titles. All I want is—"

"—is to kill Bugs," Togliatti finished for her, nodding. "That's what I've been meaning to talk to you about. You know I'm due for command of some carrier's strikegroup after this campaign." He didn't add, *If I survive.* Fighter pilots never did. "So everybody's going to be moving up one bump—including you, whether you like it or not. And you need to understand something. There's more to it than just killing Bugs."

"Yeah? Somehow, I thought that was what we were out here to do. Silly me."

Togliatti ignored the undertone of petulance, and his voice was as serious as Irma had ever heard from him when he continued.

"Yes it is—to do it in an organized fashion, so that the killing is as efficient and effective as possible. And that's what people in command positions—which you're going to be, sooner or later—are for. It's a fallacy to think that the best warrior is always the best officer. A *good* officer isn't so much a warrior as a *manager* of warriors. Random violence is just self-indulgence. It's worse than useless, because it disperses energy that ought to be focused on achieving our war aims. I'm telling you all this because when you rise in the chain of command and assume greater responsibilities—and it's your duty to do just that, whether you want to or not—you're going to have to give something up. Can you?"

Irma was silent for a space. She'd never heard Togliatti talk like this, and she sensed that this wasn't a moment for flippancy. And she knew just what he meant, for in unguarded moments of post-battle camaraderie and off-duty drinking, she'd revealed her past to him. So she emulated his seriousness.

"I . . . don't know, Skipper. I'll have to think about it."

"That'll be fine."

✧      ✧      ✧

*It was perplexing. The concentration of tonnage and firepower that the cloaked pickets reported was entirely out of proportion as a response to the destruction of a mere survey flotilla.*

*To be sure, the Enemy had been a more active explorer than the Fleet even before the Fleet's losses had curtailed its own survey efforts. The path of survival had always mandated the careful and complete development of each System Which Must Be Protected before the expanding perimeter of the Fleet's explorations risked contact with star systems which might contain fresh Enemies to threaten those Systems Which Must Be Protected. Closed warp points, especially, were logical places to halt exploration while the Systems Which Must Be Protected consolidated behind them, since such warp points formed natural fire breaks against potential Enemies.*

*That doctrine of slow and cautious expansion had, of necessity, been modified somewhat on all three occasions upon which the Fleet had encountered an Enemy whose own sphere had encompassed multiple star systems. Even then, however, the Fleet had not diverted such effort into dashing off in every conceivable direction, and now that the Fleet had been forced—temporarily, at least—onto the defensive, its exploration efforts had virtually ceased. After all, the last thing the Fleet needed was to stumble into yet another Enemy while it was already engaged against two of them. Far better to allow the Enemy to blunder into systems the Fleet had already picketed with cloaked cruisers and then backtrack him to a point of contact in his space.*

*Yet even allowing for the fact that this group of Enemies were frenetic explorers, the commitment of a force this powerful just to continue exploration of a single warp line was . . . odd.*

*Or perhaps it wasn't.*

*The Enemy survey force which had been destroyed in this system had been detected by the system's cloaked pickets when it first passed through on what clearly had been its outbound course. When the Fleet attacked it, it had been returning to its home base, which might have been for any number of reasons, ranging from the need to resupply to the discovery that the warp line it had been exploring ended—as so many did—in a useless cul-de-sac. But the dispatch of a follow-up force this powerful down a barren, dead-end warp chain would have been pointless. And the diversion of so much combat power from the known points of contact to follow up a relatively unimportant warp line whose exploration had simply been interrupted by a routine need to return to base would have made no sense.*

*Therefore, the Enemy must not think the chain was unim-portant.*

*What had the survey flotilla found?*

*It couldn't be the closed warp point through which the Fleet had entered and left the system. There was no way the Enemy could know of its existence, and even if the Enemy had deduced that it must exist, it would have been impossible for him to locate. And, in any event, the Enemy wasn't proceeding toward the closed warp point, but rather was advancing single-mindedly toward the open one that would take him to the chain's next, even more useless warp junction.*

*But whatever these Enemies' mysterious objective might be, they would eventually be returning this way, as the survey flotilla had. They could not be allowed to do so unchallenged—especially not when a force this powerful had obligingly thrust itself into a position where it might be cut off by even more powerful forces and utterly destroyed. But the immediately available forces were insufficient to entrap it on its return. Therefore, help must be summoned from elsewhere.*

*Fortunately, there was a place from which that help could come.*

# CHAPTER ELEVEN
## Chaff in the Furnace

In the words of the legendary and doubtless apocryphal Yogi Berra, it was *déjà vu* all over again.

They'd entered Home Hive One just as unobtrusively as they'd once slipped into Home Hive Three, emerging from the closed warp point into Stygian regions where a six light-hour-distant Sol-like sun barely stood out from the starfields. Then they'd formed up and proceeded sunward in a long-prepared order, toward the three Bug-inhabited planets which a chance bit of orbital choreography had placed in a neat row, at a three-way aphelion.

As he gazed into the system-scale holo display, Raymond Prescott found himself wondering if the Bugs believed in astrology. Somehow, he doubted it. But if they did, they were about to get a whole new perspective on planetary alignments as a harbinger of ill luck.

He and Shaaldaar and their staffs had discussed the upcoming operation and its execution in exquisite detail, poring over the survey data Andrew had died to get home. They had a very good notion of the daunting scope of the task which faced them, and the discussion of precisely how to go about it had waxed voluble. Indeed, given the Orion and Gorm traditions of free-wheeling debate—which were considerably more fractious than the TFN normally embraced—the debate had moved beyond free-wheeling to vociferous on more than one occasion.

The overwhelming temptation was to try to repeat what Sixth Fleet had managed to accomplish in Home Hive Three. Hopefully, the "Shiva Option," as the Alliance's strategists had decided to label it, would have the same disorienting effect here that it had had there.

Unfortunately, there'd been two major problems in relying on that strategy. First, the Bugs must have suffered a severe jolt to their confidence in the inviolability of their home hive systems after what had happened to Home Hive Three. At a bare minimum, they'd almost certainly upgraded their sensor nets in the other home hive systems, and it was unlikely that Seventh Fleet would succeed in creeping in quite as close as Sixth Fleet had managed. Given the orbital defenses and the massive mobile force Andrew had detected in Home Hive One, it was very unlikely that Seventh Fleet could land a repeat of that devastating strike without first fighting its way through everything the Bugs could throw at it.

Second, and perhaps even more important, there was no way to be certain that the "Shiva Option" would even work a second time. If what seemed to have happened in Home Hive Three was in fact a universal Bug response to massive "civilian" casualties, then breaking through to directly attack the planetary surface, even at the risk of ignoring the fixed defenses on the way in and of paying for the attack with heavy losses in the strike forces, was the only logical way to go after a home hive system. Unfortunately, there was no way to be certain the effect was universal. Or even that the effect was what everyone thought it had been in the first place, for that matter. Hopefully, one result of Operation Retribution would be to confirm the universality of the effect, but no responsible strategist could plan an attack on this scale on "hopeful." Because if it turned out that the effect *wasn't* universal, the fixed defenses would use the time consumed by the planetary attack to get their own systems fully on-line and massacre the strike wave as it attempted to withdraw.

In the end, although certainly not without regrets, Prescott had decided that he had no choice but to plan for a conventional assault intended to cripple or destroy the defenses *before* going after the planetary population centers. He wasn't the only one who regretted the logic which left him no other option, but it was a bit of a toss-up. There were at least as many staffers who were relieved by his decision as there were those who were disappointed by it.

But as Task Force 71 moved in-system, and as the recon fighters and drones probed ahead, thoughts about astrology, bad luck, and the "Shiva Option" all left his mind to make room for a single perplexing question. Where was the bulk of the massive Bug fleet presence his brother had found here?

"It's a trap," Terence Mukerji jittered at an informal staff meeting on the flag bridge. "They knew we were coming, and they're in cloaking ECM, waiting for us. Once they know we're in the system, they'll move in and seal the warp point behind us."

Jacques Bichet cleared his throat.

"There may be some reason for concern, Sir," he said, loudly not adding *Even though Mukerji thinks so.* "The Bugs do have a history of using cloaked forces to spring surprises, starting with what they did to Commodore Braun," he pointed out, and Prescott turned a carefully noncommittal face to his intelligence officer.

"Amos?"

"I disagree, Sir. It's true that the Bugs have a history of using cloak, but I don't believe they set up an ambush because they knew we were coming. If the Bugs knew that your bro— er, that SF 62 had probed Home Hive One, then they would have put a major fleet presence in AP-5, not just the light forces we encountered."

Bichet looked unconvinced.

"Maybe. But isn't it also possible that they might have decided not to do that in order to lure us deep into the system and trap us there?"

An unspoken frisson ran through the group, for Bichet had summoned up the ghosts of Operation Pesthouse, but Chung stood his ground.

"I don't think so, and not just because I think they would have tried to stop us in AP-5. Everything our scouts have reported so far indicates that the units we *can* see are at a low state of readiness, like the ones we encountered in Home Hive Three. To me, that suggests the same kind of 'cost-conscious' resource husbanding we've deduced about their defense of that system. And that sort of stance is totally inconsistent with the notion that they're keeping forces as large as SF 62 reported permanently under cloak and at general quarters. The resource demands would simply be too prohibitive, in my opinion. Admiral, I've prepared an estimate—a rough one, necessarily—of what that would cost, if you'd like to see it."

"That won't be necessary, Amos. I can readily imagine it. And I agree with you." Prescott faced the rest of staff. "I don't pretend to know where the heavy fleet elements that were in the system have gone, but I'm entirely satisfied that they're not here now. We'll proceed as planned."

He activated the holo sphere around which they stood. In the inner-system display, the green icon that was Task Force 71 split into two smaller ones, which homed in on Planets I and III. Prescott himself would lead the attack on the innermost planet, leaving the outermost—the most populous and important of the three inhabited worlds, judging from the energy emissions—to Shaaldaar. Planet II would be dealt with later.

There was no argument, not even from Bichet. There was, however, an undercurrent that Prescott had no trouble detecting. *They wonder if I'm predisposed to favor whatever interpretation of the facts allows me to get down to the business of sterilizing the system without delay.*

*I wonder if I am, too.*

*But Chung* does *make sense.*

"Ah, one other matter, Admiral." Mukerji broke the silence. "I understand why you've found it necessary to split Force Leader Shaaldaar's task group into two elements, one of them under your own direct command. But you've also split Admiral Raathaarn's and Admiral Kolchak's task groups between the two elements. I'm concerned about the complications that introduces into the command structure."

"It's a little late to be bringing it up, Admiral Mukerji," Prescott observed mildly. *Or it would be, if you were doing it for any reason except to build a case for possible later use in playing the blame game. But in that event, you'll probably be dead—proving the old adage about silver linings.* "And, at any rate, I see no alternative. It's necessary to provide each of the two attack elements with comparable fighter strength, and this is the only way to do it."

"Of course, Sir," Mukerji murmured obsequiously, and Prescott suppressed an urge to wipe his hands on his trousers.

The task force continued on its sunward course, and increasingly detailed sensor returns from the scouts and RD2s brought the system's defenses into clearer focus. Each of the three inhabited planets had the array of orbital fortresses, with a mammoth space station as centerpiece, that Andrew had reported. Indeed, it was all very reminiscent of Home Hive Three, even to the low state of readiness. Equally quiescent were the mobile forces—twelve monitors, twelve superdreadnoughts, and eighteen battlecruisers—in orbit around the third planet. Their presence there tended to confirm the identification of that world as the system's demographic and industrial center of gravity.

Prescott studied the readouts in a black abstraction that no one was inclined to interrupt. He didn't take Mukerji's funk seriously, of course. But ... where *had* they gone, those other ships that *Concorde* had detected? Thirty-five monitors and almost forty superdreadnoughts, not to mention their escorting battlecruisers, represented one hell of a lot of firepower. *Something* must have inspired the Bugs to send it elsewhere, but Prescott had been thoroughly briefed on all of the operations the Grand Alliance currently contemplated. Nothing on the schedule—except for his own offensive—should have required reinforcements that heavy. And Chung was completely correct in at least one respect: if the Bugs had been given any reason to suspect Seventh Fleet was *en route* to the system, the logical place to stop it would have been in AP-5, and none of the missing ships had been there. So where were they?

The obvious answer was that they could have gone anywhere. This system could be a staging area for any of the war's fronts, and even though the Bugs did appear to have reverted to the strategic defensive, they could have moved those ships for any number of reasons, not just in response to Allied moves. Given the Alliance's near-total ignorance of the internal warp layout of the Bugs' domain, who was to say where Home Hive One's open warp points might lead?

It was a reasonable question, but a basic stubbornness wouldn't let him simply file the matter away under the heading of "Answer Unknowable." This couldn't be an accident. There must, he felt with a certainty beyond mere logic, be some immediate significance to the absence of such an awesome assemblage of tonnage and firepower at this particular time in this particular place. And yet, like a dog without a bone or even a stick to gnaw, he lacked any solid basis for speculation. Given the unpredictable nature of the warp connections ...

For lack of any other starting point, he cleared the holo sphere and summoned up a strategic-scale view of the warp lines he did know: the Prescott Chain, proceeding from what was now officially known as Prescott's Star through the glowing little orbs of four more systems before reaching AP-5. From AP-5, it ran through four more nexi, the last of which was El Dorado with its broken string-light closed-warp connection to Home Hive One ... beyond which lay the unknown.

It called nothing to mind. The display was only a chain of lights, connecting two known points across an unknown distance with an unknown number of closed warp points on its flanks. He frowned thoughtfully at it, and then began to trace it in reverse. He worked backwards from Home Hive One to AP-5, where Andrew had met his death and where he was certain he would have to fight his own way through on his return, against whatever forces the Bugs had been able to rush through the closed warp point that system must hold. . . .

And all at once, dizzyingly, he knew.

There was one perfectly good reason why those massed formations of capital ships might no longer be in the system. He'd been correct in supposing that the Bug pickets still in AP-5 had summoned help to cover that system against his return. What he hadn't guessed then was that the help they required had been available from only one source—*Home Hive One*.

His imagination supplied another warp chain, one originating with an open warp point of Home Hive One and running parallel to the Prescott Chain, doubling back through some unknown but probably small number of intervening systems to AP-5, which it entered through a closed warp point. That closed point had allowed the Bugs to ambush Andrew there on his return leg . . . but they'd done so without any way of knowing just where he'd been returning *from*. And because they didn't know what he'd discovered for the Alliance, they'd reached, quite logically, for the closest nodal reaction force when Raymond's own, far heavier fleet crashed through AP-5.

The main Bug forces had been speeding frantically away from *this system* even as TF 71 had been advancing slowly but steadily towards it.

He brought his excitement under stern control and suppressed his instinct to share his theory with his staff and flag officers. He would have confided in Zhaarnak, had his *vilkshatha* brother been here. But he wasn't, and Prescott knew this couldn't be proved.

But he also knew that he needed no formal proof that the observed facts weren't mere coincidence. Coincidence simply wasn't that energetic. Of course, it was entirely possible that what seemed so clear to him might be somewhat less obvious to others.

No. This wasn't the time to make his staff any more doubtful about his ability to maintain professional detachment. So he'd just keep this insight to himself. And use it. . . .

✧      ✧      ✧

As they'd done at Home Hive Three, Prescott and Shaaldaar timed their arrivals at Planets I and III to be simultaneous—a simpler problem in astrogation here, as these planets were so close together at their present approach. Still, "close" was a purely relative term when it came to interplanetary distances, so—again, as at Home Hive Three—there would be a communications lag. In the present case, it would be six minutes before either admiral would know the results of the other's attack, and it would take equally long to transmit any other information between them. But there was no alternative. All indications were that telepathy was instantaneous, operating on some level of reality where the light-speed limit didn't apply, so any real-time gap would allow one Bug planet to warn the other of what was coming.

It was too much to expect that they'd be able to close to point-blank range before being detected. Home Hive Three had been an unrepeatable piece of good fortune. Nevertheless, the space stations and orbital fortresses around the two target worlds were still struggling up to whatever passed for full alert among the Bugs when the attack forces drew into range to launch their fighters and gunboats.

Of the two admirals, Shaaldaar had the more complex tactical problem, for some of the mobile units at Planet III were undoubtedly at full alert at any given time, and the others would undoubtedly power up faster than the fixed defenses. So the plan called for him to send his Gorm gunboats, with their capacity to carry far more external ordnance than the fighters, to smother those awakening warships with FRAMs before more than a few of them were able to bring their weapons on-line. Meanwhile, his fighters would swarm like locusts over the space station and orbital weapons platforms.

Prescott, faced only with static defenses, had more options, and he'd opted to divert part of his attack waves to hit Planet I's surface while its orbital defenders were still under attack. Sensor returns had revealed a surprising plethora of ground installations on the planetary surface—it was the single most striking difference between this system and Home Hive Three that they'd yet observed—so there was no shortage of targets in the hemisphere where the extra fighter assets would be employed.

Prescott was studying a holographic image of the planet and its orbiting defenses as they approached launch range and the last few minutes of the countdown ticked away. Everyone on Flag Bridge was as determined as he himself to play the "I'm calm, cool, and collected game as the pre-attack tension ratcheted higher and higher. He doubted that he was actually fooling anyone else any more than they were fooling him, but that didn't absolve any of them of their responsibility to try.

Any of them except Amos Chung, who chose that moment to approach his admiral with his habitual diffidence somewhat in abeyance.

"Sir. . . ."

"Yes, Amos?" Prescott prompted without looking away from the holographic that continued to absorb at least eighty percent of his attention.

"Uh, Sir, we're close enough now to get more detailed sensor readings of those ground installations all over the planet, and my people have just completed an analysis of the latest imagery, and—"

"Yes, Amos?" Prescott repeated. His voice wasn't exactly testy, but it had taken on a definite come-to-the-point undertone, and Chung drew a deep breath.

"Sir, it's my considered judgment that those are ground bases for gunboats. And, based on the number each of the installations— they're very standardized—could accommodate . . . Well, Sir, I think there are twenty-four hundred gunboats on that planet."

All at once, Chung had Prescott's undivided attention.

"Did I understand you to say—?"

"Yes, Sir." Chung braced himself anew. "And judging from the data downloads on Planet III we've gotten from Force Leader Shaaldaar, it looks like there are an approximately equal number of the bases on each of the other two planets, as well. His people hadn't identified them before they sent off their raw sensor download, but when I compared their take to what we'd already picked up here, it's sort of jumped up and hit me in the eye. Sir," he shook his head, "I just don't see anything else they could be."

Prescott didn't reply at first as he stared into Chung's face without even seeing the intelligence officer. Instead, for a sickening instant, the numbers swam before his eyes. *Seventy-two hundred gunboats! And there's no way we can warn Shaaldaar that he's facing a third of them—not in time, not with a six-minute communications lag. And even if we could, by the time we turn on Planet II, the twenty-four hundred there will be in space, ready to swarm over us like a river of army ants eating elephants to the bone. . . .*

The paralysis of that realization threatened to freeze him in place, but then he sucked in a deep breath and pulled himself together.

*No, there's no way to warn Shaaldaar in time. But there's something else we* can *do!*

"Commodore Landrum!" he snapped.

The *farshathkhanaak* hurried over. That wasn't Captain Stephen Landrum's official title, of course, but except in official paperwork, nobody ever called the staff officer specializing in fighter ops anything else.

"Steve," Prescott said rapidly, "alert all fighter squadron commanders that we're changing the plan. We'll drop back to our earlier tactical projections of the absolute minimum strength needed to deal with the space station fortresses. All other fighter assets will be reassigned to the surface strike. It won't be perfect, but if Amos is right about the gunboat strength down there, then our only option is to go with a partial Shiva Option . . . and pray that Home Hive Three wasn't a fluke."

Landrum's jaw dropped, and his eyes darted to the countdown clock. It showed less than two minutes remaining before launch, and Prescott hurried on.

"I know it's bound to generate confusion. That can't be helped. I also know there's no time to assign the additional fighters to specific surface targets. They'll just have to go after targets of opportunity—concentrating on population centers. Any questions?"

Landrum had plenty of those, but he knew there was no time to ask them.

"No, Sir. I'll get those orders out at once."

He departed at a run, and Prescott turned back to the holo display. The scale expanded to show the approaching Allied forces, and presently the tiny icons of fighters began to go out.

The admiral felt someone at his elbow and turned his head. It was Chung, who'd been one of the stronger advocates of going with a Shiva approach from the very beginning, and Prescott cocked an inviting eyebrow at him.

"So it looks like we get to try the Shiva Option after all, Sir," the intelligence officer said quietly.

"Not under exactly the sort of controlled test circumstances I might have preferred," Prescott agreed with a crooked smile which held no humor at all.

"No, Sir. I can see that. Still," the spook's nostrils flared as he inhaled, and he turned his head to meet his admiral's eyes, "given what happened to SF 62, I can't think of a better laboratory for it."

"Are you *sure* there aren't any more last-minute changes in plan, Skipper?" Irma Sanchez inquired as Planet I's atmosphere began to whistle around her fighter, far below the orbital fortresses VF-94 had originally been slated to attack. "After all, we've still got almost two whole minutes to the launch point."

At the moment, no one seemed to be shooting at their squadron, but not everyone could have made that claim. One of the other squadrons in their own strikegroup had been virtually wiped out by the point defense crews of a Bug OWP which had gotten its systems on-line just a little faster than any of its fellows. And the gunboats and fighter squadrons tasked to suppress the rest of the fixed fortifications were taking ever heavier fire as the Bugs fought to respond to the attack. These defenders had been given a little longer to respond than the orbital defenders of Home Hive Three, and Irma suspected that they'd been at a somewhat higher level of readiness even before they'd picked up Seventh Fleet. Whether that was true or not, Planet I's high orbitals had become a seething furnace of flashing warheads, failing shields, and exploding fighters and gunboats, which made her own momentary immunity feel brittle and profoundly unnatural.

"Can the chatter!" Togliatti snapped. "And get your targeting solutions locked in, everybody. We're going in now."

Irma complied. For all her griping, she wasn't averse to going after the kind of target they'd been told to seek out just before they'd been launched into this cluster fuck.

The whistle of the F-4's passage through atmosphere grew louder as she crossed the terminator and entered the night side, and it didn't take long to acquire her target visually. The Bug cities weren't a nighttime blaze of light like human ones. Still, Bugs did see in the visible-light wavelengths, and presumably they did like to be able to do things after dark. A galaxy of rather dim stars grew ahead of her.

The city was vast, as Bug cities tended to be. A mountain range upswelling of oddly massive towers and bulging domes that rose like some disturbing alloy of toadstools and stalagmites. Irma had seen imagery of the cities on Home Hive Three—or, at least, of what those cities once had looked like—from the operational debriefs after that attack. These cyclopean ramparts of Hell looked exactly the same, and her mind pictured the chittering, scuttling throngs swarming like maggots in their bowels while the flash and glare of the warheads hammering at the orbital defenses flickered on the outer walls like distant lightning.

The city seemed huge, indestructible and invulnerable. But the FRAM she fired into its heart was a weapon designed for deep-space combat, using the inconceivable energies of matter-antimatter annihilation to produce a blast that was terrifying even when there was no atmosphere to carry the shock wave and thermal pulse. Its designers, surely, had never imagined it being set for a ground burst on a Terra-type planet.

Irma's fighter had shot ahead at Mach 5, streaking over the city and beyond it, before the event—"explosion" was a banality—occurred. Her view-aft simply shut down, and she hauled her nose up, seeking altitude and the refuge of vacuum ahead of the expanding sphere of Hell.

Then she spared a glance to port, and another to starboard. She'd been part of the first wave to hit the surface, but others had followed. It was as if a wall of inconceivable fireballs marched across the planet's nightside, leaving burned-out lifelessness behind it—a landscape lit by firestorms and the glow of lava oozing up through the splits and cracks in the planet's skin.

She turned her eyes from the flaming planet and looked ahead. The fighter was continuing to climb, and the stars appeared.

"How're the others doing against the forts, Skip?" she asked, and there was a pause before Togliatti responded.

"They're mopping them up now. The Bugs seem to have stopped resisting effectively."

Force Leader Shaaldaar was confused.

As was always likely to be the case in an operation in which forces separated by interplanetary distances were expected to coordinate, Seventh Fleet's timing had been off. Not by very much—this was a superbly trained force which had rehearsed exhaustively in preparation for the attack—but by enough to be significant. His own task force had been forced to deviate slightly from its planned course by a Bug freighter which had chosen to bumble through exactly the wrong volume of space at precisely the wrong time. Making up the lost time had required him to use rather more drive power than he would have liked, and he suspected that the extra power had allowed a Bug sensor platform to pick him up early. At any rate, he'd been forced to launch his attack slightly later than Prescott's and from slightly further out because the emissions signatures of the OWPs protecting his target had suddenly begun to shift and change as they'd abruptly began rushing to a higher readiness state.

Because of that, Shaaldaar's intelligence people had been given somewhat less opportunity to gather and analyze data on the planetary infrastructure than Amos Chung had been granted. They were still trying to deduce the reason for the extraordinarily high number of ground bases when, suddenly, his sensor crews began reporting antimatter ground bursts on Planet I.

Shaaldaar slapped his mid-palms together in a gesture of perplexity. The decision *not* to employ the so-called Shiva Option had been made long before Seventh Fleet departed for this attack. More, it had been confirmed by Prescott himself when the two strike forces separated to close stealthily in upon their targets. So why had the Human admiral changed his mind? And if he was going to change it at all, why had he done it so abruptly—and with so little time left—that it had been impossible to advise Shaaldaar of his decision?

There had to be a reason, but what—?

"Force Leader!" Shaaldaar wheeled towards his plotting officer in surprise. He and Sensor Master Haalnak had served together for over three Terran Standard years, and he'd never before heard that degree of consternation and surprise in the sensor master's voice.

"What is it, Haalnak?" Shaaldaar dropped to feet and mid-limbs and cantered across the deck towards Plotting.

"Those ground installations, Force Leader—they're gunboat bases and they're launching now!"

Shaaldaar's blood ran cold. Of course they were gunboat bases—why hadn't he realized that himself? But if all of them were nests of gunboats, then how many—?

"Tracking reports over a thousand-plus gunboats, Force Leader!" someone else announced, and the blood which had run cold seemed to freeze. *A thousand-plus?!*

He reached Haalnak's station and slithered to a halt. The rising gunboats were a blood-red spray of icons on the plot, fountaining upward like some cloud of loathsome parasitic spores, reaching for his own gunboats and fighters . . . and the starships beyond them. The number estimate had to be too low, and even if it wasn't, it looked like all of these gunboats were coming from just one hemisphere of the planet. Gormus only knew what the numbers were going to look like when the rest of them launched!

The tide of destruction oriented itself, thrusting for the very heart of his task force, and then—

Shaaldaar stood upright, his eyes wide, as the serried ranks of death spores suddenly disintegrated. The deadly purposefulness of the gunboat tide lost its cohesion. The ones which had already launched began to behave erratically, staggering, seeming to stumble with an abrupt loss of purpose, while no more rose from the untouched surface. He stared at the chaos of what should have been an overwhelming attack, and as he did, he knew what Raymond Prescott had done . . . and why.

The lifeless ball of slag which had been Planet I receded rapidly in the viewscreen above the conference table in *Riva y Silva*'s flag briefing room as Prescott's staff took their seats. The image held a horrific grandeur as the firestorms of the bombardment blazed in visible seas of flame, wrapped around the smoke and dust enshrouded ruin of a once life-bearing world. It hovered there before them all, and as the admiral took his own seat, more than one of his officers felt a sense of dreadful appropriateness, for his place was directly under the raging hell his warriors had wreaked upon the Bugs.

"Obviously," he began in a crisp yet quiet voice, apparently the only person in the entire briefing room completely unaffected by the apocalyptic vision, "our original plans are going to require modification. Amos?"

"Yes, Sir." The intelligence officer recognized his cue and consulted his terminal for a moment. Not that he really needed to.

"We were luckier than Force Leader Shaaldaar in a lot of ways," he said then. "From the sensor records, it's pretty clear that the defenses were only just starting to come on-line when we hit Planet I, whereas the Force Leader had to fight his way in against much greater opposition. The effectiveness of the Shiva Option seems to have been pretty conclusively confirmed, however, because all effective resistance on and orbiting Planet III came apart the moment our surface strikes went in.

"That's the good news. The *bad* news is that the data record from Planet III confirms what we'd already suspected from our own experience at Planet I. There were just as many gunboats there as on Planet I, so I see no option but to conclude that there are at least as many more of them based on Planet II. Which, I must also point out, is now fully aware of our presence."

None of this was really news to any of the people in the briefing room, but it still induced a stunned silence.

"But, but, Admiral," Terrence Mukerji stammered into the crackling quiet, "surely the psychic shock that paralyzed Planet I and Planet III will also paralyze Planet II's defenders!"

Prescott permitted himself a small sigh of exasperation but restrained himself from replying directly. Instead he nodded for Chung to continue.

"Unfortunately, Admiral Mukerji," the spook said, "the 'psychic shock' to which you refer is of limited duration—as we've been aware ever since the First Battle of Home Hive Three," he added as pointedly as he dared. "Judging from our experience there, the paralysis will have begun wearing off by the time either of our attack forces could reach Planet II. Their defenses' effectiveness would probably continue to suffer some degradation, but it would be nowhere near as severe as what we experienced at Planet I and Planet III."

Mukerji paled, swallowed hard, and turned back to Prescott.

"Admiral, this is terrible! We'll be overwhelmed! And not just because of the numerical odds, either. Our advantage of surprise is gone, too, since—"

"That goes without saying, Admiral Mukerji," Prescott said quietly. "Which," he added, considerably more pointedly than Chung had dared, "is why our plans have always assumed that they'd be ready for us by the time we got around to Planet II."

"But . . . *twenty-four hundred gunboats!* None of our plans took *that* into consideration, Sir! They couldn't. It was not only unforeseen but inherently unforseeable."

"What, exactly, are you proposing, Admiral Mukerji?"

"Well," the political admiral began, obviously relishing the unaccustomed sensation of being asked for an opinion on operational matters, "this calls for a radical rethinking of our plans."

"Agreed." Prescott nodded, and a number of faces around the table wore looks of surprise . . . and suspicion. Mukerji's own jaw dropped. "In point of fact, I've already rethought them, in consultation with Commodores Mandagalla and Bichet, before this meeting. In fact, new orders have already gone out to Force Leader Shaaldaar."

Prescott activated the smaller holo sphere at the center of the table. It showed the three life-bearing—or formerly life-bearing—planets in their current alignment, and the green icons of TF 71's two elements moving away from the innermost and outermost planets towards the one between.

"We'll continue on our present, preplanned course for now," Prescott continued as the green icons kept on converging, to Mukerji's visible consternation. "Shortly before we come into tactical range of Planet II, however, both forces will change course to rendezvous here." The broken green string-lights of projected courses abruptly curved away from the target planet to illustrate the admiral's words. "The object, of course, is to draw the ground-based gunboats out, where we can engage them at long range and where they'll be without the support of Planet II's orbital defenses."

Mukerji had passed beyond consternation into a state of outright panic.

"Admiral, I must protest! It's imperative that we change course at once, and return to our warp point of entry. We must—"

"*Must*, Admiral Mukerji?" Prescott's voice was as quiet as ever, but the staffers were no longer under any uncertainty as to what lay behind that mildness. Several had begun to wish themselves elsewhere.

Even Mukerji had a momentary inkling. But then, banishing it, came the comforting recollection of his exalted political patronage. The thought puffed him up visibly.

"Yes, Admiral! I remind you that I speak for the civilian leadership of the government we serve. And I solemnly assure you that those leaders would view with grave, yes, grave misgivings any further operations in this system at the present time. There could not fail to be adverse career repercussions for everyone here. *Everyone*, Admiral."

Prescott leaned forward, and his eyes narrowed into slits in a very uncharacteristic way.

"Is that what's uppermost in your mind, Admiral Mukerji? 'Career repercussions'?"

"Of course not, Admiral!" Mukerji said, instantly and just a bit too heartily. "Naturally, my first concern is for the safety of this task force. Thanks to your sagacity, we've destroyed two of the three inhabited planets in exchange for acceptable losses. Surely it's time to ... 'quit while we're ahead' is, I believe, the expression."

"*My* first concern, Admiral Mukerji, is the completion of our mission—which is to implement General Directive Eighteen *throughout* the system."

Sweat began to pop out on Mukerji. His eyes were wild as

he sought desperately for the right combination of words to convince Prescott that he must not, could not, send the task force—including *Riva y Silva*, with Mukerji's own personal body aboard her—against the remaining planet and its fully prepared armada of gunboats, every one of them laden with antimatter and crewed by beings to whom the very concept of individual survival was foreign.

"Admiral, I assure you that what you've accomplished so far is all that anyone could expect—all that the government *will* expect! You've already won a great victory. Why jeopardize it for mere personal vengeance?"

"*That will do!*" Prescott's voice wasn't extraordinarily loud; it just sounded that way because it came from a man who *never* shouted at his subordinates. Everyone jumped, and Mukerji recoiled backwards. "I will not leave an untouched Bug-inhabited planet in this system to serve as a base for them to open a new front along the Prescott Chain, simply to spare you the unaccustomed sensation of personal danger!"

"Admiral, when we return to the Federation I will protest this outrageous treatment to higher authority. *Very* high authority!"

"I have no doubt of that, Admiral Mukerji. But for now, you're under my command, and we're in a war zone. For the remainder of this conference, you will not speak unless I give you leave. If you display any insubordination, I will place you under close arrest. If you endanger this command by cowardice in the face of the enemy, I will have you summarily shot! *Do I make myself clear?*"

Mukerji swallowed and nodded jerkily. Prescott's flinty eyes impaled him for perhaps five more seconds, and then the admiral drew a deep breath, released it slowly, and addressed the rest of his stunned staff in a normal voice.

"Commodore Bichet will now outline the tactical dispositions we'll adopt when we rendezvous with Force Leader Shaaldaar. It's going to involve reorganizing and rearming our fighters, and deploying most of our SBMHAWK4s under shipboard control. . . ."

The Bug gunboats seemed noticeably sluggish and uncertain as they moved outward from Planet II—probably residual aftereffects of what they'd undergone when Planets I and III died. But that hangover was beginning to wear off by the time they overtook TF 71 and began to close in.

All seventeen hundred and eight of the task force's remaining fighters met them head-on.

Once, in the days of reaction drives, it had been confidently asserted that there could be no such thing as a "dogfight" in space. At most, antagonists might exchange fire briefly as they flashed past each other at enormous relative velocities, or else they might match orbits and settle into a slugging match that would end the instant one side scored a thermonuclear hit. Reactionless drives, with their inertial compensators, had changed all that. And now the yellow sun of Home Hive One shone on the vastest dogfight in history.

The reactionless drive wasn't magic, however. The fighters couldn't instantaneously reverse direction, or any such fantasy. And the Bugs weren't interested in killing fighters—they only wanted to break through and get their real targets, the capital ships. Inevitably, quite a few of them did. . . .

"Let me send out my gunboats." Shaaldaar's face in the com screen wore a pleading look. "The crews have volunteered to go."

*I don't doubt that for a second,* Raymond Prescott thought. *This task force is their immediate* lomus *at present.* But deeply though he understood, he shook his head.

"I appreciate their willingness, but we need to conserve them. We'll stick with the original plan."

Shaaldaar looked for just a moment as if he were going to argue, but then he gave a curt human-style nod and turned away from his pickup. Prescott drew a deep breath, then turned away from his own com station to watch the sanitary violence in his plot while the quiet, clipped voices of communications and plotting officers and ratings rustled in the background of a cathedral-like hush.

He knew what Shaaldaar had been thinking, but he and Jacques Bichet had planned carefully for this moment, and as the icons of the incoming gunboats swept closer and closer to the far slower starships they sought to kill, that plan unfolded.

The gunboats were a ragged mass as their survivors broke past the intercepting strikefighters. Hundreds of them had already been blown out of space, and their squadron datanets were so riven and broken that it was impossible really to tell whether or not they were still suffering the lingering aftereffects of the Shiva Option. But they were Bugs. Neither disorganization nor slaughter could turn them from their mission, and they continued to close in a pulsating swarm of what were effectively manned missiles.

But as they closed, they suffered successive decimations.

First came the SBMs. The strategic bombardment missiles were the longest-ranged shipboard weapons in space, and these were fired from SBMHAWK pods, which were themselves deployed the better part of ten light-seconds out from the fleet to give them even more standoff range. The pods seemed to disintegrate as their cargoes of death streaked off towards the oncoming Bugs, and Seventh Fleet's plots glittered with the icons of outgoing missiles.

SBMs were less accurate at extreme range than capital missiles were, and they were relatively easy targets for point defense to intercept. But they also had half again as much reach, and there were hundreds of them as they slammed into the gunboats at a range far in excess of any weapon with which the Bugs might have replied. Huge fireballs blazed at the heart of the formation as warheads designed to kill starships expended themselves upon mere gunboats, and clouds of plasma and vaporized alloy, mixed with scattered atoms of what had once been organic matter trailed behind the stream of kamikazes.

And then it was the capital missiles' turn.

Shorter-ranged than the SBMs, the capital missiles carried warheads that were just as powerful, and they used the internal volume freed up by their smaller drive systems to pack in sophisticated onboard ECM, which made them extremely difficult targets for the missile defenses. A far higher percentage of them got through, and the furnace consuming the Bugs roared hotter.

*Still* the gunboats came on, and as they closed through the extended-range defenses they were met by standard missiles in sprint mode. Point defense was completely useless against sprint-mode fire, for there was insufficient flight time for missile defenses to track the incoming birds. The same velocity which made them impossible to intercept limited their own tracking time and degraded both their accuracy and their range, but they struck like unstoppable hammers from Hell, and they were backed in turn by anti-ship energy weapons, and finally by point defense laser clusters.

It was the densest, most multilayered pattern of defensive fire anyone in the task force had ever seen, and the front of the Bug formation was a solid wall of flame, a wall that glared and leapt and died, like a torch guttering in a hurricane.

To most of those who observed it, it was self-evident that nothing could come through it.

Raymond Prescott knew better. In a universe ruled by chaos theory, there was no such thing as an impermeable defense. Yet even he allowed himself to hope, as he watched the "hostile" icons that had resembled a blood-red blizzard in his plot melt away like snow flakes in a hot oven.

Not all of them melted, though—not even in that fiery furnace. Twenty-four hundred gunboats had made up that inconceivable swarm at the beginning. Less than a hundred got in close enough to launch FRAMs. Of those, only thirty-eight managed to get off a second salvo. Of those, precisely nine completed their ramming runs.

Which was quite bad enough.

Prescott kept his face immobile as the reports came in, even though every "Code Omega" was a barbed blade in his gut. Then, at last, Anthea Mandagalla reported that the data were all in, and the computer displayed them with cybernetic emotionlessness. TF 71 had lost eight hundred and sixty-two fighters, seven battlecruisers, four fleet carriers, two assault carriers, five superdreadnoughts, and—despite the tremendous wealth of defensive fire from the *Hannah Avram*-class escorts—one monitor. Five more capital ships had suffered varying degrees of damage.

"It could have been worse, Sir," Mandagalla ventured.

"I know," Prescott replied absently. And he did. Indeed, what he was thinking didn't bear uttering aloud: *Thank God Andy got us in through a door they didn't know to watch. If they'd detected us coming in, and met us with a single concerted wave of over seven thousand gunboats . . .*

He ordered himself not to shiver in front of his staffers. Instead, he turned to face them and spoke briskly.

"Anna, we'll detach two of our *Borsoi-B* fleet carriers and a squadron of battlecruisers to escort the damaged units back to the warp point. In the meantime, the rest of the fleet will proceed to Planet II."

"Aye, aye, Sir." Neither Mandagalla nor anyone else had expected Prescott to depart without finishing off the last inhabited planet, now denuded of its gunboats. Still . . . "Admiral, there are still the orbital defenses to deal with. And we've expended most of our SBMHAWKs on the fighters."

"I know," Prescott replied again. "But we still have about two hundred left, and we've got plenty of SRHAWKs. We can send out mixed salvos to confuse the Bugs' point defense."

"What about kamikaze shuttles, Sir? Those fortresses, and the space station, probably have quite a few of them, and our strike-groups have taken heavy losses."

Prescott turned to his spook.

"Amos?"

"It's our assessment, based on the size and configuration of those forts, that they only have so many shuttles." Chung spoke without hesitation, but also without much happiness. "I've already made my conclusions available to Jacques and Commodore Landrum."

Prescott cocked his head at Landrum, and the *farshathkhanaak* answered his unspoken question.

"I believe our remaining fighters can handle them, Sir." He sounded barely less unhappy than Chung had, but Prescott ignored it.

"Very well, then. Let's get down to cases. . . ."

*It was frustrating.*

*It was clear now what the Enemy survey flotilla had found that was so important: the closed warp point that had admitted the Enemy undetected into this system—a System Which Must Be Defended. Any doubt the Fleet might have entertained on that head had been dispelled once the gunboats' scanners had obtained solid data on the Enemy starships. Several of those starships' emissions signatures were perfect matches against the reports from the system the Enemy had fought his way through. There was no question that this was the same fleet, although the Enemy had somehow managed to conceal the existence of his own monitors from the picket force he'd smashed on his way here.*

*And that was what made it so frustrating, for the heavy Fleet units that should have defended this system were gone—called away to intercept this very Enemy force on its way home!*

*Naturally, courier drones had gone out as soon as the System Which Must Be Defended had come under attack, summoning those heavy units to return. But now, quite clearly, there would be nothing here to defend by the time they could return.*

*So new courier drones must be sent out, to meet the returning units at some point along the warp chain and order them to return post-haste to where they had originally been sent. There, they could at least still cut off this Enemy force as it retired.*

*It was still difficult to do things rapidly—the aftereffects of the deaths of the first and third planets lingered stubbornly. But it must be done. Otherwise, those units might miss the Enemy both here* and *at the system where the survey flotilla had been ambushed.*

*That would be . . .* intensely *frustrating.*

Irma Sanchez activated her F-4's internal hetlasers. Her eyesight was saved by the fighter's computer, which automatically dimmed her visual display as the Bug shuttle vanished with the unique violence of matter/antimatter annihilation.

As she pulled away, she allowed herself to feel a sense of satisfaction.

This had been, she had reason to believe, the last of the kamikaze shuttles. Not one of them had reached TF 71's capital ships. And the orbital fortresses that had sent them out on their forlorn-hope mission were no more, buried under an avalanche of long-range bombardment.

Shortly, the Gorm gunboats would be launched. They would spearhead the destruction of the now-naked planet that showed as a pale-blue disc up ahead. But the Terran and Ophiuchi and Orion fighters would also play a part.

She'd never really caught up on her sleep after the desperate fight with the gunboats. But the thought of what was to come filled her with an exhilaration that banished exhaustion.

The task force was headed outward towards the warp point, with the three now-lifeless planets receding astern, when Raymond Prescott's staff met once again in *Riva y Silva's* flag briefing room. This time, Shaaldaar, Kolchak, Raathaarn, and Cole were in attendance via com screens, and Prescott wasted no time in coming to the point.

"I realize that some of you are surprised that I've ordered an immediate departure, without pausing to finish off the warp point defenses."

They were all taken back by the bluntness—the more so because what he'd said was absolutely true. Long-range sensor probes had confirmed SF 62's conclusions concerning the Bug forces defending each of Home Hive One's five open warp points: thirty-five orbital fortresses of monitor-like size, plus forty-two of the purpose-built warp point defense heavy cruisers. The Bugs had sensibly declined to send those cruisers in-system to the aid of the habitable planets. Nowadays, nothing lighter than a battlecruiser had any business in a fleet engagement—and especially not when it was as slow as they were. Still, that was a lot of tonnage . . . and a lot of Bugs. . . .

Prescott smiled into their unspoken curiosity.

"Rest assured that I would have preferred to make a clean sweep. Nevertheless, we've achieved our primary objective by sterilizing the inhabited planets, and there are sound reasons not to linger here.

"First of all, we must assume that the Bugs sent out courier drones as soon as they became aware of our presence. We have no way of knowing how long their reinforcements are going to take to get here, but when they do . . . Well, we've taken significant losses, especially among our fighters."

Prescott turned to Landrum as though inviting confirmation.

"That's true, Sir," the *farshathkhanaak* acknowledged. "We started with almost two thousand fighters. We're down to eight hundred and forty-eight."

"And our depletable munitions are getting lower than I'd like to see, Sir," Commander Sandra Ruiz, the logistics officer, piped up. "In particular, our SBMHAWKs are down to three hundred and twenty Mark Threes and only forty Mark Fours. Granted, we still have three hundred and sixty SRHAWKs of all marks, and nine hundred and fifty-six RD2s that we can deploy. But—"

"I'm aware of the problem, Commander." Prescott ran his eyes around the table, and also across the row of com screens. "Given what Commodore Landrum and Commander Ruiz have just said, it should be clear why I have no desire to face fresh Bug forces in this system, here at the end of a long warp chain which, for all we know, may already have been cut behind us."

They were all silent, although Prescott's last seven words weren't really a shock. Intellectually, they all knew the danger. But Prescott decided it ought to be put into words, and he knew just the man for the job.

He turned to Mukerji—there'd been no way to avoid inviting him, after all, so he might as well make himself useful.

"Admiral Mukerji, you have a comment or questions?"

"Ah . . . I assume, Admiral, that you're referring to the closed warp point in AP-5."

"Of course. As it happens, I have reason to believe that Bug forces have in fact been dispatched there. Furthermore, I have a pretty fair idea of those forces' strength."

That got everyone's attention, especially Amos Chung's. Despite the gravity of the situation, Prescott was actually tempted to smile as every eye stared at him with emotions which varied from simple surprise to the sort of wariness only to be expected from someone who'd suddenly found himself trapped in a small room with a lunatic. He suppressed the temptation, however, and proceeded to outline the conclusions he'd reached shortly after entering Home Hive One. When he was done, they sat open-mouthed.

Mukerji surprised him by being the first to find his voice.

"Admiral, this warp chain you're postulating, running from one of Home Hive One's warp points back to AP-5 parallel to the Prescott Chain . . . You realize, of course, that it's sheer speculation."

"True, in the sense that I have no direct evidence of its existence. But the theory accounts for the absence of the system's heavy mobile units—accounts for it too well for coincidence. For now, I see no reason to stop using it as a working assumption, at any rate."

Prescott waited for Mukerji to say something about the possible political consequences if the assumption was mistaken. But the latter had learned better. Without letting the pause stretch too far, Prescott resumed.

"So, as you can all see, we can't afford to waste any of our remaining combat strength against warp point fortresses that no longer have anything to guard. Not when we'll need everything we have left to fight our way through that force, if it's in AP-5 when we get there. But there's also another aspect to consider."

"Sir?" Mandagalla inquired, and Prescott leaned forward and let his smile grow predatory.

"Remember what I said earlier about the courier drones that must have gone out from the system when our attack commenced. Well, if I'm right about where those mobile forces went, maybe one of those drones went to AP-5 to recall them. In that case, they're on their way back here now. So, if we head back without delay, we may make it through AP-5 while they're in transit!"

Actually, it was an incident in Old Terra's military history—specifically, the opening phases of World War I, four and a half centuries ago—that had made him think of it. Just before the First Battle of the Marne, the Germans, jittery about the Russian threat, had diverted four divisions to the East. Those divisions had ended up missing the decisive battles on both fronts, which had very possibly lost Germany the war. He considered mentioning it, but decided it would take too much time to convey all the background information the nonhumans would need. Instead, he watched as his staffers savored the possibility of a free run home.

Shaaldaar spoke slowly from his com screen.

"I want as much as anyone to believe in this possibility, Admiral. But if the Bug command here in Home Hive One did, in fact, recall its battle-line from AP-5 when our attack began, it must also have sent orders to that battle-line to return there when it became clear that the system was doomed, so that even if we couldn't be stopped here, we could at least be intercepted on our return."

"You're probably right, Force Leader. And if you are, it's all the more reason for us to depart without delay." Prescott became very brisk. "Commodore Mandagalla, send out orders for the task force to retire on the warp point. Commodore Landrum, it will be necessary for the fighters and gunboats to cover our withdrawal and insure that no Bug scouts are in a position to observe our warp transit. The location of that warp point is a secret I mean to see kept."

"Aye, aye, Sir," the chief of staff and the *farshathkhanaak* responded in unison.

A dispatch boat was waiting in El Dorado.

For security reasons, GFGHQ, with Prescott's and Zhaarnak's strong support, had decided against deploying the sort of inter-stellar communications network which would have permitted light-speed message transmission across the star systems of the Prescott Chain. The ICN was the backbone of the command and control systems of major star nations like the Federation and Khanate and had already been of enormous strategic advantage to the Alliance, since the Bugs, with no equivalent of it, were forced to accept far greater delays in communication. The Bugs' offsetting advantage, however, was that by never emplacing the long chains of deep-space relay satellites which sent messages across star systems, or the crewed com stations hovering at each intervening warp point to shuttle courier drones back and forth, or even the navigation buoys which courier drones required to reorient for transit without such com stations, they left no "bread crumbs" behind. There was no trail of installations which might draw a survey force's attention to a warp point, or lead an inva-sion force along the critical warp lines of their domain.

If Seventh Fleet had been operating through space the Alliance knew the Bugs had already surveyed, that wouldn't have been a factor. But in this case, the Allies had no idea how much or how little of the Prescott Chain the Bugs might have explored, and so the Strategy Board had decided to take a page from the enemy's book and put up no signposts to help them out. Which was just fine from many perspectives, but meant that Seventh Fleet's communications were far slower and more roundabout than Allied commanders were accustomed to.

Prescott had detached small, cloaked picket forces in each of the star systems through which he'd passed, both as a security measure to watch his back and also to serve as communications nodes. But such pickets had to have freedom of maneuver to do their jobs, so courier drones couldn't be programmed with known coordinates to reach them. And, for obvious reasons, sending out drones with omnidirectional radio beacons the pickets might have homed in on was ... contraindicated.

The only practical solution was to use dispatch boats—actual starships, all large enough to mount cloaking ECM, who played postman between the picket forces. Like the one which had just delivered TF 71's most recent mail.

Prescott, Mandagalla, Bichet, and Chung studied the data as *Riva y Silva*'s computer downloaded it to the flag bridge's display. Finally, the spook looked up.

"You were right, Sir."

Prescott nodded absently. It was conclusive. The AP-5 pickets had observed the arrival of a Bug force there shortly before the standard date of February 2, 2367, when TF 71 had entered Home Hive One. That force matched the "missing" part of the units Andrew had observed in Home Hive One too precisely for coincidence.

But Prescott was more interested in the *second* message from the picket commander. One of the picket ships had gotten close enough to observe the Bugs make transit and pinpoint the coordinates of the warp point through which they'd entered. Beside the excitement of that news, the confirmation of his theory was of little moment.

"They copied everything they included in our dispatches up the Prescott Chain to GFGHQ, as well," Bichet observed, and Prescott nodded.

"So no matter what happens to us, the Federation will know the locations of the Bugs' closed warp point in AP-5," he agreed with profound satisfaction.

Mandagalla admired the boss's selflessness, but found herself unable to share it.

"Uh, Sir, we've got confirmation of where they came from, but there's nothing to suggest that the Bug force from Home Hive One was *recalled* from AP-5."

"No, there isn't. But . . ." Prescott did some mental arithmetic. "There wouldn't be. The dispatch boat hasn't been here long, so any later messages, reporting the Bugs' withdrawal, would still be on the way. We should encounter them somewhere between here and AP-5. For now, we'll continue to regard it is a possibility, and act accordingly. That is, we'll proceed at the maximum speed the task force can manage. I want our seriously damaged units taken in tow by Admiral Cole's *Wolf 424*-class tugs, so they won't slow us down."

The arrangements were made, and TF 71 fared onward.

Passing through AP-7, two transits from AP-5, they encountered a second dispatch boat. The news it delivered couldn't be suppressed, and the euphoria that spread through *Riva y Silva* was palpable.

The staff was no more immune than anyone else. Mandagalla's dark face was alight with joy as she looked up from the readouts on the flag bridge.

"You were right again, Sir! They've withdrawn from AP-5! They're on their way back to Home Hive One, and—"

"Unfortunately, Anna, Force Leader Shaaldaar was almost certainly right, too. At some point before the destruction of the last Home Hive One planet, they must've been ordered to resume station in AP-5." Prescott smiled grimly. "A human commander in the same position might have let them continue back to Home Hive One in the hope of a miracle, but I don't think the Bugs believe in miracles. And even if they did, whoever was left in command of their warp point fortifications certainly would have turned them around *after* we finished off Planet II. If you'll observe the date of this message, it's within the realm of possibility that they've *already* returned to AP-5."

"Do you really think they have, Sir?" Bichet asked.

"No . . . not yet." Prescott produced a very thin smile. "But it's going to be a horse race to see whether we get there first or they get back before we do, I think."

Bichet looked another question at him, and Prescott shrugged.

"If we assume that the picket force we destroyed on our way through AP-5 immediately requested reinforcements, and that the Home Hive One mobile forces were sent off as soon as the picket force's courier drone was received there, then we can make a fairly good estimate of the transit time for my hypothetical warp chain by noting when the reinforcements actually arrived in AP-5. Of course, we don't know how many star systems are actually involved, since there's no way for us to predict the distance between warp points in any given system along the way. But what matters for our purposes is how long it would take a courier drone from Home Hive One to reach AP-5."

He leaned back in his bridge chair and rubbed his eyes wearily.

"I ran the numbers a second time, assuming that Home Hive One sent the drone recalling their mobile forces at the moment that we first were detected in Home Hive One, and the time required for the drone to make the same trip matches almost exactly. So I think we've got a pretty good idea for the length of the communication loop between Home Hive One and AP-5. And, frankly, it's not as long as I'd hoped it would be."

His smile, not much of a smile in the first place, died altogether.

"It's unfortunate that this message has become general knowledge. Anna, I want you to go have a quiet talk with the captain immediately. It's important that we prevent its content from spreading beyond the flagship."

She gave him an old-fashioned look, and he waved a half-apologetic hand.

"I recognize the limits of my control over the workings of Rumor Central," he told her wryly. "And I don't expect you or anyone else to perform miracles. But we—and I mean everyone on the staff—has to do everything possible to put a damper on the general excitement. No one will be happier than me if we do manage to get through AP-5 without a fight, but in my opinion it's almost certain that we *won't*, and I don't want an unrealistic euphoria to bite our morale in the ass when our people find out it was unjustified."

"Aye, aye, Sir," a visibly deflated Mandagalla said.

"In fact," Prescott continued thoughtfully, "given the general giddiness, we should probably keep a lid on the *good* news everyone seems to have overlooked so far in the excitement, too."

"Sir?" several staffers queried at once, and Prescott's smile was back.

"I refer to the message from Fang Zhaarnak which Rear Admiral Heath forwarded with the second dispatch boat. If he holds to his estimated time of arrival, and we do the same, he should enter AP-5 with TF 72 three standard days after we do. So that, ladies and gentlemen, is how long we're going to have to survive in that system unaided."

After being recalled to protect its System Which Must Be Defended, the Mobile Force had only completed three warp transits before receiving the word that there would shortly be nothing left to protect. So it had reversed course with all possible dispatch, and was now back in Franos, only two transits away from the system where the Enemy survey flotilla had been ambushed . . . and where the destroyers of the System Which Must Be Defended might also be caught, for they must pass through it, and all calculations indicated that they and the Fleet would arrive there at about the same time.

The Mobile Force would take the picket force here in Franos with it, so a hundred and forty-one ships would be available to close the escape hatch of an Enemy force which had, to a considerable extent, spent itself.

Still, it was unwise to underestimate the force that had seared the System Which Must Be Defended clean of life. It had cost the Fleet entirely too much to learn that lesson, but learn it the Fleet had.

So it was just as well that the relief force that had been summoned from the nearest other System Which Must Be Defended—two hundred and twelve more ships—was on its way, and should arrive while the battle was still in progress.

# CHAPTER TWELVE
## "This is Terran space!"

*I will never grow accustomed to Humans*, the newly promoted Fifteenth Fang of the Khan Zhaarnak'telmasa thought.

But no, he amended. With the help of his *vilkshatha* brother, he might very well grow accustomed to Humans.

He would just never grow accustomed to Kevin Sanders.

The Cub of the Khan—no, Zhaarnak reminded himself, the *lieutenant*, as if anyone could pronounce such an outlandish sound—had been assigned to Task Force 72 just before its departure, to serve as the eyes and ears of Marcus LeBlanc at the front. At least he hadn't actually been in Zhaarnak's fur for the most part. He'd been able to turn the young *caraasthyuu* over to Uaaria'salath-ahn, who, for some perverse reason, actually seemed to *like* him.

And besides, the small fang thought with returning frustration, the new addition to his staff was the least frustrating of the decisions that had been made for him around that time.

He grew aware that he was pacing—more accurately, prowling—the flag bridge of *Hia'khan*, first of a new class of command monitors to which the Bugs were about to be introduced. *Assuming, that is, that we ever reach them!* He suppressed the thought and ordered himself to assume the posture of assured, controlled aggressiveness that the *Zheeerlikou'valkhannaiee* expected of their commanders. It wasn't easy, and in an attempt to keep his mind off his impatience, he studied the tactical display of his task force in his private holo sphere.

TF 72 was divided into two task groups. The first was the

battle-line, commanded by Twelfth Small Fang Yithaar'tolmaa; twenty-four monitors, including *Hia'khan*, and eighteen superdreadnoughts. Thirty-First Small Fang Jaarnaa'kolaak-ahn, one of the first females of Zhaarnak's race to attain such a rank, commanded the carrier task group of fifteen assault carriers and fifteen fleet carriers, escorted by thirty battlecruisers. All were ships of the Khanate and its component the Empire of Gormus, and Zhaarnak permitted himself a moment's surge of pride.

But then his eyes strayed to the other icons in the sphere—the flock of freighters he was shepherding—and the moment ended. It was all he could do not to bare his teeth and snarl futile commands for more speed.

Out of the corner of one eye, he caught Uaaria and Sanders approaching from across the flag bridge. The Human no longer drew stares, and Zhaarnak had come to grudgingly admire the aplomb with which he handled being the only member of his species aboard the flagship. In the entire task force, come to that.

"Small Claw Uaaria, Cub Saaanderzzz," Zhaarnak greeted them. Early on, he'd observed elementary courtesy by asking Sanders if the Orion equivalent of his unpronounceable rank title would be acceptable. The Human had assured him that it would, with the grin that was the outward manifestation of his trademark insouciant self-assurance in the presence of his astronomically higher-ranking elders.

"There is no sensor indication of any Bahg presence in this system, Fang," Uaaria reported. "Any more than there has been anywhere else along the Pressssscott Chain."

Zhaarnak gave the low growl that answered to a Human grunt.

"Very good. We had not expected any, of course, this side of AP-5. Still, if they emerged unexpectedly into that system, it is not impossible they could do the same elsewhere."

"At least, Fang," Sanders said smoothly, "these precautionary scouting missions can be carried out by sensor drones, and don't entail any delay."

Zhaarnak glanced up sharply. Sanders' eyes—of that weird bluish color—met his unflinchingly. *He has recognized my impatience,* he thought. Then he had to laugh inwardly at himself. *No great feat! I have not exactly made a secret of it.*

Sanders raised his eyebrows, and his lips quirked upward.

*He has recognized my amusement at myself, as well,* Zhaarnak thought. *He is remarkably—almost disturbingly—perceptive about a race that is not his own.*

*He also has a way of inspiring frankness.*

"Yes, Cub Saaanderzzz, as you and everyone else are aware, I *am* impatient. Desperately so." Zhaarnak glowered at the display again. "What you perhaps are not aware of is the reason for my impatience. Just before we departed—after my *vilkshatha* brother was already beyond ICN range—the decision was made to use this task force to escort a convoy of freighters carrying replacement fighters for Task Force 71. I argued that speed was of the essence. But I was overruled."

Even Sanders was a bit hesitant, in the face of the glimpse he'd gotten into the depths of Zhaarnak's frustration, when he spoke again.

"Perhaps, Fang, the fighters will be badly needed after Admiral Prescott has fought his way out of Home Hive One."

"Oh, I do not doubt that the fighters will be welcomed. But the point is, we are scheduled to rendezvous with Task Force 71 in the AP-5 System at a certain time. And despite everything I have done to make up the time it cost to assemble the convoy, we will not make that rendezvous. Nor," Zhaarnak had begun pacing again, and this time he didn't even notice that he was, "has it been possible to inform Task Force 71 of the delay, because of the decision against extending the ICN along the Pressssssscott Chain. I have sent a dispatch boat ahead, but I was unable to send it off until I knew what my true schedule might be . . . which I have only recently learned. It will not arrive greatly in advance of the entire task force, and TF 71 will know nothing of the alteration in schedule until it does. I only hope Raaymmonnd'pressssssscott-telmasa is not counting on me to make the schedule of which I had advised him *before* the convoy escort mission was decided upon."

Abruptly, the intelligence officers forgotten, he whirled around and strode to the com station.

"Inform the staff that I want a report containing detailed proposals for decreasing our transit time."

No one in earshot dared to exclaim, "*Another* one?"

There was nothing quite so chilling as a starless warp nexus.

It was only there that humans ever experienced actual interstellar space and came face-to-face with the reality that the warp network generally allowed them to ignore: the absolute, illimitable, unending, soul-destroying emptiness of the universe. This was the true Void. With no nearby star to give a reference point, the mind could get lost in those vast, meaningless spaces and never find its way home again.

TF 71 was now traversing such a space—a segment of nothingness defined only by the presence of two warp points and labeled AP-6. Raymond Prescott had ordered the outside view turned off.

The briefing room holo sphere didn't even show a display of this "system." It was too mindlessly simple: two warp points, one of which they'd emerged from, and one they were approaching, beyond which lay AP-5 . . . and the Bugs.

Instead, the AP-5 System was displayed. A white light-point represented its primary star in the center of the sphere. The planets were shown, but they were unimportant. Everyone's attention was focused on the warp points, arbitrarily designated number one (through which they would enter the system), number two (the closed warp point which gave the Bugs access), and number three (leading onward along the Prescott Chain, which meant that Zhaarnak's task force would emerge from *it*). All three were in the outer system, four light-hours or more from the local sun. Warp Point One was at nine o'clock from that sun, Warp Point Two at twelve o'clock, and Warp Point Three at eleven o'clock.

"There are two essential facts to bear in mind," Prescott said, sweeping his hand in a half-circle that encompassed the holo sphere. "First, both we and the Bugs now know where all three of these warp points are. Considering this system as a battleground, there are no 'terrain features' that are going to come as a surprise to either side. And both of us have cloaked scouts already there, aware of each others' presence, watching all of the warp points and feeling each other out.

"Secondly, our options are limited by the fact that we have to proceed to Warp Point Three, and the Bugs know it."

"Why, Sir?" Landrum inquired. "Why can't we just skulk around the system and wait for Task Force 72 to arrive?"

"Think about it, Commodore. Fang Zhaarnak will be entering the system without a preliminary SBMHAWK bombardment. So if we allow the Bugs to take up an undisturbed position within point-blank range of Warp Point Three . . ."

" 'My enemy cannot help but engage me,' " Mandagalla quoted *sotto voce*. " 'For I attack a position he must succor.' "

Prescott gave her a wintry smile.

"Precisely, Commodore. Sun Tzu would understand our predicament, if not its setting." He grew brisk, and turned to Bichet and Landrum. "Have the two of you finalized the plan for consolidating our strikegroups?"

"Yes, Sir," the ops officer answered. "We'll be moving eight hundred and forty-six assorted fighters from their current carriers to the *Minerva Waldeck*-class monitors, our seven undamaged Ophiuchi assault carriers, and our two undamaged Terran command assault carriers. We've consulted with Commander Ruiz on the supply aspects."

"Complications are bound to arise from such a scrambling of personnel of different races, Sir," the logistics officer said, understating the case considerably. "But I believe we can handle it."

"I recognize the difficulties you're all facing," Prescott said, with a quick smile. "But in the sort of engagement we're going to be fighting, nimbleness and quickness will be even more important than usual. We can't afford to encumber ourselves with any vulnerable or ineffective ships. So I want the rest of the carriers, as well as our worst damaged superdreadnoughts and battlecruisers, to remain here in AP-6. They're to take up a position far from either warp point—and I mean light-hours from it."

The staffers exchanged glances. Then Mandagalla spoke hesitantly.

"Aye, aye, Sir. Ah ... that means, of course, that those ships will be left stranded here in AP-6 if ... That is ..."

Prescott smiled more broadly into the chief of staff's misery.

"I don't plan for this task force to meet with ... anything untoward, Anna."

Mandagalla smiled back briefly, but a streak of stubborn integrity wouldn't allow her to simply shut up and take the out Prescott had given her.

"Actually, Sir, I wasn't thinking of that. What I meant was ... Well, what if, at some point, a situation develops in which it becomes possible—and seems advisable—for us to withdraw from AP-5 via Warp Point Three and rendezvous with Fang Zhaarnak in AP-4? With our cripples and our empty carriers left behind here in AP-6, we won't have that option."

"We don't have it in any case, Commodore," Prescott said very quietly. Then he leaned forward and swept his hand once again through the holo sphere's display of the AP-5 system, where his brother had died. "This is *Terran* space!"

✧       ✧       ✧

Two standard days had passed since they'd entered AP-5.

They'd been two days of cat-and-mouse with the Bug battle fleet that had entered the system through its closed warp point at essentially the same time TF 71's leading elements had emerged from Warp Point One. Those hundred and forty-one Bug ships (to Prescott's hundred and forty-six) were more numerous than could be accounted for by Home Hive One's missing mobile forces alone—but that merely meant they'd picked up help along the way. Their arrival, in a virtual heat with TF 71, had proved out Prescott's gloomier suppositions.

Now, after two days of edging across the system and feeling out his opposition, he was ready to offer battle. He'd used his ships' superior speed—and the ability of his engineers to baby their military-grade engines through that kind of long-term maneuvering—to hold the range between them open, because every Allied flag officer had developed a healthy respect for the threat posed by kamikaze assault shuttles. The shuttles might be slower, and have less capacity for sustained flight than gunboats did, but with their cargo spaces packed full of antimatter, they were actually more dangerous kamikazes than the larger and faster gunboats.

Keeping as far away from them as possible was one way to blunt their effectiveness. Not only did they have less life-support endurance than gunboats did, but their speed advantage over starships was considerably lower, which meant they would be forced to risk engine burnout in order to reach and overhaul their targets. The difference between their performance and maneuvering envelopes and those of a gunboat also made it difficult to manage a coordinated shuttle/gunboat kamikaze strike, yet without the close support of covering gunboats, shuttles were unlikely to be able to penetrate the layered defense of an unshaken Allied task force. That was yet another area in which holding the range open favored TF 71, because it would give the task force's combat space patrols more depth—which equated to more time—in which to intercept and kill the kamikazes while they were inbound. For all of those reasons, fighting the action at as long a range as possible offered many advantages . . . and, unfortunately, a few *dis*advantages.

Which was the point of the present discussion.

"If we launch against their battle-line from this far out, we'll have to send our fighters in without primary packs, Sir," Stephen Landrum pointed out in respectful but clearly unhappy tones, and Prescott nodded glumly.

The Grand Alliance's possession of the strikefighter had been one of its greatest assets from the outset. The gunboat offered many formidable tactical and strategic advantages of its own, but in close combat, the strikefighter—especially in its latest marks—continued to hold the upper hand by a decisive margin. And although it was much shorter ranged than the gunboat and incapable of independent warp transit, a strikefighter fitted with extended life-support packs could attack effectively at intrasystem ranges at which kamikaze shuttles could not. Unfortunately, if the necessary life support was mounted, the available menu of offensive ordnance packages shrank dramatically.

In particular, the generating machinery for the brief but incredibly intense pulse of space-twisting gravitic energy that was a primary beam could only be miniaturized down to a certain point. Like life-support packs, primary packs were large enough to place extravagant demands on a fighter's external ordnance capacity. In fact, primary-armed fighters launched at their maximum possible range from the target couldn't carry anything *but* primary and life-support packs ... which would automatically exclude the ECM and decoy missiles that would keep them alive.

*Trade-offs!* Prescott thought, as though it were a swear word. Which, in fact, it *was* for anyone who had to agonize over optimum ordnance mixes.

"I take your point, Commodore," he said after a moment. "But if we let the Bugs think they're almost succeeding in getting close enough to launch a coordinated shuttle/gunboat attack, we can launch our fighters from beyond their theoretical life-support range, and let the Bugs continue to close the range and meet them."

Landrum blinked, and Prescott felt all of his staffers staring at him in surprise. Vice Admiral Raathaarn eventually broke the silence from his com screen.

"Darrrrring, Ssssssir. And risssssky."

"Granted. And pulling it off will require that we be quick and agile ... and that our timing be perfect," Prescott said. "That's why I had the task force strip down to the minimum possible number of units consistent with maximum possible combat effectiveness. Like everyone else, I would've liked longer for the composite strikegroups to shake down together, but we've operated together as a task force long enough that I expect them to come through when it matters.

"Of course, even under the best conditions, pulling off the maneuver I have in mind will require a certain degree of cooperation from the Bugs," he admitted. "If they realize what we're up to and turn away, they can hold the range open to one at which only our gunboats could reach them. By the same token, though, we won't really be any worse off if they pull back than we would have been if they'd never come in at all. If they turn away, we'll simply recall the fighters." He shrugged. "We'll have expended a lot of time and burned up a lot of life support, but that's about all. Well, that and we'll have to figure out another way to get at them."

"Pulling that off will require some pretty careful management between the primary-armed fighters and the support squadrons Sir," Landrum pointed out, and Prescott nodded.

"You're right about that, Steve, and I'll want you and Jacques to assist Admiral Raathaarn in working out exactly the right launch range to make it work. And I'm afraid we'll also have to place the entire task force at State One Readiness—and *keep* it there. Timing is going to be critical, so I want the flight crews for all of our fighters in their ready rooms, ready to launch on a moment's notice. And I want the launch bay crews just as ready to arm and launch their birds. Clear?"

A rumble of assent went up, but Landrum leaned close to Bichet's ear and whispered, "I hope this doesn't take too long!"

It didn't.

Irma Sanchez had begun to wonder if she and the other surviving personnel of the original VF-94 had set a record for the number of ships they'd been attached to in the course of a single campaign.

She had just gotten used to TFNS *Banshee* when the latest reorganization had landed the squadron aboard the *Minerva Waldeck*-class MT(V) *Angela Martens*. It was her first experience of a monitor, and she considered it a change for the worse. First of all, the old rule (which dated back to the wet navies of pre-space Terra, had she known it) still held true: the bigger the ship, the more junior officers got packed into a single berthing compartment. Larger berthing compartments in absolute terms, granted, but smaller per occupant. Second, to her acquired sensibilities a strikegroup of eighty-four fighters seemed just simply too damned big. Third, while she might not have gone so far as to call Commander Strikegroup 137, Commander Jason Georghiu, a prick, it was widely rumored that he had to keep his tunic's standing collar fastened up to hide his circumcision scar.

All of which had paled in comparison to the time they'd spent waiting by their fighters and launch bays, subsisting on low-residue chow. But finally the word had come, and the mass drivers had flung them out into space. To Irma, it was like a homecoming.

They'd taken fewer losses after entering the Bugs' defensive envelope than they'd dared to hope. No question about it, Vice Admiral Raathaarn knew his tactics. The fact that each of the F-4s could carry a primary pack, an ECM pack, a life-support pack, and a decoy missile—assuming that the Bugs were going to continue to cooperate by closing with the task force—had given him a degree of flexibility he'd taken full advantage of. The Ophiuchi squadrons flying behind the wavefront of Terran and Orion ones carried no primary packs at all, for they were tasked to support the Terrans and Orions with flights of additional decoys and to fend off counterattacking gunboats as the attack wave swooped in on the Bug superdreadnoughts and monitors.

Those massive ships met them with hair-raisingly dense patterns of point defense fire, especially the *Aegis*-class command monitors and *Arbalest*-class command superdreadnoughts. But Raathaarn had thought of a way to turn that defensive firepower to the Alliance's advantage. He'd had all the data Captain Chung and his own intelligence types had amassed on the command ships analyzed and found a way to identify them regardless of all the sophisticated ECM they mounted.

The Bugs, recognizing the absolute need to protect the ships whose command datalink installations made the battlegroup-level coordination of offensive and defensive fire possible, had crammed the *Aegis* and *Arbalest* ships with a horrific array of point defense and defensive missile launchers which no other unit in their inventory could match. Which meant that it didn't matter how good their ECM was if you could see how much defensive fire they were pumping out. The very strength of their defenses actually made it possible to identify them for attack.

The technique wasn't without its price tag. Over half of KONS *Kompakutor*'s strikegroup had just died to draw the fire that revealed the identity of their killer, which now lay dead ahead of VF-94 in visual range.

"All right, people," Togliatti said over Irma's headset. "It's definitely an *Aegis*—that's the word from the CSG."

Georghiu might be a lifer of the deepest dye, but nobody had ever called CSG 137 a desk jockey. He was out here in person, leading his entire strikegroup. Togliatti was only one of fourteen squadron skippers involved in the strike.

Togliatti's orders came crisply and quickly, succinctly identifying a set of tactical contingencies. Irma punched them into her computer—voice recognition software was fine and dandy in a great many contexts, but combat was not one of them. Then they were off, piling on acceleration, and their titanic prey grew rapidly in the view-forward as they stooped on it from astern.

The *Aegis* never even saw it coming.

The stupendous command ship was still preoccupied with the distracting survivors of *Kompakutor*'s strikegroup when VF-94 came screaming up from behind. One of the things fighter jocks hated most about command datalink was the way that it permitted other units of a battlegroup to pour defensive fire into the blind zones of their group mates. Before command datalink, no starship could effectively protect another from missiles or strike-fighters which had targeted it, and no ship's fire control was able to see targets that small directly astern of it, which had created the classic blind spot from which all fighter jocks were trained to attack. Now, any unit of any battlegroup could fire upon any target that *any* of its members could lock up . . . including missiles and fighters in someone else's blind zone.

Strikefighter losses had gone up astronomically as a result. Improvements in fighter ECM, decoy missiles, and defensive tactics had offset that to some degree, but command datalink had probably killed more fighter pilots than any other technological innovation in the history of space warfare. Indeed, some fighter tactic pundits maintained that it was now all a matter of cold, uncaring statistics. They argued that an unshaken battlegroup of capital ships was such a dangerous target that the only solution was to swamp it and swarm it under by sheer weight of numbers, accepting the inevitably massive casualties in order to get enough survivors into attack range to get the job done.

Irma didn't much care for that school of thought . . . and neither did Vice Admiral Raathaarn. As VF-94 and the rest of Georghiu's strike group streaked in on the *Aegis*, an entire supporting strikegroup filled the space about them with decoys and jamming. The sheer multiplicity of targets—false ones generated by the decoys, as well as genuine threats—swamped the Bugs.

Their fire control systems were probably capable of sorting out the chaos, but the organic brains *behind* those systems weren't. Individual survival instincts didn't even come into it. It was simply a matter of engaging the threats they could actually pick out from the swirling madness, and the Bugs aboard the *Aegis* chose the wrong targets. They—and, by extension, all the other units of their battlegroup—were too busy firing at *Kompakutor's* survivors (and the decoy missiles covering *them*) to see *Angela Martens'* group until it was too late.

Even tactical battlegrounds in space are immense. On the visual display, it almost looked as if VF-94 were all alone, charging single-handedly against the *Aegis*. In reality, the other seventy-eight fighters from *Martens'* Strikegroup 137 were in close support, dancing and bobbing in the complex, fire-evading pattern known to the TFN as the "Waldeck Weave." Other navies had their own variations and their own names for the Weave, but the essentials were the same for all of them, and what looked from the outside like utter confusion was actually an intricately choreographed, precisely timed maneuver which brought every single dispersed fighter together at exactly the critical instant behind the Bug monitor.

The strikegroup lost three fighters on the way in. At least one of them was lost to pure accident. In a fluke coincidence so unlikely that Irma couldn't even have begun to calculate the odds against it, a lieutenant in VF-123 actually collided with one of his own covering decoy missiles, and so proved that the Demon Murphy was alive and well. Of the other two, one fell afoul of a stray Bug gunboat which got in one screaming pass and plucked its victim out of space fractions of a second before the fighter's vengeful squadron mates killed it in turn. No one ever knew exactly how the third pilot bought it, because no one actually saw her go.

But the rest of the strikegroup was intact when it delivered a perfectly coordinated attack.

The primary packs took so long to recharge between shots that, unlike laser packs, each could effectively fire only once per firing pass. But that still meant that eighty-odd needlelike stilettos pierced the monster's vitals within the space of a few seconds. The actual primary beams were invisible, and the five-centimeter holes they punched effortlessly through the toughest armor were far too small to be seen on any visual display, but that didn't mean the damage wasn't obvious. As those deadly rapiers stabbed the leviathan to its heart, a blood trail of gushing atmosphere haloed it instantly. Water vapor, oxygen, carbon dioxide . . . Irma's blood blazed with vengeful triumph as her instruments detected the proof of internal death and destruction.

The fire of the *Aegis'* entire battlegroup faltered, losing its cohesion and focus as someone's primary fire sought out and destroyed the command datalink installation. And as they flashed on by, the fighters lacerated the huge ship with their internal hetlasers, splintering the armor the primaries had simply punched through.

Maybe the intelligence types would be able to use drastically slowed down imagery to infer the details of just exactly what happened to the monitor. But in Irma's view-aft, the rapid fire series of secondary explosions coalesced almost immediately into one, and then a short-lived sun awoke, from whose equator a disc of debris rapidly spread until it dissipated.

*Well,* she thought, *I was wondering about records. That's got to be the shortest time it's ever taken to vaporize a monitor.*

"The totals are in, Sir!" Chung was almost babbling with excitement as he and Bichet reported to Prescott. "The Ophiuchi fighters killed three hundred and seven of their gunboats, and the Terran and Orion squadrons and the Gorm gunboats got seven superdreadnoughts and four monitors. And three of the superdreadnoughts and two of the monitors were command ships!"

"That's got to hurt their battle-line." The admiral nodded soberly. "What about our own losses?"

Chung's animation faded, and Bichet shook his head.

"Sixty gunboats, Sir. And as for the fighters . . . Well, we haven't accounted for all of them yet, so I can't give you an exact figure. But we're talking almost a quarter of our total fighter strength."

Prescott nodded again, and did some mental arithmetic. Twenty or thirty fighters for a monitor—say thirty-five flight crew for a ship with a complement of three or four thousand . . . Many would have thought it the kind of loss ratio of which dreams were made. But he had to think in terms of his own available resources, which were limited. He couldn't keep losing fighters at this rate.

"Bring them back, Steve," he said quietly to Captain Landrum.

*It was clear what the Enemy was up to. In its concern to protect its critical command ships, the Fleet had never considered that those ships' lavish defensive armaments might serve to identify them. But the Enemy's single-minded targeting of them left no doubt on the matter, and the resultant losses were making it difficult to maintain datalink integrity.*

*It was equally clear that the Enemy had been maneuvering his way towards the warp point through which he had originally entered this system, all the while adroitly preventing the Fleet from closing the range and launching a coordinated strike by gunboats and shuttles.*

*Now, however, the Enemy attack craft were retiring, after expending most of their external ordnance. Perhaps this was the time to send out the gunboats.*

Jacques Bichet stiffened as the Bug fleet suddenly spawned a shoal of blood-red icons. They streamed into existence as the gunboats they represented separated from their motherships, and a solid wall of hostiles flowed across the plot towards TF 71.

"Plotting makes it more than eight hundred of them, Sir!" he told Prescott. "It must be their entire surviving gunboat strength."

"Admiral," Landrum's voice was urgent, "our fighters can turn on them now!"

"No," Prescott replied. "Order them to jettison their remaining external ordnance and return at maximum speed to rearm. Our gunboats will fight a delaying action."

"But, Sir," Landrum took his courage in both hands, "you've already ordered our capital ships to turn away from the gunboat strike—which means away from our returning fighters."

The other staffers held their breath as Prescott turned to face the *farshathkhanaak*. They knew what Landrum meant. The carriers' high-speed turn away would slow the fighters' ability to overtake them and recover to their launch bays. In turn, that would delay their return to combat . . . and require them to expend even more life support, which some of them were already running out of. Landrum might not have put that into so many words, but he hadn't really needed to, and the staff waited for the admiral's explosive reaction to the implied criticism. But Prescott spoke mildly.

"I realize that, Commodore. But if we let them turn to engage now, we'll have to hold the carriers—which means the entire task force—where they are, or the fighters will definitely have insufficient life-support to recover. If they jettison, their 'clean' speed will be enough for most of them to rendezvous with their carriers without exhausting their life support even if we continue on our present course." The inertial "sump" that made reactionless drives possible was far shallower for a craft as small as a fighter, which meant that external ordnance loads significantly degraded its performance. "They should also be fast enough to recover and rearm before the Bug gunboats can reach us—especially if our gunboats can delay them. And whether we can get them all rearmed and relaunched in time or not, we have to get them refitted with anti-gunboat munitions before we send them in."

Landrum opened his mouth, as if to protest, then closed it, because the *farshathkhanaak* knew Prescott was right. The slow-firing primary packs were virtually useless as dogfighting weapons, and a strikefighter equipped only with its internal hetlasers would be at a serious disadvantage against AFHAWK-armed gunboats. What was needed were missiles of their own, for the long-range envelope, and gun packs when it fell to knife range.

But the captain wasn't at all sure it would be possible to recover and rearm his fighters before the Bugs came in on them. The carrier deck crews in TF 71 were all veterans, and Landrum knew better than most just how good they really were. But Prescott was about to ask the impossible of them . . . and *some* of the fighters weren't going to make it home before they ran out of life support whatever happened. Their pilots' powerful locator beacons *might* be picked up by post-battle search and rescue efforts after they bailed out . . . but they might not be, too. Landrum knew there were times, especially in fighter ops, when risks had to be run, but much as the *farshathkhanaak* respected and admired the admiral, at this moment he couldn't forget that Prescott had come up through the battle-line. He wasn't a fighter pilot—had never even commanded a fleet carrier. Did he truly understand what he was about to demand from Landrum's flight and deck crews?

But then Landrum looked at Prescott's expression and knew the subject was closed.

"Aye, aye, Sir," he said.

"This is Vincent Steele, Trans-Galactic News, and I'm here, on the hanger deck of TFNS *Angela Martens*, where urgent preparations to repel an anticipated Bug attack are under way."

Vincent Steele crouched in an alcove in the battlesteel bulkhead of Fighter Bay 62 with his shoulder-mounted microcam and felt his pulse hammer while he stared out at the frantically busy Navy personnel.

He wished now that he'd paid more attention to the official

Navy briefers who'd gassed on interminably about the flight deck procedures. At least then he might have had some genuine idea of what was going on.

It would have helped if Sandra Delmore were here, too, but the brown-nosing bitch had disappeared the minute that pompous asshole Morris had ordered "all nonessential personnel" out of the hanger spaces. Stupid bastard. Just because the precious Navy had decided to annoint Sherman Morris as the captain of one of its monitors, the arrogant prick thought someone had died and made him God!

Well, Vincent Steele had news for Captain King Shit Morris. He hadn't risen to number four at TGN's prewar military affairs desk without learning how to bust the balls of people a lot more important than one miserable captain with a god complex. Lord knew he'd uncovered enough dirt on the Navy before the Bugs turned up. He was forced to admit, not without a certain degree of chagrin, that since Survey Command had fucked up the Federation's first contact with the Arachnids, the Navy had finally found something to do that actually justified all the millions of megacredits which had been wasted on it during peacetime. Of course, if Survey Command had done its job properly in the first place, this entire war might have been avoided. At the very least, the incompetent jackasses should have been able to retire through a closed warp point without showing the Bugs where it was! But, no. And this was the result.

To be honest, the thing Steele hated most about his present assignment was his producers' demand that he pander to the viewing public's current adulation of all things Navy. He'd spent his entire career trying to get the monkey of military spending off the Federation's back, and now this! It offended every ethical bone in his body to betray a lifetime's principles this way, but he had no choice. Trying to stand up to the sycophantic gushing about the Navy's courage, and the Navy's dedication, and the Navy's dauntless spirit would have been professional suicide. And being assigned to work with Sandra Delmore was the final straw. While he'd been ferreting out all of the Navy's prewar abuses of its position and misuse of its funding, *she'd* been writing asskissing odes to it as if the uniformed deadbeats who couldn't have found jobs in the civilian economy if they'd tried were some kind of paladins.

What really stuck in his craw sideways, though, was the way all of the Navy old-timers were so *delighted* to see her. Every one of them seemed to remember some little "personal interest" piece she'd done on them, or on their families, or on someone they knew, or on their *dogs*, for God's sake! They invited her to join them in their messes, bought her drinks in the O-Club, and set up special deep-background briefings for her, and they never even seemed to realize that she was nothing but a third-rate stringer. Of course, it was probably too much to expect any of those uniformed Neanderthals to recognize a serious journalist when they saw one.

But Steele's nose for news hadn't deserted him. Everybody in Task Force 71 seemed to think Raymond Prescott could walk on water, but Steele hadn't forgotten the way the Bugs had made a fool out of him at his famous "April Fool" battle. The reporter hadn't been able to make up his mind whether Prescott really was the loose warhead that people like Bettina Wister thought he was, or if he was just an unreasonably lucky screwup. The Orions certainly thought highly of him . . . which, given their history and lunatic warrior-cult "honor code," was probably a bad sign.

Up to this point, however, and almost despite himself, Steele had been leaning towards the theory that Prescott might actually be as good—in a purely and narrowly military sense, of course—as his vociferous supporters insisted. He'd done a thorough job of destroying Home Hive One, at any rate. Although, Steele reminded himself, all anyone really had to *prove* that he had were the reports and imagery the Navy itself had handed out.

But now . . .

Steele tucked himself into a smaller space, squeezing further back into the alcove in the launch bay bulkhead. Even Delmore had gotten more and more tight-faced as the two of them listened to the occasional situation reports Captain Morris had put out over the general com system for the benefit of his crew. The official press pool had been pretty much closed down for the duration of the battle—officially to keep the reporters out of harm's way, although it also just *happened* to mean no media watchdogs would be in position to report any screwups which might occur along the way. But even the reports Morris was willing to share had indicated that things were getting pretty tight.

Other people had been less reticent, though . . . and less inclined to play jolly cheerleader than the captain. Steele had spent weeks—months—working on contacts of his own aboard *Angela Martens*. Delmore might have her stooges among the officers, but Steele knew where to go if you wanted the real dirt. The officer corps always closed ranks to protect the Navy's "good name"—and their own, of course, although that was *never* mentioned. So if you wanted to get at the things the Navy didn't want you to know (which, by definition, were the ones it was most important to bring to the public's attention), you had to do an end run around the official information channels. If you looked long enough, you could always find someone who was dissatisfied enough—often over the most trivial things, but a man had to work with what he could find—to tell you anything you wanted to know.

Sometimes that someone was a disgruntled officer, sometimes it was an enlisted person or a noncom. Aboard *Angela Martens*, it was Petty Officer Third Class Cassius Bradford, a much put upon individual, who, in his own unbiased opinion, should have been at least a chief petty officer by now. The fact that he wasn't had proved a fertile source of information when Steele suggested that perhaps the support of a friendly news report or two might provide PO 3/c Bradford's career with the upward impetus it deserved. Which was how Steele had happened to learn that Admiral Hot Shot Prescott had screwed the pooch.

Again.

For the first time since his assignment to Seventh Fleet, Vincent Steele had truly come face-to-face with his own mortality, and it was Prescott's fault. *Angela Martens* was a carrier, not a battle-line unit. Even Steele knew carriers weren't supposed to get into missile range of enemy starships—that was why he'd specifically requested a carrier assignment. Oh, intellectually he'd realized that even carriers could be destroyed, but any half-competent admiral would do his best to keep the carriers out of the main fray, if only to preserve the bases from which his own fighters operated.

But that asshole Prescott had managed to get himself caught with his fighters out of position and armed with the wrong external ordnance loads while every damned Bug gunboat in the universe came charging down on TF 71! And, of course, a carrier built on a monitor hull was far too slow and clumsy to dodge kamikazes. Which meant that *Angela Martens*, as a direct consequence of Prescott's latest screwup, was about to be attacked by waves of antimatter-loaded gunboats whose sole purpose in life was to destroy her and everyone on board her ... including one Vincent Steele.

Bradford had all but pissed himself when Steele buttonholed him and the petty officer babbled out the latest news—news, which, Steele had noted, Captain Morris hadn't seen fit to put out over the net just yet. Prescott had managed to get all of them into a situation from which they could be rescued only by a miracle. The only way they could possibly beat off the waves of gunboats streaking towards them was to somehow recover their own fighters and manage to get them rearmed and relaunched before the Bugs arrived.

Which, Bradford had assured him, was effectively impossible.

Raw terror threatened to overwhelm Steele, but he'd shoved it aside. There was nothing he could do about what was about to happen, but assuming he himself survived—and despite all Bradford had said, he resolutely refused to consider the possibility that he might not—he could at least ensure that there was proof of the degree to which Prescott had screwed up *this* time.

He hadn't even considered enlisting Delmore's aid. If she'd known what he was really up to, she might well have turned him in to Captain Morris herself, given the extent to which she'd allowed herself to be co-opted by the Navy. Besides, she was a stickler for obeying every petty military instruction she received. The fact that it was at least as much her job to find out the things the Navy *didn't* want her to know as to faithfully parrot the things the Navy *did* want her to know never even seemed to occur to her. She—and the rest of the press pool—had been told the hanger bays were off limits during flight operations, and there was no way she would have accompanied Steele down here. Which was a pity. She might be a brown-nosing bitch, but she did know her way around the guts of these stupid ships a lot better than he did. He could probably have gotten here in half the time if he'd been able to count on her to help. Not to mention the fact that he would have been able to understand a lot more of what was going on with her to interpret.

But she wasn't here, so he'd just have to do the best he could without her.

He edged cautiously closer to the mouth of the alcove in which he'd hidden himself and manipulated the camera control to pan it back and forth across the scene outside it.

Despite his own sophistication (and fear), he had to admit that it was incredibly exciting to watch. He vaguely remembered the briefer who'd escorted his own small clutch of reporters around the hanger decks when they first came aboard. The young woman had seemed far too youthful for her rank as a full lieutenant—more like a teenager in uniform than a *real* officer. But someone had told him later that she was a Fringer, from one of the out worlds where the antigerone treatments were universally available, so she'd probably been quite a few years older than he'd thought at the time.

But what stuck in his mind now was the way she'd told them that a carrier's hanger deck was the most dangerous assignment in the entire Navy. He'd put it down as hyperbole intended to impress the ignorant rubes of the press, but now he wasn't so sure.

He was glad he was wearing the standard Navy-issue vacsuit he'd been issued from ship's stores. Everyone else was wearing one, too, of course—vacsuits were the Navy's standard battledress, which was probably one of the more reasonable policies it had ever decreed. Although Steele's suit bore the word "PRESS" across the front of the helmet and the shoulder blades, the label was less evident than one might have expected, especially if the person looking at it had something else on his mind. Aside from the press identification, however, Steele's vacsuit looked remarkably like that of an Engineering officer. That was because he was assigned to a life pod attached to Communications, which, in turn, was assigned to the Engineering techs assigned to Com maintenance.

At the moment, however, what was most important about his suit was that its Engineering branch color coding had sufficed to get Steele to his present position without being challenged along the way. Well, that and the fact that as he watched the steady stream of strikefighters sliding in through the monopermeable forcefield which closed the hanger deck off from space, he was profoundly happy to have a vacsuit between himself and what would happen if that forcefield failed.

He zoomed in on the returning fighters as the hanger bay tractors stabbed them and drew them into their positions. Some of them, he knew, would not be returning. No one aboard *Angela Martens* knew how many of her fighters had been lost in the battle so far, but everyone knew that at least some of them had. According to Bradford, some of those which might have been recovered wouldn't be because their pilots had run out of life-support—the consequence of yet another questionable decision of Prescott's. And some of the fighters which had come home bore the scars of battle.

He zoomed in even closer on one of them, making sure he got good imagery of the battle damage which had shredded one side of its transatmospheric lifting body. Even he knew how incredibly lucky the pilot of that fighter was to have made it back to base. The rule was that any hit which got through to a fighter and managed to penetrate the surface of its drive field was *always* fatal. In this case, however, what had gotten through had obviously been an energy weapon of some sort—probably a laser—rather than a warhead, and the hit had been a grazing one, which had somehow managed to shatter a divot out of the fighter's fuselage without taking anything vital with it.

He made sure he got good footage of the battle damage as the fighter slid past him in the grip of its tractor beam, then panned the camera across the hordes of hanger deck technicians who were converging at a run on each fighter as it was deposited on the servicing stand in its individual bay.

He held the view steady on Fighter Bay 62's deck crew as it swarmed about the fighter assigned to its care. He had to be careful to stay well back in his hiding place, because he knew for certain that they'd kick his butt out if they spotted him. Fortunately, the alcove in which he sheltered was deep enough and had enough shadows that it was extremely unlikely anyone would notice his presence. Especially not anyone who was concentrating as much on the task at hand as these people were. Despite any reservations he might still have about the Navy and the personnel who normally served in it, Steele had to admit that he'd never seen *anyone* move as quickly as the members of the deck crew he was watching.

He'd decided not to record any more voice-over just now. Not because he was afraid of being overheard—the crews servicing the fighters were making too much noise for him to worry about that, even if everyone hadn't been wearing the helmets regulations required at all times here. No, it was mostly because he really didn't have much of a clue what any of the people he was watching were doing. Maybe he could get Delmore to help him with the details later—after she finished pissing and moaning over the way he'd gotten the footage in the first place. For right now, he would just concentrate on getting as much imagery as he could. After all, he could always shape the story later. Who knew? If Prescott managed to luck out again, Steele might even turn it into still another piece praising him as a tactical genius . . . instead of lambasting him for getting himself caught with his trousers down this way.

He and his camera watched the deck crew as they flowed

around the fighter like participants in some high-tech ballet. Umbilicals were dragged out of recessed compartments in the deck and plugged into ports on the belly of the fighter. More techs disappeared underneath the fighter's fuselage with mag-lev pallets. In what seemed only seconds, they were crawling back out from under, hauling the pallets behind them, and Steele panned the camera over the external ordnance packs they'd removed. He wasn't certain exactly what type of ordnance it was, but that was something else Delmore could tell him.

The heavy canopy of the fighter slid back, and Steele swung the camera hastily back to the pilot. Unfortunately, the pilot—he couldn't even tell if it was male or female from outside its heavy combination grav-vacsuit—made no move to remove the opaque-visored helmet. Someone passed up a small container. After a moment, Steele recognized it as a zero-gee beverage bulb, and the pilot attached the strawlike drinking tube to a helmet nipple.

Steele grimaced. Maybe a little bit of that sort of thing could be used as a human interest angle, but it wasn't what he was here for, and he turned back to the deck crew.

Two of the techs had crawled up on top of the fighter, plugging still more umbilicals into ports behind the opened canopy, and another trio of them were undogging access panels on either side of the nose and directly beneath the needle-sharp prow. Once again, Steele wasn't all sure what he was seeing, although he seemed vaguely to remember something about the "internal hetlasers" which were part of the latest generation Navy fighter's armament. The techs seemed to be inspecting and adjusting whatever was inside the panels, which wasn't all that interesting, so he tracked back around to the ones with the pallets.

They were shoving the pallets up against a bulkhead. Normally, Steele knew, the Navy was downright fanatic about always properly securing gear, but right now, haste was obviously more important than dotting every "i" and crossing every "t." One of the techs working on the hetlasers (if that was what they were actually doing) had already narrowly missed being squashed. He might not even realize it, given his absolute concentration on his own task, but one of the mag-lev pallets had missed him by less than a meter as it was dragged back out of the way. Steele suspected that regulations would normally have prohibited having both sets of technicians working away at once in such a confined space, but this wasn't a day for "normally," and the pallet-towing techs only pushed their charges as far to the side as they would go. Then they used a pair of portable tractor grabs to hoist the ordnance packs off them before they turned and started across the bay, almost directly towards Steele.

Steele felt a moment of consternation. There was no way he could evade detection if they walked right up to him, and that seemed to be exactly what they were going to do. But then his consternation eased. As busy as everyone was, he might even be able to talk his way off the hanger deck without their ever summoning an officer to turn him in to. And even if he couldn't, what were they going to do to him? It wasn't as if anyone could convince a jury that he was a spy for the *Bugs*, after all! Besides—

He'd switched his helmet microphone out of the circuit to his external speakers when he began filming. The camera had been able to hear him just fine through the internal circuit, and there'd been no point in making any noise which someone might have heard. But he'd left the external audio pickup live so he could hear what was happening around him.

He'd just reached for the wrist-mounted control panel and switched the internal microphone back on when he heard something over the external mike.

It came from behind him, and he turned in surprise.

Irma sat in her cockpit, nerves still jittering from the excitement and adrenaline of combat. Sitting here, her suit umbilicals still attached to the fighter's life support systems, while the service techs swarmed over the bird was a direct violation of about two billion regulations. Breaking regulations, in itself, normally didn't bother Irma very much, but *these* regulations, she approved of, for the very good reason that they were expressly designed to keep her butt alive. All sorts of things could go wrong while life support systems were purged, flushed, and replenished. Then there were the altogether too many interesting things that could happen when the depleted super conductor rings were replaced with a freshly charged set . . . without completely powering down the systems in the process. Of course, no one aboard the entire carrier would care very much if one of the weapons techs somehow managed to deactivate the antimatter containment field on one of the FM-3 missiles they were supposed to mount on her bird's hard points. After all, the explosion of one of those missiles inside the *Martens* would blow them all to Hell so quickly that they'd never even realize they were dead.

Normally, she didn't worry about things like that. But "normally" it took a minimum of almost thirty minutes to completely service and rearm an F-4 . . . and according to Togliatti, they were going to do it in ten. Which meant every safety margin The Book insisted upon was being completely ignored. Not just here in Bay 62, but everywhere aboard the MT(V).

As she watched the service techs moving in a sort of disciplined frenzy, she decided that she was undoubtedly safer sitting right where she was—possible unscheduled life-support surges or not—than she would have been out there in the middle of all that moving equipment.

She'd just finished the electrolyte-laden drink the crew chief had passed her when the screams began.

Vincent Steele didn't recognize the sound behind him. If he had, he might have been able to move in time. But instead of immediately flinging himself out of the way, he turned in place just as the hatch cover irised open . . .

. . . and discovered that the "alcove" in which he'd hidden himself was the hatch end of the high-speed magazine tube which delivered fighter ordnance to the bay.

There were six FM-3 missiles on the transfer pallet. Each of them was four meters long and sixty centimeters in diameter, and the pallet was traveling at well over two hundred kilometers per hour.

All things being equal, the reporter was unreasonably lucky that it only hit him at the mid-thigh level. He was equally lucky in the quality of the medical services aboard *Angela Martens*, and in the training of the corpsman who was there almost before the pallet finished severing his left leg entirely and crushing the right one into paste.

In the end, the Navy even paid for both his prosthetic legs.

Irma Sanchez swore vilely as the mass driver's tractors picked her fighter up and settled it into the guides. The *Martens'* strike-group was launching in whatever order it could scramble back into space, and VF-94—which ought to have been one of the very first, given its experience level—was eleventh in line, and all thanks to that idiot reporter! Togliatti had held the rest of the squadron until she was ready, rather than peel her out of the squadron datalink, and she knew why he had. This was a maximum effort mission. If she'd lost her place in VF-94's net, they would have plugged her in with some cluster of stragglers from other squadrons. Georghiu wouldn't have had any choice—they needed every fighter they had, and they needed veterans with her experience even more. But the chances of her surviving combat in a furball like this with squadron mates she'd never flown with and who hadn't flown with her would have been virtually nonexistent.

So because an asshole of a newsie had been somewhere he had no business being, the entire squadron was launching late . . . and the only place worse than flying lead in a strike like this was to come in as Tail-End Charlie.

Prescott and his staff were still on the flag bridge, anxiously examining the statistics, when the last of the fighters came straggling back.

The rearming had been carried out—barely—and the already exhausted pilots had gone out to face gunboats that outnumbered them three-to-two. But their superiority at dogfighting had more than compensated, and they'd killed most of the attackers well short of the battle-line. Most . . . but not all. And the survivors had concentrated on TF 71's monitors, following their own ripple-fired FRAMs in as they sought self-immolation. Three monitors had been destroyed, along with three battlecruisers that had sought to screen them.

But the Bug gunboats had been wiped out. And TF 71 still had three hundred and sixty-one fighters left.

Bichet turned eagerly to Prescott.

"Admiral, this is our chance! The Bugs don't have any gunboats left for cover. If we rearm the fighters with FRAMs and—"

Landrum's eyes flashed. Like many of the fighter jocks, he'd initially looked askançe at an operations officer whose background was exclusively battle-line. Since then, Bichet's demonstrated adaptability had laid his doubts to rest, and they'd worked well together. But the old preconceptions still lay dormant, stirring to life at certain times. This was definitely one of them.

"In case it's escaped your notice, Commodore," he said sharply, "our fighters have just taken heavy losses—in the course of two major actions, with barely a break between them. The pilots aren't robots, whatever you may think."

"I'm well aware of that—without the need for sarcastic reminders!"

"That will do." Prescott's quiet interjection killed the nascent shouting match instantly. "Steve is right, Jacques," he went on, deliberately avoiding the formality of rank titles. "We need to conserve our fighters to protect us from kamikazes. Furthermore . . . Well, we also need to consider something that none of us has cared to bring up."

"Sir?" Mandagalla asked.

"I think it's a given that while Home Hive One was the nearest source of major Bug forces to interdict us, they must have summoned reinforcements from further away, as well. We have absolutely no way to know how long those reinforcements will take to get here. So while Task Force 72 *will* be here in about another standard day, additional Bug forces could arrive first. If they do, we'll need our remaining fighters.

"So," the admiral continued, meeting the eyes of his suddenly sobered staffers, "instead of launching a fighter strike, we'll stop maneuvering to hold the range open, and close with them."

He smiled grimly at the stunned expressions that confronted him.

"I imagine the Bugs will be as startled as you are," he observed. "Which is one reason for doing it. But there are others. First, the Bugs' battlegroup organization has been weakened by their losses in command ships. So we're not likely to have a better opportunity for a successful battle-line duel. Second, I'm no longer concerned with keeping ourselves interposed between the Bugs and Warp Point Three, since they haven't established themselves there and TF 72 is only one day out." Again, the subtle but undeniable emphasis. "So, if there are no questions, let's get the orders out."

The staff broke up with a muted chorus of aye-aye-sirs, but as the operations officer started to turn away, Prescott spoke to him as though it were an afterthought.

"Oh, Jacques. A word in private, please. . . ."

The flag bridge air was tight with tension that couldn't be vented aloud.

The Bugs had refused battle, edging back toward Warp Point Two, and Prescott had followed, knowing that Zhaarnak was due at any time.

But two more days of maneuvering had passed, and now every pair of eyes on *Riva y Silva* seemed to hold the same unspoken question: *Where is Zhaarnak?*

Prescott found himself less and less able to meet those eyes.

*It's partly my fault*, he thought in an inner torment no one was allowed to see. *I've kept reassuring everyone, building up their expectations. Everyone knows an exact arrival time can't be predicted for a voyage as long as Task Force 72's. But people have forgotten that because I was so determined to give them a definite, well-defined light at the end of the tunnel.*

*And besides . . . where is Zhaarnak?*

He shook off the thought and gazed at the system-scale holo display. That didn't help.

*I've let myself be drawn too close to Warp Point Two,* he admitted to himself. *Dangerously close. If only I had some recon drones on the other side of that warp point!* Wry self-mockery drove out his self-reproach. *If wishes were horses . . .*

Decision came. He straightened up.

"Anna."

"Sir?"

"I believe it's time to open the range again and stop seeking engagement."

"Yes, Sir." Mandagalla kept her relief out of her voice with a care that couldn't have made it more obvious. "I'll tell Jacques—"

In the main plot, the icon that represented the closed warp point ignited into a flashing hostile scarlet.

The flag captain must have seen it, too, because without a perceptible pause, the General Quarters alarm began to wail. Prescott didn't even notice.

"Tactical scale!" he snapped, and the display zoomed in on the warp point. The scarlet resolved itself into the rash of a mass simultaneous gunboat transits.

Prescott and his chief of staff made an eye contact that carried a wealth of unspoken communication. It was the long anticipated Bug reinforcements, doubtless well-informed by courier drone of TF 71's current position. And the task force's fighters, awaiting the battle-line engagement Prescott had been seeking, were in ship-killing mode.

"Have the fighters rearmed, Anna," he said with a calmness he didn't feel.

Irma Sanchez came through the hatch at a dead run. (That was *another* thing she didn't like about monitors. They were so damned big, it took longer to get from the ready room to the launch bays.) Bruno Togliatti had only just beaten her into the long, open passageway connecting the squadron cluster of launch bays where VF-94's four remaining fighters lay ready for space.

"We didn't need to hurry so much, after all," he gasped, catching his breath and gesturing at the fighters. Techs were still swarming over them, and she saw gun packs replacing laser packs. "They're reconfiguring the external ordnance for gunboat hunting."

"Jesus H. Christ!" Irma leaned back against a bulkhead and ran a hand through her short bristle of black hair. "What a goddamned cluster-fuck!"

But despite the change in orders, the other two surviving pilots had barely arrived when the leading CPO gave Togliatti the thumbs-up and they sprinted for their fighters. Irma went through her checklist while the deckies plugged in her support suit's umbilicals, then closed her helmet as the mass-driver tractors lifted her fighter and settled it in place. Ahead of her was the monopermeable forcefield, and beyond that was only the star-studded blackness while the rumbling of other squadrons' launches vibrated through the ship's structure like distant, prespace freight trains.

Then it was VF-94's turn. Togliatti was off first, then the g-force pressed Irma into her seat as the mass driver flung her through the forcefield. There was the usual instant of queasy sensations—departure from the ship's artificial gravity, and passage through the monitor's drive field, both almost too brief to be perceived—and then the brutal mass of *Angela Martens*, so different from the slender lines of a proper carrier, was tumbling away in the view-aft. Irma reoriented herself with practiced ease as the fighter's drive took hold. Then she looked at her tactical display.

She tried not to be sick.

Raymond Prescott was looking at the oncoming gunboats, too.

Even with the interpenetration losses they'd taken in the course of their mass simultaneous transits, there were more Bug gunboats than TF 71 had faced before—and it was facing them with far fewer fighters.

Fortunately—*and no thanks to me*, Prescott berated himself—the task force had been just barely far enough from Warp Point Two for the fighters to rearm and launch before the gunboats could reach it. Now they and the gunboats were meeting in a swirling frenzy of dogfights.

But the outnumbered fighters couldn't stop them all. More and more got through, and ships began to suffer the devastation of

FRAMs salvos followed by kamikaze runs. And some of them began to die....

"Incoming!"

The blood-chilling shriek of the collision alarm screamed in his ears as Prescott and everyone else on the flag bridge slammed their crash frames and sealed their helmets. They'd barely done so when TFNS *Irena Riva y Silva* began reverberating as though from blows of the gods' pile-driver.

It finally ended, and Prescott—unlike some others—retained consciousness. He almost wished he hadn't as he stood amid the scurrying damage control crews and observed the tally of Code Omegas.

*Three Gorm monitors,* he forced himself to recite, *and four of their superdreadnoughts. An Ophiuchi assault carrier, and both of our command fleet carriers....* And it was worse than it looked, because a number of the other surviving units were even more heavily damaged than the flagship.

And, to complete the vista of despair, the Bug capital ships had followed their gunboats through the warp point, in wave after wave, to join those already in the system. Together, they outnumbered TF 71 by more than two-to-one. And they were closing in.

"Try and reorganize around the losses, Anna," Prescott said quietly. "Priority goes to the battle-line; we'll need their point defense. Jacques," he turned to the ops officer, "keep us between the Bugs and the carriers. I'd like to withdraw our fighters and get their datanets reorganized, too, but I can't. The Bugs are bound to launch kamikaze shuttles any minute now, and we'll need the CSP to cover against them."

As if he'd overheard the comment, Stephen Landrum spoke from the direction of the main plot.

"Admiral, they're starting to launch their suicide shuttles."

Irma Sanchez had been fighting too long and too desperately. And then she'd seen the distant fireball, and heard the screech of static, that meant Bruno Togliatti was dead. And now she had nothing left to give to this hopeless, meaningless battle.

But then she heard a voice in her headset—oh, yes, it was Lieutenant (j.g.) Meswami, the young puke who'd been bragging after Home Hive One. Now his voice held a quaver.

"Lieutenant, a whole flight of shuttles has gotten through! We can't intercept them! And they're heading for *Martens!*"

*Why the fuck is he telling me this?* Irma wondered dully. Then it came to her. Togliatti's new ops officer had also bought it. *I'm the senior pilot left.*

She checked her tactical. The kid was right, so she shut out her exhaustion and her grief.

"I think we can get back there in time to be some help," she responded. "Form up on me."

And, for a while, there was nothing in the universe but the need to kill those shuttles.

Raymond Prescott had watched as the tatters of his strikegroups fended off the kamikaze shuttles. Now he drew a deep breath, looked briefly up from the plot, and nodded to Mandagalla and Bichet.

"It's time to start falling back," he said quietly. "Put us on a course for Warp Point Three."

At some point during the chaos, Mukerji had come onto the flag bridge. Prescott was usually able to effectively exclude him from it at General Quarters, even though he couldn't be kept out of formal staff conferences in the briefing room. Now his sweat-slick face lit up with hope.

"Does this mean you plan to withdraw to AP-4, Admiral?"

"Absolutely not, Admiral Mukerji. Have you forgotten the ships we left behind in AP-6? What do you think will happen to them if we abandon this system and leave them cut off?"

"But, Admiral, *all* of us will die if you *don't* retreat up-chain!"

"Commodore Mandagalla," Raymond Prescott said in a voice of cold iron, all the time holding Mukerji's eyes, "let me clarify my previous orders. We will fall back toward Warp Point Three on an oblique angle, with a view to allowing the Bugs to get between us and the warp point."

What followed wasn't really silence—there was still too much damage control work going on for that. When Mukerji finally spoke, his near-whisper was barely audible.

"You're mad!"

"And you, Admiral Mukerji, are under arrest for insubordination," Prescott replied pleasantly. Mukerji gaped at him in disbelief, but Prescott ignored him and turned his attention back to the plot.

Mukerji looked around the flag bridge helplessly, as if unsure exactly what to do with himself. None of Prescott's staffers would meet his eye, and he started to turn towards the elevators, then stopped and turned back to Prescott, his sweat-streaked face working with a panic that included more now than the simple fear of death.

If Prescott was even aware of the vice admiral's existence, he gave no sign of it as he stared fixedly into the display which showed the data codes of the task force, angling more or less towards the violet dot of Warp Point Three . . . and the scarlet rash of Bug capital ships, starting to slide in between those two icons. Mukerji's own eyes dropped to the same icons, watching them with the same mesmerized horror with which he might have watched his executioner honing the guillotine's edge, and an agonizing silence stretched out. Even the last of the damage control parties seemed hushed as TF 71 deliberately sailed straight into a death trap from which there could be no escape.

And then, all at once, Prescott seemed to see something he'd been watching for in the display. He straightened up, motionlessness buried in a sudden dynamism.

"Jacques, Anna! Implement the course change we discussed."

"Aye, aye, Sir."

The ops officer began to fire off a series of orders. Mukerji listened unbelievingly, but there was no mistake. On the display, the task group's icon began to turn onto the heading Bichet had just ordered—a heading *away* from Warp Point Three, and into the depths of the AP-5 System.

Mukerji stared at the admiral, as if Prescott were a cobra . . . or the very madman the vice admiral had called him.

The Bugs began to change course in pursuit, presenting their sterns to Warp Point Three, and Mukerji finally found his voice once more.

"Admiral," he began hoarsely, "I—"

Then, suddenly, the warp point began to flash with green fire . . . and Mukerji's mouth closed with a click as the first Orion carriers emerged.

After a stunned moment, the flag bridge erupted into a pandemonium that no one tried to control.

Tiny green icons began to speed ahead as the emerging carriers, barely taking time to stabilize their launch machinery after transit, began to send out massive waves of fighters.

"Given the shortness of the range," Prescott mused aloud, "I imagine that each of those fighters is carrying two primary packs." He turned back to his chief of staff and his ops officer. "Anna, you and Jacques should start getting our course reversed. We may be able to get back there in time to trap some of the Bug elements between us and Task Force 72."

"Aye, aye, Sir!" Mandagalla replied with a huge grin, and Mukerji shook himself.

"How—?" he began, then clamped his mouth shut once more as Raymond Prescott turned an icy eye upon him.

"I knew Fang Zhaarnak was coming, Admiral," the Seventh Fleet commander said in a voice of frozen helium. "In fact, you may recall that I mentioned that, a time or two."

"But you never mentioned *this*!" Mukerji spluttered, pointing accusingly at the display.

"Not to the task force at large, no," Prescott agreed, his tone as frigid as ever. "There was no reason to, and I'd decided not to continue to insist that Zhaarnak would get here in time, since . . . certain persons had begun to question my confidence. But that didn't mean that *I* ever doubted he'd be here, so two days ago, I had Commodore Bichet dispatch a courier drone to Commodore Horigome."

Almost despite himself, Mukerji nodded. Commodore Stephanie Horigome flew her lights aboard TFNS *Cree*, the *Hun*-class cruiser which was the senior ship of the six-ship battlegroup of cloaked pickets stationed in AP-4.

"That courier drone contained a complete, detailed download on the known Bug forces in this system, to which I had appended my analysis of their probable intentions and my belief that powerful enemy reinforcements would be arriving here shortly. It also instructed Commodore Horigome to make contact with Fang Zhaarnak upon his arrival and to communicate that data to him, along with my suggestion that he send his carriers through first at the appropriate moment. Since there was no way to be certain that the Bugs weren't maintaining a close sensor watch on the warp point, I further instructed Commodore Horigome and Fang Zhaarnak not to send any courier drones confirming Task Force 72's arrival in AP-4. Instead, Commodore Horigome was to send a drone through no later than oh-seven-hundred Zulu this morning if Fang Zhaarnak *hadn't* arrived. It was essential that the Bugs not suspect we were in close communication with a reinforcing force of our own, and so Fang Zhaarnak has used RD2s to maintain a close watch on AP-5 ever since his arrival in AP-4 in order to pick the most opportune moment for transit."

Prescott showed his teeth in what not even the most charitable soul could have called a smile, and Mukerji seemed to wither.

"Unlike some people, Admiral Mukerji," he said with the scalpel-like precision of complete and utter contempt, "I had no doubt at all that Fang Zhaarnak would recognize precisely what I was doing and know precisely how to best take advantage of our maneuvers and the Bugs' response."

"Admiral Prescott, I . . . I don't . . . That is—"

"I really don't believe you have anything more to say to me, Admiral," Prescott said coldly. "I suggest that you go to your quarters . . . and stay there."

He turned his back on Mukerji and crossed to stand beside Mandagalla, watching the icons in the main plot as the Orion fighters ripped into the Bug capital ships with the devastating fury of their primary packs. Terence Mukerji stared at him for a long moment, his eyes filled with an indescribable mixture of lingering terror, shame, and hatred.

And then, finally, he turned and stumbled towards the flag bridge elevator.

*The attack craft strike from the newly arrived Enemies was a blow from which the Fleet's position in this system could not recover.*

*There was no room for doubt that the Enemy knew the location of the closed warp point. So Franos was vulnerable to attack, and there would be no one to defend it if the forces in this system perished—as they would, for with his fresh attack craft strength the Enemy would be able to annihilate them from beyond their own shipboard weapons' range.*

*There was no alternative to an immediate disengagement and withdrawal. Further losses were unavoidable, in the course of the retreat. But most would escape to protect Franos.*

"Have a seat, Lieutenant Sanchez." Commander Georghiu looked up from the printout he'd been reading as Irma sat down. "First of all, I know how you must feel about the loss of Commander Togliatti. He was a fine officer."

"Yes, Sir." *So why don't you let me go and mourn for him in private, you pompous asshole?*

"Also, you've been under his command for quite a while. I've been reviewing your record. You were with the Ninety-Fourth from the beginning of the Zephrain offensive. Your extensive combat experience stood you in good stead after Commander Togliatti's death. You did very well, getting yourself and the other surviving pilot back to the ship."

"Thank you, Sir."

"But now you and that pilot are the only survivors—and he was one of those whose disbanded squadron was merged into yours in Home Hive One. Essentially, Lieutenant, you're all that's left of the old VF-94."

Irma hadn't thought of it that way, but . . .

"Yes, Sir."

"Now, as you're aware, Task Force 72 has brought replacement fighters and pilots—sorely needed ones, if we're going to get our strikegroups even remotely back up to strength. But, given the losses we've taken, there're going to have to be some organizational adjustments. You and Lieutenant (j.g.) Meswami, along with VF-94's technical support personnel, will be reassigned to squadrons that still have viable command structures in place."

For perhaps one full heartbeat, Irma's reaction was one of relief—it's always a relief when the big news from the boss is that your own personal situation is going to remain essentially unchanged. She'd just keep doing what she always had, with some *real* military type in charge, with all the responsibility.

Then the implications of Georghiu's words hit her.

*Disband the squadron? But . . . but . . .*

"But you *can't* . . . Sir." It was out of her mouth and into the air of the tiny office before she even knew she had it inside her. She gulped and braced herself.

"It's regrettable. But it's also unavoidable—an organizational necessity. Why, the only alternative would be to put *you* in command, and give you some very green replacement pilots." Georghiu paused, and let the pause linger.

*In command? Me? Ridiculous! The Skipper's always been there to handle all the administrative red tape and all the military chickenshit.*

*But . . . I'd be the Skipper!*

At first, such a patently impossible contradiction in logic simply refused to register, and she gathered her breath for a flabbergasted refusal.

Only . . .

*Break up the squadron? That would be like killing the Skipper a second time!*

"I'd be willing to try it, Sir," she heard herself say.

Very briefly, the corners of Georghiu's mouth did something odd. *A smile*? Irma wondered. *Georghiu? No. Impossible.* Then the CSG was his usual self, and she decided it had just been her imagination.

"Understand this, Lieutenant: you'll never be allowed to keep that squadron. You're simply too junior. It's a lieutenant commander's billet, and you haven't been a lieutenant senior grade long enough for them to even consider promoting you. No, this will only be a temporary expedient, for the duration of the present campaign."

"Understood, Sir."

"Very well. I'll have the orders cut, and we'll make the announcement. And afterwards . . . I'll report to Captain Landrum that VF-94 still lives."

# CHAPTER THIRTEEN
## "You Take the High Road . . ."

The repair crews still laboring busily in *Irena Riva y Silva*'s boatbay somewhat spoiled the effect, but the Marine detachment still put on a good show. Its members snapped to attention in a mathematically perfect line of black trousers and dark green tunics as the Orion shuttle settled onto the deck, then presented arms as the hatch slid open and Zhaarnak'telmasa, *Khanhaku* Telmasa, emerged.

The fang responded to the formal military courtesies punctiliously, but his impatience was evident even through his grave demeanor to anyone who knew him well. The instant the formalities were over, the *vilkshatha* brothers clasped arms and Zhaarnak started in once again.

"I got here as fast as I could, Raaymmonnd, but—"

Prescott laughed, and spoke in the Tongue of Tongues.

"I know, brother, I know! I never doubted it for an instant. I knew a wild *zeget* could not keep you away from the fighting!" He glanced at Zhaarnak's staffers, beginning to emerge from the shuttle and descend the ramp, one familiar Orion figure after another . . . and then an incongruous human figure, walking with Uaaria. The sight surprised him into reverting to Standard English. "Say, isn't that Lieutenant Sanders, Marcus LeBlanc's man?"

"Indeed. Like the freighters, he was inflicted upon me at the last minute," Zhaarnak said sourly, and Prescott gave him a tooth-hidden grin and resumed the Tongue of Tongues.

"They may have slowed you, but my task force would be in poor case without the fighters those ships carry."

"It would be in even poorer case if the delay had kept me from

281

arriving here for another day or two," Zhaarnak growled, and to that, Prescott could think of no reply.

Sanders reached the head of the line of visiting staff officers saluting Prescott.

"Welcome aboard, Lieutenant," the admiral said, returning his salute. "I hope you've brought us an update on Admiral LeBlanc's latest conclusions."

"I have, Sir. I'm also supposed to report back to him on what's happened out here."

"Well, in that case, you and Small Claw Uaaria should get with Commodore Chung as quickly as possible. Lord Telmasa and I have some catching up of our own to do, but I'd like our 'spooks' to combine forces before we start organizing fresh staff meetings. Commodore Chung can bring you and Claw Uaaria up to date, and the three of you can prepare a joint brief for me and Lord Telmasa."

"Yes, Sir." If Sanders felt any discomfort at being included with two officers who outranked him so substantially, he showed no sign of it, and Prescott's eyes glinted.

"In fact, Lieutenant, I think I'd like a preliminary written summary by seventeen hundred hours. Take care of that for me, would you?"

"Uh, yes, Sir!"

This time, Prescott was pleased to note, the unreasonably self-possessed young man looked more than a little anxious, so he smiled pleasantly and turned to the next officer in line.

For all of his high comfort level with the Tabbies, Kevin Sanders found it something of a relief to be once more upon a human starship. For one thing, the humidity level was considerably higher, since it was set to something humans were comfortable with. For another, there were a sizable number of personnel aboard *Irena Riva y Silva* who were young, attractive, female, currently unattached, and members of his own species. He really, really liked Uaaria, and he was fully aware that her sleek, dark-hued pelt and wide, golden eyes—not to mention the delicate arch of her whiskers and the cream-colored, plushy tufts of her felinoid ears—approximated very closely to the Orion ideal of feminine beauty. He found her quite attractive, himself, but in much the same way he might have found a cougar or a jaguar attractive. On a more . . . intimate level, the return to a human-crewed ship offered far broader opportunities.

But it was quite a different matter where sheer brain power and imagination were concerned. He rather doubted that he was ever going to meet *anyone* who was superior to Uaaria in those qualities, and he tipped back in his chair in Amos Chung's private quarters and listened appreciatively as she and Chung caught one another up.

It had been obvious to Sanders from conversations with Uaaria on the voyage out that she and Chung had an exceptionally close working relationship. The fact that Uaaria clearly regarded Chung as a friend, as well as a colleague, hadn't been lost on the lieutenant either. Yet for all of that, he hadn't quite been prepared for the way in which the two of them fitted together. Uaaria was the imagination of the partnership. She possessed the ability to think "outside the boxes" to a degree Sanders had never seen in anyone else, except, perhaps, Marcus LeBlanc himself. Chung was less intuitive, but he compensated with a logical, deductive approach and an exhaustive ability to research and pull the salient facts out of any analysis. He was the one who went out and found the data that didn't fit the conventional interpretation. Once he had it, Uaaria was the one who played with the pieces until she produced a hypothesis where they did fit. And once she had, Chung was her sounding board, perfectly prepared to shoot holes in her reasoning—and to have holes shot in his own, in return—until they produced a theory no one *else* could perforate.

Both of them also possessed the ability to accept criticism without taking it as a personal attack, and to offer it in the same way. That, Sanders had already discovered, was considerably rarer than simple brilliance, and he rather suspected it was that quality, more even than their shared passion for puzzle solving, which made them so effective. And the odd thing was, that even though it had taken the most horrible war in galactic history to bring the two of them together, it was obvious that both of them were having an enormous amount of *fun* working together.

At the moment, however, "fun" was in short supply.

"We knew you had suffered severe casualties, Aaamosssss," Uaaria said quietly, her eloquent ears half-flattened in dismay. She fidgeted with the glass on the table before her. Like many Orions, she'd developed a pronounced taste for Terran bourbon. Chung himself preferred wine, but he'd been able to fix Sanders up with the sort of nice blended scotch that a mere lieutenant would have had problems affording. Now Uaaria took a sip, and her whiskers quivered in an Orion grimace. "Severe, yes. That much we knew, but we had not realized they were *that* severe. And it is perhaps as well that Lord Telmasa did not know how desperate the situation here truly was before we reached AP-4."

"They were heavy, all right," Chung sighed, which, Sanders reflected, was one of the more substantial understatements he'd heard recently. Eight monitors, eleven superdreadnoughts, nine assault and fleet carriers, fourteen battlecruisers, and eighteen *hundred* fighters—not to mention virtually every gunboat TF 71 had possessed—certainly ought to qualify as "heavy" in anyone's book.

"On the other hand," Chung went on, straightening his shoulders like someone determined to look on the bright side, "even losses that heavy were an amazingly low price for what the Admiral managed to pull off. An entire home hive system, plus the damage we did to their mobile forces. If our original estimates—and Admiral LeBlanc's," he added, with a nod to Sanders, "—are accurate, then they only have three home hives left. And we shot them up in AP-5 at least as badly as they did us."

"Indeed," Uaaria agreed. TF 72's fighters had been responsible for the final pursuit of the fleeing Bugs, and she actually had better loss and damage totals than Chung did. "Our figures are not yet definitive, but if our fighter pilots' initial claims stand up, then, combined with what your own *farshatok* accomplished before we arrived, the Bahgs lost at least a third of their total strength before they could escape. Most of those who did manage to retire through the warp point were damaged in varying degrees, as well."

"That, unfortunately, is also true of Task Force 71," Chung observed wryly, then quirked a smile. "Still, our repairs are already underway, and the replacement fighters you brought along should let us fill practically all our surviving carrier capacity. And to be honest, the most *satisfying* damage we've done the Bugs is the insight we've obtained into the strategic situation. We've pinpointed the closed warp point here in AP-5, we know that warp point is the terminus of the chain between Home Hive One and AP-5, *and* we know approximately how long it took the Bugs to get to AP-5 from Home Hive One. Assuming average in-system real-space distances between warp points, we're probably looking at a maximum of five star systems, and probably less."

"Knowing Fang Presssssscottt and Lord Telmasa, I believe we may feel confident that they will soon be taking advantage of that knowledge," Uaaria agreed with a soft, hungry purr of agreement and touched the *defargo* honor dirk at her side. Every KON officer carried one of them, but the way in which her clawed hand caressed its hilt reminded Sanders that "spook" or not, Uaaria'*salath-ahn* was an *Orion*, and for just a moment, he felt a flicker of what might almost have been pity for any enemy besides the Bugs.

"From the kinds of questions the Admiral's been asking, I'd say you've got that one right," Chung agreed. "But in the meantime . . ."

He flipped the keyboard of his personal terminal up out of the tabletop and brought it on-line. He tapped a few keys, and a hologram appeared above the table. It showed a rough, hypothetical schematic of the local warp lines when it first came up, Sanders noted. Obviously, Chung had been putting in a little work of his own on the strategic possibilities, but he cleared that quickly and brought up an index of report headings.

"Since our guest," he grinned at Uaaria and then nodded at Sanders, "has a homework assignment from the Admiral, I thought it would be only kind of us to help him pull together his term paper. And since we have a lot of information to collate, it's probably time we got started."

At that very moment, in the far more palatial quarters the Terran Federation Navy had seen fit to assign to the admirals who commanded its fleets, Raymond Prescott and Zhaarnak'telmasa had pretty much finished catching one another up on their own recent experiences. Prescott had discarded his uniform tunic, kicked off his boots, and tipped back his chair while he nursed a bottle of dark, Bavarian-style beer from the planet Freidrichshaven. Zhaarnak, who had once been as fond of bourbon as any Orion, had obviously been corrupted by his contact with Kthaara'zarthan. Unlike Uaaria's glass, the one in his hand contained vodka. The only thing that Prescott wasn't completely sure about was whether his *vilkshatha* brother was drinking it because he actually liked it, or because it was Lord Talphon's beverage of choice. Given Zhaarnak's immense respect for Kthaara, either was possible.

"And so I managed to arrive in time after all, despite all that GFGHQ's quartermasters could do to prevent it," Zhaarnak observed with unmistakable relief.

"Yes, you did," Prescott agreed in the Tongue of Tongues. "I will not pretend that I would not have preferred to see you sooner, but things worked out quite well in the end, I thought."

"As always, you demonstrate your gift for understatement."

"A modest talent," Prescott said with a small smile. Then he finished off his beer, set the empty bottle on the table, and leaned forward, with a more intent expression.

"Now that you're here, though," he went on in Standard English, "I think it's time to move on to considering what we do next."

"Raaymmonnd," Zhaarnak began in a tone of unaccustomed caution, "Task Force 71 is in no condition to—"

"Don't worry. I have no intention of charging off before our repairs are completed and the dust from the reorganization of our strikegroups has settled."

"From which I am to infer that you do intend to charge off as soon as repairs *are* completed?"

"Well, perhaps not 'charge,'" Prescott said with another smile, this time allowing a slight edge of tooth to show. "On the other hand . . ."

He popped up his own terminal and called up a rough schematic of the local warp lines very like the one Amos Chung had been working on. The familiar Prescott Chain extended from left to right in the lower half of the display, a solid green line running from AP-4 through five warp nexi before continuing on to Home Hive One as the broken line of a closed warp point. There was, however, a second dotted line—this one indicating an unknown warp chain that started at Home Hive One and moved right through two nexi with scarlet question-mark symbols, to a third which a broken red line linked with AP-5 to complete the circuit.

"We know the location of the closed warp point here, and the Bugs know we know it. At the same time, we're as certain as anyone could be that the Bugs *don't* know where the closed warp point in Home Hive One is, and I intended to take advantage of their ignorance."

Zhaarnak gazed at the display and shifted uncomfortably, and not just because he was sitting in a human-designed chair.

"Why does something about your words cause my fur to rise?" he asked, and Prescott gave his uncannily Orion smile.

"Let me ask you this, brother. Would you feel less anxious at the prospect of going directly through Warp Point Two in the face of the Bug forces we know are awaiting us on the far side at this moment?"

"Well . . ."

"Then hear me out. I intend to take Task Force 71 back to Home Hive One and start taking out the warp point defenses we left there with attacks from the rear. That should elicit a counter-attack, siphoning off some of the forces you'll be facing here. At that point, you'll lead Task Force 72 through Warp Point Two." Prescott gestured at the broken red line between AP-5's closed warp point in the unknown Bug system beyond, and the dotted red line extending beyond that to Home Hive One. "Then you can advance along this warp chain to meet me." He smiled again, this time grimly. "To quote an old bit of human doggerel, 'You take the high road, and I'll take the low road.'"

"I knew there was a reason my pelt wished to tie itself in knots," Zhaarnak growled.

"Nonsense." Prescott chuckled. "You just wish you'd thought of it first!"

"Very humorous. And what of the fresh Bahg forces which were about to dine on you when I arrived? They came from some-where—presumably one of the three remaining home hive systems. And we have no idea of the route by which they came!"

"No," Prescott agreed, "but the fact that the reinforcements arrived only at such a late stage suggests that their home base isn't on the Home Hive One/AP-5 warp chain and is almost certainly considerably farther away than Home Hive One."

"That is all extremely vague and speculative," Zhaarnak grumbled.

"But it's the best we can hope for, given the present state of our knowledge," Prescott insisted. "I think we have enough information—or, at least, short inferences—to make this worth trying."

"But, Raaymmonnd, you know how difficult it is to coordinate widely separated forces! Are you not the one who has pointed out to me time and again that my own people's taste for 'complicated' converging maneuvers by several independent forces invites defeat in detail by challenging your Demon Murrrppheeee? How would I know when to commence my own attack?"

"There's going to be an unavoidable delay while we make our repairs and redistribute our fighters," Prescott replied. "I propose to use that time to do two other things: deploy com buoys in the systems from here to El Dorado, and probe through Warp Point Two with recon drones, so as to form an accurate picture of the forces facing us on the far side. As far as the ICN is concerned, there's clearly no good reason at this point to avoid 'bread crumbs' from here to El Dorado. It's not like the Bugs won't be able to figure out how we got from there to here. With it in place, though, our communications loop will be much shorter. As soon as I identify detachments from the force facing you in Home Hive One, I'll send you word. You'll hold yourself in readiness to move as soon as you receive that word, and since I'll know just how long the message will take to reach you, I'll also know when your attack will commence."

Zhaarnak tipped his own chair back, threw back a swallow of vodka in the approved, proper Russian style, shuddered briefly, then sighed.

"Very well. I know when your mind is made up—the fact that this is the sort of 'mad, over-complicated' plan a *Zheeerlikou'valkhannaiee* strategist would devise is obviously insufficient to dissuade you. I will not protest it further *if* you will agree, on your word as a father in honor of Clan Telmasa, that the entire operation will be contingent on Task Force 71's full readiness."

"You have my word, *Khanhaku* Telmasa," Prescott assured him in the Tongue of Tongues.

"*Full* readiness, Raaymmonnd," Zhaarnak stressed pointedly.

"Of course," Prescott affirmed innocently . . . in Standard English.

Kevin Sanders found himself standing behind Uaaria and Captain Chung as the staff meeting broke up. Prescott's proposed strategy had landed in the middle of the staffers like a bombshell. Even Captain Mandagalla had seemed taken aback, and Force Leader Shaaldaar had been more than a little dubious until Prescott assured him—with a sidelong glance at Zhaarnak which Sanders had fully understood—that the operation wouldn't begin until TF 71's damages had been fully repaired.

The one member of Prescott's staff who'd appeared completely unsurprised by the proposal was Amos Chung, which had given Sanders furiously to think, especially in light of the warp chart Chung had been studying. At the moment, however, the lieutenant had something else on his mind. Something much more pressing, given the very confidential briefing he'd received from Admiral LeBlanc before being sent here.

"Excuse me, Commodore," he said to Chung, with a diffidence that was quite out of character as Prescott's staff spook recalled it. "Ah, if I may ask . . . Well, I can't help being a little curious. I didn't see Vice Admiral Mukerji at the meeting."

"Admiral Mukerji," Chung replied, in a voice which was just that little bit too expressionless, "is confined to his quarters, Lieutenant."

Even Sanders blinked at that, although now that it was said, he had to admit it was unfortunately close to what he'd already suspected. He started to ask another question, then paused. He intended to acquire the information, one way or another, before he left the flagship, but Chung's tone suggested that perhaps he should seek another information source.

Fortunately, such a source was close at hand, for Uaaria'salath-ahn clearly didn't share her human colleague's reticence in this particular case.

"I have already heard the story, Aaamosssss," she said, and one lip curled to reveal a needle-sharp and fully functional canine. She glanced at Sanders. "Ahhdmiraaaal Muhkerzzhi displayed gross insubordination on the flag bridge at the critical moment of the recent battle, and Fang Pressssscott placed him under arrest for it."

Chung grimaced at the female Tabby's words, but not as if he were angry. It was more a case of someone who regretted the washing of the dirty family linen in public. Then he sighed and nodded, as if in recognition that the story was bound to become public knowledge sooner or later.

Sanders went absolutely poker-faced, looking back and forth between his two superiors. Then he cleared his throat.

"I see, Sir. May I ask if the Admiral has decided how he intends to proceed? Will he convene a court-martial?"

"Given Mukerji's rank," Chung said in a distasteful tone, obviously choosing his words with great care, "and the potential . . . conflict of interest in the Admiral's dual role as convening authority and principal in the case, I believe he intends to send Mukerji back to Alpha Centauri to await trial." The intelligence officer clearly disliked discussing the case at all, but by the same token, he seemed to realize that who he was really discussing it with—by proxy, at least—was Marcus LeBlanc. "I believe he plans to do so on the first occasion he has to dispatch a non-combatant ship to Centauri."

*Since he can't very well stuff him into a courier drone,* Sanders thought behind a face whose blandness matched Chung's.

"I see, Sir," he repeated. "And, since any such trial would probably require the Admiral's testimony, Admiral Mukerji may well spend some considerable time at Alpha Centauri awaiting it."

"Quite possibly, Lieutenant," Chung said in a tone clearly intended to politely but firmly close the discussion. Uaaria, however, wasn't prepared to abandon the topic just yet.

"It appears that Fang Pressssscott has found a way to rid himself of the political officer your government saddled him with," she remarked.

"Yes ... a very risky way, politically speaking." Chung sighed— with good reason, Sanders thought. "Mukerji has powerful patrons ... and he'll undoubtedly start pounding their ears with *his* 'version' of the facts the instant he arrives in Alpha Centauri."

Uaaria's ears flattened and she gave the sibilant hiss of serious Orion irritation.

"It is all beyond my comprehension. A coward like Muhkerz-zhi is not worthy to roll in Fang Pressssscott's dung! Among the *Zheeerlikou'valkhannaiee*, such a *chofak* would long since have been killed in a duel. Assuming that anyone would soil his claws with his blood!"

Chung blinked, clearly a bit taken aback, despite his long acquaintance with her, by her vehemence, but Sanders only nodded.

"Yes, I know, Claw. You've got better sense than we do in that respect," he said, and realized as he spoke that it wasn't all diplomacy on his part. Since shipping out with Zhaarnak's task force, he'd experienced total immersion in the Orion warrior culture. Never subject to any xenophobic tendencies, he'd never thought of himself as a xenophile, either. Now he was beginning to wonder.

But most of his consciousness was occupied with composing his report to Admiral LeBlanc.

Marcus LeBlanc's eyes strayed, not for the first time, towards the strategic holo display that floated in the air of Kthaara'zarthan's office.

It wasn't what he was supposed to be focusing on, and he knew it. Nevertheless, his gaze kept wandering to the little spark that represented Zephrain. The display showed Alliance-controlled systems in green, and to LeBlanc the icon of Zephrain glowed with the light of jade eyes, haloed with an insubstantial swirl of flame-red hair.

Almost three standard years had passed since he watched Vanessa Murakuma depart from the terrace of this very building, seeming to recede into a distance greater than that which yawned between the stars. They'd communicated regularly for more than two of those years, as she'd done Kthaara's bidding and honed Fifth Fleet to a fine edge out in the remote Romulus Chain, awaiting Bug invaders who never came. Then, finally, had come the half-promised summons, offering her command of Sixth Fleet in place of the Prescott/Zhaarnak team that had moved abruptly on to Seventh Fleet in the wake of Andrew Prescott's last fight and the astrogation data it had brought home.

The offer to take over Sixth Fleet had been unexpected in every sense, LeBlanc knew. She'd expected to take Fifth Fleet with her when she moved on from Justin, but the JCS had decided that Justin continued to require a mobile fleet presence to back up the mammoth fixed fortifications which had been erected there. So if she wanted an offensive command, she was going to have to leave the fleet she'd spent literally years training.

In the end, she'd accepted the new assignment. Probably only because she knew that she'd be leaving Fifth Fleet in the hands of recently promoted Admiral Demosthenes Waldeck. Relative of Agamemnon Waldeck or not, Demosthenes was every inch a TFN admiral . . . and one of the few people Vanessa would trust to look after her people for her. And so she had set off to her new posting, to begin all over again, although at least she'd been able to take her entire staff along with her.

She'd passed through Alpha Centauri on her journey to Zephrain, and LeBlanc had had a tantalizingly brief time with her—so brief that it had left his hurt intensified rather than assuaged. Gazing at that little green icon was like tugging at a scab.

*And,* he told himself sternly, *it's not what I'm here for. I'm supposed to be offering my alleged insights on Sanders' report.* He turned back to the other two beings in the office.

"Well," he philosophized, "at least Prescott didn't heave Mukerji into the brig."

Sky Marshal MacGregor, however, was in no mood to be mollified.

"Thank God for that! There's going to be enough hell to pay when Mukerji arrives here and all this comes out—especially by me, for having sat on Sanders' report!"

"Maybe not, Sir," LeBlanc ventured. "Sanders says he's going to work on trying to get Prescott to accept some kind of face-saving compromise so it won't come to a trial. Perhaps the whole thing will blow over by the time the current election is over and the politicians have stopped trying to outdo each other in claiming credit for Prescott's victories—the parts of the report you *haven't* suppressed."

Kthaara'zarthan looked across his desk at the two Humans and ordered himself not to smile—his sadistic sense of humor had limits.

"The matter of Muhkerzzhi is doubtless worrisome. Possibly even dangerous. But what is interesting is confirmation of the 'psychic shock' effect on the remaining Bahg occupants of a system when vast numbers of them die with the speed at which lavishly employed antimatter weapons can depopulate planets."

"Yes, Sir," a suddenly more animated LeBlanc affirmed. "Now the effect has been demonstrated conclusively, including its instantaneous-propagation feature. The establishment physicists are still in deep denial over that last bit. They insist that telepathy must be limited to the sacrosanct velocity of light."

"My nose bleeds for them and their dogmas," MacGregor muttered. "The important thing is that this 'Shiva Option' offers an advantage we can exploit, at least in systems where there are enough Bugs available to kill."

"If Uaaria and Chung are correct, there are only a few such systems—the home hives. But once we take those systems, the war is effectively over."

"And now we've taken out two of the five." MacGregor finished LeBlanc's thought for him. "That *has* to hurt them. It has to have an effect on their war-fighting capability."

For a moment, all three were silent, each with his or her own thoughts. To his surprised irritation, LeBlanc found himself contemplating the fact that he and MacGregor had both used that sanitized bit of militarese "take out" for the extermination of an entire system population. *Well, why not?* he thought defensively. *Does a word like "population" even apply to a lifeform like the Bugs?*

"You know," he said, hesitantly but audibly, "this is the first time in history that genocide has been used as a means to a tactical end."

"Exterminating Bugs is no more 'genocide' than eradicating any other vermin, or wiping out disease bacteria with an antibiotic!" MacGregor declared, echoing LeBlanc's own earlier thoughts but without his faint ambivalence.

"In any event," Kthaara put in firmly, "General Directive Eighteen disposes of all such considerations, as far as we are concerned.

Our rulers—your Federation and my Khan—have decreed the extirpation of the Arachnid species. By carrying out their command, we satisfy our honor as well as fulfilling our duty. If we can do so in such a way as to give us a tactical advantage, so much the better. And Fang Presssscott's campaign has brought our ultimate objective measurably closer."

"And I'm firmly convinced that the operation's next phase will bring it even closer," MacGregor declared. Sanders' report had, of course, also included Prescott's daring plan for a two-pronged offensive by himself and Zhaarnak.

"So you have no inclination to disapprove Fang Presssscott's plan?"

"Of course not! Quite aside from the fact that Prescott's achievements put him in a special class, the Federation has always had a tradition of giving its admirals wide latitude in fighting wars on the frontier."

"If it didn't," LeBlanc interjected, "there probably wouldn't *be* a Federation by now. Nobody can micro-manage military operations across interstellar distances, as much as certain politicians wish they could." *And some senior admirals*, he added mentally, but decided no useful purpose would be served by voicing the thought.

"That's not to say there aren't causes for concern in Sanders' report," MacGregor cautioned. "One is the condition of Task Force 71's strikegroups. Superficially, they look good: Fang Zhaarnak took enough replacements out there to fill all the carrier capacity Prescott has left. But those replacement pilots are green, while Prescott's suffered heavy losses among his more senior people. He's got lieutenants commanding entire squadrons of newbies!"

"I am sure he took those matters into account when assessing his task force's ability to carry out the operation." Kthaara sounded serene.

"A more fundamental worry is the Bugs' tactics, as Prescott's people have observed them," LeBlanc put in. "Especially the number of gunboats and assault shuttles employed in the kamikaze role. It appears that the Bugs have hit on the most cost-effective approach to system defense, given their total disregard for the lives of their own personnel."

"But," MacGregor protested, "it requires *vast* numbers. I thought you agreed with Captain Chung and Small Claw Uaaria that the Bugs are beginning to feel the economic pinch."

"I do, Sir. But that doesn't mean they can't continue to produce loto of kamikazes. Lots and *lots* of kamikazes. By a conservative estimate, they can turn out almost fifty squadrons of gunboats for the price of a single *Awesome*-class monitor! Not to mention the fact that it takes almost three years to build a replacement monitor and only about two *months* to build a replacement gunboat. From every perspective, that makes them a much more readily replenished combat resource. And while assault shuttles are a little more expensive than that, they can be built even more rapidly than gunboats, and they're also more lethal in the suicide role. That's especially true when they're being used in the large numbers Prescott has faced—the 'Bughouse Swarm,' as Captain Chung's dubbed it."

"And," Kthaara continued, "Fang Presssscott's experience with this tactic over the last few months has enabled him to devise counter-tactics, has it not? Cub Saaanderzzz' report indicates as much."

"Well . . . yes." MacGregor paid out the admission as grudgingly as stereotype held that her ancestors had paid out shillings. LeBlanc nodded in cautious agreement.

"Very well. In view of all these factors, and of the gradually widening technological gap between us and Bugs, I think it is time for us to rise above our engrained skepticism and consider the possibility that we may have reason to be confident of ultimate victory."

Silence descended once again. Neither of the humans had wished to tempt fate by uttering those particular words. But now the famously unsuperstitious Kthaara had done it for them, and there was something almost frightening about his daring.

"I believe you're right, Sir," LeBlanc ventured. "I also believe we have a long way to go . . . and that the price will be high." Once again the green spark representing Zephrain caught his eye, and he thought of who might be part of that price. "Horribly high."

"I had no wish to imply otherwise, Ahhdmiraaaal LeBlaaanc. In the words of one of the two or three politicians in Human history for whom my old *vilkshatha* brother had any respect, this is not the beginning of the end. It is, at most, the end of the beginning."

# CHAPTER FOURTEEN
## Familiar Space

From El Dorado, Raymond Prescott cautiously probed Home Hive One with recon drones. They confirmed that the Bugs hadn't located the closed warp point—and, indeed, had evidently given up trying to find it, for all their starships were gone. All that marred the system's lifelessness were the thirty-five immobile fortresses, attended by forty-two heavy cruisers, that guarded each of the five open warp points.

Only when he'd assured himself of that did Prescott lead his smaller but battle-hardened task force back into the system where they'd fought so hard before. And, in the absence of any data as to where the open warp points led, he'd picked one of them at random to begin his work of destruction.

None of the warp point defense forces individually possessed the power to seriously inconvenience him. So he smothered that first one under an avalanche of firepower, sent recon drones to peer at what lay on the far side of the warp point, and then moved on to the next one.

They'd repeated the process there, and were still just outside the second warp point's newly acquired nimbus of debris, when Amos Chung approached Prescott on the flag bridge.

"Ah, Amos, have you analyzed the RD2s' findings?" Prescott was as courteous as everyone expected of him, but there was no concealing his impatience to have done with this warp point and proceed to the third one.

"Yes, Sir. The star at the other end of the warp line is a blue giant."

"Hmmm." The relationship between the warp phenomenon and gravity was still imperfectly understood. But it was a fact that massive stars were more likely to have warp points, and to have them in greater numbers, than were less massive ones. (Nobody had been traveling the warp network long enough to answer the interesting question of what happened to those warp points when such a star attained its not too remote destiny and went super-nova.) Thus, blue giants were less rare in the universe familiar to spacefarers than they were in the universe at large, where they constituted only a small fraction of one percent of all stars. And this was no astrophysical research expedition.

"No planets, of course," Prescott thought aloud. There never were.

"No, Sir."

"Very well, then. I think we can—" The spook's tightly con-trolled expression brought Prescott to halt. "Is there something else you want to tell me about that star?"

"Yes, Sir. As you know, the computer's programmed to auto-matically check these RD2 readings against all the systems in its database—which means all the systems the members of the Grand Alliance have on file. It's a rather simple job for a computer, despite the sheer number of such systems."

"No doubt."

"Now, no two stars are really identical, even if they belong to the same spectral class. Each one has a uniquely individual—"

"I'm not altogether unacquainted with these matters, Amos."

"Uh . . . of course not, Sir. Well, Sir, the point is . . . *it's Pest-house, Sir!*"

A moment of dead silence passed. When Prescott finally spoke, he didn't waste air by asking Chung if he was sure.

"Are you aware of the implications of what you've just said, Amos?" he asked instead, very carefully.

"I believe so, Sir." Chung sounded more assured now that he'd finally blurted it out. He handed Prescott a datachip. "In fact, I've taken the liberty of preparing a flat-screen representation of those implications."

Prescott inserted the chip into a slot in the arm of his com-mand chair. The small screen that extended from the arm came to life, showing the Prescott Chain and the hypothesized Home Hive One/AP-5 chain that paralleled it. Everyone in Seventh Fleet's command structure had become completely familiar with that. But now a new warp line extruded itself from Home Hive One to Pesthouse. As Prescott watched, a warp chain grew from the latter system—the Anderson Chain, as Ivan Antonov had dubbed it as he'd advanced along it to his death. Like a living organism, it grew through four systems, warp connection after warp connection. Then it reached the fifth system: Alpha Centauri. From there, eight other strings of light pushed out, one to Sol and the others to as much of the Terran Federation as the little screen had room to show.

"So," Prescott said, as much to himself as to Chung, "for the first time in this war, we've 'closed the circle'—traced a chain of warp connections from the Federation all the way through Bug space to another Federation system."

"Yes, Sir—and that Federation system's Alpha Centauri itself!" Chung's excitement was now on full display. "Uh, shall we . . . that is, shall I inform Commodore Mandagalla—?"

"No. I know what you're thinking, Amos. But I have no intention of rushing back into Pesthouse just because we can. As you'll recall, the Bug forces that ambushed Admiral Antonov in that system converged from several directions. I have no desire to be trapped the same way. So for now we'll continue to execute our original plan, as Fang Zhaarnak is expecting. In the meantime, though, I want you to do two things."

"Sir?"

"First of all, prepare a full report for dispatch to AP-5 without delay. I imagine Lieutenant Sanders and his boss will find it very interesting." Prescott's eyes traced the glowing string-light of the Anderson Chain to Anderson One, where massive Bug forces stood in deadlocked confrontation at the warp point leading to Alpha Centauri. "Very interesting indeed."

"Yes, Sir. I would think so."

"And secondly, I want you to make these findings generally known to the task force's personnel." Prescott raised a hand as Chung started to open his mouth. "I think we can disregard need-to-know considerations just this once, Amos. These people—the people who smashed Home Hive One—have a *right* to know. Oh, and don't bother spelling out the fact that one of the Bug forces that trapped Second Fleet must certainly have come from Home Hive One. They'll have no trouble figuring that out for themselves."

All at once, Chung understood. And a feeling of deep, grim satisfaction—a feeling of having partially avenged Ivan Antonov and the tens of thousands who'd died with him—spread through the Intelligence officer, as it would shortly spread through all of Task Force 71.

"Aye, aye, Sir," he said quietly.

They were *en route* from what everyone was now calling the "Pesthouse Warp Point" to the next stop on their itinerary of destruction when the wide-ranging, carefully cloaked scouts flashed the report Prescott had been waiting to hear.

He called an informal conference of the operational "core" staff—Mandagalla, Bichet, Landrum, Chung, and Ruiz—on the flag bridge, with the task group commanders in attendance by com screen. It wasn't the most convenient possible way to do things, but it *was* the only way to exclude Mukerji. Prescott still wasn't sure why he'd let Sanders talk him into accepting a fulsome apology and dropping all charges against the political officer. It surely wouldn't stop Mukerji from seeking revenge later. But if the contemptible *chofak* wasn't going to be charged with anything, then logically he had to be returned to his originally assigned duties. Which, unfortunately, meant finding ways to keep him out of the way while the real work got done by the real officers assigned to Seventh Fleet.

He and his staffers stood around the system-scale holo sphere, and gazed at the same display of Home Hive One they'd viewed on their earlier visit—except, of course, that the three innermost planets were no longer keyed as "inhabited." The electronically-present task group COs had the same imagery in their own spheres, and, like Prescott, they were intently focused on the only icons that were truly important now: the ones representing the warp points.

Prescott studied those six icons. They'd been assigned numbers, and the closed warp point through which they'd come was number four. Its icon glowed in splendid isolation in the sphere, six light-hours from the local sun. The open warp point designated as number five was only seventy-two light-minutes from that sun, on a bearing sixty degrees counter clockwise from the closed warp point's. The other four open warp points were rather tightly clustered—as interplanetary space went—in a region between sixty and ninety degrees further clockwise, at distances from three and a half to six light-hours from the sun. Prescott had elected to begin with the latter group, leaving Warp Point Five to be dealt with on his return swing. So far, they'd obliterated the defenses of Warp Point One—the Pesthouse Warp Point—and Two, and were proceeding towards Three.

But everyone's eyes were on the bypassed Warp Point Five, which now flashed balefully on and off with "hostile" scarlet.

"The scouts were able to get fairly detailed readings on the gunboats' simultaneous transits," Chung summarized. "Even after interpenetration losses, there are well over eighteen hundred of them. They're proceeding on an intercept course—courier drones from the Warp Point Five defense force must have kept them up to date on our location. And now the first heavy units are beginning to transit."

None of the staffers, Prescott noted with satisfaction, had gone glassy-eyed at the number of gunboats racing toward them. After the last few months, such figures were no longer shocking.

"Well," Bichet observed to the meeting at large, "now we know which warp point leads to AP-5."

"And," Landrum added, "we can let Fang Zhaarnak know we've drawn the Bugs here as planned."

"That conclusion," Prescott said quietly, but very firmly, "and that course of action, are both premature, gentlemen. Until the Bug capital ships complete transit, we'll be in no position to positively identify them as the force our recon drones observed on the other side of AP-5's closed warp point. For now, we'll concentrate on our immediate concern: the gunboat strike now converging on us."

"Yes, Sir," the ops officer and the *farshathkhanaak* murmured in crestfallen unison.

"One poinnnt on that sssubject, Admiral," an Ophiuchi voice said in Standard English from one of the com screens. To anyone familiar with his race, Admiral Raathaarn's discomfort was obvious. "I realizzzze our tacticallll doctrinnnne hasss allllready been disssssscussed. But—"

"Yes, Admiral, it has," Prescott cut him off. He had no desire to be rude, but he knew he had to put his foot down. "I'm well aware that the Ophiuchi Association's fighter pilots are willing—no, eager—to uphold their matchless reputation and be in the forefront of the coming battle. But it's precisely because of the *Corthohardaa's* acknowledged preeminence that I must withhold them to deal with any kamikaze assault shuttles the Bugs may try to sneak past our defenses while our Terran and Orion fighters are occupied with the gunboats. We simply cannot afford to let anything as heavily loaded with antimatter as a shuttle kamikaze slip through, and unlike gunboats, shuttles can't be engaged with standard antistarship weapons. That's why we're going to adhere to the plan as already framed. We'll keep the range open as they approach, and deal with them at long range with a combination of fighters and second-generation close-assault missiles."

He half-worried that he might be laying it on a little too thick, since the Ophiuchi were undoubtedly the least militant members of the Grand Alliance. They had no true organized military tradition of their own, in fact, which was why they'd adopted the rank structure—and even the Standard English rank titles—of their Terran allies during the Second Interstellar War. But if there was one thing which could turn even the cosmopolitan, pacific Ophiuchi into fire breathers, it was their pride in their strikefighter pilots' prowess. The *Corthohardaa*, or "Space Brothers," were one of only two bodies within the Ophiuchi Association's military who had a special, distinguishing badge: the stylized *Hasfrazi* head which the Terrans called the "Screaming Eagle." (The other branch to be so distinguished was the *Dahanaak*, or "Talon Strike," units, the equivalent of the Federation's Marine Raiders, whose emblem was a stylized representation of an attacking assault shuttle.) It was a standing joke among their Terran allies that the *Corthohardaa* were downright Tabby-like in their combativeness and sense of invincibility. Not even the *Taainohk*—the "Four Virtues"—which formed the basis of the Ophiuchi's characteristically dispassionate philosophy seemed able to temper it.

Or perhaps the *Taainohk* actually *explained* it, the admiral reflected. *Queemharda*, the first leg of the *Taainohk* required an Ophiuchi to truly know himself, to know both his strengths and his weaknesses. *Naraham* required him to develop a detached ability to stand aside from all distractions in the pursuit of the other virtues, while *quurhok*, or "place knowing," required each individual to recognize and fulfill his appointed function in life. And the fourth virtue, *querhomaz*, or "self determination" was the absolute determination to achieve *qurrhok*. So given the fact that the Ophiuchi were the best natural strikefighter pilots in the known galaxy, perhaps it was not only natural but inevitable that the *Corthohardaa* should—to paraphrase the TFN's human fighter jocks—all insist that they had "great *big* brass ones."

There were times when that could be a very useful thing. There were also times when the Ophiuchi urge to demonstrate their prowess could be a decided pain in the ass, and this had the definite potential to be one of them.

Prescott regarded Raathaarn for a moment, decided that the

hammer he was using was about the right size, and turned to his logistics officer for the clincher.

"Commander Ruiz, I believe our stocks of SBMHAWK4s armed with CAM2 are still adequate?"

"Yes, Sir," Sandy Ruiz replied confidently. "The *Wayfarers* have an ample supply on board." Most of the freighters of Seventh Fleet's fleet train were still in AP-5 with Zhaarnak, but Prescott had brought along the *Wayfarers*, built on battlecruiser hulls and intended to keep up with survey flotillas, as ammunition ships.

"Very good. And your Ophiuchi fighter pilots, Admiral Raathaarn, will be our last line of defense against any gunboats that get through everything else." Raathaarn looked slightly mollified. "So now, let's get down to details. . . ."

The image of the strikegroup's briefing officer faded from the holo stage of VF-94's ready room. Irma Sanchez stood up and faced her five pilots.

To the left was Anton Meswami, now her executive officer. She still had trouble thinking of that title in connection with the j.g. and not spluttering with laughter. But then she looked at the four replacements, and by comparison it became almost believable.

*Jesus!* she thought. *Thank God I was never that young!*

*And now I suppose I have to say something.*

"All right. You heard the man. The task force is going to turn away and send us and the Tabbies in to intercept the gunboats. We'll have some support in the form of SBMHAWKs with CAM2 packages. But it'll be mostly up to us. That's the plan because the people who have all the facts know that we can do it."

An uncertain murmur ran through the ready room.

*What's the matter? Isn't that the kind of thing the Skipper would have said?*

*But I keep forgetting: I'm the Skipper. The only one these kids have ever known.*

*So I'll have to be myself.*

"You've probably all heard the jokes going around," she resumed in a more conversational tone of voice. "Like the one about how they've had to add potty training to the curriculum at Brisbane."

The laughter was uncertain, with an undercurrent of resentment. But the miasma of unfocused fear was suddenly gone.

"Yeah," she continued. "All the lifers in this strikegroup—to say nothing of all the ship's company pricks on this goddamned fat-assed monitor—think you people are a big joke. And you know what? They think *I'm* a joke, too—that I haven't got any more business commanding the squadron than you've got being in one. They think VF-94's idea of flying in formation is two of us going in the same direction on the same day!"

All the uncertainty was gone, and the resentment had come fully into its own, but with no sullenness about it. Their laughter was as real as their anger.

"Well, it happens that I know better. We had a chance to train together back in AP-5, and I know what you can do, green as you are. And now, we're going to prove it to everybody. We're going to prove it by killing so many Bugs that they'll have to take us seriously. And we're going to come back from all that Bugs-killing alive, because we're going to do it the *Navy* way, by the numbers." *My God, is this me talking?* she wondered with a small part of her mind. "Is that clear?"

"Yes, Sir," they chorused.

"What's that? I can't hear you."

It wouldn't have played with people who'd been around a while. But these pilots weren't far removed from OCS.

"Yes, SIR!"

Irma leaned forward to face Ensign Davra Lennart, who'd had some problems keeping up with rapidly changing tactical configurations.

"Ensign, do you think you're up to it?"

"I . . . I think so, Sir," Lennart said, and Irma smiled.

"I understand Sergeant Kelso is still at Brisbane, Ensign," she said, and Lennart's eyes grew round.

"You mean she was there way back when *you* were, Sir?"

"Hell, they built the place around her! Yeah, she was my drill instructor, too. And I'll bet I can guess what she used to tell you: 'Lennart, when I give the command 'About face,' I want to hear your pussy *snap!*' "

It wasn't really much of a guess, as Irma merely had to substitute the name. But Lennart's jaw dropped, and the gales of laughter swept the last vestiges of tension from the ready room. Irma let the guffaws die down, then spoke seriously.

"Well, that's all behind you now. Out here, all that counts is doing the job. And I know you can all do it. You can do it because you have the training, because you have the motivation, and because if any one of you doesn't do it, I'll personally tear him or her a new asshole.

"Now, let's suit up!"

*Sorry, Skipper . . . Bruno, I mean,* Irma thought as the ready room emptied. *I know that wasn't the way you would have done it. But I had to do it any way I could—any way that will make VF-94 live up to your memory today.*

Prescott kept his expression one of calm satisfaction as he read the final tally. He hoped none of his staffers had heard his long, relieved sigh.

The fighters had done better than he'd let himself hope. They'd knifed into a gunboat wave that dwarfed those they'd faced four months earlier in AP-5, and killed and killed and gone on killing. Behind them had been the waves of SBMHAWK4 pods with their loads of CAM2s. Little more than two hundred of the gunboats had gotten through that outer barrier—only to be blasted apart by the short-range fire of still more CAM2s, this time from the capital ships' external ordnance racks, as they entered the inner defensive envelope.

The close assault missiles were the capital missile-sized equivalent of a sprint-mode standard missile—a weapon which streaked in at velocities too high for point defense to engage it effectively. Like a normal capital missile, it carried a significantly heavier warhead than missiles fired from lesser launchers, and it also had a longer effective range than standard sprint-mode missiles. It had originally been designed as a means to give capital missile-armed warships, like the TFN's *Dunkerque*-class battlecruisers, a weapon to use in close-in combat. Once it was available, it hadn't taken long for the Navy to recognize the increased effectiveness which an interception-proof missile could provide for its standard SBMHAWK pods, and the combination had proved deadly to any defending unit in close proximity to a warp point. The use of SBMHAWK pods under shipboard fire control was also one way to permit battle-line units to lay down heavy volumes of missile fire on incoming gunboat waves at extended range, and the CAM2's ability to pierce even starships' point defense like an awl made it an ideal gunboat-killer.

Fifteen gunboats had lasted long enough to perform the horribly familiar FRAM ripple-launch, followed by a suicide run. They'd taken TFNS *Banshee* with them, which hurt. But no other ship had suffered more than superficial damage, if that.

"Your fighter pilots did very well, Commodore Landrum," he said formally. "Including the young, inexperienced ones."

"Thank you, Admiral. I'll convey that to the CSGs, if I may."

"By all means." Prescott turned to the holo display, now set on system scale. He gave a command, and it zoomed in on Warp Point Five and the array of scarlet icons deploying slowly away from it in support of the fortresses. "It's possible, ladies and gentlemen, that the Bugs don't consider the gunboat strike to have been a total waste."

"Sir?" Mandagalla sounded puzzled. "I realize that they think of gunboats—and their crews—as expendable pawns. But eighteen hundred of them certainly outweigh *Banshee* and our fighter losses."

"We also had to expend more depletable ordnance that I would have liked," Sandy Ruiz mumbled with the pessimism that went with a logistics officer's billet.

"All true," Prescott acknowledged. "But I suspect that the main objective was simply to keep us occupied while the heavy forces completed their transit into the system. If that's true, they've succeeded."

No one remarked on the mind-set behind such a sacrifice for such an objective. They'd all been fighting Bugs so long that it was no longer a subject for shock, or even for comment.

"But," Prescott continued, "we've also achieved an objective. Amos, am I correct in supposing you've positively identified these hostiles as belonging to the forces facing Fang Zhaarnak?"

"You are, Sir," the spook replied, and indicated the icons in the sphere: twenty-five monitors, thirty-two superdreadnoughts, twenty-five battlecruisers. "It's the same strength as the organic mobile force that's been shuttling back and forth between this system and AP-5 since the start of the campaign. Analysis of the exact mix of ship classes confirms it."

"Very well. We'll dispatch an ICN message immediately to inform Fang Zhaarnak that we've succeeded in drawing away part of his opposition, and ordering him to commence his offensive."

"In the meantime, Sir," Bichet inquired, "shall we advance toward Warp Point Five?"

"Why should we, Jacques?" Prescott asked with a smile. "I'm in no hurry to engage them. The longer we can put off an engagement, the longer we keep them tied down in this system. Furthermore, it would be to our advantage to draw them out to engage us, away from the support of the Warp Point Five fortresses."

The staffers exchanged glances which contained several emotions, of which the uppermost was relief. Not that they'd dreaded

seeking battle—that was a formidable Bug force, but over the
past eight months they, along with the rest of TF 71, had gained
an absolute confidence in themselves and their commander. No,
their feelings concerned that commander himself. They hadn't
been certain Raymond Prescott was psychologically able to forego
an opportunity to seek battle with his brother's killers, however
advantageous such restraint might be.

Prescott read their thoughts, and he smiled again.

"Rest assured, ladies and gentlemen, I have no intention of
waiting passively. As you may recall, we have unfinished business
in this system."

"The *other* warp point defenses, Admiral?" Mandagalla queried.

"Precisely. We were, I believe, *en route* to Warp Point Three
before the recent attack. I believe we can now resume our interrupted schedule."

*It was intolerable. The Enemy was simply continuing the oblit-
eration of the other warp point fortresses, ignoring the Mobile
Force altogether. This placed the burden on the Fleet to either
take action or remain in the role of a mere spectator to the
destruction.*

*Fortunately, the Mobile Force could draw on the gunboat and
small-craft reserves of the systems along the chain through which
it had passed. That provided sufficient assets to constitute as many
as three suicide formations, each theoretically capable of dealing
with these Enemies.*

*So the Mobile Force refused to let itself be lured away from the
warp point through which it had emerged. Instead, it would send
those formations to pursue the Enemy wherever he might roam in
the system.*

"They would have been smarter to combine all their gunboats
and pinnaces into one irresistible force at the outset, Sir," Stephen
Landrum opined.

Prescott nodded in agreement. The kamikaze formations—or
what was left of them—were belatedly doing just that. He and the
*farshathkhanaak* were gazing into the holo sphere and watching
three red icons crawl together and merge.

The Bugs' idea, Amos Chung speculated, had been for the
three swarms of deadly midges to herd TF 71 away from the
remaining warp point defenses and toward the waiting jaws of

the heavy units at Warp Point Five. If so, it hadn't worked.
Prescott had adroitly maneuvered away from them to prolong
the chase, keeping his battle-line out of reach while sending
long-range fighter strikes to repeatedly savage his pursuers.
He'd whittled their strength down by as much as two-thirds
while giving his fighter pilots more experience at this kind of
combat.

But now they'd finally gotten wise. . . .

Prescott straightened up suddenly.

"I believe it's time to let them catch us," he told Landrum. "They
can probably do so anyway, now that they're going to concentrate
on it single-mindedly."

"You mean, Sir—?"

"Yes. Fang Zhaarnak's acknowledgment arrived just a little while
ago. In real-time, he's about to launch his attack." Prescott turned
matter-of-fact. "Our tactical doctrine will be unchanged. Please
call the rest of the staff."

"Aye, aye, Sir." Landrum started to turn away, then paused.
"Uh, Admiral, despite their losses, that's a more formidable force
of kamikazes than the one that hit us last time. Our fighters are
going to sustain more losses—and more of them are going to get
through to hit our ships."

"I realize that, Steve. But that's unavoidable. And . . . every
gunboat we destroy here is one less gunboat Lord Telmasa will
face."

# CHAPTER FIFTEEN
## ". . . and I'll take
## the low road."

Zhaarnak'telmasa exploded out of AP-5 behind a storm front of SBMHAWKs and SRHAWKs.

His most recent flights of RD2s had confirmed his *vilkshatha* brother's inference: one of the two mobile forces in the system had departed and now confronted TF 71 in Home Hive One. So TF 72 faced only (!) the second one—twenty monitors, sixty-seven superdreadnoughts, thirty-six battlecruisers, and seventy-five light cruisers—and by now the Bugs had learned to keep their starships well back from warp points that could suddenly belch forth torrents of SBMHAWKs. But the fixed warp point defenses were still very much in place: twenty-four massive orbital fortresses covered by two thousand laser-armed deep space buoys, shielded by four thousand patterns of mines and hiding amid six hundred ECM buoys. Zhaarnak intended to scorch the warp point's surrounding space clean of those defenses as though with a giant blow torch.

He had a new tool for the scorching. This was to be the debut of the new HARM2—an SBMHAWK-carried homing antiradiation missile. In addition to its SBMHAWK capability, it was able to home in on the later generation deception-mode ECM emissions as well as fire confusion ones. Everyone hoped it would be the answer to the clouds of ECM buoys the Bugs loved to deploy around warp points.

As *Hia'khan* emerged from the warp point into the maelstrom, a flood of data began to pour in from the ships of the initial waves that had preceded the flagship—mostly assault carriers and Gorm *Toragon*-class gunboat-bearing monitors. Kevin Sanders took a moment to glance across the flag bridge at Zhaarnak, who was stroking his whiskers with a smooth, almost caressing motion.

"Unless I'm mistaken, that's a look of great satisfaction," he murmured to Uaaria.

"So it is," the female Orion spook agreed. "He is observing the success rate of the HARM2 against the third-generation ECM buoys. He has a keen personal interest in the matter."

All at once, Sanders remembered the "April Fool" offensive Zhaarnak had led out of Zephrain. He also remembered that Orions did not enjoy embarrassment.

"Yes, I can see how those buoys might be rather a sore subject with him."

Uaaria gave him a quelling, slit-pupiled glare, and he hastily resumed his study of the data. Zhaarnak had assumed that the Bug capital ships wouldn't be sitting atop the warp point. Hence the composition of his first waves, which were now advancing sunward through the rapidly dissipating debris of the fortresses. Those monitors and CVAs, with their gunboats and fighters, were intended to counter the kamikaze gunboats and small craft that could be expected, sooner rather than later. So far, the Fifteenth Fang's predictions were proving out.

Sanders turned his attention to the system display.

Their warp point of entry lay five light-hours from the yellow Sol-like primary. The RD2s had detected only one other fortress-cluster of the precise composition that the Bugs—consistent to a fault—assigned to warp point defense. That consistency, Sanders reflected, certainly simplified the choice of where to go next. Unfortunately, that warp point was even further from the local sun than this one . . . and on a diametrically opposite bearing.

Between the two warp points, the inner planets warmed themselves around the hearth of the primary. One of them, Planet III, was life-bearing. From its energy emissions as reported by the RD2s, Uaaria and her subordinates had inferred a medium-sized population of no more than a few hundred million. This, clearly, was no home hive system. A colony, no doubt. Maybe a relatively new one, given the Bugs' propensity for multiplying up to the kind of ugly limits once prophesied by Malthus, who'd underestimated humankind's blessed disinclination to carry *anything* to its ultimate logical conclusion.

At any rate, even if there weren't tens of billions of Bugs here, there were Bugs. Acting on General Directive Eighteen and his own inclinations alike, Zhaarnak ordered the task force to shape a course for the inhabited planet.

Waves of gunboats and small craft began their suicidal attacks—if a word like "suicidal" was really applicable to a race with no sense of individual self preservation. Losses began to mount.

And yet . . .

Sanders had begun to notice it himself just before Zhaarnak stalked over to the intelligence station.

"Their capital ships are refusing battle," the Orion stated, leaving implicit his demand for an explanation.

"Yes, Sir," Uaaria acknowledged. "They are drawing back, keeping out of range, sending in their suicide craft." She gestured at the tactical display, from whose outer margin yet another swarm of tiny hostile icons was sweeping inward. "From the numbers of gunboats and small craft we are encountering, I gather that few such have been withdrawn from the system. Perhaps they think they do not need to commit their battle-line."

Zhaarnak made a dismissive gesture.

"Nevertheless, there is a Bahg-inhabited planet in this system. It is unheard of for them to restrict themselves to standoff suicide attacks when such a world is threatened."

Uaaria and Sanders exchanged glances. Neither had any answer.

*It was true. There was no possible doubt.*

*The system that had dispatched the Mobile Force—the most powerful of all the Systems Which Must Be Defended—had flatly refused to send any additional units to reinforce it.*

*It was unprecedented. It was an affront to the natural order of things. But it was also true.*

*No explanation had been offered, of course. But none had been needed. The entire Fleet knew that the long-accumulated Reserve had become dangerously depleted. This war had dragged on far longer than the Planners had ever contemplated, and the expense of sustaining it now had to be borne by only three Systems Which Must Be Defended, rather than the original five. Under these circumstances, the losses during the course of the present campaign had stretched to the limit even the massive Fleet which had been built up against the inevitable future meeting with the Old Enemies—the Old Enemies who had now reappeared (fortunately unbeknownst to*

these New Enemies) and placed yet another burden on the already
overextended resources of the Systems Which Must Be Defended.

It was easy to recall the Old Enemies here in Franos, for one of
this system's four warp points led to Telik, where the Fleet's advance
against those Enemies had halted so long ago. It had halted for
want of anywhere else to go. A closed warp point, of course. The
Old Enemies had managed to conceal its location as they pulled
out of Telik, and that had been the end of the Fleet's first war with
them. And that potential avenue of attack had, so far, remained
quiescent in the present war.

But these recollections were irrelevant to the present problem:
the stark reality that the Mobile Force was on its own, and could
expect no help in defending this warp chain, with its five systems
and three inhabited worlds.

Nor was that the worst of it. The Enemy was advancing inexorably
towards this system's colonized planet. Even if the Mobile Force drew
back into the envelope of that planet's orbital and surface-based
defenses, it might not be able to stop the attackers before they seared
the surface with antimatter fire, especially if they made that their
primary objective. And then . . . This was no World Which Must Be
Defended, but there was no guarantee that the sudden annihilation
of its population or a large percentage thereof would not have the
kind of effects that had now been observed repeatedly. Precisely
where the numerical threshold lay was, as yet, unknown.

The Mobile Force dared not run the risk of being left in a helpless state of stunned disorientation, to be disposed of at the Enemy's
leisure. Then there would be nothing left to defend Franos, for
the other Mobile Force was tied down in what had once been a
System Which Must Be Defended, securing the other end of this
warp chain.

No. From every standpoint, the indicated course of action was to
withdraw, leaving the local defenses to take as high a toll as possible
and preserving the Mobile Force to protect Franos. This system's
population was smaller than either of the two inhabited worlds
further along the chain. And it was, of course, expendable.

It would have been hard to say whether Kevin Sanders or
Uaaria'salath-ahn looked more exhausted after the endless, running battle that had snarled its way across the system.

Aboard a Terran warship, Sanders would have been in a vacsuit,
but the Tabbies were a bit less compulsive about such things.
*Hia'khan's* flag deck was at the very center of her stupendous

hull, and any damage which got through to it—particularly in the absence of any primary beam-threat—would have to virtually dismantle the entire ship first. Under the circumstances, the officers on that flag deck had decided, the efficiency-enhancing advantages of working in a "shirt sleeve" environment outweighed the risk of being killed by sudden depressurization.

The lieutenant harbored a few doubts about that particular line of logic, but he had to admit that it did have a tendency to reduce crew fatigue under normal circumstances. Of course, these circumstances were scarcely "normal," and his usual spruceness had disappeared into a discarded uniform tunic, a loosened blouse collar, shoulders that sagged, knees that had lost their spring, and hair that had taken on an undeniably oily look. None of the Orions on the flag deck seemed to have noticed when he shed his tunic—not surprising, perhaps, given the fact that none of them wore clothing at all, except in hostile environment conditions.

Even if she'd noticed, however, Uaaria wouldn't have commented on his disheveled state, for she shared it to the full. Orions, as a species, were even more fastidious about their personal grooming than the terrestrial cats which they so reminded humans of, and Uaaria was more fastidious than most. But now patches of her plushy fur were plastered with sweat, her whiskers drooped, and the usual natural musky scent which clung to her—and which Sanders normally found rather appealing, in a primal sort of way—had become something much stronger.

But he paid no more attention to her haggardness than she paid to his, for their attention was concentrated solely on the system-scale holo display at the flag bridge's intelligence station as they watched the icon of the Bug battle-line.

"They're really doing it," the human breathed as they watched that icon move past the inhabited planet, not stopping to close ranks with the planet's defenders but proceeding without a pause on a course for the warp point on the far side of the yellow sun.

"They are withdrawing," Uaaria said unnecessarily. "I never believed they would simply leave that planet to its fate."

"But not, unfortunately, defenseless."

The two intelligence officers started at the voice. Zhaarnak was standing behind them, looking over their shoulders at the display. His own matted, disheveled fur would have been shocking to anyone who knew the Orion obsession with staying well groomed—unless that person also knew what he'd been through as his task force had moved inward.

The Bug ships had moved with them, but well ahead, keeping the range open and sending wave after wave of kamikazes back to lash the task force. The need to reverse the vector of the ships that launched them meant little to gunboats and small craft with reactionless drives. And the rapidly widening gulf between them and their motherships meant even less, for theirs were one-way missions. They'd targeted the monitors and assault carriers, Zhaarnak's most valuable ships, but also the ones most capable of defending themselves and absorbing damage. The months of waiting in AP-5 had allowed the Orion fighter pilots and Gorm gunboat crews to assimilate the lessons in anti-kamikaze tactics that Raymond Prescott's task force had paid such a high tuition to learn, and now they put those lessons to use. Still, losses had mounted steadily, and everyone had expected the Bug starships to turn and fight at any time, or at least to stand at bay near Planet III and add their firepower to its fixed defenses.

But now those starships were receding sunward and beyond, on course for the warp point through which they would exit this system. Task Force 72, momentarily without the suicidal swarms that had tormented it so long, approached Planet III.

And Zhaarnak had spoken the truth. That planet's titanic space station loomed amid an array of seventeen monitor-sized orbital fortresses. And on the surface, sensor data indicated the presence of six vast installations, mostly buried but extruding the launch ramps for four hundred gunboats and a hundred pinnaces each through the planet's crust. Already, new waves of kamikazes were on their way to take up where those of the mobile force had left off.

Zhaarnak watched stolidly as his fighters wore those waves down. Even as *Hia'khan* came under attack, he remained expressionless, watching his ships take the losses that had to be expected from the ones that got through. By the time it was all over, that toll had risen to five monitors, seven superdreadnoughts, and two Gorm assault carriers. Many other ships had taken hits, though in most cases (including the flagship) the damage wasn't serious.

The Fifteenth Fang turned away from the screen on which the carnage was tallied. He activated an intercom speaker near the intelligence station and spoke to his chief of staff, still at the auxiliary control station he'd occupied since general quarters had been sounded.

"Rearm the fighters," he ordered without preamble. "The standard mix of FRAMs and ECM packages for planetary assault."

"'Planetary assault,' Fang?" Uaaria ventured after he'd received acknowledgment and turned back to the intelligence displays. She indicated the tactical one, in which the icons of the orbital fortresses still glowed inviolate. "What about those?"

"They can wait, Small Claw. The fighters will bypass them, covered by ECM, and blanket the planet's surface with antimatter warheads."

To Sanders, Zhaarnak's tone, mild though it was, suggested that he didn't particularly desire further discussion. Uaaria, however, was an Orion, and Federation naval officers had been astonished many times since their first experiences with the Tabbies, by the—to humans—extreme freedom junior officers enjoyed in speaking their minds to their superiors. Some Terran observers were astonished that the prickly, honor-conscious, duel-fighting Orions could possibly tolerate such a situation.

Sanders, who'd seen more of Tabby interaction on this voyage than most humans saw in a lifetime, thought he'd figured out how it worked. In the end, it all went back to the honor concepts which were so central to all Orion life and to that unique bond whose manifold facets the Tabbies subsumed under the word *farshatok*. The chain of command and the deference patterns of a society which was hierarchical—indeed, feudal, in human terms—were as inflexible as iron, yet they enshrined a complex, interlocking weave of responsibilities, rights, and obligations between commander and commanded. To the Orion mind, an officer's subordinates could no more be denied the right to offer their own viewpoints for his consideration than a hand could survive without its fingers.

And so Uaaria faced the second in command of Seventh Fleet and said, "Fang, I understand your intention. But I can offer no assurance that the Bahg population here is large enough for its destruction to produce the effect you desire."

"You have not been asked to, Small Claw. We will determine the answer experimentally. We need to know whether that which the Humans have dubbed the 'Shiiivaaa Option' is, in fact, an option at all in systems less heavily populated than the home hives. That is one reason I am proceeding as I am—the other being that I would rather deal with those fortresses *after* their crews have been reduced to a state of psychic shock, if it is possible to do so."

This time, Zhaarnak's tone made it clear that the subject was closed. And just as the *farshotak* relationship gave Uaaria both the right and the responsibility to caution her commander even when he didn't wish to be cautioned, so that same relationship required her to submit and hold her tongue once the caution had been issued and Zhaarnak had made his decision anyway.

The intelligence officer flicked her ears in a graceful gesture which combined continuing reservations on her part with an acknowledgment of Zhaarnak's right of command and her acceptance of what he'd ordered.

Lord Telmasa gave her an approving glance, as much for having said her say as for having accepted his decision, and returned his attention to the display as the experiment in slaughter began.

The answer wasn't long in coming. The fighters took a certain percentage of losses from the fortresses' fire, despite their ECM cover. But then the FRAMs plunged downward through the planet's atmosphere, and the wavefront of fireballs began to advance across the continents like a forest conflagration, leaving nothing but charred lifelessness . . . and the fortresses' fire slackened, and grew sporadic and wild.

Murmured comments buzzed around the flag bridge. Zhaarnak made no response, letting his body language say he'd known it would work all along and not letting his relief show. Instead, he gave a curt series of orders, and his battle-line began to close in on the fortresses, behind a wall of SBMHAWK4s.

After it was over, Sanders pointed at the icon of the space station, now attended only by drifting wreckage.

"Fang," he said in tones of uncharacteristically diffident inquiry, "do you intend for the capital ships to proceed and deal with that? Or will you order the fighters rearmed?"

"Neither, Cub Saaanderzzz. I do not believe it will be necessary to engage the space station at this time." The young Human's reaction to this stereotype-shattering lack of bloodthirstiness was obvious, and brought a smile to Zhaarnak's face.

"The station has no capacity to project force into deep space," he condescended to explain. "And its shipyards are useless with no planetary population or industrial infrastructure left to furnish raw materials. So I see no reason to risk further losses—especially among our fighters—in reducing it. It can be left to . . . die on the vine, as I believe the Human expression goes."

Abruptly, his mood changed to grimness.

"No—we will wait here only long enough to send our carriers back to AP-4 in relays, to replenish our strikegroups from the stockpiles we have established there, and send a report to

Raaymmonnd'presssssscott-telmasa. As soon as he indicates that the time is right to do so, we will proceed towards this system's other warp point."

"Through which," Uaaria put in quietly, "the last of their starships departed shortly before our planetary strikes began to go in."

"Naturally. They had no other exit from the system. That warp point must lead further along this warp chain. The word of what has happened here will reach the Bahgs at its other end, in Home Hive One, quite possibly before our report gets there. It will be interesting to observe the result."

*The last elements of the Mobile Force had completed transit into the Franos system, and the courier drones were off, bearing the news to the other Mobile Force, three systems away.*

*It wasn't hard to predict the action that would be taken on the basis of that news. It was unavoidable, even if it courted potential disaster.*

*The new attack represented a more immediate threat to Franos than the sparring match at the other end of the warp chain. So the second Mobile Force would pull back one warp transit closer to Franos, even though it would mean giving up the Fleet's presence in the lifeless remains of what had been a System Which Must Be Defended—and the system which was this entire warp chain's only link with the rest of the Fleet. The two Mobile Forces would then be truly on their own.*

*The isolation would not necessarily be permanent, of course. The remaining Systems Which Must Be Defended would undoubtedly organize a counteroffensive as soon as possible, to reopen contact.*

*Still, it was far from an ideal option.*

*But options were becoming more and more limited.*

# CHAPTER SIXTEEN
## Keeping Up the Pressure

"That's the last of them, Admiral."

"Thank you, Jacques," Raymond Prescott acknowledged the ops officer's report courteously, although it hadn't really been necessary. The admiral had watched in his plot as the last of the scarlet icons representing the Bug capital ships he'd expected to have to fight had merged into that of Home Hive One's Warp Point Five, and vanished.

The battle with the belatedly combined flotilla of gunboats and kamikazes could have been worse, though they'd taken the monitors *Amos Huss* and *Torvulk* with them and damaged a number of other ships before the combination of Allied fighters, gunboats, anti-fighter missiles, and CAM2s had blown the last of them to plasma. But then, shortly thereafter, their motherships had begun to exit the system.

"What you think it means, Sir?" Mandagalla asked.

"I think, pending confirmation via the ICN, that Fang Zhaarnak's assault has succeeded. They're pulling this force back so it can be closer to the front he's just opened up—shortening their defensive lines, as it were." Prescott glanced at Chung, and the intelligence officer nodded in agreement.

"Well, Admiral," Bichet ventured, "I suppose this leaves us free to finish what we started."

"Eh?" Prescott looked up from the plot. His attention had been focused on Warp Point Five.

"Wiping out the rest of the system's warp point defenses, Sir," Bichet amplified.

316

"Oh, that." Prescott straightened up. "Yes, I suppose we might as well. We have to remain in the system anyway, while we replenish our fighters. Steve, I want you and Vice Admiral Raathaarn to organize relays of carriers to go back to AP-4 for replacements."

"Aye, aye, Sir."

"And, yes, Jacques, while that's progressing, we can finish sanitizing the system. *But . . .*" Prescott paused for a meaningful eye contact with each of the staffers in turn. "I want one thing clearly understood. The destruction of the warp point fortresses was never anything but a means to the end of drawing part of the Bugs' mobile forces here. In that, it's succeeded. But we must persist with the same strategy of whipsawing the Bugs between this task force and Zhaarnak's, which means it's necessary for us to keep up the pressure on them." He turned to the chief of staff. "Anna, we'll start sending RD2s through Warp Point Five immediately. As soon as our fighter losses have been made good, we'll advance through that warp point."

Mandagalla swallowed.

"Sir, I must point out that we have a number of damaged units—"

"We'll perform as much repair work as possible in the time we have. But to repeat, we *cannot let up*. We must advance without pausing any longer than absolutely necessary. Zhaarnak's relying on it, and he's held up his end of this operation. We have to hold up ours. Do I make myself clear?"

A mumble of assent ran through the staff.

The system beyond Warp Point Five proved to be a distant binary, a K-type orange star and a red dwarf, each with its own small planetary family. The viewscreen in *Riva y Silva*'s flag briefing room was set to show the outside view, and now the light of the primary component flooded the room at second hand.

It was a subdued staff that met in that sullen light.

The battle had been a grim one. It might have had a very different conclusion, but for the way the Bug mobile force had depleted its gunboat and small craft strength in Home Hive One, leaving the capital ships to face Task Force 71 unsupported. But those capital ships, unlike the ones Zhaarnak had faced, had stood and fought. Chung was still setting up and knocking down theories to account for the difference. It was, Prescott suspected, a matter of small import to the crews of the eight capital ships and five carriers who had died in the course of the savage fighting that had snarled across the system for several days.

Fortunately, this system, like the one Zhaarnak had broken into, had held a medium-sized Bug population. So the task force had fought its way grimly in-system from the warp point through which it had come, crossing 5.4 light-hours to the innermost planet. There, while still fending off desperate attacks, Prescott had managed to get a fighter strike through to the planet's surface—with the now dreadfully familiar results. The afterglow of the last antimatter fireballs had still hung in the planet's dead air as the task force turned savagely on the disoriented Bug starships.

Few of those starships had escaped. Those who had, had fled even further sunward to a nearby inner-system warp point, obvious as such from its defenses, an array of fortresses identical to that which the task force's SBMHAWKs had reduced on its way into the system. There they'd vanished into warp transit, leaving Task Force 71 to nurse its wounds and contemplate its next move.

"The message to Fang Zhaarnak has been dispatched, Admiral," Mandagalla reported. "And our emergency repairs are proceeding."

"Good." Prescott turned to Chung. "Amos, have you had a chance to study the probe returns from Warp Point Three?"

Sending those RD2s through had been Prescott's first order of business after the battle. As in Home Hive One, they'd assigned numbers to the system's warp points. The one through which they'd come was number one; number two was the inner-system warp point through which the tatters of the Bug mobile force had departed. RD2s had ventured through it after them, and reported the usual array of warp point defenses and the neutrino spoor of another medium-sized planetary population. That left number three, even further from the primary than number one and on a bearing ninety degrees away from it. Prescott's eyes had seldom strayed from that icon.

"I have, Sir," the spook responded. "It's a red dwarf, with no evidence of any artificial energy emissions. Nor are there any Bug defenses. It's empty, Sir."

"Thank you." Prescott surveyed the entire staff. They looked uncomfortable. He would have expected nothing else, for Task Force 71 was advancing into the unknown, and for these people that was a situation calculated to conjure up the ghosts of Operation Pesthouse.

"The question now is whether Warp Point Two or Warp Point Three leads further along the chain towards Zhaarnak," he said. "Jacques?"

The ops officer cleared his throat.

"Admiral, I know the RD2s don't have the range to conduct a real warp point survey of the system beyond Warp Point Three. But that system's emptiness suggests that it's a dead end. At the same time, I'd certainly expect the Bug survivors to retreat toward their fellow Bugs—the ones opposing Fang Zhaarnak—by the most direct possible route. And they fled through Warp Point Two. My vote is for that one."

Prescott considered Bichet's argument for a moment, then nodded.

"Thank you. But before we decide, I'd like to ask Amos if he's been able to reach any further conclusions about the length of this warp chain." The admiral turned to the spook. "The important question, of course, is how many more systems lie between us and TF 72?"

Chung spread his hands eloquently.

"Admiral, I don't know. We can lop at least another five light-hours off the total real-space distance, and possibly as much as nine light-hours, depending on whether the warp point we really want is Warp Point Two or Warp Point Three," he pointed out, and Prescott nodded again. "Unfortunately," the intelligence officer continued, "that's *all* we can say with any certainty. Judging from our analysis of the time their mobile forces and courier drones seem to be taking to shuttle back and forth, the total real-space distance between Home Hive One and AP-5 is about twenty-four light-hours, which means that we're a maximum of nineteen light-hours from AP-5 as we stand right now. My best guess would make that no more than another three warp nexi between here and AP-5, which would mean two between us and TF 72, assuming Fang Zhaarnak has indeed taken the next system on his list. But that's *only* a guess."

Bichet pounced.

"That reinforces the case in favor of Warp Point Two," he said firmly. "There isn't anything on the far side of Warp Point Three, much less the starships and fortresses there'd be in a system where they were preparing to make their stand against Fang Zhaarnak."

Chung looked uncomfortable. Intelligence officers were restricted line, ineligible for command in deep space—a caste distinction that lingered on, as real as it was unacknowledged. Worse, Chung's date of rank made him junior to Bichet. But he swallowed only once before speaking up.

"Granted: we know that the system is *not* the one in which we'll make contact with Fang Zhaarnak. But it would have to be an extraordinarily long distance between warp points for a single nexus to connect our present position to TF 72's. I believe there must be at least one more . . . and that we're looking through Warp Point Three at that additional system."

Bichet began to reply sharply, but Prescott shushed him with a gesture.

"Your reasoning, Amos?"

"First of all, Admiral, as the Bug remnants were retiring toward Warp Point Two, they dispatched courier drones across the system toward Warp Point Three. We detected their drive signatures. Why would they have sent courier drones into an uninhabited dead-end system?"

Bichet looked far from convinced, but his skepticism began to take on an overlay of thoughtfulness.

"Why," he countered stubbornly, "would they bottle themselves up by retreating into a cul-de-sac system?"

"I suggest," Prescott said quietly, before Chung could respond, "that the question supplies its own answer, Jacques. They hoped to draw us after them in a time-wasting detour that would allow them to concentrate against Zhaarnak. Failing that, they probably hope to make us hesitate to advance through Warp Point Three by threatening our rear. Fortunately, too few of them escaped to pose a credible threat."

"I gather, Sir," Mandagalla ventured, "that you've decided on Warp Point Three."

"Yes. I want you and Jacques to prepare a detailed operational plan for an advance through it as soon as the emergency repairs are completed."

"And as soon as we've sent carriers back to AP-4 for replacement fighters," Landrum prompted hopefully, but Prescott didn't take the cue. He looked over the entire meeting, but his eyes lingered on Landrum and on the com screen framing Raathaarn's avian face.

"I made my position clear back in Home Hive One," he said levelly. "We must maintain the momentum of our advance, without letup. All other considerations are secondary. Since I said that, we've put one more system between us and AP-4, which measurably increases the time it would take to ferry fighters forward from that system."

Landrum began to look alarmed, for he could see where the admiral was leading. He gestured for leave to speak, but Prescott continued inexorably.

"Furthermore, after our carrier losses here, our surviving fighters can fill the great majority of the hanger bays we have left. Isn't that true, Steve?"

Caught off guard, the *farshathkhanaak* answered automatically.

"It is, Sir. Eighty-two percent of them, to be exact."

"That's what I thought. And in light of those factors, I've decided to resume our advance without pausing to replenish our fighter strength."

The staffers' shock, combined with their realization that the admiral hadn't even remotely invited discussion, left silence to reign unchallenged in the briefing room. Raathaarn, not physically present—and, in any event, far nearer to Prescott in rank than most of those who were in it—finally broke it.

"Addmirrrallll—"

Prescott raised a hand—his artificial one, some recalled.

"One moment, Admiral Raathaarn. I have an additional reason for making that decision." He spoke a quiet command to the computer, and the main flat display screen lit with the same warp line chart Chung had shown him back in Home Hive One, extended now to show this system and the two the recon drones had probed from it.

"As I said, I don't believe the few Bugs who escaped through Warp Point Two constitute a serious threat to our rear. Nevertheless, there *is* a potential threat to it." He used a light-pencil to indicate the warp chain that stretched from Home Hive One to Alpha Centauri—the Anderson Chain. He left the dot of light resting on the Pesthouse System, and resumed, ignoring the *frisson* that ran through the compartment.

"Bug forces converged on Pesthouse to ambush Second Fleet," he said quietly, and he glanced at his staff. Aside from Landrum, all of them had been with him and Task Force 21 throughout that hideous ordeal. "One of those forces came from Home Hive One . . . but the others came from somewhere else. Bugs from that 'somewhere else' may move in behind us and reoccupy Home Hive One at any time."

Prescott suppressed a wintry grin as he saw Terence Mukerji's face go ashen. Having accepted the political admiral's apology (*Why*, he wondered, not for the first time, *did I ever let Kevin Sanders talk me into that?*), he could hardly exclude him from full staff conferences like this one. At least Mukerji had learned caution and seldom spoke up, but now terror overcame that caution.

"Ah, Admiral, are you saying . . . that is, do I understand that you believe the Bugs have led us into a trap?"

"Not really, Admiral Mukerji. I don't seriously believe that they would have sacrificed the planetary population here just to bait a trap. Admittedly, they abandoned Harnah to Admiral Antonov to help bait the trap they sprang on Second Fleet. But if there's any truth to our assumptions about the economic straits in which they now find themselves, then I think it's unlikely that they'll be quite as . . . cavalier as they were about writing off industrial capacity. But we can't ignore the possibility. For that matter, there might not be any deliberate 'trap' involved in it—they might simply have been unable to produce a sufficiently reinforced mobile component to hit us before we got this deep.

"In any event, we have to allow for the possibility that a strong Bug force could appear in Home Hive One while we're busy ferrying fighters through it. And what do you suppose a force like that would do to the unescorted carriers doing the ferrying?"

Mukerji wasn't encouraged. He started to wipe his brow, thought better of it, and looked around the room. Some of the expressions he saw suggested that he wasn't the only one just waking up to the full strategic implications of their new astrographic knowledge. That emboldened him to speak up again.

"Admiral, this is *terrible*. If the Bugs do reoccupy Home Hive One in force, we'll be isolated here in this warp chain, cut off from the Federation, with no path of retreat!"

"Admittedly, we're in a somewhat vulnerable position compared to Task Force 72, which has a clear, unthreatened route back to Federation space," Prescott acknowledged. "And *that*, ladies and gentlemen, is precisely the point."

He leaned forward, and all at once his face wore an intensity that was out of character even now, and would have been far more so before his brother's death.

"The way out of the potential danger we face is very straightforward. We'll advance along this chain until we break through whatever lies between us and Zhaarnak's task force. I'm confident all of you understand this. But I want it clearly understood by every squadron commander and every ship captain in Task Force 71, as well. We *will* resume our advance as soon as our repairs are made, and those repairs *will* be completed as rapidly as possible. See to it that they know that . . . and that I will accept no excuses."

With the sole exception of Anthea Mandagalla, none of Prescott's staffers, even the ones who'd been with him through the hell known as Operation Pesthouse, had ever really known Ivan Antonov. They'd been too junior then. But now, all at once, they understood what the old-timers meant. They hadn't understood it before, looking at their short, compact, quiet-spoken admiral. But now they did, even though he still hadn't raised his voice.

*In retrospect, it had probably been a mistake for the Mobile Force to stand and fight where it had, in a system with a colony planet.*

*The reasons had seemed compelling enough at the time. The Fleet had developed a new sensitivity to losses of industrial capacity, and of the noncombatant population that sustained it. And not one, but two, colony planets had been at stake, including the one in the system in which what was left of the Mobile Force was now bottled up. The Fleet, after all, would have no function if it did not at least* attempt *to defend the remaining population centers. Furthermore, the Enemy's advance from both ends of this warp chain had left so few systems that a forward defense had seemed advisable.*

*Nevertheless, it was now clear that the Mobile Force should have made its stand one system further along. Granted, there were no warp point defenses there to lend their support. But there was also no population in that barren system for the Enemy to annihilate, and so leave the Mobile Force in an ineffectual torpor.*

*But it was too late for regrets. The decision had been made. And now even the fallback strategy had failed. The Enemy was declining to be lured into following the survivors into this dead-end system—effectively lost anyway, in economic terms, now that it was isolated—and thus delaying his advance. Instead, that advance was continuing inexorably towards the empty system that was next along this warp chain.*

*There was nothing there to resist the Enemy. And beyond lay Franos.*

✦    ✦    ✦

Irma Sanchez told herself that VF-94 had been unreasonably lucky.

The squadron had come through the battles in Home Hive One without losing a single pilot. Not many could say as much. For a while, she'd thought the charm would hold through the slugging match in this system.

Maybe, she thought, that was the problem. Maybe she'd gotten too cocky, and relaxed the extra effort she'd always made to keep an eye on Davra Lennart and yell at her any time she seemed to drift out of the squadron's latticework of mutually protective fields of fire.

But, she repeated to herself, VF-94 was doing a damned sight better than the task force as a whole, to have come this far and lost only one pilot.

*The first one it's lost since I assumed command . . .*

Desperately: *What's that expression again? Oh, yes: an acceptable loss ratio. Yes, that's right. Have to keep thinking that.*

*How many times did the Skipper . . . did Bruno go through this?*

*And how many times will I have to go through it?*

*Maybe it's only like this the first time.*

*Please, God, let that be true.*

She forced her mind out of its black abstraction of raging thoughts as she strode along the passageway. The task force was forging outward towards the warp point through which the Brass had decreed that it would advance, and this would be their last briefing before transit. Up ahead was the familiar angle in the passageway just short of VF-94's ready room. She heard voices around the corner, and paused to eavesdrop.

"Hey, XO," the voice of Ensign Liang asked, "is it true this next system is going to be a cakewalk? That there aren't any Bugs there?"

"Why don't you settle down and wait for the briefing?" Meswami replied from the pinnacle of his superior maturity. Irma managed to stifle a laugh. "I'm sure the spooks will give us the straight word."

"Ha!" It was Ensign Nordlund. "Always a first time for everything!"

"Yeah," Liang muttered darkly. "Their brilliant theories are probably why we didn't get a replacement for Davra."

"Nobody else got any replacements either," Meswami reminded them sternly. "Don't ask me why. That decision was made at

higher levels—a *lot* higher. Probably Admiral Prescott himself."
That quieted them, and Meswami resumed briskly. "And now, let's
go on in. Even if the spooks are full of shit as usual, you know
the Old Lady will give it to us straight."

There was a mumble of assent. They filed into the ready room,
leaving Irma in a state of irritated puzzlement.

*What the hell are they talking about?* she wondered. *Who's the
Old Lady?*

It wasn't until later that it hit her. It was later still before she
recovered.

# CHAPTER SEVENTEEN

## "We'll do whatever we must, Admiral."

The lifeless red dwarf system really had held no organized resistance, and Task Force 71 had proceeded unmolested across the 3.6 light-hours that separated its warp point of entry from the only other warp point in the system.

Furthermore, as Prescott's lead elements closed in on that second warp point, the RD2s he'd dispatched through it had sent back the news he'd hoped for: the system beyond—a white star with a distant red dwarf companion—was the system where he and Zhaarnak would meet.

There was no possible doubt. The system matched the one Zhaarnak's RD2s had probed from the other side, as described in the reports he'd sent to Prescott. In addition to the expected warp point defenses, it held mobile forces corresponding in composition to those Zhaarnak had reported he still expected to have to face. Only now those forces were divided, for they had two warp points to cover. It would be unwise to rely too heavily on the colossal gunboat losses the Bugs had sustained in the recent battles, for the primary star's third planet gave off neutrino indications of the largest industrial base yet encountered in this warp chain—not in the same category as the home hive systems, but undoubtedly capable of cranking out large quantities of small vessels in short order. However, the losses in bases from which to operate those craft couldn't be so quickly made good. And the division of the Bugs' defensive assets was certainly hopeful.

All those factors were in Prescott's mind as he met with his staff. So was the fact that, in the teeth of his expectations, the Bugs had *not* appeared from somewhere along the Anderson Chain to pour through Pesthouse, reclaim Home Hive One, and isolate his task force. He was careful not to let his face and manner reveal to anyone his amazement that it hadn't happened . . . or his fear that it still might.

He grew aware that Chung had concluded his summary of the drones' findings. He opened the floor for comments, and a single throat was loudly cleared. The lack of any other response made it impossible not to recognize the throat-clearer, and Prescott suppressed a sigh.

"Admiral Mukerji?"

Mukerji had shaken off the jitters he'd experienced before they entered the system. Now he drew a deep breath and spoke like a man delivering a carefully prepared speech, a man who knew that his argument would be prejudiced by the very fact that he was the one presenting it.

"Admiral, these findings prove you were right. We are, indeed, looking from another direction at the same system Fang Zhaarnak faces. I therefore consider it likely that your other theory was *equally* well founded."

Prescott held the political admiral's eyes for a moment, and met only blandness. Mukerji was taking pains to construct a case too reasonable for Prescott to reject out of hand without laying himself open to the charge of personal bias.

"What 'other theory' is that, Admiral?" he inquired, knowing full well the answer.

"That Bug forces may appear in Pesthouse at any time, and move in to occupy Home Hive One. Indeed, I feel safe in saying that we're all somewhat puzzled that they haven't already done so."

Looking at the other staffers' faces, and the task force commanders' in the screens, Prescott saw no disagreement. Indeed, he felt none himself.

"Furthermore," Mukerji continued, still cautious, but visibly encouraged by Prescott's silence, "this task force and Fang Zhaarnak's have both suffered an unavoidable erosion of fighting power in the course of advancing to this point. And what we've just heard from Commodore Chung makes it clear that we're facing formidable defenses here. Now, surely, is a time for caution—a time to secure the gains we've made."

*Not,* Prescott noted, *"the gains we've made through your sagacious plans," or anything like that.* Mukerji was getting cagier. He'd carefully avoided any hint of overt flattery, or appeals to political self-preservation, or any of the other arguments he'd learned were counterproductive.

"What, precisely, are you proposing, Admiral Mukerji?"

"Simply this, Admiral: that instead of pressing on to the next system at this time, we pull back to Home Hive One, and that Fang Zhaarnak be ordered to join us there. Naturally, both task forces should leave warp point covering forces. But by sealing off this warp chain at the Home Hive One end with our combined fleet, we'll accomplish two things. First, we'll keep the system we're now facing isolated and neutralized, until fresh forces in overwhelming strength can be brought up along the Prescott Chain to reduce it. And secondly, we'll be in a position to protect the entire Prescott Chain while those forces are advancing along it."

*And third,* Prescott thought, *we'll secure this task force—meaning you—from any nasty surprises coming up behind us from Pesthouse through Home Hive One.* But the fact that danger to Task Force 71 also happened to be a personal danger to Mukerji didn't make it any less real. Did it?

He surveyed the room and the com screens.

"Comments, ladies and gentlemen?"

Anthea Mandagalla looked acutely uncomfortable.

"I must agree with Admiral Mukerji, Sir." She left off the arguably disrespectful qualifier *regretfully.* "I'm particularly disturbed by what Amos has told us about the way the Bugs are redistributing their fortresses to reinforce the warp point defenses we're facing." She turned to Chung. "I gather that still more are on the way."

"They are, Sir," the spook replied. "The RD2s report others being tractored in from across the system, presumably from other warp points which aren't immediately threatened. Still others are on the way to the warp point only eighty-four light-minutes from the one through which we'll enter—which confirms our identification of that warp point as the one where they're expecting Fang Zhaarnak, although we were already pretty sure of that on the basis of what *his* RD2s have reported."

He indicated the flat-screen system display, and the two warp points that lay less than ninety light-minutes apart, about 5.8 and 4.4 light-hours, respectively, and on the same approximate bearing from the system primary.

"Fang Zhaarnak's initial probes detected twelve fortresses of that warp point. The Bugs customarily allocate identical fixed defenses to all the warp points in a given system, so presumably that was the force level in place at *this* warp point, as well, at that time. Now, as I said earlier, we're looking at *twenty* fortresses . . . all more than monitor-sized. In addition, there are the almost two thousand deep space buoys I mentioned. Our RD2s weren't in a position to survey Fang Zhaarnak's warp point, of course, but I would be very surprised if they haven't been beefed up to the same degree."

A muttering ran around the room. Heads nodded.

*I wish I knew my history better,* Prescott thought. *Which American president was it, centuries ago, who put a crucial question to his cabinet? All nine of them voted in the affirmative. And he said, "That's nine ayes . . . and one nay. The nays have it unanimously."*

*But I can't put it that way, can I? Never mind Mukerji. All these other splendid people, who've been with me through years of hell, deserve an explanation.*

*Especially considering what I'm going to have to tell them afterwards . . .*

So he spoke deliberately.

"There's certainly a case for Admiral Mukerji's proposal to consolidate our fleet in Home Hive One and wait for fresh forces. But we're not going to do it." He ordered himself not to feel amusement or satisfaction at the way Mukerji's expression rose and then fell.

"I have two reasons for that decision. First of all, we have no way of knowing how great a force the Bugs will bring through Pesthouse against Home Hive One when they finally get around to it, as we're all agreed they eventually will. They ought to have done it already, and we dare not assume that their delay has been for lack of resources. It could just as easily mean that they're taking the time to amass a truly crushing superiority. If that's the case, we'll need a second line of retreat. Breaking open this warp chain is the only way to provide it.

"Second, we know the system ahead of us has more than just the two warp points. The fact that they have additional defenses they can redistribute to meet immediate threats proves that. But *where do those additional warp connections lead?* What reinforcements could they bring through those connections? We have no way to know."

Mandagalla filled the silence.

"Sir, there's no indication that system has been significantly reinforced."

"No, there isn't. But *would* there be, necessarily?" A wintry smile. "Remember, we're working from recon drone data. And I, of all people, am not likely to forget what the Bugs can do with third-generation ECM!"

His smile softened.

"Relax, people! I don't really believe that's what's happening here. I don't think any possible application of cloaking ECM could hide really massive forces from the swarms of RD2s we and Task Force 72 have both been expending. After all, the Bugs know the system is threatened from two separate directions. And we aren't the only ones who can't be certain about potential threats; for all they know, our side has massive reinforcements advancing along the Prescott Chain in Zhaarnak's wake. Under the circumstances, it would be logical for them to pour in any reinforcements they could and hold fast on both warp points. If we break into the system, it will become a war of movement in which our superior speed and our fighters will give us the advantage—which they won't in a warp point action. And that kind of saturation defense would involve forces so massive that, to repeat, our RD2s would probably have detected them regardless of ECM."

Prescott saw the relief spread through the room. He let it live for a couple of heartbeats, then leaned forward and spoke in a very different tone.

"But even if we assume such reinforcements aren't present, there's no guarantee that they couldn't arrive later. Remember, we know nothing about the warp lines beyond this system's other warp points. Suppose one of them leads to another of the remaining home hive systems by a very long and circuitous route. That would explain why reinforcements haven't arrived yet—but it would mean they were *going* to arrive. The question is when.

"Accordingly," Prescott resumed after a brief interval of dead silence, "we'll press the attack as we originally intended. Given the fact that the warp point defenses we're going to be facing are strong, and getting stronger, time is of the essence. We will, however, take the time to communicate our operational plan to Zhaarnak, along with orders to commence his attack just before ours is scheduled to go in. The purpose, of course, is to draw some of the massive gunboat reserves we know that system is capable of producing towards him in order to give us a window of opportunity."

"Aye, aye, Sir." Mandagalla's lack of enthusiasm was palpable. Her ancestry was African with a dash of French, lacking even a tincture of Japanese, but Prescott knew precisely the words she was thinking: *Leyte Gulf.* Those were words burned into the brains of all TFN officers, schooled in the perils of plans requiring precise coordination of widely separated fleet elements. It wasn't so much because of any wet-navy traditions as it was a result of finding a purely Terran teaching example of the perils of the sort of complex, converging operations the Khanate of Orion had been so fond of employing in its first two disastrous wars against the Federation.

"I must point out, Sir," the chief of staff went on, "that while the two warp points are unusually close together as warp points go, they *are* eighty-four-plus light-minutes apart. So the lag for any communications between them will be almost an hour and a half, and—"

"Rest assured, Commodore," Prescott said, his tone unusually formal, almost stiff, "Lord Telmasa won't fail us. Remember, his task force's fighter strength is closer to intact than ours, and he's had time to replenish his supply of SBMHAWKs. Furthermore..."

All at once, Prescott was at a loss for words. How to convey to these people, not one of whom belonged to the *Zheeerliko u'valkhannaiee,* the absolute mutual trust implicit in the oath of *vilkshatha*? And, on a less esoteric note, over the years of shared fleet command he and Zhaarnak had acquired an ability to read one another's minds that had nothing to do with telepathy. And besides... Prescott's lips quirked briefly upward as he contemplated the irony and remembered the lecture Zhaarnak had delivered to him when he'd first proposed this entire campaign to him. His *vilkshatha* brother had conscientiously cautioned him in terms not unlike those Mandagalla was using now. And, to his credit, he'd actually meant it... more or less. But if the truth be known, the Orions secretly reveled in complex operations like this.

He suppressed an inappropriate smile and started over.

"Take my word for it, Anna, we can count on Task Force 72. Zhaarnak will do his part. We only need to worry about doing ours." Prescott's flash of amusement—all too rare these days—guttered out, for he could no longer put off breaking this to them.

"In light of the urgency of bursting open our line of communication with the Prescott Chain, and the Federation beyond, it's necessary to adapt our warp point assault tactics. Accordingly, we'll expend our entire remaining SBMHAWK and AMBAMP stocks in the initial bombardment. The first wave to go in after the bombardment will consiot of relatively expendable battle-cruisers and fleet carriers.

"And that wave will go through in a simultaneous transit."

Prescott paused. For a while, there was no response beyond a generalized puzzlement as to what he was waiting for. Then his words began to register visibly, one thunderstruck face at a time.

"I realize," he resumed, "that we've never used this tactic before. I'm also aware that we've been accustomed to regard it as epitomizing the Bugs' appalling alienness from our own races. I myself have often thought—and said—as much. So I understand what you're feeling. But I've also come to understand that such an attitude is a luxury we can no longer afford. We must relearn the same lesson war has taught our ancestors throughout history: you cannot fight an enemy without becoming more like him. The more repugnant the enemy is, the more unpalatable that truth becomes—and the more necessary victory becomes, regardless of the means that must be used. In the case of *this* enemy, we're fighting for the very survival of our various species. In the face of such a moral imperative, all other ethical considerations shrink into insignificance. I will let *nothing* deter me from doing *whatever* it takes to eradicate the plague we're fighting! Do I make myself clear?"

None of them had ever heard Prescott speak like this, and no one even considered protesting or arguing. After a moment, though, Mukerji spoke very cautiously.

"Ah, Admiral, may I ask . . . Well, that is, will you ask for volunteers to crew the ships of the first wave?"

*You had to get on record with that, didn't you?* Prescott silently asked him. *Very important to insulate yourself from any future political consequences of this, in case there's an inquiry later.*

He opened his mouth, but before he could respond, Anthea Mandagalla stunned everyone present by stepping out of line in at least two ways. She not only answered Mukerji, who outranked her, but did it in place of Prescott, who outranked her even more. Not that she seemed in any mood to worry about improprieties.

"Certainly not, Admiral! Every one of those people—every member of the TFN and its allied services—understands what goes with his or her uniform. They all know warp point assaults are part of the ordinary, expected hazards for *everyone*—regardless of rank." The last three words were a little pointed, but they were true. Howard

Anderson himself had chiseled that into the marble of the TFN's traditions, a century and a half ago. "Furthermore, we all take it as a given that the Bugs have substantial numbers of kamikazes available. Any losses we take from interpenetrations will probably be less than those we'd sustain if we didn't get our first wave through the warp point and into that system as quickly as possible."

At any other time, Mukerji might have reacted by indignantly protesting the chief of staff's "insolence." Uncharacteristically, he replied directly to her.

"But if the operation goes according to plan, Fang Zhaarnak's earlier attack will draw them away."

"The *immediately available* ones, Admiral. But a 'proper' warp point assault might well give them time to deploy fresh waves of kamikazes before we can get into the system and turn the battle into one of movement. I'm confident that our personnel understand the reasoning behind this—especially coming from . . ."

Mandagalla's voice trailed off, and if it had been possible, she would have blushed. She'd almost forgotten herself, almost spoken of those personnel's willingness to do this, and more, if asked to by Raymond Prescott. But anything that smacked of flattery was as foreign to her as it was repugnant to Prescott.

Force Leader Shaaldaar's basso came from the direction of the com screens like a rumble of distant thunder.

"I concur. And it is *not* completely without precedent. As you all may remember, on the occasion of our second incursion into Home Hive Three, my Gorm gunboat crews willingly performed a simultaneous mass warp transit. *Synklomus* mandated then that they do whatever the exigencies of war required in defense of their larger *lomus*. That same consideration applies here—with even greater urgency."

"But those were gunboats! We've never done it with starships. Besides, these are—" Mukerji jarred to a halt, stopping just short of saying, *Human crews, not Gorm.* He turned hastily to Prescott. "So, Sir, as you can see, there *are* unprecedented aspects to this. Perhaps, under the circumstances—"

"No, Admiral Mukerji. Commodore Mandagalla and Force Leader Shaaldaar are right. We'll do whatever we must, Admiral. *All* of us."

It had been expected that the two Enemy forces would attack the Franos system simultaneously. It seemed the logical thing to do, and it was clear enough that they were in communication with each other. It had therefore been somewhat surprising when one of them—the one that had come directly from the system where the survey flotilla had been ambushed—had commenced its assault, while the one which had advanced from the destroyed System Which Must Be Defended sat unmoving.

Tactical doctrine, however, had superseded perplexity, and the Fleet had responded as per contingency plans as the Enemy's ships had begun transiting in their usual manner, following the customary preliminary bombardment with the crewless missile-launching small craft of which he was so fond. Massive waves of gunboats and shuttles from the warp point's combat space patrol had swept down on them, and the holocaust of combat had raged with all its familiar ferocity.

As it became apparent that both Enemy forces weren't attacking simultaneously, the Fleet had seen an unanticipated opportunity to defeat them in detail. The attacking Enemy force, by itself, appeared to have sufficient firepower to blast its way into the system through both the combat space patrol and the starships and fortresses awaiting it. But as the preliminary reports accumulated, it became apparent that the attack force most probably was not powerful enough to defeat all of the Fleet's mobile combat resources if they could be brought to bear upon it. And the Enemy's failure to coordinate simultaneous assaults gave the Fleet the opportunity to concentrate all of those resources against a single attacker.

New directives went out quickly. The warp point fortresses, already two-thirds destroyed by the preliminary bombardment, were abandoned to their fate. They would wreak whatever additional damage they could, but the mobile units which had been assigned to support them withdrew, falling back in the direction of the second warp point which must be defended. And as those starships retreated, the starships on the warp point the Enemy had so inexplicably failed to exploit simultaneously, moved to meet them.

The gunboats and kamikazes which had been deployed to cover the attack warp point continued to spend themselves in ferocious attacks upon the Enemy. His own gunboats and small attack craft were now in the system, engaging the kamikazes in savage dogfights, and the massive gunboat reserve—which had stood ready to respond to attacks on either or both of the two threatened warp points from a central position—moved to support them.

A fresh gunboat force was dispatched from the inhabited planet to replenish the Reserve. Those gunboats had been intended for the

*final, close-in defense of the planet in the event that the Enemy
succeeded in fighting his way into the system. Now that the opportunity to prevent him from doing so had been offered, however, they
would be needed to replace the losses the reserves were bound to
take in crushing the single attacking force.*

*The Mobile Forces moving away from the quiescent warp point
launched all of their own shuttles and gunboats to reinforce the
combat space patrol covering it. It was always possible that the
Enemy had intended to exploit both warp points at once and that
his failure to do so represented only a failure in coordination, not
in strategy. If that were the case, then the standing CSP must be
reinforced in case a second, belated attack should materialize. In
that event, it was unlikely that the CSP could actually stop the
second assault, but the waves of gunboats and kamikazes would at
least be able to inflict massive attritional damage on the Enemy as
he entered. And if the united starships, supported by the reserves,
could engage and destroy the first attacking force in isolation, then
the Fleet's surviving units and the fresh gunboats from the planet
would turn upon the second, severely battered force.*

*There was no assurance of victory, yet following the Enemy's serious
error, the projections had suddenly become far more favorable.*

Raymond Prescott stood on the flag bridge of *Irena Riva y
Silva*, and his face was carved from stone as he studied the latest RD2 data. The range to Zhaarnak's warp point was too great
for the drones to provide detailed reports, but the detonation of
antimatter warheads and laser buoys would be obvious enough.

They would also be ninety minutes old when the drones
detected them and returned to TF 71 with the word that
Zhaarnak'telmasa and his *farshatok* were fighting for their
very lives a mere light-hour and a half away across the star
system . . . and God only knew how far apart between the star
systems from which both halves of Seventh Fleet converged
upon *this* system.

Prescott knew when the attack was supposed to begin, and he
looked again at the time. If everything had gone precisely according
to schedule, Zhaarnak had begun his assault twelve minutes ago.
And if that were the case, then in another seventy-two minutes,
Prescott and TF 71 would have proof of it, and—

"Admiral!" Jacques Bichet looked up from his own console and
beckoned urgently at the main plot. "We just got a fresh drone
wave back, and it's reporting something very strange, Sir."

"'Strange' in what way, Jacques?" Prescott asked, striding across the flag deck towards the plot.

"I'm not really certain, Sir," the ops officer replied. "But according to the drones, all of the Bug mobile units have begun moving directly out-system from our warp point toward Fang Zhaarnak's."

"What?" Prescott's eyebrows rose in surprise. "Are we picking up any evidence that Zhaarnak began his attack early?" he demanded.

"No, Sir. Our drones haven't detected any indications of combat."

"Then why should they be pulling their starships away from our warp point?" Prescott wondered aloud, and turned to look at Amos Chung.

"I don't know, Sir," the intelligence officer responded. Then he frowned. "Unless . . ."

"Unless *what*?" Prescott prompted with an unusual testiness as the spook's voice trailed off. Chung looked up at the sharpness of the admiral's tone, then shook himself.

"Excuse me, Sir. I was just thinking. We've pretty much established that the Shiva effect transmits itself at greater than light-speed. We haven't seen any evidence of an actual FTL *communication* ability between their military units, but perhaps that's because we never *looked* for it, since we 'knew' no one had one."

"You mean you think the force on the other warp point has . . . telepathically informed the one on our warp point that it's under attack?" Bichet was obviously trying to keep his incredulity out of his voice.

"I suppose it's possible that that's what's happening," Chung said. "On the other hand, I'd think that if they were capable of the sort of complex FTL communication which would be required for tactical coordination we would have seen evidence of it before now. Unless we have seen it and just didn't recognize it because we knew it was impossible . . ."

He shook himself again, obviously tearing himself away from the fascinating possibilities by sheer force of will, and turned back to Prescott.

"On the other hand, they might not need that sort of communication ability to explain this, Sir. The casualties TF 72 would inflict in a warp point assault obviously wouldn't approach the threshold required to trigger the Shiva effect, but the impact might be sufficient for the Bugs on our warp point to sense them, even at this range."

"So what you're suggesting," Prescott said, "is that our Bugs may know that Zhaarnak is killing *his* Bugs even though their sensors can't pick up any more proof of it than our drones can?"

"I think it's certainly *possible*, Sir," Chung replied, then waved at the master plot's report of the departure of the guardian starships. "But whatever's causing it, it certainly looks like the distraction effect of the Fang's attack is already being felt."

Prescott grunted in agreement, and his mind raced. His own attack had been scheduled to begin exactly two hours after Zhaarnak's. That interval had been calculated in order to give the Bugs the opportunity to detect Zhaarnak's arrival and then get themselves at least thirty minutes out of position from TF 71's warp point before his own task force made transit. But if the Bugs were already responding to TF 72's assault, then his own attack could be moved up correspondingly. And the quicker he got his units through the warp point, the sooner his own diversionary effect would pull some of the pressure off Zhaarnak. . . .

He watched the plot change as a fresh flight of RD2s made transit. The Bug starships were clearly continuing their movement towards the other warp point. At the same time, the icons representing the defending CSP were denser and heavier than they had been, so apparently the Bugs were reinforcing their covering gunboats and kamikazes as partial compensation for the withdrawal of their starships. Which was what he'd anticipated they would do, although he hadn't expected them to do it this soon.

And it was also what he'd planned his tactics to take advantage of. He turned back to Bichet.

"We're moving up the assault, Jacques. If they're going to pull off the warp point sooner than we expected, we might as well take advantage of it."

*The Fleet's starships continued towards rendezvous with one another. As expected, the Enemy's assault force had successfully blasted its way through the protective minefields and reduced the warp point fortresses to rubble. The original warp point CSP had also been effectively destroyed, although it had managed to inflict serious damage before its own extermination. Now the massed power of the reserve gunboats and shuttles was hurtling towards the intruders, and soon the recombined Mobile Force would be able to bring its full strength to bear in support of the kamikazes. And—*

*Then everything changed as the familiar trans-warp point bombardment exploded out of the* second *warp point.*

*There was no way for the Fleet to know whether the staggered attack sequence was, in fact, a failure in coordination or something which the Enemy had planned in advance. It was certainly possible that his irritating warp-capable sensor drones had detected the Fleet's redeployment and that he was responding to it, whether he'd planned to do so or not.*

*But whatever he'd planned, he would still find his second attack force being ground away by the kamikazes just as his first had been. Even if the second force managed to fight its way into the system, the Fleet had a significant head start. By the time he could complete transit in his usual cautious way and reorganize, his starships—many of which would undoubtedly be slowed by combat damage from the kamikazes—would be too far behind to overtake the reunited Mobile Force before it engaged the first attack force and—*

*Wait!*

*No! This was contrary to the Enemy's normal procedure!*

The gunboats and small craft left to guard the warp point shuddered in torment under the lash of the SBMHAWKs which came thundering through it. The CAM2s were particularly deadly to the gunboats, slashing out in lethal shoals of destruction no point defense system could stop. The antimatter-loaded shuttles were too small, their emissions signatures too weak, to be locked up by the sprint-mode capital missiles, but there were far fewer of them to begin with.

Gunboat squadron datanets crumbled under the threshing machine fury of the bombardment, and the searing wavefront of plasma and EMP rolled outward, drowning sensor systems and fire control in waves of interference. Even as the gunboats and small craft reeled under the assault, AMBAMPs came vomiting through the warp point, spawning antimatter submunitions that fanned out like dragonseed. The deadly spores infiltrated the minefields, then detonated in a crashing wave that seared the mines from the face of the universe. And to complete the deadly preparation, still more SBMHAWKs hurled still more CAM2s at the fortresses. Their point defense was no more effective than the gunboats' had been, and the tidal wave of warheads destroyed nine of them outright and reduced the eleven survivors to battered, half-destroyed wrecks.

For the brief moments that lethal bombardment required, the

environs of the warp point blazed as brilliantly as any star. Yet vicious as the explosions were, and brutally though the fortresses had been maimed, the CSP survived. It was shaken, confused—not even Bugs could take that sort of sudden, overwhelming explosion of violence *without* being shaken—but it was still there, and it had always known an attack just like this one was possible. And so, however disorganized it might be, every unit of it knew precisely what tactical doctrine required of it.

The gunboats—which had gone to evasive maneuvers the instant they detected the first SBMHAWKs—turned back towards the warp point, riding through the rapidly diffusing clouds of plasma while they prepared to concentrate vengefully upon the long chain of invading starships which must follow on the heels of the bombardment. The kamikaze shuttles, on the other hand, actually backed off the warp point just a bit. *Their* tactical doctrine required them to observe which starships required that they expend themselves against them, and which the gunboats could destroy with conventional FRAM attacks. Besides, their proper function was to destroy monitors and superdreadnoughts, not to waste themselves upon lesser craft.

But tactical doctrine abruptly became a weak reed in the face of Task Force 71's modification of its own doctrine.

Fifty-two battlecruisers and twelve fleet carriers flashed into existence.

Two of the carriers and six of the battlecruisers flashed out of existence, just as abruptly and far more violently, as they interpenetrated. But the other fifty-six Allied ships survived, and their abrupt, mass appearance took the already confused defenders completely by surprise. The Bug CSP which had expected to hurl itself upon one individual target after another, in rapid succession, suddenly found itself forced to pause, however briefly, to allocate targets to its units.

And that delay, brief as it was, was fatal.

The surviving carriers made transit in a tight, hairpin curve which carried them directly back into the warp point, remaining in realspace only long enough to launch over three hundred fighters. Then they disappeared back to the far side of the warp point, as quickly as they'd come—so quickly, indeed, that the kamikazes were able to catch only two of them, and failed to destroy even those.

Unlike the fighter platforms, the battlecruisers had come to stay. The Bugs had long since realized that the Allies' carriers were far more valuable strategic targets than any main combatant starship. As always, they'd concentrated their efforts on attempting to catch the carriers, but in this instance the carriers simply weren't available as targets long enough. And by the time the defenders realized the carriers were going to escape them, the battlecruisers' fire control systems and point defense had been given time to stabilize.

The CSP found itself confronted not by the isolated, transit-befuddled targets it had anticipated. Instead, it confronted intact battlegroups, with every weapon and defensive system fully on-line. Even the capital missile-armed battlecruisers, the long-range snipers who normally had no business at all in the short-range slaughter of a warp point assault, were deadly foes against gunboats. They'd made transit with full external ordnance racks of CAM2s, and they salvoed all of them in a devastating wave of destruction. Then they went to rapid fire with their internal launchers, hurling a steady stream of additional CAM2s into the gunboats' teeth.

Their energy-armed consorts, like the TFN's *Guerriere* class, with their heavy broadsides of force beams and hetlasers backed up by AFHAWK-firing standard missile launchers, left the gunboats to the BCRs and turned their own fury on the kamikaze shuttles. The kamikazes were as surprised as the gunboats, and the fire which ripped into them was devastating. A handful of them got through; the majority were dry leaves trapped in the heart of the furnace.

And even while the battlecruisers poured their devastating fire into the harrowed ranks of the CSP, the strikegroups added their own fury to the inferno. Half of them were armed to kill gunboats and shuttles, and they piled into the CSP with deadly effect. The remainder were armed with maximum loads of FRAMs, and they ignored gunboats and shuttles alike to swarm over the air-leaking wrecks of the surviving fortresses. A single pass was more than sufficient to reduce those fortresses to clouds of expanding vapor, interspersed here and there with droplets of alloy which had merely been liquified. Over a third of the squadrons tasked to hit the fortresses were forced to abort their attack runs because they no longer had targets.

The battlecruisers and fighters didn't achieve their goals without losses and damage, yet the total price they paid was far lighter than the one they might have faced in a traditional attack. And when the remainder of TF 71 made transit less than fifteen minutes later, there was no effective opposition.

The titanic monitors, accompanied by the lesser sisters of the superdreadnoughts and the carriers, shook down into battle formation and moved off across the system to trap the defending starships between the anvil of TF 72 and their own looming hammer.

The lovely blue curve of the planet they now knew was called Franos showed through the atmosphere curtain as Zhaarnak's shuttle eased into *Riva y Silva*'s boatbay.

Prescott averted his eyes from its beauty and concentrated upon the shuttle. So did everyone else.

The recombined task forces of Seventh Fleet had required barely an hour of close combat to crush the defending Bug battle-line between them once they'd brought it to battle. Nothing in the system could realistically have hoped to stop the Allied fleet after that, but there'd still been grim work to do as the Bug mobile force made its last stand and fresh—though diminishing—waves of kamikazes had come in through a third warp point. Prescott had hastily reorganized his fighters in a way that was now so familiar as to cause minimal dislocation, concentrating them on the smallest possible number of carriers and sending the empty carriers to the now-accessible AP-4 to pick up replacements. Then, behind an umbrella of fighters, they'd advanced grimly through everything the Bugs could put in their path. They'd taken losses, of course. But the outcome had never really been in doubt, and a reduced but consolidated Seventh Fleet had closed in on Planet A III to exercise the Shiva Option once more.

Then, as the recon drones probing ahead of them had surveyed that planet closely, they'd become aware of a complicating factor. . . .

Prescott's mind returned to the present as the shuttle's hatch opened and he saw his *vilkshatha* brother in the furry flesh for the first time since the two task forces had parted in AP-5. The blue planet formed a backdrop to their greetings, and Zhaarnak noticed the way that Prescott's eyes strayed towards that gorgeous spectacle.

"It still troubles you, does it not, Raaymmonnd?" he asked quietly, and Prescott smiled wanly.

"Does it still trouble *you* that we didn't go ahead and sterilize it anyway?"

"No. *I* would have done it," the Orion said with bleak honesty. "But I have come to understand that the honor code of Human warriors like yourself will not permit the extermination of a sentient race—even when a Bahg population on the same planet has reduced it to slaves and meat-animals. I do not say I fully understand why that should be so. For one of the *Zheeerlikou'valkhannaiee*, death would be regarded as a gift from the gods themselves if it freed us from such a state, and I do not think my people would wish to live if they must look back upon having been so reduced. Yet I believe that the Human proverb—'Where there is life, there is hope'—applies in this instance, at least in *your* people's eyes. I accept this. And, on another level, I understand that any failure on my part to accept it might have adverse repercussions for the Alliance."

"That," Prescott said, "is one way to put it."

He recalled the days of Operation Pesthouse, four years past, when the discovery of Harnah had taken them all into the regions of nightmare. In retrospect, it was hard to see just why it had been so shocking. It had merely been a logical extension of what they'd already known about the Bugs. But they hadn't wanted to follow that logic out . . . not when they knew there were Bug-occupied human planets. It had been more comfortable to suppose that on such planets the Bugs had simply indulged in an orgy of eating until the food supply was gone. But that had never made much sense. Humans, after all, were farmers and ranchers, and so were Orions. And Ophiuchi. And Gorm. So it should have been obvious to any one of the Alliance's member species that Bug "farmers" would preserve breeding stock. But they'd been unwilling to see the obvious until they'd had their noses rubbed in it, until they'd viewed the vast pens that held the descendants of the builders of Harnah's ruined cities: food animals who could *understand*. . . .

Now they'd encountered it again, here at Franos.

Prescott didn't even know what the local natives looked like. The only reason he even knew what they had once called their planet was that the information had been gleaned from engravings on the ruins of ancient, pre-Bug public buildings which had been explored by remote orbital and air-breathing sensor platforms. The information had been included with the earliest reports, and they'd needed something to call the system in official correspondence, so there'd been no way for him to avoid that bit of knowledge. But he had been able to avoid learning more than that, and so he'd taken the specialists' word for the natives' sentience and resolutely concentrated his own attention upon other matters. It was, he supposed, a sign of weakness in himself. He couldn't bring himself to care.

They'd fought their way past the planet and looped back to the warp point between their warp points of entry—Warp Point Three, they'd designated it, the one that had spewed forth all the reinforcing gunboats. Prescott had ordered up all available mines and other defenses to seal it shut. He'd had no idea what lay beyond it, and Seventh Fleet had lacked the strength to try to find out. Instead, he'd turned back to his unfinished business here in Franos.

Waves of fourth-generation SBMHAWKs had obliterated Planet A III's orbital installations, and surgical fighter strikes had excised its space ports and planetary defense centers. Now the planetside Bugs, though still shielded from direct attack by their hundreds of millions of hostages, were isolated and impotent. To assure that they stayed that way, Prescott had already assigned a carrier battlegroup to remain in orbit around the planet.

Now the *vilkshatha* brothers turned their backs upon the beautiful blue world whose surface had seen so much horror and headed for the elevators to the flag bridge. It was a lengthy trip in a ship the size of *Irena Riva y Silva*, and an outsider might have been surprised that they passed it in silence. It wasn't the silence of two warriors lost in the black abstraction of their own thoughts as they contemplated the fate of Franos' inhabitants. It was the comfortable—and comforting—silence of two who had become in truth the brothers their oath had made them. Neither of them would have been prepared to put it into words, but both of them sensed the truth that Kthaara'zarthan had recognized in them from the beginning: they'd become far more than the mere sum of their parts. Formidable as either of them would have been alone, the interweaving of their strengths had made them a deadly weapon in the arsenal of the Grand Alliance. All of that was true, but what mattered to Raymond Prescott and Zhaarnak'telmasa at this particular moment was that each of them was once again united with the being they knew beyond any shadow of doubt would die to protect his back . . . or to avenge him.

The elevator reached its destination, and a knot of staffers stood respectfully up from a terminal as they entered the flag bridge.

"As you were," Prescott told them, then raised an eyebrow at his chief of staff. "Anna, have you finished the compilation I requested?"

"I have, Sir," she said, and indicated a screen where the total ship losses of Seventh Fleet since its arrival in AP-5 ten standard months before were displayed in an appropriate blood-red.

Fourteen monitors. Twenty-three superdreadnoughts. Nine assault carriers. Thirteen fleet carriers. Thirty-one battlecruisers. Three thousand and seventy-six fighters. Four hundred and twelve gunboats.

"Ah, Admiral," the chief of staff ventured, "if you'd like to see the figures for personnel casualties—"

"That's all right, Anna," Prescott said mildly. "Later, perhaps."

The silence resumed.

"Admiral," Chung finally broke it, "on the basis of confirmed kills, I've come up with totals of the Bug ships we've destroyed over the same period, to . . . set against this."

Without waiting for permission, he activated another screen.

There was a low chorus of gasps as the figures appeared: ninety-one monitors, one hundred and fifty-eight superdreadnoughts, one hundred and sixty-one battlecruisers, and eighty-three light cruisers.

"These figures may be regarded as minimal," Chung said into the silence. "They don't include gunboats, because the total for those is literally incalculable. We can only estimate the number we've destroyed—and the lowest estimate is forty thousand." The gasps were louder this time. "Nor do they include the warp point fortresses or the orbital defenses of four populated systems."

Bichet did a quick mental calculation.

"Even without the fixed defenses, and without the gunboats, the ship losses are over six to one in our favor. And the tonnage ratio is even better."

"All of which," Zhaarnak said after a moment, "pales into insignificance beside the annihilation of every living Bahg in five systems—including a home hive system."

"Yes." Prescott nodded slowly. "That's all true. At the same time, let's not deceive ourselves. Anna doesn't have to give me precise figures for me to know we've probably lost almost as many people as Second Fleet lost at Pesthouse. And more than half our ships are fit only for the shipyards, even if we do have to keep them on-line for now with emergency repairs. We've already run a projection of how long it will be before the fleet is ready for further offensive operations, and it comes out to a standard year and a half."

He glanced at Mandagalla for confirmation, and she nodded

unhappily. But then something seemed to thaw in him, and he surprised them all with a warmer smile than they'd believed he was still capable of.

"Nevertheless, Seventh Fleet has performed in such a manner that I'm honored to have commanded it. Ladies and gentlemen, I declare Operation Retribution at an end. For now, the initiative is in the hands of Admiral Murakuma and Sixth Fleet, at Zephrain."

# CHAPTER EIGHTEEN
## Closing the Net

Admiral Vanessa Murakuma allowed her gaze to linger a moment longer on the featherleaf branches outside the window of the office that had been Raymond Prescott's, in the slanting afternoon rays of Zephrain A. Then she swung her swivel chair back to face her visitor.

"Well, Lieutenant Sanders, you've had quite a journey."

"I have that, Sir," the famously insouciant intelligence lieutenant agreed. He looked appropriately disheveled, but of course that was only from just having been whisked from the space port to this office the instant his shuttle had touched down. It had nothing to do with the truly immense voyage that had gone before: from Home Hive One to Zephrain by way of Alpha Centauri.

*Speaking of Alpha Centauri . . .*

"How is Rear Admiral LeBlanc?" Murakuma asked in a carefully neutral voice.

"Quite well, Sir. He sends his best regards. In fact, he asked me to deliver a personal message." Sanders reached inside his tunic and withdrew a datachip security folder—supposedly not to be used for mere private correspondence. Murakuma's scrutiny of his foxlike features turned up nothing but bland propriety—except, possibly, a very slight twinkle in his blue eyes.

"Thank you, Lieutenant." She reached out, took the folder, and, with an inner sigh, put it in a drawer. *Business before pleasure. . . .*

Sanders seemed to be having the same thought.

346

"Of course, I was only at Alpha Centauri very briefly," he prompted.

"Ah, yes. And you'd departed from Seventh Fleet just after Admiral Prescott shut down Operation Retribution. We've only just learned of that via the ICN here. I gather that the Joint Chiefs had some reason for sending you off again after barely letting you catch your breath."

"Yes, Sir. I've also brought *official* correspondence from them." Sanders patted the briefcase at his side. It looked unremarkable, but it was constructed of the same molecularly aligned composite as powered combat armor, and it incorporated a computer system whose miniaturization was just beyond cutting-edge. "Specifically, new orders for you and Sixth Fleet."

"Oh?" Murakuma kept her voice level. *Could this be it?* "Your duties aren't normally those of a simple courier, Lieutenant."

"No, Sir. I'm to report directly to Admiral LeBlanc on the state of this front, just as I was previously doing when attached to Seventh Fleet."

"Well, I can certainly find a place for you in Lieutenant Commander Abernathy's organization." Despite two promotions since the days when she'd been Marcus' painfully young understudy, Marina Abernathy was still very junior for her position as Murakuma's staff spook, which she'd been ever since her mentor had been called back to Alpha Centauri. She had, however, gotten over most of her youthful insecurity, and she should be able to cope with Sanders. "In the meantime, though, I gather that you're also supposed to give me some of the background to these orders. Am I correct in assuming that your recent experience with Seventh Fleet has something to do with your knowledge of that background?"

"You are, Sir. If I may...?"

Taking Murakuma's assent for granted, Sanders opened the briefcase and activated the flat display screen on the inside of its top. A warp line chart appeared, filling the right-hand side of the screen. Murakuma recognized it before Sanders explained.

"As you know, when Admiral Prescott entered Home Hive One for the second time and commenced his destruction of the warp point defenses, he probed each of those warp points."

"And discovered that Home Hive One is connected to Pesthouse and the Anderson Chain," Murakuma agreed, leaning across her desk to trace that warp chain with a slim finger, all the way to Alpha Centauri and Sol, which were as far as this little display extended. "It's a pity he wasn't in a position to do anything about it, but given the Bug forces holding the intervening systems and our ignorance of how many warp points in those systems might serve them as avenues of attack . . ."

She shrugged, and her face clouded with the memory of Operation Pesthouse.

"Yes, Sir. But he sent RD2s through *all* of Home Hive One's warp points, not just that one." Sanders indicated the wheel-spokes extending from the hub that was Home Hive One. "None of the others turned up anything even remotely as interesting . . . including this one." Sanders pointed at the undistinguished dot of light at the end of one of the spokes. "Nevertheless, as a matter of course, all the data was sent to Alpha Centauri.

"Now, you're also aware that back when Admiral Prescott and Fang Zhaarnak were here in Zephrain commanding Sixth Fleet, there was a period after the 'April Fool' offensive in '65 when the situation in Home Hive Three was very fluid and unsettled—a war of raids and counter raids. The Bugs weren't bothering to watch Home Hive Three's other warp points very closely—"

"They still aren't," Murakuma interjected. "My own probes indicate that they only have serious defenses at Warp Points Four and Six, as Survey's gotten around to designating them. Warp Point Four is the one connecting to Zephrain."

"Well," Sanders continued, "Admiral Prescott took advantage of that inattention at the time. In the course of his raids, his ships carried a lot of RD2s into Home Hive Three, and he was able to send at least a few through the system's warp points and get back some data on what lay beyond them. That data, naturally, was also sent back to Alpha Centauri."

Sanders gave the briefcase a command, and another warp line chart appeared, on the left side of the screen, showing Zephrain, Home Hive Three, and the warp lines radiating out from the latter, terminating in the little dots representing the systems Prescott's probes had discovered.

"It was only recently—while I was on my way back from Seventh Fleet, in fact—that the two sets of data got correlated."

Another murmured command, and the two charts moved together on the screen until two dots—one of them connected to Home Hive One, another to Home Hive Three—touched, and merged into one.

"You mean—?"

"Yes, Admiral. They're one and the same system. Spectrographic analysis of that star—it's a red giant, by the way—leaves no room for doubt on that score."

"Well, well . . ." Murakuma leaned back in her chair and steepled her fingers. "In addition to being one transit away from Home Hive Three, Zephrain is also only three away from Home Hive One." Her eyes remained on the screen with its now-unbroken pattern of warp connections, but they seemed focused on something far more distant. "Another piece of the puzzle."

"That's a good way to put it, Sir. Bit by bit, we're learning the layout of Bug space. Frustratingly little, so far. But—"

"But enough to account for the orders you're bringing me," Murakuma finished for him.

"Very perceptive, Sir." It wasn't the sort of thing lieutenants usually said to admirals. But Sanders' position as the Joint Staff's messenger was an anomalous one, and Murakuma possessed her soul in patience as he fell into lecture mode.

"As you've pointed out, Admiral Prescott was in no position to do anything with the new astrographic knowledge he'd acquired. We're as sure as we can be of anything that the Bugs have only three home hive systems left, but we don't know how big a 'support structure' of secondary colonies each of them has. The fact that Seventh Fleet found half a dozen such colonies that apparently existed to supply Home Hive One with resources is fairly discouraging. It suggests maybe fifteen to twenty remaining Bug systems—fewer than we once assumed, but still a lot, any or all of which could lie along the flanks of the Anderson Chain."

He ran a finger along the light-string from Home Hive One to Alpha Centauri, with its branching warp lines trailing off into unknownness.

"Now, I'm only repeating common knowledge when I tell you the Alliance is gradually assembling a new force—to be known as Grand Fleet—at Alpha Centauri for a massive push through Pesthouse to Home Hive One. But in the meantime, we need to get support to Admiral Prescott without delay. And since we've built up Zephrain's logistics capability, as well as its defenses—"

"I believe I'm one step ahead of you, Lieutenant," Murakuma interrupted.

"No doubt, Sir." Sanders patted the briefcase again. "The details are here. But in essence, you're being directed to seize control of Home Hive Three, destroy the remaining Bug warp point defenses—destruction of their mobile forces is secondary to that—and proceed to link up with Admiral Prescott."

Murakuma leaned forward, not troubling to conceal her eagerness.

"So we're finally going to kick the Bugs out of Home Hive
Three permanently. Good! That will end the threat to Zephrain
once and for all."

"And, by extension, the threat to Rehfrak," Sanders nodded.
"That's an added benefit of the plan—and one reason why the
Orions, including Lord Talphon, pushed hard for it."

Murakuma leaned back again, all thoughts of slapping Sanders down for his informality even further from her mind than
before.

*So, finally, I'm to go on the attack, for the first time in five
years. . . . For the first time since Justin.*

*Five years of sitting on the defensive, first at Justin and then here,
honing Fifth Fleet and then Sixth Fleet to a fine edge in preparation to stand off a counteroffensive that never came.*

*The ghosts still visit me, sometimes. I thought they might stop
after I left Justin. But I suppose distance doesn't matter to them.*

*No, they have to be exorcized. With fire.*

Their first inkling of unpleasant surprises came after they'd
entered Home Hive Three, leaving the drifting debris that had
been the warp point defenses astern.

Murakuma's extended RD2 reconnaissance from Zephrain had left
her uncertain of the strength of the defenses she would face—some
of those fortress readings were bound to have deep space buoys
lurking behind them, spoofing the drones with third-generation
ECM. So she'd taken no chances. Her initial bombardment had
saturated *all* of them with the new HARM2 missiles, which had
homed in unerringly on the DSBs, leaving the *real* fortresses
standing alone against the subsequent SBMHAWK storm.

Those SBMHAWKs had been less numerous than they might
have been if Murakuma hadn't had to withhold a large reserve of
the fourth-generation ones as anti-gunboat insurance. But they'd
carried the new warheads that the physicists' prim disapproval
had been powerless to keep people from calling "shaped-charge
antimatter." The name might be nonsense, but the extremely dense,
open-ended antiradiation field formed in the microsecond before
detonation, had performed as advertised in its combat debut,
channeling all those inconceivable blast and radiation effects on
a single bearing. It had burned through the shields and armor of
the great immobile fortresses like a war god's blowtorch. Granted,

it was ill-adapted to dealing with small, nimble targets like the gunboats that teemed around the warp point . . . but that was what the SBMHAWK4s and SRHAWKs were for, and the few Bug gunboats that survived them had done so only to be swarmed under by Murakuma's own Gorm-piloted gunboats.

So now Sixth Fleet proceeded, intact, towards the location of the Bug deep-space forces, as reported by the RD2s, on as direct a course as possible.

Murakuma observed that progress from the flag bridge of TFNS *Li Chien-lu*. The green icons in the holo sphere were neatly arranged into three task forces. *Li* herself was part of Admiral Janet Parkway's TF 61, along with five other monitors, thirty-six superdreadnoughts, twelve battleships, and twelve battlecruisers. Force Leader Maahnaahrd's TF 62 was also a battle-line formation—but Gorm-crewed in its heavier units, and therefore faster—with six monitors, twenty-three superdreadnoughts, and fifteen battlecruisers. TF 63, under Eighty-Seventh Small Fang Meearnow'raalphaa, supplied fighter cover from twenty-three assault carriers and twenty-two fleet carriers, escorted by twenty-six battlecruisers. A tenuous shell of Gorm gunboats screened the whole interlocking series of formations.

Murakuma's satisfaction dimmed as she turned to the larger-scale display in which her fleet shrank to a mere three task force icons and the hostiles were little more than a vague scarlet blur up ahead. Her recon drones, constantly pounced on by roving Bug gunboats, had been unable to provide a detailed threat profile.

*So*, she told herself, *we'll just have to be ready for anything. . . .*

"Has Fang Meearnow acknowledged?" she asked her chief of staff.

"Yes, Sir." Leroy McKenna was a captain now and gray was starting to invade his skullcap of short, kinky black hair. "All his CSGs have reported their squadrons armed with anti-ship ordnance but standing by to rearm for anti-kamikaze dogfighting if necessary."

Good." McKenna's steadiness always had a calming effect on Murakuma, and if anything, the chief of staff was even steadier now that Demosthenes Waldeck was no longer around. McKenna had learned to work smoothly, even closely, with Waldeck, but he was also a Fringe Worlder who'd never been able to completely rid himself of his prejudice against Corporate Worlders—especially ones with surnames that were bywords for plutocracy.

Murakuma had never blamed McKenna for his feelings, because she knew exactly what the Corporate Worlds had done to the chief of staff's once affluent family. But she'd also known Demosthenes for close to fifty years, and she knew that whatever other members of his sprawling family might be, there was no finer officer in the TFN's black and silver. Eventually, even McKenna had been forced to admit that in Demosthenes' special case. But hard as he'd tried—and Lord knew he *had* tried!—the mere fact that Demosthenes was related by blood to someone like Agamemnon Waldeck had been a hurdle McKenna had simply been unable to completely overcome.

*Just as well Demosthenes stayed in Justin*, Murakuma reflected. The thought was no reflection on her former second in command who'd succeeded to command of Fifth Fleet. Quite the reverse, in fact. But it was a realization that she needed her chief of staff as free as possible of the one single source of instability in his character.

She dismissed the thought and turned back to the display. Too bad the returns on the Bug battle-line were so indistinct. . . .

Craft Commander Mansaduk—his official rank was "Son of the Khan" when he was required to have a rank-title for some administrative purpose or other, but it was only an "acting" rank, to borrow a useful concept from the Humans who were now part of the extended *lomus*—shifted his hexapedal form. A lengthy patrol like this seemed even lengthier in the cramped accommodations of the gunboat, but Mansaduk was used to it. And he ordered himself not to let his attention waver, lest his gunboat's portion of the elaborate multiplex pattern of sensor coverage become a window of vulnerability for the fleet.

He also ordered himself not to voice the thought to his sensor operator. Chenghat knew his duties, and unnecessary reminders might be taken as a reflection on his sense of *synklomus*. Another Human concept—*chickenshit*—came to mind.

No, he would hear from Chenghat if anything untoward appeared on the gunboat's sensor readouts.

In fact, he knew it before the sensor operator spoke. His head came up as the *minisorchi* awareness weaving back and forth between him and every member of his crew jangled with sudden tension. He'd already begun moving over to stand behind the sensor operator's hobbyhorselike "chair" to look over his double shoulder at the red blips that had appeared—and were appearing in greater and greater numbers, like a spreading rash, now that Chenghat knew where to look.

They'd crept around the fleet's flank under cloak. And now they'd just about maneuvered into its blind zone.

In some corner of his mind, as yet uninvaded by shock, Mansaduk reflected that at times like this the notorious Gorm indifference to what their allies regarded as normal standards of military punctilio had its uses. He turned to the communications operator—only a few feet away, as was everyone else on the little control deck.

"Bypass ordinary channels," he ordered. "Go directly to Force Leader Maahnaahrd's flag communications operator. This *must* be communicated to Fleet Flag without delay."

"Bring the Fleet to a heading of zero-three-zero! I want our broadsides to those hostiles!"

Captain Ernesto Cruciero knew better than to protest when Vanessa Murakuma's voice crackled in command mode.

"Aye, aye, Sir," he acknowledged. But after the helm orders had begun to go out, his natural conservatism asserted itself.

"Sir, maybe we should investigate the data a little further before we commit the entire fleet to a major course change on the basis of a single gunboat's report," he suggested.

Murakuma spared a moment to study Cruciero's dark, hawk-nosed face. Ever since replacing Ling Tian as her ops officer, he'd demonstrated certain qualities with impressive consistency. One was intelligence and an analytical approach to planning operations. Another was the moral courage to argue forthrightly with the chief of staff and even with the fleet commander in support of his views, as he was doing now. But another was a certain lack of flexibility. Give him a definite, inarguable objective, and his technical competence was second to none. But put him in a fluid situation with a multiplicity of potential threats, and the very analytical ability which made him such an effective planner could become a liability. His instinct was almost always to hold his initial course until he'd been able to consider any sudden, unanticipated threat carefully. Whether there was really time for that or not.

"No, Ernesto. Those—" she indicated the scarlet fuzz-ball of indistinct hostile icons which the fleet's base vector was now swinging away from "—are ECM3-equipped buoys simulating capital ships to suck us in while their real deep space force works its way around us under cloak. Thank God for that Gorm gunboat! As it is, we just barely have time to get turned around before they get into SBM range."

"CIC makes it less than two minutes, Sir," McKenna put in. His black face held an ashen undertone.

Murakuma felt the way the chief of staff looked. McKenna hadn't completed the thought, nor had he needed to. Another two minutes, and the Bugs would have launched from within Sixth Fleet's blind zone. Now, at least, any missiles would fly into clear point defense envelopes.

*Sheer luck. After five years, what made me think I still had it in me to command a fleet in combat?*

She dismissed the useless self-doubt and turned away from the plot.

"Commodore Olivera," she told her *farshathkhanaak* formally, "rearm the fighters. I think we can expect kamikazes."

*The ploy had come tantalizingly close to complete success, and even while falling short, it had left the Fleet in an advantageous position, in relatively short range of an Enemy fleet which was only now awake to its presence, and which was in the process of changing course. The small attack craft would be denied the kind of long-range dogfighting they preferred.*

*Now, clearly, was the time to launch every available gunboat and small craft.*

*Furthermore, the Fleet's lighter starships—sixty battlecruisers and seventy-eight light cruisers—should simultaneously be committed to a headlong attack. Those ships were too vulnerable to the Enemy's firepower to survive in a battle-line action. They were, therefore, expendable. Whatever damage they could inflict would be useful. And they might cripple enough ships to force the Enemy to slow down, allowing the Fleet's fifty-three superdreadnoughts to close the range*

Murakuma and her staff were still on *Li*'s flag bridge, which they'd left only to answer calls of nature, when the final reports of the defensive action filtered in.

In what had become standard Alliance tactical doctrine, the Ophiuchi fighter pilots had concentrated on the kamikaze small craft while the human and Orion pilots dealt with the gunboats. But the late detection of the threat, the need to delay the fighters' launch until they could be rearmed for dogfighting, and the absolute necessity of intercepting the kamikazes short of the battle-line, had sent those pilots into action under a huge disadvantage. There'd been no time for careful planning and squadron briefings, no time for CSGs to meticulously assign targets and zones of responsibility. Strikegroups and individual squadrons had been vectored into head-on, least-time interceptions which stripped away at least half of their normal combat advantages, and their losses had been painful.

But those pilots had also turned in the sort of superb performance that too many of the Federation's political/media class never acknowledged. Despite everything, they'd stopped all but one of the kamikazes short of striking a target directly. (The monitor *Danville Sadat*, lost with all hands—a fact the newsies would, of course, report with ghoulish attention to detail.) Sixty-two other gunboats had survived long enough to ripple-fire their FRAMs . . . but the swarms of pursuing fighters had forced them to do so from extreme range. So only (!) two Terran assault carriers had died, and two other ships had suffered severe damage.

But then, while the fighters were still engaged with the gunboats and small craft, a wave of battlecruisers and light cruisers had swept in—super-kamikazes, far more resistant to fighter attack at the best of times.

This hadn't been the best of times. The fighters, still armed for dogfighting, and not for anti-shipping strikes, had been forced to turn their battle weary attention to the new targets and to attack from knife-range, using only their internal lasers—and all too many of them had died in the antimatter fires of those ships' suicide-rider fighter traps. Again, the fighters had performed magnificently, but a few dozen Bug cruisers had gotten through them despite all they could do.

Not that it had done the Bugs much good. Murakuma's cruiser screen had been waiting for them, supported by long-range missile fire from the battle-line. Even command datalink hadn't enabled the light ships to survive the avalanche of missiles, and not one of them had succeeded in ramming. But some had died at ranges close enough for their huge internal antimatter warheads to inflict damage even on capital ships.

Now Murakuma stood, exhausted, and emotionally spent, and read the tale of that damage on the readouts.

"It could have been worse, Sir." Coming from McKenna, it wasn't the fatuity it might have been from some people.

"Yes, it could have." Murakuma stopped herself short of saying anything more. She didn't want to acknowledge how relieved she was, not to McKenna, and perhaps not even to herself. She gazed at the display a moment longer, then drew a deep breath. When she turned back to the chief of staff, she'd shaken off the worst of her fatigue.

"Now, then," she said briskly. "We'll detach our worst damaged ships and leave them here with a screen of battlecruisers and a fighter CSP while we close with their battle-line."

She indicated the main enemy force—the *real* one—in the holo sphere.

"Our fighter cover's been seriously weakened, Sir," Olivera pointed out.

"I know. But our battle-line's practically intact, and their kamikazes have shot their bolt." Murakuma wore an expression the staffers hadn't seen on it for a long while. They'd all known her too long to be fooled by her fragile appearance anyway, but now they were reminded anew that a bird of prey is also fine-boned. "It's been some time since we and the Bugs have fought a good old-fashioned line-of-battle engagement without significant fighter or gunboat involvement. I believe I'd like to try it. And we have the tactical speed to force engagement."

The monitor *Irena Riva y Silva* grew in the shuttle's forward ports, gleaming faintly with the feeble reflected light of the orange local star.

There'd been some debate about who should go to see whom after Sixth Fleet entered the system. Some had felt Raymond Prescott should come to *Li Chien-lu* and pay his respects to Murakuma, who was, after all, senior to him.

In Murakuma's mind, though, there'd never been any doubts. This was Prescott's system by right of conquest, bought by Seventh Fleet with blood. She was the newcomer, and she would make the ritual request for permission to enter.

*Not that we haven't paid some blood ourselves,* she thought as *Riva y Silva* continued to grow, displaying the daunting blend of massiveness and intricacy that characterized capital ships of space. The meeting of the battle-lines had cost her three battleships, and other ships had suffered various degrees of damage. But the Bug deep space force had perished in a cataclysm of massed missile salvos, with only three of its ships escaping into cloak and evading destruction. Afterwards, Murakuma had taken her fleet across the system Raymond Prescott and Zhaarnak'telmasa had depopulated in the very first application of the Shiva Option to Warp Point Six. It was the sole fortified warp point remaining . . . until its defenses, too, died beneath the missile-storm, and in all the Home Hive Three System, only humans and their allies lived.

The sequel had been anticlimactic. Sixth Fleet had proceeded through the undefended Warp Point Five and the equally undefended red giant system beyond—the one whose identification had revealed the very possibility of this operation. Then they'd pressed on through the equally lifeless emptiness of Home Hive One, and her advance elements had fired courier drones through that system's Warp Point Five to greet Seventh Fleet . . . and the circle had been closed.

*No*, Murakuma told herself as the boatbay entrance gaped in *Riva y Silva*'s side to swallow up her shuttle. *It's not closed yet. Soon, though.*

The shuttle settled to the deck. She stood up, adjusted her tunic, and descended the ramp to face a Marine honor guard and an array of officers headed by a man she'd last seen in Kthaara'zarthan's office on Nova Terra, over three standard years before. A short man, rather nondescript-looking when viewed from a distance, who stepped forward to greet her.

"Welcome aboard, Admiral Murakuma."

"Thank you, Admiral Prescott." They shook hands . . . and the circle *was* closed.

The moment lasted perhaps a human heartbeat. Then Prescott's hazel eyes twinkled.

"Well, Kthaara *did* say he'd find an offensive command for you!"

# CHAPTER NINETEEN
## Operation Orpheus

Zhaarnak hadn't been present for Murakuma's arrival. He'd been back in AP-4 at the time, reviewing the battle damage repairs. But since then, he'd returned to Bug-10, as they were calling it in accordance with the system of designation Seventh Fleet's astrographic specialists had devised for the new systems that Operation Retribution had uncovered. Now the three of them were relaxing in Prescott's quarters.

"Well," said their host, whose family tradition reached back to the wet navies of pre-space Old Terra, "I believe the sun is over the yardarm."

Zhaarnak gave the chopped-off growl that answered to a human snort. Murakuma suspected he'd heard the expression once or twice.

"*Which* sun?" he inquired, with a gesture that encompassed the binary star system outside *Riva y Silva*'s hull. The monitor flagship, not surprisingly given the nature of Seventh Fleet's composition, had the latest version of the Alliance's translation software. The electronically produced voice in Murakuma's earbug still lacked the ability of a human translator to interpret the finer nuances of the Tongue of Tongues, but it was far better than any of the others she'd encountered. It actually recognized and indicated the Tabby's amusement, but she noticed that that amusement didn't stop him from accepting a drink. She was a bit surprised by his choice of beverage, however. The Khanate had long been a major export market for the region of North America still known as Kentucky, but Lord Telmasa apparently preferred vodka.

She sipped her own Irish and studied Prescott. She'd heard of his reaction to his brother's death, and she'd half expected to find a congealed-lava sculpture of a human soul. *Of course,* she told herself, *I never really knew him before Andrew's death—barely met him, in fact. And he's had time to get over it. . . .*

And yet, she felt she could sense something of what lay behind the stories she'd heard. It wasn't that his affability was a mere façade. It was perfectly sincere—as far as it went. But now it enclosed something that hadn't been there before. She still hadn't seen him under circumstances calculated to summon that something up. And yet . . . *I remember laughing out loud the first time I heard someone compare him to Ivan Antonov. The mental image was just too droll. But now I wonder.*

Her eyes wandered to the private work area that abutted on Prescott's living quarters. Even in this day of reactionless drives, and even for full admirals, space vessels were penurious of personal elbowroom. The desktop computer terminal was too small to incorporate its own holo display, for example. But the warp network lent itself to two-dimensional representation, and the flat liquid-crystal display screen showed a pattern Murakuma recognized—for the most part.

"I see you've got your computer trained to show the new designations you've assigned to the systems out here."

"Yes." Prescott stepped over to join her. "We have to do something to keep them straight."

The systems of the warp chain between AP-5 and Home Hive One—Prescott's "high road"—and the ones disclosed by RD2 probes through the warp points no Allied task force had yet to transit had each been dubbed "Bug" followed by some arbitrarily assigned number. The display showed everything from Zephrain to AP-5, and Murakuma saw that the red giant system through which she'd passed between Home Hive Three and Home Hive One was now Bug-04. She also noted that the system into which the enemy survivors had fled from Bug-10, and where they presumably still lurked, was Bug-11. Bug-12 lay between here and Franos, and beyond Franos was Bug-14. Other such designations were appended to the various systems connected with Home Hives One and Three. And yet . . .

She pointed at three red dots, one of them connected to Home Hive Three by the string-lights of warp lines and the other two similarly linked to Home Hive One.

"You haven't gotten around to assigning designations to those?"

"Oh, those." Murakuma had no difficulty recognizing Prescott's eagerness to spring a surprise. What she wasn't in a position to recognize was how unusual that eagerness had become since his brother's death.

"Well, we've learned something new about the systems, which suggests they need something more distinctive," he said, and paused significantly. But Murakuma declined to rise to the bait, and he resumed before the pause could lengthen. "First of all, we sent RD2s through Bug-04's third warp point—the one other than those you used to enter and leave the system. It turned out to lead to *this* system."

He indicated the unnamed red dot already connected to Home Hive Three. Another red string-light appeared between it and Bug-04, and the three dots formed the points of a triangle.

"Hmmm. Interesting," Murakuma allowed. "But—"

"At the same time," Prescott overrode her, "we decided to launch a raid—a reconnaissance in force—from Home Hive One. Our RD2s had determined that one of the two unexplored systems connected with it was heavily defended, but that the other one had nothing but a screening force of their slow picket cruisers." He pointed at the middle dot of the three. "So our raiding force was able to get loose in the system, do a little quick-and-dirty surveying, and fire RD2s through the two warp points they turned up. And where do you suppose those warp lines led?"

The impression of pulling a rabbit from a hat was unmistakable now, and Prescott grinned as Murakuma watched two additional string-lights grow outward from that middle system to the other two.

"So," she breathed. "They're another chain. . . ."

"The 'Orpheus Chain,'" Prescott agreed, and shrugged as she arched an eyebrow at him. "No special significance. It's just that our fleet Survey types belong to the school that prefers names from the grab bag of Classical mythology." He gave another command, and the names "Orpheus 1," "Orpheus 2," and "Orpheus 3" appeared in red beside the three dots, from right to left. Serious again, he pointed to Orpheus 1.

"None of our RD2s have penetrated far enough into the system to search for additional warp points. But the heavy fixed defenses, and the substantial battle-line force backing them up, suggest that it's the gateway to more Bug population centers."

"Perhaps another home hive system," Zhaarnak rumbled.

"We can't know that," Prescott cautioned his *vilkshatha* brother, then turned back to Murakuma and continued in measured tones. "I think all we can say for certain is that the evidence suggests that there are fairly major Bug populations somewhere along this chain. Coming up with anything more definite than that would require a serious, manned survey effort, at the very least, and that would require a heavy naval covering force." He shrugged. "For now, we can't think in terms quite that ambitious. Our current emphasis has to be on extending our defensive perimeter—our 'glacis'—around our present position. I've been thinking in those terms ever since Sixth Fleet arrived."

"Because Seventh Fleet is still below strength," Murakuma finished the thought for him.

"True," Prescott admitted. "And it's also worrisome that we still have enemy holdouts in Bug-11—" he indicated the system beyond Bug-10's third warp point "—and the system where the Bug survivors fled from Franos."

"The gunboat raids from those systems have not allowed us to forget about their existence," Zhaarnak put in dryly.

"Nevertheless," Prescott maintained, "we can contain that problem—especially with the help of the carriers that have recently arrived from Alpha Centauri."

Murakuma nodded. She'd been advised of the Joint Chiefs decision to dispatch seventy Terran light carriers and thirty Ophiuchi escort carriers to help buttress Seventh Fleet's rear-area fighter platforms. Those ship classes had been viable battle fleet units in the days of the Third Interstellar War and (though less so) the Theban War, but they were simply too light to survive in today's battle-line combat environment. They could still carry fighters, though, and enough of them could cover the warp points beyond which those bothersome Bug holdouts lurked, staying well back themselves but maintaining fighter patrols that tracked down and obliterated the gunboat incursions in extended running battles.

"Still," Prescott admitted, "we are, as you observed, still repairing our damaged units back in AP-4. We're hoping to get some of them back into action in a month—"

"Based on what I have just seen there," Zhaarnak interjected dourly, "two months might be more realistic."

"—and substantial reinforcements are on the way. But for now, I think Seventh Fleet had best stand on the defensive."

"Sixth Fleet," Murakuma observed quietly, "has essentially completed its repairs."

"I'd thought of that." Prescott looked up to meet her eyes.

"And," Zhaarnak added, "it would lend our bridgehead here more depth if we could secure control of that chain."

A moment of three-way eye contact passed, with no further conversation, nor any need of it. Then Murakuma turned back to the screen and spoke matter-of-factly.

"Tell me more about the defenses of the Orpheus systems."

*The System Which Must Be Defended, threatened from two directions, was now isolated from all contact with its two remaining fellows. But there was no way the Enemy could know that. This new offensive must be simply an effort to extend the zone of occupied systems.*

*If so, it was succeeding, despite the ploy that the Fleet's light picket force had attempted in the first system to come under attack and despite the Mobile Force's attempt to take the attackers in the rear after they'd turned aside to deal with the empty system further along the chain.*

*Of course, the Mobile Force had had to act alone in seizing that opportunity. The System Which Must Be Defended, understandably cautious in its present extremity, would release no forces for operations beyond the system where the Mobile Force was based, one warp transit away. To venture further along the warp chain, it was felt, was to risk being cut off from the one remaining source of supply.*

*But however understandable that caution might be, it didn't change the fact that the Mobile Force, on its own, had lacked sufficient gunboats to make the stroke a decisive one. And now it was back in this system, facing an imminent attack. At least the System Which Must Be Defended had promptly replenished its gunboat strength, and was prepared to commit its massive battle-line if needed to hold* this *system.*

As she stood on *Li Chien-lu's* flag bridge, Vanessa Murakuma thought back to the briefing she'd gotten from Prescott's spook Chung and reflected on what she was about to face in Orpheus 1.

*Twice as many picket cruisers as either of these last two systems,* she thought. *And the deep space force is nothing to sneeze at: thirty-three superdreadnoughts and seventy-five battlecruisers. At least they've expended their gunboats.*

*Or have they?*

Sixth Fleet had transited from Home Hive One to Orpheus 2

behind an SBMHAWK and AMBAMP bombardment that she'd hoped would clear the way through a gunboat combat space patrol considerably heavier than the system's picketing force-level would have led one to expect—evidence for Zhaarnak's notion of a home hive system further up the line?—and leave her crewed vessels with little to do. It hadn't quite worked out that way. *Why,* she'd wondered, *doesn't it ever quite work out that way?*

The Bugs had reacted with their usual stereotype-shattering adaptability to the Alliance's use of HARMs to kill their decoy buoys. They'd refitted large numbers of their *Director*-class warp point defense cruisers to mount advanced deep space buoy control systems, and deployed their ECM3 equipped buoys in multiple shells. One shell was active at all times; but if the SBMHAWK-launched HARM2 took out too many of those active buoys as they ate their way in toward the *real* starships, then the cruisers were tasked to bring up still more buoys, giving the whole system a reactive feature.

But Murakuma, wary of ECM-related dirty tricks such as Prescott and Zhaarnak had recounted to her, had sent in RD2s in the wake of the last SBMHAWKs to assess the bombardment's effect. They'd reported altogether too many surviving targets. So she'd expended practically every SBMHAWK she had left on a second bombardment before transiting, and then exterminated the surviving twenty or thirty cruisers at the cost of damage to only a handful of her ships.

She'd found herself in possession of the lifeless red dwarf system. With nothing to detain her in Orpheus 2, she'd sent her damaged ships to Zephrain for repairs, accompanied by freighters she'd borrowed from Prescott with orders to bring back fresh supplies of SBMHAWKs.

The unexpectedly high rate at which she'd expended the warp-capable missiles had been some cause for concern, although the situation would have been far worse before she'd broken through to Seventh Fleet from Zephrain. Neither she nor Prescott had ever specifically mentioned it, but she knew both the *vilkshatha* brothers had to be immensely relieved by the shortening of their supply lines. Munitions, as such, hadn't been a problem since the end of the first year of the war. Even Leroy McKenna, with his hatred of all things Corporate World, had to admit that the incredible industrial base the Corporate Worlders had managed to build up over the past century had come fully into its own since the Bugs had made their presence known. Murakuma would never have admitted it to her chief of staff, whose prejudice against the industrial magnates who owned the Corporate Worlds needed no reinforcement, but the unscrupulous and increasingly overt ways in which Agamemnon Waldeck and his ilk manipulated the Federal laws and fiscal policy for their greedy self-interest sickened her. But however they'd done it, the stupendous manufacturing capacity of their worlds was all that had saved the Federation—and probably its allies, as well—from something far worse than mere destruction.

It was that capacity which had permitted the TFN to rebuild itself after Operation Pesthouse, and to provide the entire Grand Alliance with expendable munitions which were fully interchangeable between any of its member navies. And, for that matter, to find the yard space to build entire monitors for the less industrially capable Khanate. Now that the new assembly lines which had been set up when the war began had fully hit their strides, the fighters and missiles and SBMHAWK pods required to meet the Bugs in battle without resorting to their own self-immolating expenditure of life were literally pouring into the military's depots.

Unfortunately, merely producing the weapons didn't automatically get them to the front, where they were needed. That was the job of freighters and supply convoys, and the sheer length of the lifeline stretching between Seventh Fleet and its source of supplies meant that Prescott and Zhaarnak had been forced to be extremely sensitive to their ammunition expenditures.

But Sixth Fleet's long-time base at Zephrain was only a single warp transit from the major commercial nexus of Rehfrak. Once the Khanate had become confident that Zephrain could hold against any potential Bug counterattack from the ruins of Home Hive Three, the Rehfrak warp point had been opened to Sixth Fleet's supply convoys, and Zephrain had been built up into the second largest naval base ever built by the Terran Federation. The stockpiles of ammunition, spare fighters, and every other imaginable requirement for war fighting which had been built up in Zephrain were more than ample to support the operations of Sixth and Seventh Fleet, alike.

Yet however short and convenient their new supply line might be, the weapons still had to be physically moved from Zephrain to where they were required, and waiting while the freighters made the round trip between there and Orpheus 2 had at least given her time to decide where to turn next.

Her real objective was Orpheus 1, where she knew major Bug forces awaited her. She would have preferred to leave Orpheus 3 to die on the vine, isolated as it was by her occupation of

Orpheus 2 . . . assuming that it was, in fact, isolated. But because she couldn't be *certain* that that system held no warp connections to yet more Bug-inhabited planets, she'd had no choice but to go ahead and occupy it at least long enough to find out.

The operation had proved an easy one, and the planetless red giant known as Orpheus 3 had turned out to have no warp points—or, at least, no *open* ones—other than the three they already knew about. So she'd turned back towards Orpheus 2 . . . only to encounter courier drones bearing the news that the Orpheus 1 deep space force had made its move.

The Bug superdreadnoughts and battlecruisers had brushed aside the light screening force she'd left in Orpheus 2, but remained there only long enough to empty their gunboat racks before returning to their bolthole of Orpheus 1. The almost six hundred gunboats had then screamed across six light-hours to the warp point through which Murakuma must return from Orpheus 3.

Much as it irked her to acknowledge it, the Bug maneuver had very nearly worked. Less than a thousand gunboats could never have destroyed Sixth Fleet, but they *could* have inflicted serious damage upon it, especially striking from ambush as it made transit through a warp point it believed to be secure. Obviously, that was precisely what the Bugs had had in mind, but the courier drones from her screening force had reached her just ahead of that onrushing wave of death, and she'd begun her return transit in time . . . barely.

*All right, so maybe God* sometimes *remembers which side He's supposed to be on,* she admitted grudgingly, recalling the haste with which she'd rushed the fleet through that warp point and into a defensive posture. Her hurriedly launched fighters had burned their way through the masses of gunboats. But, as always, no defense was totally kamikaze-proof. Only one superdreadnought had actually been destroyed, but two monitors, an assault carrier, and three fleet carriers had been sent limping to Zephrain.

Despite her losses, Murakuma remained confident that she could deal with the Bug forces in Orpheus 1 as soon as she'd completed emergency repairs and brought up fresh SBMHAWKs. Still, the experience had been sufficiently chastening to make her decide a little misdirection was in order.

Which was why she now stood on *Li*'s flag deck in Home Hive One, waiting at that system's Orpheus 1 warp point with the bulk of Sixth Fleet and listening to the report from the elements she'd left in Orpheus 2.

"Force Leader Maahnaahrd confirms that he's prepared to fire his first wave of SBMHAWKs into Orpheus 1 according to plan," McKenna concluded.

"Very good." Murakuma nodded. Maahnaahrd's SBMHAWKs were loaded exclusively with HARM2s, and her plan called for him to launch them in extended waves, over a period of several hours, beginning in—she checked the chrono—twelve standard minutes. Maahnaahrd's confirmation of his readiness had taken almost eight hours to reach her, even with the ICN she and Seventh Fleet had been busy laying, so there would be no way for him to tell her if he somehow missed the schedule after all, but the Gorm flag officer was utterly reliable, and she cherished no qualms about that side of the operation. Whether it worked or not was something else, of course.

The idea was for the Bugs to conclude that Maahnaahrd's lengthy bombardment was the prelude to a serious attack, intended to clear away the decoy buoys in order to allow the true defenses to be targeted, and she ordered herself to stay calm—or, at least, to project a calm image—as she awaited the news she hoped to hear. Since the Orpheus 1-Home Hive One warp point was nine light-hours from the one at which Sixth Fleet currently waited, however, that news wasn't going to come any time soon.

Nor did it. In fact, just over ten hours had passed before Marina Abernathy, with Kevin Sanders in tow, brought her the report she'd waited for.

"Admiral, the RD2s report substantial movement of gunboats in Orpheus 1—movement away from our warp point to the system. They also report that the Bugs' mobile forces are moving in the same direction."

"Which is the direction of the Orpheus 2 warp point," Sanders finished for her—an impropriety to which Murakuma, in her excitement, was oblivious.

"So they've fallen for it!" McKenna exclaimed. "They're sending everything they've got to meet Maahnaahrd's 'attack.'"

"Absolutely!" Ernesto Cruciero agreed. "Which means they're leaving the door wide open for us!"

"But we're not going through it just yet." Murakuma told him rather more sedately, and her amusement at the ops officer's frustrated eagerness was tempered by sympathy. "We'll let their battle-line get a little further away, first."

But she didn't make Cruciero fidget much longer before she

gave the order, and waves of SBMHAWKs—this time a serious attack, and not a feint—leapt for the warp point.

Sixth Fleet's starships proceeded more slowly in the missiles' wake. They emerged, with *Li Chien-lu* not far behind the van, into a volume of space blasted clean of the mines and laser-armed buoys that had covered it, and the ECM3 buoys that had pretended to be still more of the latter. Murakuma, now well aware of the deception, had disdained subtlety in her response to it. Given the massive supplies of SBMHAWKs available in Zephrain, she'd simply poured enough of them through the warp point to wipe out *everything* on the far side.

But the Bug picket cruisers, outside the immediate kill zone about the warp point, had survived the missile-storm which had annihilated the fixed defenses. That was a mixed blessing, however, because cheating death only meant that they found themselves standing alone against the entire strength of Sixth Fleet as Murakuma's chain of stupendous capital ships emerged into Orpheus 1.

They closed in anyway, clearly hoping to overwhelm the transiting ships in detail with missile fire. But they were slow, and by the time they could draw into missile range, Sixth Fleet's leading waves had reoriented themselves and gotten their datalink back on-line. Against the datalinked point defense of capital ship battlegroups, the heavy cruisers' missile fire was as futile as hail against a metal roof. So, with the horribly familiar suicidal passionlessness, they commenced their ramming runs.

The battle was intense but brief. The cruisers were slow, and not very maneuverable, but the space around the warp point was congested. Worse, they chose as their targets ships of the following waves, the ones which were still coming through and whose internal systems hadn't yet stabilized after the grav surge of transit. Even slow and clumsy kamikazes could get through against such befuddled targets, unless they were stopped short by active defenses.

Murakuma's massive, firepower-heavy ships blasted the cruisers out of existence as they closed, but some of them managed to get through, anyway. They cost Sixth Fleet two superdreadnoughts and heavy damage to one monitor, but painful as those losses were, they were far lower than the fleet might have suffered without the distracting effect of Maahnaahrd's decoy attack.

Now, as she waited for the remainder of her ships to make transit, Murakuma was able to pause and take stock.

She was 3.4 light-hours from Orpheus 1's red giant primary, and on a bearing that the computer placed at about two o'clock in the holo sphere. The Orpheus 2 warp point lay 5.4 light-hours from that sullen central fire, at seven o'clock. *Not quite diametrically opposite to us*, she reflected, *but close enough.* The Bug deep space force had been proceeding in that direction, preceded by a cloud of gunboats. Now it was pulling up, clearly not avoiding battle, but keeping a certain distance.

She turned away from the display and waved for McKenna to join her.

"I want to begin the next phase as soon as all elements have completed transit," she told him. "We'll head for the deep space force—but we'll keep a fighter screen out at all times. And tell Anson I want his combat space patrols to be prepared to counter kamikaze attacks from *any* direction."

"Sir?" McKenna looked puzzled by her emphasis.

"Think about it, Leroy. We wiped out as many gunboats as those capital ships could carry back in Orpheus 2. But now they've got a full complement of them again. For my money, that confirms Zhaarnak's belief that there's at least one more warp point somewhere around here, leading to some major Bug population center. Now that we're loose in the system, they're bound to call in more reinforcements. I want that fighter screen out. And I also want recon fighters probing in every direction."

*So the Enemy had entered from an unexpected direction. The courier drones hastily dispatched to the System Which Must Be Defended had made that clear to the Fleet's directing intelligences.*

*Clearly, the replacement gunboats already sent to that system would not suffice. The System Which Must Be Defended would have to intervene in more emphatic fashion.*

*Unfortunately, any such intervention would come through a warp point lying at the same bearing from the local star as the one through which the Enemy had entered—and almost twice as far out from it. And the Enemy was already headed inward, in pursuit of the system's defenders.*

The Bug deep space force found itself in the position that awaited *any* Bug mobile force which failed to hold a warp point against a stronger Allied fleet. Its slower capital ships were simply unable to avoid interception, even in a stern chase. Nor could they control the range of an engagement when they were brought to action. Vanessa Murakuma had used that advantage ruthlessly when her brutally outnumbered Fifth Fleet had stood alone against the juggernaut in defense of the Romulus Chain at the very beginning of the war.

Now, she used it again.

Anson Olivera's fighter squadrons waited, with the confident deadliness which had been trained into them in Zephrain and polished in combat in Home Hive Three, as the Bug gunboats made their runs. By now, it was as stylized as a kabuki play. Both sides knew their opponent's strengths and weaknesses, and both could predict how the other would respond far more often than not. The gunboats came roaring in, determined to break through to the Allied starships in hopes of at least inflicting sufficient damage to slow them and equalize the speed differential. And the fighter pilots of Sixth Fleet met them head-on, at extreme range, equally determined that they would not.

Fireballs began to blossom in the visual display as missiles reached out from either side to pluck victims from space. The fronts of the converging formations were picked out in antimatter fireflies that flashed with brilliant, dreadful beauty against the sooty black of the endless vacuum. It was a sight Vanessa Murakuma had seen far too many times since she'd first met the Bugs in battle in the starless K-45 warp nexus before Justin. As she saw it once more, she felt the pain of every flight crew she'd lost in every battle since, yet she couldn't look away. Those brief, poignant funeral pyres—for Bugs, as well as humans and their allies—drew her eyes like magnets which she literally could not turn away from.

But there was one enormous difference between Orpheus 1 and K-45. Then she'd been hideously outnumbered, able only to delay the juggernaut, not to stop it, and forced to pour out the lives of her men and women like water to accomplish even that. But this time . . . this time *she* held the force advantage, and she heard the ghosts of Justin, the ghosts of her own dead, the ghost of her daughter, as eyes of pitiless jade watched the moving waves of flame meet. Saw the fire converge, crest . . . and die as her fighter pilots slashed the last of the gunboats out of existence.

"Recall your pilots, Anson," she heard herself say, so calmly, so dispassionately. "Get them reorganized and rearm them for an anti-shipping strike."

✧    ✧    ✧

*The Enemy's small attack craft had annihilated the gunboats. That had been expected, but the fact that this time not a single one of them managed to penetrate the Enemy's defensive screen was a disappointment.*

*Still, they'd accomplished their primary goal. The System Which Must Be Defended had accepted that it must intervene decisively in this system. Its battle-line was preparing to make transit, but moving such a powerful force would take time, and the battle-line had declined to send its own gunboats ahead lest their arrival alert the Enemy of its approach.*

*So it was the task of the Mobile Force to keep the Enemy's attention focused firmly upon itself for as long as possible. The Enemy must be enticed into pursuing it, thrusting himself deeper and deeper into this system until it was too late for him to escape. Thus the gunboats had been committed to the attack less in the hopes that they would actually inflict damage, than in hopes that the Enemy would waste time destroying them . . . precisely as he had.*

*Now it was the Mobile Force's turn to do the same thing.*

"We'll do this cautiously, Ernesto," Murakuma told her ops officer. "We hold all the cards now, so you and Anson—" her eyes flicked to her *farshathkhanaak's* face "—will coordinate the fighter strikes carefully. I don't want any avoidable losses, any lives thrown away because someone gets overeager. Remember, the object is to overload their point defense so we can get through with shipboard missiles strikes, not to feed our squadrons into a sausage machine making close attacks."

"Understood, Sir," Olivera replied, and there was more than simple acknowledgment of an order in his tone. Vanessa Murakuma had never been a fighter pilot, but she was, perhaps, the strikefighter community's most beloved flag officer. Perhaps it was because her husband had been a member of that lodge, or perhaps it was simply because of who and what she herself was, but Murakuma had always agonized over her fighter losses, and that was something the fighter jocks appreciated deeply.

Every fighter pilot knew that, in the final analysis, he represented an expendable asset. He might not care for that knowledge, but he could hardly pretend he didn't know it . . . or that it was unreasonable. Flight crews might require long and arduous training, but an F-4 carried only a single pilot. Even the F-4C command fighter carried only a crew of three. A maximum effort strike by a TFN assault carrier's entire group exposed less than sixty individuals to the enemy's fire.

So, yes, the jocks understood that any admiral with a gram of sense would far rather expose—and expend, if necessary—that strikegroup than risk the loss of, say, a battlecruiser with a crew of over a thousand.

Vanessa Murakuma was no different from any other flag officer in that respect. What made her unlike some was that she never became callous about expending them, never became comfortable with the term "acceptable loss rate." She *cared*, and while she was just as capable of committing them to high-casualty strikes as she was of exposing herself to similar risks, she never lost sight of the need to minimize losses. And because the flight crews knew that, they would run risks for her they would never willingly run for someone else.

The Admiral looked at him a bit oddly, almost as if she sensed something of what was running through his mind, but he only returned her gaze levelly. After a moment, she inhaled and nodded.

"Very well, gentlemen. Let's get it done."

*The Enemy clearly had decided to use his range and speed advantage as ruthlessly as the Fleet would have used it, had the positions been reversed. Normally, that would have been . . . frustrating. Today, it was precisely what the Fleet wished him to do. True, it would prevent the Mobile Force from exacting anything approaching an equivalent level of loss, but such a long range engagement would also, of necessity, be slower than a close action. The outcome might never be in doubt, but it would take time for the Enemy to kill all of the Mobile Force's starships, and time, really, was all the Mobile Force was fighting for.*

*The Mobile Force watched the first waves of small attack craft arrowing in while the Enemy battlegroups closed to extreme missile range behind them, and prepared to expend itself as slowly as possible.*

The battle with the Bug mobile force was still raging when Murakuma received word of what was sweeping in from behind her.

So far, Sixth Fleet had administered a most satisfactory drubbing to the mobile force, destroying a third of its ships outright and damaging most of the rest. But there were still a lot of Bugs to kill, and they were being stubborn about it.

That was perfectly all right with Murakuma, who infinitely preferred to expend missiles instead of people. Yet even as the intensity of the battle rose and fell with successive fighter strikes, she'd found it difficult to keep her attention focused on it. She kept waiting for the news she was sure had to come, and wondering what portion of the sky it would fall out of. Now Cruciero's urgent voice interrupted her abstraction.

"Admiral, the recon fighters have detected incoming hostiles. CIC is getting the data into the computer, and it should be appearing—"

As if on cue, a scarlet dot with an attached vector-arrow winked into life, and Murakuma gazed at it through narrowed eyes as her staffers crowded around.

"So," she said after a moment, "the warp point was further out from the star than ours, but on just about the same bearing. We've been heading directly away from it the whole time."

"Yes, Sir," Cruciero confirmed. "And we've been leading these new arrivals on a stern chase."

"Things might have gotten hairy if they'd already been in-system to back up their battle-line here," McKenna remarked.

"But they weren't," Murakuma replied with more serenity than she felt, and looked at her intelligence officer. "Have the scouts been able to provide any data on the composition of this second force, Marina?"

"Yes, Sir," Abernathy replied. "CIC is breaking down the initial take right now, and more data's coming in every minute. It should be appearing on the boards any time."

It did, and silence descended.

"My God," Olivera finally said softly as the data scrolled across the display and they digested the numbers. Twenty-four monitors, a hundred and two superdreadnoughts, sixty battlecruisers, and a hundred and five light cruisers. Plus—

"The scouts haven't been able to provide an exact total for the gunboat screen," Abernathy said in a voice which only seemed shockingly loud. "But we're looking at a minimum of fifteen or sixteen hundred."

"Ernesto," Murakuma said quietly into the renewed and intensified silence. "If we continue on our present course to the Orpheus 2 warp point, can we reach it before they intercept us?"

Cruciero seemed caught flat-footed, but Kevin Sanders, standing in the middle distance, rescued him.

"Actually, Admiral, I've just run a projection based on the

maximum speed their ships can manage over that distance. The relative positions of the warp points will allow them to cut the angle on us and close the range, but, no, they can't catch us."

"Not even with our monitors slowing us down?"

"No, Sir. We've got a good head start." Even the insouciant Sanders recognized that he was on thin ice, intruding into the domain of operations as he was, which may have explained how he managed to restrain himself from reciting the platitude that a stern chase is a long chase.

"Their leading groups of gunboats should just barely be able to catch up with us, though," he added instead.

"Our fighters can handle gunboats," Olivera declared.

"Very well." Murakuma summoned up a smile. "In that case, ladies and gentlemen," she said with studied understatement, "I believe it's time to shut Operation Orpheus down."

*The Enemy had detected the System Which Must Be Defended's deep space force too soon.*

*Had it been any part of the Mobile Force's original plan to survive, the Enemy's sudden alteration of course might have been welcome. Under the circumstances, however, it could only be considered a disaster. The projections indicated that the Deep Space Force's starships would be unable to overhaul the Enemy before he could escape, and there was nothing the Mobile Force could do to prevent that. Most of its surviving ships were battered, air-leaking wrecks. Many had no effective weapons left, and even those which did were utterly incapable of overtaking the swifter Enemy, or even of staying in missile range of him when he chose to break off.*

*And so the Mobile Force could only watch as the Enemy it had paid so dear a price to delay went speeding off towards safety.*

*It was most inconvenient.*

Sixth Fleet's starships raced through space towards the warp point which spelled safety. Behind them, recon fighters and Gorm gunboats formed a watchful sensor shell, tracking the hurricane of gunboats which hurtled after them in pursuit.

There was something particularly nerve wracking about watching that massive blur of scarlet icons creep closer and closer in the plot. For the moment, however, there was no immediate danger, and the starships' crews went about their duties with disciplined calm. Those ships which had taken damage in the engagement with the original Bug mobile force took advantage of the break in the action to make repairs. Aboard the carriers, deck crews serviced the fighter squadrons as they were recalled from the CSP. Fighter missiles and gun packs replaced the anti-ship ordnance they'd been carrying. Pilots took the opportunity to gulp down hasty hot meals and hit the heads, then reassembled in their ready rooms for quick briefings before they hurried back to the launch bays, climbed into their cockpits, and waited.

And all the while, the pursuing cloud of scarlet death crept closer, and closer, and closer. . . .

*It was unfortunate that the Enemy's small attack craft had detected the Deep Space Force's approach soon enough to break off and run. Such an outcome had always been possible, of course—that was one reason the Deep Space Force had been reluctant to commit itself initially. Revealing its existence—and its strength—to the Enemy had been a calculated risk, taken only because an opportunity to cut off and completely destroy this invading fleet had presented itself.*

*That risk had failed. The Enemy was going to escape, and now he knew the Deep Space Force existed. He would be prepared for it when he finally moved against the System Which Must Be Defended, which would materially increase his chance of defeating it.*

*But at least the gunboats might be able to overtake him short of his warp point of escape. They couldn't possibly destroy such a force, but if they could catch it, they could bleed it.*

"All right, people," Captain Anson Olivera said over the fleet flight control net while he gazed into his master plot. Sixth Fleet's starships continued to speed onward, into the depths of Orpheus 2 and directly away from the warp point they'd just transited. But even as they fled, the icons of the carriers and the Gorm capital ships spawned a diamond dust of even tinier icons.

Olivera watched those little chips of light gather themselves, settling into the precisely arranged formation of a combat space patrol directly atop the warp point.

"We all know what to do," Sixth Fleet's *farshathkhanaak* told his glittering galaxy of lights. "Now do it."

*The Enemy formation had disappeared through the warp point before the gunboats could overhaul it. After so much had been risked and revealed in order to attack it, it was . . . unacceptable to allow it to escape intact.*

*At least the gunboats were hard on the Enemy's heels. And unlike the Enemy's small attack craft, gunboats were warp capable.*

Anson Olivera's pilots were waiting.

The Allied gunboats opened fire first. Unlike their Bug counterparts, who were armed to kill starships with short range FRAMs, the Gorm gunboats carried standard missiles on their ordnance racks. They opened fire from far outside the effective range of any weapon their enemies mounted, and those missiles carried far better penetration aids than had been available at the beginning of the war. Point defense could still stop them, of course, but that assumed point defense was available.

It wasn't.

Just like any starship, a gunboat's internal systems were subject to the grav surge of warp transit. For a brief, helpless moment, the Bugs *had* no effective point defense, and a forest of fireballs glared in their formation as the Gorm missiles slammed into them like blows from the Thunder God's hammer. The window before the Bugs' point defense came back on-line was brief, but the Gorm made the most of it—and even after the point defense came back up, a high percentage of their missiles got through.

After so many years of warfare, the Allies had amassed an enormous body of operational data on the Bugs. They used that data now. Carefully programmed tactical computers aboard the command fighters which led each strikegroup analyzed the seemingly total chaos of the Bugs' transiting formation, and within that chaos, found underlying order. Individual gunboat squadrons could be identified by the formations in which they flew, once one knew what to look for. The command fighters' computers knew. So did the ones aboard the Gorm gunboats, and targets were assigned with merciless precision.

Survival in a deep space dogfight depended upon many things. Individual pilot ability and training were highly important, of course. So was experience. But most important of all was teamwork. That was why pickup squadrons assembled out of random pilots unaccustomed to one another's individual strengths and weaknesses tended to be less effective in anti-shipping strikes and had low survival rates in fighter-on-fighter combat. But the underlying bone and sinew of deep space teamwork was the datanet which tied the individual units of the squadron together into a single, cohesive fighting force. And what made that fighting force dangerous was its ability to concentrate its full combat power against a single target or small, carefully selected group of targets.

Which was why the Gorm crews deliberately split their fire between multiple squadrons. Any Bug gunboat they could kill was worth destroying, but killing a squadron worth of gunboats out of several different squadrons was more effective than simply destroying a single squadron in its entirety. Taking them from many squadrons reduced the combat power of *each* of those squadrons in the same way that the picadore's darts weakened the bull before it faced the matador.

Of course, there were a great many "bulls" in the Bug formation . . . but there were also a great many matadors waiting for them.

The picadore Gorm pulled up and away as they fired the last of their missiles, and then it was the strikefighters' turn. There were no suicide pinnaces in this formation, because pinnaces couldn't have kept up with the gunboats in their long, high-speed run after Sixth Fleet. And because there were no pinnaces or shuttles, this time the Ophiuchi pilots who found themselves held in reserve, again and again, to pick off kamikazes short of the battle-line, were free to join their Terran and Orion allies in the gunboat hunt.

They led the way now, stooping upon their prey as their long-ago ancestors had stooped upon living prey in the air of the Ophiuchi homeworld. They volleyed their own missiles as they closed, ripping the heart of the Bug formation with blinding glares of cleansing fire, and then they followed the missiles in, gun packs and internal lasers blazing.

They sliced through the Bug formation, already disordered and riven by the missile fire directed upon it by the Gorm, like a whirlwind, and space burned in their wake, littered with the broken debris which had been Bug gunboats. But the Ophiuchi, like the Gorm who'd begun the engagement, were selective in their slaughter. Like the Gorm, they took their victims from different squadrons, killing mercilessly and further eroding the ability of those squadrons to kill their allies . . . or to defend themselves in turn.

And then it was the rest of the CSP's turn.

The Terran and Orion pilots who formed the overwhelming backbone of Sixth Fleet's total fighter strength roared down on the shaken gunboat formation like the wrath of God. Their missiles went in front of them, spreading out in a lethal cloud that enveloped the Bugs and blotted them from the face of the universe. And then, like the Ophiuchi, they followed their missiles in.

To an untrained eye, the plot before Anson Olivera was pure chaos, with no more order than the forest fire of nuclear and antimatter explosions blazing in stroboscopic spits of fury in the visual display. But Olivera's eye was trained. He knew precisely what he was looking at, and a fierce sense of pride and vengeful hunger raged behind his disciplined façade as his *farshatok* ripped into the Bug formation which had outnumbered them by almost two to one.

It wasn't really a contest. Some of his pilots died. Losses were particularly heavy among the Ophiuchi who led the main interception, who lost almost fifteen percent of their pilots. However skilled they might have been individually, they'd also faced the heaviest and best coordinated defensive fire of any of the strike-groups. But their attack runs were decisive. Coupled with the damage the Gorm had already wreaked, they broke the back of the Bugs' squadron organization, and the Terran and Orion pilots took vicious advantage of the opening which had been created for them. Sixth Fleet lost no gunboats in the interception, and its total fighter losses were under a hundred and fifty.

The Bugs lost one thousand six hundred and twelve gunboats. Only seventeen of them got close enough to attack Sixth Fleet's battle-line. Only five of them scored shield hits with FRAMs.

None of them rammed successfully.

"Yes," Raymond Prescott nodded. "I agree. Continuing to run toward the Orpheus 2 warp point was exactly the right decision. And I can't help thinking that it exemplifies the kind of tactical flexibility we have and the Bugs seem inherently incapable of duplicating. If anything is going to win this war for us, that's it."

"On a slightly less metaphysical level," Zhaarnak put in, "it must have been gratifying to give the Bahg gunboats such a bloody nose, to use your charming Human idiom."

Murakuma grinned and took a sip of her drink. The whiskey caught the orange light of Bug-10's primary sun, flooding in through the wide, curving armorplast viewports of *Riva y Silva's* flag lounge. That lounge was empty, but for the three of them.

"Yes, Fang. We barely made it through into Orpheus 2 ahead of them, and they barreled through after us without even slowing down. I understand our personnel are calling it the 'Great Orpheus Turkey Shoot.'"

"Yes," Prescott, one of whose ancestors had claimed two air to air victories in the battle which had prompted the allusion, agreed. "I can see how they might—even if some of your in-laws might not particularly appreciate it, Admiral Murakuma. So none of the gunboats lasted long enough to complete their ramming runs?"

"Not successfully. And as nearly as we can tell, no more than a dozen or so of them even got away. We assume that the few who did are the reason the Bug capital ships didn't make transit after they finally lumbered up."

"You are undoubtedly correct," Zhaarnak allowed. "I, for one, am never truly happy when the Bahgs demonstrate something approaching tactical wisdom, but I am forced to concede that they do so upon occasion."

"More often than I'd like," Murakuma agreed. "Still, how much 'wisdom' does it take to stay on your own side of the warp point when you know an entire fleet worth of strikefighters is waiting to ambush you on the far side . . . and that your own ships are too slow to overtake the enemy you're chasing even if you survive the ambush?"

"Truth," Zhaarnak admitted, and stroked his whiskers thoughtfully. "We must now assume that the third warp point in Orpheus 1 definitely leads to another home hive system, however. Nothing less could support a force as large as the one you detected."

Neither human could muster any grounds for contradicting him. For a space, they all nursed their drinks in silence. Finally, Prescott drew a deep breath and leaned back in his comfortable chair.

"You're correct, of course," he told his *vilkshatha* brother, "but that can be left for the future. We'll have to go back to Orpheus 1 eventually, but the fact that we hold both Orpheus 2 and Home Hive One gives us two avenues of attack and requires them to divide their forces to cover both of them."

"Truth," Zhaarnak agreed. "Operation Orpheus accomplished a great deal."

"And," Murakuma said, returning the courtesy, "Seventh Fleet wasn't exactly idle while it was going on."

"Well," Prescott acknowledged with just a trace of complacency, "we'd been wanting to eliminate those holdouts in Bug-11 for some time. The damaged ships we're getting back into service, coupled with our fighter reinforcements, meant we could finally do it."

"Unfortunately," Zhaarnak added glumly, "the same was not true of the system beyond Franos' Warp Point Three."

"Remind me to light a fire under astrography," Prescott told him in an annoyed tone that failed to mask a deeper frustration. "It's about time they assigned that system a designation."

Murakuma took another sip of her drink, this time to hide a smile. Marina Abernathy had already briefed her on Seventh Fleet's abortive attempt to force its way through Warp Point Three. Prescott and Zhaarnak had been able to smash the fixed defenses on its far side with a smothering wave of SBMHAWKs, but the sheer number of gunboats which had supported those defenses had prevented them from doing much more. They'd managed to get RD2s through for a fairly detailed look at the system's astrography, but they'd been forced to abandon any thought of sending manned units through when they saw the hordes of gunboats those same drones had detected.

"I still think we should have pressed on," Zhaarnak growled. "We could have taken that system!"

"Perhaps, brother," Prescott said, speaking in the Tongue of Tongues, as he often did when Zhaarnak was like this. "But it would have meant heavy losses—which we can ill afford at present if we are to . . ."

His voice trailed off into a silence of mutual understanding, and Murakuma's gaze sharpened, and darted from one of her companions to the other.

"You two," she stated, "are up to something."

"Well, we *do* have a proposal," Prescott admitted. His tone held a complex freight of meaning: acknowledgment that Murakuma outranked both of Seventh Fleet's joint commanders, and realization of how little that had proven to mean between them. "As you know, the repairs in AP-4, plus our reinforcements, have pretty much gotten Seventh Fleet back up to strength. At the same time, Sixth Fleet took *some* losses in the course of Operation Orpheus. So we feel it's time for you to revert to a defensive stance while we undertake the next offensive."

"Whose objective is . . . ?"

"Pesthouse."

It was as though that one word had fallen from Prescott's lips into a well of silence. *So we're going back there,* Murakuma thought. For the barest instant, resentment flared in her, fueled by the realization of what returning to Pesthouse meant—above and beyond its strategic significance—and the suspicion that this pair of *vilkshatha* brothers wanted to exclude her from it.

But only for an instant. Only until she remembered who'd

led Second Fleet's bleeding, fighting withdrawal from that nightmare . . . and realized how very right it was that that same man should lead the Alliance's return there.

"Lieutenant Sanchez, reporting as ordered, Sir."

Irma didn't know why Commander Georghiu had sent for her. VF-94 had certainly held up its end of the Bug-11 operation, suffering no losses and racking up a score that solidified her kids' reputation as the best gunboat-killers in Strikegroup 137. *Among the best in Seventh Fleet,* she told herself. Not that she would have dreamed of telling *them* that. Encouragement of cockiness was the last thing fighter pilots needed. Heads that swelled had a way of getting blown off.

She had a pretty good idea of what this was about, though. She'd been expecting the summons for a long time. Now it seemed to have finally arrived, and she wondered why her emotions were so mixed.

"Sit down, Lieutenant." The CSG blew out his cheeks as if to pump up his pomposity. "As you doubtless recall, on the occasion of your assumption of acting command of VF-94 following Commander Togliatti's death, I explained that the appointment was only a temporary one. Fighter squadron command is, after all, a lieutenant commander's billet, and you hadn't even been a lieutenant senior-grade very long."

"Yes, Sir." *Yep, I was right. This is it. It had to happen. In fact, when I accepted command, it was the light at the end of the tunnel. I knew that sooner or later they'd send some lifer to take the responsibility off my shoulders.*

*And, damn it, it is a relief. Isn't it?*

*So why aren't I happy?*

"At the time," Georghiu continued, "I never expected the arrangement to last as long as it has—sixteen standard months now." Irma nodded unconsciously; she hadn't either. "But other positions have always seemed to have higher priority whenever senior officers with the right qualifications were available, and . . . Well, during that time, the squadron's performance has been . . . satisfactory." Georghiu looked as if pronouncing the word hurt his face. "Furthermore, I'm advised that a change in command at this time might do more harm than good in terms of the squadron's morale."

*Yes, I suppose the relief and the happiness will come later, when it's sunk in.*

*But . . . Hey, wait a minute! What's he saying?*

"I have therefore," Georghiu droned on, "recommended to Captain Landrum that, for organizational reasons, an accelerated promotion may be in order. In fact, I did so some little time ago. And he concurred. But of course it had to go through BuPers, and I wanted to wait for confirmation before informing you."

*This can't be right!* The leaden lump of depression in Irma's gut was gone, expelled by something akin to panic. *It can't! Only lifers make lieutenant commander. That's a law of nature.*

"Uh, excuse me, Sir, but are you saying—?"

Georghiu's face gave the same odd quirk she'd seen on it once before, sixteen months ago. In anyone else, it might have been suspected of being a very brief smile.

"Your promotion won't become official for a few weeks. But I think we can go ahead and make the announcement that your appointment as commanding officer of the Ninety-Fourth is no longer provisional." Again, that almost invisibly quick facial twitch. "I think you'll agree that it will be almost anticlimactic by now."

"Uh, yes, Sir," was all she could think of to say. Afterwards, she had no clear recollection of being dismissed and bumping into the frame of the hatch as she left the office.

*What's the matter with me?* she wondered. *I was depressed before, and now . . . I don't know what I feel.*

*What do I really want?*

She rounded a corner . . . and almost ran into the knot of figures waiting beyond it. Meswami was in the front. Behind him were Liang and Nordlund and the other pilots, crowding the narrow passageway. All of them were grinning from ear to ear.

*Figures,* she thought resignedly. *Even in a ship the size of this goddamned monitor, Rumor Central always gets the word first.*

# CHAPTER TWENTY
## Return to Pesthouse

While Sixth Fleet had been carrying out Operation Orpheus and Raymond Prescott and Zhaarnak'telmasa had been conducting their tidying-up operations beyond Bug-10 and Franos, other elements of Seventh Fleet had been busy.

They'd probed aggressively out through Home Hive Three's Warp Point One, and on through the lifeless binary system beyond that warp point. They'd pressed on, against virtually nonexistent opposition, to the blue giant they'd dubbed Bug-05. Unlike most massive stars, it had possessed only one other warp point . . . and that one had led to Pesthouse.

And now the bulk of Seventh Fleet was flowing through Home Hive Three toward that system.

*The Enemy had surely identified this as the warp chain from whose far end others of his kind had once advanced towards disaster. But of course he wasn't—couldn't be—aware of what his seizure of control of it would mean.*

*It was just as well that he wasn't.*

*The directing intelligences of the three remaining Systems Which Must Be Defended were, however, all too aware. It would mean that each of them would be on its own, isolated from the other two.*

*But there was little the other two could do to help. They had their own commitments. One was still bogged down in what amounted to its own private war with the Old Enemies. Another was responsible for the defenses of the long-quiescent warp chain where the first contact with the New Enemies had occurred. No, the Deep Space*

*Force must stand alone. And its defensive problems were complicated by the number of avenues of advance open to the Enemy.*

*True, one of this system's four warp points was almost certainly of no concern, even though it led to a system the Enemy had scouted with his tiny automated probes. No amount of scouting could have detected the closed warp point to which it connected in that system. But the Fleet was no longer prepared to make assumptions about the surprises this unpleasantly resourceful Enemy might spring. It had not, after all, expected the Enemy to discover closed warp points admitting him to two separate Systems Which Must Be Defended, either. The Enemy's success in that regard might suggest that the Fleet's decision against aggressive exploration by its own units had been in error, but that was a matter which could be considered later. What mattered now was that it was remotely possible that one of the Enemy's all but invisible probes had managed to detect a cloaked system security picket as it made transit from that system to this one through the closed warp point. Accordingly, it could not be absolutely assumed that the Enemy didn't know of all three separate routes by which he might enter this system.*

*Under the circumstances, it was tempting to withdraw to the next system along the chain, abandoning this position for one with only a solitary warp point to defend. But that system held the most direct route linking the other two Systems Which Must Be Defended. If it fell, too much else would also be lost.*

*No, a stand must be made here. The available static defenses would be divided among the threatened warp points—even the one leading to the closed warp point, in the absence of absolute certainty of the Enemy's ignorance. So would the cruisers. But the Deep Space Force itself would be kept together, and positioned to cover the warp point connecting to the most recently devastated System Which Must Be Defended. That was the most direct route for the Enemy to take. Besides, it was the warp point closest to the one through which the Deep Space Force must withdraw if necessary to avoid being trapped here.*

*Not that the Fleet intended to be driven away. This Enemy might be unpleasantly resourceful, but he would find that certain new defensive doctrines had been introduced by the Fleet, as well. . . .*

Ghostlike in its silence, mountainous in its mass, another monitor slid past the armorplast transparency in *Riva y Silva*'s flag lounge. Vanessa Murakuma had long since stopped trying to keep track of how many millions of metric tonnes of death she'd watched depart for Bug-05.

Task Group 72.4—a light covering force of twenty-one light carriers escorted by an equal number of light cruisers under Vice Admiral Keith al-Salah—would remain here in Home Hive One. The rest of Seventh Fleet was streaming toward Bug-05 in an awesome procession which *Riva y Silva* herself would presently join. Intellectually, Murakuma realized that what had paraded before her within visual range was only a small fraction of the stupendous total: sixty monitors, thirty-six superdreadnoughts, twenty-two assault carriers, thirty-four fleet carriers, ninety-eight battlecruisers, and eleven light cruisers. And that didn't even count the freighters and tugs of Vice Admiral Alexandra Cole's Support Group.

She became aware that Zhaarnak'telmasa had joined her at the viewpoint. And his thoughts had evidently been running parallel to hers.

"It would seem," he remarked through her earbug's translation program, "that, however much our confidence in it may have been shaken at times, the Alliance's initial faith in the supremacy of the Terran Federation's industrial capacity was not misplaced." His voice held understandably mixed emotions.

"It's difficult to imagine," Murakuma said, as much to herself as to the Orion, "that this operation is just half of a two-pronged attack on the same warp chain."

Before Zhaarnak could reply, Prescott entered the lounge.

"Sorry I was called away. What were you two just saying?"

"Oh," Murakuma turned away from the spectacle beyond the armorplast, "I was just recalling the other offensive Kthaara'zarthan is planning from Alpha Centauri. I understand he's named the combined plan Operation Ivan."

"Of course," Prescott nodded. "After all, Admiral Antonov was his *vilkshatha* brother."

"And," Zhaarnak deadpanned, "I am reliably informed that he comes closer than most Human speakers of Standard English to an accurate pronunciation of its name."

"*I* am informed," Prescott shot back, "that First Fang Ynaathar'solmaak has laid down the law to him on the subject of taking personal command of that offensive."

"Truth. Kthaara is now under direct orders from the Khan to keep his graying pelt at Alpha Centauri, where it belongs."

"I don't imagine he's very much fun to be around, just now," Prescott mused.

Murakuma ignored most of the byplay.

"I understand how he feels. I ought to be coming along with you two."

"We have been over all of that repeatedly, Vaahnesssa," Zhaarnak chided.

"Yes, yes, I know." Murakuma told herself firmly that he wasn't really being patronizing to a superior officer. But she must not have entirely succeeded in keeping her irritation out of her voice, for Prescott spoke up in his patented oil-on-the-waters tone.

"The important thing isn't who's commanding each of the two operations, but the fact that there *are* two of them. We've built up to the point where we can use multiple threat axes to whipsaw the Bugs with separate fleets."

"We could do so even more effectively if half our combat strength was not moldering away in systems far from the war fronts," Zhaarnak said sourly.

Neither human responded immediately. It was a sore point. Early in the war, when the nature of the threat was finally recognized by the politicians, Bettina Wister and others of her ilk—not all of them human—had created an atmosphere in which disproportionately large forces had to be kept tied down in static defensive positions. It might not have made military sense, but it had been a political necessity.

For the Federation, it still was.

The Khanate of Orion had responded in similar fashion earlier in the war, and with even greater justification, following the Kliean Atrocity's four billion dead. But the Orions were a warrior people, and the Khan had long since begun systematically reducing the nodal response forces he'd scattered about his domain in the horrifying wake of Kliean. The Federation had not, and for a depressingly simple reason. If the relatively sensible people now running the Federation didn't take care to soothe the popular jitters, they'd be out, and the Liberal-Progressives would be in. The potential consequences of *that*, at this particular historical juncture, didn't bear thinking about.

Zhaarnak read his companions' thoughts, and the chance to rub it in tempted him beyond his character.

"I believe a Human military historian of the last pre-space century once observed that a democratic government will always put home defense first."

Prescott and Murakuma avoided the slit-pupiled Orion eyes.

Zhaarnak's words made uncomfortable hearing, however much one might privately agree with them.

"Still and all," Prescott insisted, "the fact remains that we can do it anyway. And if there's anything to our spooks' latest speculation, it's entirely possible that the Bugs have already done their worst."

"What speculation?" Murakuma asked.

"That's right, you wouldn't have heard about it yet. Well, Uaaria and Chung—with some input from Lieutenant Sanders, before he returned to Alpha Centauri—have had a chance to study the rubble of the Bug infrastructure in Home Hives One and Three. It's enabled them to refine their earlier conclusions. Now they're convinced that they've figured out the secret of the mammoth Bug fleets we faced at the beginning of the war."

"I'm all ears," said Murakuma, who had better reason than anyone else to remember those desperate early days.

"They claim those fleets must have been the product of a century of stockpiling. The Bugs were evidently thinking in terms of a short, *extremely* high-intensity war, so they built up an enormous reserve fleet to support their attritional tactics."

"But . . . a war with *whom*?" Murakuma demanded in perplexity. "They didn't even know we existed. Surely not even Bugs would make that kind of effort against some hypothetical enemy they *might* someday run into!"

"The possibility of such a threat must have been a very real one to them," Zhaarnak said in a measured voice. "Surely they could see that the existence of the aliens they had subjugated implied the existence of other aliens elsewhere—perhaps more advanced ones."

A silence descended, and Zhaarnak looked uncomfortable in the face of the ghost he'd summoned up. The problem of those subjugated—what a mild word!—races was something about which none of them liked to talk or even think. But Zhaarnak's discovery of Franos had brought it back to trouble their sleep. And in the path of Kthaara's projected offensive lay Harnah, where the Alliance had first seen the fate that awaited races conquered by the Bugs.

Murakuma had never been to Harnah, and although she sometimes thought it might be cowardly of her, she never intended to go there. Especially not after Justin. Most of the millions of civilians she'd lost there had at least gone to their horrible deaths with merciful quickness, but she still remembered the handful of brutally traumatized, filthy, broken-eyed survivors who'd seen everyone else devoured. Strangers. Friends . . . family . . .

Her dreams were hideous enough without seeing an entire species which had been turned into intelligent meat animals for generations.

Prescott *had* been there, and the imagery Second Fleet's orbital reconnaissance platforms had brought back had been just as terrible as the scenes he was certain Murakuma was visualizing. Especially the footage of Bugs actually feeding.

That was why *he* had never been to visit Franos.

"We don't know that for certain, Vanessa," he said now, hastening to haul the conversation back on course. "Maybe Bugs *would* invest such an effort against a purely hypothetical threat. Then again . . ." He shook his head. "No, never mind."

"What?" Murakuma prompted.

"Well . . . Have you considered the possibility that they've already met another enemy besides us? An enemy they expect to meet *again*?"

"That would account for their stockpiling," Zhaarnak mused, after a moment's silence.

"It would, but we're speculating beyond our knowledge," Murakuma said firmly. "And I've got to get back aboard *Li* in time to depart for Bug-10."

"That's right," Prescott agreed. "We've let ourselves talk altogether too much shop when we were supposed to be having a stirrup cup, as it were."

They raised their drinks.

"Here's to—" Murakuma began, then hesitated. "I was about to toast Operation Ivan, but that's just the name for Kthaara's show. What are you calling Seventh Fleet's end of the operation?"

"Actually," Prescott admitted, "we haven't given it a name. Let's just call it the return to Pesthouse."

Three glasses clinked together.

Theoretical physicists continued to ridicule the very concept of simultaneity as applied across interstellar distances. As a practical matter, however, every bridge in the TFN had a display—which no one had ever succeeded in proving wrong—which showed the current local time at Greenwich, England, Old Terra. So Raymond Prescott knew when the clock in that remote place struck 10:30 A.M., August second, 2368. And, knowing how reliable Keith al-Salah was, he knew that at that precise instant the

SBMHAWK bombardment was going in from Home Hive One to Pesthouse.

He turned from the digital clock to the holo display of the Pesthouse System, as though to remind himself of why that bombardment was commencing from Home Hive One and not from here in Bug-05, where he and Zhaarnak waited with the overwhelming bulk of Seventh Fleet. It was a display uncomplicated by planets, for Pesthouse was a blue giant. Such massive stars generally had many warp points, so there might well be more than the four they knew about. But they'd been able to draw some conclusions from the layout of those four, and the location of the Bug mobile force.

All four of the warp point icons lay in the lower right-hand quarter of the sphere. Warp Point Three, roughly three light-hours from the star at a bearing of six o'clock, led to an unknown terminus and was, for the moment, unimportant. Warp Point One, a like distance out, but at three o'clock, was the one leading to the next system up the Anderson Chain (Anderson Four, as Ivan Antonov had named it) toward Alpha Centauri. It was evidently the Bugs' escape route, given the fact that the mobile force had positioned itself nearby—as interplanetary distances went—to cover Warp Point Four, 3.8 light-hours out at four o'clock, which led to Home Hive One. From there, it was difficult to see how they could be cut off from their bolthole of Warp Point One . . . least of all by an attack from Bug-05, which must enter through Warp Point Two, the furthest from the blue giant of the four at 5.6 light-hours and lying at a five o'clock bearing.

So Prescott and Zhaarnak weren't basing their plans on trapping the mobile force before it could escape to Anderson Four. Still, it would be *nice* if they could do so.

That was why they now waited in Bug-05 while the SBMHAWK-storm from Home Hive One was—they hoped—convincing the Bugs that the main attack would come through Warp Point Four. Better still would be if it drew a gunboat counterattack through that warp point, to be pounced on by the fighters of al-Salah's light carriers . . . but only after detecting the two hundred deep space buoys whose deceptive ECM was counterfeiting heavy starships poised to attack.

Unfortunately, there was no way Prescott and Zhaarnak could know about that. They could only wait until the prearranged time—10:00 P.M. GMT—and then launch their own bombardment into Pesthouse. They only took the time for a single massive wave of SBMHAWKs, then immediately began pushing their monitors through.

As *Riva y Silva* emerged into Pesthouse, Prescott found himself gazing at the system display and visualizing what must have happened five years before.

*Yes, now I see how they did. A force from Home Hive Three must've entered Pesthouse through Warp Point Two, just as I'm doing now. Another must've come directly from Home Hive One, through Warp Point Four. What about the third force that appeared here? Maybe it came through Warp Point Three, from some system we don't know about yet.*

*No wonder they were so eager to lure Second Fleet here.*

*God, what suckers we were!*

*No, that's not fair. There was no way Antonov or any of us could have known. We thought we'd recognized what we were up against, but we hadn't. Not really. Not then. And because we hadn't, who could have dreamed that even Bugs would go to such lengths, sacrificing whole flotillas as bait? Abandoning entire planetary populations they had the firepower to defend just to suck us into a trap? All our decisions were rational, given the information we had.*

*Tell that to the ghosts hovering in this system and all the other systems along the trail of death back to Alpha Centauri.*

Some of the people on Prescott's flag bridge wondered why his eyes had grown so very cold. The senior members of his staff, who'd been to this system with him once before, did not.

But the moment passed as the initial trickle of reports swelled to a torrent.

The preliminary bombardment had done its work. The single wave of carrier pods had been programmed with a staggered firing sequence, the HARM2 missiles taking out the ECM-generated phantom targets first and leaving the actual fortresses and defense cruisers exposed for the rest. But there was even better news: the Bug mobile force still seemed to be regarding this attack as a feint, refusing to react to it. Instead of bothering his subordinates with useless orders to do what they were already doing, Prescott ordered himself to appreciate the priceless gift of every minute that went by with the Bug starships still fully engaged against Warp Point Four and his own ships deploying into Pesthouse in a steady stream.

It was easier said than done, as he awaited al-Salah's courier drones, hoping that one of them at least would have broken past the Bugs into Pesthouse space with tidings of what was going on at Warp Point Four.

When those tidings finally arrived, they banished the last of the ghosts from his mind.

Al-Salah's SBMHAWKs had been less effective than might have been hoped, for the Bugs had adopted a new readiness posture—inexplicably overdue, in the opinion of the Allies' analysts. All their units within SBMHAWK range of warp points now lay inside clouds of buoys equipped with fire-confusion ECM, which had significantly degraded the accuracy of the pod-launched missiles. But however little actual damage it had done, the missile-storm had achieved its objective. It had fixated the Bugs' attention on Warp Point Four, through which they'd dispatched a gunboat counterattack. And now the mobile force sat on that warp point in all its awesome might, awaiting the two hundred phantom capital ships the gunboats had reported waiting in Home Hive One.

*Yes!* Prescott thought, trying not to exult. *Let them squat there while we head for Warp Point One!*

But, of course, it was too good to last. Hours crept past while Seventh Fleet ground ponderously across the light-hours towards Warp Point One and scouting gunboats sped towards Warp Point Four to establish direct observation of the Bugs there. Prescott knew it was foolish, but as the time trickled away with no report that the Bugs were moving, he allowed himself to hope that they would just sit there, mesmerized by al-Salah's deception, after all.

But they didn't. By the time the first report came back across the three light-hours from Warp Point Four, the mobile force had already been under way for at least two hours, and it had only sixty percent as far to go. Its slower speed meant he'd be able to bring it into fighter range before it escaped from the system, but unless it decided to let him, his battle-line would be unable to engage it.

He gazed as expressionlessly as possible at the mobile force's scarlet icon as it began to move in response to the scouts' reports even as Chung approached him diffidently.

"They seem to have finally caught on, Sir. They're moving off on a course calculated to keep us from cutting them off short of Warp Point One. And they've launched a gunboat strike towards us."

"I see." Prescott gave a command, and the master plot

reconfigured to "tactical" scale, showing the stupendous power of the mobile force, with the red streaks of gunboat formations beginning to race away from it to meet Seventh Fleet.

*Good,* Prescott thought as he watched those streaks. Well aware that their battle-line was outweighed, he and Zhaarnak had counted on being able to first wear down the Bug gunboat strength with their fighters, which would free those fighters to seek out to the *Aegis* and *Arbalest*-class command ships.

"Anna," he said quietly to his chief of staff, "tell Steve to get our fighter cover deployed."

But the gunboat wave had covered only a few light-minutes before it turned back, refusing engagement in a most un-Bug-like manner. It was an anticlimax Prescott didn't care for at all.

Worse was to come.

"They're doing *what*?" Jacques Bichet demanded at the hastily convened staff conference.

Amos Chung was clearly unhappy, but he stood his ground.

"I know it's unprecedented. But you can understand their reasoning. They can read the figures as well as we can, so it must be clear to them that they're not going to be able to reach Warp Point One before we can hit them with multiple fighter strikes, given our speed advantage. So they've decided to send in a spoiling attack to push us further away from the warp point."

"But they had a gunboat strike heading for us earlier, and they recalled it," Landrum protested.

"My guess is that they recalled it before it was clear to them that they couldn't maneuver past us without entering our fighter envelope," the spook replied. "And they probably decided they didn't want to send their unsupported gunboats into a fighter envelope as strong as the one this fleet can put out, given what seems to be their new sensitivity to losses." Chung paused briefly, but his better nature triumphed, and he didn't remark on the apparent confirmation of his and Uaaria's theories. "So instead, they're sending *this* in."

Chung didn't need to point at the display. Every pair of eyes turned to the unique formation it showed: a tight sphere of baleful scarlet "hostile" light-points, like a bloody snowball hurled at Seventh Fleet.

"The Bugs," Chung said into the silence, "detached every one of their battlecruisers and light cruisers, and sent them at us in this globular formation. At the same time, they put all their assault shuttle kamikazes in the center of the globe. And finally, they wrapped their gunboats *around* the globe, an outer shell within the battlecruisers' protective missile range."

"Not a particularly easy formation to attack." Mandagalla's tendency to understatement had a way of emerging under what many considered the most inopportune circumstances.

"No, it isn't," Prescott agreed with commendable restraint as he looked at the sidebar listing the forces within that globe: a hundred and sixty-two cruisers of all types, all of them faster than his own battle-line, covering hundreds of antimatter-loaded kamikazes, and covered in turn by over two thousand gunboats.

Zhaarnak'telmasa, aboard Task Force 72's flagship *Hia'khan*, was looking at the same display, and had heard Chung's words without noticeable time-lag. Now he spoke from the com screen.

"Raaymmonnd, we are going to have to respond to this."

"Yes," Prescott sighed. "And we'll have to hold the range open as long as possible while we do it." *Reversing course and allowing the Bug battle-line, slow as it is, to reach Warp Point One ahead of us. Which, of course, is precisely what they want. But we never did count on trapping it in this system. Did we?*

"In the meantime," he went on, "this is how I propose . . ."

VF-94 launched as part of the vastest assault wave Irma Sanchez had ever seen or imagined: four thousand human- and Orion-piloted fighters and six hundred Gorm-crewed gunboats. The huge strike soared towards the oncoming Bugs, and behind it came a solid screen of battlecruisers.

Yet something was missing. Even as they approached the onrushing, multilayered sphere of Bug vessels, that something was a subject for com chatter.

"Hey, Skipper," came Liang's nervous voice. "I was talking to a guy in VF-88 before we launched, and he says he heard that they're holding back the Ophiuchi fighters because—"

"Can it!" Irma snapped. "When *you* make admiral, then you can start worrying about decisions like that. For now, just pull up and get your ass into proper formation!"

"Aye, aye, Sir."

Liang's deviation from the squadron's formation had been so minor that it would normally have gone unremarked. But Irma was irritable because she shared the general uneasiness at the absence of the Ophiuchi, acknowledged even by the Tabbies as the Alliance's best natural fighter pilots—and, unlike the others, couldn't say so out loud. Snapping at Liang had to substitute.

Commander Georghiu's voice invaded her consciousness, calling for his squadron skippers to sound off.

"All right, people," he said after the last of the acknowledgments, "we're coming up on Point Griddle. Synchronize on my mark."

Irma couldn't help smiling at the code word as she complied. That glowing sphere of hostiles on her HUD *did* resemble a snowball. *Couldn't have been Georghiu who thought of it*, she reflected.

But then, as the count wound down and she gave the order to attack, the tiny display began to blossom with myriad tiny red pinpricks—*AFHAWKs*, she thought automatically—that separated from the battlecruisers of the intermediate layer and sped outward through the surrounding gunboats.

"Skipper—!"

"Yeah, I know." Her own fighter's computer had already screamed "Incoming!" at her. "Evasive action, everybody! And follow me in!"

She rolled her fighter inward with practiced ease, to engage the gunboats while letting the computers fend off the AFHAWKs. *Like trying to fight a karate bout with a swarm of bees buzzing around your head*, she thought. *And no Ophiuchi. . . .*

Then they were in among the gunboats, and there was no more time for thought.

Liang was the first to die.

Raymond Prescott kept his face expressionless as he watched the loss figures add up.

*We've gotten spoiled*, he told himself. *I can't even remember the last time we lost more fighters than the Bugs did gunboats in an engagement like this.*

It had been the AFHAWKs from the Bug battlecruisers, of course. But in spite of them, in spite of everything, the fighters had smashed the Bug formation's outer gunboat layer. Now their survivors were returning to be rearmed, and the battlecruiser screen was placing itself in the Bugs' path.

Those battlecruisers were BCRs of the Terran *Dunkerque-C*, Orion *Prokhalon II-B*, and Gorm *Bolzucha-C* classes, able to dance away from heavier foes while delivering blows with the capital missiles that constituted their exclusive offensive armament. They needed that agility now, lest the Bug formation get close enough to crush them beneath the weight of its hoarded kamikazes. Their need to stay away from the kamikazes meant that they couldn't stop that formation's inexorable progress. They could, however, inflict losses entirely out of proportion to the twenty-seven of their own who died in the missile exchange. More important by far, they weakened the formation's integrity, for every Bug battlecruiser slowed by engine damage was left behind. So it was a badly weakened globe of Bug cruisers that finally delivered the kamikazes within striking range of Seventh Fleet's battle-line. In the cold, remorseless calculus of combat, Prescott was willing to accept the loss of well over a quarter of his total battlecruiser strength for that result.

He dragged his attention back to Jacques Bichet's most recent report.

"The Bug light cruisers—particularly the *Epee*-class and suicide-riders—are still trying to press home attacks. But our own cruiser screen has stopped all of them well short of the battle-line. It looks—"

What it looked like to the ops officer would remain forever unknown, for at that moment the shrunken Bug globe-formation in the display dissolved.

It really was that abrupt. The carefully husbanded kamikazes at the center of the now almost nonexistent battlecruiser shell joined with the remaining battlecruisers and streamed toward Seventh Fleet's battle-line in a crimson tide of death.

"Commodore Landrum," Prescott said quietly to the *farshath-khanaak*, "inform Vice Admiral Raathaarn that it's time to commit the Ophiuchi fighters."

"That's the last of their light cruisers, Sir," Mandagalla reported wearily.

Prescott nodded. Four hundred fighters with fresh Ophiuchi pilots had massacred the Bug kamikazes before a single one of them had reached Seventh Fleet's battle-line. After that, it had been a simple matter to eradicate the unsupported Bug cruisers from long range. And yet . . .

"What about their heavy units?"

Mandagalla's weariness seemed to deepen.

"They're still in the process of transiting through Warp Point One, Sir. Of course, there's no way we can get there in time to—"

"Of course." The Bugs' attack might not have so much as scratched the paint of Prescott's heavy units, but it *had* bought time for their battle-line to escape to Anderson Four before his badly disorganized strikegroups could get themselves sorted back out and swarm over them.

He dismissed his disappointment with a headshake. At a cost of twenty-nine battlecruisers (plus another six seriously damaged), three hundred and two gunboats, and 2,781 fighters, Seventh Fleet had secured Pesthouse.

Zhaarnak agreed with his conclusions as the two of them conversed later via com screen.

"The loss ratio was overwhelmingly in our favor, Raaymmonnd. They lost well over three hundred cruisers of all classes. Of course, our own battlecruiser losses are disturbing."

"Especially given that we've just seen a demonstration of how essential a battlecruiser screen is against their new kamikaze formation. We're going to have to be a little stingier with ships of that class in the future."

"That could hamper our tactical flexibility," the Orion said glumly.

"Truth. But . . ." Prescott straightened up. "Never mind. There are still the warp point fortresses to worry about. Let's get them cleaned up. I want every living Bug out of the system."

"Of course."

Zhaarnak, who hadn't been at the *First* Battle of Pesthouse, looked at Prescott, who had. Very few people who hadn't survived Second Fleet's agony in Operation Pesthouse could have understood what was happening behind Raymond Prescott's round-pupiled Human eyes, but Zhaarnak'telmasa had been at Kliean. His task force had been driven out of that system . . . and he'd commanded another, far more powerful task force, when Third Fleet fought its way back in and discovered that two entire core world planetary populations had been annihilated. So, yes, he understood what taking this system meant to his *vilkshatha* brother as he watched Prescott's gaze shift to the outside view of the spaces lit by Pesthouse's blue giant star.

The ghosts were still there. But now they were appeased.

"Yes," Raymond Prescott said after a moment. "By all means, let's finish sanitizing the system."

# CHAPTER TWENTY-ONE
## Who are those people?

Kthaara'zarthan might be under a direct personal command from the Khan to leave Operation Ivan to others and remain in the Alpha Centauri system. But—so he reasoned—nobody had said he had to stay dirtside on Nova Terra.

So it wasn't *quite* disobedience when he came almost four light-hours out, to the vicinity of the closed warp point behind which Anderson One lurked. And now, with the prowling gait age had finally begun to stiffen, he moved through the passageways of *Hiarnow'kharnak*, flagship of the newly organized Eighth Fleet.

As he entered the conference room and acknowledged its occupants' greetings, Kthaara consoled himself, as he often did, with the thought that it wasn't everyone who had *two* First Fangs to execute his plans in his stead. Not that the Humans called Ellen MacGregor that, of course. The Sky Marshal was to remain here with a weakened Terran Home Fleet, supported by a massive shell of mines, fortresses and buoys, to secure Alpha Centauri—and Sol behind it—while Ynaathar'solmaak led Eighth Fleet through the closed warp point and down the Anderson Chain to meet Seventh Fleet.

Those two weren't the only ones in the conference room. Marcus LeBlanc had beaten Kthaara here by hours, which meant he'd had time to study the news that had brought both of them rushing out from Nova Terra.

"Well, Ahhhdmiraal LeBlaaanc?" Kthaara prompted as he lowered himself onto the cushions, less smoothly and more cautiously than he once had.

LeBlanc cleared his throat.

"As we all know, Sir, the Bugs have long since figured out what our second-generation recon drones are for—although they haven't duplicated them yet, for reasons which, inevitably, remain obscure. And, unfortunately, even the stealthiest drone isn't completely invisible if you know what to look for. So now they routinely patrol their warp points heavily, and we have to send enormous waves of RD2s through to assure the survival of any of them. Continuous, ongoing RD2 surveillance is a thing of the past."

"Yes, yes," muttered MacGregor, who lacked the patience of the two Orions, descendants of pouncer carnivores. "Get to the point."

"Of course, Sky Marshal. The point is that on November 5, 2368, Terran Standard—yesterday—Eighth Fleet got its latest glimpse of the far side of this closed warp point. Only this time, the RD2s had no trouble getting back and reporting. Which is directly attributable to what they reported: that the Bug fleet covering their end of this warpline was in motion *away* from the warp point. What's more, that fleet was in the process of launching what we calculate to be the bulk of its gunboat strength!"

First Fang Ynaathar'solmaak, to whom this was not news, leaned forward as though getting closer to pouncing.

"And what conclusions do you draw from this? Why should they be fleeing toward the next system along the Aaahnnderrssson Chain, when we have not yet even attacked? And why would a withdrawing fleet launch its gunboats? Most of my task force commanders believe it is some kind of trick."

"I can't say just exactly what they're up to, First Fang. But I can say this: our initial interpretation of their course was mistaken." LeBlanc placed a tactful emphasis on the word "our," as opposed to "your intelligence people's." He activated a holo of the system of Anderson One's primary star—the distant red-dwarf companion didn't count, and neither did the lifeless planets. The warp point connecting with Alpha Centauri lay six light-hours from that star, at eleven o'clock. By contrast, nestling only thirty-six light-minutes from that orange fire at twelve o'clock was the one that led to Anderson Two—like everyone else, LeBlanc shied away from using the name "Harnah," bestowed on that system by its natives, once civilized, now barely sentient after God—or His opponent—knew how many generations as meat-animals. The two warp points had been designated Three and One respectively.

"At first, it was assumed that they were heading toward Warp

Point One," said LeBlanc. "But it turns out that their course isn't quite compatible with that. It *is* compatible with *this* destination." He indicated the third warp point icon, 3.6 light-hours out at three o'clock.

"Warp Point Two," MacGregor mused. "We never seem to think about that one."

"That undoubtedly had something to do with the fact that no one considered it as a possible destination, Sky Marshal. Nevertheless, as you can see, while the two courses are fairly close . . ."

"Yes, yes—I'm not questioning your analysis." MacGregor peered at the display intently. "What do we even know about Warp Point Two?"

"Nothing, Sky Marshal. It was surveyed during the course of Operation Pesthouse. Admiral Antonov dispatched a survey flotilla through it—Survey Flotilla 19, to be exact—as he continued to advance along the Anderson Chain. It was dispatched early enough in Pesthouse that it was beyond communications range when the Bugs sprang the trap, of course, so there was never any hope of recalling it when they closed in behind the Admiral. Which, unfortunately, means that any data the flotilla had amassed on further warp connections beyond Two was lost right along with it."

"Of course," MacGregor echoed. She studied the conjectural course. "They've got a long way to go."

"Yes," Ynaathar agreed. "Almost four light-hours. Which means that, whatever they are going there for, they are already too far away to support the fixed defenses at Warp Point Three." He turned eagerly to Kthaara. "Whatever it is they think they are doing, they have in fact presented us with a unique opportunity."

"Yes!" agreed MacGregor. "Without their battle-line to support them, their fortresses are vulnerable—we can blow them to dustbunnies! And First Fang Ynaathar can probably get Eighth Fleet into that system to stay. But we have to move *now*."

"But are you prepared to do so?" inquired Kthaara.

"Task Force 83, under Force Leader Haaldaarn, is unfortunately engaged in exercises, too far away to be recalled in time," Ynaathar admitted.

"Forty fast superdreadnoughts," mused Kthaara, who had Eighth Fleet's order of battle memorized. "He will be missed."

"Truth. But we cannot wait. And the rest of Eighth Fleet is, indeed, ready."

"But the staff work—?"

Ynaathar smiled. He wasn't as old as Kthaara—*So few are*, the latter thought ruefully—and at this moment he seemed positively young.

"Do not be concerned about that, Lord Talphon. Our staffs set to work on this as soon as the drones' report was verified."

For an instant, the resentment that had been smoldering in Kthaara threatened to ignite. But only for an instant. *After all*, he reminded himself, *why should he even have to ask me?* Operation Ivan was Ynaathar's show—that had been made clear enough. And as First Fang, Ynaathar was his service superior.

And yet it wasn't that simple. Kthaara chaired the Joint Staff of the Grand Alliance, of which the Khanate was a part. Ynaathar and MacGregor might have already made up their minds that they were going to seize the inexplicable opportunity the Bugs had offered them with both hands, but they understood the need for coordination among allies. Their request for Kthaara's presence hadn't been an empty gesture, still less an insult. This had to be cleared with him.

"Very well," he said after only a moment's pause. "I concur. You should proceed as soon as possible. Which means," he continued briskly, rising to his feet, "that I should be returning to Nova Terra at once."

"One request, Lord Talphon," said Ynaathar. He turned to LeBlanc, who had risen with Kthaara. "Ahhdmiraaaal LeBlaaanc, I believe your subordinate Lyooo . . . Leyowoo . . . Cub Saaanderzz accompanied you here."

"Why, yes, First Fang. He's still closeted with your intelligence people, trying to make some sense of the RD2 findings. I was just on my way to collect him."

"My request is that you not do so. I would like him attached to my staff for the duration of this offensive."

Nonplussed, LeBlanc looked from Ynaathar to Kthaara and back again.

"But, First Fang, Lieutenant Sanders has only recently returned from temporary detached duty with Sixth Fleet—and *that* came hard on the heels of a similar assignment with Seventh Fleet!"

"Precisely the point, Ahhdmiraaaal. He has had much experience acting as your alter ego. And I know Lord Talphon cannot spare *you*." Ynaathar grew more somber. "What is happening in Aaahnnderrssson One is bizarre even for Bahgs. This disturbs me. I need an intelligence officer with experience in making sense of Bahg behavior."

Kthaara turned to LeBlanc. "Ahhdmiraaaal . . . ?"
"I'll break it to him, Sir."

*It had finally happened.*

*And at the worst possible moment, as things continued so inexplicably to unravel.*

*The destruction of two of the five Systems Which Must Be Defended had been bad enough. But then the New Enemies had cut one of the remaining three off from all outside contact. So in effect there were only two left. And only two fragile lines of communication linked those two. And now the New Enemies were unwittingly threatening two systems through which those lines of communication ran.*

*And—the final blow—the Old Enemies had fought their way through to one of those systems, as well.*

*If those systems fell, the Fleet would no longer exist as such. Instead, there would be three separate fleets, each with its own System Which Must Be Defended, each alone in the cosmos with no knowledge of how the other two fared—an unthinkable logical contradiction.*

*Furthermore, the New Enemies and the Old Enemies would at last know of each others' existence, and doubtless join forces. This must not be.*

*So, from every standpoint, there'd been no alternative. The Deep Space Force must hurl its full strength at the Old Enemies before they could establish themselves in this system beyond any possibility of being dislodged. With that decision, it had departed from its station, leaving the fixed defenses and the mobile warp point defense to watch the warp point beyond which the New Enemies crouched.*

*But the New Enemies had chosen that very moment to send through a cascade of their robot probes.*

*The intelligences which directed the Fleet shared nothing like their enemies' belief in fate, or karma, or even the Demon Murphy. Yet as the probes poured through the warp point the Deep Space Force had just left, something very like those beliefs flickered at the edge of their awareness. Unfortunately, the Deep Space Force had already been far beyond any range at which it might have changed plan and course and returned to defend the warp point. It had had no choice but to continue on its current mission, and the New Enemies had seized the opportunity without delay, smashing the fortresses and burning swathes through the buoys and mines with the assorted*

*weapons their warp-transiting launch pods spewed forth in such*
*abundance. Now their ships had followed and were shaking them-*
*selves out into their organizational components: thirty-one monitors,*
*eighty-four superdreadnoughts, seventy-eight battlecruisers, sixty lesser*
*cruisers, and forty-four carriers for their small strike craft, twenty*
*of which belonged to the superdreadnought-sized variety.*

*It was unquestionably a more formidable force than the one the*
*Old Enemies had put into this system. So it became imperative to*
*obliterate the latter before the New Enemies could intervene on their*
*behalf. The Deep Space Force's gunboats and assault craft would*
*continue on their assigned course.*

Admiral Francis Macomb, TFN, broke the stunned silence.
"Who *are* those people?!"

Ynaathar turned to the bank of com screens which held the
faces of his task force commanders. Macomb, commanding TF 81,
Eighth Fleet's primary battle-line component, was a crusty war-dog
of the old school, outspoken to a fault. Trust him to blurt out
what everyone was thinking. The only surprising thing was that
his ejaculation hadn't contained two or three obscenities.

Ynaathar, however, felt he owed it to his position to maintain
a façade of imperturbability.

"Unknown, Ahhdmiraaaal. All our drones have been able to
tell us is that the Bahg mobile force is engaged against a fleet of
unknown origin. Is this not correct?" He turned to a bewildered-
looking knot of intelligence officers. Kevin Sanders, with questionable propriety, spoke up first.

"Correct, First Fang. We haven't a clue as to who the unknowns
are, but at least we can give you a rough count of their order of
battle by ship types: twelve monitors, sixty superdreadnoughts,
sixteen assault carriers, twenty fleet carriers, sixty battlecruisers
and forty-eight heavy cruisers."

"A formidable force," Fifth Fang Shiiaarnaow'maahzaak, commanding Task Force 82, commented.

"But not in the same class as ours," Vice Admiral Samantha
Enwright, CO Task Force 85, added.

"No, Sir," Sanders confirmed. "Which is probably why the Bugs
are trying to defeat it in detail before turning on us. They're sending in what appears to be their entire complement of gunboats
and kamikazes. Our analysis doesn't give the strangers a high
probability of survival."

"I should think not," Ynaathar murmured as he studied the

statistics of the tsunami of death sweeping down on . . . whoever it was that had emerged from Warp Point Two. He reached a decision and turned to face the com screen holding the Ophiuchi face of his carrier commander. "Ahhdmiraaaal Haaathaaaahn, am I correct in believing that our fighters, if launched without delay, can intercept the Bahg gunboat strike before it can reach the unknowns?"

Haathaahn recovered quickly, and responded after a hurried consultation with someone outside the pickup. "Ittt woulllld be exxxxtremely clossssse, Firsssst Ffffang. Nnnneedlesssss to ssssay, it woulllld require the fightttters to operrrrate at exxxxtreeme rrrrange, evvvven withhhh maxxxximummm lllllload llllife sss-support paccccks."

"Get them so loaded at once, then."

"You mean, Sir—?" Macomb's dangling question spoke for them all, and Ynaathar flicked his ears affirmatively.

"Yes." he met all four task force commanders' eyes, one com screen at a time. "I assume, at least provisionally, that anyone fighting the Bahgs is a potential friend of ours. On the strength of that assumption, I am prepared to commit Eighth Fleet to the unknowns' support."

No one commented, and Ynaathar saw no disagreement in the screens. He also saw no great regret over the fact that he, and not they, bore the burden of such a decision.

It was, Commander Thaamaandaan decided, difficult to fight a battle and readjust one's reality structure at the same time.

The weariness of a long flight in a fighter's cramped quarters didn't help.

Eighth Fleet's fighter strike had come close to its goal of catching the Bugs' gunboats and kamikazes before they could engage the enigmatic fleet which was their target. Indeed, considering that the fighters had had to cross almost four of the light-hours the Humans had made standard for the Alliance, the closeness was rather remarkable. But the unknowns had launched their own fighters with unexpected promptness, and those fighters had come to grips with the Bugs shortly before Thaamaandaan and his fellows could join the battle. So it had worked out well after all, in that the Bugs were now caught between two fires.

But it gave Thaamaandaan food for thought which he had little time to chew as he led his squadron into the maelstrom of battle.

That the Ophiuchi fighter pilots were the best in existence had been acknowledged for so long that it had assumed the dignity of a natural law. The *Corthohardaa* weren't insufferable about the advantage they derived from their evolutionary heritage; that would have been bad form. They merely took it as axiomatic.

Now, Thaamaandaan saw, they'd never be able to do so again. These strangers used their fighters like a *hanaakaat* master used his talon spur. Their dogfighting skill was such that he had to believe they were, to an even greater extent than his own race, born to it.

But as the range closed the sensors revealed something even more disconcerting. These fighters that had appeared so unexpectedly out of the infinite depths of the galaxy were replicas of the human-designed F-3 that Thaamaandaan himself had piloted a scant four years ago, before the F-4 had superseded it. *Exact* replicas.

But now he was in among the Bugs himself, and there was no time to ponder these matters. There was only time for killing and staying alive.

Ynaathar's trademark *sang-froid* was somewhat in abeyance.

In his holo sphere, the vast dogfight was a snarling, writhing pattern of fighters, gunboats and kamikazes, like some multicolored poisonous scorpion thrashing about as it tried to sting itself to death. But he could spare it little attention. The Bug capital ships had turned at bay, and Eighth Fleet, with its fighters otherwise engaged, had had no choice but to meet them ship to ship. So a titanic battle-line engagement now rose to crescendo, echoing on a larger scale the battle still raging between the unknowns and the remnants of the Bugs' Warp Point Two defense force.

Thus far, *Hiarnow'kharnak* hadn't sustained any hits in the bizarre, three-cornered battle. Ynaathar almost wished it had. At least it would have taken his mind off the rising tally of ships which *had* been damaged . . . or destroyed.

But the loss ratio was still in Eighth Fleet's favor. And the battle the strangers were fighting against the fixed defenses had not only started earlier; it had also been one-sided from the first, once the Bugs' mobile forces were prevented from intervening directly. Ynaathar was confident that they would soon be in a position to come to his own fleet's aid.

He wished he was equally confident that they would be inclined to do so. Their motivations were as enigmatic as everything else about them and might or might not include gratitude.

There was, of course, no point in even trying to establish communication with them at this point. Even at their leisure, getting past all the incompatibilities of technology, protocols and language would be a lengthy and tedious job. In the midst of a battle . . . ! No, there would be plenty of time later—

"First Fang," the communications officer diffidently interrupted Ynaathar's thoughts, "we are being hailed by the unknown fleet's flagship."

Ynaathar stared. "Did I understand you correctly?"

"Yes, First Fang." The communications officer's whiskers were aquiver with suppressed excitement and perplexity. "They are using *Terran* protocols—several years old, but nonetheless recognizable."

Ynaathar ordered himself to come out of shock.

"Acknowledge, and put them on," he ordered, then turned in the direction of the intelligence station. "Cub Saaanderzz, we are about to establish contact with the unidentified fleet. Please join me, as I believe your insights may be helpful."

"Aye, aye, Sir," said Sanders, just as the screen awoke.

Ever since entering this system and detecting those enigmatic strangers, they'd all given free rein to their imaginations. But none of the unheard-of lifeforms they'd visualized would have been as stunning or unexpected as what the screen now revealed.

"This is Rear Admiral Aileen Sommers, Terran Federation Navy, commanding Survey Flotilla 19," said the early-middle-aged human female in TFN black-and-silver, speaking like one finally delivering a message rehearsed over and over in the course of years—a message she'd doubted she would ever have the chance to utter. "I wish to report my flotilla's somewhat belated completion of the mission on which it departed this system approximately five and a half standard Terran years ago." She turned and beckoned, and a second being entered the pickup—smaller than herself, sandy-furred but vaguely batlike to Sanders' eyes with its large folded wings. It raised a four-digited hand in what was presumably a greeting, and Sommers resumed. "I also wish to report, in my capacity as *de facto* ambassador from the Terran Federation to the Star Union of Crucis, that the Grand Alliance has a new member."

# CHAPTER TWENTY-TWO

## "I suppose we must approve. . . ."

"Well, Warmaster," Aileen Sommers said as they emerged from the conference room, "now *you* know what it's like to be an ambassador."

"Yes—an officially accredited one," Warmaster Robalii Rikka, now ambassador from the Star Union of Crucis to the Terran Federation, the Khanate of Orion and the Ophiuchi Association, shot back rather pointedly.

Sommers silently acknowledged the accuracy of the barb. But she couldn't help being struck by the irony of Rikka's appointment to a diplomatic position. "Diplomatic" was one of the last words she would have thought of applying to the warmaster, a fighting admiral with a reputation for being aggressive to a fault. He'd justified that reputation not long since, at the Second Battle of Skriischnagar, when he'd smashed open the road to Pajzomo—and, beyond it, the warp chain along which SF 19 had once fled, leading back to Anderson One and thence to Alpha Centauri. But his desire—no, his *need*—to slaughter as many Demons as possible had pushed his innate boldness almost over the edge into rashness. It was a need his family line came by honestly, and it was what gave him so keen an edge as the Star Union's sword. But it was also a two-edged weapon, and his losses had been so heavy that he'd only narrowly avoided the unthinkable calamity of the destruction of his entire force of two Grand Wings. Afterwards, he'd taken stock of himself and brought his lust for vengeance more firmly under the command of his training and discipline.

Still, there was something irresistibly amusing about the thought of Rikka as a *diplomat*.

He'd done rather well, though, with the help of the multispecies Star Union political staff that had accompanied First Grand Wing on its long offensive. That offensive had brought it, not without bitter fighting along the way, at last to Anderson One, whence SF 19 had departed so long ago . . . only to find it in Bug hands. Sommers and Hafezi had passed some of the worst moments of their lives as they'd contemplated the implications of that—and the size of the tidal wave of gunboats and kamikaze shuttles roaring down on them. But then exultation had banished their despair as Alliance forces had entered the system from the Alpha Centauri warp point and joined with First Grand Wing to grind the Bugs out of existence.

The victory hadn't come cheaply. First Grand Wing had lost four monitors, fourteen superdreadnoughts, five assault carriers, seven fleet carriers, eighteen battlecruisers and twelve heavy cruisers. Neither had Eighth Fleet escaped unscathed: six of its monitors, eight superdreadnoughts, three assault carriers, five fleet carriers and eleven battlecruisers were now cosmic detritus, while numerous other ships were damaged to varying degrees. But no living Bug remained in the Anderson One system. Which had been just as well on several levels. Sommers' lengthy explanations of just who her new friends were had left First Fang Ynaathar and his staff so thunderstruck that Sommers rather suspected their combat efficiency was well below maximum.

Once those explanations were completed, however, Ynaathar hadn't hesitated for a moment over what to do next. He'd sent them back to Alpha Centauri and this space station, where Ambassador Rikka and his political types had just finished a hectic round of preliminary talks with Alliance officials, by the fastest means possible.

"Are you coming down to the planet with us?" Rikka asked her, gesturing through a nearby transparency at the companion-planet Eden, rising over the cloud-swirling blue curve of Nova Terra.

All at once, Sommers' good spirits vanished like a pricked bubble.

"No, Warmaster. I've been ordered to report in person to Sky Marshal MacGregor, here on the station. My military superiors want an accounting of my actions over the last five and a half years."

"I can well imagine that they do," Rikka said judiciously. "Still, I understand the news media and the political leadership are anxious to have you on the planet without delay, for the purpose of public appearances."

Feridoun Hafezi joined them just in time to hear Rikka's remark. He grinned whitely in a beard that still held considerably more pepper than salt.

"That, Warmaster, is precisely the point. The word's gotten out, and the story's become a sensation down there. The Sky Marshal wants to debrief her before she goes groundside and the circus begins."

"I doubt if your governmental leaders are particularly happy with the delay," Rikka opined mildly.

"That's one way to put it. The politicos all want to get their pictures taken with her. Next election, they'll claim credit for the fact that we've suddenly got a new ally against the Bugs."

Sommers shot Hafezi a glare. *Keep it in the family, Feridoun!*

Rikka looked twenty centimeters up and met her eyes.

"I can't advise you on how to deal with the situation in which you find yourself, as it is completely foreign to my experience. I am not, however, unacquainted with the bureaucratic mindset. If you should find yourself in difficulties over any arguably irregular actions you've taken over the last few years..."

He hesitated awkwardly, then shrugged his wings in a gesture which mingled the combination of apology and the decision.

"I realize that you're uncomfortable when my own people or our fellow citizens remind you that without the gifts of technology and the training in its use which you gave us, we would never have survived the coming of the Demons. We have no wish to embarrass you, but I am prepared to remind the responsible authorities—through channels, naturally!—of your unique and crucial role in forging the alliance with the Star Union. And to let it be known that my government would...take a negative view of any action against you."

A moment passed before Sommers could speak.

"Thank you, Warmaster," she said then. "But the Alliance is more important than my career. I must ask you not to do anything that would jeopardize it. And now..." She took a deep breath and drew herself up. "I have an appointment with Sky Marshal MacGregor."

*Sky Marshal MacGregor.* Sommers was still getting used to that, although early in the course of her hurried catching-up she'd learned what had happened to Ivan Antonov and Hannah Avram and so many others.

"Let me come with you," Hafezi said, and his voice held a number of things. Military propriety wasn't one of them.

"No, Feridoun. The order only mentioned me—it didn't say anything about bringing my chief of staff. Anyway, I was in command. The responsibility was mine." She glanced around. For the moment, no one else was around except Rikka. She took Hafezi's left hand in her right and gave it a quick, hard squeeze. Then she turned on her heel and strode off down the passageway.

The lump in her stomach seemed to grow heavier as she passed through the outer offices. It assumed the proportions of an ancient iron cannon ball as the door to the sky marshal's private office loomed ahead.

"Er, excuse me, Admiral," said the yeoman accompanying her. "This way, please."

"But isn't this . . . ?" Sommers gestured toward the door with MacGregor's name on it.

"Actually, Sir, they want to see you over here in the briefing room."

*They?* Sommers thought as she walked through the indicated door . . . and then stopped cold.

Sky Marshal MacGregor was there, all right, seated at a table along with four others of various species. Sommers' body, acting without orders from her forebrain, came to the most rigid position of attention she'd achieved since the Academy. *Who the hell do I report to?* she wondered frantically. She settled for focusing her eyes on a spot between MacGregor and the silvered-sable Orion at the head of the table and rapping out, "Rear Admiral Sommers reporting as ordered, Sir!"

"Please be seated, Ahhdmiraaaal Saahmerzz," purred Kthaara'zarthan. "You have, I believe, already met Sky Maaarshaaal MaaacGregggorr and First Fang Ynaathar'solmaak. Permit me to introduce Ahhdmiraaaal Thaarzhaan and Fleet Speaker Noraku, who represent, respectively, the Ophiuchi Association and the Empire of Gormus on the Grand Allied Joint Chiefs of Staff—which I have the honor to chair."

Sommers managed to mumble something as she lowered herself into a chair across the table from the awesome array of rank.

Kthaara seemed to read her mind.

"You probably were not aware that the entire Joint Chiefs of Staff were present here on this station. The fact has not been publicized. You see, you have become something of a celebrity, what with your miraculous return from the dead years after your flotilla was given up for lost." He gave a soft, rippling growl that Sommers—who hadn't seen an Orion in five and a half years and was still readjusting to the race—belatedly recognized as the equivalent of a human's nasty chuckle. "So if we had waited for you on the planet, it might have been too late. We wanted a chance to talk to you informally, before turning you over to the tender mercies of your politicians and news media."

MacGregor muttered something, which Kthaara ignored. He resumed with renewed seriousness.

"Let me emphasize the word 'informally.' This is not an official board of inquiry. Whether any such proceedings are indicated is a matter for your own Human service, not the Alliance. We merely wish to let you orally supplement the report you tendered to First Fang Ynaathar in Aahnnderrssson One."

Ellen MacGregor leaned forward, a movement unsettlingly reminiscent of the way a force beam projector's business end extruded itself from the hull for action.

"To put it another way, we kidnapped you so we could hear in your own words just what the *hell* you've been doing out there in the name of the Terran Federation and its allies."

"Before we proceed," came Noraku's soothing basso, "I for one would appreciate an update from Admiral Sommers on the more recent stages of the Crucians' war with the Bugs, as I fear that my briefing on the subject was cut short by my hurried departure for this station. I am familiar with Survey Flotilla 19's escape from the Bugs, its first contact with the Star Union, and the early stages of the war, including the Bugs' conquest and colonization of the Rabahl system and the check the Crucians—with your help—administered to them at the battle of Rey ... Rey. . . ."

"Reymiirnagar, Fleet Speaker," supplied Sommers, grateful for the reprieve. "That was the *First* Battle of Reymiirnagar, where the Crucian fighters got their baptism of fire. The Bugs came back, of course, a few months later. But we held. By that time the Star Union had deployed a lot more fighters. Their pilots were green, but even a green Crucian pilot is ... well, you have no idea!"

"Actually, I do," Ynaathar put in, "having observed them in action in Aaahnnderrssson One. So in my case, at least, you are—how does your Human expression go? Expounding religious doctrine to the temple singers?"

"Close enough," MacGregor allowed impatiently. "Go on, Sommers."

"After Second Reymiirnagar, the Star Union was able to go on the offensive. Our initial objective was to reestablish communication with the Zarkolyan Empire, which the Bugs' advance had cut." Sommers was unconscious of her own shift to the first person, but she became conscious of the bewildered looks on some of the faces across the table, especially Noraku's.

"Allow me," Kthaara said. Sommers' report had already been downloaded into the secure data section of the space station's computer net. Now the Chairman of the Joint Chiefs gave an oral command in ripply-snarly Orion, and a holographic display of the Star Union's warp network appeared on the room's screen. Sommers studied that pattern, now so familiar to her, and picked up a light-pencil.

"The Zarkolyans' primary point of contact with the Star Union was through a closed warp point here, in the Giizwahn system," she began. "A secondary one, at the end of a long supply line, was over *here*, at Jzotayar—"

"What's the story on these Zarkolyans, anyway?" interrupted MacGregor. "Are they Star Union members or not?"

"They were in the process of amalgamation when Survey Flotilla 19 arrived. The disruption of their lines of communication didn't exactly help. But at the same time, they . . . proved themselves. You see, in addition to their physical oddity—" Sommers didn't elaborate; if they hadn't already seen holos of the trilaterally symmetrical, multitentacled egg-layers they soon would, and nothing short of that could truly convey their weirdness "—they're very different from the Crucians psychologically and socially. To put it unkindly, they're a bunch of stereotypical money-grubbing capitalists, with no military tradition. However, they're an industrial powerhouse, and if they weren't warlike to start with, they've certainly gotten warlike enough lately to hold up their end."

"Close acquaintance with the Bugs tends to have that effect on people," MacGregor remarked drily.

"Too true, Sir. The Telikans are an even better example."

A brief, uncomfortable silence fell. By now they all knew of that race's tragedy. Sommers, however, had had far longer than they had to become accustomed to it, and she didn't allow the silence to linger.

"The Telikans' original homeworld was almost uniquely pacifistic and nonviolent," she said. "But now . . . well, let's put it this way: if I were the Bugs and had to be at the mercy of *somebody*, I'd rather have it be anyone in this room than a Telikan!"

"Quite a transformation," Noraku observed.

"Indeed, Fleet Speaker. The tiny Telikan minority of the Star Union's total population now accounts for over eighty percent of their fleet's ground-assault troops. The racial Crucians are unsuited to that kind of thing." Sommers smiled reminiscently. "The Telikan social pattern is matriarchal—the females are at least half again as large and strong as the males—and any Telikan field commander is addressed as the *talnikah*, or 'battle mother.' But our xenologist who first translated the term was Ophiuchi, and in Standard English his translation got garbled into something our Marines—having seen them in action—decided was actually better: 'combat mama.'"

The nonhumans—even Kthaara—looked blank. But MacGregor had to choke back a guffaw.

"I'll bet your grunts even use that in official paperwork by now," she chortled. Then she remembered herself and forcibly banished her huge grin. "Ah, continue, Sommers."

"Uh, yes, Sir. After retaking the Menkasahr warp nexus and rolling up the Giizwahn System, we reestablished contact with the Zarkolyans and learned they hadn't just been hiding behind their closed warp points. They'd been raiding through Jzotayar, disrupting the Bugs' supply lines to their forward base at Rabahl—which, by then, had become what you might call the Bugs' Zephrain. Our next objective, in conjunction with the Zarkolyans, was the warp chain from Reymiirnagar to Pajzomo."

"The system where you had initially encountered the Crucians," Noraku put in.

"Yes, Fleet Speaker. At Skriischnagar, Warmaster Rikka opened the way to Pajzomo . . . at considerable cost." Sommers' eyes momentarily clouded over with dark memories, for she'd been at Skriischnagar and knew what lay behind those dry words *considerable cost*. "In fact, we had to slow the operational tempo down a bit afterwards due to the Star Union's losses. But a coordinated offensive by us from Skriischnagar and the Zarkolyans through Jzotayar finally took Pajzomo. That accomplished the first objective of our offensive: to cut Rabahl off from Bug space completely. It's still there, tremendously strong but now isolated. We'll take it eventually."

"And the *other* objective of the offensive?" Kthaara asked mildly, and Sommers swallowed, knowing she could procrastinate no longer.

"After Pajzomo was secured, Warmaster Rikka and First Grand Wing—accompanied by me and Captain Hafezi, my chief of staff, with the remainder of my people remaining behind to serve as cadres—advanced from that system, following Survey Flotilla 19's old route in reverse. The objective, of course, was to break through to Alpha Centauri so that we could . . . uh, formalize the Star Union's membership in the Grand Alliance."

"Ah, yes." Kthaara exuded an air of finally coming to the point. "The membership that you had already taken it upon yourself to offer them."

Sommers had always heard that the actual arrival of a moment one has dreaded for years is never truly as bad as one has feared. *The hell it isn't*, she thought as the leaden lump reappeared in the pit of her stomach.

"That's correct, Sir. In my capacity as commander of a Survey Flotilla temporarily out of communication with higher authority, I exercised the broad discretionary powers granted by Article Twenty-Seven, Section—"

"I'm aware of that regulation" MacGregor leaned forward again in the same alarming way. "I'm *not* aware of any regulation that empowers Survey commanders to call themselves 'ambassadors'—or to treat a newly contacted polity as an ally, with all that implies regarding security of classified information. Are *you* aware of one, Admiral?"

Sommers knew how unflattering the sheen of sweat on her face must be in the room's lighting. It really ought, she reflected, to be the least of her worries.

"Ah, no I'm not, Sir. But—well, the Star Union is a sovereign power, and they treated me as the Grand Alliance's representative for purposes of diplomatic protocol. It was a practical necessity if the alliance was to go forward."

"And," Kthaara said mildly, "you made the decision—on behalf of the Khan'a'khanaaeee, among others—that this alliance was worth whatever irregularities were necessary to bring it about?"

The force of absolute conviction stiffened Sommers' resolve and steadied her voice.

"Yes, Sir, I did. I was among beings who'd saved my life and the lives of my entire command—absolute strangers to them at the time. Beings who were fighting for their existence against the Bugs . . . and even then I had some inkling of what that meant, having heard rumors about what Admiral Antonov had found on Harnah."

Since returning, she'd learned those rumors had been true. It was a bit of knowledge she had *not* shared with Rikka. Still less had she shared it with Warmaster Garadden, Rikka's second in command. . . and a racial Telikan. They continued to believe that the Telikan homeworld's agony had at least been quick. She knew better now, and her voice wavered momentarily as she looked inward on the vistas of nightmare. Terrible as they were for her, she knew they would be infinitely worse for the beings she'd come to know as friends, not just allies in a war, and it was an agony she simply could not inflict upon them. But then she blinked those nightmares away and met the row of eyes across the table.

"Now we all *know* what the Bugs are. That's why we have a Grand Alliance. Not just to defend our own particular races from the Bugs but to *destroy* them before they eat the universe hollow of everything individual consciousness has brought into it. The capacity to love—and, yes, to hate, because some things *ought* to be hated. The capacity to recognize beauty and sometimes even create it. Most of all, the capacity to make moral choices—including the ultimate choice of sacrificing that very individual consciousness in the name of what all of us recognize, in one form or another, for what it is: honor. All of our races, however different, have those things in common. *And so do the Crucians!* They're part of what the Grand Alliance exists to keep alive in the universe. I did what I did because I *couldn't* do otherwise. What else would any of you have done?"

Abruptly, Sommers stopped. In the ringing silence, the realization of what she'd said caught up to her.

*Well,* she thought in the midst of a strangely relieved calm, *I can always do something else for a living.*

The rustling purr of an Orion sigh finally dispelled the silence, and Kthaara'zarthan flattened his ears in his race's gesture of resigned melancholy.

"Well, let me make certain I am clear on the facts as they seem to stand. On your own initiative, without any authority whatever, you released the Alliance's latest classified military technology to a hitherto unknown interstellar polity and committed the Alliance to support that polity against the Bahgs—"

"Yes, Sir," Sommers murmured.

"—all for no better reason than to save the lives of the person-nel under your command, force the Bahgs to fight on a second front, split the enemy's attention and spread his resources thinner, and add another industrial base almost as large as the Khanate to the Alliance's support structure?"

"Yes, Sir. . . ." *Huh?*

Kthaara leaned back and sighed more deeply.

"Well, under the circumstances, I suppose we must approve your actions." His slit-pupiled eyes held a twinkle that transcended species. "Sky Maaarshaaal, do you concur?"

"Oh, I *suppose* so. Only . . ." MacGregor looked at Sommers, and sternness dissolved into a huge grin that made her face almost unrecognizable. "Don't let it happen again!"

"I'll try not to, Sky Marshal," Sommers said in a small voice.

# CHAPTER TWENTY-THREE
## The Last Roadblock

The staffers and subordinate commanders crowding *Hiarnow'khar-nak*'s flag briefing room rose respectfully as Ynaathar'solmaak entered. The First Fang didn't notice. Instead he stared aghast at the screen, where the planet Harnah showed in all its blue loveliness.

*What* graaznaak-*brained idiot left the outside view on? The sight of that planet is* not *what we need! And of course it would be out of the question for me to order it turned off now. All I can do is try to ignore it.*

So he made the best of a bad situation and proceeded to his place at the table with a mumbled "Please be seated." They did so, led by the trio directly across from him: Warmaster Rikka, who'd asked for this conference; his Telikan second in command, Warmaster Kazwulla Garadden; and Aileen Sommers.

Even though Ynaathar considered himself—not without reason—a cosmopolite, it was never easy to read the body language of aliens, especially of aliens whose species one had only recently encountered. Despite that, he could tell that Rikka and Garadden were in the grip of some strong emotion, sternly controlled—an emotion rising, in Garadden's case, to the level of waking nightmare. Equally obvious was an element of strain between Rikka and Sommers that hadn't been there before, a certain stiff, self-conscious separateness in the way they sat side by side.

"This meeting," Ynaathar began, "has been convened at the request of the commanding officer of Task Force 86."

That was First Grand Wing's designation within the

organizational context of Eighth Fleet. Rikka had accepted it with every appearance of good grace, and Ynaathar was certain it had nothing to do with whatever was bothering the Crucian. It was certainly an appropriate designation, given the sheer size of Eighth Fleet, and the warmaster had clearly recognized the need to fully integrate his own command into the far larger Allied force structure in a way which would minimize communications and command bottlenecks.

At the same time, Ynaathar was beginning to realize that the Crucian "task force" was a strategic asset whose value far exceeded its mere tonnage. The SBMHAWK bombardment of the Anderson One warp point fortresses had reduced them effectively to rubble, and no major Bug fleet units had been committed to the defense of the system. But that didn't mean they'd been unopposed, and the gunboats and kamikaze shuttles based on Harnah had swarmed to meet them. The Crucian fighter pilots were eager to upgrade to the specially modified F-4s the Federation was already putting into production to suit their own life support and body form requirements, but what they could do with the "obsolete" F-3s was an eye opener. They'd cut their way through the Bug gunboats and small craft like a laser scalpel, and Ynaathar knew their efforts had substantially reduced the casualties Eighth Fleet would otherwise have suffered.

Which made Rikka's obvious unhappiness even more distressing to the fang. He watched the warmaster's folded wings quivering, as if he was constantly forced to restrain their need to unfold in agitation, and hoped this meeting wasn't going to be as bad as he feared it might.

"As all of you know," he continued after a moment, "our recon fighter screen has reported that the only starships still in Aaahnnderrssson One are the thirty warp point defense cruisers in orbit around the planet." He neither named Harnah nor indicated the blue globe floating serenely in the screen behind him as he went on. "Our sensors have confirmed that the starships are tied into the planetary defense nets, which, of course, means they would be able to use the planetary point defense installations to support their own anti-missile defenses if we should decide to attack them in a . . . conventional manner."

He paused, considering his circumlocution, and decided it was time to stop worrying about awakening ghosts.

"Now, in the absence of a thorough reconnaissance of this

system we have no way to be certain that there really are no additional Bahg starships in it. They could be lying in cloak, waiting to come in behind us. And ever since our experience in Operation Pessssthouse, we have known better than to discount the threat of Bahg traps."

An uncomfortable muttering ran through the room, but Ynaathar had expected it and continued calmly.

"As we all know, Second Fleet did not bombard Harnah when it passed through this system in the course of Operation Pesssst-house—and we all know the reason why. That reason has lost none of its force. But that was before we knew what the abrupt annihilation of a large Bahg population does to the remaining Bahgs in the local planetary system. In light of what we now know, we must seriously consider the possibility of exercising what has become known as the 'Shiiivaaa Option.'"

Ynaathar gestured toward the commander of Task Force 82.

"Fifth Fang Shiiaarnaow'maazaak has proposed that, after taking out Harnah's orbital fortresses and cruisers, we position SBMHAWK carrier pods in a dense orbital pattern around the planet, to be activated if we come under attack from additional, heavy Bahg mobile forces, searing the surface clean of life and thereby stunning and disorienting our attackers."

He ran his eyes over the room. It held a variety of expressions.

"Needless to say, the ethical implications cannot be ignored. I am sure Fifth Fang Shiiaarnaow is as sensible of them as any of us." Actually, Ynaathar wasn't sure of any such thing. Shiiaarnaow was a reactionary who fancied himself a warrior of the old school. "But before we turn to this issue, I invite Warmaster Rikka to address the meeting."

"Actually, First Fang, it was on this very issue that I wished to make my views known."

Rikka straightened up and, in the very limited space available to him, fluttered his folded wings back and forth a few times in what Ynaathar suspected was the equivalent of a Human or an Orion drawing a deep breath.

"I first learned of the 'Shiva Option' while at Alpha Centauri," the warmaster began. "When we entered this system and I learned there was a Demon planetary population of billions here, I asked one of my human liaison officers why we even hesitated to use it. That was how I learned . . ." All at once, Rikka's self-control gave way and he whirled on Sommers. "Why did you never *tell* us?"

Sommers stared back at him for several agonizing seconds, then spoke from the depths of obvious misery.

"I didn't know myself, until our return to Alpha Centauri. Oh, there'd been rumors about Harnah, just before my survey flotilla departed. But that was all: rumors!"

"You could have shared those rumors with us."

"I didn't really believe them . . . because I couldn't *let* myself believe them! Remember, there are human colonies that have been under Bug occupation since the early days of the war."

"But after we arrived at Alpha Centauri, you learned that the rumors had been true all along, and *still* you said nothing!"

"All right, damn it!" flared Sommers. "Yes, I could have told you. But would you really have *wanted* to me too? Are you sure you really would have wanted to know? You . . . and Garadden?" A low sound escaped the Telikan warmaster. Ynaathar's interpreter earpiece—aside from the personnel of the original SF 19, no one in the Alliance had had time to learn Crucian, so SF 19 had downloaded its own translation software to the flagship's computers—didn't translate it. But Sommers needed no translation, and something seemed to go out of her.

"Cancel all that bullshit," she muttered. "Yes, I should have told you. Call me a coward if you want to. I can't argue."

Rikka also subsided.

"I, too, have been uttering grazing-animal excrement. I understand why you didn't tell us, and it has nothing to do with cowardice—a thing no one in the Star Union would ever accuse you of. No, you knew only too well how we would react. You knew how you yourself had reacted, knowing that the Demons had held certain Human worlds for a few of your years. And you thought to yourself: 'But a *hundred* years. . . ?'"

Ynaathar had been getting ready to reprove Rikka and Sommers for the impropriety of their exchange. Now he felt no inclination whatsoever to do so. For he, too, understood.

He cursed himself for not understanding sooner.

He had no excuse. He'd reviewed Sommers' report, and talked to the Crucian representatives. So he'd known, as a matter of dry historical fact, the way the First Crucian-Arachnid War had ended, a century before. He'd even known—on the same bloodless level—that the closed warp point through which the Crucians had withdrawn had been located in the home system of the Star Union member-race known as the Telikans. He'd known all that. He'd just never *felt* it.

*What is wrong with me?* he wondered. *Have the last nine years so surfeited us with horror that we have lost the capacity to notice it? That one who calls himself a warrior of the Zheeerlikou'valkhannaiee could not even think about the implications . . . or realize how any being sworn to the defense of his—or her—people would react to such news?*

*If so, that is not the least of the things the Bugs have robbed us of.*

Garadden's hands twisted together. They were surprisingly humanlike—the most humanlike thing about her. To Humans, she resembled an animal known as a koala bear—sheer coincidence, for the koala was a mammal, while the Telikans laid eggs—but with arms that hung almost to ground level when she stood up to her full 1.7-meter height. Humans, Ynaathar had heard, regarded koalas as irresistibly cute. There may have been some, although he hadn't met any, who thought that about Telikans. But *nobody* thought it of Garadden.

"One of the children the retreating Crucian fleet evacuated from Telik was my direct maternal ancestor," she said without looking up, in a voice of acid-etched lead. "When those children were thought old enough for the truth, they were told what everyone in the Star Union *believed* to be the truth. That is the myth that has sustained us ever since: our families purging the planet's databases of all reference to the closed warp point, leaving us and the rest of the Star Union safe to someday avenge them, and then sitting down to wait for the Demons to arrive, bringing a death which, however obscene, was at least quick."

Garadden rose to her feet, gray fur bristling, and her voice grew louder and harsher. *No, not cute at all,* thought Ynaathar.

"Now we know the real truth. We know the agony went on for generation after generation. We know that Telik today is not a world of honored ghosts, but of meat animals that *know*. And that those meat animals are our cousins!"

Garadden looked like she was going to be sick. In any other circumstances, it would have astonished anyone who knew her. But Ynaathar didn't find it incongruous at all. He belatedly recalled—*as I have been belatedly recalling a great many things,* he reproached himself—that the Telikans were herbivores. Garadden had been speaking of things even more horrifying and revolting for her than they would be for an omnivorous Human, and far more so than for a carnivorous Orion.

Rikka also stood, a diminutive form beside his massive second in command, but radiating no less horror —— or fury. He glared around the room, letting his eyes linger on every other officer present before he finally brought them to rest on Ynaathar.

"*All* members of the Star Union—not just Telikans—are as one on this point. We cannot countenance the idea of killing the Demons' victims along with the Demons. Nor can we allow ourselves to be associated with such an act!"

Ynaathar met the Crucian's eyes. Rikka had retained enough diplomatic poise to not state the obvious corollary of his own words: that the alliance had no future if Ynaathar did this thing. And Ynaathar, of course, could hardly utter it aloud either.

"Thank you for your forthright expression of the Star Union's position, Warmaster Rikka," he said instead. "For my own part, I regret the breakdowns of communication and failures of sensitivity that led us to this unfortunate misunderstanding. Now that I understand your viewpoint, and appreciate the horror that lies behind it, I fully accept your argument."

Rikka and Garadden resumed their seats amid a general relief that was as palpable as it was unvoiced, and Ynaathar turned a subtly pointed look on the Task Force 82 commander.

"Fang Shiiaarnaow, I presume you will wish to withdraw your proposal."

Shiiaarnaow hesitated, and for a horrible instant Ynaathar was afraid the crusty warrior was going to ruin everything. Traditionally, the honor code of the *Zheeerlikou'valkhannaiee* had held that, while it was the duty of the warrior caste to defend the Khanate's civilian populace, even some of those citizens were expendable if the harsh necessity of war required it to defend the Khanate as a whole. And Shiiaarnaow was just the being to indulge in some totally inappropriate huffiness along those lines at this of all moments. But when he finally spoke, it was with his very best attempt at diplomacy.

"Of course, First Fang. We all share our allies' fury and revulsion at what these *chofaki* have done. And, at any rate, the issue is hardly a vital one here in Harnah, where there is no major enemy fleet element to oppose us. But . . ."

Again, Shiiarnaow paused. Then he spoke unswervingly, and Ynaathar found himself reluctantly recalling the Human expression *big brass ones.*

"There will be other systems where populations like the Harnahese—and, yes, the Telikans—still exist in their millions among the Bahg billions. What if we encounter a massive concentration of defensive power in such a system? Are we to unconditionally deny ourselves the option of disorganizing and befuddling the Bahgs in such a situation? Will our Crucian allies insist that we abide by their principles at *any* cost, no matter how many avoidable casualties it entails?"

"I respect your viewpoint, Fang," Rikka replied heavily. "But *you* must respect the fact that for us this is more than a 'principle,' which is how my translator renders your term. It is a cultural and religious imperative!"

"But," TF 85's Vice Admiral Samantha Enwright protested in a deeply troubled voice, "we're talking about beings degraded almost below the level of sentience, Ambassador. They're the end products of generations of ruthless selection in favor of individuals willing to go on living and reproducing in the full knowledge of what awaited them and their children. Forgive me, Warmaster Garadden, but might death not be a mercy for them? A release?"

"I will *not* accept that death or continued animalism are their only alternatives," Garadden ground out. "They can be . . . rehabilitated. And no, I don't expect it to be easy. It will take a heartbreaking effort. But we *must* make that effort!"

The commander of Task Force 81 looked up, and his expression surprised Ynaathar. Admiral Francis Macomb was what one might call a human equivalent of Shiiarnaow, and Ynaathar would have expected him to give the Orion his full-throated support. But he looked uncharacteristically troubled.

"Warmasters, I understand what you're saying. From the bottom of my heart, I understand it! But *how* can we liberate a subjugated population on a world like this?" Macomb's usual persona returned with a bark of scornful laughter. "When Admiral Antonov first discovered Harnah, there was a lot of talk about some kind of gene-engineered bioweapon that would wipe out the Bugs without harming the native life forms. Typical! As far back as the twentieth century, we humans got into the habit of expecting a high-tech 'silver bullet' for every dilemma. But it came a cropper in the end."

There was much nodding of heads, and the various nonhuman equivalents thereof. In retrospect, the failure of the bioweapons research was no surprise. Galactic society was far less advanced in that area than a twentieth-century Terran would have expected. The reason was simple: fear. The kind of fear that had assumed the stature of a full-blown cultural taboo. Everyone knew that tailored microorganisms could mutate beyond their creators' control faster than you could say "Frankenstein." Humans knew it in their forebrains, from theoretical studies and computer models. Orions knew it in their guts . . . from what had actually happened to their original homeworld.

"So," Macomb continued, "if we want to selectively exterminate the Bugs on a planet like Harnah while sparing the natives, we're going to have to do it the old-fashioned way: put our Marines down into the mud. Now, the only time we've gone toe-to-toe against the Bugs on the ground was during Admiral Murakuma's counteroffensive in the Romulus Chain. I've talked to General Raphael Mondesi, who commanded the landing force—he's at Alpha Centauri now, in a staff billet. So I have some conception of what it's like."

Macomb hesitated, and sought for the words that would give these people a glimpse of the hell Mondesi had evoked for him. In the end, he knew, no one who hadn't seen it for himself could possibly grasp the full implications, but he went ahead and tried anyway.

"It's not like fighting a normal enemy, one whose spirit you can break by hurting him enough," he said. "It's more like fighting a force of nature—like a hurricane or a tidal wave, but one with a *brain*. One that can think and plan and adjust its responses in the face of resistance. One made up of millions of units that individually *just don't care* whether they live or die! And it's not just the warriors. They can use the workers to screen their warriors' assaults—to soak up our fire until they can get across any kill zone we could set up. And on a planet like Harnah, there are billions of them. *Billions!* Do you have any idea what that *means*? Any idea of the losses our Marines would take?"

There was a dead silence as everyone in the room tried to see through the eyes of those Marines—necessarily limited in numbers, for even the Grand Alliance's spacelift capacity was finite. It would be like staring up at a towering tsunami of malignant, insensate protoplasm.

"The position is, undeniably, a difficult one, First Fang," Rikka said into the silence at last. "We fully grasp the implications of what we're insisting on—the sacrifices we're asking of your personnel. And we are prepared to make you an offer as an earnest of our commitment."

"An . . . offer?"

"Yes First Fang. I make it in my capacity as ambassador. But Warmaster Garadden has asked to speak for me—as, I believe, is fitting."

Garadden stood up again.

"Our proposal is this," she said. "If the other members of the Grand Alliance will pledge to refrain from bombarding Demon-occupied planets with subjugated native populations on their surfaces, the Star Union will pledge in return to furnish a minimum of fifty percent of the ground-assault forces necessary to take any such planets."

At first, Ynaathar wondered if the translator software had rendered the Telikan's words correctly.

"Ah, Warmaster, did I understand you to say—?"

"You did, First Fang. I refer not to a ceiling, but a *minimum* of half the total landing force for the entire Alliance for every planet like Harnah."

Sommers stared up at Garadden. Clearly, this was news to her.

"But . . . but the Star Union Ground Wing is far smaller than either the Federation's Marine Corps or the Khanate's Atmospheric Combat Command—much less *both* of them!" she protested, her expression horrified. "And it consists overwhelmingly of racial Telikans, drawn from the small refugee population base. Garadden, were you listening to Admiral Macomb? Do you realize we're probably talking about *millions* of casualties?"

"Yes," Garadden replied simply. Her muzzle wrinkled in her race's smile. "You see, we take our convictions in this matter very seriously."

Silence fell yet again. A different sort of silence, this time.

"As far as the Grand Alliance as a whole is concerned," Ynaathar said at last, "this will of course have to be ratified by the Joint Chiefs of Staff. But pending their decision—as to which I have little doubt—I undertake on my own initiative to abide by the agreement you have proposed. In other words, there will be no bombardment of Harnah by Eighth Fleet." He looked around the very subdued conference room, letting his gaze linger pointedly on Shiiarnaow. "Is there any further discussion?"

There was none.

"Good," said Ynaathar with finality, "for we must turn to other matters. In particular, I fear the unanticipated lack of opposition in this system may have disturbing implications. Indeed, it may invalidate some of the basic assumptions behind our entire joint operation with Seventh Fleet."

*The Fleet waited.*

*There was very little else it could do, for the united strength of*

*the New Enemies and the Old had effectively completed the destruc-*
*tion of all those thousands of warships which had been laboriously*
*built up after the Old Enemies' long ago disappearance. Now the*
*combined Enemies stood poised to smash the last link between the*
*remaining Systems Which Must Be Defended, and the Fleet lacked*
*the strength to drive those Enemies back. It could only await their*
*attack and hope that the division between the Enemy forces and*
*their points of contact would create a lapse of coordination which*
*would permit the Fleet's surviving united strength to fall upon one*
*of them and crush it in isolation.*

*It was in the fading hope of such an opportunity that the Fleet*
*had chosen not to resist the Enemies' intrusion into the most recent*
*system to fall. The decision had not been an easy one. With the*
*loss of two Systems Which Must Be Defended and their supporting*
*satellite systems, every productive population center had become*
*critically important to the Fleet's continued operations, yet there*
*had never really been any other possible choice, for that system*
*could be dispensed with. That in which the Mobile Force which*
*had once defended it now stood could not. Nor could the one in*
*which the only other Mobile Force the Fleet retained now waited*
*to face its allotted share of the Enemies' warships.*

*In a way the Fleet had never contemplated, those systems, too,*
*had become Systems Which Must Be Defended. They simply could*
*not be lost, for if they were, they would take with them any hope*
*of coordinated action between the old Systems Which Must Be*
*Defended. And at least they were directly linked, without any*
*intervening warp junctions to separate them, which provided at*
*least the possibility of rapidly reinforcing one Mobile Force with the*
*other to achieve the sort of crushing superiority which had eluded*
*the Fleet for so long. That superiority would give the Fleet victory,*
*if it could be achieved. If it couldn't be, the only possible outcome*
*was defeat, and if the Fleet lost here, then any hope of ultimate*
*victory—or survival—would be equally lost.*

*Which would be most unfortunate, indeed.*

"You know," Raymond Prescott remarked, gazing somberly into
the glowing display before him, "this is more your sort of operation than mine, in a lot of ways."

"Indeed?" Zhaarnak walked over to stand beside him, letting his
own eyes rest on the glittering icons and light-strings of warp lines
stretching from Pesthouse to Centauri.

"Of course it is," Prescott said with a small, tight smile. "If there's one thing we humans pound into our midshipmen in their tactical courses, it's the KISS principle!"

"Aye, yes!" Zhaarnak purred a chuckle. "'Keep It Simple, Stupid.'" His Orion accent mangled the Standard English indescribably. "What a delightfully Human concept! Although," he sobered considerably, "one which has certainly demonstrated its soundness under certain circumstances."

"That it has, brother," Prescott said in the Tongue of Tongues. "On the other hand, your own traditions have their place, as well, much as some admirals I know would like to deny it. Still, this sort of complicated coordination of operations is something the *Zheeerlikou'valkhannaiee's* instincts are far more comfortable with."

"Truth," Zhaarnak agreed. "Yet whether we are more 'comfortable' with it or not, there are times when there is no other road to victory. Just as your Fang Aaahnnderrssson taught us in the Wars of Shame that there are times when your own warriors' ways are the only road. Which," he added quietly, "does not make me one bit less . . . anxious than you, brother."

Prescott nodded soberly. He was well aware that Zhaarnak wouldn't have made that admission so freely to any other human, but there was only too much justification for any anxiety his *vilkshatha* brother might feel.

On the scale of the display, the glittering icons representing Seventh and Eighth Fleets were mere centimeters apart in the Anderson One System and Pesthouse, respectively. Only the crimson stars of Harnah, Anderson Three, and Anderson Four separated them. A mere three warp transits, and the two fleets—with over seven hundred and twenty starships, thousands of fighters, and hundreds of gunboats between them—would join forces and, in the process, secure total control of the Anderson Chain. Only three.

A civilian, looking at that display, would see instantly that only a tiny step remained, that only the tiniest gap lay between those forces. And, although the astrophysicists' best guess was that Harnah and Anderson Four lay something like a hundred and three light-years from one another in real-space terms, the civilian would have been correct, for light-years meant nothing to the starships which plied the crazy quilt of the warp lines.

Or not usually, at any rate.

But this time wasn't usual, for between Pesthouse and Anderson One lay not simply three star systems, but two massive Bug fleets, each dedicated to smashing any intruder foolish enough to come within its reach. And because those sullen Bug warships waited there, the light-years between Pesthouse and Anderson One meant a very great deal, indeed, for any message from Eighth Fleet must be relayed by the ICN from Anderson One, back to Centauri, through a score of additional star systems and starless nexi to L-169, and thence down the length of the Prescott Chain, through Home Hive One, to Pesthouse. Even with light-speed transmission relays across every one of the intervening star systems, that message would take literally weeks to reach its destination. The "shortcut" across Zephrain helped a little, but not enough to make any real difference, and that made the coordination of the step across that "tiny gap" physically impossible.

Unfortunately, Zhaarnak's observation that no other approach was possible was damnably acute. Those three star systems *had* to be taken, at whatever risk or cost, and so the strategists had no choice but to coordinate on the macro scale what could not be coordinated on the micro scale. Which was, of course, the reason for Zhaarnak's—and Prescott's—anxiety. According to the plan painstakingly worked out and communicated over the weeks between Centauri and Pesthouse, Seventh Fleet was to time its attack on Anderson Five to commence on March 11, 2369, Terran Standard Reckoning, exactly five days after Eighth Fleet began its assault on Harnah ... and there was absolutely no way to confirm that First Fang Ynaathar's attack had actually begun on schedule.

Prescott drew a deep breath and chided himself—again—for his doubts. Of course there was no way to confirm it, yet there was no real need to, either. If one thing in the universe was certain, it was that Eighth Fleet had begun its attack on time. Ynaathar's proximity to Centauri assured him of completely secure support down a far shorter supply line than the long stretch of systems which lay behind Seventh Fleet. It was possible, even probable, that there'd been last-minute changes to his projected order of battle, additions and subtractions alike from the list of forces which he'd forwarded to Prescott, but the ships, personnel, and munitions for his attack had been assembled, and Ynaathar and every one of his flag officers was only too well aware of how critical it was to distract the Bugs. Given the enemy's interior position, the Alliance had no choice but to force him to split his attention between two separate threats at opposite ends of the section of the Anderson Chain he still controlled, and Eighth Fleet knew it.

Just as Prescott and Zhaarnak knew that their own attack on Anderson Four *must* begin on schedule to provide the counter-balancing diversion Ynaathar would require to reduce the odds against *him*. And at least Seventh Fleet was once again at full strength and ready for the challenge it faced.

The human allowed his eyes to move from the warp links to the endless lists of task forces, task groups, squadrons, strikegroups, and battle divisions which filled the data display, spelling out the sheer, ponderous might of the force he commanded. Sixty monitors, forty-six superdreadnoughts, twenty-five assault carriers, thirty-one fleet carriers, thirty-one battlecruisers, twenty-one light carriers, and twenty light cruisers, all supported by more than forty-four hundred fighters, and over seven hundred and fifty gunboats. The stupendous firepower under his control was, as he and Zhaarnak had demonstrated only too grimly—sufficient to sterilize entire planets, yet Eighth Fleet was even more powerful. It had only half as many monitors as Seventh Fleet, but four times the superdreadnoughts and battlecruisers as compensation, and its more numerous assault and fleet carriers, coupled with the proximity of Centauri, more than balanced the twenty-one CVLs of Vice Admiral al-Salah's TG 72.4.

Surely that crushing mass of destruction had to be enough, properly handled, to smash even the soulless, uncaring ranks of death which were a Bug fleet!

Of course it was, he told himself flatly, and his eyes hardened as he remembered his brother and all the men and women—human and nonhuman alike—who had died under his command since the Battle of Alowan to reach this moment. He no longer quailed under the weight of his blood debt to those thousands upon thousands of warriors and the billions of civilians who'd died under the monstrous tsunami of the Bugs' ravenous omnivoracity. It was a burden he'd been given no choice but to learn to bear, just as Ivan Antonov had learned, but Raymond Prescott knew the great secret Antonov had tried so fiercely and with so much success to hide.

Whatever one might learn to bear, one could never learn to *forget*. That much he understood perfectly when he looked into Vanessa Murakuma's eyes and saw the shadows and darkness no one else seemed to recognize. And those memories and that debt, and the cold, savage hatred for Andrew's death, came to him now as he inhaled once more and then turned to look into the slit-pupiled, alien eyes of the being who had become not

just his comrade in arms but the brother Andrew had never
known . . . and who shared Raymond Prescott's determination to
avenge his death.

"You should return to your ship, brother," he said quietly in
the Tongue of Tongues, his expression calm, almost serene. "We
will begin the attack in three standard hours."

"May our claws strike deep," Zhaarnak replied, equally quietly,
and Prescott nodded and laid a hand briefly on the Orion's broad,
powerful shoulder.

"May our claws strike deep," he agreed.

*It had worked.*

*The decision against opposing the attack of the New Enemies
who had been joined by the Old had exposed the approaches to
no less than two Systems Which Must Be Defended to potential
attack, but it had also disordered the Enemies' battle plan. It was
obvious that the two Enemy fleets had intended to attack in close
coordination, staggering their assaults just enough to draw the
Fleet into committing against the first threat before the second
revealed itself. But the Fleet's withdrawal had caught the Enemies
off-balance, instead.*

*Half of the Mobile Force which had been withdrawn before the
first Enemy thrust stood in place, prepared to delay any thrust on
his part. But the other half sped to join the other Mobile Force
as it fell back before the second Enemy attack. The joint forces of
two Systems Which Must Be Defended raced to rendezvous and
throw themselves upon the second Enemy force, the one which had
already slain two other Systems Which Must Be Defended, and for
the first time in far too long, the Fleet knew that victory lay within
its reach. Three hundred and fifty warships, headed by sixty-three
monitors and ninety-six superdreadnoughts, reached out to wrap
their tentacle clusters about a mere hundred and eighty Enemy
ships and crush the life from them, and the unsuspecting Enemy
continued blindly towards them.*

Raymond Prescott stared at the plot and tried not to be sick.

The master holo sphere was set to system scale, and Anderson
Four's primary was a yellow dot at the center of a system Prescott
remembered only too well. Just over five light-hours from it, at
nine o'clock, was Warp Point Three, through which Seventh Fleet
had entered the system from Pesthouse, blowing away the defenses
with minimal loss and proceeding across the system toward Warp

Point One, which led onward along the Anderson Chain. That was a long haul, for their destination was four and a half light-hours from the primary on an almost diametrically opposite heading of two o'clock. Warp Point Three, whose terminus was still unknown, lay on a bearing of eight o'clock, at 5.6 light-hours.

But Prescott had eyes for none of that, much less for the system's lifeless planets. Like everyone around him on *Riva y Silva*'s flag bridge, he could only stare at the swarming red "hostile" icons that his wide-ranging recon fighters had revealed.

The Bug deep space force in this system, pulling back ahead of Seventh Fleet, was bad enough: thirty monitors, sixty-six superdreadnoughts, ninety-six battlecruisers, and seventy-eight light cruisers. But he and Zhaarnak, though expecting a stiff fight, had pressed on into the system, confident of their ability to take that force. Until the new Bug forces had appeared, bearing down from Warp Point One. A detailed force breakdown was impossible as yet, but at least thirty-five monitors, forty-five superdreadnoughts, and sixty-five battlecruisers had streamed in from Anderson Three, where they were supposed to be fully engaged in the defense of Harnah. Nor was that the end of Warp Point One's capacity to spew forth death, for an estimated five hundred oncoming gunboats had now been detected behind that daunting array of capital ships.

Finally, the quiescent icon of Warp Point Two behind them had erupted with the scarlet of still more gunboats. Their number was unknowable as yet, but there were tides of them, streaming in from what Prescott was now sure must be one of the three remaining home hive systems.

All those converging red icons seemed to swim before his eyes, and he stared into a nightmare from which there would be no awakening.

*Well, now we know how it happened. This system and Anderson Three are the conduits from at least two of the home hives. And now we're here, just like Second Fleet was. . . .*

Amos Chung cleared his throat softly.

"Sir, it appears that they're using the same tactical disposition they did in Pesthouse."

He indicated the icon of the deep space force that had now turned on them. Then he gestured at an auxiliary plot with its tactical display. Yes, Prescott reflected. It was the same globular juggernaut of battlecruisers, light cruisers, gunboats, and kamikaze small craft.

He stared at them for a handful of endless heartbeats, then inhaled sharply, almost spitefully. He faced his sense of paralysis and drove it back into its kennel as he pulled himself ruthlessly together. This was _not_ Operation Pesthouse all over again. Battle-hardened though Second Fleet had been by the time it reached Pesthouse, its temper couldn't have begun to match that of the blade _he_ wielded. Seventh Fleet stood behind him, its monitor battle-line immeasurably more powerful than Second Fleet's had been, forged and hammered beyond common conception in the crucible of history's bloodiest series of campaigns and calm in the knowledge that the Bugs could be beaten. And he and Zhaarnak had made the decision to bring along the light carriers, not generally regarded as viable battle fleet units but able to augment the combat space patrol of fighters.

They would need them now.

"Raise Lord Telmasa, and the task force commanders," he told the communications officer quietly. "Put them on screens in the flag briefing room." Then he gestured to his staffers to follow him and strode into the adjacent compartment with its array of com screens.

"Evidently," Zhaarnak began without preamble, "First Fang Ynaathar's attack on Harnah did not distract the attention of the enemy forces in Aaahnnderrssson Three after all."

"Evidently not," Prescott agreed. If either of them doubted that the attack had taken place, he did not voice those doubts. Instead, Prescott turned to all of the flag officers watching him from their individual screens. "Ladies and gentlemen, I think it's time for us to activate Case Doppelganger."

If there was anyone in Seventh Fleet who felt no trace of panic as word of the odds against them spread, then that "anyone" had to be a lunatic. But if anyone in Seventh Fleet was about to let panic paralyze him, there was no sign of it as the fleet's personnel responded to its commander's orders.

Case Doppelganger was the product of endless hours spent gaming out possible responses to the Bugs' globular kamikaze formations in the tactical simulators aboard _Irena Riva y Silva_ and _Hia'khan_. As the name suggested, it was in many respects an adaptation of the Bugs' own concept—in this case, a tight globe of mutually defending capital ships, packed as closely as their own drive fields and the need to allow for evasive maneuvers would permit.

There was plenty of time to assume the formation as the enemy attack forces swept towards Seventh Fleet across light-hours of vacuum, and Captain Stephen Landrum and the *farshathkhanaaks* of each separate task force briefed their pilots carefully. Those fighters would sweep outward from the fleet's globe, engaging and weakening the kamikazes and gunboats while the globe ran before them.

It was all about defense in depth to bleed the Bugs as they closed and then meet them with the most murderous close-in defensive fire into history of space combat.

Now all that remained was to see if it worked.

*Clearly the Enemy had been as completely surprised as the Fleet could have hoped. If he hadn't been, he would never have continued onward with a force so much weaker than that waiting to destroy him.*

*Yet as the Fleet's strike elements swept towards him, it became evident that he had adapted his own doctrine once again. The Fleet had never before seen the spherical formation he'd adopted, yet it quickly recognized the similarity between it and the Fleet's own new attack formation. From its own experience, the fleet was fully aware of the defensive effectiveness of such an arrangement, and the Enemy's decision to turn away from his pursuers would make it even more effective. The strikes were faster than his battle-line, but the need to include cruisers and battlecruisers in their defensive shells limited their speed advantage to barely fifty percent. That meant they could overtake the Enemy only slowly, and while they did so, his small attack craft would hammer at the formation's defenses.*

*That was regrettable. Yet the small attack craft could venture into their own attack range only at the expense of casualties, and as they were ground away, so would be the Enemy's ability to wear down and fend off the next attack formation.*

Stephen Landrum watched his strikegroups go in again and again and again. They were good, those pilots, possibly the most experienced and best trained in the history of interstellar combat, with the sort of kill ratios that fighter pilots throughout history could only have dreamed of.

But good as they were, there were only so many of them, and the Bugs had devised a formation which denied them at least half their usual advantages in combat. If the strikefighters wanted to attack the gunboats and the kamikazes who represented the true threat to their starships, they must first run the gauntlet of the massed anti-fighter missile batteries of the *Bugs'* starships.

And they did.

They did it over and over again. The glare of nuclear and anti-matter warheads, the invisible death of x-ray lasers, the sudden mid-word interruption of deep-space death . . . By now, they were only too familiar to Landrum and every other fighter commander in Seventh Fleet. And if they were familiar to the COs, how much more common were they to the fighter jocks who lived and died through them? Yet not one strikegroup balked, not a single squadron hesitated.

The first of the Bug attack globes was clearly visible in the visual display now. Not the ships themselves. No one could have picked them out even yet. But Seventh Fleet's personnel didn't need to see the ships.

They could see the explosions that marked the deaths of humans, Orions, and Ophiuchi, as well as Bugs. The explosions that wrapped themselves around the outer perimeter of the globe and turned it into a solid sphere of brimstone come straight from Hell as it rumbled dreadfully onward in Seventh Fleet's wake.

After a while, Raymond Prescott had found, one passed beyond fatigue into a state of heightened awareness.

It was something he'd experienced before, of course. He was, after all, one of the two most experienced combat commanders in human history. It had shaken his perception of the universe when he realized that he and Vanessa Murakuma now had actually seen more—and more intense—combat even than Ivan Antonov. Of course, fighting Bugs either gave one experience quickly or killed one . . . when it didn't do both of those things at once.

Yet for all the dreadful history of combat and slaughter which lay behind him, he'd never experienced anything to surpass this.

He'd lost track of how long it had been since he'd left the flag bridge. He ate meals brought to him there, and disposed of their end products in facilities a few steps away. But sleep was something dimly remembered, a fading memory of some prior life, recalled only when it appeared in the form of an irresistible temptation he nonetheless had to resist.

*But why resist it?* an inner voice he didn't want to hear asked. *What's the difference? Death is death, regardless of whether or not you're awake when it comes. And it's coming.*

He shook himself as if to physically throw off the incubus of despair.

The fighters had done their magnificent best, but some of the gunboats and shuttles had broken through. A screen of battle-cruisers and light cruisers had interposed themselves—and the bodies of their crews—between them and Seventh Fleet's main body. Almost seventy of those ships had died. But the Bugs had come on with something beyond their normal indifference to losses—something that Prescott, had he been talking about any other race, might have called desperation. At least two hundred gunboats and a hundred kamikaze assault shuttles had broken through and plunged into the battle-line's final defensive envelope with fighters still on their tails.

There were no reliable figures on how many of them had completed their attack runs—nor did Prescott need them. The figures that mattered were those of the ships they had taken with them into death: eight monitors, twelve superdreadnoughts, and eleven light carriers. And, of course, the people. Prescott was still coming to terms with the fact that he would never hear Force Leader Shaaldaar's rock-steady basso again. Vice Admiral Janos Kolchak had died with *his* flagship, as well. Twelfth Small Fang Yithaar'tolmaa's *Howmarsi'hirtalkin* had survived, but the small fang's own remains were somewhere in the twisted mass of wreckage that comprised most of his flagship.

And yet, Prescott kept forcing himself to remember, the battle-line had mostly survived. The Bug deep space force originally assigned to this system had evidently underestimated the extent of that survival, for it had pressed on without waiting for support from the massive Bug formations coming in from Anderson Three. That miscalculation had almost certainly saved Seventh Fleet—for now, at least. That and its own battle-forged toughness. It had met the incoming Bug starships with a hurricane of missiles, wrapping them in a shroud of purifying antimatter flame that swept them from the continuum. But the Allied battle-line had paid with fourteen more of its own monitors to do it, and the number of other ships destroyed or damaged was in the usual proportion.

And now the monstrous array of fresh capital ships from Anderson Three was closing inexorably in, its BCRs racing ahead of the slower monitors and superdreadnoughts in their haste to begin finishing off the crippled prey. And Zhaarnak was comming him.

He turned to the com screen, and the *vilkshatha* brothers looked at each other. Each of them saw the memory of Alowan and Telmasa in the other's eyes and knew how precious the shared years which had passed since that unexpected reprieve had been to both of them. Yet there seemed little to say. There was no need for them to put what they felt into words . . . and there was certainly no point in saying that the next fight would be Seventh Fleet's last, for they both knew it.

So instead, Zhaarnak turned to practicalities with a briskness that anyone familiar with his race would have recognized as a mask for despair.

"We must reorganize our battle-line, Raaymmonnd."

"Yes." Prescott looked again at the loss totals, then looked away. "Our task force organization has pretty much vanished. We'll abandon our worst damaged ships and scuttle them, so they won't slow up our withdrawal. I've already got Anna and Jacques at work forming new battlegroups around whatever command ships are still alive."

"Can we manage such a fundamental restructuring in the midst of battle?"

"We can." Prescott's tone held no doubt, only certainty. Only a force as superbly trained and battle-tried as Seventh Fleet could even have considered plugging units from different Alliance members into the same datagroups on the fly. Prescott knew that, and the pride was like ashes in his mouth.

"I want those BCRs to encounter the kind of coordinated missile fire they're not expecting," he said. "Maybe it'll give them pause."

"We will also need to reorganize our strikegroups to cover the withdrawal."

"Truth. Raathaarn and Stephen are working on it, but it's going to involve even more organizational improvisation. We'll base all of the surviving fighters on Terran carriers because they're the best equipped to meet multispecies life-support requirements."

*And because the surviving Terran carriers alone have ample hangar space for every one of the fighters we still have left,* he left unsaid.

"Very well. I will have Small Fang Jarnaaa coordinate with Claw Laaandrummm."

There was little left to say. Zhaarnak said it anyway.

"It has been a good hunt, brother."

Prescott gazed into the screen at the brother he would almost certainly never see in the flesh again. This electronic image would have to do, and in a way he knew Zhaarnak would have understood, it was Andrew to whom he spoke, as well.

"Truth, brother. A good hunt. Our claws struck deep indeed."

TFN safety regulations imposed strict limits on the number of sorties a given fighter pilot could fly in a given time. In Seventh Fleet's present pass, those regulations—like so much else—had long since gone by the boards.

Several times, Irma Sanchez had almost yielded to the enormous army of exhaustion, sleeplessness, stress, and grief for her gallant, too-young pilots. Meswami had been the latest to go—she'd let herself feel it later. Pink-cheeked Rolf Nordlund was now, by default, the XO of a "squadron" reconstituted out of ingredients from three species. And Irma was still skipper, senior to Cub of the Khan Mnyeearnaow'mirnak, Lieutenant (j.g.) Eilonwwa and the two human pilots who'd been foisted on her.

That, she reflected, was probably what had kept her from simply letting go: the problem of running this motley crew that still went by the call-sign "Victor Foxtrot Niner-Four." That, and the small blue-eyed face that occasionally floated up to the surface of her mind amid all the fatigue and horror—for what kind of universe would Lydochka inhabit after all this was over?

A snarl of Orion brought her back to the present. She'd never learned the Tongue of Tongues. Eilonwwa understood it, however, and could speak Standard English with his own race's extended consonants. Irma wondered what she'd do if the Ophiuchi bought it.

This time, though, she didn't need Eilonwwa's services as a translator, for she had a pretty good idea what Mnyeearnaow was talking about.

"I see them, Lieutenant," she cut in as Eilonwwa began to interpret. It was yet another formation of kamikaze shuttles, stooping like raptors on Seventh Fleet's dwindling battle-line. She rapped out a series of commands. At least Mnyeearnaow could understand Standard English, and he kept formation as well as anyone in this *ad hoc* squadron as they altered course and went to the attack.

Their external ordnance was long gone, and hadn't been all that copious to start with, given their need to carry extended life-support packs for this endless patrolling. But their F-4s' internal hetlasers jabbed and thrust, turning antimatter-laden assault shuttles into expanding miniature suns. But the kamikazes went into evasive action, and fresh formations of gunboats appeared to complicate the tactical picture.

A scream of static and a brief fireball, and Irma winced. *Johnson*, she thought. *Or was her name Jackson? God, I can't even remember, I've known them so few hours.*

But then the last kamikaze was free of them, and only Mnyeearnaow was in a position to intercept it. The Orion swooped in . . and didn't fire.

Irma heard the snarling, mewling voice in her headset and cursed her inability to understand. "Eilonwwa—?"

"He sayss hiss firrring mechanisssm hass mallllfunctionned, Ssir," the Ophiuchi fluted.

"Mnyeearnaow," Irma snapped, "pull up! That's a direct order."

But the Orion's fighter continued to close with the shuttle that now had nothing between it and the battle-line.

"Goddamn it, don't pretend you can't understand me!" Something caught Irma's eye. The computer had deduced the kamikaze's target: TFNS *Irena Riva y Silva*.

*Fleet Flag* she thought automatically. *Maybe Mnyeearnaow's seen it too.*

"Mnyeearnaow," she yelled, "talk to me!"

The Orion voice finally sounded in her headset—but only in a howling, quavering war cry that sent primal ice sliding along her spine. And then fighter and shuttle met at a combined velocity that was an appreciable fraction of light's. Irma's outside view automatically darkened; the flash wasn't why she had to squeeze her eyes tightly shut and blink them rapidly a few times.

Then they were past the gunboats and into the clear. Irma let herself take a deep breath among the clean stars for a moment while receiving the survivors' acknowledgments, then braced herself for the gunboats to resume the engagement.

Only . . . they didn't.

Bewildered, Irma wondered if she'd heard something. But no, the sudden break in the battle-pattern had triggered a sense deeper than hearing. Yet to her or any veteran it was practically audible.

Nordlund must have "heard" it, too.

"Uh, Skipper—?"

"Yeah, Rolf . . . er, XO. Resume our patrol pattern. I don't know where they've gone, but I'm not arguing."

✧　　✧　　✧

"No, Ahhdmiraaaal Maaaacomb," First Fang Ynaathar said flatly, "we will *not* probe the warp point first."

"But, First Fang—" TF 81's commander began, and Ynaathar forced himself not to snarl. It wasn't easy, and only the fact that he'd fought shoulder to shoulder with Macomb and knew the Human was no *chofak* but as true a *farshatok* as the First Fang had ever known made it possible.

"There can be no other decision," Ynaathar cut off the TFN commander of Eighth Fleet's battle-line. "You know as well as I that Fang Presssssscottt and Fang Zhaarnaak commenced their attack precisely on schedule. And if the Bahgs have chosen not to defend Harnah, then it can only have been to employ their warships—and their gunboats and kamikazes—somewhere else. We cannot allow them to combine against Seventh Fleet and crush it in isolation!"

"Sir, I agree completely with your analysis of the Bugs' actions and probable intentions," Francis Macomb said respectfully. "It's the logical thing for them to have done, if they're willing to simply write Harnah off. But they've certainly proven in the past that they can do the unexpected. If they have more strength than our analysts believe they do, they may have elected to repeat their Pesthouse strategy and draw us forward so they can cut *us* off from retreat, not Seventh Fleet. Or they may have already defeated Seventh Fleet and be prepared to turn their combined strength in our direction if we continue to advance. I fully accept that we have no choice but to advance anyway. I'm only pointing out that we've carried out no detailed reconnaissance of this warp point and that we have no existing operational plan for an advance beyond Harnah into Anderson Three. Sir, we're not *prepared* for this operation. If we push ahead too hard and too fast, we may put ourselves into precisely the same situation we're afraid Seventh Fleet's already in."

Ynaathar gazed at the Human face on his com screen and heard the echo of Operation Pesthouse in Macomb's voice. It was understandable, the First Fang thought, for the ambush of Second Fleet was the sort of traumatic shock from which few warriors ever fully recovered. The loss of so many ships—and of Ivan Antonov and Hannah Avram—had cost his Terran allies something else, as well. It had cost them much of that calm assumption of ultimate victory which had so infuriated so many of the *Zheeerlikou'valkhannaiee* before the present war, much of that mantle of invincibility they'd won largely at the expense of the KON.

Under some circumstances, Ynaathar admitted to himself, he might have taken a certain grim satisfaction in the humbling of that pride, for it had been the Humans who had humbled the pride of the *Zheeerlikou'valkhannaiee* in the Wars of Shame. But that had been before the Bugs burst upon Human and Orion alike. Before they had fought and died as *farshatok* before the faceless, implacable menace which had come out of the Long Night to murder both their species. And before Ynaathar'solmaak had realized what a priceless asset that Human confidence and almost innocent arrogance truly was.

And because all of that was true, the First Fang chose his words with care.

"There will be no more debate, Fraaaaancisssss," he said, and if his voice was calm, it was also unflinching. "Seventh Fleet depends upon us—*Fang Pressssssscottt* depends upon us—and we will not fail them. This is not Operation Pesssthouse, my friend . . . nor will we allow it to become such. Your reservations are noted and acknowledged. They have much merit, but that merit must be set against our responsibilities to Seventh Fleet. The decision to advance immediately into Aaahnnderrssson Three without further reconnaissance is mine, and I assume full responsibility for it."

He held Macomb's eye for perhaps two breaths, and then the Terran officer nodded.

"Yes, Sir," he said crisply.

"Thank you," Ynaathar replied quietly, then straightened. "Prepare the SBMHAWKs and stand by for transit."

*Disaster.*

*It had never happened before. It could never happen. Yet it had, and the Fleet—*

*No. Not the Fleet, for the impossible action had destroyed forever that which had been "the Fleet." That which had always fought as one being, with one awareness and only one purpose, had broken at last under the strain which could no longer be endured, and from one, it had become two. Or perhaps even more than that.*

*The ships which had first flung themselves upon the second Enemy attack watched in something for which those who crewed them had no word. Another type of being might have called it shock, or disbelief—possibly even betrayal. But these beings had no terms for those concepts, and so they had no way to describe it or categorize it, or even to understand it clearly. Yet even in their confusion, they recognized the shattering of the Unity which had always been theirs and which had bound them eternally to the same inexorable Purpose.*

*In that moment, however dimly, the beings aboard those starships and at the controls of those gunboats and suicide shuttles which still survived recognized in the sudden appearance of the combined forces of the Old Enemies and the New the same moment of final desperation they had brought to every other species—save one—they had ever encountered. For in that moment, the Mobile Force which had been sent forth by the System Which Must Be Defended in which the New Enemies had first been encountered, broke off without instructions from the Fleet. Indeed, broke off against the orders and the plan which had sent it here in the first place. It responded not to the threat to the Unity and the Purpose, but to the threat to its own System Which Must Be Defended, and so it abandoned the attack. Deserted the Unity to fall back in desperate defense of its own single fragment of that Unity . . . and so abandoned the Purpose that Unity served.*

*It could not happen.*

*Yet it had.*

"No, First Fang." Raymond Prescott's exhaustion detracted not at all from his obvious resolution, and he spoke in the Tongue of Tongues with careful emphasis. "I cannot entertain such a proposal."

Ynaathar stared across the table of his private office.

The orange light of the Anderson Three binary shone through the viewport, and Prescott knew precisely what the First Fang was thinking. Not that understanding could undermine the adamantine power of his determination.

He and Zhaarnak had brought what was left of Seventh Fleet here to Anderson Three after the Bugs' inexplicable withdrawal from Anderson Four. By then, Eighth Fleet had finished off the system defenses, and the Bug mobile forces had vanished into cloak, presumably to slip out through this system's unexplored Warp Point One. Both *vilkshatha* brothers had been properly grateful for their deliverance. But now . . .

"Fang Pressssssscottt, look at the loss figures!" Ynaathar protested with an edge of respect which might have seemed odd to a human, coming from a superior officer to one of his juniors. "Seventh Fleet comprises barely more than an oversized task force now. The only reasonable course is to dissolve it and merge its units into Eighth Fleet."

"Seventh Fleet is more than just an organization chart, Sir," Prescott replied, still in the Tongue of Tongues. "It is more than just a total of ships and personnel. It has come to . . . to *mean* something that transcends all that. I admit that we are in no shape to fight again, at present. We should return to Alpha Centauri for refitting and reinforcement. But I will resist any move to dissolve Seventh Fleet, by all the means in my power. That includes going to Alpha Centauri and personally appealing to the Joint Chiefs. It also includes, as a last resort, resigning my commission if my arguments are unavailing."

Zhaarnak leaned forward.

"And I, First Fang, will go further. I will go all the way to New Valkha and put the case before the Khan himself. I will make it a matter of the *Zheeerlikou'valkhannaiee's* honor . . . and of his."

"Do you understand what you are saying?" Ynaathar breathed. *And does your* vilkshatha *brother realize what it would mean? That if you test the* Khan'a'khanaaeee's *own honor in this matter and he decides against you only your death will maintain* your *honor?*

But then the First Fang looked at Raymond'prescott-telmasa's hard, set Human expression and knew that *this* Human understood perfectly.

"Yes, First Fang," Zhaarnak replied to the question flatly, "for it *is* a matter of honor. Seventh Fleet has become my *farshatok*. Breaking it up would be a greater wrongness than I would care to live with."

Ynaathar regarded the two fathers in honor of Clan Telmasa, sitting there in their haggardness—and in their mantle of legend—and recognized defeat.

"Very well, I agree," he capitulated. "I will so advise the Joint Chiefs, and I believe they will concur."

"No, Commander."

Commander Jeanne Nicot looked up sharply.

"What did you say, *Lieutenant* Commander Sanchez?"

Irma remained steady under the new CSG's glare. Commander Georghiu's atoms were scattered through the spaces of Anderson Four, and Irma was still trying to understand her own feeling of loss. In retrospect, there was something almost endearing about his stuffiness, which had lacked Nicot's hard edge.

"Sir, you know our record, so you know how much the

Ninety-Fourth has been through. Hell, we've been down to less than this—down to me and Lieutenant Meswami, in fact." She swallowed the lump of memory and pressed on. "Now there are *four* of us: me, Lieutenant (j.g.) Nordlund, Lieutenant (j.g.) Eilonwwa, and Ensign Chen . . . I mean Chin."

"Three," Nicot corrected. "You can't count Mister Eilonwwa. These mixed squadrons were strictly a desperation expedient. Come to think of it, you only got Mister Chin as part of the same emergency consolidation. So it's really down to you and Mister Nordlund—who, as you know, has even less business being an executive officer than . . . Well, the point is, do you really think you can put VF-94 back together with some green replacements?"

Irma met Nicot's eyes unwaveringly.

"I've done it before, Sir."

"Hmmm . . . So you have." Nicot flipped through some sheets of hardcopy. "There's quite a bit about you in the records I inherited from Commander Georghiu. He thought highly of you," she said, and Irma's facade collapsed into a pile of astonishment.

"He *did* . . . Sir?"

"Yes, in his own way—although I don't think he ever knew quite what to make of you. At one point, he refers to you as a 'character.'" Nicot shook her head dismissively. "Well, if you think VF-94 is still viable . . ."

Irma decided to press her luck.

"It would help, Sir, if we could keep Chin. And . . . it would help even more if we could keep Eilonwwa."

"We've been through that," Nicot snapped irritably. "Come on, you know it's out of the question! The different dietary requirements, the variant life-support specifications—"

"Our fleet and assault carriers have had Ophiuchi squadrons along with Terran ones ever since the Zephrain offensive, Sir. They have a lot of experience handling whatever logistical complications that causes. Maybe VF-94 could be transferred to one of those carriers." *And get us off this goddamned monitor at last,* Irma forced herself not to add. Belatedly, it occurred to her that Nicot might take the idea as a personal affront, but the CSG gave no sign of it if she had.

"So now we're supposed to accommodate Seventh Fleet's entire strikegroup organization to VF-94's convenience? You *do* think a lot of yourself, don't you Sanchez?"

"I think a lot of the squadron, Sir. So should anyone who knows its record."

"Commander Georghiu's estimate of you wasn't exaggerated, Sanchez," said Nicot coolly. Then, unexpectedly, she smiled. "All right, I'll make the suggestion to Captain Landrum. Maybe something can be arranged."

"And about Mister Eilonwwa, Sir . . . ?"

"Yes, yes, that too—although I'll be amazed if you get your way on that." Another small smile. "On the other hand, if this idea does go through, I won't be getting a chance to know you better. I'm almost sorry about that. Almost."

# CHAPTER TWENTY-FOUR
## "Some cripple!"

Restless, Vanessa Murakuma got up, threw on a sheer robe and walked to the open window. The morning light of Zephrain A streamed in, and a breeze off the Alph River caused the robe to flutter, caressing her slender body.

"Do you have any concept of how erotic you look?" Marcus LeBlanc inquired from the bed, and Murakuma gave a fairly delicate snort.

"Not bad for an old broad, I suppose."

"Spare me the false modesty." That, in fact, was precisely what it was. Murakuma couldn't take credit for the generations in low gravity that had produced a body form not unlike the elves of myth, nor could she take credit for the development of the antigerone therapies which kept her looking physically so much younger than her calendar age. But she wasn't unaware of her good fortune, and she *did* take the trouble to keep herself in condition.

Besides which, of course, now she knew Fujiko was alive after all—still inaccessible, somewhere in the far reaches of the Star Union of Crucis, but alive. LeBlanc, after the years of separation, could see the rejuvenation more clearly than she could herself.

She returned to the bed and settled in beside him.

"It's almost time," she murmured.

"Yeah, I know. You've got to go. One or the other of us *always* has to go. Are we ever going to get more than a few days at a stretch together?"

"We're lucky you're here at all."

"True," LeBlanc allowed, not particularly mollified. "But damn it, I should be going with you to join Sixth Fleet at Orpheus 1, not staying here at Zephrain!"

"That's not exactly our decision," she reminded him gently.

The Joint Chiefs had finally come to the realization that Prescott, Zhaarnak, and Murakuma, in their remote detached commands, were too far from Alpha Centauri for any kind of realistic turnaround on intelligence questions. The occasional Kevin Sanders junket was no substitute for ready access to the best possible intelligence information and analysis. And the organization LeBlanc had trained was by now quite capable of functioning without him. So the decision had been made to station him in Zephrain, to serve as a local resource of Bug expertise for Sixth and Seventh Fleets.

Now, of course, with the entire Anderson Chain in Alliance hands, that rationale had lost much of its validity as far as Seventh Fleet was concerned. So LeBlanc had argued—not entirely without ulterior motives—that it would make better sense to attach him to the staff of the one commander still operating in isolation from Alpha Centauri. He'd then proceeded to learn an immemorial truth: military orders are so hard to change that they often outlive the circumstances that caused them to be issued.

"Kthaara said something about not wanting to risk me with Sixth Fleet," LeBlanc groused. "Gave me direct orders to stay at Zephrain, in fact. Come to think of it . . ." He trailed off, then sat up straight as suspicion reared its ugly head. "Say! You don't suppose he's so bitter about . . . Well, I know they say misery loves company, but surely he wouldn't . . . Would he?"

"Kthaara? No!" Murakuma smothered a laugh.

"Anyway, I suppose it's just as well. They could just as easily have canceled the whole thing and kept me at Alpha Centauri. It probably helped that they wanted to send somebody anyway, to deliver your new orders."

"Yes." Murakuma sat up straight, and the room's atmosphere underwent a sudden change.

"You still have reservations about the plan, don't you?"

"Damned right I do! Everything about it *oozes* overconfidence—even that stupid code name GFGHQ's assigned to it. 'Operation Cripple' indeed!"

LeBlanc smiled at her vehemence. The "cripple" the code name referred to was the home hive system Sixth Fleet's RD2s had detected beyond Orpheus, which Murakuma had been ordered to attack.

"Well, your drones have established that there's a lot of industrial capacity in that system—"

"You might say that!" Probing through Orpheus 1's Warp Point Two, the RD2s had reported a binary system of two bright F-class stars. The secondary star, currently two hundred and fifty light-minutes out, was too remote for examination. But the primary had no less than *three* inhabited planets, each of them pulsating balefully with the intense energy signature of a heavily industrialized Bug world.

"And yet with all that capacity," LeBlanc pressed on, "they've made no attempt to dislodge Sixth Fleet from their doorstep at Orpheus 1. Headquarters thinks that means they *can't*, that they lack the mobile firepower."

"Of *course* they do!" Murakuma said with withering sarcasm. "It all just evaporated in the solar wind."

"Not quite," LeBlanc replied, suppressing an urge to smile while he wondered if there was anyone else she would have felt comfortable enough to vent with this way. "In fact, the theory is that between you, Seventh Fleet, and Fang Ynaathar, the mobile forces assigned to that system must have taken quite a beating."

"That's Headquarters thinking if ever I heard it. Have they even considered the fascinating little possibility that for all we know that system may have warp connections to both of the other two remaining home hives?"

"Maybe it does," LeBlanc said, still in devil's advocate mode. "But, by the same token, that could mean a lot of strength has been bled off from it to help those other home hives try to hold the Anderson Chain. You have to admit, your RD2s have detected very little in the way of heavy mobile forces."

"Which proves exactly nothing. The Bugs have been patrolling that warp point so heavily the drones haven't been able to penetrate any distance beyond it. Just because we haven't *detected* an ambush—"

"Relax!" LeBlanc sat up beside her. Their knees didn't quite touch. "I'm just pulling your chain. The fact is, I happen to agree with you. GFGHQ is suffering from a bad case of 'victory disease.' You'd think the losses in Operation Ivan would have cured it, but . . ." He trailed off into a brooding silence before resuming. "You're not going to protest it, though, are you?"

"No. I'll follow their orders. But that doesn't mean I have to share their cockiness. I've got a few precautions in mind."

"Yes, I know you do." LeBlanc brooded a moment longer. "I ought to be going with you," he repeated mulishly.

"No," Murakuma smiled, but her voice was very serious, "you shouldn't. You probably don't remember what we said to each other once—"

"—on a terrace on Nova Terra, looking out to sea, almost five years ago," LeBlanc interrupted, and she turned her head to stare at him.

"So you *do* remember! Then you must understand."

"No," he said flatly. "I didn't understand then, and I still don't. It's not your responsibility to keep those you care about alive, Vanessa."

"You're right: you don't understand. Can't you see? It's not a matter of some sort of moral responsibility, Marcus. It's *fear.*" She turned her head and met his eyes unflinchingly as she finally admitted the truth and put it into words for them both. "It's bad enough having to function in the face of death, even though I've had to learn to do it. But if *your* life were on the line at the same time . . ."

And he did, indeed, see. He just didn't want to admit it, and so, without any words—he could think of none, anyway—he took her in his arms.

*With the always fragile line of communication long since cut, it was impossible to know whether the other two remaining Systems Which Must Be Defended were still in contact with one another. Nor did it make any practical difference at the moment. This system was uncompromisingly thrown back on its own resources and those of the systems which serviced it.*

*Fortunately, those resources were far from inconsiderable. This, after all, was the most densely populated and heavily industrialized of all the Systems Which Must Be Defended. The enemy had no way of knowing the full extent of that population and industrialization, for none of his probes had gotten close enough to the secondary stellar component to detect the two fully developed planets that orbited it, for a total of five Worlds Which Must Be Defended. They could produce gunboats and small craft in virtually any desired quantity, to support the twenty-five monitors, seventy-two super-dreadnoughts, seventy-two battlecruisers, and ninety light cruisers that stood behind the massive warp point defenses.*

*Arguably, however, the most valuable resource of all was the Enemy's strategic ignorance. He had no inkling that more of his own kind lay three systems away in the* opposite *direction, where they had faced the Fleet, stalemated, for so long. A coordinated two-front offensive would have been very difficult to deal with.*

*And this time, that strategic ignorance would be matched by tactical ignorance.*

*The Fleet had gone to great lengths to counter the Enemy's intensely inconvenient robot probes. It had smothered the space around the warp point with continuously patroling gunboats and armed small craft. Furthermore, it had pulled those capital ships not on full alert status well back from that warp point, and powered their drives down to standby level, rendering their emissions effectively undetectable.*

*And, of course, the Enemy couldn't possibly imagine the number of gunboats and small craft that crouched on the planetary surfaces. Or the new innovation with which those gunboats had been supplied.*

Vanessa Murakuma permitted herself a grim smile when the sensor reports of awakening Bug starship drives began to light up TFNS *Li Chien-lu*'s flag bridge threat board. She visualized Marcus, back on Zephrain, smiling the same way at the confirmation of their suspicions. . . . But no, he'd be too eaten away by worry to smile about anything.

At least he'd be pleased that their shared skepticism had led her to proceed cautiously into the system—now identified as Home Hive Two from analysis of the orbital fortresses through whose wreckage they were currently advancing.

There'd been forty-eight of those immense constructs, to say nothing of ninety-six defensive heavy cruisers and thirty suicide-rider light cruisers, all surrounded by a veritable haze of mines—eight thousand patterns of them—spangled with thirty-three hundred deep-space buoys. Murakuma had had no intention of rushing in against such defenses. She'd emplaced over half her total inventory of mines around the Orpheus 1 side of the warp point in thin shells which would have been largely useless against capital ships. But by accepting a lower density, she'd been able to emplace them in much greater *depth*, which would provide an attritional shield to absorb and blunt any gunboat counterattack. Then she'd committed her SBMHAWKs in careful waves, provoking the Bugs into activating shell after shell of ECM-equipped buoys and then sweeping them away with further waves of HAWK2-equipped missiles. Now, with her battle-line making transit against the crippled fortresses and the remnants of the cruisers, she still held a substantial emergency supply of SBMHAWKs in reserve.

It might be a good thing she did, she reflected, for the sensor readings continued to pour in, and the figures mounted and mounted. It wasn't so much the total numbers and tonnage opposing her—daunting though those were—as it was the Bugs' closeness to the warp point. And they were getting even closer, closing in for a point-blank duel.

"They were lying with their drives stepped down to almost nothing," Leroy McKenna stated, echoing her own thoughts.

"It would appear," Murakuma remarked, "that we've been had."

"I wasn't going to put it that way, Sir—" the chief of staff began.

"Nor should you," Murakuma cut in briskly. "Because it's inaccurate. *I've* been had. But at least most of our capital ships have already completed transit and our CSP is out." She glanced at Anson Olivera for confirmation of the last, and the *farshath-khanaak* nodded emphatically. "Good. If they want a toe-to-toe slugging match, I'm not averse to it."

She spoke loudly enough to be sure everyone nearby heard her, but it wasn't just bravado. She knew the quality of her personnel.

"And now, Captain Delbridge" she resumed, speaking into the intercom to her flag captain, "please sound General Quarters. This won't be long in coming."

*The initial portion of the plan had worked.*

*Unfortunately, there were no perfect solutions to the problems the Fleet faced. Unlike starships, gunboats and small craft could not cloak, and the Fleet had begun to appreciate at least some of the advantages the Enemy's warp-capable missile pods bestowed upon him. Those advantages had become more pronounced as the Fleet's supporting resource base was carved away and the Enemy's industrial advantage became more and more overwhelming. In the final analysis, no combat space patrol of gunboats was survivable in the face of the unending hurricane of missile pods the Enemy could pour through a warp point, especially since the introduction of the missiles which point defense couldn't intercept.*

*The only way gunboats or small craft could be hidden from the Enemy's sensors—and so from destruction—was to hold them entirely beyond sensor range of the warp point or to retain them on the external gunboat racks and in the internal boat bays of starships which could cloak. Unfortunately, if they were held beyond sensor range, then they were also beyond any range at which they could immediately intervene against an Enemy incursion. But if they were held on the racks and in the bays of their motherships, only the number which the mobile units had the capacity to support would be available.*

*Faced with this dilemma, the Fleet had decided that some gunboats and kamikazes would be superior to none. And so, as the Enemy advanced inward from the warp point and the starships of the Deep Space Force brought their drives on-line and revealed themselves, a mass wave of small craft erupted from them.*

No one in Sixth Fleet was surprised by the sudden appearance of the gunboats and kamikaze assault shuttles. Indeed, if there were any grounds for surprise, it was that the Bugs hadn't made a greater effort to coordinate the swarms of gunboats which must be just beyond sensor range with the commitment of their starships.

*But I suppose it's not really that surprising after all,* Murakuma thought as she watched the icons of the Bug small craft dashing towards her battle-line. *After all, how much coordinating could they do? Their capital units are still slower than ours, so the only way their battle-line could reasonably hope to intercept ours is to catch us within relatively close proximity to the warp point, before we have time to disappear into cloak and use our speed to dance rings around them. But if they'd kept their gunboats close enough to the warp point to intervene, then they'd have been in our sensor envelope and we could have sent the SBMHAWKs after them.*

Which was all very interesting, no doubt, but didn't change the fact that she had to deal with the scores of gunboats and hundreds of shuttles coming straight down her throat.

Anson Olivera's fighter squadrons went to meet them, and the plot was suddenly speckled with thousands of even tinier icons as anti-fighter missiles and gunboat-killing FM3s crossed between the two forces. Scarlet "hostiles" began to vanish in appalling numbers, but a handful of the bright green "friendlies" went with them, and the Bugs' success at hiding their starships meant the kamikazes had only a very short way to go, as distances went in deep-space combat.

Fortunately, these Bugs weren't employing the globular version of the "Bughouse Swarm" formation which had given Seventh Fleet so much difficulty. The defensive fire from the gunboats and the scores of pinnaces scattered among the assault shuttle kamikazes was bad enough, but at least Murakuma's fighters didn't have to break through a solid barrier of ship-launched AFHAWKs before they could even get at their true targets. It was possible that that was an indication that this home hive system had been completely cut off from its fellows long enough that whichever Bug lord high admiral had devised the new doctrine had been unable to communicate it to them. Murakuma reminded herself not to put too much faith in any such assumption and checked the seal on her vacsuit, then locked her shock frame as the first gunboats broke past the CSP.

*It was as well that the Fleet had never placed a great deal of reliance on the Deep Space Force's gunboats and kamikazes. When there was no great expectation of success, there was no great disappointment when all that was achieved was failure.*

*At least the attacking small craft had forced the Enemy to expend some depletable munitions, and a few score of his small attack craft had also been destroyed. It would have been preferable to achieve at least some damage to his starships, but the Fleet had no option but to settle for what it could get.*

*In truth, the Fleet had no great expectation that the Deep Space Force would defeat the Enemy. The Enemy's numbers were too great, and his entry warp point was too close at hand. At best, the Deep Space Force might drive him into retreating from the system, yet the Fleet was far from fully convinced that that would be the best possible outcome. After all, if the Enemy managed to disengage intact, the Fleet would only have to fight him again. In the end, the decision to stand at the warp point had been made less on the basis of purely military considerations than on the necessity of preventing the Enemy from getting deep enough in-system for his sensors to tell him what it was he truly faced in this System Which Must Be Defended.*

*His ignorance was the Fleet's greatest single strategic asset, and so the Deep Space Force was committed at the earliest possible moment. If it succeeded in driving the Enemy back whence he'd come, well and good. If it failed, then the true backbone of the defenses would deal with him. Of course, the entire Deep Space Force would be dead by then, but the probability of its destruction*

*was a paltry price to pay for the possibility of maintaining the
Enemy's ignorance.*

The Bug battle-line had used the attack of its gunboats and
kamikazes to close with Sixth Fleet. Murakuma's capital ships
couldn't use their superior speed to pull away from the enemy
when they were busy using that same speed in desperate evasive
maneuvers to avoid kamikazes. As a result, the Bugs were able
to draw into SBM range before the final, despairing wave of
kamikazes was blown apart short of the monitors.

But that was fine with Murakuma. Even with the diversion of
their kamikazes, the Bugs were unable to close much beyond the
very fringe of the SBM missile envelope. They could hurt her at
that range, but they couldn't *kill* her—not quickly, at any rate—and
as soon as the last of the attacking small craft had ceased to exist,
Sixth Fleet began opening the range once again.

But not by too much. She drew her starships out of range from
the Bug battle-line, and while she was doing that, her carrier flight
deck crews rearmed her fighters and her CSGs reorganized their
squadrons around the thankfully few holes the Bug gunboats had
blown in their tables of organization. She waited a few moments
longer, in hopes that the Bugs might be tempted into sending
their BCRs in unsupported. But it would appear that the enemy's
increased sensitivity to losses was at work. Or perhaps it was
simply a recognition that no battlecruiser in the universe could
survive within the missile envelope of an unshaken monitor battle-
line long enough to achieve anything at all. Vanessa Murakuma
would never understand the way Bugs thought, and she was just
as glad that was true. But it would appear that even *Bugs* could
choose not to expend themselves for no return at all.

*Well,* she thought. *If they won't come out, we'll just have to go
in after them.*

"Ernesto," she said quietly to her ops officer, "tell Anson to kill
the command ships. Then execute Case Rupert."

*Had the beings which crewed the Fleet's ships been capable of
such an emotion, they might have felt despair as their sensors
blossomed once again with the fresh spoor of hundreds of small
attack craft. The fact that the Enemy had opened the range once
more—and had stopped opening it just before he relaunched his
attack craft—told the Deep Space Force what he was about.*

*Unfortunately, there was nothing the Deep Space Force could do about it . . . except to kill as many of the Enemy as possible before it died itself.*

Anson Olivera's strikefighters screamed straight into the teeth of the Bug battle-line's horrific array of defensive firepower. Deadly though a fighter could be, it was a frail and tiny thing when thrown all alone against the unshaken wall of devastation those sullen Bug leviathans could project.

Which was why Case Rupert did nothing of the sort.

Oh, the fighters led the way, but the rest of Sixth Fleet came right behind them. Entire squadrons of fighters salvoed nothing but decoy missiles into the Bugs' defensive envelope, providing hundreds of false targets to lure fire away from the real attackers. Fighter ECM did its bit, as well, fighting to deny point defense laser clusters and AFHAWKs the ability to lock their targets up, and intricate evasive maneuvering—the Waldeck Weave—made them even more difficult to hit. But what truly cleared the way for them was Vanessa Murakuma's decision to take her starships into the Bugs' long-range missile envelope right along with them.

Her monitors and superdreadnoughts flushed their XO racks, sending stupendous volleys of antimatter-armed SBMs and capital missiles straight for the Bugs. Those missiles howled down upon their targets like lethal hammers, and the Bugs had no alternative but to honor the threat. Fending off that torrent of destruction diverted their point defense almost entirely from the strikefighters, cutting the totality of their anti-fighter firepower by almost fifty percent.

The battle-line paid a price to open the door for the fighters, for if it could hit the Bugs, then the Bugs could hit it, and warheads began to go home. Shields flashed and died as the hearts of small, violent stars exploded against them. Most of the Bug missiles concentrated on the battle-line, but here and there an enemy battlegroup decided to vent its fury on easier prey and an entire monitor or superdreadnought battlegroup vomited its entire missile broadside at a single battlecruiser squadron.

No battlecruiser could survive that sort of punishment, and Murakuma's jaw clenched as the Code Omega transmissions began to sound once again.

But offering her ships as targets had accomplished its goal. Olivera's F-4s went howling in to point-blank range. Dozens of them died, despite anything decoy missiles, ECM, or diversions could accomplish. But if dozens perished, hundreds did not, and once again, the sheer volume of the Bug command ships' defensive firepower stripped away their anonymity.

Taut-voiced CSGs vectored their squadrons in on the suddenly revealed targets, and the unstoppable power of the primary pack ripped straight to the hearts of their gargantuan foes. Command datalink installations died under the pounding of those vicious stilettos, and the coordination of their battlegroups faltered.

And that, of course, was the other reason Murakuma had closed on her fighters' heels. She would allow no time for the Bugs to recover from the disorientation as the voices of their command ships were silenced forever. She would give them no respite, no opportunity to reorganize. She would seize the instant of their nakedness mercilessly, and as any battlegroup faltered, at least two battlegroups of her own focused a tornado of missile fire upon it.

Bug monitors writhed like spiders in a candle flame, and Vanessa Murakuma watched them burn with eyes of frozen jade ice.

Afterwards, it was hard to believe the head-on clash had been so brief.

Every combat veteran knows the protracted nature of time in battle, and Murakuma had thought herself long since beyond astonishment at it. But now the old "that *can't* be right" sensation was back in full force. Surely so much carnage, of such intensity, couldn't have been crammed into a mere thirty standard minutes.

She shook the feeling off, annoyed at herself. She also blocked out the noise of the damage control teams, the residual ringing in her own ears, and all the other distractions as she concentrated on the incoming reports.

It had been a holocaust, but at least the loss ratios were heavily in Sixth Fleet's favor. She watched the list of damaged and destroyed ships and tried—without success—not to think about all of the lost and ruined lives hiding behind that passionless electronic display. She made herself watch until the report scrolled downward to the very end, then drew a deep breath, turned, and beckoned to Leroy McKenna.

The chief of staff crossed the flag deck to her, his helmet in the crook of his left arm, and she nodded to him.

"Please get with Ernesto about this," she said, waving a hand at the damage reports she'd just perused. "I want to cull out the most heavily damaged ships and send them back to Orpheus 1, and I want proposals for reorganizing our battlegroups around our losses. And tell Anson I want recon fighters out as soon as possible." She managed a wan smile. "Our fighters have been a bit occupied," she said with studied understatement, "and the lack of fresh reconnaissance is making me just a little nervous."

*The destruction of the Deep Space Force was, no doubt, regrettable. But, viewed in one way, it could be regarded as an advantage. It would induce overconfidence in the Enemy, who would assume that his hardest battles in this system were now behind him.*

*It was also unintendedly advantageous that the formations of gunboats and small craft from the planets of the secondary stellar component were still far behind the more closely based ones. When the Enemy detected the first wave of planet-based craft speeding toward him, he wouldn't recognize the full magnitude of the threat. For that wave represented only a third of it. . . .*

"Did you say *eight* thousand?"

Marina Abernathy swallowed, hard. But the intelligence officer didn't wilt under the admiral's regard.

"Yes, Sir. I know the original report said two thousand gunboats and kamikazes. The first fighter to detect them immediately turned back into com range and transmitted that report. But the rest of his squadron stayed out there, and now they've detected three more formations, each as large as the first."

"I see," Murakuma acknowledged, and nodded slowly.

Her acknowledgment was the only sound and motion on the shock-frozen flag bridge, and she turned to McKenna, who was as pale as it was possible for him to get.

"I wonder how much more there is to be detected?" she said in an almost conversational tone.

"Sir?"

"We keep forgetting about that secondary component," she pointed out with a touch of impatience. "It's another class F main-sequence star, and even though they're usually not old enough to have life-bearing planets, Component A here obviously *is*, and both components of a binary star system coalesce at the same time. So Component B could have another heavily developed planet—or more than one of them, given the wide liquid-water zone around a bright star like that. We really have no idea of the total resources we're facing here. And if those idiots at GFGHQ—"

She chopped herself off and shook her head irritably. This time her impatience was with herself.

"That doesn't matter. Eight thousand of them are quite enough. It's time we got ourselves back to Orpheus 1."

"Thank God we hadn't penetrated any further from the warp point before we picked up the trailers," McKenna muttered, and Ernesto Cruciero looked up from a computer terminal.

"You're right about that, Sir," the ops officer agreed fervently. "Two thousand we could take, and I'd have advised doing just that. But eight?" He shook his head. "But even if we start pulling back immediately, we're already in too deep to be able to exit this system before they can reach us. We'll be right at the warp point when they do, but they're still going to catch us short of Orpheus 1."

"I know." Murakuma gazed at the system display for a few seconds, then inhaled and turned to her *farshathkhanaak*. "Our fighters are going to have to do what they can to keep those kamikazes off us, Anson."

*In retrospect, it might have been better after all if the system's entire twenty-four thousand planet-based gunboats and their supporting small craft had been in a position to arrive as one overwhelming wave. Even the ones the Enemy had sighted had been enough to send him instantly into a course-reversal which might well take him back out of the system before the wave could reach him, and he'd deployed his small attack craft to cover the retreat.*

*Those craft would, of course, concentrate on the antimatter-loaded small craft which posed the most deadly threat to the capital ships. They always did. This time, however, they were in for a surprise.*

*They've done it again*, Anson Olivera thought, watching in horror as his plot told the tale.

Like Admiral Murakuma, Olivera had faced the Bugs from the very beginning of the war. He still didn't know how he'd survived the unbelievable butchery of the strikegroups in the desperate fight to defend the Romulus Chain. He'd never blamed Murakuma for the losses the squadrons had taken, and in all fairness, all the rest of Fifth Fleet had been hammered almost equally as hard. It was just that someone aboard a superdreadnought still had a chance of coming home if his ship took a hit; a fighter jock didn't.

Which was why Fifth Fleet had suffered well over three thousand percent casualties among its fighter pilots.

Anson Olivera had no idea why *he* hadn't been one of those casualties, and there were times when the phenomenon the shrinks called "survivor's guilt" kept him up late at night. But it had never hit him as hard as it did at this moment.

*I ought to be out there*, he thought numbly, cursing his own relative safety as he manned his station in Sixth Fleet PriFly, the nerve center of its fighter ops coordination and control, and listened to the broken bits of panicked combat chatter coming back from his pilots through the bursts of strobing static.

An isolated corner of his mind wondered, almost absently, why it still seemed so surprising whenever the Bugs introduced a new technological surprise. It wasn't as if they hadn't done it often enough, God knew. But somehow, it still seemed . . . unnatural for an unthinking force of nature to innovate.

Which didn't keep them from going right ahead and doing it anyway.

No doubt the intelligence types would get together with BuShips' R&D experts to figure out exactly how they'd done it, but that would be cold comfort for all the pilots Olivera was losing . . . and about to lose. What mattered at the moment was that somehow the Bugs had engineered an ECM installation capable of jamming fighter datalink down into something small enough to mount on a gunboat. To the best of Olivera's knowledge, no one in the Alliance had ever even considered such a possibility. Certainly, no one had ever suggested it to him. And no one had ever evolved a doctrine for how a fighter squadron suddenly deprived of the fine-meshed coordination which spelled life in the close combat of a dogfight was supposed to survive the experience, either.

The space around the warp point was a hideous boil of exploding warheads and disintegrating fighters and gunboats. The term "dogfight" had taken on an entirely new meaning as individual fighter pilots, deprived not just of datalink, but of almost all communication, found themselves entirely on their own on a battlefield that covered cubic light-seconds. The mere concept of visual coordination was meaningless in deep-space, and from the fragments Olivera and his assistants could piece together, even the fighters' individual onboard sensors seemed to be affected by whatever it was the Bugs were using.

It was fortunate that the starships of Sixth Fleet were outside the jammers' apparent area of effect. And it was even more fortunate that Sixth Fleet's fighter squadrons were as finely honed and trained as any in space. Good as Seventh Fleet was, Olivera had always privately believed his own pilots were at least as good or even better, and as he listened to the slivers of chatter he could hear, he heard them proving it. Yes, there was panic and confusion—even terror—but these were men and women, whatever their species, who'd been tried and tested in combat and never found wanting.

Nor were they wanting today, and Anson Olivera tried not to weep as he watched their icons vanishing from his plot and pride warred with grief, for not one of them vanished running *away* from the enemy.

The protracted late-afternoon light of Alpha Centauri A was slanting through the windows of Kthaara'zarthan's office when Ellen MacGregor unceremoniously entered it.

"You've read it," she stated, rather than asked.

"Yes. I have only just finished." Kthaara put down the last hardcopy sheet of Vanessa Murakuma's report on Operation Cripple.

The Sky Marshal plopped herself down on one of the scattered cushions Orions favored—she'd acquired a taste for the things, even though Kthaara always kept chairs for human visitors.

"We fucked up," she said succinctly.

"As ever, your directness is refreshing." The response was completely automatic. Kthaara's mind was entirely on what he'd just read.

"Murakuma warned us we were talking out our asses," Mac-Gregor pointed out after a pause, bringing Kthaara back to the present. "And she was right. Although not even her crystal ball was up to predicting a gunboat-portable device for jamming data nets!"

"No," Kthaara agreed. "Of course, she was hardly alone in that. Still, the concept requires no fundamental theoretical break-throughs, and we no longer have any right to feel surprise at Bahg inventiveness."

None of which, thought the pilot who'd made his own name in the elite ranks of the Khan's strikegroups, had been any comfort to Murakuma's fighter pilots when they suddenly found themselves operating as unsupported individuals. *On the other hand, there were so many targets it must have been hard to miss. . . .*

MacGregor read his thoughts and smiled grimly.

"Murakuma says seventy-five percent of her pilots made ace that day. Ah, that's an old Terran expression dating back to the days of atmospheric combat with hydrocarbon-burning airfoils. It means—"

"I know what it means," Kthaara said quietly.

Those fighter pilots' ferocious resistance had probably saved Sixth Fleet from annihilation. But given the numbers they'd faced and the technological surprise that had been sprung on them, it had been inevitable that some of the Bugs had gotten past them. Not in hundreds, but in thousands.

It was only by the grace of the gods themselves—coupled with Murakuma's wisdom in falling back as soon as the first reports of the incoming strike reached her—that her starships had been almost back to her entry warp point and the reserve SBMHAWK4s she'd left in Orpheus 1. The courier drones she'd sent ahead to the control ships she'd left with the missiles had sent the pods flooding back in the opposite direction, targeted for gunboats.

Their CAM2s had winnowed the attackers down to numbers the capital ships' defensive armaments could deal with, but by the time it was over, every one of Murakuma's capital ships had suffered at least some degree of damage . . . and the *second* wave of kamikazes had been screaming in. She'd barely had time to recover her remaining fighters and evacuate the surviving personnel from the ships too heavily damaged to escape. Then she'd funneled the rest through the warp point into Orpheus 1 space.

The pursuing Bugs had followed—straight into the precautionary minefields she'd left behind. That, combined with the massed fire of Sixth Fleet's surviving starships and desperately relaunched fighters, had stopped them. Barely.

"Murakuma's going to need months to make repairs," MacGregor observed dourly.

"Truth. Nevertheless, we can count ourselves fortunate." Kthaara shook off his brooding. "We cannot count on good fortune to come to our rescue in the future. We must not underestimate that system's strength again."

"No. Murakuma makes the same point in her report—rather forcefully."

"Indeed she does. I suppose she can be forgiven for waxing a bit . . . idiomatic towards the end."

"That's one way to put it." MacGregor picked up the final page of the hardcopy and chuckled grimly as she quoted. "'Some *cripple!*'"

# CHAPTER TWENTY-FIVE

## "I feel them still."

KONS *Eemaaka* loped across the last few light-seconds to her destination, and Admiral Raymond Prescott stood silently on her flag bridge with Zhaarnak'telmasa and watched his *vilkshatha* brother with carefully hidden concern. The *Kweenamak*-class battlecruiser was a lowly vessel to fly the lights of not one, but two, fleet commanders, but she was also one of the minority of Seventh Fleet's units to escape Operation Ivan completely undamaged. With so much of the rest of the fleet down for repairs, *Eemaaka* at least offered the advantage of availability. She was also fast enough for Prescott and Zhaarnak to make this trip within the time constraints the repair and refitting of Seventh Fleet imposed. And it was entirely appropriate for them to use an Orion vessel.

Neither of them was particularly happy about leaving the responsibility for the necessary repairs in other hands, even when those hands belonged to their own highly trained and reliable staffs. But neither of them had even considered not making this trip, either. The request for their presence had come directly from Third Great Fang Koraaza'khiniak, and although it wasn't an order, it had carried an honor obligation which would have made any possibility of refusal unthinkable.

Yet now that they were here, Prescott felt the waves of remembered pain radiating from his *vilkshatha* brother, and he reached out to lay his flesh and blood hand on the Orion's furred shoulder.

The CIC master display was configured in astrographic mode,

showing the layout of an entire star system. The portion of that star towards which *Eemaaka* was headed was dotted with the frosted light icons of a massive military fleet, but it wasn't those light codes which held Zhaarnak's attention, and Prescott heard him draw a deep breath as his eyes rested upon two other icons. They were the symbols for two oxygen-nitrogen planets, well within the liquid water zone of the brilliant white system primary, but they weren't the welcoming green of the habitable worlds they ought to have been. Instead, each planet was represented by a small, blazing red sphere of light surrounding the four interlocked triangles which served the Orions as the ancient trefoil symbol served humanity.

The symbol which would mark those planets on Tabby astrogation charts for the next several thousand years.

"I feel them still," Zhaarnak said, very quietly, and Prescott's grip on his shoulder tightened. "Four billion. Four billion civilians."

"I know," Prescott said in the Tongue of Tongues, his voice equally quiet. "I hear them, as well. But you had no choice, Zhaarnak. You know that as well as I do . . . just as you know how many other lives you saved by falling back."

"Perhaps." Zhaarnak gazed down at the Orion-style flat-screen display for several more seconds, then shook himself. "You speak truth, brother," he said then, "although you would be more accurate if you added the modest part *you* played in stopping the Bahgs in Alowan and in retaking Telmassa. Yet there are times when truth is cold comfort, and I wonder what the ghosts of Kliean would say of my decision to leave them to the Bahgs."

"They are the ghosts of *Zheeerlikou'valkhannaiee*," Prescott replied, "and they know what choice you had to make and how much it cost you. Just as they know there was no way you or anyone could have predicted what the Bugs would do when they retreated from this system."

"I think you may be too kind to me," Zhaarnak told him with a small ear flick of grim amusement. "The Bahgs had not bombarded planets into nuclear cinders in the past, true, but that was only because they had never been given the opportunity to destroy what were obviously major industrial and population centers which they could not retain in their possession. No, Raaymmonnd." He shook his head in a human gesture of negation he'd picked up from his *vilkshatha* brother. "Whatever the rest of the *Zheeerlikou'valkhannaiee* may think, I knew when I ordered Daarsaahl to fall back from Kliean what would happen to the planets here. I think that I tried to fool even myself into believing we could retake the system before the Bahgs could . . . devour more than a small percentage of the total population. But that was a lie I told myself because I had to."

The Orion inhaled again, then turned his back resolutely upon the display and met the human admiral's eyes levelly.

"You are correct, of course, Raaymmonnd. I had no choice, not with so many more billions of civilians behind me, but I knew I had signed the death warrants of Zhardok and Masiahn when I withdrew from the system. I could not have prevented their destruction if I had not withdrawn. I know that, too. But there are times even now when they come to me in the night and I wish with all my heart that I had died with them."

"It may be selfish of me," Prescott said after a moment, "but I, for one, am delighted you did not. It would be a colder and a lonelier war without your claws to ward my back, Clan Brother."

"Or without yours to ward mine," Zhaarnak agreed, reaching up to rest one clawed hand briefly and lightly upon the human hand on his shoulder. "And do not mistake me, Raaymmonnd. I know full well that the dead who reproach me live only in my own heart and mind. They are the scars of my soul, and I must bear them, as a warrior bears the scars of his flesh—without ever forgetting, but without permitting sorrow and grief to paralyze me or prevent me from making other decisions out of fear." His ears flicked again, this time in an expression of wry irony. "I think, perhaps, only Vahnessssssa could truly understand."

"You may be right," Prescott replied after a brief, thoughtful pause, still speaking Orion. "I never really considered her stand at Sarasota and Justin from that perspective." He waved one hand. "Oh, I knew there had to be at least some 'survivor's guilt,' but I was like everyone else. I saw only the lives she saved and how hard—how brilliantly—she fought to retake Justin. But she sees it from the other side . . . just as you see it here. She sees the lives she could *not* save, and it is that which puts the ghosts in her eyes."

"We have each of us paid our own tolls to loss and grief and regret, brother," Zhaarnak said. "This is not a warrior's war. Not one in which one may take honor from matching strength to strength against a foe worthy of respect. It is a war against a plague, a pestilence. Against creatures who massacre entire worlds . . . and who give us no choice but to do the same to them. I cannot forgive the Bahgs for that, and most of all, I cannot forgive them for filling me with the hatred which makes the 'Shiiivaaa Option' something to be embraced."

Koraaza'khiniak, Lord Khiniak, stood in the enormous, echoing boat bay of KONS *Kinaahsa'defarnoo*. The *Hia'khan*-class monitor was vastly larger than the battleship *Ebymiae* aboard which he'd flown his lights when last he met with both Raymond Prescott and Zhaarnak'telmasa. That was as it should be, for she was also the flagship of a far more powerful fleet than he'd commanded then. But for all of that, he felt a remembered echo of that other meeting as he watched the cutter from *Eemaaka* settle into the docking arms.

Bagpipes wailed and the side party snapped to attention as the *vilkshatha* brothers whose presence he'd specifically requested emerged from the cutter and saluted the boatbay officer. This was a ship of the *Zheeerlikou'valkhannaiee*, and so Zhaarnak requested permission to come aboard for both of them, and Koraaza stepped forward to greet them in person as permission was granted.

"Welcome, Fang Zhaarnak, Fang Presssssscottt," he said, and offered each in turn the flashing claw slap of an Orion's warrior greeting. "We are all most happy to see you, and I am especially happy to see you looking so much better than when last we met in Telmasa, Fang Presssssscottt."

"Thank you, Great Fang," Prescott replied. "It is hard to believe, sometimes, that it has been over seven standard years."

"If it is hard for you," Koraaza said, "it is even harder for me and for my *farshatok*. It seems at times that everyone has forgotten we even exist!"

"That seems to be the nature of war, and especially of this one," the Human said. "The only options seem to be boredom or sheer terror."

"Truth," Koraaza agreed. There were not many, even of the *Zheeerlikou'valkhannaiee*, to whom he would have admitted he could ever feel terror, but Raymond'prescott-telmasa was one of them. He considered that thought for a moment, then brushed it aside and gave his guests a fang-hidden Orion smile.

"In this case, however," he told them, "I hope you will forgive me if I admit that my invitation to you was made at least partly in hopes of transforming my fleet's boredom into something more lively."

"The possibility had crossed our minds, Great Fang," Zhaarnak said dryly. "Neither of us is quite so . . . inexperienced in the machinations of fleet commanders who must deal with the inertia of Fleet Headquarters as we were when last all three of us met."

"Good!" Lord Khiniak gave a grunting chuckle-purr. "I would not have you think I do not value your presence for many reasons, but I am glad both of you understand all of my motives. It would never do to have lured you here under false pretenses!"

"There is little fear of that, Great Fang," Prescott assured him.

"I am relieved to hear it, Fang Presssssscottt. But there will be time enough to deal with my ulterior motives later. For now, Third Fleet is prepared to pass in review to commemorate this anniversary of our reconquest of this system. You and Fang Zhaarnak would do me great honor if you would join me on Flag Deck for that evolution, and afterward, I would value your impressions of the maneuvers my staff has laid on."

"The honor," Prescott said sincerely, "will be ours."

"In that case," Koraaza said, "let us go. The Fleet awaits us."

The word for Third Fleet, Raymond Prescott decided, was "impressive." He'd known all along that Lord Khiniak's fleet area had held a lower priority for the new construction which had flowed with ever increasing force towards his own and Zhaarnak's commands. The fact that the Tabbies simply didn't have the industrial plant to build as many monitors as the Federation and that Third Fleet was effectively a pure Orion and Gorm command meant that Koraaza's task groups were heavily biased towards lighter ship types. Third Fleet's official order of battle—which wasn't entirely present even now—listed a total of two hundred and sixty-seven ships of all classes, but only six were monitors. Over a quarter of Koraaza's strength lay in his sixty-eight superdreadnoughts, which—along with eighty-nine battlecruisers—constituted fifty-eight percent of his total hulls. Of course, it was a Tabby fleet organization, so it boasted far more total fighters than its twenty-four carriers and twenty-eight light carriers would have suggested . . . particularly since five of Koraaza's monitors were the big, monitor-hulled *Shernaku*-class carriers, each of which embarked no less than a hundred and thirty-two strikefighters. In fact, its mobile units alone carried almost three thousand fighters and almost four hundred Gorm-crewed gunboats, and the orbital bases covering the Shanak-Kliean warp link provided a reserve of over five thousand more fighters from which losses might be replaced.

Even with the oversized fighter components typical of Orion fleet mixes, Third Fleet was weaker than Seventh Fleet had been before Operation Ivan, especially in the sluggers of its battle-line. Yet as he and Zhaarnak had watched Koraaza and his staff put the fleet through its paces in a complex series of week-long maneuvers, Prescott had realized that Third Fleet's fighting power should not be assessed in terms of tonnages and weight of broadside alone.

The Orion naval tradition, dating as far back as there'd *been* an Orion Navy, had seen a warship not so much as a platform for weapons as as a *single* weapon in its own right. It was an ideal better suited to light warships, and best of all to fighters, which helped explain why the Tabbies had never truly been happy with superdreadnoughts and battleships. But it was also an ideal which had never been abandoned for those heavier ship types, either. It was far more difficult to infuse a crew the size of a capital ship's with the sort of elan and sense of unity which could be created aboard smaller ships, and the Orions recognized that, but that recognition didn't prevent them from trying to achieve it anyway.

As Third Fleet had come very, very close to doing.

Prescott knew, as only one could whose forces had survived Operation Retribution and Operation Ivan, what that meant in terms of its fighting power. His and Zhaarnak's own Seventh Fleet and Vanessa Murakuma's Sixth Fleet were the most superbly drilled and battle-hardened naval forces he'd ever hoped to see. They were certainly more efficient and effective on a ship-for-ship and task force-for-task force basis than Eighth Fleet . . . or had been, at least, before the brutal casualties of Operation Ivan. To admit that was not to in any way denigrate Eighth Fleet or the part it had played in Ivan, either. Murakuma had been given literally years to put together her command team and staff before their transfer to the already superbly drilled fighting machine he and Zhaarnak had created in Zephrain before her arrival. Since taking over, she and her staff had turned Sixth Fleet's subordinate commanders and crews into virtual extensions of her own central nervous system.

He and Zhaarnak had been given less time to build Seventh Fleet, but they'd also possessed the huge "advantage" of forging their command teams in the very furnace of battle. Eighth Fleet had been allowed neither the years of training time which Sixth—and Fifth—Fleet had been granted, nor honed and polished in the unforgiving crucible of combat, and so it had been inevitable that First Fang Ynaathar's command should lack the incomparable temper those fleets had attained.

But Great Fang Koraaza had also been given years to train and drill his forces, and the grim and silent charnel houses of Zhardok and Masiahn had provided all the motivation any fleet commander could have desired. Even the Gorm—or perhaps *especially* the Gorm—of Koraaza's command were filled with a white-hot flame of determination to repay the Bugs in full and bitter measure for the atrocity of Kliean, and the fact that Third Fleet consisted solely of Orions and Gorm had prevented any tiniest dilution of that incandescent purpose. That single ambition unified them all, from the Great Fang to the lowliest rating aboard his lightest vessel, and it showed. Third Fleet was a rapier in the hand of a fencing master, and in some ways its lack of monitors might actually make it more effective. It was faster, unfettered by the slow and ponderous might of a heavier battle-line, and its maneuverability and flexibility were perfectly suited to the fighter-oriented Tabbies and the fast capital ships which had always been the hallmark of the Gorm.

It was impossible for anyone to say with complete assurance how any unblooded warship or force of warships would respond to the reality of battle before the actual test, but Raymond Prescott had no doubt that Third Fleet would acquit itself in a manner to make Varnik'sheerino himself proud.

Assuming, of course, that it was ever allowed to do so.

" . . . and so we have emphasized training in both the assault mode and in more mobile and far-ranging operations," Koraaza said. He leaned back on the low cushions on his side of the Orion-style briefing room table and showed just the tips of his fangs in a predator's smile. "We have given particular attention to the techniques you and Ahhdmiraaaal Murrraaahkuuuuma evolved for dealing with the 'Bahghouse Swarm.' The fact that neither we nor the Bahgs have been in a position to commit our full strength to battle has given us much time to refine our approach. Unfortunately, it does not appear that Grand Fleet Headquarters is prepared to allow us to put our training into practice."

"That conforms with my own impression, I fear," Prescott said after a moment, and glanced at Zhaarnak, sitting at his side.

"And mine," his *vilkshatha* brother confirmed. "I believe that both Lord Talphon's and Fang Ynaathar's instincts are to give you leave to begin offensive operations, Great Fang, but the advice of their planning staffs is another matter."

"That, unhappily, is not news to me," Koraaza told them. "I was, of course, delighted to learn of the existence of the Star Union and of its readiness to fight at our sides against the Bahgs. Nonetheless, the sudden introduction of the Union's forces into the strategic equation provoked a complete upheaval in the war plans and calculations of everyone in Centauri. No doubt the two of you are even more aware of that than we here in Kliean, but the same impetus which inspired GFGHQ to accelerate the timetable for Operation Eeevaan also caused it to divert many of our scheduled reinforcements to Eighth Fleet. I do not begrudge Fang Ynaathar the strength he required to carry that operation to a successful conclusion, yet I deeply regret the manner in which the diversion of warships has set back our own schedule."

"I am afraid I am less fully familiar with events here in Kliean and in Shanak than I ought to be," Prescott admitted.

"That is fully understandable," Koraaza said. "It is not as if you and Fang Zhaarnak had not had matters of your own to consider!"

"Truth," Prescott agreed. "Nonetheless, it is my understanding that you were able to pinpoint the location of the Bugs' closed warp point in Shanak almost a full standard year ago."

He made the statement a question, and Koraaza flicked an ear in agreement.

"Indeed. The Bahgs have obviously been too hard pressed—by your own actions, in no small part—to attempt any further offensive operations along the Kliean Chain. No doubt the fate which befell their earlier offensives also had much to do with that, but at the same time, the strength of our response and the richness of their prize here in Kliean must have suggested to them that this line of advance would have led them to further important systems. Perhaps that is the reason they did not revert to a completely passive posture in Shanak. I do not pretend, of course, to understand how what passes for intelligence among Bahgs operates, but I suspect that they could not quite bring themselves to totally abandon any possibility of resuming the offensive should our own fleet dispositions present them with an opportunity to strike. I can think of nothing else which would have inspired them to continue operations in Shanak at all."

"Not even Admiral LeBlanc is prepared to suggest how Bug analysts—assuming that they *have* analysts—would approach such a situation," Prescott said. "Nonetheless, I think you are probably correct. Certainly if they intended to stand solely upon the defensive, it would have been pointless for them to operate in Shanak."

Zhaarnak gave a grunting purr of agreement, and Prescott knew that his *vilkshatha* brother was thinking about the botched survey update of Shanak which had led directly to the Kliean Atrocity. Least Claw Shaiaasu's entire survey squadron had perished in a hopeless, suicidal charge straight into the teeth of the Bug battle fleet which had driven Zhaarnak's hopelessly outnumbered command out of Kliean. It had been the final, despairing stroke of a warrior who knew he was totally over-matched by his foe, but for all its determination and sacrifice, it had required far less courage of Shaiaasu and his personnel than Zhaarnak's decision to fall back on Telmasa had required of him. In a sense, it had been almost an act of cowardice, for under the honor code of the Orions, it had expiated Shaiaasu's "guilt" for having led the Bugs to Kliean in the first place.

It hadn't really been the least claw's fault. Prescott never doubted that Shaiaasu had followed his orders to insure he and his squadron weren't spotted and tracked by any Bug starships. Unfortunately, it was far easier to order someone to avoid detection than it was to carry out that order against hostile vessels hiding in cloak at the moment their sensors detected your own drive fields, and that was almost certainly what had happened to Shaiaasu. It was entirely possible that the least claw had allowed himself to be just a bit casual about his procedures in the case of Shanak, but that was understandable enough, for he'd had no prior reason to suspect that Shanak was unique in the experience of both Orion and Terran galactic exploration. Many systems contained closed warp points, but to date, only Shanak contained *only* closed points. Of course, it was conceivable that there were dozens of similar star systems, and that possibility had been the subject of a great deal of lively speculation over the last seven years. Unfortunately, there was no practical way to test it. By the very nature of things, a closed warp point couldn't be detected. Which meant that the only ways to know a star system contained more than one of them were to find the additional closed point from its open end . . . or to see someone else make transit through the closed point you didn't already know was there.

And that was undoubtedly precisely what had happened to Shaiaasu.

The consequences for Kliean had been catastrophic, and if not for the desperate backs-to-the-wall stand which had brought Zhaarnak and Prescott together for the first time, the catastrophe would have been far wider and more terrible still. The four billion dead of Kliean could all too easily have become thirty or even forty billion before the Khanate assembled a fleet strong enough to meet the Bugs head on. Only the sacrificial gallantry of his and Zhaarnak's crews had enabled them to hang on by their very fingernails until Koraaza could relieve the pitiful wreckage which had been all that remained of their commands.

But Koraaza *had* relieved them, and he'd carried on from their bridgehead in Telmasa to retake the gutted Kliean System, then pressed forward to retake Shanak, as well. He'd paid a high price in ships and lives to drive the enemy out of Shanak, but the Bugs had been in a perfect position to cut their losses and their exposure. After all, the Alliance had no idea how to locate the closed warp point which had given them entry into Shanak in the first place. All they had to do was retire from the system and stay retired to effectively climb down the rabbit hole and pull the hole in after themselves, precisely as the Star Union had done in the case of Telik.

Only the Bugs hadn't done that. They'd continued to probe Shanak with light forces, creeping stealthily about under the protection of their cloaking ECM, no doubt in an effort to keep tabs on the Alliance's actual strength in the system. Koraaza was probably correct about their motivations, although Prescott wasn't about to allow himself to draw any hard and fast conclusions about how Bugs thought. Still, the only possible explanation for their behavior which he could conceive of was that they'd hoped the Allies might somehow be stupid enough to reduce their strength in Shanak and Kliean to a level which would permit them to launch a fresh attack. No doubt a human or Orion strategist would have entertained the same possibility, however wistfully, but given how completely the Bugs had been driven back upon the defensive themselves, they surely ought to have recognized that the likelihood of any such blunder on their opponents' parts was minute.

Whatever had or hadn't passed through whatever Bugs used or didn't use for brains, they had, in fact, continued their stealthy probes, and their scout cruisers and Third Fleet's light picket units had fought their own long, bitter war of ambush and counter-ambush. Cloaked cruisers and battlecruisers had stalked one another through the useless yet strategically vital star system's depths with implacable determination. The Bug ships had sought ceaselessly to determine Third Fleet's dispositions, and the Orion and Gorm pickets had striven with equal determination to track the Bugs to their hidden entry warp point.

And finally, fourteen months ago, the Orion battlecruiser *Basnkykhan* had succeeded in doing just that.

She hadn't survived her success, but her captain had known his business and been fully aware of the critical importance of his discovery. He'd gotten his courier drones off before the first Bug gunboat had come into range to detect their drives, and so he and his crew had gotten their priceless data home despite the total destruction of their ship.

"I have not had the opportunity to actually discuss the situation here in Kliean or in Shanak with any of Lord Talphon's planners," Prescott said after a moment. "My impression, however, is that they believe the Bugs probably failed to detect *Basnkykhan*'s courier drones. Coupled with the fact that she had already begun to retreat, probably before they even knew she was there, they may not have realized she ever managed to track one of their vessels through the closed warp point in the first place."

"That is indeed essentially what they think," Koraaza agreed. "Their view is that if the Bahgs do not realize that their bolthole has been discovered, there is no compelling reason to hasten an attack through it. Undoubtedly, the Bahgs have been preparing their defenses on the far side of the warp point ever since we retook Shanak from them, but GFGHQ believes the security of a closed warp point will have inspired them to give fortifying it a lesser priority, particularly in light of the greater threats they have faced along other axes of advance. The fact that the Bahgs have continued to operate their scouting vessels in Shanak, entering and exiting through their closed warp point only with extreme caution and stealthiness, is seen as further supporting evidence for that thesis."

"And the theory is that we should let sleeping *zegets* lie?" Zhaarnak suggested with a wry twitch of his whiskers.

"In part," Koraaza conceded, "but, to be fair, *only* in part. I believe GFGHQ intends ultimately to allow Third Fleet to take advantage of *Basnkykhan*'s discovery and launch our attack through Shanak. What most concerns me are two points. First, the fact that all of my *farshatok* are as prepared and ready to strike *now* as they ever will be and that every day which passes threatens to dull the keenness of their edge through overtraining or frustration. Second, and even more importantly, I do not share the analysts' faith that the Bahgs are unaware that *Basnkykhan* pinpointed their warp point.

"I have, of course, done all I may to encourage them in their ignorance, assuming that they are in fact ignorant in the first place. My survey ships continue to 'search' assiduously and to track every Bahg vessel we detect. Indeed, I have lost two more battlecruisers since *Basnkykhan*'s destruction as a direct result of our persistence in such operations.

"Despite this, my staff and I have come to the conclusion that we dare not ignore the possibility that the Bahgs' operations are a mirror image of our own. As we seek to convince them we continue to search for the closed warp point because we do not know where it is, so—we suspect—do they maintain the same operational patterns in an effort to deceive us into thinking that they do not know we have already located that point. Needless to say, there is no way we could possibly prove our theory without actually firing recon probes through the warp point to determine what defenses, if any, they have erected against us. Since doing that would absolutely confirm our knowledge of the warp point's coordinates, we dare not do anything of the sort until we are prepared to commit immediately to a full-scale assault through it."

"And GFGHQ is so busy concentrating on other fronts just now that it has no interest in permitting you to test your theory," Prescott said.

"Precisely. My strength continues to build, although at a slower than projected rate due to the diversion of units originally earmarked for Klian to Operation Eeevaan and its follow-up operations," Koraaza said. "Nonetheless, we remain considerably below the force levels the Strategy Board has specified as the minimum necessary for us to begin offensive operations through Shanak. As I have said, I understand the logic which has led to that decision, but—"

"—but if your theory is correct, then every day your attack is delayed increases the losses you are likely to take when you are finally permitted to attack," Zhaarnak finished for him.

"Precisely," Koraaza said again, flattening both ears for emphasis. "I believe it is highly probable that they have assigned a higher priority to fortifying the far side of the warp point ever since *Basnkykhan* located it. Valkha only knows how powerfully they have already fortified it, but I do not care at all for the thought of giving them still more time to improve their defenses even further. Moreover, the power of the attack force they originally committed against Kliean and Telmasa, coupled with how quickly and powerfully they reinforced that force, has always suggested that at least one of their major star systems lies within relatively close proximity to Shanak. If that is correct, then I believe it is important to take the offensive as quickly as possible and so, hopefully, force still more dispersal of whatever strategic reserve remains to them. Every additional dispersion on any front can only weaken them further on *every* front now that we have obviously driven them back onto the defensive."

"You make a strong case, Great Fang," Prescott said after a moment. "Of course," he went on dryly, "Zhaarnak and I are also mere fleet commanders whose opinions are of strictly limited value to the *droshkhouli* who slave over their analyses under the dreadful conditions which exist on Nova Terra." Zhaarnak and Koraaza produced matching purr-chuckles of amusement, and Prescott grinned at them. Then he sobered.

"In seriousness, Great Fang, I understand both your concerns and the opportunity you sense, and I think I share your conclusions, as well. Am I correct in assuming that you wish for Zhaarnak and me to present those conclusions to Lord Talphon and Sky Marshal MacGregor?"

"You are," Koraaza admitted. "I realize that technically you and Lord Telmasa are mere fleet commanders yourselves, but as I believe a Human writer observed several of your centuries ago, some animals are more equal than others." The Orion admiral chuckled again at Prescott's obvious surprise at his reference. As the Human's reputation as a student of Orion history, culture, and philosophy had spread among the officers of the Khan, a certain competition to beat him at his own game had sprung up among some of them, and Koraaza took considerable pleasure from the knowledge that he'd just scored a telling point in that contest.

"I know Lord Talphon and the Joint Chiefs of Staff give full attention to my own reports and suggestions," the Third Fleet commander went on more seriously after a moment. "But I also know that any senior flag officer's views and conclusions are inevitably shaped and colored by the fashion in which their staffs present their own analyses to them. To be honest, what I hope is that the personal relationships the two of you have developed with the Joint Chiefs and, especially, with Lord Talphon will lend additional weight to your views. I feel sure that an exposition of your views would go far to cut through that inevitable layer of insulation between field commanders and commanders in chief, assuming you are willing to support my own conclusions and arguments."

"It is possible you overestimate the extent to which we have the ear of the JCS," Prescott replied wryly. "Even if you do not, anything we say must be properly presented if we hope to overcome that insulation you have mentioned. And I would like the opportunity to fully explore the evidence and analysis which have led you to your conclusions before committing myself to support them."

"Of course," Koraaza agreed instantly. "I would not expect you to endorse my ideas without the fullest opportunity to test my evidence and my logic."

"In that case, speaking for myself, and assuming that—as I feel confident will be the case—I share your conclusions after studying the data, I would be honored to speak in their favor to Lord Talphon and the rest of the Joint Chiefs," Prescott said seriously.

"And I," Zhaarnak agreed. He gazed at his *vilkshatha* brother for a moment, then turned his eyes to Koraaza. "All you have said makes excellent sense to me, Great Fang. And there is another point, one I feel certain Lord Talphon, at least, will recognize. *Vilknarma* for Kliean is due and overdue, and what place could be more fitting than this from which to exact it? What attack more appropriate than one upon the very systems which dispatched the ships which murdered our worlds?"

He raised one palm and extended the knife-edged claws of his predator ancestors, and his steady eyes never flickered as he closed his fist, sinking those claws into the heel of his hand to draw blood. Then he opened his hand once more, showing the blood upon his claws, and his voice was very, very quiet.

"I have told my brother that I hear the dead still, Great Fang, and so I do. I hear the terror of the cubs, the sorrow of their dams, and the rage of their sires. I have heard them in my dreams and, if I listen carefully, in my waking thoughts, as well, and I hear them now. But now they are no longer ghosts, crying out in protest at their own deaths and the murder of all they loved. Now they are the voice of vengeance, the voice of the *Zheeerlikou'valkhannaiee*, crying out from the very stones, and I, too, will be their voice."

He closed his hand once more, his eyes burning into Koraaza's, and his ears were flat to his skull.

"I will speak for you before the Joint Chiefs, Great Fang, and in my voice they will hear Kliean, and the fury of the *Zheeerlikou'valkhannaiee* will sweep over the Bahgs like the very fists of Valkha Himself."

# CHAPTER TWENTY-SIX
## "Take them at a run."

"Well. Lieutenant Sanders, isn't it?" Vice Admiral Winnifred Trevayne pronounced it *lef*-tenant. Her medium-dusky coloring, a throwback to some twentieth-century Jamaican ancestor, was the only thing about her that wasn't stereotypically British. "What do you hear from Admiral LeBlanc, out at Zephrain?"

"Nothing lately, Sir." Kevin Sanders' usual insouciance was somewhat in abeyance. The Director of Naval Intelligence didn't exactly encourage informality, even among those well acquainted with her and close to her in rank, and Sanders was neither. "I and the rest of First Fang Ynaathar's staff have only just arrived."

"Of course. You had to come all the way from Anderson Four. I've been here less than two local days myself." Trevayne didn't get to Alpha Centauri often, but she'd made a special trip out from Old Terra for this conference, which promised to be crucial. Matters were coming to a head.

"I see the Sky Marshal gesturing for me, Lieutenant. And you'd best rejoin the First Fang's staff." With a final nod, Trevayne turned on her heel and crossed the GFGHQ formal conference room.

Sanders watched her go, then gazed around the room. It was much as he remembered it from the time he'd sat here with Marcus LeBlanc, nearly six standard years earlier. The light of Alpha Centauri A was even streaming in through the tall windows at about the same afternoon angle. But this was Nova Terra's spring, and the light wasn't the same dismal winter grayness.

As before, the top brass sat at the oval table: the Joint Chiefs and Ynaathar. Their staffers sat behind them, backs toward the

474

wall. Trevayne was so close behind MacGregor that she was almost within the magic circle that shimmered—invisibly, to the uninitiated—around the table. Sanders sighed and took his own place, well back from Ynaathar.

In accordance with ritual, everyone rose as Kthaara entered— even Ynaathar, who technically outranked him. To Sanders, who hadn't seen him in a long while, the signs of Orion aging were unmistakable: the gait had grown too stiff to be called a prowl, and the fur too silvery to be called black.

"As some of you are aware," Kthaara began after the formalities were concluded, "I had hoped Fangs Presssssscottt and Zhaarnak would be present for this conference. Unfortunately, they are still *en route* from Shanak, where they have been consulting with Lord Khiniak. However, they have sent a dispatch ahead. It raises an issue which I would like to place at the head of our agenda."

He paused for a moment, then glanced sharply at Admiral Curtis Treadman and Fang Haairdaahn'usaihk, the senior permanent Terran and Orion members of the Joint Strategy Board. Neither of them seemed particularly pleased to find themselves the focus of his attention, but they returned his gaze steadily, and he gave a small Orion smile before he turned back to his colleagues.

"Fang Presssssscottt and Fang Zhaarnak have both informed me that they completely share Lord Khiniak's conclusions and his recommendations. In particular, Fang Presssssscottt's despatch emphasizes his belief that Lord Khiniak is entirely correct to fear that the Bahgs realize that we now know the location of their entry warp point and are making preparations to receive any attack from Shanak. I realize—" he glanced once more at Treadman and Haairdaahn "—that the consensus here at Centauri remains that the Bahgs do *not* know we have pinpointed their warp point. Further, I am aware that there is no hard evidence to prove or disprove the possibility, and I am familiar—as are we all—with the analyses of their dispositions in Shanak which argue that they do not.

"I am, as always, impressed by the thoroughness and energy with which the Strategy Board and its analysts have examined this entire question, and we are all painfully well aware that trying to determine how the Bahgs 'think' is . . . problematical, at best. Nonetheless, I am also impressed by the arguments Fang Presssssscottt and Fang Zhaarnak have presented. As Fang Presssssscottt points out, while it is essential that we do not allow ourselves to be misled by imputing our own thoughts and motivations to the Bahgs, it is equally essential that we do not simply conclude that they are completely inscrutable and unknowable. He agrees with the Strategy Board that it is best to rely on analysis of hard data rather than upon an evaluation of enemy intentions, but he points out that the data must be considered from all angles. And alien as the Bahgs have proven themselves, they face essentially the same physical and material constraints we do.

"He therefore respectfully suggests that the Joint Chiefs reconsider the timetable for Third Fleet and accede to Lord Khiniak's request that we bring forward the date of his attack from Shanak. Would anyone care to comment?"

It was obvious how Kthaara himself felt on the matter, Sanders decided. And it was clever of him to emphasize *Prescott's* position, since it neatly undercut at least some of the impression that he was pushing a purely Orion perspective. Having watched Prescott and Zhaarnak operate, the lieutenant felt certain the *vilkshatha* brothers had deliberately drafted their recommendations in a way which gave precedence to the human partner's views, as well, in order to help Kthaara do exactly what he just had. But that didn't necessarily mean the decision was going to sail smoothly to a preordained rubber-stamp conclusion, and Fleet Speaker Noraku gave the basso rumble that was the equivalent of a human clearing his throat for attention.

Over the years, the Gorm had more and more emerged as the voice of caution on the Joint Chiefs. He'd also proven more and more willing to stake out positions independent of Orion ones. Indeed, there were rumors that Noraku had been the main advocate within the JCS for the Strategy Board's view of the position in Shanak, and Sanders sensed the tension which suddenly focused upon the fleet speaker.

"I have, of course, reviewed the despatches from Admiral Prescott and Fang Zhaarnak." As always, Noraku's tone was measured and thoughtful, and he cocked his head as if to consider Kthaara's expression. "I share the Strategy Board's view that it is best to err on the side of caution in analyzing the Bugs' intentions. Certainly we have all discovered that it's wiser to limit ourselves to analyses which depend upon known physical deployments and the capabilities those deployments and the enemy's known strength make possible rather than attempting to predict what they *may* do in a given situation. This has been my view in regard to the war in general and, especially, in respect to Shanak and Third Fleet."

Sanders carefully hid a frown of disappointment he was much too junior to go around showing in such senior company. Noraku had the definite sound of a being laying the groundwork to disagree with the Chief of the Joint Chiefs, and the lieutenant suspected it was a mistake. He had a lively respect for both Raymond Prescott and Zhaarnak'telmassa, and he felt certain Marcus LeBlanc would have supported them if he'd been present.

"Nonetheless," Noraku went on after a moment in exactly the same tone, "in this instance, I believe I must agree with Lord Khiniak, Admiral Prescott, and Fang Zhaarnak." Sanders managed not to blink in astonishment, and even from his distant position, something in the massive Gorm's body language suggested that the fleet speaker was rather enjoying the reaction he'd just drawn. Even Kthaara seemed surprised, but Noraku allowed no indication of amusement to color his voice or his manner as he continued.

"It's always wise to consider the viewpoint of the actual commander on the spot," he rumbled, "and Lord Khiniak's arguments have been, I believe, both cogent and persistent. This is not a sudden 'inspired guess' on his part, but rather the product of long and careful consideration. As for Admiral Prescott and Fang Zhaarnak, their reputations obviously speak for them. They are aggressive and bold, true, but they're also thinkers who have, I believe, demonstrated that they've come as close as anyone can to divining the essential principles which guide the Bugs' strategy. I am, therefore, disposed to support the recommendation that Third Fleet's operational schedule be advanced as per Lord Khiniak's request."

There was a moment of complete silence as the Gorm finished delivering his bombshell and then sat back in his saddlelike "chair" with an air of imperturbability which Sanders, at least, found distinctly irritating. But then Kthaara shook himself and turned his head to look at each of the other members of the JCS in turn, with one ear cocked in the Orion equivalent of a raised eyebrow. No one said a word, although it seemed to Sanders that MacGregor was having a hard time not grinning broadly.

"Very well," Kthaara said after a moment in a tone of calm finality. "It would appear we are agreed. I will have Lord Khiniak's orders prepared and dispatched. And now, let us turn to the original subject of this meeting: the timetable for Eighth Fleet's attack on Home Hive Four."

At once, Sanders perceived a change in the room's atmosphere. The debate on Lord Khiniak's request had aroused no great acrimony, but now the discussion was entering territory in which positions had been staked out and were bristling with emotional defenses. Looking at Ynaathar's back, Sanders could see it stiffen—the First Fang could sense it too. So could Robalii Rikka and Aileen Sommers, sitting close to him, and Noraku cleared his throat once more.

"I understand, of course, the desirability of eliminating Home Hive Four," the fleet speaker said. "And I also understand that it lies beyond Anderson Four's second warp point, judging from Eighth Fleet's analysis of the wreckage in that system. But the fact remains that we have no idea how many systems lie between Anderson Four and Home Hive Four. We would be going in blind."

"Perhaps not altogether, Fleet Speaker," Kthaara said. He turned to Ynaathar. "First Fang, would you like to respond?"

"Yes, I would, Lord Talphon. As would Warmaster Rikka. He has a particular stake in this, as he will now explain."

The Crucian shifted his folded wings back and forth slightly, drawing breath. His words reached his listeners through their translators, in their various native languages.

"Now that Lieutenant Sanders has supplied us with your intelligence data on the technological characteristics that identify the different Home Hives, we've been able to compare them with our own databases. The results are unambiguous: the Demon forces fighting the Star Union have all come from Home Hive Four."

There was a stir around the table. This was news to everyone but Kthaara and a few others.

"Well and good," Noraku's deeply reverberating voice replied. "But I wonder, Warmaster, if you may be allowing that discovery to prejudice your judgment. No offense intended—"

"None taken," Rikka interjected.

"—but you may be predisposed to favor aggressive action against what you now know to be the *particular* Bug system that has been your people's nemesis. And, at any rate, how does this relate to the problem of determining Home Hive Four's location?"

"Cub Saaanderzz," said Ynaathar. "If you please. . . ."

Sanders stood and walked to the controls at the far end of the table from Kthaara. An immaterial warp line diagram appeared above the gleaming tabletop. It showed Alpha Centauri at the upper left corner, with the Anderson Chain extending below it to Anderson Four, whence a branching warp line led to a system designated Bug-21 under the new system, beyond which a broken string-light straggled out to the right, into the unknown. From Anderson One, another series of system-icons linked by string-lights grew out to the right: the warp chain Rikka had followed from the Star Union to Alpha Centauri.

Using a light-pencil, Sanders indicated the second system of that chain.

"As you will recall, ladies and gentlemen," he began, "Warmaster Rikka's forces encountered stiff fighting here, in Bug-25, on their way to Alpha Centauri. The Bugs withdrew essentially intact, however, proving that the system has a closed warp point—which, unfortunately, wasn't located." He touched the controls, and Bug-25 sprouted another of the dashed string-lights, pointing downward.

"A dissssturrrrbing datummmm," Admiral Thaarzhaan fluted.

"Indubitably," Rikka admitted. "However, I left a force there to watch for any Demon incursions and, hopefully, follow them to the closed warp point. Lieutenant Sanders, please continue."

"Yes, Warmaster. Our analysis of the data on the Bug ships involved in that fight confirms, to no one's surprise, that they came from Home Hive Four." Sanders gestured vaguely at the blank area of the display, toward which the two broken lines pointed from different directions. *Here there be dragons*, he thought, recalling the unexplored areas of Old Terra's ancient maps. "But, more to the point, certain *individual* Bug ships that fought Warmaster Rikka in Bug-25 turned up later in Anderson Four."

"Can you be certain of that?" rumbled Noraku.

"Yes, Fleet Speaker. Comparison of Warmaster Rikka's data with First Fang Ynaathar's leaves no room for doubt. They were the same ships. And the elapsed time between their two appearances was short enough to suggest that the warp chain they followed from Bug-25 through Home Hive Four to Bug-21 can't be a very long one."

"In other words," Ynaathar took up the thread, "there cannot be many warp transits between Anderson Four and Home Hive Four. It is my personal belief that there are only two, that Home Hive Four lies just beyond Bug-21."

"You're asking us to stake a great deal on your 'personal belief,' First Fang." Noraku's tone wasn't truculent, but it held profound skepticism. "Even assuming you're correct, we have no up-to-date intelligence concerning what you would have to face in Bug-21. After all, you haven't been probing it with RD2s recently."

"Truth, Fleet Speaker. We have refrained from doing so in

order to lull the Bahgs into a false sense of security. However, we did some probing in the immediate aftermath of the fighting in Aaahnnderrssson Four, so we can speak with some confidence on the warp point defenses. These consist of eighty heavy cruisers of the *Danger* and *Derringer* classes, twenty *Estoc*-class suicide-rider light cruisers, thirty-two thousand patterns of mines, and slightly over eleven thousand deep-space buoys of various configurations."

Thaarzhaan stirred, with a rustle of feathers, on the framework that served his species as a chair. To anyone familiar with the Ophiuchi, as Sanders was, his ambivalence was blatantly obvious.

"Butttt you havvvve no conccccception whhhhhhhatever of the deffffffenses of Hhhhome Hhhhhive Ffffour itssssselffff!"

"That is not precisely the case," Kthaara put in. "No direct observational data, true. But I believe our intelligence analysts have been able to draw some inferences. Is that correct, Sky Marshal MaaacGregggorr?"

Ellen MacGregor looked as torn as Thaarzhaan, and she spoke with uncharacteristic hesitancy.

"Vice Admiral Trevayne, the Director of Naval Intelligence, is here, and she's had time to consult with the specialists on New Atlantis Island. Admiral, would you elaborate?"

"Certainly, Sky Marshal." Winnifred Trevayne had a way of tilting her head back and peering down her long, straight nose that not everyone found endearing. "Thanks to Warmaster Rikka, we now have access to the Star Union's data on the Bug losses on that front—specifically, Home Hive Four's losses, as we now know them to be. Coupling those with the observed Bug losses in the Anderson Four fighting, and assuming resources of the same order of magnitude as those of the home hive systems we've been able to observe, the analysts have concluded that Home Hive Four must have expended virtually its entire starship strength."

A Gorm laugh sounded rather like a short blast from a foghorn. Noraku produced one, then turned to Kthaara.

"That, Lord Talphon, is the kind of thinking that almost lost us Admiral Murakuma and Sixth Fleet at Home Hive Two! What if Home Hive Four has also produced tens of thousands of gunboats and small craft? Eighth Fleet could likewise find itself facing more than it could handle. No, I say we should wait until Seventh Fleet is in a position to support the attack, in accordance with the original plan."

Aileen Sommers leaned forward. Her status here was ambivalent. A mere rear admiral, she wasn't even one of Ynaathar's task force commanders—Rikka's official reason for being present. But her self-bestowed, never-ratified position as "ambassador" gave her a unique standing which had made it out of the question to exclude her from this conference.

"In point of fact, Fleet Speaker, Sixth Fleet's experience in Home Hive Two is the very reason we're advocating prompt action against Home Hive Four. Remember, Seventh Fleet is still undergoing major repairs and reinforcement. At one point, I believe, there was serious discussion of disbanding it altogether and incorporating its remnants into Eighth Fleet. If we're to strike quickly, Eighth Fleet must do it unaided. And consider: Home Hive Two had been under a threat a single warp transit away ever since Admiral Murakuma completed Operation Orpheus. Presumably, it began at that moment to concentrate on gunboat production, with the results we all know. Home Hive Four, on the other hand, has been facing the threat of a direct attack for a considerably shorter period—even assuming, as I and everyone in Eighth Fleet does, that it lies just beyond Bug-21. So the longer we wait, the more time it has to mass-produce kamikazes."

A silence settled over the room. Sanders used it to unobtrusively retreat to his position in the rearmost row of seats.

"Lord Talphon," MacGregor finally said, "we're admittedly dealing with a long chain of inferences here. But in my opinion, we face much the same situation here, although for different reasons, that Lord Khiniak faces in Shanak. Assuming First Fang and Warmaster Rikka are correct about the length of the warp lines in question—and I think they probably are—then the possibility of giving Home Hive Four more time to build up the kind of defenses Admiral Murakuma faced is decisive. We can't wait for Seventh Fleet. We must go in now."

"I agrrrrrree," said Thaarzhaan, his indecision hardening into quiet resolution.

Noraku watched the defection of the waverers without expression, then turned to Ynaathar.

"In the end, First Fang, it comes down to this. Are you confident of Eighth Fleet's ability to fight its way through Bug-21's defenses and on to Home Hive Four without pausing? Are you *that* confident of the intelligence estimates and of your own conviction that you will have only one more warp point to get through?"

"I am."

"Very well. Lord Talphon, I withdraw my objections."

"So be it." Kthaara gave his carnivore's smile. "We are agreed, then. We shall, in the Human phrase, 'take them at a run.'"

# CHAPTER TWENTY-SEVEN

## "And then there were two."

"It was well that you held back a reserve of SBMHAWKs, First Fang," Robalii Rikka said.

"It is still more fortunate, Warmaster, that you suggested sending a wave of gunboats into this system ahead of our ships."

Ynaathar's courtesy was equal to the Crucian's. It was even sincere, and Rikka's image in the com screen inclined its head in acknowledgment. Ynaathar's gaze wandered across *Hiarnow'kharnak*'s flag bridge to the big screen, currently set to simulate the naked-eye outside view. This lifeless system's primary—a red dwarf three and a half light-hours distant, and lying aft in any case—wasn't visible, of course. Neither was the wreckage their initial SBMHAWK bombardment had left of the warp point defenses.

Their estimate of the fixed warp point defenses had proven accurate, and the SBMHAWKs they'd allocated had been sufficient. However, they'd had no current information on mobile units, and the ninety-six heavy cruisers and twenty suicide-rider light cruisers might have proven troublesome for the first wave. But, at Rikka's suggestion, Ynaathar had let gunboats lead the advance, and they'd provided the information that had enabled Ynaathar to target his reserve SBMHAWKs. In addition to the gunboat losses, it had required the expenditure of more of his total SBMHAWK inventory than he'd planned on. But it was a basically unscathed Eighth Fleet that was now proceeding toward the system's other warp point, a mere forty-eight light-minutes outward from the primary, and no Bug mobile forces barred its way.

Though he lacked any hard data to back up his opinion, Ynaathar was convinced Home Hive Four lay on the other side of that warp point. He doubted very seriously that he would continue to advance unopposed.

*This had come at the worst possible time.*

*This System Which Must Be Defended, true to its accustomed role of concentrating on the Old Enemies, had feared that the closed warp point in the system through which those enemies had passed had been located. The Fleet's cloaked scouts had skirmished with the Old Enemies' pickets there, and there was no guarantee that one of the scouts hadn't been tracked. So the Deep Space Force, its battle damage only just repaired, had been dispatched two systems in that direction, to guard against any incursions. And now the attack had come from the* opposite *direction—the Old and New Enemies in league, now only one warp transit away from the System Which Must Be Defended.*

*The Fleet was doing what it could, of course. The Deep Space Force had been summoned back with maximum urgency, and the available mobile forces in the system the enemy had entered—thirty-seven battlecruisers and thirty suicide-rider light cruisers—were now shadowing the enemy's advance, cloaked against detection.*

*They wouldn't be alone for long. Even now, with the enemy still too remote to observe its emergence from warp, the massed small-craft strength of the System Which Must Be Defended was transiting to attack.*

It had been a long time since Ynaathar had left the flag bridge. But he sternly ordered fatigue to heel and remained where he was, for he was awaiting a certain report.

The incoming kamikazes had dispelled his last doubts that Home Hive Four lay immediately ahead—nothing less could have dispatched those massed formations. He'd ordered Eighth Fleet's entire fighter strength, barring a small reserve, sent out against them, overruling the caution of Admiral Haathaahn, his carrier commander. He'd soon had second thoughts, for the Bug battlecruisers shadowing him had seized their opportunity, dropping out of cloak and leaping to the attack behind the wavefront of their own gunboats and suicide-riders. None of them had gotten past Eighth Fleet's screen of battlecruisers and Crucian heavy cruisers, but in the absence of fighter support that screen's losses had made Ynaathar give the flattened ear flick that answered to a human wince.

Nevertheless, he didn't regret his decision to commit practically all his fighters against the waves of kamikazes from Home Hive Four. Those kamikazes had been burned out of the continuum before reaching the screen. And better still, their vector had been plotted and analyzed, and it narrowed the search for their warp point of entry to a very small volume as interplanetary spaces went. Now Ynaathar awaited word from the *Hun*-class scout cruisers of Survey Squadron 234, which had been attached to Eighth Fleet for this very purpose.

It didn't take long. Even as Kevin Sanders approached with the dispatch, Ynaathar saw the warp-point icon flash into being in the holo sphere, and its precise coordinates appeared on the board. He gave orders to prepare the RD2s.

"As you can all see," he said later to a hastily assembled meeting of his core staff, with the task force commanders attending via com screen, "while only a few RD2s returned, their findings leave no room for doubt. This is Home Hive Four."

He didn't speak in crowing tones—it was foreign to his nature, and at any rate these officers had all agreed with him from the first. The system display the task force commanders could all see in the master plots on their respective flag bridges merely confirmed what they'd believed.

The two innermost planets of the yellow star the RD2s had found were inhabited, and to the drones' esoteric senses they'd blazed with starlike intensity, for theirs was the electro-neutrino output of worlds industrialized the way only Bugs industrialized them, and they nestled amid a firefly-swarm of lesser emission-sources: the fleets of freighters that were a Home Hive's circulatory system. Detecting those planets had been no great problem, for the drones had emerged from a warp point in the inner system, only one light-hour from the G-class primary.

"The promptness with which we located the warp point," Ynaathar continued, "has given us a priceless advantage. We need not spend as much time surveying as we normally would. We can press on and, perhaps, catch them off balance."

"*Yes*, by Valkha!" Shiiaarnaow'maazhaak exploded. The Task Force 82 commander, must, Ynaathar thought, imagine himself back in the good old freewheeling days before the Khanate had encountered the Terrans—one of whom, Francis Macomb, now gave a growl of agreement.

Robalii Rikka shifted his folded wings back and forth.

"I understand the force of this argument," the warmaster said. "And yet . . . we expended more SBMHAWKs than anticipated in breaking into this system. It's a pity we have no replacements for them."

Shiiaarnaow looked about to burst, but to Ynaathar's relief he kept his response more or less within diplomatic bounds.

"We *cannot* wait for more SBMHAWKs to be brought up! We must sink our fangs into these *chofaki* while they are still stunned by the rapidity of our advance."

"Otherwise," Macomb declared, "we piss away the very advantage the First Fang just mentioned."

"Agreed," Rikka conceded.

"Ideally," Force Leader Haaldaarn, commanding Task Force 83, put in, "I would like to have more complete reconnaissance of that system. The RD2s revealed no Bug capital ships. Perhaps they're waiting in cloak."

"They also might not *be* there," Shiiaarnaow shot back.

"A risky supposition," Haaldaarn rumbled.

"Nevertheless," Rikka said, "if true, it offers us a golden opportunity. Despite my earlier reservations, I am inclined to seize that opportunity." The Crucian's eyes shifted to something outside the com pickup. They all knew he was looking at the holo display of what was, to him, the very home of the Demons. When he turned back to the pickup, he wore a new expression . . . and by now they were all familiar enough with his species to be chilled. "I would like very much to enter that particular system—especially inasmuch as the 'Shiva Option' can be applied there without compunction."

Ynaathar looked at the screens and saw no inclination for further discussion.

"Very well. Lord Talphon directed us to 'take them at a run.' That is precisely what we are going to do."

*The small-craft attack had proven ill-advised. In addition to expending a goodly proportion of the available strength in such vessels—strength which was sorely needed now—for no result, it had evidently enabled the Enemy to locate the warp point and commence his attack in less time than had been allowed for.*

*True, in his haste the Enemy had attacked with fewer of his warp-capable missile pods than usual, and the defensive cruisers had survived to inflict significant losses on the starships that had followed—almost annihilating the first two waves, in fact. But there was no disguising the fact that the Enemy fleet—a very substantial one by any standard, even with its losses—was now loose in the System Which Must Be Defended. And the Deep Space Force, although it had returned at maximum speed as per its orders, had only just begun entering the system at the time the attack began.*

*The real problem, of course, was the location of the warp points. The one through which the Deep Space Force had returned lay about as far from the system primary as such phenomena normally occurred, while the enemy was emerging directly into the inner system—closer to the primary than either of the life-bearing planets, in fact. The Deep Space Force was hastening sunward, but the enemy could force engagement with it before it reached the inner system. Datalinked with the innermost planet's massive space station and its attendant orbital fortresses, the Deep Space Force might have been in a good position against an enemy bereft of those troublesome missile pods. As it was, however, the situation was . . . unsatisfactory.*

Once again, Ynaathar could only visualize the drifting debris that his fighters had left of the three monitors, fifty-four super-dreadnoughts, twenty-six battlecruisers and ninety light cruisers that had finally straggled in from a warp point six light-hours distant from the local sun. Not one of them had even made it into weapons range of his battle-line, and neither had any of the depleted stock of gunboats and small craft the planets had sent out to support them.

And, at any rate, that was history. His attention was focused on the little blue disc in the big screen that was Home Hive Four I.

He glanced at the holo sphere, where the planet appeared as a scarlet icon seven light-minutes from the primary, as did its sister planet, not quite in opposition to it and orbiting at ten light-minutes. He focused on the tiny cluster of green icons approaching that latter red beacon.

"Warmaster Rikka should be almost in range of Planet II, Sir," a voice said from behind him, echoing his thoughts in Standard English, and Ynaathar smiled as usual at the Human tendency toward unnecessary verbalization. They'd been social animals longer than the *Zheeerlikou'valkhannaiee*, who'd become pack hunters at a fairly late stage of their development towards tool-using.

"So I see, Cub Saaanderzz," he acknowledged to the young Terran intelligence officer, still present in the same ill-defined staff capacity.

Robalii Rikka was someone else whose status was ambiguous. He was the representative of a remote but powerful ally as well as being one of Ynaathar's task force commanders. Besides, he commanded a very large task force—so large it was subdivided into two task groups, one of which accounted for roughly a third of Eighth Fleet's fighter strength. When Ynaathar had detached Rikka's Task Force 86 and the main carrier force, Task Force 84, and sent them against Planet II, he'd placed the Crucian in overall command. Admiral Haathaahn of TF 84 had made no protest, and Ynaathar was convinced he'd done the right thing. But, he admitted to himself, he missed Rikka's counsel now that the carrier force was sixteen light-minutes away on the far side of the local sun.

He turned to the com screens holding the faces of those task force commanders with whom he *could* converse via lightspeed radio waves.

"Warmaster Rikka is, as far as we know, nearly in position," he stated. Neither he nor any of his listeners voiced the platitude that no one could be sure, when the latest signal from Rikka's command was over sixteen minutes old. "We will therefore proceed to the outer envelope of Planet I's defenses as planned."

There was no discussion to speak of. Eighth Fleet's main battle-line moved into position and began to probe Planet I's defenses with long-range missile fire that those defenses were quite capable of shrugging off. Ynaathar had expected nothing else. His purpose was not to seriously harm the planet or its orbital works, but merely to be in position to take advantage of what he expected to happen when Rikka's fighters struck Planet II.

Robalii Rikka was equally unable to be certain of where Ynaathar was—and equally confident that he was where he was supposed to be—as he watched his fighters streak away towards Planet II.

Planet II shone a brighter but paler blue than Planet I, as it was a relatively chilly world and the arrangement of its continents allowed much of its water to be locked into polar caps. Actually, they'd determined that Planet I was no prize either—a hot, humid world rather like pre-space Humans had sometimes visualized their neighbor Venus. Not that conditions on either had stopped the Bugs from filling both with populations of fairly respectable size even on their standards, meaning of obscene size on anyone else's.

Aileen Sommers moved to his side. There'd been a time when he'd felt uncomfortable about Humans standing too close to him. They were so *big*—even Sommers, who was of only average height for a female though exceptionally sturdy. It no longer bothered him, especially in her case.

"That space station and those fortresses may have expended their gunboats, but they can still put out a lot of beams and anti-fighter missiles," she muttered.

"True," Rikka agreed. "But our entire ordnance mix has the sole purpose of allowing enough of the fighters to get through the defensive envelopes."

Sommers nodded reluctantly. An unprecedented percentage of the fighters carried ECM packs, and the use of decoy missiles was equally lavish.

"It should be enough," she admitted, still sounding less than happy.

"And," Rikka continued, "if your people's experience in other home hive systems is any guide, getting a sufficient number of the fighters through to the planet itself should be enough."

Sommers met his eyes—large, dark, altogether unhuman. She'd thought she knew him. But something in him had changed—or, perhaps, only intensified—since he'd learned of the "Shiva Option." And at this moment, with that planet's Bug-choked surface beckoning, he was clearly uninterested in casualties . . . uninterested to a degree that made her wonder if she'd ever really known him at all.

Fourth Nestmate Rozatii Navva flexed his feet convulsively as he wrenched his fighter away from yet another missile. It was a habitual Crucian reaction to danger. Their feet, with opposable "thumbs" like their hands, were capable of manipulation but were really better adapted for crushing. The race had been using those feet as weapons for its entire evolutionary lifetime, and Navva instinctively sought to grasp the Demons who'd already claimed the lives of two of his squadron's pilots.

But he suppressed his instincts, consciously relaxing his feet. His orders were clear. The titanic space station—clearly visible, especially to the remarkably acute Crucian eyesight which counterbalanced a sense of smell even worse than that of Humans—was not the target. Neither were the twenty-seven more-than-monitor-sized fortresses that wove a tracery of orbits mathematically calculated to cover all approaches to Planet II with overlapping fields of fire.

No, his was one of the FRAM-armed squadrons whose role was simply to dash between those fortresses, trusting to the ECM-bearing escorts and the decoy missiles to keep them alive long enough to get within range of the planet. It hadn't worked for the leading elements of the fighter strike, few of which still flew. But the escorts had soaked up more and more of the defensive fire, and now the planet was looming up ahead in Navva's view-forward, close enough for its icy, arid bleakness to be visible.

It was, Navva thought, about to get even bleaker.

He didn't devote much of his mind to the thought, of course. He was a thoroughgoing professional and a seasoned veteran, one of the first to train with the fighter technology the Humans had brought to the Star Union . . . and one of the few of those first to still remain alive. As such, he kept his consciousness focused on checklists, instrument readouts, threat indicators, and the disposition of the other three fighters that remained under his command. But he was still a Crucian, and the planet ahead meant something more to him than it did to his Human and Orion and Ophiuchi comrades. It was as much a place of dark myth as of dry astrophysics, the very Hell from which Iierschtga, evil twin of Kkrullott the god of light, had sent his Demons to torment his brother's children.

Then they were through, and Navva's reduced squadron took its place in the comber of death that began to roll across the surface of Planet II.

The rationalistic high-tech warrior who was Rozatii Navva was now functioning like an automaton, leading his squadron across the terminator into darkness as it swooped toward the planetary defense center that was its target. His innermost self stood apart, and watched with a kind of dreamy exaltation as the unintercept-able FRAMs flashed planetward to burn a reeking foulness out of the universe.

He had time for an instant's fiery elation when the warheads released their tiny specks of antimatter on the surface and the darkness erupted in blue-white hellfire. Then his two selves came crashing together and fell into oblivion as a point-defense missile already launched from the surface found his fighter.

He never knew that missile was one of the last effective defensive actions taken by the Bugs in Home Hive Four.

"*Yes!* It's happened!"

First Fang Ynaathar ignored Kevin Sanders' youthful enthusiasm as he calmly studied the computer analysis of the Bugs' reaction to his long-range probing of Planet I's defenses. It told him what he wouldn't learn from Robalii Rikka's report for another sixteen minutes: that the fighter strike on Planet II had gone in as scheduled, and that billions of Bugs had abruptly died.

"So it appears," he acknowledged quietly. He turned to his assembled core staff. "The observations of Fangs Presssssscottt and Zhaarnak in two other home hives stand confirmed. The same kind of stunned confusion has clearly overtaken the Bugs here, and done so simultaneously throughout at least the inner system. We will not allow it time to wear off. We will proceed with our primary contingency plan and move our battle-line into Planet I's defensive envelope for close-range bombardment in a single firing pass."

"Ignoring the orbital works, First Fang?" someone queried.

"That is the plan," Ynaathar stated firmly. "Our primary targets are the planetary defense centers."

His orders were carried out. Eighth Fleet's "firing pass," employing strategic bombardment missiles, capital missiles and standard missiles in succession as it approached closer and closer, eventually brought Ynaathar's battle-line within CAM2 range before it broke free of the planet's gravity and receded outward.

By the time Ynaathar received Rikka's report that only a few million Bugs remained alive on Planet II, none of them at all were alive on Planet I.

Kevin Sanders was seriously behind on his sleep.

The wildly varying rotational periods of planets tended to have that effect on interstellar voyagers, far beyond the "jet lag" Terrans had begun to experience in the late twentieth century. And Ynaathar had exercised the worst possible timing in dispatching him to Alpha Centauri with a personal report to the Grand Allied Joint Chiefs of Staff.

But he forced himself to remain alert as he stood in the light of Alpha Centauri A, streaming through the wide window of Kthaara'zarthan's office at a time every weary fiber of his body said—no, screamed—was three in the morning after a couple of sleepless nights. It wouldn't do to fall on one's face in *this* company.

"So," Fleet Speaker Noraku rumbled, "the First Fang took no further action against the orbital constructs?"

"No, Fleet Speaker. He felt they weren't worth the expenditure of any additional ordnance, orbiting depopulated planets incapable of supplying them."

"It's possible that the space stations have fully self-sustaining lifesystems which will keep their personnel fed," MacGregor objected.

"True, Sky Marshal . . . though it's highly unlikely that the fortresses do. But in both cases, lack of basic maintenance will eventually render them incapable of even what the Bugs consider minimal life support."

"That could take some time," Kthaara commented.

"First Fang Ynaathar's position," Sanders said in measured tones, "was that the same lack of maintenance will reduce their defensive capabilities to total impotence before it results in their starvation. So if we grow impatient, we can simply wait until that eventuality and eliminate them with great economy. Either way . . . Well, Admiral Macomb quoted an old Terran proverb and said they can be left to die on the vine."

Kthaara's tooth-hidden smile showed his Standard English was up to that one.

"So be it. I agree with the First Fang." He shifted his body—stiffly, Sanders, noted; when old age caught up with Tabbies, it tended to catch up abruptly—and turned to look at the holo display that now filled a full end of the spacious office.

It was no wonder the display had grown like ivy, for it depicted all the war fronts, incorporating all the new astrographic information that Prescott, Zhaarnak, and Murakuma—the "Three Musketeers" of the Grand Alliance, as wits had begun calling them—had won. In all that labyrinthine complexity, Sanders instantly recognized one particular icon: the dull reddish-black one, like a burnt ember, that represented a now-lifeless home hive. There were two of them.

Kthaara spoke a command to the computer, and a third one appeared.

Ellen MacGregor spoke grimly into the silence. "And then there were two. . . ."

# CHAPTER TWENTY-EIGHT
## "We're going back."

As they walked along the curving passageway just inside *Li Chien-lu's* outer skin, they passed a viewport. Beyond it, the light of Orpheus 1 glinted off ships which, to their practiced eyes, were clearly too small to have any business in this brutal new era's battle fleets.

The sight was enough to set Marcus LeBlanc fuming.

"Goddamn all politicians to hell! But no; as usual, it isn't really them who belong there, it's their cretinous constituents. Not even Bettina Wister could do any harm if the voters weren't such goddamn silly sheep! When I think of all the heavy ships that are tied down when they're needed at the front—!"

Vanessa Murakuma smiled. She was still buoyant with the recorded message that had finally gotten to her through the long and tortuous communication line from deep in the Star Union of Crucis.

"Well, you can't really blame people for worrying about home defense. If the Bugs can find a closed warp point into Alpha Centauri, they can appear anywhere. Even civilians understand that much."

"That's exactly the point—and exactly what even Heart World civilians ought to be able to grasp . . . if certain politicians and their pet so-called admirals weren't so busy feeding them sound bytes instead of accurate analysis! To provide total security for everybody, we'd have to keep forces equal to the combined Bug fleets in every inhabited system in the Alliance at all times!"

"Shhhh! Don't say that so loudly." Before LeBlanc could reach critical mass, Murakuma turned serious. "Just be thankful that all these light carriers were available. You might also," she continued in a subtly different tone, "be thankful that you finally got permission to come this far forward."

"Hmmm . . . There *is* that." LeBlanc was still forbidden to accompany Sixth Fleet when it set out into Bug space, but he'd managed to wheedle GFGHQ into letting him come as far as Orpheus 1. He pondered that accomplishment with a certain undeniable complacency, and he was in a visibly better mood when they reached the briefing room. Murakuma's staff and task force commanders stood as they entered.

"As you were," Murakuma said crisply. "As some of you already know, we're fortunate to have Admiral LeBlanc here from Zephrain. He's been studying the data from our incursion into Home Hive Two five months ago. Admiral LeBlanc, you have the floor."

"Thank you, Admiral Murakuma," LeBlanc replied formally. (Everyone refrained from cracking a smile over the exchange of formalities.) He activated a holo of the Home Hive Two binary system, with the two star-icons a little over a meter and a half apart.

"Fortunately," he began, "one of the last waves of Bug kamikazes appeared on Sixth Fleet's scanners just before you completed your withdrawal from the system. I say fortunately, because it provided fuller data on the vectors involved. Your own intelligence people's studies of those data have been invaluable."

He inclined his head in the direction of a smiling Marina Abernathy. The pat on the head was intentional. Abernathy had been flagellating herself for the past five months over inaccurate threat estimates.

"Our analysis leaves no room for doubt: that wave—and, unquestionably, others—came from Home Hive Two B. So we may infer that Component B has one or more inhabited planets of its own."

"Besides the three around Component Alpha." Leroy McKenna looked and sounded faintly ill.

"Indeed, Commodore," LeBlanc nodded, still in formal mode. "This system is as heavily developed as any of the other home hives we've observed—probably more so."

Ernesto Cruciero stared at the hologram, his eyes dark.

"I wonder which of these systems their species actually evolved in?" he half-murmured.

"Do you suppose they even remember?" Marina Abernathy

asked very softly. Eyes moved towards other eyes, then slipped away uneasily. A silence fell, and hovered there, until LeBlanc cleared his throat to banish it.

"Well, at any rate," he went on a bit more briskly, "this helps explain why Home Hive Two was able to produce gunboats and small craft in such enormous numbers. The good news is that we believe your previous incursion left their starship strength crippled—at least in the heaviest classes, which can't be replaced in five months or anything close to it."

He raised a hand as if to ward off skepticism.

"Yes, I know: we're getting into speculative territory here. And we can't ignore the possibility that they can bring in reinforcements through some warp point we know nothing about. But I've already gone on record with the opinion that another shot at Home Hive Two is worth the risk *if* an answer to the kamikaze threat can be found."

"And we believe we have such an answer," Murakuma said, leaning forward in her chair, "in the form of the *Mohrdenhau*-class light carriers which have become available." She inclined her head in the direction of Eighty-Seventh Small Fang Meearnow'raalphaa, who'd previously commanded TF 63, Sixth Fleet's heavy carrier task force. Now he'd turned that command over to Thirteenth Small Fang Iaashmaahr'freaalkit-ahn, one of the highest ranking female officers in the entire KON, and taken over the newly formed TF 64: eighty *Mohrdenhau*-class CVLs, escorted by sixty cruisers of various sizes.

A prewar class, the *Mohrdenhaus* were rather low-tech, and hence apt to be underappreciated by the cutting-edge-happy TFN. It was also a quintessential Orion design: an uncompromisingly pure carrier with twenty-four fighter bays crammed into a hull no larger than a heavy cruiser's, which left very little room for anything else . . . including the ability to absorb punishment. Its life expectancy was measured in minutes after it came within weapons range of enemy capital ships. But it was never intended to be there. Instead, the Khanate had used it as a frontier picket . . . which was why its designers had somehow made room for a cloaking ECM suite. More recently, it had been used to secure the Allied fleets' lines of communication. Now, with those lines secure enough and the Bugs sufficiently on the defensive (apparently) to justify a little less caution . . .

*And the Khan released them, not having to appease the kind of popular hysteria that scum like Agamemnon Waldeck and Wister promote so they can exploit it*, Murakuma thought with a subversive bitterness she hadn't allowed Marcus to see. Then she shook off the mood and chided herself sternly. *Of course we ought to have a whole flotilla of the big Terran carriers that're sitting around in the nodal systems, neutralized by our own politicians as surely as the Bugs could hope for. And of course we shouldn't have to rely on fragile Tabby designs that're out of date where everything but their ECM and their crews' guts are concerned, instead. But instead of crying into your beer about it, you ought to be giving thanks to whatever gods you worship that you've got those eighty fragile ships and their nineteen hundred-plus fighters.*

"So," she said aloud, "even though we all know the *Mohrdenhaus* are far too light for a warp point assault, they can provide anti-kamikaze cover once we're in Home Hive Two—where, based on Admiral LeBlanc's findings, we have some new ideas on how to proceed. Those ideas will be detailed in the staff briefings."

She paused for a moment, and then spoke in a voice whose quietness left no question about her assumption of undivided responsibility for the decision.

"We're going back in."

*The buoys with which the Fleet had seeded the space surrounding the warp point were set continuously on deception mode. Naturally, the enemy would be awake to the possibility that this was the source of the readings being picked up by his robotic probes. But he would be hesitant to rely on that possibility, assuming—as was only natural—that the Fleet would have summoned all available forces to the defense of such a manifestly crucial system.*

*It was unfortunate that the Enemy's apprehensions were unjustified.*

*There were no such forces. This System Which Must Be Defended was isolated from all other prewar population centers except one rather small one a single warp transit away. And not only was that system of no material help, it was actually a drain. For beyond it lay a system in which yet another Enemy force had lain for so long, awaiting its chance. That threat must also be guarded against.*

*And, perhaps even more importantly, the Enemy must never learn that this star system held not three warp points, but* four. *The food source which had very briefly attained the status of Enemy on the far side of that fourth, closed warp point, had chosen a most inopportune moment to reveal itself. It was fortunate, indeed, that its technology had been so much cruder than that of the Fleet's current*

*Enemies. Indeed, it had been cruder than the technology of the Old Enemy at the time of the first war. Nothing heavier than a gunboat had been required to crush the food source's feeble resistance in space, although it had proven unusually difficult to subdue on the surface of the world the Fleet had taken from it.*

*Had the food source made its presence known even half of one of the primary Worlds Which Must Be Defended's years earlier, the Fleet would have regarded its emergence with complete satisfaction. As it was, there'd been insufficient time to prepare a proper grafting from this System Which Must Be Defended. A population with all of the critical elements had been transported to the new planet, but the new world had a harsh and demanding environment, and the Fleet couldn't be certain that the transported population had sufficient depth and redundancy to survive in the face of unforeseen contingencies. Nonetheless, the decision had been made that no further population or resource transfers would be made to the System Which Must Be Concealed. Unthinkable as it once might have been, that single, newly conquered world might well have become more important than all of the prewar Systems Which Must Be Defended combined, and no risk could be run of inadvertently revealing the warp point which led to it to the Enemy's stealthy robotic spies.*

*If the worst befell the Systems Which Must Be Defended, perhaps that single grafting, in time, might grow into yet another System Which Must Be Defended. If that happened, then the new System Which Must Be Defended must be more cautious than its predecessors had been. It must never return through its warp point of arrival again, and it must prepare itself for the possibility that it would yet again meet the present Enemies at some distant future time.*

*It was a pity that this System Which Must Be Defended was uncertain whether or not any of its courier drones had reached its sisters with word of the existence of this new and fragile daughter. Perhaps the surviving, isolated splinters of the Fleet might have taken some . . . consolation from the knowledge. And perhaps not. The survival of such a delicate sapling in such a cold and hostile universe was far from certain, as, indeed, the straits to which the fully developed Systems Which Must Be Defended had been reduced demonstrated only too well.*

*But at least the Enemy had no way of knowing that the System Which Must Be Concealed existed, either—just as he couldn't know that his second fleet also threatened this System Which Must*

*Be Defended. If he had known, he could have mounted a coordinated two-front offensive. Even as it was, the Fleet's resources had to be kept divided, to guard against both threats. And those resources were seriously depleted. In addition to the destruction it had wrought on the warp-point fortresses of the System Which Must Be Defended, the Enemy's last incursion had—as the Enemy probably suspected—wiped out the entire available inventory of monitors. More were under construction, of course. But that took time . . . probably more time than the Fleet had.*

*Matters weren't entirely unsatisfactory, however. The last incursion had, after all, been repulsed, and the gunboat and small craft losses had been made good since. It was therefore possible to station the bulk of the superdreadnoughts—a hundred and two, out of the available total of a hundred and forty-four—in the other system, where they would join the undepleted array of seventy-two orbital fortresses in a posture of close-in warp point defense. The gunboats and small craft should be able to deal with any future direct attack on the System Which Must Be Defended, using the jammer-aided tactics the enemy had previously seemed to find troublesome.*

Vanessa Murakuma released a quiet sigh as *Li Chien-lu* completed transit and the damage reports from the first waves began to light up the board. Leroy McKenna heard her, and gave her a crooked a smile of shared satisfaction.

"A lot of damaged units," the chief of staff murmured, "but very few destroyed outright."

They'd gotten into Home Hive Two more cheaply than Murakuma had allowed herself to hope. The RD2s had reported a starship total compatible with Marcus LeBlanc's projections. Naturally, they'd considered the possibility that some of the ships were electronic ghosts conjured by ECM3 buoys, but Murakuma had placed absolutely no reliance on that. She'd spent SBM-HAWKs as if the multi-megacredit pods were mere firecrackers, and the avalanche of warheads had blown away the twenty-three fortresses the Bugs had been able to emplace since her previous visit. The CAM2-armed SBMHAWK4s had annihilated the few suicide-riders covering the OWPs and wrought havoc among the patrolling gunboats, and the kamikazes on hand had been able to inflict only the limited damage Murakuma and McKenna were now observing with relief. Quite evidently, the SBMHAWKs had made a clean sweep of the starships.

As the computer analysis of the wreckage began to accumulate, it became clear that they'd more than done so.

"So," Marina Abernathy said, bending over a terminal as the admiral and chief of staff looked over her shoulder, "most of those capital ship readings *were* bogus."

"You'll never hear *me* complaining about wasted SBMHAWKs," McKenna growled. "That's what they're for."

"Still," the intelligence officer mused, "you have to wonder: where are the ships the Bugs *could* have had here?"

"I'm sure Admiral LeBlanc will be intrigued." Murakuma smiled briefly at the thought of Marcus, back in Orpheus 1, a slave to orders. "But I take your point, Marina. They must have other deep-space forces somewhere in the system, so we'll exercise caution. Leroy, we'll wait here until all our units have transited, and I want the heaviest possible fighter CSP out at all times. While Anson is getting that organized and deployed, we'll send our cripples back and reorganize our battlegroups around lost units."

"Aye, aye, Sir."

"And then . . ." Murakuma's smile returned, but this time it was very different. Predatory. "We'll execute Operation Nobunaga."

In a war against an enemy with whom no communication was possible, the security rationale for giving operational plans irrelevant or even nonsensical code names no longer obtained. But military habit died hard. And, she told herself, Tadeoshi would have appreciated this one: Oda Nobunaga, the sixteenth-century Japanese warlord who, time and again, had left his enemies choking on his dust by attacking unexpected objectives.

"I'd love to know," she said, aloud but more to herself than to her staffers, "what the Bugs will think—if that's what they do—when they analyze our course."

*This was . . . unexpected.*

*The remaining units of the Mobile Force—the ones which hadn't been stationed at the warp point and so had survived the initial bombardment—were continuing in cloak. Rather than squander themselves in an attack against an Enemy whose tonnage and firepower were exceeded only by the caution with which he proceeded, they were conserving their gunboats and small craft to assist the thousands of such craft even now speeding out from the planetary bases to meet the invaders.*

*All very well, and according to doctrine. Only . . . the Enemy had set course for the system's secondary star!*

*The Mobile Force would pursue, of course. But it couldn't possibly catch up, given the Enemy's head start and superior speed. The waves of planet-based gunboats would be able to intercept, despite being slowed by the inclusion of shuttles and pinnaces in their formations, but their attacks might not be as well coordinated as might have been hoped.*

Home Hive Two B blazed in the view-forward, an F-class white sun barely less massive and less hot than Component A, now little more than a zero-magnitude star in the view-aft at almost two hundred and fifty light-minutes astern. Given the geometry of the star system, Component B lay approximately 9.2 light-hours from the warp point to Orpheus 1. At *Li Chien-lu*'s maximum sustainable velocity of just over three percent of light-speed, the direct trip would have taken four and a half days. Allowing for the need to stay well clear of the inner system of Component A—which, unfortunately, lay directly between the warp point and the secondary component—the actual transit time had been well over six days.

It was about the longest trip anyone could have taken within the confines of a single star system, binary or not, and this one had seemed even longer than it was as one wave of planet-based kamikazes after another had smashed into Sixth Fleet.

But this time Sixth Fleet at least knew about the Bugs' new jammer technology—its dangers, and also the ease with which its emissions could be detected and locked up by fire control, once the Allied sensor techs knew what to look for. Operation Nobunaga had incorporated defensive doctrine based on that knowledge. Murakuma had formed her capital ships into concentric protective screens around the fragile carriers, then dispatched her fighters to engage the kamikazes at extreme range. The fighter strikes, rather than press home to point-blank dogfighting range, had launched their missiles at extreme range, which kept them outside the jamming envelope and permitted each squadron to coordinate its fire in precise time-on-target salvos. They'd concentrated on the readily identifiable emissions signatures of the gunboats carrying the jammer packs, and although the gunboats' point defense had degraded the effectiveness of such long range fire, enough of it had still gotten the job done.

Once the jammer gunboats had been savaged, the strikegroups fell back to their carriers to rearm. By then, the range had fallen, and Murakuma had maneuvered to hold it open as long as possible with a view to giving them more time to relaunch and continue their work of destruction. Those maneuvers accounted for much of the extra time which had been required for the voyage.

The fighters had gone back out to meet the attack waves coming in on the fleet, and, with the jammer packs effectively taken out of the equation, they'd been able to close for a conventional dogfight without worrying about the loss of their datanets. They couldn't stop those oncoming waves—King Canute couldn't have done that. But the kamikazes were depleted and disorganized by the time they entered the battle-line's missile envelope.

Murakuma kept telling herself that Sixth Fleet's losses were well within the acceptable parameters for this stage of Operation Nobunaga. It didn't help.

At any rate, she couldn't let herself think about it. She had a decision to make.

She turned away from the viewscreen and studied the holo display of the Home Hive Two B subsystem. They'd been close enough for some time to get sensor readings on the inhabited worlds—yes, *worlds*, plural. Planets II and III blazed with high energy emissions, bringing the binary system's total to five—easily the most heavily populated and industrialized system in the known galaxy. In particular, Planet BIII, which Sixth Fleet was now approaching, evinced a population as massive as any yet encountered in Bug space. It lay on a bearing of two o'clock from the local sun at a distance of fourteen light-minutes, guarded by the customary enormous space station and a coterie of twenty-four more massive OWPs. Fortuitously, it was also close to the somewhat less massively developed Planet BII, ten light-minutes from the primary at three o'clock.

"In essence," Marina Abernathy was telling the assembled core staff, "the Bug deep-space force has fallen so far behind that it's no longer a factor in the tactical picture. In fact, it's not even bothering to stay in cloak anymore. But two more really scary waves of kamikazes are bearing down on us."

The staff spook indicated the threat estimates on the board. No one felt any need to comment on the totals—they were all growing desensitized to numbers that once would have left them in shock. But Ernesto Cruciero leaned forward and studied the estimated time to intercept.

"It appears," he said carefully, "that we have time to finish rearming our fighters, carry out the strike on the planet, and then get them back aboard, rearm them again, and launch them to meet this threat."

Despite the painful neutrality with which Cruciero had spoken, Anson Olivera glared at him, as the TFN's *farshathkhanaaks* had a tendency to glare at operations officers.

"That, Commodore," he said with frosty, pointed formality, "is what's known as 'planning for a perfect world.' What if the attack runs into trouble getting past those orbital fortresses? And even if it doesn't, you're asking a lot of our fighter pilots." *As usual,* his tone made it superfluous to add.

Cruciero's retort was halfway out of his mouth when Murakuma raised a hand, palm outward. Both men subsided and waited while the admiral spent a silent moment alone with the decision she must make.

It didn't take long before she looked up.

"Anson, if we hold the fighters back to defend the fleet and then launch the planet-side strike later, they'll have to face kamikazes piloted by Bugs who're at the top of their forms," she said. "But if we exercise the 'Shiva Option' on that planet first, the kamikazes will be a lot easier to deal with. And either way, the forts and the space station are still going to be there when we go in against the planet. I know it's cutting it close . . . but we're going to do it. Continue loading the fighters with FRAMs."

Despite the reservations it was their *farshathkhanaak's* responsibility to feel, Anson Olivera's pilots knew precisely what they were about. More than that, they understood their Admiral's logic. That didn't mean they liked their orders; it only meant that they knew they would have liked any other set of orders even worse, under the circumstances.

The FRAM-loaded F-4s spat from their launch bay catapults, bellies heavy with the destruction they bore, and grim-faced pilots of three different species looked down upon the blue-and-white loveliness of the living planet they'd come so far to kill. Somehow, seeing how gorgeous that living, breathing sphere was made the reality of the Bugs even more obscene. Their very presence should have obscured the heavens, covered itself and all its hideous reality from the eye of God in a shielding, evil-fraught gloom. But it hadn't, and the assassins of that planet's distant beauty settled themselves in their cockpits as they prepared to bring the sun itself to its surface . . . and bury it in eternal night.

The massed fighters, the total strength of every strikegroup in Sixth Fleet, settled into formation. Flight plans and attack patterns were checked a final time and locked into the computers. The hundred or so CAM2-armed SBMHAWK4s Vanessa Murakuma had reserved for this moment deployed with them and locked their targeting systems on the orbital fortresses. There weren't enough of them to destroy the fortresses, but their warheads would suffice to batter the forts and . . . distract them as the fighters streamed past.

Anson Olivera watched his plot, watched his pilots as they finished forming up and dressed their ranks with the precision of veterans who knew the value of careful preparation from painful personal experience. He tried not to look over his shoulder at the master plot, which showed the ominous scarlet icons of the incoming kamikaze strikes sweeping towards Sixth Fleet from behind. Like his pilots, he understood the logic of their orders, but this was going to be close.

He suppressed the need to snap orders at them to hurry up. They were already moving as rapidly as they could. If he tried to make them move faster, it would only engender confusion which would actually slow the entire process, and he knew it. Which didn't make it any easier to keep his mouth shut.

But then, finally—almost abruptly, it seemed, after the nerve-gnawing tension of his wait—they were ready. He made himself pause just a moment longer, running his eyes over the status lights and sidebars in one last check, then nodded and keyed his mike.

"All flights, this is the Flag," he said clearly. "Execute Nobunaga Three."

The last dawn came for the billions of beings on the world below.

*One question, at least, was settled. This horrible disorientation, like all telepathy-related phenomena, might halt at the edge of the interstellar abyss, but it had no difficulty propagating across the gulf between the components of a distant binary system.*

*There were far more of the small attack craft than had been expected, as they were augmented by almost two thousand operating from a swarm of ships smaller than any normally seen in the Enemy's battle fleets—no larger than the Fleet's warp point defense cruisers, in fact. The Enemy had committed practically all of them to a single massive strike that had ignored the fire from the orbital works and, at a single blow, virtually depopulated the third planet of the secondary sun. The ensuing psychic shockwave had hit the onrushing waves of gunboats and small craft well before*

they reached their objectives, stunning them into a state of ineffectual disorganization. The small attack craft, returning from the
smoldering sphere of radioactive desolation that had been a World
Which Must Be Defended, had slaughtered them.

Now the Enemy was proceeding toward the nearby second planet.
It must be left to its own devices. Once, that would have been
unthinkable for any World Which Must Be Defended. But now
there was no alternative. The waves of gunboats and small craft
still following the enemy could accomplish nothing. They must be
recalled, for they were in no condition to fight a battle now, and
when the Enemy killed the second planet, the effect of the psychic
shock would only be intensified.

Yet writing off the secondary sun's second planet carried with it
an additional complication. The new wave of confusion wouldn't
affect only the gunboats and small craft in proximity to the Enemy.
It would wash over the entire system and its defenders, even before
the effects of the first one had even begun to wear off. The Fleet
couldn't be certain what would happen when two such shockwaves
hit in such close temporal proximity. There was simply no experience on which to base any estimate, just as there'd been no warning
that such an effect could be produced at all until the Enemy had
proven it could. It was entirely possible that the second shockwave
would not only extend but intensify the effects of the first.

And if that happened, and if the effects persisted while the Enemy
returned to the primary sun . . .

There could be no further indecision. A force which had not been
exposed to those psychic impacts was needed, and needed badly.
And there was only one such force available.

"The recon fighter's report is confirmed, Sir," Ernesto Cruciero
reported. "Heavy Bug forces have entered this system from Warp
Point Three."

He indicated the Warp Point icon in the holo display of the
Home Hive Two A subsystem. They'd known of it only by inference from the array of fortresses around it. Naturally, they had
no idea where it led.

Now Vanessa Murakuma glared at that icon. It lay four light-
hours out from the local sun on a bearing of seven o'clock—about
ninety degrees clockwise from the course Sixth Fleet was following towards that sun. Then she looked at Cruciero's threat
estimate. *No monitors,* at least, she reflected. *But over a hundred
superdreadnoughts . . . !*

Sixth Fleet had made its way back from the now-lifeless planets of Home Hive Two B unopposed, for the Bugs were clearly avoiding battle. The staff had spent the voyage arguing the pros and cons of staying and finishing the job by sterilizing Component A's three Bug-infested worlds, whose defenders were still showing unmistakable signs of residual grogginess. The pros went without saying. But, Abernathy had insisted, the Bugs still possessed thousands of kamikazes. And, while Sixth Fleet had lost mercifully few capital ships outright, the strikegroups and the battlecruiser screen had taken losses that left Murakuma unhappy about the thought of facing those kamikazes.

Still, her heart had been tugging her toward the "pro" side.

Now, though . . .

"I fully understand the impulse to stay and burn this system clean of the last Bug," she told the staff. "In fact, that's my own inclination. But this changes things. We'd be able to make it across the inner system to Warp Point One without being intercepted by this new force, wouldn't we, Ernesto?"

Cruciero nodded.

"I doubt if they'd even try, once it became apparent we weren't going for the inhabited planets," he said, and his tone was ambivalent. Like Murakuma, he'd been wavering.

"We should be able to exit the system without any opposition except maybe occasional stray kamikaze formations we can brush aside," Abernathy agreed. There'd never been any question about where she stood. Ever since Sixth Fleet's earlier disagreeable surprise in the system, the spook had been inclined to err on the side of caution.

"Very well." Murakuma straightened up. "We're calling it a day. Leroy, please inform the task force commanders."

"Aye, aye, Sir."

Murakuma turned away and studied the holo sphere again as the staffers hurried about their duties. No one could dispute that she'd made the prudent decision, and none of the staffers had even shown disagreement in the body language she'd come to know so well.

*So,* she wondered, *why do I feel this doubt—almost a sense of regret?*

# CHAPTER TWENTY-NINE
## Ghosts of Kliean

"I am sorry to disturb you, Sir, but I think you should see this report."

Third Great Fang of the Khan Koraaza'khiniak, Lord Khiniak, sat up on his bed pad as Claw of the Khan Thaariahn'reethnau entered the cramped sleeping cabin. The small, spartan compartment was located immediately off *Kinaasha'defarnoo*'s CIC, and the great fang had discovered that it was entirely too conveniently placed. The monitor's designers had intended it for the emergency use of a flag officer during sustained maneuvering and combat, not as someplace for a fleet commander to spend every night. He supposed some might argue that his decision to essentially move himself permanently into the cabin for the immediate future might be less than fully reassuring to some of his personnel, and he was certain that the proximity to CIC, Flag Bridge, and Plotting wasn't doing good things for his own regular and undisturbed sleep patterns.

Despite that, he had no intention of changing his routine. From the moment Lord Talphon's official permission to proceed with his long-planned offensive had arrived in Shanak, he'd been an impatient *zeget* on a fraying leash, and he didn't particularly care that his behavior meant his officers and crews had to be fully aware of that fact. In fact, he *wanted* them to be aware. Wanted them to share his own focused, almost feverish sense of exalted anticipation.

And they did. Lord Khiniak doubted that anyone outside Third Fleet, with the exceptions of Raymond Prescott and

Zhaarnak'telmasa, had anything like a true grasp of what his command had become over the seven dreary standard years of waiting in this accursed star system. It was the ambition of any officer of the *Zheeerlikou'valkhannaiee* to train his warriors as *farshatok*—that term the Humans translated, accurately but incompletely, as the "fingers of a fist." Of course, Human fists were blunt, clawless instruments, but the sense came through. But Third Fleet had gone beyond that. His personnel were not simply *farshatok*, not simply a band of warriors who fought with perfect unity, teamwork, and ferocity, but *vilka'farshatok*, warriors of a single clan—of one blood, whatever their birth or clan affiliation. Even the Gormish units of his command had been touched by Third Fleet's eagerness to avenge Kliean, and so Lord Khiniak had no fear they would misinterpret *his* eagerness as anxiety or uncertainty.

Unfortunately, despite the permission he'd been given to mount his longed-for attack, he wasn't free to proceed with operations the way he truly wished to. Given a more perfect universe, he would have restricted himself to a single recon drone probe of the closed warp point. Just enough to secure the data he required to program his SBMHAWKs before he launched his entire fleet at the Bugs' throats. In the long run, any risks involved in that approach would almost certainly have been offset by the fact that it would have allowed him to retain the element of surprise.

But there were other factors to consider—the same factors, in many ways, which had driven Zhaarnak'telmasa to fall back from Kliean before the Bugs' initial onslaught. Although Lord Khiniak and his crews regarded themselves as an offensive weapon, they could never forget that their true function for seven endless Human years—almost fourteen of their own—had been to stand as a barrier between any additional Bug attacks and the heavily populated star systems which lay beyond Kliean and Telmasa. Certainly, the Strategy Board hadn't forgotten, and Fang Kthaara's permission to proceed hadn't arrived completely free of strings.

Koraaza'khiniak suspected that Kthaara had been forced to attach those strings largely for political considerations, but to his own sensitive nostrils some of them carried the definite scent of Fleet Speaker Noraku's caution, as well. In fairness, few beings in the explored universe were less politically motivated than Noraku, and while Koraaza often found the Gorm representative's deliberate, phlegmatic approach to problems even more maddening than he found most Humans, the Third Fleet commander was forced to concede that this particular set of strings wasn't entirely senseless.

Given the fact that the Bugs clearly had been forced more and more heavily onto the defensive, it was impossible even for him to argue that an attack from Shanak was essential. Valuable and extremely useful, yes; essential, no. Koraaza believed fervently that his proposed offensive would help shorten the war, but he wasn't blind to the fact that his thirst to engage the enemy was as much the product of his people's code of honor as of cold, strategic analysis. The one didn't invalidate the conclusions of the other, yet the *Zheeerlikou'valkhannaiee* had learned the hard way (which—he conceded in the privacy of his own thoughts—was the way in which they seemed to learn *all* of their lessons) that the pragmatism of their Gorm allies and their one-time Human foes was just as important as honor when it came to planning military operations. And, pragmatically speaking, it was far more important to the Alliance that Third Fleet prevent any possibility of a last-ditch Bug offensive out of Shanak than it was for that same fleet to launch an offensive of its own.

If that was true, then it only made sense—however much he resented it—to be certain before any offensive was launched that it was in a position to succeed without risking the destruction of Third Fleet's protective barrier. Which explained both the substantial reinforcements GFGHQ had somehow managed to pry loose from the rear area pickets and also the very specific orders from Centauri which had required him to conduct a thorough reconnaissance of the warp point defenses—if any—awaiting him on the far side of the warp point in the system which the Alliance's astrographers had designated Bug-06.

Bug-06, his probes had quickly revealed, was a largely useless binary system with a K-4 class primary and a dim ember of a red dwarf secondary component. The two-star system boasted a total of ten planets, one of them inhabited, and a single massive asteroid belt, but it was obvious that it could have been only a staging point for the massive forces which had streamed forward to murder Kliean and to threaten Alowan and Hairnow with matching destruction seven years earlier. The relatively small (by Bug standards, at least) population of the K-4 star's innermost planet was far too tiny to have supported such an attack . . . or the massive Bug fleet which hovered now within two light-minutes of the closed warp point's far terminus.

The drone probe data had to be taken with a grain of salt, as a Human might have put it, given the Bugs' demonstrated ability to use deception mode ECM effectively. Even allowing for that, however, it was clear to Koraaza that his earlier suspicion that the Bugs realized perfectly well that the Alliance had determined the warp point's location had been accurate. At least seventy massive Type Six OWPs hovered within missile and beam range of the warp point through which any attack must come, supported by forty-plus heavy and light cruisers, at least ten thousand patterns of mines, and thousands of laser buoys, all liberally seeded with jammer and deception-mode ECM buoys. Which didn't even include any of the hundred-plus superdreadnoughts, their supporting battlecruisers and cruisers, and the hordes of gunboats and suicide small craft which undoubtedly stood ready to assist them in repelling any attack.

In light of the way in which Operation Retribution and Operation Ivan had obviously stretched the Bugs' available strength to and beyond the breaking point, even Koraaza had been surprised by the numbers of starships detailed to defend what clearly was at best a secondary system. On the other hand, the presence of so many mobile units might well serve as further support of his theory that one of the "home hive" systems stood in relatively close proximity to Shanak. If there were only one or two stars between Shanak and one of the Bugs' core population concentrations, then this "secondary" star system would be of crucial importance despite its unprepossessing appearances. Not only that, but the Bugs had discovered by now, if they hadn't already known, what happened when the "Shiva Option" was applied in a heavily populated system. They must realize as well as the Alliance that they simply could not allow a bombarding fleet into range of a major population center without effectively writing off every military unit in the same star system. Which meant the pressure to defend such perimeter systems as Bug-06 must be even greater than ever.

None of which had made the forces arrayed against Third Fleet any more palatable. Despite the firepower massed to cover the warp point, Koraaza was confident he and his *vilka'farshatok* could fight their way into the system with acceptable losses. The problem was that there was no way to predict what additional forces the Bugs might hold in reserve. Losses which would be acceptable under other circumstances would become intolerable if the Bugs turned out to have had the resources and cunning to bring up an even more powerful fleet and hide it in cloak somewhere beyond the units the recon drones could see. It was extremely unlikely, given how hard-pressed they were on other fronts, but the shattering experience of Operation Pesthouse continued to loom in the back of every Allied strategist's thoughts. If the Bugs were able and willing to sacrifice the OWPs and their immediate supporting warships as bait, inflicting attritional losses on an attacker in a "losing" battle that lured the attacker into position to be crushed by an even more powerful fleet waiting in ambush, then a quick riposte through Shanak and Kliean could win them enormous prizes.

It was that same thinking, in no small part, which had inspired GFGHQ to come up with the reinforcements headed towards Shanak. Although Koraaza was far too good an officer to turn up his nose at the offer of additional forces, he had to admit that he was of two minds in this instance. On the one hand, such a substantial increase in his order of battle would be highly welcome. On the other, any newcomers, however well-trained and motivated, would be just that—newcomers.

Few civilians, and, unfortunately, not all flag officers, truly understood the extent to which any effective fleet was a single living, breathing organism. Oh, if a Navy had fundamentally sound doctrine, uniform training standards, and officers who made it their business to see that both of them were firmly adhered to, then there was no reason—in theory—why a fleet or task force organization couldn't simply be made up of randomly selected units and committed to battle. But theory, as always, had a distressing tendency to come up short when confronted with reality.

There had been altogether too many occasions in history, Human as well as that of the *Zheeerlikou'valkhannaiee*, when there'd been no option but to assemble such scratch forces, commit them to action, and pray for the best. On occasion, they'd actually produced victory, but that virtually never happened when they faced competent opposition, and the reasons were simple. In battle, it was absolutely essential that cohesion and the unity of purpose be maintained, and that an entire fleet act in unison with a clearly understood objective. That was true from the very highest level of strategic planning down to—and perhaps even more especially at—the tactical level of individual squadrons and starships. Teamwork, training, mutual confidence, and the knowledge that when an order was given both he who gave it and he who received it understood it to mean exactly the same thing. . . .

Those were fundamental keys to success, and to commit a fleet which lacked them to battle was to send it against the foe with its claws broken and one hand tied behind its back. That was the very reason that Zhaarnak'telmasa and Raymond Prescott had been forced to hold so long and so desperately in Alowan and Telmasa seven years earlier before Koraaza brought Third Fleet to their relief. His ships had come from every conceivable source, piled together in whatever order they had arrived, and he'd had no choice but to hold them at the sector capital while he drilled them mercilessly until they could at least all get underway, on the same course, on the same day.

And that was the reason his current reinforcements were, to some extent, what the Humans called a "double-edged sword." Their firepower would be most welcome, but unlike his *vilka'farshatok*, they wouldn't be completely familiar with his plans and his thoughts or the procedures of his existing fleet. Nor would it be possible to truly integrate them into Third Fleet's structure in the time available, and so they would bring weaknesses as well as strengths.

But whatever impact the reinforcements' arrival might have, they weren't here yet. Koraaza wasn't categorically forbidden to begin his attack without them if the Bugs' dispositions in Bug-06 offered him an opportunity. At the same time, he was well aware that he was *expected* to defer any offensive until they joined him. Any great fang was also expected to exercise his own judgment, but if he began operations before his entire assigned force had assembled and things went poorly, more than enough critics would emerge to explain to him precisely how he'd failed his Khan and his people.

It had seemed any such quandary was unlikely to arise, however. Koraaza was confident his analysts would eventually be able to determine what the Bugs were actually up to with a reasonable degree of certainty. Thanks to the Humans, there was no shortage of recon drones, and since his orders had already cost him the chance for strategic surprise, he was prepared to expend the drones in any required numbers before he committed his warriors to an attack. And he remained confident that the analysts' final conclusion would support his own theory. But until that happened, he was bound by the letter of his orders to proceed with all deliberate caution. Which meant Third Fleet would sit here, sending massive waves of drones through at staggered intervals while its covering fighters pounced upon and annihilated any Bug gunboat that dared to show itself in Shanak space, until Koraaza's honor permitted him to conclude in good faith that he could launch his own attack without jeopardizing the security of the populated systems behind him.

It appeared that it would require weeks to reach that point, during which time the Bugs would be given every opportunity to prepare for his obviously impending offensive. The fact that it would also give time for the arrival of his own reinforcements had struck him as no more than partial compensation for alerting the Bugs to the incipient threat, but there'd been nothing he could do about that except prowl around CIC and Flag Bridge like an irritated *zeget* to "encourage" his tactical officers' efforts.

Unless, of course, Thaariahn's diffident interruption of his sleep meant something important had changed.

"What is it you wish me to see?" he asked his operations officer as he brushed the sleep from his eyes.

"We have just recovered the latest probe volley, Sir," Thaariahn replied, and held out an electronic message board. Koraaza took it, but he never lowered his eyes from the claw's face, and one ear cocked in question.

"The Bahgs' ECM continues to generate hundreds of false sensor images," Thaariahn said, answering the unasked question, "but this data—" he gestured at the pad Koraaza now held "—appears to indicate that their entire mobile force is withdrawing."

"*Withdrawing?*" Koraaza repeated sharply, and Thaariahn flicked both ears in agreement.

"The sensor readings are unambiguous, Sir. It is, of course, possible that this represents some sort of ruse or deceptive maneuver on their part, but CIC's confidence is high. A follow-up probe volley has already been dispatched on my authority to confirm the original readings, but I do not expect its findings to alter CIC's present evaluation."

The effort the claw made to restrain his own enthusiasm was obvious, despite his deliberately measured tone, but he was far too professional to allow overconfidence—his own, or anyone else's—to lead Third Fleet into a Pesthouse-style ambush. Koraaza approved heartily, and he concentrated on matching his ops officer's restraint as he keyed the message board alive and studied its contents.

There was no way to know what had caused the sudden change in the enemy's long-standing defensive deployments, but as Thaariahn had said, the readings themselves were certainly clear enough. Whatever the Bugs were up to, they didn't appear to be wasting any effort on subtlety. They hadn't even attempted to conceal their departure. Indeed, the suddenness with which they'd brought up their drives and the engine-straining speed at which they'd sped off across the star system had all the earmarks of an emergency departure.

"It would appear that you and CIC are correct, Thaariahn—at least as far as the fact of the Bahgs' starships' departure is concerned," Koraaza said after a moment. "As you say, however, the question of precisely *why* they have been so obliging as to suddenly withdraw by far the more effective portion of their defensive force is quite another consideration."

"Truth, Sir," the ops officer agreed. "But whatever their motive, it seems they have presented us with the opportunity we have sought. Assuming, that is, that this is not an elaborate effort to bait some sort of trap for us."

"A possibility no one is likely to overlook after what happened to the Humans' Second Fleet," Koraaza acknowledged. "And one which assumes added weight given the fact that our own reinforcements have not yet arrived. By the same token, however, we cannot allow ourselves to worry our way into ineffectiveness. Nothing is ever truly certain in battle . . . except that he who attempts to avoid all risk will never attain decisive victory."

He switched off the pad, laid it aside, reached for his uniform harness, and stood.

"You have done well," he told his ops officer. "I will join the duty watch in CIC until your fresh probe volley returns and its data can be processed. But you, I fear, will have other duties while I await that information."

"Other duties?" Thaariahn cocked both ears, and Koraaza gave a purring chuckle as he buckled his harness.

"Indeed, Claw Thaariahn. I realize it will require some hours of frenzied effort on your part, but I want the Fleet brought to immediate readiness and a complete SBMHAWK bombardment plan ready for implementation the instant I give the command!"

*The timing couldn't have been worse.*

*The Fleet had feared all along that the Enemy would eventually launch an attack through the closed warp point which had allowed the Fleet to destroy two of the Enemy's Worlds Which Must Be Defended. The Fleet certainly would have done so in his place . . . once it discovered the location of the warp point, and it had long seemed likely the Enemy had done just that. There'd been no way to be certain, but careful analysis had suggested that the one battlecruiser which was known with certainty to have been in position to detect the transit of one of the Fleet's scout cruisers had probably done so . . . and gotten its courier drones off before it could be destroyed.*

*That possibility had not eased the Fleet's strategic constraints. According to prewar doctrine, the Fleet ought to have assembled a massive shell of orbital fortresses and minefields to cover the open end of the warp line the instant the presence of an enemy beyond it became known. That was especially true for a warp point which simultaneously lay in such close proximity to a System Which Must Be Defended and offered a potential route by which the Enemy might be attacked in turn. The only way to ensure that a closed warp point was never detected was never to use it, but the rich prizes which the Fleet had already gained through its use strongly suggested that still richer ones remained to be gained as soon as the Fleet could revert to offensive operations. Yet there was no way to know when such operations might become feasible without maintaining a scouting presence beyond the warp point, and that meant scout ships had no choice but to make transit on a semi-regular basis.*

*Under prewar doctrine, the risk of revealing the warp point's location had been more than justified by the opportunity, yet the proximity of a System Which Must Be Defended absolutely mandated that the strongest possible defenses be emplaced. Unfortunately, the massive losses which all components of the Fleet had suffered in its unrelenting battles against the most unpleasantly resilient New Enemies and Old Enemies had forced some compromise decisions. The New Enemies' passive stance in the system beyond the closed warp point had suggested at least a possibility that they would remain passive—that the losses their Worlds Which Must Be Defended had already suffered had driven them completely onto the defensive here, as had been the case on the front on which the New Enemies had initially been contacted at the war's beginning. Moreover, the fact that it was a closed warp point whose location the Fleet was reasonably certain was unknown to the Enemy automatically reduced its place in the hierarchy of threats the Fleet had suddenly found itself forced to confront. But most significantly of all, the Fleet simply could not fortify every threatened point on the lavish scale prewar doctrine had required. There hadn't been sufficient resources for that—not if combat losses were to be replaced and the new starship types and the new gunboats were to be constructed in sufficient numbers—even before the Enemy had successfully destroyed the first World Which Must Be Defended.*

*The huge Reserve which had been built up between the last contact with the Old Enemies and the first contact with the New had been gone even before the New Enemies finally determined the location of the closed warp point. Now almost all the new construction starships were also gone. Sixty percent of the shipyards which had built both the Reserve and the new Fleet were gone, as well, and so were the workers, and the foundries, and the asteroid mining ships which had supported them. And so, even with the total resources of the System Which Must Be Defended this Fleet component was assigned to protect, there was no real possibility of erecting the proper fixed defenses. Yet there was also no option but to mount the strongest possible defense here, where the attackers couldn't possibly strike the Worlds Which Must Be Defended and so cripple the starships and fortresses attempting to protect them.*

*Since the gunboats and suicide craft must be retained in the System Which Must Be Defended, the only real alternative had been to build up the strongest fixed defenses possible—largely by dismantling existing OWPs in the System Which Must Be Defended and transporting them here to be reassembled—and to station the Fleet's main remaining starship strength here to support them while relying upon massive numbers of lighter units to protect the System Which Must Be Defended from the other direction.*

*Ultimately, there was no way to hold this system against the numbers the Enemy could bring to bear upon it, and the Fleet knew it. Yet what other option did the Fleet have but to try? The actions of the Enemies, Old and New alike, clearly demonstrated that their fleet had adopted precisely the same logic the Fleet had, which at least simplified the Fleet's menu of strategic choices. When the only possible alternative to victory was extinction, surrender and strategic withdrawal were no longer options worthy of consideration.*

*At least the Fleet had known it enjoyed one enormous advantage, for there was no way for the Enemy to know that the System Which Must Be Defended was simultaneously threatened from two separate directions. Or so the Fleet had believed.*

*Now that no longer seemed so certain. The sudden introduction of the tiny robotic spies through the warp point had finally resolved any ambiguity over whether or not the Enemy knew its location. It still seemed impossible for there to be any way in which the Enemy could have extrapolated the warp lines which converged in the System Which Must Be Defended, yet the Fleet had been . . . anxious in the wake of the first attack on the System Which Must Be Defended. The original deployment plan hadn't been altered, since no better alternative offered itself, yet the Enemy's habit of launching widespread offensives, now here, now there, had accustomed the Fleet to thinking in terms of attacks carefully timed to strike the Fleet at the most inopportune possible moments. Whether or not the Enemy realized that he had two possible avenues by which to approach the System Which Must Be Defended, the possibility that he might launch separate, near-simultaneous attacks upon it—even by accident—had deepened the Fleet's anxiety.*

*And now this. The frantic messages from the System Which Must Be Defended left the mobile units no choice. There was no point in maintaining a grip on this unimportant star system if the System Which Must Be Defended was lost, and only the mobile forces here could possibly provide an unshaken force with which to defend the remaining Worlds Which Must Be Defended. And so the starships and their attendant gunboats had begun their high-speed run back to the System Which Must Be Defended . . . just as yet another flight of the Enemy's drones transited the warp point.*

*The Fleet hesitated almost imperceptibly, torn between the reflex to return to the defense of the warp point and its imperative orders to race to the rescue of the Worlds Which Must Be Defended. But that hesitation was brief, meaningless. The only reason for the Fleet's existence was to protect the Worlds Which Must Be Defended. That was not its primary task; that was its only task, and so the withdrawal continued despite the opportunity the retreat offered to the Enemy beyond the closed warp point.*

*It was all a matter of timing.*

Koraaza'khiniak gazed at the icons in his master plot and felt the eyes of his task force commanders upon him. They weren't physically present in *Kinaasha'defarnoo*'s CIC, yet he knew their attention was intensely focused upon their own duplicate plots and the displays of the com links which joined them to his flag bridge. And as he felt those eyes, he sensed the matching eagerness which blazed behind them.

*It is still too early,* he made himself think. *Lord Talphon's reinforcements are still en route. Their arrival will increase my nominal combat power by at least twenty-five percent, and suddenly that no longer seems such a "minor" consideration! And yet . . . and yet . . .*

He very carefully didn't look over his shoulder at the com screens which would have shown him his commanders' faces and expressions. This was his decision, and his alone, and so he would make it alone. And truth to tell, even as he conscientiously considered all of the reasons against attacking, he already knew what that decision would be.

"Your pardon, Great Fang," Thaariahn said quietly, appearing suddenly at his elbow. "The SBMHAWK bombardment plan you requested has been completed."

"It has?" Koraaza never looked away from his plot, but he sensed Thaariahn's ear flick of agreement.

"It has, Sir. Small Fang Kraiisahka has worked out the details and is prepared to deploy the pods at your command."

"I see." Koraaza hid a small smile at Thaariahn's studiously uninflected statement. Kraiisahka'khiniak-ahn was both his most junior and perhaps his most promising task force commander. She was also his daughter-in-law, of whom he was inordinately fond. The Khanate had none of the Federation's official disapproval of nepotism (which, Koraaza had long since concluded, was far more a matter of appearances than substance, even among the inexplicable Humans), yet Kraiisahka had made it respectfully but firmly clear that she intended to win any commands or advance-ment on her own merits. In general terms, Koraaza agreed with her. Senior command slots were too important to be handed to anyone who hadn't proved his—or her—ability, whoever he or she might happen to be related to. On the other hand, such matters of principle could be taken too far, and so he'd made it quietly clear to Thaariahn that he expected his operations officer to keep a distantly protective eye on her. Since she was senior to the ops officer and possessed a temper even the most charitable would have described as fiery, Thaariahn's assignment had not been an enviable one.

"Show me the details," the great fang said after a moment, and the claw tapped a series of commands into the master plot.

Koraaza watched the icons flash through the projected deploy-ment and launch and grunted in satisfaction. Given the heavy ECM environment into which the SBMHAWKs would be emerg-ing, Kraiisahka had opted for what would almost certainly be proven a massive case of overkill where the orbital fortresses and relatively immobile heavy cruisers were concerned. It would cut deeply into Third Fleet's store of the warp-capable missiles, but he'd amassed huge numbers of them and he heartily approved of her logic. Better to use more than were strictly necessary than to use too few and suffer avoidable losses during the break-in. That was a lesson he'd learned the hard way—and at the cost of far too many lives—when he first retook this system so many years before. Zhaarnak'telmasa had made that point to him at the time he'd planned his original assault, but Koraaza had still been too accustomed to thinking in terms of the Khanate's tight prewar fiscal constraints. The cornucopia of the Human Federation's production capabilities had long since loosened them ... and the lives he'd paid would have driven him to break them even if they hadn't loosened.

He reran the plan twice more, then looked up and turned at last to the com screens and his waiting flag officers.

"I approve Small Fang Kraiisahka's proposed bombardment plan," he said formally. "Small Fang," he looked directly at his daughter-in-law, "you will begin pod deployment immediately. The attack will begin thirty-five minutes from now."

The grim, massive OWPs waited silently amid the protective embrace of the minefields, energy platforms, and ECM buoys. The light of the system primary was wan here, touching the hulking fortresses with only the feeblest of glows against the eternal dark of the diamond-chip immensity of space. It was a region of cold and dark, well suited to the beings who crewed those ominous defenses.

But then, suddenly, the cold and dark were touched by something else. Only the OWPs' sensors saw the first, invisible flicker of movement as the initial wave of missile pods made transit, but what had been invisible to the organic eye became a wall of sun-bright fury as the wrath of Hiarnow'khanark, the ancient war god of the *Zheeerlikou'valkhannaiee*, and his death messenger Valkha reached out for the beings who had murdered so many of their people. Dozens of the transiting pods interpenetrated and vanished, building that wall of fire as they immolated themselves in space-wracking spits of dragon venom, but even as dozens perished, hundreds upon hundreds survived.

The Bugs aboard those doomed fortresses and the handful of slow, obsolete warp point defense cruisers which had been left to support them had just long enough to realize that the Ghosts of Kliean had come for them.

And then the surviving pods launched.

Koraaza'khiniak studied his display with grim, vengeful satisfaction. Kraiisahka's bombardment plan had consumed over half of Third Fleet's total supply of warp-capable munitions. More were available from his stockpiles in Hairnow and the systems further up the warp lines, and although it would take time to bring them forward, Koraaza felt no temptation to complain. The massive wave of SBMHAWKs had blasted every fortress out of existence before the first Allied starship made transit. They and the other specialized missiles had blotted away every cruiser, and virtually all of the waiting gunboats, as well, despite everything the Bugs' ECM could do, and Third Fleet had flowed steadily into Bug-06 without the loss of a single starship.

It had been a very Human-style attack, the great fang thought to himself, but the thought held only profound satisfaction, not complaint. The *Zheeerlikou'valkhannaiee* had learned to adopt those tactics which worked from enemies and allies alike, and that was good. But even as they adopted the techniques of others, they'd remained themselves, and it was time for Koraaza's *vilka'farshatok* to demonstrate what that meant.

"We are getting back the first detailed reports on the planet, Sir," Thaariahn informed him. "Our initial assessment appears to have been accurate. The new drone reports indicate that the orbital defenses are minimal—one space station of no more than moderate size, and no more than half a dozen orbital fortresses, the largest considerably smaller than any we confronted here."

"Is there any sign of planet-launched gunboats?" Koraaza asked.

"None at this time," Thaariahn replied. "I suppose it is possible that they are retaining them until we close with the planet, but that would not be consistent with anything we have seen out of them in the past."

"No, it would not," Koraaza said thoughtfully, combing his whiskers with the claws of his right hand while he considered the master plot. He paid particular attention to the projected course of the Bug starships. They had never wavered from their original heading and continued to stream away from Third Fleet at their maximum speed, which raised several interesting questions.

Why had they fallen back from the warp point in the first place? Especially when the steady flow of recon drones from Shanak must have confirmed that an attack was imminent? Surely only some dire emergency somewhere else could account for such a maneuver after so long spent patiently and obviously awaiting that attack. The most logical explanation to suggest itself to him was that some other Allied attack had presented a threat to a more important objective somewhere else. Unfortunately, given his total ignorance of how the warp lines beyond this system related to one another, it was impossible to make any sort of guess as to what that objective might be.

But that left three other intriguing considerations. First, where exactly was the warp point for which they were bound? They'd attempted to go back into cloak, but the long-range recon drones had managed to hold them, and now recon fighters shadowed them cautiously, covered by no less than six strikegroups of escort fighters. Given the energy signatures starship drives radiated at the Bugs' current speed, not even the best ECM in the galaxy would be able to hide them from the exquisitely sensitive sensors of his scout craft. So wherever they were headed, he should be able to track and pursue them.

Which led naturally to the second consideration—how long would it take them to reach their exit warp point? His own entry point lay just over a hundred light-minutes from the system primary in what the Humans would have called the "four o'clock" position. The single habitable world was barely four light-minutes from its cool star in the "seven o'clock" position, which placed it just over two light-hours from Third Fleet's present location, while the Bugs' starships were headed away from his command on a bearing of approximately six o'clock and had already put almost a light-hour between them. That, unfortunately, was the sum total of his knowledge of the system's astrography. He knew how long it would take him to reach and attack the planet, but he had no way of knowing whether he could execute the Shiva Option before the Bugs fled through their destination warp point and thereby avoided the psychic shockwave.

Without that knowledge, the decision between attacking the planet and going in immediate pursuit of his fleeing enemies in hopes of following them through the warp point before they could fully prepare themselves to receive his attack was a difficult one. Worse, the Bug population in this system was relatively small, and that was the third and final consideration, for he was far from certain the Shiva Option could produce sufficient casualties to generate the disorientation which resulted from the destruction of larger populations.

He combed his whiskers for a few more moments, then reached his decision and turned to a communications tech.

"Connect me to Small Fang Kraiisahka."

"At once, Great Fang!"

The tech was as good as his word, and Koraaza smiled as Kraiisahka appeared on his com screen.

"Your bombardment plan succeeded handily, I see," he observed. "Congratulations. You did well." He allowed his pride in her to show in his smile and the set of his ears, but, mindful of her determination not to rely upon connections of blood and family, he was careful to actually say no more than that.

"Thank you, Great Fang," she replied formally. Koraaza fully recognized that she was at least as deadly as any other officer under his command, yet he couldn't set aside the thought—inappropriate though he knew it to be—that she was also as cute as a kitten. Not that he permitted a trace of that thought to color his manner.

"Now," he continued, "we must proceed to the next stage. I believe that under the circumstances, it is time to activate Zhardok Three." A shadow of disappointment flickered through Kraiisahka's eyes, but she was clearly unsurprised, and he felt a fresh surge of pride as she waited calmly and without protest for her orders. "You will return to Shanak with your task force," he told her, "and use your carriers to ferry the fighter reserve through to this system. I will detach your organic strikegroups and assign them to Small Fang Huaada. As you transport each wave of the reserve into Bahg-06, you will equip them with life-support packs and send them to join Huaada, as well."

"As you command, Great Fang," Kraiisahka acknowledged levelly.

Eleventh Small Fang Huaada'jokhaara-ahn commanded Task Force 33, the main carrier force of Third Fleet. Her twenty-four fleet carriers and their escorts were only slightly more numerous than Kraiisahka's own Task Force 34, but Kraiisahka's most powerful units were her twenty-eight *light* carriers, and they carried less than seven hundred strikefighters, compared to the thousand-plus aboard Huaada's big carriers. Perhaps more to the point, Huaada's ships were not only larger, they were much tougher and more survivable, and Kraiisahka knew it. Her own task force, as she'd also known from the beginning, was little more than a ferry command, suitable for the transportation of fighters through warp points but with no business anywhere gunboats and kamikazes could get at them. The fact that Koraaza had permitted her to plan and execute the SBM-HAWK bombardment which had blown Third Fleet's way into the star system was already more than she'd realistically expected, and she took her demotion to freight hauler with calm dignity.

"The last two waves of the reserve," Koraaza continued after only the briefest of pauses, "will *not* be sent on to Huaada, however. Instead, you will retain them here under your own command and proceed against this system's inhabited planet." Her eyes widened, and almost unconsciously, she came to the position of attention. He held her gaze steadily, fully aware of the surprise and pride which filled her in that moment. "You will," he told her quietly, "execute the Shiiivaaa Option against that planet."

"Of course, Great Fang!" she replied, and the acknowledgment was a promise that she would not fail the trust he'd reposed in her.

"Very well, Small Fang," he said. "I will expect a report of your successful completion of your assignment within the next forty standard hours."

"Yes, Sir!"

He flicked his ears at her in a gesture which mingled approval, expectation, and dismissal, and returned his attention to Thaariahn as the com screen went blank.

"You heard?"

"Yes, Sir." Thaariahn seemed somewhat less enthusiastic than Kraiisahka had been, and Koraaza suppressed a small chuckle. His operations officer was a meticulous and methodical soul. He understood the logic of what Koraaza intended, but its improvised nature offended his inherent sense of neatness.

Well, it wasn't precisely the way Koraaza would have preferred to proceed in a more perfect universe, either. Unfortunately, in the universe in which Third Fleet actually lived, he had too few fighter platforms to transport all of the fighters available to him. At the same time, it was likely that he would require every fighter he had when he finally ran the retreating Bug starships to ground. If he'd been able to await the arrival of the remainder of Lord Talphon's reinforcements, his carrier strength would have more than doubled. In the absence of those additional carriers, however, the only way to get the fighter strength he needed far enough forward to be of any use was to use the technique the Humans called "hot bay." By rotating fighters through his available carriers' hanger bays in succession he could effectively triple the number of fighters each of those carriers could support. The downside was that it would place an enormous strain upon his maintenance and service crews, not to mention the pilots themselves, since two-thirds of his total fighter strength would have to be in space at any given moment. And it also meant he would be forced to use a carrier shuttle technique to transport his total strength through the next warp point, which could pose some severe problems, particularly if it proved necessary to retreat quickly.

Still, the ability to send almost six thousand fighters into action was worth a few inconveniences and potential problems, especially if he and his *vilka'farshatok* encountered what the Humans had dubbed the Bughouse Swarm.

"Very well, Claw," Koraaza'khiniak told his ops officer. "Let us place the remainder of the fleet in motion. I doubt that it will be possible to overtake the enemy before they make transit, but there is at least the possibility that Small Fang Kraiisahka will be able to execute the Shiiivaaa Option before they leave the system. If so, I would very much like to arrive close enough upon their heels to take advantage of their confusion."

"At once, Sir."

Lord Khiniak returned his attention to the master plot while Thaariahn's crisp directives sped outward from his flagship.

*The ghosts are not yet satisfied,* he told the fleeing light codes of his enemies, recalling a conversation with Zhaarnak'telmasa and his *vilkshatha* brother. *But they will be. Oh, yes. They* will *be.*


*The Fleet raced onward, and if the beings who crewed its ships had been anything remotely like what their enemies called individuals, and if those individuals had believed in anything greater than the omnivoracity of their own species, the passages and compartments of those vessels would have been filled with furious protests against fate or whatever might have served them as a god.*

*The Enemy who had so savaged the System Which Must Be Defended wasn't following the course which had been predicted for him. True, he was returning from the secondary component of the system, but he wasn't headed directly for the remaining Worlds Which Must Be Defended. Instead, he'd chosen a course which would ensure he could retreat to the warp point by which he'd first entered the system . . . before the Fleet could intercept him. The Fleet could scarcely complain if the Enemy chose not to kill those worlds, but his maneuvers meant the Fleet would be unable to bring him to action.*

*Worse, the withdrawal of the mobile units from the warp point in this system had greatly facilitated the successful incursion of the second Enemy force. Given the flood of warp-capable missiles which had poured through the warp point, it was certainly possible that the mobile units would have been destroyed along with the*

*fortresses had they not withdrawn, but that didn't alter the fact
that the Fleet now had no choice but to flee from a force which it
might otherwise have met in deep space battle with at least some
prospect of victory. Not when the Enemy was in position to wipe
all life from this system's inhabited world and so paralyze and
disorganize the Fleet.*

*No. All the Fleet could do now was to continue to run, hop-
ing it could reach the warp point and make transit to the System
Which Must Be Defended before this fresh force of New Enemies
was able to carry out the attack which would disrupt and disable
the last intact force remaining to defend it. And at least enough
time had elapsed for the gunboats and kamikazes in the System
Which Must Be Defended to recover from the death shock of the
Planets Which Must Be Defended which had already died. So when
the Fleet did make transit, it was probable that there would be at
least some support for it.*

*Any other species might have reflected upon the bitter irony
which had sent the Fleet racing from one position towards another
only to find itself caught between them and unable to intervene at
either at the critical moment. But the beings which crewed the Fleet
weren't like any other species. They were as immune to irony as
they were to the concept of love or pity, and so the Fleet continued
its headlong flight from one hopeless battle towards another, and
there was only silence in the dark bowels of its ships.*

"Here they come!"

Koraaza could overhear the chatter of combat reports from
his fighter pilots to *farshathkhanaak* Raathnahrn quite clearly.
The small claw of the Khan's command station was scarcely ten
paces from Koraaza's own, and the great fang listened tautly as
the intensity of combat mounted.

The visual display was a chaotic pattern of brilliant, short-
lived stars as Third Fleet's fighter strength slashed and tore at the
incoming hurricane of gunboats.

"Break left, White Three! *Break left! Break—*" The squadron
commander's frantic warning to one of his pilots ended with the
knife-sharp abruptness of thermonuclear death, and Koraaza's grip
on the arms of his command chair tightened.

This avalanche onslaught wasn't what he'd anticipated. The
mobile units from Bug-06 had continued to flee at their maximum speed even as Kraiisahka and her task force closed in
on the inhabited world they'd abandoned. Third Fleet had cut

the distance between them almost in half before the first Bug starship disappeared abruptly through the warp point less than one standard hour before Kraiisahka's initial attack went in, but Koraaza's command had been unable to overtake them in time to prevent their successful withdrawal from the system.

He'd known that the enemy's escape from the consequences of the Shiva Option would permit it to mount an effective warp point defense, which meant his own losses would be much, much worse than they might have been, but he hadn't hesitated. This was what Third Fleet had come for—to follow the enemy wherever he fled, to meet him in battle, and to destroy him utterly. And the only way to do that was to pursue through the warp point whose location he had so considerately revealed.

Yet the Bugs hadn't done the expected. Koraaza had paused long enough for a single recon drone volley when he reached the warp point in turn, and the drones' reports had galvanized him back into immediate motion. The Bugs showed no intention of defending the warp point; instead, the starships he'd followed from Bug-06 had continued to flee at their best speed. They were already far enough from the warp point that the recon probes had experienced the utmost difficulty in locating and tracking them. But they hadn't quite managed to slip entirely out of detection range, despite their ECM, and Koraaza had no intention of allowing them to do so.

Once again, Third Fleet achieved the unheard of and made transit through a Bug warp point in the presence of the enemy without losing a single starship. There weren't even any OWPs to protect it, although it was surrounded by extensive minefields which ought to have been seeded with fortresses. The only reason Koraaza could come up with for the absence of those fortresses was that they'd been removed to cover some other, more immediately threatened warp point. If the Bugs were becoming as strapped for major combat units as all of the intelligence reports suggested, then they were probably short of OWPs, as well, and they must be moving those they still possessed to cover their most vital spots.

But Third Fleet's unprecedented immunity hadn't lasted long. The first long-range strike against the fleeing Bug starships had roared out, with murder in its pilots' eyes, but before they could make contact with their targets, the recon fighters covering the flanks of the attack formations had picked up the incredible tidal bore of gunboats thundering in to the attack.

It was the first time Koraaza or any of his personnel had seen the "Bughouse Swarm" with their own eyes, and the sight had been almost more than he could credit. He'd thought he was intellectually prepared for the reality. He'd been wrong. No one *could* be prepared until they'd actually experienced it, yet the sheer, stunning impact of that onrushing tide of destruction hadn't paralyzed him. Nor had it paralyzed his *vilka'farshatok*. They'd planned and trained to face precisely this threat ever since Raymond Prescott and Zhaarnak'telmasa first encountered it, and his pilots reacted with the instant precision of drilled, bone-deep response.

No one in Third Fleet had ever seen a dogfight a fraction as intense as the one which erupted as their strikefighters met the gunboats head-on. The Bugs had enjoyed the advantage of knowing they would encounter fighters, and they'd armed their gunboats accordingly, with heavy loads of anti-fighter missiles. The AFHAWKs had taken a grim toll of the Orion fighters, but the pilots of those fighters had sound doctrine of their own and no one in the explored galaxy—with the possible exception of their new Crucian allies—was better than an Orion in this sort of combat environment. The loss rate was entirely in Third Fleet's favor. Indeed, well over a thousand gunboats had been blown out of existence in return for scarcely two hundred fighters, but some of them had still gotten through, and *Kinaasha'defarnoo* and the *Shernaku*-class MTVs, as the largest units in Third Fleet's order of battle, had drawn the full brunt of their fury. But that, too, had been anticipated in Koraaza's battle plans and training. Third Fleet had turned its monitors into kamikaze traps, surrounded by escort vessels especially trained to coordinate with the strike-groups specifically tasked for the short range defense of the huge carriers and the fleet flagship.

No Human admiral—with the possible exceptions of Raymond Prescott or Vanessa Murakuma—would have as much as considered such tactics. TFN doctrine was explicit and unyielding on this point: fighters were responsible for long-range interceptions; starships were responsible for the close range defense against fighters or kamikazes. Above all, one kept one's own fighters out of the envelope of one's own AFHAWKs, because the possibility of friendly fire casualties became a virtual certainty if one did not.

But Orions weren't Humans. Neither Koraaza nor any of his staff officers or subordinate commanders had even considered such tactical restrictions, and because they hadn't, they'd done something no Human had ever attempted—they'd actually devised and implemented a tactical doctrine in which their own fighters operated in the very heart of their starships' defensive fire. It wasn't easy, and it didn't come without cost, for the Humans were right. The fanatical emphasis Third Fleet had placed upon training its fighter defense officers for this moment paid enormous dividends, but not even that training could prevent "friendly fire" from claiming over two dozen of the defending fighters.

Yet while those two dozen fighters and another thirty destroyed by Bug missiles were dying, the massed fire of starships and fighters destroyed another three hundred-plus gunboats. Only nine of the kamikazes actually got through, and the massive size which had marked the monitors as targets to be swarmed out of existence stood them in good stead, for their equally massive shields and armor shrugged off the impacts without significant damage.

But although the exchange rate had been overwhelmingly favorable to the Alliance, the reports of still more gunboats streaming in while the ships Third Fleet had pursued from Bug-06 halted their flight and turned to come back at Third Fleet in company with the fresh gunboat threat promised that that could change.

Koraaza settled himself more firmly in his command chair, watching his plot through slitted eyes as the incredible density of hostile icons swept towards him. He had complete confidence in his *vilka'farshatok*'s ability to defeat even this threat, but even the most confident and courageous warrior could feel wrenching pain at the price his *farshatok* would pay for their victory.

"Great Fang!"

Koraaza's head snapped around at the sudden shout. In all their years together he'd never heard Thaariahn raise his voice on duty, and sheer surprise held him for just an instant. But then he felt an even greater sense of surprise as he realized it wasn't fear he heard in his ops officer's voice. It was astonishment. Perhaps even . . . delight. And that was insane at a moment like this.

But Thaariahn seemed completely unaware that he'd just taken leave of his senses, and his very whiskers quivered as he waved a clawed hand at his own display.

"Great Fang!" he repeated. "Look at this—*look!*"

"Look at *what*, Claw of the Khan?" Koraaza demanded.

"The report from Astrography, Sir!"

"What about it?" Koraaza's attention was fixed upon the incoming threat. He truly didn't have time for the distractions of routine survey findings, although he supposed that Thaariahn's ability to focus on such matters at a time like this said a great deal for the claw's powers of concentration.

"Sir, we *know* this system," Thaariahn told him fiercely. "We have enough data now to positively identify it."

"We *what?*"

The operations officer's last statement had been enough to pull Koraaza away from the tactical plot even at a moment like this. Nor was the fleet commander alone in his reaction. At least a dozen officers turned to peer at Thaariahn in momentary astonishment before the reflexes of relentless training snapped their eyes back to where they were supposed to be.

Koraaza, on the other hand, could look anywhere he damned well pleased, and he stared at his ops officer in shock.

"We know this system," Thaariahn repeated. "Sir, it's Home Hive Two!"

"*Valkha!*" Koraaza breathed softly, and then his wide eyes narrowed. "No wonder they pulled their mobile units out of Bahg-06! Ahhdmiraaaal Muraaaaaaakuma's offensive must have succeeded in breaking through as planned—and she must have inflicted major damage on whatever forces the Bahgs had stationed here to resist her. That is why they required reinforcements—any reinforcements!—even if it meant allowing us into Bahg-06!"

The outriders of the fresh gunboat storm burst upon the perimeter of Third Fleet's combat space patrol and silent vacuum burned afresh with plasma pyres as fighters and gunboats ripped and tore at one another. The urgent tempo of the combat reports rose once more about Koraaza, and he shook himself free of his sense of wonder.

He sat back in his command chair, watching the plot as his warriors and the Bugs slaughtered one another, and his mind raced. .

Yes, Murakuma must have succeeded at least partly in her attack on the system. At the same time, she couldn't have succeeded in full, for the gunboats racing in to attack Third Fleet showed little sign of the disorientation inflicted by the Shiva Option. That wasn't to say there'd been *no* planetary bombardment, of course. It was entirely possible that Murakuma had managed to completely destroy one or more planetary populations and that the defenders had simply had sufficient time to recover from the shock before his own fleet arrived.

But it was also possible Murakuma's fleet had been badly

defeated, or even destroyed. That was unlikely, because if the Bugs had managed to do that out of their locally available forces, there would have been no need for them to summon the force he'd followed here from Bug-06. Yet it was obvious that whatever else had happened, Murakuma was no longer operating here in Home Hive Two. If she had been, the Bugs would be continuing on their course to protect their inhabited planets from *her*, not turning on Third Fleet in full fury.

He wished, suddenly and passionately, that he'd paid more attention to the routine brief on Murakuma's intentions. There'd been no reason he should have, really. After all, no one in the entire Alliance had even suspected that he and Sixth Fleet had been planning to attack exactly the same objective! But even though his recollection of her plans and objectives was much less complete than he might have liked, he knew enough of her reputation and past accomplishments to feel confident that if she'd been forced out of the star system, she'd withdrawn on her own terms and in her own good time.

Which, he decided, was an example he would do well to emulate.

"We will fall back to Bahg-06," he told Thaariahn, and sensed a ripple of shock spreading out from him. He understood it, and he allowed his eyes to sweep the rest of the flag bridge before he returned his attention to the operations officer.

"We will defeat this next wave of gunboats," he said confidently. "I have no doubt whatsoever of that, nor do I doubt that our *vilka'farshatok* will manage to defeat and destroy the Bahg mobile units if we engage them fully. But we will take losses if we press the battle at this time. At this moment, we have the strength to hold Bahg-06 against *anything* the Bahgs can throw against us, and I do not choose to take losses among our *farshatok* by pressing on in ignorance of what Sixth Fleet may already have accomplished here. There is no need for us to encounter what-ever forces remain in the star system by ourselves—not when we already know a second way into it. So we will fall back one system, and there we will dig in once more while we report what we have discovered to GFGHQ."

Understanding began to spread about him, replacing the sense of shock which had preceded it, and he bared his fangs in a hungry, predatory smile.

"We have honored our ghosts well this day, clan brothers and sisters," he told the flag bridge personnel. "We have brought them

their first *vílkñurmu*, and we have already accomplished more than
Lord Talphon anticipated we might when he agreed to allow us
to attack. But now we know where our attack leads—that our
axis of advance provides another route directly into one of the
only two home hive systems which still remain to the Bahgs. I
do not think the Strategy Board will overlook the importance of
Third Fleet a second time! And perhaps even more importantly,
we know now that this—*this!*—is the central system from which
the ships who murdered Kliean came.

"We will return, clan brothers and sisters," he said, and his low
voice was more than a mere promise and his eyes blazed. "We
will return, and on the day we do, our vengeance for Zhardok
and Masiahn will be complete."

# CHAPTER THIRTY
## Unfinished Business

"Actually, First Fang," Kthaara'zarthan said, "this is unexpected. When I requested that Waarrrmaaaasterrr Rikka return to Alpha Centauri for consultation, I never meant to imply that *you* needed to accompany him. Evidently I failed to express myself with sufficient clarity."

Ynaathar'solmaak gazed at the uncharacteristically flustered Chairman of the Grand Allied Joint Chiefs of Staff from across the latter's desk.

"You made yourself pellucidly clear as always, Lord Talphon. But Waarrrmaaaasterrr Rikka is one of my task force commanders—one in whom I have absolute confidence. As a matter of honor, I feel obligated to stand beside him if he is to be summoned onto the rug, as the Humans say."

"That's 'called on the carpet,'" Sky Marshal Ellen MacGregor supplied from her chair to Kthaara's left. "And he *hasn't* been!"

"Absolutely not," Kthaara agreed emphatically. "I remind you, First Fang, that Waarrrmaaaasterrr Rikka is more than merely the commanding officer of one of Eighth Fleet's task forces. He is also the de facto representative of an allied power to the Joint Chiefs of Staff. It is in this latter capacity that I have requested his presence here to discuss questions of strategic coordination, so that he can convey our concerns to the Star Union's Khan."

"The *Rhustus Idk*," the subject of the discussion corrected, shifting his folded wings back and forth a couple of times with a soft rustling sound. "And he is in no sense a monarch, but rather a chief executive chosen by the *Niistka Glorkhus*—the legislature."

"Sort of like the Federation prime minister," Aileen Sommers chimed in helpfully, earning a glare from the MacGregor for her pains.

"Thank you, Waarrrmaaaasterrr, Ahhdmiraaaal," Kthaara said with an urbane inclination of his head. "At any event, I hope you will be able to make him understand our position on the projected Telik operation."

"I surmised that Telik was to be the subject of this conference, Lord Talphon," Robalii Rikka sat up straighter on the species-compatible chair that had been provided. "That was the reason I asked Rear Admiral Sommers to accompany me in the hope that she can help me make *you* understand the . . . unique significance this objective holds for us. Unfortunately, it was out of the question for me and my second-in-command, Wingmaster Garadden, to simultaneously absent ourselves from First Grand Wing—excuse me, from Task Force 86. As a racial Telikan, she could have offered a valuable perspective."

"No doubt. However, I am already conversant with the history involved. Be assured that I and the other Joint Chiefs fully appreciate what the liberation of Telik has meant to the Star Union for a standard century."

"Ah, but you may not be aware of our excitement when you shared your most recent astrogation data—the data you'd acquired since Admiral Sommers' departure—and we saw the Franos System. What we were looking at wasn't immediately apparent to us. Only when we correlated your data with our own did the identification leap out at us. For we know the systems around Telik, the battlegrounds of our first war with the Demons."

Kthaara nodded in a very Human gesture which had become second nature to him after his long association with the species. It was more than merely habit in this instance, however, for it was a gesture he was confident Rikka would recognize after his long association with Aileen Sommers, whereas the ear-flick his own species used might not yet have acquired that ease of recognition.

Now that the Alliance had finished comparing the Crucians' astrogation data bases with its own, as well, the same correlation had become clear to its astrographers. Given that Raymond Prescott and Zhaarnak'telmasa hadn't had any of that data at the time, their decision not to advance from Franos to Telik had been perfectly logical. Unaware that there was any . . . domesticated species in the system to rescue—had the Alliance at the time had any policy for dealing with such situations in the first place—they'd seen no reason to divert from their main axis of advance against a warp point whose defenses they knew to be quite formidable.

Of course, they hadn't known about the closed warp point connection to the Star Union, either.

"For generations," Rikka went on, leaning forward with an intensity which caused the highest officers of the Grand Alliance to recoil almost physically, "we've lived with the knowledge that we could put a fleet into Telik at any time, without having to fight our way through a defended warp point . . . and that the risk was so terrible that we didn't dare to. *Now we do!*"

Kthaara gave the low, fluttering purr that meant the same as a human's nervous throat-clearing.

"Yes, of course, Waarrrmaaaasterrr. We are aware of Telik's history, and share your excitement over the new strategic possibilities. After all, we knew we were going to have to deal with the unfinished business of Telik sooner or later. The more economically it can be done, the better."

"But," MacGregor put in, "Telik isn't going anywhere."

"That is the essence of our position," Kthaara agreed. "There is no need to launch the attack immediately. Not while the Star Union is still heavily committed to our joint campaign against the home hive systems—and to the reduction of Rabahl."

Rikka's wings folded momentarily a little tighter in his equivalent of a Human's wince. There seemed no end to the task of cutting out the cancerous ulcer in the Star Union's vitals that was Rabahl, nor to the flow of blood from that surgery.

"It is precisely that type of wastefully brutal warp-point warfare that we plan to avoid in Telik, Lord Talphon," he said.

"But why not wait? There is no urgency. Wait until elements of the Allied fleets are available to reinforce you."

For a space, Rikka seemed to be organizing his thoughts—though the others hadn't known his race long enough to be sure. When he spoke, only Sommers recognized the effort he was putting into keeping his tone level.

"There may seem no urgency to you. You cannot understand what Telik means to us. It's too foreign to your experience, for which you should count yourselves fortunate. And I appreciate your offer of support. More, I realize that your concern and desire to minimize our own casualties by asking us to wait until you can provide that support is entirely sincere. But, as you yourselves have in effect admitted, that would take time, given your priorities. Those priorities are entirely understandable—that's your war. And we are more than willing to join in it, as my command has done and will continue to do. But Telik is part of *our* war—a war that began long before yours."

"But do you have the strength to reduce Telik on your own?" MacGregor asked bluntly.

"Our heaviest forces are, as you've pointed out, engaged against Rabahl or assigned to my Grand Wing. But we've built up a reserve of carriers and lighter battle-line units. We'd planned to use them in the Rabahl campaign. But knowing what we now know, we've assigned them to Wingmaster Shinhaa Harkka's Fifth Grand Wing, to be used against Telik . . . immediately."

Aileen Sommers looked back and forth between Rikka—calm as stone and just as immovable—and the two across the desk, who were visibly searching for the combination of words that would move him. She swallowed a time or three, then cleared her throat diffidently.

"Sky Marshal, Lord Talphon, I believe we must respect the Star Union's position on this."

They stared at her—the totally unofficial "ambassador" who still personified the Terran Federation in Crucian eyes—and she hurried on before they could remember she was also a mere rear admiral.

"It goes beyond military calculations. I know we've all heard about their century-old pledge to the Telikans. But I wonder if any of us really grasp what it means. It's . . . it's . . ."

*What do I think I'm doing?* she wondered desperately. *I'm a Survey officer, not a philosopher!*

"Lord Talphon, I'm sorry to say that I'm not really sufficiently familiar with Orion philosophy to find an exact parallel, but it's like our Human idea of the 'social contract.' It's central to their vision of what they are—what they *mean*—as a society. Now that they believe they have a fighting chance to redeem that pledge, they *have* to try. To do otherwise would be to . . . betray themselves."

In the hush that followed, Sommers felt oddly calm. *What the hell? Considering how far I've wandered from the orthodox career pathway over the last few years, they'll never promote me again anyway.* She waited for Kthaara or MacGregor to speak. But to her surprise, it was Ynaathar's snarling, skirling Orion voice that broke the silence.

"I agree with Ahhdmiraaaal Saahmerzzz. She suffers from

that curious Human reluctance to speak openly of honor which has sometimes misled the less perceptive members of the *Zhe eerlikou'valkhannaiee*, to their subsequent regret. But honor is precisely what we are dealing with here, and unlike the Ahhd-miraaaal, I *am* sufficiently familiar with the philosophy of the *Zheeerlikou'valkhannaiee* to find the parallel she seeks."

The First Fang, the highest ranking serving officer of the Khan's unified military services, looked Kthaara'zarthan straight in the eyes.

"It is a matter of *shirnask*," he said. "Not of the Star Union as a government, but of its warriors—and of *all* of its citizens—as individuals."

Kthaara sat back suddenly, and MacGregor's expression changed abruptly. Sommers was much less familiar with the precepts of the Orion honor code than the Sky Marshal had become over the last half decade, but even she knew that *shirnask*—the absolute, unwaveringly fidelity to his sworn word—was the ultimate and fundamental bedrock of any Orion's personal honor. To be called *shirnowmak*, or oath-breaker was perhaps the second worst insult any Tabby could be offered.

"We do not ask them to violate their oaths, First Fang," Kthaara said very quietly, "and if by any word, deed, or expression it has seemed that such was my intention, then for that insult to our Allies' honor, I offer personal apology. Our concern is solely that it is not possible for us to provide them with the heavy battle-line support we deem necessary for the liberation of Telik at this time, and we fear that without such support, their losses will be heavy. It is as *farshatok* to *farshatok* we speak, urging only that they hold their claws until we may strike at their side."

"I understand that, Lord Talphon," Ynaathar replied gravely, while Rikka and Sommers sat silent. "And I believe Waarrrmaaaasterrr Rikka also understands it. Yet their oath does not bind them to act when they may do so safely. It binds them to act as soon as they *can*. To delay beyond that moment would open them not only to the charge of *shirnowmak* but also to the charge of embracing *theermish*."

If MacGregor's face had stiffened when Ynaathar mentioned *shirnask*, it went absolutely expressionless when he said the word "*theermish*." *Theernowlus*, which Standard English translated as "risk bearing," was the fundamental Orion honor concept which went so far to explain the near fanaticism with which the Tabbies embraced the strikefighter. *Theernowlus* required that any Orion expose himself to the risk involved in the execution of any plan or strategy he might have devised. To send others to bear that risk while he sat by in safety was the ultimate betrayal of the *farshatok* bond. There might be instances in which the orders of a superior or some other obligation or insurmountable physical obstacle prevented him from doing so, and in those instances he was not personally guilty of *theermish*—or "risk-shirking"—but even in those instances, his honor code denied him any credit for the success of that plan or strategy, however brilliant it might have been.

"And finally," Ynaathar went implacably onward, "the oath each officer of the Star Union swears when accepting his commission requires him to embrace any sacrifice to liberate Telik at the *earliest possible moment*. And so, Lord Talphon, any delay on their part if they believe—in their own considered judgment—that they have the capacity to reclaim that star system at last, would be to commit *hiri'k'now*."

The First Fang said the final word in an absolutely neutral tone, but MacGregor inhaled audibly, and Kthaara flinched. *Hiri'k'now* was the violation of *hirikolus*, the liege-vassal military oath which bound every serving Orion officer personally and directly to his Khan. There was no worse crime an Orion could commit. Anyone guilty of it became *dirguasha*, "the beast not yet dead"—a clanless outcast and an animal who might be slain by anyone in any way.

"I tell you this," Ynaathar went on, "not to charge you with urging the Waarrrmaaaasterrr to commit such offenses, but because I believe you were not aware of all of the implications inherent in any consideration of the liberation of Telik. I was not myself aware of them, of course, before the Waarrrmaaaasterrr became *farshatok* as a task force commander in Eighth Fleet. The *Zheeerlikou'valkhannaiee* paid a heavy price—and, knowingly or unknowingly, gravely insulted the honor of the Humans—by failing to grasp the complexities of their honor code or its points of congruity with our own when first they were our enemies, and then our allies. I will not be guilty of the same blindness where the Star Union is concerned."

Kthaara and MacGregor looked at one another, and then, in unison—almost as if it had been rehearsed—the Human shrugged ever so slightly and the Orion's tufted ears flicked straight out to the sides. Then Kthaara looked back at Ynaathar and Rikka.

"Thank you for explaining the aspects of the situation which our ignorance had prevented us from fully considering, First Fang," he said gravely, and then gave his race's tooth-hidden carnivore smile, to which decades of association with Humans had lent a new and very individual quality. "And whatever our concern over the possible casualties of an ally might have been, we can scarcely prevent the Star Union from taking any action it pleases, can we? Telik, as Waarrrmaaaasterrr Rikka has reminded us, is part of *their* war. We can only attempt to urge caution, and if caution is secondary—or tertiary—to the requirements of the situation, let us turn to the practicalities of how we *can* contribute to maximizing the operation's chances of success."

"First of all," MacGregor, said "we need on-scene Alliance liaison with the Crucian attack force."

"No problem there, Sky Marshal," Sommers grinned. "As you know, the old Survey Flotilla 19 is scattered all around the Star Union to serve as training cadres and technical support. We've got people with Wingmaster Harkka at Reymiirnagar. They're headed by one of my best officers: a survey specialist who's developed some new sidelines. She's very junior for the job, as most of our people are. But her family name is one to conjure with in the TFN."

Any volume of interplanetary space was like any other, Lieutenant Commander Fujiko Murakuma thought. And the local sun, tiny across the 5.8 light-hours that separated it from the closed warp point from which they'd emerged, was a perfectly typical late type G.

But she knew better than to say that to Wingmaster Shinhaa Harkka, or to any of the other Crucians on the flag bridge. And she definitely wasn't about to say it to any of the Telikans. They all stood—none were still seated—and stared at the viewscreen in a silence which Fujiko would not have dreamed of breaking, any more than she would have interrupted a religious ceremony at which she was a guest.

Instead, she glanced at the system-scale display. The icon of Fifth Grand Wing glowed alongside that of the closed warp point, on an eight o'clock bearing from the primary. Far across the system, well over two hundred light-minutes from the primary at a bearing of four o'clock, was the system's solitary open warp point—Warp Point One, as it had been designated by the Alliance survey personnel whose RD2s had surveyed it from Franos—beyond which Vice Admiral Eustace Sung waited with the seventeen Terran light carriers and nineteen even smaller Ophiuchi escort carriers of Task Force 93. Telik itself was the second planet; its six-light-minute radius orbit had currently brought it to a five o'clock bearing.

But Fujiko only had eyes for the scarlet threat icons, reflecting the reports of the stealthed recon drones Wingmaster Harkka had already sent fanning out from his command. So far, those drones fully substantiated the downloads the ICN had relayed to GW 5 from Admiral Sung's most recent probes through the warp point. And the tale they told seemed to confirm their hopes so completely that she dared not tempt fate by voicing it.

Captain Mario Kincaid, TFMC, clearly felt no such inhibitions.

"Did it, by God!" he breathed as he gazed over her shoulder at the plot's report that every known Bug unit in the system was either at Warp Point One or in orbit around the planet. So far as GW 5's most carefully watched sensors could reveal, not a single Bug picket was in a position to note its arrival. "The damned Bugs must never've been able to nail down even an approximate location for the point!" Kincaid finished.

Fujiko sniffed, but eschewed any observations about people with a flair for stating the obvious. She should, she reflected, be grateful that the Marine had displayed the uncharacteristic restraint to speak barely above a whisper and not shatter the moment their Crucian allies were enjoying.

Kincaid, in her opinion, was a "cocky Marine" straight from Central Casting. He even affected the close-trimmed mustache favored by male officers of the Marine Raiders. *Of course*, she thought with a touch of malice for which she knew she ought to be ashamed of herself (but wasn't), *that might have something to do with the fact that he* isn't *a Raider.* Survey Flotilla 19 hadn't included any of those elite ground-assault troops, only the ships' Marine detachments. But all Marines liked to fancy themselves Raiders—including a young first lieutenant whose duties hadn't normally included anything more macho than ceremonial honor guards and routine security aboard TFNS *Jamaica*.

None of which would have bothered Fujiko, except for a certain unfortunate communications delay shortly after contact with the Federation had been reestablished. BuPers had transmitted a raft of overdue promotions . . . and Kincaid's had arrived a few standard days before hers. So for one brief shining moment—as viewed from his standpoint, anyway—they'd been equal in rank.

He'd attempted to capitalize on that status with a haste and a lack of subtlety calculated to uphold the Marine image. The attempt had, to put the matter with exquisite tact, been less than successful. Subsequently, it was through sheer bad luck that they'd both been assigned to Fifth Grand Wing. Fujiko had no intention of being the first to break the scrupulously correct behavior they'd both observed since.

*Anyway,* she told herself, *his mustache is so light you can barely see it. I'm surprised he's old enough to grow one!*

*In a way, though, it's too bad he hasn't made a better job of that mustache. He isn't really all that bad looking otherwise. That narrow waist and that tight little—*

*Stop that, you twit! He's a conceited, insufferable prick on a testosterone overdose! Just look at that self-satisfied smile of his!*

*Although sometimes it's a kind of nice smile. Boyish.*

*I said* stop *that!*

She turned with relief as Shinhaa Harkka approached.

"No sign of any activity in response to our emergence, Wingmaster," she said unnecessarily, simply to be saying something.

"No, there isn't. No surprise, really. Nevertheless, it's good to have confirmation of our supposition that this closed warp point is still unknown to them."

"Right, Wingmaster," Kincaid said, smiling. "They've got nothing on this side of the local sun—nor any reason to, from their standpoint. We can be on top of the planet before they even know we're here! This could be a virtually bloodless walkover, if it wasn't for—"

All at once, Kincaid's smile froze into embarrassed immobility.

*Nice going, Mario!* Fujiko thought, mentally gritting her teeth, but Harkka took no apparent offense.

"You're quite correct, Captain Kincaid. Nonetheless, the existence of the Telikan population *is* a fact, and it renders the so-called 'Shiva Option' out of the question . . . as you are, of course, aware."

"Of *course*, Wingmaster," Fujiko and Kincaid chorused.

"That," Harkka continued, with no sign of amusement that was visible across the gulf of species, "is the very reason we've ruled out the use of antimatter warheads against surface targets. Telik is to be a test case for dealing with Demon-occupied planets with native sentients. And we of the Star Union have, you might say, a special motivation to find a solution to this hithertofore intractable problem. We believe that, with the help of your Terran

BuResearch, we may have done so." He faced Kincaid. "As liaison officer assigned to our landing force, you'll be able to render a full report on how successful we've been."

Kincaid drew himself up an extra centimeter or two—not the most tactful thing for a human to do around Crucians—and his smile was back in full force.

"Yes, Sir!"

*Ever since the Enemy had occupied the Franos System, it had been assumed that Telik was next. But after the initial probes, no attack had materialized. It was puzzling. Those whose business it was to speculate about such things had suggested that might have something to do with the Enemy's inexplicable reluctance—observed on several occasions—to apply maximum force to planets with food sources which had previously exhibited tool-using behavior. But the hypothesis remained unproven.*

*At any rate, the most recent reconnaissance through the warp point suggested that the Enemy forces in Franos consisted entirely of light starships configured to carry small attack craft—useful for deploying those craft in a defensive role, but quite unable to survive a warp point assault.*

*So Telik remained isolated but unthreatened. The Fleet would, of course, continue to build up forces to a level limited only by the availability of crews. And a large percentage of the planet-based gunboats and small craft would be kept, on a rotating basis, at the warp point to help cover against any possible surprise attack. But there was no need for any special—*

*But wait. . . . What was this latest sensor reading . . . ?*

*No!*

The jubilation on the flag bridge at the initial strikes' success had been muted by the fact that it wasn't unexpected. Tension aboard GW 5's cloaked starships had been high as they crept cautiously across the light-minutes, concealed within the cloak of invisibility of their ECM. It had been hard for the Crucian fighter pilots to sit in their launch bays and rely on remote probes rather than their own recon fighters, but Harkka had been determined to keep his presence in the system unknown until he reached strike range of his objective. And unlike starships or recon drones, strikefighters couldn't conceal their drive signatures in cloak.

The wingmaster's caution had paid off. His unsuspected carriers had crept so close to Telik before launching that their fighters had gone in completely undetected until it was too late to mount any effective defense. They'd used their primary packs and standard nuclear warheads as precision instruments, taking out the planetary defense centers without inflicting any appreciable losses on the Telikan livestock—Fujiko gagged on the word—but also without the wholesale immolation of the Bug population in antimatter fires that would have induced psychic shock in the remainder.

No such restraints obtained in space. After the annihilation of the planetary kamikaze nests, the fighters had rearmed with antimatter loads and gone after Telik's titanic space station. But that delay had allowed the station to bring its awesome array of weapons on-line, and now the last vestiges of giddiness had departed the flag bridge as the loss figures rolled in.

Shinhaa Harkka turned away, and his expression was cast in cold iron.

"We must break off the attack," he said, and the two humans stared at him with looks of astonishment and—in Kincaid's case—pained disappointment.

"Wingmaster?" Fujiko queried.

Junior officers didn't generally rate explanations from a full admiral, which was what "wingmaster" meant. But the thinly spread SF 19 people had grown accustomed to filling roles three or more rank levels above their own, and the Crucians had grown accustomed to treating them accordingly.

"I cannot allow my fighter strength to be further depleted at this time. Our intelligence analysis, based on observations from the strike on the planetary defense centers and also the reports of our reconnaissance fighters, indicate that a substantial percentage of the planet's gunboat strength was at Warp Point One, reinforcing the mobile units there against the threat they *expected* to face. Thus, the Demons retain a substantial deep-space capability. Which is on its way here."

Fujiko glanced at the system-scale display. Yes, the scarlet icon of the deep space force was moving away from its station, on a course to intercept the planet's orbit. Her eyes went to the board showing the estimated composition of that force: only one monitor, but ten superdreadnoughts, twenty battlecruisers, and a hundred and six light cruisers. And a swarm of gunboats from the warp point defense force was *en route* to rendezvous with them.

"Wingmaster," Kincaid said, pointing at the latter, "they've weakened their warp point defenses. If we can get drones through to

Franos, maybe Admiral Sung can step up the timetable and break into the system. He's got six hundred F-4s to reinforce us!"

"But," Fujiko reminded the Marine, "he's got no heavy ships—just light carriers and escort carriers. They wouldn't last a minute in a warp point assault against the defenses the Bugs still have in place." She indicated the breakdown of those defenses: forty orbital fortresses, a hundred and eleven heavy cruisers, and sixteen suicide-rider light cruisers, to say nothing of over twenty-eight hundred armed deep-space buoys and eight thousand patterns of mines. "And," she continued, "he's got no SBMHAWKs to blast him a path through all that, because—"

"Because of the haste with which we of the Star Union organized this offensive," Harkka finished for her calmly.

"The demands of other fronts also played a part, Wingmaster," Fujiko assured him, attempting to dilute the implied criticism.

"No doubt. However, the fact remains that Admiral Sung's task force can't support us until it gets into the system—and it can't get into this system until we clear the way for it."

"Catch-22," Kincaid muttered *sotto voce.*

"Because of that," Harkka continued, "we must fight the Demon deep space force before we can turn our attention to the planet— and I prefer to do so well away from any surviving planet-based kamikazes. Excuse me while I give the necessary orders."

The wingmaster started to turn away . . . but then he paused, and his gaze lingered on the viewscreen, with the little blue dot that had been his race's seemingly unattainable goal for a standard century.

Fujiko had years of experience in dealing with Crucians. But even without it, she could have read Harkka's mind: *So near and yet so far. . . .*

Kincaid cleared his throat.

"It's only a temporary delay, Wingmaster. We'll be back as soon as we've established control of the system. The Bugs down there are living on borrowed time."

*Well, well!* Fujiko thought, impressed in spite of herself, and Harkka gave a gesture of pleased gratitude.

"Thank you. You're very understanding. And I understand *your* eagerness to turn to our real purpose in coming here." He turned away, now all business.

"I didn't think you had it in you, Captain," Fujiko murmured, and Kincaid's grin reawoke.

"Why, thank you, Commander, for what I *suppose* was a

compliment. By the way, shouldn't you be calling me 'Major'? After all, we're aboard a ship, and—"

"The Crucians don't have that tradition," Fujiko cut in coldly. "And it wasn't so much a compliment as an expression of surprise at your lapse into sensitivity—from which, I'm sure you'll recover."

"Oh, the wingmaster was right. He and I understand each other."

The Marine's eyes strayed, and he looked at the blue dot of Telik in much the same way Harkka had.

And Fujiko, too, understood. For Kincaid, that planet represented the chance to finally take part in a planetside assault out of the Marine legends on which he'd been weaned—a chance this mass butchery misnamed a war had offered in all too short supply. Of course, an excellent chance of being killed went with it . . . but only for other people. Like all young men, he was immortal.

"Maybe you do, at that," she said, in a tone very different from the one he was accustomed to hearing from her.

Not that Bugs thought that way, but those in the Telik System had very little to lose.

They came on in the now-familiar "Bughouse Swarm," with the starships englobed by gunboats and small craft, and those thousands of kamikazes made a threat which Fifth Grand Wing had to take seriously. Shinhaa Harkka commanded an impressive number of ships, but the mix of types was decidedly on the light side by the standards of today's battle fleets: no monitors, only four assault carriers, and twenty-four superdreadnoughts, as contrasted with twenty fleet carriers, sixty battleships, forty-two battlecruisers, and ninety of the heavy cruisers the TFN deemed too small for front-line service.

But if the Bugs had even greater motivation than usual—or would have, if they'd been any other race—so did the Crucians. This was the climactic moment of their history, the apocalyptic hour for which they and their parents and grandparents had spent a century preparing themselves. Fujiko had expected Harkka to broadcast some inspirational speech before battle was joined. He hadn't. It would have been superfluous.

And now she and Kincaid watched in a mixture of awe and horror that silenced even the Marine's volubility.

"This isn't war," Kincaid finally breathed. "It's . . . something else."

Fujiko nodded without being conscious she was nodding. The inborn skill of the Crucian fighter pilots was in evidence, as always, but this time it wasn't being employed in the service of rational military calculation.

"If there were a way they could eradicate every Bug *cell* in this system, they'd try to do it," she said softly.

"Without regard to losses," Kincaid agreed in an equally hushed voice.

Harkka had sent Fifth Grand Wing's entire fighter complement screaming ahead of his ships. But it wasn't so much a shield as a spear. The fighters tore into the layers of gunboats and small craft enveloping the Bug ships, burning a hole like a red-hot poker through insulation, opening a path for the ships.

There was to be no question of any long-range missile bombardment in support of the fighters, as per normal Terran or Orion tactical doctrine. No, the remaining fighters spread out, holding back the walls of the passage they'd opened against the swarming kamikazes outside it, and the two Terrans rode the flagship *Fahklid-23* into that tunnel of flame, racing toward the insanely close-range beam-weapon duel that the Crucians, with one will, sought like a sexual consummation.

Afterwards, Fujiko had only the most disjointed memories of that time of thunder.

She knew it had been real, though. Her body gave proof enough, for it ached all over. *Fahklid-23* had staggered under repeated impacts that had overloaded her inertial dampers, and they'd been tossed about in the crash frames that had prevented broken bones but not bruises. And the acrid stink of the drying sweat trapped inside her vacsuit told her she had, on some level, felt more fear than she'd been aware of, caught up as she'd been in the Crucians' near-exaltation of bloodlust.

*If you can smell yourself, then everybody else can smell you, too,* she quipped to herself wearily. Actually, she was doing *everything* wearily just now. But she fended off the encroaching demands of sleep and made herself study the display.

Fifth Grand Wing was traversing the asteroid belt that girdled Telik's sun at a fifteen light-minute radius, forging outward toward Warp Point One. There would be more Bug-killing to be done there, but it would be anticlimactic. And after the fortresses were no more, Admiral Sung would bring Task Force 93 through. . . .

"Damned good thing, too," Kincaid said, reading her thoughts. He looked more recovered than Fujiko felt, but his expression was unwontedly serious. "We can really use those fighters after the losses we've taken."

"That's for sure. When we return to Telik, the Warmaster's decided—thank God!—to stand off and take out the space station with fighter strikes. And we'll need cover against any surviving kamikazes that might be lurking around."

The last wisps of Kincaid's fatigue evaporated, and his eyes lit up.

"Yes . . . when we return to Telik!"

Fujiko observed his eagerness with amusement—and with a trace of an emotion whose exact nature she found frustratingly difficult to define, but which included worry.

# CHAPTER THIRTY-ONE
## "We're going home."

Most humans would probably have seen something funny about a room full of koala bears in military uniforms rising to attention.

Captain Mario Kincaid, TFMC, didn't. Like everyone else in Survey Flotilla 19, he'd come to know the Telikans.

Admittedly, they *did* look rather like gray-furred koalas, albeit large and long-armed ones. And while their clothing belonged to no human sartorial tradition, it was obviously a uniform. The multi-species Star Union allowed a variety of tailoring that accommodated its full bewildering range of bodily forms. But rank insignia and color schemes were universal, and the officers who stood respectfully as Pinionmaster Haradda Brokken entered wore the black with green trim of the Ground Wing.

And they were all Telikans. The race accounted for a disproportionate percentage of the Ground Wing—the Star Union's planetary-assault arm, for which the Crucians themselves were physically unsuited. But they made up *all* of the force that was to commence the liberation of Telik. Nobody in the entire Star Union had disputed the rightness of that.

As for Kincaid, he contented himself with a certain satisfaction that they were coming to attention for Brokken with a snap that would almost—not quite, of course—have won the approval of his OCS drill instructor. The Telikans derived no such tradition, nor any military fetishes of any sort, from their own planet-bound history of matriarchal herbivorousness. Encountering the Bugs had done wonders for their pacifism, however, and now that they had a role model in the Terran Federation Marine Corps, the only equivalent of the Union Ground Wing they'd ever known, they'd taken to its customs and usages with the enthusiasm of neophytes. Indeed, Marine officers as high-ranking as these wouldn't have been coming to attention like recruits, even for a lieutenant general, which was approximately what "pinionmaster" meant. (SF 19's linguists had had to reach a bit for Standard English equivalents of some of the Crucian rank titles.)

Brokken, though, was too old a dog to learn the new Terran tricks. She merely waved her officers back to their seats, without saying "as you were" or some such. Then she drew herself up to her full one hundred and seventy-five centimeters—tall for a Telikan, even a female—and gripped the sides of the lectern.

"This is our final conference. Wingmaster Harkka has declared the Telik System secured. Our Terran allies have taken over the responsibility for maintaining fighter cover and hunting down any surviving Demon craft that may still be lurking in the outer system. So, with uncontested control of orbital space now firmly established, we have the go-ahead to commence planetary assault operations."

There was no sound. An emotion for which "anticipation" was too drab a word communicated itself throughout the large chamber without the need for vocalization. Even Kincaid felt the tingle. He wondered what the Telikans felt.

They were aboard one of the transports which had joined Harkka's battered fleet in orbit after the Bug space station had finally died under long-range bombardment. An interorbital shuttle had brought Kincaid here from the flagship. He'd been *en route*, with the big blue marble of Telik below, before guiltily realizing that in his excitement he'd barely noticed Fujiko Murakuma's uncharacteristically gentle farewell.

*I suppose I must've said something back*, he told himself. *But I can't for the life of me remember what.*

Once he'd arrived aboard the transport, he hadn't been surprised to find Brokken already there. The transport had no command-and-control facilities, but none were needed. The pinionmaster wasn't going to direct this assault from orbit. As *talnikah*, or field CO, she was going down—age, rank, and all—with her troops. That was how the Union Ground Wing's combat mamas—it had been a long time since any Terran Marine had used the officially approved translation "battle mothers"—did things. And even if it hadn't been, Kincaid very much doubted that even a direct order could have kept Brokken in orbit, gazing down at the world of her ancestors while others fought for it.

Now she activated a holo display of that world, and they all studied the symbology that adorned it. Black crosses marked the sites of the Bugs' former planetary defense centers with grim finality. But the room's attention was focused on certain green circles scattered about the planet's fertile areas.

"As you all know," Brokken resumed, "the objective of our initial landing is to secure the Telikan population centers." Naturally, she didn't use any such term as *ranches.* "We believe our ten divisions, spearheaded by the Special Landing Force, will suffice for this purpose, given the Star Wing's success at mapping the locations of these . . . concentrations from orbit." She met Kincaid's eyes—the only non-Telikan eyes in the room. "And, of course, given the tools with which our Terran allies have supplied us."

Kincaid replied to her look with a smile and an inclination of his head which he hoped conveyed his appreciation. At the same time, he found himself wishing Fujiko were present. *She* would have produced something elegantly diplomatic like . . .

"BuResearch merely acted on the Union Ground Wing's creative suggestion, Pinionmaster," he said.

*Not bad, if I do say so myself,* he thought as Brokken inclined her own head in acknowledgment. *I even remembered to use her rank title. I haven't earned the right—yet—to address her as* talnikah.

Still, a stubborn honesty made him admit that he'd merely said what he knew Fujiko *would* have said. And besides, it was no more than the truth.

The Ground Wing had been deeply impressed by the TFMC's hypervelocity missiles—as Kincaid knew, having been one of those who'd introduced them to the concept. Essentially, the HVM was simply a tiny, man-portable drive coil that could accelerate to a perceptible fraction of light-speed in effectively zero time. In pre-drive-field days, when six or seven thousand meters per second had been recognized as the maximum velocity any material projectile could attain in Old Terra's atmosphere before burning up from fiction, the notion would been self-evidently preposterous. But the HVM could sustain a drive field for the infinitesimal fraction of a second in which its flight time was measured. On impact, with its inconceivable kinetic energy concentrated by the field even as it yielded it up, it needed no warhead.

It wasn't new technology. In fact, it had been around for the better part of a century and a half. But, the Union Ground Wing had innocuously asked, was there any reason why a larger, more powerful version of the same system couldn't be built . . . and used from orbit?

A lot of people in the Federation were still kicking themselves as they wondered why nobody had ever thought of that before.

*Maybe Fujiko's right*, Kincaid reflected. She'd spoken, in one of their rare unguarded moments, of the way a society suddenly introduced to a more advanced technology could sometimes produce fresh insights on that technology's potential applications. She'd cited her father's ancestral nation on Old Terra, but Kincaid could never remember its name.

Be that as it might, BuResearch had responded with a will, developing the prototype of the kinetic interdiction strike system, or KISS, and putting it into production in time for this offensive by adapting existing small-craft drive coils. True to the "if it works, it's obsolete" philosophy Terran engineers had espoused for the last four centuries, they were already promising a more capable and flexible version. But the Star Union hadn't been disposed to wait.

Brokken punched in a new command, and large-scale maps of the target areas appeared on the room's flat screen.

"You already have the coordinates of your assigned landing zones." Another command, and cross-hatchings marked the LZs. "Talonmaster Voroddon, I assume that your Special Landing Force is ready."

Nanzhwahl Voroddon came to attention, which only brought his head up to a hundred and twenty centimeters. Gender equality was one of the social changes that had overtaken the Telikan diaspora, for the race's once submissive males had demanded—and gotten—the right to join in what Captain Hafezi had once called the *jihad* against the Demons. It was still unheard of, however, to find one holding a rank equivalent to major general and commanding what amounted to a special forces division—Fujiko had once said something about a "glass ceiling," which Kincaid hadn't understood, history not being exactly his subject. He decided it was safe to assume that Voroddon was one very tough and capable Telikan male.

The Union Ground Wing's divisional organization was much like the TFMC's, and had been even before they'd encountered SF 19. In Terran terminology, each division had three regiments, each consisting of three battalions: one powered combat armor, one light infantry, and one a mix of special weapons and vehicles, most notably armored skimmers. By detaching one powered armor battalion from each of her ten divisions, Brokken had created the equivalent of an overstrength division that was all powered armor, and put Voroddon in charge of forging it into the Special Landing Force that would hit the ground first.

"Yes, *Talnikah*," the talonmaster replied to her question.

"Excellent." Brokken was a female of the old school, and there was something in her voice and body language that was . . . not "patronizing" or "protective," exactly. Just not quite what it would have been if Voroddon had been female. "After you've secured the landing zones, the subsequent waves will commence their descent, under heavy fighter cover. I will accompany them—as will our liaison officer."

Kincaid ordered himself not to pout. They'd been over this before, and he couldn't really dispute the decision's logic. Still . . .

"I would welcome the opportunity to participate in the initial descent on the surface, Wingmaster."

"I have no doubt of that, Captain Kincaid, and I mean no reflection on your courage. Rather, I speak of political reality. It's out of the question to risk the Terran Federation's observer in the first wave."

"Of course, Wingmaster." *Besides*, Kincaid admitted to himself, reluctantly and just a little bitterly, *I'm not really a Raider. Voroddon doesn't need somebody to nursemaid.*

"Very well, then. You all have the detailed operational timetable in your own data files."

Brokken paused. She'd never been given to drama. But, just for a moment, she stepped out of character long enough to lean forward, hold all the other large dark Telikan eyes with her own, and speak the simple sentence they and their exiled ancestors had been waiting a Terran century to hear:

"We're going home."

It was the stench that hit Kincaid first.

Over the centuries, space travelers had become blase about the variety of planetary environments the warp points had made accessible. Of course, it helped that most people—even most military people—normally experienced none but Earth-like worlds. The necessary parameters of a life-bearing planet allowed for only a limited range of variation. Within that range, no one but the rawest of newbies even commented on gravity, sunlight quality, atmospheric pressure, color of vegetation, nearness of horizon ... or odors.

Kincaid had expected it to be the same here. Telik was a perfectly Earth-like world: a little closer to a somewhat less luminous sun, its moon a little smaller and further out, but nothing really noticeable. He was telling himself that as the assault shuttle grounded and its hatch sighed open to admit rather hot, humid air—they were in the subtropics, and it was this hemisphere's summer. He hitched up his battle dress and began to follow Brokken and her staffers outside. There was the inevitable adjustment to a somewhat different air pressure, and he drew a breath before opening his mouth to pop his ears. . . .

Sheer, desperate determination not to lose face before the Telikans prevented him from throwing up.

*What godawful chemical have they* got *in this atmosphere, anyway?* he wondered from the depths of his nausea. His head spun, and he nearly lost his balance. He steadied himself against the short solid bulk of a Telikan in the crowded aisle—he hadn't noticed before just how crowded it was—and mumbled an apology through teeth that were tightly clenched to hold the rising tide of vomit behind them in check. *And why the hell didn't they* warn *me?*

But then he noticed that the Telikan to whom he'd apologized didn't look all that well herself.

And he finally recalled where he'd smelled such a fetor before.

Once, as a young second lieutenant, he'd pulled some groundside time on the noted beef-producing planet of Cimmaron. On a certain hot day, he'd chanced to come near what the locals called the *stockyards*.

This wasn't really the same, of course. Telikan shit didn't smell precisely like the bovine variety. But there was the same effect of too much of it, produced by thousands and thousands and thousands of herd animals packed into too small a space, listlessly defecating whenever and wherever the need took them and uncaringly leaving it for the heat to work on.

Emerging from the hatch into the open air should have been a relief from the shuttle's stuffiness. But the odor was even worse. And there was the *sound.* . . .

Looking around, Kincaid located its source. To the west, the land rose toward a mountain range. There, through the swathes high-tech firepower had torn in the subtropical vegetation, he could glimpse in the middle distance a kind of smudge against the foothills: a series of vast enclosures and low buildings. Something else he remembered from Cimmaron came from that direction: the collective sound of multitudes of dumb, doomed animals. But this wasn't really that kind of mindless lowing. The thousands of throats that produced it were Telikan ones, possessing the same kind of vocal apparatus as his comrades-in-arms because they belonged to the same species. And it held a subtle, indescribable, and deeply disturbing undercurrent of sentience, of something that cattle would mercifully never know.

The staffers around him looked even sicker than Kincaid felt. He reminded himself of the human colonies the Bugs still held after a mere few years . . . and his gorge rose again. He looked frantically around for something—anything—to concentrate on instead.

The sky was clear, and combat skimmers crisscrossed in their patrol patterns. At higher altitudes, armed assault shuttles did the same. Still more shuttles were descending in a steady procession, pouring the follow-up waves into the secured landing zones as rapidly as possible. On the ground, the entire perimeter was a hive of activity as Brokken's forces dug in. Nearby, although the Telikans didn't go in for formal honor guards, a number of Voroddon's troopers were in evidence.

The concept of powered combat armor wasn't new to the Union Ground Wing. SF 19 had found them using versions reminiscent of Theban War-era models in their clunky massiveness. Now they wore sleeker, more nearly form-fitting ones—Telikan-tailored equivalents of the TFMC's "combat zoots," as they'd been dubbed long ago by some aficionado of twentieth century popular culture. Now Voroddon, in battle dress himself, at the moment, advanced through a loose formation of zooted troops, clearly for security rather than for show. He gave Brokken the fist-to-chest salute of a race whose arms were so long they'd have done too much damage with their elbows if they'd tried the Terran kind.

"Welcome, *Talnikah*. I apologize for . . ." Voroddon gave a vague, all-encompassing gesture. "I would have preferred to direct your shuttle to a landing site further away from—"

"Don't worry, Talonmaster. Safety considerations were naturally paramount. Besides, we'd all have had to experience it sooner or later anyway." Brokken glanced westward at the obscene blot on the landscape, and hastily looked away again. "Are matters progressing satisfactorily . . . over there?"

"Well enough. We've gotten an organization in place. Unfortunately, I've had to detail more of my troops than I'd planned to for guard duty there, simply to prevent stampedes. You see, they're very . . . confused. The idea of beings shaped like themselves with the kind of powers that, by definition, only the Demons possessed is simply outside their frame of reference. We've had to deal with some actual . . . well, not resistance; they were too frightened for that. More a matter of terrified reluctance to leave their pens. And we haven't wanted to hurt them by forcing them."

Kincaid thought back to half-forgotten military history classes and recalled what the terrorism-ridden late twentieth century had called the "Stockholm Syndrome." This was worse. Much worse.

"Well," Brokken assured Voroddon, "now you'll be able to turn that sort of duty over to the regular infantry, and the specialists."

"Thank you, *Talnikah*! In addition to the diversion of power-armored resources, it's been hard on my personnel's morale. There are so many. . . ." Voroddon's expression wavered, and he tried again. "So many little ones."

*Of course,* Kincaid thought. *Among the Telikans, it's always been the males who've brooded the eggs the females laid . . . and raised the young.*

He watched as Brokken, in a spontaneous gesture, reached down and gave Voroddon's shoulder a hard, steadying squeeze.

The moment passed.

"Well," Brokken said, "let's proceed with the briefing I'm sure your staff has prepared for me."

"Of course, *Talnikah*. My headquarters bunker is this way."

As they walked across the newly cleared area, Kincaid hastened ahead of the gaggle of staffers—no great feat for a human, since Telikans' legs were short even in proportion to their stature—and drew abreast of the two flag officers.

"I presume there are no new reports from other landing zones?" he overheard Brokken ask.

"No. The situation's essentially unchanged since you departed from orbit. As you know, our initial landings enjoyed complete tactical surprise. That, and our fighter cover, enabled us to secure all our initial objectives."

"Yes, you did well. But what about the Demons?"

"We've been able to interdict everything they've thrown at us from long range. As of now, their behavior is as expected from the records we've all seen of the Terrans' experience in the Justin System. They're moving toward all the landing zones in massive columns, concentrating for what we anticipate will be coordinated planetwide counterattacks."

Kincaid spoke up, his privileged status as liaison officer empowering his natural *chutzpah*.

"One thing I don't understand, Talonmaster. Knowing those columns' location from orbital surveillance, why haven't you called in KISS strikes on them?"

He gestured upward toward low orbit, where a dozen *Buurtahn*-class ships—minelayers built on battlecruiser hulls—traced a pattern calculated to maintain coverage of the landing zones. One of the KISS system's virtues was that, like mines, the projectiles could be deployed from simple cargo holds, each of which could accommodate five thousand of them. And each *Buurtahn* had fifteen such holds.

"If we strike them too soon," Voroddon explained, "they'll disperse so as to present less tempting targets. No, we want them to complete the concentration of their forces." An odd, dreamy look came over the talonmaster. "Oh, yes, indeed we do."

They were in the command bunker when the attack rolled in—and the prepared fire zone beyond the perimeter quite simply exploded.

The outside view polarized automatically before Kincaid's eyes could be more than temporarily dazzled, as opposed to permanently blinded. At perceptibly the same instant, the concussion almost threw him and the bunker's other occupants off their feet. Steadying himself, he turned to peer through the dust that suddenly hovered in two bands—one just beneath the bunker's ceiling, the other at floor level—at one of the visual displays that showed what was happening at another of the LZs, on Telikan's nightside, as viewed from low orbit.

Ever since the hypervelocity missile had first been introduced, people had been remarking that it looked the way pre-space Terrans had assumed a "death ray" would look. Actual lasers didn't; they left a crackling trail of ionized air that was visible, at least at night, but the effect was pretty unspectacular—those old science-fiction fans would have been sadly disappointed. An HVM, though, tearing through atmosphere at c-fractional velocity, was to all appearances a solid (if momentary) bar of lightning, dazzling in the dark.

As Kincaid watched, the trail of KISS projectiles a *Buurtahn* had left as it orbited were activated, going instantly to just under ten percent of light-speed. Such velocity was, of course, not perceptible as motion. Instead, as the hundreds of drive coils entered atmosphere, a dazzling curtain of fire seemed to appear. Where that curtain's hem touched the nighted planetary surface, that surface erupted in a line of terrible white light, far too intense to be called mere "flame."

Kincaid turned back to the outside view, where the aftereffects of the same kind of bombardment were dying down sufficiently to permit damage assessment. Each KISS strike released the kinetic energy of a tactical nuke—but precisely targeted, and without the radioactive contamination that made wholesale use of nuclear and antimatter weapons out of the question on worlds like Telik. The areas around the Ground Wing's lodgements had been seared as clean of the local ecology as they had been of Bug attackers—but that ecology would grow back, unmutated.

The Bugs wouldn't.

Brokken looked out at the swirling tonnes of dust that hid the devastation beyond the perimeter. The abruptly released thermal pulse had birthed almost cyclonic winds, which continued to howl outside the bunker, drowning out the terrified wailing of the thousands of rescued Telikans in the shelters into which they'd been herded.

"Talonmaster Voroddon," she said in a voice of flint, "as soon as outside conditions permit, we will advance as planned. Please ask your communications officer to put me in contact with Wing-master Harkka."

Brokken's entire ten divisions were now dirtside, and without waiting for the reinforcements beginning to arrive in the system—a multiracial ground force that would eventually number over a million—she went on the offensive behind a rolling barrage of KISS strikes that obliterated the Bug population centers and smashed any troop concentration that stood in the way.

Still the Bugs came on in their silently suicidal way, which not even years of familiarity could fully rob of its power to horrify. The warriors came intermingled with millions of workers, a mass of mute, uncaring flesh in which much of the Ground Wing's firepower was uselessly absorbed. They poured in nuclear warheads in attempts to swamp the defensive energy-weapon fire by sheer numbers, for even one nuke could do horrible damage if it got through. And any time their ground forces managed to come to grips with the Telikans, the latter had to fight them in the old-fashioned way, for under such circumstances not even KISS could be targeted precisely enough. The Ground Wing was prepared to accept a certain number of casualties from friendly fire, but however determined they might be to achieve victory at any cost, they weren't Arachnids.

So Brokken's forces advanced in open order to avoid offering tightly bunched targets for nukes, under air cover from combat skimmers and assault shuttles with HVM pods. The powered-armor troops led the advance, backed by armored fighting vehicles. The light infantry, in regular battle dress and unpowered body armor, followed; they had no business in the front lines against massed Bugs, as the TFMC had learned at Justin.

Brokken herself rode in Voroddon's divisional command vehicle, comparable to the TFMC's Cobra. Kincaid was there, too, studying a planetary holo display in which the green of the secured areas was steadily expanding as the offensive rolled on, and would keep expanding until Telik was a globe of emerald. But the expansion was uneven, for fighting was still heavy.

All at once, that heavy fighting left the realm of the abstract as the forward units reported contact with a fresh Bug force, better concealed than most. KISS support was called for, and blast shields clanked into place around the viewports barely in time to shut out of the glare as the Bugs' rear elements died. But the leading waves came on, already far too close to be targeted with something as . . . energetic as KISS, and a phalanx of the heavily armed and armored helicopters the Bugs favored rose from camouflaged sites in the subtropical forest to support them.

Orders went out as the command vehicle ground to a halt behind the ground fighting that erupted ahead. Assault shuttles screamed in, cutting swathes through the helicopters with HVMs. But that kept them from the work of lacerating the oncoming waves of Bugs on the ground with anti-personnel cluster-bombs. Likewise, the special-weapons units were kept busy interdicting the tactical missiles that sleeted overhead with their cargoes of nuclear death. It was left to the Telikan grunts to bear the brunt of the ground assault, and a tidal wave of Bugs crashed into them.

*No,* Kincaid corrected his thought, *not Bugs. Demons. That's how they see them.*

*And who's to say they're not right?*

His mental paralysis shattered into a million shards of panic as the cry came: "*Incoming!*"

One of the Bug helicopters had gotten through, only to take a glancing hit from one of the nearby fire support teams. Now it was visible above the trees, trailing smoke and losing altitude . . . and getting larger, for it was headed straight for the command vehicle.

"Get out!" someone shouted.

Kincaid scrambled to obey, but staggered back as he banged his helmet on the overhead—always easy to do in this Telikan-designed jalopy. He shook his head to clear it, and flung himself through the hatch. He emerged into the hellish noise and rotor-wash of the descending chopper, which smashed into the command vehicle just as he hit the ground a mere few meters away. He landed with a numbing force but managed a clumsy, sliding roll and staggered shakenly to his feet.

Bugs poured forth from the broken chopper as though in some obscene childbirth.

Aliens were nothing new to Kincaid, and he'd spent the last few years getting acquainted with whole new species he'd never imagined. But now, seeing the Bugs firsthand, he felt something even the optopoid Zarkolyans had never aroused in him: a dizzying, gut-wrenching sense of *wrongness*, as though he were looking at something that had no business existing in any sane universe.

Bugs and Telikans ripped each other apart at point-blank range, where the latter's zoots availed little against armor-piercing rounds, and he fumbled for his side arm. But his desperately grasping hand found only empty air where the holstered pistol should have been. He must have lost it when he hit the ground, and he watched in horror as a Bug bore down on a crumpled figure on the ground he recognized as Brokken. Someone else put a shot into the Bug, but it didn't even seem to notice as it continued to advance on its six flashing legs, charging towards the helpless pinionmaster, and there was nothing Kincaid could do.

But Voroddon was there, too. The range was too short for weapon fire. Instead, the zooted talonmaster flung himself bodily on the Demon, and, grasping two of the appendages, heaved in opposite directions.

Any other time or place, Kincaid would have been sick as the Bug's carapace parted, torn open by the myoelectric strength of the zoot's "muscles," and a gush of fluids and internal organs washed over Voroddon.

But then a second Bug was there, bringing a weapon into line. As Kincaid staggered forward in what seemed slow motion, a burst of fire ripped through Voroddon and his victim alike.

Without thinking, Kincaid reached for his boot and unsheathed his combat knife. He flung himself across the last few meters, driving the knife into what he remembered from long-ago briefings was a vulnerable point of the body-pod. The Bug writhed, and one of its hard, segmented legs lacerated his left thigh. He gasped in pain, but drove the knife deeper and yanked viciously upward. The nauseating fluids that had drenched Voroddon spurted before he could finish his gasp, and he choked on them. For a time, he could do nothing but be sick, again and again. Luckily, he landed on top of the dying Bug, rather than vice versa.

By the time he got shakily up, it was over. Zooted Telikans stood among a scattering of dead Bugs, and Brokken was limping over to that which had been Voroddon. She knelt over the crumpled talonmaster, lying half under a Bug carcass that would have crushed him but for his armor. She waved a medical orderly away and sank awkwardly to the ground, where she gazed for a long, silent moment through the male Telikan's blood-spattered faceplate. Very gently, she touched the side of the helmet. Then she finally accepted help in rising to her feet and turned to face Kincaid.

"I regret placing you in danger, Captain. But I can't be sorry you were present, for I owe you my life."

"Think nothing of it . . . *Talnikah*."

Neither Brokken nor any of the other Telikans made any objection.

A Terran month passed before the surface of Telik was deemed sufficiently secured for Wingmaster Haradda to land there. Not every Bug on the planet was dead—it would probably take a long time indeed to hunt them all down, through every nook and cranny of a planet of the size of Old Terra, and they would live on far longer in the monster stories this world's infants would be told, but the warrior caste's resistance had been broken.

The shuttle landed on the outskirts of what had once been Telik's planetary capital. Not that there was anything to see—the vegetation had had a century to take over the ruins a nuclear strike had left of the city, and only historical records had enabled them to locate the site from orbit. But the symbolism was there.

As Harkka descended the ramp, Brokken stepped forward with only the slight stiffness that still remained in her walk. She saluted with great formality, but her words went far beyond any military punctilio in their very simplicity.

"Welcome home, Wingmaster."

Afterwards, Harkka's staff followed the wingmaster out of the shuttle. Fujiko Murakuma was with them.

She spotted Mario Kincaid among Brokken's staffers, and hurried over. What she saw as she neared the Marine took her aback. He seemed far more than a month older.

"Well," she cracked, "you got your wish. Even picked up a wound!"

"So I did," he said shortly, and she cocked her head.

"What's with you? No adolescent attempt at a pass? I should probably feel insulted! Besides, I should think you'd be jumping for joy under the circumstances."

A wraith of Kincaid's old impudent grin awakened.

"Yeah, I suppose I should. In fact, I *definitely* should be happy for the Telikans, and I am. It's just . . . well, we took casualties. A lot of casualties."

"Yes, I know." Fujiko bit her lip, and her brow furrowed. "I know, and I shouldn't have been flippant. But . . ." All at once, she could no longer contain her excitement. "Mario, don't you understand the implications of what's happened here?"

"Uh . . . you mean the way the Bugs became less combat effective toward the end? Yeah, that's news the Alliance is going to want to hear," he agreed.

It turned out that the Shiva Option effect didn't actually require the *instantaneous* annihilation of massive Bug populations. The effect appeared to be cumulative, and began to snowball once a certain threshold was reached, although there was still some question about how many millions of deaths that threshold required.

"Oh, yes," Fujiko replied. "That's certainly new data. But don't you *see*? The important thing is that KISS performed as advertised! The Crucians and Telikans have found the answer to the moral quandary we've been in ever since Admiral Antonov discovered Harnah!"

Enlightenment came, and Kincaid's private darkness began to lift.

"You mean the question of what to do about Bug planets with surviving indigenous sentients?"

"Yes! We no longer have to choose between nuking a planet till it glows or suffering unacceptable losses on the ground. The Bugs can't hide behind populations of hostages any longer!" Fujiko could no longer contain herself. Face shining with a fierce joy, she grasped him by the shoulders and spoke with an intensity that—he forced himself to remember—was a product of her need to share what she'd just realized with someone of her own species. "Oh, Mario, for the first time I know—not just hope or even believe, but really *know*—that we're going to win this war, and win it without having to damage our souls!"

"Our souls," the Marine said slowly, the clouds closing over his sunny smile once again, "may already be more damaged than we know."

She looked at him sharply. This wasn't like him. Not at all, but she forbore from trying to jolly him. *What do I know about it? How can I know the things he's seen down here?*

She gazed at him a moment longer, and then—somehow—the right words were given to her, and she flung out an arm and swept it around a half-circle that took in all of Telik.

"It's over here, Mario," she told him softly. "That's the point. Soon, it's going to be over *everywhere*. This war is finally coming to an end. The Telikans, and their children—and *all* our children—are going to live in a universe cleansed of the Bugs!"

Kincaid's private clouds parted again. This time they stayed parted.

# CHAPTER THIRTY-TWO
## Cushion Shot

To Vanessa Murakuma, the 4.8 light-hour-distant dot of white brilliance that was Home Hive Two A as viewed on emergence from Warp Point One was getting to be an old . . . not "friend," certainly, but perhaps the word "acquaintance" was permissible.

In one respect, though, this transit from Orpheus 1 was different from her previous two. It was almost unopposed.

Not altogether, of course. As her probes had indicated, the Bugs had abandoned any hope of mounting a full-dress crustal defense after the losses they'd taken in starships and orbital fortresses. But they'd continued to patrol the warp point with planet-based gunboats—lots of them, many equipped with jammer packs.

But Murakuma had anticipated that. She'd employed SBMHAWKs with devastating prodigality, then sent her own gunboats from Force Leader Maahnaahrd's Task Force 62 through to deal with the survivors before allowing her starships to commence transit.

So Sixth Fleet stood in these now-familiar spaces undepleted in its starship strength: eleven monitors, seventy-one super-dreadnoughts, eighteen battleships, thirty-four assault carriers, twenty-four fleet carriers, and seventy-six battlecruisers in the three primary task forces. Small Fang Meearnow's *Mohrdenhau-*class light carriers provided additional fighter support, and were escorted in turn by ten battlecruisers, thirty light cruisers and twenty destroyers. Also under Meearnow's command was Commodore Paul Taliaferro's Task Group 64.1: eleven *Guerriere-C*-class command battlecruisers, thirty-one combat tugs of the *Turbine-B* and *Wolf 424* classes (built on battlecruiser and battleship hulls respectively), and twenty-four massive freighters, including nine of the *Krupp-A*-class mobile shipyards.

Murakuma smiled as she contemplated Taliaferro's command. The Bugs might well wonder what such an oddly constituted formation—all those command ships in a task group that didn't even include any other combatants—was doing amid a battle fleet. They'd have a while yet to wonder, but it would become clear in the end. Essentially, the rest of Sixth Fleet was here to protect TG 64.1 as it set up what Murakuma had had in mind when she'd quipped to her staffers—human, so most of them had understood—that "it's time for a cushion shot."

Her smile deepened as she recalled the hardcopy that rustled against her rib cage where it lay inside her tunic. Indeed, it was all she could do to avoid chuckling at Fujiko's references to a certain Marine captain—references whose disdain was exceeded only by their frequency. The message's Terran Standard date was December 9, 2369, for Fujiko had sent it from Telik just after the liberation of that tragic world. Now that the Star Union was hooked into the local interstellar communications network at the Telik-Franos warp point, that message had taken less than one full standard day—twenty-three hours and twenty-two minutes, to be precise—to reach her across the real-space light-minutes between the light-year-distant stars. It was more wonderful than Murakuma could have expressed to have her daughter so close, figuratively speaking, at last, but she didn't allow herself to dwell upon it at this particular moment. She had other things to think about, for it was now late December and Sixth Fleet was here in Home Hive Two again, for what they confidently hoped would be the last time, awaiting Third Great Fang Koraaza's Third Fleet and wondering—

"Where *is* Third Fleet?"

Murakuma sighed at Leroy McKenna's irritable ejaculation. This wasn't the first time she'd heard it, from the chief of staff and others as well, and she set her persona on "soothing" mode.

"Remember the time lag, Leroy. We're thirty-six light-minutes away from Warp Point Two."

"I haven't forgotten, Sir. But we've been here long enough—especially with our recon fighters deployed in the direction of Warp Point Two—to have picked up Lord Khiniak's signal, if he were here to send it."

"Communications between us and Third Fleet have been incredibly roundabout even with the ICN. Yes, the plan called

for both fleets to enter this system simultaneously. But..."
Murakuma stopped herself short of the patronizing lecture on
military history Tadeoshi would probably have delivered, with
emphasis on the words "Leyte Gulf." McKenna was well aware
of the difficulty of coordinating widely separated forces. "If Lord
Khiniak had really made transit at precisely the same time we
did, it would have restored my faith in miracles! Let's give him
a little longer before we start panicking."

"Aye aye, Sir," McKenna clearly wasn't happy, but just as clearly
he understood the force of Murakuma's argument.

Murakuma sensed the unhappiness, but it wasn't blatant enough
to merit a rebuke. Instead, she leaned close enough to speak
privately.

"I *know* he'll come, Leroy. And so do you."

"How long do we wait, Sir?" McKenna's question might have
been regarded as truculent. Murakuma knew it wasn't. The chief
of staff was raising a legitimate point.

"I'll decide that. For now, we'll use the time to shake down the
fleet and resolve any organizational issues that may exist. When
Third Fleet appears, we'll be *ready*."

"Aye aye, Sir."

In the end, it took less time than Murakuma had feared
before the signals of Lord Khiniak's emerging ships began to
impinge on Sixth Fleet's electronic consciousness. Ignoring the
excitement around her, and carefully concealing her relief, she
turned to the flag bridge's system-scale holo sphere, where the
green icon of Third Fleet was blinking into life at Warp Point
Two, a hundred and twenty degrees counterclockwise from Warp
Point One's bearing and 4.2 light-hours from the primary. The
incoming data indicated that Koraaza'khiniak was encountering
the same kind of limited resistance as she had, and was dealing
with it in the same way. No surprise. RD2 findings and logic
alike had suggested that the Bugs wouldn't try to contest the
warp point. No, they'd pull back within medium-to-close range
of the three inhabited planets and exact the highest possible
price from any who violated those spaces.

Not that Murakuma and Koraaza had any intention of paying
it. That was what Taliaferro was here for with his curiously constituted task group. And it was why the Bugs were about to watch,
with whatever degree of surprise they were capable of feeling, as
the two invading fleets proceeded toward their rendezvous—*away*
from those planets.

Murakuma's eyes went to the halo of tiny lights that girdled the central sun-icon—a very wide halo, well outside the orbits of the inhabited planets. Twenty-four light-minutes was uncommonly far from a sun to find an asteroid belt; normally, a Jupiter-sized gas giant coalesced just outside the outermost limits of the liquid-water zone, gravitationally aborting planet formation just inside it and leaving a trail of planetoidal rubble to mark what would have been the orbit of an unborn world. But, as astronomers had been learning for centuries, the rules of planetography were made to be broken. The brutally massive Home Hive Two B had somehow formed at a forty light-minute orbital radius, and the result was the stream of glowing dust motes in the sphere towards which Sixth and Third Fleets were bound. When they met, Murakuma would assume overall command of the combined fleets—a truly massive array of killing machinery with the addition of Third Fleet's two hundred and forty starships.

Leroy McKenna followed the admiral's eyes and read her thoughts.

"I wonder what the Bugs will think?" he murmured.

*The staggered arrival of the two Enemy forces, while somewhat unexpected, was of no material advantage to the Fleet given the decision to make no attempt to contest the outer system. Instead, the Deep Space Force was to interpose itself between the invaders and the inner planets.*

*Except . . . the enemy wasn't advancing toward those planets.*

*His unexpected behavior had been the source of much perplexity. Eventually, the indecision had been resolved, and the planet-based gunboats and small craft launched, with the first Enemy force to enter the system as their objective. But the delay had enabled the later-arriving force to approach rendezvous close enough to lend the support of its small attack craft. An unacceptable number of craft had been expended for no significant result.*

*Now, however, the directing intelligences of this System Which Must Be Defended had regained their accustomed equilibrium. There would be no more ill-coordinated attacks. All available gunboats and small craft would be consolidated into a single, massive strike which must surely overload the Enemy's defenses.*

"And so, Great Fang Koraaza," Murakuma concluded the prear-ranged spiel, "pursuant to orders from the Grand Allied Joint Chiefs of Staff, I assume overall command of Third and Sixth Fleets."

"Acknowledged, Ahhdmiraaaal Muhrakhuuuuma," Koraaza'khiniak replied with equal gravity.

As a practical matter Murakuma had been exercising command throughout the battle they'd just concluded. But now her flagship *Li Chien-lu* and Koraaza's *Kinaahsa'defarnoo* had finally approached close enough to permit the little ceremony to proceed without irritating time-lags.

The disparity in sustainable speeds between the Bugs' gunboats and shuttles had—not for the first time—been a priceless gift to the Allies. And while the oncoming clouds of kamikazes had employed jammer packs lavishly, the Alliance's fighter pilots had by now worked out the tactics for dealing with them. They'd picked off every jammer they could identify from long range with third generation fighter missiles, then closed in to knife-range, slashing through those seemingly inexhaustible formations with hetlasers and gun packs, then coming around to slash again.

Eventually the Bugs had grasped that limiting their kamikaze mass's speed to that of the slower shuttles simply enabled the Allied starships to avoid being overtaken. So they'd sent the gunboats streaking ahead at their maximum velocity, leaving the shuttles to follow as best they could. But that had enabled the Allied battle-line to concentrate its tremendous wealth of defensive fire on the unsupported gunboats, burning vast numbers of them out of the plenum before they could complete their ramming runs. Still more were blown apart by the fighters that snapped at their heels.

As always, some of those multitudes had gotten through—more than enough, for Vanessa Murakuma's money. But her gaze held steady as she studied the totals of ships damaged or, in a few cases, destroyed outright. It had to be considered an acceptable loss ratio, given how few gunboats of the attack wave had made it back to their planetary bases.

The shuttles had fled back there, too. Lagging behind the gun-boats, they—or, rather, whoever or whatever did their thinking for them—had seen the futility of pressing on with an independent attack on ships they'd have had difficulty overtaking in any case. So, along with a second, as yet uncommitted wave of gunboats, they'd retired to the planets which they knew to be the Allies' objectives, evidently concluding that they need only wait for the Allied combined fleets to enter their effective attack envelope, as they must do sooner or later in order to reach those objectives.

It was, Murakuma reflected, a perfectly logical conclusion on their part. It just happened to be wrong.

"So, Ahlildiiihaal," Koraaza's voice from the com screen brought her back to the present, "matters are now in the doubtless capable hands of your Small Claw Tahlivver."

Murakuma chuckled inwardly. Koraaza, without the spelling to mislead him, came closer to pronouncing Paul Taliaferro's surname accurately than most humans who didn't come from the region on Old Terra's North American continent known as Virginia.

"Indeed, Lord Khiniak—as soon as we can locate enough asteroids that meet his somewhat exacting requirements," she agreed, and Koraaza favored her with a tooth-hidden smile.

"I, too, am not altogether unacquainted with the foibles of engineers. But we have an entire asteroid belt to choose from. Shall we proceed?"

*The case for abandoning the outer system to the Enemy had been an unexceptionable one. If the speed differential between gunboats and shuttles made it impossible to coordinate a single overwhelming attack as planned, the obvious solution was to draw all available resources of both sorts back around the Worlds Which Must Be Defended, where the Enemy must come to them and would surely be swamped by sheer numbers. Viewed in that light, there was no need for undue concern over the fact that the Enemy's carriers for their small attack craft had vanished into cloak in the outer system.*

*However, the Enemy's subsequent behavior had continued to refuse to conform to expectations. It was extremely difficult for the Fleet's scout craft to penetrate the dense shells of small attack craft the Enemy was maintaining about his starships. And, lacking a foothold in the asteroid belt itself, the Fleet possessed no sensor stations in position to substitute for that lack of reconnaissance with direct observation.*

*Still, the essential facts seemed clear enough, judging from the handful of fragmentary reports from the few gunboats which had gotten through and lived long enough to send back any data at all. In contrast to the usual pattern of events, the Enemy was preparing for a protracted campaign by constructing bases on three of the largest asteroids and six smaller ones. The defensive installations being emplaced on those asteroids were certainly consistent with the hypothesis.*

"Coming up on Sledgehammer Three, Commodore."

Paul Taliaferro, sitting in the position from which he'd

unceremoniously displaced the copilot, grunted something unintelligible. The pilot expected no better in the way of a response, accustomed as she'd become to the commodore's preoccupied taciturnity, so she went on piloting.

Taliaferro wasn't quite the surly misanthrope his reputation suggested. Indeed, he occasionally wished he possessed more of the social graces whose lack—in the opinion of many, including and especially his former wife—helped account for his failure to rise above the rank of commodore. He just didn't have the time for them . . . nor, to be honest, the motivation. When manipulating and reshaping the inanimate physical universe through engineering, there was generally one best way to do a thing, and that was that. It was so straightforward! None of the irritating ambiguities and irrationalities with which humans insisted on complicating their lives. Often they actually seemed to *resent* having the path of maximum efficiency pointed out to them as succinctly as possible. He wondered why.

It was different, though, with Admiral Murakuma. She *understood*! Or at least she listened with appropriate attentiveness, and with none of the unreasonable resentments that he'd always found so hard to understand. True, she sometimes smiled in a way that left him vaguely puzzled on the rare occasions when he noticed it. But she'd presented him with such an *interesting* problem. Even better, she'd provided him with the authority and the tools he needed to do his job, and then left him alone to do it. Bliss!

Now the asteroid they'd dubbed Sledgehammer Three was visible in the shuttle's lights, waxing to fill the viewport whose presence was the reason Taliaferro had appropriated the copilot's seat. He studied the asteroid with care, for this was his last stop on his last inspection tour of it and its two mates, and of the lesser asteroids designated Hammer One through Six.

Sledgehammer Three was a rugged sphere almost four hundred kilometers in diameter. As far back as the twentieth century, it had been recognized that above a certain minimum mass an astronomical body's own gravity would prevent it from retaining a grossly irregular shape. Only four of Sol's asteroids were above that minimum. Here in Home Hive Two's fifth orbital position, though, it was pretty clear that the unborn planet would have been a true whopper if it had succeeded in clumping together. In spite of a vastly greater radius, this asteroid belt was as dense as Sol's, and held far more giant members. The three Sledgehammers had been easy to find, the six smaller rocks for the mere Hammers effortless.

Then had come the toil of constructing the installations which Taliaferro now observed. Over a hundred robotic point-defense emplacements dotted Sledgehammer Three's wild and barren surface. Also, buried deep under the crevasses and craters, were the command datalink facilities that would enable Taliaferro's eleven *Guerriere-C*-class command ships to coordinate the three Sledgehammers' defensive fire. The six Hammers mounted proportionately lighter defensive works.

All of that, however, was secondary, meant only to keep these asteroids in existence long enough to fulfill their destiny. Only one engineering work on Sledgehammer Three really mattered—the one that couldn't be given a trial run.

"Get me Commander Lin," Taliaferro muttered. The pilot had barely complied before he leaned forward and snapped into the grille. "What's the word on that flaw in the pusher plate?"

"We're not certain there *is* one, Sir," Lin Yu-hsiang replied from his temporary command post on the surface of Sledgehammer Three. "When it comes to constructing Orion drives, we don't exactly have much experience—and having to stop what we're doing to answer questions about it doesn't exactly help!"

The pilot blanched, expecting thunderbolts. But Taliaferro actually chuckled—partly in recognition of a kindred spirit, and partly at what had become a standing joke in TG 64.1. When the name for what the task group was constructing had reached the Tabbies, they'd thought they were being honored. No one had had the heart to tell them that the name dated back to a time centuries before humanity had dreamed their race existed.

Nuclear pulse propulsion—"Project Orion"—had been a product of the twentieth century, one of many notions for liberating the infant Space Age from the dismal mathematics of chemical rocketry. Conceptually, it set some kind of record for brute-force crudity: detonate a series of nuclear explosions behind you and let them *kick* you forward! Naturally, it required a massive shock-absorbing plate for your vehicle's rear end. Worse, however, it had faced insurmountable political obstacles in a world understandably jittery about allowing anyone to send up spaceships packed full of what were in effect hundreds of small nuclear weapons. But for a time it had seemed to offer the best hope for reaching the outer planets and—especially after the Bussard ramscoop had come to grief on the hard facts about the interstellar medium in Sol's vicinity—the stars.

Then had come the unanticipated breakthrough into reaction-less drives, and the Orion concept had gone the way of Jules Verne's giant cannon. At the same time, the idea of "dinosaur killers"—asteroids used as kinetic-energy weapons against planets—had joined reaction drives in the dustbin. It just wasn't practical to enclose an entire asteroid in a drive field. And tractoring such an object would have no effect except to rip the tractor-beam projectors out of ships that instantaneously took on velocities measured in percentages of *c*.

No, it couldn't be done with reactionless drives . . . but Vanessa Murakuma had wanted it done anyway. When she'd put the problem to Taliaferro, he'd automatically snorted that it was preposterous. Then he'd gone off and thought about it, to the near-exclusion of eating and sleeping. And when he'd put his solution before her, she'd backed him to the hilt, selling the idea to a skeptical Joint Chiefs of Staff.

Taliaferro's moment of amusement passed.

"I tell you what, Commander," he said. "You've got precisely as long to decide whether there's a problem—and, if there is, to fix it—as there is between now and Sledgehammer Three's scheduled ignition."

"But . . but, Commodore—"

"But me no buts, Commander. I've just finished checking out all the other asteroids, and *they* all report that they're ready for ignition. The first of them, Hammer Four, is due to light off in—" Taliaferro glanced at his wrist chrono "—thirteen minutes and a little less than twenty seconds. After that, there's no turning back. I'm damned if I'll stop the clock now to wait for you to get your act together!"

"Commodore, I protest!"

"Protest all you want to, Yu-hsiang—later. But right now, if I were you I'd get busy on that pusher plate. Sledgehammer Three *is* going to get kicked out of its orbit on schedule, and if you're still there at the time . . . well, it ought to be an interesting trip to Planet III, especially with fusion bombs going off under your ass!"

Taliaferro cut the connection while Lin was in mid-splutter, and turned to the pilot.

"All right, get us back to *Alfred*. And raise Fleet flag."

While he waited, Taliaferro studied a two-dimensional schematic

of the Home Hive Two A System out to and including the asteroid belt. Sheer habit, for he'd long since memorized it. Still, he
gazed at the little lights of the nine asteroids which TF 64.1 had
transformed into weapons. They were strung out over forty-odd
degrees of the belt's circumference, a curving scimitar of death.
That was where they'd been found, and it had been out of the
question to move them together, for the same reason their drives
couldn't be tested: an Orion drive in operation was something the
Bugs could hardly fail to notice. So they would start moving in
staggered order starting with Hammer Four, each asteroid lighting
off its drive as the others came up level with it on the hyperbolic
orbit that would send them careening across the inner system,
terminating at one of the three scarlet planet-icons on the display.
Sledgehammer Three, the tip of the scimitar, would be last, so
Lin actually had a fair amount of time left. *Just as well,* Taliaferro
thought. *I wouldn't really leave him there. Probably.*

He'd barely finished reporting to Murakuma across the light-
minutes when a multi-megatonne fusion fireball awoke a few
score meters behind Hammer Four, its brilliantly defined shock
wave surging toward the asteroid but never quite touching it.
Then another . . . and another . . . and slowly, ponderously, Hammer
Four began to move out of its immemorial orbit, trailing what
looked (or would have looked, to anyone who'd braved the sleet
of gamma rays) like a trail of small suns connected by a stream
of glowing gas.

Operation Cushion Shot had begun.

*It had taken an appreciable amount of time for the realization
of what was happening to sink home through layers of unexpectedness—not a fatal delay, perhaps, but certainly a disadvantageous
one. But there was no longer any room for doubt. The orbits into
which those asteroids had been moved could be projected without
difficulty, and all of them intersected at the point that would then
be occupied by the third planet. Calculating the kinetic energy such
impacts would release was equally simple. And the Fleet knew only
too well what would happen to the system's remaining defenders at
the instant that planet's population died.*

*Abandoning the outer system to the Enemy had been an error.
That it was an error grounded in flawless logic was no excuse.
Neither was the totally unprecedented nature of what the Enemy
was doing.*

*There was, however, a positive aspect to the situation. The asteroids could be deflected from their courses—or, in the case of the smaller ones, actually broken up. It would not be easy, but with antimatter weapons it could be done. And the Enemy must be as aware of that fact as the Fleet was, so his freedom of action was limited by the need to defend those incredible kinetic projectiles as they followed their immutable hyperbolic courses in free fall, at a velocity which, while high on the standards of normal interplanetary bodies, was practically stationary to vehicles using reactionless drives.*

*There could be no further thought of waiting in defensive posture on and around the planets. Those asteroids must be intercepted as far away as possible. All available gunboats and small craft must be fitted with antimatter loads and launched immediately. And the Deep Space Force must go with them.*

"Well, we expected it, Sir."

"So we did," Vanessa Murakuma replied to Leroy McKenna's observation. The response was purely automatic. Her entire consciousness was focused on the approaching Bug formation—a classic "Bughouse swarm."

Yes, she *had* expected it. Not even an idiot or a politician could harbor any remaining doubts about the Bugs' capacity to reason from observed data—or, at least, to perform some process that filled the same function as reasoning. They understood what that formation of asteroids meant, and they were committing everything they had left to what they knew was their final stand against apocalypse.

She studied the readouts on the mobile force that trailed behind the tens of thousands of kamikazes: sixty-seven superdreadnoughts, fifty-two battlecruisers and a hundred and thirty-four light cruisers. At least there were no monitors; evidently intelligence was correct in supposing that the Bugs had had insufficient time to complete any new ones since she and Lord Khiniak had made their last, regrettably uncoordinated incursion into this system.

Her eyes went to the holo sphere on whose scale that formation shrank to a single scarlet icon, moving to intercept a cluster of tiny green lights representing the asteroids and the combined fleets' battle-line, together with the fighter screen spread before them by Small Fang Meearnow'raaalpha's eighty light carriers.

Finally, she let her gaze rest on another emerald icon, near the inner fringes of the asteroid belt—one which she hoped and believed appeared on no similar displays aboard the Bug ships whose course it was paralleling.

Anson Olivera approached. The *farshathkhanaak* had had his eyes on that remote green icon from the first.

"Admiral, we've gotten another call from Fang Koraaza's staff. They want to know if it's time to—"

"Not yet. A little longer, I think." Murakuma had a multitude of figures, actual and projected, at her fingertips. But in the end it came down to a matter of *feel*, complicated by the need to factor in communications time-lags.

Still, Olivera only had a minute or so longer to fidget before Murakuma straightened up abruptly.

"All right, Anson," she said crisply. "Signal Small Fang Iaashmaahr."

The signal flashed across the light-minutes to Iaashmaahr'-freaalkit-ahn, commanding her own Task Force 63 and also Third Fleet's TF 33—thirty-four assault carriers and forty-eight fleet carriers, which had gone into cloak and maneuvered among the asteroids until they were in position to cover the Bugs' anticipated course. The signal was received, and thirty-four hundred primary-pack-armed fighters launched undetected.

They couldn't remain undetected quite long enough to reach their targets, of course. The ships of the Bugs' deep space force managed to launch their gunboats into the path of the fighter strike, and other gunboats hastily detached from the "Bughouse swarm" joined them. But that desperately erected barrier could barely even slow Orion and Terran and Gorm pilots who smelled blood. One Bug starship after another died in a stroboscopic cluster of fireballs, and the com frequencies rang with cries of triumph in three languages, from three different sets of vocal apparatus.

Then the fighter strike was through, emerging into clear space and sending reports flooding into the databases of Fleet flag.

"It worked, Admiral!" Ernesto Cruciero exclaimed. "The data are incomplete, of course, but most of the deep space force ships were either destroyed outright or damaged so severely they won't be able to keep formation . . . and wouldn't be much use if they could!"

Murakuma permitted herself a brief smile at the ops officer's enthusiasm.

"Very good, Ernesto. Convey my congratulations to Small Fang Iaashmaahr—and also my desire that she expedite the recovery of her fighters so she can rendezvous with us as quickly as possible." Cruciero and Olivera both looked somewhat crestfallen. "Let's face it, gentlemen. Crippling the deep space force, while certainly desirable, was really something of a sideshow. *That's* the real threat." Murakuma pointed at the innocuous-looking ruby icon that represented clouds of antimatter-laden gunboats and shuttles. "And we're going to need Iaashmaahr's fighters very badly to deal with it."

There was a basic inelegance to it: the Allies had to defend the asteroids and the Bugs had to neutralize them, and both sides knew it. All of which left little scope for finesse.

Iaashmaahr's carriers remained in cloak for their run to rejoin the rest of the combined fleets, so they had the benefit of one more undetected launch. Those fighters, and the nineteen hundred others from Small Fang Meearnow's *Mohrdenhaus* (whose usefulness even the Terrans were coming to appreciate), went out to meet the Bug kamikazes in a dogfight whose scale was exceeded only by its desperation.

As always, the fighters cut great gashes through the massed Bug formations. And, as always, they couldn't possibly kill enough of those endless, uncaring hordes. Like water pouring through a collapsing dike, streams of kamikazes closed in on the asteroids.

The battle-line slid in, interposing itself, suffering hideous losses as it burned away hundreds more of the kamikazes. Vanessa Murakuma lay in her command chair crash frame, trying to disassociate her mind from her bruised body as *Li Chien-lu* shuddered from hits that sent even a monitor's mass reeling. It was all she could do. She'd already given sufficient orders: stand and fight.

Again, many of the attackers broke through—into a latticework of death around the asteroids, whose defensive installations were directed by Taliaferro's command ships. And again, not all the kamikazes could be denied their rendezvous with death. Two of the smaller "Hammer" asteroids were shattered into pieces which wouldn't even stay on trajectories that would bring them into collision with Planet III to burn up in its atmosphere, for their fragments—unlike their intact sisters—were no longer accelerating down their precisely calculated track. But not even the ultimate violence of antimatter annihilation could break up the big planetoids.

At last it was over, and Murakuma and her staff surveyed the readouts of carnage.

"Their remaining kamikazes are falling back to Planet III to regroup," Marina Abernathy concluded.

"We need to do the same thing," Murakuma pointed out, and turned from the intelligence officer to address the ops officer and the *farshathkhanaak*.

"Ernesto, Anson, I want a schedule for our carriers with undamaged drives to shuttle back to Orpheus 1 and Bug-06 in relays for replacement fighters. We have a long way to go, and the Bugs will be back."

She proved to be right. The Orion drives had kicked the asteroids into fairly flat hyperbolas involving far less transit time than the years simple Hohmann transfer orbits would have taken, and those same drives continued to accelerate them steadily. But on the standards of this era's spacefarers, the pace was a veritable crawl. There was plenty of time for the Bugs to return to the attack, again and again. But they did so with steadily weakening forces, for this system was on its own. They inflicted losses, which the combined fleets grimly took. They disrupted or deflected all but two of the "Hammer" asteroids. They even managed to alter the orbit of Sledgehammer One, sending it careening harmlessly aside.

It wasn't nearly enough.

They were all feeling drained as they stood on *Li Chien-lu*'s flag bridge and watched Home Hive Three A III die.

The Bug attacks had come with greater and greater frequency as doom had drawn closer to the planet—but they'd also grown weaker and weaker. In the end, the Bugs had nothing left to throw at the onrushing asteroids, which had gradually picked up speed as they'd fallen down the sun's gravity well and, eventually, the planet's. By now they were moving at what the pre-reactionless-drive era would have accounted a very high interplanetary velocity.

They watched the view on the big screen, downloaded from recon fighters that were continuing to shadow Sledgehammer Three. Gazing at that rugged spheroid—even more rugged now, after all the hits it had taken—Murakuma contemplated the inappropriateness, verging on banality, of the popular term "dinosaur killer." *That* asteroid, which had slammed into Old Terra's Yucatan peninsula sixty-five million years ago, was estimated to have been a mere ten kilometers in diameter, rather like the two "Hammer" asteroids that continued to follow the monster in the screen, like lesser sea creatures in the wake of a whale. And it had almost certainly been traveling a lot more slowly. If the thing she was now watching had struck Earth, neither she nor any other life form of Terran origin—not even a microbe—would now exist.

Leroy McKenna was calling out the minutes to impact in a leaden voice. She didn't listen. Instead, she watched Planet III grow and grow in the screen. Presently, the fighters swerved away to stay out of range of the planet-based defenses, and the panorama expanded.

A seemingly small, artificial-looking object appeared, glinting in the planet's reflected light. She'd been told to expect it. By sheer coincidence, Sledgehammer Three was going to sideswipe the planet's space station on its way down. That station was as titanic as all such Bug constructs, but its mass was as nothing compared to the falling planetoid, and the pyrotechnics of its death were disappointing. The asteroid, trailing a scattering of debris that had been the space station, dwindled in the distance against the clouded bluish backdrop. It had probably been deflected a bit, but not enough to matter this close to the planet.

"Minus ten seconds," McKenna intoned, his voice even deeper than usual.

Time crept by. At minus three seconds, an extraordinary thing happened. The swirling cloud-patterns of Planet III abruptly vanished, replaced by concentric rings rushing away from the black dot that had suddenly begun to glow redly with the heat of friction. Sledgehammer Three had entered atmosphere like a three-hundred-kilometer cannonball, generating a shock wave that blew a hole in the air as it went.

Murakuma had only two seconds to absorb that spectacle. Then Sledgehammer Three crossed the terminator into darkness. A protracted second later, a blinding fireball erupted on that nighted surface, impossibly huge given the fact that it was a planet they were looking at. The night vanished as thermal pulse drove a shock wave that overwhelmed the earlier one, pushing outward in all directions from that inferno of an impact-point. Following it across the oceans came hundred-meter walls of water that would, in another hour or so, flood the coastal plains, finally expending their last efforts against the highest mountain ramparts. The earthquakes erupting along every fault line on the planet passed unnoticed. So would the glowing sleet of red-hot rock as the gigatons of debris that had been blasted into space returned in an hour or so; there would be no living eyes to see it, no living organisms to be immolated in the heat.

The impacts of the two surviving "Hammer" asteroids were barely worthy of comment. Sledgehammer Two, when it arrived, was sheer redundancy.

Murakuma finally turned to face the strangely silent flag bridge and the people who'd just witnessed the greatest single act of destruction ever unleashed by sentient beings. She spoke like a machine.

"Commodore McKenna, convey my personal congratulations to Commodore Taliaferro on the success of Operation Cushion Shot. And please raise Fang Koraaza. Given the total depletion of this system's kamikaze assets and the psychic effect the remaining defenders must now be experiencing, I believe we can proceed to reduce the other inhabited planets by . . . conventional means."

Lord Khiniak and his staffers came aboard *Li Chien-lu*, to full military honors, as the combined fleets orbited around the lifeless hulk of Planet IV. There was now the leisure to indulge such niceties.

As she led the Orions into the flag lounge, Murakuma's eyes strayed to the calendar display on the bulkhead, with its Terran Standard equivalency: January 23, 2370. It was so easy to lose track.

A little over a standard year since they'd entered this system. Operation Cushion Shot hadn't been quick. Neither had it been cheap. Even the Orions looked very sober as they contemplated the losses they'd taken in the battles that had swirled around that phalanx of asteroids. Nearly thirty-two percent of the combined fleets' starship strength. Two hundred and four ships—seven monitors, forty-five superdreadnoughts, twenty battleships, nine assault carriers, eighteen fleet carriers, nineteen light carriers, thirteen heavy cruisers, twenty-two light cruisers and sixteen destroyers—had died that those inconceivable projectiles might reach their destination. So had forty-two percent of all fighters engaged. It was a loss total that would have been beyond prewar comprehension.

But . . .

"So, Ahhdmiraaaal Muhrakhuuuuma," Koraaza interrupted her brown study. "Is it confirmed?"

"Yes, Lord Khiniak. We had plenty of time to scout the outer system during the preparation of the asteroids, and found nothing. Commodore Abernathy is prepared to state categorically that every Bug in this system is dead. I propose we dispatch a courier drone so informing the Joint Chiefs of Staff."

Koraaza gave a long, rustling purr of a sigh. "So. One home hive is left."

"Don't forget the Bugs' base at Rabahl," Murakuma cautioned, recalling Fujiko's messages.

"I have not. But according to the latest message traffic, our allies of the Star Union are preparing the final assault on that system. It will no doubt be a major operation, yet they clearly consider it a matter of no immediate urgency."

"True." Fujiko had intimated as much. "They've invested Rabahl thoroughly. It isn't going anywhere, and the Crucians want to completely assimilate the new technologies they've gotten from us before going in."

"So," said Koraaza once again. "We can safely leave our allies to deal with the Bahg defilers of their own worlds. For us, there remains but one great task. Both our fleets, and those of Fangs Zhaarnak and Pressssssscottt will come together and meet at last." The slitted pupils in his amber eyes narrowed, and all at once the cosmopolite Murakuma had thought she'd known was no longer there behind those eyes. "It will be a gathering of warriors beyond anything in legend. I imagine that even Lord Talphon will be there, for he owes a *vilknarma*, a blood-balance for the death of his *vilkshatha* brother. Surely the Khan will relent and allow him to be personally present at the killing of the last Bahgs in the universe."

# CHAPTER THIRTY-THREE
## Full Circle

Marcus LeBlanc caught sight of a familiar figure across the great room through the rays of Alpha Centauri Alpha-light that slanted through the tall windows.

"Kevin!"

"Admiral! How are you—?" Kevin Sanders began, then remembered himself and started to come to attention.

"To hell with that!" LeBlanc strode up and shook hands with his one-time protégé, whom he hadn't seen in a year and a half. "I didn't know whether you'd be coming here with First Fang Ynaathar or not. It's good it to see you."

"Likewise, Sir. You're looking very well, if I may say so." Which was true, even though there was a little more salt and less pepper in LeBlanc's beard than there had been. Zephrain clearly agreed with him. *That, and being close to Admiral Murakuma*, Sanders added to himself with an inner chuckle. "Oh, and congratulations on your richly deserved promotion, Sir."

LeBlanc mumbled something insincerely self-deprecating. The conventional wisdom that promotions come fast in wartime actually held true for the combat branches—but not necessarily for intelligence and other restricted-line types, who weren't permitted to get the all-important tickets of command in space punched. Sanders, for example, was still a lieutenant. LeBlanc's sleeves, though, now bore the one wide silver-braided stripe and two narrow ones of a vice admiral—about as high as a spook could normally go.

"Not much has changed here, has it?" LeBlanc asked, changing the subject as he looked around the room. "How long as it been. . . ?"

"Five years and eight months, Terran Standard," Sanders replied instantly. Then he grinned. "That wasn't really a feat of quick recall. In fact, just before you arrived, I was thinking back to the last time we were here."

"Yes. . . ." The shadow of a wind-blown cloud of memory crossed LeBlanc's consciousness as he recalled that grim time after the inconceivable catastrophe in Pesthouse, when the successful defense of the "Black Hole of Centauri" had seemed merely a reprieve.

"Anyway," Sanders piped up, unable in his mercurial way to sustain *any* single mood for long, "one thing's the same: the tonnage of rank in this room. Do you think the floor will collapse?"

LeBlanc chuckled and looked around. The Joint Chiefs were here, with the exception of their Chairman. So were Raymond Prescott and Zhaarnak'telmasa, seemingly surrounded by a nimbus of legend. So was Ynaathar'solmaak, in whose train Sanders had arrived. The First Fang had also brought Robalii Rikka with him to speak for the Star Union in these councils. Rikka, in turn, had brought the commander of a task group that had only recently joined Task Force 86, as he'd long since become resigned to hearing First Grand Wing called. The newcomer drew stares even in this company: a radially symmetrical, three-armed triped—all of those limbs tentacular—whose mouth was set atop a disc-shaped body at a height of 1.3 meters, surrounded by three eye-stalks which provided a 360-degree field of vision. Xenobiological dogma, confirmed across almost five centuries of interstellar exploration, held that the evolutionary logic of tool-using mandated a bilaterally symmetrical form, bipedal or—in rare cases—centauroid. But even though Admiral Dar'sahlahk was a living affront to conservative xenobiologists, everyone else welcomed his presence. The Zarkolyans had paid a disproportionate price in the early fighting against Home Hive Four, and they had a debt to exact from the Bugs. Even the Orions understood that, however little else they had in common with that mercantile-oriented race.

Sanders sometimes thought that the paradox of the Zarkolyans' shift in orientation over the past few years supplied its own answer. A culture with a warlike tradition might have had more of a . . . well, sense of proportion about what they'd experienced. The Zarkolyans hadn't, and they'd taken to militancy in response to those experiences with the unleavened enthusiasm of the neophyte.

"There are still a few late arrivals yet to come," the lieutenant observed blandly, following LeBlanc's gaze around the crowded room and well aware of which late arrival the new-minted vice admiral was awaiting.

Then a side door opened to admit the combined staffs of Third and Sixth Fleet, just in from Home Hive Two. Vanessa Murakuma and Koraaza'khiniak entered side by side, but the former stopped dead when her eyes met LeBlanc's across the room.

LeBlanc muttered something that might have been "excuse me" and departed, leaving Sanders smiling.

As if the admirals' arrival had been a signal, the impending arrival of the Chairman was announced, and everyone hurried to his seat. Just as before, the high brass sat at the oval central table, with the staffers placed well back from it, and LeBlanc, despite his promotion, reluctantly took his place among the latter just before Kthaara'zarthan entered and everyone stood.

Intellectually, Sanders was aware that the Orions had no equivalent of the human antigerone treatments. Their natural spans were considerably longer than those of humans, which might explain some of the reason they didn't, and for some of them, a vague taint of dishonor attached to such research. The lieutenant also knew that once the Orion aging process set in, it proceeded with what humans found to be startling rapidity. But he hadn't seen the JCS chairman in some time, and he couldn't help being taken aback. Kthaara's pelt was ashen, like some ebon wood burned over by the fire of time. He'd grown gaunt, and could no longer manage the characteristic gliding Orion prowl—half-attractive and half-sinister to human eyes—but walked with a stiffness to which he imparted an awesome dignity.

Sanders looked around at the other Orions in the room. He'd come to know the race well, and now he read their body language. *The pack elder has entered the circle of the fire—a mighty hunter, who's lived to such an extraordinary age that they know they're in the presence of great skill, or great luck, or maybe the great favor of Valkha. Even sophisticates like Ynaathar and Koraaza feel it; they're back at that campfire along with all the others, and they're unconsciously showing it.*

Kthaara lowered himself carefully into his chair, and everyone else followed suit. When he spoke, his voice had lost some of its resonance, but none of its firmness.

"Thank you all for coming. I especially welcome Ahhdmi-raaaal Muhrakhuuuuma and Great Fang Koraaza'khiniak, the conquerors of Home Hive Two. What they have done there has set the stage for this conference." Kthaara's pause seemed longer than the heartbeat it was. "We are here to plan the concluding campaign of this war."

For a moment, time hung suspended as all in the room sought in their own various ways to decide how to react to the words they'd sometimes doubted they would ever hear, to the imminent disappearance of what had been the central fact of their lives for a decade.

*Will we know how to come to terms with the absence of this war?* Sanders wondered. *Is it even possible we may actually* miss *it?*

*In a pig's ass we will!*

Kthaara raised a clawed hand to halt a low sound that had begun to rise from his audience.

"Do not misunderstand me. There will remain some work to be done afterwards. Worlds like Harnah and Franos will have to be dealt with, now that our allies of the Star Union have shown us how planets with hostage indigenous populations can be retaken. And, of course, the Star Union will have to complete the reduction of the Bahg stronghold at Rabahl—an operation for whose support we have already earmarked ten percent of the Grand Alliance's available units. But all of that will be in the nature of what Humans call 'mopping up.' Ahhdmiraaaal LeBlaaanc, who returned from Zephrain several local days ago and has had time to review and correlate the latest astrographic data, will present our reasons for believing this to be the case. Ahhdmiraaaal?"

LeBlanc stepped to a podium-*cum*-control console that had been set up at the opposite end of the table from Kthaara. He manipulated the controls, and the windows polarized to darken the room. Then a holographically projected display screen appeared against the wall behind the Chairman, showing a warp chart in the standard two-dimensional way: rather like a circuit diagram, or an ancient railway switching board, without any foredoomed attempt to approximate the real-space relationships of the stars in question.

It was the largest such display that most of them had ever seen, at least indoors. It had to be, to hold more warp lines and warp nexi than any of them had ever seen before on one chart.

Most of them recognized it for what it was even before LeBlanc spoke.

"Since securing Home Hive Two," he began, "Third and Sixth Fleets have probed through that system's warp points. Their findings have answered the last questions we had. We now know the warp layout of Bug space in its entirety. Here it is."

Everyone stared at that display, and especially at the five icons they'd all come to know as representing home hive systems. Four of them glowed sullenly with the dismal dark-red of clotted blood, meaning that they'd been burned clean of life in accordance with General Directive Eighteen. Only one—Home Hive Five—still glowed like a malevolent scarlet eye.

After a moment, though, people began looking elsewhere for other, secondary hostile-system icons, both living and dead. Presently, a low murmur began, and, finally, Raymond Prescott gave it voice.

"You mean—? Well, I'll be damned!" he turned in his chair and looked to where Amos Chung and Uaaria'salath-ahn sat, looking stunned. "When you two broached your theory about the Bugs back in late '64, did you expect *this*?"

"No, Sir," Chung admitted. "We believed that each of the five Bug sub-groupings Lieutenant Sanders had identified represented a small group of intensively industrialized systems. Since then, we've had to constantly revise our estimate of the number of those systems downward as more and more of Bug space was revealed. But we never dreamed that the *entire* Bug industrial infrastructure was concentrated in the five home hive systems, with only a few other occupied systems to support them with resources."

Sky Marshal MacGregor gave her head a slow shake of the wilderness.

"But how can that be *possible*?" She twitched a shoulder in an almost irritated shrug. "Granted that the home hives are over-populated and overdeveloped beyond any nightmares we've ever had and that the whole concept of a 'standard of living' is foreign to the Bugs. Granted even that their single-mindedness is literally beyond our comprehension. But . . ." She shook her head again. "How could five industrialized systems—*any* five industrialized systems—have supported the overwhelming fleets we faced at the beginning of the war?"

"I believe I know the answer," Robalii Rikka said. "After their first war with the Star Union, the Demons began building up reserves in anticipation of a subsequent meeting. We ourselves did the same—but their buildup was far greater, due to the factors you just mentioned. Then they encountered the Terran Federation. So you, not us, had to face those reserves." Rikka looked somber, for he'd studied details of those desperate early battles in the Romulus Chain. "Truly, we owe you a debt above and beyond the new technology that Admiral Sommers brought to us. You bore the brunt of what was intended for us—and wore it down, at terrible cost to yourselves."

Eileen Sommers squirmed uncomfortably in her place seated among Ynaathar's staffers. She looked around at the hectares of silver braid, stars, and other gleaming and gemmed insignia which made it painfully clear just how junior a mere rear admiral was in a room like this. But then she cleared her throat.

"We can't take undeserved credit, Warmaster. We were fighting for our own survival, not for the Star Union's. In fact, we didn't even suspect that you existed."

"Perhaps. But the fact remains that those inconceivable fleets would have overwhelmed us if we'd had to face them in the fullness of their strength. We feel ourselves in your debt, even if you don't regard us as your debtors. Which is why my Grand Wing is remaining under First Fang Ynaathar's command, as an integral part of Eighth Fleet, rather than returning to the Star Union to participate in the Rabahl operation. We wish to contribute what we can to the eradication of the home hive whose forces you first encountered. We feel there is a . . . fitness about it."

"You are correct," Kthaara said. "Honor is a concept which our cultures may express differently, but we all possess it in some form—it is what sets us apart from the less-than-*chofaki* we fight. And honor, however each of us understands it, demands that all our races be present for the completion of the *vilknarma*. Which leads me to a related matter."

The aged Orion turned to Prescott.

"Fang Presssssscottt, you honored me with the suggestion you made in connection with the final assault on Home Hive Five."

"Every other fleet commander has endorsed it, Lord Talphon. I was merely the first to voice what everyone feels."

"I appreciate that. Nevertheless, as I explained at the time, my orders from the Khan required me to reject it. Since then, however, I have made a direct appeal to the Khan, and he has been gracious enough to rescind his previous command. So I now take this opportunity to announce that I will assume direct personal command of Grand Fleet for this operation."

Kthaara raised his hand once more, this time to quell the incipient applause, and turned to Vanessa Murakuma.

"Ahhdmiraaaal Muhrakhuuuuma, if you are agreeable, I will fly Grand Fleet's lights from *Li Chien-lu*."

He made a remarkably creditable attempt at pronouncing the name of Sixth Fleet's flagship, and all eyes went to the slender, flame-haired human woman. The politics of the choice were obvious: if an Orion was to command the operation, balance required that he do so from a ship of the other superpower. But far more was involved in this decision than mere politics, and everyone knew that, too. Vanessa Murakuma was the first naval officer in the history of the galaxy to actually stop an Arachnid offensive—an offensive launched with all of the massive, crushing superiority of the reserve to which Robalii Rikka had just referred. The senior officers in this conference room knew far better than most just how impossible a feat that had been, just as they knew that the juggernaut she had somehow battered to a halt had come from Home Hive Five. It was entirely fitting—indeed, inevitable—that *her* flagship should carry Grand Fleet's commander-in-chief for the final home hive assault, and Sanders stole a glance at LeBlanc, who was looking at his lover and grinning like an idiot with pride.

"I—" Murakuma began, then stopped and almost visibly got a grip on herself. "I mean, I would be honored, Lord Talphon," she said. "Thank you."

Sanders decided that if she hadn't genuinely been taken by surprise, the galaxy had lost a great actress when she'd opted for a military career.

"Excellent. And now, Ahhdmiraaaal LeBlaaanc, please continue."

LeBlanc activated a flashing cursor that pointed to the solitary balefully red gleam. A warp line connected it with Anderson Three, the system where the first units of Grand Fleet was even now beginning to converge. The string-lights of the Romulus chain grew from its other side.

"There's still a vast Bug war machine in the systems between Home Hive Five and Justin, still facing Fifth Fleet. But there's no need to fight it. Home Hive Five is the Arachnids' last remaining resource base. After it falls, the forces confronting the Romulus Chain can be left to die on the vine. We estimate it will take six months to a year before lack of maintenance renders them incapable of offering meaningful resistance. It might take somewhat longer, depending on the extent of their forward-deployed stockpiles, but the ultimate result will be the same however long it takes."

"All well and good," Fleet Speaker Noraku rumbled. "But in

the meantime, what of the opposition we will face in Home Hive Five?"

"We're presently conducting RD2 probes from Anderson Three. They're incomplete as yet, and it will take additional time to analyze the findings. If I may, I'd like to defer my response until that work is complete."

"I agree," Kthaara interjected. "We should await definitive findings. In the meantime, we will turn our attention to the routing of our fleets to Anderson Three."

From some standpoints, Sanders reflected, assembling an attacking force before knowing what it was going to have to go up against might have seemed an odd way of proceeding. But in this case it made perfect sense. They were going to have to go into Home Hive Five regardless of what it had in the way of defenses, and Anderson Three's Warp Point One was the only way to get there. It was simple to the point of crudity.

*But,* his familiar imp whispered, *remember what Clauzewitz said about the simplest things often being very difficult.*

When next they all met, a standard month later, they did so under the orange light of Anderson Three A.

That light was dim indeed, for they were just over four and a half light-hours from the small type K main-sequence star, at the warp point where Grand Fleet lay waiting. A procession of VIP shuttles brought the senior officers of all the component fleets aboard *Li Chien-lu,* where they were met with full formality in the cavernous boat bay.

It was unlikely that any of them, even the representatives from the multispecies Star Union, had ever seen an honor guard quite like the one awaiting Vanessa Murakuma's guests. It was a very large honor guard, because every race of the Grand Alliance and every available member species of the Star Union was represented in it. Three-meter Gorm centaurs; tall, slender, fiercely crested Ophiuchi, koalalike Telikans; bat-winged Crucians; naked-skinned Terrans; sleek-furred Orions; even the late-arriving Zarkolyans . . . all of them were there. Uniforms—for those who wore them—were immaculate. Terran Navy and Marine brightwork gleamed, Orion metalwork and jewels glittered and flashed, the formal leather harnesses of the Ophiuchi were polished to eye-watering brightness, and brutally utilitarian Gorm uniforms stood as a drab background for the martial splendor . . . and, in the process, made their own implacable statement of purpose.

In its own way, and very deliberately, that honor guard was a microcosm of the entire war . . . and its cost. Its members were clearly aware of that, and the polished precision of their drill suggested that they'd spent the entire past month working out and practicing the choreography which fused their intensely different military traditions (or lack of them) into a single harmonious whole.

Afterwards, the gathered flag officers of Grand Fleet filed into the flag briefing room, with its wide, curving armorplast viewport.

The lights dimmed, the better to see the tactical-scale holo sphere in the compartment's center. It showed the formations of ships that lay poised to pass through the violet circle of the warp point. Third, Sixth, Seventh, and Eighth Fleets were now assembled in their full combined might: eighty-one monitors, two hundred and eighty superdreadnoughts, nineteen battleships, seventy assault carriers, eighty-one fleet carriers, a hundred and thirty-four light carriers, and two hundred and sixty battlecruisers. The lighter supporting ships—almost a hundred and fifty in all—were beneath notice in a haze of green icons that would have been beyond the belief of any prewar admiral. And there was an additional thicket of smaller, even more numerous icons between the starships and the warp point: fifty-three hundred SBMHAWKs, twenty-four hundred SRHAWKs, and two thousand AMBAMPs, lying in wait to clear the way through the defenses waiting beyond it.

Marcus LeBlanc stepped forward after they were all seated and focused on the display.

"Despite the heavy losses our RD2s have suffered," he said rather heavily, "we now feel that we're in a position to report on everything in Home Hive Five within sensor range of the warp point."

He manipulated controls, and the sphere changed. The violet circle remained, but the soul-lifting array of green vanished, leaving a blackness into which a scarlet rash spread rapidly as he spoke.

"First of all, the warp point is englobed by a hundred and sixty-eight orbital fortresses of the *Demon Gamma*, *Devastation Gamma* and *Devil Gamma* classes. All of them are of roughly the same tonnage: about a quarter again that of our largest monitor. We've also detected a hundred and forty-four of their defensive heavy cruisers, of the usual mix of classes, and ninety *Epee*-class suicide-rider light cruisers. In addition, the warp point is surrounded by thirty-two thousand patterns of mines, presumably antimatter-armed."

The compartment was one great hiss of indrawn breath, a sound that was surprisingly similar in all of the Grand Alliance's constituent races, and LeBlanc pressed on hurriedly.

"The warp point is also covered by something in excess of eleven hundred deep-space buoys, armed with a characteristic Bug mix of independently deployed energy weapons. Indications are that the majority of them are bomb-pumped lasers, but we can't say that with certainty."

"Is that all?" Force Leader Noraku asked with what, in any race but the Gorm, would have been suspected of being sarcasm.

"Er . . . not quite, Force Leader. The Bugs have also mounted a combat space patrol of several hundred gunboats on the warp point. Since they must know by now that our SBMHAWK4s can wipe out any CSP they can mount, we assume that they've done so for the purpose of forcing us to use up enough SBMHAWKs to do precisely that. They've supported the gunboats with a dense deployment of kamikaze small craft."

LeBlanc indicated the force readouts, and the silence deepened until Raymond Prescott finally broke it.

"What about their deep space force?"

"Unknown, Admiral. They're evidently holding their capital ships well back from the warp point, and our RD2s have been unable to obtain any definitive readings. The same, of course, applies to the planetary defenses. However . . ."

LeBlanc adjusted more controls, and the warp point became a violet dot at the very limits of the holo sphere as the scale expanded to include the entire inner system. It was a layout which had become only too familiar to them all since the ill-fated day when TFNS *Argive* had entered Home Hive Five and lifted the veil of Hell. But LeBlanc thought it worth refreshing everyone's memory, and he sent a cursor flashing over the innermost three orbital shells.

"When assessing the possible force levels of this system," he said quietly, "it should be remembered that Planet II contains a population and industrial base unthinkable for anyone but Bugs. It is, quite simply, the most heavily industrialized single planet that any member of the Grand Alliance—including the Star Union—has ever encountered, with a *minimum* population of something over thirty-five billion. None of the other planets in this system are quite up to Planet I's standards, but Planet III is actually a *binary*, both of whose worlds are very heavily developed on any normal standards, and Planet I is just as heavily industrialized in its own right. Think of Sol plus Alpha Centauri. Then add Galloway's Star. Then double it. That's the industrial muscle at the heart of this single star system. Given that, we must assume that the deep space force is a formidable one, and that the close-in defenses of these planets have been built to whatever scale the Bugs deemed desirable. Ladies and gentlemen, there is no practical limit to what could be waiting in the inner system."

He looked up from the sphere, meeting the collective weight of all those eyes. And then, with startling abruptness, he sat down.

Kthaara leaned forward, silhouetted against the blazing starfields beyond the viewport.

"Now," he said, as quietly as LeBlanc had spoken, "you all know what we are facing. You also know that it is essentially what we expected—and that our plans have been laid with precisely such a contingency in mind." He turned to Admiral Dar'sahlahk. "All members of the Alliance appreciate the role the fleet of the Zarkolyan Empire has agreed to play in those plans," he said.

It was difficult to read the facial expression of a being who, in the usual sense, had no face. Nor could the translator convey much in the way of emotion. Still, the software was fairly sensitive to emphasis, and it was clear that the Zarkolyan admiral was speaking in no casual tone.

"We are honored to be given that role, Lord Talphon. It was with just such an eventuality as this in mind that we designed our *Kel'puraka*-class battlecruisers, and the personnel who crew them are fully aware of the implications of that design philosophy."

"Very well, then. As this is our last conference before commencing the operation, I will now open the floor for discussion."

There was surprisingly little. Everyone knew the plan, and all that remained was the usual tug of war over resource allocation. Even that was soon concluded, and the participants filed out, leaving Kthaara seated in the starlight.

He stood up slowly and turned to face the viewport. For a time, he gazed out in silence. Then he became aware that he wasn't entirely alone. He turned back to the room, still dimly lit, and his dark-adapted eyes made out the figure standing in the shadows.

"Ahhdmiraaaal Muhrakhuuuuma?"

The fragile looking, slender Human female—Kthaara knew the

race well enough to know how far she deviated from the physical norm—stepped forward into the starlight.

"Pardon me, Lord Talphon. I was just recalling the last time I offered you the hospitality of a flagship of mine. You, and Ivan Antonov."

Kthaara felt the years roll away, and he gave a long, rustling Orion sigh as the memory flowed over him.

"So long ago," he said, and gave a deliberately Human nod. "I, too, remember it well. And I also seem to recall hearing that Sky Maaarshaaal Avraaam . . . discussed that invitation with you. My impression was that she felt that Eeevaan and I were old enough to know better than to transform an inspection trip into one final ride together on the war-trail." A purring Orion chuckle escaped him. "In fact, I believe that Eeevaan told me that after she finished explaining that to him at some considerable length, she intended to explain the same thing to *you*."

"That's one way to put it!" Murakuma said, with her own species' chuckle. "She must have rehearsed all the way from Alpha Centauri to Justin, because once she got there, she tore an extremely painful and well-thought-out strip off of my hide for letting the Chairman of the Joint Chiefs and a relative of the Khan endanger themselves like that."

She grinned, but then, abruptly, a dead emptiness opened in her heart. Her eyes strayed to the viewport and the spaces of the Anderson Chain, where Hannah Avram had died along with so many thousands of others. Her grin vanished, and Kthaara's slit-pupiled eyes softened as he read her change of mood.

"But, after reprimanding you, she presented you with your race's highest decoration for valor, did she not?" he asked gently.

"Yes," Murakuma's hand strayed unconsciously to her breast, and the ribbon of the Lion of Terra. "Yes, she did," she said in a voice almost too small to be heard, and Kthaara smiled.

"We all have our dead to mourn, Ahhdmiraaaal. My own recollections go back much further than that: to the Theban War, when I was young enough to be *truly* foolish. Ah, what a blood-mad *zeget* I was then, burning to avenge my cousin's treacherous death! Ahhdmiraaaal Antaanaaav gave me the chance to seek that vengeance, even permitted me to fly a fighter in one of his strikegroups. And he and I became *vilkshatha* brothers."

"And now you're seeking vengeance again." It was a statement, not a question, and Murakuma held the old Orion's eyes with hers. "I'm curious about something, Lord Talphon. In all the planning for this operation, I notice you've never once considered the possibility of using 'dinosaur killers' in Home Hive Five, like Lord Khiniak and I did in Home Hive Two."

"No, I have not, have I?" Kthaara maintained a blandly inscrutable silence for a heartbeat or two, then relented. "There is really no mystery. I do not devalue that approach, and I am sure your Small Claw Tahlivver would be more than willing to repeat his exploit. But, as you discovered in Home Hive Two, even your 'cushion shot' option is subject to interception by a defending fleet. In the end, we would have to confront their mobile forces and their gunboats and kamikazes whatever we did, and unlike Home Hive Two, Home Hive Five has not been stripped of its fleet by previous incursions. And, as you know better than most of us, it takes a great deal of time. I want to *finish* this war, and finish it quickly. I believe the force we have assembled here can do that."

"Of course." Murakuma nodded. "I understand. And yes, we *will* finish it for you."

She stood straighter, gave a respectful nod, and left him. Kthaara watched her go, and then turned back to the viewport, now alone. Only he wasn't truly alone, for the Anderson Chain held other ghosts besides that of Hannah Avram.

*I did not tell her the full truth, Eeevaan'zarthan. She would not have understood. She might even have thought that I was impugning her honor. In that, she would have been quite mistaken. What she did in Home Hive Two was not dishonorable. It merely would be* wrong *at this moment. It would be vermin extermination, not vengeance.*

*Admittedly, there can be no true* vilknarma, *no blood-balance, for all the Bugs in the universe would not balance you.*

*Nevertheless . . .*

Kthaara's eyes went to LeBlanc's holo display of Home Hive Five. The four inhabited planets still glowed redly.

*Nevertheless, brother, I can at least provide you with an impressive, if belated, funeral pyre.*

All was in readiness. In the master plot on *Li Chien-lu*'s flag bridge, the swarming green icons seemed to coil as Grand Fleet poised to strike.

"Lord Talphon . . . ?" Leroy McKenna diffidently indicated the countdown that was crawling through the last few minutes.

"Yes, I see," Kthaara acknowledged with a small nod to the

chief of staff. His eyes met Vanessa Murakuma's in a moment of shared knowledge. Then he turned to the com pickup that was hooked into the flagship of every fleet, every task force, and every task group.

*Anyone expecting a bloodthirsty oration is going to be disappointed,* Kthaara thought. The way of the *Zheeerlikou'valkhannaiee* was to use few words, but heartfelt ones, at the important moments in their lives. The more important the moment, the fewer words with which it should be diminished. And so Kthaara'zarthan, *Khan-haku* Talphon, fourth cousin of the *Khan'a'khanaaeee*, Chairman of the Combined Joint Chiefs of Staff of the Grand Alliance, and Commanding Officer of the Alliance's Grand Fleet, gave the order which launched that fleet against the final home hive system in existence after the fashion of his people.

"Proceed," he said quietly.

# CHAPTER THIRTY-FOUR
## The Vengeance of Kthaara'zarthan

*The end could not be long delayed.*

*The Fleet stood at bay in defense of the final System Which Must Be Defended, and the massive waves of robotic probes the Enemy had sent through the warp point again and again and again promised that its wait would not be much longer.*

*Introspection was not something to which the beings who crewed the Fleet were given, nor—in any sense humans or any of their allies would have understood—were hope, or happiness, or despair. Yet those units of the vast, corporate hunger which had spawned the Fleet who were responsible for analysis and strategic planning understood what had happened . . . and what was about to happen.*

*Not fully, of course. Those analysts had no equivalent of the emotions, the terror and hate, which drove their Enemies. They didn't understand love, or the ferocity broken love and loss-born vengeance could spawn. They served colder imperatives, ones in which the things which made their Enemies what they were—individuals—could have no place, for theirs was not a society of individuals, it was . . . an appetite. An omnivoracity, whose every facet and aspect rested upon a single, all-consuming compulsion: survival.*

*Survival at all costs. At any cost. Survival which had no other objective beyond the mere act of surviving. Survival which would inspire nothing but survival: not art, not epic poetry, not music or literature or philosophy. Not ethics. And certainly never anything so ephemeral and yet so central to all their Enemies were as honor.*

*And because that single imperative was all the Fleet's analysts truly understood, they could never grasp the entirety of what drove*

592

*their enemies. Not that they would have cared if they had been able to grasp it. What mattered motivation, in the end? Their own imperative would have demanded the same action, although they would never have been so wasteful as simply to exterminate potential food sources if there was any way to avoid it. But emotionless, uncaring survival was a harsh and demanding god, and the analysts who had preceded those who now served the Fleet had given dozens of other species to it as its sacrifices. In the end, those sacrifices had been in vain. Indeed, although the analysts were far too alien to their Enemies to ever visualize the concept that any other course of action might even have been possible, those sacrifices were what had made the present disaster inevitable. The complete impossibility of coexistence—the all or nothing appetite which had driven something which could never truly be called a "civilization" to the very stars—left no other option, no other possible outcome, than this one.*

*That much, in their own way, the analysts grasped. The greater must overwhelm and devour the lesser. That was the law of the universe, the only path of survival, and their kind had enforced that law against every other species it had ever encountered, with a cold, uncaring efficiency which couldn't even be called ruthlessness, for the existence of "ruthlessness" implied the existence of an antitheses, and the analysts' kind could imagine nothing of the sort. Yet they'd always understood that he who could not eat his Enemies must, in turn, be eaten by them, and so they'd always known this moment must come if they failed to conquer.*

*And they had failed.*

*It was easy—now—to look back and trace the course of their failure, yet even now, on the brink of their final defeat, it was impossible for those analysts even to consider having followed any different course of action. Oh, yes—there were minor changes they might have made, a swifter response to overcoming the technological advantages of their Enemies, perhaps. Or possibly a less profligate expenditure of the Reserve in the early, all-out offensives of the war. Perhaps they might have diverted the resources of more than a single System Which Must Be Defended to the destruction of the Old Enemies . . . or perhaps they might have diverted less, in order to concentrate more fully against the New Enemies. Or—*

*There were many such possibilities, yet in the end, all were meaningless beside the one possibility which had never existed for a moment: the possibility of never beginning the war at all. Even now, the recognition that their automatic, instinctive response to the discovery of yet another sentient race might have been in error was impossible for the analysts to grasp or even consider.*

*They were what they were, and they'd done what they had done because what they were had been incapable of any other action, any other response. And so, in the final analysis, they weren't even "evil" as those who'd gathered to destroy them understood the term, for "evil" implied a choice, a decision between more than one possible course of action. And because the analysts had never been able to envision the possibility of choice—because they couldn't do so even now—they felt no guilt as they awaited the destruction of the final System Which Must Be Defended. Not for what they'd done to other species, and not even for what they had brought down upon their own. It would have been like expecting a whirlwind to feel a sense of blame, or a forest fire to feel remorse.*

*And yet, for all the monstrous gulf which separated them from their Enemies, the analysts shared, however tenuously, two emotions with those Enemies. In their own cold, dispassionate way, they knew despair. The despair which had swept over the citizens of Justin, of Kliean . . . of Telik. The despair which knew there was no escape, that no last-second miracle would reprieve the Worlds Which Must Be Defended or turn aside the fiery doom their species' own actions had laid up for it.*

*And even in their despair, they knew one other fragile emotion: hope. Not for themselves, or for the System Which Must Be Defended, but rather for the System Which Must Be Concealed. For the single star system of which the very last courier drones to reach them from a murdered System Which Must Be Defended had whispered, and which might someday attain once more the status of a System Which Must Be Defended.*

*In time, perhaps, the System Which Must Be Concealed would wax powerful once more. Indeed, it must do so, if it survived at all. And perhaps, in some far distant day, the analysts which served the System Which Must Be Defended would return to this area of space—wiser, better prepared, knowing what they faced—and secure the survival of the new System Which Must Be Defended and its daughter Systems Which Must Be Defended in the only way that was certain: by destroying all possible competitor species, root and branch. And perhaps those future analysts would not return here. Perhaps they would seal off the warp point behind themselves and avoid these Enemies—forever, if that were possible, and for as long as possible, if it were not.*

*The present analysts couldn't know the answers to those questions. Nor, to be honest, did they much concern themselves with them, for they weren't questions these analysts would ever have to answer.*

*The questions they faced would be answered shortly . . . and forever.*

The first scene of the last act commenced with an eruption of SBMHAWK carrier pods into Home Hive Five in the now-familiar pattern. First came the HARM-armed wave to take out the decoying ECM-equipped deep space buoys. Then came a truly massive wave armed with SBMs and CAM2s, targeted on the Bug gunboats, fortresses, and defensive cruisers.

That far, all went according to well-established doctrine. But what came next was something else altogether.

The Gorm were stereotypically a stolid, imperturbable race. As often happens, stereotype held a grain of truth.

Gunboat Squadron Leader Mansaduk, for example, had never been affected by the disorienting sense of wrongness that seemed to overtake his Orion comrades-in-arms and Terran allies at the instant of passing through a warp point—at least not to the same extent. Oh, he felt it, of course; no brain, organic or cybernetic, was immune. He just didn't let it upset him. So normally, he approached transit with serene equanimity.

Not this time, though. He looked left and right beyond the outer corners of his curving viewscreen and watched the wall of gunboats of which his was a part. They were clearly visible to the naked eye, for this was an exceptionally tight formation on the standards of space warfare. It had to be for what it was about to do.

"Approaching transit," Sensor Operator Chenghat reported in a voice which, like his *minisorchi*, was a little too tightly controlled, and Mansaduk turned his gaze straight ahead. The warp point was, of course, invisible.

*Well,* he told himself, *if it happens, it should be the quickest possible form of death.*

Before he'd even finished the thought, the universe seemed to turn itself inside out, and they were in Home Hive Five. The largest simultaneous warp transit the Allies had ever performed—every one of Grand Fleet's gunboats, in fact—was over.

Stroboscopic flashes to Mansaduk's left and right marked the deaths of gunboats that had interpenetrated. There were a great many of them.

The Squadron Leader took dispassionate note of the fact that he was still alive. A quick glance at his display showed him that one of his squadron's gunboats wasn't, but there was no time to feel anything. No time to do anything but give the orders which sent his surviving gunboats to their places in the wave rushing toward the Bug kamikazes.

The gunboats' ordnance loads were configured for killing small craft. The CAM2s had cleared away all of the opposing gunboats of the Bug CSP. All that were left were the assault shuttles and pinnaces, which were enormously more vulnerable missile targets. Fighter missiles would have been highly effective against such vulnerable targets; the all-up, shipboard AFHAWKs a gunboat could carry were even deadlier, and the intolerable glare of nuclear and antimatter warheads ripped at the guts of the kamikaze cloud.

At first, the kamikazes simply tried to avoid the gunboats which were killing them. Their purpose was to kill transiting starships, and to do that they must survive, not waste themselves in combat against mere gunboats. But they must also somehow remain within attack range of the warp point, and they couldn't do that if they were dead. And so, as the gunboats' kill totals climbed and climbed, the massed kamikazes had no choice but to turn upon them. Exchanging one of their own number for a gunboat was hardly cost-effective, but the Bugs had no choice but to expend some of their number if the rest were to survive to perform their real function.

A vicious fight snarled around the warp point as the better-armed pinnaces of the kamikaze cloud flung themselves upon the gunboats. Mansaduk watched the suicide shuttle that had been his gunboat's latest target flare into a momentary sun, then took advantage of a brief lull to study the readouts. The kill ratio was very much in the Allies' favor, for a gunboat was a small, nimble target, difficult for a kamikaze to catch. But against the numbers the Bugs had to waste *no* kill ratio could truly be considered "favorable," and Mansaduk began to feel an anxiety that would have surprised his non-Gorm acquaintances. His eyes strayed towards the view-aft. *Isn't it time yet. . . ?*

Then, with no warning, as was the nature of such things, it happened . . . and once again the warp point was marked by the firefly-flashes of simultaneously-transiting vessels materializing in the same volume of space. There were fewer fireflies this time, but bigger ones, because now *starships* were making transit.

The first wave consisted of Zarkolyan *Kel'puraka-B* and *Kel'junar-B*-class battlecruisers, crewed by beings whose fiery hatred for the Bugs was an elemental force, untempered by any tradition of dispassionate military professionalism. The original *Kel'puraka* and *Kel'junar* classes had been extraordinarily well-defended against missiles and kamikazes, with four advanced capital point defense installations each, which made them better adapted to warp point assaults than most battlecruisers. But the "B" refits, while retaining the original designs' defensive power, incorporated a truly radical offensive departure: the elimination of *all* normal missile launchers in favor of massed batteries of the new "box launcher" systems, effectively converting what had been conventional BCRs into highly *unconventional* specialized kamikaze killers.

The entire design concept was a calculated risk; the box launchers were slow and awkward to reload, for they lacked the sophisticated ammunition-handling equipment that made up so much of the mass and volume of conventional launchers. Because of that, the box launchers had to be loaded one round at a time, from outside the ship, with its drive field down. But the advantage of the "box launcher" was that multiple missiles could be simultaneously loaded into each box . . . and fired in one, massive salvo. And the very absence of the reloading equipment of other launchers meant that three times as many box launchers could be mounted in the same internal volume. Which meant that a single battlegroup of five *Kel'puraka-B*s and one *Kel'junar-B* command ship could belch forth four hundred and thirty-five anti-fighter AFHAWKs in a single coordinated salvo.

They did, and as they fired, each battlegroup became the center of a spreading cloud of fiery death. Their missiles raced outward, like the blast wave of some stupendous explosion, and its crest was a solid, curving wall of kamikazes vanishing into the plasma-cloud death of their own massive loads of antimatter.

The Zarkolyans blasted enormous swathes through the ranks of suicide shuttles before the Bugs understood what they were dealing with. Then the kamikazes, as though in response to a single will, turned on the new attackers. Six of the battlecruisers who'd survived transit died, but most of the pressure was removed from the gunboats, which proceeded to torment and distract the kamikazes. Those gunboats had expended their own AFHAWKs, but they retained their internal weapons, and they took vicious advantage of the kamikazes' distraction. And while they did, the surviving battlecruisers withdrew through the warp point to reload their box launchers in the safety of Anderson Three.

As they withdrew, the main body of Grand Fleet began to transit—one at a time, led by more Zarkolyans. This time they were *Shyl'narid-A*, *Shyl'tembra*, and *Shyl'prandar*-class superdreadnoughts, the larger cousins of the *Kel'purakas* which had preceded them. They embraced precisely the same design philosophy, but with five times as many launchers each, and the defenders of Home Hive Five had never seen anything like them. The kamikazes turned once more, swinging back from the gunboats to leap upon these bigger, clumsier, more vulnerable targets . . . and the superdreadnoughts belched death into their faces like the blasts of some war god's titanic shotgun.

Mansaduk's squadron was down to only two gunboats by the time they broke through into the clear and saw those advancing behemoths. A quick glance at his HUD showed the surviving kamikazes regrouping for an attack on the new threat—the one they'd been intended to face. He had no need to look at his crew. Unlike his inanimate instruments, their *minisorchi* was woven with his; he knew what they felt.

"No, Chenghat," he said, his eyes still on his HUD. "Not just yet. We have work to do here before we can follow the battlecruisers back. We must give the superdreadnoughts our support. *They* won't have the option of retiring to rearm."

*The Fleet tallied the losses of the warp point defenders with profound dissatisfaction.*

*Ultimately, there'd never been any realistic hope of preventing the Enemy from gaining entry to the System Which Must Be Defended, of course. The introduction of those extremely irritating warp-capable missiles had seen to that. Still, the Fleet had hoped to exact a far higher price of the invaders as they made their assault transits. Unfortunately, this Fleet component hadn't known of the new battlecruiser and superdreadnoughts classes. Sensor data shared with all of the Systems Which Must Be Defended by the System Which Must Be Defended which had been charged with the war against the Old Enemy suggested that the new classes came from the Old Enemy's fleet components, but no report had indicated that they would be capable of such massive salvos of AFHAWKs, and their appearance in simultaneous transits—coupled with the Enemy gunboats' earlier transits—had wiped out far more of the combat space patrol and kamikazes than projections had allowed for.*

*Still, total gunboat losses had been barely eighteen hundred, less than seven percent of the Fleet's total gunboat strength in this system, and thousands upon thousands of planet-based kamikazes remained to replace those lost on the warp point. The Fleet's Deep Space Force's starships were outnumbered by more than three-to-one by the Enemy units now in the System Which Must Be Defended, and the balance of firepower was even worse than those numbers suggested, for over half of the Deep Space Force's total starships were mere light cruisers. But even now, those ships could call upon the support of the planet-based kamikazes and almost twenty-four thousand more gunboats, and some of those gunboats carried the new, second-generation jammer packs. Clearly, the Enemy's total combined attack craft strength was less than half that—indeed, current estimates suggested it was less than ten thousand—and they were supported by little more than a thousand gunboats after their losses during the initial assault.*

*The odds against the Fleet were thus formidable, yet not truly impossible. The Fleet's greatest weakness lay in the disparity in the speeds of its component units and the tactical constraints that disparity imposed, but its numerical advantage in gunboats, properly applied, offered an opportunity to offset that weakness. Coupled with the new jammer technology, the Fleet estimated that it actually had one chance in three of inflicting sufficient damage to induce the casualty-conscious Enemy to break off short of the Worlds Which Must Be Defended.*

*This time.*

Kthaara'zarthan and Vanessa Murakuma stood side by side on *Li Chien-lu's* flag bridge, watching Grand Fleet take form in the plot.

It was, inevitably, a somewhat diminished array. As usual, the destabilizing effects of warp transit had degraded the accuracy of the defensive fire that had met the kamikazes. Ten monitors and a dozen superdreadnoughts of the leading waves had either been destroyed or sent limping back to Anderson Three. But they'd absorbed all the damage the Bugs had been able to inflict. The carriers, coming afterwards, had entered unmolested and were now deploying a fighter cover of unprecedented strength. Behind that shield, the remainder of Grand Fleet was streaming in and coalescing into its prearranged formation with practiced ease.

*As well it should,* Murakuma thought. This operation was unprecedented in numbers and tonnage, but in nothing else. It was the kind of offensive which nearly a decade's experience had rendered almost—not quite—routine. From any prewar viewpoint,

Grand Fleet's experience level would have been as awe inspiring as its size.

"Do you suppose the Bugs will have any technological surprises waiting for us?" she asked Kthaara.

"Surprises, by definition, are unpredictable," the Orion said philosophically. "The possibility cannot be denied. We have learned to our cost that the Bahgs are capable of inventiveness, and in their present straits they must be innovating under the lash of desperation—if, indeed, they are capable of feeling such a thing as desperation. Nevertheless, our precautions should suffice against any plausible threat."

Gazing at the solid phalanxes of green lights forming up on the plot, Murakuma couldn't disagree. For all of Kthaara's eagerness to end the war in one grand, sweeping act of vengeance, the canny Orion refused to neglect the Allies' hard-learned tactical doctrines. The massive battle-line would advance in-system behind a cruiser screen, its flanks covered by clouds of fighters. That advance, toward the teeming planets whose destruction would cripple any further resistance, would force engagement upon what must be a badly outnumbered deep space fleet. True, the DSF would surely be preceded by a *lot* of planet-based kamikazes. But, again, the Allies were used to that, she reflected, then looked up as Leroy McKenna walked across to her and Kthaara.

"Lord Talphon, Admiral, the last units have transited successfully."

"Excellent." Kthaara straightened up. "Please let me know the instant all commands have reported readiness to proceed. It is time to finish this."

Lieutenant Commander Irma Sanchez had thought she was prepared for the oncoming wavefront of death.

VF-94 had launched from TFNS *Hephaestus*, the assault carrier on which the squadron was now embarked, and taken its place in Grand Fleet's fighter cover. To minimize pilot fatigue, that cover was maintained by squadrons in rotation, and this was VF-94's shift. It was almost over, and Irma was allowing a certain blue-eyed face to peek into her consciousness. She'd managed to get leave a couple of months earlier, but hadn't been able to stay for—was it possible?—Lydia's twelfth birthday. That was a few standard days from now. . . .

"Sssssskipperrrrr—"

The voice in her helmet was that of the recently promoted Lieutenant Eilonwwa. Irma was still amazed by her good fortune at having kept him. The multispecies fighter squadrons Seventh Fleet had cobbled together amid the retaking of Anderson Three had been emergency expedients only, as Commander Nicot had told her at the time, and by now none were left . . . except VF-94. Commander Conroy, *Hephaestus'* CSG, subscribed to the if-it-ain't-broke-don't-fix-it philosophy.

Eilonwwa was currently on the squadron's outermost flank, and he'd picked up the downloaded readings from the recon fighters first. But now Irma's fighter was displaying them for her. She managed to acknowledge Eilonwwa's transmission as she gaped at the readings. *That* can't *be right! Can it?*

"Heads up!" Commander Conroy's voice was crisp yet completely calm, almost conversational, on the command circuit, but Irma knew he, too, had read the tale of those tens of thousands of kamikazes roaring down on Grand Fleet in formations whose density was without precedent in space warfare—even in *this* war. He fired off a series of orders, and *Hephaestus'* component joined the wave of fighters that curved inward to support the cruiser screen and, it was hoped, envelop its attackers.

The forward squadrons began to salvo their FM3s, and Irma wondered if they were even bothering to pick targets. There was no real need, after all. Anything fired into that mass of small craft was almost bound to hit something, and the missiles' short-ranged seekers would probably do as good a job of finding something to kill as the overloaded tactical computer of whatever fighter launched them.

Fireballs began to glare all along the cliff face of that moving mountain of suicidal death. It was incredible. They were actually so close together that an exploding kamikaze's antimatter load could take out two—even *three*—additional small craft by simple proximity. It was worse than shooting fish in a barrel; it was like dynamiting them in a fish bowl!

And yet, if you could accept the sacrificial logic of massed kamikaze attacks in the first place, then that hideous hurricane of exploding small craft made perfectly good sense. Yes, the fighters could kill anything they could see, but the Bug formation was so dense, so compact, that the strikegroups could see only a tiny fraction of them at a time, and while they were killing the ones they could see, the others were sweeping closer and closer to the Fleet at over twelve percent of light-speed.

That was why the protective fighters had to envelop them, had to capture them in a net of coordinated crossfires and finely sequenced squadron-level pounces.

But there were too many attackers to envelop, and no time to work around the perimeter. There was time only for each squadron to salvo its missiles head-on . . . and then follow them straight into that maw of destruction. It was sheer, howling chaos, with absolutely no possibility of centralized direction. Strikegroups came apart, shredding into individual squadrons—sometimes individual fighters—as they fought for their own lives and the life of the battle-line.

But they were used to that, had been ever since the Bugs introduced their gunboat-mounted jammer packs. Nor did it matter much; there were plenty of kamikazes for everyone to kill. Enough, and more than enough.

"All right, people," Irma said as she finished her formal orders and VF-94's spot in line flashed closer at a combined closing speed of over .25 *c*. "Try to keep some kind of formation and watch each others' backs. But mostly . . . *kill the bastards!*"

And then they were in among the vastest dogfight in history, and there was plenty of killing for everyone.

Even for veterans of the war against the Bugs, there was something horrible about the way the seemingly illimitable ranks and columns and phalanxes of gunboats and small craft advanced. There was absolutely no tactical finesse. This was an elemental force that existed for the sole purpose of reaching the screen, and passing through it to the capital ships and carriers.

*They know—in whatever weird way they "know" things—that this is their last stand,* Irma thought in some sheltered recess of her mind, even as she blew two kamikazes out of the plenum, so close together and in such rapid succession that the fireballs merged. *And we know this is the last real battle we'll have to fight. That's why there's a kind of madness about this carnage . . . from* both *sides.*

Then the tatters of the Bugs' first waves came into contact with the screen, and it became clear that there was going to be something else about this battle that was unique.

"Report! I want answers!" Leroy McKenna's strain broke through his usually rock-steady surface as he snapped at the staff intelligence officer. Murakuma decided that this wasn't the time to reprove him. Instead, she concentrated on trying to match the studied imperturbability that Kthaara'zarthan radiated as he stood beside her.

Marina Abernathy glanced up, then exchanged a few more hurried words with a knot of specialists before she turned to face the chief of staff.

"It's clear enough, Sir—we just never anticipated it. The Bugs have developed and deployed a system analogous to the jammer packs they've been using against our fighters. But this version disrupts the datalink systems of *starships.*"

"But . . . but there's nothing bigger than gunboats out there!" McKenna waved at the master plot showing the oncoming torrent of tiny red lights that was coming up against the cruiser screen . . . and suffering far fewer losses from its fire than it should have. "They can't carry second-generation ECM on something that small!"

"They're not. It's a much weaker system than that, with what seems to be a maximum range of not more than two light-seconds—probably closer to one and a half. But within that range, it has the same effect."

Murakuma decided it was time to step in.

"Does it radiate an easily detected emissions signature, like the earlier generation jammer packs?"

"According to the preliminary reports, it does, Admiral."

"Very well, then." She turned to Ernesto Cruciero and pointed to the teeming plot, where the swarms of emerald fighters were still snapping at the heels of the masses of kamikazes. "Ernesto, get with Anson. Our fighters must understand clearly that their first priority is detecting and killing the jamming gunboats."

"Aye, aye, Sir. We'll pass the word—and it looks like several of our strikegroups are already doing just that, on their own initiative."

Murakuma nodded. She would have expected no less.

"I agree we need to kill the jammers," Abernathy put in, "but the destruction of the jamming system does *not* imply instantaneous restoration of the datalink it was jamming. It's going to take at least a little time to put the net back up, so no matter what our fighters can do. . . ."

The spook left the thought unfinished.

"Both points are well taken," Murakuma acknowledged formally. "But however well it works—or doesn't—it's still the only game in town. Send the orders, Ernesto."

"Also, Ahhdmiraaaal Muhrakhuuuuma," Kthaara said, speaking

up for the first time, "it would be well to alert all fleet commands to what the battle-line can expect. They are already at General Quarters, of course. But . . ."

He indicated the plot, where the scarlet ocean was beating against the dam of the cruiser screen. The dam was already starting to spring leaks.

"The battle-line," the old Orion resumed, "including, needless to say this ship, should prepare for heavier kamikaze attacks than we had anticipated."

The battle rose, if possible, to an even higher pitch of insanity. The cruisers of the screen, many of them now fighting individually rather than as elements in the precision fire control of datagroups—poured out fire in a frenzy of desperation. Fighters corkscrewed madly through the dense clouds of kamikazes in grim efforts to seek out and destroy the jamming gunboats.

There weren't as many of those last as might have been expected from earlier experiences with the first-generation jammer packs. Probably, it was a new system the Bugs hadn't had time to put into true mass production. But great as that mercy might have been, there were still enough of them to make a difference. For all the frantic efforts of the fighters and the cruisers of the screen, more and more kamikazes broke through and hungrily sought out the massed formations of monitors and superdreadnoughts, and the carriers sheltering behind them.

Most especially, they hunted the command ships—like Seventh Fleet's *Irena Riva y Silva*, a ship by now almost as legendary as the admiral whose lights she flew.

A thunder god's hammer smashed home, and the entire world rang like one enormous bell. Even in the shelter of his armored, padded command chair and its restraining crash frame, Raymond Prescott momentarily lost consciousness as the latest kamikaze impacted.

That was the wrong word, of course. It wasn't the direct physical collision that not even a monitor could have survived. The last-ditch point defense fire had prevented that, and it very seldom happened in space war anyway. But what had happened as the searing ball of plasma reached out and slammed into the flagship's drive field was bad enough.

Prescott dragged himself back to awareness, shaking his head inside his sealed vac helmet. The reverberations of the kamikaze's death throes echoed through his brain, making it impossible to think quickly or clearly, but his eyes sought out the plot and the data sidebars that detailed his command's wounds out of sheer spinal reflex. But then his attention was pulled back away from them as his private com screen awoke with the call he'd ordered be automatically patched into it if it came.

"Raaymmonnd!" Zhaarnak'telmasa's voice was as torn by static as his image was shredded by interference. "You must abandon ship immediately! The Bahgs have realized you can barely defend yourself now. They are closing in from all sides!"

Intellectually, Prescott knew his *vilkshatha* brother was right. But there was a difference between what intellect recognized and what the wellsprings which made a man what he truly was demanded.

"All right. But first I want Admiral Meyers and his staff to get off." *Riva y Silva* was doubling as Allen Meyers' flagship for Task Force 71. "After that—"

Amos Chung had always been bad about delaying the moment he helmeted up. That probably explained the blood streaming down from his lacerated scalp . . . and it certainly explained how he overheard the *vilkshatha* brothers' hurried conversation.

"Admiral Meyers is dead, Sir!" He shouted over the whooping of the emergency klaxons, the screams of the wounded, and the creaking groans that arose from the ship's savaged vitals. "Direct hit on secondary Flag Plot! And the same hit buckled the escape pod tubes from Flag Bridge! We'll have to use the elevators!"

"All right," Prescott said to Zhaarnak as he unlocked his crash frame and sat up, then turned to Chung. "Amos, tell Anna—"

"She's dead, too, Sir," the spook said harshly.

For a moment, Prescott sat amid pandemonium, head bowed, unable to move.

"*Raaymmonnd!*" The voice from the com unit was the yowl of a wounded panther.

"Incoming!" someone shouted from what was left of Plotting.

"Come *on*, Sir!" Chung pleaded. Jacques Bichet joined him. Together, they dragged the admiral physically to his feet and started him towards the hatch. After a few steps, he started moving under his own power. Soon, he and Bichet were helping Chung.

They'd just gotten into the elevator and started toward the boatbay when the next titanic sledgehammer smashed into the wounded ship.

✧          ◊          ✧

Irma Sanchez blinked away the blinding dazzle of the fireball. *Well, the Ninety-Fourth was the only multispecies squadron,* she thought, seeking with bitter irony to hold her grief back out of arm's reach where it couldn't hurt her.

But there was no time to mourn Eilonwwa. She'd broken free momentarily of the battle pattern, where she could at least take stock. They'd stayed with the kamikazes as the latter passed through the collapsing cruiser screen, and on towards the battle-line. Now some of those gargantuan ships were close enough to be naked-eye objects.

She managed to study her HUD through muffling layers of fatigue. The nearest one—a *Howard Anderson*-class command monitor—was an atmosphere-haloed wreck, shedding life pods, shuttles, and pinnaces as it signaled its distress. Then she noticed the ship ID: it was *Riva y Silva,* flagship of her own Seventh Fleet. With the years of experience that made the fighter an extension of her own body, she wrenched the little craft into the kind of tight turn that only inertia-canceling drives made possible.

The Code Omega arrived just as her viewscreen automatically darkened.

Not even the shuttle's drive field saved it from the shock wave that rushed out from the bloated fireball astern where *Riva y Silva* had been, and small craft carried only the most rudimentary inertial compensators. It was hard to see—the secondary explosion inside the elevator shaft had damaged his helmet visor badly, and the HUD projected on the inside of the scorched, discolored armorplast showed strobing yellow caution icons for at least a quarter of his suit's systems. But Raymond Prescott could see as well as he needed to when the brutal buffeting was over and he knelt beside the motionless form of Amos Chung. The intelligence officer's shattered visor showed the ruin inside only too clearly.

He heard a voice over his own helmet com. The com seemed to be damaged, like everything else about his vacsuit, and it took him a second or two to recognize it as the young voice of the shuttle's pilot.

"Admiral . . . everyone . . . our drive's gone, and there's a gunboat coming in fast! Stand by for ejection!"

Prescott obeyed like everyone else, out of the sheer auto-response of decades of training. But even as he sat, his eyes were locked once more upon that uncaring, damnable HUD and the blazing scarlet icon of his suit's location transponder. Even with a working transponder, the chance that an individual drifting survivor would be detected by search and rescue teams—assuming there was anyone left to worry about SAR—were considerably less than even. Without one, there was no chance at all.

Raymond Prescott stared at the blood-red death sentence, and a strange, terrible calm flowed through him. The death that every spacer feared more than any other, if he were truly honest. The fear of falling forever down the infinite well of the universe, alone and suffocating. . . .

He began to reach for a certain valve on his vacsuit.

It was only because she was following the gunboat that Irma Sanchez detected the crippled shuttle. She pressed on after the Bug, crushed back into her flight couch by the brutal power of the F-4's drive. Grayness hovered at the corners of her vision, but it wasn't acceleration alone that bared her teeth in a savage grin.

There was no time for a careful, by-The-Book attack run. The only way she was going to be able to get any kind of targeting solution was by coming insanely close.

The damage the shuttle had already taken must have affected the circuitry. The pilot's first attempt to eject his passengers and himself failed.

Surprise at that stayed Prescott's hand.

Someone screamed. The gunboat was lining up on them. Prescott prepared for a quick death instead of a slow one.

Then the pilot yelled something about a fighter.

The F-4's computer screamed audible and visual warning as a Bug targeting radar locked the fighter up. Irma knew where it was coming from. There was no more time—no time for a proper target lock from her own fighter. She laid the shot in visually, the way every instructor at Brisbane had told her *no one* could do, and her internal hetlasers stabbed out with speed-of-light death.

In the fragment of an instant before it erupted into a ball of flame, the gunboat birthed its own, slower-than-light death darts.

The second time, it worked. With a g-force that almost induced blackout (and finished off his suit com once and for all), Raymond

Prescott was out into the starry void, just in time to be dazzled by the gunboat's death.

His rank meant his was the first seat in the sequenced ejection queue, and the old-fashioned explosive charge hurled him outwards. But even it was damaged; it fired erratically, its thrust off-axis, and the starscape swooped and whirled crazily ... and then the shuttle blew up behind him.

A fresh stab of grief ripped through him. So much grief. Grief for all the men and women who'd never gotten off of *Riva y Silva* at all. Grief for Amos Chung ... and for Jacques Bichet and the other shuttle passengers he knew were still sitting in their seats, still waiting for their turn in the queue. Still waiting, when the dead man without a transponder had already been launched because he was so "important" to the war effort.

The charge stopped firing, and his hands moved mechanically, without any direction from his brain as he unstrapped from the seat. He thrust it away from him almost viciously and watched it go pinwheeling slowly off across the cosmos. There was a huge, ringing, silent nothingness within him—one that matched the infinite silence about him perfectly—as he watched, as well as he could through his damaged visor, while the seat vanished into the Long Dark that waited for him, as well.

Strange. Strange that it should come to him like this, in the quiet and the dark. Somehow, he'd always assumed it would come for him as it had for Andy, in the flash and thunder and the instantaneous immolation of matter meeting antimatter. In the fury of battle, with the men and women of his *farshatok* about him. Not like this. Not drifting forever, one with the legendary Dutchman, the very last of the *farshatok* who'd planned, and fought, and hoped beside him for so many years.

His vacsuit had never been intended for extensive EVA. Its emergency thrusters' power and endurance were strictly limited ... and they showed another yellow caution light in his HUD. It made no difference, of course—not for a single, drifting human in a vacsuit with no transponder—but he reached for the thruster controls, anyway. The life support of his damaged suit was undoubtedly going to run out soon enough, yet it was important, somehow, that he exercise one last bit of self-determination before the end.

He tapped the control panel lightly, gently, almost caressingly, and the thrusters answered, slowing his own spinning tumble.

When the end came, he would choose a single star he could

see through his damaged visor, fix his gaze upon it, and watch as the darkness came down at last.

Somehow, Irma had managed to punch out in time.

She had no idea how. Nor did she have any true memory of the death of the faithful little fighter which had served her so long and so well as it ate the Bug missile. Now, as she tumbled through space, amid the horror of vertigo, she clung for her sanity's sake to the thought of the extremely powerful transponder every fighter pilot's vacsuit contained.

Actually, a pilot's suit had a number of goodies that went beyond the standard models that everyone aboard a warship wore in combat—and not just its greater capacity to absorb body wastes before overloading with results best not thought about. For one thing, it had a considerably more powerful thruster system than a standard suit.

That thought drove through her brain at last, and she forced control on herself and used the thrusters to stop the tumbling. Then she shut them off. No need to waste the compressed gas. She had nowhere in particular to go. If anything was going to save her bacon, she told herself philosophically, it was the transponder, not the thrusters. Not that it was likely to. She'd probably survive for the short run, for the battle had receded, turning into a distant swarm of fireflies. But that had a downside: no one was close enough for her half-assed helmet com to communicate with, and the odds of anyone coming close enough to pick up even her transponder signal were slim, to say the very best.

So she simply drifted. There was nothing else to do. She drifted for a long time. Eventually, she stopped looking at her helmet chrono. Periodically, she took sips of the nutrient concentrate the suit's life support system dispensed, with no great enthusiasm—the stuff would keep you alive, but it tasted like puke. Mostly, she let her mind wander listlessly through the landscape of memories.

Then, after some fraction of eternity, she spotted another vacsuit.

*Somebody from the shuttle, maybe?* she wondered. *If so, he's probably dead already.*

*But if he isn't . . . That's a standard vacsuit, but from this close, I ought to be able to pick up even its dip-shit transponder code. Assuming it was transmitting. So it must not be. And with no transponder, he's got no chance.*

Without further thought, she maneuvered herself into the right alignment and activated her thruster pack.

The gas was nearly gone when Irma was still about fifty meters short of the other suited figure. She cut the thrusters and let herself coast onward. She managed to snag the other suit *en passant*, and they tumbled on together in a clumsy embrace for a few seconds before she was able to use the last of the gas to halt the sickening motion.

*Well, that's just dandy! No more thruster.*

Irma brought her helmet into contact with the other's for direct voice communication with a certain resentful emphasis. She gazed through the helmet visor, but whatever this poor bozo had been through, his suit hadn't gotten off unscathed. It was so badly scorched she couldn't even make out the rank insignia, much less the name which had once been stenciled across the right breast, and there were spatters of what had to be blood daubed across it. The enviro pack didn't look any too good, either, although at least the external tell-tales were still flashing yellow, not burning the steady red of someone who would no longer need life support at all. Even the visor's tough, almost indestructible armorplast was heat-darkened. She could barely see into it at all, but she caught the impression of open eyes, looking back at her, so at least the guy was alive and conscious.

"You all right?" she demanded.

"Yes, more or less." The answering voice was badly distorted by the transmitting medium of their helmets, but it sounded a little old for regular space crew. Not weak, or shaky. Just . . . like it ought to be accompanied by gray hair.

"Thank you—I think," it went on. "You must be a fighter pilot, from the looks of your suit."

"Yeah—Lieutenant Commander Irma Sanchez, commanding VF-94. If," she added bitterly, "there's any VF-94 left to command."

"So you have a chance of being found, by someone tracking your transponder. And now *I* have that chance, too. Yes, I *definitely* thank you, Commander. By the way, I'm—"

"Can the thanks, Pops," Irma cut him off rudely. "I just pissed away my ability to maneuver—not that it was doing me much good. And before that, I'd gotten my fighter blasted out from under my ass to save that shuttle you were on. So don't thank me, all right? I wasn't doing you a favor. I was just being stupid—as usual!"

The old-timer didn't seem to take offense. Instead, the poorly transmitted voice only sounded thoughtful.

"VF-94 . . . yes, I seem to recall. On *Hephaestus*, right? And aren't you the last of the human squadrons to have non-human pilots?"

"We *were*. We had an Ophiuchi pilot—a damned good one. But he's dead now."

For no particular reason, the reminder of Eilonwwa knocked open a petcock which had been holding back a reservoir of hurt, and now it poured out in a gush of rage.

"He got killed just like everybody gets killed who deserves to live! Like my lover—we were in the Golan System, when the Bugs came, do you know that? He stayed. So did the parents of a little girl I took with me in the evacuation. And now they're Bug shit! Do you understand that? And now I'm in the goddamned fucking military so I can kill Bugs. I've killed them and killed them and *killed* them, and there's just no fucking end to them, and I'm fucking sick to death of it!"

She jarred to a sudden halt and sucked in a deep, shuddering breath as she realized she'd been screaming into this inoffensive middle-aged guy's helmet.

"Sorry, Pops," she said uncomfortably. "Didn't mean to blast your eardrums."

"Oh, that's all right. And yes, I think I do understand. I've lost friends myself. I just lost a lot of them, when *Riva y Silva* went. And before that . . . I lost my brother."

"Shit. I shouldn't have dumped that load on you."

"That's all right," the man repeated. "But tell me: what about that little girl? What happened to her?"

"I adopted her. It was all I could do, especially after . . . after losing the child I was carrying."

"I'm sorry."

"Anyway," Irma went on, "she's going to be twelve in a few days. I haven't been able to see all that much of her, just whenever I can get leave. And every time I do, it's been so long that . . . well, it's as if . . . Hell, there I go again. Why am I telling you all this?"

"Possibly because I'm the only other human being available," the man said, and she could have sworn she heard something almost like a smile in the distorted voice. "Anyway, I'm glad you have. It reminds me of why we're doing what we're doing."

"Huh?"

"You see, you're wrong about one thing. There *is* an end to the Bugs. It's right here, in this system."

"So? It's not like it'll make any difference to you and me. Face it: transponder or no transponder, the odds are about a million to one against our being rescued. Nobody's going to come looking for survivors out here in the middle of all these cubic light-minutes of nothing."

"It's possible that you're being too pessimistic," the old-timer suggested in an odd tone, almost as if he were chuckling over some private joke. Which was just a bit much out of somebody in a suit that was about to crap out in the middle—literally—of nowhere at all.

Something scornful was halfway out of Irma's mouth when her communicator suddenly pinged with a deafening attention signal.

The shuttle's crew was made up of Tabbies, but there was a human lieutenant aboard. He was already speaking to the middle-aged man as they cycled Irma through the inner hatch of the lock. Her fellow castaway had his helmet off and his back to her as the lieutenant finished what he was saying.

"—and he's waiting for you now, Sir."

*Hmmm . . .* Irma reflected. *That "Sir" sounded awfully respectful. Pops must outrank me. Maybe I shouldn't have lipped off quite so much.*

"Thank you," the man said to the lieutenant and bent over the cabin com screen, which displayed the image of an Orion. Incredibly, he began speaking in what sounded awfully like the howls and snarls the Tabbies called a language.

*I always thought humans couldn't do that,* she thought.

"What's been happening?" she demanded of the lieutenant. "I've been out here a long time."

"The kamikazes hurt us, Sir," the youngster said, "but not enough to even the odds when the Bug deep space force arrived. That was what they must've hoped for, but they crapped out. Our battle-line was still fast enough to hold the range open, and we blasted them out of space without ever closing to energy range."

"But what about their suicide-riders?"

"Yeah, *they* had the speed to close with us. And we took some losses from them. But only a few of them managed to break through without fire support from their capital ships."

He shrugged. "Like I say, we got hurt—but every single one of their ships is either dead, or so much drifting junk nobody's ever going to have to worry about it again."

Irma sagged against a bulkhead with relief. Then, with the important questions taken care of, another one occurred to her.

"But if the Fleet's still headed in-system, how the hell did you find us? What were you doing back here?"

"You've *got* to be kidding!" The lieutenant stared at her with a stunned incredulity that made him forget her rank. "D'you think Fang Zhaarnak was about to let us call *this* search off?"

"Fang Zhaarnak?" Irma stared back in confusion. "What does he have to—?"

But then the older man wrapped up his alley-cat-like conversation with the Orion in the com screen—who, Irma now noticed, wore the very heavily jeweled harness of exalted rank—and turned to say something to *her*. And as he did, she finally saw his face clearly—the face she'd seen in more news broadcasts then she could count. The face she'd seen before the First Battle of Home Hive Three when the admiral commanding Sixth Fleet in Zephrain had announced to his personnel, including a young fighter pilot consumed with rage and the need for vengeance, that they were going to kill the very first home hive system to die.

"Oh, shit," she said in a tiny voice, and Raymond Prescott smiled at her. There were ghosts behind those hazel eyes, she thought numbly, yet that smile held a curious warmth. One that didn't fit well with the stories she'd heard about him since his brother's death.

"I just asked Fang Zhaarnak to inquire into the status of VF-94, Commander. You'll be glad to know that three of your pilots made it back to *Hephaestus*."

"Thank you, Sir. Uh, Admiral, I apologize for—"

"For heaven's sake, don't apologize! As you pointed out—rather forcefully, as I recall—you saved my life. And that wasn't all you did for me."

"Sir?"

"You reminded me of something I'd lost sight of, in the world of large-scale abstractions I inhabit, and in . . . becoming what I became after my brother was killed. You reminded me of why we're fighting this war—the real reason. And it's very basic and very, very simple. We're fighting it for that little girl of yours."

After a moment in which the background noises of the shuttle seemed unnaturally loud, Prescott grew businesslike.

"We're on our way to rendezvous with Fang Zhaarnak's flagship. Grand Fleet's regrouping for the final advance in-system. In the meantime, our carriers are going to go back to Anderson Three to pick up replacement fighters from the reserves there. We still have some work to do."

Irma straightened up.

"Sir, if possible I request to be returned to *Hephaestus*."

"After what you've been through? No one will expect you back immediately, and Fang Zhaarnak's people are already informing *Hephaestus* that you survived. At least take time to get checked out physically."

"I'm fine, Admiral. And . . . if we're going to get a couple of replacement pilots, I'll need all the time I can get to integrate them into the squadron before we tackle the planets."

Prescott nodded, and smiled.

"I believe we can probably arrange that, Commander."

Kthaara'zarthan stood on *Li Chien-lu*'s flag bridge, a motionless silhouette against the viewscreen whose starfields now held two new, pale-blue members: the twin planet system occupying Home Hive Five's third orbit, seemingly almost touching each other at this distance.

Vanessa Murakuma didn't disturb him. Instead, she turned to her chief of staff.

"Are the ship losses in yet, Leroy?"

"Yes, Sir. As expected, they were very light in this latest action. So the earlier figures are essentially unchanged."

She thought of what lay behind McKenna's emotionless words. Twenty-nine monitors, thirty six superdreadnoughts, five assault carriers, twenty-one fleet carriers, forty-one battlecruisers, and thirty-three light cruisers. They'd also very nearly lost Raymond Prescott when his flagship died; would have, if it hadn't been for some fighter jock.

But Leroy was right. Virtually all those ghastly losses had been sustained in the earlier battle with the deep space force and its massive wavefront of kamikazes . . . and the Bugs had shot their bolt in that battle. When Grand Fleet had reached the inner system, it had found relatively few gunboats and small craft remaining. And the Allies' surviving carriers had been able to launch full complements of fighters to meet those kamikazes at extreme range.

So few of them had gotten through that the cruiser screen, even after the laceration it had taken earlier, had blown them apart with almost contemptuous ease.

Kthaara turned slowly, as though reluctant to give up his contemplation of those twin bluish lights.

"Have all the fighters recovered?"

"Yes, Sir. Some of the carriers have already finished rearming their groups; all of them should be done within another twenty minutes." There was no need for McKenna to report the nature of that rearming, for it was preplanned: FRAMs, fighter ECM, and decoy missiles.

"Excellent." The old Orion drew a deep breath. "Our fighter losses in the latest action were so light that I believe we can proceed with the first of our operational models. Do you concur, Ahhdmiraaaal Muhrakhuuuuma?"

"I do, Sir," she said formally. The other models had postulated a fighter strength so badly depleted that it could deal with only one of the twin planets at a time.

"Very well." Kthaara turned back to the viewscreen, and spoke in the Orion equivalent of a whisper. "Do it."

*There was very little of the Fleet left, but what there was knew it had failed.*

*The Enemies had been brutally wounded, but they hadn't been broken. Perhaps the Fleet had taught them too well over the years of warfare, for there'd been a time when such losses would have caused them to break off. Or perhaps not. The Enemies must know as well as the Fleet did that this was the last of the Systems Which Must Be Defended, after all.*

*It didn't truly matter. The long survival the Fleet had guarded for so many centuries was about to end, and there was no longer anything the Fleet could do about it. Not really. All that remained was to kill as many Enemies as possible before the death of the first World Which Must Be Defended destroyed any possibility of organized resistance. It wasn't much. Indeed, there was no logical point in it at all. Yet for a species for which coexistence was not even a concept, for which the possibility of negotiations or surrender did not even exist, it was the only action which remained, however pointless.*

There was no subtlety to it.

The fighters screamed down on the twin planets, ignoring the space stations and the almost fifty fortresses in low orbit about each of those doomed worlds. Speed was their only armor as they shot past those orbital defenses.

Nor did they slow down to maneuver into position to attack specific dirtside objectives, which would have given the fortresses time to complete targeting solutions. No, there were enough fighters to render any sort of tactical precision superfluous in a mission whose sole purpose was planetary depopulation. They just came in at full speed in a single pass, allowing the planets' gravity wells to whip them around in the classic slingshot effect, and simply dumped their FRAMs before pulling up and swerving away. It didn't even matter whether the missiles struck land or ocean; tsunami was as good a killer as any.

The spectacle was downloaded to *Li Chien-lu*'s main flag viewscreen. They watched as the faces of both planets erupted obscenely in boils of hellfire. It was the final application of the Shiva Option.

When it was over, Kthaara'zarthan received reports of the losses the fighters had taken. They weren't inconsiderable. But . . .

"Shall we send the carriers back to Anderson Three for more replacements, Sir?" Murakuma asked.

"I think not. Given the well established impact on the Bahgs' mental cohesion of this—" he waved a hand in the general direction of the two dead planets "—I believe that even understrength strikegroups can deal with the remaining planets."

"What about the orbital works here, Sir? They're untouched."

"They have ceased to matter. Leave them to die—we will not sully our claws. Set course for Planet II."

Irma Sanchez had managed to get away from the throng that had greeted her on her return from the dead, and actually caught a little rest as *Hephaestus* returned to Anderson Three. But then two unbelievably young pilots had arrived in VF-94's ready room, and she'd spent the return trip to Home Hive Five in a frenzy of improvisation that left her wondering if being lost in space had really been so bad after all.

Then had come the attack on the twin planets—shrieking past the orbital fortresses at a velocity that made them look like slingshot pebbles whizzing past, with the target planet zooming up with startling rapidity before she'd released her FRAMs. It had all been too quick.

But then had come Planet II. They'd been able to take that a little slower, because the Bugs in *those* fortresses had been in the grip of whatever it was that gripped them when billions of their fellows went abruptly into the flames.

And now it was time for Planet I.

*The last one*, she thought as she saw it growing in the fighter's little viewscreen. The reality hadn't hit her until now. *Forty billion Bugs, the spooks say. The* last *forty billion in the universe. Shouldn't I be feeling something? Is it possible that this has become routine?*

But, she realized, so suddenly that it was like some abrupt revelation, she'd emptied her cup of rage long ago. Once, approaching this planet, she would have seen Armand's face, and the sickening fury would have come roaring up like boiling acid. But now she remembered the words of Raymond Prescott, and the face that rose up in her mind's eye was that of a blue-eyed eleven-year-old girl.

*No,* she corrected herself, glancing at the chrono, with its date in Terran Standard. *Not eleven anymore.*

Then they were in, past the sluggishly responding fortresses.

*Happy birthday, Lydochka,* she thought as she sent her FRAMs streaking down. The now familiar fiery wall of antimatter fireballs walked across the planet, cauterizing the universe, burning away something that could not be allowed to blight any more young lives.

Afterwards, there was a long silence.

# EPILOGUE

"So," Robalii Rikka said, "I suppose my carefully rehearsed farewell speech must go to waste. I'll be seeing you again before very long, in the Star Union."

"Yes, Warmaster," Aileen Sommers replied. "The Legislative Assembly's confirmation came through today. There's still some paperwork left to unravel in the Foreign Ministry, of course."

"After which you will resume your position as ambassador from the Terran Federation to the Star Union—this time with proper accreditation," Rikka couldn't resist adding. "I must say it was a remarkably intelligent decision—" the Crucian stopped just short of saying *on the standards of your human politicians* "—given the unique status you hold among us. You are the logical choice. Oh, by the way, congratulations on your promotion."

"Thank you, Warmaster," she said with a grin . . . after a pause of her own just long enough to confirm that she knew perfectly well what Rikka had left unsaid, even though her agreement must remain equally silent. "They did it just minutes before retiring me. The whole business was a matter of hustling me from one office to another on the same floor. I think their idea was that a retired vice admiral would seem more impressive than a retired rear admiral."

"So you'd think the same logic would apply to her military attaché, wouldn't you?" Feridoun Hafezi asked rhetorically. "They ought to have made me at least a rear admiral for the job. But no, the best they could do was commodore!"

"You're still on active duty," Sommers reminded him. "So in your case they have to play by the rules."

"Still . . ." Hafezi muttered darkly into his beard, and Rikka gave Sommers his race's smile.

"The esteem in which you're held in the Star Union has nothing to do with courtesy ranks. But if your rulers' *belief* that it does has caused them to give you a long-overdue promotion, then far be it from me to disillusion them."

"So the right thing gets done for the wrong reasons," Hafezi said, this time with a trace of *genuine* bitterness.

"In this universe," the Crucian pointed out gently, "the right thing gets done so seldom that it ill behooves us to be overly particular about the reasons when it does." He gave the slight flexing of his folded wings that presaged a return to formality. "I can delay no longer. Farewell for now."

Rikka departed, leaving the two humans alone in the lounge just inside the outer skin of Nova Terra's space station. They stood at the transparency and watched the light of Alpha Centauri A glint off the flanks of the Crucian ships. First Grand Wing, also known as Task Force 86, was preparing to return to the Star Union, where work still remained to be done.

After a moment, Hafezi spoke a little too casually.

"Well . . . have you thought about it?"

"Yes," Sommers said softly.

"And—?"

Sommers turned to face him. She looked the very picture of desire at war with a lifetime's stubborn determination to face the practicalities.

"There are a lot of problems, you know," she said.

"Such as?"

"We don't really have enough time before we leave for the Star Union."

"Yes we do. And even if we didn't, we could do it there. In fact, maybe you could do it yourself. Can't an ambassador perform marriages?"

"Be serious! There's also . . . well, we haven't had a chance to talk to your family. What are *they* going to think?"

"I believe they'll approve. And even if they don't . . . well, I hope they do, but if they don't it changes nothing."

"And what about you?"

"*Me?* Haven't I made clear enough that I couldn't care less about—"

She stopped him with the lightest touch of her fingertips to his mouth. She finally smiled.

"Are you sure you've thought everything through? For instance, I outrank you. You'll have to do as you're told."

"Me and a few billion other men," Hafezi remarked, and gathered her into an embrace.

Vanessa Murakuma gave Fujiko a final hug.

"So long for now. I know you're in a hurry, with that Marine captain of yours—Kincaid, is that his name?—waiting."

"He just asked to show me a few sights here, Mother," her daughter explained painstakingly. "He was here on Nova Terra once, you see, and . . . and he's most definitely *not* 'my' Marine captain! In fact, he's conceited and self-absorbed and insufferable and . . . and what was that?"

"Only something from Shakespeare, dear. Get going—you'll be late."

She watched until Fujiko had vanished down the corridor, then hurried to the nearest drop shaft. She was nearly late herself.

Ellen MacGregor's office commanded a magnificent view of the Cerulean Ocean from its lofty altitude. The Sky Marshal didn't seem to be enjoying it. She directed Murakuma to a chair with a grunt, then held up a sheet of hardcopy and spoke without any preliminary niceties.

"What, exactly, is *this*?"

"I think it's self-explanatory, Sky Marshal. I'm resigning my commission."

"So it's true—I got one of these from Marcus LeBlanc just yesterday. You and he really are planning to retire to . . . what Fringe World hole is it?"

"Gilead, Sky Marshal," Murakuma said, and MacGregor shuddered.

"This is preposterous. Your resignation is *not* accepted."

"I believe I'm within my rights, Sky Marshal. I've obtained definite legal opinion to the effect that—"

"Oh, spare me that!" MacGregor glowered for a moment, then relaxed. "See here, let's try to work out a compromise that'll accommodate both your, uh, personal agenda and the good of the Navy."

Murakuma's antimanipulation defenses clanked into place at the last five words.

"I'm willing to listen, of course," she said very, very cautiously.

"Excellent. I've been doing some consulting, too, and I believe we could offer you permanent inactive status. Oh, I know, it's unusual. Unique, in fact. But it could be done. And," MacGregor's genes made her add, "the money would be better than your retirement pay."

"Hmmm . . ." Murakuma subjected the Sky Marshal to a long, suspicious look. She saw only blandness. "But then you could reactivate me any time you wanted," she pointed out.

"Oh, *no!* It would be strictly your decision whether or not to accept any reactivation *request.*" MacGregor emphasized the last word.

"I'd have that in writing?"

The Sky Marshal looked deeply hurt. "Of *course.*"

"Well . . ." *I'll have to look this over, but if she's not snookering me . . . well, what harm can it do? I'll never accept reactivation.* "May I have a day or two to think it over?"

"Certainly—two *Terran Standard* days." The emphasis was perceptible. MacGregor wasn't likely to forget about this twin-planet system's godawful sixty-two-hour rotation period.

"Thank you, Sky Marshal." Murakuma stood, and MacGregor dismissed her with an airy wave and an expression behind whose benignity ran the mental refrain: *Got her! Got her!*

Murakuma returned to the first floor and proceeded to the main meeting room. A briefing had just broken up, and Marcus LeBlanc was chatting with Kevin Sanders as she approached.

"Lieutenant," she greeted Sanders. "I understand you're departing for Old Terra sometime soon."

"That's right, Admiral. I'm being attached to the DNI's staff."

"Well, Admiral Trevayne is fortunate to get you."

"Thank you, Sir. She's assigning me to the . . . the office that specializes in the Khanate." That was about the closest anyone, even the famously irrepressible Sanders, could come to admitting out loud that the Federation spied on its allies.

"So you'll be working for Captain Korshenko," LeBlanc observed.

"Yes, Sir. In fact, I'll be going back with him. I'm not sure he exactly wanted it that way. He seems to think I'm a little . . . well, unorthodox."

"Where *do* people get their ideas?" Murakuma wondered, deadpan.

"Can't imagine," LeBlanc intoned with equal solemnity, and Sanders cleared his throat.

"Well, must be going, Sir. Admiral Murakuma," he said, and departed jauntily. The other two waited until he was out of earshot before they laughed.

After a moment, they went out onto the terrace where they'd always seemed to find themselves whenever the winds of war had swept them both to Nova Terra.

"So," LeBlanc began, "have you talked to her?"

"Yes. She had a proposal."

"Oh, God! Please don't tell me you let her—"

"No, no, no! I only told her I'd think about it. Just let me bounce it off you—"

Kthaara'zarthan turned his head without surprise as someone walked up from behind him. Two someones, actually, and he smiled at them—the expression remarkably gentle for a warrior of his race and reputation—and then turned back to the painting. Silence hovered as the newcomers stood beside him in the quiet, late night gallery. It was long after hours, but the museum's board had been most gracious when he asked them to permit him one final visit before his departure from Terra.

"It is a truly remarkable work," he said finally, his voice quiet as he gazed at the enigmatic Human-style smile which had entranced viewers for over eight Terran centuries.

"Truth," Raymond'prescott-telmasa agreed, equally quietly. He didn't add that Kthaara was one of only a small number of Orions familiar enough with human expressions and emotions to realize just how remarkable a work it truly was.

"She knows something the rest of us do not," Zhaarnak'telmasa said, and Prescott smiled at his *vilkshatha* brother. It was different, that smile of his, since the destruction of Home Hive Five. Warmer. More like the smile Zhaarnak remembered from before his younger brother's death, but touched as well with some of that mysterious serenity which hovered about the painting Kthaara had been admiring.

The younger Orion returned his own attention to the portrait and considered how much he himself had changed in the years since Raymond had taught him the true meaning of honor—of his own honor, as much as of his *vilkshatha* brother's. How odd, he thought yet again, that it had taken a Human to make him realize what the *Farshalah'kiah* truly meant. Not because he hadn't already known, but because, in his pain and his shame for his retreat from Kliean, he'd allowed himself to forget.

"I wonder," he went on after a moment, "if she would share her secret with us?"

"There is no secret, younger brother," Kthaara said, and pretended not to notice the way Zhaarnak's shoulders straightened at his form of address. "Not truly. She smiles not because of any secret knowledge forbidden to the rest of us, but simply because she remembers what we too often forget."

"And that is?" Prescott asked when he paused.

"That life is to be lived," Kthaara said simply. "She is eight of your centuries dead, Raaymmonnd, yet she lives here still, upon this wall, revered by your race—and by those of mine who have the eyes to see—because she will never forget that. And because by recalling it, she keeps it alive for all of us."

He turned away from the painting, slow and careful with the fragility which had come upon him, and he was no longer the tall, straight, ebon-furred shadow of death he'd been all those years ago when he and Ivan Antonov had first met. So much. He had seen so much as the years washed by him—so much of death and killing, so much of triumph and of loss. And now, at the end of his long life, he finally knew what he had truly seen along the way.

"We are warriors, we three," he told them, "yet I think there have been times in this endless war when we have . . . forgotten the reason that we are. I was thinking, as I stood here alone, of other warriors I have known. Of Eeevaan, of course, but also of others long dead. Some of the *Zheeerlikou'valkhannaiee*, but even more of those who were not. Of Annnngusss MaaacRorrrrry, who I met on your world of New Hebrrrrideeees during the war against the Thebans, Raaymmonnd. And, even more, perhaps, of Ahhdmiraaal Laaantu. Do you know his tale?"

"Yes," Prescott said. Every TFN officer knew the story of First Admiral Lantu, the Theban commander who'd fought so brilliantly against the Federation in the opening phases of the Theban War. The admiral who'd led the forces of "Holy Mother Terra" to one stunning triumph after another and fought even Ivan Antonov to a near draw. And the greatest "traitor" in Theban history.

"I hated him," Kthaara said quietly. "I blamed him for the death of my *khanhaku*, for it was units under his command who destroyed my cousin's squadron in the very first battle of the Theban War, and they did so by treachery. Looking back from today, it would be fairer to say he did so in a surprise attack, but I did not know—then—that Laaantu believed he was already at war against the *Zheeerlikou'valkhannaiee*, and so I was consumed by my hatred for his 'treachery.' Indeed, it was my need to seek *vilknarma* which first brought Eeevaan and me together. But in the end, Laaantu taught me the true duty of a warrior, for he betrayed all he had ever known, the faith in which he was raised, even the *farshatok* whom he had led into battle, because he had learned what none of them knew—that the 'Faith of Holy Mother Terra' was a lie. That the *chofaki* who ruled his people had used that lie to manipulate them for seventy of your years and then to launch them in a war of conquest. It was a war they could not win—not in the long run—and Laaantu knew what a terrible price would be exacted from his people if they fought to the bitter end. If their false leaders refused to surrender and Eeevaan was forced to bombard his world from orbit. And so he joined his enemies and aided them in every way he could, fighting to defeat his own people. Not for any personal gain, but because only by defeating them quickly and with as few Human casualties as possible could he hope to protect them from the consequences of their rulers' actions.

"And when I realized what he was doing, and why, I could no longer hate him, mightily though I tried. Oh, how I *cherished* my hate! It had kept me warm, filled me with purpose and the passion of rage, and in the end, the killer of my *khanhaku* had taken even that from me, for he had reminded me that the true warrior fights not from hate, but from love. Not to destroy, but always and above all to preserve. Do you understand that, Raaymmonnd?"

"Yes," Prescott said softly, thinking of a fighter pilot and a little girl . . . and of his brother. He looked into Kthaara'zarthan's ancient eyes, and his own hazel gaze had softened.

"I do not counsel any warrior to forget wrongs which cry out to be avenged, or to foreswear *vilknarma*," Kthaara said, "and certainly I do not equate the Thebans—or Laaantu—with the Bahgs. But the essential point is about *us*, about who we are and why we chose the Warrior's Way, and not about who we fight against. And as Shaasaal'hirtalkin taught so long ago, he who cannot relinquish the comfort of his own hate damns only himself in the end, and he who fights only in the name of destruction is the death of all honor holds dear. It is life we are called to defend. The life—" the wave of a clawed hand indicated the portrait on the wall "—she represents. The love of life which is all the secret hidden in her smile."

He gave a soft, purring chuckle and looked at the two younger officers. Raymond Prescott, who'd already been named the commander of Home Fleet, which meant his elevation to Sky Marshal, probably within the next ten years, was virtually assured, and Zhaarnak'telmasa, whose career in the service of the Khan would surely match that of his *vilkshatha* brother. They were very different from his own younger self and the basso-voiced "Ivan the Terrible" who'd sworn that same oath so many years before . . . and yet they were also so much alike that his heart ached as he gazed upon them.

"More years ago than I wish to remember," he said softly, "Eeevaan told me of how Fang Aandersaahn had watched over his own career, of the pride the fang had taken in his accomplishments, and of the example he had set. It was, he said, as if when Fang Aandersaahn arranged his assignment to command against the Thebans, he had somehow passed on to him some secret fire, some spark. As if Eeevaan had been given charge of a treasure more precious than life itself."

He smiled in recollection of his *vilkshatha* brother, the expression both sad and yet filled with cherished memories, and then he inhaled deeply.

"And now, Clan Brothers, that treasure has passed to me . . . and from me, to you. It is what brought all of our peoples together in this Grand Alliance—what taught us to trust and to fight as *farshatok* where once there was only distrust and suspicion. And for all its power, it is a fragile fire. There will be those, Human and *Zheeerlikou'valkhannaiee* alike, who will wish to step back, now that the menace of the Bahgs is no more. Our leaders will turn from the war which has cost so much, in both lives and treasure. They will seek to put it behind them, to rebuild its ravages, and that is as it should be. But when they do, when they must no longer remember the desperate need which brought us together, they will give openings to those who wish to step back, to forget that we ever became *farshatok*. They will try to return to the days of suspicion and distrust, and to some extent, at least, they will succeed."

He smiled again, sadly, and reached out to rest one clawed hand on each officer's shoulder.

"It will not happen at once, and I think I will be gone before it does, but it *will* happen, Clan Brothers. And so I charge you to guard our fire—the true fire of the *Farshalah'kiah*. Your fire and mine, Fang Aandersaahn's and Eeevaan's. Remember not just for yourselves, but for those who will come after, and in the fullness of time, pass that same treasure to your successors, as I have passed it to those who have succeeded Eeevaan and myself."

"We will, Clan Lord," Zhaarnak promised quietly, and Prescott nodded.

"Good," Kthaara said very, very softly, and his hands squeezed once. No longer young, no longer strong, those hands, and yet in that instant, infinitely powerful. "Good," he repeated, and then drew a long, deep breath and shook himself.

"Enough of such solemnity!" he announced with sudden briskness. "My shuttle leaves in less than an hour, but there is time enough for us to share one last drink—and one more glorious lie each—before I depart!"

He laughed, and they laughed with him, then followed him from the gallery. Behind them, she hung upon the wall, still smiling with all the deep, sweet promise of life.

"But, *Agamemnon*," Bettina Wister protested, "you *know* Admiral Mukerji could *never* have done the *dreadful* things that woman accuses him of!"

Assemblyman Waldeck looked at his nasal-voiced colleague with expressionless contempt and wondered if she'd actually bothered to view Sandra Delmore's report. Probably not, he decided. At best, she'd had one of her staffers view it and abstract its "salient features" for her.

Waldeck, on the other hand, *had* viewed it, and he had no doubt whatsoever that it was essentially accurate. The only question in his mind was who'd leaked the damning information to the press.

*LeBlanc*, he thought. *It was probably LeBlanc. He knew vice admiral was as high as any intelligence analyst was ever likely to go, and besides, he's retiring. One of his spies or informants probably reported it to him at the time, and he's just been waiting for the right moment to use it. It's exactly the sort of thing he would do.*

". . . and even if it were *true*," Wister continued, "he was *only* doing his duty. That *awful* woman can call it 'cowardice' if she wants to, but I call it simple prudence. Of *course* any responsible military officer who knew what the policy of his government was would try to *restrain* a uniformed thug like Prescott who was *clearly* taking unwarranted risks with the fleet committed to his allegation and its personnel. And as for the *ridiculous* charge that he was 'insubordinate'! Why, if I'd been there, I'm sure *I* would have called that myrmidon 'insane'!"

"Bettina," Waldeck said, much more calmly than he felt, "Prescott is hardly one of my favorite people, either. And, like you, I've always found Terence has a proper appreciation for the relationship between the civilian authorities and the military chain of command. But it could certainly be argued that calling the commander of a major fleet actually engaged in battle against the enemy insane in front of his entire staff and flag deck command crew represents a case of . . . questionable judgment."

"But Prescott *is* insane!" Wister shot back so stridently Waldeck winced. "The people may not realize it *now*, but they will! I'll make it my special task to see to it that the truth about his *bungling* of the so-called 'April's Fool' battle—*and* at the Battle of AP-5, as well—is made a part of the public record! '*War hero,*' indeed! Why, he might as well be one of those horrid Orions himself!"

Waldeck opened his mouth . . . then closed it. Sometimes a man simply had to know when there was no longer any point trying to explain, and this was one of them. Mukerji had been a useful tool for decades, but the only thing to do with any tool was to discard it when it broke. And thanks to Sandra Delmore's reports, Mukerji was definitely a broken tool.

At this particular moment the Terran electorate—including Wister's mush-minded constituents—were convinced that Raymond Porter Prescott had single-handedly defeated the entire Bug omnivoracity . . . and probably killed the last Bug emperor in hand-to-hand combat. The fact that any halfway competent flag officer could have defeated the Bugs with the immense material superiority the Corporate Worlds had provided was completely lost upon the hero-worshipping proles, and they would have no mercy on anyone who dared to trifle with the object of their veneration.

It was a pity, really, but there it was. That blind adulation was the true explanation for the fury which had swept that electorate when Delmore's "exposé" of Mukerji's . . . confrontation with Prescott broke. If a few more years had passed, the Heart World sheep would have forgotten all about any sense of indebtedness to Prescott. But they hadn't, and as the public denunciation swelled, the rest of the media—sensing blood in the water, and not particularly caring whose blood it was—had picked the story up with glee. They could be counted upon to keep it alive for months, at the very least.

Unless, of course, the Naval Affairs Committee took action against the source of the public's discontent. Which would necessarily mean tossing Mukerji off the sled before the wolves caught it.

The real question in Waldeck's mind was what to do about Wister. He'd been able to sit on her during the war, but her present stridency wasn't a good sign. The idiot really believed the nonsense she spouted, and the last six or seven years of being forcibly restrained from airing her idiocy in public appeared to have pushed her over the edge. She seemed unable to understand that the mere fact that the war was over wasn't going to automatically and instantly restore the universe she'd inhabited before the Bugs came along. And like any petulant, spoiled adolescent who wanted back the world in which *she* had been the center of everything that mattered, she was perfectly prepared to pitch a public tantrum until she got her way. Which could have...unpleasant consequences for her political allies.

No, he decided. She'd been another useful tool, but, like Mukerji, she was scarcely irreplaceable. Of course, it would have to be done carefully. In fact, it might be that the Delmore story offered an opportunity to kill two birds with a single stone. If he handled it right, he could distance himself from the Mukerji fallout by making it appear that *Wister* had been the political admiral's patron. And if he gave her enough rope in the public hearings, let her babble away in public the way she was now, he could confidently count on her to destroy any credibility she might have retained if she or Mukerji tried to deny the relationship. And when Chairman Waldeck found himself "forced" by the mounting examples of Mukerji's incompetence and cowardice to turn against his political protector Wister—more in sorrow than in anger, of course...

It was always so convenient to have someone else one could use as the anchor to send one's own unfortunate political baggage straight to the bottom.

He considered the proposition for a few more seconds, then nodded mentally, and turned to Wister with an expression of thoughtful concern.

"Protecting Mukerji against these charges will be politically risky, Bettina," he told her in a carefully chosen tone.

"Protecting him against the *vicious* accusations of a violent, bloodsoaked *butcher* like Prescott," Wister shot back, completely ignoring the fact that Raymond Prescott had yet to make a single public statement in the case, "is the Right Thing to Do!"

"I didn't say it wasn't," Waldeck said in that same artfully anxious voice. "I only meant that it would require someone willing to put his—or her—political career on the line in defense of his political principles."

"I have *never* hesitated for an *instant* to stand up for the things in which I *believe!*" Wister declared, and Waldeck was careful to keep any sign of elation from crossing his face.

"Well, in that case," he told her with admirable resolution, "I'll have the Committee staff began assembling evidence in the matter immediately."

The Sanchez house, a rambling retirement villa, crowned a bluff looking eastward to Orphicon's Naiad Ocean. Ramon and Elena had occasionally considered selling the place. They weren't getting any younger, and their granddaughter—for their daughter had made clear to them that the blond toddler she'd brought through hell and adopted was precisely that—had always had a hair-raising love of playing along the edge of the cliff whose foot the waves lapped at high tide. Even now, just turned twelve, she often went there alone and looked out to sea as though waiting for someone.

This time, she really was.

Lydia Sanchez—born Lydia Sergeyevna Borisova on a world called Golan A II, about which the grownups always avoided speaking—stood on the bluff under a sky as blue as her eyes and as vast as all heaven, silent amid the screeching of the Terran-descended seabirds. The wind stirred her hair and sent her lightweight shift flapping against her slender no-longer-quite-child's form. She didn't notice the chill. Her mother was late.

Yes, her mother—the only mother she'd ever truly known. Oh, there'd been a woman once, whose face Lydia sometimes glimpsed fleetingly in her dreams. A woman who'd sung her to sleep with lullabies about the witch Baba Yaga, and the Firebird, and Vasilisa the Brave. A woman who'd called her Lydochka.

She never heard that diminutive here; Orphicon's ethnic stew contained few Russian ingredients. No, there was only one person who ever called her that. . . .

"Lydochka!"

She whirled around and saw a figure running up the pathway from the house—a figure whose TFN black-and-silver was already opened at the collar in its wearer's haste to get it off.

"Mom!" she squealed, and ran into an embrace that lasted and lasted, the black hair mingling with the blond.

When Irma Sanchez could finally force words past a constricted throat, all that came out was, "Oh God, honey, I'm so sorry I missed your birthday!"

Lydia giggled.

"Oh, that's all right, Mom." She tried to hug Irma even harder, but recoiled with an "Ouch!" She looked down at that which had jabbed her. A little golden lion gleamed against the midnight tunic.

Lydia looked up—not very far up, for she was already almost as tall as her mother. She'd known about it, of course—her grandparents were practically inarticulate with pride. But now she found she didn't know what to say.

"Uh . . . it's very pretty, Mom."

"Pretty? Yes, it is, isn't it?" said Irma, very softly. She lifted up the golden lion, hanging from its varicolored ribbon. It flashed in the sun.

Lydia was puzzled, for her mother's eyes were focused far away. She had no way of knowing how far—in time as well as in distance, and beyond the veil that sunders the living from the dead. The dead went by names like Eilonwwa, Meswami, Georghiu, Togliatti . . . and Armand. And then there was Armand's unborn child, to whom Irma could not even give a name, for they'd never chosen one. They'd had all the time in the world.

With a sudden, violent motion, Irma tore the medal from her tunic, ripping the nano-fabric. She reached back like a discus thrower and, with all the wiry strength in her, flung the Terran Federation's highest decoration for valor out over the cliff. It caught the sun, glistening as it fell. The splash, far below in the surf, could not be seen.

Lydia stared at her mother, round-eyed.

"What did you do *that* for, Mom?"

Irma took a deep, shuddering breath.

"Because it's *over*, dear. That—" she gestured out to sea "—that was part of something I had to do. Something called war—something horrible. The only excuse for it is that sometimes it's the only way to stop something even more horrible. But even that doesn't change the fact that it's all about misery and pain and death and sorrow and loss and . . . and . . . and it's *over!*"

Lydia continued to stare, and tried to understand.

"Do you mean it's true, what everybody's been saying? That the Bugs aren't going to come after all?"

"That's right, Lydochka. The Bugs are never going to come."

Arm in arm, mother and daughter turned and walked along the pathway to the house, under the clean sky.

# INSURRECTION

# GALE WARNING

*"Politics is the womb in which war is developed."*
General Karl von Clausewitz, *On War*

Ladislaus Skjorning frowned at his watch and re-scanned the sparsely-peopled late-night anteroom of Federation Hall, but there was no sign of Greuner. It was unlike him to be late, and, from the code phrase, his news was urgent, so where *was* he?

Someone tapped him on the shoulder, and he turned slowly, one hand moving unobtrusively to the small slug thrower in the sleeve of his loose tunic of Beaufort seawool. A man faced him in the conservative informal dress of New Zurich's upper classes—but it wasn't Greuner. Greuner was a little man; this fellow rivaled Skjorning's own 202 centimeters, and, unlike many Corporate Worlders, he looked fit and mean. Ladislaus eyed him with hidden distaste, and the muzzle of the invisible slug gun settled on the newcomer's navel.

"Mister Skjorning?"

"Aye, I'm to be Skjorning." Ladislaus' deep voice sawed across the thin New Zurich accent like a doomwhale catcher through fog.

"Mister Greuner sends his regrets."

"Not to come?" Ladislaus asked slowly, broad face expressionless as scorn for his uncouth dialect flared in the Corporate Worlder's mocking eyes. He plowed on like an icebreaker, pandering to the man's contempt. "Would it chance he's to be sending a wording why not?"

"Illness, I believe." The Corporate Worlder's mouth was a thin slash of dislike as he eyed the bearded giant. Skjorning was a

Titan for any world—especially a heavy grav planet, even one whose chill temperatures favored large people—but the one huge hand he could see was a laborer's, thick-knuckled and scarred by a childhood with the nets and a young manhood with the purse seines and harpoons.

"Not to be serious, I'm hoping," Ladislaus said sadly.

"I'm afraid it may be. In fact, I believe he's decided to return to New Zurich for ... treatment."

"I'm to see. Well, grateful I'm to be for your wording, Mister—?"

"Fouchet," the tall man said briefly.

"Aye, Fouchet. Remembered to me you'll be, Mister Fouchet." Skjorning turned away with a bovine nod, and Fouchet watched him enter a deserted washroom. He started to follow, then stopped and turned on a scornful heel. Whatever Greuner might have thought, that thick-witted prole was no danger.

The washroom door eased slowly open behind him, and one brilliant blue eye followed his retreating back. The slug gun eased back into its sleeve clip regretfully, and Skjorning stepped out of the washroom.

"Aye, Mister Fouchet," he said softly, barely a trace of accent coloring his voice, "I'll remember you."

Fionna MacTaggart looked away from her terminal and rubbed her eyes wearily, then glanced at the clock and allowed herself a crooked grin. Old Terran days were tiresomely short for someone reared to the thirty-two hour Beaufort day. The air was bothersomely thin, and the gravity was irksomely low, but one could grow used to anything, including feeling tired at such a ridiculously early hour. She rose and poured a cup of Terran coffee, one of the only two things about the motherworld she would truly miss when she finally returned to Beaufort for good.

A chime sounded, and she crooked a speculative eyebrow and pressed the admittance key. The door hissed open, and Ladislaus Skjorning towered on the threshold, his blue eyes bright with annoyance. ·

"Damn it, Chief!" Mister Fouchet would never have recognized his tone. "You're *still* not checking IDs!"

"No, I'm not," Fionna said coolly. "Not inside our own enclave, anyway. Nor am I meeting guests at the door with a laser in my hand." She shook her head with mock severity. "Sometimes I think all this security nonsense is going to your head, Lad."

"Do you, now?" Ladislaus sank into one of the recliners, his anger ebbing, and closed his eyes wearily. Fionna's face tightened with sudden concern. "I wish our friend Greuner shared your opinion."

"He didn't show?" Fionna knelt on the recliner next to him and massaged one taut shoulder.

"No," he said softly.

"They got to him, is it?" she asked, equally softly.

"Aye. Hustled him back to New Zurich—I hope. But there's little to be putting past a Corporate Worlder who smells gelt, Chief." She felt him relaxing as her strong fingers dug the tension from him, then frowned and stopped massaging, leaning her forearms on his massively muscled shoulder.

"You're right, Lad. I just wish I knew what he had for us!"

"I feel the same," Ladislaus rumbled, allowing himself a frown, "but let's be grateful for what he already gave us. He turned from his own to be helping us because he thought it right; now I've the thinking he's to be paying for it soon and late."

"I know, Lad. I know." She patted his shoulder, smiling contritely, and he felt a surge of guilt. It was hard enough heading a Fringe World delegation without your own people snapping at you. Besides, Fionna was right to worry. The one clue they had to Greuner's message was the phrase "Gale Warning," and that was the code he and the little man had arranged to indicate a major Corporate World offensive against the Fringe.

"I did pick up something a mite useful," he proffered as a peace offering. "The name of the new New Zurich bully boy, I'm to be thinking. Fouchet. A tall, mean son-of-a sand-leech with a face like boiled blubber."

"He's their new security chief?" Fionna asked, eyes narrowing.

"Chief, you know they're not to be using such titles! They're not so crude as that—he'll to be called Computerman's Syndic or some such. But, aye, he's the one. And had he just a little more curiosity or a little less brain—mind, I'm not sure which it was—it's squeezing Greuner's information from him I'd be the now."

"Lad," Fionna said sternly, "I've *told* you we can't operate that way! They already call us 'barbarians.' What do you think they'll call us if you start acting like that?"

"Aye? I don't have the thinking it's to mind me the much," Ladislaus said, laying the accent with a trowel. "It's maybe 'Corporate Worlder' they're to call me if I have the doing of their own against them. And where's the difference to lie? Yon Corporate Worlder flays his whales with money, Chief; *I'm* only after the doing of it by hand."

Fionna started to reply tartly, then stopped. She and Ladislaus had grown up together on the cold and windy seas of Beaufort, and she knew it irked him to play the homespun fool for men like Fouchet—but she also knew he recognized the advantages of his role. During his time in the Federation's navy, Ladislaus had acquired a cosmopolitanism at odds with the Innerworld notion of a Fringer, though, like anyone, he tended to revert to the speech patterns of childhood under stress. The slow Beaufort accent had drawn attention even in the Fleet, where such idiosyncrasies were far from rare, and Lad had learned the hard way to speak excellent Standard English. But his sense of humor had stood him in good stead, and he'd also learned to ape the stereotype so well few of his victims ever realized they were being hoodwinked. He found his hayseed persona useful as head of security for the Beaufort delegation, and he usually enjoyed it. Yet it seemed this latest episode had cracked his normal shield of humor. He'd evidently become closer to Greuner than she'd thought . . . and he was *right*, damn it! The little banker had jeopardized his career, certainly, and possibly his life, to help worlds he'd never even visited—and now he'd pay for it. She felt a sudden hot stinging behind her own eyes, and her hands squeezed his shoulder in silence until she felt the new tension run slowly out of them both once more. . . .

A low, murmuring rumble filled the chamber, and Fionna Mac-Taggart looked across from her console at the tall podium in the center of the vast hemispherical room. It stood over two hundred meters from her seat in the center of the Beaufort delegation, separated from the ranked tiers of delegates by a floor of ebon marble shot with white veins like tangled skeins of stars. After twenty-five years in the Assembly—twenty of them as head of her planet's delegation—Fionna had learned the bitter, sordid realities of the Federation's government, but the Chamber of Worlds still took her breath away. She wished she could have seen it when the Assembly had lived up to its promise, but not even the present's gangrenous partisanship and exploitation could diminish the grandeur of the ideal this chamber had been built to enshrine.

Her eyes swept over upward-soaring walls hung with the flags and banners of scores of planetary systems, all dominated by the space-black Federation banner with its golden sunburst and the blue planet and white moon of the homeworld. The air stirred coolly against her skin as she adjusted her hushphone headset over her red hair. Ladislaus was going to be late if he didn't get a move on.

A tiny light glowed on her panel as the Sergeant at Arms warned her a member of her delegation was on his way, and she looked up, hiding a smile as Skjorning lumbered down the aisle. Thank God none of their constituents ever visited Old Terra! They'd have a fit if they ever saw the role Ladislaus had assumed so well.

The big man sidled bashfully through the crowd in a state of perpetual embarrassment, then sank gratefully into the chair at Fionna's left hand and leaned forward to fumble clumsily with his hushphone.

"Any clues, Lad?" she asked softly.

"No, Chief." Ladislaus' lips barely moved. "Only the code, and it's a seaharrower's own luck *that* much got to us."

Fionna frowned and nodded in agreement. She started to say something more, but the echo of a soft chime cut her short.

The Legislative Assembly of the Terran Federation was in session.

Fionna fidgeted uneasily as the opening formalities filtered past her. She could see the Galloway's World delegation from where she sat, and Simon Taliaferro wasn't in his usual place. The New Zurich delegation was less than ten meters away, and she noted sinkingly that Oskar Dieter wasn't with his fellows, either. Whatever Greuner had tried to warn them of, those two would be at the heart of it. Her fingers flew over her information console, keying their names and punching up a cross index of the committees on which they sat, for she'd learned long since that it was in the closed committee meetings that the Corporate Worlds wove their webs.

The screen lit, confirming her memory. Both men were from populous worlds; combined with their personal seniority in the Assembly and the "representative membership" committee rules the Corporate Worlds had rammed through twelve years ago, that gave them membership on dozens of committees . . . including shared membership on Foreign Relations and Military Oversight. She frowned. Not only was each a member of both, but Taliaferro chaired Foreign Relations and Dieter chaired Military Oversight. It was an ominous combination.

The Clerk finished the formalities of the last session's minutes and stepped aside for David Haley. By long tradition, the Speaker of the Legislative Assembly was a citizen of Old Terra, and Fionna, listening to his beautiful Standard English as he turned the Assembly to business, wished his office still had the power it once had held. Unlike most of his Heart World fellows, Haley had traveled to the Fringe; he knew the hostility and hatred for the Corporate Worlds festering on the Fringe Worlds—and what was happening under the false cordiality of the delegates' relations. Unfortunately, there was little he could do about it.

"Ladies and Gentlemen of the Assembly," Haley said, "the Chairman of the Foreign Relations Committee has requested a closed session of the Assembly sitting as a committee of the whole. Are there any objections?"

Fionna keyed her console and saw Haley glance down as her light pulsed on his panel. Then he looked out over the sea of faces to the Beaufort delegation, and his face vanished from the giant screen behind the podium, replaced by Fionna's, though his image continued to stare up from the small screen before each delegate.

"The Chair recognizes the Honorable Assemblywoman for Beaufort," he said, and Fionna's headset beeped to indicate a live mike.

"Mister Speaker, this is highly irregular," she said quietly. "I would ask why the Chairman of the Foreign Relations Committee feels the need for a closed session? And why we were not informed in advance?"

The face on her console screen was clearly unhappy. Haley was too experienced to show his emotions openly, but the assemblymen were too experienced not to read him anyway.

"Ms. MacTaggart, I can only tell you that the Chairman of the Foreign Relations Committee and Minister of Foreign Affairs Assad jointly have requested the Assembly's attention to a matter of grave import. That is all the information I have. Do you wish to object to the request for closure?"

Fionna certainly did, but it would accomplish little, since she would know no more about Taliaferro's plans after blocking the secret session than she did now. Damn him! Despite the warning, he'd managed to keep her completely in the dark!

"No, Mister Speaker," she said softly. "I have no objection."

"Is there any debate?" Haley asked. There was none, and the Speaker gaveled the Assembly into secret session.

✧   ✧   ✧

The chamber buzzed with side conversations as the Sergeant at Arms and his staff escorted the news people out. The great doors boomed softly shut, and sophisticated anti-snooping defenses were set in motion. There would be no way for the outside world to discover what was said or done here unless a delegate leaked the word.

Such "accidental leaks" were far from uncommon these days, though they once had been. As the Fringer population base had slowly grown to challenge the Corporate Worlds' domination of the Assembly, the campaign of secret slander and counterslander had taken on vicious overtones. Initially, the Outworlders had been at a considerable disadvantage, but Fionna was almost saddened by how well they'd learned to play the game since. Only this time, leaks wouldn't be enough. Greuner's disappearance proved that.

Two new figures appeared beside Haley. One was Oskar Dieter, though he was as careful as ever to stay in the background. The other was Simon Taliaferro, possibly the man the Fringers hated most of all.

Taliaferro could have been prime minister, but his position as head of his delegation was more useful, and he would have been forced to resign it to accept the premiership. On the other hand, he could never have been president, for that largely gelded office was still decided by direct election. As heir to one of the ship-building dynasties which had used political power to cement its stranglehold on the Outworlds' commerce, he could never have carried enough of the popular vote. Ninety percent of all Federation cargo moved in hulls owned by Corporate World shipping magnates, yet over sixty percent of the Federation's systems lay in the Fringe and Rim. Which was why Taliaferro was hated . . . and why he was prepared to embrace any expedient to stave off the rapidly approaching day when the Fringe's delegates would be numerous enough to demand an accounting for two centuries of economic exploitation.

"Ladies and gentlemen," Haley said, "the Chair recognizes the Honorable Simon Taliaferro, Delegate for Galloway's World and Chairman of the Foreign Relations Committee. Mister Taliaferro."

"Thank you, Mister Speaker." Taliaferro's dark face was incongruously jovial on the huge screen, and Fionna's lips curled with dislike. It was like a badly crafted disguise, she thought. A threadbare mask for the ruthless brilliance under that jolly exterior—yet the rules of the game required one to pretend his bonhomie was real.

"Members of the Assembly," Taliaferro said, "I bring you great news! After months of negotiation, I can now tell you that perhaps the most momentous departure in the history of the Galaxy has been proposed. President Zhi and Prime Minister Minh have received a direct communication from the Khan of the Orions, borne by a fully empowered plenipotentiary." He paused for effect, knowing he'd gathered the eyes and ears of every delegate. "The Khan proposes nothing less than the amalgamation of the Terran Federation and the Khanate of Orion!"

His voice rose steadily through the last sentence, but it was almost lost in the roar which burst forth at the word "amalgamation," and Fionna was on her feet, one fist clenched on the top of her console.

"*No!*" she shouted, but her voice was lost in the uproar. It was just as well, she realized a moment later. She was the leader of the Fringe Caucus. She must appear calm and reasonable. Above all, reasonable! Yet such a proposal would be intolerable to her constituents, and the Corporate Worlds knew it. In fact, only those fat-headed, liberal-minded, bureaucracy-worshiping Heart Worlders could be so blind as to think the Fringe *wouldn't* fight this!

Her eyes narrowed as she sank back into her seat. Of course the Corporate Worlds knew, and Taliaferro's obvious delight made cold, ugly sense as her mind once more began to work with its wonted precision.

How was the huge population of the Khanate to fit into this new, amalgamated monster? Were the Orions suddenly to find themselves enfranchised to vote for the first time in their history? It had taken over a century of slow, painful population growth in the outworlds to earn the delegates to challenge the Corporate Worlds. With such a huge influx of votes, the Assembly would have no choice but to cut the representational basis . . . which would just coincidentally gerrymander the sparse Fringe population out of the representation it had finally gained.

Just who, she wondered, had proposed what to whom? Had the Orions conceived this on their own? Or had the Corporate Worlds "suggested" it to them? Or had they, perhaps, simply misled the Khan's ambassadors into thinking the proposal would be joyfully accepted throughout the Federation? There were too many possibilities and too few answers—yet.

She pressed her call button. Haley's panel must be bloody with scores of red attention lights, and she almost hoped Taliaferro would refuse to yield to her. But he would, if only to give her the opportunity to cut her own throat, and, in a way, it would be a relief to take a stand, whatever the outcome. She had no choice but to voice the Fringe's position . . . and it was time, part of her cried, to have done with careful maneuvering. It was time to speak from the heart.

"Mister Speaker," Taliaferro's amplified voice cut through the uproar, "I yield temporarily to the Honorable Assemblywoman for Beaufort!"

The background noise died instantly as Fionna appeared on the giant screen, and her green eyes flashed fire.

"Mister Speaker," her voice was clear and strong, "I must tell the Honorable Assemblyman for Galloway's World that he has made a grievous error if he expects every Federation citizen to greet this proposal with loud hosannas! No one in the Federation has more respect for the Orions than we of the Fringe. We have fought against them and beside them. Fringers have died fighting to the last at their sides to defend their worlds, as well as our own, from genocidal butchery. We admire their courage, their fortitude, their sense of honor, and their spirit. They have their own claims to greatness: the first race to hypothesize the possibility of warp travel; the first to create a stellar empire; and the first to recognize the inevitable end result of blind militarism and turn away from it. But, Mister Speaker, they are *Orions*—and we here represent the *Terran* Federation! We represent a society forged, in part, in combat *against* the Orions, one which has made for itself a place second to none in the known Galaxy. And, Mister Speaker—" her long anger and frustration burned in her throat as she hurled the final words at Taliaferro "—the Fringe will *never* consent to this so-called amalgamation!"

She sat down abruptly, and the Chamber of Worlds went berserk.

Soft, somehow mournful music swirled like the sea as Fionna stood at the head of the receiving line, smiling and gracious despite her exhaustion. The last week had been a nightmare, and only the extravagance of her personal exertions had held the Fringe bloc together. It wasn't that any delegation favored the proposed amalgamation; the reverse was true—they were angry with her for not taking a more extreme position.

But if twenty-five years in the Assembly had taught her anything,

It was that the Heart Worlds didn't understand the Fringe. The Corporate Worlders knew their outworld cousins and enemies far better than the motherworld and its oldest colonies did, though she suspected not even the Corporate Worlds fully realized the fulminating anger they were fanning. But the Heart Worlds were too far removed from their own frontier days. They'd forgotten what it was like to know that any outside attack must come through *their* systems to reach the heart of empire. As they'd forgotten—if they'd ever known—what it was to have their commerce, the lifeblood of their societies, manipulated and exploited by predatory merchants with a yen for power.

And because they had forgotten or did not know, they were a terrible danger to the Fringe. Fionna had seen the "new liberalism" of her Heart World colleagues. The Heart Worlds had it too good, she thought bitterly; they were too content, too ultracivilized. The Corporate Worlds could convince them the Fringe really was peopled by uncouth barbarians but little removed from outright savagery. Worse, they could be convinced to do what was "best" for the Fringe—even if it killed the object of their kindness!

Knowing that, she also knew it was imperative to convince the Heart Worlds of the Fringe's maturity ... or at least open-mindedness. The position she'd taken was the strongest she could take. The firebrands who longed to denounce the Corporate Worlds openly, to point the accusing finger where it so richly deserved to be pointed, would play straight into Taliaferro's and Dieter's hands, but only one Fringer could convince them of that. Fionna MacTaggart wasn't a vain woman, yet she knew no one else among the Fringe delegates had the prestige and power base she'd built against this very day.

Of all the Fringe Worlds, Beaufort, perhaps, most despised Corporate Worlders. Beaufort's heavy gravity had not been kind to its colonizers, despite their selection for high pressure tolerance, yet there had been fierce competition for space on the colony ships. The rebels of the Corporate Worlds, those who could no longer tolerate their roles as cogs in the vast machines, had seen in Beaufort a world poor enough and distant enough to be secure from manipulation and control. They'd gone to Beaufort to escape, and many had died there—so many BuCol actually closed the planet to immigration for almost sixty years.

Fionna's parents and grandparents had spoken of those bitter years. The gene pool was small; the environment was harsh; and

BuCol's Corporate World bureaucrats had not gone out of their way to help. Those six decades of isolation had produced the dialect the Innerworlders mocked—and left a burning hatred in the hearts of the people who spoke it.

But then the unsuspected pharmaceutical potential of the Beaufort doomwhale had rocked Terran medical science, and suddenly the Corporate Worlds and the Assembly were filled with concern for the colony they had ignored for so long. The Corporate World combines had moved in, and the Corporate World nightmare had come for the people of Beaufort once more.

Yet cold, hostile Beaufort had trained them well, and the planetary government moved quickly to regulate doomwhaling and exclude the Corporate Worlds, unmoved by threats of economic reprisal. There was little anyone could do which the Corporate Worlds hadn't already done, and, for the first time in over a century and a half, Corporate World plutocrats were forced to dance to the economic piping of a Fringe World.

They'd hated it, and it was Beaufort's successful resistance to their penetration which gave her delegation such prestige. Beaufort had proved the Corporate Worlds could be stopped; now it was time to prove they could be pushed back, and Fionna MacTaggart had dedicated her professional life to that goal. Yet there was only one of her, and she was tired . . . so very, very tired. Beyond each confrontation, another loomed, and she faced each a little more diminished, a little more weary.

She shook herself mentally, banishing the dark thoughts. It had been a bad day—perhaps that was why she felt so somber. Or perhaps it was this reception. It had been scheduled before Taliaferro dropped his bomb, and canceling it now was out of the question, but it was a strain to be polite to the Corporate Worlders as they arrived. Still, she thought with a sudden flicker of amusement, it might be equally hard on them.

She glanced at her watch. Another ten minutes and she could find herself a drink and begin to circulate. That might help. It was always easier to deal with people in small, intimate groups rather than in formal, antagonistic public forums. Then she looked back up and bit off a curse as Oskar Dieter entered with his now-constant shadow, Fouchet.

She felt Ladislaus materialize by her side. Dear Lad! He played the buffoon for the Innerworlders, but his fellow Beauforters knew his worth. Indeed, she sometimes wished she didn't know him quite so well. It would have been nice to lose herself in an affair with someone with his strength and integrity, but any liaison with him would have felt incestuous.

Dieter paused at the head of the reception line, and his dark eyes glittered. Fionna didn't like Dieter; she never had, and she knew the feeling was mutual. Unlike Taliaferro, Dieter was a poor hand at hiding his emotions, and she'd flicked him on the raw often in debate. He resented that, and resented it all the more because she was a woman. The Constitution might outlaw sexual discrimination, but New Zurich's unwritten law enshrined it, and she suspected Dieter found her an insult to his prejudices, as well as to his ambitions. Still, there were amenities to be observed, and she held out her hand with a smile.

"Mister Dieter."

"Ms. MacTaggart." He bowed slightly, ignoring her hand, and his voice was cold, his eyes scornful. Fionna's palm itched.

"A pleasure to see you, sir," she made herself lie. "I understand you will be taking a major role in tomorrow's debate?"

"Indeed," he said. "And so, I hear, will you. Playing your usual obstructionist role, I presume."

Conversation slackened, and Fionna felt Ladislaus tighten beside her. She touched his hand unobtrusively.

"I prefer, sir, to consider my role as that of a constructive advocate for the Fringe Worlds," she said, equally coldly. "We, too, have a right to present our point of view and to contend for our values and dreams."

"Values and dreams? *Fringe garbage!*" Dieter flushed suddenly, his voice hissing, and Fionna's eyes widened. Good God, what ailed the man? One simply didn't say things like that at formal receptions!

"Yes, Mister Dieter," she heard herself say, "we, too, have our dreams and aspirations—or will the Corporate Worlds take even those from us?"

Ripples of silence raced outward. Fionna dared not turn to see the effect of the acid exchange, yet neither dared she retreat. It was one thing to appear reasonable; it was quite another to appear weak.

"We have no desire for them," Dieter sneered. "You speak very prettily in debate, for a *Fringe Worlder*, Madam, but the Assembly will not be blind to your barbarism and xenophobia forever. You and your kind have stood in the path of civilization too long!"

He almost spat the last words, and suddenly she smelled his breath. Reefgrubs! He was almost in orbit on New Athens *mizir*!

The drug was well known for the euphoria it evoked, but it was a dangerous way to relieve stress. It depressed inhibitions to the point of nonexistence, and sometimes that produced something all too much like induced paranoia in a small yet significant percentage of its users . . . and Dieter was obviously one of them. How could he be so stupid as to meet her in this condition? But whatever madness possessed him wasn't her worry; responding to his attack was.

"We may be barbarians, sir," she said, and her voice rang clearly in the silence, "but at least we have the advantage of you in manners!"

Dieter's face twisted as the crowd murmured approval. Even through the haze of *mizir* fumes he could sense the incredible blunder he'd made. But recognizing it and retrieving it were two different things, and his fuddled brain was unequal to the task.

"*Slut!*" he hissed suddenly, thrusting his face close to hers. "You've aped your betters for too long! Get home to your stinking little ball of mud and make babies to play in the muck!"

Fionna and her guests froze. Enmity between political leaders was nothing new, but this—! No one could quite believe Dieter was so lost to self-control, yet his words hung in the supercharged air like a subcritical mass of plutonium, and they waited breathlessly for the explosion.

It came. Ladislaus Skjorning's huge right hand lashed openpalmed across Dieter's face.

The New Zuricher rebounded from the blow, crashing into Fouchet, blood bursting from the corner of his mouth. He stared at Ladislaus for a moment of terror, then clawed himself upright, gobbling curses while Fouchet's hand darted inside his tunic. But Ladislaus wasn't yet done, and Fionna's world reeled about her as his quarterdeck rasp cut through Dieter's fury.

"You're to meet me for this," he grated.

Dieter's mouth snapped shut as a warning battered at the *mizir*. He was in the Beaufort enclave; the enclaves enjoyed extraterritoriality; and on Beaufort, dueling was an accepted fact of life. He stared at the giant before him, and for the first time he understood the difference between a patiently plodding ox and a charging bull.

"I—I—" He fought for words. "This is . . . is preposterous! Barbaric! You can't be—"

"Aye, we're to be called barbarians," Ladislaus agreed grimly, "but it's to meet me you'll be for all of that."

"I—I won't!" Dieter gasped desperately.

"No?" Ladislaus wrapped one hand in the New Zuricher's tunic, and muscles bred to a gravity a third again that of Old Terra's rippled as he lifted him from the floor. "You've the right to be calling barbarians, but not the guts to be facing one, have you? But it's on Beaufort soil you are the now! It's Beaufort law has the ruling of it here."

"Let him go, Skjorning!" It was Fouchet, his hand still inside his tunic, and Ladislaus' blue eyes moved coldly to the security man's tight face.

"Chief?" the big Fringer said softly.

"Mister Fouchet," Fionna's voice rang through the horrified room, "You are legally on the soil of Beaufort, and as chief of her delegation, I will thank you to remove your hand from your tunic—empty."

Fouchet eyed her contemptuously, then paled. Three grim-faced Assembly lictors stood behind her, stun batons in hand and a hard light in their eyes. He hadn't seen them appear, but he knew whose orders they would obey in this room.

His hand came out of his tunic—empty.

"Thank you," Fionna said icily, then touched Ladislaus lightly on the arm. "Put him down, Lad," she said quietly.

For a moment it seemed the towering blond giant might refuse, then he slammed Dieter back onto his feet, and the Corporate Worlder swayed. Fionna's eyes were emerald ice, but her voice was colder.

"Mister Dieter, you have been challenged to honorable combat by Ladislaus Skjorning. Do you accept the challenge?"

"I—*No!* Of course not! It's—"

"Be silent!" Fionna's voice whiplashed across his spluttering and shocked him into silence. "Very well. You have declined the challenge—as is your right. But as representative of Beaufort on Old Terra, it is my duty to inform you that you are no longer welcome on her soil. Leave. If you ever return, you will be forcibly ejected."

Dieter stared at her like a gaffed fish, the mottled red print of Ladislaus' hand the only color in his white face. He looked desperately around the circle of hostile faces, and he found no support. Not a man or woman present questioned Fionna's decision. He opened his mouth.

"One word, *Mister* Dieter," Fionna said softly, "and I will ask these lictors to escort you from the premises. Now leave!"

And Oskar Dieter turned to stumble away through the crowd.

Fionna couldn't fault Lad—except, perhaps, in that the challenge had rightfully been hers to give. Such behavior was not tolerated on Beaufort, nor most other Fringe Worlds. Sparse societies in alien environments tended to be armed, and insults carried a stiff price. Yet even if she couldn't question his act, she regretted the impact she expected it to have.

But the actual impact surprised her. The Corporate Worlds might have convinced the Heart Worlds the Fringe was uncouth, but not even they dared argue that a society's customs could be challenged with impunity. That sort of intolerance would have destroyed the Federation long since, and no Heart Worlder hesitated to condemn Dieter's behavior. Not even the excuse that he'd been drugging (acceptable on most Heart Worlds, though not in the Fringe) could mitigate his unforgivable boorishness. So far as the Heart Worlds were concerned, the whole focus of the Corporate-Fringe World debate had been shifted by a single instance of supremely bad manners.

The Fringers' reactions were even more startling. She'd expected a ground swell of anger she would never be able to control; instead, she got a tightening of ranks and an upwelling of ever stronger support. The hatred she'd expected was there, but it was controlled by respect for her and Ladislaus.

Dieter's stupidity had strengthened her prestige with Fringer and Heart Worlder alike, and the Corporate Worlds lost ground steadily in debate. The amalgamation issue was far from resolved, but under her leadership the Fringe had emerged as a moderate and reasonable entity, and as the days passed, she felt the pendulum swinging in her favor.

Simon Taliaferro's joviality was in abeyance, and his eyes were cold as Oskar Dieter and Francois Fouchet entered his office.

"You idiot!" he flared. "How could you *be* so stupid?!"

"I—I wasn't myself," Dieter muttered. "I was provoked!"

"Provoked, hell! You were glitter-dusted to the eyeballs, that's what you were! Look at *these*"—he slammed a fist on the sheaf of printouts on his desk—"and tell me it was worth it!"

"Mister Taliaferro," Fouchet's calm voice cut the superheated tension like an icicle, "we're prepared to stipulate an error was made, but fixing blame won't solve our difficulties. Clearly you have something to tell us; equally clearly it isn't something you much care for. Very well. Tell us, and let's see if we can't find a way to retrieve the situation."

Fouchet's coolness seemed to calm Taliaferro, and he drew a deep breath. Then he let it hiss out and squared his shoulders.

"You're right, Francois," he said finally. "I'll say no more about the . . . episode. But the consequences are out of all proportion, I assure you. These—" he thumped the printouts again "—tell it all. A week ago, we had them; today, they're rolling us up like a rug."

Dieter mopped his forehead with a tissue and said nothing. In one terrible week he'd fallen from the Corporate Worlds' second most powerful leader into a sort of limbo. Every insider knew Fouchet spoke for New Zurich now, and most expected Dieter to be recalled so Fouchet could replace him officially. He was ruined, and his eyes burned into Fouchet's back as he remembered who had encouraged him to glitter-dust that evening . . . and provided the drug that was so much more potent than he normally used.

Dieter knew all about *mizir*'s side effects. He'd never before actually experienced the level of reaction he had at the reception—and he wouldn't have even there if the drug had been of its normal potency, he thought grimly. Still, he'd known how it might combine with stress. Yet he hadn't let that stop him. Partly because of Fouchet's subtle yet effective encouragement, but also because he knew not even *mizir* could make a man say what he didn't actually feel. It might affect his perceptions, cause him to . . . take things wrongly, but his reactions to those perceptions were his own. Which was why his statements had shocked him even more, perhaps, than they had Fionna MacTaggart. Because he knew they'd reflected his true feelings . . . and revealed no mere political animosity, but a virulent, *personal* hatred he hadn't even known existed.

But Fouchet had known. Fouchet had maneuvered him, yet accusing him would be worse than useless. If there was anything the Corporate Worlds had less use for than a fool, it was a dupe.

"Those projections are confirmed?" Fouchet asked, and Taliaferro nodded. "But, of course, they're based on certain givens, aren't they?"

"Any projection is, but there's not much room for change in the parameters. What it boils down to is that we've lost the high ground. In a straight debate over something as emotional as amalgamation, they'll probably beat us—even without the reapportionment issue. God! To think of a brainless lummox like Skjorning bumbling into the *only* thing that could hurt us this way!"

"I'm not so sure he is brainless," Dieter offered in a subdued voice.

"Of course you're not," Taliaferro sneered. "That'd make your little fiasco look better, wouldn't it?" Dieter wilted under the savage irony. "But he *is* a fool. He reacted with his muscles, the way he always does, and it just happened that this time it was the best thing he could do—or the worst, depending on your viewpoint!"

"But it comes down to Skjorning and MacTaggart, doesn't it?" Fouchet murmured thoughtfully, recapturing Taliaferro's attention.

"Eh? I suppose so—not that *he's* too important. It's MacTaggart. She's spent a quarter-century building a power base. She's got the best political brain in the whole Fringer crowd, and they know it—that's why they follow her lead—but her control was slipping. Another few days and I'd've moved the vote, and every projection said she'd lose the firebrands on the floor. Well, the hotheads are hotter than ever, but she's got more authority than ever, too. They'll never break with her now."

"No, I can see that," Fouchet said slowly, "but if there were some way to remove her from the equation?"

"Without MacTaggart, they'd attack us like wolves," Taliaferro said simply, "and that'd be just as good as their scattering like sheep. But we can't touch her. She can't be bought, she can't be blackmailed, she can't be intimidated, and she's headed the Fringe Caucus for fifteen years. After last week, she might as well be in God's hip pocket!"

"True," Fouchet said, his lips curving slowly, "but accidents do happen, don't they? And Granyork isn't like a colony world. Why, we're right in the middle of the Northeast Corridor Conurbation, and that's a sort of jungle Fringers aren't well equipped to deal with. . . ."

"What are you *saying*?" Dieter's horror cut the sudden silence like a saw. "You can't possibly suggest—"

"I didn't hear Mister Fouchet suggest a thing, Oskar," Taliaferro said coldly. "I only heard him speculating idly on matters totally beyond our control. And, of course, he's quite right. If Ms. MacTaggart were to suffer an . . . accident, it could only help us on the floor. Unless, of course, our enemies were able to . . . invent . . . a connection between her accident and us."

"Oh, of course," Fouchet agreed. "Of course."

Fionna MacTaggart considered the face in her mirror critically. It wasn't quite as young as she still liked to think of herself, and she'd never been—in her opinion—a beauty, but her image had nothing to apologize for. She nodded companionably to herself.

"Just you and me, girl," she said softly. "No one else has to know how hard we worked for that, do they?"

She chuckled and reached for her small evening bag. God, it felt good to be going somewhere besides to another floor fight! But the Corporate Worlds were on the defensive now. Now *they* were fighting to delay the vote, though she didn't really know what they hoped to achieve; delay only strengthened her hand at this point. No doubt they planned something devious, and equally no doubt Ladislaus or one of the others would figure it out if she didn't. But for now she felt younger than she had in weeks, and she looked forward eagerly to the night's entertainment. True, the thin Old Terran atmosphere detracted a bit from her enjoyment, but the strength of the performance more than compensated. Opera had been born on Old Terra, and in her opinion it still achieved its highest expression here.

She glanced into her bag at the chunky, snub-nosed two-millimeter needler and debated leaving it behind, for if it was small, it was still heavy. And it wasn't as if she were headed into the back islands. Granyork was the epicenter of the ultracivilized Heart Worlds. Still, she knew how Lad would react if she went unarmed . . . She sighed and closed the bag.

She keyed her bedside terminal and the screen lit briefly with an attention pattern, then with Ladislaus' face.

"All set, Lad," she told him cheerfully. "Would you have the car sent around, please?"

"Aye . . . if you're not leaving your little toy behind," he said suspiciously.

"Me?" She laughed and clunked the bag solidly against the terminal. "See, Daddy?"

"Laugh if you will," he said with a slight grin, "but I rest easier knowing you're armed, Fi."

"I know, Lad." She was touched by his use of her name, for Ladislaus was always careful to call her "Chief" to avoid any impression of taking advantage of their lifelong friendship. "I may think you're a little paranoid, but you're the man I chose for security chief. If you want me in a combat zoot with a grenade launcher, that's how I'll go."

"I know you mean it for a joke, but it's happier I'd be for it," he said, only half-humorously. "Still, it's the offalbirds are on the rocks the now, it's to be seeming. So go—have a good time, Chief!"

"Why, thank you, Lad," she cooed, batting her eyes. "I certainly shall." She touched the button again, and the terminal blanked.

Twenty minutes later, Ladislaus' terminal hummed once more, and he looked up from his report with a frown, for he'd left orders not to disturb him. Then he looked again, and his brow furrowed. It was an outside call on his priority number, and his eyes widened as he touched the acceptance key and Oskar Dieter's sweating face filled the screen.

"Please excuse the intrusion, Mister Skjorning!" Dieter took advantage of his shock, speaking quickly to wedge a toe in the door. "I had to call you. I have . . . have vitally important information for you."

"Do you, now?" Ladislaus' voice was cold, but his mind raced. Under Beaufort's code, Dieter no longer existed as far as he was concerned, and he could imagine nothing they might have to discuss. Yet the Corporate Worlder had to know he would feel that way, so it followed that there *was* something important here—but what?

"Yes. I—I don't know who else to give it to," Dieter sounded desperate, and Ladislaus suddenly noted how low-pitched his voice was. Was he afraid of being overheard?

"And what's that information to be?"

"B—before I say any more, you have to promise to keep its source confidential," Dieter said feverishly, wiping his brow.

"I'm to be but a simple fellow. What's—"

"*Please,* Mister Skjorning! You may have convinced the others—indeed, you play the part very well—but must we continue to pretend?"

Ladislaus' eyes narrowed. So a Corporate Worlder had finally bothered to pierce his mask. Yet it seemed Dieter had little interest in sharing his deductions with his fellows . . . not if he was honestly seeking to impart some sort of sensitive information. . . .

"All right, Mister Dieter," he said. "You have my word."

"Thank you, Mister Skjorning!" Dieter drooped with relief, yet now that he had Ladislaus' promise, he seemed to find it difficult to go on. Ladislaus could almost feel the painful physical effort with which he screwed up his courage.

"Mister Skjorning, I—I made a fool of myself the other night. I know it and you know it, but I swear to God I had no idea where it would lead!"

"What are you talking about?" Ladislaus' brows knitted. Could the man be drugging even now?

"I wrecked a lot of plans," Dieter said in a fast, frantic monotone. "I'm sure you know what I mean. But I never realized just how . . . how *desperate* some of my colleagues have become! They're going to kill her, Mister Skjorning!"

Dieter seemed to sag, as if simply voicing the words lifted a great weight from his shoulders, but Ladislaus was totally at a loss for an instant. Then it penetrated.

"Are you serious? They're going to *assassinate* Assemblywoman MacTaggart?!"

"Yes! That is—I think so." Dieter squirmed in fresh uncertainty. "All I really know is that there was a lot of talk. You know—hypothetical discussion about how 'convenient' it would be if something happened to her. I—I tried to oppose it, but I don't have the influence I had. . . ."

"Who's going to do it and when?" Ladislaus snapped.

"I'm not even positive they *are* going to do it," Dieter said anxiously. "I think . . . I think it's Francois Fouchet's project. I don't know when or how."

"Is that all you have for me?"

"Yes. Except . . . except Francois said something about how dangerous Granyork can be."

"My God!" Ladislaus paled and reached for the disconnect, then paused, his eyes on the wretched man before him. "Mister Dieter, I thank you. What was between us is no more."

Dieter's miserable expression lightened slightly as he recognized the formal renunciation of challenge.

"Thank you," he whispered. "And for God's sake, don't let them kill her! I never dreamed—" He stopped and chopped his hand at the pickup. For a moment, he became the man he once had been. "Enough! Protect her, Mister Skjorning. And tell her . . . tell her I'm sorry."

"I will. Good night."

Ladislaus cut the circuit and immediately punched for another, staring at his watch. With any luck and normal Granyork traffic, Fionna had not yet reached the Met.

"Goodness, Chris, I don't believe we've ever made such good time," Fionna remarked as the ground car slowed.

"I think you're right, Chief," the young security man agreed, his eyes flickering over the smartly dressed crowd before the opera house.

"Good. I hate finding my seat after the house lights go down."

Chris Felderman opened her door and she stepped out, picking her way through the crowd towards the huge front doors behind him.

"Stop, thief!"

Fionna and Felderman swung to face the shout as a running man suddenly burst from the crowd and snatched at the purse of the wife of Hangchow's chief delegate. His course carried him close to Fionna, and she punched her bodyguard's shoulder sharply.

"Stop him, Chris! That's Madam Wu's purse!"

"Yes, ma'am!" Felderman lunged after the thief, his long legs gaining ground quickly, and Fionna watched for an instant, then felt something like a chill on the nape of her neck. She turned, and her eyes widened as she saw two men approaching her. She'd never seen them before, but something in their purposeful expressions woke a warning deep inside her. She felt an instant of helpless panic as a terrible premonition struck—replaced in an instant with icy calm.

She knew better than to turn and run. There was no time to resummon Chris. The thoughts flicked through her brain like lightning, yet her reactions were even faster. Her hand darted into her bag. Her fingers found the butt of the needler. She didn't try to draw the weapon; she simply raised the bag and pistol together.

The killers were from the world of Shiloh. They hadn't expected their target to be armed; still less had they allowed for the reaction speed a high-grav planet instills. But they could not mistake her movements, and they were the best money could buy.

The thunder of two compact machine pistols buried the high, shrill whine of the needler.

Fionna was lying on the sidewalk. It hurt—God, how it hurt!— and she whimpered a little at the terrible pain. She lay in a puddle of something hot, and she felt a gentle hand under her head, raising it to slip some sort of cushion behind it.

She opened her eyes. It was Chris Felderman leaning over her, she thought confusedly. But why was he crying?

"Chris?" The voice was hers, but she'd never heard herself sound so weak. Something dribbled down her chin, and she realized it was blood. She felt only a distant curiosity at the thought.

"D—Don't try to talk, Fionna. *Please!* The medics are coming."

"M—medics?" She blinked at him. A mist was rising from the pavement, obscuring her vision, and the temperature had fallen. Then she understood, and she managed a weak smile. "Don't think . . . it'll matter . . . much," she whispered.

"It will! *It will!*" Chris sobbed, as if saying it could make it so.

"May—maybe." She knew better, but it struck her oddly detached brain as needlessly cruel to tell him so. "What about—?"

"Dead!" he whispered fiercely. "You got 'em both, Chief!"

"G—good." The mist was much thicker, and she was much, much colder. Yet the darkness beyond the mist seemed suddenly warm and inviting. It wouldn't hurt so much there . . . but she had something left to say, didn't she? She cudgeled her fading brain, then her bloody mouth smiled up at Chris. Two police floaters screamed to a halt, but she ignored them as she gripped his hand.

"G—give . . . Lad . . . my love," she murmured. "And . . . tell him . . . tell him . . . I got them b—"

The light went out of her universe forever.

Ladislaus Skjorning sat in the Chamber of Worlds like a boulder of Beaufort granite, and the black-draped seat beside him was less empty than his soul.

He'd failed. He'd failed his planet and himself, but, far worse, he'd failed Fionna. Chris Felderman thought the failure was *his*, but Ladislaus knew. The entire surviving Beaufort delegation was in shock, but the others had managed somehow to keep going. Not Ladislaus.

He remembered their childhood on windy, purple seas under the orange Beaufort sun. Remembered sailing and fishing, the first time she stood for office as a seaforcer, the day she convinced him to seek the new Assembly seat. "I need someone to watch my back, Lad," she'd said, and for ten years he'd done just that—until he let her go out onto a street on the birthworld of Man to be gunned down in her blood like an animal.

His teeth ground together on the agony of memory, and suddenly a single, clear thought stabbed through his brain like an ice pick.

The Federation wasn't worth Fionna's life.

Four and a half centuries of human history had come down to this, he thought bitterly, looking at the banner-hung walls and marble floors. To this holodrama showpiece, this mausoleum dedicated to dead ideals and housing a government whose members connived at murder.

His broad face went grim. Fionna was gone, and with her went her dream. There would be no transition, no gradual change. Without her, the Fringe bloc was leaderless, headless, already splintering in rage as the local authorities sought uselessly to link the dead assassins to someone—*anyone*—but the tracks were well buried.

The killers had been Fringers, not Innerworlders, but the Outworlds knew who'd hired them. Ladislaus had Dieter's confirmation, though his oath meant he couldn't use it. His fellows didn't need it, for the Fringe knew its enemies well. Yet there was no proof, and without proof, there was no guilt. Without guilt, there was no punishment; and without punishment, the Fringe would shatter in incoherent fury and be swept aside by the Corporate World machine. He saw it coming, and he was glad. *Glad!*

He rose and pressed his attention button, and there was a moment of silence as the delegate from Xanadu looked down from the giant screen and recognized who sought recognition.

"Mister Speaker," the delegate said slowly, "I yield to the Honorable Assemblyman for Beaufort."

Ladislaus Skjorning's grim face appeared on the master screen, and the chamber fell silent. In ten years, he had never sought the floor.

"Mister Speaker!" His voice was harsh, with little trace of his habitual accent, and he felt a stir around him as he put aside his mask at last. "I would like clarification on a point of law, Mister Speaker."

"Certainly, Mister Skjorning," Haley said, his face compassionate.

"Mister Speaker, am I not correct in believing that many years ago—in 2357—Winston Ortler of Galloway's World was accused of murdering his Old Terran mistress?"

A silent gasp rippled through the Assembly, and Simon Taliaferro's face twisted in fury while Haley stared at Ladislaus in
shock.

"Am I not *correct*, Mister Speaker?"

"Yes . . . yes, you are. But no formal charges were ever filed—"

"Precisely, Mister Speaker." Ladislaus' face was bleak. "No formal charges were filed—just as no formal charges have been filed
over the death—the *assassination*—of Fionna MacTaggart. But in
the earlier case, I believe, there was substantial evidence of guilt,
was there not? Is it not true that his colleagues ruled that, as an
assemblyman, he was immune from prosecution for *any* crime
under the Constitution?"

"Yes, Mister Skjorning," Haley said softly. "I am very much
afraid that was the case." He drew a deep breath and gripped
the dilemma by its horns. "May I ask the purpose of your questions, sir?"

"You may." Ladislaus drew himself up to his full height, towering over the other assemblymen like an angry Titan. "It is only
this, sir; just as there was no prosecution then, there will be none
now. Because the men who murdered Fionna MacTaggart *are in
this very chamber!*"

The Chamber of Worlds exploded as the words were spoken
at last. The Speaker's gavel pounded, but Ladislaus grabbed the
volume control on his console and wrenched it to full gain. His
mighty bass roared through the tumult, battering the delegates'
ears.

"Fionna MacTaggart was murdered by the political machine
headed by Simon Taliaferro!" Confused shouts of outrage and
approval echoed from the floor, but Ladislaus thundered on.
"Fringe World fingers pulled those triggers, but Corporate World
money bought them! It may never be 'proved,' but Francois
Fouchet planned her murder because she stood in the Taliaferro
machine's way!"

His savage words shocked the Assembly into silence at last,
but for a handful of shouted denials from the Corporate World
seats, and Ladislaus slowly turned down the volume.

"But let it pass," he said very softly, his amplified voice echoing in the silence. "We of the Fringe have learned our lessons
well. We cannot turn to this Assembly for justice; the Assembly
is the tool which *took* our rights. But let that pass, too. Let all
of it pass. It doesn't really matter any more, because when you
killed Fionna—" his eyes burned across at the New Galloway

delegation "—and when these other Innerworlders *let* you kill her, and demanded no accounting, you also killed this Assembly. You're dead men's shadows in a hall of ghosts, and you will wake one morning to find that you are all alone here. . . ."

His voice trailed off, and an icy hush hovered as he started to turn away. But then he paused. His fists clenched at his sides, and when he turned back to the pickup the muscles in his cheeks stood out like lumps of iron in a face reduced to elemental hatred by loss and rage.

"But happen to be one last service this putrid Constitution have the doing of for Fionna," he said thickly. "Happen to be a Fringe Worlder can claim a *Corporate* Worlder's protection!"

They were still staring at him in confusion as he vaulted the low railing of his delegation's box. Members surged to their feet as his long legs flew over ten meters of marble to the New Zurich box.

Fouchet saw him coming and lunged up, his hand snaking into his coat, but Ladislaus was too fast. Muscles trained in a gravity thirty percent greater than Old Terra's—almost forty percent greater than New Zurich's—hurled him into the New Zurich delegation, and his right hand locked on Fouchet's wrist. His fingers closed like a vise, twisting, and Fouchet screamed as his wrist shattered like crushed gravel.

Ladislaus jerked the moaning Corporate Worlder to the front of the box, his left hand scything a New Zurich aide contemptuously aside, and his bull voice roared through the tumult.

"Happen to be"—he shouted, tears streaming down his bearded cheeks—"even a Fringe Worlder can find justice if he make it for himself!" His left hand gripped the back of Fouchet's neck while the entire Assembly rose to its feet in disbelief. Two lictors raced towards the box, but they were a lifetime too late. Fouchet shrieked as steely fingers tightened, but Ladislaus' bull-throated roar battered through all opposition. "Happen to be your stinking Constitution give *me* immunity for *this!*"

And he snapped Fouchet's neck like a stick.

# COUNCIL OF WAR

"My friends!" Simon Taliaferro raised his glass and beamed at the men and women seated around the conference table. "I give you victory!"

Agreement rumbled as glasses were lifted and drained, but Oskar Dieter left his on the table and felt dull, smoldering anger burn in the pit of his belly. His eyes were narrowed to knife-hard sharpness as they sought to strip away the false joviality which always shrouded Taliaferro's inner thoughts. How had he worked so long with him without realizing exactly what he was?

"Yes, my friends," Taliaferro continued, "much as I regret the death of Francois Fouchet, his murder—his *martyrdom*—has assured our victory. I received the latest projections this morning," He beamed at them like a fond uncle. "Within two months—three at the outside—our majority will be sufficient to assure approval of the Amalgamation!"

The rumble of approval was even louder, and Dieter felt a chill breeze whistle around the corners of his soul. The Amalgamation was but the first step of the plan he and Taliaferro had worked out years before, but Dieter had always regarded it as a theoretical exercise, a sort of "what if" in case the opportune moment ever arrived. He'd never really believed that they would succeed. Nor would they have . . . without murder.

He stared into his glass. The media, with its customary voracity for sensationalism, had arrived even before the medical examiner, and Dieter's heart chilled as he recalled the pathetic figure lying almost neatly in the wide, dark pool of blood. The assassins hadn't bled as much as she; men who die instantly bleed very little.

Dieter had watched those news shots with a sort of self-flagellating fascination. He'd tried to prevent it, but his efforts had been too little too late, and for all that he'd striven to stop it, it was also his unforgivable stupidity which had made the act inevitable . . . and stripped him of the power to forbid it.

He looked up from his glass with a bitter half-smile. Fouchet's death had restored him, however temporarily, to the ranks of the Corporate World autocrats on Old Terra. He lacked the power and prestige which had once been his, but there was no one else to speak for New Zurich, so his fellows had been forced to accept him once more, at least until the New Zurich oligarchs replaced him. Yet he was an outcast, now; more so even than they realized. He understood the dreadful attraction he held for them—the near hypnotic fascination of a tainted man whose career lay in wreckage. But they seemed unaware how deep the taint truly went.

"Of course, we all regret the terrible events which led to this," Taliaferro was saying smoothly, "but one cannot deny that the entire crisis is tailor-made for our needs."

"Maybe," Hector Waldeck rumbled. The chief delegate from Christophon was a choleric man, and his face flushed as he spoke. "No doubt the Amalgamation will pass, Simon, but what about Skjorning? The bastard's a damned savage! He ought to pay for what he did, by God!"

Dieter's mouth twisted behind his hand as others murmured agreement. They were all so sanctimonious about Skjorning's act—what about what *they* had done? They knew the truth about Fionna's death, yet Waldeck was so smugly self-righteous he could demand punishment for Skjorning!

He sighed, anger tempered by shame as he realized that once he would have shouted as loudly as any. He glanced around the angry, self-important faces, seeing them as they were at last, now that he was no longer part of them, and it was like looking into a terrible mirror. They were no more truly "evil" than he himself. Like him, they played by the only rules they knew, and they played the "game" well. That was the problem. For them, it was *only* a game, a vastly exciting contest for the wealth of a galaxy.

They were manipulators and users because it had never occurred to them to be anything else. The Legislative Assembly was no government; it was a tremendous, fascinating toy, a machine whose buttons and levers disgorged ever more wealth, ever more power, and ever more intoxicating triumphs. And the people who were crushed in the production of those triumphs weren't real to them, had no existence in the real world.

Sorrow filled him. The Corporate Worlds had spent trillions of credits and decades of political effort to master that machine, and when the growing Fringe population threatened their control, they'd moved ruthlessly to crush the opposition—all as part of "the game." For all the time and effort they spent plotting and planning, they were even blinder than the insulated Heart Worlders, for they saw Fringers only as obstacles, not as people, and certainly not as fellow citizens. They saw them as pawns, dupes—cartoon caricatures cruelly drawn by habitual contempt and denigration. As *things,* not people . . . and *things* were made to be broken and trampled underfoot if they got in the way.

"No, Hector," Taliaferro said firmly. "We don't want to punish him—though I certainly share your outrage!" He managed to sound quite sincere, Dieter thought bitterly, and revised his earlier estimate. Some of these people *were* evil, however you defined the term. "But despite what we feel, we must remember that Skjorning's accusations can be made to work for us rather than against us. We need to use him, not indict him."

"Crap," Waldeck said harshly. "I want that murderous bastard stood up against a wall and shot! We need to teach these barbarians a lesson—especially the Beauforters!"

Dieter saw a few sardonic smiles. Christophon's medicinal combines had tried hard to move in on the doomwhaling industry, and Beaufort's government had slapped them down with a sort of savage delight. Waldeck's fellow oligarchs hadn't taken that well, nor had they cared for the loss of prestige they'd suffered.

"No, Hector," Taliaferro repeated more forcefully. "In fact, I intend to oppose any effort to try him on civil charges. We need him gone, true, but we can arrange that without a civil trial—and we damned well better after the insane charges he made in the Chamber! If we come down as hard as he deserves, his supporters will scream it's part of a cover-up, and some of the Heart Worlders might believe it. Besides, if we can send him home in disgrace, it'll undermine the Fringe far more effectively, not to mention the approval our forbearance will win from the liberals."

"But—"

"Listen to me, Hector," Taliaferro said sharply. "All our projections say that as soon as Skjorning's gone, scores of Fringer delegates will resign in protest. They'll take *themselves* out of the picture and give us an absolute majority. But if we make him a martyr the Fringe'll close ranks to 'avenge' him. It'll be as bad as having MacTaggart back!"

"I don't like it," Waldeck grumbled.

"Nor do I, but the Amalgamation is what matters."

"Is it?" Dieter was more surprised than any of the others to hear himself speak. Eyes swivelled to him, filled with a sort of cold curiosity, but Taliaferro's eyes weren't cold. They were fiery with contempt.

"Of course it is, Oskar," the Gallowayan said, sweet reason sugarcoating the disdain in his voice. "You worked as hard as anyone else to arrange it." His tone added the unspoken qualifier "before you lost your touch," and Dieter flushed. But his chin lifted, and he looked around with a sort of calm defiance which was new to him.

"I did," he said quietly. "Before I saw what it's going to cost."

"What are you talking about?" Amanda Sydon's harsh-voweled New Detroit accent grated on Dieter's ears, and he eyed her with distaste. Sydon was a cobra, every bit Taliaferro's equal. And then he remembered his drugged insult to Fionna. Was his damned prejudice speaking again? But, no, there was no comparison between Fionna and Amanda Sydon. They both happened to be women, but Fionna had also happened to be human.

"You know what I'm talking about, if you'd care to accept the truth, Amanda," he said quietly.

"The truth," she sneered, "is that the Fringe won't even know what hit it for at least ten years—if they manage to figure it out then! With our majority, *we'll* control the post-amalgamation reapportionment. We'll gut them, and they'll stay gutted for fifty years!"

"Fifty?" Dieter allowed himself a chuckle. "Amanda, you obviously don't know as much about the demographics as you think." He felt spines stiffen as he threw his challenge into her teeth, filled with a courage based for a change on conviction rather than convenience. "It won't be fifty years, dear. If the Fringe population curves hold steady and the borders continue to expand, it'll be more like a *hundred* and fifty years."

He glanced at Taliaferro amid a hiss of indrawn breaths as the others heard the true figures for the first time, and the fury burning behind the fixed joviality amused him. So Simon hadn't wanted his minions to know the full extent of his ambition? Was he afraid even they might see the result?

"Dear me, Amanda—didn't Simon mention that?" Dieter's

voice was harsh in the semisilence. "He should have, because the Fringers have waited two hundred years for their representation to match ours. They'll certainly run a worst-case projection and realize they're facing at least another century of powerlessness. How do you think they'll react to that?"

"How *can* they react?" Taliaferro scoffed. "They won't have the votes to stop it."

"Precisely," Dieter said flatly. He drew a deep breath and rose, his gaze burning over the faces around him. Guilt over Fionna's death and over the part he'd played—intentionally and unintentionally—in bringing the Federation to this pass supported him. It wasn't enough that he'd only played the game. Games were for children; adulthood carried the duties of adulthood. Angry self-loathing gave him a sort of visionary strength, and he suddenly knew how Cassandra must have felt. Yet he had to try, if only to prove to himself that once he'd had the right to sit in the same chamber as Fionna MacTaggart.

"Listen to me, all of you," he said softly. "We can do it. We can use Skjorning to break the Fringe and then ram reapportionment through whatever opposition is left, but are you all too blind to see what will happen then?"

"Tell us, Oskar, since you seem so prescient," Taliaferro sneered, no longer hiding his contempt.

"All right, Simon. I *will* tell you," Dieter said, his voice sad. "War."

"War!" Taliaferro's laugh was harsh. "With whom, Oskar? That penniless bunch of ragged-assed barbarians? Hell, man, the Taliaferro Yards alone can build more hulls than all the Fringe Worlds put together! Not even Fringers could be stupid enough to buck that much firepower!"

"Can't they? Simon, I chair Military Oversight. I know what I'm talking about. They can fight, and they *will*. They'll be ready enough if you only railroad Skjorning out of the Assembly—" he saw frowns of distaste at his deliberately honest choice of verb "—but that isn't all you'll be doing. This amalgamation is an antimatter warhead, man! The mere *threat* of enfranchising the Orions will drive them berserk. And it won't be 'barbarian xenophobia,' whatever you tell the Heart Worlds. It'll be a cold sober appreciation of what adding that many non-Terran voters will do to their representation."

"So what?" Taliaferro shot back. "Let some of them try to secede! We'll squash them like bugs, and it'll *prove* they're barbarians!

The Heart Worlds'll be as eager as we are to expel them from the Assembly—for good!"

Cold shock knifed through Dieter. Not surprise, really; perhaps he'd guessed Taliaferro's real intent all along and simply chosen not to face it.

"My God," he said softly. "You *want* a war."

"Nonsense!" The denial was just a bit too quick, a touch too offhand. Some of the others were clearly shaken by Dieter's charge, and Taliaferro made himself smile. "It won't come to a war, no matter what you think. The absolute worst may be a police action or two, and we've had those before, haven't we, Hector?" He winked at the Christophon delegate, and the reminder of the food riots on Christophon, three hundred years past, woke a rumble of nervous laughter. "But nobody's left the Federation after a police action," Taliaferro went on persuasively, "and that's all it can be. The Fringers don't have a fleet *or* the means to build one; *we* have both. All I'm saying is that if they're that stupid, it'll only strengthen our position in the long run."

Dieter saw Taliaferro's words sink home. They were the words his allies wanted to hear, the ones that told them everything was fine, that they still controlled "the game." He'd jolted them, but not enough to break Taliaferro's hold. They would follow him despite anything a political has-been said, and Dieter swallowed an angry rebuttal.

"You're wrong, Simon," he said. "Even assuming all we get is a 'police action or two,' the damage will be done. You've all forgotten that the Federation exists only because its citizens *want* it to exist. When enough of them stop wanting it to live, it will die."

He shook his head, feeling their disbelief and rejection.

"No doubt you'll all do exactly as you wish," he said heavily, "but I warn you now—I'll oppose you, both here and on the floor."

The tension in the room suddenly doubled.

"Go ahead!" Taliaferro snarled, his face dark with rage. "If not for your stupidity, we'd already have carried the amalgamation vote! So go on, damn you! We'll still be here when you're a memory—and you know it!"

"Perhaps so, Simon," Dieter said sadly across the immense breach between them. "And you're probably right about whether or not I can stop you. But when you turn the Federation into armed camps which can never live in peace again—" his eyes were live coals as they swept the silent room "—remember I told you it would happen. And when it does, I'll be able to say I tried to stop it . . . What will *you* be able to say?"

"You're almost as eloquent as Skjorning," Taliaferro sneered.

"No, Simon," Dieter's quiet voice sliced back through the silence, "I'm nowhere near as eloquent as he is—but I'm just as accurate."

Taliaferro made a contemptuous gesture, but even under his anger there might have been just a trace of uncertainty. Dieter didn't know, but if Taliaferro did feel any lack of confidence, it wasn't enough. Dieter looked at the stony faces and knew he'd failed. He'd tried to convince them, but they refused to hear; now he could only fight them.

He closed his briefcase, the sound loud in the breathless hush, and walked to the door through the silence, and hostile eyes burned his back. He knew he'd just sealed his political fate, but what mattered was that he would make his fight on the Assembly floor . . . and lose.

He closed the door gently behind him, and the corridor was as empty as his future as he walked slowly to the elevators. He felt the approaching defeat in his bones, but he'd forfeited his career the night he insulted Fionna and discovered he was not the man he'd thought himself to be, and the floor fight would be his Gethsemane. His self-destruction could never expiate his guilt, but perhaps it would let him face Fionna's memory with a sense of having done his best. With a sense of having stood up on his hind legs and said "I am a man—with a man's duties and a man's right to destroy myself for what I know is right."

Oskar Dieter stepped out into the night of Old Terra under a blanket of stars—a man without a future, but one who held his chin high again at last.

# CHANGE OF ORDERS

Captain Li Han, commanding officer of TFNS *Longbow*, shrugged as her tunic's seams slid back off the points of her shoulders and the dragonhead flash of her planet dipped low. She should have stood over that tailor with a club! He wasn't used to dealing with officers who massed just over twenty-six kilos, and it showed.

The intraship car slowed and Han banished her frown, squaring her cap on her sleek black hair. The trick, they'd explained at the Academy, was never to notice that anything was wrong. If *you* didn't, *they* didn't. Assuming, of course, that the Protocol Procedures profs were correct.

The door hissed open on the boatbay, and Han watched the side party snap to attention beside her cutter as the electronic bosun's pipe shrilled. There were few non-Oriental faces in *Longbow*; she was homeported on the Fringe World of Hangchow and her crew reflected her ethnicity, and even those few were from other Fringe Worlds. There was not a single Innerworlder in *Longbow*'s complement, and Han sometimes wondered if any of her personnel ever guessed just how and why that had come to pass.

She hoped not. She hoped they would never have to know.

She shook herself mentally and stepped from the car. Hangchow ran to about ten percent more gravity than the one standard G all TFN ships maintained—enough to make the one-gravity field restful (and to produce a musculature which at least gave her a little more body mass, despite her height)—and Han moved with a dancer's grace, hiding a familiar wry smile as she passed through the side party. The top of her cap was below shoulder level on the sideboys, and she wondered if they found her small size amusing? Probably. Han's diminutive size dogged her career like a shadow. She'd probably always be remembered as the small-est midshipman ever to enter the Academy, rather than as the woman who graduated with the honor sword by her side, but the fact that she stood just under 119 centimeters hadn't kept her from showing the whole pack her heels, she thought cheerfully. And captain's rank in Battle Fleet at thirty-seven was no mean accomplishment, either.

She returned the salutes, and the cutter's hatch slid shut as she dropped into the cushioned chair. And so, she thought, off to another scintillating courtesy call . . . but this one might be more important than most.

The cutter idled clear of *Longbow*, and Han allowed herself a moment of pride as she studied her command through the port. The huge, ungainly bulk of Skywatch Three, the orbital headquarters of Galloway's World System Defense Command, made a perfect foil for the battlecruiser's elegance. Light from the system's G4 primary glittered on *Longbow*'s graceful flanks and turned her recessed weapons bays into sooty ovals of shadow, hiding the deadly devices crouching within. Even the clutter of external ordnance hardpoints and the massive housings of her drive pods seemed graceful and balanced. Other ships carried heavier armaments, or more defense, but none matched the speed, maneuverability, and power blended in *Longbow*'s sinister beauty.

Han sighed and looked away. Beautiful, yes, but still a killing machine. A weapon of war to engage and destroy humanity's enemies. It passed belief that Navy personnel might someday have to decide just which *humans* were enemies.

Air screamed past the cutter's hull as it skipped into Gallo-way's World's atmosphere, and the little boat banked gently as it headed for the Yard's landing pads. Han watched the Jamieson Archipelago grow, amused as always by the anomaly which left the Fleet's fourth largest shipyard the only Navy base in existence without a name. It was just "the Yard," as it had been since the First Interstellar War, when Galloway's World was *the* navy yard for the Federation—just as the sprawling kilometers of dependent housing around it were simply "the Reservation." There were larger bases now— Zephrain for one—but no other planet rivaled the sheer numbers of hulls which emerged from the military and civilian building slips of Galloway's World.

The cutter swooped over the innocent weather domes that hid the Yard's missile silos and projector pits. As a rule, the TFN

preferred to defend inhabited planets with orbital forts, sparing civilians the incidental destruction attendant upon modern
combat, but there was no point pretending about the Jamieson
Archipelago. The Yard alone made the island chain a priority
target for any enemy, and the Yard wasn't alone. It crowded
shoulder-to-shoulder with the Taliaferro Yard; the Kreuger Space
Works; Vickers-Mitsubishi-Galloway's World; General Dynamics
of Terra; and a dozen other major building centers. Coupled with
the orbital facilities where the ground-built components were
assembled, the Archipelago represented the largest concentration
of industrial might in the known galaxy.

The cutter dropped quickly for its landing circle, and Han
watched the ground rush up to meet them, but her thoughts were
on her meeting with the Port Admiral. She drew a deep breath,
concentrating on the mental discipline that calmed the pulse, and
glanced at her watch. Right on the tick. Good.

"Good afternoon, Captain Li." The yeoman in the outer office
smiled respectfully as the tiny captain entered. "Please have a seat.
Admiral Rutgers' last appointment is running a little over."

Han settled in a comfortable chair and checked her watch
again, hoping Admiral Rutgers wasn't going to be tied up long.
She was due to ship out for Christophon in two hours, and there
were always last-minute details to crowd a departure time. It was
well known that Port Admirals' whims had much the same force
as direct decrees from God, but that never seemed to help when
the admiral at the other end wanted to know where you'd spent
that extra hour or two.

The door slid open and Han glanced up—then came quickly
to her feet at the sight of a vice admiral's sleeve braid. The tall,
dark-faced man with the neat beard nodded to her.

"Captain."

"Admiral Trevayne."

"Another penitent here to see the Admiral, Captain Li?"

"No, sir." Han hid a smile. "Just a courtesy call before
departure."

"Ah!" Trevayne nodded and turned away.

Li Han regarded his broad shoulders thoughtfully. Now what
did that "Ah!" mean? There was something hidden behind it; she
could almost taste it. Did he know something she didn't? Possibly. Quite possibly. Trevayne was a marked man in the service:
the youngest man ever to command a monitor battlegroup, and

no question that he was headed for CNO and possibly even Sky Marshal before he was done. If there was any loose information floating around, it would have come to his ears long since. Rumor credited the man with an uncanny ability to read the future. Was he reading it now?

Han didn't know him well enough to be certain, though she knew his son quite well. It was always easier to know one's juniors than one's seniors, but even if it hadn't been, Lieutenant Commander Colin Trevayne of the scout cruiser *Ashanti* was a highly . . . visible personality within the Fleet. Centuries of tradition decreed that the Federation's widely diverse military people *must* be nonpartisan. In a sense, accepting a TFN commission was to take a vow of political celibacy—or so it had been until very recently—and Ian Trevayne honored that tradition. Colin, however, was as fiery as his father was calm and controlled. His outspoken sympathy for the Fringe put him firmly in the "Young Turk" camp, and Han wondered if rumor exaggerated the rift between father and son.

The yeoman's panel beeped gently, and he spoke into his hush-phone, then listened briefly.

"Admiral Trevayne, Captain Li; Admiral Rutgers would like to see you both, if you please," he said, and Han felt her eyebrows rise. There *was* something in the wind! She waited courteously for Trevayne to lead the way into the inner sanctum, and her nerves were strung to fever pitch.

Fleet Admiral William Rutgers was a bulky man of indeterminate ancestry, and Han smiled warmly as a paw like an Old Terran bear's enveloped her tiny hand in greeting. Rutgers, once her father's chief of staff, had been her own fifth-year tactical instructor almost fifteen years ago.

"Thank you both for being patient," he said, sitting back down and waving them to chairs. Han waited until Trevayne sat before she followed suit. It was just a little awkward to be so junior to the only other two people present . . . especially after coming straight from her own ship, where she was mistress after God and even that precedence was a bit blurred.

"Patient, Bill?" Trevayne chuckled. "Junior officers are always patient—or they bloody well better learn to pretend they are!"

"Except for the ones like you, Ian," Rutgers said, shaking his head in mock sadness.

Trevayne laughed easily. His elegant frame—no problems with *his* tailoring—was seated casually, almost carelessly, right ankle on left knee. To sit like that in the presence of an admiral, you had to *be* an admiral. But Trevayne had something else, something beyond even his membership in one of the "dynasties" of the Federation's Navy. His rapid rise wasn't due solely to birth or brilliance. Han's father had been an admiral before his retirement, and his father before him, yet she lacked that not-quite-arrogant "something else." Charisma, perhaps?

But from what source? He was a man who valued style and flair, and one who carried it off with ease, yet that wasn't explanation enough. It came to her suddenly that Trevayne had been reared to lead even as she had, but in a society which openly acknowledged and accepted such expectations. He *expected* to be a leader, and because he expected it of himself, others expected it of him, as well. His undoubted brilliance simply confirmed the wisdom of those mutual expectations.

"Well, today I have good reason for being in a hurry," he said. "Tomorrow is Courtenay's birthday, and I haven't picked out a present yet. And your godson is shipping out tomorrow on *Ashanti*." His jaw clenched for an instant, as if with sudden hurt. "I'm supposed to have lunch with him . . . lunch and—" he added, looking straight at Rutgers "—a much-needed talk."

Han carefully did not take note of the pain in her senior's dark face.

"I'm sorry, Ian," Rutgers said, suddenly serious. "You'd better delegate the shopping to Natalya. As for Colin . . . I know things are touchy just now, and I'll try to leave you time for lunch, but I may not be able to. Your leave's been canceled."

Han sat straighter and felt her face become masklike. Vice admirals' leaves were not cut short on whims.

"I see." Trevayne's face was very calm as he studied the Port Admiral, Too calm. It was a mask, too, Han realized sadly; everyone wore masks these days, even in the Fleet. "And might one ask why, Admiral?"

"One might," Rutgers said grimly. He glanced over at Han for a moment. "I asked you two to come in together to save a little time; what I have to say will affect you both. On the other hand, I trust that I don't have to remind you both that what's said here *stays* here. Clear?"

Both his juniors nodded.

"All right. As you know, the Assembly's been in a furor ever since the MacTaggart assassination. And it didn't help a bit when Skjorning murdered Fouchet! I—"

He broke off and glanced at Han, then smiled unwillingly and shook his head.

"Captain, I seem to recall a certain midshipman's expression which generally indicated disagreement. Why am I seeing it now?"

"Disagreement, Admiral?" Han shook her head. "Not disagreement. It's just that I find it difficult to condemn Assemblyman Skjorning."

"Who said I condemned him? I only said it didn't help, which it didn't. Mind, I'm not saying the same thing wouldn't have happened if he'd held his hand; I think it would have, in fact. But it's happened now, and it's up to us to pick up the pieces."

"Yes, sir."

"What 'pieces' d'you mean, Bill?" Trevayne asked, his eyes narrowing.

"I wish I knew," Rutgers sighed, running a hand over his hair. "I take it you're both reasonably informed on events on Old Terra?" They nodded, and he continued. "Well, things are coming to a head. The Assembly has decided to impeach Skjorning."

"It's not as if they really have a choice, Bill," Trevayne pointed out, "but it doesn't automatically follow that the impeachment will be sustained."

"Oh, you're so right, Ian," Rutgers said softly, and pulled out a classified binder. He slapped it down on his blotter and pressed his thumb to the lock. Scanners considered for a moment, then released the latch, and he pulled out a sheaf of yellow security paper.

"This," he said, "is an ONI evaluation of the situation as of three weeks ago. It arrived today . . . by courier drone."

Han's inner tension clicked higher. Galloway's World was a Corporate World, tied into the communications net the Corporate Worlders had used to deadly effect against the Fringe for decades. No com beam could be driven through a warp point, but it was quite possible to build deep-space relay stations within star systems. All messages had to be physically carried through warp points aboard ships or small, unmanned courier drones, but once through, they could be transcribed and transmitted to the next warp point. Yet such systems took time to emplace, and they were incredibly expensive, both to build and maintain.

The Corporate Worlds had capitalized upon that. In the spirit of "generosity," their delegates had declared that it was only proper that each system should be responsible for its own relay networks rather than making them a charge upon any other system, and, since they controlled the Assembly, the Assembly had agreed. But the Fringe Worlds, of course, were too poor to build and extend the relay nets to *their* worlds. *All* of their messages must travel by ship or drone, which—just coincidentally—meant that it was far, far easier for Corporate World politicos to confer with their homeworlds. They could send a message and get a response in days; the same process took months for a Fringer delegation, and that explained a great deal about the smoothly oiled precision of the Taliaferro Machine.

But if ONI had sent this data by drone, it meant whoever had sent it didn't trust the relays. It wasn't all that unusual for classified data to be sent physically rather than risk interception, but Admiral Rutgers' tone and expression told her *this* drone was more important than most.

"Indications are that the Taliaferro crowd doesn't plan to challenge the Ortler precedent," the burly admiral continued grimly. "Rather than push for Skjorning's civil trial on Old Terra, they're going to expel him from the Assembly and send him back to the Kontravian Cluster under Lictor escort. As Taliaferro puts it—" he thumbed through the Naval Intelligence report for the passage he sought, and his voice was harsh as he read aloud "—'Let us send the barbarians among us back to the Fringe where they belong!'"

Han felt her face blanch. No wonder Trevayne's leave had been canceled! When the Fringe heard about *this*—!

Rutgers watched her calmly, and she returned his gaze levelly. He shook his head.

"Han, someday you may be able to keep me from guessing what you're thinking. Until that day comes, I wouldn't waste the effort, if I were you."

"Sir?"

"You know precisely what I mean. This—" he tapped the piece of paper "—is probably the stupidest brilliant political maneuver in human history. And, my dear, you know it as well as I do."

"As the Admiral says," she said in a colorless voice.

"One day, Han," Rutgers mused, "you'll try the china doll trick once too often." Despite her concern, Han's lips twitched, and he grinned at her. Then he sobered.

"This is also—" he said slowly, tapping the paper again "—going to make a bad situation much, much worse. Amalgamation and reapportionment would be terribly hard for the Fringe to swallow under any circumstances, but when you add the MacTaggart assassination and what they're going to see as a calculated and contemptuous rejection of justice . . ."

"I should bloody well think so!" Trevayne said. "Talk about a cat among the pigeons!"

"I know, Ian. I know. But ONI thinks it's going to happen."

"But it hasn't happened yet, has it?"

"No, but it will, Ian. It's only a matter of time, and what matters to us right this minute are the Fleet orders which came in the same drone. They're the reason your leave's been canceled, and why you, Captain, aren't going to Christophon after all."

He pinched his nose wearily. "In all my days in the TFN, I have never received orders quite like these," he said soberly. "As of now, the Fleet's primary mission has been changed 'for the duration of the current political crisis,' as our instructions so neatly phrase it. Our new mission is to play fireman across the width and breadth of the Federation when this gets out."

"Good God, Bill," Trevayne said mildly. "They have to be out of their minds. They *do* realize the Federation is over fourteen hundred light-years across, don't they? How do they expect us to be everywhere we'll have to be?"

"They don't. Intelligence has identified a dozen critical systems and clusters with an exceptional potential for disaster. Our immediate concern is to place a battlegroup or two to cover each of them as a show of force."

"Against our own people, sir?" Han asked softly.

"Against *anyone*, Captain," Rutgers said heavily.

"If you'll pardon my saying so, Bill," Trevayne said quietly, "that's an excellent recipe for disaster if something does go wrong. Since you're talking to us, I assume you mean Battle Fleet units, not Frontier Fleet."

"I do," Rutgers said. "Frontier Fleet's spread too thin as it is—Frontier Fleet is *always* spread too thin." And, Han thought sadly, too many of Frontier Fleet's officers were too sympathetic to "their" sectors' needs to be "reliable." "So we're dispersing some of Battle Fleet to the trouble spots; a little less than half our active units, to be precise."

"And if the balloon goes up, we won't have concentration of force anywhere," Trevayne pointed out.

"I know that. You know that. Probably the Joint Chiefs know that. The Assembly, unfortunately, doesn't know it and doesn't *want* to know it. And we, as you may recall, work for the civilians."

"Yes, sir."

"Thank you. Now, Ian, your battlegroup is headed for Oster-man's Star. I want you to ship out before nineteen hundred zulu today."

"Yes, sir."

"You, Captain Li, will sign for this binder. You will personally deliver it to Fleet Admiral Forsythe and attach your ship to his command. He'll give you further orders at that time."

"Yes, sir."

"All right." Rutgers rubbed the binder and drew a deep breath. "I'm going to say something I really shouldn't say. I'm going to tell you that I think the Assembly's lost its mind and that when—not if—the shit hits the fan, it's going to be up to us to scrape it off our faces and salvage something from the wreck. We're the Federation Navy, and the Federation Navy has never fired on Terran civilians. I'd like to keep it that way. But if it comes to it—" his eyes burned into Han's and then swivelled slowly to Trevayne "—remember that we are the *Federation* Navy."

There was a moment of silence, and Han felt something like guilt as she returned her old teacher's regard.

"Very well." Rutgers rose to signal the end of the interview and held out his hand again. "My yeoman has your orders. Pick them up and carry them out. And may God have mercy on us all."

Li Han reclined in lotus position in the center of her cabin carpet. By planet-side standards, her cabin was small and cramped; by Navy standards, it was luxuriously large; and by anyone's standards, a proud Hangchow government had furnished it with elegant taste. Her eyes drifted to the priceless fifth-century lacquered screen hiding her safe, and the thought of what lay within it undermined her ability to find tranquillity.

She sighed and rolled out of the lotus. There was no point pretending, and it was a bad habit to pretend to relax. She flowed to her feet and considered more stringent exercises, but activity wasn't the anodyne she needed now. Her doubts demanded resolution.

Yet there was nowhere for a captain to turn when troubled by doubt. Junior officers could discuss their fears; enlisted people could do the same. Even admirals could talk with other admirals, or at least their flag captains. But captains' absolute authority during their months-long voyages robbed them of that luxury. God was the only person to whom a wise skipper admitted her doubts. Infallibility. Her lips quirked at the thought. That was what a captain must radiate. Absolute confidence.

Han had never made any secret of her own apolitical loyalty to her homeworld, and though, like most Fringers, she'd studied politics closely, she wasn't a political person. Or, at least, she hadn't *been* a political person. Like every child of Hangchow, she'd learned at an early age that the Corporate Worlds controlled her people's economic destiny, yet she had always believed the Legislative Assembly would somehow safeguard their political rights . . . until she'd gained her fourth ring and become privy to the inner workings of the policies the Fleet sometimes enforced. Her first deployment as captain had based her ship on New Detroit, and, for the first time, she'd realized how totally the Corporate Worlds controlled the Assembly.

Even then, she'd believed time and demographics were on the side of the Fringe; now it seemed the Corporate Worlds were determined to turn back the clock and disenfranchise her people. They even had a precedent, for the Reapportionments of 2184 and 2240 had done exactly the same thing, if for somewhat different reasons.

Han had not been a political person, but she had been and still was a direct one. She never lied to herself. When the first doubt appeared, she'd dragged it ruthlessly into the open, examining it pitilessly.

To her surprise, the light of day did not kill it. Indeed, it thrived in the sunlight, and her suspicion-sharpened eyes saw things she'd never noticed before. And as a direct person who accepted the Fleet's admonition to be prepared, Han had begun to consider what she—Li Han the woman, as well as Li Han the captain—would do if the unthinkable happened. What was her duty? Where did her loyalty lie if the madmen on either side pushed the Federation beyond its strength? Her conclusions had shocked her, but she was what she was. She could be no other; and being what she was, she had acted.

Captain Li Han, TFN, woke frequently these nights—woke praying that the Federation she loved and served would survive the storm lashing across it. But if the day came when the Federation toppled under the hurricane, she also knew what she would do . . . what she would have to do.

"Challenge from the flagship, sir."

Han glanced at her executive officer and then at the plot

displaying the might of Task Force Seventeen. Eight monitors, eight superdreadnoughts, six assault carriers, two fleet carriers, ten battlecruisers, dozens of cruisers, and scores of destroyers, Marine transports, repair ships, colliers . . . It made an imposing sight on the tactical display. More firepower than the TFN had committed to many campaigns of the Fourth Interstellar War—certainly more than had ever been deployed in a single battle since that war. And all this panoply of war, she thought sadly, was to overawe the citizens of the Federation, not to defeat their enemies in battle.

"Standard acknowledgment, Chang," she said.

"Yes, sir."

The message reached out across the emptiness to the task force. There was a communications lag of over two minutes at this range, even as *Longbow* loped towards Task Force Seventeen at ten percent of light speed.

"Reply from Flag, sir. We are to take position in company with *Flintlock*. Captain to report aboard *Anderson* as soon as convenient. One query: do we have dispatches on board?"

"Reply affirmative, Exec." She pressed a stud on her command chair arm console. "Boatbay," she said.

"Boatbay, aye," a voice replied in her mastoid battlephone.

"Chief Ling, this is the Captain. I need my cutter in twenty minutes."

"Yes, sir. She'll be ready to flit."

"Thank you, Chief."

She killed the circuit and returned her attention to the plot, watching the tiny blips blink from the red-ringed circles of unidentified ships to the green-ringed dots of known units as *Longbow*'s computers sorted out their transponders. One dot was circled in gold—TFNS *Howard Anderson*, the monitor flagship—and it swung to the center of the plot as *Longbow* headed straight for her. Han studied it a moment, then punched up identities on the others, looking for familiar faces among their commanders.

*Anderson*'s skipper she knew: Captain Willis Enwright, Fleet Admiral Forsythe's handpicked flag captain and one of the most brilliant of the many Fringe World officers in the Fleet. Nor was he the first such in his family—*Anderson*'s sistership, the *Lawrence Enwright*, was named for one of his ancestors. Captain Simon Hodah had her, Han remembered with a warm smile. Simon was ten years her senior, but they'd been close friends since Han's middie cruise as his assistant astrogator. There were other names and faces out here to be remembered. Vice Admiral Traynor in command of one of the superdreadnought battlegroups; Vice Admiral Eric Hale, commanding the other. Vice Admiral Analiese Ashigara, a Fringe Worlder from Hokkaido, flying her lights aboard the assault carrier *Basilisk*. Vice Admiral Singh, Forsythe's second in command, flying his lights aboard Hodah's ship.

Meetings between this many Fleet units were rare, and it felt good to see the light codes, to remember the men and women in the tight-knit Navy community. They were professionals one and all; brothers and sisters of the sword, dedicated to the pure service of the Federation's ideals.

Or that was the idea. That was the Navy's credo, even if its members were merely human and often fell short of the ideal. Han's smile faded as she weighed herself against the standards of the Fleet, and she wondered how many of those others she knew were doing the same thing over there behind the weapons and armor, behind the armor of their eyes?

She shook her head and rose.

"You have the con, Exec," she said formally. "I'm going to my quarters for a quick shower before I report to the Admiral."

"Yes, sir."

Commander Tsing Chang took the command chair as the captain left the bridge. His eyes flicked over the readouts as the intraship car's doors hissed quietly shut. Only then did he allow himself a glance at the blank doors which had hidden his tiny captain. Did she really think no one else on board had guessed what she was thinking? He returned his attention to the tactical plot, his face expressionless, his mind busy behind his dark eyes.

"Greetings, Captain Li." Fleet Admiral Stepan Forsythe held out his hand, and Han could not help comparing his dry, frail grip with the firm, hairy clasp of the last fleet admiral she'd met. Stepan Forsythe was William Rutgers' physical opposite in every way, she thought. He was slender, stoop-shouldered, showing his advanced age in his lined face and thinning hair. Forsythe was a living link with the days of the Fourth Interstellar War, and Han knew he was due for retirement soon. His body was old and frail, for he was one of the rare individuals who responded poorly to the antiaging therapies, but keen intelligence and willpower glinted behind his gray eyes.

"Thank you, sir," she said, returning the clasp.

"You made a fast passage," Forsythe continued, waving her

to a chair and touching the security binder on his desk as if to restrain a venomous serpent.

"We tried, sir."

"Yes. Well, would you like a drink while I glance through this?"

"No, sir. Thank you."

"Very well. If you'll excuse me?"

Han arranged her cap very precisely on her knees and sat quietly as the old admiral opened the binder and extracted the sheets of closely printed material. He read slowly, carefully, but no change of expression betrayed his thoughts. Perhaps the contents were less of a shock to him than they'd been to her. Perhaps he'd gone even further than she in analyzing the crisis, or perhaps he simply had access to more information than a mere captain.

Forsythe sighed and turned the final page at last, then jogged the sheets neatly back into order. He returned them to the binder and pressed a stud on his console, glancing into the screen as it lit.

"Willis? Would you come to my quarters, please?"

"Yes, sir."

Forsythe cut the circuit and smiled tautly at Han. "I realize you probably don't know any more than is contained in these documents, Captain Li, but I'd appreciate it if you'd give Captain Enwright and myself the benefit of your firsthand impressions. We're rather isolated out here, and neither of us has had any personal contact with the Innerworlds in almost a year."

"Of course, sir," Han said, hiding her discomfort.

"Thank you. We—ah! Here's the captain."

Han rose quickly as Willis Enwright entered the cabin with a hurried stride. That was one of the things she associated with Enwright—quickness, speed, almost haste. It was as if he resented the dawdling pace of time and wrestled with every second for the maximum utility he could wring from it. It made for a thorny personality, but it also made him a superb captain and would someday make him an equally outstanding admiral.

"Han!" He squeezed her hand warmly. "Good to see you again. How are your parents?"

"Mother is as beautiful as ever; Father is as handsome." Han smiled. "What else is there to say?"

"I suppose that does just about cover it," Enwright agreed with a grin. He dropped sloppily into a chair, and Han seated herself again, glancing at Forsythe for his reaction to Enwright's informality. The old admiral only smiled at his flag captain. Then his expression tightened.

"Willis, Captain Li has brought us some disturbing information." He slid the binder across the desk. "Want a look?"

"Why?" Enwright shrugged. "No doubt the Assembly's done something else foolish. They've specialized in that for years, or we wouldn't be out here, sir."

"Foolish or not, they're still the duly constituted government," Forsythe said, the slight edge in his voice suggesting that this wasn't the first time he and Enwright had struck sparks on the subject. "However—" Forsythe shook his head "—I have to agree that this time they really have been foolish. Look at this." He opened the binder and handed Enwright the top sheet, and the captain's face tightened.

"Foolish isn't the word, sir," he said quietly, his humor vanished. "My God, if this goes through the whole Fringe will go up in smoke . . . and I don't know as how I'll blame them, either." He read further, then whistled. "Jesus! If they *do* expel Lad Skjorning, the shit will really fly, Admiral!"

"Precisely," Forsythe said frostily. "And if, as you so quaintly put it, the shit *does* fly, whose job is it to quiet the situation back down?"

"Ours," Enwright said, his voice troubled.

"Ours, indeed, Captain." Forsythe turned back to Han. "Captain Li, is it your impression this evaluation is essentially accurate?"

"Well, sir," Han said carefully, "Admiral Rutgers certainly seemed to think so when he spoke to me." She shrugged. "But you probably know more about it from his dispatch."

"His dispatch, like many things these days, is written on many levels." For just an instant, Forsythe showed every year of his advanced age. "It seems we're afraid to be totally open even in secure communications."

"It's because no one wants to face it, Stepan," Enwright said. "But we have to. The Federation is on the verge of civil war."

It was the first time someone had come right out and said it in Han's presence—trust Willis to be the first. She watched Forsythe, but the old admiral had his expression well in hand.

"On the verge is not the same thing as actively at war, Willis," he said quietly. "It's our job to see it doesn't go that far."

"Agreed," Enwright nodded. "But what if it's a job we can't do, sir?"

"There is no job the Fleet can't do!"

"Sir, Fringers aren't Arachnids or Rigelians—or even Tangri or Orions. Dealing with aliens may come down to a matter of firepower more often than we like, but it doesn't bother the Fleet much. That's our job, after all. But firing on our own people?" Enwright shook his head sadly. "With all due respect, I'm not sure the crews could do it."

"It won't come to that," Forsythe said. "We'll make transit out immediately for routine maneuvers in Kontravian space. Not even the Beauforters are crazy enough to start something with a task force this size overhead."

"Probably not," Enwright said softly. "But what if it's already started, sir? I've served with Lad Skjorning. He's no hothead, but once he makes up his mind, not God nor the devil can change it."

"Skjorning is only one man, Willis."

"But if they send him home, he'll be the most important 'one man' in the entire Kontravian Cluster, sir. He's inherited all of Fionna MacTaggart's prestige, as well as his own, which was already pretty considerable."

"Admiral," Han said diffidently, "Captain Enwright has a point. I don't know if you realize just how critical Skjorning has become. If the Assembly expels him, hundreds of Fringer delegates will resign in protest."

"Then they're fools!" Forsythe snorted. "They should stay and fight!"

"That's easy for us to say, sir," Enwright pointed out gently. "We've been safely isolated here in the Fleet. We're more like one of the old monastic fighting orders than a representative segment of our society, and we certainly haven't personally faced the Corporate World political machine. Its manipulation of the Assembly has become so blatant no Fringer delegate had any doubts left even before MacTaggart was murdered. Now the writing's on the wall, as far as they're concerned. They're tired of fighting within a system that won't let them win, sir."

"But if they persist in this madness they'll force an open break! They're playing right into the hands of this sort of manipulation." Forsythe tapped the binder. "Don't they *see* that?"

"With respect, Admiral," Han said, "they're too angry to care."

"And do you share their anger, Captain Li?" Forsythe asked softly.

"Yes, sir, I do." It was the first time a superior had asked her that, and Han found it almost a relief to answer openly.

"Stepan," Enwright's quiet voice drew the admiral's eyes away from her, "most of the Outworlders in the Fleet share Captain Li's feelings. You're not a Fringer, so maybe you don't see it that way, but the Fringers *do.* That's why I'm so concerned about this 'show of force' business. If it comes to a real confrontation, there's no telling how the Fleet will react. More than sixty percent of our personnel *are* Fringers, Stepan."

"They are also sworn members of the Federation's armed forces," Forsythe said levelly. "If the time comes, they'll remember that." He waved a hand briskly, as if to dispel the tension which had sprung up. "But we're going to the Kontravian Cluster to make certain it never comes to that."

"Yes, sir," Enwright said, leaning forward in his chair, "and with the admiral's permission, I'd like to make a suggestion."

"Of course." Forsythe watched Enwright thoughtfully.

"You're absolutely right on at least one point, sir; the best way to make sure nothing happens is to create a Fleet presence in Kontravian space before any explosion. I suggest that we detach Admiral Ashigara's carrier group and the battlecruisers and send them on ahead. They're fifty percent faster than the monitors. At flank speed, they could reach the Kontravian Cluster almost three months before the rest of the task force. That'd give us that much more time before the Kontravians can do anything rash."

Forsythe swivelled his chair slowly back and forth, considering, and Han watched him closely. Willis was right. The sooner they got warships into the cluster, the better. Even the most fervent Fringe sympathizer in the Fleet would be willing to nip trouble in the bud *before* it reached shooting proportions.

"No, Willis," Forsythe said finally. Enwright looked prepared to argue, but Forsythe waved a hand gently. "I'm glad you're thinking in terms of prevention, but if we send a detachment ahead the whole idea of a routine visit goes out the airlock. And I think you overestimate the depth of feeling in the Cluster. I don't question your reading of the Fringe leadership, but there's a deep reservoir of loyalty to Old Terra among the population. We'll get there before their leaders push them into anything truly rash."

"Stepan," Enwright said, "please don't equate loyalty to the motherworld with loyalty to the Assembly! Fringers see them as two separate entities."

"Perhaps," Forsythe said testily, "but there's enough overlap to offset any rashness, I think. And the last thing we can afford is to look as if we *expect* a break. No, Willis. We'll do it my way."

Han held her breath and wondered if Enwright would push it. She glanced at the captain, reading the worry in his face, but he held his tongue.

"That's settled, then," Forsythe said with the same finality. He glanced at his desk chronometer. "I see it's just about time for dinner, Captain Li. Will you dine with us?"

"I'd be honored, Admiral," she said, accepting the change of subject, and rose to follow her superiors from the cabin, glancing back at the sealed security binder on the desk as they left.

A cold breeze blew through her bones as she passed the Marine guard and the cabin hatch closed behind them. Admiral Forsythe was a good man, a loyal man—one who cared about *all* the Federation's citizens. Yet she had a premonition that a terrible mistake had just been made.

# HOMECOMING

The wrenching stress of warp transit echoed in every inner ear aboard the starship *Capricorn*, though liners never transited warp points at the same speed as warships lest their delicate (and paying) passengers lose their breakfasts. The moment of indescribable tension passed into memory as *Capricorn*'s momentarily addled electronic systems recovered, and her deck plates trembled gently as her powerful drive sang back up to maximum, for *Capricorn* was a fast ship, with a reputation to maintain.

Ladislaus Skjorning stepped out of his cabin into the carpeted passages of first class. After months of travel, he no longer bothered to glance over his shoulder at the calm, expressionless face of the Assembly lictor gliding a pace behind him. In all the long, dreary days of shipboard existence, Ladislaus had not even learned the man's name, not that it mattered. One lictor was very like another, he'd found; none permitted mere humanity to hamper the discharge of his duty.

He frowned at his own derisive thought, for he knew it was unfair. From the Lictor General down to the rawest first-year recruit, the lictors had no planetary loyalties and ground no partisan axes. They were servants of the Assembly, with Federation-wide citizenship so no single world could challenge their devotion to it. But fair or not, Ladislaus could see his anonymous shadow only as an extension of the Assembly.

A familiar throb of rage touched him as he recalled the farce the Assembly had called an "impeachment." He'd never attempted to deny his guilt; indeed, Wu Liang, Hangchow's chief delegate and Ladislaus' advocate, had based his entire defense on the Ortler Decision, claiming the same immunity for his client, and

684

so underlined the defiant Fringe insistence that his act had been neither more nor less than an execution and thrown the Corporate Worlds' hypocrisy back into their teeth.

Ladislaus had known how thin a thread his life hung upon, but hatred had supported him, feeding on the vituperation the Corporate Worlds heaped upon him and stoked by his cold appreciation of the skill with which the Taliaferro Machine used the Fringe's own fury to destroy it. The decision to expel him like a pariah—to send him back to the Fringe as if that were the one proper dumping ground for "barbarians"—had cut like the flick of a whip, and it had driven the Fringe berserk. Delegate after delegate had risen to denounce the Corporate Worlds, and the Heart Worlds had heard only their incoherent fury. They had not chosen to recognize the manipulation which spawned that rage, and Ladislaus had watched the Innerworld delegations recoil from the Fringers' passion, accepting the damning Corporate World caricature as truth.

He'd seen it sound the death knell of compromise, and he'd felt only a grim eagerness to go back out among the sane worlds of the distant stars and begin what must be begun.

Yet he'd also felt a sort of admiration for the handful of moderates who had fought to stem the furious tide of history. It had been overshadowed by his own impatience, his own awareness that the dream they sought to preserve had already died, but it had been real. And he'd admired no one more than he had Oskar Dieter.

How many other delegates had felt his own astonishment when the slim New Zuricher begged for moderation and reason? When he, as head of Fouchet's own delegation, moved to drop all charges against Fouchet's killer? When he met Simon Taliaferro headlong in the furious debate, fighting with every ounce of parliamentary skill to save both Ladislaus and the Assembly? It had been a doomed battle, but he'd refused to surrender and a few—a tattered remnant—of the erstwhile moderates had rallied to his banner, as if they, like Ladislaus, recognized the true stakes. . . .

He shook free of the past and made his way into the lonely first-class lounge. He was *Capricorn*'s last first-class passenger, for Beaufort was the end of her run—the last, ultimate end point of the Federation, in a sense. Many worlds lay still further out, but Beaufort was the end of the warp lines into the Kontravian Cluster, a lonely world, ignored by the magnates who moved and shook the Federation until the doomwhale had suddenly beckoned profit.

Ladislaus parked himself in a lounger under one of the magnifying screens as the ship swept towards the planet of his birth. Already he could make out the orbit port, tiny with distance as it waited with shuttles and cargo. Ships like *Capricorn* were creatures of the void, fated never to taste atmosphere, and before the days of doomwhaling there had been no orbit port at Beaufort. Only the tramp freighters, adapted for atmospheric travel, had come here then, gleaning a fragile profit in waters too shallow to attract the huge combines like the Taliaferro Line or even the chartered mail packets of the Mobius Corporation.

Beyond the orbit port loomed the vast, purple bulk of Beaufort, and he stared at it with hungry eyes. He could almost taste the iodine-rich wind, almost feel the heavy pull of gravity. Huge clouds covered half the visible planet, and he smiled. There was heavy weather in the Hellbore, and heavy weather on Beaufort was like heavy weather nowhere else in the Galaxy. Most of the planetary surface was water, the deep, purple, surging water of home. Except for the small southern continent of Grendelsbane, the limited habitable land masses were found only in the loose necklaces of islands threaded around the watery sphere. Some of the islands were huge, by Terran standards, but they were still islands, the peaks and plateaus of sunken mountains rearing sheer and indomitable from the cold, cold seas. Man had shaped those islands into homes for himself and his children, but Beaufort had shaped Man, too. The granite of its stony archipelagoes was in the Beaufort soul, and Ladislaus longed to touch the surface of his world, longed to draw the strength of that bedrock presence within himself once more.

Yet first he must face his failure. He'd gone to Old Terra as Chief of Security; he returned a broken man, derelict in his duty and expelled from the Assembly. And if the people of Beaufort were compassionate and understanding in ways which far outreached the Innerworlders on their safe, tamed planets, Beauforters also did their jobs. On a world where gravity, pressure, and the sea all conspired against the human intruder, there was only one fully acceptable excuse, and that was death. Ladislaus understood that side of his people, for it made them what they were even as it had made him what he was, and he dreaded their silent disapproval almost as much as he dreaded his own sense of failure.

He sat motionless for long hours as the orbit port grew and

grew. They passed the bulk of Beaufort Skywatch, spartan and pure in the black and white blazonry of Fortress Command, and he watched a light cruiser slide past *Capricorn*, her white hull and blue Frontier Fleet markings gleaming under the distant light of Beaufort's sun. The stylized galactic lens of her service glistened like silver on her forward hull as she altered course and slashed away with all the arrogance of her greyhound breed, and Ladislaus wondered what so heavy a Fleet unit was doing here.

Beaufort's massive moon cleared the edge of the planet, looming huge and lovely in the sun's reflected light, for Beaufort's Bowditch was bigger than Old Terra's neighbor Mars, with a .5 G gravity and nearly enough atmosphere to support life. It was one of the universe's more bitter jokes that Beaufort—a planet almost too massive for Man—should possess a moon not quite massive enough for him. Ladislaus could still recall his initial shock upon seeing Old Terra's Luna and realizing what a miserable lump of rock had given birth to the white moon on the Federation's banners. And as for the ridiculous little ripples Old Terra called "tides"—!

Then *Capricorn*'s drive died at last. The tractors of the orbit port reached out, and the liner shivered as they snubbed away her last motion and rolled her, aligning her with the huge, flexible docking tubes. Within minutes, she would be secured, her cargo and personnel ports open, and Ladislaus rose slowly. He turned and left the lounge, with the lictor like an expressionless ghost behind him.

The shuttle dropped away from Beaufort Orbit Port like a seashrike striking at nearcod, and Ladislaus sat silently, watching out a port. The shuttle's wings configured back, their leading edges glowing as the pilot skimmed atmosphere to dump orbital velocity. He watched them extend slowly as the shuttle's speed dropped, the orange glow fading as the heat bled away into Beaufort's cold air, and their speed dropped still further, until the engines took over, pushing them the last few hundred kilometers to the Beowulf Archipelago . . . and home.

The sprawling island of Kraki came into sight, the modest spaceport dead center in its star-shaped mass. It was a small port, by Innerworld standards, and few attempts had been made to gloss over the gaunt functionalism of early days. Beaufort wanted its spaceport grim and cold.

The shuttle touched down, and Ladislaus felt an icy pang of

dread as he looked out at the unexpected throng awaiting him. They ringed the shuttle pad, coats and clothing whipped by the bitter wind of Beaufort's spring, hair flying in the near gale. The shuttle rocked uneasily until the grapples engaged, holding her against the wind, and only then did Ladislaus rise and walk towards the opening hatch. Cold air invaded the shuttle, and he shrugged into his seawool coat as the familiar wind whined beyond the hull.

The lictor followed, and Ladislaus eyed him curiously. He'd been guard and protector in one, his simple presence extending the protection of the Assembly over Ladislaus to shield him from arrest and extradition, but his had been a silent presence. No word of welcome, no word of condemnation or approval, had ever passed his lips, and Ladislaus wondered if he meant to change that now that his duty was discharged. But he merely followed Ladislaus silently to the hatch and stopped. From the moment Ladislaus' foot touched Beaufort soil, he would need no protection, and the lictor watched calmly, silently, as Ladislaus stepped through the hatch without a backward glance.

The damp cold of Beaufort's dense atmosphere slapped his bearded cheeks, and the heavy hand of gravity dragged at his bones. He hadn't been home in five years, and almost he had forgotten how it felt to be his proper weight. He walked down the gangway, moving carefully until muscles and reflexes could adjust to the thirty percent jump over *Capricorn*'s artificial gravity, and the crowd pressed closer around the foot of the ramp. He saw his father and brother looming above the forest of heads like giants, and then his foot touched the soil of his homeworld, and for just an instant the shock of homecoming vibrated through him like an icicle of relief.

He turned towards his father and stopped. A slender woman stood before him, the colorful plaid of the Beaufort-circling Mac-Taggart Clan's chieftain blowing from her shoulders. Age had not dulled the flying red of Dame Penelope MacTaggart's hair, yet she looked frail and slight as the eternal Beaufort wind sang about her. She stood with all the dignity and strength of her authority, and Ladislaus stopped before her, feeling suddenly gross and huge as he confronted the calm, emerald eyes in which pride and composure glistened over a sea of sorrow.

"Dame Penelope," he said softly, his deep voice frayed by the wind.

"Lad," she said quietly.

"I—" He broke off and swallowed, feeling the familiar burning behind his eyes once more. "It's sorry I'm to be, Dame Penelope," he said humbly. "Warned I was, but too late. Gone she was, before I was knowing, but it's to be my fault. I owe a life."

His head bent and he felt the crowd stiffen as he spoke the formal acknowledgment of blood guilt. In a Beaufort court, such an admission was tantamount to accepting sentence of death. This was not a court of law, but Ladislaus had still given his life into Dame Penelope's hands, to do with as she willed. He sensed the shock of the crowd, yet even that admission was too little to express the depth of his guilt.

"Ladislaus Skjorning, I am hearing you," Dame Penelope's voice rang through the wind in formal response, and Ladislaus raised his eyes to her face, its graceful planes so like Fionna's. "But to be telling me this, Ladislaus Skjorning—was it not that both the killers died by her hand? And was it not that you it was caused her to be armed? Was it not that you had warned her? Was it not that you protected her for ten long years before they had the killing of her?"

Ladislaus' face was grim as her questions underscored his ultimate, unforgivable failure, but he nodded.

"Then, Ladislaus Skjorning, do not be telling me you owe a life!" Dame Penelope's voice cut the tension like a knife. "It's proud we're to be—proud of my daughter, who did not go alone to death, and of you, the man who made it so! There's to be no blood debt between you and the MacTaggarts, Ladislaus Skjorning, for it's one of our own you're to be, my son!"

Ladislaus' head came up, and tears tracked his bearded cheeks as Dame Penelope's strong arms reached around his waist and she laid her proud head on his massive chest, her last words burning in his heart like new hope. They were the formal words of adoption, and the foster tie she offered meant almost more than blood on cold, harsh Beaufort. His hands fluttered helplessly over her slight shoulders, feeling the strength of Beaufort in them, and he bent his head, his blond beard mingling with the windblown red of the MacTaggarts.

"It's a daughter you've lost, Mother Penny," he said softly, his great voice choked, "a debt no man can pay. But it's a mother you're to be to me, and I a son to—" His voice broke before he could complete the formal phrase, and Dame Penelope drew his face down against her shoulder, tears cutting her own cheeks before the crowd of her neighbors.

"Ah, Lad, my Lad," she murmured in his ear, stroking his heaving shoulders, "it's always a son you've been to me—did you not know it?" And she led him to his father's side.

Seapine burned on the huge hearth. The dried, treelike kelp glowed with a clear, blue flame, and Ladislaus was grateful for the rolling heat, for his blood was thin by Beaufort standards, and he was still shaken by the emotional catharsis he'd endured. Firelight flickered across the metal and stonework with which the people of Beaufort brightened their homes, and the dancing light rippled like sun off water. His father sat across the hearth, his craggy face, sculpted by sea and wind into a cliff of character, gilded by the fire. Ladislaus' brother Stanislaus sat behind him, even taller and broader than he in his seawool tunic with the crossed-harpoons shoulder badge of the master doomwhaler, and Dame Penelope sat beside Sven Skjorning.

Ladislaus let his eyes rest on her and remembered his own mother, Ireena Skjorning, thirty years dead, and her unborn daughter with her. Even with the best of medical science—which Beauforters had not been offered before the doomwhale brought them wealth—Beaufort's high gravity and hostile environment exacted a high price of its women. Beaufort weeded its people mercilessly; only the strong survived its unyielding harshness.

"It's to be good to be having you home, Lad. I was feared they were to have your life, as well." Sven Skjorning's voice was even deeper than his son's, and bitter with hate. He'd given a son to the Federation already, dead in the destruction of his heavy cruiser.

"I had the same thinking for long," Ladislaus agreed soberly, "but it's too smart they're to be for that, Father, and they're to place their harpoons with care. They *let* me go, because it's to suit their purpose to paint us as barbarians and themselves as 'civilized' men!"

His face twisted, and he felt the same fury simmering in his audience.

"Sven," Dame Penelope said into the silence, "it's too long we've been waiting." Her voice was cold as the Beaufort sea. "Too many have had the giving of too much, and what's it to be bringing us? Shame and oppression, Sven Skjorning!"

Ladislaus nodded unconsciously, watching his father with burning eyes. Sven Skjorning stared into the heart of the fire, and his face was hard.

"Aye," he said slowly, "you've the right of it, Penny—as always.

Thirty years past I gave Ireena my word, but if she'd lived, it's to agree with you she'd be, I think."

Ladislaus straightened in his chair. His father stood high in Beaufort's sparse community, but for thirty-three years he'd honored his promise to his dying wife, throttling the hatred which had burned in his heart since the death of his eldest son. The heavy cruiser *Fearless* had died for one reason only: a Corporate World merchant prince had possessed the political power to demand her service as an escort for a "vital" cargo during the height of a Tangri raid.

"It's our children they're to be taking," he rumbled like slow-flowing magma. "Our wealth they cannot touch, our rights they've had the taking of long since—but no more of our children will they be having!" He looked up from the fire, and his eyes were as bright and blue as the flames. "A son from me, a daughter from you—enough! It's to be ending!"

His fist slammed the thick arm of his chair, and the expensive wood cracked under the blow.

"I've the same thinking, Father," Ladislaus said softly, "but it's to be careful we must. The Federation's arm is long, and it's the Corporate Worlds have the owning of that arm the now."

"And we're to do nothing?" Sven Skjorning demanded dangerously.

"No, Father. But it's to speak to others before the government I must. It's to be taking time, and when we strike, it's to be with care."

"You're to be talking treason," Stanislaus said softly.

"Aye," Ladislaus replied levelly, "and past time for it, too."

"No argument from me," Stanislaus said, "but to be thinking what it's to mean to Beaufort if you fail, Lad."

"I have," Ladislaus said bleakly. "Stanislaus, it's to be better to die than accept some things. There's no stomaching more—I'm not to be standing by any longer. Can you be seeing that?"

"Aye, Lad, of course," Stanislaus said simply, gripping his brother's shoulder, "but it's to be sure *you* do before you have the starting of a war upon your head. For you're to see it's *you* must have the doing of it here."

"I know," Ladislaus said softly. "God help me, I know."

The planetary government of Beaufort was not the sprawling bureaucracy that was the Federation, or, for that matter, any of the Innerworld governments. There were fewer than

six million people on the planet, and the Beaufort Assembly
reflected the sparseness of its population base. There were only
fifty-six members, all told, and for the most part they were
the elders of the great clans which had formed in the Years
of Abandonment. The social and survival requirements of an
environment humanity was never bred to face had created a
paternalistic order, a semifeudalism, that carried over into its
political processes, as well.

Yet Ladislaus had never felt more nervous in the Chamber of
Worlds. The conference room didn't even hold the full Assembly—
only its leaders sat around the rectangular table, their eyes calm
and dispassionate upon him.

Three weeks of cautious, private conversations had brought
him here. Despite his care not to involve the government in his
discussions, it seemed the government had decided to involve
itself. Now he gazed at the people in the room—President Bjorn
Thessen, President Pro Tem Knute Halversen, crucial committee
chairmen—and waited for the inquisition to begin.

"Ladislaus," President Thessen said finally, "you've been meeting
with influential people in the short time you've been home. We're
wondering why you haven't asked to meet with us."

Ladislaus tightened inwardly at Thessen's Standard English.
Since the days of the Abandonment, the dialect of Beaufort had
become a badge its people wore consciously. It was their declaration of defiance to the worlds which had ignored them in their
hour of need, and while almost any Beauforter could speak barely
accented Standard English, most would see themselves damned
and in Hell before they would . . . except in official settings, where
the planetary government's members felt they somehow stood in
the presence of their Old Terran ancestors. So if Thessen chose
to speak Standard English, it meant he spoke as President of the
Beaufort Assembly . . . an officer charged to preserve and maintain
the Federation.

"Forgive me, President Thessen," he said softly. "I wanted to
sample public opinion before I spoke to you officially."

"And why was that?" Thessen wondered slowly. "Could you be
thinking of seizing power from us, Ladislaus?"

"No!" Genuine horror sharpened his voice. "It was only—"

"Enough," Thessen said with a headshake. "Excuse our doubts,
but we're a suspicious lot these days. Blame it on the times. At
any rate," he added with a wintry smile, "we chose you for the
Assembly because you've a quick mind and strong will, like your

father. We can't very well complain because you act accordingly. But now that you're here . . .'

Thessen straightened, an age-spotted hand touching a document before him.

"You probably won't be surprised by this, Lad." He handed the single sheet over, and Ladislaus ran his eyes down it, then raised them to Thessen's face with renewed respect. As delegation security chief, he'd thought he knew all their avenues of information, but their intelligence network obviously reached further than he'd believed possible. What he held was a memo signed by Simon Taliaferro himself.

"It's no surprise, no," he said quietly.

"We've read your reports—and Fionna's. Is this memo accurate? Will the Amalgamation pass, do you think?"

"Like a doomwhale through nearcod," Ladislaus said flatly.

"Aye, I had the fearing of that." Thessen's Standard English lapsed briefly, then he shook himself.

"You should know, young Lad, that *Capricorn* brought a writ of extradition from Old Terra. I sent it back marked 'opened by mistake'—" a mutter of harsh laughter filled the room "—but you're right; Fionna's murder is but the beginning. I've viewed the chips of that 'impeachment.'" The old man's face wrinkled with disgust. "It's clear there's no reasoning with them. Except, perhaps, this man Dieter, of all people. How say you, Lad?"

"Dieter?" Ladislaus frowned. "I'm thinking he's a good enough man . . . but he's only one man. Aye, he insulted Fionna, but he was drugging, and . . . in a way, that may have been the making of him. But whether he's to be surviving . . ."

He broke off with a shrug.

"So no matter what he feels, there's little he can do, eh?"

"Aye. It's Taliaferro has them in his grip the now, and it's a mad seashrike with a mouthful of blood that man's to be. There's to be no stopping him!"

Ladislaus jerked himself to a stop, a little abashed by his own vehemence.

"Then, young Ladislaus," Thessen asked slowly, "what's to be done? Fionna spent twenty-five years seeking our rights. Was it all for naught?"

"Not for lack of trying," Ladislaus said grimly. "No one ever fought harder than Fionna. You know—you *all* know—she wanted no more than justice, no more than a transition. If even *one* Corporate World had reached out a hand to her—!"

"But fail we have?" Thessen pressed quietly.

"Aye, Mister President," Ladislaus said heavily. "We have."

"And it's that message you've been sharing with others, is it?" Thessen's old eyes were keen.

"Aye." Ladislaus looked up almost defiantly. "It's not to make any difference what wording I share, Mister President. You're to know that. And even if you're not to—" he drew a deep breath and committed himself "—it's to tell them I must."

"I see." Thessen's voice was very level. He glanced at his colleagues, and Ladislaus felt the tension. What he'd said was treason.

"Young Lad," Thessen said finally, "it's not quite fair we've been with you. This group—" he gestured around the table "—is more than just the leadership of the government. This—" he tapped the memo "—is no more than a part of what we've done. Are you, then, prepared to tell us the Federation is doomed? Is it to defy all of us you are? Knowing we're to have information even you're not to know?"

"Aye, Mister President. If so I must, then it's to defy you I will be doing! Fionna had the giving of her life for her dream, but her dream had no life of its own. I'm not to be seeing more! It's to be enough of our blood they've had the taking of! It's to be war they're waging, a war of 'laws' and 'writs' and 'reapportionments.' Well, to *give* them their war!" He was on his feet, blue eyes flashing, and his voice was rolling thunder in the chamber. "To give them a *bellyful* of war—and not with words!"

He choked himself off abruptly. Whatever he felt, whatever he thought, these were the leaders of his people. It was not proper to raise his voice to them, and his temerity shamed him. Yet he was resentful, too; resentful of their slowness, resentful that age and high position blinded them to what he saw so clearly.

He sank back into his chair, watching Thessen glance once more around the gathered faces. Here and there a head nodded slowly, wordlessly, and Ladislaus felt his heart sink at the slow confirmations.

"Ladislaus Skjorning," Thessen's voice was deeper and more powerful, his old face flushed, "it's to be too long you've had the living amongst Innerworlders!" The Beaufort dialect penetrated, and Ladislaus raised his head. He stared at Thessen's bearded face, and the old man smiled slowly. "Did you have the thinking it's to be only you to know these things, Lad?" The president shook his head. "We've had the thinking of such thoughts for long now, and we've had the preparing for it, as well. You're to make no rebellion against *us*, Lad Skjorning, for we're to be before you. Aye, young Lad—if it's to make war they are, then it's to make war *we* are, as well!"

Ladislaus gaped at the old man, and the pieces suddenly fell together. The copy of the memo, the channels of information, the persistent questioning—he'd come into this chamber convinced he alone saw what must be done, only to find they'd already seen it!

"We've had the making of our plans for long," Thessen said slowly, "yet we're to be old, Ladislaus. We're to be worn and tired—we're not to have the strength and youth for this. But it's to see *you* do. So to tell us, young Lad—will it be you who has the leading of us?"

"Aye," Ladislaus said softly. There was no hesitation in him, only the grim, cold certainty that it was for this moment he had been born and trained, and he looked around the circle of old faces, seeing the same bitter determination in the wise eyes and lined faces looking back at him. He nodded his head slowly, and when he spoke again, it was to swear an oath.

"Aye," he repeated. "It will be that!"

# SECESSION

Fleet Admiral Stepan Forsythe looked up from his paperwork as his communicator lit with the face of his staff communications officer.

"Yes, Mister Qwan?"

"Sir," Lieutenant Doris Qwan said carefully "we're picking up something from a Mobius Corp mail packet. A transmission, not a courier drone."

Forsythe cocked an eyebrow. A transmission meant they were in the same system as the packet, but why transmit at all? This system was uninhabited and far outside the Innerworld relay nets; logically there was no one to hear the message, except for the unmanned recorders in the warp point nav beacons.

"What sort of message, Lieutenant?"

"I . . . don't really know, sir. May I play it off for you?"

Forsythe nodded, and his screen flickered abruptly, then steadied with the image of a lean, uniformed man. The twisted-loop collar insignia of his firm was overlaid by the crossed starships of a Federation mail carrier's captain, and his dark, strong face was tense, almost frightened.

"This is Captain Donald Stiegman, Federation mail packet *Rising Moon*, TFMP-11329. The following information *must* reach government authorities as quickly as possible. Stand by to receive coded

696

data; this is a Class One Priority signal." Forsythe stiffened. Class One Priority was assigned only to threats to the very existence of the Federation, and his finger stabbed the emergency buzzer on his desk as the screen dissolved into a blur of static. The image danced insanely for perhaps ten seconds, then cleared, replaced by Captain Stiegman's worried face. "Reverse course immediately. Do not enter the Kontravian Cluster. Get that message out. Stiegman, message ends."

Forsythe's cabin door opened as Captain Enwright and Commodore Samsonov hurried in past an astonished Marine sentry. They slid to a halt, faces anxious, but Forsythe motioned them to silence. He watched the screen blank briefly before the message repeated itself, then gestured both men to chairs and punched the override to recall Lieutenant Qwan.

"It's a loop, right, Lieutenant?"

"Yes, sir, with an 'all ships' header. We've been in-system over an hour without hearing a thing, so I think we caught his first transmission. I'd guess he came through from Bantu and started transmitting the moment he hit normal space."

"I see. Anything on that coded sequence?"

"No, sir. I'm afraid the computers haven't broken the scramble yet, much less the code. I think he's using mail service protocols, sir."

"Very well. Keep on it and do what you can." Forsythe felt little hope. Mail service codes were at least as good as the Fleet's codes.

"Yes, sir. Any response?"

"Not yet. I'll get back to you."

Forsythe turned to his juniors. Enwright's expression was thoughtful and waiting; only someone who knew him well would recognize the questions burning in his hazel eyes, but the curiosity in Gregor Samsonov's wrinkled forehead and hooded brown eyes was more evident. Forsythe smiled a wintry smile as he nodded to his flag captain and his chief of staff.

"Gentlemen, it seems we have a mystery."

"Mystery, sir?" Trust Willis to ask the first question.

"You know as much as I do, Willis. You heard the message. Reactions?"

Enwright sat very erect. "A few points seem obvious, sir."

"Indeed?" Forsythe cocked his head. "Enumerate, please."

"Yes, sir. First, he doesn't have any drones or he'd've sent the message direct to a Fleet base. Secondly, whatever the message is, it's both urgent and hot. If it wasn't urgent, he wouldn't be transmitting; if it wasn't hot, he'd transmit in clear. Third, he's worried about pursuit. He's not in range of our scanners, so we sure as hell aren't in range of his. That means he's transmitting blind and hoping someone hears. Couple that with his injunction to clear out fast—" He shrugged. "He must be afraid there're bandits on his tail, and he's warning any unarmed civil ship to stay clear of them.

"And those three points, sir," he finished levelly, "lead to a fourth: he's absolutely right to declare a Priority One emergency."

Forsythe drummed gently on his desk. It was a mark of Enwright's true stature, he thought, that there wasn't even a trace of 'I told you so' in his voice. He glanced at his chief of staff.

"Gregor?"

"I'm afraid I have to agree, sir," Samsonov said unhappily.

Forsythe sighed heavily, feeling the full weight of his years, then nodded and managed a bleak smile.

"Well, I'm afraid I agree, too. It seems you gentlemen were right to urge me to split the task force."

It was a bitter admission, but he made it calmly, then turned to his communicator and punched up the flag deck. The screen lit with Lieutenant Qwan's face, and he could just see his operations officer behind her. He smiled to himself. Commander Rivera must have heard about his summons to Samsonov and Enwright.

"Lieutenant. Commander." His voice was as gravely courteous as ever. "Task Force orders, Commander. We will increase to flank and close the Bantu warp point. Detach the battlecruisers and Admiral Ashigara's carriers—send them ahead of the battle line."

"Yes, sir," Rivera said crisply.

"Lieutenant Qwan, inform Admiral Ashigara of the situation and see to it she gets a copy of *Rising Moon*'s message. Then I want a message transmitted to *Rising Moon* immediately. Message begins: Fleet Admiral Forsythe, CO TF 17, to Captain Donald Stiegman, master, TFMP *Rising Moon*. Message received—give him the time, Doris. My force headed to meet you at max. Estimate rendezvous with my advanced screen in—" he raised an eyebrow at Enwright.

"Call it nineteen hours, sir."

"In approximately nineteen standard hours, Lieutenant," Forsythe continued to Qwan. "Courier drone with your transmission dispatched. Good luck. Message ends. Got it?"

"Yes, sir. It's on the tape."

"Good. Send it standard civil service code, no scramble."

"Yes, sir."

"Thank you, Doris." Forsythe switched off the communicator and turned back to Enwright and Samsonov. "And now, gentlemen, let us give some thought to our circumstances." He smiled his bleak smile again. "Somehow I feel certain even my delicate touch will not suffice to make them any worse."

Vice Admiral Analiese Ashigara, slim and severe in her black and silver uniform, sat on the flag bridge of TFNS *Basilisk* and watched the bright dot of the mail packet on her display. She glanced at a com rating.

"Anything from the patrols, Ashworth?"

"No, sir. They're a hundred and fifty light-seconds out, and they report nothing detectable in scanner range."

"Thank you." She glanced at her operations officer. If the recon fighters' exquisitely sensitive instruments weren't picking up anything, then there was nothing to pick up. "Recall them, Commander Dancing."

"Aye, aye, sir."

"Communications, raise *Rising Moon*."

"Aye, aye, sir."

There was silence on the bridge—the silence of a professional team aware of the dangers of unnecessary chatter—as Admiral Ashigara leaned back in her command chair and waited. Suddenly the main screen filled with the image of a dark, lean face wreathed in a huge smile of relief.

"Captain Stiegman, I am Vice Admiral Analiese Ashigara. I assume you have a reason for declaring a Priority One message condition?"

"I wish to hell I didn't," Stiegman said in a rich New Antwerp accent. "All hell's broken loose out here, ma'am, and no mistake. If you don't mind my asking, where's Admiral Forsythe?"

"He is following with the battle-line, Captain." Ashigara said. "I expect him in approximately six hours."

"*Battle-line?!* Thank God!" Stiegman seemed to sag towards the pickup. "You don't know what's going on out here, Admiral! They're crazy! They—"

"Captain Stiegman," Ashigara cut him off, "I appreciate the strain you're obviously under. I would request, however, that you say nothing more over an open channel. I will, with your permission, send my cutter for you so that you can deliver your message to me in person. And confidentially."

"Yes." Stiegman inhaled deeply. "Certainly, Admiral. Send your cutter at once. The sooner I can tell someone else, the better, by God!"

"Well, Captain Stiegman," Admiral Forsythe said as he handed the man a drink. "I have the essentials of your story from Admiral Ashigara." He sounded too calm, he thought. The Galaxy was collapsing around his ears, and he sounded too calm about it all. "I don't yet have all the details, however, and I'd appreciate it if you'd summarize for my staff, as well."

"Summarize, Admiral?" Stiegman drained half the glass in a single gulp. "Gladly. In fact, I'll be delighted to let someone else worry about it for a while."

His slowly easing tension wasn't lost on his listeners, and they hunched closer to him as he began.

"It started about a month ago," he said slowly. "I put into Bigelow with a mail consignment—they break it down on Hasdruble for transshipment to the rest of the cluster—and they told me my departure clearance and return cargo would be delayed a day or two." He shrugged. "Two days is a long layover, but I've had longer, so I didn't think much about it.

"But a few hours later, the port master called me up again—something about a viral infection and they couldn't find one of the people who'd been exposed. He agreed the odds were against their plague carrier being on board, but SOP required a search of the ship. Well, I wasn't too pleased, but nobody wants to chance another plague outbreak, so I agreed."

He paused and stared down into his drink. When he looked back up, his eyes were hot.

"But it wasn't any damned medical inspection party they sent aboard my ship," he grated. "It was an entire platoon of Marines—or they wore Marine combat zoots, anyway." He relaxed his muscles with a visible effort. "But they were already aboard before I realized they weren't medics, and no one in his right mind argues with a platoon of zoots, whoever's inside 'em."

He shook his head slowly, remembering.

"They were polite as hell—I'll give the bastards that! But they posted two men in each drive room and two more on the bridge, and they told me—*me*, the skipper of a Federation mail packet, damn 'em!—that they had to 'detain' me." His lips twisted.

"Wouldn't say why or for how long. Wouldn't say *anything* else. Just stood there and waited for their reliefs."

He growled something under his breath and finished his drink. Forsythe personally refilled the glass, to his obvious relief, and he sipped again, more slowly.

"Anyway, they had us. I tried getting a message out when I saw a Frontier Fleet cruiser on my screens, but they were on top of me in seconds. No nastiness, you understand—just another guard suddenly appeared in the com section and they stripped off our drones in case I got any smart ideas about using *them*.

"At first, I thought it was some kind of mistake, but then I figured out the whole orbit port was in on it—whatever 'it' was. And at least some of those 'Marines' really *were* Marines. I'm sure of it. I considered piracy, a real medical emergency—hell, even a port-wide outbreak of mass insanity! But I never once considered what was really happening."

"And that was, Captain?" Willis Enwright prompted when Stiegman paused once more.

"Treason, Captain," the mail packet captain said harshly. "God-damned, old-fashioned, dyed-in-the-fucking-wool treason! The whole damned system's decided to 'secede' from the Federation!"

The blood drained from Lieutenant Qwan's face. Enwright's features only tightened slowly, but Samsonov looked as if he'd been punched in the stomach and Rivera looked murderous. Only Forsythe seemed unaffected—but, then, only he had seen Admiral Ashigara's scrambled transmission.

"I see, Captain Stiegman," he said quietly. "And their objective, obviously, was to keep *Rising Moon* from letting the cat out of the bag?"

"Exactly. Took us a while to put it together, Admiral, but there had to be some contact between my tech crews and the port service personnel.

"Near as we can figure it, it all began a month or so after Ladislaus Skjorning got home. Nobody's sure whether it was his idea or whether it was his whole damned planet's notion, but Beaufort's where it started, and whoever planned it must've had one hell of an organization! Given the way the warp lines run, Beaufort's at the bottom of a sack; all the rest of the cluster sort of drains down to 'em. They knew what that meant, too, because they didn't start *on* Beaufort; they started *from* Beaufort."

" 'From Beaufort'?" Enwright repeated.

"They sent out 'emissaries,' Captain. God only knows what kind of underground's been cooking away out here, but they sure as hell knew who to talk to where, and they sent out people like Stanislaus Skjorning and Dame MacTaggart. Hell, no wonder people listened! I'm a Fringer myself; I know how hot tempers are running out here since the MacTaggart murder. But goddamn it to hell, there's no excuse for a full-scale civil war!"

"A war, Captain?" Rivera did not—quite—sniff. "What do they plan to use for a navy?"

"Damned if I know," Stiegman said frankly, "but it's going to take a fleet—and I mean a *fleet*—to change their minds."

"How so, Captain?" Samsonov asked.

"Because they're not stupid, however crazy they are. They stage-managed it perfectly. Just one day everything is peaceful and fine; the next, Killiman Skywatch is in mutinous hands."

"*Killiman Skywatch?*" Rivera half-rose. "Good God, man, do you know what you're *saying*?"

"Damn right I do." Stiegman seemed almost gloomily satisfied by Rivera's reaction. "I don't know how they did it, but I know they had Killiman, and I'm pretty sure they had Beaufort. Don't know about Bigelow—they were playing it mighty close to their chests in Bigelow, which could mean they didn't have Bigelow Skywatch—but Bigelow's the only way into the cluster, so it could just mean they were being careful in case of visitors."

"Even if they have Skywatch," Samsonov said, thinking out loud, "there's still the Frontier Fleet orbital base. No armament to speak of, but there's a Bigelow-based cruiser squadron. They might not want—"

"Exactly, Gregor," Forsythe cut in, and Samsonov broke off as he remembered a civilian was present. "Captain Stiegman," the admiral went on, "did you at any time monitor . . . unusual, shall we say, com traffic between the orbit port and Skywatch or the Fleet base?"

"Never," Stiegman said flatly, "and we kept a good listening watch."

"I see. And how did you finally come to escape, Captain?"

"We were lucky—or maybe they got careless. My engineer contacted a buddy in the orbit port and suggested most of the Fringers in our crew were on their side and ready to mutiny against me with a little help from their 'Marines.' Stiegman shrugged. "They went for it. Guess I'm a better actor than I thought. At least, the 'fight' between me and a half dozen others and the 'rebels' in the crew seemed to convince 'em. Fair amount of shooting to tear up the bulkheads, chief engineer stopping me at gunpoint just before I wrecked the drive—that sort of thing. Nobody hurt, thank God!"

"Very neat," Forsythe congratulated him. "And after the 'mutiny'?"

"Locked me up in my own brig," Stiegman said cheerfully. "Well, not a 'brig,' really; mail ships don't run to those. But one of our secure cargo holds worked just fine, and then *Rising Moon* was a good rebel ship. Took 'em a few days to feel sure of it, then they pulled the Marines off. Needed 'em elsewhere, I gather."

"I see. And then?"

"We waited another few days, behaving like perfect little rebels till we were pretty sure they believed it. Then we powered the drive real slow—told 'em it was an equipment test—and ran for it."

"You ran for it," Samsonov repeated. "Why didn't you contact Bigelow Skywatch or the Fleet base?"

"Because if either of 'em *were* rebel controlled, stopping in com range'd be a real good way to get our ass shot off. Besides, there were Frontier Fleet units in-system. If they were loyal, well and good—but if they weren't? *Rising Moon*'s fast, but not that fast. If we were going to have light cruisers on our tail, I wanted all the start I could get!" Stiegman grinned wearily. "We made transit so fast nobody's eaten since, and our backup astrogation computer's *still* pitching fits!"

"I see. And then you headed for Innerworld space?"

"Not directly. Actually, I was headed for Heidi's World. Figured to check in with the Frontier Fleet base and come back loaded for bear. Never figured on meeting half the Navy this far out!"

"I understand, Captain." Forsythe forced the warmth of approval through the winter of failure in his voice. "But I'll take care of that with a courier drone. I'm afraid I'm going to have to commandeer your vessel."

"Why not?" Stiegman grinned wryly. "I'm getting used to it by now."

"Then I want you to head for the Fleet base at Cimmaron to carry my dispatches and your own account directly to Vice Admiral Pritzcowitski. He'll know what to do from there."

"Glad to." Stiegman finished his drink and set it aside, his face thoughtful. "And may I ask what *you* plan to do, Admiral?"

"You may," Forsythe said with a wry smile, "but I'm afraid I haven't really decided, yet."

"I see." Stiegman rose. "In that case, I'll get back to my ship, with your permission. But, Admiral—" he met Forsythe's eyes levelly "—I'd recommend some caution. You haven't talked to these people; I have. They're serious, mighty serious." He shrugged uncomfortably. "I haven't seen your intelligence reports, but this is my normal run. I've felt the tension growing out here for months, and I can tell you this—the Fringe is a nuke about to go off, Admiral."

"I know, Captain Stiegman. I know."

There was a brief silence after Stiegman's departure. Forsythe and his juniors stared down at the carpet, wrapped in thought. Finally the old man raised his head.

"Captain Stiegman," he said, "is a most resourceful man."

"Yes, and he's got guts," Enwright's voice was tighter than usual, "but I can't help thinking he was a little too lucky, sir."

"In what way, Willis?"

"He got away with it," Enwright said bluntly. "No one fired on him and no one chased him. If they had, they'd've caught him. A packet's fast, but so is a light cruiser—and a cruiser's armed."

"True. But if they haven't taken the Fleet base or Skywatch, the rebels couldn't have fired on him—assuming they had anything to fire with—without alerting those installations."

"No, sir. But why didn't either of those bases ask *Rising Moon* where she was going and why? Don't tell me she had departure clearance!"

"A point. You're suggesting, then, that the rebels control everything? The entire cluster, fortifications and all?"

"We can't know that, sir. I'd say they hold Bigelow, but the rest of the cluster?" Enwright shrugged. "Still, it seems probable. *Rising Moon* may have jumped the gun on them, but they let her go. And since Bigelow's only six transits from Heidi's World, that must mean they figure they're about ready anyway. Or close enough they didn't feel they had to blow away an unarmed mail packet just to keep us in the dark a little longer, at least."

"I see. But assuming you're correct, where do we go from here? Gregor?"

"I don't know, sir," Samsonov said frankly. "I'm no Fringer—I don't pretend to know how these people are thinking. But even if Willis is right, they couldn't have known TF Seventeen was coming. They must figure on at least another three months before anyone can turn up; and if they're expecting a relief from Heidi's World, they're only expecting Frontier Fleet units—not monitors and assault carriers."

"Gregor's probably right, sir," Enwright said, "but remember our discussion with Captain Li. Everything I said then still holds true."

"I know you think it does, Willis," Enwright said. "You may even be right. God knows I don't want to go down in history as the first Navy commander to fire on other Terrans! But I don't see that we have any choice. If Bigelow Skywatch *isn't* in rebel hands, it's going to need all the help it can get, and the same is true of the Fleet base, the repair yards in Killiman—the entire cluster, for that matter."

"Admiral, please," Enwright's voice was urgent, "send in a few destroyers first. Find out what's happening before we barge in in force. The cans will have the entire task force behind them—and they can say so. That should stop any itchy trigger fingers long enough for a parley."

"With respect, Admiral," Rivera said harshly, "I think that would be a mistake. If Bigelow Skywatch is still loyal, it could touch off the very incident Captain Enwright wants to avoid. Take the entire task force. *Show* them the odds, and they'll cave in."

"Don't delude yourself, Commander," Enwright said coldly. "If these people've gone this far, they're ready to go further. The actual presence of the task force won't achieve anything except to up the stakes for everyone!"

"Perhaps," Forsythe said softly, "but if the entire task force is there, we can be certain anything that happens is over quickly, Willis."

His heart ached at his flag captain's look of desolation.

"Face it, Willis," he said gently. "We can't afford delays. There's no way to keep this quiet—we can't even try to; we need to warn the other Fleet bases, warn the government, warn *everyone*—and the word is bound to leak. We need to be certain a *resolution* follows the news as quickly as possible, or other Fringe Worlds will be tempted to follow suit. You know that as well as I do."

Enwright looked away from the thin, troubled face with the wise old eyes. Yes, he thought, some of the other Outworlds will follow suit if the Kontravians aren't stopped. But this was the wrong way to do it. He knew it was the wrong way. Or did he? Was that the TFN officer in him, or was it the Fringer? His intellect, or the confusion of his loyalties? He looked back.

"Please, sir. Talk to them first."

"I'll talk to them, Willis." Steel showed through Forsythe's compassionate tone. "But from the flag bridge of this ship with the task force behind me." He rose, terminating the meeting. "Gentlemen, check your departments. I want a complete status report in one hour. We will then formulate our precise plans."

His staff saluted and left. Willis Enwright walked slowly to the hatch and paused, then turned back to his admiral, his face older than his years.

"Sir, what if they don't surrender? What will you do if they fight?"

"Do, Willis?" Forsythe felt the cold of interstellar space blow down his spine. "I'll honor my oath to defend and preserve the Constitution—any way I must."

"You'll open fire, then," Enwright said almost inaudibly.

"If I must," Forsythe said steadily. "I don't want to. I'll tell them I don't want to. But I have orders to execute and four centuries of history to defend. Unlike them, I have no room to make personal choices, do I?"

"I suppose not, sir," Enwright said quietly. "But consider this, I beg of you. What you see as a personal choice may not seem like one to others." He seemed to be trying to tell Forsythe something, but the old admiral was too worried and heartsick to hunt for the meaning.

"I understand that, but I don't have an option. No one can ask more of any man than that he do his duty as he sees it." He shook his head sadly. "No matter how painful it is."

"Yes, sir. I hope we *all* remember that," Enwright said quietly. Then he drew himself up and gave Forsythe the sharpest salute the admiral had ever seen from him. He stepped through the hatch, and it closed behind him.

# DUTY

"Captain Enwright and Admiral Forsythe are both *dead!*"

The gasping words came hoarse over the com channel, but the screens were blank with electronic hash. Commander Windrider didn't recognize the distorted, faceless voice. Who was it? Had they ever met?

"They're *all* dead on flag bridge!" the voice went on desperately. "There's fighting everywhere ... crew quarters ... officer country ... power rooms. ... We need *help*, for God's sake! We—"

The snarl of a laser pistol slashed across the words and the voice went silent. The blinking light codes on Windrider's fire control screens chilled his blood, and his hands clenched on the gunnery console of the monitor *Enwright* as the flagship fell away, the first mutiny in the Federation Navy's history raging on her command bridges and in her drive rooms.

Jason Bluefield Windrider couldn't believe it. No, he told himself grimly, he could believe it; he just didn't want to. Mutiny was an obscenity to a man like him, but he understood the mutineers. Not long ago, some of them would have been guests in his quarters, discussing the crisis, wondering where their true duty lay. It seemed they'd decided aboard *Anderson*.

He looked into the strained faces of his control team. They knew what was happening aboard the flagship—but what could they do about it? For that matter, what could *he* do? He and his ratings sat at the very core of a tremendous hull, 285,000 tonnes of alloy and armor wrapped around their fragile bodies and sensitive instruments. They were *Enwright*'s fighting brain, controlling the power to vaporize a planetoid or sterilize a world, and soon they might have to perform actions which would scar their souls. He didn't know what the men and women of his crew would decide. He was certain of only one thing; he himself was about to face a moment of truth he did not believe he could endure.

The communicators muttered, ghostly voices blurring in his battlephone implant as frantic commanders conferred, afraid to expose their inner convictions, yet compelled by duty and training to act decisively.

And that was their true curse, Windrider thought savagely. Navy training and their own inclinations forced them to *act*. They weren't *politicians* (the word was a vicious epithet in his thoughts) who could confer and debate and duck responsibility. When you put on Navy black and silver, you put your judgment on the spot. "An imperfect response *now* is a thousand times better than recognizing the perfect response too late." That was what the Academy taught—but there were *only* imperfect responses to this!

Windrider shook his head angrily. The universe was crumbling before his eyes and he was *philosophizing*? Yet what else could he do? He, too, had "reacted" long since, but his had been a hypothetical decision, one he'd hoped never to face. One he'd *believed* he would never face, because he had dared not believe anything else. But now its hungry breath was in his face, hot and stinking as a pseudopuma's.

It wasn't *fair*! Hadn't the bureaucrats *known*? Were they so blind to human needs and loyalties they hadn't even *considered* what might happen out here?

But of course they had. That was why the Marine contingents aboard the transports consisted almost entirely of Innerworlders.

Yet the politicos had miscalculated, he thought grimly. They'd guessed at the hatred they were about to unleash, but not how quickly the flames would erupt. Their planned show of force was supposed to nip rebellion in the bud, on the ground. They'd never dreamed the Kontravians might seize their local orbital defenses and Frontier Fleet squadrons or have the guts to defy TF 17's might after they did. Besides, the Navy's monumental dependability was the bedrock of the Federation; it had never occurred to them that the Fringers in the Fleet might be as conscious of planetary loyalties as any Corporate Worlder. So they hadn't "sanitized" the Fleet as they had the ground forces. Perhaps they couldn't have, really, given the high proportion of Outworlders in the Fleet. Only a few ships had "reliable" Innerworld crews. Most had heavy Fringe contingents; some were completely Fringer-crewed. Now their officers were caught between their oaths and the dreadful prospect of turning their weapons on fellow Fringers, and it was intolerable. Faced with the unfaceable, Enwright had acted, Forsythe had reacted, and laser fire had gutted *Anderson*'s flag deck. But they were only the first casualties; Windrider could already taste the blood to come, and it sickened him.

"Captain! Admiral Singh is coming up on the all-ships channel!"

"Throw it on the big screen, Mister Sung."

Li Han held her face calm and her voice level as she waited for the screen to light, but she felt her bridge crew's tension. Even her imperturbable executive officer showed the signs; Tsing Chang's breathing was harshly audible.

Thomas Singh had always struck Han as belonging to an earlier age. The neatly trimmed beard in fashion among the Fleet's male officers somehow contrived to look fierce and predatory on Singh, and never more so than now. His dark eyes flashed, and the lips under his hooked nose were tight. When he spoke, his voice was harsh and cold.

"Ladies and gentlemen, I will be brief. Captain Willis Enwright and others aboard the flagship have mutinied against the lawful orders of their superior officers and against their oaths as officers and enlisted personnel of the Federation Navy. I will not permit this to spread! I believe Admiral Forsythe to be dead, and I hereby assume command. All Marine detachments will report to the armories and draw full combat equipment." Han tensed, and a soft sigh ran around her bridge. "Marines from the transport group will board *Anderson*. Any individual participating in this disgraceful violation of the Fleet's trust will be arrested to await tr—"

"No!"

Despite her iron control, Han jerked as the single word cut across Singh's cold voice. She thought it had come from one of her own people . . . until Singh whipped around to stare behind him. Then he was flinging himself aside, dropping towards the deck, and a laser bolt slashed across the pickup. His command console flared—plastics burning, metals melting—and the snarl of lasers continued for a fractional second before someone's fire incinerated the entire command station.

Han's eyes jerked to her tactical display, and her heart froze as data codes began to blink and change. Mutiny flashed through

the task force like a nuclear blast as Fringer after Fringer realized what loosing Corporate World Marines on their fellow
Outworlders meant.

The sleek carrier group flagship *Basilisk* slid to one side, drive
faltering as she convulsed internally. Her flight group was entirely
Fringer, and now the pilots joined the Outworlders of the ship's
company against their fellow crewmen. Ever since the Theban War
officers and senior ratings went to action stations with side arms;
now those weapons created holocaust within her compartments
and passages . . . and she was but one ship among many.

"Captain?" Tsing's normally passionless voice questioned, and
Han felt his eyes, felt the burning questions in the minds of her
bridge personnel. It was against this cataclysmic instant of ruin
that she had prepared for all these months; against this decision
that she'd selected her crew, trading ruthlessly on past debts and
owed favors. Now her handpicked personnel looked to her, tense
and straining as attack dogs, their fear and confusion checked
only by their trust in her.

And how strong was that trust? They were Federation officers, trained and sworn, yet they were also Fringers. How could
she—how could *anyone*—hold them in a moment like this? For
an instant, she felt as small and frail as her appearance suggested, but her finger touched a stud on her chair arm, and
she heard Tsing's breath hiss as her com panel lit with the face
of Captain Wang Chung-hui, commander of *Longbow*'s Marine
detachment.

Wang's cheeks quivered under her level regard, but there was
no strain in *her* face, he thought almost resentfully. What was
she about to demand of him? He knew his duty . . . but he, too,
was a Hangchowese.

"Major Wang," Han's voice was cool, and Wang felt a stab of
near hysterical mirth. There could be only one "captain" aboard
a warship, yet it was typical of Li Han to remember a point of
etiquette and give him his courtesy promotion at a time like this.
She was the smallest person in *Longbow*'s complement; she was
also the largest.

"Yes, sir?" he said hoarsely, and his heart sank as he realized
that when she ordered it he and his men would don their combat
zoots and board *Anderson*, blasting down anything in their path.
Not because of duty or Admiral Singh, but because Captain Li
had ordered them to.

"You heard Admiral Singh, Major," Han said softly.

"Yes, sir."

"Report to the armory, Major." Wang's heart plummeted. "Draw combat gear for your men, then post guards on the boatbay and all auxiliary hatches. Nobody leaves this ship. Is that clear?"

"Sir?" Wang blinked. Guard the boatbay and hatches? *Seal* them? Then she wasn't . . ."Yes, *sir!*" Wang barked, and the salute he threw her would have done credit to the commandant of the Corps.

"Thank you, Major." Han broke the circuit, her face still calm, despite the sweat beading her hairline. She continued to ignore her bridge crew, forcing herself to remain oblivious of the holstered lasers riding at every hip as she touched another stud.

"This is the Captain," she said, ignoring the normal preambles of an all-hands announcement, and speakers throughout the ship rattled with her measured voice. "You know what's happening." She drew a deep breath. "Now I'll tell you what's going to happen in *Longbow.* We are not going to obey Admiral Singh's orders." She felt her bridge crew twitch in near convulsive reaction. "I am your commander. As a sworn officer of the Federation Navy, I have no choice but to obey my lawful superiors, just as you have none but to obey me. Yet some orders cannot be obeyed, and Admiral Singh's are such orders. I cannot order you to mutiny"—she used the word deliberately—"but understand this: the only way *Longbow* will assist in suppressing the outbreak aboard *Anderson* is by mutinying against *me.*"

She paused, tasting the shock and confusion in some of her officers, the burning determination in others. She felt weak and shaken, as if her body were a hollow shell filled with air, and wanted desperately to lick her lips, but she didn't.

"I intend," she went on, her voice clear and strong, "to place this vessel at the service of the Kontravian Cluster. Any who disagree with that decision are free to leave. Report to Major Wang at the boatbay—without weapons. That is all."

She released the stud and turned her chair slowly, meeting Commander Tsing's eyes squarely before she let her gaze sweep her other officers. Every holster was sealed. No one spoke in encouragement or condemnation. That wasn't the Hangchow way, she thought almost whimsically. But there was a way to gauge their true feelings.

"Lieutenant Chu?"

"Yes, sir?" Her navigator sounded breathless, but there was snap in his voice.

"Lay off a course to place us between *Anderson* and the rest of the task force, Lieutenant Chu."

"Aye, aye, sir."

And that was all there was to it.

Commander Windrider watched *Basilisk* peel off the edge of the formation—and she was only the first. The monitor *Prescott* slid drunkenly aside as fighting wracked her command deck and navigation spaces before the drive could be cut. The destroyers and cruisers of the screen went berserk as their complements turned on one another, and garbled scraps of chatter told him the fighting had become general aboard *Enwright*, as well. Only one ship was under complete command. He watched his display as a single battlecruiser shot out of the scrambling formation to hover between *Anderson* and her consorts. The data codes gave her identity, and her shields were up, her weapons on line.

"Alert! Alert!" A computer voice wailed, then choked off, replaced by Captain Hodah's voice, and Windrider smiled bitterly. There was no taped message for this madness.

"This is the Captain! All persons resisting their lawful superiors will cease immediately or face summary courts-martial for mutiny! Marines will lay aft to the boatbay and prepare to board *Anderson* pursuant to the orders of Admiral Thomas Singh. Any person resisting execution of this order will be *stopped*. Marine officers are instructed to use weapons immediately in any case of resistance. This is a direct order—and your final warning!"

Windrider blanched. Hodah was a calm, humane man; for him to turn the Marines against his own people with a virtual license to kill—and to announce it for all to hear—must mean he felt the situation could get no worse. And what the hell had happened to Admiral Singh? Why wasn't *he* on the com?

A strident buzzer shrilled, and his eyes widened. The passages outside fire control were depressurizing . . . and that could happen only if someone deliberately spilled atmosphere! God! The blast doors and armored bulkheads were slamming shut, sealing fire control even more tightly. With zero pressure beyond and atmosphere within, it would be impossible to open those doors from outside—and blasting them open would take hours . . . or a nuke. Had Hodah done it to keep mutineers away? Or had the mutineers done it to isolate fire control from the loyalists? But the deck plates still pulsed to the rhythm of the drives, so Hodah had secured the power plants, or slaved their controls to the bridge. Was the power gang alive, or breathing space? What was *happening* out there? Who controlled what in the lunatic asylum which had once been a capital ship?

One of his ratings jerked on his gauntlets and reached for his helmet, and Windrider stabbed him with an angry stare.

"Where do you think *you're* going, Bearclaw?"

"B—but, sir! Those are our *friends* out there! We've got to do *something*!"

The missile tech was a product of Windrider's own world, an Amerind from Topaz, and his words tore at Windrider's soul. He felt sweat under the tooled leather band at his temples and remembered the scent of the evergreen *tomash* trees above his home.

"What you're going to do, Bearclaw," he said harshly, "is stand away from that hatch and sit down."

Bearclaw sat slowly, and his crewmates looked away in confusion. What was Windrider doing? Where did their own officer stand? The click of plastic and metal jerked their eyes back as he laid his laser on the console.

"No one enters or leaves this compartment without my permission," he grated. "*No one.* Is that understood?"

He met each of his subordinate's eyes in turn, pinning them with a brown, bitter glare until they nodded. Then he turned back to the targeting screens, sick at heart at what he'd just said, and sicker still at what he might yet have to do.

Red lights flared on status boards as whole computer sectors fell out of circuit. Shot out or cut, it made no difference to his own command station. They could cut the drives, they could cut the data net, they could blow the bridge to atoms; as long as *Enwright* had power, *he* controlled her weapons.

But what of it? He asked himself that with all the pent up bitterness and helplessness—and fear—which filled him. It had seemed so simple in the bull sessions. Nothing violent. Just a refusal to fire if the time came. Passive resistance. Not this! Never this mindless murder of fellow Navy men and women who were only doing their duty as best they understood it!

His battlephone beeped a priority code, and he punched a console key, shifting to a secure intraship battle channel. It was Hodah.

"Commander." The captain sounded harassed, but his voice was still crisp. "These damned mutineers must have planned this ahead of time. They've taken the armory and most of the Marines' quarters—we can't even get to the combat zoots, much less the boatbay! We still control the drive, and I think we still hold the power rooms, but I don't dare release the remotes to find out. I've confirmed the loss of auxiliary fire control and CIC, and all contact with flag bridge went out five minutes ago. We had a shoot-out in plotting, too, and there was a godawful explosion in datalink control right after we lost touch with flag bridge. I hold the command deck, and I've got armed Marines on the bridge elevators, but all I've got left up here for battle control is the auxiliary nav tank. Have you got all that?"

"Yes, sir." Windrider felt sweat matting his eyebrows.

"All right. It comes down to this, Commander," Hodah grated. "I can still move this ship, but that's *all* I can do. You're the only man who can target and fire her weapons. So tell me, Commander Windrider—are you prepared to do your duty?"

"My duty, Captain?" Windrider hesitated, his face ashen, then answered firmly. "Yes, sir. I'm prepared to do my duty."

"Then understand this, Commander," Hodah said softly. "Admiral Forsythe is dead, and Admiral Singh was apparently killed when they took out our flag bridge. Admiral Traynor may be dead; we've lost all contact with *Vesuvius*, so I have to assume she's either dead or a prisoner. I've got contact with Admiral Hale, but the mutineers have all the engineering spaces in *El Chichon*; he can't even maneuver. Admiral Ashigara apparently went over to the mutineers aboard *Basilisk*, so as near as I can figure it, Hale's the senior man left, and he's given me orders to terminate the fighting aboard *Anderson*—fast. Maybe we can bring the whole task force back to its senses if we get some Marines in there quickly. But Captain Li and *Longbow* are in the way, and they've threatened to destroy the first boat launched against *Anderson*. I've got two superdreadnoughts from Admiral Hale's group, and one attack transport is prepared to go in, but they can't launch until *Longbow*'s neutralized . . . one way or the other." Windrider heard the pain in his voice and remembered the evening Captain Li had dined aboard as his guest. "I'm going to give Li one last chance to move aside," Hodah said quietly. "If she refuses . . . Then, Commander, it's all up to you and your team."

"I—understand the situation, sir," Windrider whispered.

"Good. Switch to the intership channels, Commander. I want Captain Li to hear us if I have to pass you orders."

"Yes, sir." Windrider shifted channels and ran his fingers over the cool plastic console, feeling the latent destruction and understanding Hodah's pain too well, for Windrider, too, knew Li Han's reputation.

Han stared into her com screen at Simon Hodah's worried, angry face, reading the fear and fury in his eyes and wondering if he saw the pain in hers. His mouth was a slashed wound and his voice was harsh.

"Captain Li, you are in violation of the Articles of War. You will surrender your command and person at once, pursuant to the orders of Vice Admiral Eric Hale. You will heave to and await my boarding party. Officers designated by myself will relieve you of command and place you under close arrest to await trial. This is a direct order, logged and taped. You may authenticate with Admiral Hale."

"Captain Hodah," Han said softly to her old friend, "I must respectfully refuse your order."

"You have no authority to refuse!" Even the rage in Hodah's voice couldn't hide the pleading under his fury. "Now cut your shields and get out of my way, Captain, or by the living God, I'll blow you apart!"

Han looked around her bridge crew. Every set of shoulders was tense, every face knotted with tension, but not a voice protested as she turned back to her superior officer. God, she was proud of them! Yet her heart ached at matching their courage against their own fellows. It was such a waste—such a tragic, stupid waste—yet all of them were caught in the conflicting webs of duty, loyalty, and trust. Did her people suspect how much strength she drew from them? Or did they think they drew theirs from her?

She glanced down at her plot almost idly, watching data codes flash as weapons and tracking systems came alive aboard the trio of capital ships, and the deadly threat of those weapons was her reality. Her mind flickered over her life, remembering the things she'd done, recalling those she'd meant to do. How would her father react to this? What of the children she'd always known she would someday bear?

She raised her eyes once more to Simon's. She knew him so well. He *would* fire—indeed, she would leave him no option—and when *Enwright* and the superdreadnoughts fired, *Longbow* would die. No battlecruiser ever built could survive that concentration of fire at this range.

She hadn't anticipated when she handpicked her crew that she had chosen them only to die with her, yet Hodah's margin for error was razor thin. *Longbow*'s destruction would clear the path to *Anderson*, but it was a deadly expedient which might well recoil upon him, for it would give every mutineer his options, spell out the full, deadly consequences of resistance. It might awe them into surrender, but she thought not.

Her face was calm as the death of her ship and crew looked back at her from Hodah's eyes. It was unfair. It was cruel. Yet in a sense, it was also the sublime completion of her life. She drew a deep breath, hoping no one would notice.

"Go to hell, sir," she said very gently.

The deck shivered as *Enwright* moved deliberately towards the slim, defiant *Longbow*, and the Corporate World-crewed superdreadnoughts *Nanda Devi* and *Pentelikon* moved in beside her, shields glowing. The transport *Chief Joseph* slid in behind them, but she was unimportant in the confrontation of Goliaths, and Windrider's fingers flew over his own console even as his mind tried to reject the firing setup he was creating. Horror froze his subordinates into shocked, speechless immobility as the target codes appeared on their monitors, and he heard Han's reply and waited in a private hell for the words he knew must come.

"Fire Control!" Hodah's voice pounded in his brain.

"Yes, sir?" He was astounded he could sound so calm.

"Lock on all weapons. Prepare to fire at my command."

"Aye, aye, sir. Locking on now."

His fingers pressed the commit keys, and red lights glowed as weapon bays opened. Massive beam projectors snouted out and missiles slid into their launchers, backup rounds dropping silently into the loading trays. The ranked missiles riding the external racks woke to malevolent life, and sweat burned his eyes. He was sealed in a cage of ice and fire, for he was both a Fringer and a Federation officer. What *was* his duty? It mattered, and his uncertainty was agony as his hands hovered above the firing keys.

"Captain Li, this is your last chance!" Hodah snapped.

"Go ahead, Simon!" Li Han's voice was harsh at last, almost as if she were deliberately goading her old friend. "Fire and be damned!"

"Very well, Captain." Hodah's voice was as cold as space. "You leave me no choice. Fire Control, you have your orders. Open fire—*now!*"

Windrider's hands trembled on the deadly snakes of his firing keys and he blinked his eyes, fighting to focus. *Longbow* and the superdreadnoughts were virtually shield-to-shield, floating in his targeting screens at suicidal range, the battlecruiser small and alone, frail despite her weight of armor and weapons.

Visions and sounds filled his mind. Memories of his homeworld. The final parade at the Academy. Men and women he knew in the ships on his control screen. Men and women waiting to die when he touched those keys. All of them flashed through his mind, and his hands were paralyzed. He couldn't do it. God help him, he couldn't *do* it!

"Damn it, Windrider! Open fire!" Hodah roared, his own grief flogging his fury. "Do your duty, man!"

The word "duty" flared in Windrider's mind like a bomb, and he jerked spastically.

"Aye, aye, sir," he said very softly, and his eyes flicked over the targeting codes, a professional double-checking his work even in his anguish. Then his fingers tensed, and *Enwright*'s weapons spoke.

The world of the com channels shattered around him, battered by the roar of a hundred furious, denouncing voices and as many more that bellowed with triumph. A tide of destruction ripped from *Enwright* in a fury of beams and the impassioned streaks of missiles, and devastation rocked the vacuum as her weapons found their targets—Windrider's targets. Shields flared and died. Plating split, ruptured, disintegrated, vaporized. Atmosphere fumed from a gutted hull, and Jason Windrider clung to his sanity with bleeding fingernails while tears streamed down his cheeks and TFNS *Nanda Devi* died under his fire.

# THE MARK OF CAIN

Naomi Hezikiah felt out of place in *Pommern*'s command chair, for a heavy cruiser was not normally a lieutenant commander's billet, and even the thin Bible in the breast of her vac suit was scant comfort as she contemplated what was about to happen.

She punched up communications, and a painfully young ensign answered her. Yet another sign of the times; it should have been at least a full lieutenant.

"Anything from the flagship, Harvey?"

"No, sir." The young black man shook his head in mild surprise. "Standing orders are to maintain com silence, sir," he reminded respectfully.

"I know." Naomi probed the ensign's face for any uncertainty and started to say more, but she'd set her hand to the plow, as Elder Haberman would say. To every thing there was a season . . . even to this, she supposed drearily. So she made herself smile, instead. "Carry on, Ensign."

"Aye, aye, sir," the com officer said, and the screen blanked.

Naomi leaned back and closed her eyes. All she wanted was to be back on cold, bleak New Covenant. But she couldn't be there—and after what had already happened . . . after what was *about* to happen . . . not even New Covenant would want her back. She remembered Abraham and prayed silently for God to send another ram before the blade fell. But he wouldn't.

Her mind went back over the past, terrible two weeks that had started so wonderfully. She and Earnest had had the medic's official report; they'd actually been discussing ways to finagle their assignments so she could take her maternity leave at home on New Covenant when the scrambled transmission came over the relay net. An entire Battle Fleet task force—not just a battle-group, a *task force*—taken by its own personnel. Casualties had been heavy, and the few ships which remained loyal had been hunted down and captured or destroyed before they got far. But not before they got their courier drones away.

Commodore Prien had been a fool. Naomi's eyes stung as she remembered the kindly old man, a Heart Worlder who couldn't believe his own squadron might follow suit. He'd actually broadcast his decision to return to base immediately . . . and why. He should have known what would happen—and it had happened within hours. Desperate men and women had met, and the Fringers among his crews had risen against him.

But not all of them. No, not all of them. The meetings had been too clandestine, too hurried. Everything had been improvised by isolated groups, trusting no one outside their own little band. Not until the first mutineer drew his weapon could anyone know who stood where outside whatever tiny group *they'd* discussed it with, and the loyalists had fought back furiously. The carnage had been more savage than she would have believed possible; there were laser scars on the bulkheads around her, and the victorious mutineers had barely half the personnel they theoretically needed.

And when the fighting ended, Naomi found Earnest sprawled over his fire control panel, laser in hand, and two dead mutineers before him.

She had barely been able to read the funeral service through her tears. Had he known they were on different sides? Would he have fought beside her if he'd known? Or would his stubborn sense of duty, the courage she loved so much, still have ranged them against one another?

She didn't know. She couldn't know, for Earnest had died, and she had inherited command of a heavy cruiser . . . and even Elder Haberman would never be able to convince her that God could forgive her.

Not that the Elder would have the chance, she thought mordantly, glancing at the nav tank. She would have the opportunity to plead her case before the Lord herself all too soon, for the pulsing pattern of the nav beacons was clear in the tank, and her astrogator turned to her.

"Thirty seconds to transit, Captain," he said quietly.

"Very well," Naomi nodded curtly. "Carry on."

"Aye, aye, sir."

And so it was official. Toshiba wasn't going to relent.

◊          ◊          ◊

"We have no choice," Captain Victor Toshiba had told his "captains." "We're too deep in Innerworld space. We'd never make it to the Fringe if we just ran, and we've burned all our other bridges. We all know why we did it, but that doesn't matter. We're all of us—every one of us—mutineers."

He'd scanned his subordinates' faces, reading their despair, but his eyes were determined as he went grimly on.

"We're walking dead, ladies and gentlemen. Face it. Accept it and use it, because we're just as dead whether we spend our lives profitably or not. There's one, and only one, thing we can do for the Fringe now." His finger had stabbed the crazy quilt of warp lines in his nav tank. "Galloway's World. *That's* what we can give the Fringe . . . by taking it away from the Federation!"

Naomi had stared at him in horror, yet she was his senior "captain."

"But, sir," she'd said softly, "we don't begin to have the strength to seize Galloway's World. Surely you're not suggesting . . . ?"

"That's precisely what I *am* suggesting," Toshiba had said coldly. "We can gut the shipyards if we get in unchallenged. It's gone too far to stop now. It's war, Commander, war between the Fringe and the Innerworlds, and we both know who holds the industrial trumps. Can we stand by while the Corporate Worlds beat our people to death? No! We're going to hurt them—hurt them *now* and hurt them *badly*. We're going to buy time for our people, the one way we can." He'd paused, as if steeling his own nerve. "The only way: a nuclear strike on Galloway's World."

Naomi had wanted to vomit. They were the TFN, sworn to *defend* humanity against mass murder! And yet, wrong as he was, he might also be right. They *were* doomed, and they owed their people a chance. She remembered the winter wind howling around the dome on New Covenant and knew she could kill to defend the civilians of her world. But could she kill *other* civilians for them? She'd looked up and her lips had parted, but Toshiba's voice had marched on ruthlessly, forestalling her objections.

"I know there are bound to be heavy casualties—civilian casualties. The Jamieson Archipelago is the most densely populated area of the whole planet. Only an idiot could think you can nuke a target like that and *not* kill civilians; only a liar would tell you you could.

"But I also know what we're defending—and so do you! Our own homes, our own societies . . . the kind of societies that let humans be *people*, not just well-fed, two-legged domestic animals producing for Corporate World masters!"

His vehemence had shaken them all, and Naomi had felt her resistance waver. Then he'd paused and looked at them sadly. When he resumed, his voice was very soft.

"I know what you're thinking. Do we have the right to do this, even in self-defense? I don't know how you'll answer that, but I know how *I* will. They say a flower will grow toward sunlight even through ceramacrete, and perhaps they're right. But . . . what if *everything* is covered with ceramacrete? What if the flower finally breaks through, but there's no one left who can recognize a flower when he sees one?"

Naomi had bent over her hands, feeling his eyes on the crown of her head as his will beat against her, and realized how pivotal her own decision was. They'd endured one mutiny—perhaps they had another in them yet. But the first had cost her too much. Whatever God demanded of her, it couldn't be another spasm of the bloodshed which had taken Earnest. Her head remained bent, her eyes locked on her fingers, and the moment for rebellion passed.

"We've got a good chance of pulling it off," Toshiba had said softly as Naomi silently withdrew her opposition. "No one knows we've mutinied. We can put into Galloway's World for new orders, carry out the strike, and run. It's even possible"—he'd tried to sound as if he meant it—"some of us may get home. We're fast and well-armed; we may be able to split up and avoid action. But"—his voice had grown somber once more—"that's not what's important. Whether we can get away or not, we *have* to do it."

And every rebellious officer in his cabin had nodded silently.

"Transit in five seconds," Astrogation said softly. "Four . . . Three . . . Two . . . One . . . Transit!"

Naomi flinched as the indescribable surge of warp transit gripped her. She knew it was impossible, but in that instant she thought she felt the child within her. Thank God Doc Sevridge had understood. Losing her command would have left her a mere spectator, and no matter what her private purgatory, she had to *do* something. So he'd wiped the pregnancy report from the data banks with a tired smile.

"Might's well carry mutiny to its logical conclusion," he'd said. . . .

"I have a challenge, Captain!" The voice in Naomi's implant jerked her back to the present. "Standard query for ID and purpose."

"Stand by, Gunnery," she said through dry lips, watching the warp point forts on her tactical display. "Commodore Toshiba will roll the tape any minute now. Then we'll know." Her anxious eyes moved to a secondary screen as the carefully crafted composite of Prien's recorded messages went out over the com channels. It was good, she thought distantly. The electronics boys had done a bang-up job. But was it good enough?

". . . so after the fighting," the dead commodore said from the screen, "we patched up our damage and headed here. Commodore Jacob Prien, Tenth Cruiser Squadron, Frontier Fleet, awaiting orders."

"Good report, Commodore. Excellent!" The florid-faced admiral in the reception screen had a strong Fisk accent. "We had some trouble here, too, when the news first hit, but the local reservists turned the trick. We've got our heel on the scum now, and we're keeping it there! Shape your course for Skywatch Three. They'll have new orders cut by the time you get there."

"Aye, aye, sir," the recorded composite said. "Commodore Prien, out."

"And thank God for that," someone muttered as the admiral disappeared.

Naomi heard but didn't respond. If God were truly kind, that fathead would have been suspicious. They would have had to fight or flee well clear of the planet. She knew she could die happily in a ship-to-ship action, and she found that she'd been secretly hoping for just that.

She watched the plot as *Kongo* led the squadron in-system. *Revenge* and *Oslabya* fell in astern, followed by Naomi's own ship and then the two DDs. It all looked harmlessly normal, but *Pommern*'s battle board glowed a steady scarlet. All but the shields. They still blinked green and amber, for to raise them would raise questions, as well.

The hours dragged endlessly past, Galloway's World looming slowly before them, and Naomi considered the bitter irony which brought *Pommern* back to the yards which had birthed her in a terrible act of matricide. No one down there would spare a thought for the holocaust lurking in the belly of her ship, she thought bitterly. Fleet missiles were to protect them, not kill them.

And then, finally, Skywatch Three loomed close aboard of them, and she gritted her teeth, watching her board, waiting for what she knew must come.

It came. Command codes flashed over the data net from *Kongo*. The squadron's shields slammed up. Hetlasers swiveled in their bays. As one ship, drives and engines slaved to the flagship, they charged the orbiting fortress, minnows against its bulk. The external ordnance racks belched their deadly loads, joined by the internal launchers, and Naomi Hezikiah was a spectator as the Tenth Cruiser Squadron, TFN, blew Skywatch Three to half-vaporized rubble in less than thirty seconds.

The com channels went wild as incredulous loyalists realized what was happening. Naomi's battlephone hummed and whined as hastily tuned jammers came on line, fighting to shatter the squadron's datalink, but the cruisers drove onward, drives howling at max as they arrowed towards the planet.

The first defensive missiles lanced out to meet them, and Naomi watched her display as point defense stations spewed counter missiles against them and space burned with detonating warheads. They were fast on their feet, those gunners, but where were the beams?

"Communications seizure attempt!" her com officer shouted, and her battlephone shrieked into her mastoid for a fraction of a second before the filters damped the sound.

"Data net jammed," the ensign snapped.

"Independent targeting," Naomi ordered, feeling her shock frame tighten about her. *You should be my husband,* her brain screamed at the gunnery officer, but she strangled the thought as she scanned the battle plot. "Take those destroyers ahead of us. We have to hold them off the flag."

"Aye, aye, sir!"

Naomi found it easier to cling to her sanity as her ship's weapons moved independently at last, reaching out to rake the oncoming ships with hetlasers and missiles. *Kongo*'s own ECM must be jamming the tincans' data net, for their point defense was late, and *Pommern*'s fire tore the lead ship apart.

But missiles were getting through among the squadron as their own point defense stations went to independent control. She winced as a direct hit smashed at *Pommern*'s outer shields. *Kongo* was taking hits, too, and so was *Oslabya*, but not so many as *Revenge*. Naomi watched the second cruiser shudder in torment as her shields went down and the first warhead ripped at her drive field and mangled her armor.

"Shields one through three down," Gunnery reported. "Incoming missiles tracking *Kongo* from astern, sir. There's somebody on our ass. Somebody *big*. Those are capital missiles."

"Understood," Naomi said coldly, and under her crisp surface, a little girl recited ancient words. "*Yea, though I walk through the valley of the shadow of death . . .*"

She shook free of the thought. She'd wanted a ship-to-ship action; perhaps she had one.

"New course!" she snapped. "Bring us around on a reciprocal. Let the Commodore deal with those cans—we've got bigger fish to fry!"

*Pommern* snarled around in a tight turn. Even through the drive field, she felt the lateral motion as her ship fought inertia and momentum.

"Communications!" she barked. "Advise the Commodore of our heading and intent."

They steadied on course, and the author of the capital missile fire was before her.

"Battlecruiser at eleven light seconds!" Gunnery yelped. "Computer reads her as the *Kris*."

Naomi knew her well. She'd served on her as a lieutenant—an eternity ago. Homeported on the Yard, and no doubt as fanatically Corporate World as her own madmen were Fringer.

"Gunnery," she said softly, "there's your target. Maneuvering, I want a random evasion course and I want it now. We're up against some heavy metal; let's be where it isn't!"

The acknowledgments came, and she watched her missiles going out as the range closed. More capital missiles scorched in, but they were no longer targeted on *Kongo*. *Kris* had accepted *Pommern*'s frail challenge.

"*Kongo*'s opened fire on the planet, sir! Track looks good for the Taliaferro Yard!"

Naomi shut it out. She no longer wanted to think of the two cities clustered tight against the Taliaferro Yard, of the civilians with seconds to live. She no longer wanted to think of the mark of Cain she wore. She pressed one palm over the Bible in her vac suit and sealed her helmet as they entered laser range, and *Pommern* shook and quivered to the fury of missiles and counter missiles bursting around her hull.

"Missiles away from *Oslabya*, sir! Tracking for the Yard!"

But Naomi's attention was riveted to her gunnery officer.

"Laser range!" he announced, and here it came. The deadly

energy sleeted from the battlecruiser and howled around *Pommern*'s hull.

"Second strike off from *Kongo! Revenge* launching now!" Naomi wasn't listening. She was watching her screens as her own lasers raved defiance at *Kris. Pommern*'s gunnery had always been good, she thought sadly as armor vaporized on the battlecruiser. Better than any capital ship's in the Fleet, Earnest had always said.

"*Oslabya*: Code Omega!" communications reported. So Lieutenant Jolson's first command was no more. Well, he'd soon have company.

"Oh, dear God!" Naomi's eyes jerked toward her white-faced scanner rating. "*Oslabya*'s missiles must've been under shipboard control, sir! They're going to a standard dispersion pattern!"

Naomi's heart chilled as she stabbed a quick look at Battle Two. It was true. With her computers out of the circuit, *Oslabya*'s missiles were spreading to cover the target with maximum devastation, and what was supposed to be a precision strike had become an atrocity. They were only tactical nukes, but they'd land all over the Reservation and dependent housing. . . .

"Good hits on target." Gunnery's almost droning report jerked her eyes away from the horror unfolding on Battle Two. "She's streaming air, sir!"

And then *Kris* found the range.

*Pommern* screamed as the lasers raped her. Naomi had always known ships had souls—she felt it now, in her own soul, as the cruiser's armor puffed to vapor and vanished under the radiant energy.

"Forward launchers gone!" Gunnery's professional calm had disappeared. "Laser One destroyed!"

Naomi turned towards him, but she never completed her order. *Kris* found them again, her hetlasers knifing through armor and plating and flesh. Naomi gasped involuntarily as air screamed from the holed compartment and her suit puffed tight, and *Pommern* lurched as a drive room died, and then another. She was toothless and naked, but *Kris* was badly hurt herself, and the Jamieson Archipelago was a forest of poisonous mushrooms as Toshiba blasted the shipyards and the battlecruiser's crew's homes and families burned.

Naomi looked away from her looming executioner, her own eyes burning as *Oslabya*'s missiles laid their artificial suns across the Navy base. How many were dying down there? How many whose husbands and wives and fathers and mothers wore the same uniform as she? Yet they were only a few more deaths against the civilians dying around the other yards. How many would there be? A million? Two million? Three? Against that kind of devastation, what could a few thousand Navy dependents matter?

*Kris* slid alongside at point-blank range, and Naomi watched almost incuriously in an outside screen as the battlecruiser's surviving hetlasers swiveled across her ship. *Kris* poured fire into the gutted, mutinous cruiser.

Naomi had a tiny fraction of a second to see the end of her bridge explode into vaporized steel. Only a fraction of a second before the fury came for her—but long enough to feel the mark of Cain in her soul again and know that death would be sweet. . . .

# DISASTER

"Mister Speaker," Simon Taliaferro said somberly, "I take little pleasure in being vindicated in such fashion." He looked around the Chamber of Worlds and shook his head sadly. "We should have known it would come, I suppose, when so many Fringe World delegates resigned their seats to protest the 'severity' of a decision far more merciful than just. Barbarism, Mister Speaker—the acts of little, frightened minds which must not be allowed to destroy all the Terran Federation stands for."

Oskar Dieter sat quietly, listening to the beautifully trained voice, and wished he possessed some of the same histrionic ability. But he didn't; all he could do was tell the truth, and where was the appeal of truth when lies were so convincingly presented?

"I ask you, Ladies and Gentlemen of the Assembly," Taliaferro went on, "where is the reason in *this*?" He waved his hard copy of the report which had originated this secret session. "Even if, as I do not for an instant believe, amalgamation is an unmeant threat to the Fringe Worlds' representation, is *this* the way to contest it? Where are the Fringe World delegates, ladies and gentlemen? Where are the petitions? We see none of them. Instead we see *this!*"

He crumpled the sheet of paper contemptuously, and Dieter winced as the theatrical gesture evoked a spatter of applause.

It was sadly scattered applause, for the Chamber of Worlds was sparsely populated, the blocks of assemblymen and women separated by the empty delegation boxes of Fringe Worlds no longer represented here.

The Fringer delegations had been small, but there were many Outworlds, and their absence cut great swathes through the

727

larger, less numerous Innerworld delegations. And it was Simon
Taliaferro and others like him who had created this absence,
Dieter reminded himself, staring at the heavyset Gallowayan with
a hatred it no longer shocked him to feel.

"They've made no effort to oppose amalgamation," Taliaferro
went on. "They haven't even bothered to discover whether or not
it has in fact been ratified! They have fastened upon it—fastened
upon it as a cheat and a pretext for *treason*, and let us not delude
ourselves, my friends! The act of the Kontravian Cluster is treason,
and when Admiral Forsythe has brought these traitors to their
knees, we must show them that the Federation is not prepared
to brook such criminality."

Here it came, Dieter thought grimly. Taliaferro had spent forty
years maneuvering for exactly this slash at the Fringe's jugular.

"My friends," Taliaferro said soberly, "we must face unpleasant facts. The Kontravian rebels are not the only treasonously
inclined members of the Fringe. If we falter, if we show weakness or hesitation, the Federation will vanish into the ash heap
of history. Only strength impresses the immature political mind.
Only strength and the proven will to use it! We must demonstrate our will power, whatever it may cost us in anguish
and grief. We must punish ruthlessly, so that a few salutary
lessons will prevent the wholesale bloodshed which must assur-
edly follow weakness.

"I therefore move, ladies and gentlemen, that we draft special
instructions to Fleet Admiral Forsythe and all other commanders,
instructing them to declare martial law and empowering them
to convene military courts to try and punish the authors of this
treason. And, ladies and gentlemen, I move that we inform our
commanders that the sentences of their courts martial *stand
approved in advance!*"

Dieter was on his feet in a heartbeat, fists clenched in shocked
outrage. He'd known Taliaferro was ruthless, prepared to provoke
civil war to gain his own ends—but *this* was simple judicial
murder!

His fury turned icy as the full implications registered. If one
could only be as conscienceless as Taliaferro himself it was almost
admirable. Killing the Beaufort "ringleaders" would, at one stroke,
remove the Fringe leaders best able to oppose him, inflame the
extremists on both sides, and stain the hands of the Assemblymen
with blood. Even if their ardor cooled, even if they later realized
Taliaferro had used them, they would be his captives. They would

share his guilt, and so would perforce becomes his accomplices in future crimes, as well.

Dieter forced himself to use his anger, burning the fury from his system and replacing it with frozen calm. He must speak out, must inject an element of opposition and carry at least a minority with him, so that when the fit passed there would be *someone* free of Taliaferro's blood guilt.

He drew a deep breath and touched his attention button as David Haley opened debate on Taliaferro's motion.

"The Chair recognizes the Honorable Assemblyman for New Zurich," Haley said, and Dieter heard the relief in his voice.

"Thank you, Mister Speaker."

Dieter's huge face stared out over the delegates, showing no sign of his inner turmoil. How should he address them? With fury, denouncing Taliaferro as a madman? Or would that merely brand him another hothead? Should he, then, try cold logic? Or would that stand a chance against the hysteria Taliaferro had been fanning for so many months? Derision, perhaps? Would mockery achieve what head-on opposition could not? He shook his thoughts aside, knowing he must play it by feel.

"Ladies and Gentlemen of the Assembly," he heard his own stiffness and prayed no one else did. "Mister Taliaferro proposes to recognize the depth of this crisis by enacting extraordinary legislation. He argues—and rightly so—that this is a moment to show strength. The Federation has withstood many external threats, yet today we face an *internal* threat to our very existence. Indeed, Mister Taliaferro may well be too optimistic, for he overlooks the composition of our military. As chairman of the Military Oversight Committee, I can assure you there are enough Fringe Worlders in the military to make the ultimate loyalty of our own armed forces far from assured."

He felt the surprise as he admitted even a part of the Gallowayan's arguments. The Dieter-Taliaferro enmity had been a lively topic of Assembly gossip for months, and he knew the wagers in the anterooms were heavily against him. But they'd reckoned without the years of favors he'd desperately called in among the hierarchy of his homeworld. And without the recorder his briefcase had concealed during his final, parting-of-the-ways meeting with the Taliaferro Machine's leadership. He'd hung on, emerging as Taliaferro's only real opposition, and though his Assembly membership still hung by a thread, that thread grew steadily stronger as his warning penetrated deeper into the fundamentally conservative minds of the bankers who owned New Zurich.

His secretly made recording had helped immensely, for he knew some of the New Zurich syndics shared his private opinion that Taliaferro was no longer sane. They were willing to keep him on as a counterweight—at least until they knew whether the Gallowayan would succeed. And if Taliaferro did, Dieter knew, he would be the sacrificial lamb offered by the New Zurich leaders as they sought rapprochement with Galloway's World.

He shook such thoughts aside and forced his mind back to the present. His increasingly frequent woolgathering mental side-trips worried him.

"Yes, ladies and gentlemen, Mister Taliaferro is quite correct— and he is also entirely *wrong*. He would have you believe the only strong reaction is to crush the rebels, that the only strength is the iron fist of repression. Ladies and gentleman, there are more strengths than the whip hand! Let us acknowledge that this is an unprecedented crisis. Let us admit that what we face is mass treason—treason not of a single person, or a single clique, or even a single world, but of an entire cluster! And let us ask ourselves *why* eight star systems and eleven inhabited worlds and moons would *simultaneously* take such a drastic step! Has some mysterious madness gripped them all? Or is it, perhaps, much as we would hate to admit it, *we* who have driven them to it?"

He paused, feeling the hovering resentment like smoke. Some would hate him for opposing their carefully laid plans, and others for saying what they themselves had thought without admitting. Only a tragically small few would understand and support him. But it had to be enough. It must be.

"Ladies and Gentlemen of the Assembly, I oppose this motion. I oppose the creation of kangaroo courts whose only possible verdict can be death. I oppose the institutionalization of the fracture lines splitting our polity at this critical moment. Let us demonstrate that we are strong enough to be reasonable and wise enough to be rational. Let us show the Fringe that we're willing to listen to grievances and, for a change, to act upon them. It is time for compromise, ladies and gentlemen, not for judicial murder."

He sat down abruptly, feeling his last two words ringing in a sudden silence that proved some, at least, had heard. But not enough, he thought grimly. Not enough.

Indeed, he was surprised only by the extent of his support, for as delegate after delegate rose to speak, almost a third supported him. He would have wagered on less than a quarter, and he was gratified to see so much sanity, even as he recognized his failure to stop Taliaferro.

The motion passed by slightly less than a two-thirds majority, and a license to kill was dispatched to the Federation's far-flung commanders.

Dieter prayed they would have the moral courage to ignore it.

"Chief! Mister Dieter! Wake *up* sir! *Please* wake up!"

The grip on Dieter's shoulder wrenched him awake, and his hand darted under the pillow to the pistol butt which had become so unhappily familiar in the past fourteen months. The weapon was out, safety catch released, before his sleep-dazed mind recognized Heinz von Rathenau, his security chief.

Rathenau stepped back quickly, and Dieter lowered the needler with a twisted grin and a shrug of apology. Since the first attempt on his life, he'd found himself uncomfortable without a weapon to hand.

"Yes, Heinz," he said. "What is it?"

He glanced at the clock and winced. Four A.M. He'd been asleep less than two hours.

"A priority message, sir." Rathenau looked desperately unhappy in the light of the bedside lamp. "From the Lictor General's office."

"The Lictor General?" Dieter rose quickly, shrugging into a robe even as he headed barefooted for the door. "What priority?"

"Priority One, sir."

"Oh, God! Not again!"

Dieter bit off further comment as he walked quickly down the hall beside Rathenau. The armed New Zurich Peaceforcers at the elevators snapped to attention as Dieter passed, and Rathenau noticed that his normally affable superior didn't even acknowledge the courtesy.

They reached the communications room, and Rathenau stopped outside as Dieter stepped through the heavy security door. His predecessor would have walked through at Dieter's elbow with a calm assurance of his right to be there, but Rathenau felt no desire to appear even remotely akin to Francois Fouchet. Fouchet had mistaken Dieter's trustfulness for weakness . . . and paid for it, Rathenau thought with grim satisfaction. For himself, he would follow Oskar Dieter back to New Zurich without a murmur when the axe fell. It wasn't often a Corporate World security man found himself serving a chief worthy of personal loyalty.

Dieter shut the door without sparing Rathenau a thought. He had eyes only for the flashing red light on the panel, and his blood ran cold. The last time he'd seen that light had been three months ago to receive news of the Kontravian secession.

He presented his eye to the retinal scanners, automatically suppressing the blink reflex. It took thirty seconds to satisfy the brilliant lights; when he finally read the message, he wished it had taken thirty years.

He stared at the screen, his mind encased in ice. God, he thought. Please, God. Why are You letting this happen?

But there was no answer. There would be none.

He rose finally, like an old, old man, switching off the communicators and wishing he could switch off his mind as easily. He opened the door and saw young Rathenau's face tighten at his own expression.

"Chief?"

"Heinz—" Dieter's hands moved for a moment, as if trying to recapture something that was irretrievably shattered.

"What is it, Chief?" Rathenau's voice was much softer, almost gentle.

"Wake the others, Heinz." Dieter drew a deep breath, but the oxygen was little help. "Get everyone assembled in conference room one in—" he glanced at his watch "—twenty minutes. Tell them to forget dressing."

"Yes, sir. May I ask why, sir?"

"I'm afraid you'll have to wait for the briefing. There'll be an emergency session at 0600 hours, and I have calls to make."

"Yes, sir."

Rathenau watched Oskar Dieter move brokenly down the corridor, and his heart was cold within him.

The Chamber of Worlds was hushed, wrapped in a silence it had not known in decades—if ever. Dieter looked around the shocked faces and wondered if even the Battle of VX-134 had produced such an effect. Howard Anderson's battle had been Man's first with a rival stellar empire; this news was worse.

He glanced up as Taliaferro walked briskly to his seat. He wanted nothing else in the Galaxy so much as to see Taliaferro's expression, to read the emotions in the dark, arrogant face of the man who'd orchestrated this disaster. The man whom he, God help him, had *helped* create this catastrophe.

Taliaferro dropped into his chair almost as the chime struck, and Dieter understood. He'd timed his late arrival to preclude any buttonholing, but how would he deal with it? How would he manage *this* session?

"Ladies and Gentlemen." David Haley's voice sounded as if it had been pulverized and glued unskillfully back together. "Ladies and Gentlemen of the Assembly, the Legislative Assembly is in session."

He paused and cleared his throat, his face pale in the vast screen.

"I am certain all of you have been apprised of the reason for this emergency session. However . . . however, for those of you who may not be fully informed, I will summarize."

His hands trembled visibly as he adjusted his terminal, but Dieter was certain he didn't really need any notes. Like himself, he no doubt found the information burned into his quivering brain.

"On February 12, 2439, Terran Standard Reckoning," Haley said slowly, as if seeking protection in the formality of his phrasing, "Task Force Seventeen of the Terran Federation Navy Battle Fleet entered the system of Bigelow in the Kontravian Cluster for the purpose of suppressing the secessionist elements therein. It was hoped—" his voice broke, then steadied. "It was hoped this force was strong enough to overawe the rebels. It was not. The Kontravians refused to surrender, and, after the failure of lengthy negotiations, Fleet Admiral Forsythe moved against them."

He drew a deep breath, and a strange strength seemed to possess him, the strength which comes only to those who have faced the worst disaster they can conceive. When he continued, his voice was cold and clear.

"Task Force Seventeen," he said quietly, "no longer exists. Apparently—the message is not entirely clear, ladies and gentlemen—but apparently mutiny first broke out aboard the flagship. It spread. Within a very short space, virtually every ship was involved. Most—" he drew another breath "—went over to the Kontravians."

They'd known, but the shock which ran through his audience as the words were finally said was actually visible. Dieter looked away from Haley, fixing his gaze on Taliaferro, willing the man to show some reaction, but the Gallowayan had himself under inhuman control.

"There was some fighting between loyal and mutinous elements," Haley continued. "Our only information comes from a courier drone from the superdreadnought *Pentelikon*. The drone carried an Omega message." The chamber was utterly still; Code Omega was used only for the final communication from a doomed ship.

"As nearly as we can determine," Haley said into the hushed silence, "the entire task force—minus those units destroyed in the fighting—went over to the Kontravians or was subsequently captured. As of the time *Pentelikon*'s drone was dispatched, the count of survivors was approximately as follows: eight monitors, six superdreadnoughts, seven carriers, eleven battlecruisers, twenty-one heavy and light cruisers, forty-one destroyers and escort destroyers, and virtually the entire fleet train. At least six destroyers, three light and heavy cruisers, one carrier, and two superdreadnoughts were destroyed in the fighting.

"Ladies and Gentlemen," the Speaker said very quietly, "this means, in effect, that there are *no* loyal survivors from the entire task force."

The silence grew, if possible, even more complete. Most of the delegates were staring at Haley's image in horror. Very few seemed capable of coherent thought—and that, Dieter thought, was what was desperately needed now.

He was reaching for his own attention button when the sound of another bell cut the air. Haley glanced down at his panel, and an edge of uncontrollable bitterness crossed his face, but when the Speaker spoke, his voice was as impersonal as ever.

"The Chair recognizes the Honorable Assemblyman for Galloway's World."

Dieter leaned back as Taliaferro appeared on the screen. His face was taut, but any sense of guilt was well hidden as he looked out over the depleted delegations for a long second, then spoke.

"Ladies and Gentlemen of the Assembly," he said sadly, "this is the most horrible, damnable news ever to come before this Assembly. Not only have the traitors not been suppressed, but the madness has infected even our own Navy! The Terran Federation Navy, the most loyal, the most courageously dedicated fighting force in the history of Man, has been touched by the insanity of treason!"

He shook his head in eloquent disbelief.

"But we must not allow shock and shame to paralyze us," he continued after a brief, sorrowful pause. "However terrible the news, it is our responsibility to act and act promptly. Consider, my friends—the Kontravian traitors have acquired the equivalent of their own navy out of this. The ships of Task Force Seventeen will be turned against us, the legitimate government of the Federation. Threats of force and force itself may be used against us by these damnable traitors! Our defenses are strong; it is unlikely any rebel attack will penetrate Innerworld space, and our loyal commanders will surely move quickly to prevent the spread of this insidious rot, but we must accept that some additional fraction of the Fleet may join this contemptible attack upon us. I have said before—and this Assembly has agreed with me—that this is a time for strength, and so it is. Our only option, ladies and gentlemen, is to show our steel, our determination that this criminal conspiracy shall not succeed! We must mobilize the rest of Battle Fleet. We must call in every loyal ship, every loyal military man and woman. We must crush the heart out of the Fringe World conspiracy! We must show these barbarians that *we*—not *they*—are the representatives of civilized humanity! And with God's help, we *will* show them that! We will defeat them, and we will hunt down and execute every traitor who has dared to raise his hand against the might and dignity and justice of the Terran Federation!"

A roaring ovation sealed his words, and Dieter shuddered. Damn the man! Damn him to *hell*! This disaster demonstrated the fundamental, destructive insanity of his entire self-serving policy. It should have stunned him. Instead, with a few brief words and a simplistic appeal to patriotism and pride, he had the Assembly eating out of his hand! Bile rose in Dieter's throat and, for the first time, he allowed himself to wonder if such an Assembly was even worth saving.

He bowed over his hands in defeat. He'd tried. As God was his witness, he'd *tried.* But he'd failed, and the Taliaferros and Waldecks and Sydons had inherited the Federation . . . or whatever smoking ruins would be left. He felt hot tears behind his eyes and turned in his chair. He would have no more of it. He would resign his seat, leave them to their madness. . . .

A hand touched his shoulder, and the concern and desperate faith in Heinz von Rathenau's eyes stopped him. Of all the New Zurich delegation, Heinz saw most clearly. He *understood*, and as Dieter saw the faith in those green eyes, he could not leave it unanswered. He owed it to Heinz, to the Federation, and most of all—God help him—to Fionna MacTaggart.

"Chief?" Rathenau asked softly. "Are you all right?"

"Yes, Heinz." Dieter rested his hand on the fingers gripping his shoulder and squeezed gently. "Yes, I'm all right now. Thank You."

He saw Rathenau's confusion and hoped the young man would never realize just what that "thank you" meant. But whether young Heinz ever did or not, all that mattered now was the battle which must be fought. And as he thought of Heinz, as he thought of Fionna and of Taliaferro's greed, anger returned. He wasn't like Taliaferro, but for today, just for this morning, it was time to take a page from Taliaferro's book. His hand stabbed the button, and the attention bell chimed softly.

"The Chair," David Haley's amplified voice cut through the hum of excited conversation, "recognizes the Honorable Assemblyman for New Zurich."

Dieter stood in the ringing silence and knew the Chamber of Worlds was agog with curiosity. How would he respond? How could he possibly continue to oppose Taliaferro now that they faced a life and death struggle for survival itself? But he let his bitter eyes sweep over them for long, long seconds before he finally spoke, and when he did, his voice was a whip.

"You *fools*," he said coldly, and the Assembly recoiled, for no one spoke to them in that flat, bitingly contemptuous tone! Dieter felt their anger and let it feed his own as he leaned into the pickup.

"Can't you see what this *means*? Are you all so blind you can't recognize reality just because it happens to clash with your comfortable image of yourselves as the last bright hope of humanity? By God, you don't *deserve* to survive! Think of the *date*, you idiots! Task Force Seventeen mutinied *three months ago*! Who knows what's happened since?"

His words shattered the rising anger like a lightning bolt. They'd lived with the reality of the Fringe's slow communications all their lives, had learned to use their faster communications for ruthless advantage, yet until he threw the date in their faces, they hadn't even considered the time element. But now the implications were before them, and their palms were suddenly slick with fear.

"Yes," Dieter sneered. "It takes a long time for courier drones to come that far—and who knows where other drones were sent? *We* have one from a single unit of the task force. Do you seriously think that was the only drone launched? Do you seriously think other Fleet units haven't heard by now? Sixty percent of the Fleet is Fringer. *Sixty percent.* Can none of you understand what that means? *We* don't have the numerical advantage in the civil war you've provoked—*they do!*"

His words unleashed the ugly, snarling pandemonium of terror. For over a year, he'd hammered away, warning them, pleading with them, and all but a minority had ignored him. *They* controlled the Fleet. *They* spoke with their every word backed by the suppressive might of the Federation's military. And now, suddenly, they saw the nightmare at last, and the man who'd warned them, who'd earned their contempt for his weakness, had been right all along.

Dieter's voice thundered above the tumult.

"*Yes!* Yes, flog the Fringe! Ignore their legitimate complaints! Call them barbarians because they're more honest, more desperate than you are! And now see what you've created! God help me, I helped you do it—now I must bear the same guilt as you, and the thought makes me *sick.*"

"But what are we going to do?" someone yelled. "My God, what are we going to *do?*"

"Do?" Dieter sneered down at him. "What do you *think* we're going to do? We're going to fight. We're going to fight to save what we can, because we have no choice, because the only alternative is the utter destruction of the Federation—that's what we're going to *do*. But understand this, all of you! The days of contempt for the Fringe are over. Fight them, yes. But never, *never* call them 'barbarians' again! Because, ladies and gentlemen, if they really *are* barbarians, we're doomed."

His words plunged them back into silence. A fearful, lingering silence.

"We're doomed because they have Task Force Seventeen, ladies and gentlemen, and by now they have other ships. By the time we can get our own courier drones to the Fringe, they may have all of Frontier Fleet—perhaps even the Zephrain Fleet base."

He felt the sudden whiplash of terror that thought woke in the delegates who knew what it meant, but he hammered the point mercilessly home.

"I know what that means, and so should you. Weapons research in the data base of Zephrain Research and Development Station. Research on weapons which may outclass anything this galaxy has ever seen—and it lies in the *Fringe*, ladies and gentlemen, not in the Innerworlds."

He glared at them, and his voice was cold.

"And if they act as what you've called them—if they truly are barbarians and choose to seek vengeance rather than relief—they will not use those ships and weapons in self-defense. Oh, no, ladies and gentlemen! If the Fringers are barbarians, you'll find those ships *here*, striking the Innerworlds, and you'll find those weapons turning your precious planets into cinders."

He hissed the last word, and its chill ran through his audience like a wind.

"So get down on your knees," he finished. "Get down on your knees and pray you were wrong."

He cut the connection with a contemptuous flick. Silence roared about him, and he was heartsick and frightened, yet he could almost feel Fionna at his shoulder, and knew he had finally paid the first installment on his debt.

A bell chimed.

Dieter looked up and saw what he'd known he would. Simon Taliaferro was pressing for recognition, his shoulders hunched, his face bitter. He had no choice but to respond, and Dieter knew that if his security showed the tiniest chink, he himself was a dead man.

"The Chair," Haley said, "recognizes the Assemblyman from Galloway's World."

Taliaferro appeared on the screen, and his face shocked Dieter. The compelling strength had waned, and the arrogance was mixed with desperation. It struck him suddenly that Taliaferro had actually never considered this possibility. That he, too, had missed the significance of the drone's date. That he'd brushed aside Dieter's warnings about the Fleet simply because his blind, overweening confidence had never considered the chance of failure.

But though Dieter might hate him, Simon Taliaferro had cut his way to power with courage as well as conspiracy, and he gathered his shaken will to respond.

"Ladies and Gentlemen of the Assembly," he began, his formal courtesy somehow pathetic after Dieter's contempt. "My friends. The Assemblyman for New Zurich—" he drew a deep breath. "The Assemblyman for New Zurich may be right. Perhaps we have lost more Fleet units since the . . . mutiny. But it changes nothing. *Nothing!*"

He shouted the last word, and suddenly he seemed to find fresh strength. Dieter recognized the signs. Like himself, Taliaferro was unleashing his anger, letting fury sustain him.

"We are still the Federation, and they are still barbarians! Even if they have every ship in Frontier Fleet, even if they have every dispersed unit of Battle Fleet—even if they have the Zephrain Fleet base itself!—what of it? Before they can injure us, they must come to us, ladies and gentlemen! They must fight their way through Fortress Command. They must deal with the remaining strength of Battle Fleet. They must deal with the Reserve, ladies and gentlemen. Fifty percent of Battle Fleet—*fifty percent*—is in mothballs! How will they deal with that when we mobilize it? Even if they have Zephrain, surely the base personnel—person-nel rigorously screened for loyalty and integrity—destroyed the facilities before they could be taken! And what will they use for shipyards? They have only a few, scattered repair bases and small civilian yards. *We* hold the Fleet shipyards! *We* hold the major construction facilities!"

Dieter felt the shaken Assembly take courage from Taliaferro's words. Couldn't they recognize the counsel of despair when they heard it?

"Let them come against us, ladies and gentlemen! It will prove I was right—that *we* were right—when we called them barbar-ians! Driven to it? *Poppycock!* This is a coldly calculated act of treason. This is—*must* be—the end product of a long and careful conspiracy! We've driven them to nothing—but we *will* drive them. We will drive them to destruction and retribution! Our worlds are safe behind our fortifications, their worlds will lie open to our attack when the Fleet is fully mobilized! Let us teach them the true meaning of war, my friends! Let us cauterize this cancer of conspiracy in the only way they understand—with the flames of war and iron determination!"

It took all Dieter's strength to keep his dismay from his face. He'd shaken Taliaferro, but the Gallowayan was rallying his forces, and without the Outworlds not even a unified bloc of Heart Worlds and the few Corporate World moderates could fight the political steamroller Taliaferro controlled.

"And if it's a long war, what of it?" Taliaferro demanded hotly. "We've fought long wars before and come back to victory. We will do it again! We have the strength to crush these traitors—it's only a matter of mobilizing that strength! My friends! As chief of delegation for Galloway's World, I place the combined building capacity of the Jamieson Archipelago—the greatest concentration of industrial might in the Galaxy—unreservedly at the service of the Terran Federation! Let us see how the rebels like *that*!"

A roar greeted his words—the desperate roar of a panicked crowd which suddenly sees salvation. Dieter hammered his call button, but Taliaferro ignored him as he ignored Speaker Haley's urgent, amplified pleas for calm, smiling fiercely out at the shouting, clapping delegates. He'd done it. He'd salvaged victory and his career from the very teeth of disaster.

And in that moment of heady political triumph, the sealed doors flew open and the Sergeant at Arms raced down the aisle, followed by the red cloak of the Lictor General. A shockwave of quiet fanned out from them, and Taliaferro's fierce grin faded as he saw them.

The two men hurled themselves up the steps to Haley's side, and only later did Dieter come to recognize the blind providence—or the brilliance of David Haley—which had left the Speaker's mike open. Every ear in the Chamber of Worlds heard the message the Lictor General gasped into Haley's ear.

"A message from Galloway's World, sir! It-it's terrible! Skywatch HQ is gone! A dozen destroyers blown apart! At least a quarter of the mothballed units wiped out! And the Jamieson Archipelago!"

"What about the Archipelago?" Haley's question was sharp.

"Gone, sir! The yards, the Fleet base, half the Reservation—just . . . gone, sir. It was a nuclear strike. . . ."

The Lictor General's voice trailed off as he realized the microphone at his elbow was live, but no one noticed. Every eye was on Simon Taliaferro as he swayed, his swarthy face pale, his eyes blank, and stumbled silently away.

# ATROCITY

The furrows stretched out behind Fedor Kazin's lurching tractor—miles and miles of furrows, hungry for Terran wheat, waiting for spikeweed sprigs. The one to feed Innerworld bellies, he thought sourly, and the other to liven their dreams, and which did they value more, eh?

Yet whatever they paid him, it wouldn't be enough... again. Not with the shipping fees those Corporate World *vlasti* extorted from the Fringe. For thirty years he'd harvested his wheat and spikebalm, and *still* he was perpetually in debt to the shipping lines.

He glanced up at the clouds. His grandfather had always claimed Novaya Rodina's steppes were almost as beautiful as Old Russia's, but for the color of the sky. Fedor wouldn't know; he'd seen only recordings from the motherworld, and he'd always suspected they touched the things up a little—surely no sky could be *that* blue!—but he knew his own sky well. He only hoped he finished his plowing before the storm struck.

Thoughts of the weather turned his mind to the storm ripping through the entire Federation. He couldn't believe the tales coming out of Novaya Petersburg! Did those madmen think they were all back in the days of the tsar? That the Federation was run by Rasputin? And who were *they*, these men who called themselves 'Kadets' once more? Kerensky? Trotsky? Fedor had no more love for the Corporate Worlds than the next man, but the Federation was the *Federation*! It had risen from the flames of Old Terra's Great Eastern War and reached out to the stars, protecting its people as it placed them on worlds light-years from their birthworld. It was the Federation of Howard Anderson and

Ivan Antonov. Four centuries it had stood—what were a hundred years or so of mistakes against that? And Novaya Rodinans were Russians: they knew a thing or two about endurance.

But these crazy Kadets—! Madness! Even if they succeeded, where would his wheat go? There had to be *some* form of foreign exchange—and who in the Fringe needed foodstuffs? What Fringe farming world could sell Novaya Rodina the manufactured goods she needed?

So Fedor plowed and sowed, for the day would come when the crazy men realized they couldn't succeed. It might be necessary to chastise them a little first, but in the end the Federation would take them back. And when it did, Fedor Kazin would have a crop ready, by God!

He looked up as thunder muttered and the squall line in the east swept closer. He wasn't going to finish today after all: best to stop at the end of this furrow and head home. 'Tasha would have supper waiting.

Pieter Tsuchevsky looked around the quiet room at his fellow Kadets. So this was how it felt to be a rebel. He'd never really wanted to be one. He doubted any of the others had. But it was inevitable for those who controlled the old government to call their opponents "rebels." He'd known that from the start, just as he'd known where his first public expressions of discontent might lead.

They'd led here—to the men and women who had declared themselves the new Duma of Novaya Rodina and stated their determination to withdraw from the Federation . . . not without fear and trembling. There was something almost holy about the Federation, but a government was only a government, and surely its function must be to make the lives of its people better, not worse. The purpose of an elective assembly *couldn't* be to murder its own members!

Pieter had never met Fionna MacTaggart, but he'd corresponded with her over the light-years, and even from her recorded messages he'd felt the intelligence and determination which had made her the Fringe's leader. Had she done her job too well? Was murder the fate small minds always reserved for great minds they could not silence? He didn't know, but from the morning the news arrived, he'd known the Federation was doomed. Anything that rotten at its core deserved to die, and die it would.

If only communications were less chaotic!

Novaya Rodina had been supplied with a relay system during the Fourth Interstellar War, but the system had been much more important to the rest of the Federation then. The planet's most famous son, Ivan Antonov, had commanded the Grand Alliance's fleets during the critical, early days of desperate resistance to the Arachnids, and a lot of Fringe systems had been tied into the net for purely military reasons. But the postwar Assembly had given maintaining the *civilian* relays a far lower precedence, especially after the Corporate Worlds began manipulating the Assembly so blatantly, and, one by one, the Fringer components had been allowed to fall into disrepair. Fleet communications continued to move with reasonable speed, but only the far slower courier drones remained to service the civilian—and political—needs of worlds like Novaya Rodina.

And even those drones had become notoriously unreliable since the Kontravian Mutiny. No doubt many nav beacons had been shut down or destroyed, but it went further than that. The Corporate Worlds handled a tremendous percentage of the total drone traffic, just as they monopolized the freight lanes. Almost certainly they were tampering with the drones to keep the "rebels" disorganized.

Well, if he were in their position, he would probably do the same. But in the meantime, it left him with the devil of a problem! He cleared his throat, and the eyes around the table returned to his face.

"So there you have it, comrades," he said slowly. "The Federation has declared martial law and suspended *habeas corpus* . . . among other rights. And we—you and I, my friends—we are all rebels." He shrugged. "For myself, I realized this must come, but possibly some of you did not. So it is only fair that we reconsider what we have done, I think. We've made our gesture, voiced our protest. Is that all we wish to do? If so, we'd best dispatch a courier drone with apologies and renewed protestations of loyalty at once! But if we don't, if we continue as we've begun to follow the lead of the Kontravians, God alone knows where we shall end."

"Pieter," Magda Petrovna stroked her prematurely silvering hair, "you say you knew this would come. Do you think we were all fools, Pieter Petrovich?" She smiled in gentle mockery. "How noble of you to give us a choice! But tell us—what will *you* do when we all run crying home to *babushka* Terra?"

A soft laugh ran around the table, and Pieter smiled unwillingly; but he also shook his head.

"This is no laughing matter, Magda. This is life and death. Oh, we hold the cities and universities, but the farmers and ranchers think we're mad. They won't raise a hand if it comes to a fight—and we've little chance of defeating the Federation if they would!"

"Mega shit!"

The tart remark could come only from one man, and Pieter's eyes twinkled as he turned to Semyon Jakov, the single *megaovis* rancher in their Duma. The old man's blue eyes were fiery as he puffed his walrus mustache, looking as fierce as one of his huge, vaguely sheeplike herdbeasts.

"No way we could beat the Federation, no," he snapped, "but we won't be fighting the Federation—only an Innerworld rump, and well you know it, Pieter Petrovich Tsuchevsky! And they won't even have the full Navy. Damnation, man, the Kontravians took a task force—a *task force*—in one snap! D'you honestly think they haven't lost *more* ships? I wouldn't be surprised to hear they've lost half the Fleet by now, Pieter!"

"True, Semyon, but Novaya Rodina is no Navy base. There were no ships for *us* to seize; it was pure luck Skywatch supported us. They could've blown our leaky old tubs out of space—and those are still the best ships we can scare up. No, Semyon Illyich, whatever the Kontravians may have taken, *we* can't fight what the Federation can send here."

"But why send anything?" Tatiana Illyushina asked plaintively. "We're not exactly the richest of the Fringe Worlds!"

"No, Tatiana," Magda said gently, "but we *are* what the Fleet manuals call a 'choke point.'"

The others listened carefully. Semyon Jakov had been a Marine for fifteen years, but Magda had reached the rank of captain in Frontier Fleet before resigning in protest over the Assembly's policies.

"A choke point?" Tatiana asked.

"An especially valuable warp nexus," Magda explained. "The way the warp lines lie, some systems control access to several others. The Corporate Worlds are mostly on early choke points of the Federation. That's why they're so powerful; every ship to the Heart Worlds has to go through choke points they control."

Tatiana nodded. When it came to the *economic* implications of the Corporate Worlds' galactic position, every Fringe schoolchild understood.

"Well, the same thing makes choke points militarily important,"

Magda said "If Novaya Rodina goes over to the Kontravians, we'll block a whole section of the Fringe off from the Federation; they'll have to take this system before they can attack the others. But if we remain loyal to the Federation, the Fleet will have several possible avenues of attack into Fringe space to choose from, you see?"

"But . . . but in that case, they're *certain* to come here—aren't they?" Tatiana asked very quietly.

"They are," Pieter told her gently, "and soon, I think. They wouldn't have sent this—" he waved the official message form gently "—if they didn't mean to back it up. There's some pretty stiff language in here; if they planned on talking us back into the Federation, they'd've taken a more flexible initial position."

"I agree," Semyon said harshly, "and I say—fuck 'em! Let them come! There's twenty million people on this planet. It'd take half the Corps to hold us down!"

"Except that only eight million or so of them are actively on our side," Pieter begun, but Magda interrupted.

"It doesn't matter anyway, Semyon Illyich," she said with an affectionate smile. "Just because you grunts spend *your* time crawling around in the mud doesn't mean the Fleet does! They don't care about planets, only warp points and the normal space between them."

"So? They still need someplace to base ships!"

"Certainly," Magda nodded, "but what if a monitor drops into orbit and zeros a few missiles on Novaya Petersburg? Or Novaya Smolensk? You think we shouldn't surrender to keep them from firing?"

"Well . . ."

"Exactly, you old cossack!" Magda punched the old man's arm lightly.

"Are you saying we should just give up?" Jakov demanded incredulously.

"Did I say that? Certainly not! We've already sent off our own drones, so the rest of the Fringe knows what's happening. I'm only saying that if it comes down to ultimatums, we'd better decide what we'll do ahead of time. I don't want to believe a TFN commander would fire on civilians; it goes against all we've been taught. But he might. And I want us to know *now* what we're going to say to him to keep any itchy finger off the button."

"So what you're saying, Magda," Pieter cut in pacifically, "is that we should continue as we have, possibly even to fighting in

space, but that if it's a choice between bombardment and surrender, we should surrender?"

"Exactly." Magda's face was unusually grim. "I don't like it any
more than you do, Pieter—or you Semyon. But what alternative
do we have?"

"But what'll happen to us if we surrender?" Tatiana asked. "I
don't mean the rest of our people, I mean *us*, right here in this
room?"

"Hard to say," Magda said with a shrug. "There's never been a
case like this, and it's not as if we're the only planet to secede.
I'd think the government would have to follow a fairly lenient
policy—especially with any of us 'rebels' who surrender—if they
have any hope of ever healing the break. Unfortunately, we can't
depend on that."

"They might execute us?" Tatiana asked faintly.

"They might," Magda agreed calmly. "Of course, even under
martial law, any death sentence has to be confirmed by the civilian
authorities. I'd think that confirmation would be unlikely."

"All right," Pieter said suddenly. "I propose a vote. All those
in favor of declaring our immediate surrender?" There was no
response, although several uneasy glances were exchanged. "All
those in favor of continuing as we have but surrendering to avoid
bombardment?" A chorus of affirmatives ran round the table.
"Very well, the ayes have it."

Fedor Kazin watched the fields soak. Another day, at least,
before he could resume plowing. Well, there were advantages to
bad weather. Such as sitting with 'Tasha on a spring morning
instead of bouncing around in his poorly sprung tractor. If only
it weren't for those crazies in Novaya Petersburg! He had half a
mind to go talk to them himself.

He frowned and glanced over at his wife. Maybe he should.
After all, here he was cursing their stupidity, but had he done
anything to change their minds? They might just not realize
how others felt. And old Semyon Jakov was one of them . . . and
Andrei Petrov's girl, Magda. They were good people. Maybe he
could make them see reason?

Of course, 'Tasha would have a fit if he took himself off to the
city and left her and the boys alone with the planting. On the other
hand, if this madness wasn't settled, there wouldn't be a market
come harvest, now would there? He filled his pipe with Orion
tobacco (his one true luxury), and the pungent smoke curled up

around his ears. Yes, the idea of going to Novaya Petersburg to confront the Duma . . . it definitely bore thinking on. . . .

Admiral Jason Waldeck, of the Chartiphon Waldecks, regarded his subordinates so coldly they shifted uneasily under his glare.

"I don't want to hear any more crap about poor misunderstood Fringers!" he snapped. "They're mutineers and traitors—and that's all! That bastard Skjorning should've been shot. Might've nipped the whole damned thing in the bud!"

His officers remained prudently silent. Admiral Waldeck had never been a good man to cross, and it was far more dangerous now. News of the Kontravian Mutiny was still threading its way through the Fleet, but one consequence of it was already clear: moderation was not in great demand among TFN commanders. Indeed, any "softness" might well be construed as treason by the angry (and frightened) cliques of "reliable" Innerworld admirals.

"I don't give a good goddamn why they're doing what they're doing," he grated. "We've got to stop them, and Fleet's shorthanded as hell after the mutinies, especially in capital units and carriers. Hell, we've lost so many pilots there won't even be fighter cover for most operations! So it's up to us—understood?"

"Yes, sir," his juniors murmured.

"Good. Now, I don't expect these hayseeds to put up much resistance, but if they try, I want some examples made."

" 'Examples,' sir?" one officer asked carefully.

"Yes, Captain Sherman—examples. If anyone wants to fight, let 'em. Don't give them a chance to surrender till you've burned a few bastards down."

"But, sir . . . why?"

"Because these traitors have to learn the hard way," Waldeck said grimly. "The Assembly's finally gotten its head out of its ass, and we're under military law now. That means *my* law. And I'm going to teach these proles a little lesson in obedience. Is that *clear*, gentlemen?"

It was clear. They might not much like it, but it was clear.

"All right, then, Commodore Hunter, here's your first objective."

The cursor in the chart tank settled on a warp nexus, and Commodore Hunter squinted at the tiny letters. "Novaya Rodina," they said.

❖     ❖     ❖

"It's confirmed, Commodore. From the drive strengths, they have to be warships."

"I see." Magda Petrovna nodded as calmly as she could. They'd hoped someone would turn up from the Kontravians or one of the other Fringe systems before this, but Asteroid Four watched the warp point to Redwing, and Redwing was part of The Line, one of the fortified Terran-Orion border systems whose mighty orbital forts had remained loyal to the Assembly. She looked around her crowded bridge wryly. It only remained to see what strength the Fleet had scraped up. Her collection of armed freighters might—possibly—hold its own against light units, and Novaya Rodina's Provisional Government had short-stopped two mutinous light cruisers headed for the depths of the Fringe. But that was all she had; that and Skywatch.

She sighed. Unless the mutinies had hit really hard, there was no point even hoping. A single fleet carrier—even a light carrier—would eat her entire force for breakfast, and she hated to think what a few battlecruisers might do! But the worst of it was that she didn't *know*. Except for Skywatch, none of her units had long range scanners; without those, she could form only a vague impression of what was headed for her.

"Query Asteroid Four for exact drive strengths," she said suddenly.

"Sir," the commander of her cruiser flagship said as they awaited an answer, "those miners don't have the equipment for precision work—and an hour-long transmission lag doesn't help. Why not take *Jintsu* and *Atlanta* out and see for ourselves?"

"I appreciate your spirit, Captain," Magda said, peculiar though it felt to call a mere lieutenant "Captain" onboard a light cruiser, "but we can't take our only cruisers into scanner range all by themselves . . . and if we took the freighters with us, we couldn't run if we had to."

"Yes, sir." Lieutenant Howard blushed as he realized his commodore had just tactfully advised him to let her tend to her own knitting.

"Asteroid Four says they *think* they're all strength twelve or less, Commodore," her com officer finally said dubiously.

"Thank you. Any incoming messages from them?"

"No, sir. Nothing."

That was bad, Magda thought. No surrender demands? Did that mean they were unaware they were being scanned? Or that they had a pretty good notion of what she had and figured she meant to fight no matter what they said? And did she intend to fight? Exactly what had they sent against her?

Well, now, if they *were* strength twelve or less, then almost certainly there was nothing out there larger than a cruiser. If only Asteroid Four could relay the information directly onto *Jintsu's* cramped battle plot!

"We've got an amplification from Asteroid Four, Commodore. They make it three at strength eight to twelve and three strength six or below. They sound confident, too."

All right, Magda—think, girl! Strength six drives were destroyers. Strength twelves *could* be light carriers, but she doubted it. Too many fighter jocks were Fringers. Assume they were all cruisers . . . a heavy and two lights? They might make it a standard light battlegroup, if the CA were a *Goeben*. . . .

"Ask Asteroid Four if—"

"Commodore," her com officer's voice was very quiet, "they just went off the air in midsentence."

Magda closed her eyes. No messages, and they just casually polished off an unarmed listening post *en passant*. That sounded more like Orions than the TFN, but it resolved her dilemma. They'd drawn first blood; if she had any chance at all, she'd fight.

She thought furiously. Against command datalink, her own forces were at a severe disadvantage. The enemy ships would think, move, and fight as a single, finely meshed unit; her ships were not only more lightly armed, but they'd have to fight as individuals. On the other hand, she had over a dozen armed freighters, and her two light cruisers formed a datagroup with Skywatch, as long as they were in range—and Skywatch was a lot bigger than any CA, especially a *Goeben* with all that armament sacrificed in favor of data net equipment. Of course, if it *was* a *Goeben*, she'd also mount jammers to take out Magda's own datalink at close range.

All right, Just suppose she had them figured right—what did she do with them? They'd be in missile range of the planet in eleven hours, or she could go out to meet them. If she went out, she lost Skywatch; if she stayed, she lost maneuvering room. Decisions, decisions.

She drew a deep, unobtrusive breath and nodded to Lieutenant Howard.

"Captain Howard, the flotilla will assume Formation Baker. We'll wait for them here."

"Yes, sir," Howard's voice wasn't especially enthusiastic, and she felt a twinge of sympathy. Light cruiser captains were imbued with the notion of maneuver and fire—they hated positional battles.

"If I'm right," Magda said slowly, "there's a *Goeben* out there, Captain. I want maximum firepower laid on her as soon as we can range on her. If we can break their data group—and keep their ECM from breaking *ours*—we'll have a good chance. They'll outclass us ship for ship, but we've got the numbers. If we don't break them—" She shrugged.

"Yes, sir." He sounded more enthusiastic as he digested her plan. God, what she wouldn't give for a properly trained staff! But in another sense, she wouldn't trade these people for anything. They might be mutineers and traitors, but they'd put their lives on the line just to get here. There would never be any reason to question their devotion, and maybe enough of that could make up for their rough edges.

"Skywatch has them on scanners, Commodore!"

Magda jerked awake in her command chair as her chief scanner rating's voice burned into her dozing ears.

"Coming up from data base now, sir . . . Flagship's definitely a *Goeben*. She's *Invincible*, sir, and she's the only heavy! The other cruisers are strength nines—light cruisers! They're . . . *Ajax* and *Sendai*, sir!"

Thank God! They had a chance, but their losses were still going to be awful. She turned to Howard.

"Captain Howard, tune in your datalink. If those bastards don't say something soon, Operation Borodino is about to begin."

"Aye, aye, sir!"

The hours of waiting were suddenly minutes, flitting past like raindrops. Magda watched her plot, almost praying for a surrender demand. But there was nothing, and the range continued to drop.

"Enemy force launching missiles," her fire control officer said suddenly. So there it was. They didn't even *want* to negotiate.

"Stand by point defense," Magda said coolly. "Targets?"

"Tracks look like Skywatch, sir."

"Very well. Lay our own missiles on *Invincible*."

"Aye, aye, sir."

"Open fire!"

*Jintsu* quivered as her external ordnance let fly, and Magda's plot was suddenly speckled with flecks of light as *Atlanta* and

Skywatch flushed their external racks at the oncoming cruiser, as well. She felt her lips thin over her teeth. Even command point defense was going to have trouble with *that* lot, and she wondered if the loyalist commander knew Skywatch had taken delivery of antimatter warheads just before the mutinies? If he didn't, he'd be finding out shortly.

But incoming missiles were sleeting in at Skywatch, and there were a lot of them. Point defense crews aboard the cruisers and fortress tracked the incoming fire while battle comp sorted out the clean misses from the salvo, but there weren't many; orbital forts weren't very elusive targets. Then the small laser clusters trained onto the probable hits. Counter missiles zipped out, and for seconds space was wracked with brilliant flares of detonating warheads.

"Hits on *Invincible*!" Gunnery screamed. "One . . . three . . . *five* of them, sir! She's streaming air!"

But Skywatch's blip was pulsing, too, as missiles slipped through to impact on the big fort's powerful shields. Magda gripped her lower lip between her teeth, waiting as the brilliant dot flickered and flashed. Then the report came in.

"Eight hits on Skywatch, sir—all standard nukes. Took out most of her shields, but she's still in business!"

"Good!" Magda ignored the informality of the elated report. "Captain Howard, *Jintsu* and *Atlanta* will engage *Invincible* at close range. Captain Malenkov will come with us. The remainder will engage targets of opportunity among the enemy formation."

"Aye, aye, sir!"

The rebels lurched into motion. Only Malenkov's three big freighters could even hope to stay with a warship . . . the others were much too slow, and Magda had no choice but to turn the engagement into one huge melee and hope.

The two forces closed to energy weapon range, and the TFN loyalists were taken aback by the rebels' reckless courage. Those lumbering freighters were sitting ducks . . . but they were so god-damn *big*! They soaked up force beams and hetlasers as they bumbled into range for their own light armaments, and what they lacked in datalink they made up in determination and sheer volume of fire.

Commodore Hunter realized Admiral Waldeck had made a serious error in assuming they would face only local yokels. There *had* to be Fleet regulars or reservists over there! Well, the hell with standing orders! His own orders went out: break through and get free, then stand off with missiles where his datalink would do him the most good.

But as his ship merged with the milling freighters, Magda's careful briefings took effect. No one tried to *destroy* his vessels; instead they concentrated on battering down shields and armor just far enough to get at the datalink. As soon as a ship fell out of the link, fire shifted to someone else.

Commodore Hunter cursed as the first ship dropped out of his net. They were stripping away his coordination, and if his outnumbered units had to fight as individuals among that many enemies, they wouldn't stand a chance! But he didn't have much choice, because two light cruisers were lunging straight for him.

He watched in something very like awe as the rebel ships soaked up the fire from his own lights, homing on his wounded flagship. He saw hits going home all over them . . . both of them were streaming atmosphere . . . and *still* they came on. One suddenly staggered and yawed aside as she took a direct hit on a drive pod, but she hauled back on course and kept coming. He barked an order, and *Invincible* tried to turn away, but her crippled drive faltered. He looked back into his plot and swallowed as *Sendai* blew in half and the rebel cruisers closed to half a light-second, energy weapons aflame.

"Abandon ship!" he screamed—but he was too late. *Jintsu's* het-lasers zeroed in on his command deck with uncanny accuracy, and a burst of finely focused X rays tore him and his staff apart.

The battle collapsed into a mad, whirling ball of snapping ships. *Atlanta* exploded in a massive fireball, followed by *Ajax*. The surviving loyalists began a limping withdrawal, and a dozen gutted freighters drifted helplessly in their wake, glowing from the hits they'd taken . . . but there was a dead destroyer to keep them company. Skywatch streamed air through a dozen huge rents, but her energy weapons were still in action—some of them—and her missiles pursued the two retreating destroyers.

"Break off the engagement, Captain Howard," Magda Petrovna said wearily. He looked at her in surprise. *Jintsu* was hard hit, but half her weapons were still in action. "If we chase them and we're dead unlucky, we might catch them, Captain. Just us. We're the only ship that could."

Howard's face lit with understanding. "Yes, sir," he said.

"And send a message down to the planet," Magda said, looking at her battle plot. Better than half her "fleet" had been destroyed in the short, savage action, and all the rest were damaged. "Tell them we won—I think."

"And you mean to tell me," Admiral Waldeck said icily, "that a handful of armed freighters shot an entire light battlegroup to hell?"

The white-faced lieutenant commander across his desk stared straight ahead. Spots of color burned on his cheeks, but his voice was controlled.

"Not precisely, sir. There were also two Fleet cruisers and a class-three fort, if you'll remember. With antimatter warheads."

Waldeck flushed with fury. His lips worked, and the commander thought he'd gone too far. But the admiral gradually regained control.

"All right, Commander, the point is well taken," he said coldly. "But the fact remains that in the first engagement against rebel forces, we lost virtually an entire flotilla. Your ship will be out of action for months, and I doubt *Cougar* will ever fight again."

"Yes, sir."

"*We* were supposed to teach *them* a lesson!"

"Yes, sir."

"Well, by God, we *will* teach them one!" Waldeck punched up a com link to his flag captain. "Captain M'tana, the task force will move out in one hour. We're going to Novaya Rodina!"

"Yes, sir."

"And you, Commander," Waldeck returned his attention to the unfortunate in front of his desk, "are going to come along and see what three battlecruisers do to your precious rebels!"

"Well, Pieter Petrovich, that's that." Magda raised her glass of vodka in a tired toast. "After all the repairs we can make out of local resources, the 'Novaya Rodina Fleet' consists of one crippled light cruiser, one crippled OWP, and four crippled freighters. We *might* be able to hold this system against a troop of Young Pioneers."

"I see." Tsuchevsky's face was lined and tired. He was appalled by their losses; only Magda and Semyon had really had any concept of what a fleet action was like. "What do you think the chances are that the Kontravians will get here first?"

"Poor," Magda said grimly, refilling her empty glass carefully. "The Rump was surprised by the mutinies, but it still has an intact command structure and better communications. What do we rebels have? A handful of planets that are partially organized and tied together only by courier drones; it'll be a while yet before we can get beyond that point and start throwing task forces around."

"So all those people died for nothing," Pieter said sadly.

"Maybe, maybe not. You can't run your life on Russian melancholy and the second sight, Pieter Petrovich, and we know what would have happened if we *hadn't* fought. Still, I admit I'll be surprised if we have time to do much of anything else before the next TFN force arrives, and this time it'll be a battlegroup worth the name." She shrugged, but her voice was softer when she went on. "We did our best, my Pieter. Maybe we should have surrendered if they'd given us a chance, but they just opened fire."

"I know." He swiveled his chair to look out the window at the bright spring morning. "Well," he said heavily, "if they come back in force, we have no option but to surrender. Agreed?"

"Agreed," she sighed. "Those are good people up there, Pieter. I don't want to see them die uselessly."

"All right. Will you see to the communication arrangements, Magda?"

"I already did," she said with a tired smile. "After all, that's why I'm commodore of our magnificent fleet, isn't it?"

"Hush, Magda." Pieter grinned slowly. "Now *you're* being maudlin! Drink your vodka and cheer up. Things could be worse."

"What do you mean, going to Novaya Petersburg?" Natasha Kazina put her hands on her hips and glared at her husband. "Who do you think you are? Vladimir Lenin? You're maybe going to bore from within like a mole and topple the government?"

" 'Tasha, you *know* why I'm going—me and Vlad Kosygin and Georgi—we need to be sure those people understand what they're doing to us."

"Really?" Her voice dripped sarcasm. "And you think they don't already? Idiots! Firing on a Terran Fleet! Next thing you know, there'll be missiles on the cities, and there you'll be, playing *Menshevik* in the middle of it!"

"Hush, 'Tasha! You know I agree with you—but maybe they aren't all idiots, no? There are good people mixed up in this, *our* people. Let me go see them. Let me try to convince them they're wrong."

"Argue with the rain! It pays more attention!"

"Natasha, I'm going, and that's an end to it. Sure the Federation has problems, but this isn't the right answer! If I don't try to tell the Kadets that, I won't be able to sleep nights."

"Ahhh! Men—you're all idiots!" Natasha exclaimed, throwing up her hands in disgust. "But go! Go! Leave me and the boys to see to the planting! Just don't come crying to me when they don't listen!"

"Thank You, 'Tasha," Fedor murmured, kissing her cheek gently. "I knew you'd understand."

"Get out of my sight!" she told him, but her eyes twinkled as he backed off the porch. "And don't forget to bring home some new dress material!" she admonished in a parting shot as he climbed into Kosygin's chopper and it chirruped aloft.

Alarms whooped as the ships emerged from transit, and Magda watched her display in silence. At least they'd been able to mount proper instrumentation out there: no helpless miners to be vaporized this time! But the story her scanners told was heartbreaking. Ship after ship slid out of the Redwing warp point; three battlecruisers, two heavy cruisers, five light cruisers, and *fifteen* destroyers. God, it was an armada, she thought wearily, and tuned her communicator to Tsuchevsky's priority channel.

"Yes, Magda?" His eyes were puffy. She'd waked him up, she thought. Waked him from a sound sleep to face a nightmare.

"They're coming, Pieter," she said sadly.

"How bad is it?"

"If I order a shot fired, it will be as good as executing every man and woman in my fleet."

"All right, Magda," he said softly. "I understand. Patch me through to their commander, if you can. I'll handle it from here."

"I'm sorry, Pieter Petrovich," she said very quietly

"You did your best, Magda. Time was against us, that's all."

"I know," she said heavily, and turned to her com officer.

Pieter Tsuchevsky stared into the screen at Admiral Jason Waldeck, TFN. The admiral's cheek muscles were bunched, and Pieter shivered as he realized the man had *wanted* a fight.

"Admiral, I am Pieter Petrovich Tsuchevsky of the Provisional Gov—"

"You, sir," Waldeck cut in coldly, "are a traitor, and that is *all* you are!" Pieter fell silent, staring at him, and the admiral went on implacably. "I understand the purpose of this communication is to arrange your surrender. Very well. All ships in space will land immediately at Novaya Petersburg Spaceport. Any armed vessel incapable of atmospheric flight will lower its shields and await boarding by one of my prize crews. The same applies to what's left of Skywatch. Is that clear?"

"Yes." It took all of Pieter's strength to get out the strangled word, and Waldeck made no effort to hide his own savage satisfaction.

"As for your so-called 'Provisional Government,'" he sneered, "you will surrender yourselves to me as soon as my ships planet. There will be no exceptions. Anyone who resists will be shot. Is *that* clear?"

"Yes," Pieter managed once more.

"It had better be. I will see you aboard my flagship in three hours." Waldeck cut communications curtly, and Pieter stared at the blank screen for long seconds as he tasted the ashes of defeat.

"Look at that!" Fedor Kazin gasped as the chopper swooped past the spaceport after a ten-hour flight. The others turned and looked—and looked again. Novaya Petersburg Spaceport had never seen such a concentration of shipping. Fedor's index finger moved slowly from ship to ship as he counted.

"... twenty-three ... twenty-four ... twenty-five ... Twenty-five! And those big ones—are they battlecruisers, Georgi?"

"Yes." Georgi Zelinsky grunted. "My God, it's all over! There wouldn't be any grounded battlecruisers if it weren't. They're about the biggest warship that can enter atmosphere at all, and they have to take it mighty easy when they do. No commander lands them any place he might have to get out of in a hurry."

"Look!" Fedor said excitedly. "All the hatches are open—see? And over there! Look at all the *people!*"

"Yeah," Vlad said, squinting into his teleview. "All in uniform, too. Looks like they must've stripped the crews off the ships."

"They wouldn't do that," Georgi disagreed. "Not all of them. There has to be a power room watch on board."

"Yeah? Well *look* at 'em! They didn't leave many on board."

"You're right there." Georgi tapped his teeth, his mind going back over the decades to his own five-year hitch in the Navy. "Looks like they've mustered all hands for some reason. And over there—what's that?"

"That" was a long snake of civilians winding its way out from the city. Vlad swooped low over their heads. There were thousands of them.

"What do you think is going on?" he asked.

"Damned if I know," Fedor said slowly, "but I think better we should land and find out, no?"

"I think yes," Vlad agreed.

The helicopter landed quickly, and as the three farmers hurried over to the edge of the crowd something nibbled at Fedor's awareness. They were already merging into the front ranks of the long snake when he realized what it was.

"Look—no guns!" he whispered.

"Of course not," Georgi said after a minute. "They must've declared martial law while we were in the air. Martial law means no civilian guns."

"Well what about *us*?" Vlad whispered, tapping the heavy magnum automatic at his hip. It was a clumsy weapon, but Vlad was old-fashioned; he preferred a big noisy gun that relied on mass and relatively low velocities.

"I recommend," Georgi said, unbuttoning his coat and shoving his laser pistol inside, "that we get them out of sight—fast!"

Fedor tucked his own pistol (a three-millimeter Ruger needler with a ninety-round magazine) under his coat, then turned to the nearest townsman.

"What's happening, *tovarich*?" he asked softly.

"You don't know?" the townie looked at him with shock-hazed eyes.

"I just landed, *tovarich*. Came all the way from Novaya Siberia to talk to this Provisional Government."

"*Shhhhh!* Want to get yourself arrested, you fool?!"

"Arrested? For *talking* to someone?" Fedor blinked in astonishment.

"The whole bunch of 'em are under arrest," the city man said heavily. "We're occupied."

"Well, what're you all doing out here, then?"

"Orders," the townie shrugged. "I don't know. They landed two hours ago and went on the city data channels. Somebody named Waldeck—he says he's the new military governor. He ordered the head of every household in the city to be out here by seventeen hundred . . . he didn't say why."

"*Every* head of household?" Fedor blinked again at the thought.

"Right. So here we are."

Fedor looked up as the long column shuffled to a halt and began to spread. Anxious-faced Marines in undress uniform, armed with autorifles and laser carbines, dressed the crowd, but something was wrong here. Those men looked worried, almost frightened—but they'd *won!*

"*Hsst!* Look at those shoulder flashes!" It was Georgi, whispering right in his ear. "Not a Fringer among 'em!"

There was a great sigh from the crowd, almost a groan, and he looked to one side. More Marines were herding a group of fifty or sixty men and women into an open space between two of the battlecruisers. The newcomers were manacled, and when he looked more closely he recognized Magda Petrovna and Semyon Jakov among them.

"The Provisional Government!" someone whispered. "All of them—and the defense force officers!"

Fedor shook his head, trying to understand, and wiggled his way into the very front rank, staring over at the prisoners. He knew Magda well—he'd danced at her parents' wedding, too many years ago—and it angered him to see her chained like an animal. All right, so she'd broken the law! But she'd been provoked. It might have been wrong of her, but she'd only been doing what she believed she must!

There was another stir as the Marines drew back from the prisoners and formed a line between them and the crowd. They faced the prisoners vigilantly while the Navy personnel formed two huge blocks, separated by about ten meters, and a party of officers strode briskly down the open lane.

Fedor was no military man, but even he could figure out the tall man with all the sleeve braid was an admiral. But he wondered who the other officer—the black one arguing with the admiral—was? Whoever it was, they were going at it hammer and tongs. Finally the admiral gave a curt headshake and said something loud and angry, but Fedor was too far away to hear....

"Admiral, you can't do this!" Captain Rupert M'tana said yet again. "It's illegal! It violates all their civil rights!"

"Captain," Waldeck said savagely, "I will remind you—for the last time—that this planet is under martial law. And no one—I repeat, *no one*—rebels against the government, kills Navy personnel, and gets away with it on my watch! Especially not ignorant, backworld Fringe scum!"

"For God's sake, Admiral!" M'tana said. "You—"

"*Silence!*" Waldeck whirled on the dark-skinned officer, and his eyes snapped fire. "You will go to your quarters and place yourself under close arrest, Captain M'tana! I'll deal with you later!"

"I'm your flag captain," M'tana began angrily, "and it's my duty to—"

"Major," Waldeck turned coldly to a Marine officer. "You will escort the captain to his quarters!"

"Yes, sir!" The major had a thick DuPont accent, and his eyes were very bright. He saluted sharply, then jerked his head at M'tana as the admiral turned on his heel. M'tana could almost taste the Navy crews' confusion, but the Marine major tapped the butt of his laser meaningfully, and the flag captain knew it was hopeless. Sagging with defeat, he allowed the major to lead him away.

Waldeck didn't even watch him go. He had other things on his mind, and he mounted an improvised platform and turned to face the crowd of murmuring civilians. He gripped a microphone, his eyes bitter as he stared at them. The only way to avoid more bloodshed was to rub these stupid proles' noses in what happened when they rebelled. He looked at his own massed crewmen. Yes, and show *them*, too. Let them see what awaited those who defied them. He raised the mike.

"People of Novaya Rodina!" Fedor's head snapped around as the massively amplified voice roared. "You have rebelled against Federation law. You have harbored and abetted mutinous members of the armed services. Such actions are treasonous."

Fedor flinched from the harshness of the admiral's voice. Treasonous? Well, maybe technically—but a man could stand only so much. . . .

"By the authority of the Legislative Assembly, all civil law on this planet is hereby suspended. Martial law is declared. All public gatherings are banned until further notice. I now announce a curfew, to take effect at 1900 hours. Violators will be shot."

Fedor blanched. *Shot!* For walking the street?

"Before you stand the leaders of your rebellion against legitimate authority," Waldeck went on coldly. "As military governor of this planet, it is my responsibility to deal with these ringleaders."

He paused and glanced contemptuously at the prisoners.

"The Federation is just," he said then. "It extends its protection and support to those who obey our laws and justly deserved punishment to those who defy them.

"Now, therefore, as military governor of Novaya Rodina, I, Admiral Jason Waldeck, Terran Federation Navy, do hereby sentence these traitors to death!" A great silence gripped the crowd. "Sentence—" Waldeck finished harshly "—to be carried out immediately!"

Fedor couldn't believe his ears. This couldn't happen! Not in the Federation! It was a nightmare! It was ... it was an *atrocity*!

He stared at the scene before him, unable to comprehend, as two Marine privates took Pieter Tsuchevsky by the arms. He moved slowly, as if in shock, but held his head high. As he and his guards moved away from the group, two more privates singled out Tatiana Illyushina. The slender young woman drooped in their hands as she realized she would be next, yet she fought for control and tried to stand erect.

Paralysis gripped Fedor. He was suspended in disbelief, unable to think, barely able to breathe. He watched numbly as Tsuchevsky was turned to face the crowd. Six Marines with autorifles marched smartly out and took position before him, weapons at port arms.

"Firing squad!" a Marine officer shouted. "Present arms!"

Weapons clattered.

"Take aim!"

Butt plates pressed uniformed shoulders. Fedor felt something boiling in him against the ice, but still he could not move.

"Ready!"

The pressure building in his throat strangled him.

"Fire!"

Six shots rang out on semi-automatic.

It all happened in slow motion. Fedor saw Tsuchevsky's shirt ripple, saw great, red blotches blossom hideously as the slugs tore through his body, and Pieter Petrovich Tsuchevsky, Chief of the Duma, President of the Provisional Government of Novaya Rodina, jerked at the impact, then toppled like a falling tree.

And as he hit the ground, the pressure in Fedor Kazin burst. His sustaining faith in the Federation died in an agony of disillusionment, and his hand flashed into his coat.

"*Nooo!*" he screamed, and the heavy needler came free.

For one instant he faced them all alone, one man with a pistol in his hand and rage in his heart. Then the pistol rose. It lined on the burly admiral as he turned angrily towards the single voice raised in protest.

He never completed his turn. The needler screamed, and Admiral Jason Waldeck's uniform smoked under its hypervelocity darts. He pitched to the ground seconds behind Tsuchevsky, and the crowd went mad.

Fedor never knew who struck the first Marine, but the guards never had a chance as the screaming, kicking mob went over them. Here and there an autorifle spoke, a laser carbine snarled. The Marines didn't die easily, and they didn't die alone—but they died.

Fedor wasn't watching. He was racing across the open space, needler in hand, dashing for the guards who were already training their weapons on the helpless prisoners. He slid to a halt, bracing the needler with both hands as a laser bolt whipped past him, thermal bloom scorching his hair. A guard saw him and turned, his jaw dropping, but too late. A stream of needles spat from the weapon, and the guards went down like autumn wheat before Fedor's reaper.

Screams and shouts were everywhere. Weapons fired. Men and women beat Marines to death with fists and feet. Navy personnel scattered—only senior ratings and officers were armed, and they were outnumbered by hundreds to one. They fought desperately to bring their weapons into play, but they hadn't known what Waldeck intended, and they were just as shocked as the civilians. Their minds needed time to clear and adjust, and there was no time.

Fedor ran to the manacled prisoners.

"Are you all right?" he bellowed as Magda Petrovna picked herself up off the ground. She stared at him for a moment with burning eyes, then nodded sharply and snatched up a dead Marine's laser with her chained hands. Her voice rang out over the tumult.

"The ships!" she screamed. "Take the ships!"

Some of the crowd heard. They seized the weapons of their fallen enemies and fell in behind her, and their discordant yells coalesced into a single phrase, thundering above the bedlam.

"*The ships!*" they roared, and foamed forward in an unstoppable human wave behind a mutinous ex-captain and a farmer who had wanted only justice.

# IRONY OF POWER

Oskar Dieter blinked wearily and fingered the advance. The strains of a New Zurich waltz filled his office, but the soft music was at grim variance with the data on his screen, and he sighed and leaned back, pinching his nose and trying to shake himself back to a semblance of freshness.

It was hard. Catastrophe had followed disaster with monotonous regularity for months, and in his nightmares endless trains of courier drones whizzed towards Sol, packed with tidings of fresh calamity.

What was happening in the Fringe was bad enough, but affairs on Old Terra were little better. The Assembly had been stunned by the Taliaferro suicide, but not Dieter. His fellow Gallowayans might put it down to grief over the Jamieson Archipelago—which *was* a tragedy of staggering proportions—but Dieter knew better. Understanding, the terrible realization that the "game" had become real, had driven Simon's hand. Dieter almost pitied him . . . but only almost, and his face hardened as he wondered yet again how many others would die before the madness ended.

Yet Taliaferro's death only compounded the Federation's plight. His had been the dominating presence behind the Corporate World bloc for over thirty years, and now that superbly engineered machine was flailing itself to destruction . . . and threatening to take the Federation with it. The desperate survivors were haunted by guilt they could not admit even to themselves and terrified of its consequences. The succession battle was the most vicious Dieter had ever seen, yet whoever finally won would inherit only a corpse.

It wouldn't be very much longer before the ground swell of public opinion rolled over the politicos. Already the first combers were crashing through the Chamber of Worlds; a few more disasters, and it would become impossible for them to cling to power, and—

His communicator chimed, and he reached automatically for the button, eyes narrowing as he recognized the neatly groomed face of Oliver Fuchs, President Zhi's executive secretary.

"Good morning, Mister Dieter," Fuchs said politely. "Would it be convenient for you to meet with the President in his office this evening? At eighteen hundred, perhaps?"

"Why, of course, Mister Fuchs," Dieter replied slowly, and his thoughts raced. "Ah, might I ask what the President desires?"

"I'm sorry, sir, but he wishes to explain that to you himself," Fuchs said with a pleasantly diffident smile.

"I see," Dieter said even more slowly. "Very well, Mister Fuchs. I'll look forward to asking him in person."

"Thank you, sir. I'll tell him to expect you," Fuchs said, and the screen blanked.

Dieter sat and stared at it for a long, long time, and his mind was busy.

Fuchs was waiting in the Anderson House foyer when Dieter arrived at the presidential residence at 17:45. He whisked the visitor into an elevator with the skill of a veteran maitre d' and filled the short ascent with utterly inconsequential small talk, but Dieter noted a strange intensity in the secretary's eyes. Curiosity, or evaluation, perhaps. Whatever it was, it only added to the tension hovering within him.

The elevator deposited them outside Zhi's office, and Fuchs opened the old-fashioned manual doors and stood aside, waving him through, then closed them quietly behind him.

The office was a large room—huge, by Innerworld standards— furnished with all the sumptuous luxury due the Federation's head of state. To be sure, the power of the man who occupied it had waned over the decades, but the trappings of authority remained. And they weren't entirely a façade, Dieter reminded himself. Prime ministers came and went, but the president provided the state's stability, and he still represented the popular choice of the majority of the Federation's myriad citizens.

But Dieter had been here before, and his attention was not on the rich carpets and indirect lighting. It was drawn inevitably to the cluster of people sitting around the President's desk.

Zhi himself was a small man, shorter even than Dieter, though more sturdily built. He rose as Dieter approached, and his hand-clasp was firm, but his face bore the stigmata of strain.

"Mister Dieter," he said. "Thank you for coming."

"Mister President," Dieter returned noncommittally, glancing at the others, and Zhi smiled wryly.

"I believe you know most of these people, Mister Dieter," he murmured, and Dieter nodded, then bowed slightly to the group, his mind whirring with speculation.

Sky Marshal Lech Witcinski, commander-in-chief of the Terran military, responded with a curt nod, half-raising his burly body from his chair. His uniform was immaculate, and his blunt, hard features showed surprisingly little sign of the tremendous strain focused upon him.

Not so the man seated beside him. David Haley had aged appreciably in the past weeks, but his smile of welcome was far warmer than it once had been.

Dieter returned it in kind, then raised an eyebrow at the sharp-eyed man at the Speaker's left. Kevin Sanders, he thought musingly. Admiral Kevin Sanders, retired, one-time head of the Office of Naval Intelligence. Now wasn't *he* an interesting addition to this gathering? Even seated, Sanders managed to exude a sense of mingled composure and agility, like a lean, gray tomcat, and his amused eyes gleamed as if he could read Dieter's mind. And perhaps he could. Far more esoteric powers had been ascribed to him during his career.

The single person Dieter didn't know wore the space-black and silver of a vice admiral, and he felt a stir of admiration as he looked at her. Long, platinum hair rippled over her shoulders, and her eyes were a deep, almost indigo blue. She was certainly the most attractive flag officer he'd ever seen, he thought wryly, and held out his hand to her.

"Good evening, Admiral—?"

"Krupskaya, Mister Dieter," she said in a soft, clear voice. "Susan Krupskaya."

"Enchanted," he murmured, raising her hand briefly to his lips, and her own lips quivered in an amused smile.

"Well, then," Zhi said briskly, reclaiming Dieter's attention and waving him to a chair, "to business."

"Of course, Mister President. My time is yours," Dieter said, seating himself, and Zhi's sardonic smile surprised him.

"In more ways than you may suspect, Mister Dieter," he said softly, and Dieter's eyebrows crooked politely.

"I beg your pardon?" he said, but Zhi didn't respond directly. Instead he nodded to David Haley.

"Mister Dieter—Oskar—" the Speaker said, "I'm afraid we have you at a bit of a disadvantage. You see, the Minh Government has resigned."

Dieter managed to hide his surprise—barely. The government had fallen? Why hadn't he already heard? And how in the Galaxy had they kept the press from finding out?

"It won't be announced at once," Haley continued, "because, under the circumstances, it seems vital to follow the news with the immediate announcement of the formation of a new government." Dieter nodded. The last thing they needed was a prolonged ministerial crisis.

"Which brings us to you, Mister Dieter." President Zhi took over once more. "You see, when I asked Prime Minister Minh and Speaker Haley to recommend a successor to form a new government, they both suggested the same man: you."

This time Dieter's surprise was too great. His jaw dropped, and he stared at Zhi in disbelief. *Him?* He was a pariah, repudiated by his own long-time allies! They couldn't be serious!

"Mister President," he said finally. "I-I don't know what to say. I'm honored, but—"

"Indulge me a moment, Mister Dieter," Zhi said quietly. "Officially, I'm not supposed to have opinions in these matters, but, to speak frankly, there are no other choices. You, more than most, are aware that the Minh Government has been totally discredited. Indeed, the situation is worse even than you know, but the critical point—politically speaking—is that anyone else is unacceptable. To put it bluntly, Simon Taliaferro's associates are all tainted by their support of his policies, yet they remain a very potent force in the Chamber of Worlds. If we're to find an alternative to one of them, it must be someone who can gather support from both the Assembly moderates *and* the public. Someone like you."

"But, Mister President! I—"

"Oskar," Haley cut back in, "think a moment. You're a Corporate Worlder, yet you openly opposed Taliaferro's excesses. The Corporate World moderates will follow your lead, and so will the Heart World liberals. That gives you a power base, and the Taliaferro crowd can't very well oppose you without refocusing attention on their own mistakes."

"And, Mister Dieter," Witcinski put in, "you enjoy the support of the military." Dieter looked at him in astonishment, and the sky marshal shrugged. "I know. That's not supposed to be a factor, but we all know it will be. Your position on the Military Oversight Committee gives you a background knowledge which may be invaluable. And, if I may speak completely candidly, the Fleet views you as a moderate. As Prime Minister, you'd be tremendously reassuring to the bulk of the officer corps."

"*But,*" Zhi said warningly, "that same reputation is a two-edged sword. You *are* a moderate, and we need moderates, but we have a war on our hands. If you accept this office, you'll have to demonstrate that you're a war leader, as well."

"And how would I be expected to do that?" Dieter asked, eyes narrowing.

"By forming an all-parties cabinet," Haley said quietly, and Dieter nodded slowly.

Of course. Minh's government was associated solely with the extreme Corporate World interests, which was why it had to go. But its replacement must command broad support, and the only way to do that would be to combine all elements. Part of him quailed at the thought of exerting mastery over such a disparate gathering of interests, but he understood. And he was beginning to see why Zhi had turned to him.

"Mister President," he said finally, "why did the government resign at this particular moment? May I assume Admiral Sanders' presence has some bearing on that point?"

"You may," Zhi said heavily. He tugged at an earlobe and frowned. "I've asked Admiral Sanders to return from retirement and reassume direction of the Office of Naval Intelligence."

Dieter nodded mentally; he'd suspected as much. Whatever the immediate cause of the secession, the speed with which the Fringe had closed ranks behind the Kontravians spoke volumes for the degree of clandestine communication which must have been established long since among the Outworld governments. Yet no whisper of any of it had reached the Assembly, which pointed to a massive intelligence failure.

"I see." He regarded Sanders thoughtfully. "In that case, with your permission, Mister President, I'd like to ask Admiral Sanders a few questions before I give you my decision."

"I assumed you would. That's why I arranged to have the military represented," Zhi said dryly, waving a hand to proceed.

"Thank you. Admiral, I suspect the situation is even worse than most of my colleagues realize. Am I correct?"

"That depends, Mister Dieter," Sanders said carefully, "on just how bad they think it is. Off the cuff, however, I would have to say yes."

"Enlighten me, if you please."

"All right." Sanders eyed him measuringly. "Sky Marshal Witcinski could probably give you better figures on precise Fleet losses, but ONI estimates that in addition to TF Seventeen, at least fifteen percent of Battle Fleet has gone over to the rebels. Many additional units in Innerworld space have mutinied and attempted to join them, but we've been able to stop most of them. The cost in loyal units—" he met Dieter's eyes levelly, and Dieter felt an inner chill "—has been high.

"At the same time," he went on even more dispassionately, "we don't really know what's happened to Frontier Fleet. No drones are getting through to us from any of our bases in the Fringe, which, since the rebels control the intervening warp points and Fleet relays, may or may not mean they've changed sides. On a worst-case basis, we're estimating the loss of at least ninety percent of Frontier Fleet."

Dieter was staggered, though he tried to hide it.

"Fortunately," Sanders continued, "our large Innerworld bases have remained loyal and the rebels have to set up their command structure from scratch, which gives us time to activate the Reserve while they get themselves organized. On the whole, and given the greater mass of Battle Fleet's capital units, the tonnage balance probably favors the rebels by as much as thirty percent, but the ratio of firepower is a bit in our favor when Fortress Command is allowed for."

"I see. And Zephrain RDS?"

"Unknown, Mister Dieter," Sanders admitted. "The only hopeful news is that one of our Battle Fleet battlegroups *may* have gotten through to it."

"May?" Dieter asked sharply.

"May. Vice Admiral Trevayne's BG Thirty-Two was cut off at Osterman's Star when the mutinies began, and we've received an official Orion complaint of a TFN border violation at Sulzan, about four transits from there. In all probability, that was Trevayne, and if it was, and if he managed to avoid internment, and *if* the Orion district governor at Rehfrak was willing to let a force that powerful pass through his bailiwick, then he *may* have reached Zephrain. Unfortunately, the Orions have since closed their borders completely. Any sort of confirmation from them will be a long time coming."

Sanders shrugged, and Dieter nodded again. He'd met Ian Trevayne exactly once, when he appeared before the Oversight Committee, but the incisive man he remembered just might have taken a chance on violating Orion space . . . and he would have known exactly how important Zephrain was.

"But that's only the present situation," Witcinski said, breaking the brief silence. "It doesn't address the future."

"No," Sanders agreed, "and that's really Susan's area."

He nodded to Krupskaya, and her dark blue eyes met Dieter's as she took her cue.

"As you know," she said, "the Innerworlds have a tremendous industrial advantage over the Fringe, but more than seventy percent of all our warships came from Galloway's World."

Dieter felt his nerves tighten. He'd known this was coming, but that made it no more palatable.

"The Jamieson Archipelago attack may have been a mistake, politically speaking," Krupskaya continued, "since its 'barbarism' has generated such widespread shock and repugnance among the Innerworlds, but militarily it was brilliant. They knocked out more than ninety percent of the civilian yards as well as the Yard and all Reserve units mothballed there. We estimate that it would take two or three years for the rebels to set up any substantial yard capacity of their own, but *we* need time to rebuild Galloway's World. We can put the facilities there back into service faster than we could build new yards and their infrastructure on other planets, but it will be at least eighteen months—more probably two years—before we can even begin laying down new ships there.

"Which means, Mister Dieter, that—assuming the rebels *have* seized most of our bases in the Fringe—our current building capacity gives us no more than a twenty percent advantage over them. We believe we can expand existing yards faster than they can build new ones, but for the foreseeable future we're going to have to be very, very careful about risking losses, particularly, in light of their long construction times, among our heavy units."

"I see," Dieter said again, and another silence fell. God, it was even worse than he'd feared.

"But you asked why the government resigned," Zhi said finally. "Beyond the obvious erosion of its majority—of which, I'm sure, you are aware—and general military situation, we've suffered yet another reverse."

Dieter wondered if he really wanted to hear any more bad

news, but he nodded for Zhi to continue. Yet it was Witcinski who took over again.

"This morning, we received a message from Admiral Pritz-cowitski at Cimmaron," he said. "He and Admiral Waldeck had initiated local operations to suppress the rebellion in the immediate vicinity. Unfortunately, their first effort, directed against Novaya Rodina with light units, was badly defeated by some sort of jury-rigged defensive force. Admiral Waldeck proceeded at once with his entire task force to retrieve the situation. As of the time Admiral Pritzcowitzki's message was dispatched, Admiral Waldeck's next scheduled report was seventy-two hours overdue."

Dieter closed his eyes. It got worse and worse. No wonder Minh had resigned! When the Assembly learned all that he'd just learned, Minh would be lucky to escape impeachment.

"So that's the situation, Oskar," Haley said quietly. "We've had our differences, but I hope you know how much I've admired you in the past few months—and that I hate to ask this of you. But we need you."

Dieter didn't even open his eyes, and behind his lids he saw every agonizing step which had led him and the Federation to this pass. The military position was grimmer than even he had feared, and he knew how the Assembly would react when they discovered the truth. The existing fury over the "sneak attack" and "massacre" at Galloway's World would mix with panic. The war fervor which already gripped the Innerworlds would intensify rather than ease as they drew together in the face of danger—and so would the extremity of the Federation's war aims.

If he accepted Zhi's request and formed a government, it would be a war government. It could be nothing else, and he would have to prove his own determination to achieve victory or go the way Minh had already gone. It would be the final, bitter irony of the political odyssey he'd begun when he broke with Simon. He, who had thrown away his career in an effort to preserve the peace, would be elevated to the highest office of the Assembly and charged with fighting the very war he'd tried to prevent!

"I realize we're asking you to make bricks with a very limited supply of straw, Mister Dieter," Zhi said, even more quietly than Haley, "but Speaker Haley is right. We *need* you. The Federation needs you—as the one man who may be able to form a stable government and as the one prime minister who may be able to control the extremism already rampant in the Assembly."

Dieter winced, for that was the argument he'd most feared to face. Zhi's violation of the president's traditional neutrality in such matters only underscored the point; if any of Taliaferro's old associates took the premiership, any chance for moderation would vanish . . . and he still had not paid his debt to Fionna.

He drew a deep breath. His wildest dreams had never included becoming prime minister—and certainly never like this! And yet, ironic as it was, he had no choice. He opened his eyes and looked at President Zhi.

"Very well, Mister President," he sighed. "I'll try."

# DECLARATION

"Novaya Rodina, eh?" Ladislaus Skjorning watched the blue and white planet as the crew of the TFNS *Howard Anderson* brought their ship into orbit. "I take it you're finding this a strange spot for a convention of traitors, Admiral Ashigara?"

His eyes touched briefly upon the empty right cuff of the woman standing beside him. Analiese Ashigara was every bit as taciturn and unyielding as her severe exterior and precise Standard English suggested, but he felt a strange kinship for the hawk-faced woman with the almond eyes and white-streaked hair who'd given a hand for her beliefs.

"I would have expected the convention to convene on Beaufort," she said calmly. "Beaufort is, after all, the home of the rebellion." It was like her, Ladislaus thought wryly, that she never resorted to euphemisms.

"Aye, I can see why you might be thinking that, but Beaufort is too far from the frontiers. We've no command structure at all the now, and until we've had the creating of one, we're to need the shortest courier drone routes we can be finding. Novaya Rodina's well located for that."

"Yes, I can see that. But I think perhaps there is more to it than that, Mister Skjorning."

"Aye, there is. As you've said, Beaufort's to be a logical place—if it were a Kontravian rebellion we're after having. But we're after making this a Fringe-wide movement, so holding our convention somewhere else should be helping along a sense of unity, you see. I've the thinking it's Beaufort's to be the capitol of whatever it is we're to have the building of, but it's not the place to be declaring what we are."

771

"That seems sensible," Ashigara said, nodding slowly.

"Aye. But there's to be another reason. Have you had the hearing of the term 'bloody shirt,' Admiral Ashigara?"

" 'Bloody Shirt'? No, Mister Skjorning, I cannot say that I have."

"It's to be an old Terran political term, Admiral, and what it's to mean is appealing to emotions on the basis of lost lives and hatred." Ladislaus' face was grim. "It's not a tactic I'm proud to be using, but it works; and Novaya Rodina's after being the best place to be doing it."

Analiese Ashigara shook her head slowly. "I am more happy than ever to be a simple Fleet commander, Mister Skjorning. My mind does not work the way this business of creating a government appears to require."

"Don't be feeling any loss over it," Ladislaus said very quietly. "It's not to be something I ever thought to have the doing of, either."

He fell silent, watching the planet a moment longer, then left the bridge, and Admiral Ashigara turned her attention to the final approach maneuvers of her undermanned task force. No, she thought. She did not envy Ladislaus Skjorning at all.

The horde of delegates crowded the huge auditorium, their rumbling voices filling it like a solid presence, and the surviving Duma stood behind Ladislaus on the stage, surveying their visitors with slightly dazed eyes.

Magda Petrovna stood at his elbow, her mobile face quite still. Only Ladislaus knew she intended to resign from the Duma to accept a commission in whatever they were going to call their navy, and only Magda sensed how much he envied her freedom to do just that. But it wasn't freedom for her; it was flight.

She knew her own strengths: a flair for organization, levelheadedness, moral courage, and compassion. But she also knew her weaknesses: blunt-spokenness, a tendency towards autocracy with those unable to keep up with her thoughts, and a well-developed capacity for hatred, and she felt that hate within her now, though few of her friends saw it or recognized it as the inevitable by-product of her compassion.

She'd been able to accept her own sentence of death, but not the brutality of Pieter's murder. Not the cruelty which had nearly snapped Tatiana Illyushina's sanity. That had been too much, yet as long as she'd believed only Waldeck's madness was responsible, she'd maintained a degree of detachment.

But then the provisional government had found the special instructions from the Assembly in his safe.

Waldeck need not have acted on them, but giving men like him such an option was like giving a vicious child a charged laser, and she would never forget that the Assembly had done so. She would never be able to flush the hatred from her mind if ever she must deal with that government. Besides—she felt herself smile affectionately—there was a better choice to head the Duma now. Well, two, perhaps, but Fedor would kill himself first! No, only one person had emerged from the day of the riots as Pieter's true successor, and that person was Tatiana Illyushina.

Magda glanced at the slim young woman. Daughter of one of Novaya Rodina's very few wealthy families, Tatiana had never faced the hard side of life before the rebellion. Then the earthquake shocks had come hard and fast, but Tatiana, to her own unending surprise, had met them all. Her oval face was still as beautiful, she looked as much like a teenaged child as ever, but there was flint behind those blue eyes now. Flint and something else, something almost like Magda's own compassion, but not quite.

But now, as acting Duma President, Magda had been granted a unique moment in history, and she stepped up to the lectern at Ladislaus' tiny nod. She drew a deep breath, and her gavel cracked on the wooden rest under the microphone. The sound echoed through the auditorium.

"The first session of this convention of the provisional governments of the Fringe will come to order," she said.

"Well, Ladislaus, what do you think?" Magda refilled their vodka glasses and hid a smile as he picked his up cautiously. "Will it work?"

"Aye, I'm thinking it will." Ladislaus sipped his second glass far more slowly as Magda threw back her own in approved Novaya Rodinan fashion. "It's not as if any of us have the thinking we can go back again."

He looked meaningfully around the small gathering of the Convention's crucial leaders.

"But it doesn't necessarily follow we can act together," Tatiana said. "Agreeing to hate the Corporate Worlds, yes." She smiled tightly. "But we're all so different! What else do we have in common?"

"Don't be underestimating the strength of hate, Ms. Illyushina." Ladislaus' answering smile was bleak. "But that's not all we're to be having. I'm thinking we're to have a better understanding of what the Federation is supposed to be than the Rump has. We're agreed in that."

"True." Magda's cold voice raised eyebrows, but she leashed her rage and leaned back. Then she laughed. "Has it occurred to anyone else that *we're* not the radicals? We're the conservatives—*they're* the ones who've played fast and loose with the Constitution for over a century!"

"Aye, so Fionna had the saying, often enough," Ladislaus nodded. "And we've no hope of building something really new—not in the time we're to have. So it's something old we must be building on."

"So *that's* why you brought this along," Li Kai-lun mused, tapping the sheets of facsimile on the table and nodding slowly. His reaction pleased Ladislaus. Hangchow's diminutive chief convention delegate was not only her planetary president but a retired admiral, as well. His support—political and military—would be literally priceless in the weeks ahead.

"Aye." Ladislaus ran a fingertip over the ancient lettering. "It's a federal system we're needing, Kai-lun. Centralization was the Corporate Worlds real error. It's to give the government the most power, but it's to concentrate too much authority in one place—and even with relays, slow communications are to make it clumsy in responding to crises . . . or people."

"Agreed," Li said, then smiled. "And at least *this* constitution's got a good track record. If I remember my history, the United States did quite well for itself before the Great Eastern War."

" . . . and if fight we must, let it be under a common standard! I move to appoint a committee to select a suitable device for our battle flags."

The stocky delegate from Lancelot swirled the brilliant cloak of his hereditary rank and sat, and Magda sighed. She found the barons and earls of Durandel rather wearing, but he might have a point—even if he was inclined towards purple prose.

"Very well. It has been moved that we appoint a committee to design a flag for our new star nation," she said. "Is there a second?"

"I second the motion, Ms. Chairman." Magda blinked as Li Kai-lun spoke up. Now why was *he* supporting a motion which could only waste precious time and energy? She shrugged mentally. Undoubtedly he had a reason.

"Very well. It has been moved and seconded that we appoint a committee to design a flag. All those in favor?" A rumble of "Ayes" answered. "Opposed?" There was not a sound. "The motion is carried. Mister Li, would you be so kind as to take charge of the matter?"

"Of course, Ms. Chairman."

"Good. Now, to return to our agenda. . . ."

"But why, Ladislaus?" Tatiana demanded. "We have so many other things to do, why waste time designing a *flag*, of all things?"

"Well," Ladislaus rumbled, "you might be noticing who Kai-lun had the recruiting of for his committee."

"What? Who?" Tatiana asked, but Magda laughed suddenly.

"*Now* I understand! Very neat, Lad! And how did you put Baron de Bertholet up to it?"

"Jean de Bertholet isn't after being the worst sort, Magda. It's on our side he is, and he understands entirely."

"Well *I* don't," Tatiana said.

"You would if you'd seen the membership of that committee," Magda chuckled. "Between them, Lad and Kai-lun have shunted most of the 'noblemen' in the Convention off to a harmless flag-designing mission."

"Aye," Ladislaus nodded. "Not that I really think they're after creating a new hereditary aristocracy for us all, but it's not to be hurting a thing to be certain of it when the Constitution's debated, now is it?"

"Ladislaus," Tatiana said sternly, "you're an underhanded, devious man."

"Aye," Ladislaus agreed calmly. "That I am."

"Ladislaus," Magda said, "I'd like you to meet Rupert M'tana."

Ladislaus looked up from his paperwork and frowned at the dark-skinned officer. M'tana returned an equally measuring look, and Ladislaus propped one elbow on a chair arm.

"Captain M'tana," he rumbled thoughtfully, "you're to be the senior prisoner, I'm thinking?"

"Yes, sir. I was Admiral Waldeck's flag captain."

"I see." Ladislaus' lips twisted in distaste despite himself.

"Just a moment, Lad," Magda said quietly. "I think, perhaps, you don't entirely understand. At the time of Pieter's execution, Waldeck had placed Captain M'tana under close arrest."

"Aye?" Ladislaus' blue eyes returned to M'tana's face, even more thoughtful now. "And why might that have been, Captain?"

"I . . . disagreed with his decision, Mister Skjorning."

"I see," Ladislaus said in an entirely different tone. He waved at two chairs and M'tana and Magda sank into them. "I've memory enough of my time in the Fleet to be understanding how far you must have pushed him, Captain. But, if I may have the asking, what's to be bringing you here?"

"The captain has a suggestion, Lad—a good one, I think," Magda said. "He approached me with it because we're both Navy or ex-Navy and we've come to know one another pretty well."

"Ah?" Ladislaus cocked a bushy eyebrow. "And just what is it you and the captain are after cooking up here, Magda?"

"It's like this, Lad. Like Beaufort, we had a number of . . . friends in various places in the Innerworlds. We spent years cultivating that network, but now that actual fighting's begun, we're cut off from it."

"Aye," Ladislaus nodded. "We're to have the same problem at Beaufort."

"Right. Well, Captain M'tana may have come up with a way to put part of our network back on line."

"Have you, now?" Ladislaus bent a hard look on M'tana. The captain shifted slightly in his chair but met it unflinchingly.

"Yes, sir. Understand something, Mister Skjorning. I'm an Innerworlder—a Heart Worlder—but when my people settled Xhosa, they didn't exactly do so completely voluntarily. I think we knew something about oppression, then, but we've forgotten since. We should have remembered, and that means we have a responsibility here. I don't want to see the Federation torn apart; in that respect, at least, you and I will never agree. But what I want and what's going to happen are two different things. There's no way to paper over the cracks this time—too much blood's already been shed.

"So as I see it, I can either join my fellow prisoners in refusing to give you any aid while we wait hopefully for repatriation and—with luck—another chance to contribute to the killing, or I can help you people. Not because I love your rebellion—I don't—but because the sooner the Federation realizes it can't win even if it defeats you militarily, the better."

"I see." Ladislaus grinned slowly. "Captain, I've the thinking I'm to like you—and I'm betting that's not to matter a solitary damn to you. But you've the right. It has gone too far for healing. So how is it you're to be helping?"

"What Captain M'tana suggested to me," Magda said, "ties in with our plans to allow correspondence between prisoners and their families. We'll give him the codes and address of our contact on Xhosa and his 'letters home' will reopen our best conduit."

Ladislaus studied M'tana's face, seeking some sign of treachery, any intent to betray. He saw exactly nothing.

"You're to have the knowing, Captain," he said quietly, "of the penalty if the Federation is ever to be finding out about this?"

"I do," M'tana said flatly. "But I know—now—what the Assembly's done to you people, and my oath is to the Federation, not just its government. If I can help shorten the war and reduce the killing, I have to do it. Besides—" he looked uncomfortable "—I don't enjoy killing Terrans, Mister Skjorning, not even ones who are technically traitors."

"I see," Ladislaus said yet again. Then he added slowly. "Let's have the discussing of the details, then, Captain...."

Stanislaus Skjorning waited patiently as the armed guard checked his ID. Some of the brand new Republic's citizens were already muttering darkly about "imperial trappings" and "new aristocracies," but for most, the memory of Fionna MacTaggart's assassination was still too recent, too raw. And here on Novaya Rodina, there was the Tsuchevsky murder, as well. Like Stanislaus, most people were more than willing to put up with armed security and ID checks to prevent still more murders.

"Thank you, Lieutenant." The guard handed his ID folio back. She wore the uniform of a Federation Peaceforcer, but the Federation patch had been removed from the right shoulder and replaced with the plain, unrelieved black shield Novaya Rondina had adopted in memory of Pieter Tsuchevsky. "The President is expecting you."

"Thank you, Sergeant." Although Stanislaus had left the Beaufort System only three times in his entire life before this trip, his deep voice carried only a hint of his older brother's famous accent. Of course, he had less need to make a statement about who he was than Lad did these days.

"The elevator is through the foyer and to your left," the Peaceforcer said helpfully, pressing the button to open the powered door. "And," she smiled faintly, "inside security's got us on visual now. You're cleared all the way through to the dining room."

"Thank you," he repeated with another smile, and stepped through the open door.

The elevator delivered him quickly and smoothly to the eighth floor of what had been Novaya Petersburg's best hotel. Of late, the Sherevenko Arms had been renamed "Convention Hall," and its suites were packed to the bursting point with delegates from other worlds. The staff had taken it in stride and was managing—somehow—to maintain the Sherevenko's reputation for attentive service, but he noticed raw fiber optic cable runs running along the tops of the corridors' panelled walls. The Constitutional Convention's technicians had been busy upgrading the hotel's communications systems for over two weeks now.

Another guard glanced at him alertly as he approached the dining room door, but the sentry only nodded as he stepped past, and Stanislaus' lips quirked in a wry smile. He wasn't exactly the hardest person in the galaxy to recognize, he supposed. Like Ladislaus, he had the Skjorning nose, and he was a good six centimeters taller than even his brother.

"Stanislaus!" Ladiuslaus Skjorning rose with a smile as his brother entered the private dining room. He walked around the table to shake hands, then threw both arms around Stanislaus in a bear hug. "Father wrote me you were to be coming, but his wording never said you were to be here this quickly!"

"My orders came through sooner than expected," Stanislaus said, hugging back. He clapped his older brother on the back, then stood back, hands on Ladislaus' shoulder and examined his face carefully.

"You're to be looking more worn than I'm liking, Lad," he said quietly.

"Aye?" Ladislaus' smile went crooked, and he shrugged. "I've the hearing there's to be a lot of that going about these days. And will be, for quite a while, I'm to be thinking."

He started to say something else, then changed his mind with another shrug and turned Stanislaus to face the other two guests sitting at the table. "Stanislaus, be known to President Li Kai-lun of Hangchow and to Ms. Tatiana Illyushina, President of the Duma. Kai-lun, Tatiana, this is to be my baby brother."

"It must be something in the Beaufort water," President Li murmured, gazing up at Stanislaus' towering centimeters as he shook hands. "But how do you all avoid nosebleeds at that altitude, Ladislaus?"

"Pay no attention to him, Lieutenant Skjorning," Illyushina said sternly as she shook hands in turn. "He's been making sizeist remarks ever since he arrived."

"Has he, now?" Stanislaus' smile broadened as he took in the Duma president's blue-eyed beauty. "Well, it's used to it we are, the both of us. I've the thinking that envy can be an ugly thing."

Li laughed, and Ladislaus shook a finger at his brother.

"You'll not be setting my diplomatic efforts back that way, Stanislaus. Even if it *is* to be truthful you are!"

"That's all right, Lad," Li said, dark eyes glinting wickedly. "I know something the lieutenant doesn't. And, secure in my secret information, I intend to await his well-deserved comeuppance with gleeful anticipation."

"You do, do you?" Illyushina looked at Li speculatively. "And what sort of 'secret information' would that be?"

"If I told you, it wouldn't be secret anymore, would it?" Li said smugly.

"I tried, Lieutenant!" she told Stanislaus with a chuckle, "but I'm afraid he was too smart for us."

"Well, as to that," the corners of Stanislaus' eyes crinkled with amusement as he smiled down at her, "I wouldn't be so very sure he really is to know something I'm not." He shook his head, then looked back at Li. "I've already gotten my orders, Mr. President," he said, Beaufort accent vanishing completely.

"Drat," Li said comfortably.

"Orders?" Ladislaus repeated, looking at Stanislaus speculatively as he waved his brother into a chair between his own and Illyushina's.

"Aye." Stanislaus settled a bit carefully into the chair. Furniture on most worlds wasn't built with the bulk of a Skjorning in mind . . . as he had already rather abruptly discovered since his arrival on Novaya Rodina.

"What President Li meant," he continued as the chair creaked but stood up manfully to the strain, "is that I've been assigned to the Marine detachment aboard *Longbow*."

"You have?" Illyushina frowned. "But you just got here, didn't you?"

"This morning," Stanislaus agreed, unfolding his napkin and draping it across his lap. "From what they tell me, though, the Navy's been raiding the crews which came over more or less

Intact for cadre for other units. Which means they have to find replacements for the transfers somewhere."

"Then I'm thinking they'll just have to be making do with such as you, and a sad thing it's to be, too," Ladislaus sighed, but there was a twinkle in his eye.

In fact, Stanislaus had held a captain's commission in the Beaufort Peaceforce, and one of his few trips off world had been to spend eighteen months on active duty as a Federation Marine as part of his training. Where, as Laidislaus knew perfectly well, he had received glowing evaluations from all of his superiors and promises of rapid promotion if he would accept a regular Marine commission.

"Aye," Stanislaus agreed mournfully. "Still," he brightened visibly, "I understand Captain Li runs a taut ship. She won't let anyone pick on me, I'm sure."

"Oh, of *course* not!" President Li agreed.

"Well, if it's assigned so quickly you're to be, the more reason for us to be snatching what time together we can," Ladislaus said more seriously. "How long are you to be having before reporting?"

"*Longbow*'s out on maneuvers at the moment," Stanislaus said. "I understand she's due back in sometime the day after tomorrow, and I'm to report on board when she enters orbit again."

"That isn't very long," Illyushina observed. Stanislaus looked at her, and she shrugged. "I mean, you won't have time to see much of my planet before they drag you back off it again, Lieutenant."

"Aye," Stanislaus said, and sighed gustily. "Still and all, I'm to be thinking as how, with time to be so short and all, it might be more of it I could be seeing with a local guide to be showing it to me." He looked earnestly at the head of Novaya Rodina's government. "Would you be knowing where I might be finding such, Ms. Illyushina?"

"Well, Chang?" Commodore Li Han tipped back her chair in *Longbow*'s briefing room as she regarded her chief of staff. Commander Robert Tomanaga, her new battlegroup operations officer, sat beside Tsing, and the pair of them were flanked by Lieutenant Commander Esther Kane and Lieutenant David Reznick, Han's staff astrogator and electronics officer.

"Commander Tomanaga and I have gone over the Fleet ops plan, sir," Tsing replied. "We'll know better after we run it on the tac simulator, but for now, it looks solid."

"You agree, Commander?" Han turned her eyes to Tomanaga.

"Yes, sir. Oh, we could use more weight of metal, but quality counts more than quantity." He grinned, and Han frowned mentally, bothered by his brashness and wondering if her worry was justified. Tomanaga was certainly qualified on paper; but *all* of her staff officers were qualified "on paper," with no real experience in their new positions. Nor did *she* have any, and with an inexperienced staff under a commodore who was herself as green as grass . . . She hid a shudder and nodded calmly.

"Run it down for us, Commander," she said.

"Yes, sir. First, I'd like to put our own operation in perspective to the overall situation. Our operational problems are complicated enough, but we *think* the Rump's are worse. So far, about seventy percent of Frontier Fleet has come over or been taken by our units, and it looks like we've got about twenty percent of Battle Fleet, too, but our forces are scattered all over the Fringe. With only drones for communication, concentrating them for operations is going to take time and, for the immediate future, our units here at Novaya Rodina constitute Admiral Ashigara's full disposable strength."

Han stifled an urge to hurry him up. There was time, and it was better to be sure her entire staff understood Fleet HQ's viewpoint.

"Admiral Ashigara's intelligence people estimate that the Rump has suffered losses we don't know about, and that fighter losses have probably been *extremely* high because so many fighter jocks were Fringers. That's a bit speculative, sir, but it matches our own experience. At any rate, the Rump is undoubtedly strapped for striking forces, but has the advantage of an intact command, better communications, and the interior position; they can move what they have from point to point faster than we can shift around the periphery.

"Our own immediate strategic need is to secure our frontiers before the Rump begins to recover, for which purpose Fleet plans a series of attacks on choke points. Our own operation against Cimmaron will cut off four separate Rump axes of attack,"

He touched his panel, and the briefing room lights died. A hologram appeared over the table, and light from the tangled warp lines glittered briefly in his eyes as he picked up a pointer.

"Here's Cimmaron," he touched a tiny light dot. "Only two transits away via Redwing, but Redwing's covered by The Line.

'The forts are cut off now, but Fleet prefers to isolate them rather than attack them."

Han felt a mental nod circle the table. No one wanted to tangle with *those* forts.

"So," Tomanaga went on, "we'll go from Novaya Rodina to Donwaltz—" his pointer hopped from star to star as he spoke "—to MXL-23 to Lassa to Aklumar to Cimmaron—a much longer route, but one we own as far as Aklumar. Because of its length, we're going in with only carriers, battlecruisers, and light units, since battle-line units would slow us by thirty percent. On the other hand, there are no fortifications at Aklumar—thanks to the Treaty of Tycho—and they won't know we're coming, so we ought to retain the advantage of surprise until the moment we hit Cimmaron."

He laid the pointer aside and brought the light back up.

"Our best analysis of the defense is a guess," he admitted, showing an edge of concern at last. "The Fleet base's fixed defenses are negligible, but Cimmaron Skywatch is quite heavy: eleven type-four orbital forts, three covering the Aklumar warp point. Before the mutinies, there was also a strong OWP-based fighter force, and despite Fleet's estimate, there's no guarantee they haven't brought their fighter strength back up. They must be as aware of Cimmaron's strategic value as we are, so the system undoubtedly has priority for reinforcements."

He paused to let the numbers sink in, then went on.

"What *we* have, after essential detachments, is two battlecruiser groups (ours and Commodore Petrovna's) and four carrier groups with approximately three hundred fighters embarked, plus escorts. The balance of force should be with us, but our edge is slim and we don't have any superdreadnoughts or monitors. Without them, the battlecruisers will have to keep Skywatch occupied until the carriers can stabilize their catapults and launch."

All of them knew what that meant. Type-four OWPs were big and powerful, stronger than most superdreadnoughts. It was statistically certain some of the battlecruisers wouldn't be around to see the fighters launch.

"That's the bare bones of the plan," Tomanaga continued after a moment. "We're transporting several hundred crated fighters to hold the system once we have it, because half the carriers will have to pull out for Bonaparte and the Zephrain operation while the rest move on Gastenhowe. Other attacks should clear up additional choke points at the same time, but Cimmaron and

Zephrain are the really critical ones. We need more depth to protect Novaya Rodina, and Fleet wants to deal with the research station as soon as possible."

"Thank you Commander," Han said quietly as he finished, then looked around once more, evaluating reactions.

Captain Tsing looked merely thoughtful, but he was a bulky, impassive man, virtually incapable of revealing much emotion. He was always simply Tsing—unreadable, phlegmatic, and utterly reliable.

Tomanaga looked confident. It was, after all, an ops officer's job to exude confidence, and certainly one could not dispute the neatness of the plan . . . assuming one could subordinate one's own survival to the other objectives. It seemed Tomanaga could do that—which could be a flaw in an ops officer. Best to keep an eye on him.

Lieutenant Commander Kane's eyes were intent, her lips pursed as she toyed with a lock of short-cut chestnut hair. Han had watched her jotting notes as Tomanaga spoke; now her stylus ran down the pad, underscoring or striking through as she rechecked them. Han put a mental question mark beside Kane's name, but she was inclined to approve.

She turned finally to Lieutenant (junior grade) David Reznick, by far the youngest member of her staff, and perhaps the most brilliant of them all. At the moment, he was frowning.

"You have found a difficulty, Lieutenant?"

"Excuse me?" Reznick looked up and blinked, then flushed. "Could you repeat the question please, Commodore?"

Han hid a smile. It was difficult not to feel maternal towards the young man. "I asked if you'd found a difficulty,"

"Not with the ops plan, no, sir, but I'm a little worried about the electronics."

"Ah?" She regarded him thoughtfully.

"Er, yes, sir. *Longbow* wasn't designed as a command ship. We squeezed everything in by pulling those two heavy launchers, but the whole datalink setup is jury-rigged. It's put together with spit, prayers, and a lot of civilian components, sir, and we're spilling out of the electronics section. If we have to slam the pressure doors, we'll lose peripherals right and left."

"But the system does work?"

"Uh, well, yes, sir. Works fine. The thing is, if we start taking hits the whole shebang could go straight to shi—um, that is, the system could go down, sir."

Han couldn't quite hide her smile, and Reznick flamed brick red before his sense of humor rescued him. Then he grinned back, and Han's last real concern vanished as a chuckle ran around the table. The chemistry was good.

"Very well, David." She drew a pad and stylus toward her. "Give me a worst-case estimate and let's come up with ways around it."

"Yes, sir." He opened a thick ring binder and flipped pages. "First of all Commodore . . ."

"But, Lad, you got *your* Constitution adopted, and we're adopting *your* Declaration," Li Kai-lun said reproachfully. "The least you can do is endorse the flag you asked me to design for you!"

Ladislaus looked sourly at the sinuous, blood-red form coiled about the ebon banner's golden starburst. Except for the star—and the wings on the snakelike doomwhale—it looked remarkably like the Beaufort planetary flag.

"I'm thinking it won't be so very popular with the others," he rumbled.

"You round-eyes are always seeing difficulties," Kai-lun teased. "It's really childish of you. Why not just learn to accept your karma?"

"Because my 'karma's' probably to be a short rope when they see this, you old racist!"

"No, no!" Kai-lun disagreed. "It's only right that the symbol of Beaufort should adorn our banner, Ladislaus—the committee was unanimous on that. And for those who need a little symbolism, we've added the star and wings to indicate the sweep and power of our new star nation. You see?"

"Were you ever being a used-skimmer salesman?" Ladislaus asked his small ally suspiciously.

"Never."

"Ah. I had the wondering." He thought for a moment, then grinned. "All right. It's glad I'll be to be seeing the old doomwhale, anyway."

"Good." Kai-lun rose and headed for the door, then stopped to smile over his shoulder. "Actually, you know, that—" he waved at the banner "—is a symbol of good fortune."

"Eh? I've never had the hearing of the doomwhale being *that*!"

"Ah, but when you put wings on it, it's *not* a doomwhale."

"No?" Ladislaus' suspicions surged afresh. "What's it to be, then?"

"Any child of Hangchow knows that, Lad." Kai-lun smiled. "It's a dragon, of course."

"Lieutenant Skjorning, reporting for duty, sir!"

Stanislaus Skjorning braced to attention—mindful of the overhead—in the tiny shipboard office assigned to Major Wang Chung-hui, CO of TRNS *Longbow*'s Marine detachment.

"Stand easy, Mr. Skjorning," Wang said, and tipped his chair back as he contemplated the towering giant who had strayed into his office. Wang was tall for a Hangchowese, but he doubted his head would have reached as high as Skjorning's shoulder if they'd both been standing.

Stanislaus dropped into a stand easy position, hands folded behind him, and returned the major's scrutiny levelly. He'd already noticed that, despite the new Admiralty's raids on *Longbow*'s crew, non-Oriental faces remained in a distinct minority in her company. And even without that, or his relationship to the Republic's President, his size would have made him a marked man aboard her. He was accustomed to that, but he wondered exactly how Wang was going to approach it.

"So, Lieutenant," Wang said after a moment, "you're our new platoon leader."

"Yes, sir," Stanislaus replied crisply.

"And I see from your records that you served eighteen months with the Five Three Ninety-Eighth. That would have been Colonel Howell, wouldn't it?"

"No, sir. Colonel Howell took the regiment just after I left. Colonel Jouvet had the command while I was with it."

"Charles Jouvet?" Wang asked. "From New Zurich?"

"Yes, sir."

"My, my." Wang smiled crookedly. "And how did you and the Colonel get along, Lieutenant?"

"As well as any Fringer got along with him, sir." Stanislaus gave a thin smile of his own. "I don't think he much cared for any of us, and it showed. But he had the same standards for everyone—Fringer, Corporate Worlder, or Heart Worlder."

"Yes, he did," Wang agreed. "And he apparently thought rather well of you, despite your origins. I see here that it was strongly recommended that you be offered a transfer to the Regulars. Which wouldn't have happened if your CO hadn't endorsed the notion."

"Colonel Jouvet did mention that he thought a regular commission would be a good opportunity for me, sir," Stanislaus replied. "I thanked him, but they needed me back on Beaufort."

He did not add that his decision to return home had been influenced by his oldest brother's death in action and his father's determination to give no more of his children's lives to the Federation.

"Well, if Martinet Charlie thought that highly of a Fringer, you must have been something else, Lieutenant," Wang observed. "So I suppose we should be glad to have you."

"I'll certainly try to pull my weight, sir," Stanislaus said, "but I've spent over ten years as a reservist. There are bound to be some rusty spots. And just looking over the manuals, I've already noticed several equipment mods and upgrades that never made it out to Beaufort."

"It's like riding a bicycle, Mr. Skjorning," Wang told him. "I'm sure it will all come back to you quickly. And if it doesn't, I'm *positive* we can find someone to, ah . . . mentor you until it does."

Stanislaus managed not to wince. From what he'd already seen of Wang, he was sure the major's confidence wasn't misplaced. Which, given the number of "rusty spots" he knew needed buffing up, meant his next few weeks were going to be interesting ones.

Wang smiled again, as if he'd read the thoughts passing through Stanislaus' mind, and pressed a button on his com.

"Sir?" a voice responded almost instantly.

"Sergeant, Third Platoon's new CO has graced us with his presence. Would you ask Captain Ju to join us in my office?"

"Aye, sir," the voice replied.

No more than forty seconds passed, and then the office hatch slid open once more and a compact, immaculately uniformed Marine stepped through it.

"You wanted me, sir?" he said to Wang, and the major nodded.

"Ju Chang, meet Stanislaus Skjorning. He's Lieutenant Shang's replacement. Lieutenant Skjorning, Ju Chang. He has Able Company, but we're shorthanded enough that he's wearing two hats. He's commanding First Platoon, as well as the Company, and he's been holding down Third, too, pending your arrival. Which makes him the man to get you settled in and up to speed ASAP. Yes?"

"Yes, sir!" Stanislaus braced back to attention, and Wang nodded.

"Very well, gentlemen. Go do something useful," he said, and nodded at the door.

" . . . and this is where you'll bunk," Captain Ju said, and rapped twice on the attention pad beside the hatch.

"It's open," a voice said over the speaker beside the pad, and Ju hit the admittance button. The hatch slid open, and a slim, dark-haired young man in a lieutenant's uniform turned the swivelled station chair at a small, cluttered desk to face the opening.

"Lieutenant Bao Jai-shu, meet Lieutenant Skjorning," Ju said dryly. "He's your new bunkie."

"Jesus," Bao said, climbing out of the chair with an easy smile and craning his neck to peer up at Stanislaus. "Tell you what, Lieutenant. I just decided you get the bottom bunk. I'd rather climb a ladder every night than risk having you fall on me!"

Stanislaus smiled back down at him, and Bao held out a hand. The big Beauforter gripped it, careful not to break anything, and Bao chuckled.

"Jai-shu has Second Platoon," Ju explained. "They never leave the ship—they man Point Defense Two at Battle Stations—so don't let him fool you into thinking he's a *real* Marine."

"You cut me to the quick yet again, sir," Bao said reproachfully, giving Stanislaus a toothy grin.

"Sure I do," Ju told him, shaking his head. Then went on. "Stanislaus is taking over the Third," he said. "Major Wang turned him over to me, and I want to take him around myself, but I've got a meeting scheduled in about four minutes with Gunny Malthus. How about getting him settled in here until I can get back and pick him up again?"

"Can do, Skipper," Bao agreed cheerfully. "In fact, they already delivered his gear."

He waved at the locker and field ruck placed neatly at the foot of the unmade bunk against the cabin's after bulkhead.

"Is that everything, Lieutenant?" Ju asked, arching an eyebrow at Stanislaus, and the big Beauforter shrugged.

"I brought along my own vac suit and zoot, sir. Somehow people seem to find it a bit difficult to fit me out of standard equipment." Stanislaus kept his expression deadpan, but Ju chuckled in understanding. "They told me the Armorer wanted to check out the zoot—it's an older model, not really standard issue—before he cleared it, so I'm guessing it's down in the shop somewhere.

And Engineering's doing the same for the vac gear. But this is everything else."

"You do travel light, don't you?" Ju said.

"Back home, I spend most of my time on a doomwhale catcher, sir." Stanislaus shrugged. "Compared to a cuddy on the boats, this—" he gestured at the cramped cabin "—is a palace. So doomwhalers learn to travel light, if they don't want their crewmates tossing their gear over the side some dark night to clear deck space."

"Well, don't let *this* 'crewmate' take advantage of you," Ju said, jerking a thumb at Bao. "He'll spread out and fill the entire cabin if you let him, but half this palatial space is yours."

"Oh, I'm minded that there's not to be a problem," Stanislaus said slowly, grinning as he dropped briefly out of Standard English. "It's fine we'll be getting along, the Lieutenant and me, I'm sure."

He laced his fingers together in front of him, flexed massive shoulders, and cracked his knuckles loudly.

"Won't we, Lieutenant?" he finished genially.

Commodore Petrovna looked very calm in her new uniform, but she knew every officer of the new Republican Navy could see her on the all-ships hookup, and her warm voice was hushed with a sense of history.

"Ladies and Gentlemen of the Fleet, I introduce to you the President of the Republic of Free Terrans, Ladislaus Skjorning."

She vanished, and Ladislaus Skjorning appeared on the screen. His face was composed, but his blue eyes were bright—and hard. He sat behind a plain desk, and the crossed flags of the newborn Terran Republic covered the wall behind him.

"Ladies and gentlemen," his deep voice was measured, his famed Beaufort accent in complete abeyance, "fourteen years ago, I, too, was a serving officer in the Fleet of the Terran Federation. As one who once wore that uniform, I know what it has cost each of you to stand where you now stand, and I share your anguish. But I also share your determination and outrage. We have not come here lightly, but we have taken our stand, and we cannot and shall not retreat from it."

He paused, picturing the officers and ratings—including his brother—watching his image, hearing his voice, and for just a moment it seemed that he stood or sat beside each and every one of them. It was a moment of empathic awareness such as he had never imagined, and it showed in his voice when he continued.

"Ladies and gentlemen, it is you who will fight for our new nation; many of you will die for it. It's not necessary for me to say more on that head, for whatever else history may say of you, it will record that you were men and women who understood the concept of duty and served that concept to the very best of your ability. However, since it is you who will bear the shock of combat, it is only just that you know and understand exactly why we are fighting and what we are fighting for. It is for this reason I asked Admiral Ashigara for this all-ships hookup tonight.

"I am about to record our first official message to the Federation's Assembly, and I wish you to witness this communication as it is recorded. I suppose—" he permitted himself a bleak smile "—that this is an historic moment, but that isn't why I wish to share it with you. I wish to share it because of who you are and what you will shortly be called upon to do.

"We represent many worlds and many ways of life. We spring from a single planet, but the diversity among us is great. We do not even agree upon the nature of God or the ultimate ends of our ongoing evolution. Yet we agree upon this: what has been done to us is intolerable, the systematic looting and manipulation of our economies and ways of life by others is not to be endured, and *no* government has the right to abuse its citizens as the government of the Federation has abused us. And if that agreement is all we share, it is enough. It's more than enough—as your presence in your ships, as your willingness to wear the uniform you wear, demonstrates. We may not share the same view of God, but before whatever God there is, I am proud to speak these words for you, and humbled by the commitment you and your worlds have made to support them."

He looked down at the concealed terminal built into his desk—not that he needed it; what he was to say was written in his heart and mind as surely as in the memory of his computer—then glanced up once more.

"Some of you will recognize the source of these words. Many may not, but, I think, no one has ever said it better—and their use may help the Federation's citizens to understand our motives despite their present government's self-serving misrepresentation."

He drew a deep breath and faced the pickup squarely, forcing his shoulders to relax. When he spoke once more, he appeared completely calm. Only those who knew him well saw the anguish which possessed him.

"To the Legislative Assembly of the Terran Federation," he

began calmly, "from Ladislaus Skjorning, President of the Republic of Free Terrans, for and in the name of the Congress of the Republic of Free Terrans.

"When in the course of human events, it becomes necessary for one people to dissolve the political bands which have connected them with another, and to assume among the powers of the Galaxy the separate and equal station to which the laws of nature and the usages of justice entitle them, a decent respect for the opinion of all races requires that they should declare the causes which impel them to the separation."

He drew another deep breath, his voice rumbling up out of his chest, powerful and proud and defiant, yet somehow reverent as he spoke the fierce old words, newly adapted to changing circumstances.

"We hold these truths to be self-evident: that all sentient beings are created equal, that they are endowed with certain unalienable rights, that among these are life, liberty and the pursuit of happiness. . . ."

The survivors of the coming battles might see that recording many times in the course of their lives, yet never again would they see and hear it as it was made. They were joined with Ladislaus Skjorning, floating in the heart of a crystal moment, temporarily outside the bounds of space and time. Never before had so many men and women so intimately charged with the defense of a cause been joined in the moment of its annunciation; perhaps it would never happen again. Yet for all that they shared it as it happened, few could ever recall hearing the exact words Ladislaus spoke. What they remembered was the strength of his deep voice, the emotional communion as he forged words to hold their anger and frustration and their inarticulate love for the government they could no longer obey. They heard the list of abuses not with their ears, but with their souls—and they knew, knew now in their very bones, that the breach was forever. They could never return to what they had been, and in that instant of unbearable loss and political birth, the Terran Republic's Navy was forged on the anvil of history as few military organizations have ever been.

". . . We must, therefore," Ladislaus went on, drawing to the close of his message, "acquiesce in the necessity which denounces our separation, and hold you, as we hold the whole of the sentient races of the Galaxy, enemies in war, in peace friends.

"Now, therefore, the representatives of the Republic of Free

Terrans, in general congress assembled, appealing to the Supreme Judge of the Universe for the rectitude of our intentions, do, in the name and authority of the good people of these worlds, solemnly publish and declare that these united worlds are, and of right ought to be, a free and independent nation; that they are absolved from all allegiance to the Legislative Assembly of the Terran Federation, and that all political connection between them and the Terran Federation is and ought to be totally dissolved; and that as a free and independent state, they have full power to levy war, conclude peace, contract alliances, establish commerce, and do all other acts and things which independent states may of right do."

He stared into the pickup, his face carved from stone, and behind his eyes he saw the crumpled body of Fionna MacTaggart—the final, unforgivable indignity to which the Fringe Worlds had been subjected—and the closing words rumbled and crashed from his thick throat like denouncing thunder.

"And for the support of this declaration, with a firm reliance on the protection of divine Providence, we mutually pledge to each other our lives, our fortunes, and our sacred honor."

# OFFENSIVE

*"A man can die but once; we owe God a death..."*
William Shakespeare, *Henry IV*, Part II

TRNS *Longbow* was five hours out of Novaya Rodina orbit as Commodore Li Han stood beside Captain Tsing Chang in the intraship car, her face tranquil, and worried over what she was about to discover about her crew.

The new Republican Navy was desperately short of veterans. Of the sixty percent of the Fleet which had been Fringer, roughly ninety percent had favored mutiny, but the furious fighting had produced casualties so severe the Republican Navy found itself with less than half the trained personnel to man its captured ships.

Figures were even worse among the senior officers. Admiral Ashigara was, so far at least, the most senior officer to come over to the Republic. Others might have joined her, but the carnage on most of the flag decks had been so extreme none of them had survived. Which explained Han's indecently rapid promotion ... and also why she found herself wearing two hats. She might be a commodore, but experienced Battle Fleet skippers were at such a premium that she had to double as CO of the *Longbow*—not that she minded that!

Fortunately, they'd picked up a few unexpected bonuses, as well, such as Commodore Magda Petrovna. Han didn't know her as well as she would have liked, for Petrovna had been indecently busy on Novaya Rodina, splitting her time between the Convention and her new command, but the prematurely graying woman had certainly proved herself at the Battle of Novaya Rodina. Her choice of Jason Windrider as her chief of staff only strengthened Han's respect for her. She felt no qualms about going into action with Commodore Petrovna on her flank.

The car stopped on the command bridge, and the officer of the deck stood as they stepped out. The other watch-keepers stayed seated as per her standing orders. Some captains preferred for their bridge crews to indulge in all the ceremonial rituals whenever they came on the bridge; Han preferred for them to get on with their jobs.

"Good afternoon, Exec," she said to Commander Sung.

"Good afternoon, sir. Commodore Tsing."

Han shook her head mentally at the titles. She was commodore of BG 12, but also *Longbow*'s captain. For squadron purposes, she was properly addressed as "Commodore," but when acting as *Longbow*'s CO, she was properly addressed as "Captain." Just to complicate matters further, Tsing was now a captain—but there could be only one "Captain" aboard a warship, so Tsing was properly addressed as "Commodore," since courtesy promotions were, by definition, upward. Thus there were occasions on which they would both properly be addressed as "Commodore," but only Han would ever be addressed as "Captain," which meant that from time to time a "captain" outranked a "commodore" aboard *Longbow*. Not surprisingly, Sung, like most of her crew, took the easy out and addressed her only as "Sir" unless there was absolutely no alternative or it was completely clear which hat she was wearing.

"I have the con, Exec," she told Sung, sliding into the command chair.

"Aye, aye, sir."

The short, slender commander stepped quickly back behind the chair, waiting.

"Mister Chu, how long to transit?"

"Approximately forty-three standard hours, sir."

"Very good." She swung her chair toward the exec. "Commander Sung."

"Yes, sir?"

He looked nervous. That was a good sign.

"It's been a while since our last comprehensive drills," she said calmly. "Don't you think we might spend a few hours brushing the rust off?"

Sung Chung-hui had dreaded this moment. *Longbow*'s casualties had been the lowest of any ship in TF 17, but the new Republican Admiralty had raided her ruthlessly for experienced cadre. He'd managed to hang onto barely half of her original bridge crew, and losses below decks had been worse. He'd done his best to fit the many replacements into his team, but all too many were on "makee-learnee," and he shuddered to think of the next few days.

He glanced at Tsing, but the former exec seemed thoroughly fascinated by the display on the main plot. No help there. He drew a deep breath.

"Whenever you wish, sir."

"Then sound general quarters, Exec," Han said, and Sung breathed a silent prayer as he pressed the button.

The word, Han thought as she worked up lather, was "horrible."

She raised her face to the shower spray and the water dragged at her long hair. It really wasn't all that bad, considering, she told herself as she rinsed. Unfortunately, war left no room for "considering." With nukes flying around your ears, there were only adequate crews—or dead ones. She remembered the fine-tuned instrument she and Tsing had made of *Longbow* before the mutiny and shook her head, but the present arthritic uncertainty wasn't Sung's fault. He hadn't had time to work up the new drafts, and he'd actually done quite well in the time he'd been given.

She finished rinsing and reached for a towel.

She and Sung were going to be unpopular over the next few days. At least she'd managed to hang on to most of her point defense crews—that was about the only department which had performed with a flourish—but damage control was terrible and engineering was no better. She couldn't fault Sung's initial concentration on gunnery and maneuvering, but gunners and coxswains alone couldn't make *Longbow* an effective fighting machine.

She wrapped the towel around herself sarong fashion and sat before her terminal. It was Sung's job to bring the crew up to her standards. Under the iron-bound traditions of the service, her ability, even her right, to interfere with his handling of the problem was limited. But she was also the captain. The ultimate responsibility was hers, and she and Sung both knew how new to his duties he was. She could stretch the point a bit, she decided, without convincing him he'd lost her trust.

She punched up the intraship memo system slowly, considering how to begin. Her fingers poised over the keys, then moved.

To: CDR Sung C.
From: CMDR Li H., CO TRNS LONGBOW
RE: Exercises conducted this date

Drills conducted by all departments indicate only point defense and maneuvering personnel fully competent in assigned duties. Engineering performance was far below acceptable standards, and general crew performance leaves much to be desired. I therefore suggest:
(a) series of intensive exercises of all hands in . . .

The words appeared with machinelike speed as *Longbow's* drive pushed the ship ever closer to battle, and Commodore Li Han, wet hair plastered to her bare shoulders, felt her mind reaching out to meet the test to come.

Stanislaus Skjorning sat stoically beside Bao Jai-shu in the briefing room aboard *Longbow*, waiting for what promised to be a thoroughly unpleasant afternoon.

"At least the Navy pukes screwed up worse than we did," Bao said philosophically.

"Yeah, sure," another Marine lieutenant said. She grimaced. "Easy for you to say. *You* got to keep your entire platoon intact. No wonder you aced *your* sim!"

Bao was about to reply when the briefing room hatch slid open.

"Attention on deck!"

Feet scraped on the decksole as the assembled officers and senior noncoms snapped to attention with rather more alacrity than even Marines normally displayed. Major Wang strode briskly down the center aisle between rows of his stiffly braced subordinates to the briefing officer's raised platform, set his uniform cap very neatly on the corner of the lectern, and turned to face them.

He did not, Stanislaus noted glumly, invite them to stand easy.

"I suppose," the major began in a dangerously conversational tone, "that there must have been somewhere, in the entire history of the Corps, a performance more pitifully inadequate than the one I've just witnessed. A scrupulous search of the database, however, has failed to turn that performance up. More to the point," he smiled, with absolutely no humor at all, "I have been made aware that *Captain Li* has never witnessed one. And, as she has been so kind as to share her firsthand impression of our performance with me, I feel it only fair that I should share it with *you*."

"I thought you Hangchowese were supposed to be inscrutable," Stanislaus complained as he and Bao headed down the passage towards their cabin. Bao glanced up at him, one eyebrow crooked, and Stanislaus snorted. "I've had the seeing of doomwhales with more blubber left than yon Major was to be leaving on the lot of us!"

"Major Wang does have a modest gift for the language," Bao agreed. "I'd like to know exactly what the Captain had to say to him, though. Whatever it was, it inspired him to new heights."

"Aye, so you might be saying."

"Actually, you got off fairly light compared to some of the others," Bao observed. "As, of course, did I and my superbly trained—*and* commanded!—platoon," he added modestly.

"For such a wee, tiny fellow, you've an ego the size of a good-sized moon, don't you just?" Stanislaus replied, blue eyes glinting as he smiled down at his roommate.

"I suppose it's the curse of all great men," Bao agreed with a gusty sigh. Then he laughed. "I've known the Major for almost two years, Stanislaus. He was pissed, all right—no question of that. But he recognizes the value of a well-timed tantrum, and that one was a beaut. He's going to be right behind us, kicking us in the ass just the way he promised, but he knows why we screwed up just as well as we do."

"Maybe," Stanislaus half-agreed. "But truth to tell, Jai-shu, I'm not used to screwing up quite that badly, whatever the reason."

"*You* didn't screw up at all," Bao replied. "As a matter of fact, I suspect the Major was a lot more pleased with your performance than he was prepared to let on. It wasn't your fault Hsu's squad screwed the timing on your sim. Hell, he's not even in your platoon, but it was his screwup that stacked your people up behind him in front of that strongpoint! And you may have noticed that the Major gave Captain Ju a particularly detailed analysis of First Platoon's . . . shortcomings. Besides, he only put you on point in the simulation to see how well you'd do."

"And?" Stanislaus prompted as Bao paused.

"And I noticed—even if you didn't—that he's tasked Third Platoon as the ship's lead ground element. *After* the sim. Which he wouldn't have done if he didn't think you'd performed, um, *adequately*, shall we say?"

Stanislaus grunted noncommittally as they reached their cabin and Bao opened the hatch.

"Seriously," Bao said as he opened his locker and stowed away his cap, "you did damned well for somebody who just took over a brand new platoon, Stanislaus."

"If I did, it's mostly because Huang held my hand."

"Sure," Bao snorted as Stanislaus opened his own locker. "Look, I'll agree you were lucky you got to keep Huang, at least. He's one of the best platoon sergeants I've seen. But if you don't think *he* was testing you just as much as the Major was, then you're not as smart as I think you are."

There was probably something to that, Stanislaus conceded mentally as he laid his own cap on the top shelf of the locker. And the more he thought about it, the more willing he became to grant that Bao's analysis of how his platoon had come to take seventy percent casualties in the simulation might contain at least a few grains of truth. But still—

"My goodness! What *do* we have here?"

The question snapped Stanislaus' attention back to Bao, and his heart sank. The other lieutenant was grinning wickedly as he reached past Stanislaus' elbow—he was far too short to reach over his towering new friend's shoulder—for the holo cube beside his cap.

Stanislaus' first instinct was to slam the locker shut, hopefully surgically removing the intruding hand in the process. Unfortunately, the damage was already done.

"You do work fast, don't you?" Bao observed, turning the cube to catch the overhead light on Tatiana Illyushina's smiling face. "Of course, if *I* had the sort of political connections you've got, you'd never have a chance with her, you know."

"Of course I'd be having a chance," Stanislaus told him, reaching out and removing the cube from his hand. Bao's eyes twinkled wickedly, but he wisely made no effort to resist as Stanislaus reclaimed his property. "Because if you were to be going anywhere near her, it's sad I am to be saying as how you'd be suffering a serious accident, little man."

"You wouldn't *really* hurt me, would you?" Bao said plaintively, looking up at Stanislaus in a remarkably good imitation of a puppy.

"Of course not," Stanislaus reassured him kindly. "It's all over it would be, and the ashes ready to scatter, before you were feeling a thing."

Han sniffed at Tsing's pipe smoke. Few spacers smoked, and she hated cigarette smoke, but though she would never admit it, she rather liked the smell of Tsing's pipe blend. Not that liking it kept her from scolding him over the filthy habit in private.

She glanced across the small table at Lieutenant Reznick and Commander Sung, noting the wariness in Sung's eyes. The past weeks had been a foretaste of hell for him, but he'd done well. *Longbow*'s newcomers had slotted smoothly into place and even the abandon-ship drill had gone quite well, though she hadn't seen fit to tell Sung so. It wasn't nice, but it had inspired him to maximum effort.

"Well, Chang," she said finally, "could this crew zip its own shoes without supervision?"

"Just about, sir." Tsing blew a beautiful smoke ring and glanced at Sung, "Just about."

Sung's face fell, and Han shook her head reproachfully at Tsing.

"Actually, Exec," she said, "I think you've done very well. There are still a few rough spots, but all in all, we've got one of the most efficient ship's companies I've seen."

"Thank you, sir!" Sung's face lit with pleasure.

"And just in time, too," she went on.

She touched a button and a hologram of the local warp lines appeared above the table.

"We'll make transit to Lassa in about an hour, gentlemen," she said calmly. "Eighty-one hours after that, we'll be ready to fire probes through into Aklumar for a last minute report."

"Yes, sir." Tsing passed the stem of his pipe through the warp line between Lassa and Aklumar. "That ought to be an interesting trip."

"Not as 'interesting' as the one to Cimmaron," Han reminded him. "It had better not be, anyway!"

She tapped the table gently, then turned a calm face to Sung.

"Chung-hui, I asked you to join us because I'm going to depend heavily on you and Chang. I'll have to coordinate the battlegroup and fight *Longbow*, as well, and I can't do it unless you both understand exactly what I plan. You'll both have to exercise a lot of discretion in what you report to me and what you act upon yourselves, so I want us to have a very clear mutual understanding of the operation. Fair enough?"

"Yes, sir."

"Good. Then here's the first point; we're going into Cimmaron before Commodore Petrovna because the Rump data base won't list us as a command ship." Sung nodded; *Longbow* hadn't *been* a command ship the last time the Rump saw her. "On the other hand, our datalink has cost us two capital missile launchers, so we'll hold back our external ordnance when the others launch. We'll use the racks to hide our lack of internal launchers, because if they realize we're the command ship they'll go for us with everything they've got."

"Yes, sir. I understand."

"Good. Second, I want everything on line when we transit into Aklumar, no matter what the probes show. I hope we won't find anything to worry about—we *don't* need a Second Battle of Aklumar."

This time both Sung and Tsing nodded. Aklumar had witnessed the climactic engagement of the First Interstellar War, but the last thing they wanted was a clash to alert Cimmaron.

"*But*," she went on, "if I were commanding Cimmaron there'd be at least a picket at Aklumar to watch for exactly what we hope to do. And if there is—" she brought up a schematic of the Aklumar warp junction "—he'll be right here." She touched the image. "Placed to dash down the warp line as soon as we enter scanner range. So we have to make sure we don't enter scanner range until we've dealt with him."

"Sir?" Sung sounded uncertain.

"If the Admiral agrees, we'll go in cloaked," Han explained. "We'll close with him and—hopefully—pick him off before he knows we're there."

"But, sir, the battlegroup doesn't have cloaking ECM."

"No, but we do, and so do scout cruisers. We'll form a three-ship data group with two of them and clear the way for the rest of the task force."

"Unless," Tsing observed with the mild air of a man who'd made the same point before, "they've posted a light carrier, sir. A couple of long-range recon fighters on patrol, and we'll never get close enough."

"We've been over that, Chang, and I still don't expect it, not with so much of Frontier Fleet coming over. They'd never risk a fleet or assault carrier on picket duty, and all the lights were in Frontier Fleet. They can't have many of them left."

"You're probably right, sir, but it's my job to point out problems. And here's another: they might use a scout cruiser of their own."

"If they go by The Book, that's exactly what they'll do," Han agreed, "but they can't have many of them, either. If they do, the whole ops plan goes out the lock anyway. If they're cloaking, the probes won't spot them and they'll have just as good a chance to hide from us as we have to hide from them. Which gives them the advantage, of course, since their whole job is to run away while we try to locate and destroy them. But there's only one way to find out, isn't there?"

"You might ask Admiral Ashigara to send in a squadron of fighters to check it, sir," Sung suggested hesitantly.

"I might," Han agreed dryly, "if fighters carried *any* ECM."

"Sorry, sir. I should have thought of that." Sung sounded abashed.

"Don't worry about it." Han smiled. "But we're going to have to deal with this ourselves, so be certain plotting and gunnery are ready. We'll have to be quick to stop them from launching a courier drone."

"Yes, sir."

"All right. Now—" she switched to a schematic of Cimmaron "—this is where we're *supposed* to run into trouble. Commodore Tsing, Commander Tomanaga, and I have spent quite a while discussing how to handle this, Exec, and I want you to understand what we're up to. SOP would bring us in last to protect the command ship from the opening salvos, but the Rump knows The Book, too. Commander Tomanaga suggests we come in first, since that's the last place they'll expect the flagship, but I've decided to come in third. Lieutenant Reznick here tells me our datalink won't stand much pounding, so I don't want us out too early, just as I don't want us in the standard flag slot. We'll rely on the shell game approach—they'll know we have a command ship, but not which one it is . . . I hope. If we can force them to disperse their fire looking for us, we may survive until BG 11 comes through and offers so many targets they *have* to divide their fire. Understand?"

"Yes, sir."

"Good. And instead of a tight, traditional globe, we're coming in in line abreast for the same reasons—*everything* will be directed towards keeping them guessing."

"Yes, sir."

"And there's another point, one which relates to our datalink." Han turned to Reznick, who flushed slightly under her calm regard; it was amazing how readily he colored up. "Because we may lose our command data net so quickly, I want alternate standard datalinks set up between our units as a priority. If we lose the command net, I don't want any delays in dropping into smaller groups, Lieutenant."

"Yes, sir."

"All right. Now, here's the final point for you, Exec—you won't be on the command deck when we enter Cimmaron."

"Sir?" Sung blinked. "But that's my duty station! I—"

"It is normally," Han cut him off calmly, "but this isn't normal. We don't have a flag bridge, and I have to be able to see battle plot. That means the flag will be on the command deck. If a single hit takes out me, Commodore Tsing, *and* you—" she shrugged.

"I see." Sung still sounded unhappy, and Han found it hard to blame him. "But where *will* I be, sir? Auxiliary fire control?"

"No, Commander Tomanaga will be there. I want you with Mister Reznick in command datalink." She caught him with a level stare. "Understand this, Commander. If the command deck buys it, you're suddenly going to inherit an entire battlegroup, because yours will be the only ship with command datalink capability. Hopefully Commander Tomanaga will still be around to advise you, but I can't even promise you that."

"I see, sir." Sung licked his lips, then nodded firmly. "I see."

"I'm glad you do, Chung-hui." She glanced at her watch. "All right—let's get back to the bridge." She killed the holograph and tucked her cap under her arm, facing them as they rose. "But remember, gentlemen, up to now, it's been a matter of seizing choke points where we happened to have mutinying units and cleaning up undefended systems. That's over now. We're going to fight for everything we get from here on out, and I want the Republican Navy to be just as dedicated and just as professional as the *Federation* Navy. This is a civil war, and passions are running high on both sides, but there had better not be any Jason Waldecks under *my* command. These aren't Arachnids we're fighting—they're Terrans. I expect you to act accordingly."

Then she turned, and they followed her silently from the briefing room.

✧     ✧     ✧

"Good afternoon, Commodore Li." Admiral Ashigara regarded Han from her com screen, and Han watched her left hand play with her empty right cuff in the nervous gesture she'd developed since Bigelow. "We have the data from the Aklumar recon probes. It would seem—" the admiral permitted herself a thin smile "—your concerns were well founded. The probes report a single unit, probably a heavy cruiser, guarding the Aklumar-Cimmaron warp point."

"I see," Han said. "But there's not one on the Lassa-Aklumar point?"

"No," Ashigara said softly, and Han knew her admiral had considered the same point she had. It would have made a calculating sort of sense to post a second picket. The nearer watchdog would have virtually no chance of surviving any attack from Lassa, but her very destruction would insure a warning for the defenders of Cimmaron.

"I have decided to approve your plan, Commodore," Ashigara went on after a moment. "I will detach *Ashanti* and *Scythian* to accompany *Longbow*, and your force will make transit in two hours. The rest of the task force will follow eight hours later, in standard formation at half speed. We will remain beyond scanner range until you engage, but once you do, we are committed. Either you will destroy him before he dispatches a warning, or you will not. In either case, therefore, the task force will assume Formation Alpha and transit to Cimmaron immediately, without reconnaissance. There would be little time to evaluate the results of a probe recon even if we could send probes through without giving the warning we desire to prevent the picket from sending, so there is no point in delaying the inevitable."

"I understand, sir," Han said, hoping she sounded equally calm.

"Very well, Commodore. *Ashanti* and *Scythian* will report to you shortly. Good hunting."

"Thank you, sir," Han said, and the screen went blank.

"All stations report closed up, Captain."

Lieutenant Chu was clearly more nervous over filling in for Sung than he was over the prospect of being blown to atoms, Han noted wryly.

"Thank you, Lieutenant." She glanced at a side screen which held the faces of Sung and Reznick. "Are you ready, gentlemen?"

"Yes, sir," Sung said. "Data net is operational and ECM is active."

"Very well. Let's go, Mister Chu."

"Aye, aye, sir!"

*Longbow* quivered as her drive engaged, and Han felt a familiar queasiness as the grav-damping drive field warred briefly with the artificial shipboard gravity. There had to be a better way to do such things, she told herself absently, but her attention was on Battle One.

The battlecruiser nosed into the warp point to Aklumar, and her entire hull writhed as the tidal stress of transit twisted her. It was a brief sensation, but one which could be neither forgotten nor described to anyone who hadn't felt it, and Han gritted her teeth against the sudden surge of nausea. Some people claimed not to mind warp transit, or even to enjoy it. Some people, she thought, were liars.

The tactical display shimmered as delicate, shielded equipment hiccupped to the transit stress. Then the image steadied as the computers stabilized, and she was staring at a blank screen. Within the range of *Longbow*'s scanners, space was empty.

She felt herself relax as the emptiness registered. She'd expected it, but the confirmation was still a vast relief. Now all she had to do was sneak up on the ship watching the Cimmaron junction.

"All right," she said softly, leaning back. "I want a *sharp* watch. We should come into scanner range in—" she glanced at the chronometer "—sixty-four hours and ten minutes, but if he's decided to move, we may meet him much sooner and where we don't expect it. So stay on your toes."

Her bridge crew made no reply, and she nodded in satisfaction. So far, she told herself, toying with the seal of her vac suit, so good.


"You know, Lieutenant, I thought right up to the last minute that we were going to have to down check Hanbo's zoot, but it looks to me like we're actually ready, after all," Sergeant Huang said, as he and Stanislaus finished the equipment checklist.

"Aye, so it does," Stanislaus agreed. He input his electronic signature on the battalion armorer's certification of the suit of powered armor in question, and tipped his chair back. He sat gazing at the neat lines and columns of characters on the display for a few more seconds, then sighed and closed the file.

"I think our people are ready, too, Sir," Huang said, and

Stanislaus hid a mental smile at the sergeant's just-that-too-casual tone. Third Platoon's senior noncom couldn't very well ask the platoon's commanding officer if *he* was ready.

"As ready as we can be, Tse-lao," Stanislaus agreed, after a moment. "There's going to be some dry-mouth, whatever happens, but over all, I'm satisfied. Very satisfied. And," he smiled slightly at the short, blocky sergeant, "we all know who I have to thank for that, don't we?"

"No idea what you're talking about, Lieutenant," Huang replied.

"Of course not," Stanislaus said with a slightly broader smile. "Well," he continued in a brisker tone, "in that case, I'd say we're done here, Sergeant Huang. I'll see you at final equipment check."

"Aye, aye, Sir," Huang acknowledged. He pushed back his own chair, stood, came very briefly to an abbreviated position of attention, and left.

Stanislaus watched the hatch slide shut behind him and allowed his smile to become still broader. He'd been extremely lucky to draw Huang Tse-lao as his platoon sergeant. Huang was almost half-again Stanislaus' own age, and he'd spent the better part of twenty standard years learning to do his job very well indeed, even by the standards of the Marine Corps. He couldn't have been very happy to receive a brand-new platoon commander less than two months before *his* platoon (and whatever officers might think, the platoon *always* belonged to its senior noncom) went into combat, but he hadn't let that faze him. Instead, he'd dug in and gotten Stanislaus squared away in record time, and between them, he and Stanislaus had run Third Platoon ragged over the past six weeks.

Along the way, the platoon's personnel had found their own ways to test their new lieutenant's mettle, just as he'd been testing theirs, and he hoped they were as satisfied as he was with what they'd discovered. He wished passionately that they had still more time to shake down together, but despite their abbreviated settling in period, the platoon was a smoothly functioning, well integrated machine. A machine Stanislaus Skjorning had been neatly inserted into by Huang Tse-lao. The fact that Stanislaus had always had an excellent memory for names and faces, and that doomwhaling was probably one of the galaxy's half-dozen or so riskier occupations hadn't exactly hurt, either. A master doomwhaler had to be alert, flexible, and as close to immune to panic attacks as any human being was ever likely to become. And he also required a sense of situational awareness at least as acute as any long-term combat veteran's. Anyone who failed to develop those qualities was ... unlikely to survive long enough aboard the doomwhale catchers to earn his master's shoulder patch.

Which didn't make Stanislaus any more immune to the anxiety of a junior officer about to lead *his* people into combat for the first time than anyone else.

He grimaced at the thought. Of course, if the intelligence pukes were right, the people of Cimmaron were going to regard the Republican Navy's arrival as a liberation, not a conquest. The troops which had been dispatched to Cimmaron to assure that it remained "loyal" to the Rump were another matter entirely, but assuming that the Republic won the naval engagement for the system, any ground forces would be at a hopeless disadvantage. If they had a grain of sense, they would recognize the inevitable, and Stanislaus' "combat mission" would turn into little more than an alert, wary occupation, instead.

Murphy might have other ideas, but even so, Stanislaus suspected he would enjoy his time on the planet more than he would enjoy his spectator's role in the upcoming naval battle. Unlike Bao Jai-shu, who would be fully occupied with his duties in *Longbow*'s point defense, Stanislaus and his entire platoon would be sitting helplessly, strapped into an assault shuttle in *Longbow*'s boat bay while they waited to go dirt side. It would keep them out of the Navy types' way, and he supposed that—in theory, at least—it would give them the best chance available of getting out if something unfortunate happened to the ship. But he was bitterly envious of the fact that his friend would actually have something to *do*—besides sweat, of course—during the battle itself.

Still, a man couldn't have everything in this imperfect universe. And if dropping out of an assault shuttle onto a planet garrisoned by Corporate World Marines might not be exactly the safest thing he could be doing, it probably wasn't any riskier, when all was said, than going after a wounded forty-meter doomwhale in shallow water. Less, actually. And, if he was going to be honest, he couldn't deny that he felt more than a trace of eagerness, as well. Not to kill people, and certainly not to see any of *his* people killed, but to test himself. *Prove* himself. A man didn't become a doomwhaler if he didn't relish challenges ... or if the thought of conflict and danger was likely to deter him. And after the endless catalogue of manipulation, abuse, and murder the Corporate Worlds had heaped upon the Fringe, there could be no fitter challenge, no better cause, than this.

His people were owed a debt, and Stanislaus Skjorning intended to collect it in their names.

"There she is, sir," Lieutenant Chu said, and Han nodded as courteously as if she hadn't already seen the small, red dot. A moment passed; then small, precise data codes flashed under the blip and it turned orange, indicating a cruiser class vessel. The red band of an enemy identification continued to pulse around it, but *Longbow*'s computers knew her now, and a quick search of the database provided her name, as well.

"She's the *Swiftsure*, sir," a scanner rating announced.

"Thank you, de Smit," Han said calmly, and watched the icon creep slowly across the display as her small squadron slid stealthily closer. She glanced at Battle Two, checking her own formation. Even *Longbow*'s scanners couldn't have located *Ashanti* and *Scythian* with certainty if they hadn't known exactly where to look. Now it remained to be seen whether or not *Swiftsure*'s scanners would detect them as they closed to missile range. The odds against it were astronomical, but it was possible. . . .

"Commodore, we're coming into extreme range." It was Lieutenant Kan, her gunnery officer. "I have a good setup."

"Stand by, Mister Kan."

Han watched the tactical display unblinkingly, her expressionless face hiding her flashing thoughts as she considered. The range was long, but all three of her ships carried external loads of capital missiles, so she could fire now, banking on the fact that the motionless *Swiftsure* was an ideal, nonevading target. But the scout cruisers lacked *Longbow*'s more sophisticated fire control, so their accuracy would be poorer, and missiles were sublight weapons. Firing at longer ranges meant longer flight times and gave *Swiftsure* a better chance to detect their approach in time to get a drone off. On the other hand, the closer her ships came, the more likely *Swiftsure* was to detect *them*, which made deciding exactly when to fire a nice problem in balanced imperatives.

Han felt herself tightening internally, but her bridge crew saw no sign of it. She made herself lean back in her command chair. Ten light-seconds. That was the range at which detection became almost inevitable. She glanced at the tactical display. Eleven light-seconds . . .

"Open fire, Mister Kan," she said quietly, and *Longbow* twitched as she flushed her external ordnance racks.

The missiles lifted away, drives howling as they slammed across the vacuum between Han's squadron and her victim at sixty percent of light speed. She watched the speckled lights on her display as the missiles arrowed towards their target, and her brain concentrated on *Swiftsure*'s icon, watching like a hawk, hoping the doomed cruiser would die unknowing. But another part of her hummed with a sort of elated grief.

The missiles bore down on *Swiftsure*, and Han heard a murmur of excitement around her. Clearly their enemy had never suspected their proximity—even her point defense was late and firing wide. Only three missiles were stopped by her desperate, close-in defenses; the others went home eighteen seconds after launch in a cataclysmic detonation brighter than the star of Aklumar.

The dreadful fireball died, sucked away by the greedy emptiness, and Han stared at her display, her heart as cold as the void around her ship. There was nothing left. No courier drones—no escape pods. Just . . . nothing.

She stared at Battle One for perhaps five seconds, and somewhere deep within her was a horrified little girl. She was a warrior. This wasn't the first time she'd participated in the death of another ship and its crew. But it was the first time she'd struck down fellow Terrans from the shadows like an assassin. She'd given them only warning enough to know death had come for them. Only enough to feel the terror . . .

She knew her success would save hundreds of her comrades when the Battle of Cimmaron began, but knowing did nothing to still her shame or the shocked sickness of triumph crawling down her nerves.

She turned her command chair to face Lieutenant Chu.

"Take position two light-seconds from the warp point on the task force approach vector, Mister Chu, then get the XO racks rearmed." Her face was serene. "We'll wait here for further orders."

"Aye, aye, sir," Lieutenant Chu said. He hesitated a moment, but his enthusiasm was too great to resist. "That was beautiful, sir. Beautiful!"

"Thank you, Lieutenant," Han said coolly, and her eyes met Tsing's. He regarded her steadily, his face unreadable as he reached for the pipe lying on his console. He stuffed it slowly, and Han looked away.

✧     ✧     ✧

"Battlegroup formed up for transit, sir."

"Thank you, Commodore Tsing."

Han drew a deep, unobtrusive breath, tasting the oxygen in her lungs like wine, and felt *Longbow* gathering her strength about her. Her beautiful, deadly *Longbow*, ready to plunge through the maelstrom of transit, eager to engage her foes. And suddenly Han, too, was eager—eager to confront her enemies openly. She allowed herself a last glance at the long, gleaming line of light beads stretched out astern of her battlegroup, then touched a stud.

"Flagship." The voice in the implant behind her ear was brisk and professional, but she heard the tension blurring its edges.

"Commodore Li," she identified herself. "BG 12 ready to proceed."

"Very well, Commodore." Han recognized the harsh voice of her admiral. "Execute your orders."

"Aye, aye, sir. Commodore Li, out." She turned her head slightly, glancing at Commander Tomanaga and Lieutenant Reznick on her com screen. "You heard the lady, gentlemen. Full military power, Commander Tomanaga."

"Aye, aye, sir!"

Tomanaga's face split in a sparkling grin of mingled tension and anticipation. His fingers flew over his command panel, and program codes flashed from his terminal to the datalink equipment sprawled across the electronics section. Reznick watched them flicker across his monitor, ready to reenter them if any of his delicate circuitry suddenly died, and Commander Sung sat beside him, feeling unutterably useless away from his station on the bridge.

Battlegroup Twelve awoke. The individuality of its ships vanished into the vast, composite entity of their data net. Drives snarled, snatched awake by signals flowing from Tomanaga's computer, harnessed and channelled to Han's will, and the battlegroup hurled itself at the warp point.

Han held her breath as the line of ships flashed towards the small, invisible portal—the tiny flaw in space which would hurl them almost two hundred light-years in a fleeting instant spent somewhere else. Only one ship at a time would enter that magic gateway, for death was the penalty for ships which transited a warp point too close together. Two ships could emerge from transit in the same instant, in the same volume of normal space—but only for the briefest interval. Then there would be a single, very violent explosion, and neither ship would ever be seen again.

Now BG 12 led the Terran Republican Navy's first offensive, and the battlecruisers struck at the warp point like a steel serpent. TRNS *Bardiche* vanished into the whirlpool of gravitic stress like a fiery dart, followed by *Bayonet*, and then it was *Longbow*'s turn. Han drew one last breath, her mind focused down into a tight, icy knot of concentration, and *Longbow* leapt instantly from the calm of Aklumar into the blazing nightmare of Cimmaron.

"Incoming Fire!" Kan snapped. "Missiles tracking port and starboard."

Damn, those gunners had been fast off the mark! Their missiles must have been launched even before they'd seen *Longbow*—launched on the probability that someone would be coming through from Aklumar to meet them. Thank God *Swiftsure* had been less alert! If the forts had been granted any more warning . . . if they'd had their energy weapons on line . . .

More missiles flashed towards her ships. She ignored them. There was nothing she could do about them. They were Kan's responsibility, his and the point defense crews'; she had responsibilities of her own, and through the blur of battle chatter and the soft beeping of priority warning signals she heard Tsing hammering his keyboard as he and Tomanaga and Reznick fought to restabilize the net and feed her the data she needed.

There! The display cleared suddenly, the icons of her battle-group clear and sharp, and they were all there! Dwarfed by the massive, crimson dots of the forts they might be, but they had all survived, and suddenly the data net had them. Missiles flashed away as their XO racks flushed. Brilliant detonations wracked the space around the fortresses, hammering their shields like Titans, and Han heard Kan's whoop of triumph. Their missile crews had been far more alert than their point defense gunners, she thought grimly. The first massive salvo went in virtually unopposed, and one of the forts was suddenly streaming atmosphere through shattered armor and plating.

But missiles were still screaming towards BG 12, and Han saw the icons of her ships flash crazily as Skywatch's warheads crashed among them. *Longbow*'s datalink took control of BG 12's point defense systems, dragooning them into a tight-woven network in defense of the entire battlegroup, and Han caught a brief impression of her two escort destroyers as their missile defenses flared like volcanoes against the incoming tide of destruction.

But not all of it could be stopped.

"Signal from *Bardiche*, Commodore! Code Omega!"

Han's eyes darted to her lead ship, the one in the spot Tomanaga had wanted for *Longbow*. The ancient, inverted horseshoe—symbol of death for the ships of Terra—flashed across her icon, brilliant precursor of her doom. Then her dot vanished, and Li Han no longer commanded four battlecruisers.

"Close the range, Commodore Tsing. Missiles to sprint mode. Stand by to engage with hetlasers."

"Good hits on target two, sir!" Lieutenant Kan's voice rang in Han's ears. He had precious little time for reports, for it was his panel, feeding through the datalink, which controlled the gunnery of the entire battlegroup, but he was right. Target two was an air-streaming ruin, its remaining weapons no longer synchronized with its fellows.

"Two's datalink is gone, Gunnery," she said, amazed at the calm sound of her own voice. "Drop it. Concentrate on one and three."

"Aye, sir. Fire shifting now!"

"*Falchion*'s out of the net, sir!" Tsing reported sharply.

"Tell her to withdraw," Han said, not even looking up from Battle One. Without the protection of synchronized point defense, *Falchion* was helpless before the hurricane of missiles slashing in upon her. Her only hope was to break off. If she could. If the forts would let her go.

Time had stopped. Han's ship lunged around her, squirming desperately through the fortresses' fire. Half her battlecruisers gone already, and the engagement had only begun! She heard her voice, cold as ice, belonging to a stranger as it rapped out orders, fighting for her ships' survival with every skill she had been taught, every intuition she had been given by God. And it wasn't enough.

She knew it wasn't enough. *Longbow* lurched as another missile slammed into her shields—and another. Where was Petrovna? Where was the rest of the task force? Surely she and her people had been fighting alone for *hours*!

"*Falchion*—Code Omega," Communications reported flatly.

"Scanners report enemy fighters launching! ETA of first strike ninety seconds!"

"Abort standard missile engagement," she heard herself say. "Stand by AFHAWKs. Take the forts with beams, Chang."

"Aye, aye, sir."

*Longbow* lurched indescribably, and Han's teeth snapped together through her tongue. She tasted blood, and dust motes hovered in the air.

"Direct hit, sir! Laser Two's gone! Heavy casualties in Drive Three!"

"Initiate damage control. Tracking, anything on BG 11?"

"*Battleaxe* is emerging now, sir!"

Thank God! Help was coming. If she could just hold on—

*Longbow* twisted, writhing as force beams pummeled her. The shields were down, and armor and plating shattered under the assault. Han felt her ship's pain in her own flesh as the shock frame hammered her, bruising her savagely through her vac suit. The bridge lighting flickered and flashed back up, and she heard the deadly hiss of escaping air.

"Vac suits!"

She snapped down the faceplate of her own helmet. It was too much. The price they were paying was too high.

"Here come the fighters!"

Han saw them on Battle One, sweeping in from port in a wave. They were too tight, showing their inexperience in the massed target they gave her gunners—but there were so *many* of them!

"Engage with AFHAWKs," she said coldly.

David Reznick no longer watched his monitor. He was too busy with his servos, fighting the mounting destruction of his jury-rigged equipment. Repair robots scuttled through forests of cables like metal beetles, bridging broken circuits, fighting the steady collapse. He was dimly aware that Commander Sung had taken over the backup monitor as he himself strove desperately against the inevitable. The vibration was even worse than he'd feared, yet somehow he kept the net on line despite the terrible pounding.

Then it happened. He was never certain, afterwards, exactly what it felt like. One moment he was crouched over his remotes, directing his army of mechanical henchmen—the next a wall of fire exploded through the compartment. He heard the screams of his datalink crew, and the air was suddenly thick with the stench of burning flesh.

He slammed down his visor in blind reflex, choking and gasping as his suit scrubbers attacked the smoke, and blinked furiously against the tears, fighting to see through the flames. He got only a glimpse of his monitors, but it was enough. There was no hope of restoring the net, and the heel of his hand slammed down on the secondary datalink. There was no response. The system was dead, and *Longbow* was on her own.

He whirled to another console, jerking a red lever, and his suit whuffed out as blast doors slammed and emergency hatches blew. The fire died instantly, smoke, oxygen, and fuel alike snatched away by vacuum, and only then did he wonder why he'd been left to throw the switch. That was Commander Sung's job—

He looked down and retched into his helmet. Less than half Sung's body lay there, and the fragment which remained was shriveled into something less than human. Reznick sobbed and dragged himself away, nostrils full of the smell of his own vomit as he crawled across the gutted compartment through the shattered circuitry and molten cables. Surely *someone* was still alive?

"Datalink gone, sir! Point Defense One no longer responds! Main Fire Control's out of the circuit! Heavy casualties in Auxiliary Fire Control!"

Han merely nodded as the litany of disaster crashed over her. *Longbow* was dying—only a miracle could save her ship now. She glanced at the plot, frozen in the instant her scanners went out. One fort was gone and one was badly damaged, but the third remained. Magda Petrovna was here, furiously engaging the remaining fortifications, and it looked as if all her ships were intact. And Kellerman's carriers were launching; she'd seen the tiny dots of strikefighters going out even as her display locked. But BG 12 was gutted. *Bardiche* and *Falchion* were gone, and *Longbow* was savagely mauled. She had a vague memory of an Omega report on *Yellowjacket*, and it horrified her to realize she couldn't remember when the escort destroyer had died.

"Withdraw, Mister Chu," she said harshly. "There's nothing more we can do."

*Longbow* turned to limp brokenly away.

Han's shock frame broke as a massive concussion threw her from her chair. She turned in midair like a cat, landing in a perfect roll and bouncing back onto her feet in an instant. Lieutenant Chu was draped over his console—it took only a glance at his shattered helmet and grotesquely twisted spine to know she could do nothing for him. Lieutenant Kan heaved himself out of the ruin of his fire control panel, one hand slamming a patch over a hissing hole in his vac suit sleeve. Tsing was there, and five ratings. The rest of her bridge crew was dead.

She was still turning towards Tsing when the drive field died. There was no way to pass damage reports to what remained of her bridge, but she needed no reports now; the loss of the field meant the next warhead would vaporize her ship. There was no time for fear or pain or loss. Not now. Her chin thrust down on the helmet switch, and her voice reached every living ear remaining aboard her ship.

"Condition Omega! Abandon ship! Abandon ship!" she said, her voice almost as calm and dispassionate as when the action began. "Aban—"

*Longbow*'s fractured hull screamed as another force beam ripped across her command section, shattering plating and flesh. The shock picked Han up and hurled her against a bulkhead, and darkness smashed her under.

An angry giant kicked Stanislaus Skjorning squarely in the spine as the assault shuttle hurtled out of the boatbay under full emergency power. Commodore Li's calm Code Omega was still sounding in his ears when the shuttle launched, and a deep spasm of grief went through him as he remembered how he'd envied Jai-shu's duty station in Point Defense Two.

Han's vision cleared. She felt hands on her arms and looked around dazedly. Tsing held her left arm, Kan her right, and the thunder of their suit packs came to her through their bodies as they fought for their lives and hers. She tried to reach her own pack controls, but she was weak, numb, washed out. They were risking their lives for her, and she wanted to order them to save themselves, but she had nothing left to give. She could only stare back at the gutted, shattered ruin of her splendid ship, her beautiful ship, her tremendous, vital, living *Longbow*, dying behind her. Point Defense Two was still in action, its Marine crew ignoring her bailout order as they fought to delay the moment of destruction—to give their fellows time to clear the lethal zone of the impending fireball, and tears clouded her eyes as she watched their hopeless battle. She should be with them. She should be there with her people. And how many of her other people lay dead within her beautiful, broken ship? How many of her family had she left behind?

The question was still driving through her as the missile struck. It took *Longbow* amidships—not that it mattered to the defenseless hulk. Han had a brief impression of fury and brilliance and light before her helmet polarized and cut off her vision. Then the fireball reached out to claim her, and there was only darkness.

# STRONGPOINT

"Amber section! Heavy weapon at three o'clock! *Three o'clock low! Thr—!*"

Stanislaus killed his armor's jump gear instantly. He plummeted downward, slamming to the ground amid the rubble of what had once been a small specialty shop of some sort. The wreckage was too blasted and burned for him to estimate what wares it might have sold, but he had other things to worry about at the moment, anyway.

He stared at the moving icons on his heads-up display. The green and red fireflies of friendly and hostile units crawled across the HUD, but it was cluttered with the shadowy outlines and wire drawings (where available) of the surrounding residential and commercial towers. Details were almost impossible to make out, and the fact that so many of the *extremely* solidly built buildings contained their own power sources and masses of still-functioning machinery—air-conditioning, lift shafts, lighting, powered doors, computer nets—made it far worse. All of those background emissions provided enough electronic "noise" to hide even powered armor from enemy sensors if its wearer shut down his own active sensors and nonessential systems.

Stanislaus' mouth twisted in a bitter grimace as he located Corporal Tso Chiang's icon. The corporal's shouted warning had been in time for the rest of this section to hit dirt and find cover in the steadily spreading wreckage of the city of Selkirk's Landing. But there hadn't been time for Tso to follow suit. The quartet of heavy auto cannon on the third floor of the two hundred-floor tower one block to the east must have spotted him at the same instant he'd spotted them. A burst of superdense forty-millimeter penetrators took him almost center of mass, and not even a combat zoot could stand up to that. The icon strobed amber while Stanislaus' armor's knees were still flexing to absorb the shock of landing. By the time they'd straightened again, the icon had flashed the black-crosshatched scarlet of a dead man.

*He shouldn't have sky-lined himself.*

The thought flashed through Stanislaus' mind, but even as it did, he knew it was unfair. This nightmare of urban terrain was the worst imaginable arena for combat . . . especially when both sides knew there were still thousands of civilians huddling out in the middle of the insane carnage. All too often the only options were to go over an obstacle—which always threatened the consequences which had just claimed Tso's life—or try to bull right through the intervening structures when any hallway or stair could hide a Rump marine with a flechette gun or a plasma lance.

Or some terrified huddle of civilians trying frantically to stay out of both sides' way.

"Amber Three, Gold One," he said harshly over the platoon's tactical net. His zoot's CPU recognized the call sign and automatically routed the signal to Private O'Grady. "Amber Two is down. You're it. Acknowledge."

"Gold One, Amber Three," O'Grady's soprano came back almost instantly. "Confirmed, I've got Amber Section."

Stanislaus grunted in bleak satisfaction. Despite her unlikely name and painfully fair coloring, Estelle O'Grady was a third-generation citizen of Hangchow. Unlike Stanislaus, she spoke perfect Chinese as well as Standard English, and she'd been with the *Longbow* detachment for over two standard years. He hated to lose Tso for a lot of reasons—including the two sons back on Hangchow who would never see their father again—but O'Grady was solid. The section would be in good hands.

As long as it lasted, at least.

He punched up the most detailed schematic he could get of the tower which had killed Tso and tried not to think about how many people he'd already lost while he worked on deciding what to do next.

It was all so goddamned *stupid*. Admiral Pritzcowitski, the Rump system commander, had tried to do the smart thing. As soon as he'd realized Sky Watch had lost control of the space around the planet, he'd ordered the system's ground forces to lay down their weapons and surrender. Like the vast majority of humanity's planets, Cimmaron possessed no heavy planetary ground-to-space weapons or planetary defense centers. Defending inhabited worlds was the job of orbital weapons platforms. Without such weaponry or fortifications, there was no way the planet's defenders could hope to stand off the Republican Navy more than briefly, and if they refused to surrender, under the Federation's own rules of warfare, the Republic would be fully justified in employing orbit-launched kinetic weaponry or even old-fashioned tactical nukes against them.

But the garrison the Rump had dispatched to Cimmaron to keep a lid on its "rebellious" citizens had been carefully selected. It was overwhelmingly Corporate Worlder, and better than half of its officers had rejected the surrender order. Stanislaus had no idea what they thought they could accomplish. Probably, they figured—correctly—that no Republican admiral would resort to weapons of mass destruction on a heavily inhabited planet if they deliberately chose their positions in the midst of its civilian population. And maybe they were so stupid they actually thought they could hold out long enough for a Rump fleet to fight its way through and relieve them. Or maybe they just hoped to kill as many "rebels" as they could before they were killed themselves.

It didn't really matter what they *thought* they were doing. The consequences were that only two of the three assault shuttles *Longbow* had managed to launch before her destruction had survived the man-portable antiaircraft missiles which weren't supposed to be fired as they approached the landing zone after Pritzcowitski's formal surrender of the system. Major Wang had been on the shuttle that exploded in midair, and Captain Ju had been severely wounded barely fifteen minutes later when the LZ came under heavy fire. Which was how Stanislaus Skjorning had found himself in command of everything that was left of *Longbow*'s Marine detachment.

Brigadier Lyman, the Republican ground commander, was only marginally less happy about that than Stanislaus himself, but there wasn't much either of them could do about it. Lyman had done what he could, attaching *Longbow*'s orphans to Major Urowski's company from TRNS *Snaphaunce* to form an improvised, truncated battalion. The brigadier had hoped Stanislaus' people could be pulled back as Urowski's reserve, but the situation was too chaotic, the fighting too vicious. Urowski had had no choice but to throw *Longbow*'s survivors into the cauldron.

"Snaphaunce One, Longbow One," he said. It felt ridiculous—and presumptuous—to identify a mere lieutenant as the commander of a battle cruiser's entire Marine detachment, but he didn't have much time to reflect on that at the moment, either.

"Longbow One, Snaphaunce One," Urowski's voice came back almost instantly. "Go."

"Snaphaunce One, Longbow is taking heavy fire from—" he doublechecked the terrain tags on his HUD "—Building Oscar-William-Three-Eight. Western wall. Can we bypass?"

"Longbow One, negative," Urowski said flatly. "I repeat, negative. Snaphaunce's left flank is also taking fire from the same building. We've tried two assaults, but they've got even more weapons dug in on the south wall, and we've got to cross plazas on both sides of the street before we can even get to the tower. We're taking heavy losses, Lieutenant, and they're using the tower as a roadblock on Central Avenue. We've got to punch them out, and bad as it may be from your side, it looks like the west wall has the least defensive firepower."

Stanislaus closed his eyes. He'd been afraid Urowski was going to say something like that.

"Snaphaunce One, Longbow One. I understand, sir. Do I have any support assets?"

"Negative, Longbow One. Everything we have is already committed. We'll have some shuttles rearmed for support strikes and on call, but not for at least another twenty minutes. We don't have that long to wait; they've got enough heavy weapons on the east wall to massacre anyone moving down Central, and Colonel Trevallion needs to get down Central to the hoverport fast, before they get dug in still deeper there. Besides, I don't think airstrikes are going to help much in this situation."

"Snaphaunce One, Longbow One copies negative support. We'll just have to do the best we can with what we have. It's going to take me a few minutes to get organized, though."

"Longbow One, you can have all the time you want . . . as long as it's not more than ten minutes," Urowski replied.

"Snaphaunce One, Longbow One copies. Ten minutes." He managed not to swear only because he knew Urowski couldn't have liked giving that order much more than Stanislaus had liked hearing it. "Longbow One, out."

He glared at the HUD for another thirty seconds, then grunted as he made up his mind.

"Gold Two, Gold One."

"Gold One, Gold Two," Huang Tse-lao responded instantly.

"Gold Two, you heard?"

"Aye, Skipper," Huang said. At Stanislaus' direct instruction, the noncom had been monitoring all transmissions between Stanislaus and Urowski.

"Then you know it's going to be a stone bitch," Stanislaus said grimly.

"What we've got is what we've got, Skipper." Stanislaus could almost hear Huang's shrug. "How are we going to handle it?"

"There's not much room for finesse." It was Stanislaus' turn to shrug. "We can use this little shopping plaza for cover—" he dropped a command into his CPU, and his zoot's tactical display obediently used a flashing cursor to indicate the three-quarters-demolished row of shops on Huang's display "—until we get within forty meters or so. We do that, then go in with a rush. But we've got to do something about those damned cannon first."

"That's a big affirmative, Skipper," Huang said harshly. He and Tso had been friends for many years.

"I think the best way to handle it," Stanislaus went on, "is for you to take Third around to the left, here." He dropped another cursor into Huang's display. "While you do that, I'll take First Platoon down the center. Amber of the Third can provide covering fire—O'Grady's already in position for that. Then—"

"On the tick," Estelle O'Grady said softly over the section's free-flow tactical net. Anything from higher authority would instantly suppress the local net, but aside from that it gave her all the advantages of face-to-face conversation with the seven Marines she'd just inherited command authority over. "Not until the lieutenant gives the word."

"Can't be soon enough," someone muttered. O'Grady's HUD IDed the speaker as Jo Binyan, the section's second grenadier.

"It'll be when it'll be," she told him.

"I know. I just want payback for Chiang," Jo said, and even though she knew he couldn't see her, O'Grady nodded in agreement. They *all* wanted payback, she thought coldly. And not just for Chiang.

She glanced around the Selkirk's Landing skyline and grimaced. It had been a fairly nice little city, once, she thought. Not much compared to an Innerworld city, maybe. Or even Hangchow, for that matter. Probably not more than a couple of hundred thousand residents. But now the drifting smoke made it difficult to tell how attractively it had once been laid out and landscaped. Most of the fires were fairly well contained, but one or two of them had clearly gotten out of hand, especially down along the riverfront, and she tried not to think about the civilians who'd lived in the green belt along the river.

"All sections," Lieutenant Skjorning's deep voice rumbled across her com. It was amazing how calm he sounded. "We'll do this on my mark, people. Stand by.... *Now!*"

O'Grady triggered her weapon. Amber Section was Second Squad's heavy weapons team, and O'Grady's "rifle" was actually a belt-fed twenty-five-millimeter cannon. Its caliber was smaller than the ones which had killed Tso, but its muzzle velocity was higher ... and so was its rate of fire. Her armor vibrated as the belt hissed out of the ammunition tank mounted behind her shoulders, and the ceramacrete façade of the tower across the street from her firing position exploded in dust.

But O'Grady's weapon was actually the *lightest* one Amber Section was firing at the weapons emplacement which had killed its leader. Jo's grenade launcher coughed rhythmically, and incandescent spikes of brimstone flared savagely as the plasma grenades detonated. Combat zoots could do a lot to protect the person wearing them, but there were limits in all things. And powered armor couldn't protect the basic structure of the building. Amber Section's merciless fire blew a crater into the face of the tower—one that belched smoke, dust, flames, and debris.

Stanislaus hit his jump gear as O'Grady's fire hammered the face of the tower. The Rump Marines had separated their cannon's firing positions, and no doubt they'd dug them in as deeply as they could. But they hadn't gotten enough dispersion, and they couldn't dig in deeply *enough* and still have useful fields of fire. He didn't have time to stand around and gawk, but he got a good enough look to know that anyone who'd been manning one of those cannon was either dead or cowering in any hidey-hole they could find.

Even that brief glance upward was almost more than he should have spared. Like all of his surviving Marines, he was covering the distance between his start position and the tower in prodigious, low-trajectory jumps. The problem was that low-trajectory jumps didn't give much margin for clearing obstacles like ornamental walls and fountains, and it was actually harder to land, recover, and jump again on a low trajectory than on a high one. Stanislaus experienced one of the pitfalls of low-trajectory urban power jumps when he cleared a marble-faced planter box and landed squarely in the middle of a big, multi-jet fountain.

Water flew everywhere, but that didn't bother him at all. What *did* bother him was that the floor of the fountain's basin was a good meter lower than he'd anticipated. It wasn't that much of an unexpected drop, but the basin was also honeycombed with plumbing to feed the fountain jets, and Stanislaus' zoot gyros whined in protest as they fought to keep him upright when his right foot abruptly stopped moving.

They almost pulled it off, but he slammed down on his right knee, better than hip-deep in the water. He recovered quickly, but somebody with an assault rifle or a flechette gun opened up on him as he scrambled back to his feet. Hypervelocity projectiles turned the fountain's water into a dense fog. They also whined, screamed, and howled as they skipped off of Stanislaus' zoot.

He swore viciously and hit his jump gear again—hard. It blasted him out of the fountain on a sharper trajectory than he'd really wanted, but being a moving target was more important than keeping as close to the ground as possible. He needed out of that bull's-eye before someone turned up with something heavier.

More fire chewed up the tower's side plaza—spewing dust, this time, not mist—and something big, heavy, and high-velocity slammed into Stanislaus' left shoulder. It drove him forward and down, and he barely managed to tuck an armored shoulder under before he hit. The impact sent him skittering across the plaza pavement like a berserk bowling pin, and he grunted at the impact, even through the zoot's inertial damping systems, as he crashed into the tower's outer wall and came to an abrupt stop.

He showed himself up into a sitting position, breathing hard, and triggered a quick diagnostic. The zoot's pauldron had survived the impact, whatever it had been. It was badly dished, and the zoot computer dropped a flashing red caret into the corner of his HUD to remind him not to expose the weakened area to any more fire than he could help, but he was effectively intact. Which was more than he could say for his rifle.

He grimaced and drew his "sidearm." There'd been some raised eyebrows aboard *Longbow* at his nonstandard choice of backup weapons, but no one had chosen to object after they saw his range simulations scores with it. The sawed-off plasma carbine was a vast improvement over the old, original single-shot weapons, but only someone in a zoot could survive the back blast and thermal bloom of firing the thing. It was relatively short ranged, and had a maximum magazine capacity of only five rounds, but not even a zoot could survive a direct hit from it. Unfortunately, he'd never expected to use the thing *indoors*, and he made a fervent mental note to liberate something a bit less fractious from the first Rump Marine he encountered.

He took a quick look at his HUD, and his mouth tightened. Three more green fireflies had turned amber, and one had turned red, but it looked like all the survivors were across the fire zone, and a couple of Marines from First Platoon's third squad turned up beside him. At least he had someone to watch his back now, he thought. And now that he did, all they had to do with their two understrength platoons was clear a two hundred-story building, about whose interior architecture they knew nothing at all, of a completely unknown number of opponents with equally unknown weapons capabilities.

*Nothing to it*, he told himself, and slammed an armored, exoskeleton-powered foot through the glass doors in front of him.

None of them had ever experienced anything like it.

There weren't that many of the Rump holdouts in the tower, really. No more than two or three dozen of them, Stanislaus estimated. But every one of the bastards had a combat zoot, and they'd obviously raided the heavy weapons locker before they chose the position for their strongpoint, because the auto cannon on the west wall were the *lightest* of the weapons they'd dug into prepared firing positions around the tower's perimeter. But given their relatively low numbers, they didn't have enough people to keep all of them manned at once, and as they realized Stanislaus' people had broken into the tower, they were forced to pull off the perimeter weapons to deal with their attackers.

That was undoubtedly a godsend to Major Urowski's people *outside* the tower, Stanislaus thought bitterly, but it didn't help *his* people one bit. And unlike Stanislaus, the defenders obviously did have a fairly good idea of the building's layout. They were waiting on stair landings, around corners, covering lift shaft doors, and Stanislaus' people had already used almost all of their sensor remotes before they ever got this far. Without remotes to toss around blind corners or lob up a stairwell, the quarters were so tight and the sensor interference so severe that at least half the time the only way *Longbow*'s Marines discovered one of those waiting ambushes was when the ambushers opened fire.

Stanislaus' hard-clenched jaw muscles ached as still more of his people went down. Most were "only" wounded, thanks to the protection of their zoots. But not even a zoot was much help when someone poked his helmet cautiously around a blind corner and someone else, in another zoot, blew that helmet off his shoulders with a plasma lance.

It was insane. The defenders couldn't win, not in the end, whatever they did. They *had* to know that. But they didn't seem to care, and they'd stockpiled plasma lances, grenade launchers, and even *rocket* launchers to use *inside* the tower. The destruction was unbelievable. Modern towers like this one were almost unbelievably tough for civilian construction, and he had no doubt the basic structure was going to survive whatever he and the defenders might do. But its interior walls had never been designed to resist that sort of fire even momentarily. Even major structural girders disintegrated like shattered glass when they took hits from shoulder-launched rockets designed to destroy heavy armored vehicles. Stanislaus supposed he should be grateful the lunatics had at least not opted to use HVMs. Apparently, even they had no desire to set off the equivalent of a low-yield tactical nuke inside the same corridor as themselves.

But that was about the *only* heavy weapon Stanislaus and his depleted fire teams failed to encounter as they fought their way savagely up, up, ever upward. Walls disappeared. Fire suppression systems tried—and failed—to extinguish the conflagration raging steadily upward with the combat. They were civilian systems, and their designers had never dreamed for an instant that they would be called upon to deal with bursts of plasma or the deliberate use of flamethrowers.

The tower's central, loadbearing core survived more or less intact, but as more and more of the less essential interior partitions were shattered, the tower itself became a chimney. A blast furnace. Air roared in through the shattered façade, sucked into the maw of the fires raging like some huge, unchecked beast, and the combatants hunted one another through the vestibule of Hell. Even combat zoots found the temperature levels hard to handle, and as the furnace blazed hotter and hotter, the chance of anyone surviving even a tiny breach in his armor essentially disappeared.

But ultimately, despite any advantages of position and their own undeniable, if totally misplaced, ferocity and determination, there simply weren't enough defenders for a building the tower's size, and as they took losses, their ability to cover multiple axes of approach crumbled. It didn't come easy, and it didn't come cheap, but *Longbow*'s survivors found themselves flanking defensive strongpoints more and more rapidly as the defenders' numbers dwindled.

In the end, the final handful of Rump holdouts were pinned down on the tower's hundred-and-eighty-first floor.

"Good to see you, Skipper," Sergeant Huang said as he and Stanislaus finally met face-to-face on the hundred-and-eightieth floor.

"The same to you," Stanislaus replied, and then his eyes widened in surprise as he checked the time. Surely they'd been fighting their way up this tower for *days* now, but according to his chrono, less than two hours had passed since Corporal Tso was killed. Two hours, in which a full twenty percent of his remaining Marines had been killed or wounded. At this rate, he'd be back down to the single platoon he was supposed to be commanding in another hour and a half.

"What now, Skip?" Huang asked, gazing up the broad, triple stairwell to the next floor. The air was so thick with smoke that even their thermal imaging systems were half-blinded, but Huang could make out the bodies of three Marines—one Republican and two Rump—tangled together on the smoldering treads of the central stair.

"We go up after them," Stanislaus said grimly. "And we don't take any fucking chances."

Huang looked at him, and Stanislaus gestured at the body-laden stairs with the grenade launcher he'd found to replace his rifle.

"I gave them the option of surrendering," he said harshly. "Those two said they wanted to accept. And when Hwang went up to collect their weapons, one of them shoved an armor-piercing grenade up against her chest and detonated it." His expression was grim, even harsher than his voice. "They don't get another chance to do that, Tse-lao."

Huang looked at him for another moment, then nodded.

"I can live with that," he said almost conversationally.

"Good." Stanislaus showed his teeth in a smile that belonged on something out of the Beaufort depths, then waved a hand at the lift shafts beside the stairwell.

"I don't see an easy way to do this, Tse-lao," he said. "I can't get a good read through the floor and all the other interference, but I'm pretty sure there can't be more than four or five of them left, at most. Unfortunately, that's still enough for at least one of them to be covering the stairs and each of the lift shaft banks we've found. And I'm pretty sure we've found them all, because if we hadn't, they'd be beating feet out of here by now."

Huang nodded again. The remaining handful of defenders had to know what was going to happen to them. Fanatic or no, if they had a way out, they would already have taken it—if only in hopes of linking up with others of their kind to continue their resistance.

"Since that's the way it is," Stanislaus continued grimly, "and since they obviously aren't interested in surrendering, the way I see it our only real option is to launch an attack straight up the stairs. They can't cover all three flights without spreading out, and the stair wells are wide enough that we can at least come at them more than one at a time each way. But I'm not real interested in paying the price an assault up the stairs is going to cost if we press it all the way. So what I'm figuring is that we push them hard enough to make them honor the threat. If they don't pull people off the lift shafts to hold us here, we'll bull through and take them out frontally. If they *do* pull people off the lift shafts—which I think they will—that's when *you* take what's left of Third Platoon up the shafts and hit them from behind."

"Skipper, I think that I should—"

"Then you think wrong," Stanislaus said flatly. "You're going up the shafts; *I'm* going up the stairs."

Huang looked like a man who clearly wanted to argue harder, but he clamped his mouth shut and nodded curtly, instead.

"Good," Stanislaus said again, softly, and smacked him on one armored shoulder. "Get your people in position. Let me know when you're ready."

"Gold One, Gold Two. We're ready when you are, Skipper."

"Gold Two, Gold One. All right, Tse-lao. On our way." Stanislaus looked around once more, then nodded to himself. "All right, people," he said. "Let's do it. *Now.*"

His Marines opened fire instantly. They'd expended a lot of ammunition on their way to this point, but they also had been liberating replacement rounds from dead Rump holdouts and their own wounded and dead, and a firestorm of destruction roared up the stairwell. Grenades sailed up through the storm front of flechettes and penetrators, and the grenadiers bounced them skillfully off the walls, sending them ricocheting around the bends in the stairwells.

It seemed impossible for anything to survive in the face of that much firepower, but return grenades came rattling and bouncing down the stairs in reply. They exploded mostly harmlessly, although they ignited fresh fires all around Stanislaus' Marines, but they constituted a grim warning that there were still live defenders waiting up there.

"First Team, move!" Stanislaus snapped, and a trio of armored Marines leapt for the center of the three stairs, moving as quickly as their jump gear allowed. They got as far as the first landing and wheeled to their left, firing up the narrow gut of the stairwell. More fire shrieked back down at them, and one of them went down, yet another firefly blinking from green to red on Stanislaus' HUD.

"Second and Third Teams!" Stanislaus barked, and six more Marines charged the other two stairs.

As Stanislaus had hoped, First Team had drawn the attention of at least some of the holdouts. The defensive fire down the flanking stairwells was much lighter, especially on the left-hand stair. In fact, Second Team got all the way to the second landing before there was *any* defensive fire on that side.

"Fourth Team!" Stanislaus said harshly, and went forward himself, leading his fourth assault group up the center stair in First Team's wake.

A grenade plunging from above bounced off his helmet and exploded behind him, sending yet another of his people down. Then he was on his belly beside First Team's two survivors, firing his own launcher steadily up the stairs. His people were taking a murderous weight of fire, but it was unaimed. They were throwing too much of their own fire up the stairs for the defenders to expose themselves to fire back accurately. They were still taking some losses, and they couldn't keep it up forever without shooting themselves dry, but it wasn't the massacre Stanislaus had been afraid he might be sending his people into.

He started working his way up the next flight of stairs on his belly. Even as he did, he knew it was the wrong move. He was the Marines' commanding officer. It was his job to coordinate, to *manage* the battle and impose control on it, not to get his idiot self shot playing "Follow me!" But this was—had to be—the final strongpoint in this entire damnable tower. That made this the last of the endless assaults they'd made to reach this point, so there was no point worrying about what happened next. And Stanislaus Skjorning couldn't—not wouldn't; literally *could not*—send his people up that stair before him.

Somebody at the head of the stairs decided to expose himself, and Stanislaus cringed as a burst of aimed fire slammed into the back of his armor. The armor held, but a shrill audio alarm sounded as the already weakened section behind his left shoulder took more damage. He could feel the heat of the furnace roaring about him seeping through the damaged section. It wasn't anything the zoot couldn't handle—yet—but if he took *another* hit there . . .

And then, suddenly, the fire roaring *down* the stairwells abruptly ceased. There was still shooting going on—a lot of it—but it was no longer aimed at Stanislaus and his assault teams. His HUD was suddenly speckled with a dozen green fireflies on the floor above him, and he bounded to his feet.

"*Come on!*" he bellowed, and hit his jump gear one last time.

The prodigious bound send him up the final flight of stairs like an old-fashioned rocket. It was, he realized, an incredibly stupid stunt which should have made him a sitting duck for any defender. But Huang's sudden thrust up the lift shafts had worked. The Rump fanatics had more immediate things to worry about as deadly accurate fire ripped into them from the rear, and they wheeled to face the shocking, unanticipated attack from behind them . . . just as Stanislaus erupted from the stairwell, already firing.

It was a gymnasium, a corner of his mind noted. A big, open space, almost as badly on fire as the floor below, with the charred carcasses of exercise equipment looming up amid the bodies and the cases of ammunition the holdouts had stockpiled here. But only a fragment of his attention applied itself to the architecture. All the rest of it was focused on killing his enemies before they killed any more of his Marines, and he got off three grenades while he was still in midair, then touched down, still firing.

After two hours of murderous combat which had reduced the entire tower to a seething volcano of internal fires, it was all over in less than seven seconds from the time he hit his jump gear.

There were no Rump survivors.

"All right, people." Stanislaus managed to keep most of his own exhaustion out of his voice as he looked around the survivors of *Longbow*'s company. It had entered Cimmaron with two hundred and six officers and enlisted personnel; the fifty-seven survivors, less Amber Section, fitted into the fire-gutted gymnasium around him easily.

"We've got the tower," he went on, "such as it is and what's left of it. But there's still the rest of the city out there. Let's get this area policed up. Tse-lao, make sure we've found all the wounded—theirs, if any, as well as ours. Fuchien, you're in charge of sorting through all this ordnance. We burned a hell of a lot of ammo on the way in, so let's reammo from what we've got here, as much as we can. Shu, your squad has perimeter security. Let's move, people."

As Huang and the other two noncoms set about executing his orders, Stanislaus walked across the burning gymnasium to the tower's outer wall, looking for a clear transmission path for his com. He found a three and a half-meter breach in the wall and stepped into it.

"Snaphaunce One, Longbow One," he said wearily.

"Longbow One, Snaphaunce One. What's your situation?"

"We have the objective. I'm down to roughly sixty effectives, and low on ammo, but we've captured a good bit of ordnance. I'll need a little time to reorganize before I c—"

"Skipper."

Stanislaus' sentence chopped off in mid-syllable at the single word from behind him. It came over his priority dedicated link to Huang Tse-lao, but that wasn't what jerked him back around from the hole in the wall. No. What jerked him back like a garrotte about his throat was the raw, bleeding anguish in the sergeant's tone.

"What?" he asked quickly. Huang was bent forward, as if his zoot's "muscles" had somehow failed, and he carried something in his arms. Stanislaus couldn't see see the small bundle clearly, but the sergeant was hunched over it.

"Longbow One, Snaphaunce One," Major Urowski's voice said over his com. "Longbow One, your transmission was interrupted. Say again all after 'reorganize.'"

Stanislaus heard him, but it was only noise, without meaning as he tried to understand what had happened to his sergeant.

"Skipper," Huang half-sobbed. "Skipper . . . it was—Oh, sweet Jesus! This was a *school*, Skipper."

Stanislaus Skjorning's heart seemed to stop. He looked around the gymnasium almost automatically, and for the first time noticed how small most of the equipment was. Realized the stature of the people it was sized to fit.

He stepped forward, and Huang raised his helmeted head, staring at him through his battle-scarred visor while tears ran down his face. The sergeant held out his arms, and a saw-edged blade of agony went through Stanislaus as he recognized Huang's "bundle" at last as the small, horribly burned body of a little girl.

"Dozens of them, Skip," the sergeant said hoarsely. "My God, my God—there are *dozens* of them, all huddled together in a classroom back there, all *dead!*"

Stanislaus' soul cringed at the thought. *They must have been up here, on the top floor, when those fucking lunatics decided to turn their building into a fort,* he thought. *Did the bastards even know they were here? Did they* care? *And what does it* matter? *My God, what they must have gone through before we killed them all in the end.*

"Tse-lao," he said. Then stopped and cleared his throat. He reached out and put both armored hands on the sergeant's shoulders.

"Tse-lao, we didn't—*you* didn't—do this. We didn't choose where those Rump bastards decided to fight from. *They* did, and in defiance of their own system commander's orders *not* to fight."

"But, Skipper—" Huang began, his voice harrowed with the agony of grief, horror, and guilt.

"We didn't *know*, Tse-lao. We *couldn't* know. And—" Stanislaus drew a deep breath and gently, very gently, took the tiny, pitiful body in his own armored arms "—there's nothing we can do for them now."

Huang stared at him, mouth quivering, and Stanislaus laid the dead girl carefully on an exercise bench.

"I know, Tse-lao," he said quietly. "I *know* exactly what you're feeling. But there's still hundreds of bastards just like the ones in this tower out there." He jerked a hand in the direction of the breached wall. "They need us—and I need *you.*"

"I—" Huang paused, then straightened. He drew a deep, shuddering breath, and nodded inside his helmet. "I understand, Skipper. I'll . . . be all right."

"No, you won't, Tse-lao," Stanislaus said. "And neither will I. But we'll deal with it together, later. All right?"

"Aye, aye, Skipper," Huang said in a stronger voice.

"Good." Stanislaus gripped his armored shoulder again for a moment. "But one thing we can do. Every one of them goes downstairs out of this fire with us. I promise you. That much at least we can do for them and their families."

"Yes, sir. I'll take care of it."

"Good," Stanislaus said again, and turned back to the hole in the tower wall.

"Snaphaunce One," he said, and a part of him was horrified by how calm, how . . . intact, his voice sounded in his own ears, "Longbow One. Sorry about the interruption, Major. My people just found some . . . civilian casualties up here. We'll be bringing them out with us. Now, what I was saying, is that I'm going to need a little time to reorganize around my casualties. I estimate—"

Lieutenant Stanislaus Skjorning, Terran Republic Marines, went on speaking crisply, clearly, doing his job, while deep inside he wept.

# CASUALTY

Li Han woke unwillingly. There was something horrible, she thought in drowsy terror. Something waiting—

She opened her eyes to a pastel ceiling and brilliant sun patterns, dancing and leaping as the window curtains fluttered, and relief filled her.

It had been a bad dream. She raised a hand to her forehead. A nightmare. If it had been real, she'd be dead. And she wasn't even . . .

Her hand slid over her forehead, and her eyes widened in horror, for she had no eyebrows. Her hand moved higher, trembling with the tactile memory of long, sleek hair . . . but there was no hair.

The discovery slashed away her drowsiness, and ivory-knuckled fists clenched. It had happened, and tears burned as her broken heart railed at a universe cruel enough to spare her from her beautiful *Longbow*'s destruction.

But long years of mental discipline chided the extravagance of her grief. The universe moved as it would; it was neither kind nor cruel, and all it asked of her was that she play her own part against its vast impartiality. Her pale lips murmured mind-focusing mnemonics, channeling grief in a technique which had served her well over the years, but this time it took over an hour to approach calm.

Yet calm came at last, and her eyes opened once more. She was in a hospital, she thought, turning to the window. On a planet with a small, warm sun that could be neither planetless Aklumar nor cool, barren Lassa and so must be Cimmaron. Which meant that the Republic had won . . . or lost. She smiled with a ghost of real humor as she pondered the question. Was she a victorious hero in a conquered hospital? Or a miserable POW, doctored by her captors? There was only one way to find out, and she reached for the call button, dismayed by the languid, weary weakness of her muscles.

Her door opened within seconds, and she turned her naked head slowly, blinking against tears and light dazzle, as a woman in nursing whites entered. It took endless seconds to clear her eyes enough to read the tiny letters etched across the nurse's medical branch caduceus. "TRN," they said.

So they'd won; no Rump commander would permit POWs to wear the Republic's insignia, and her eyes closed again as relief ate at her frail reserves. Then she felt cool fingers in the ages-old, feathery touch as her pulse was checked and forced her eyes back open, staring up into a plain, serene face.

"How—" Her throat was dry and she felt a sudden surge of nausea, but she tried again, grimly. "How long?" she husked, and the rusty croak which had replaced her soprano appalled her.

"A little over a week, Commodore," the nurse said calmly, and offered her a tumbler of half-melted ice. She held the plastic straw to Han's cracked lips, and Han sucked avidly, coughing as the water ran down her desiccated throat. It was only when the nurse finally removed the straw, gently disengaging Han's weak fingers from their almost petulant, childlike grip, that her words penetrated.

*A week!* Impossible! And yet . . .

"A week?" she repeated, cursing the haziness of her thoughts.

"Yes, Commodore," the nurse said serenely, and touched a switch. The bed rose under Han's shoulders, and she clutched suddenly at the side rails, eyes rounding in pure astonishment as vertigo flashed through her.

"Too much?" The nurse released the button quickly, but Han shook her head almost viciously. She was a naval officer, and no hospital bed was going to make *her* whoop her cookies! The nurse watched her a moment, then shrugged and held the button down until Han sat bolt upright, wondering dizzily if her pride was worth such physical distress.

But the vertigo slowly diminished. The bed still seemed to curtsy gently and nausea still rippled, but it was better. Perhaps if she told herself that often enough she would even believe it. She focused with some difficulty on the nurse's nameplate.

"Lieutenant Tinnamou—"

"Yes, Commodore?"

"Mirror?" Han husked. The lieutenant's eyes remained serene, but Han saw the doubt and forced her hurtful lips into a smile. "I—can handle it."

"All right." The nurse produced a small mirror. It seemed to weigh fifty kilos, but Han managed to raise it and peer at the stranger it held.

Her eyes were huge holes in a thin, gray-green face, sores covered her lips, and dark mottled patches disfigured her complexion. Her hairless skull seemed obscene and tiny on the bony column of her neck, and her collarbone was a sharp ridge at the neck of her hospital gown.

Rad poisoning. She'd seen it before, but, her detached, dizzy mind decided calmly, she'd never seen anyone look worse and live. Her brain went back to that final nightmare instant of consciousness, seeing her helmet polarize again. Close, she thought. Her impression of the fireball reaching out for her was all too close to the truth.

"Captain Tsing?" she asked hoarsely. "Lieutenant Kan?"

"Both alive, Commodore," Lieutenant Tinnamou said briskly, reclaiming the mirror. But she laid it conveniently on the bedside table, and Han felt pathetically grateful. The gesture seemed to imply confidence in her ability to endure what it had shown her.

"H-how bad?" She gestured weakly at herself.

"Not good, sir, but you'll make it. I'd rather let your doctor give you the whole picture."

"When?"

"He's on his way now," the lieutenant said. "I expect—ah!"

The door hissed open and a small, cherub-faced man bounced in, smiling so hugely she wondered whether she was more amused by his antics or resentful of his abundant energy.

"Good morning, Commodore Li!" he said briskly, and her eyes widened at the harsh, sharp-edged vowels of his New Detroit accent. They dropped almost involuntarily to his uniform insignia.

"Yes," he grinned wryly, "I'm one of those damned loyalists, Commodore. But then—" his smile turned gently mocking "—uniforms don't matter much to us kindly healers. I can find you a good, honest rebel if you like, but I'm really quite a good doctor."

His ironic tone touched something inside her, and her cracked lips quivered.

"Much better!" he chuckled, crossing his arms and looking down at her. "I'm Captain Llewellyn, by the way. Pleased to meet you at last. I've been in and out for the last week or so, but you've only been out."

"How bad?" Han asked hoarsely.

"Could be worse," he said frankly, "but not a lot. It was all touch and near-as-damn-it-go, actually. At the moment, you weigh about eighteen kilos."

She flinched, but her eyes were steady, and he nodded approval.

"You were lucky it was only a nice, clean fighter missile," he went on. "On the other hand, you'd already have checked out of our little hotel if you'd had the shielding of an escape pod. I understand the bridge pods were buckled and your crew got you out just in time, as it were."

"H-how many?" she husked.

"From the bridge?" He looked at her compassionately. "Five—counting you." She winced, and he went on quickly. "But overall, you did much better. Over half your crew got out safely."

Her lips twisted. He was right, of course; fifty percent was a miraculous figure. But if over half had survived, almost half had not.

"As for you, you got an awful dose, but your chief of staff seems to have unusual rad tolerance. He got you and your lieutenant picked up and hooked to blood exchangers in time, but even so, it was a rough forty-eight hours. We've managed to scrub you out pretty well, and the cell count looks okay, but it was tight, ma'am. Really, really tight."

"Don't look much like I made it anyway," Han rasped.

"Ah." Llewellyn nodded. "You *are* a bit the worse for wear, Commodore. We doctors should, after all, be honest. But you'll improve quickly now we can get you *off* the IV's and put a little weight back on you." He examined her face critically and rose briskly. "But for now, I want you to go back to sleep. I know, I know—" he waved aside her half-voiced protests "—you just got here. Well, the planet isn't going anywhere, and neither are you. We've got you scrubbed out, but you have seven broken ribs, a cracked cheekbone, a fractured femur, and a skull fracture—just for starters. I'm afraid you're going to take a while healing up from *that*."

Han blinked at him, wondering where the pain was. They must have her loaded to the gills with painkillers, she decided, which helped explain her wooziness. His last words seemed to echo around a vast, dark cavern, and she realized dimly that the cavern was her own skull. She blinked again and let herself sink into the lightheadedness. The sun patterns on the ceiling danced above her, weaving the pattern of her dreams. . . .

The next few days were bad. Han was sick and dizzy, and she hated her surrounding forest of scrubbers and monitors. The instruments were silent, but she knew they were there—probing and peering for the first sign of uncorrected damage. They were part of the technology which kept her alive, and she hated them because they were part of what confined her to her bed.

It took long, hard effort to attain her normal calm, and it slipped away abruptly, without warning. She hated her loss of control almost as much as she did her weakness, and that loss showed when Lieutenant Tinnamou refused to let her visit Tsing Chang.

Han tried reason. It didn't work, so she pulled rank, only to find that medicos are remarkably impervious to intimidation. And finally, she resorted to a hell-raising tantrum which would have shocked anyone who knew her and, in fact, shocked her—but not as much as the flood of tears which followed.

That stopped her dead. She fell back on her pillows, exhausted by the expenditure of emotion, and her emaciated form shook with the force of her sobs. She turned her face away from the nurse's compassionate eyes, and the lieutenant frowned down at her for a moment, then stepped out into the hall.

Han heard the door close with gratitude, for her reactions both shamed and frightened her. How could she exercise command over others if she could no longer command herself?

But then the door opened again and someone cleared his throat. Her head snapped back over, and Captain Llewellyn looked down at her, his cherub's face incongruously stern.

"I suppose, Commodore, that we could call this 'conduct unbecoming an officer'—but I'm old-fashioned. Let's just call it childish."

"I know," she husked and turned her head away again. "I'm sorry. Just—just go away. I-I'll be all right. . . ."

"Will you, now?" His voice was sternly compassionate. "I think not. Not, at least, until you accept that you're merely human and entitled as such to moments of weakness."

"It's not that," she protested, scrubbing her eyes with balled fists like a child. "I . . . I mean . . ."

"Yes, it is," he said gently. "I've checked your record, Commodore. Sword of honor. Youngest captain in Battle Fleet. Stellar Cross. Headed for the War College, but for the current . . . unpleasantness. And that's only the official record. There's also your crew."

"My—crew?" It popped out involuntarily, and she bit her tongue, cursing her crumbling self-control.

"The survivors have had our visitors' desk under siege ever since your arrival. If I hadn't put my foot down, you'd've been buried under well-wishers—which, since *I* don't want you plain buried, I'm not about to permit! But my point is simple: amassing that record and winning that loyalty says a lot about your personality." His voice grew suddenly gentle. "You're not used to being helpless, are you?"

Han turned away, horribly embarrassed, but his question demanded an answer. And she owed him one for keeping her alive, she supposed fretfully.

"No," she said shortly.

"I thought not. Which explains exactly why you're reacting this way," he said simply, and Han turned back towards him.

"Perhaps," she said levelly, "but it doesn't help that you haven't told me everything, either, Doctor."

Llewellyn's face stilled at the accusation, and his eyes narrowed.

"Why do you think that, Commodore?" he asked finally, his tone neutral.

"I don't know," she confessed bitterly, "but you haven't, have you?"

"No." His simple response surprised her, for she'd expected him to waffle. But she'd done the little Corporate Worlder an injustice, he was as utterly incapable of evading a direct question as she herself.

"And what haven't you told me?"

"I think you know already," he said quietly. "You just haven't let yourself face it. I'd hoped you *wouldn't* for a while, but you're more bloody-minded than I thought," he added, and a door opened in her mind—a door she had been holding shut with all her strength even as she hammered against it.

He was right, she thought distantly. She did know. Her hand crept over the blankets across her belly, and he nodded.

"Yes," he said gently, and her teeth drew blood from her lip.

"How bad is it?" she asked finally, her hoarse voice level.

"Not good," he said honestly. "A high percentage of your ova are sterile; others are badly damaged. On the other hand, some are perfectly normal, Commodore. You can still bear healthy children."

"At what odds?" she asked bitterly.

"Not good ones," he met her eyes squarely, his voice unflinching, "but you know about the problem. It wouldn't be difficult to check the embryos and abort defectives at a very early stage."

"I see."

She looked away, and Llewellyn started to reach out, then stopped as he recognized the nature of her withdrawal. She wasn't dropping deeper into depression; she was merely digesting what she had been told.

He stared down at her helplessly, tasting her anguish and longing with all his heart to comfort her. Yet he sensed something more than anguish under her sick, weakened surface, something pure and almost childlike in its innocent strength, like spring steel at her core. This was a woman who knew herself, however imperfect her self-knowledge seemed to her.

He sank into a chair, knowing she would turn back to him shortly, that his departure would shame her, watching the taut, bony shoulders relax. And as he watched the wasted body unknot, he felt himself in the presence of a great peacefulness, as if she were but the last link in an endless chain, able to draw on the strength of all who had gone before her. He'd already recognized the years of self-discipline behind her serenity, yet now his empathy went deeper, sensing the gift of freedom her parents had given her so long before, and he wished desperately that more of his patients could be so.

Her head moved finally, the delicate skull under the fine, dark fuzz shifting on the pillow, and she spoke quietly.

"Thank you, Doctor. I wish you'd told me sooner—but maybe you were right. Maybe I needed to wait for a little while."

"No, I was wrong," he said humbly.

"Perhaps. At any rate, now I know, don't I? I'll have to think about it."

"Yes." He rose unwillingly, shocked to realize that he wanted to stay within the orbit of her strength, then shook himself and smiled faintly. "Should I send Lieutenant Tinnamou back in? I think she's a bit concerned you might have, er, exhausted your strength."

"Is she?" Han's weary face dimpled. "I hadn't realized I knew so much profanity, but I'd rather be alone for a bit, Doctor. Would you give her my apologies? I'll apologize in person later."

"If you like," he said, relieved to see her smile at last, "but we kindly healers know sick people aren't at their best, Commodore."

"Please, call me Han," she said, touching his wrist with skeletal fingers. "And I *will* apologize to her. But not just now."

"Certainly. I'll tell her—Han." He twinkled sadly at her and touched his nameplate. "And my name is Daffyd."

"Thank you, Daffyd." She smiled again and closed her eyes. He left.

It took hours to truly accept it. The actual fact was not surprising—not intellectually. Somehow Han had assumed it wouldn't happen to *her*, but she'd always known it could. It was unfair, but then so was biology.

She felt tears on her cheeks, and this time felt no shame. Her life had been so orderly. She'd faced her need to excel in her chosen field, known that pride required proof of her competence. And, as a woman, the pressure for early achievement had been great, for she was not just a Fringer; she was Hangchowese, born to a culture which thought as much in generations as individuals. So her schedule had been set; she would achieve her rank, and then take time for the children she wanted.

She rolled her head on the pillow, agonized by a loss even more poignant because she had never possessed what had been lost. The pain was terrible, but the awful moment of realization was past. All she must do now was face it. All she had to do was cope with the unbearable.

It would have been different if she were an Innerworlder, she thought sadly, for the crowded Innerworlds restricted access to longevity treatments. But Han had been born on a Fringe World blessed with adequate medical technology, one where the antigerone therapies were generally available. At thirty-nine, she looked—and was—the Innerworld equivalent of perhaps twenty, and the differential would grow as time passed. She had expected another fifty years of fertility . . . fifty years which had been snatched away. For a moment, she almost envied the Innerworlders' shorter spans. They would have had fewer lonely years, she thought in a surge of self-pity.

She frowned sadly. Llewellyn was a good man, despite his homeworld, but his every word of comfort only underscored their differences. There were too few people in the Fringe. Alien gravities and environments inhibited fertility—it took generations for the biological processes to readjust fully, and no woman of Hangchow would even consider conceiving a child with a potentially lethal genetic heritage. For them, babies were unutterably precious, the guarantee of the future, not burdens on a crowded world's resources. Intellectually, Han could accept Llewellyn's words; emotionally they were intolerable.

She shook her head slowly, feeling the pain recede as she faced the decision. There was only one she could make and be true to herself and her culture, she thought, and knowing that defeated the pain.

But nothing would ever dispel her sorrow.

Time passed slowly in a hospital. Seeing days slip past without activity to fill them was a new experience for Han, and she felt events leaving her behind. Her battlegroup was disbanded as *Bayonet* and *Sawfly*, the last surviving units, were repaired and transferred to other squadrons, and even her surviving staff was on the binnacle list. Tsing Chang would be returning to duty only shortly before Han herself, and Esther Kane had never cleared *Longbow*. Robert Tomanaga would live, but he would be busy learning to walk with one robotic leg for months to come.

Only David Reznick had survived unhurt.

He was the sole visitor she was allowed for two weeks, and meeting him again was perhaps the saddest of her few duties, for if he was physically unscathed, his coltish adolescence was gone. He'd been forced to mature in a particularly nasty fashion, and she was only grateful it had not embittered him. Indeed, she felt a certain subtle strength within him, the strength of a man who has been so afraid that he will never be that frightened again. She hoped she was right, that it was strength and not the final, fragile ice over a glaring weakness. She was in poor shape when he called on her, and the visit was so brief she could scarcely recall it later, yet she felt her judgment was sound.

But her staff's losses reflected her people's casualties as a whole, and she grieved for them. There were over four hundred dead from *Longbow* alone, and it had taken all her will to remind herself that almost five hundred of her people *had* escaped.

Yet no one at all survived from *Bardiche* or *Yellowjacket*, and only twelve from *Falchion*. She supposed historians would call the operation a brilliant success, but twenty-eight hundred of her people had died, and it was hard to feel triumphant as she brooded over her dead in the long, lonely hours.

Yet endless though the days seemed, she *was* improving, and she received concrete proof of that in her third week of convalescence. A chime sounded, her door opened, and her thin face blossomed in an involuntary smile as she looked up from her bookviewer and saw Commodore Magda Petrovna.

"Han!"

Magda reached out to grip her hand, and her concerned eyes surveyed the ravages of Han's illness. But they were also calm, and Han recognized a kindred soul in the lack of effusive, meaningless pleasantries.

"Come to view the nearly departed, Magda?"

"Exactly. Mind?"

"Of course not. Sit down and tell me what's happening. It's like pulling teeth to get them to tell me anything in this place!"

Magda scaled her cap onto an empty table and brushed back her hair. The white streaks flashed in the window's sunlight like true silver, and for just a moment Han was bitterly envious of her healthy vitality.

"Not too surprising," Magda grinned. "It's a Rump hospital, and they wouldn't like to talk about a lot of what's happening."

"I think you're doing Captain Llewellyn an injustice," Han said gently from her pillows. "I don't think he worries about his patients' uniforms. He certainly couldn't have been kinder to me."

"Then he's an exception," Magda said tartly. "Most of 'em look like they smell something bad when we walk into a room. Hard to blame them, really. Their defense wasn't anything to be particularly proud of."

"No?" Han's mouth turned down. "They did well enough against me, Magda. They destroyed my entire battlegroup."

"No they didn't, Han. Oh, they hurt you, I don't deny that, but *Bayonet* and *Sawfly* came through practically untouched. And my God, what you did to them! All my group had to do was clean up the wreckage, Han—you and your people won the battle."

Han shook her head stubbornly and said nothing.

"You did," Magda insisted. "The poor Rump pilots were so green they never stood a chance once Kellerman got his fighters launched, and the local population was with us. Some of the planetary garrison tried to hold out, and there was some pretty ugly ground fighting with the holdouts. But they never had a chance, with us controlling the orbitals, and it was over in less than a day. But if you and your people hadn't smashed those forts up before they came fully on line—" She shivered elaborately.

"They did well enough against me," Han repeated with quiet bitterness.

"No argument. But they were the only vets Skywatch had, and their only Fleet units—one battlecruiser and a half-dozen tincans—hauled ass as soon as they realized we were in force." She grinned suddenly, her humor so bubbling it reached through even Han's depression. "You should hear what old Pritzcowitski has to say about *them*! They'd better pray *he* never writes an efficiency report on them!"

"I can imagine," Han agreed, and amazed herself by laughing for the first time since the battle. It felt so good she tried it again, feeling Magda's approving eyes upon her. "You're good for me, Magda."

"Fair's fair," Magda said, shaking her head. "If you hadn't done your job, I wouldn't be here. They went for *Snaphaunce* with everything they had as soon as they saw her—fortunately, you hadn't left them much."

"I'm glad."

"So was I. Oh, by the way, I checked on your Captain Tsing on the way up here. He's madder than hell the doctors won't let him come see you, but he's doing fine. In fact, he even kept some hair."

"Thank God!" Han said quietly. "And Lieutenant Kan?"

"A little worse than Tsing, but he'll be fine, Han."

"Thank you for telling me."

"Well, I hope someone would tell *me* if the position were reversed!"

"So the rest of the Fleet got off light," Han mused.

"Yep. In fact, Admiral Ashigara's already headed for Zephrain, and Kellerman's carriers are off to join our monitors and move on Gastenhowe."

"Then why aren't *you* gone?" Han asked.

"I, my dear, am senior officer commanding Cimmaron—at least for now. They added a cruiser and light carrier group to my battlecruisers, then uncrated those fighters . . . and most of Skywatch surrendered intact when they saw what you did to one detachment."

"I see." Han pursed her lips thoughtfully. "Not bad for a lowly commodore, Magda. I'm glad for you."

"You are?" Magda smiled warmly. "Thanks—but I'm only *your*

deputy. You're still senior, so as soon as you're up, the command is yours. So get yourself well and relieve me, Commodore!"

"I'd say the job was in good hands," Han said.

"Thanks, but I'll be glad to turn it over to someone else, believe me. And in the meantime, if you don't mind too much, there's someone out in the hall who'd like to see you. My chief of staff."

"Then invite him in! I haven't been allowed *any* visitors, Magda, and I still haven't thanked him properly for saving my ship at Bigelow."

Magda smiled and stepped back out into the corridor to collect Captain Windrider. Han watched his gaze move over her hairless skull and wasted face and wondered if her appearance shocked him, but he only smiled.

"Good morning, Commodore. You're looking better than I'd expected."

"Better?" Han shook her head. "Were you expecting a corpse, Captain?"

"No, just someone who'd come a little closer to being one."

"Well, I suppose I came close enough, at that," Han agreed, and patted her bed. "There's only one chair, so one of you has to sit here."

She half-expected an awkward pause as Windrider took the chair and Magda perched on the bed, but these were fellow professionals; they knew the risks, and they could speak of them unself-consciously. But more than that, she realized, she was profiting from how comfortable they were with one another. She knew they'd never met before Windrider became Magda's chief of staff, yet they seemed far closer than the mere professionalism of a smooth command team could account for. It was a personal sort of closeness, one that carried them over any bumps in their conversation without a pause.

The more she listened to them, the more aware she became of the almost telepathic nature of their communication. They used a sort of shorthand, with single words replacing entire sentences, yet seemed totally unaware of it. But they reached out to her, as well, and she found herself opening up to others as she never had before. She wondered later if physical weakness had somehow eroded her normal reserve, but she suspected the answer was far simpler than that: Magda Petrovna.

Han watched Magda, feeling the way she drew both Windrider and herself towards her. Not since she'd been a little girl in the presence of her own mother had Han felt such an aura of peace, and at this moment in her life, she could feel only gratitude, for she well knew how desperately she needed it. She allowed herself to relax completely—so completely that she barely noticed when the conversation turned to her injuries.

She never could recall the exact words in which the information slipped out, but she never forgot Magda's expression. The brown eyes were soft, but they were also warm and supportive. Few people have the gift of offering complete sympathy without undermining the ability to deal with pain. Magda, Han realized, did.

"It's confirmed?" Magda asked gently.

"Yes." Han felt her mouth twist and straightened it, drawing her serenity about her once more. Magda's support offered her strength, and she nodded. "I have about one chance in sixty of conceiving a normal child."

"Shit." Windrider's single, bitter word might have undercut her self-control, but she saw the anger in his dark, lean face and eyes. Anger over her loss, utterly unencumbered by self-consciousness. In that moment, he became her brother.

"Have you decided what to do?" Magda's face was serene, and Han felt she would have reached down to smooth her hair, had she still had hair, as she asked the question.

"I've arranged to have my tubes tied." She shook her head wryly. "Daffyd took it worse than I did, though he tried to hide it."

"I imagine," Magda patted Han's sound thigh gently. "Funny how irrational we Fringers are, isn't it?" She smiled and patted her again, then glanced at her watch and rose. "Damn, look at the time! Your 'kindly healer'—" Han grinned at Llewellyn's favorite phrase "—muttered something about firing squads if we wore you out. And you're looking a little peaked to me, so we'd better clear out. But we'll be back, won't we, Jason?"

"Sure thing, Boss." Windrider patted one thin hand, squeezing it as he rose. "Don't worry, Han. We'll mind the store until you come back."

"I'm sure you will." She watched them head for the door and then raised her voice slightly. "Thank you for coming. And—" she found the words surprisingly comfortable for one normally so reserved "—thank you for being you. It . . . helped. It helped a lot."

"Tubewash!" Magda chuckled, tucking her cap under her arm

as Windrider opened the door. "Just an excuse to get dirtside, Han!"

She sketched a casual salute and stepped through the door, followed by Windrider. It closed behind them, and Han stared at it thoughtfully. Then she let herself settle back into her pillows as the familiar drowsiness returned.

"I'm sure it was, Magda," she whispered softly, lips curving in a smile. "I'm sure it was."

# REDEMPTION

"Welcome to Cimmaron, Madame Vice President!"

"Thank you, Commodore," Tatiana Illyushina replied with admirable gravity, just as if she hadn't known the silver-haired woman in the uniform of the Republican Navy for virtually her entire life.

"If you'll come this way," Magda Petrovna continued courteously, waving at the scarlet carpet runner between the motionless ranks of the Marine honor guard, "there are other people who will be almost as happy to see you as I am."

"Of course, Commodore Petrovna," Tatiana agreed, and stepped forward as the Navy band struck up "Ad Astra," the Terran Republic's chosen anthem.

"And thank God *that's* over!" Tatiana said the better part of four hours later as she flung herself untidily into a huge, comfortable armchair in her assigned VIP suite. She looked more like a teenager than ever, Magda reflected, as she parked herself sideways, leaning back with both legs across one of the chair's armrests.

"If Lad had leveled with me about how much feathers and fuss were going to be involved with this job, I never would have taken it!" the Vice President continued astringently.

"Of course you wouldn't have," Magda agreed so affably that Tatiana half-straightened in the chair to dart a suspicious look in her direction. "I'm sure you'd be much more content just sitting home on Novaya Rodina, probably darning socks or knitting cute little caps for the troops."

"Not exactly the most respectful possible attitude, there, Commodore," Tatiana said, flopping back with a little-girl grin.

"Then don't do that 'poor-little-me' number with me, young lady."

The slight twinkle in Magda's brown eyes undermined the severity she projected into her tone, and Tatiana laughed. But then she sighed, turned to put her feet on the floor, and straightened up with a much more serious expression.

"I hadn't expected to see quite so much damage, Magda," she said quietly.

"And we hadn't expected to inflict it," Magda agreed. Her mouth thinned with anger for a moment. "The only good thing I can say for the bastards who decided not to obey Pritscowitzki's surrender order is that almost every one of them managed to get himself or herself killed in the process."

"Almost?" Tatiana repeated.

"We have about a dozen of them in custody," Magda told her.

"That wasn't in any of the reports I saw before I headed out here." Tatiana's voice was decidedly firmer than it had been, and Magda wondered if the young woman realized just how much she'd actually grown since Pieter's murder. That was still the voice of the girl Magda had watched grow up, but it was also the voice of a woman who had grown accustomed to responsibility . . . and to holding others accountable for the discharge of *their* responsibilities.

"Because we hadn't realized who they were when I sent those reports off," Magda said. "These aren't the lieutenants and noncoms who were doing the actual fighting, Tatiana. They're some of the field grade officers who coordinated the resistance. When we overran the actual fighting positions, they jettisoned their uniforms and tried to pass themselves off as civilians to avoid the net."

She showed her teeth in a cold little smile.

"It didn't work. We picked them up in ones and twos over the last week or so as we've started making real progress on organizing the civilian population."

"What have you done with them?" Tatiana asked.

"For now, I've got them confined in solitary. As for what we do with them in the end, I think that's going to be a political decision, Tatiana. I know what I'd *like* to do with them." Her normally warm brown eyes were frozen as she looked steadily at her Vice President. "So far, by our count, the civilian death toll is somewhere in the neighborhood of six thousand, and every one of them was killed in fighting which never would have happened if these people hadn't chosen to violate the legal order of their superior officer to surrender. Under Federation law and the Articles of War, refusal of a direct legal order is a capital offense. Given how many people they got killed, I don't think there's very much chance that a court-martial would choose to show clemency in this case, either. But—"

"But every single officer and enlisted person in the Republic's armed forces is currently violating the 'legal orders' of their *Federation* superiors," Tatiana finished for her.

"Exactly." Magda grimaced. "From everything we can tell, it looks like Heart World public opinion is still a bit lukewarm—or, at least not incredibly optimistic about the eventual outcome—when it comes to supporting the Rump war effort. But that's not the case on the Corporate Worlds, which is where every one of these people is from. If we shoot them, or hang them, however justifiable our actions, the Corporate World propaganda machine will have a field day with it."

"They'd claim it was an atrocity," Tatiana said sourly. "Just like they did that strike on Galloway's World."

"Not quite the same," Magda disagreed. "I'm afraid the Galloway strike probably *was* an atrocity, however we want to slice it, Tatiana. I understand why whoever did it did it, of course. And no one is ever going to be able to claim the Archipelago and The Yard weren't legitimate military targets. But it was a nuclear strike on an inhabited planet by members of the Federation's own military. We can't deny that, and, to be honest, it was a godsend for the Corporate World propagandists."

Tatiana looked for a moment as if she intended to argue, but then she shrugged.

"Point taken," she conceded. "And I suspect, to be honest, that when the Rump finally gets around to declassifying the actual damage estimates and casualty counts, we're going to find out it was one hell of a lot worse than anything that happened here on Cimmaron. But just to keep the record totally straight, the *Republic* had nothing at all to do with that strike. We didn't order it, we didn't authorize it, and we didn't know a damned thing about it until the Rump media started reporting it."

"Of course not. But nobody in the Corporate Worlds is going to admit that. For that matter, the civilians probably don't even realize that that was the way it had to have been. But right now, as far as we know, we have a lot more Rump prisoners of war than they have of our people, and all of us, on both sides, are still trying to feel our way into some sort of code for the treatment of other *human* POWs. It's not," she said dryly, "something we've had to pay a great deal of attention to over the last few centuries.

"So, if we shoot these people as they so richly deserve, are we going to provoke retaliation against our own people in Rump hands? That's the immediate, tactical concern that I and other members of the military are probably going to have. But on a more fundamental level, if we're going to argue that our decision to reject what were certainly legal orders when they were given was a valid one, as a matter of conscience, then unfortunately, I think we're on shaky ground to deny at least the theoretical validity of that argument as a defense for these people's actions."

"Point taken," Tatiana said again. She leaned back once more in her chair with a heavy sigh. "I wish just one thing about this civil war of ours could be simple and straightforward!"

"I don't think civil wars come in that flavor."

"No. No, they don't." Tatiana shook her head and considered what the other woman had said for several seconds, then shrugged.

"All right, Magda. I'm sure Lad and the Congress are going to make any final decisions about your prisoners. For right now, though, on my authority, you are *not* to consider them prisoners of war at all. Lad may overrule me, but until he does, I want no legal precedent that could be used to argue that they come under the protection of the uniforms they abused. As far as *I* am concerned, they're terrorists, murderers—not soldiers. I intend to argue that they should be held as common criminals and prosecuted as such, under the civil law code of the planet where the murders were committed, after the conclusion of hostilities."

"The Rump is almost certain to insist that they be included in any future prisoner exchanges." Magda didn't sound as if she disagreed, only as if she were noting potential difficulties. "If nothing else, the *Corporate Worlds* are going to insist. They'll probably make it a case of 'protecting' their citizens from legalized murder at the hands of us barbarians."

"At the moment, my response to that is to go ahead and let them insist all they want. I'll recommend allowing contact with them, but only through civil lawyers serving as their defense counsel in a civilian court. And I'll also recommend that we make it very plain that we have no intention of proceeding with their prosecution until the termination of hostilities and that after we've won, they will be fully entitled to representation by counsel of their choice—from the Rump, if that's what they want."

"It's going to be a can of worms however we approach it," Magda said heavily. "And it may well be something we'll run into on other worlds, again, before this thing is over. Off the top of my head, I'd say what you're proposing makes sense. As the acting Cimmaron CO, I'll endorse it officially if you want me to."

"I think that would probably help," Tatiana said. "On the other hand, you might want to wait until your opinion is asked for. I don't see any way Lad, at least, won't ask for the input of the military commander on the spot, and if you wait until you're asked, it may seem less like I put you up to it before I ever sent my recommendation in. I suspect that some of the Senators and Congressmen are already a little unhappy over the 'Novaya Rodina clique's' undue influence on the formulation of national policy, so let's not throw any more fuel on the fire unless we have to."

"I hadn't thought of that," Magda said, eyeing the young woman with even more respect. Then she shrugged slightly.

"At least a partial change of subject, Madame Vice President," she said, then paused.

"What sort of change of subject?" Tatiana asked warily.

"It's about your request to tour the worst damaged areas. I don't think it would be a very good idea to proceed the way you've suggested."

"Magda, the citizens of Cimmaron are Fringers, and the Republic is a Fringer government—one the local planetary government has already asked to join. And I, as you may recall, am the Vice President of the Republic. I *need* to see the damage, the losses they suffered, with my own eyes. Because of my office and my responsibilities to the people of this planet, and because *I*—me, individually, on a personal level—need to see it. And, politically, so that the Cimmarons *know* that I've seen it, and that the Republic takes what happened here very seriously."

"I don't disagree," Magda replied. "I only said I have reservations about the way you've suggested *making* your tour. You need more security than your plan is allowing for, Tatiana."

"I'm not some Inner World machine politician!" Tatiana said hotly. "I don't need an entire posse of security people, armed to the teeth, between me and our own people!"

"Yes, you *do*." Magda's voice was so firm that Tatiana blinked at her.

"You're not back on Novaya Rodina," the commodore continued

in that same no-nonsense tone. "These people don't know you the way people back home do. To them, you're still just as much an outsider as the Corporate World Marines who had their boots on the backs of their necks. Maybe—no, certainly—almost all of them think of you as a different *kind* of outsider, but they've been through a lot in the last couple of months. The best of them are going to be wary, and some of them are going to blame *us* for the deaths of family and loved ones. Yes, the bastards I've got in lockup are the ones who decided not to surrender, but *we're* the ones who decided to attack the planet. For that matter, in a population this size, there have to be Rump sympathizers. Maybe it's only a tiny percentage of the total population, but that's still a very large absolute number. And all it takes is one Rump loyalist, or one unstable person who's lost a husband, or a wife, or child and has access to a gun, for the Republic to need a new Vice President. And I," she finished in a tone of vast understatement, "wouldn't like that very much."

"Neither would I, when you put it that way," Tatiana admitted with a crooked smile. "And your solution is?"

"My solution is tighter security." Magda grimaced. "To be perfectly honest, what I'd *like* to suggest would be that you forget about it completely. Unfortunately, your political arguments are valid, and I know from personal experience just how stubborn you are. So my compromise solution is to assign you a bodyguard of Marines and lay on some fairly visible overhead security with armed skimmers prominently on display. If it will make you feel any better, I'll have the Jarheads drape the skimmers with some nice, festive bunting and pretend they're a parade in honor of your visit, but I *want* that security in place before I let you out on the street, young lady!"

"My, doesn't *that* sound like fun," Tatiana said with a grimace of her own that was only half-humorous. "I can just see myself now, marching along with some suspicious, hard-nosed Marine hanging over my shoulder like an anchor."

"Oh," Magda said with a lurking smile. "I think we can probably do a little better than that for you."

" . . . and that over there used to be the Weston Tower, Madame Vice President," Councilman Higgins said. He gestured at the huge structure, now little more than a charred shell, and his voice was heavy. "That one was particularly ugly, I'm afraid."

Tatiana glanced at him. He sat next to her in the open skimmer's middle row of seats, and his expression was as grim as his tone of voice. Selkirk's Landing was the heart of his constituency in the Cimmaron planetary legislature. That was what had won him the seat he occupied now . . . and, she was sure, explained his dark emotions.

She looked over her shoulder at the Marine captain sitting in the jump seat behind her. She'd been both delighted and more than a little irritated by Magda's choice of nursemaids. If she'd been permitted to make the choice herself, it would have been exactly the same one, but the slight, knowing smile Magda had bestowed upon her when she produced the newly promoted Captain Skjorning had been maddening. Not a surprise, really. Novaya Rodina was the sort of world where everyone knew exactly who everyone else was seeing. Just . . . maddening.

She was certain Stanislaus had been pleased to see her. The light in his blue eyes had given that much away, at least. But he wasn't the man she remembered from Novaya Rodina. That man was still inside there somewhere, and she saw occasional flashes of him, but only like brief sparkles of light behind the barred shutters of the grim, haunted eyes of the man he had become. Now his face was expressionless as a stone wall, and that very absence of expression on the face whose smiling gusto for life had implanted itself so deeply in her memory, was like the blow of a fist.

He wasn't even looking at her. For that matter, for the first time since they'd set out, he didn't seem to be watching their flanking armored Marines or the armed skimmers hovering above them at higher altitudes, either. He was staring at the building—the one Higgins had identified as the Weston Tower—and his jaw was clenched.

"I've seen a lot of ugly things since my arrival, Mr. Higgins," she said, turning back to the Cimmaron legislator. "A lot of tragic, heartbreaking things."

"I know you have, Madame Vice President." Higgins, too, was staring at the burned-out building, but he shook himself and met Tatiana's gaze. "But the holdouts turned that building into a strongpoint . . . without evacuating the school on its upper floors."

"Oh, my God," Tatiana whispered, and he nodded slowly.

"Wasn't your people's fault," he said heavily. "No way any of them could have known there was a school up there. Or that the lunatics shooting at them hadn't at least evacuated the children. But we lost two hundred. Two *hundred* kids, Madame Vice President. Not a one of them over the age of ten standard years."

A tear Tatiana knew was completely genuine sparkled at the corner of the man's eye, and he shook his head.

"Some of our people, the parents especially, are . . . pretty bitter over it," he said. "Who can blame them? Their *children* are dead, and the only people still alive for them to hate are your Marines. They'll get past that part of it, eventually—most of them, at any rate. They'll understand who was really responsible for it. But right now, the wound's still too fresh, the pain's still too sharp."

He sighed, watching the building as the skimmer moved steadily past it. Then he shook himself and managed a smile. It wasn't much of a smile, but at least he was trying.

"This next bit doesn't bother me anywhere nearly as much," he told her, pointing at the better part of an entire square block of burned-out buildings. "This whole block belonged to the Masaryk Corporation, out of New Detroit. They've been evading taxes and siphoning money out of the Selkirk's Landing economy for as long as I can remember. Rebuilding *this* block is going to be a pleasure!"

Tatiana nodded, smiling back at him, but she didn't even see what he was pointing out to her. Her attention was fixed on Stanislaus Skjorning's profile as the bearded Beaufort giant's eyes remained locked on the looming tombstone of the Weston Tower.

The sun had set, and the cool, early fall night was settling in over the balcony terrace of Tatiana's suite as she sat down to supper. It was the first time all day that she'd truly had any time to herself, and she looked across the table at her sole dinner guest.

He hadn't wanted to be there. If she hadn't seen the pain in his face, she would have been hurt by his efforts to avoid the invitation. But as Magda Petrovna had observed, Tatiana Illyushina had grown. She refused to allow him to evade her, and so he sat facing her across the snowy white tablecloth and glitter of crystal and china.

The food and the service were superb; she'd expected that. What she hadn't expected, despite the deep and obvious changes in Stanislaus, was that he would be virtually silent throughout the meal. That hurt, too, but she simply pretended not to notice, pretended to concentrate on her own excellent dinner, just as he was pretending to concentrate upon his.

Until the dessert dishes had been removed and they were left with only their wine glasses, at least.

He looked around, then, with the first obvious uneasiness she'd seen out of him. Well, she reflected, that was probably wise of him.

"Tell me, Stanislaus," she said quietly.

He twitched as if she'd touched him with a live wire. His eyes jerked up from the wine glass in his hand, and despite everything she'd already seen, all of her suspicions, she was shocked by the fear she saw in them. *Fear*—the one thing no one would ever have expected from any Skjorning, she thought.

"To be telling what?" he asked.

"Don't pretend that you don't know what I'm talking about," she said gently. "I've been with you all day. You haven't made a single joke, haven't produced a single real smile, haven't said any of those absurd, wonderful things you always say. You're a ghost, Stanislaus—the ghost of the man I met on Novaya Rodina. And I want that man back. I want him back now, here. And you're going to tell me where he's gone so I can bring him back."

She stopped and cleared her throat, surprised at the way tears had fogged her voice, prickled at the backs of her eyes.

"Tatiana—" he began, then closed his mouth. Jaw muscles bunched, and he looked away, over the terrace's rail at the sparkling lights of First Stop, Cimmaron's planetary capital. From here, in the gathering dark, all they could see were the lights, sparkling with the purity of Heaven's own stars. The damage, the wreckage left by the fighting which should never have happened, was invisible, but both of them knew it was there.

"Lass," he said finally, still looking away, "don't ask me to be telling you. It's—It's not to be something I'd want you to be carrying with you. Bad enough that I—"

He cut himself off, chopping one hand in the air between them.

"I can't do that," she told him softly, and he looked at her, obedient, manifestly against his will, to the unwavering determination of a voice as stern as Beaufort bedrock. "I thought you were only going to be someone to have a good time with for a few days before you shipped out," she continued. "And I did—have a good time, I mean. But that wasn't all that happened, and I don't think it was all that happened for you, either, Stanislaus. And I won't—I *can't*—walk away from that, or from *you*. If it hurts you,

I'm sorry. But I'm not going away, and I'm not letting you go away from me. So tell me. You've got to tell someone."

"I . . . I can't," he said, and his voice was hoarse.

"I didn't see what you've seen here, Stanislaus," she said with an odd, quiet serenity. "I doubt I can even imagine what you saw here. No, I'm sure I can't—I saw your face when Higgins was telling me about the school." His nostrils flared, and he flinched as if she'd just punched him. "But I saw Pieter Tsuchevsky shot. I *knew* they were going to shoot me next. And I saw Marines—Marines in the uniform of *my* Federation—murdering people I'd known from the day I was born. I saw them firing into the crowd, and I saw that crowd go over them like the sea, Stanislaus. I saw them in some cases torn apart—*literally* torn apart—by the bare hands of my neighbors, my friends. So no, I can't imagine what you've seen here, but I think I can at least begin to understand, to share it with you, if you'll just let me in. And knowing that there *is* someone to share it with you . . . that's important, Stanislaus. That's *so* important."

"But—"

"Start at the beginning," she told him, still with that note of implacable, serene command. "I've cleared my schedule for the entire night. So take your time. But start now."

He looked at her squarely for the first time since she'd begun speaking, and she kept her own expression calm and attentive as she saw the tear trickling down his right cheek. For an instant longer, he wavered. But then he closed his eyes, his shoulders seemed to sag visibly, and he sat back in his chair.

"It wasn't to be this way," he began finally, slowly. "Not like this. But after we'd broken into the system, after they'd had the killing of *Longbow*, Brigadier Lyman assigned us to the occupation of Selkirk's Landing."

He inhaled deeply.

"We'd the wording that the planet had surrendered," he continued, "and—"

Tatiana Illyushina sat there in the chill of the gathering night and listened as Stanislaus Skjorning surrendered his pain to her one slow, anguished syllable at a time.

The larger of Cimmaron's moons was high overhead, shining down on a city which had largely turned off its lights and gone to sleep. But on one terrace balcony, the lighting still burned dimly as a young woman sat on the long, padded bench against the terrace's outer parapet. A tall, broad shouldered Marine captain lay stretched out on the bench, his head resting in her lap, and her hand lay gently on his huge chest.

Stanislaus' face was no longer the armored mask he had shown that Tatiana from the moment of her arrival on Cimmaron. The mask was gone, crumbled into ruin, and if the face which had hidden behind it was older, more worn, than the one she remembered from Novaya Rodina, at least it belonged to the same man once more. She stroked his chest gently, her hand scarcely moving, and she knew her own face showed the tears she'd shed as he told her about the people he'd lost, the people he'd killed . . . those tiny, broken bodies in the flaming charnel house which had been a school. It was the children, she knew. That was what had threatened to destroy him. And the fact that he'd *known* that it truly wasn't his fault, hadn't meant that it wasn't his *doing*.

But they'd survived that. He'd gotten it out, shared it with her, and he'd been right about the horror she would feel, the grief. But she'd been right about his need to let her in so that he was no longer alone with the crushing weight of those murdered children. And now, hours later, in the hard-won tranquility that came after the storm, they floated together in the quiet hollow of the night's hand.

"Look at the moons, Stanislaus," she murmured. "Aren't they beautiful?"

"Aye, they are that," he agreed. "A mite on the small side, they're to be, for a proper moon, but beautiful."

"You and Lad!" She laughed softly and hit him on the chest with a small fist. "To hear the two of you talk, every single thing on Beaufort is bigger and better than anywhere else in the known universe!"

"Bigger, aye. That they're to be, I'm thinking. But better?" He shook his head. "Not always better, and right this minute it's in my mind that it may just be Novaya Rodina has the most beautiful sight I've ever had the seeing of."

"What are you talking about now?" she asked, but her voice was low, soft, and her eyes softened as he reached up one hand to touch her cheek gently.

"I'm thinking you're to know that already, love," he said very, very softly, and something inside her trembled as he called her "love" for the first time.

"I don't know how you passed the Marine physical with vision that bad," she said, and he shook his head.

"No, love. It's past the time for us to be hiding behind jokes. It was a dark place I'd gone to, and it's the light of you that's to be bringing me back from it again. So let's not be pretending any longer, you and I."

"It'll never work, you know," she told him . . . in the voice of someone who believed exactly the opposite. "You're from Beaufort; I'm from Novaya Rodina. I've never seen a body of water larger than a pond in my entire life—not close up and personal. And you—! I can just see you as a *megaovis* rancher on Novaya Rodina!"

"Somehow, I'm doubting that you're to be one bit less stubborn than me," he said. "And that being so, aren't you thinking that it's to be a mite silly to be dwelling on niggling little details like that? Besides, you're to be Vice President, and Congress has already had the deciding that Beaufort's to be our capital." He smiled, a smile that was more than a shadow of the infectious grin she remembered. "So I'm to be having the inside track, I'm thinking."

"You do, do you?"

She arched her eyebrows, then laughed suddenly. The sound was throaty and low, and it bubbled with a sort of wicked joy. Of relief, and the feeling of life in her veins. She thumped his chest again, and then she pushed at him—a bit like a miniature poodle pushing at a great dane.

"Get up!" she told him peremptorily. "Come on, you big lummox—on your feet!"

"And what's this to be about?" he demanded as he climbed to his feet once more, towering over her.

"It's about taking unfair advantage," she told him tartly, looking up at him in the moonlight with laughing eyes. "You're so damned complacent about getting me to Beaufort. Well, you may be right. But in that case, Captain Skjorning, I intend to acquire a few unfair advantages of my own."

"Such as?" he inquired, smiling back down at her, and she took one of his hands in both of hers and started towards her suite, towing him behind her, like a catcher boat towing a doomwhale.

"As I believe I may have mentioned earlier," she told him, "I've cleared my schedule for the *entire* night."

# DRUMBEAT

*"Courage above all things is the first quality of a
warrior."*

General Karl von Clausewitz, *On War*

Zephrain, as humans rendered the name bestowed by its Orion
discoverers, was a distant binary system. Component B, an orange
K8 star, swung ponderously around its yellow G5 companion
in an orbit of over fifty percent eccentricity, coming as close as
three light-hours at periastron. Both stars had small families of
planets, and extensive asteroidal rubble marked the hypothetical
orbits of stillborn gas giants which would have formed but for the
gravitational havoc wrought by each star on the other's planetary
system.

Zephrain A-II was Earthlike—a small, dense world with abundant
liquid water and free oxygen. Named Xanadu by a humorously
inclined Terran Survey officer, A-II was home to a thriving human
population, but Zephrain RDS was on Gehenna, Planet A-III—a
lifeless, nearly airless ball of sand not much better than Old Terra's
neighbor Mars—precisely because the station must inevitably be
the primary target in the system. Since Howard Anderson's day,
the TFN had believed that "combat should be kept out in space
where it belongs," or, if not in space, at least on worthless planets
no one would miss when the planetbusters arrived.

And that, thought Vice Admiral Ian Trevayne, was a very fine
policy against aliens who would lose no sleep over the incidental
genocide of whole human colonies. But in a war between humans,

857

there were arguments for placing targets like Zephrain RDS next to a city or two. Or would that have given the Terran Republic pause, after all? Certainly the murderous bastards had already shown their willingness to inflict noncombatant casualties, he thought bitterly.

The Terran Republic! Trevayne recalled a cynical query concerning Old Terra's Holy Roman Empire: in what respect was it holy, Roman, or an empire? He almost voiced the thought to the older man beside him, but he knew he would have gotten a look of incomprehension and polite disinterest. Vice Admiral Sergei Ortega was no history buff.

At any rate, there were more urgent matters at hand. Like persuading Ortega to stay aboard this ship.

They stood on the flag bridge of the monitor *Zoroff*, Trevayne's flagship. Accompanying her in orbit around Xanadu were the other ships of the battlegroup he'd brought through the chaos of insurrection to Zephrain. He still couldn't contemplate the journey without a feeling of awe that he had actually gotten away with it.

Battlegroup Thirty-Two had been stunned when news of the first mutinies arrived from the Innerworlds, but Trevayne had foreseen the storm and taken precautions. His personnel, even the Fringers, knew and trusted him, and his captains had been loyal to a man (or woman, as the case might be). The few outbreaks had been quelled with a minimum of bloodshed.

Only then had there been time to come to terms with the *other* news the light cruiser *Blackfoot* had brought. News of the bloody raid on Galloway's World, BG 32's home port, which had gutted the Federation's largest shipyards and destroyed, among other incidental items, Admiral's Row, where Natalya, with seventeen-year-old Courtenay and thirteen-year-old Ludmilla, had awaited his return. . . .

Doctor Yuan, *Zoroff*'s chief medical officer, had explained the "denial phase," when tragedy remains merely unacceptable. Luckily for BG 32, Trevayne had still been in that state when a rebel fleet followed *Blackfoot* through the same warp point.

His orders had come with a methodical precision as ship after ship emerged from transit. There were too many to fight—but none had been monitors, and nothing lighter than a monitor really wanted to *catch* a monitor. That natural hesitancy to invite self-immolation had given him the chance to disengage and run, but there were few places to run as the Fringe went mad. He remembered the weary progression of systems: Juarez, Iphigenia, Lysander, Baldur—where he'd hoped to break back to the Inner-worlds only to meet a rebel carrier group which cost him both scouting cruisers. Baldur had been bad. It was at Baldur that he'd realized he was completely cut off from the Innerworlds, his only choice to stand and fight or head into Orion space.

The Orion commander at Sulzan had been a fool, and Trevayne was grateful for it. The Khan's official policy of neutrality should have meant internment for any TFN refugee, but Small Claw Diharnoud'frilathka had dithered long enough for Trevayne to transit out for the district capital at Rehfrak. The District Governor was no fool, but he, too, had turned a blind eye as BG 32 passed through. Probably, Trevayne suspected, because of the Khan's vested interest in an Innerworld victory . . . though BG 32's firepower might have been a factor, as well. Whatever the reasoning, the governor had allowed him to leave via the one warp point he'd really wanted: the one to Zephrain.

Zephrain, gateway to the region known as the Rim. Zephrain, the largest naval base humanity had ever built. Zephrain, where—to his relieved surprise—the Federation's writ still ran.

The people of Xanadu shared the same political and economic grievances as other Fringe Worlds, and they contemplated the proposed Federation-Khanate amalgamation with equal revulsion. But militant loyalty was bred into them, for their system had borne the brunt of the Fourth Interstellar War. Every man, woman, and child in the Zephrain System had been an expendable frontline soldier against an enemy who saw humans as culinary novelties. Between them and the Arachnids there had been only one shield: the Federation's ships. The Federation was nearly a religion to these people, and they had not been prepared to entertain a schism.

Isolated by rebellion from the rest of the broken Federation, they'd formed a loyalist provisional government. Since Admiral Ortega, commanding the Frontier Fleet elements at Zephrain, had found himself equally isolated from his superiors, he had placed his forces at the disposal of the provisional government. He was neither brilliant nor imaginative, but his integrity was absolute and he had the seniority. Trevayne had placed himself under his command.

But once the desperate race was won, what had happened came crowding back like a slow, dreary drumbeat to which the rest of his life was mere counterpoint. The realization that only Colin was left to him. Colin . . . whom he had last seen as an angrily retreating back.

He remembered the quarrel with merciless clarity. Colin had declared his sympathy for the Fringers, and Trevayne reacted with fury. And that, he thought, was because his son had blurted out things he himself felt but could not say, so that he'd been reduced to sputtering like an idiot about "Your oath . . ."

"My oath," Colin had shot back, glaring at him with Natalya's blue eyes, "is to the Federation, not a bunch of greasy Corporate World political hacks! Can't you *see*, Dad? The Federation you and I swore our oaths to died with Fionna MacTaggart!"

"That's enough!" Trevayne had roared. "D'you think I don't know the Fringe Worlds have grievances? But neither those grievances *nor anything else* can justify shattering over four centuries of human unity!"

So it had gone: the sterile repetition of incompatible positions and the final, angry parting. Now the only anger Trevayne had left was reserved for the fate which had kept him in deep space as a junior officer for most of Colin's boyhood. Only later, with more time in port, had he found that which is given to a parent but once: to rediscover the universe while first watching a child discover it. And he'd found it with Courtenay.

Trevayne made one last try as he and Ortega left the flag bridge.

"Damn it, Sergei, *Zoroff*'s command facilities are far better than *Krait*'s, and incomparably better protected. It doesn't make sense to keep fleet command in something as fragile as a battleship—and you bloody well know it!"

Ortega smiled wearily. He followed Trevayne's advice on most things, but on this he had his heels dug in and there was no moving him.

"Ian, *Krait*'s been my flagship ever since I've been out here. Most of my people are from the Rim, and we've gotten to know one another, they and I. But if I transfer to *Zoroff*, no matter why, they'll think I don't trust them anymore . . . and they won't trust me. Things are chaotic enough; let's disturb routine as little as possible."

He paused for a moment, then resumed as if reluctantly.

"And don't start again on my allegedly indispensable personal acquaintance with the key people in the provisional government. We both know the Rim is still pretty volatile and that we'll probably have to proceed under martial law in one form or another."

"Now *you're* underestimating these people," Trevayne demurred. "They know better than most what war is about, and they put together the provisional government because they're loyal. So you *are* important because of your connections with it. Why, your daughter's one of its founders! There's no need to bypass it. Let's just give it a chief executive who represents the Federation and has extraordinary powers for the emergency. My legal officer and I have come up with a precedent: a captain who assumed emergency powers as temporary military governor of the Danzig System during the Theban War and was upheld afterward. We'll declare you—oh, say Governor-General of the Rim for the duration."

He held up a hand against the objections that were halfway out of Ortega's mouth.

"If the Assembly doesn't like it, they can say so when contact is reestablished. But for all we know, Sergei, the Rim is all the Federation that's left. Old Terra could have fallen into a black hole last month, and we'd have no way of knowing it. We're on our own out here, and we'd better start acting accordingly. *That's* why you're so bloody important . . . because you're one of these people's own, at least by adoption!"

Ortega opened his mouth, then closed it. Finally he shook his head.

"For God's sake, Ian, you're moving too fast for me again! Let's at least defer this until the immediate threat is past."

The "immediate threat" was, of course, the rebel attack that must come, sooner rather than later. Not because of the mammoth building and refitting facilities. Not even because Zephrain held the "Gateway," the warp point which was the Rim's only practicable link with the rest of the Federation. What made Zephrain unique was the R&D Station, where two generations of brilliant minds had happily turned out the blueprints for a whole new order of military technology. They'd been cheerfully oblivious to the fact that none of it was being produced. (Who wanted a new arms race with the Khanate of Orion?) But what they'd never seemed to notice was that their quest for a heavier, longer-ranged missile had brought them innocently to the threshold of a gravitic engineering revolution that would transform more than just warfare. The memory banks of Zephrain RDS were a womb wherein a whole new era gestated—and Trevayne would unflinchingly perform a thermonuclear abortion if he saw the station about to fall into rebel hands.

Zephrain RDS was the key to the Rim. If enough of the new weapons could be put into production—and the Zephrain Fleet base was one of the two or three places in the Federation where it might be done—then the Rim would survive. And, knowing that, Trevayne and Ortega had to assume the rebels *also* knew it and would act to prevent it.

The intraship car reached *Zoroff*'s boatbay, and the two admirals emerged, a study in physical contrast. Ortega was short and slightly overweight, his stocky frame and broad, high-cheekboned face reflecting his Slavic and Mesoamerican ancestry. Trevayne was tall, lean, and very dark, an Englishman with more than a trace of the "coloured" genes that the departing empire had bequeathed to the island's population in the late twentieth century. His hair was beginning to thin on top, but unlike some (including Ortega) he'd made a good job of growing the short, neat beard currently in vogue among male TFN officers. The latter caused him more satisfaction (and the former more annoyance) than he cared to admit.

"After I get back from the exercises, let's both visit Xanadu for a few days," Ortega said. "You've been ship-bound too long, Ian—getting a touch of bulkhead fever, I'd say." He grinned toothily. "Besides, I want to introduce you to some of the people in the provisional government—especially Miriam." His face took on the expression it usually wore when he spoke of his daughter: a mixture of pride and bewilderment. "She's been wanting to meet you."

"I'd be delighted," said Trevayne, not sounding particularly delighted. Ortega noticed the lack of enthusiasm and smiled again.

"You may as well resign yourself, Ian. She's like you—she tends to get her way. It's almost unnatural how much like her mother she is."

They proceeded towards Ortega's cutter, and Ortega paused as the Marine honor guard clicked to attention.

" 'Governor-General'!" he snorted. Then, with a sudden twinkle, "Well, at least it got your mind off trying to keep me aboard *Zoroff*!"

The next day found Trevayne in the small staff briefing room adjacent to *Zoroff*'s flag bridge with his chief of staff, Captain Sonja

Desai, while his operations officer, Commander Genji Yoshinaka, described the exercises planned for the next few days. Captain Sean F. X. Remko, *Zoroff*'s CO, attended via com screen from his command bridge. Part of Trevayne's brain listened to the briefing, but another part considered his three subordinates.

Desai listened to Yoshinaka with her usual thin-lipped lack of expression. Looking at her dark, immobile face, a blend of Europe and India, Trevayne knew she would never be a charismatic leader, but her brilliance was acknowledged even by those—and they were many—who disliked her.

Remko's ruddy, brown-bearded face nodded in the com screen as he followed Yoshinaka's comments. Trevayne could easily visualize the workings of the burly flag captain's mind. Remko was a battlecruiser man by temperament, but he performed his present duties with aggressive competence. He was a fighter, a man whose sheer guts and ability had carried him from a childhood in the Hellbroth, the worst slum on New Detroit—a planet noted for its slums—to his present rank despite the prejudice his buzz-saw accent engendered.

Yoshinaka was gesturing at the clustered display lights that represented all of Ortega's Frontier Fleet strength, except those units keeping watch over potential trouble spots throughout the Rim, as they floated near the Gateway and its fortresses in preparation for exercises with Zephrain Skywatch. Like Trevayne, the ops officer was that rarity in the TFN, a native Old Terran, and that distinction had always formed a bond between them. It was an unspoken bond—not much ever had to be spelled out for Yoshinaka. He was a deft, subtle man who stayed in the background. No one but Trevayne fully recognized the unobtrusive ops officer's importance to what Yoshinaka himself called BG 32's *wa*, a word inadequately translated into Standard English as "group harmony."

Remko suddenly turned a scowling face to someone outside the screen's pickup. He listened a moment, his scowl fading into tense understanding, then broke in on Yoshinaka.

"Priority signal from Skywatch, Admiral! Missile pods are beginning to transit the Gateway! The minefields are taking some out—but not many!"

Trevayne looked quickly at the display unit. Clearly Ortega had gotten the same message. Some of the yellow and orange lights in the tank—his faster cruisers and destroyers—were already accelerating away from the red lights of his capital ships.

"Captain," Trevayne clipped as he rose from his chair, "sound general quarters. Commodore Desai, we're leaving orbit immediately and proceeding to the Gateway under maximum drive."

He strode onto the flag bridge, Desai and Yoshinaka on his heels, as a com rating looked up with a signal from *Krait* that confirmed the orders he had anticipated.

Beneath his decisiveness, Trevayne was amazed that the rebels (he would *not* call them "the Terran Republic") had managed to organize their attack so soon. But then he saw the intelligence center's preliminary analysis of the forces emerging from the Gateway even as the last wave of pods launched their clusters of homing missiles to seek out the orbital forts. They were in less strength than he would have anticipated, particularly in carriers. Perhaps they were attacking before they were quite ready. And perhaps they didn't realize BG 32 had arrived? His lips curved wolfishly at the thought.

The fortresses were taking a terrible beating—not surprisingly, in light of how close to the point they'd been deployed. Trevayne hadn't liked that, but one had to work with what one had, and those forts were armed with heavy batteries of primaries. It was, in his considered opinion, a criminally stupid design philosophy, given what sprint-mode SBMHAWKs could do to any platform. No doubt it had made sense to the overly clever theorist in his safe office back on Old Terra who'd ordered its adoption . . . and who was not, unfortunately, present to share in its test by fire. But there'd been no time to even contemplate changing their armament, and the short effective range of their weapons dictated the range at which they could be deployed, so he and Ortega had been forced to settle for beefing up their missile defences as much as possible and hoping.

It was obvious that the platforms were taking murderous punishment and heavy casualties, despite the missile defense upgrades, but their primaries—those that survived to fire—were doing their intended job. Trevayne hated the exorbitant cost in lives and material, but he had to admit that they were pulling a lot of the attackers' teeth, and Ortega's battleships were launching long-ranged strategic bombardment missiles. To which they inevitably would soon be receiving a reply in kind. In fact, the first rebel missiles were already spitting back, and a high percentage of those missiles were targeting the respective flagships, for both side's fire control could pick out targets on a "first name" basis. It would not, Trevayne thought sourly, be a healthy war for the top brass.

BG 32 was still beyond scanner range of the Gateway. In some commands, the fact that the only hostile warp point into the system was beyond scanner range might have led to a certain laxness in the scan ratings: not in BG 32. Trevayne expected maximum scanner capability whenever the ships were at general quarters, and his captains had learned that his standing orders were best taken seriously. Thus it was that Sonja Desai, her usually immobile hatchet face animated by excitement, exclaimed:

"Admiral, we've picked up a trio of cloaked assault carriers! Now that we've isolated them, we should be able to catch any escorts. . . . Yes, they're coming in now: two fleet carriers and a light cruiser. The cruiser must be a scout, since she's carrying third-generation ECM. Distance just over eighteen light-seconds, heading . . ."

She rattled off the figures, then her head jerked up to dart a startled look at her admiral.

"Admiral, they're on a course about seventy degrees from ours, converging rapidly, and they seem to be coming from somewhere around Zephrain A!"

But Trevayne's mind had already gone to full emergency overload as he assimilated the data and its implications. There was only one possible answer: a defense planner's worst nightmare—a "closed" warp point. The only way to locate a closed warp point was to come through it from the normal warp point at the far end. Obviously the rebels had done just that, undoubtedly with cloaked survey probes, and now that they had the defenders' attention riveted by their great, noisy frontal attack, they'd sent this lot in through the back door neither he nor Ortega had suspected existed.

Yes, it made sense—whether they knew about BG 32 or not. Carriers to get up close undetected and launch a massive fighter attack from the rear, and a scout cruiser's scanners to provide "eyes" without using easily detected recon fighters. And the buggers should have gotten away with it. The chance of long-range scanners picking up a cloaked ship at this distance were minute.

Yet they *had* been caught . . . but long-range scanners were *passive* . . . it'd be some seconds before they tumbled to the fact that they had. . . .

An unholy glee pushed the dull drumbeat from his consciousness. The sods had their ECM set for cloak, and it took time to shift ECM modes. As far as fire confusion was concerned, those ships were mother-naked! Now that they'd been spotted at all, they might as well not even *have* ECM! But they didn't know that yet! If he attacked now—*before* they realized and launched . . . !

The stream of thoughts and conclusions ripped through his mind in so small a fraction of a second that his stream of orders never even hesitated.

"The battlegroup will alter course to intercept the carrier force. Commence firing with SBMs—*now*." They were still outside normal missile range—but not SBM range. "Implement anti-fighter procedures."

BG 32 reoriented itself. The four Brobdingnagian monitors lumbered into a tight, diamond-shaped formation with their two escort destroyers positioned to cover their blind zones. The attached recon group (a light carrier with two escort destroyers) took up position astern and launched all three of its fighter squadrons. AFHAWK missiles slid into their shipboard launchers. And before the maneuver was even completed, the monitors twitched and shuddered, expelling a cloud of lethal strategic bombardment missiles from their external racks. The deadly swarm of missiles flashed away, closing on the rebel ships.

"We're getting some individual IDs, Admiral," Desai reported as her screen flickered with sudden data. "The CVAs are *Gilgamesh*, *Leminkanien*, and *Basilisk*, sir. CVs *Mastiff* and *Whippet*, and . . ."

She sucked in her breath sharply and stopped dead.

Trevayne heard the hiss and turned toward her in concern. Her face was even more frozen than usual, and her eyes were haunted as she looked up at him over the terminal.

"What is it, Sonja?"

"Admiral," she said, very quietly, "the scout cruiser is *Ashanti*."

Every officer on the flag bridge either personally knew or had heard of Trevayne and what had happened to his family—and that Lieutenant Commander Colin Trevayne was executive officer of TFNS *Ashanti*. Heads turned and eyes looked at the admiral.

"Thank you, Commodore," Trevayne said levelly. "Carry on, please."

Yoshinaka glanced quickly at the command bridge com screen, seeing the pain in Remko's dark eyes. Years before, struggling upward through the tight, almost hereditary ranks of the peacetime TFN, the flag captain had encountered Innerworld senior officers who'd barely troubled to conceal their snobbery and others who'd displayed their enlightened social attitudes with forced, patronizing tolerance. And then Lieutenant Commander Sean Remko had found himself serving a flag officer who quite simply didn't give a damn about where Sean Remko had been born or how he talked.

And now, watching Remko stare from the com screen at that same officer, Yoshinaka understood the inarticulate flag captain's need to offer Trevayne something.

"Sir, the carriers are what matters. A scout doesn't have enough armament to hurt us much . . . and the missiles are still under shipboard control . . . it ought to be possible to . . ."

Trevayne also understood, but he turned to the screen and calmly cut Remko's stammering short. "Fight your ship, Captain," he said.

Then he settled back in the comfortable admiral's chair. The drumbeat was back, but he ignored it. There were decisions to be made in the next few minutes, and there was no time for anything else. No time to examine the new sensation of being utterly alone in the cosmos but for the cold companions Duty and Self-Discipline. No time for grief, or self-hatred, or nausea. Plenty of time for all of that, later.

# ALLIANCE

Xanadu averaged slightly warmer than Old Terra, and its axial tilt was less than fifteen degrees, giving it short and mild seasons. Prescott City, on the seaboard of the continent of Kublai, lay just inside the northern temperate zone and was enjoying a typical winter as Ian Trevayne stepped from his shuttle. The day was blustery but only mildly cool; the chill was in his soul.

He spent a moment acclimating himself. (Weather of any sort was always a little startling to a man who spent most of his working life in artificial environments, and the 0.93 G gravitation was perceptibly different from the TFN's statutory one G.) Then he crossed the ceramacrete to greet Genji Yoshinaka. The dapper ops officer saluted and fell in beside him.

"Good afternoon, Admiral. Your schedule's been arranged for the evening. In the meantime, your skimmer is waiting. The pilot is a Prescott City native; he says Ms. Ortega's address is a good kilometer from the nearest public landing platform, so I've laid on a ground car to take you the rest of the way."

Trevayne looked around him. Low clouds scudded rapidly across a sky of deep blue crystal. For the first time in months, he made a completely impulsive decision.

"Cancel the ground car, Genji. I'll walk."

Yoshinaka, struggling to keep pace with his long-legged boss, was startled. In the week since the engagement people were beginning to call the Battle of the Gateway, Trevayne's days had been regimented almost to the second. It was inevitable, of course, especially given the new responsibilities which had fallen to him when Sergei Ortega had died with his flagship. But Yoshinaka understood why the admiral had attacked his work with such furious energy. There were too many ghosts, and Trevayne sought to hold them at bay in the only way he knew. Knowledge made his impulsiveness, his willingness to waste time, all the more startling. But, then, Yoshinaka reflected, the admiral had never been a predictable man.

Trevayne had visited Xanadu before, but only for brief conferences at the base itself. Now, for the first time, he looked down from the skimmer and saw the planet's chief city not as an abstraction to be defended, but as a bustling urban sprawl. He couldn't recall what Prescott City had been called when it was founded during the Fourth Interstellar War—probably something else outré from Coleridge. The old name didn't much matter anyway, for it had soon been renamed in honor of Rear Admiral Andrew Prescott, whose statue and column dominated the lawn before Government House, and his older brother, Fleet Admiral Raymond Prescott. It was a fitting tribute to the two brothers who had done so much to win that war: Andrew, the survey officer who had died to provide the Terran/Orion alliance with the information it needed to win that war, and Raymond, who had commanded the fleet which had done so much to forge that victory. There were persistent rumors that the Zephranese had wanted to use Raymond Prescott for their statue, but Raymond had survived the war and gone on to become Sky Marshal, and no one had quite dared to suggest such a thing during his lengthy life. By the time he died, Andrew's statue had become a comfortable and treasured part of Xanadu's history, and no one had even suggested making a change.

Well, making a change of *statues*, anyway. Trevayne's mouth twisted with the wry grimace that now served him for a smile. He hoped Winston Churchill had been wrong about the bad luck that attends nations which change the names of their cities.

It was hard to quarrel with Xanadu's choice of the name, though. Time after time, the war had brought large-scale space combat to this system. At the touch of the destructive energies those battles released, a living planet would wither like a leaf in a flame. Thanks to Andrew and Raymond Prescott, the people of Xanadu had finally awakened one morning and known they could live and bear children without that fear.

Until now, Trevayne thought, and the bile rose in his throat. Now the fear was back, but this time it was fear of the rebellious ships of the TFN itself, the TFN which for centuries had stood between *all* the worlds of Man and that horror! As Sergei had stood. . . .

His controlled face tightened as his vivid imagination pictured the loathsome mushroom clouds once more. Only the consuming demands of responsibility had kept him functioning under the shocks of the mutinies and the deaths of his wife and daughters. And then Colin. . . .

His mind shied away from the thought like a wounded, skittish horse. In the aftermath of battle, Trevayne had deliberately filled the little free time he might have had with a hectic round of self-imposed duties. Such as this one: a call on Sergei's daughter to express his condolences. It ought to fill the time between now and tonight's round of appointments and paperwork. And the time wouldn't be totally wasted. She was, after all, politically influential.

The wind gusted as he turned into Miriam Ortega's street, and he cursed as he nearly lost his cap. Then the gust died and he straightened his cap, glancing around at his surroundings.

The street skirted the broad estuary of the Alph, running down to a seawall and the azure, white-capped harbor. This was one of Prescott City's oldest residential districts, and the houses were on the small side but well-built, mostly of stone and wood, as first-wave houses tended to be. High-rises and fused cermacrete came later, as did the premium on space which would have doomed the large old native trees surrounding the houses. The architecture was vaguely neo-Tudor, and he suspected it had developed locally; it certainly fit the materials and the setting.

He drew a deep, lung-filling breath of the salt-tinged air and decided he'd been right to take the time to walk. Sensory deprivation was an ever-present danger in space; it had probably begun to catch up with him. In the midst of artificiality, the mind tended to turn inward on itself. His native Old Terra might be out of reach, but here he could at least touch the soil of a world humans had made their own.

A few children were at play, and at the sight of them a shadow chilled his mind just as the low-flying clouds periodically blocked out the warmth of Zephrain A. A small boy looked up and smiled at him. Trevayne hurried on.

Miriam Ortega's house wasn't far from the seawall. He stepped through the old-fashioned gate in the low, stone wall along the street, noticing the faint rime of salt clinging to the seaward stones. He climbed the steps and rang for admittance, and the door swung open.

The woman in the doorway was in her middle to late thirties, he decided. She was of medium height and rather sturdy build, with thick black hair pulled back in a severe style which accentuated her high cheekbones. Those cheekbones reminded Trevayne of Sergei, but the rest of her features, including the strongly curved nose, seemed to owe more to Sergei's late wife. Ruth Ortega had been from New Sinai, and her genetic heritage was strong in her daughter's face. Miriam Ortega, he thought, was no beauty.

"Ms. Ortega?"

"Yes. You must be Admiral Trevayne. Your yeoman called earlier today. Won't you come in?" Her voice was husky but firm. Though she seemed somber, there was no quaver.

She led him down a short hallway to a sitting room whose large, many-paned window overlooked the street. Though not messy, the room looked very lived-in. It was lined with old-style bookshelves, and an easel with paints and brushes stood near the window. A desk sat to one side, built around a functional data terminal and utilitarian tape and data chip racks.

"Do you paint, Ms. Ortega?" He gestured briefly at the easel.

"Only as an off-and-on hobby. No real talent, I'm afraid." They sat down and she lit a cigarette. "I'm going to give it up this summer—smoking, that is, not painting. Right now, though, I seem to need all the bad habits I've got to see me through."

Trevayne was uncomfortably reminded of his reason for coming. He cleared his throat.

"Ms. Ortega, the last time I talked to your father, he spoke of you. He said he wanted me to meet you. I deeply regret that we're finally meeting under these circumstances. But please accept my condolences for your loss. Believe me, I share it. Your father was, in many ways, one of the finest officers I've ever served under."

*God,* he thought. *I didn't intend to sound so formal; it's almost stilted. But what can one say? I've never been at my best dealing with human tragedy. Including my own.*

Miriam Ortega inhaled smoke and let it trickle out.

"You know, Admiral, I think Dad was a bit disappointed to have produced possibly the most unmilitary offspring in the Federation, but I managed to soak up enough of his attitudes to understand him. However easygoing he sometimes seemed, he felt very strongly about certain things. One of them was the Federation, and another was his concept of what TFN service meant.

He used to quote some ancient saying about placing your body in harm's way, between the horror of war and those you're sworn to protect. He could imagine no higher calling."

Her face had worn an inward look, but now she looked up at Trevayne and he could almost feel the unconquerable vitality she radiated. When she spoke again, her voice was still controlled, but the words were vibrant.

"Dad died the way he would have wanted to. I can't deny I'm grieving for him, but at the risk of seeming callous, I can't honestly say I feel sorrow. Sorrow isn't big enough . . . there's no room for pride in it!"

Trevayne was startled by how closely she'd paralleled his own earlier thoughts. But beyond that, he suddenly wondered how he could have thought this woman unexceptional-looking even for a moment. She wasn't conventionally pretty, no; but her face was a strikingly vivid and expressive one, uniquely her own. She was like no one else.

For an instant he wanted to reach out to her and tell her of his own loss. She was the sort of person who inspired confidences. But no, he had no right to burden her with his problems. And he wasn't sure he was ready to expose his own wounds.

"I know you were close to your father," he said. "I recall him mentioning that you moved out here when he was first posted to Zephrain."

"I suppose my closeness to him was a form of overcompensation. I didn't see much of him when I was young—he was in space a lot, and Mother played a much bigger role in raising me. Whenever he was around, he did his best to turn me into a tomboy." Her mobile features formed a rueful smile. "Some would say it took. Anyway, you're right about my coming out here. It was just after my divorce. I was in the mood for a change of scenery, and Mother had died just before he was out-posted; he was still taking it pretty hard."

She broke off for a moment, drawing on her cigarette. Her face was briefly thoughtful before she shrugged and looked up again.

"I had a law degree from New Athens and reasonably good references, so I was able to establish myself here on Xanadu. I found I liked it here. What started as a 'stay close to Dad' sort of thing turned into something else entirely, in a sense. I landed a position with one of the better firms—Bernbach, de Parma, and Leong—and suddenly I was one of the old hands. That doesn't take long here in the Rim, you know. And our firm's always been heavily into local politics, which is how I ended up involved in the formation of the provisional government."

Trevayne nodded, though he suspected that wasn't the half of it. Suddenly she looked self-deprecating and waved her cigarette dismissively.

"Here I am running off at the mouth about myself when I've got the most famous man in the Rim sitting in my living room! Just bringing your battlegroup all the way out here made you a hero to these people, you know. Since the battle, you've become even more of one, if that's possible! I'm probably boring you stiff. . . ."

"No, no," Trevayne denied. "Far from it. In fact, you were just coming to something I need to know more about. I'm still not too clear about the origins of your provisional government."

"No?" She regarded him thoughtfully for a moment. "How much do you know about Xanadu's history, Admiral?"

"Only the bare-bones outline from the handbook, I'm afraid."

"Then you know Xanadu was settled during the Fourth Interstellar War when the Navy built the Fleet base. What you may not realize is just what that meant for the makeup of our population. There was a tremendous amount of military construction going on eighty years ago, and that required a large labor force. People came from all over the Federation, and today's population is about as racially mixed as you'll find anywhere. Which—" a sudden smile "—is probably one reason I fit in so well! Anyway, the point is that this isn't one of the planets settled by closeknit ethnic or national groups. To govern themselves, this polyglot crew needed a simple pyramidal structure to interact on. Xanadu is divided into prefectures, which are grouped into districts, above which are provinces. Each prefecture elects a representative to the district assembly. The district assemblies each select one representative to the provincial assemblies, which each send one member to the Planetary Council. There's also a popularly elected president, who appoints the judiciary. There's a lot more to it, of course, but that's the basic idea."

As democratic systems went, Trevayne reflected, it owed more to the French than to the American model.

"Actually, it's worked pretty well," she said. "The planet has taken on a sort of uniformity in diversity. The Xandies are probably on the way to developing what the anthropologists call a 'planetary ethnicity.' " Seeing his puzzled look, she elaborated.

"People from Xanadu are called 'Xandies.' It's not a slur," she added quickly. "We call ourselves that." He noted the shift from third to first person.

"Anyway," she continued, "the pro-rebel party here was extremely small and—partly as a result of being so alienated from the Xandy mainstream, I suppose—extremely militant. Right after word of the mutinies arrived, a gang of fanatics tossed a bomb which killed the President and several high-ranking members of the government . . . not to mention a good number of innocent bystanders." She grimaced. "The chief conspirators fled off-planet and got as far as Aotearoa. I was a member of the delegation sent to arrange their extradition, and, in the course of the discussions, it became clear that we needed some sort of inter-system authority to deal with any further terrorist acts locally, since we were completely isolated from Old Terra. The result was the provisional government, which includes Zephrain and several of the nearer systems—the most populous and highly developed ones in the Rim. Brilliant improvisation!" She beamed at him in mock self-satisfaction. "Dad's support gave it some teeth, but it's still pretty chaotic."

"Yes. Your father and I talked about this. As I see it, the problem is that the Rim is on its own indefinitely. We need a Rim-wide provisional government, if only to perform the kind of day-to-day functions that the Federation always provided. But it isn't only day-to-day matters . . . we've handed the rebels a setback, but we haven't heard the last of them. And it's only a matter of time before the Tangri Corsairs take advantage of this civil war to start raiding again."

He rose and began pacing as he went on.

"I said to your father that we may as well be all the Federation that's left . . . and I wasn't just being dramatic. We're isolated to an extent that no one in the government has ever dreamed of, much less planned for! Thank God we've got a loyalist provisional government to work with."

He stopped suddenly in the middle of the room and looked at her and realized that she'd been watching him intently.

"Ms. Ortega, a while back you said something about not wishing to seem callous. Well, neither do I. But I must tell you that what I said earlier about sharing your loss was meant not just on a personal level. The fact is, I'd planned to have your father, as TFN senior officer, declared emergency governor-general of the Rim systems. It's legally defensible, but without support from local leaders, it would probably do more harm than good. With the contacts he'd built up in his years out here . . ." His voice trailed off.

"Sorry," he said. "Didn't mean to get carried away. And it's all a matter of might-have-been now that he's dead."

Miriam Ortega's expression had become even more intent. Now her eyes flashed.

"No! It still makes sense—beautiful sense, politically as well as militarily. Your idea of a 'governor-general' is perfect. He'd represent the Federation, so he'd provide a focus for loyalist sentiment. And he'd give the provisional government exactly what it lacks: a strong executive. And . . . we've got the perfect man for the position."

Trevayne looked at her levelly. "Me," he said, slightly more as a statement than a question.

"It's got to be you," she said emphatically. "As the ranking TFN officer in the Rim, you're the only possible choice. And remember what I said earlier; your prestige couldn't be higher."

Neither of them had really noticed the courtesy call turning into a political conference, but that, Trevayne realized, was exactly what it had become. He'd already reached the same conclusions, but he'd needed to hash out the problems and objections with someone. And in the loneliness of supreme command, there had been no one.

"I can't do it alone," he began. "I don't know these people. . . ."

"But I do," the woman said flatly.

Two pairs of dark-brown eyes met, and they were allies.

"I can't just make the proclamation out of the blue, though." He resumed his pacing. "That would defeat the whole purpose of involving the Rim leadership. I need to meet the key people in this provisional government and arrange for a statement of solidarity from them to follow the announcement. And we need to set up an interim legislative assembly to handle inter-systemic statutory matters. Just the inflation that's bound to overtake a wartime economy will require a mass of bread-and-butter amendments to practically all Federation statutes that specify monetary amounts. . . ."

"Good point," Miriam interjected. She cocked her head to one side and looked at him. "I must say, for a professional military man you seem to have quite a good grasp of these things."

"I've read a little history." He gave a deprecatory half-smile. "But as I was saying, I need to meet with the loyal leadership unofficially, so it probably wouldn't be a good idea to do it at Government House. . . ."

"Why not here?" she asked.

Trevayne stopped in midpace. "Why not, indeed? Can you contact the people I need to talk to?" She nodded. "As to when . . . my schedule isn't too flexible. I don't know how much longer I'll be able to stay dirtside." No more than a few days, he thought. Maybe after the trip to Gehenna. . . .

"How about the day after tomorrow, at 1000 hours?"

"Day after tomorrow?" he echoed faintly, staring at her.

"Well," she said reasonably, "these people are scattered all around the planet. I may not be able to get them all together by tomorrow."

He nodded slowly. It was a new sensation for him to find himself caught in someone else's slipstream.

"We won't have time to bring in anybody from off-planet," she was saying, "but at least Bryan MacFarland—he's an Aotearoan—is already in Prescott City. And, of course, Barry de Parma—he's a senior partner in my firm and he's got a finger in every political pie on the planet. And . . ."

"Make a list. I'll need a briefing on each of them. It shouldn't take too long to . . ." His voice trailed off as he looked at the clock. "Bloody Goddamned hell!" he exploded. "Er . . . excuse me." She choked down a laugh as he adjusted his wrist communicator. "Genji?"

"Admiral? I was trying to decide whether or not to call you."

"Genji, I'm going to be at Ms. Ortega's a bit longer than I expected. You'd better postpone tonight's appointments. And don't schedule anything for day after tomorrow, at least not in the morning or early afternoon."

Two days later, they were once again alone in her sitting room, this time among a litter of scattered chairs and heaped ashtrays. He waved a hand vaguely before his face, as if to brush away the canopy of tobacco smoke. Aside from the chairs and ashtrays, the room was much as before, except for the cloth that covered the easel.

"Well," Miriam said, "I think you've done it."

"You had as much to do with it as I did," Trevayne demurred.

"No, it was you. You didn't just win them over to the idea, you overwhelmed them with it. When you announce the Rim

Provisional Government, they'll come through right on schedule—and they'll do it because they know you're right. We'll reconvene the current provisional government as a sort of committee of the whole to organize the Rim Legislative Assembly, then invite all the Rim systems to send representatives."

"Good. In fact, I'd like you to move ahead on setting that up right now, but the public announcement is going to have to wait a week or so."

"A week?" She cocked her head to one side thoughtfully. "No problem. I'll go ahead and get the messages out—they're going to take a month or so to reach some of the more distant systems—but why wait that long for the initial announcement? The provisional government can be ready to go in two or three days."

"I know. But for now I have to go to the R&D Station, which means a flight to Gehenna, of course. My chief of staff is organizing a project out there—one that's at least as important to the survival of the Rim as what we've started at this end."

"Oh? Ready to start producing new weapons?"

"How the devil did you know that?" Trevayne stared at her, reminding himself once more never to underestimate this woman.

"What else would you be doing on that dust ball?" she asked dryly. Then she shook her head at him. "Don't worry—I won't mention a word to anyone. But every Xandy knows what Zephrain RDS has been up to for the last forty years or so, you know. Not that it matters too much, I suppose; it's hardly likely to get into the rebel news channels, now is it?"

"I suppose not," he admitted with a reluctant smile. "On the other hand, good security is as much a set of mind as anything else, so I'd rather not discuss it just now. And I'd appreciate your keeping mum about it."

"Don't worry, I will," she assured him.

"Thanks." He glanced at the clock and stood, picking up his cap. "I've got to go—my shuttle's waiting at Abu'said—but I'll be in touch directly I get back. I'll want your help on the finishing touches to the proclamation."

"Try and keep me away from it!" She also rose, facing him. "You know, I really believe we're going to pull this off."

"So do I. It's not easy to feel pessimistic around you! Besides, I was impressed by your colleagues. I thought I hit it off particularly well with the MacFarland chap."

"Yes, I was sure you'd like him. He even sounds like you."

Trevayne almost choked. That God-awful Anzac twang?! Then he threw back his head and laughed for the first time in far too long. She blinked at him in momentary startlement, then burst out laughing, too. And then his elbow brushed the easel, and the cloth slipped off.

"Oh, shit," Miriam said quietly.

Trevayne gazed at the charcoal sketch for a long moment, his laughter dying, his face turning thoughtful. Then he eyed her quizzically.

"Do I really look that grim?"

"Yup," she replied, not quite her usual brassy self, but standing her ground. He took a closer look.

"I suppose I've never thought of myself as looking that . . . harsh."

" 'Harsh' isn't the word I'd use. 'Tough' comes closer. You've got the sort of face that shows absolutely no vulnerability. And—" her voice was suddenly both gentle and bold "—that's a pity, because I think you're a very vulnerable man in a lot of ways. One who's been hurt." She stopped abruptly, as if she had surprised herself.

Trevayne looked at the sketch a moment longer, absorbing the closed-off expression her charcoal stick had captured and feeling her words sink under the edge of his armor. Then he turned to face her.

"Yes, I have . . ." he began, then stopped. Once more, he wanted to speak of how badly he'd been hurt. But he had to leave. Besides, he knew now that he would tell her everything when he saw her again . . . and, he realized with dawning surprise, that was enough. What really mattered was knowing there was someone he could talk freely to after so long.

"Ms. Ortega . . ."

"Miriam."

"Miriam. As I said, I'll be in contact when I return. And . . . I'll look forward to talking again."

"So will I, Admiral Trevayne."

"Ian."

"Ian." She smiled her vivid smile. They shook hands.

He left and walked up the street. There was a brisk wind off the harbor once more, but the day was cloudless. Some of the same children were playing along the street, and the same small boy smiled at him.

He smiled back.

# SEPARATION OF POWERS

Genji Yoshinaka had never seen Sonja Desai so angry. To be honest, he couldn't swear he'd ever seen her display so much of *any* emotion.

"The Admiral must be out of his mind!" she muttered through clenched teeth. "No," she continued, answering herself before Yoshinaka could get a word in, "of course he's not. But we all know what a strain he's been under...."

"Now, Sonja," Yoshinaka interrupted, all diplomacy, "you know the political rationale for what the Admiral is doing. We've discussed it often enough since arriving in the Rim. And if you feel so strongly about it, why didn't you voice your objections to him when he was on Gehenna?"

"Oh, yes, I've heard all the political arguments, and I'm only to happy to defer to the Admiral's judgment on *that* sort of thing." Her voice held an infinity of exasperation with politics and the other incomprehensible interactions of her fellow humans. "But," she continued, suddenly almost venomous, "I always assumed we were talking about some ceremonial parliamentary talkfest that would give the local political gasbags an outlet for their self-importance while we get on with the important work. I never dreamed that we were going to be expected to take the farce seriously!" She glared across the room at the cluster of civilians ... and, it seemed to Yoshinaka, at one of them in particular.

The room she glared across was deep in the heavily shielded core of Government House in Prescott City. The shielding—like the architecture, which was what public buildings had looked like in the days of the Fourth Interstellar War—reflected the structure's origins. Its security aspects had been largely habit, given an enemy from whom nuclear warheads were more to be expected than espionage, but they'd made this particular conference room the natural site for Trevayne's first joint meeting with both his military staff and the leaders of the newly inaugurated Rim Provisional Government. Both groups now stood awaiting him . . . and, as if by gravitational attraction, had clumped themselves into opposite corners of the large chamber.

The thought of security got Desai off to a fresh start.

"Damn it, Genji," she said, low-voiced and intense, "I don't really mind the idea of setting up a civilian government for the Rim; I suppose I wouldn't even *want* us to have to carry the whole burden of administration, which we would under martial law. But I simply can't believe that the Admiral really plans to grant security clearances to the members of this 'Grand Council' who're directly connected with the war effort. Is that even *legal*?"

"Matter of opinion," Yoshinaka opined. "He's doing it while wearing his Governor-General's hat, which puts it in what might tactfully be called an ill-defined area of the law. As he's fond of saying, the Cabinet can tell him if they don't like it—after contact is reestablished."

Desai waved a hand impatiently. "That's not really the point anyway. You haven't been out to Gehenna, but you know what's at stake here. We're not talking about some kind of minor engineering refinements! We're talking about a whole new order of technology!" She paused and took a breath. "I've got to make him *see* that we don't dare compromise security on this thing . . . not after what's happened on Gehenna."

Yoshinaka nodded soberly. He could understand her feelings, after what she'd been through mere days before. But, as always, he found her intensity oppressive. She had no lightness in her. And this vehemence wasn't like her at all.

"I've got to make him *see*!" she repeated. "Surely it must be clear now that he can't trust these . . . colonials!"

Yoshinaka was shocked. Abrasive Desai might be, but he'd never heard a remark even remotely like that from her. It didn't even make sense; her own ancestors hadn't exactly evolved from the primordial ooze of Nova Terra! And Sonja Desai *never* talked nonsense. What was her problem?

He drew himself up slightly. (He still had to look upward at her, as he did at most people.) "I think," he began, in his best conversation-closing voice, "that the Admiral is committed to the course he's taken, Sonja. And I think you missed your chance to talk him out of it when you had him to yourself on Gehenna. And I *definitely* think that, in spite of what's happened since then, it would do far more harm than good to raise the point at this time, in this company. I strongly advise against it."

Desai's rejoinder was lost forever as an old-fashioned double door swung open and an usher intoned "The Governor-General!"

Trevayne was wearing an expensively tailored civilian suit, making clear which of his figurative "hats" he was wearing. The point was not lost on the officers and politicians as they took their places on opposite sides of the large conference table. The glance he shared with Miriam Ortega, on the other hand, went unnoticed by almost everyone.

"Please be seated, ladies and gentlemen," Trevayne invited, all affability. They did so, military crispness opposite civilian casualness, and Miriam absently lit a cigarette.

"Filthy habit," Desai muttered to Yoshinaka, just below the threshold of public audibility. Miriam, almost directly across the table from her, raised a single eloquent eyebrow and blandly put out the cigarette.

Introductions and other preliminaries completed, Trevayne turned to specifics.

"We all know what's occasioned this meeting," he began, "and I know everyone shares my relief that Captain Desai is able to be with us." A murmur of agreement ran around the table. Trevayne resumed, addressing Desai. "Sonja, I apologize for having to bring you here from Gehenna on such short notice, particularly straight from sickbay." He indicated her left arm, still immobilized even though the wound was, by the standards of modern medicine, minor. "But we need your input, as you were closer to the incident than anyone . . . closer than you would have liked, I daresay!"

Desai didn't share in the general chuckle. "Thank you for your concern, Admiral," she replied. "But there is one preliminary point which I feel it is my duty to raise before the discussion enters areas of sensitive military information. I refer to the matter of security . . . especially in light of what has just happened on Gehenna."

Yoshinaka groaned silently.

Everyone at the table—everyone in the Zephrain system, for that matter—knew what had happened, only hours after Trevayne had left Gehenna to return to Xanadu and announce the formation of the Provisional Government. The security advantages of

an uninhabitable planet were part of the reason Zephrain RDS
was located on Gehenna. But, inevitably, a city had grown up,
under domes and burrowed beneath Gehenna's reddish sands,
in response to the presence of the Station and a fair number of
miners . . . a city whose lower levels had sheltered a surprisingly
well-organized rebel underground with carefully developed plans
to sabotage the Station.

Still, the rebels had moved before they were quite ready, unable
to resist the temptation of bagging Trevayne during his inspection tour. Desai's media disinformation concerning his departure
schedule had prevented that, at least. He'd been in space when the
rebels had struck, heavily armed and using access codes obtained
by blackmail of certain key personnel.

Of course, they hadn't expected a walkover. The vicious, utterly
unexpected boarding actions of the Theban War had cured the
TFN of its habit of relegating small arms—and training in their
use—to the Dark Ages and to such present-day Dark-Ages types as
Marines. Side arms were now part of the service uniform . . . but
they were laser side arms, ideal for space but subject to many
inherent limitations on the ground, which was why hand-held
laser weapons had never entirely supplanted slugthrowers. The
rebel attackers had used slugthrowers . . . and anti-laser aerosol
grenades. Surprise had been nearly total, and the Station's upper
levels had, for a time, resembled a scene from Hell. Desai herself
had been caught in a surrounded office block, where she'd had
good use for the personal combat training she had detested and
never expected to use. But Marine quick-response teams had been
on standing alert for Trevayne's visit and hadn't quite had time to
stand down. Reinforcements had arrived—in combat zoots—before
any crucial data or equipment had been destroyed, and no attackers were believed to have escaped. Damage had been extensive,
however . . . especially to Desai's temper.

"And so," she concluded her description of the attack, "our
schedules have been set back by weeks. I think this incident
reveals a *very* serious security problem involving . . . certain elements of the Rim populations." The civilian side of the table was
utterly quiet.

"I wonder," Desai finished, looking straight at Miriam, "if the
Grand Councilor for Internal Security would perhaps care to comment on the fact that this conspiracy arose among the civilian
population of Gehenna . . . without being detected."

At the head of the table, Trevayne frowned. Sonja was obviously in one of her moods . . . but he'd thought she had understood the necessity of tact in dealing with the Provisional Government. And she was being utterly unfair; Miriam hadn't even *held* the internal security portfolio at the time the attack took place, much less while it was being prepared. There hadn't been a Rim Provisional Government to hold it in!

But he couldn't dress Desai down publicly, for any of a number of reasons, not the least of which was that Miriam *had* to handle this on her own if she was to command any sort of respect from the military people. So he held his tongue and let her respond.

"First," she said, slowly and deliberately, to the room at large, "let me say that I share the Governor-General's relief that Captain Desai escaped serious injury, and that I deeply regret the casualties that occurred . . . casualties that might have been avoided if our people had been given a free hand to investigate certain early leads which were duly passed on to Navy security on Gehenna. Correct me if I'm wrong, Captain Desai, but I believe that this information was what led you to take the very sensible precaution of leaking a false itinerary for the Governor-General's tour."

She gazed levelly at the naval officer, and Desai's eyes might have hardened just a tiny bit more. But she refused to rise to the bait, and after a moment, taking her tight-lipped silence as confirmation, Miriam continued.

"Jurisdiction over the civilian population of Gehenna has always been unclear. The Navy considers the entire planet a military reservation, and regards civilian law-enforcement officials as being there more or less in an advisory capacity. This is unfortunate, as local people with an intimate knowledge of local conditions would have access to sources of information beyond the normal compass of Navy security. They would be in a better position to ferret out the small lunatic fringe that I can't deny exists, and whose very powerlessness (as I've mentioned to the Governor-General) makes it more apt to reckless acts of violence. The solution is to give my new organization, representing the loyal mainstream of the Rim, full authority to police our own few renegades."

A confident rumble arose from the civilian side of the table. Miriam sat back and, after a moment's hesitation, lit a cigarette. She didn't—quite—blow the smoke in Desai's direction.

"Well," Trevayne said, stepping in to fill the gap before Desai could speak, "I think Ms. Ortega has raised some valid points. At the very least, we need to address the jurisdictional question posed by the civilian habitats on Gehenna . . . which, of course, didn't exist when the RDS was founded. Comments, anyone?"

Discussion proceeded without anything provocative from Desai. Trevayne, relieved, exchanged a quick smile with Miriam. No one but Yoshinaka noticed that Desai grew even stiffer than was her wont.

"I don't think your Captain Desai likes me very much."

Trevayne waved a negligent hand as he and Miriam walked together down the corridor after the meeting had broken up.

"Oh, don't feel singled out," he said airily. "I'm afraid Sonja's like that with everyone. It's just the way she is. Don't give it another thought."

"Maybe," Miriam replied dubiously.

# HONOR

"Begin," the judge said, and Lieutenant Mazarak unleashed a short, straight lunge in sixte.

Han's wrist flicked, brushing the blade to the outside, arm extending in a quick riposte in the same line. But he shortened to parry and fell back, and she followed, her mind almost blank as hand and eye and reflex carried the weight of her actions.

Back and forth, blades grating and slipping, dreamy thought coming in a curiously flecting pattern. Few Hangchowese bothered with the ancient dueling sword, especially in its Western forms, and Han had never considered it herself until she'd been wounded. Yet it seemed she possessed a natural aptitude, and the elegant converse of steel suited her.

She disengaged and Mazarak pursued, pressing her cautiously, yet Han felt he was more defensive-minded, and she believed she had a better sense of point. She feinted above his hand, dropping her point to go in under his drawn guard, but he parried like lightning and riposted in octave. She put his point aside—barely—with a counter-parry, and he tried a quick double disengage in sixte. But she was ready, seizing his blade and carrying it low and outside in a quick bind that flashed instantly into a fleche. Her epee snaked home as she passed to his left, and the scoring light lit.

"*Touché,*" the judge intoned, and they drew apart, breathing just a bit more heavily and saluting as they prepared to reengage for the next point.

Han emerged from the salle, mask in hand and epee under her arm, shaking her sweat-damp hair. She hadn't had it back all that long, and she rather enjoyed the feeling.

"Han," Magda Petrovna said, "that's got to be the silliest sport ever invented."

"Come now, Magda! Its origins were anything but silly."

"Maybe." Magda tucked a proprietary arm through Jason Windrider's. "But I'll settle *my* quarrels decently . . . with pistols at twenty meters, thank you!"

"Russians have so little soul," Han mourned. "It's fun, Magda. Not like judo, but I had to get back in shape somehow, and I thought I'd try something new." She shrugged. "I like it."

"Well, it certainly seems to've gotten you back on your feet, Admiral, sir," Jason Windrider teased.

"It does, does it, *Commodore*?" Han asked deflatingly.

Windrider stroked his new insignia and grinned. "Just trying to keep up, Admiral. And you and Magda haven't had your stars all that long."

"No, we haven't," Han said more somberly, glancing at the heavy braid on Magda's cuff.

When she was in uniform, her own sleeves matched Magda's these days, and it made her uneasy. She'd been confident enough when they made her a commodore—but that was before Cimmaron.

Yet the Republic had no choice. It had paid heavily in ships and personnel for its string of victories, and disproportionately so in the flag officers aboard their easily identified command ships.

Nor had all of them died victorious. There were still no formal avenues of communication between the Republic and the Rim Systems, but Vice Admiral Trevayne (and what a shock to discover he was not only alive but in Zephrain!) had supplied a casualty list, and there were few Republican survivors. Neither Analiese Ashigara nor Colin Trevayne was among them, and Han wondered how Trevayne could live with what he'd done. The question held a dread fascination, for he, at least, had demonstrated just how far duty and honor could carry a person.

But the Republic's heavy butcher's bills explained the rapid promotions. Han had been a commodore for less than eighteen months, and ten of them had been spent as Daffyd Llewellyn's patient. What he'd been pleased to call a "fractured" femur had required massive surgical reconstruction, and the antigerone therapies had their disadvantages. To stretch the life span, they slowed the biological clock—including healing speeds. The quick-heal drugs which were part of the doomwhale's pharmaceutical cornucopia could offset that, but not after such rad poisoning as

Han had survived, which had made her a semi-permanent fixture at the hospital, though she'd bullied Llewellyn into out-patient status the moment she began therapy.

Magda had been only too glad to turn over the Cimmaron command. And, having experienced the restrictions of a dirtside appointment for the last eleven months, Han didn't blame her at all.

"At least you look healthy enough jumping around with that ridiculous thing." Magda's teasing voice pulled Han back from her thoughts.

"Thanks. BuPers thinks so, too—I got confirmation of my new status yesterday, and I'm back in space next month! I'm going to miss Chang, though."

"I imagine so," Magda agreed, and Han hid a smile as her friends exchanged glances. She knew they both resented the fact that Windrider's promotion made him too senior to remain Magda's chief of staff even while it delighted them both as proof of his professional reputation and future.

"Who's replacing him?" Magda asked after a moment.

"Bob Tomanaga. He's cleared for active duty again, too."

"Tomanaga?" Magda repeated.

"I know—he worried me once, but I was wrong. It's just the way Bob is. He can't seem to be discouraged or even detached no matter what." Han shook her head. "I don't know why he's so round-eyed."

"Certainly not," Windrider agreed, grinning disrespectfully.

"Well," Han paused by her waiting skimmer, "back to the salt mines. You two will join me for supper, won't you?"

"I will," Magda agreed with a slight pout, "and Jason *may*. His group's spacing out with Kellerman, you know."

"I'd forgotten."

Han frowned, rummaging through her orderly memory. Kellerman was slated to carry out another probe of the rear approaches to the Rim Systems, amid the star systems wrecked from end to end during the titanic clashes of the Fourth Interstellar War. Not that anyone expected much to happen there. Only a handful of habitable planets had survived ISW 4, and most of them had become protectorates of the Star Union of Crucius, not Terran or Orion possessions.

The Crucians still labored under their generations of dedication to the destruction of the Arachnids, which had made them the natural stewards of the brutalized survivors of the "Bugs' " sentient meat animals. It wasn't even a matter of humanity or the Orions shoving an unwanted responsibility off onto someone else, because the Star Union had actually wanted that heartbreaking responsibility. And they'd discharged it well, Han thought. Indeed, there was a great deal to admire about the Star Union.

But, like the Khanate, the Crucians had declared neutrality when their Human friends began trying to kill one another. Han suspected that the Crucians were rather more distressed over it than the Orions (the Tabbies, after all, had a millennia-long history of civil wars of their own), but that only emphasized their insistence upon maintaining complete impartiality. That very impartiality, however, was invaluable to the Republic, however, because of their control of the star system they had renamed Zeklar. Zeklar had once been called Anderson One, and it was only two transits away from Sol itself. It was also the shortest connection between the Rim and the Innerworlds . . . or would have been, if the Crucians' neutrality hadn't closed that avenue tight. And unlike the Orions, the Crucians were not about to make any exceptions for anyone, so that road was *staying* shut.

With Zeklar closed, what ought to have been a deadly threat to the Republic had become very much a secondary theatre. The lifeless warp lines there were ill-suited to sustained operations, and neither Han—nor anyone else, it seemed—expected much to come of the probes. But there'd be enough skirmishing to satisfy the newsies, and the Fleet was stretched thin at the moment. The Rim had been demoted to secondary status while the frontline systems were stabilized and the new shipyards got into production.

"It's all right, Magda," she said finally. "Anton and the dockyard are squabbling over *Unicorn*'s repairs. He's not going anywhere without his flagship, and the yard won't turn her loose for at least another forty hours. You'll both have time for supper."

"And for a little something else, God willing," Windrider murmured as he opened the hatch for Han. His eyes twinkled wickedly, and Magda actually blushed. "But we *will* be there for supper, Admiral. Won't we, Admiral?"

"Unless I brig you for disrespect," Magda growled, and tossed Han a salute. "Bye, Han. See you this evening." And the skimmer swept away.

"Well, Chang, I guess this is goodbye."

"Yes, sir." The bulky captain faced her over her desk, cap under one arm, unreadable as ever, and Han studied him carefully. They liked and respected one another, but there was an inner core to him which she had never cracked. Not that it mattered, she thought with sudden affection. However he ticked, he was the most utterly reliable subordinate a woman could want.

No, not subordinate. Assistant. Better yet, colleague.

"Chang, I won't embarrass you by saying how much I'll miss you," she said slowly, "but I *will* say that *Direhound* couldn't find a better skipper. And—" she looked into his eyes "—that no one ever had a better chief of staff."

"Thank you, sir," he said. "It's been a pleasure, Admiral. I—" He broke off suddenly, and gave a tiny shrug.

Han nodded, surprised less that he'd stopped than that he'd spoken in the first place. It was like him, she thought. So very like him.

"Very well, Captain." She held out her hand with the traditional blessing. "Good fortune and good hunting, Chang."

"Thank you, sir," he said gruffly, gripping her hand hard.

She squeezed once, then stepped back as Tsing turned to leave. But he halted at the door of her office and placed his cap very carefully on his head, then turned and threw her an Academy-sharp salute.

Han was startled. Navy regs prohibited headgear indoors dirt-side, and it was officially impossible to salute without it. But her own hand rose equally sharply, and Tsing turned on his heel and vanished.

Good bye, Tsing Chang, she thought wistfully. You never doubted me during the mutiny. You fought with me at Cimmaron. You saved my life. I suppose that's all I really need to know about you, isn't it . . . my friend?


"Well, Admiral," Robert Tomanaga crossed Han's office without even a limp to betray his prosthetic leg, "it's a new staff, but it looks good."

"Not entirely new. We've got you and David from the old team. That's a pretty good survival rate, considering."

"I suppose so, sir," he agreed, but his tone was a clear rejection of her implied self-criticism, and she shook her head mentally. Bob Tomanaga's voice and face were as communicative as a printed message and it felt strange to always know precisely what he was thinking, but right now he meant what everyone meant whenever she let her guard down. No one else seemed to think the casualties might have been lighter . . . if only she'd been more clever.

She put the thought aside and leaned back in her chair, considering her new staff. Aside from Reznick, now a lieutenant senior grade, whom she'd been determined to have, she hardly knew any of them, but Bob was right: they looked good.

Her new ops officer, Commander Stravos Kollentai was small, slight, and arrogant—the perfect fighter jock—but his efficiency reports were excellent and he radiated an aura of almost oppressive energy and competence. Her astrogator, Lieutenant Commander Richard Heuss, was a quiet fellow with fair hair and eyes like gray shutters. He said little, but his navigation was beautiful to see.

And finally there was the new staff slot filled by Lieutenant Irene Jorgensen: battlegroup intelligence officer. Fleet had decided to once again remove the intelligence function from the ops officer's jurisdiction. That had happened before, during ISW 4, but the traditionalists in the service had never been happy about it. They'd returned intelligence to its subordination to ops with indecent haste following Raymond Prescott's retirement. Han had never understood exactly why, but there were always internal factions and cliques within the Navy, ready to engage in "turf wars" at the drop of a hat, and the spooks had lost that round.

Unfortunately, the type of war they were fighting had resurrected the overwhelming logic in favor of intelligence's independence. And, Han thought with a small mental smile, the *Republican* Navy hadn't had as long for its factions and cliques to become set in ceramacrete. Still, even to Han, it felt strange to have the spooks speaking for themselves on the staff again after so long. On the other hand, the tall, scrawny lieutenant who filled the slot on *her* staff hid a lurking humor behind her muddy brown eyes and appeared to have a computer memory bank concealed somewhere about her unprepossessing anatomy.

"Have the official orders come through yet, Admiral?" Tomanaga asked, breaking her train of thought.

"Yes. Admiral Iskan will relieve me tomorrow and we'll move out to *da Silva*."

Thank God. She'd been half-afraid the Admiralty would leave her here now that Cimmaron had been upgraded into what was clearly an admiral's billet even for the admiral-starved Republic.

"I see." Tomanaga frowned. "Any word on our destination, sir?"

"Not officially. But Fleet Ops whispered something about Rigel."

"Rigel, sir?" Tomanaga blinked.

"I think Fleet wants to keep an eye on Admiral Trevayne," Han said slowly, swinging her chair gently. "We're still not sure what happened, you know. I think someone's running a little scared over Zephrain RDS."

"Stupid of them, sir, if you'll forgive me," Tomanaga said.

"Oh? And on what do you base that pronouncement, Commander?"

"I don't think any 'mystery weapon' did in Admiral Ashigara, sir. The ops plan relied too much on surprise and ECM, and they screwed up when they tried a pincer. All it gave them was lousy coordination. That's why the diversion got chewed up when the main attack went wrong."

"And how did it go wrong?"

"I'm not certain," Tomanaga admitted, "but the survivors all agree BG 32 wasn't involved in the Gateway fighting till close to the end—so Trevayne must've been busy destroying the carriers. But carriers are faster than monitors, and Admiral Ashigara's fighters had at least as much effective firepower as BG 32. Of course, she didn't expect to see him there any more than he could have been expecting her, but if she'd had time to launch her birds, she should have been able to stand off and hammer him. The fact that she didn't means that somehow or other he spotted her despite her ECM—probably when he was already in SBM range, at least, of her carriers—and clobbered them before she got the fighters off. It's the only answer I can think of, sir."

"So it was bad luck?"

"Maybe," Tomanaga said, "but it was compounded by bad planning. They should've concentrated in Bonaparte and taken everything in through the new warp point to pin the *defenders* against the Gateway. Then we'd've had tactical command exercised in one place over only one force that could've withdrawn down a single warp line. As it was, both COs were out of contact and neither could cut and run as long as that might leave the other unsupported—a classic example of defeat in detail, *triggered* by bad luck, but not caused by it."

"You could be right," Han admitted, for she'd pondered much the same thoughts herself. "But why not new weapons, as well?"

"The time factor, sir. I don't care if Trevayne is a special emissary from God Himself, it takes time to turn research into hardware. That's why we should hit them again now—immediately. Forget the border. We've got the Rump on the run; keep them there with feints and go for Zephrain now, before they really do get new hardware on line."

"I'm inclined to agree, Bob. Unhappily, grand strategy is the First Space Lord's job. And whether you're right or not, it makes sense to picket the old Rigelian and Arachnid systems, whatever the Rim is or isn't up to."

"Agreed, sir, but a monitor battlegroup with carrier support is hardly a 'picket.' It's a vest-pocket task force, and one cut for a mighty big vest. We'd be better employed striking directly at Zephrain rather than worrying about what they may do to us." Tomanaga sounded unwontedly serious, even worried. "If we *don't* hit them pretty quick, we may find ourselves up against exactly what we're afraid of right now. Give Trevayne time to get the new systems on line, and . . ."

He shrugged eloquently.

"Consider your point made," Han said softly. "Write up a staff appreciation and we'll sit on it long enough to see where they send us. If we wind up out near Rigel and we still agree you know what you're talking about, we'll update it and fire it off. Fair enough?"

"Yes, sir."

"Good. Meanwhile, tidy up here and we'll transfer out to *Bernardo da Silva*."

"Yes, sir."

Tomanaga left, and Han frowned pensively down at the desk she would delightedly turn over to Jack Iskan in two days, wishing she disagreed with her chief of staff.

"Another day with nothing to report, sir." Tomanaga sounded disgusted. "I don't see why they're so damned mesmerized by the need to picket the Rim. Go in now and smash 'em up fast—take some casualties if we have to, but get it over with—and we won't need to scatter a quarter of our available strength out over the damned approaches."

Han tried and failed to imagine Tsing Chang unburdening himself with equal frankness. It was strange how well she got along with someone so different from Tsing. Just as strange as to remember that she'd once distrusted Tomanaga's enthusiasm.

"Well, Bob, we've sent off your appreciation," she said calmly.

"In fact, we've done everything we can short of taking it upon ourselves to attack single-handedly."

"I suppose so, sir," Tomanaga agreed sourly, "but the crews are beginning to go stale."

"I know."

Battlegroup 19 had maintained its long, slow patrol of the old Rigelian warp lines, with an occasional foray into dead Arachnid space, for almost five months without a sign of the enemy. They'd encountered a single Tangri battlecruiser, but the horseheads had shown admirable restraint and declined to match themselves against four monitors, two fleet carriers, two light carriers, and four escort destroyers.

Yet that very boredom had been a godsend for Han, and she would have been the first to admit it. Patrol duty wasn't glamorous, but at least it let someone a bit skittish over reassuming a space command ease back into it. Her worries had faded as she grappled with her new responsibilities, and she could look in her mirror now and recognize herself again.

"Well," she said finally, "let's find something to occupy them, then." She swiveled her chair down and frowned—her equivalent of raging consternation—and tapped her terminal. "You've seen this from *Shokaku*?"

"That freighter, sir?"

The light carrier's recon fighters had found the remains of a freighter drifting erratically around the primary of the Orpheus One System.

"Yes. Does anything about it strike you as odd?"

"You mean aside from what she was doing there to begin with?"

"Exactly. There are no inhabited planets in Orpheus One System. In fact, aside from Shanak and Franos and Telik—both of which belong to the Star Union—there aren't any inhabited worlds within four transits of Orpheus, and haven't been since the Alliance dusted the Arachnids out eighty years ago. I suppose her skipper *might've* been taking a short cut between Shanak and Rehfrak by way of Zephrain, since it was a Rump registry vessel, not a Tabby. But it's hard to believe anyone would try that, even assuming he could talk the Tabbies into *letting* him, and I doubt he could. Not when he had a sub-charter from Admiral Trevayne in Zephrain. That made her an official belligerent, and the Tabbies would never have let her pass through their space. But I can't think of anything else he'd be doing unescorted on this side of Zephrain, either, especially this close to Tangri space. Surely everyone knows they've been using that closed warp point in AP Five! They were doing that occasionally even before the Civil War distracted us from the area, and Trevayne's not stupid enough to route a ship through here. Even assuming she'd have anywhere to *go* out this way."

"But she's here, sir, and she *was* looted."

"True," Han nodded. "But did you examine the passenger list *Shokaku* pulled out of her computers?"

"Well, no, sir. Why?"

"They recovered the bodies of all twenty-five crewmen," Han said.

"So? The horseheads don't take prisoners, sir."

"True. But the passenger and crew sections were undamaged. Whoever attacked raked the drive and command sections with primaries and needle beams, then looted the holds and finished off the crew in the process."

"Yes, sir. Typical Tangri work."

Tomanaga was puzzled. Clearly his admiral had noticed something he had missed.

"Except this, Bob. According to the passenger manifest, there were fourteen young women aboard that ship. So where are *their* bodies?"

"What?" Tomanaga rose and moved to her desk. "May I, sir?" he asked, laying his hand on the swiveled terminal.

"Certainly."

He turned the screen and peered at it thoughtfully, mind racing.

"It doesn't make sense," he muttered. "Only the women are missing."

"Exactly. And the Tangri have never shown any particular interest in kidnapping young, female Terrans."

"Yes, sir. So it had to be someone with a use for them. . . . What about ransom? Were any of them wealthy?"

"On a tramp freighter?" Han shook her head. "Navy nurses and doctors from Zephrain."

"So whoever hit her didn't hail from the Rim, either." Tomanaga frowned. "I don't like it."

"Neither do I. Nor, I suppose, did those passengers and crewmen."

"Sorry, sir. I meant I don't like the implications. Whoever did it isn't based at Orpheus—we swept the place with a fine-toothed comb. That means some bunch of *Terrans* is involved in inter-system raiding. And that, sir, means there's a joker in the deck. If we spot anyone, we can't know whether it's the Rim or these pirates."

"Perhaps." Han cleared her screen and a warp chart flickered to life. She tapped it with a stylus. "Here's our patrol area. Here's Orpheus One." She touched a light dot to one side of their patrol area. "Now, everything Rimward of Orpheus *Two* belongs to the Rim, and whoever it is can't operate from there, because both sides watch those warp points like hawks. And he can't operate from here—" her arcing stylus indicated their patrol area "—or *we'd've* spotted him. But that leaves this warp network over here, see?" She tapped the screen. "It connects with Orpheus from the back, through the closed warp point in Bug Eight . . . and it also extends all the way to here. . . ."

"My God! Right into our rear areas!"

"Precisely. I don't know who they are or where they came from, but someone is raiding civilian traffic from a base somewhere along this warp network. There's nothing much out here but outposts and mining colonies—no heavy traffic, sparse populations, slow commu-nications. Most of the 'colonies'—such as they are, and what there is of them—are less than fifty or sixty years old, emplaced since ISW Four. They could be almost anywhere. Take over a mining colony and the nav beacons and you control all communications with the system. Who's to know you've done it?"

"Then we'd better get a drone off immediately, sir."

"Agreed. But what then? It'll take two months just to reach Cimmaron. Then two more months for Admiral Iskan to reply or relay it—four months, minimum, for whoever it is to go on doing whatever they're doing. No, we have to deal with it ourselves."

"But, sir, this area—" he indicated the suspect warp lines "—is outside our patrol area. It'd take us—what, five weeks?—just to get there, and it'd mean abandoning the picket. I don't think the Admiralty would like that."

"The Admiralty isn't out here, Bob: we are. We won't take the entire battlegroup, anyway. We'll take one other monitor, *Shokaku*, and two of the cans and leave the rest here under Commodore Cruett. I suppose I could detach Cruett, but it's my responsibility if decisions have to be made."

"Yes, sir. But—"

"Bob, we're going. We're supposed to prevent things like this, war or no war. Understood?"

"Yes, sir."

"Good. Then get together with Stravos and rough out a set of orders for Cruett. And ask Dick to lay out the best search pattern for us. I don't want to be gone any longer than we have to be."

"Aye, aye, sir."

He left and Han cocked her chair back once more, studying the star map and disliking her thoughts.

TRNS *Bernardo da Silva* plowed slowly through space, accompanied by her sister monitor *Franklin P. Eisenhower* and the light carrier *Shokaku*. Two escort destroyers watched the rear while *Shokaku*'s recon fighters swept the detachment's projected track and flanks, and Rear Admiral Li Han sat on her palatial flag bridge, fingers steepled under her clean jaw line, contemplating her empty plot.

A month of cruising the suspect warp lines, and nothing. Was she on the wrong track? Had she made a major error—one that validated her earlier fears over her judgment? Her face was calm as she silently reviewed her discussions with Tomanaga, her endless perusal of dry facts with Irene Jorgensen. The data was there, she decided once more; only her response to it was suspect.

A bell chimed, and she roused, cocking an eyebrow at the com section as David Reznick bent over the battle code printer. He tore off the message flimsy and turned to her.

"Signal from *Shokaku*, sir. One of the fighters is onto something."

"I see." Han scanned the message. "Doesn't say much, does she?"

"No, sir. But her fighter's going in for a closer look. Shall I sound action stations, sir?"

"Not yet, Lieutenant. We're a good three hours behind those fighters—we'll have time. Excuse me a moment."

Han summoned up the com image of Samuel Schwerin, her flag captain.

"Good morning, Sam," she greeted him. "*Shokaku*'s fighters have picked up something—no telling what yet—on our line of advance. They're going in for a closer look, but it'll take us about three hours to catch up with them, so I thought we might advance lunch to get it out of the way if we have to go to action stations."

"Certainly, sir. I'll see to it immediately."

"Thank you, Sam."

Reznick's printer chimed again as Han signed off, and she waited patiently. If using coded whisker lasers delayed communications, it also eliminated the chance of message interception and greatly reduced the likelihood of long-range detection. Then Reznick handed her the message, and her face tightened almost imperceptibly as she read it. She turned to Lieutenant Jorgensen.

"Irene," she said quietly, "punch up your shipping logs and double-check for me, please. According to *Shokaku*, this is what's left of a *Polaris*-class liner. I'm afraid it may be *Argosy Polaris*."

"Yes, sir," the lieutenant was punching keys, watching the data come up. "*Argosy Polaris*, sir. Two hundred passengers and a priority medical cargo. Reported overdue at Kariphos ten months ago."

"Damn," Han said softly.

"It's the *Polaris*, sir," Commander Tomanaga confirmed grimly, studying the drifting hulk on his screen. "Somebody ripped hell out of her, too. Must've been quick and dirty to keep her from even getting a drone away. Look at that."

His finger indicated the relatively small punctures riddling the command section of the big liner.

"Primaries and needles," Han said flatly. "They knew she was armed—not that her popguns would've helped much. So they closed in, tractored her, and blew her command and com sections before she could yell for help."

"But how did they get close enough? And what's she doing way out here? We're six transits off the Stendahl-Kariphos route."

"I don't know how they fooled her master," Han said, "but getting her here wouldn't be hard. There's no damage to her drive pods. They just blasted the command deck and then gave whoever was left his options: surrender or see two hundred passengers vaporized. After that, they used the engine room controls to bring her out here so they could loot her at leisure. Not the approved technique, but workable as long as they were in company with someone with intact nav capabilities."

"Sounds reasonable." Tomanaga's words were calm; his face and tone weren't. "But it was sloppy to leave her intact. They should've blown her fusion plants or dropped her into the primary to hide the evidence."

"No, Bob. This is a lonely spot, and that's a hundred thousand tonnes of ship. Lots of spares and replacements to be scavenged out of her."

"Of course." Tomanaga shook his head. "Shall I send in the examination teams, sir?"

"Yes. And call away my cutter. I'm going too."

Han swam down the passage of the dead liner, her powerful lamp illuminating the splendid furnishing of first class—marred in spots by laser burns and occasional scars of pure vandalism. The raiders must have damped the power before they depressurized the hull, for the blast doors stood open. She'd seen one grisly corpse—a crewman dead of explosive decompression—and she was coldly certain they'd dumped atmosphere intentionally to kill any fugitives.

She turned a corner and spun gracefully, landing on her magnetized boot soles beside the Marine search party which had summoned her. Two troopers were busy sealing a transparent bubble to the bulkhead around a closed hatch.

"Afternoon, Admiral."

Major Bryce saluted her, and she returned his salute, then shifted her magsoles to the deckhead, hanging like a weightless bat to watch over the shoulders of the work detail.

"This is the only hatch holding pressure, Major?"

"Yes, sir. We checked out all the others and came up empty"—he seemed unaware of his own grim double entendre—"but there's atmosphere on the other side of this one."

"How much longer, Major?"

"We've just about got her sealed in, sir." He gestured at the plastic airlock. "Soon's we get a little pressure in there, we'll crack the hatch. Not that it's going to make any difference to whoever sealed it."

Han nodded slowly within her helmet. After ten months, no one could possibly survive beyond that hatch.

"Ready, Major," a sergeant said.

"All right, Admiral," Bryce looked at Han, "would you like to go in?"

"Yes, Major. I would."

"Very good, sir."

Bryce managed things smoothly, and Han found herself sandwiched between the looming combat zoots of a pair of Marine corporals as one of them fed power to the hatch from her zoot pack. The hatch slid open, and the plastic lock creaked as its over-pressure bled into the cabin. The corporals moved awkwardly to either side to permit Han to enter first, and she pushed off through the hatch.

It was a tomb.

The first things she saw in her helmet lamp were the rags and plastiseal packed into a pair of ragged holes; one of the primaries that took out the command deck had passed through this cabin. Someone had kept his wits about him to patch those holes so quickly, and the angle of the punctures might explain why the cabin hadn't been searched—they just about parallelled the passage outside, and the single beam had probably pierced at least a dozen suites. Much of first class must have died practically unknowing, and the raiders had probably assumed this cabin's occupants had done the same.

Her evaluation of the patches took only seconds; then she saw the bodies, and her lips twisted with rage.

Children. They were *children*!

She counted five of the huddled little shapes, peacefully arranged in the beds as if merely sleeping, and saw the body of a single adult—a young woman—at a desk to one side. A candle stub was glued to the desk with melted wax, and her head was a shattered ruin, wrought by the heavy-caliber needler death-locked in her hand.

Han looked away and felt her belly knot. There was no nausea—only a cold, deadly hatred for the beings who had wreaked this slaughter of the children she would never bear.

She mastered herself and bent over the stiff corpse of the unknown woman. There was an old fashioned memo pad mag-sealed to the desk, and Han eased it gently loose. Then she turned back to the lock.

"Dump the air, Major," she said, and for the first time she hated herself for sounding serene under pressure. "And transport the bodies to *da Silva.*"

"Yes, sir." Bryce sounded wooden, and she realized he'd been watching his minute com screen; he'd seen everything his corporals' pickups had seen. "We'll be taking them back to Cimmaron, sir?"

"No, Major," Han said quietly. "It won't help their loved ones to see *this*. We'll try to identify them and then bury them in space."

"Yes, sir."

"I'm returning to the flagship, Major."

"Yes, sir. Shall I assign an escort?"

"No, Major. I'd rather be alone, thank you."

"Yes, sir."

Han looked up as Tomanaga entered her cabin. He'd seen the pictures of that cabin and knew his admiral well enough to sense the fury behind her calm demeanor, and he took the indicated chair silently, feeling his way through the storm front of her rage.

"You wanted me, sir?"

"Yes," she said calmly. She tapped the memo pad. "I'll want you to drop this off with Irene. It may be useful."

Tomanaga studied her covertly. Her face was as calm as ever, yet she radiated murderous fury. Only belatedly did he realize what it was. Her dark eyes, usually so tranquil, were deadly.

"Yes, sir," he said quietly.

"In the meantime," Han went on carefully. "I'd like to tell you what it is. *This*, Commander, is a record of what that young woman endured."

"Is there any ID on the attackers, sir?"

"There is," she said coldly. "Allow me to summarize. Her name was Ursula Hauser, and she was a second-year student at New Athens—a philosophy major." Despite her hard-held control, Han's mouth twisted before she could smooth it. "A philosophy major," she repeated softly. "According to her notes, her cabin lost integrity almost immediately, but Ms. Hauser was a quick thinker, and she managed to patch the holes.

"Then, over the intercom, she heard the boarders killing the passengers, Commander Tomanaga." She looked up, her black eyes pits of flame. "They lined them up, sorted out the ones they wanted to keep—the young, pretty women—and slaughtered the rest in number three hold.

"But Ms. Hauser was determined they wouldn't get all the passengers. She knew a little about small craft, so she decided to try to steal a cutter and escape. She was on her way to the boatbay when she came across five terrified children from third class, running for their lives from one of the raiders. She stabbed him to death . . . with a carving knife from the first class galley." She paused, and Tomanaga felt his pulse in his temples. "She took his weapon, but she knew now that they were between her and the boatbay, and while they might let *her* live, they would certainly kill the children. So she did the only thing she could and looked for a hiding place.

"She was certain they knew their primaries had depressurized her whole cabin block, so she took the children back to her cabin, hoping they would be overlooked and she could get them to the boatbay after the raiders left. But then they dumped the air, and there she was: locked into her cabin with five children, no power, no vac suits, no airlock, and no way out."

Han's voice trailed off and she looked away from Tomanaga's pale face, speaking so softly he could barely hear her.

"So she did what she had to do, Commander. She fed each of those children a lethal overdose of barbiturates from her cabin medical stores. And when she was quite certain they were all dead, she sat down at the desk, recorded all of their names, finished her memo . . . and shot herself." Han stroked the pad. "She was nineteen, Bob."

A long silence fell. Robert Tomanaga had never personally hated any enemy in all his years of service, but at that moment he knew exactly what hate was, and he understood the old, hackneyed cliches about "killing rages."

"But, sir," he sought a professional topic, something to push the sick hatred away, "how did they catch the ship? *Argosy Polaris* was fast—nothing but a fighter could have overhauled her if she'd had any sort of start. Surely her master didn't allow an unidentified ship into weapons range in the middle of a civil war!"

"No," Han said coldly. "He allowed a Republican cruiser patrol to close with him."

"Oh my God. No. . . ." Tomanaga whispered.

"Precisely. Obviously somewhat modified; they've replaced at least some of the hetlasers with primaries. But that was how he identified them to his passengers when he hove to. I doubt he ever learned his mistake."

"Sir, what—?"

"What are we going to do, Commander?" Han laid the pad aside almost reverently, and when she looked up, her eyes were carved from the obsidian heart of hell. "We're going to find them, Commander Tomanaga. We're going to find the vermin who did this, the vermin who used the honor of the Fleet to cover themselves. And when we do, Commander, I only hope they live long enough to know who's killing them!"

"Admiral! We're picking up something on the emergency distress channel!"

Han straightened in her command chair. Two weeks had passed

with no sign of the pirates, but the possible hiding places had been narrowed methodically. Now there were only a handful of systems it could be, and Siegfried, on the far side of the next warp point, was one of them.

"Get a bearing, David," she said with the special serenity her staff had learned to expect in moments of stress. "Bob, send the group to quarters."

"Aye, aye, sir!" Tomanaga snapped, and the high-pitched shrilling of the alert wailed through the massive ship. Han hardly heard it.

"Got it, sir! Oh-one-niner level, two-eight-eight vertical. Looks like a standard shuttle transmission."

"Thank you. Bob, raise Captain Onsbruck. I want one fighter squadron to take a close look; hold the other two back for cover. This could be legitimate or a trap, so tell the pilots to take no chances."

"Aye, aye, sir."

"Thank you." She punched buttons, and Schwerin's face appeared on her com screen. "Captain, until I know exactly what we've got, you will halt the flagship and the battlegroup ten light-seconds short of the signal source."

"Aye, aye, sir."

"Thank you." She cut the connection and turned back to Tomanaga, and the lean chief of staff shivered at the hunger in her normally tranquil eyes.

"And now, Commander," she said softly, "we wait."

". . . know how important it is," Surgeon Commander Lacey told his admiral firmly, "but these are very sick people, sir! Another two days—" He shrugged. "You'll just have to use the statements they've already made."

"Very well. Thank you, Doctor."

Han switched off the intercom and looked around the briefing room at the taut, angry faces. The battlegroup's COs attended via com links to their command decks and looked, if possible, even grimmer than her staff.

"Lieutenant Jorgensen," she said, "you've been correlating the survivors' statements. What conclusions have you been able to reach?"

"Everything they've said is consistent, Admiral," Irene Jorgensen twisted a lock of hair around an index finger, "and according to them, the pirate commander is an Arthur Ruyard. Our prewar data base lists him as CO of the *Kearsarge*, a Frontier Fleet cruiser. Apparently he seized Siegfried by declaring support for the rebellion; once he controlled communications he dropped that pretense, and he's been raiding commerce—ours, the Rim's, even the Orions'—ever since."

"Oh my God!" Captain Janet MacInnes of the *Eisenhower* groaned. "Not the bloody Tabbies, too!"

"I'm afraid so, Captain," Jorgensen said, "but they've said nothing about it. I suspect they've chosen to take their losses and deal with the raiders on their own rather than provoking a possible incident because of the Khan's desire for neutrality."

"All right," Han brought the discussion quietly back to immediate problems. "What's your best force estimate, Lieutenant?"

"Sir, they appear to have the heavy cruisers *Kearsarge* and *Thunderer* and the light cruisers *Leipzig*, *Agano*, and *Phaeton*. There are also five or six destroyers and a prewar squadron of system defense fighters operating from Siegfried III."

"But *Leipzig* and *Agano* were destroyed in action against a Rim destroyer flotilla!" Alfred Onsbruck objected. "I saw copies of the Omega drones."

"I don't doubt it," Captain Schwerin said. "Lieutenant—" he turned to the intelligence officer "—I'll bet none of his ships are listed as current members of the Republican Navy, are they?"

"They aren't, sir. *Leipzig* and *Agano* at one time *were* Republican units; none of the others were ever listed as having come over."

"There you are," Stravos Kollentai said crisply. "Ruyard started with only his ship, then picked off the others from either the Rim or us—probably pretending to belong to the same side until he got close enough to spring the trap." He paused and rubbed his nose. "What bothers me is his crews. I hate to think he found that many potential pirates in uniform!"

"He didn't," Jorgensen said. "Two of his first prizes were TFNS *Justicar* and *Hammurabi*—convict ships. According to our survivors, that's where the bulk of his personnel come from."

"I see. And just who are these 'survivors,' Lieutenant?"

"There are seventeen, sir: seven men and ten women. The men worked in Siegfried's mining operations before the war, as did two of the women. The others were aboard ships Ruyard's men captured. I understand—" Jorgensen's plain face twisted with distaste "—that Ruyard intends to found a dynasty. He's been collecting women to 'entertain' his crews, but the prettiest of them are earmarked for his 'nobility.'"

A savage, inarticulate sound came from Han's officers.

"How did they escape?" Kollentai asked after a moment.

"The 'fleet' was out on a raid and they stole an ore shuttle in for repairs—it had a bad drive, but they preferred to take their chances. They made it through the warp point, but then their drive packed in. They drifted for over a month before activating their beacon."

"That," Onsbruck said quietly, "took guts."

"Indeed," Han agreed. "And thanks to them, we know one thing Irene hasn't mentioned yet." She smiled thinly at her subordinates. "This Ruyard doesn't trust any of his prisoners aboard ship for any reason."

"Now isn't that nice of him," Captain MacInnes said softly.

"I see your point, Admiral," Onsbruck said, "but even if we can blast them without worrying about civilian casualties, we have to be in range to do it. And we've got a problem there."

"Agreed." Han nodded with a tight smile. "Commander Kollentai and Commander Tomanaga have given the matter some thought, however. Bob?"

"Thank you, sir." Tomanaga faced Onsbruck, even though he was addressing them all. "Essentially, our problem is that although either one of our monitors outguns their entire 'fleet' by a factor of five, all of their ships are faster than we are."

"Exactly, Commander. So how do you propose to make them stand still for us?" Onsbruck could have sounded scornful, but he didn't.

"Commander Kollentai thought of the answer, sir. Deception mode ECM. We'll come in openly, but what they'll see will be two battlecruisers—*da Silva* and *Eisenhower*—and three destroyers—*Shokaku*, *Black Widow*, and *Termite*. Even though the 'battlecruisers' will out-mass anything they have, they won't expect any fighters and their total firepower will be far superior to what they believe we have."

"And if they send scouts out to check from close range?" Schwerin asked.

"According to the escapees, this Ruyard sticks with what works. He closes with his entire force before he drops his mask because his victims are less likely to balk if he gets in close, and, if they do, he's got the close-range firepower to deal with them. The chance to add two 'battlecruisers' to his force should suck him right in where we want him."

"But if it doesn't?" Schwerin pressed.

"Then we'll just have to do our best, sir. Their fighters can't run; they're restricted to Siegfried III. As for the mobile units, long-range strikes from *Shokaku* should nail at least both heavies before they can transit out. That's better than nothing, sir."

"But not enough." Han's voice drew all eyes back to her, and her face was as cold as her voice.

"We don't talk about it, ladies and gentlemen," she said, "but each of us—even those who only joined up after the mutinies—is here because we believe it is our duty to protect our worlds and our people. That is the *only* acceptable reason for wearing the uniform we wear, and it is also something which, I hope and believe, we continue to share with the TFN."

She looked at them. One or two looked a bit embarrassed—especially David Reznick—but no one disagreed.

"The commanders of these ships have violated that purpose. They are mass murderers and rapists, but they are also outlaws against us. Against *this*." She touched the collar of her uniform. "Against our honor."

She paused once more, and her eyes burned.

"No one—*no one!*—is entitled to do that. The law sets only one penalty for their actions, just as there is only one penalty which can wipe away the dishonor they have brought to our uniform."

She looked at her subordinates once more, seeing her own anger in their faces. Only Tomanaga seemed to fully understand the shame she felt, but all of them shared her fury.

"And that, ladies and gentlemen, is the penalty we will enforce upon them," she finished grimly. She leaned back, her face once more calm, her voice once more serene. "It is my intention to enter Siegfried and attack within the next six hours. Carry on, ladies and gentlemen."

"There, sir," Tomanaga murmured as the enemy light codes crept onto the plot. "Still at extreme range, but they're closing. . . ."

Han nodded, watching the light dots of the piratical cruisers drift slowly closer, the red bands of hostile ships flashing around them. She picked out both heavies and all three of the lights, accompanied by the white dots of four destroyers.

"Data base can't identify the heavies, sir," David Reznick reported. "They've been altered and refitted too much—looks like the missile armament must have been downgraded in favor of primaries, wherever they got them. But I've got good IDs on the lights: *Phaeton, Agano,* and *Leipzig.* Two of the lineans are *Pike* and *Bengal,* but we don't know the others. Range is fifty light-seconds and closing."

"Thank you, David. Try to raise them, please."

"Aye, aye, sir."

There was a brief silence in response to *da Silva*'s hail, then the screen lit with the image of a thin-faced, scholarly looking man who matched the data base pictures of Arthur Ruyard.

"I am Rear Admiral Li Han, Terran Republican Navy, commanding Battlegroup Nineteen," Han told him. "And you are?"

"Commodore Dennis Khulman, commanding the Twentieth Cruiser Squadron," the thin-faced man replied after the inevitable transmission lag, and Han's eyes did not even a flicker at the lie.

"What brings you out here, Commodore?" she asked with just the right trace of curiosity.

"I was about to ask you that, sir." Ruyard/Khulman smiled. "We're on a standing patrol out of Klatzenberger by way of Tomaline, Admiral. And you?"

"Out of Novaya Rodina via Jansen, Schulman, and Kariphos," Han lied equally smoothly. "We didn't expect to see Republican units out this way."

"No, sir. We didn't either," Ruyard/Khulman agreed.

"Well, I suppose we'd better rendezvous and exchange news, Commodore," Han said, watching the other ships creep closer on her plot.

"Of course, sir. But you'll pardon me if I keep my shields up until we do?" Ruyard/Khulman allowed himself a deprecating shrug. "Can't be too careful out here, sir."

"I certainly agree, Commodore," Han smiled, black murder in her heart.

"Thank you, sir. I make our rendezvous in approximately eighteen minutes at our present speeds. Is that acceptable?"

"It is," Han nodded. "I'll expect you for dinner, Commodore."

"Thank you, sir. I'm looking forward to it."

Li Han cut the communication and smiled savagely at the blank screen.

"Fifteen light-seconds, sir," Reznick reported.

"Very well. When we drop to twelve light-seconds, cut the ECM."

"Cut the ECM, sir?" Reznick was startled into asking the question.

"That's correct, Lieutenant," Han said calmly. She wanted Ruyard to know what he faced. She punched up *Shokaku*. "Captain Onsbruck?"

"Sir?"

"Prepare to launch fighters when our ECM goes down."

"Aye, aye, sir!"

"Thank you."

Han leaned back and watched the outlaw ships inch closer at their reduced speed. Even now Ruyard/Khulman's preplanned surrender demand would be ready, but her message would go out first. The last message he would ever have, she thought coldly: the dropping of her deception the instant before she fired.

She remembered her cold-blooded destruction of the *Swiftsure* at Aklumar and recognized the similarity, yet the resemblance was only superficial. *Swiftsure*'s people had been enemies, but they had been honorable foes, worthy of a far better end. These enemies were scum.

"Thirteen light-seconds, sir," Reznick reported softly. "Standing by to disengage ECM. Disengaging . . . *now!*"

The battlegroup's ECM died, and the monitors and carrier stood revealed. Han watched the fighters spitting from *Shokaku*'s catapults, but only with a corner of her eye. Her attention was on the dots of the enemy.

"Sir! Message from *Kearsarge!*" Reznick sounded startled. "They want to surrender, sir!"

Ruyard was fast on his mental feet, Han thought grimly. He knew he couldn't outrun her missiles, so he wasn't even trying. He was banking on the fact that the Terran Navy—Federation or Republican—always gave quarter if it was asked for. It might be another trap or simply another example of his using the Navy's honor against itself. She watched the last of the fighters launch, and her face was bleak and cold.

"Captain Schwerin."

"Yes, sir?" Schwerin responded, his voice neutral.

"Open fire, Captain," Rear Admiral Li Han said softly.

# WAR WARNING

Leornak'zilshisdrow, Lord Sofald, Sixteenth Great Fang of the Khan, and District Governor of the Rehfrak Sector by proclamation of *hirikolus*, appeared on the Orion passenger liner's com screen, and Ian Trevayne looked for the first time at the being who had held his life in his hands thirty-one standard months before. Studying the tawny-furred, felinoid face, he noted admiringly that Leornak's whiskers were spectacular even by the standards of well-endowed Orion males. Rumor had it that the Orions approved of the current Terran fashion of growing beards; they felt it lent human faces a certain much-needed character.

Leornak smiled a fang-hidden carnivore's welcome and spoke, producing a series of sounds suggesting cats copulating to bagpipe music, then paused. Like many high-ranking Orions, the governor understood Standard English well, but the Orion vocal apparatus was poorly suited to produce humanlike sounds. The problem was mutual, of course, which was one reason humans persisted in calling Orions "Orions." The thoroughly inaccurate label—assigned by ONI when Terrans first learned of the three-star-system, fourteen-warp-point nexus near the Great Nebula in Orion which was the heart of the Khanate—was far easier to pronounce than *Zheeerlikou'valkhannaiee* . . . and even that was but a crude approximation of what the Orions called themselves.

Trevayne shook the inconsequential thoughts aside as the translator on Leornak's jeweled harness used his ship's sophisticated computers to produce pedantically exact English, complete to properly interpreting Leornak's formal tone and nuance.

"Welcome to Rehfrak, Admiral Trevayne. I am glad for the opportunity to meet you in person—although you will understand that the welcome must be entirely unofficial. I trust you are not in quite so much of a hurry as you were on your last visit?"

Trevayne smiled back, careful to hide his own teeth as good manners demanded. As an Englishman, he could appreciate studied understatement.

"No, Governor, this time I'm not trying to make good an escape—which I managed only as a result of your good offices. But, as you so rightly point out, these proceedings are unofficial—and, in my case at least, clandestine. The sooner I can meet with my government's representative, the better for all concerned."

"Of course, Admiral. He has already arrived and is here aboard my flagship, *Szolkir*." With further exchanges of courtesies, arrangements were made for Trevayne to be picked up by one of *Szolkir*'s cutters.

Trevayne watched Leornak's flagship gleam in the reflected orange light of the gas giant she orbited as the cutter approached her. Like all Khanate officers with sufficient pull, Leornak flew his lights aboard one of the *Itzarin*-class assault carriers. The Orions and the Terran rebels were as one in the prestige they accorded strikefighters and the starships which carried them, he thought dryly. In fact, for all their noisy anti-amalgamation invective, the Fringe Worlders were a lot like the whisker-twisters in many ways. Some twentieth-century wit had observed that the really great hatreds are between peoples that are alike and can't stand to admit it. Apparently that held as true between species as between human groups.

Trevayne gazed at the lovely killing machine and smiled faintly. After the next battle, the Khanate, as well as the "Terran Republic," would have some reassessing to do. He watched the cutter dock, and his mind slid back in time to the day, almost exactly a standard month before, when his journey had truly begun. . . .

Trevayne sat in a familiar conference room in Prescott City and looked around the table at the Grand Council of the Rim Provisional Government, which people were beginning to call the Rim Federation—though not in Trevayne's presence!

His Councilors were chosen by the Legislative Assembly from among its own members. Their function, in theory, was to advise the Governor-General; in practice, they governed the Rim when Trevayne was in deep space, which was often.

It was all very novel to these Outworlders, but Trevayne had read enough history to know he'd set in motion a reenactment of the birth of parliamentary government in his native England seven centuries before. In fact, this was what cabinet government was *supposed* to be like, for there were no structured parties in the Rim. That, he thought glumly, would come later, along with organized voting blocs, mass-media electioneering, and the rest. And would the people of the Rim, having tasted home rule, be willing to give it up when (the word "if" did not even cross his mind) the Federation won the war?

He looked at each Councilor, and at one in particular. To some extent Miriam Ortega owed her rise to the memory of her father, but that was only a part of it—and, after the early days, a small part, overshadowed by her own intelligence and force of personality.

Her eyes met Trevayne's. They'd been lovers for over a year.

He looked away, sweeping the other Councilors with his gaze once more.

"Ladies and gentlemen," he began, "I've called this meeting to confirm the rumor: we've received, through the Orions, a reply to our message to the Federation!"

He waited for the inevitable hubbub to die down. The Rim's only warp connection with the Innerworlds (other than those in rebel-held space) was the very circuitous one through the Khanate by which Trevayne's command had reached Zephrain. Afterwards, the Khan had closed his frontiers to *all* human entry. Even the raw materials purchased by the Innerworlds travelled only in Orion hulls, and only after a long and frustrating period of indirect negotiation had the Orions agreed to carry one message for Trevayne and to bring back one reply.

"All the Orions will say," he resumed, "is that the Federation is sending a representative to Rehfrak, which is as far as they'll let him come, in one standard month. They'll allow me to go to him—alone, secretly, in one of their own unarmed civilian craft. I'm frankly amazed that they're willing to violate their self-imposed neutrality even to that extent."

"Do I understand, sir, that you intend to accept this, uh, invitation?" Barry de Parma, chairman pro tem of the Grand Council, looked shocked at Trevayne's nod. "But the risk! You're indispensable—"

"The Orions," Miriam Ortega cut in, "favor the Federation. They're neutral only because they know overt help from them would give our side an 'alien' taint." She smiled wryly, knowing that much of the resentment felt by the rebelling Fringe Worlds was shared by the people of the Rim, including some in this room. The Corporate Worlds had been wrong to accuse the Fringers of "xenophobia," but there was no doubting the Outworlders' grim determination to remain independent of the Orions. She hid a sigh of impatience with her fellow Councilors, saying only, "They have no motive for treachery."

"Precisely," Trevayne agreed, "and as for my . . . classified knowledge," he added, knowing they all took his meaning, "I'm not a technician, and no hard information could be got out of me. Besides, we have no reason to think they know there's any to get."

He changed the subject before any cautious souls like de Parma could spot the gaping holes in his rationalization.

"Now, about security. Obviously, this jaunt can't be a matter of public knowledge." They all nodded, knowing how their people would react to the news that the Provisional Government was having any dealings whatsoever with the Tabbies. "Officially, I'll be on exercises with the Fleet, and all transfer operations will be in the hands of people I can trust."

"What if you're gone an unusually long time?" De Parma looked glum. "What if questions come up for debate in the Assembly?"

"Don't let them," Trevayne replied cheerfully. "You're here because together you can control the Assembly. As a countryman of mine named Disraeli, who had some small experience in these matters, once said, 'A majority is the best repartee.' "

Miriam gave him a glare beneath which a smile flickered. "You and your quotes! No one out here can ever be sure you're not making them up!"

He smiled at her. "Would that I were so creative!"

Trevayne came back to the present as the cutter's hatch opened. A proudly overconscientious young Cub of the Khan, whiskers almost visibly atwitch with curiosity, led him to what would have been called the wardroom in a human capital ship, but no military courtesies were exchanged. The wardroom was under heavy guard, but when Trevayne entered only two individuals rose to greet him. He recognized Leornak at once, and the human beside him looked vaguely familiar. Trevayne felt he ought to recognize the man, but he couldn't quite place him.

"Welcome to *Szolkir*, Admiral," Leornak greeted him.

"Thank you, Governor."

Trevayne watched Leornak's tufted ear twitch as his computer translated the Standard English into Orion. It was an impressive performance, but the Orions had always been exceptionally good with computers and cybernetics—not that they had all the answers. Like the Federation, they'd been persistently thwarted in their efforts to create an artificial intelligence which didn't go promptly insane on them. Still, they made much more use of voice-coded software, even aboard warships, than Terrans did.

Of course, their language and vocal apparatus gave them a considerable advantage there. There were no Orion homonyms, and Orion voice patterns were even more readily identifiable than human patterns, which made computer authentication much simpler. More importantly, perhaps, Orions tended to express strong emotions—like excitement and fear—with visual cues, not voice cues. To date, the Federation had been unable to devise a voice-coded software package which could cope with human stress patterns without requiring a prohibitive amount of storage space. Trevayne himself had been a gunnery officer aboard the superdreadnought *Ranter* the last time BuShips had tried to introduce voice-cuing into Fleet use, and he still shuddered at the memory of *that* fiasco.

Leornak reclaimed his attention with a graceful gesture at his human guest. "Allow me to present an old colleague and sometime opponent, Mister Kevin Sanders, representing the Prime Minister of the Terran Federation."

Of course! Trevayne shook hands with the tallish, slender man, whose sharp features and gray Vandyke gave him a foxy look. He was well over 120, Trevayne remembered; in an age before longevity treatments, he might have been a sprightly and well-preserved sixty. Like Trevayne, he wore conservative civilian clothing.

"Good to see you back on the active list, Admiral Sanders," Trevayne said after the initial greetings. "Last I heard, you were still engaged in ruining the image of retired officers."

Sanders' merry blue eyes twinkled upward into Trevayne's somber dark-brown ones, and he chuckled.

"Strictly speaking, I'm no longer an 'admiral.' True, I was dusted off and brought back to ONI after the insurrection—for some reason, there were quite a lot of early retirements about then. But I resigned my commission last year to become a minister without portfolio in the Dieter Government—a liaison of sorts between the Cabinet and the intelligence community."

He noted Trevayne's raised eyebrows at the words *the Dieter*

*Government*, but he said nothing. Privately, he was impressed by how well Trevayne had controlled the surprise he must have felt.

"But," he concluded, "that's more than enough about me. It's a privilege to meet you, Admiral, and also a pleasure. For one thing, I once had the privilege of serving under your great-grandmother, when *she* was head of ONI. And for another, we're both members of a rare breed out here: I'm also from Old Terra."

"Yes," Trevayne said. "I know."

"Oh?" Sanders' gaze grew a trifle sharper. "How?"

Trevayne indulged himself. "I've always been fascinated by the variations with which we native English-speakers still manage to enliven what's become a universal trade language," he said with a professorial air Miriam would instantly have recognized. "You, sir, are a North American—from either the old Canadian Maritime Provinces or the Tidewater area of the old American states of Virginia and Maryland, I'd say. The two dialects are almost identical, you know."

Sanders managed to keep his aplomb, saying only, "The latter is correct." He wasn't at his best dealing with people as clever as himself, a deficiency he ascribed to lack of opportunity for practice.

Leornak's grin grew and his whiskers quivered slightly as he regarded the two humans. "Kevin," he said to Sanders, "I had a feeling this meeting would be a salutary experience for you. Unfortunately, I have duties to attend to and I must leave, as much as I am enjoying this. And you gentlemen doubtless need a degree of privacy—but I shall expect you for dinner afterwards."

Trevayne felt a momentary uneasiness at the invitation. Terran and Orion biochemistries were close enough to make such shared social events practical, but humans found some Orion culinary practices . . . disturbing. His queasiness died quickly as Leornak's slit-pupiled eyes laughed at him. Of course—a confirmed old cosmopolite like Leornak could be expected to defer to his guests' sensibilities by avoiding such customs as munching live specimens of that species which had always reminded Trevayne of hairless mice.

After the door closed behind Leornak, the Terrans sat at a low table on the cushions which served Orions in lieu of chairs, and Sanders poured from the bottle he and Leornak had been sampling. Bourbon, Trevayne thought dourly, had become so popular among upper-crust Orions that it was one of the Federation's

major export items. Why the bloody hell hadn't the Tabbies had
the common decency to take a liking to fine, malt Scotch?

He raised the glass, returning Sanders' brief salute, and drank.
Then, somewhat fortified, he asked the question he had not cared
to ask in Leornak's presence.

"Ah . . . correct me if I'm wrong, but did I understand you to
refer to the *Dieter* government?"

"Why, yes," Sanders answered with a look of bland innocence.
"I noticed you seemed surprised," he added. *Damn the man!*

"Well," Trevayne said carefully, "my last news from the Innerworlds was just before the mutinies. You must admit, at that time
Mister Dieter's political star wasn't exactly in the ascendant." The
single time he'd met Dieter, the man had struck him as a typical,
blindly avaricious Corporate World political hack. "It's just seems
a trifle . . . odd, from my perspective out here."

"Admiral, never underestimate Oskar Dieter," Sanders said.
"Simon Taliaferro did, and it cost him."

Trevayne blinked at the other's sudden seriousness. Clearly
there had been some changes in the Innerworlds!

"But," Sanders went on more lightly, "the Admiralty's briefing
chips will bring you up to date on background events and time
is short, so allow me to discharge myself of my instructions and
deal with the present and future."

He set his glass aside to open an old-fashioned briefcase with
an extremely modern security system.

"And so to business, Admiral . . . all of it pleasant business for
you. You're now a Fleet Admiral, and all the field promotions
you've made are retroactively confirmed. As is your assumption
of the title 'Governor-General.' In fact, I should have greeted
you as 'Your Excellency,' which is how the protocol experts have
decided a governor-general should be addressed."

Trevayne gave the older man what he hoped was a quelling
glare, but it was difficult to tune up the full voltage against a
man more than twice his age. And he suspected that even at full
bore, his expression would have had little effect on Sanders, who
only grinned and continued as flippantly as before.

"There was a little more trouble about this Rim Legislative
Assembly of yours. No provision for it in the Constitution, after
all . . ."

"There's also nothing in the Constitution about an insurrection
that isolates part of the Federation from Old Terra," Trevayne cut
in. "These people remained loyal when all the rest of the Fringe

revolted—and, I might add, despite their systematic abuse by the Corporate Worlds. Their loyalty is a priceless resource—we'd be wasting it if we hadn't involved them in their own defense!"

"*Pace,* Admiral!" Sanders raised a hand. "All was ratified. Oh, a few politicos are afraid you're setting up as an autonomous warlord out here, but of course they keep quiet about it. They want to stay in office!" He chuckled, then paused at Trevayne's puzzled look, but understanding dawned quickly.

"Of course! How could you know? The fact is, you've become something of a legend, Admiral. The original reports of your flight from Osterman's Star into Orion space captured the public imagination, especially since no one even knew if you'd survived. Then when the news broke that you were not only alive but had rallied the Rim and given the Rebels a bloody nose, to boot—well, I can hardly overstate the reaction. The Federation has produced precious few victories and even fewer victorious commanders. When an authentic hero turned up, there was no shortage of Corporate World money to publicize him."

Sanders' eyes danced. He'd watched happily as Trevayne's embarrassment grew visibly. Now he gently administered the coup de grace.

"You'll be pleased to know, Admiral, that you're the subject of a lavishly financed, hugely successful holodrama mini-series entitled *Escape to Zephrain.* You were played by Lance Manly, only slightly aged for the role."

He sat back and listened with pure pleasure while Trevayne swore in six languages for a full minute without repeating himself. He waited until the new fleet admiral had run out of breath, if not obscenities, before he continued with a toothy grin.

"I've brought chips of the entire series, Admiral. The government feels it will enhance civilian morale in the Rim. . . ."

But Trevayne's habitual self-control had reasserted itself. "I'll take personal custody of those chips, if you don't mind." And cycle them through an airlock at the first opportunity! "But don't keep me in suspense any longer, damn you! How is the war going?"

Sanders was suddenly serious. "Not well. The rebels have gained control of all the choke points connecting their systems to the Innerworlds—without, I'm sorry to say, very much hindrance. You may not realize how extraordinary Admiral Ortega's and your success in holding your forces together really was, Admiral. The government put the Navy in an incredibly vulnerable position, and when the shooting started, the Fleet simply disintegrated before our eyes. Before we got the news about Zephrain, we'd estimated that ninety percent of Frontier Fleet had gone over—now we've revised that to just over eighty percent. But what really hurt was losing over fifty percent of Battle Fleet's active units."

"*Fifty percent!*" Even this man could be rocked by some revelations, Sanders noted. "Sweet mother of God, man!"

"Fifty percent," Sanders confirmed grimly, "but that doesn't mean the rebels got all we lost."

His face suddenly looked every day of its age, and Trevayne leaned back against his cushions.

Of course. It had to have been like that, or those Battle Fleet monitors already would have taken Zephrain away from him. He closed his eyes in brief pain as he contemplated the grim scenes that must have occurred within the Federation as scattered, mutinous battle-line units went down under the fire of their own service—and took their share of loyal ships and crews with them.

"So they had both the time and strength to grab their choke points," Sanders went on after a moment. "Not only that, but by now they've had time to set up a few yards of their own. So far we haven't seen any heavy capital ships among their new construction . . . but give them time. They'll get to it. They got too much breathing space, and crushing them is going to be long and bloody. And, of course, there's always someone waiting to step in as soon as there's an opening. Like the Tangri. I noticed in your report that you've had a few brushes with them out along the Rim?"

"One or two," Trevayne agreed calmly. "Not very many, though. I adopted an argument they understood, and they've left us alone since."

"Really? I've had some experience of the Tangri myself, Admiral. I'm afraid I'm not familiar with an 'argument' they pay any attention to."

"Oh, but you are, Mister Sanders." Trevayne chuckled dryly. "As a matter of fact, I believe you were present in the Lyonesse System when the same argument was propounded once before." His better nature triumphed just before he added, "That was before my time," and he ended with a simple, "I estimate three percent of their raiding force got home."

"Ah!" Sanders nodded. "It's a pity the Federation has always been too easygoing to use that argument more often. Still, I suppose the plutocrats have been more concerned with squeezing the

Fringers. And they have other worries now. There was even some wild talk about bringing Battle Fleet home to 'stand shoulder-to-shoulder in defense of the homeworld!' But, of course, that was before they really understood the Fringe's objectives. The rebels want to secede, and for that they only have to hold what they've already got, not add more stars to it. Except—" he looked sharply at Trevayne "—for the Rim. They want that. And now they feel they can take it."

He patted the briefcase. "I've brought ONI's analysis for your perusal. The prognosis is: you can expect a really massive attack on Zephrain within sixty standard days. The question is: can you hold?"

Their eyes locked as Sanders silently asked the question that could not be asked aloud aboard an Orion warship. Have your people managed to transmute the theoretical data at Zephrain RDS into the kind of hardware that will even the odds you'll face?

Trevayne understood. And he knew that if Leornak had any conception of what was truly at stake, all the possible "diplomatic repercussions" in the Galaxy would not assure his own safety. Leornak would have to try, even though torture was notoriously unreliable, even though all TFN officers were immunized to truth-extracting drugs, and even though the limitations of hypnosis were still essentially what they had been in Franz Mesmer's day.

So he answered simply, "Yes."

They settled back on their cushions and sipped their bourbon, two men who understood one another perfectly, and Sanders smiled his impish smile again.

"Well, Admiral, I'm confirmed in my view that the government acted wisely in ratifying your actions. That's the one advantage of a plutocracy: it can sometimes be frightened into doing the sensible thing." He caught Trevayne's disapproving look and deliberately misinterpreted it. "Oh, yes, of course the good Leornak is bugging us . . . but only for his private amusement and the edification of his own superiors. And while those superiors would rather do business with *us*, they don't have much emotional investment in this war. Not like those of us who're out to avenge the blood of kith and kin, as it were."

He stopped suddenly, looking uncharacteristically uncomfortable.

"Apologies, Admiral. That was an inappropriate thing to say. Of course I know about your family."

But Trevayne hardly heard him, for in the corridors of his memory, a long-shut door swung open.

It had been sixteen years before, with his younger daughter Ludmilla newly born. He'd taken his family to Old Terra for the first time. They'd visited England, of course, and Moscow. And like all human visitors to the birthworld, they'd journeyed to Africa where the Temple of Man exploded up over Olduvai Gorge in arches and spires that soared towards infinity while *homo erectus*, captured forever in the masterpiece of the twenty-second century sculptor Xentos, gazed at the lights in the night sky and wondered. . . .

But the image that haunted him still was from the Mediterranean island of Corfu, whose mountains meet the sea to subdivide beaches into ancient coves where squinting, sun-dazzled eyes can sometimes momentarily glimpse Odysseus' galley rounding a headland. Until the day of his death, he would never be able to think of his older daughter Courtenay without seeing a four-year-old girl on the beach at Corfu, the brilliant sun conjuring reddish glints in her chestnut hair . . . followed swiftly by the dissipating radioactive dust which, for a little while after the missiles struck, must have colored the dawns and sunsets of Galloway's World.

He allowed himself five twenty-nine hour Xandy days in Prescott City after his return from Rehfrak. On the sixth day, he awoke and walked to the open window to gaze out into the high summer of Xanadu's northern hemisphere. Imported elms mingled with native featherleaf and falsepine across a well-tended lawn crystalline with dew, and creatures that weren't quite furry birds flew overhead in the early morning light of a sun just too yellow to be Sol. He sniffed the cool air, already sensing the heat the day would bring, and there was a strange stillness in his heart.

He heard a stirring behind him as Miriam reached for him in her sleep and, finding his side of the bed empty, awoke. She smiled sleepily.

"For God's sake, Ian," she murmured. "Put some clothes on if you're going to stand at the window. At least spare what little's left of my reputation."

He smiled. Their affair was the worst-kept secret in the Zephrain System, if not the entire Rim. In fact, he'd been considerably relieved when he viewed the mischievous Sanders' wildly overdone HV chips (which had since mysteriously vanished) and found no mention of Miriam. He sat down on the bed and kissed her forehead gently.

"Go back to sleep," he whispered. "No need for you to get up yet. But I have to leave."

She was fully awake now, and her smile departed. "I suppose it's useless to tell you again that any of your new-minted admirals—Desai, Remko, any of the rest—are competent to act as your in-space commander? Or to remind you of your importance to the Rim?" She caught herself before saying "the Rim Federation."

He thought ruefully of his last conversation with her father. "My 'importance' ends the day the rebels break through," he answered grimly. "The Rim lives or dies with the Fleet. I may as well do the same."

"Ian," she smiled again, "you're full of shit, as usual. I'm a Navy brat, remember? I know the real reason you're going."

Of course they both knew the unwritten (and therefore unbreakable) rule that required any TFN commander who could manage it to be in space with his personnel in battle. Howard Anderson had been aboard one of those twenty-third century battlewagons, now so quaint-seeming, at Aklumar. Ivan Antonov and Raymond Prescott had ridden their flagships into the meat-grinders of Lorelei, Pesthouse, and Home Hive III. And Sergei Ortega had flown his lights to the end in *Krait* at the Battle of the Gateway. . . .

Miriam looked up at the swarthy, invulnerable face and ran her fingers through the close-trimmed, slightly graying beard. Few who knew him saw any reason to dispute the common judgment that he was "complex" and "inscrutable"—some might even add "sinister." She alone had come to know his face lied, that his complexity, seen whole, resolved itself into concentric rings of defense around the dull hurt at the center of him.

Miriam's lovemaking was no more passive than anything else about her, and she pulled him down to her, kissing him. "You don't have to leave just yet," she said softly, "and God knows how long you'll be gone. . . ." And, for a time, nothing existed for either of them except the other.

Afterwards, she sat on the bed among the tangled sheets, hugging her knees and smoking as she watched him dress and groom himself meticulously. Yes, she thought, even the surprising personal vanity fits the pattern. It was a part of the fortifications.

What she did not know, what she would never know, was that without her he was alone with his hurt.

Then he turned back to her, totally familiar and yet almost a stranger in his uniform. They kissed once more, lingeringly, and it was time for him to go.

"You realize, of course," she said with mock severity, "that while you're gone, in addition to being miserably horny, I'm going to have the Devil of a time keeping the Grand Council in harness."

He paused at the door and grinned innocently. "Well," he began, "in the words of a noted pre-space Chinese philosopher . . ."

He managed to beat the hurled pillow through the door.

# CONDUIT

Kevin Sanders hardly noticed the Marines guarding the prime minister's residence. He hadn't been on Old Terra many hours, and he was far more concerned with smelling unrecycled air and seeing more than a handful of faces in one place.

He glanced at his watch as the elevator whisked him to the penthouse. He was running slightly late, but political meetings, he'd learned long ago, were very like social gatherings; it was better to arrive late—even by a large margin—than early by the smallest.

The elevator doors opened, and he stepped out to be met by a tall, fair-haired young man.

"Evening, Heinz. I take it they're awaiting me with bated breath?"

"More or less, Admiral Sanders."

Sanders sighed. Heinz von Rathenau, Dieter's personal security head, was the only member of the New Zurich Delegation to follow him—officially, anyway—into the prime minister's residence, and he seemed incapable of forgetting the titles people had once acquired—or "earned," as he put it. Sanders suspected him of incurable romanticism.

"Shall I go on in, Heinz?"

"Of course, sir. Conference Room Two."

"Thank you."

Four people sat around the polished crystal conference table. Sanders nodded pleasantly to Sky Marshal Witcinski and Chief of Naval Operations Rutgers and bestowed a special smile on Susan Krupskaya, his successor at ONI, then half-bowed to the prime minister.

Dieter was the least impressive of them all, physically speaking, but his was unquestionably the dominant presence. Which was no small trick, given the wealth of experience his military subordinates represented. Either Sanders' first impression of Dieter had been sadly mistaken, or else the man had somehow grown to meet his moment. He suspected the latter, but he was none too sure his suspicion didn't stem from his own dislike of admitting mistakes.

"Mister Sanders." Dieter did not rise, but his courteous greeting gave the impression he had. "I'm glad you were finally able to join us."

"Thank you, sir." Sanders hid a smile. "I'm sorry—I am running a bit late." He didn't mention that he'd walked rather than take a ground car.

"Quite all right," Dieter said. "Man must walk before he can run, I suppose." He smiled pleasantly. "But you're the man of the hour, after all—or, at least, the man who's met him." He leaned back and waved at a chair. "Let us hear your report, Mister Sanders. Please."

"Yes, sir." Sanders laid his briefcase on the table and snapped its security locks. Reinforced titanium sheathing gleamed dully on its inner surfaces as he extracted a folder of holo chips and laid them on the table.

"This is the official report, sir. But I gather you want an . . . ah, off-the-cuff summation?"

"Precisely, Mister Sanders. Your summations are always so enlivening."

"Thank you, sir. I strive to please."

"I'm sure." Dieter opened an inlaid cigar box and waited while Sanders selected and lit one. Then he cleared his throat gently. "Your summation?"

"Yes, sir. Frankly—" Sanders eyes swept the group, his customary levity absent "—we're damned lucky. I was prepared for a determined man, but not for the one I met. In my considered opinion, the Governor-General will hold the Rim Systems if any living man can do it."

"A strong endorsement, Kevin," Susan Krupskaya said quietly.

"Is it?" Sanders suddenly grinned impishly. "Let's just put it this way, Susan—he puts Lance Manly to shame."

"So you're confident he can hold Zephrain?" Witcinski asked somberly.

"I am. More importantly, *he* is. Mind you, we couldn't talk openly on board an Orion carrier, but when I asked him if he could, he answered with one word: 'Yes.' "

"That sounds like Ian," Rutgers said.

"Yes. The Governor-General *does* seem rather, ah, formidable," Sanders agreed. "And he clearly feels he has the firepower he needs . . . plus the locals' full-blooded support. At least," he chuckled dryly, "he defended them most vehemently against a few carefully dropped aspersions."

"That sounds like him, too," Rutgers said.

"And it brings up another point," Witcinski pressed. "Forgive me, Bill—I certainly don't wish to impugn the honor of an officer who's accomplished what he has—but there *has* to be some temptation towards empire-building in his position."

"I suppose so—for some," Sanders broke in before Rutgers' anger could find expression. "Sky Marshal, you no doubt know that Admiral Trevayne lost his wife and daughters on Galloway's World?"

"Yes," Witcinski agreed guardedly.

"Well, sir," Sanders said quietly, "he's lost his son now, too." He watched the sudden pain in Rutgers' broad face, then eyed Witcinski.

"I'm sorry to hear it, Mister Sanders," the Sky Marshal said gruffly, "but how does that answer my question?"

"His son," Sanders said very softly, "was aboard one of the ships BG 32 destroyed in the Battle of Zephrain." He kept his eyes on Witcinski as Rutgers gasped in dismay. "I submit, sir, that neither you, nor I, nor anyone else has the right to question his loyalty after that."

"No," Witcinski said slowly, "I don't suppose so."

There was no apology in his voice, only understanding, but Sanders was content. Witcinski was very like Trevayne—a little harder, perhaps, a little narrower . . . certainly less imaginative. But in one respect they were identical: neither ever apologized for doing what he felt was necessary.

"And your estimate of the military situation, Kevin?" Rutgers' voice was flat, its impersonality covering his own pain.

"The Governor-General provided a force summary, but it's not exhaustive. We were both aware that Fang Leornak was certain to read his report—one way or another." Sanders shrugged and grinned again, dispelling much of the lingering solemnity. "Leornak and I are old friends, so I made his job a little easier by leaving the report on my desk when we went to supper."

"You did *what*?" Witcinski stared at him.

"Of course I did, Sky Marshal," Sanders said cheerfully. "It was only courteous."

"Courteous?!" Witcinski glared at him, and Sanders smiled.

"Please, Sky Marshall!" He waved an airy hand. "The Orions certainly know as much about Zephrain RDS as Admiral Krupskaya and I do about Valkha III. Which is to say each side knows the other has a facility where all that nasty weapons research has carefully not been carried out for the last sixty years. Leornak is a civilized old cat, by his lights, but if he thought he had any chance to discover the contents of Zephrain RDS, he'd have no option but to try—a point, by the way, of which the Governor-General seems well aware. As long as Leornak can tell the Khan there's no evidence of such data being transmitted, he can avoid the unpleasant and diplomatically catastrophic necessity of . . . acquiring it." He shrugged. "So I made it easier by giving him access to the recorded data, since I felt confident Admiral Trevayne was too wise to record anything incriminating. Now Leornak can assure the Khan that no sensitive data was transmitted . . . which meant, incidentally, that the Governor-General and I could leave his flagship."

"My God!" Witcinski shook his head. "I think you actually enjoyed it!"

"My dear Sky Marshal! Why else would anyone *become* a 'spook'?" Sanders permitted himself another chuckle.

"But you do have a strength estimate?" Rutgers pressed.

"Certainly. The full data is in the report. Fortunately, few capital ships were actually lost at Zephrain. His damaged units have been repaired, and apparently he's undertaken a program of new construction, as well. . . ."

Sanders' voice trailed off in deliberately tantalizing fashion.

"New construction?" Rutgers frowned at him. "What sort?"

"A new group of monitors—he says." Sanders' voice was quite neutral.

"Says?" Krupskaya asked sharply. Trust Susan to be the first to pounce, he thought wryly.

"Let's just say I think he finessed some clues past the Orions—which takes some doing with a wily old whisker-twister like Leornak."

"Clues, Mister Sanders? What sort of clues?"

"Just this, Sky Marshal—he's building *only* monitors, each of which is tying up the full capacity of a Terra-class space dock, and he's named the first of them *Horatio Nelson*."

"What? What sort of name is that for a monitor?"

"Precisely, Sky Marshal. Monitors are named for TFN heroes, yet this ship isn't. The Orions probably won't give it a thought—after all, our nomenclature is as confusing to them as theirs is to us—but a nonstandard name suggests a nonstandard class, no? Coupled with the building capacity devoted to each of them and the fact that he doesn't seem to feel the need for carriers—" Sanders raised one hand, palm up.

"I see." Witcinski scratched his chin. "I believe you have a point, Mister Sanders."

"So Admiral Trevayne has a sizable conventional force, plus whatever unorthodox vessels and weapons he may be building," Dieter mused. "And on that basis, he feels confident of defeating anything the rebels can throw at him." He nodded slowly. "My friends, I think that may be the best news since this whole sorry disaster began. If he's right—if he *can* hold—it may be time for us to consider Operation Yellowbrick." He glanced at his two senior military commanders. "Comments, gentlemen?"

"Really, Kevin," Susan Krupskaya chided as she poured scotch into his glass, "you should watch the way you talk to the Sky Marshal."

"Why?" Sanders yawned and stretched, looking briefly more catlike than an Orion. "Has he noticed something?"

"Kevin, you're a clever man, not to mention devious and underhanded, but the Sky Marshal is cleverer than you think. He may not waste time on decadent things like social amenities, but he's quite well aware you enjoy twitting him."

"Nonsense! That man's not 'well aware' of anything that doesn't mount shields, armor, and energy weapons!"

"Oh, no? That's not what his war diary says."

"*War diary?*" Sanders sat up and frowned at her. "You've been tapping the confidential war diary of the military commander-in-chief, Susan?"

"But, Kevin," she batted her eyelids demurely, "you always said that anything someone considers worth keeping a secret is probably worth knowing. Besides, he's a Fringer; it seemed like a good idea to check him."

"But if he catches you at it," Sanders said warningly, "not even Dieter's going to be able to save your shapely ass."

"No?" Krupskaya grinned a trifle crookedly. "Why do you think

I warned you he's cleverer than you think? Here's my last intercept from his diary." She tossed him a sheet of facsimile.

"Ah?" Sanders glanced at the transcript and began to chuckle. After a moment, it became full-throated laughter, and he raised his glass ungrudgingly to the absent sky marshal. All it said was: "My Dear Vice Admiral. I trust you and Mister Sanders have enjoyed being on the 'inside.' L. Witcinski."

"And he accused *me* of enjoying it!"

"And he was right, you old reprobate!" Krupskaya shook her head wryly. "I'm still not certain how he caught me, but he thinks you put me up to it."

"Well, I suppose I did, in a sense," Sanders agreed lazily. "After all, I taught you everything you know."

"Not quite everything," she said dryly. "And before you start blowing your ego out your ears, I have something for you. Here." She handed him a sheaf of pages.

"Ah! An excellent job, Susan. Excellent!"

"Sure." She shook her head at him. "Kevin, what are you up to? Here's proof that Captain M'tana and Alistair Nomoruba are feeding information to the rebels, and you won't let me do a thing about it! Damn it, they've been doing it for over two *years* now!"

"So they have." Sanders finished the first sheet, nodded to himself and crumpled the paper, breaking the security coating, then tossed it into the ice-bucket at his elbow. The sheet touched melted ice-water and vanished as he turned to the second page.

"I've done a lot for you, Kevin," Admiral Krupskaya said sternly, "and I'll probably go right on doing it, but you owe me an explanation. I don't mind putting my career on the line, but sitting on this may violate my sworn oath as an officer."

"Sweet Susan," Sanders said soothingly, "the skill has not yet deserted these palsied old fingers. This old eye has not yet lost its keenness. This old ear has not yet—"

"Spare me a full catalog of decrepit organs that are still more or less functional," she interrupted rudely. "What you're saying—in your thankfully inimitable style—is that *you* know what you're doing?"

"Precisely."

"Kevin," she said with unaccustomed severity, "I'm no longer a wet-nosed snotty in your operation on New Valkha. I have my own duties—and I've run about as for with this as I intend to without an explanation."

"Ah, but your baby fat made you such a charming ensign," he said gently. "Still—" he weighed the angry fondness flashing in her eyes and shrugged "—perhaps it *is* time for the wily old master to enlighten his round-eyed, admiring disciple."

"Kevin—!"

"*Pace,* my dear!" His eyes still gleamed, but his voice was serious, and she settled back to listen. "Consider: I first tapped into this conduit less than a month after the POW letter exchanges began, correct?"

"Yes."

"Fine. And at the time, the information passing through it, while undoubtedly useful, wasn't precisely Galaxy-shaking. Correct again?"

"Yes."

"Well, as I taught you in the dim mists of your youth, my love, one *never* tampers with a conduit unless the information passing through it is of deadly importance. Instead, one monitors it, traces it, and, above all, makes certain it carries information in apparent security, thus preventing the ungodly from tinkering up something one *doesn't* know about to replace it. This is spook basic training manual stuff, is it not?"

"Yes, Kevin," she sighed. "But why not tell *anyone* about it?"

"My sweet, a secret is a secret when only one person knows it; anything else is simply more or less compromised information. Dear, toothsome Susan! I wouldn't have told *you* if you hadn't been moving into the worry seat at ONI!"

"And if you hadn't needed my help to stay tapped in!"

"That, too, of course," he admitted graciously.

"All right. I can accept that. But look at some of this stuff, Kevin! Details of the communications with the Orions to set up your trip. Or here—" she pointed at another sheet "—details of Cabinet meetings, for God's sake! We're talking heavy duty data, Kevin. This is no longer Assembly gossip!"

"And quite interesting it is, too," Sanders agreed brightly.

"Damn you, Kevin! Don't evade me! Why can't I even tell *Heinz* that someone *inside the Cabinet* is passing priceless data to the enemy?"

"Priceless?" Sanders finished the last page of the intercepts and watched it curl into nothingness in the ice-bucket. "Perhaps, and perhaps not."

He stirred the clear water and clinking ice with an idle forefinger.

"No 'perhaps' about it!" Krupskaya snorted.

"Actually, you know, there is," he corrected gently. "Consider this, my dear—everything you've picked up from the Cabinet is purely political. There hasn't been one scrap of military intelligence."

"That's true," she agreed slowly, her tone suddenly thoughtful.

"Now," Sanders purred, "who has access to all *this*—" he tapped the bland water in the ice-bucket "—but *not* to military data? The same Cabinet meeting which discussed sending me to the Orions also discussed our entire naval strategy, yet there's not a word of that in here. Surely that would be worth more to the rebels than, for example, Prime Minister Dieter's requests for opinions on granting the 'Republic' limited belligerent status?"

"Selective information," she said softly, nodding her head. "But why? You're right; it's valuable, but less valuable than military intelligence."

"Ah, but is it?"

"Damn you," she said without rancor. "Don't start your damned double-think on me now!"

"I'm not. But who does it have value for? The recipient . . . or the sender?"

"I don't pretend to understand that one—yet. But I will, I promise you!"

"I'm sure you will," he soothed, his smile taking the offense from his words. "You were always my best student, or you wouldn't be sitting where you are now. But unlike you, my love, I already know our mole's identity."

"And you don't intend to share it with me?" she said resignedly.

"No, Susan, I don't," he said, his suddenly flat tone contrasting sharply with his normal urbanity. Then he smiled again. "But it's a *lovely* game, my dear! I know—but does he know that I know? And if he does, does he know that I know that he knows that I know? *Ad infinitum,* of course."

"Kevin Sanders," she said acidly, "if I didn't trust you more than my own mirror, I'd have you in irons under babble juice therapy this second!"

"And, my dear," he purred, "if I didn't trust you—and *know* that you trust me—I would never have recommended you to run ONI, now would I?"

Susan Krupskaya laughed and shook her head. "Hold out your glass, you rotten old bastard," she said affectionately.

✧     ✧     ✧

"Here. The latest information for Captain M'tana."

The tall man took the record chip and tucked it inside his tunic beside his holstered needler. He frowned.

"You seem displeased." The observation was made gently, but there was a chuckle in the voice.

"No, sir. It's just . . . just . . ."

"Just that it goes against the grain to pass things to rebels?"

"Well, yes, sir," the courier said unhappily.

"But we don't give them any military data, now do we? Just political information to let them know what's happening in the Cabinet and Assembly."

"Yes, sir, but—"

"But me no buts." The voice hardened slightly. "The 'rebels' are Terrans, too, you know. Possibly better Terrans than we are. It can't hurt to give them this information—and someday it may do a great deal of good for them to know precisely what the government *really* thinks."

"Yes, sir," the tall young man said, and turned away with the priceless—if nonmilitary—intelligence tucked into his tunic. He would see to it Nomoruba got the information without a clue as to its source. Heinz von Rathenau might not understand the motives of the Terran Republic's most highly placed spy, but he knew he could never question them.

After all, Oskar Dieter *was* the prime minister.

# FORTRESS

Ian Trevayne stood on the flag bridge of his new flagship, in orbit around Xanadu, and watched the great curve of the planet on the big screen. That blue, cloud-swirling loveliness woke the home-calling of his blood, and his eyes swung toward the constellation Xandies called the Hexagon. There, the astronomers asserted, lay Sol.

How far was Sol from Zephrain? The question was a fascinating one for the theoretical astronomers (whose current best guess was seven hundred light-years), but of no significance whatsoever to the working spacers who traveled the mad ingeodesics of the warp lines. Yet Trevayne contemplated the sheer distances involved more often of late, deliberately dwelling on the immensity of space and time as a sort of tonic when his spirits flagged. For huge though the universe might be, Man's very presence here, in this system, was the best measure of his own stature. Seven centuries from Earth Trevayne had come, as the lonely radiation of light rode the vacuum. Surely after such a voyage as that he could accomplish what duty demanded.

He shook himself and dismissed that thought to consider the ship he rode. Shortly before the war, the Zephrain Fleet base had laid down a prototype fortress, larger even than a monitor and with far more mobility than the usual OWP's station-keeping capabilities. As far as Trevayne was concerned, anything mobile, however slow and clumsy, was a ship, and after completing it with major modifications, he'd given it a name. It was now TFNS *Sergei Ortega*, and it was the largest self-propelled structure ever wrought by *homo sapiens*—but not for long. The militant energy of the Rim had come together with the scientific wizardry slumbering at Zephrain RDS and birthed the five mammoth constructions that orbited alongside *Ortega* in various stages of incompletion, overshadowing even her bulk. Destroyer-sized construction ships slid between their massive ribs; tractored barges piled high with steel and beryllium and titanium from Zephrain's mammoth smelters shuttled back and forth among them; and fierce, tiny constellations of robotic welders lit their bones. Only one was even partially operational, but he'd at least decided on a name for that one: TFNS *Horatio Nelson*. When Miriam had asked who that was, he'd told her she could bloody well look it up.

He thought of those gargantuan monsters—he would, he supposed, probably call them supermonitors—and of the wholesale refitting of the other Fleet units, and, not for the first time, he was awed and even a little frightened by the Faustian dynamism of the Rim society. He never realized (no one did, except Miriam Ortega, and she only dimly) that it was he who had tempered that unique human metal into the terrible weapon now poised to strike.

It struck on the twenty-third standard day after Trevayne had been piped aboard *Ortega*.

Genji Yoshinaka (a captain, now, and Trevayne's chief of staff) scanned the reports of SBM carrier packs coming in from the closed warp point near the photosphere of Zephrain A—the "Back Door," as it had come to be called—then looked up to meet Trevayne's eyes as they realized they'd won their first gamble. They'd counted on the rebels rejecting another pincer after their earlier disaster and made their own deployment accordingly. Their mobile units—now officially listed by the TFN as Fourth Fleet—covered the Gateway, but the orbital forts which once had protected it did not. They'd been repaired, refitted, and towed across the system to join the handful of new forts protecting the Back Door. There was a reason for that redeployment, and the rebels were about to discover it.

Trevayne spoke a few quiet words, and the orders went out, setting in motion long-prepared contingency plans, both in space and on Xanadu. The fleet uncoiled itself from the Gateway in response, reaching out on the flag plot like gleaming tendrils of light. And on the planet, sirens screamed and civil defense teams sprang into orderly action. Kevin Sanders' briefing might stress the rebels' promise to avoid further strikes on populated worlds so long as the Federation did likewise, but Ian Trevayne would take no chances. There would be no mass murder on Xanadu.

He watched his secondary plot—the one tied directly into the Back Door fortresses—and his hard smile tightened as a crazy quilt of explosions erupted about the warp point. The hordes of tiny robotic spacecraft with their loads of homing missiles were taking a beating, he thought coldly. SBMHAWK carriers had always been largely immune to minefields, for it was hard for the hunter-killer satellites to target something so small, and harder still for them to catch the agile, wildly evading pods before they stabilized their launchers and fired. That was what made them so deadly against fixed defenses like OWPs . . . until Zephrain RDS had supplied an answer: a new mine with vastly improved tracking systems and a far higher attack speed. Their attack radius was shorter than for conventional mines, and their lighter warheads were largely ineffectual against shielded and armored warships, but they were deadly against the unprotected SBMHAWKs.

Their shorter range required denser patterns and there had been insufficient time to build enough for both warp points. But Trevayne and his staff had reasoned that the rebels would prefer the Back Door to the long-established Gateway defenses, and placed their limited supply accordingly.

"Skywatch says the new mines took out ninety-plus percent of the missile pods before launch, Admiral," Yoshinaka reported crisply. "Operational orders transmitted to mobile units and acknowledged. All ships closed up at action stations and redeploying towards the Back Door. All civil defense procedures implemented on Xanadu."

"Thank you, Commodore," Trevayne acknowledged formally, his eyes on the main battle display. Any moment now, he thought. . . .

The rebels received the first of several surprises as their lead units emerged to find their attack warp point still covered by heavy OWPs. Vice Admiral Josef Matucek, commanding the Republican van, watched in horror as his superdreadnoughts transited into a holocaust of close-range beam fire. Shields flared like paper in a furnace as the heavy batteries of energy weapons—energy weapons which should have been blasted to rubble by the torrent of SBMHAWKs—ripped his ships apart.

It was incredible! How had they *survived*? And having survived, where was that hurricane of force beams *coming* from?

Every Terran fortress designer was imbued with the necessity of balancing force beam and primary beam armaments—the former to batter down shields and armor at close range when the capital ships came through; the latter to lacerate the hangar bays of the carriers in the follow-up waves—but those forts couldn't possibly mount anything *but* force beams! There was no room for anything else, and their heavy fire gutted the leading Republican ships. Fragile datalink systems collapsed in electronic hysteria under the pounding, and the superdreadnoughts had to fight as individuals, surrounded by those demonic fortresses like mastodons besieged by tigers.

But superdreadnoughts were tough. Eight were destroyed outright, and a dozen more were crippled, half-demolished, hulls glowing with the energy bleeding into them from the defenders' force beams, but they struck back hard. Their crews were every bit as courageous, every bit as determined, as the defenders, and they blew a gap in the in-system edge of the defensive ring. Neither Matucek nor many of his people lived to see it, but the follow-on wave of carriers found a hole wide enough to offer escape from the full fury of the distance-attenuated force beams.

They charged through it—only to reel in shock as every surviving fortress cut loose with the same incredible number of *primaries* and taught the Republican Navy the power of the "variable focus" improved force beam refined from the theoretical data at Zephrain RDS. Stressed field lenses allowed the same projector to operate in primary mode, projecting a beam which was tiny in aperture and brief in duration compared to a regular force beam. And while, like all primaries, it lacked the wide area effect of the force beam, it was a weapon to which electromagnetic shields, metal armor, and human flesh all offered equal resistance—that is to say, none at all.

The vicious beams stabbed through the carriers, crippling electromagnetic catapults and, all too often, the readied fighters, as well, and the first carrier wave staggered aside, toothless, their riddled fighter bays useless.

But even the improved force beam required a cooling period between primary-mode shots, and the rebel commander turned the full fury of his fleet upon the remaining fortresses. The Book called for intact forts to be bypassed, for the follow-up waves to flood through the holes opened by SBMHAWKs and the assault waves to draw out of range of the surviving energy weapons, but that was impossible here. Admiral Anton Kellerman threw the surviving ships of the first wave into the teeth of the big forts, and the primaries' slow rate of fire proved decisive. They died hard, but they died . . . and took half a dozen more superdreadnoughts (and six assault carriers which had no business—by The Book—in such an engagement) with them into death.

Trevayne watched grimly as the relayed scanner images recorded the destruction of Zephrain Skywatch. He'd known from the first that this was the probable outcome of a truly determined assault—and so had the Skywatch crews. He wondered how many of his personnel had died with their fortresses. Not so many as would normally have been the case, but far more than he would find it easy to live with. He'd done his best to reduce the death toll by employing as much automation as possible, but there had to be some human brains behind the robotics. There had been, and most of them had been volunteers. He only hoped the specially designed escape pods built into the fortresses had saved more than a tithe of those extraordinary people.

It might have been different if he'd dared to marshal Fourth Fleet behind Skywatch. The firepower of his mobile units, coupled with that of the forts, would have smashed the rebel attack into dust—but someone had had to cover the Gateway in case he and Yoshinaka had guessed wrong.

He studied his display narrowly, wishing for the thousandth time that even one of his supermonitors was operational, but only the immobile, half-finished *Nelson* was even partly so. Another thirty standard days might have changed that, but he had to fight with what he had, and, as he watched Anton Kellerman gather his shaken units back into some sort of formation amid the drifting rubble of Skywatch, he wondered grimly if it was enough. He'd been confident when he told Sanders he could hold Zephrain, but ONI had underestimated the rebel attack strength by at least a factor of three. Too many of those ships out there weren't listed in his flagship's data base. New ships, the fruit of the shipyards Sanders had warned him about.

But Skywatch had done bloody well, and that had to be a very shaken rebel commander. Virtually all of his superdreadnoughts had been crippled or destroyed outright, and his carriers had suffered heavily. He had to be wondering what fresh disaster awaited him from Zephrain's Pandora's Box, and if he could just be convinced that what awaited him was even worse than it actually was . . .

He watched a small rebel force line out for Gehenna while a second, larger one headed directly for Xanadu and his own forces, and wondered what the rebel commander would do with his surviving strikefighters? The Book called for a close-in launch to avoid as much AFHAWK attrition as possible, but he might be shaken enough to launch at extreme range. Trevayne hoped not, for that was the one thing he truly feared.

He encouraged the enemy's adherence to The Book by holding back his own fleet—including the monitors of BG 32, commanded now by Sonja Desai and very different from any other monitors in space. There were a few monitors in the rebel fleet. They must have been the rear guard, protected from the first crushing embrace of action because their long building time made them so hard to replace. But his primary interest lay with the surviving carriers as *Ortega* shivered, moving into a slightly wider orbit in company with BG 32. *Ortega* and Desai's monitors were datalinked to the immobile *Nelson*; they couldn't leave Xanadu without dropping the partially operational supermonitor out of the net, and he needed *Nelson*. He needed her badly, and he had to suck those carriers into range of her weapons before they launched. . . .

Anton Kellerman watched the plot aboard his CVA flagship *Unicorn* and wondered just what Trevayne was playing at. He'd once served under the Rim commander, and the one thing Trevayne had never seemed was hesitant. Yet he wasn't moving forward to engage. True, he was badly outnumbered—by at least three-to-one in fighters, Kellerman judged—but still . . .

It was possible he wanted to engage close to Xanadu for a very simple reason: he could have based hundreds of strikefighters on the planet. Yet those stupendous, half-completed hulls drifting in orbit above the Fleet base seemed to argue that he couldn't have built *too* many fighters. Could it be they'd caught him with his pants down? Was it possible that, despite the long delay, he wasn't ready for them?

Kellerman hoped so. His own people were badly shaken. Few of them had ever imagined an opening phase such as they'd just endured; none had ever actually witnessed its like. He settled deeper into his command chair, watching his plot, wondering, and the gleaming diamonds of his battlegroups crept across it toward the waiting wall of Trevayne's warships.

✧　　　✧　　　✧

The fleets were still beyond the range at which combat could even be thought of when the rebels received their next surprise.

As a lieutenant, Ian Trevayne had commanded the corvette *Yangtze*. That starship had been only a little larger than any one of the launchers which now awoke on *Ortega, Nelson*, and Sonja Desai's monitors. *Ortega* and *Nelson* each mounted five of them; *Zoroff* and her sisters mounted only three each, and they'd sacrificed ninety percent of their normal armament to squeeze them in. It was a desperate expedient which deprived Fourth Fleet of the solid, close-in punch monitors normally provided, and Trevayne had hoped to reconvert the standard monitors as the supermonitors came on line. But now those launchers spoke in anger for the first time and hurled missiles forth at velocities heretofore unthinkable.

Those missiles were less physical objects than energy states as they lunged at the rebel ships. Given the relatively innocuous name "heavy bombardment missiles," or HBMs, they were twice the size of any missile ever before used in space combat. And the monstrous housings which launched them weren't mass drivers like other missile launchers; they were something else—something technicians feeling their way through an entirely new technology with no ready-made jargon had dubbed "grav drivers." Nor did those missiles rely upon conventional drives; their initial velocities actually *increased* as their new gravitic drive fields cut in.

Even at their speed, the HBMs' range was such that Kellerman's scanners had time to record their novel drive patterns before the first salvo came close enough for cybernetic brains to decree the moment of self-immolation. Forcefields within the warheads collapsed, and matter met antimatter. If the target was a small ship, the small ship died. A capital ship might absorb more than one hit—but not even the most heavily shielded and armored ship could survive more than a very few.

Admiral Kellerman was not a man to panic, and he did not panic now. At such ranges, a high degree of accuracy was impossible, and nine of the first salvo were clean misses. His point defense ignored them, concentrating on the other thirteen, and his seasoned crews stopped ten of them short of his ships' shields. But three got through, and the assault carrier *Hector* vanished in a brilliant flare of light. He winced inwardly at the prodigious power of the new weapons and ordered his fighters launched to clear the suddenly threatened "safety" of their bays. And then Anton Kellerman got his final surprise.

"Admiral!" A scanner rating stiffened at his console as the second wave of HBMs came in. He was a veteran, but his voice wavered on the edge of hysteria. "Admiral! Those misses from the first salvo are *coming back!*"

Kellerman was still turning towards him in disbelief when he, the rating, and the rest of *Unicorn*'s 180,000-tonne hull ceased to be.

A ripple of shock ran through the rebel fleet as it realized what had happened. Unlike normal missiles, these new monsters didn't simply self-destruct when they overran their targets and lost their vectors. Instead, they turned, and on-board seeking systems of unheard of power quested with insensate malevolence to reacquire the targets they'd missed and bring the HBMs slashing back around in repeated attack runs.

The Republican Navy's appetite for surprise died with its commander. Too many links in the chain of command had already been ground to powder by Skywatch's savage defiance. No one above the rank of rear admiral survived, and the terror of the Rim's new weapons was upon them. The attack force began shedding battlegroups as carriers and battlecruisers, destroyers and heavy cruisers—the ships with the speed to run—turned and fled. It didn't happen instantly, but the first desertion was like a tiny hole in a straining dike, and the ugly stench of fear was contagious. It swept the Republican command bridges like pestilence, proving that even the most courageous could be panicked by the unexpected.

The Gehenna-bound flotilla had already turned back, and would make it through the Back Door. So would the fastest ships of the main force—those with skippers ruthless enough to abandon their fellows. But for the battleships and the handful of monitors and surviving superdreadnoughts there was no escape.

Trevayne's force accelerated outwards from Xanadu, and something resembling an orthodox space battle began. *Ortega* moved ponderously with BG 32's monitors, advancing beyond *Nelson*'s datalink range; but it no longer mattered. The one thing Trevayne had feared most—sustained stand-off fighter strikes from beyond even HBM range—had evaporated with the flight of the carriers. Only two of them stood to die with the rebel battle line, and their fighters were hideously outnumbered by the fighter strength

Trevayne could bring to bear. Stripped of their supporting elements, the rebel capital ships stood no chance against the firepower he commanded—especially since his every ship had been refitted with an improved force beam armament.

More salvos of HBMs were launched, targeted with cold logic on the lighter battleships and superdreadnoughts. If any ship was to be retaken for the Federation, it would be those monitors—on that Trevayne was savagely determined. The range fell, and space was ugly with the butchery of ships and humans as whoever was in command over there fought to close to SBM range, matching futile gallantry against the deadly technical superiority slaughtering his ships with machinelike precision.

But Fourth Fleet smelled victory in the blood, and Trevayne slewed his ships away, holding the range five light-seconds beyond SBM range while his deadly salvos went out again and again. Yet another was readying when the surrender signal finally arrived. Yoshinaka's face lit and he turned to Trevayne . . . who sat in the admiral's chair and said nothing.

In default of a cease-fire order, the grav drivers flung the waiting salvo outward.

The surrender signal was repeated frantically. The rebels launched deep-space flares which dazzled visual observers and stabbed the com links with screeching static from radioactive components; there could be no mistake.

His staff officers stared at Trevayne. His face was a mask of dark iron set in an indescribable expression none of them had ever seen as he sat absorbed by the tale his battle plot told, saying nothing.

The HBMs continued to home on the monitor *da Silva*, now the rebel flagship. What, Yoshinaka wondered, must those poor bastards be feeling?

Trevayne continued to stare fixedly at the impending final carnage. And on the other side of his eyes, a little girl with chestnut hair played on a beach beside a sunlit sea, and the world was young.

Yoshinaka felt the almost physical force with which everyone else on the bridge pled silently with him to intercede.

He sighed and reached out towards his admiral, turning over in his mind the appeal he wanted to make . . . Ian, right now you're the hero of the age. Don't ruin it. And don't ruin the Rim Federation, which will always be your lengthened shadow. . . .

But, of course, that wasn't the thing to say. Instead, he touched his friend's shoulder and said, very firmly: "Admiral, they have surrendered."

Trevayne looked up, and his eyes were suddenly clear.

"Quite," he said conversationally. "Cease firing. Reassume control of the missiles and maneuver them to cover the surviving rebel ships. And have communications raise the rebel commander."

So vast was the range at which the engagement had been fought that there was almost a full minute's delay before the big com screen lit. The face upon it belonged to an officer he had known a lifetime ago, in another era.

"This is Fleet Admiral Ian Trevayne, Provisional Governor-General of the Rim Systems. Am I addressing the rebel commander?"

Fifty long, endless seconds trickled past between question and reply.

"As the senior surviving officer of this force, I can nego—" The face of the small woman in the screen was shocked, her voice dull, but she paused suddenly, realizing exactly how he had addressed her, and a flicker of pride reignited in the olive-dark, almond eyes. "I am Rear Admiral Li Han, of the Terran Republican Navy, sir!" she said sharply.

Trevayne's voice did not rise appreciably in volume, but it left no room for any other sound. "Spare me your comic-opera political pretensions, *Captain.* There will be no negotiations. Your ships will lower their shields and heave to for boarding by officers who will take command of them in the name of the legitimate Federation government. Any resistance to our boarding parties on any ship will be construed as a hostile act, terminating the present cease-fire. Is that understood?"

He stood rigidly, watching the screen, waiting as his words winged across to that other bridge, and when they reached it, it was as if he had slapped the rebel commander across the face. Fury flashed in her eyes as she remembered another time and another commander who had faced her with the same option. Yet far more than a single battlecruiser's fate hung on her decision this day, and the factors she'd gambled on then weren't present now. Thousands of Republican personnel had died already; the death of her remaining ships would achieve nothing. But Trevayne read her rage and leaned forward with a tight, merciless smile.

"I wish you would, Captain," he said, and his voice was a soft, hungry whisper.

It is not pleasant to see the beaten face of a human who accepts defeat neither easily nor often. Most on *Ortega's* bridge looked away in something akin to embarrassment as his words burned across the light-seconds. They stared at their consoles, waiting, as Li Han faced their admiral and saved the lives of her crews by forcing herself to say: "Understood."

Trevayne broke the connection and spoke in a drained, almost inaudible voice. "Commodore Yoshinaka, please take charge of the surrender arrangements. I'll be in my quarters." He turned on his heel and strode away.

He had barely stepped off the flag bridge when the cheering began, and spread, and grew until the mobile fortress rang with its echoes. He never heard it.

# BOND

*"War is fought by human beings."*
General Karl von Clausewitz, *On War*

*De facto* capital of the Rim Worlds or no, Prescott City wasn't much of a city by Innerworld standards. But it was the largest one on Xanadu, and it was large enough to have traffic problems. Ground traffic was bad enough, but the aerial traffic patterns were even worse, despite the best efforts of overtaxed controllers, human and robotic.

It might not have been so bad had the Provisional Government not established itself here. Not only had the city's population risen by almost fifty percent, but more and more military skimmers reduced its traffic patterns to chaos as they cut across them, their shrill transponder signals clearing a path through the carefully nurtured order. To the air traffic authorities, the Peaceforcer skimmer approaching Government House was only one more flaw in the jigsaw puzzle of their job.

Government House, located on a hilltop in what had been the outskirts of town two years earlier, was the city's most imposing edifice. Silhouetted against the bustling traffic of Abu'said Field, it took on an even more imposing air when the Fleet was in port. Unlike the newer buildings surrounding it, Government House dated back to the Fourth Interstellar War and the initial settlement of Xanadu. Constructed of natural materials, its façade dominated by the addition of Admiral Prescott's monumental bronze column, Government House had been built to last for centuries—and on a far larger scale than it had needed to be. For it had been more than a mere headquarters for a new planetary government. It had been a grand gesture of defiance, thrown in the faces of the Arachnids, one warp transit away.

Ian Trevayne had once told Miriam Ortega that Government House reminded him of a certain Peter the Great, who'd constructed a new capital city on the territory of a country he was then fighting for possession of that very land. Miriam, to his delight, had responded with a pithy phrase from her late mother's lexicon: Government House, she'd said, had *chutzpah*.

The Peaceforcer skimmer slid down onto the Government House roof just at sunset. (At least, Zephrain A was setting. Zephrain B remained high in the sky, glowing as a very tiny sun or a very bright star, depending on how one chose to view it.) A Marine major in undress dark-green trousers and black tunic stepped onto the roof to meet the brown-uniformed Peaceforcers who emerged from the skimmer. With punctilious formality—the two services wasted little love on one another—he took custody of their prisoner, addressing her with a noncommittal "ma'am." Whether Li Han was a captain or an admiral—or, in fact, whether an admitted rebel and mutineer was entitled to a military rank at all—involved political questions the major preferred to leave to older, wiser, and better-paid heads.

Li Han looked even smaller than usual between her two guards. They towered above her, and their combined body weight outmassed her by a factor of over five. Her cheeks were slightly sunken (the food at the prison compound was adequate, but not always appetizing), emphasizing her clean facial structure, and she moved with her habitual grace, thanks to a rigidly self-imposed exercise schedule, but she looked like a child in an adult's pajamas in her standard-sized gray prison garb. The major eyed the unprepossessing little figure with a measure of curiosity mingled with contempt—anything less like a Navy flag officer was hard to imagine.

Until she opened her mouth.

"Good evening, Major," she said crisply. "You may escort me to the Governor-General."

The major's hand was halfway into a salute before he caught himself. He managed to maintain his military bearing, but there was a brief pause before he mumbled, "This way, ma'am." He turned on his heel and led the small, ramrod-straight figure to the elevator, glaring at any of his subordinates who looked like they might even be thinking of smiling.

✧ ✧ ✧

Prisoners were rare in warfare against alien species—the only sort of war the TFN had ever fought. Not only did ship-to-ship combat generally result in the annihilation of the loser's crew, but what prisoners were taken were usually turned over to the xenologists (or their alien equivalents) rather than becoming a charge of the military authorities. Hence, the Federation's Navy's codes, both for treatment of prisoners and conduct when captured, were badly underdeveloped. As senior prisoner, Han had been forced virtually to reinvent the whole concept of a POW doctrine.

She'd been offered parole and freedom of the planet, as befitted her rank, but she'd refused, electing to stay with her fellow prisoners. The shock of defeat and—far worse—the desertion of their fellows had come hard for them. Morale had deteriorated as their sense of betrayal became resentment, directed almost as much at their own officers for surrendering as at those others who had deserted them. For Han, even less accustomed than her crews to the notion of defeat and supremely incapable of dishonoring herself by abandoning her comrades, surrender had held a particularly painful poignancy. And the situation was made still worse because her battlegroup's late transfer to Kellerman's command had left her a virtual unknown to most of her fellow POWs—an unknown who'd surrendered them all to the Rim. But she'd attacked her problems and theirs with all the compassion and ruthlessness which made her what she was. Now, nine months later, the captured Republican personnel were warriors once more.

But once the immediate personnel problems were resolved, Han found herself with nothing to do. The camp was like a well-run ship or squadron, fully capable of humming smoothly along under the direction of her exec as long as she stood aloofly behind him as the distant yet instantly available balance wheel. She'd found that being a "commander-in-chief," even of a prison camp, was even more lonely than battlegroup command.

As fall gave way to the short, mild winter of Xanadu's temperate zones, Han realized the irony of her success. She'd given her subordinates purpose and unity while she herself fretted like a captive bird against the maddening inertia and monotony of her captivity. Only once had there been any excitement to vary the soul-crushing boredom of her life.

Han's experience with governments in general, and particularly with those serving the purposes of the Corporate Worlds, had not been happy. So when she was summoned to meet a Ms. Miriam Ortega, Provisional Grand Councilor for Internal Security of the Rim Systems, she was prepared to confront yet another bored, insensitive bureaucrat.

But Ms. Ortega had begun by gracefully dismissing the camp commandant, effectively placing the entire interview off the record, which was not typical of the red tape-worshipping automatons Han associated with "government" outside the Terran Republic.

It was both a shrewd and a generous gesture, Han had thought, and felt herself warm towards the other woman. She thawed further as they discussed camp conditions and the needs of the prisoners, and it was heaven to talk to someone new after months of the same faces! Especially to someone like this irreverently intelligent woman with her earthy sense of humor. Han had worked hard for the serene devotion to duty which was hers, yet she'd paid a price of loneliness along the way. Now, as she talked with Miriam Ortega, she felt the attraction that opposites often exert, and it was hard to remember they were enemies.

When it was time for her to go, she'd risen with regret. Yet before she left, she'd fumbled to frame an awkward question, despite her fear that it might shatter the precarious rapport she'd found with her "enemy."

"Ms. Ortega, I couldn't help wondering . . . with your last name . . ."

Miriam Ortega, had stopped her, answering the question before she could complete it.

"Admiral Ortega was my father," she'd said simply.

Han had regretted the painful question, under the circum-stances, but the woman with the marvelously expressive face had continued.

"He was a man of strong principles and he died acting on them—a pretty good way to go, I think." Then, with another smile, "I hear you've very nearly done so several times!" and the thawing process was complete, the rapport no longer forced.

Han was stunned, later, to learn through the carefully cultivated guards' grapevine that Miriam Ortega was Ian Trevayne's lover. To be sure, he *had* been out of contact with his wife for over three standard years. But . . .

Han had never met Natalya Nikolayevna Trevayne, but the woman's flawless beauty had been the subject of frequent com-ment by envious male officers and ostentatiously indifferent female ones, and there had never been a whisper of a hint of infidelity in all the Fleet gossip. Surely Miriam Ortega, however striking in her own dark, very individual way, couldn't possibly be Trevayne's type! And yet . . . was it her imagination, or had a certain humorous warmth crept into the other's voice whenever she spoke of "the Governor-General"?

Then, with the onset of spring, came the summons which had taken her from the compound for the first time in half a year. Now, walking under guard through the corridors of Government House, she concentrated on looking unconcerned as she wondered why Trevayne had sent for her.

They came to the suite of offices from which Ian Trevayne ruled the Rim Systems. Han and her intelligence officers had spent considerable effort piecing together a schematic of the Provisional Government, and she sometimes thought it might have been designed by the legendary pre-space engineer Goldberg. Most of the day-to-day administration devolved on the departments headed by the members of the Grand Council, who were members of the Rim Legislative Assembly and so responsible to it. But they worked for and in the name of Governor-General Trevayne, who, even though he was the sole member of the executive branch, wasn't even a member of the Assembly, much less responsible to it. *He* was responsible directly to the Federation Legislative Assembly on Old Terra—with which he was only infrequently and circuitously in touch by some means Han had yet to uncover. It was one of those legal tangles which *homo sapiens* secretly and guiltily loves, she'd decided, but it worked . . . as her present captivity demonstrated all too well.

The major ushered her through the bustling outer offices and knocked at the Governor-General's private office doors. A voice from within called admittance, and the major pushed the old-fashioned doors open and stepped back, coming to a sort of half-attention as she passed him. He closed the doors quietly behind her, not without a sigh of regret. Normally he had no strong interest in the meetings of his superiors, but this time he couldn't quite suppress his curiosity. Somehow, he felt, any discussion between those personalities was bound to produce some very interesting by-products.

Trevayne sat behind his desk, wearing the carefully tailored civilian dress he permitted his Governor-General persona. A broad window behind him overlooked Prescott City, and a cabinet below it held two holo cubes. One showed three women—no,

Han decided, a woman and two teen-aged girls. In the other, a dark young man in the black-and-silver of a TFN ensign tried not to look too pleased with himself. She looked away and came to attention before the desk, and a brief silence ensued as she and Trevayne regarded one another and both recalled another meeting in another office.

Trevayne spoke first. "Please be seated," he invited.

"I prefer to stand, sir."

"Just as you like," he nodded, sounding unsurprised. "But please stand easy, Admiral Li."

What he'd said registered as she went into a stiff "at ease," and Trevayne smiled briefly at the minute widening of her eyes—her equivalent, he suspected, of openmouthed astonishment.

"Yes," he continued, "we've received one of our infrequent messages from the Innerworlds. It seems the government, for legalistic reasons with which I'll not bore you, has chosen to accord limited belligerent status to those worlds styling themselves 'the Terran Republic.' " He sounded as if he'd bitten into something sour. "This entails, among other things, recognition of all commissions bestowed by that . . . entity. I have, of course, no alternative but to conform to this policy." He allowed himself a wry smile. "I console myself with the thought that its purpose is 'not to confer a compliment but to secure a convenience,' in the words of Winston Churchill, with whom you may not be familiar—"

"On the contrary, Admiral," Han interrupted. "Winston Churchill was a politician on Old Terra during the Age of Mao Tse-Tung—a very eloquent spokesman for an imperial system which was already doomed."

Trevayne was momentarily speechless, but he recovered quickly and resumed. "We're also in receipt of one other bit of news which I think you'll find pertinent. The Federation has agreed to a general prisoner exchange to reclaim the loyalist personnel incarcerated by the various Fringe Worlds. As you may know better than I, that agreement was apparently stymied for quite some time by the dispute over the custody of alleged 'war criminals.' That dispute has now been resolved—or at least deferred until the end of the actual fighting. 'War criminals' will remain in custody where they are now being held until hostilities come to a close; all other prisoners are to be exchanged forthwtih. You'll be leaving Xanadu within the week."

It was Han's turn to find herself completely at a loss. Trevayne awaited her response with curiosity.

"Admiral," she said finally, "I believe I *will* sit down."

He motioned her to a chair. "You will, I trust, be able to inform your superiors that you've been well treated?"

"Yes," she admitted, still grappling with the stunning news. Then she shook herself. "In particular, I'd like to commend the compound medical staff for their skill and, even more, for their humanity." She thought of Daffyd Llewellyn on another planet, and smiled. "That quality seems to transcend political alignments—at least in the best doctors." Trevayne nodded, declining to mention the considerable care he and Doctor Yuan had given to selecting the prison camp medical staff. "And," she continued, "please convey my respects and gratitude to Grand Councilor Ortega for the interest she has taken in our welfare." She watched curiously for his reaction, but he only nodded again.

"I will. And in return, I'll ask you to convey a message for me." He gazed at her over steepled fingers. "Certain medical personnel from Zephrain, whom we'd thought lost to Tangri corsairs, were repatriated by your government before the negotiations for the present exchange had been formally begun. From them, we've learned that they were in fact captured by humans, of a sort—former TFN personnel indulging in a bit of free-lance piracy." His words could have been light. They weren't.

"Historically—" his eyes grew very hard "—brigandage by renegades purporting to represent one side or another is one of the inevitable consequences of civil wars—one of the many nasty consequences which the initiators of the breakups always seem to overlook, and for which they never accept the slightest responsibility. But I digress." His expression softened a trifle. "Please express to your superiors my thanks for repatriating our people. And," he added, leaning forward and smiling very slightly, "please accept my personal thanks for ridding the Galaxy of a particularly loathsome excrescence on the human race."

Han nodded, taken slightly aback, for she hadn't even known the doctors and nurses had been returned, though she'd urged the Admiralty to do so. On the other hand, her recommendations might have had more weight if a certain portion of the Republican Navy hadn't disapproved of her handling of the situation. If Ruyard's surrender had been accepted, they'd pointed out, the Fleet would have gained five cruisers, plus his destroyers.

She and Tomanaga had argued that her actions had been good and prudent tactics, precluding any possibility of further treachery on Ruyard's part and so terrifying the pirates still on the planet as to prevent any last minute atrocities. Nevertheless, Han had been officially censured, though the First Space Lord had told her privately that he approved her handling of the battle.

Personally, Han had never considered the episode a "battle" at all, though it was now officially called the Battle of Siegfried. From her perspective, it had been a case of vermin extermination.

Silence stretched out across the desk as Trevayne toyed with a stylus, and Han sensed an unaccustomed hesitance, even an awkwardness, on his part.

"Admiral," she asked tentatively at last, "may I go?"

"Eh?" He looked up quickly, as if caught off balance while trying to formulate a statement or question. "You may," he said gruffly.

Han stood and walked toward the doors. Then she stopped and turned back to face him.

"Admiral, if I may ask . . . why did you bring me here to tell me this, instead of simply sending word through Commandant Chanet?"

Trevayne glanced back down at his desk for a moment, seeming to gather himself. Then he looked back up at her.

"Admiral Li," he almost blurted, "were you, by any chance, involved in the raid on Galloway's World?"

Han eyed him sharply. Now why, she wondered, did he want to know *that*? There'd been some ugly repercussions over the strike, she recalled, despite the fact that every strategist had always known the Jamieson Archipelago was a primary strategic target. Still, both sides had been horrified by the heavy civilian casualties, and the raid had led to the *de facto* agreement banning nuclear strikes on inhabited planets. But why . . . ?

Understanding struck. Her glance switched quickly to the holos as she remembered a conversation in Admiral Rutgers' office, and her eyes widened in horrified understanding.

And then her gaze met Trevayne's. His eyes were almost beseeching, and he read the shocked compassion in hers. For an instant, there was an intangible bond between them.

Han needed to say something—she knew not what—to reach out to this man who'd lost so much. She opened her mouth to speak . . .

. . . and remembered the Second Battle of Zephrain, when Fourth Fleet hung beyond weapon range and the deadly HBMs kept coming in spite of her desperately repeated surrender signals. As the missiles which had already been fired looped impossibly back, closing through the storm of counter missiles and point defense lasers, joined by fresh salvos from the enemy fleet, Han had sat in her command chair, giving her orders calmly, holding her people together even as she waited to die with them.

And now she looked at the dark, menacingly bearded face across the desk and saw not a man whose family had died but the callous, murderous commander who had been willing to butcher her helpless crews.

"No, Admiral." Her voice rang in the still room. "I had no part in that heroic action!"

She watched Ian Trevayne rise, his dark face expressionless despite the terrible fire that blazed suddenly in his eyes. She watched him walk around his desk, and the furious anger of his anguish came with him. She sensed the murder in his heart, but she held herself stiffly, her own eyes hard and hating as they burned into his, refusing to flinch.

He stopped, fisted hands clenched at his sides, and muscles trembled in his arms as he fought to keep them there—fought to control the furious need to smash them into her suddenly hateful face.

And then he straightened, expelled a long breath, and was no longer a mere vessel of fury. He jabbed the button which summoned the Marine guards.

"Remove the prisoner," he told them, looking over her head. They did. And as they hustled her out of the door, she looked back, and in his face she seemed to see a reflection of herself, like a mirror of the soul. She couldn't explain the sudden surge of empathic understanding, for she herself had never felt what she saw in that face . . . except, possibly . . .

Comprehension came wrenchingly as she remembered *Argosy Polaris* and those child-bodies. And at that moment, she knew exactly how Ian Trevayne saw those to whom he'd almost done what she had done to Arthur Ruyard.

Their eyes met one more time, and for the barest instant the bond was back. But now their tenuous, shared understanding encompassed the unforgivable wrongs they'd done one another, the wrongs that were somehow a microcosm of the whole, colossal tragedy in which they were caught up. The understanding flared up between them, hideous with the deadly, conflicting tides of duty and desperation and hatred which could bring good and decent human beings to such a pass, but for only an instant . . . then it was cut off by the closing office doors.

Trevayne stared at the closed doors for a moment. Then he walked to his office's private washroom and stared into the mirror for a long, long time, as if prolonging the hideous glimpse he'd gotten into his soul.

# COUNTERSTRIKE

The prisoners had departed and spring was turning into summer when the Orion courier craft emerged from the Zephrain-Rehfrak warp point.

The commander of the picket stationed there had explicit orders covering this rare occurrence, and a brief message was smoothly transferred before the Orions departed as quickly as they'd come. The message was beamed to TFNS *Horatio Nelson* in a high-speed squeal carried by a hair-thin laser, and *Nelson's* receiving dishes scooped it out of space and beamed it down to Government House with equal security, and Ian Trevayne called an emergency meeting of the Grand Council.

"The Orions are being even more uninformative than usual," he told them. "They say only that an emissary will be arriving here from Rehfrak in less than three standard weeks. Period." He shrugged. "This will be the first time an Orion has come to Zephrain since the war began—more than that; as far as I'm aware, it will be the first time a highly placed Orion official has paid an official call on *any* section of the Federation during that time. There's no hint as to the purpose of the visit, but I'll wager it's something big. Remember, the Orions don't prize prolixity the way we do. Among them, the more important an announcement is, the more terse it's likely to be." He hoped the implication wouldn't be lost on certain overly verbal persons, but he suspected it would be. "So," he concluded, "this emissary will probably be quite a high ranking Orion. Possibly even Leornak himself."

"Or someone even higher?" queried Barry de Parma.

"There is no one higher in this part of Orion space," Trevayne said flatly. "Only five Orion military officers outrank

Leornak'zilshisdrow, but that's only part of it. Theoretically, the Khanate is an absolute monarchy, but the district governors are practically autonomous as long as they follow the Khan's policy guidelines. You might say Leornak has what we'd consider permanent emergency wartime powers, if only because of the sheer distance between him and the Khan. No, anyone higher than he would have to come all the way from New Valkha itself; and if we rate that kind of attention, God only knows what's afoot!

"At any rate, we have to decide on the nature of our welcome. I propose to greet the envoy aboard *Nelson*. It never hurts to impress the Orions—though, needless to say, I have no intention of inviting as knowledgeable an old cat as Leornak to examine our new weaponry!" They all nodded at that. "And I think we should have a high-powered political presence on board: Mister de Parma, Ms. Ortega, and Mister MacFarland."

Again, there was no demurral. De Parma, as titular head of the Grand Council, was an obvious choice. So was Bryan MacFarland, Grand Councilor for External Affairs. He'd always had little to do, inasmuch as the Provisional Government's only exchanges with other human polities had been restricted to nuclear warheads and the only nonhuman powers with whom the Rim had contact were the Orions and Crucians (whose official policy was one of non-intercourse for the duration) and the Tangri (whose permanent policy was that humans were simply an exceptionally dangerous species of prey). Now it seemed his hour might have arrived. Besides, Trevayne found him a refreshing personality. His world of Aotearoa, as its name suggested, had been settled initially by New Zealanders, but most of its subsequent immigrants had been from Australia. Now the Aotearoans were more Aussie than the Aussies—just listening to MacFarland reminded Trevayne of his tour at the Navy's strikefighter pilot program at Brisbane on Old Terra.

There was another, unspoken reason for including him, though. So far, the pressure of the war effort had kept the other Rim Worlds from resenting the disproportionate role played by Xandies in the Provisional Government, but it was only a matter of time. Trevayne intended to forestall it by involving as many non-Xandies as possible in high-level functions. Miriam, though a Xandy by adoption, wholeheartedly approved. She herself had no obvious business aboard *Nelson*, but no one questioned his decision to include her.

It was odd, he thought. In most times and places, a relationship like their never-acknowledged but widely known one would have damaged her politically. But it hadn't done so here. Perhaps, he thought wryly, it was because no matter how tightly allied they were, she never hesitated to disagree (sometimes violently) when she thought he was wrong—and her disagreements weren't always announced in private. No one could ever think Miriam Ortega's politics belonged to anyone but herself, and it showed even more strongly against the virtually unbroken deference her fellow Grand Councilors extended towards his policies.

Miriam looked up and hid a smile as his musing glance slid past her. She knew what he was thinking, just as she knew his habitual blind spot kept him from seeing the answer. Part of her fellows' acceptance came from the fact that she refused to be awed by their governor-general, but at least as much stemmed from the unique status their relationship had conferred upon her. In the eyes of the Rim population, Trevayne's standing was such that he was, quite simply, above resentment, and she, by close association with him, shared in the *mana*. Yet he would never understand the way it worked, she thought. He was too intimately acquainted with what he considered his weaknesses to accept that the Rim could see him—or her—in that light. And she'd be damned before she'd in any way suggest it to him.

The Orion cutter completed its docking sequence in *Nelson*'s boatbay, where Trevayne stood before a group that included Vice Admiral Sonja Desai, Commodore Genji Yoshinaka, and Captain Lewis Mujabi of the *Nelson* in addition to the Grand Councilors. The officers (including Trevayne) wore full dress uniform for the occasion, and each left shoulder bore the distinctive patch which Trevayne had recently authorized for the Rim armed forces: a ring of stars (one for each Rim system) surrounding the planet-and-moon of the Federation. Miriam had suggested that the stars should encircle a human hand with the *digitus impudicus* upraised to express the true spirit of the Rim. Trevayne was privately convinced she was right, but he had—reluctantly—vetoed the suggestion.

The hatch opened, and the emissary emerged.

Trevayne said, simply, "No."

"But yes!" Kevin Sanders beamed, stepping down the short gangway ramp with a spryness that longevity technology alone couldn't explain. He was, as usual, clearly enjoying himself.

Trevayne stepped forward and bent slightly so he could speak softly into Sanders' ear. "You old sod! How the hell did you talk the Orions into letting you through? No, wait, let me guess: I daresay you had your spies dredge up something in Leornak's sex life to hold over him!"

"Admiral! I am cut to the quick! I'll have you know that I've never approved of blackmail. I much prefer bribery; greed is more dependable than fear. The fact is," Sanders grinned hugely, "I brought him a case of Jack Daniels. Been keeping him supplied since the war began."

Then he became, if not serious, at least sincere. "It was necessary for a cabinet-level official to come here, Admiral, and I pulled every string in sight to be the one. May I say that's it's a pleasure to see you again? As a token of my esteem, I've brought you a case of Glen Grant."

Trevayne's face was momentarily transfigured. Then he glared. "At least have the goodness to tell me what *I'm* being bribed to do."

"All in good time, Admiral," Sanders said with another of his disarming chuckles. "For now, let's not keep the reception committee waiting."

Trevayne introduced the Gray Eminence of Terran Intelligence to the officers and politicians. Sanders bowed over Miriam's hand with courtly grace, addressing her as "Madam Ortega" and, incredibly, leaving her almost flustered. *The bugger plays the gentleman of the old school to the hilt,* Trevayne thought dourly.

Then they all moved towards *Nelson's* wardroom, where Captain Mujabi had prepared to extend his ship's hospitality. Trevayne contrived to maneuver himself and Sanders into an otherwise empty intraship car, intending to grill the unexpected visitor. But as soon as they were alone, Sanders turned to him with an expression that was half-amused and half-abashed.

"Ahem ... Admiral, do you recall the HV chips I gave you at Rehfrak?"

"Yes," Trevayne replied, caught off balance. "They've unaccountably disappeared, I'm afraid." *Please, God,* he thought quickly. *Don't let the bastard have another set!*

"I'd suspected that might happen. However, the series was such a resounding success that they've produced a sequel: *Triumph at Zephrain.* I had intended to arrange direct distribution rather than troubling you with the matter ... thus minimizing the possibility of the sort of accident which befell the original."

He paused, gauging the visible effect of all this on Trevayne.

Judging the risk of coronary arrest to be within acceptable limits, he resumed.

"But I've changed my mind after meeting Ms. Ortega. You see, she figures rather, ah, prominently in the sequel. And I can see now that the unknown actress who, for obscure reasons, was chosen to play her was badly miscast. She isn't endowed with the Grand Councilor's vivid personality and lively intelligence—however well-endowed she may be in certain other respects. So, Admiral, I think I'll let you be the judge of the production's suitability for public display in the Rim systems. Or, for that matter, private viewing by Ms. Ortega." He smiled beatifically.

Trevayne forced himself to recall a bit of folk wisdom from Sanders' part of Old Terra: He may be a son of a bitch, but at least he's *our* son of a bitch. Suddenly he grinned. He might as well, he decided, give over trying to resist the man. It was hopeless, anyway.

"Very handsome of you," he said. "Glen Grant, is it? For God's sake, call me 'Ian,' you sodding Yank!"

"All right. Talk."

Trevayne and Sanders sat in the former's stateroom. Like all spacecraft living quarters, it was compact, but it was comfortable and laid out so efficiently its efficiency was barely noticeable. Captain Mujabi, who hadn't been expecting an extra passenger for the return to Xanadu, had assigned Sanders a similar compartment. Fortunately, the *Nelson* class was designed to house admirals and their staffs.

Trevayne watched Sanders' eyes twinkle. The evening's socializing (a nearby supernova would have been less of a novelty than a visitor direct from Old Terra) had been so intense that he'd managed to pry Sanders loose only by leaving Miriam to fight a rearguard action. He more than suspected that Sanders had enjoyed every moment of his notoriety—he certainly hadn't made any effort to assist in separating himself from it!

"Talk," Trevayne repeated. "I'll not get a wink of sleep until you tell me the news."

"Well, Ian," Sanders temporized, "there was more truth than poetry to the excuse you used to haul me out of the wardroom: I *am* a bit fatigued. After all, I'm not as young as I once was. . . ."

"You'll bury us all," Trevayne said flatly. "Stop playing games, for once, and tell me exactly what you're doing out here. You may as well face the fact that you're not getting out of this stateroom until I know!"

"Very well." Sanders sighed in mock resignation. "As you've no doubt gathered, your victory at Second Zephrain changed the entire complexion of the war. As I mentioned at Rehfrak, the rebels have been pressing us hard almost from the beginning, and to date, it's always been a matter of their taking choke points away from us, no matter what minor tactical successes we've had."

He paused thoughtfully, face very intent. For just a moment, Trevayne realized, his mask was slipping.

"You know, Ian," he said slowly, "I think the Innerworlds were even less well prepared for this war than they've been thinking."

"How the bloody hell do you 'prepare' for something like this?" Trevayne asked quietly. "It can't be done."

"No, but there are ... mindsets, call them, which can make or break your ability to cope when it comes," Sanders countered. "Look at it this way. Anyone who could count knew that the Fringe, with thirty percent of the people, provided sixty percent of the Fleet—but no one really seemed to think about the attitudes which sent so many Fringers into uniform. And not just the sheer numbers of them, either; the composition of the Fringer military should have given us pause."

"You mean all the female personnel?" Trevayne asked softly.

"Exactly." Sanders eyes lit as he realized Trevayne understood precisely what he meant. "Fringe Worlds are chary with the lives of their women, Ian. They have exactly the opposite problem from that of the Innerworlds; too few people and too much planet. So every potential mother is desperately needed, and they've acquired a whole new social status as a result. Fringer women tend to be protected as their planets' investment in the future, yet over forty percent of all Fringer military personnel are women. That bespeaks a culture which places a high premium on military responsibility ... a higher premium, I'm afraid, than Innerworlders do."

"The old 'rich democracies are soft' argument?" Trevayne could have sounded mocking, but he didn't.

"In a sense. Not so much soft, though, as inexperienced. There haven't been any real penetrations of Innerworld space—except for Timor and the Alpha Centauri raid—in two centuries, Ian. Oh, there was plenty of panic during ISW Four—especially after Centauri. I was there to see it, and you're historian enough to know what I'm talking about. But the breakthrough everyone was afraid of never happened to us the way it did to the Tabbies, and once the Arachnids were history, the Innerworlds forgot their panic with indecent haste."

Sanders shook his head, old eyes staring at something only he could see, and, despite his impatience, Trevayne sat quietly, waiting until the older man inhaled sharply and shook himself.

"It never happened," he repeated. "Thank God. But because it didn't, it left the cocoon intact. Innerworlders have been insulated from the realities of warfare, and, frankly, they didn't have the initial personal commitment the Fringers had. Then they lost all those Fleet units and, as a result, all the early engagements. It shook them pretty badly. In fact, I'm afraid there was a lot of defeatism—or, no, not *defeatism* so much as fatalism. And, let's face it, public opinion's been divided on whether or not we should even be trying to hold the Fringe against its will since the shooting started. It's an . . . ambiguous war, in a lot of ways, without the sort of black-and-white, victory-or-extinction war aims and mindset of ISW Four. There was no fire in the Federation's belly for *this* war, if you'll pardon the purple prose."

He grinned, and the serious, analytical thinker vanished once more into the persona of the japester.

"But all that changed when First Zephrain convinced the Innerworlds we can win victories—and they don't even know about the new technology yet. So now the Corporate and Heart Worlds are feeling full of beans for the first time since this war began, and the rebels have been given a shock that puts *them* on the defensive for the first time. So . . ."

The light above the stateroom door flashed in a series of blinks Sanders suspected wasn't as random as it seemed. Trevayne touched the admittance stud, and Miriam Ortega stepped through the door as it slid open.

"Sorry I took so long," she said to Trevayne. There were only two chairs, so she perched on the edge of the bunk. "Barry can be long-winded at times. Hope I haven't missed too much."

Sanders cleared his throat and gave Trevayne a quizzical look, only to be answered with a bland smile.

"Ms. Ortega is cleared for 'Most Secret,' " he said. His smile broadened slightly as he added. "By me, under my emergency powers. I call your attention to the documents you gave me at Rehfrak. . . ."

"No problem with clearance, Ian," Sanders waved that point

aside. "But while I don't wish to appear ungracious, Ms. Ortega, it's my duty to question your need to know."

"Ms. Ortega is my closest ally in the Provisional Government. Whatever it is you expect out of the Rim Systems, she's going to be instrumental in mobilizing political support for it. She'll have to know sooner or later." Trevayne's face showed a trace of exasperation. "It's as I told you at Rehfrak. D'you think the Rim puts out the kind of effort that won Second Zephrain because I stand over them with a whip? Not bloody likely!"

Sanders understood. He'd noted, without comment, the patch on Trevayne's left sleeve: hardly a standard TFN shoulder flash! Fleet flashes indicated individual planets, members of the Federation—not whole multi-system political units. He glanced over at Miriam, watching her busy herself lighting a cigarette as if to stand aside from the discussion. She felt his gaze and looked up with a flashing smile.

"Just think of me as part of the furniture, Mister Sanders. My application for a Beautiful Female Spy's license was turned down when I flunked the physical. And," she added, her smile turning into something suspiciously like a grin, "please call me Miriam."

Sanders smiled back. He wanted to play no power games with these people. In theory, he spoke with the voice of the Prime Minister. But that, he acknowledged wryly, was bullshit. If Trevayne didn't happen to like an order, he had every legal right to demand confirmation from the Cabinet—which was impossible. And then they'd be back at square one. So, he concluded happily, to hell with it.

"Believe me, Miriam," he said in his most winning voice, "you'll never be mistaken for part of the furniture. And I'm grateful to Ian for giving me an out for including you in the discussion. Now, where was I?

"Oh, yes, the effect of Second Zephrain on the Innerworlds. You see, the rebels were already on the defensive, but the Innerworlds didn't really realize it. The insiders knew, of course; why should the rebels come to us anymore? They already *had* everything they wanted in Innerworld space. So they reverted to a holding stance and turned their attention in your direction, and there wasn't a lot we could do about it, especially not now that the rebel yards appear to be keeping pace with their losses in everything but heavy battle-line units. Now, however, they've run slap into your new technologies, and it's clear the new developments give the Rim a tremendous combat advantage. But that advantage doesn't apply to the Innerworlds, because there's no way to send us the data through Orion space. Oh, our R&D efforts have been spurred, of course—but so have the rebels', and, for that matter, the Orions'. In engineering matters, knowing for certain that a given thing can be done is half the battle. But even so, R&D takes time.

"So the Cabinet and Admiralty have decided to make the time lag in development an asset rather than a liability. They've decided on a coordinated attack to open up a corridor between the Rim and the rest of the Federation *now*, while only the Rim has the new weapons. The purposes, of course, are manifold, but one of the obvious ones is to hit the rebels before *they* have time to develop the same weapons and, simultaneously, to get actual samples of the technology into Innerworld hands. Once we can apply Innerworld industrial capacity to turning out the new weapons you've already developed, we'll be able to put an end to this war.

"And that, to answer your question, is why I'm here: to coordinate this end of Operation Yellowback, the campaign to reunite the loyal segments of the Federation."

"But . . ." Miriam paused. "Excuse me. I may be a Navy brat, but I'm also about as unmilitary a person as you're ever likely to meet. Still, it occurs to me that there are a dozen rebel-held systems on the most direct warp line between Zephrain and the Innerworlds, aren't there? Short of moving through Orion space, of course."

"Thirteen, to be exact," Sanders replied. "The next closest is twice that long, through the Romulus Cluster. And, yes, I know that sounds like a lot of systems to blast your way through. But if we attack from both ends simultaneously . . . well, I've lost most of my initial skepticism now that I've seen this ship. I knew about her in a general way, but nothing I'd heard or read quite prepared me for the impact. How many *Nelsons* do you have?"

"Six. Four more in a month or so," Trevayne responded absently. He'd taken on a thoughtful, brooding look while the other man had been speaking.

Sanders' well-schooled features hid his astonishment. Ten of these leviathans, constructed and manned by a thinly populated region like the Rim?! Trevayne was right: these people were . . . formidable.

The other two, he could tell, were deep in their thoughts.

Trevayne was at his most inscrutable. Miriam puffed on her cigarette and looked worried.

Abruptly Trevayne looked up, and the introspective look was gone.

"Yes," he said. "I agree. It can be done. And this damned deadlock is going to continue as long as the Federation is split into two parts, neither strong enough to scotch the rebellion. I have to say that the ambiguity you say Innerworld public opinion feels isn't very apparent out *here*, Kevin, but I can readily believe that it exists in the rest of the Federation. And if that's true, every month of delay will only create a greater subliminal acceptance of the *status quo* by everyone involved. So when is our offensive scheduled to begin?"

"The details are in my subconscious, to be retrieved under deep hypnosis by means of . . . a certain trigger word I'll tell you how to obtain later." Cautious habits die hard. "But it's about three standard months from now."

"Three months! Bloody hell, man! D'you realize what's involved? Nobody in history's ever tried to mount a sustained offensive through this many contested warp connections—not even Raymond Prescott during the Home Hive One campaign! The supply problem alone . . . we'll have to commandeer half the bleeding freighters in the Rim just to haul ammunition! And I don't suppose you have detailed information on the defenses we'll encounter along the way, now do you? *I* certainly don't! And no bloody way to get it, either—you can only send recon drones so far, you know."

"Ah, but think of the incentive you have: getting rid of me!" Sanders beamed innocently at them. "Not wishing to belabor the obvious, I haven't mentioned that I'm your permanent guest until we fight our way back to the Innerworlds. After all, it's out of the question for me to go back through Orion space now that they know approximately what your new weapons can do. I may be a technical near-illiterate, but I *have* seen some of what you've got at first hand. Leornak would hate it, but he'd have to arrange an 'accident' and go back to drinking domestic Orion booze!"

Trevayne laughed. Miriam smoked her cigarette and glanced back and forth between the two men, very thoughtfully.

There was little leisure for anyone after their arrival at Xanadu. The welter of details inundated them so completely that it was several days before Trevayne and Sanders could sit privately in Trevayne's office discussing his plans for a final fleet operational exercise.

"Are you sure you won't come along? I can promise you quite a show."

"Thank you, Ian, but the trip out here was all the spacing I can handle for a while at my age." Trevayne snorted. If Sanders had been much younger he wouldn't have left him on the same planet with Miriam.

"No, seriously," Sanders insisted. "I've been chronically fatigued lately. I think I'm still having trouble with this twenty-nine-hour day. One loses one's adaptability in such things, you know. Still, I wouldn't have missed this for the Galaxy. I was getting bored with Old Terra and the Cabinet, not necessarily in that order."

Trevayne was quiet for a moment, regarding his blotter with pursed lips as if the mention of the Cabinet had started a new train of thought. When he looked up, he spoke with some hesitancy.

"Kevin, if you don't mind my asking . . . how well do you know Prime Minister Dieter?"

"Personally? Hardly at all. He's not an easy man to know. Why?"

"Oh, I was just wondering what you think of him."

"Or," Sanders grinned, "put another way, how did the man responsible for the mess wind up as Prime Minister? Actually, it was pretty much a matter of elimination; every other Corporate World delegate was too discredited, and we're just damned lucky he was available. He's had to accept a pretty broad spectrum of ministers—all the way from Amanda Sydon as Treasury Minister to Roger Hadad from Old Terra as Foreign Minister—but he combined Defense with the premiership, and that gave him a leg up. By now, he's firmly in control and shaping up very nicely." Sanders shrugged.

"I'm relieved to hear you think so highly of him," Trevayne said slowly, "but I'm a bit concerned by this policy of what seems to be *de facto* recognition of the Terran Republic. Of course," he added, "this is all entirely off the record. Publicly, I've followed the government line to the letter. But privately . . . well, I can't help thinking that you've lost half the battle when you accept the other side's semantics. It was a mistake your ancestors and mine frequently made in the twentieth century."

"It wasn't an easy decision," Sanders acknowledged. "But there are difficulties in fighting a war when you don't recognize your opponent's legal existence. Some of them are amazing. It reminds me of the American Civil War, six centuries ago. The government of the old 'United States' never officially recognized the secessionist confederation as a separate nation, but in practice it treated it as a belligerent in a number of ways. For example, it declared a blockade, which is by definition something you do to a foreign power. The legally consistent approach would've been to simply declare the seceding states' ports closed to foreign commerce, but the only effect of that would've been to make the United States government a laughingstock."

"I know," Trevayne nodded, "but I never realized you were a history enthusiast, Kevin."

"I leave that to people like yourself." Sanders grinned with an eloquent, seated half-bow. "But there's been a lot of research into the civil wars of Old Terra lately. We don't have much recent experience to go by, so Dieter's had the archives turned upside-down for precedents."

He paused thoughtfully.

"That's one of his great strengths, you know: he's a detail man. And his other strength is his ability to face new realities squarely . . . not an easy thing to do, but, then, he's had a lot of experience since the MacTaggart assassination. Now that he's learned how, he's very much in the mainstream tradition of the Federation, of course. You know the Federation has never been a monolithic ideological state. Centralized, yes, but not monolithic; it couldn't have been, even when it was restricted to the Solar System. The rebels recognized that when they opted for such a loose, federalized system, but realists have always known the Federation could only function as a template on which diverse cultures and interests could interact and reach compromise accommodations." He stopped rather abruptly, his mischievous look suddenly returning. "Anyway, whatever else can be said of Dieter, he's unquestionably a superb judge of character. After all, he brought me out of retirement, didn't he?"

Sanders rose from his cluttered desk and stretched. He was the last one left in his offices in Government House—not surprisingly, at this hour of the night. The staff Trevayne had assigned to him had all gone home, leaving him to cope with the effects of Xandau's damned, long day as best he could. Ever since he'd arrived, he'd felt as if he'd stayed up far too late. Which, he decided, he really had in this case. He switched off the light and started to leave, but stopped on seeing the figure silhouetted in the door to the still-lighted outer office.

"Good evening, Kevin," Miriam Ortega said. "May I come in?"

"Certainly."

He turned on the desk lamp and waved at a chair, sitting back down himself. They sat on opposite sides of the bright pool of light, and Government House was quiet around them.

"To what do I owe the pleasure?" he asked, thinking this was the first he'd seen of her since Trevayne had departed for the Fleet exercise. She got out a cigarette, and he automatically reached across with an antique desk lighter. The spill of light from the small flame glowed on her bold features as she puffed the tobacco alight. Blue smoke spiraled through the island of light and vanished into the surrounding darkness.

"Well," she said around the cigarette, "I was wondering if you were ready to tell me what you weren't telling us aboard the *Nelson*."

Sanders almost dropped the lighter.

"Whatever do you mean?" he asked warily. Miriam sat back and blew smoke in his direction with a gently malicious smile uncannily like that he sometimes saw in his mirror.

"When you and Ian discussed this offensive, I couldn't help noticing a slight discrepancy between what he said and what you said," she said. "He took it for granted that reopening contact with the Innerworlds was the first step in a final campaign to force the rebels back into the fold. And you never corrected him. *But*—" she gave him the same smile once more "—you never actually said that, did you? The closest you came was . . . oh, how did you phrase it . . . 'putting an end to this war.' And it also occurred to me that you were touching just a shade emphatically on the 'ambiguous' nature of public opinion on this war. At the time, I thought it might just be the nit-picking lawyer in me, which was one reason I didn't mention it. But now I've gotten to know you better than that, Kevin. No matter how glib and charming you may be, you never say anything—or leave anything out—without a damned good reason."

Sanders savored a number of unaccustomed sensations and stalled while he collected his thoughts.

"Why else have you waited so long to mention this?"

"I've been waiting for a chance to talk to you alone. I have a strong sense that, underneath all your game-playing, you wish Ian well. So I'm giving you a chance to explain your reasons for letting him jump to a false conclusion. Especially one which is going to hurt him so badly when he finds out it's false. And," she finished pointedly, "you're still stalling."

He capitulated. "You know, Miriam, I've see enough since I've been here to realize who the real power in the Provisional Government is. Now I begin to see why. Very well, I'll make a clean breast. What I said aboard *Nelson* was absolutely true, so far as it went. The offensive *will* begin on schedule, and its objective is to open up a warp connection between the Innerworlds and the Rim. But once that's done, Prime Minister Dieter plans to offer the rebels a peace settlement based on acceptance of the *status quo.* The result will be a Terran Republic consisting of all the Fringe Worlds—except those we'll have seized to serve as the corridor we need—and a Federation shaped rather like a dumbbell." (He was speaking in terms of the layout of the warp network. If the Federation he described had been charted in actual three-dimensional space, it would have resembled a geometrician's opium dream. But she understood.) "And they'll accept it. What I said about the combined military potential of the two loyal segments of the Federation was also true."

"How do you know all this?"

"I don't—not officially. But I've worked closely enough with the PM to learn how his mind works. Also," he added with his most impish grin, "I have my own sources. Deviousness, my dear, has its uses."

"Of course," she observed dryly.

She was a strong woman, he thought. Despite her suspicions, confirmation of exactly what he'd been holding back must have been quite a shock, yet she was adapting nicely. He folded his hands neatly on his blotter and awaited her response with interest.

Miriam sat back to digest his words. As always with Sanders, it was wheels within wheels. She doubted that she could ever fully understand this sophisticated old man from a sophisticated old planet. But her instincts continued to tell her that he was fundamentally a friend to Ian, which made him at least an ally of hers.

She noticed that her cigarette had burned low and stubbed it out, selecting another one. She glared down at it for a moment. She really ought to cut back on the damned things . . . to hell with it. She lit up.

"Kevin, you must know that Ian and I are . . . close. What makes you think I won't tell him all this?"

Sanders leaned forward into the pool of light. His blue eyes were disconcertingly sharp.

"You won't tell him for the same reasons I haven't. Our mutual friend is an idealist in the truest sense. He also thinks in straight lines, something I've forgotten how to do, if I ever knew how in the first place. He can imagine no conclusion to the war except the triumphant restoration of the Terran Federation, and the truth would be . . . unacceptable to him. You're right, I have deliberately brought up the divided public opinion back home . . . and it's sailed right past him. He simply can't conceive of any war aim short of a total victory that will reinvigorate the ideal of the Federation the Corporate Worlds killed long ago."

Sanders shook his head sadly, and Miriam suddenly wondered what it must have been like for someone his age, with his brilliant, incisive mind and all the advantages of his place in the intelligence community, to watch the long, slow destruction of Howard Anderson's Federation. He'd seen literally a *century* of it, and she suspected that there'd been more than a little of the idealist in him, once upon a time. Perhaps there still was, yet that idealism had been tempered and alloyed by experience and pragmatism, and his eyes moved back to her face and focused once more.

"Accepting any other outcome would, I think, be something even you would have to bring him around to seeing only slowly. And we don't have time to do things slowly, Miriam; not if we're going to strike before the rebels find an answer to his new weapons." His eyes grew even sharper. "Since we don't have that time, he's going to be risking his life in this campaign very shortly. You have even better reason than I for not telling him anything that might impair his effectiveness!"

She glared at him. "Don't you ever get tired of manipulating people?"

"Miriam, it would take a far bigger man than me to manipulate either you or Ian. The fact is that you know I'm right. You also knew Dieter is right. The Federation simply won't work on any basis but a consensual one, and that's gone now, as far as the Fringe is concerned. Maybe they're even right to pull away before the hate that's built up curdles us *all* internally. The most we can hope for is an Innerworld/Rim unity with the Corporate World arrogance knocked out of us."

She puffed thoughtfully. "You may have a point. But unless Dieter is prepared to give up the whole idea of an Orion amalgamation, that issue is still going to be with us. I can tell you the idea doesn't sit well with the Rim—and that's just one aspect of a broader issue. You say Ian's an idealist, and God knows that's true. It's one of the reasons I love him, but it's also one of the things which makes the Rim so fanatically loyal to him. He doesn't recognize that himself, but it's there . . . and it's because we're *all* idealists out here, in a way. You've got to understand that people out here are passionately loyal to the *idea* of the Federation. But they're also passionately attached to self-government, and they see no contradiction between the two."

"Federation member planets have always had local self-government. . . ."

"Maybe so, but it's beyond that, now. The Rim is no longer a gaggle of unrelated planets. We've acquired a sense of identity—almost nationhood—by successfully defending ourselves. And the provisional government Ian's organized has given us a Rim-wide forum. You've probably heard people out here use the phrase 'the Rim Federation.' " She paused thoughtfully.

"Ironic, isn't it?" she went on with an odd half-smile. "Nobody talks about the 'Rim Federation' around Ian! The whole concept is anathema to him. As far as he's concerned, he's simply holding the Rim for the Federation—and he may be the only man in the Galaxy who could have done it." She leaned forward, and her eyes glowed as they caught the light. "But in the process of doing what's necessary—militarily and politically—for that, he's fathered a new nation! The Federation's going to have to take account of the rights, interests, and, yes, prejudices of the Rim. Otherwise, Dieter's policy will fall flat on its ass. And besides . . . I think we've earned it!"

Her voice had become a harsh clang of pride. After its echoes died away, Sanders remembered to breathe.

"I agree," he said quietly. "The postwar astrographical realities will necessitate some form of special autonomy for the Rim within the Federation. I tell you quite frankly—I'm rapidly learning better than to try to bullshit you—that the Amalgamation *will* come. There's been too much public commitment to it and too many Innerworld voters see it as a symbol of victory for Dieter to resist it even if he wanted to. But home rule should shield the Rim from most of the things people out here find repugnant about it. No doubt if our friend were here he'd find all sorts of historical precedents for it—from his own ancestors' commonwealth period, perhaps."

His eyes took on a faraway look.

"You know, this may turn out for the best. Amalgamation opens up fascinating possibilities for interspecies cultural interaction, which probably means it's the wave of the future. But at the same time, human-dominated societies will continue to have something to offer. And the Terran Republic is ... immature. It may be that your own 'Rim Federation' will incorporate the best of both worlds, especially if it can avoid the mistakes of either."

Miriam realized anew that she would never know quite where she stood with this man. There was something almost inhuman about that long a view. She wanted to ask him if he still had any parochial loyalties, any passionate attachments, any fundamental beliefs of any kind. But that wasn't how the question came out.

"Kevin, were you ever young?"

"Miriam," he suddenly flashed his toothiest grin and chuckled, "you wouldn't have *believed* me as a junior officer!"

"Attention on deck!"

The men and women in *Nelson*'s staff briefing room rose to attention as Trevayne strode in.

"Carry on, ladies and gentlemen," he said briskly, moving towards the head of the U-shaped table, and they immediately resumed their seats. He took his own place and came directly to the point. "I want to congratulate all of you on the results of the exercise. Even Commodore Yoshinaka could find little to criticize." A rueful chuckle went around the table. "I won't ask you to congratulate your personnel for me, because I plan to do so personally on the fleet-wide communication hookup at 2100 hours."

He paused, his eyes sweeping his officers. They were a mixture of his handpicked people from BG 32 and Sergei Ortega's best subordinates, welded into a team in the fires of battle. He allowed himself to consider them one by one, as if in a final testing for weak links in the chain of command.

Sonja Desai, now a vice admiral, commanded his second supermonitor battlegroup. (Trevayne himself commanded the first, in addition to holding overall command, and Vice Admiral Frederick Shespar commanded the third.) Rear Admiral Remko, now commanding the battlecruisers and their supporting craft, sat beside her. Ever since he'd received his new appointment, Trevayne thought with an inner smile, Sean had worn the look of a man who was once again in his element.

Genji Yoshinaka sat quietly at Trevayne's elbow, as he always did. Their link had grown even stronger since the Second Battle of Zephrain. Neither of them ever mentioned the incident which had caused it, but their shared understanding needed no statement.

Trevayne had persuaded him to accept promotion to commodore only by agreeing to let him stay on as chief of staff, though a captain might have filled the billet.

Vice Admiral Shespar sat at his other elbow, a dark-visaged, competent man with hard eyes who'd been Sergei's second in command before BG 32's arrival. Beyond him was Commander Joaquin Sandoval y Belhambre, another of Ortega's people, and one of the few actually born in the Rim. A fighter pilot who'd distinguished himself in the Battle of the Gateway and against the Tangri, he'd shown an unexpected gift for operational planning as a carrier group ops officer, in which position he'd caught Genji's eye.

Sandoval had brought along his intelligence officer, Lieutenant Commander Lavrenti Kirilenko, who was widely regarded as a man to be watched. Though young, he had the kind of face which, Trevayne thought, lady novelists used to call "saturnine." He also had a sardonic sense of humor, but there was a kind of purity about his approach to his profession: the amoral fascination of a chessmaster. Trevayne suspected that he had the potential to develop into another Kevin Sanders. If so, the great difference in their ages was just as well; one per century was enough.

Opposite Trevayne sat Flag Captain Lewis Mujabi, an even rarer bird than Sandoval in many respects—a Fringer whose native planet had seceded without him. In an era when more and more of the human race was blending into a nice, even shade of brown, Mujabi was so black he was, in some lights, almost purple. His people, predominantly African to begin with, had settled Kashiji, a planet near the inner edge of the liquid-water zone of a class F2 sun. Natural selection, abetted by some modest genetic engineering, had taken its inevitable course.

BG 32 itself was now commanded by Rear Admiral Maria Kim, originally one of its ship captains. Another, Commodore Khalid Khan, led another battlegroup built around monitors captured at Second Zephrain (two of which had also been added to Shespar's BG 3 to round out its lower supermonitor strength). Rear Admiral Carl Stoner, who'd commanded Ortega's Frontier Fleet carriers, filled the same billet under Trevayne.

Looking around the crowded room at these officers and the others who comprised Fourth Fleet's brain, Trevayne could barely repress a thrill of pride. He abandoned himself to the reverie for just a moment longer before he cleared his throat and continued.

"Turning to the classified folders before you, I would ask you to open them now." There was a crackle of breaking seals. "Commander Sandoval will briefly summarize."

He had stressed the adverb slightly, and there were grins around the table (not least from Sandoval himself), for the ops officer had earned a reputation as a raconteur of hilarious but lengthy anecdotes.

"Yes, sir. I'll keep it brief, sir."

There might have been just a suspicion of irony in his voice. It was hard to tell, but Genji Yoshinaka had recommended Sandoval for the job partly because he was a brilliant, irreverent soul who refused to be completely in awe of anyone or anything, including admirals. Now the dark, wiry commander, very young for his job, rose and switched on a holographic star display.

"First, ladies and gentlemen, allow me to point out that although the joint operation we are about to undertake is called 'Operation Yellowback,' we are concerned only with that portion of it called 'Operation Reunion.' "

There was a chuckle at that, and Trevayne hid his own smile. Sanders had tended towards a sort of scandalized chagrin when Trevayne had announced the change in operational designations. Sandoval and he had stood to their guns, however. Trevayne had argued that there were innumerable precedents for renaming subsections of campaign plans and that the new name had more positive morale connotations. But what had really floored the Old Terran was Sandoval's irreverently point-blank refusal to lead men and women into battle under an operational code name from a five-hundred-year-old children's story—and, no, Sandoval wasn't impressed by the fact that the story in question had always been one of Admiral Sanders' favorites.

"This operation is relatively straightforward," Sandoval went on, "although it may or may not be simple. Our only really difficult strategic decision was whether to make our breakout through the Gateway or the Back Door. Either would take us to the Purdah System, meeting the bare-bones ops plan the Joint Chiefs sent us via Admiral Sanders, but the Gateway route does so in only three transits. The Back Door takes four, and would almost certainly meet stiffer resistance, since that route leads into the Bonaparte System"—a star blinked on the display—"which contains the major rebel base from which Second Zephrain was launched. Drone probes and raids have given us pretty good intelligence on our home warp points, and based on that data, we decided on the Gateway. It'll be rough, but not as rough as Bonaparte.

"After the breakout, we hope to proceed rapidly. Our axis of advance will be through these systems." A net of warp lines lit in red as he touched a button. "There are two main problems in an offensive like this. One, of course, is supplies, especially of depletable munitions. The fleet train is accordingly of the first importance, and guarding it is going to be essential. This will become especially true as we advance, because we'll open 'sally ports' on our flanks as we bypass warp points to other rebel-held systems. It's also possible, as we all know, for commerce raiders to operate for a time within a single system, even if cut off from outside support. We consider the risk to the fleet train will not become critical, however, until we reach the Zapata System, the first major choke point on our planned route.

"And that brings us to the second major risk to our momentum: lack of intelligence. To be perfectly frank, we have no idea what system defenses we'll face after our initial breakout. Until we control more warp points, we can't even use drones, much less scouting squadrons, so we're going in blind. On the other hand, we know the rebels must have been committing the majority of their industrial capacity to shipbuilding, judging by what they used at Second Zephrain and the enemy deployment data Admiral Sanders brought us. Presumably, that means they can't have built a lot of fortifications out here, at least not behind the immediate 'front line' systems. As for Fleet units—" he shrugged slightly "—we think they were badly hurt at Second Zephrain, and we've demonstrated the efficiency of our weapons. Unless they have a radically higher number of hulls than ONI estimates, they shouldn't be strong enough to stop both us and the forces attacking to meet us."

He stopped and seated himself.

"Thank you, Commander, "Trevayne said, rising. "That's about all that can be said at this stage—and it was admirably brief." He allowed himself a slight smile as his staff chuckled. "We'll meet again tomorrow, after you've had a chance to study the plan and formulate questions. In the meantime, remember the com hook-up at 2100. I want every man and woman in the Fleet to hear me."

He strode out. The room seemed to get bigger, as rooms tended to when Trevayne left them. . . .

✧　　　✧　　　✧

Neither of them had planned it that way, yet they found themselves alone outside the elevator that would take Trevayne away.

Virtually everyone else who was to be aboard *Nelson* for Operation Reunion, including Sanders, had already left Xanadu. A floater waited on the roof of Government House to take Trevayne to Abu'said Field and his cutter. It was a trip he'd made many times, but they both knew this time was different. This campaign would, one way or another, change their lives. Win or lose, it would never be the same again.

They'd said their farewells the previous night, and they'd both dreaded any last-minute awkwardness. But with the inevitability of gravity, they found themselves facing one another outside the private VIP elevator.

"Well," he said, "I'm off." Brilliant, his superego gibed; too bloody scintillating.

"Send word back whenever you can," she said. And within her: My, how terribly clever!

They stood in silence for a moment, and then gathered each other in. They kissed with utmost gentleness.

"Miriam, I'll be back. I *promise* I'll be back."

She put her hands on his shoulders, holding him at arms' length and grinning wickedly. "Well," she purred, letting her eyes travel suggestively downwards, "I know from experience that in your case talk is *not* cheap."

He broke into a grin of his own. They hugged one another once more, hard. Then the light above the elevator door flashed. The door opened, and closed again, and he was gone.

Miriam sighed. As always, everything that mattered was left unspoken. She even understood why; as long as they were cracking wise, they were on safe ground. She turned, eyes downcast, and walked away.

Out of the corner of her eye, she saw the light flash again. She turned back, curious, as the doors slid open.

"Forget something?" she asked.

"Miriam," he stepped towards her, "I suddenly realized that . . . well, that there were things I'd left unsaid. I . . ."

She raised a hand, almost afraid, and pressed her fingers to his lips. "Hush, darling. We both know that. We've never needed to say much, have we?"

He seized her wrist almost roughly and forced her hand aside. "No! It's different now, and I can't leave without saying . . . that . . ."

His throat seemed to constrict. And then, like a dam bursting, "Miriam, I *need* you! I love you!"

And her own dam burst.

"Oh, God, Ian, I love you, too! I love you so much!"

And all the restraint of the past was less than a memory. They kissed, and it was like the first time they'd ever kissed each other.

After a little while, as stars and planets measure time, she spoke.

"What do you suppose we were so afraid of, all this time?"

He didn't answer. Another moment passed before he spoke again, almost lightly.

"You know, if we run down to the Judge Advocate General's office, we might just be able to find someone authorized to perform a marriage."

She sputtered with laughter and looked up at him, eyes shining. "Ian, you're so full of shit your eyes are browner than usual! You know you've got to go. We'll talk about this when you get back. And for God's sake, let it keep till then! Right now, you need more things on your mind like Admiral Prescott needed more Arachnids!"

He laughed, a joyful sound of final release. Then he sobered, gripping her shoulders firmly.

"Miriam, remember what I said: I . . . promise . . . I . . . will be . . . back!"

Miriam Ortega was a Navy brat. She knew, better than most, what could happen when ship met ship in deep space combat. She had already lost a father to exactly that, and she knew no one could predict exactly where the warhead or the beam would strike. And yet, she also knew that Ian Laurens Trevayne always kept his promises.

"Yes, my precious love," she whispered. "I know you will."

As the cutter left the pale-blue reaches of the upper atmosphere for the velvet-black realm of space, Trevayne gazed out the port. For the first time in years—too many years, filled with columns of numbers on phosphor screens—he really saw the universe in which he moved and worked. His gaze ranged further and further out, sweeping over the unwinking, jewel-hard stars strewn in their myriads down the roaring, mind-numbing reaches of infinity.

*God,* he thought. *How beautiful it is.*

# THE SHORTEST DISTANCE

Rear Admiral Li flinched as rolling drums assaulted her ears, then straightened her shoulders quickly. Other returning prisoners crowded the shuttle hatch behind her, and not the most jaded of them could hide his reaction to the scene.

The domed spaceport on Bonaparte's second moon was jammed with black and silver uniforms. Thousands of them! Han stared out over the sea of faces through the crashing fanfare of *Ad Astra*, the ancient twenty-first century hymn chosen as the Republic's anthem, and she was stunned.

A rear admiral greeted her with a crisp salute, and only reflex action brought her own hand up in response as she recognized Jason Windrider. His dark eyes glowed, and as the last bar of the anthem crashed out and the music died, his hand came down in a flashing arc. Han's matched it.

"Welcome home, Admiral!" He gripped her hand tightly.

"Thank you." Han swallowed, blinking burning eyes, and smiled. "Thank you, *Admiral*," she said more firmly. "It's good to be back."

"We've been waiting for you," he said warmly, "and you may as well accept the inevitable." His smile was both wicked and warm. "We're proud of you, ma'am, and you're going to have to put up with us while we show it!"

And then he was leading her down the flag-draped landing platform stair, and the roar of cheers split the bright, dome-filtered sunlight around her.

"Well!" Jason Windrider doffed his braided cap and waved at a chair. "Thank God that's over! Though I must say—" he cocked his head critically "—the Golden Lion looks good on you, Han. Sort of sets off your hair."

"Thank you," she said dryly, trying to hide her own deep emotion as she sat. She touched the Golden Lion of Terra—the highest award for valor of Republic and Federation alike. "If this is what the loser gets, I'd like to see the winner's medals!"

"You didn't lose, Han," Windrider said decisively. "You and Bob were right. We should've gone in fast and nasty, before their new forts and beams and those Godawful missiles were on line."

"Maybe," Han said, "but *I* surrendered, so I'm the one who's going to face a Board over it—and maybe a full Court."

"The Court already sat," Windrider said, suddenly grim. "On the admirals who ran out on you. I won't lie to you—some people *were* cashiered, but everyone knows you held the battle-line together in a hopeless situation and then had the good sense not to get thousands of people killed for nothing." He shrugged again. "That's more or less what the Admiralty said, in fancier language, when it recommended you—unanimously—for the Golden Lion."

"I see." Han drew a deep breath and felt the tension flow away at last.

"Do you, now?" Windrider grinned. "Actually, there's an even more tangible proof of their lordships' attitude."

"Oh?" she eyed him suspiciously. "A blindfold and a last cigarette?"

"You have an untrusting nature," Windrider said sorrowfully. Then he became more serious. "I'm afraid it's slightly non-reg, Han, and Magda wanted to give you this, but she can't make it, so I have to deputize. Here."

Han opened the small case and gasped as she saw the double stars nestled in the dark velvet. She stood abruptly, left hand rising to the single star at her collar, and her eyes were shocked.

"Yes, sir," the rear admiral said. "Congratulations, *Vice* Admiral Li!" He reached out and unpinned her rear admiral's star gently, then took a paired star from her and slid its pin through her collar.

"B-but I'm not *ready*!" Han wailed. "I was only a *captain* four years ago!" Yet she seemed unable to resist as he fastened the badge in place. "I just got back from surrendering an entire battle fleet!"

"Han," Windrider said severely, "sit down and shut up."

She sat obediently, too shaken to notice how brashly a rear admiral was ordering a vice admiral about.

"Better," he said. "Now listen to me. Every senior officer in the Fleet knows you and Bob wanted to attack earlier, and most of 'em know the panic that *really* beat us at Zephrain wouldn't have happened if you'd been senior to the bastards who—Never mind." He shook his head sharply. "But there's not a one of them who questions giving you that star. None. And no doubts will be entertained from you, either, young lady!

"Besides, we need you. Admiral Ashigara is dead, and so are Kellerman, Matucek, Ryder, Nishin, Shukov, Hyde-White, Mombora. . . ." His voice trailed somberly off, and she stared at him.

"That many?"

"And more," he confirmed. "Han, we never did have many admirals, and those we had have taken a terrible pounding; we've *got* to promote. I was a *commander* four years ago, for God's sake! If I can take my medicine and wear one star, you can damned well wear two—got it?"

"Yes, sir," she said meekly, touching her collar badges and smiling at last. "I just hope it isn't a mistake."

"Han, will you *please* get it through your radiation-jellied Oriental brain that you've got those stars—*and* that medal—because you're one of the best we've got?" She eyed him doubtfully, and he grinned. "Besides, if we don't give 'em to you, somebody might try to give 'em to *me*, God help us!"

The skimmer swooped downwards, and Han peered out at the lights blazing against the night. They marked a sprawling mansion, one-time home of the Corporate World manager of Bonaparte's largest *chesht* plantation, taken over by the Republican military when the focus of operations shifted to Zephrain.

Windrider grounded the skimmer and popped the hatches, and Han climbed out, wrinkling her nose as the reek of over-ripe *chesht* mingled with the fresh smell of marshes. It amazed her that something whose flavor had supplanted chocolate and vanilla alike in Terran estimation could smell so horrible in its native habitat.

Strange voices shrilled and clicked in the night, and wings fluttered as Bonaparte's equivalent of a bat flitted past. She glanced upward, but the two larger moons had set and the third, Joseph, was little more than a low-albedo lump of captured asteroidal rock. Its wan illumination barely brought a glow to the mists and hinted at rather than revealed the artificially precise spacing of angular machinery. *Chesht*-pickers rusting in idleness, she thought as the cool breeze off the marsh rustled the *chesht* pods. Bonaparte's F1 primary was hot, but the planet was near the outer edge of the liquid-water belt. Even high summer was cool, which suited Han well, for it produced a climate very like that of her homeworld.

Jason however, came from Topaz—a warm, dusty world with little axial tilt—and he preferred less chilly environs. He rubbed his hands briskly and tried to look patient as she sucked in the crisp air.

"All right, Jason," she smiled finally. "Lead on."

"Good!" he agreed quickly, and guided her through a double-paned door into what had been a palatial foyer before the Republican Navy took charge. A pair of Marine guards came sharply to attention as they stepped inside, and as Han noted their unsealed holsters, she suddenly realized what those angular shapes in the marsh had been: not *chesht*-pickers, but heavy armored vehicles. And the thick glass entry doors weren't glass at all, but armorplast capable of resisting medium artillery fire!

"Good evening, Admiral Li. Admiral Windrider." A Marine major saluted them. "May I see some identification?"

He subjected their ID folios to the most rigorous check Han had seen since the war began. What in God's name was going on here?

"Thank you, sir." The major returned her ID and summoned an armed orderly. "Chief Yeoman Santander will escort you to the planning room."

"Thank you, Major." Han returned his salute, then followed the silent yeoman into the house proper and down a corridor. He stopped and opened a door, raising his voice without entering.

"Admiral Li and Admiral Windrider, sir!" he said crisply, and stepped back as they passed him.

"Thank you, Chief Santander," a warm, easily recognized voice said.

"Magda! Jason didn't say you were here!"

"I know he didn't." Magda Petrovna smiled from behind her desk in the large, brightly lit room, and the paired stars on her collar mirrored Han's. "Very few people know I'm here, and they aren't talking."

"But why all the secrecy?"

"I'm about to tell you, Han," Magda said with the chuckle Han remembered so well. "After which you'll disappear, too. Where's she off to, Jason?" Brown eyes rose to smile over Han's head at Windrider.

"Vice Admiral Li is returning to Novaya Rodina for debriefing," Windrider said smoothly. "In fact, I escorted her aboard ship myself."

"You see?" Magda asked with a grin.

"No, I don't see at all!"

"It's pretty simple, really. You and I, my dear, are the Republic's last great hope." Magda's voice was humorous; her eyes weren't.

"Meaning what?" Han demanded.

"Meaning that you and I—with the help of a few souls like Jason, Bob Tomanaga, and Tsing Chang—are now the Republic's answer to Ian Trevayne."

"We're going back to Zephrain?" Han was stunned by the recklessness of the idea. "Magda, I don't think you understand just what—"

"No, Han," Magda said softly. "Trevayne is coming to us. He's staging a breakout sometime in the next five standard months."

Han sat down heavily. It had all come at her too fast, she thought dazedly. The homecoming, her medal and promotion, all the secrecy and security—now this. She couldn't have understood correctly.

"Five months." She shook her head. "Magda, it isn't possible. He doesn't have enough hulls to mount a sustained offensive—not a decisive one—now that we know what he's got and the panic factor's been eliminated, and there's no point in his taking losses for anything indecisive. Besides, those monsters of his take a long time to build—they mass over a half million tonnes *each*, Magda! He won't risk them without a decisive objective in view."

"Correct." Magda tipped back her chair and a half-smile lurked in her eyes. "But he is coming out. What could inspire him to do that?"

"Nothing," Han said, but she sounded less certain. She thought furiously for a minute, then looked up again. "Are you saying they're planning a joint operation? A simultaneous attack by the Rump and the Rim?"

"Give the lady the prize," Windrider said softly.

"But that's crazy, too," Han protested quietly. "There's no way they could coordinate. I never figured out how they get messages back and forth, but it seems pretty clumsy, however they do it."

"Right again," Magda nodded, "but let me show you something." She rose, and Han's eyes widened in amazement.

"Damn! I keep forgetting to allow for that." Magda stood back from her desk and patted her stomach with a wry frown. Her new figure, Han thought with a helpless chuckle, was *definitely* non-reg.

"What's so funny?" Magda demanded, then touched her stomach again and laughed. "*This* isn't what I wanted to show you."

"You thought I wouldn't notice?"

"No, you silly slant-eye, I just forgot you didn't know. It's all over the Fleet by now—and that cad in the corner is making insufferably proud noises over every bar on Bonaparte."

"I see." Han managed to stop chuckling, but her voice was a little unsteady. "And you don't think your timing was a bit off?"

"Hell," Magda laughed, "this little stranger is one reason I *got* this job. Everyone knows pregnant women are barred from combat. Ergo, *I'm* barred from combat, which makes my disappearance for planning purposes that much easier to explain. And as for my 'timing'—" she met Han's eyes, suddenly serious "—you're one reason for that."

Only Magda could have said that without opening her own wounds, Han thought affectionately.

"I don't want what happened to you happening to me now that I've found Jason," Magda said quietly. She reached out a hand, and Windrider was there in an instant to take it. "So I'm having at least one child before I go out to be shot at again. Besides," she smiled gently, holding out her free hand to Han, and for the first time her voice was hesitant, "this child is for you, too, Han."

"Me?" Han was deeply touched as she took the offered hand.

"Yes. We'd like—like it very much—to name her Han."

Han's grip tightened, and a seemingly endless silence stretched.

"If you can't think of a better name," she said finally, "I'd be proud. Very proud."

"Done!" Jason's brusque cheerfulness broke the spell, and Han was grateful. She drew a deep breath and blinked twice.

"But I think you were going to show me something besides my future namesake?"

"So I was," Magda said, tucking an arm through Han's and leading her over to a wall panel. She punched buttons busily, and a huge hologram filled the darkened room. Han stared at it raptly; she hadn't seen a warp map quite that large since the Academy.

Magda picked up a luminous pointer and moved to the center of the map.

"This helps with visualization, Han," she said, turning brown eyes spangled with tiny stars to her friend. "Our warp lines are green. The Rump's are red; the Rim's amber. Notice anything?"

"Besides the lack of any red-amber connections?"

"That's certainly the salient point, but I'm thinking about something else: distances. At closest, and always excluding passage through Orion or Crucian space, they're at least a dozen transits apart. So whatever they do, they're facing a long, drawn-out campaign before they get back into contact, right?"

"I'd think so, yes."

"So did we. We have, however, certain intelligence assets in the Rump. Not in the Rim, I'm sorry to say, and our very best conduit didn't give us a word of warning about it, but computer analysis of what we *do* have has picked up on something very interesting.

"First," she tucked her pointer under her arm, for all the world like a pregnant schoolteacher in uniform as she ticked off points on her fingers, "Rump construction rates have been low, which confused us until we found out why. The Galloway's World Raid did more than take out a couple of yards, Han; it took out the entire archipelago. They've recovered now, but it explains why the Rump's been so sensitive to combat losses.

"Second," she went on, "despite their desperate need for ships, they're holding them back. We didn't notice that immediately, but our raids, recon probes, and captured or otherwise compromised Rump deployment orders all indicate it. Why?

"Third, they haven't been massing them opposite Cimmaron, as we might expect. They could cut off this whole quarter of the Republic from there," she gestured at a glowing snake's nest of green warp lines "or go straight for Novaya Rodina. But where the analysis teams finally found them is over here, at a totally new Fleet base at Avalon—a system we've never even threatened.

"Fourth, and finally, we *know* how the Rim gets its messages. They come through Orion space, via Rehfrak." Magda waved a hand at Han's sharp glance. "I know, very un-neutral of them. However, we haven't objected because we wanted to see who goes where along that warp line, and it turns out the errand boy is none other than one Kevin Sanders. Does that ring any bells?"

" 'The Fox,' " Han said softly.

"Exactly. The best chief of ONI in two centuries, and currently a cabinet minister without portfolio. Obviously they need a top man for a hot potato like this, but they're sending Sanders—

probably the one person in the Galaxy who knows where *all* the Federation's bodies are buried—through Orion space whenever he goes to Zephrain. And the Orions only permit him to go as far as Rehfrak; the Governor-General comes to *him*."

"I'm sure all of this is headed somewhere?"

"It is indeed. Six months ago, Sanders was in Avalon. Then they rushed him back to Old Terra so fast they burned out a destroyer's main drive converters. Why? Because he's already gone again, making another trip . . . and this time he's going all the way to Xanadu—and staying."

"What?" Han stood straighter and frowned.

"Exactly. It took a lot of work—and luck—to piece his itinerary together, but it's solid. Now why would the Rump separate itself from its foremost spook? Unless, of course, the separation isn't permanent?"

"I see your point," Han mused.

"I thought you would," Magda said grimly. "They're sending him because they need someone with his authority, brains, and experience to coordinate their plan to hit us before we can react to the new weaponry. If they can hammer a bridge between the Rump and Rim—if the Rump's industrial plant gets the data and working models it needs—we're in deep, deep trouble."

"I see," Han murmured once more, searching the red and amber warp lines with her eyes. "They're assembling the Rump pincer at Avalon, so they're not going for any finesse beyond their hope for surprise."

"That's what we think," Magda encouraged her.

"It's the only answer," Han muttered, frowning in thought. "From Avalon, hmmm . . . ?" Her eyes narrowed suddenly and she nodded once, sharply. "There's their route, Magda—Avalon to Lomax to Hyerdahl to Thor to Thule to Osterman's Star to Tybold to Juarez to Iphigena to Zapata to Sagebrush to Purdah. From there they might go Rousseau to Ney to Bonaparte to Zephrain, or New India to Zvoboda to Zephrain. I'd bet on the New India Route—not even Ian Trevayne wants to tangle with the defenses here."

"What makes you so certain?" Magda asked, not challengingly but as if she merely wanted confirmation of her own thoughts.

"Only a fool tries to be clever when he can't completely orchestrate a complex operation, Magda. We learned that watching the Orions in the first two interstellar wars . . . and relearned it at First Zephrain. So if you can't be fancy, you be direct as possible, and that route—" she nodded at the one she'd traced out "—is the shortest distance between two points: Avalon and Zephrain."

"I think you're right," Magda acknowledged, "and you might like to know that it took the Strategy Board a month to reach your conclusions." She smiled. "But there's still a billion-credit question, Han. We don't have the Fleet units to oppose both forces at once. We have to stop one of them, then turn to deal with the other in detail, using our advantage of the interior position. So which do we oppose?"

Han blinked at her.

"You're asking me? Magda, I've been out of circulation for a year!"

"But you're also the senior commander who's really seen the Rim's weapons in action, so you can give us the best gut reaction on them. Should we worry more about quantity or quality? Because—" Magda grinned crookedly "—for our sins, you and I are going to be the Fleet commanders who do the stopping. So who do we stop, Han? The Rump or the Rim?"

Han dropped into a chair and thought long, hard and furiously.

"The Rump doesn't have any of the new technology? Just numbers?"

Magda nodded.

"And have *we* come through with any of those 'wonder weapons' people were muttering about before Second Zephrain? Do we have any surprises of our own?"

"A few," Windrider said.

"Then we have to block the Rump with secondary forces and go for the Rim with everything we have," Han said, suddenly decisive. "No matter how many hulls the Rump has, we can tangle them up in the frontier forts, mines, and local fighter bases. We can slow them up, at least, but you've never seen anything like Trevayne's new battle-line. We have to stop him, and stop him hard. If at all possible, we have to cut him up badly enough to move in and take Zephrain away from him. Even if we lose a dozen systems—or twice that many!—to the Rump, we've still got a good chance to win this war in the end *if* we can keep them away from Zephrain."

"And where do we stop them?" Magda asked tonelessly.

"Zapata," Han said crisply. "It's a critical choke point, and we can move stuff in from Bonaparte for the big engagement. Use commerce raiders on the flanks as they advance . . . pick at them . . . get them off balance and force them to overextend . . . then meet them head-on at Zapata and thank God building that monster battle-line's cut into their carrier production! It's our only chance, Magda."

"I see." Magda exchanged a nod with Jason, then turned back to Han. The tangled lights of the holo map gilded her silver-streaked brown hair with a crown of jewels, and her eyes glittered with stars. "That's another thing you and the Strategy Board agree on, and I'm glad you see it so clearly . . . sir."

Something in her voice caught Han's attention, and she stared at her friend suspiciously. No! She couldn't mean . . . !

"That's right, Han," Magda said almost compassionately. "One of the reasons I was ordered to have this little chat with you was to be certain you *did* understand the priorities. You got your second star while you were still a POW—the same day I got mine. And that means you're still senior." She held out the luminous pointer.

"Welcome to supreme command of Operation Actium, Admiral Li."

# OPERATION REUNION

Operation Reunion began with an irruption of SBMHAWK carrier pods into the Zvoboda System. One moment the Republican Navy's detection screens were blank: the next a multitude of unmanned pods transited into the teeth of the forts guarding this gateway to the Terran Republic. A few came to grief in the warp point minefields; a few more emerged in overlapping volumes of space and died with the violence the gods of physics reserve for phenomena which violate their laws. But most survived to fling their missiles at the forts, announcing the arrival of the Federation's warriors in fire and death.

Probes of the Zvoboda System had been limited to avoid alarming its defenders, but Ian Trevayne had a fairly good notion of what he would face. The Republic had erected a formidable shell of big type four OWPs around the Zephrain warp point and another around the warp point to New India, but Lavrenti Kirilenko was convinced there would be few mobile units. The forts were typical of the Republic's designs, each incorporating two squadrons of fighters; that fighter strength, coupled with the forts' own weapons, needed no support to decimate any conventional assault.

Trevayne and Genji Yoshinaka agreed with Kirilenko's assessments; hence the lavish SBMHAWK bombardment that preceded their ships through the warp point. Such a heavy employment of SBMs would seriously deplete their stores for the next assault, but there was no point planning for the next battle if they lost this one. Besides, everything seemed to suggest that Zvoboda had been so heavily fortified that the Republic could have spared little for the defense of New India.

Missiles leapt from their carrier pods, but the Republican gunners hadn't been asleep. The Rim's decreased probe traffic hadn't lulled them; rather it had confirmed their suspicions, and they'd gone on round-the-clock alert. Still, no one could be a hundred percent alert at every instant, and if point defense stopped a lot of missiles, nothing could have stopped them all.

Antimatter warheads flared against shields. Tremendous fireballs wracked the space around them. Armor glowed, vaporized, flared away. Atmosphere whuffed outward, water vapor sparkling, as the missiles savaged the forts. Yet for all their savagery, all their violence, they couldn't prevent the Republic from launching the majority of its fighters.

But Trevayne had anticipated that, and he had no intention of offering up his strictly limited carrier strength for target practice, even if The Book did call for fighters as the best defense against fighters. Instead, the ships that followed the carrier pods into Zvoboda used a tactic which was new, one so unorthodox it took the defenders totally by surprise, yet so simple they wondered why no one else had ever thought of it.

TFNS *Nelson* was the first ship out of the warp point, followed by the monitor *da Silva*. As soon as *da Silva* emerged, *Nelson* grabbed her with tractor beams and began to tow her astern. Simultaneously, *da Silva* cut her own propulsion, maintaining just sufficient drive field to interdict missile fire, and rolled to place herself stern-to-stern with *Nelson*—an unheard of position. Then another supermonitor/monitor pair emerged, and another. . . .

All strikefighter pilots knew to attack battle-line units by maneuvering into the sternward "blind zone" created by the slow and clumsy ship's drive field, where its tracking systems were useless and its weapons could not be brought to bear. But the rebel pilots, racing to implement their fundamental tactical doctrine, were slaughtered by defensive fire from the supermonitors and monitors while searching for blind zones that were, in effect, not there! They inflicted damage, of course—quite a lot, in fact. But monitors were designed to absorb and survive damage, and supermonitors even more so. The fighters were cut down before their short-ranged weapons could take decisive effect, and the big ships lumbered towards the fortresses, contemptuous alike of the fighters and mines that sought to hinder them.

The fortress crews knew what their fighters' failure meant. They'd seen the reports on Second Zephrain, and they knew all about the improved force beams Trevayne's ships mounted, but they stood to their weapons, pouring in defensive fire against the oncoming ships. Damage control parties aboard the supermonitors and monitors found their services in high demand, but not critically so, and the capital ships riddled the forts with primary-mode fire and then reduced them to tangled wreckage with "wide-angled" fire even as Sean Remko's battlecruisers savagely hunted down the few mobile rebel units.

Fourth Fleet reformed into a more conventional order of battle, complete with escort cruisers, and lumbered into a hyperbolic course across the system. Ian Trevayne sat in his command chair, listening to the reports as his crews worked frenziedly on the damage. It wasn't quite as bad as he'd anticipated, he thought. Bad enough, certainly—especially in terms of human life—but no internal damage his repair crews couldn't put right in the seventy-eight hour trip across the system. It was a case of slap-dash repairs, of course, but aside from the damage to his ships' armor, virtually full combat efficiency had been restored between the first engagement and the moment the New India warp point fortifications hove into range.

Not that he had any intention of exposing those repairs to fresh damage if he could help it. And he could help it, for the Terran Republic still had no counterweight for the HBM.

The rebel commander knew it, too, and he launched his fighters before the supermonitors came into HBM range. That saved them from destruction in their bays but exposed them to extended-range AFHAWK fire from Trevayne's screen and interception by Carl Stoner's fighters. A few broke through both missiles and defending fighters, displaying the skill and determination which were the hallmarks of Republican fighter pilots, but they were a spent force. The escorts and capital ships blasted them apart in return for trifling damage, and shortly thereafter the HBMs began to batter the fortresses.

The Republican commander had no more desire to die uselessly for a point of honor than Trevayne himself. As soon as he'd satisfied himself of all the facts (and fired courier drones out to New India with them), he surrendered.

His surrender was followed four hours later by another, rendered to the cruiser screen as Remko cleaned up the pieces. Occupation of the domed mining colony on the largest satellite of Zvoboda IV, a "brown dwarf" so massive as to be almost self-luminous, completed the conquest, and Trevayne called a halt. It was time to garrison the domes and send prisoners back to Zephrain, in addition to the usual post-battle chores.

He remained on the bridge while his ships carried out the most urgent of these—the replenishment of their magazines from the fleet train beginning to emerge from the warp point—and waited until the repair ships moved alongside to make good his most critical damage. Then he called a meeting of all ship captains aboard *Nelson* and finally left his flag bridge.

Trevayne couldn't help feeling amused by Yoshinaka's morose expression as they rode the intraship car toward the wardroom. The chief of staff was a natural worrier, and he seemed to feel duty bound to compensate for everyone else's euphoria.

"Well," he grumbled, "at least you followed my advice to hold this skippers' meeting after the first battle."

"Why, Genji-san, I always follow your advice," Trevayne said in the bantering tone he affected when Yoshinaka was in one of his moods. "Didn't I give the second *Nelson* the name you wanted?"

Yoshinaka refused to be mollified.

"Right. You named her *Togo* . . . which," he added pointedly, "you would've had to do eventually anyway, having decided to name the class after wet-navy admirals. After all, he was the greatest fighting admiral in the entire history of Old Terra." He waited, but Trevayne declined to rise to the bait. "And you couldn't have ignored him for long, either—not after copping the *first* ship in the class for your precious Nelson! But then you named ships three and four after Raymond Spruance and Yi Sun-Sin, both of whom made their reputations swabbing the decks with the Japanese! Has anyone ever told you you've got a strange sense of humor?"

"The Grand Councilor for Internal Security has mentioned it once or twice," Trevayne admitted airily.

Yoshinaka's scowl dissolved into a grin. Trevayne had been practically whistling as he was piped aboard *Nelson* on the eve of Operation Reunion, when many others had had an understandable case of dry-mouth. Yoshinaka had no idea what had passed between his admiral and Miriam Ortega, but he was grateful for it—and not just because Trevayne's cheerfulness in the face of a frontal assault through a fortified warp point had been a shot in the arm for everyone's morale.

The car hummed to a stop, and they emerged into a crowded

wardroom filled with an uproar of shoptalk as the battle was refought. The monitor skippers—already dubbed the "bass-akwards brigade" by their disrespectful fellows—were the butt of the occasion.

"Attention on deck!" Mujabi's basso profundo cut through the hubbub with ease, and all talk subsided as Trevayne and Yoshinaka mounted the improvised dais where Sandoval waited. Standing at the podium, Trevayne looked down at the array of faces, faces of every color and cast of features in which *homo sapiens* came. Outside himself and Yoshinaka, no one in the room wore the broad stripe; he wanted these men and women to be able to speak their minds freely and openly. His own deep baritone filled the room.

"As you were, ladies and gentlemen. First, congratulations are in order. Your performance in battle was exactly what I would have expected of you—and I can think of few higher compliments. In particular," he added with a slight emphasis, "the monitor commanders are to be congratulated for performing superbly under highly unorthodox conditions." That was true of everyone, he thought. Only a superbly trained and motivated fleet could have achieved the organizational flexibility these people had displayed.

"The reason for this captains' meeting," he went on, "is that we've now seen at first hand what we're up against. You're here because I want to directly answer any questions you may have, and because Commodore Yoshinaka, Commander Sandoval, and I need your feedback. So let's hear any questions or comments."

Numerous hands went up, and Trevayne recognized what looked to have been the first of them. "Captain Waldeck?"

Sean Remko's flag captain rose. He had the Waldeck look—burly, with a jowly, florid face boasting a big nose and massive chin oddly at variance with the small, pursed mouth.

"A comment, Admiral. If what we've encountered here is any indication, this operation should be a walkover. I refer specifically to the cowardice of the rebel commander. He surrendered when he still had the capability to do us some damage or at least force us to expend a lot of our HBMs on his forts. I think the inference is clear: all the rebels ever had going for them was the elan of their initial successes. Now that that's worn off, they're reverting to their natural state—rabble!"

Mujabi's face got, if possible, a bit darker, even though Waldeck had been careful to refer to "rebels" and not to "Fringers." His eyes flashed dangerously, but he was saved from the need to speak by an anonymous voice.

"Sure," it piped up from the back of the wardroom. "Just like the rabble on Novaya Rodina!"

Waldeck flushed, and his massive jaw clenched as a sound swept the wardroom. It wasn't—quite—a chuckle, but rather an inarticulate amusement too great to be entirely suppressed. For a moment he seemed about to snarl a response, but thought better of it at the last moment.

Trevayne himself was torn by several conflicting emotions. The remark was well-taken (if unkind), and he couldn't help sharing the assembled captains' amusement just a bit. Yet at the same time, the whole Novaya Rodina episode left a bad taste in his mouth.

But as far as Waldeck himself was concerned, Trevayne had tried to keep an open mind. He was born of the close-knit world of the TFN's "dynasties," with few illusions about its inhabitants, and he'd never liked Captain Cyrus Waldeck. And that, he thought, was unfortunate in a way, because for all his abrasive arrogance and snobbery, there was no question of Waldeck's competence. It was because of that competence that he'd assigned Waldeck to command the *Arquebus*, Remko's flagship. Yet he couldn't help chortling to himself just a bit whenever he thought of Waldeck, the embodiment of that clan of Corporate World magnates, directly under Sean Remko's command. Could it be that Miriam and Genji were right about his sense of humor?

"Let's not get carried away by our *own* elan, Captain Waldeck," he said calmly. "It would be the height of recklessness to assume on the basis of one battle that the rebels have lost their edge— and I remind you that the first fortress commander we engaged most certainly hadn't lost *his*. That's an attitude we'll have to be particularly wary of in the next few weeks; now that we've broken the rebel frontier, we're likely to be passing through lightly defended systems until we reach Zapata. The rebels will have to offer battle there. I don't want us to arrive for it in a mood of fatuous overconfidence."

A murmur of agreement ran through the wardroom, and Waldeck, his face once more tightly controlled, sat down. Trevayne's voice had been as pleasant as ever, but his remarks stung all the more following that fathead hiding in the rear ranks.

Waldeck surveyed his fellow captains with hidden contempt.

These people's attitude towards Ian Trevayne ran the gamut from deep respect through awe all the way to idolatry, he thought. But, of course, he hadn't assigned *them* to be flag captain to a jumped-up prole from the slums of New Detroit—the cesspool of the Corporate Worlds!

He thought bitterly of Trevayne's reputation for being above social prejudice. For Waldeck's money, that only meant he didn't feel any more superior to Fringe Worlders than he did to everyone else!

And yet, he thought, listening to Trevayne responding to questions and comments, not even his resentment made him immune to the admiral's magnetism. The man had the sort of sublime self-assurance that came from being perfectly suited to the role of leadership he'd been born to fill; people followed him because he expected to be followed, expected it with such certainty that he had no need for bombast. Well, Cyrus Waldeck would follow him, too, but with bitterness eating at his heart.

The assault shuttles were on their way once more, carrying garrison troops to the inhabited planet of the Purdah System, when Trevayne called another meeting aboard *Nelson*. It was a small gathering; Sanders, Yoshinaka, Sandoval, and Kirilenko were there, as was Ingrid Lundberg, the supply officer. Sonja Desai had come over from *Togo*, her flagship, but she couldn't stay long, for she was in charge of organizing the temporary military government of this system. Of Trevayne's closest allies, only Remko was absent; he was busy deploying forces to screen the fleet train while it licked its wounds from the latest of the raids which had occasioned this meeting.

At Trevayne's request, Lundberg began with a summary of the supply picture as the stewards poured coffee. (It was late by ships' clocks.)

"... And that's about the size of it, Admiral." She ran fingers through her auburn hair. "We lost a lot of general stores when *Falkenberg* blew up, and I'm not happy about losing all those medical stores when they crippled *Jolly Merchant*, but we've actually been fairly lucky ... so far. The munition ships have avoided any serious losses—though I'm not too happy about the missile supply." She glanced at Sandoval from the corner of one eye. "Some people seem to have the idea missiles come straight from God as needed; they don't. If we can't move colliers safely, I can't continue to meet the ammo demands of the Fleet."

"I see." Trevayne nodded and glanced at Kirilenko. "Lavrenti, what do you have for us on these raiders?"

"Less than I'd like, sir. They're using carriers and staying at extreme range. I suspect we're looking at escort carriers rather than light or fleet carriers—the attack patterns suggest small fighter groups—but whatever they are, we haven't been able to run any of them down. They obviously carry cloaking ECM, and they're as fast as anything we've got." He shrugged. "The best I can report right now is that they're losing fighters steadily, but that's not the way to stop determined commerce raiders."

"Anything more on my pet hypothesis, Lavrenti?" Sanders asked.

"I've subjected it to computer analysis and lots of plain, old-fashioned human skepticism, sir," Kirilenko said, "and I'd say you're probably right. They've set up some sort of deep-space basing facilities out there. Maybe just a couple of old freighters hiding somewhere, but *something*—and in more than one system too. They're rearming somewhere, and I'd bet they've got replacement fighters stashed out there, too. All of which supports your theory: this was carefully planned. It's no last-minute improvisation."

Trevayne's officers and advisers exchanged looks and glanced covertly at the admiral, who leaned one elbow on the polished tabletop and thought. Finally he leaned back and rapped the edge of the table with his light pencil, breaking the grip of the silence.

"Very well. Matters have gone pretty much as expected, in the sense that the rebels haven't committed major forces to defend either New India or this system. They've fought token holding actions, forcing us to expend munitions and inflicting maximum losses in a short time before withdrawing.

"We also anticipated that our advance would expose the fleet train to flank attacks through warp points leading to rebel systems off our line of advance. Again, no surprises . . . except possibly for the weight of the attacks and the fact that they're also using these deep-space bases Admiral Sanders and Commander Kirilenko have hypothesized to operate inside the systems we've reoccupied. And, of course, for the number of escort carriers—or whatever—they've committed."

He paused and looked around the table. "Now, what do these facts, taken together, mean? I realize one school of thought holds that our rapid advance means the rebellion is collapsing like a house of cards. That, I'm sure, is Captain Waldeck's view," he added with a crooked smile. "But I don't believe it. These raids show too much forethought, and they're being pressed too aggressively; we're clearly not fighting a beaten enemy. I still think the decisive battle will come at Zapata, whatever anyone else believes, but in the meantime we can expect more of the same at Sagebrush.

"Therefore," he continued, "we need to further reinforce the escort elements for the fleet train. Commander Lundberg is quite correct about the state of our missile supply—we must both restrict our expenditures and safeguard our existing supplies. For this purpose, I intend to detach Admiral Stoner's light carriers."

"Carl won't like it," Sonja Desai foretold.

"He'll ricochet off the bulkheads," Sandoval added, earning a glare from Desai.

"I know. I also know our carriers are already stretched thin, but it can't be helped. Supplies are our Achilles heel, and whoever's orchestrated the rebel strategy has grasped that fact very well." Trevayne had a pretty definite idea who that person was, but he kept it to himself. "We may as well face the fact that whenever the rebels finally decide to offer battle in earnest, they're going to greatly outnumber us in fighters. Our great strength is our battle-line." (The finest in the Galaxy, he thought, but silently; he didn't want to add to the general cockiness.) "It's more important to assure ourselves of an abundant supply of missiles—especially HBMs—for the decisive battle than it is to hoard fighters that won't, after all, be able to go toe-to-toe with their opposite numbers on even terms."

Heads nodded around the table. Then Yoshinaka spoke up.

"Admiral, another concern is the relatively heavy losses among our scout cruisers. We're not exactly oversupplied with them to begin with."

"True," Trevayne acknowledged. "Of course, you expect high losses among them due to the nature of their missions." Deep within him an old pain stirred briefly. He sternly suppressed it. "I'm thinking we ought to conserve them for now and rely on drones and recon fighters. In fact, we might make the two problems solve each other by temporarily detaching the scouts to help escort the fleet train." He held up a hand. "Yes, I know it's not what they're designed for, but with their missile armaments, they've got a lot of AFHAWK capability. Besides, I don't think the rebels are going to be expecting escorts with third-generation ECM! It could make things interesting the next time their 'vanishing carriers' pull one of their long-range raids if a couple of light cruisers suddenly drop out of cloak into their midst."

Glances were exchanged around the table as people found, to their surprise, that they liked the idea.

"Yes, sir," Sandoval said. "Of course, the scout cruiser types won't like it at first. They're a bunch of hot dogs . . . almost as bad as fighter jocks," the former fighter jock added. "But give them some rebel fighters to chew on, and maybe an escort carrier or two, and they'll come around."

"Also, Ian," Sanders put in, "we don't need them for recon just now anyway. We've already probed Sagebrush, and I gather we shouldn't need scouts there." He looked to Sandoval and Yoshinaka for confirmation. "We should be able to go through that system rather easily and quickly."

Sandoval grinned from ear to ear. "Like beans through a Gringo, sir."

Sanders spluttered into his coffee and nearly choked. Trevayne, pounding the older man on the back amid the general laughter, tried to give Sandoval the full-powered glare that had reduced strong men to jelly. He failed utterly. It was difficult to get mad at the irrepressible ops officer, and impossible to stay that way.

Impossible, that was, for most people. Sonja Desai's lips, always thin, became practically invisible, and they barely moved as she clipped out, "Admiral, if you'll excuse me I think I'd better get back to *Togo*. The shuttles should have landed by now, and the reports will be coming in." She carefully did not glare at Sandoval.

"I think we've about finished anyway," Trevayne said, and turned to Yoshinaka as Desai rose. "I'll be on the flag bridge for a while, Genji. There are still a few loose ends to tie together before I can turn in." He smiled ruefully. "Y'know, we can use robot probes for reconnaissance—don't you think someone would invent a robot admiral, too?"

After he was gone, Sandoval grinned at Desai's retreating narrow back and muttered to Yoshinaka, "I think we've already got one, sir."

"That will do, Commander," Yoshinaka replied, pleasantly but with finality. Opposites, he reflected, don't always attract.

# INFERNO

The quiet buzzer seemed raucous in the darkened cabin, and the tiny woman in the bunk opened her eyes instantly, reaching for her com key.

"Yes?"

"Message from *Maori*, sir. Rim units are emerging from Sagebrush."

"Thank you, Bob." Vice Admiral Li sat up and reached for her battle uniform. "Composition?"

"They wasted a lot of SBMHAWKs on the decoys, sir, then the battle-line came through. They're reforming now."

"Good. Ask Admiral Tsing to meet us on Flag Bridge."

"Yes, sir."

Han sealed her vac suit, and lifted her helmet from the bedside table. Her cabin door opened silently, and the Marine sentry snapped to attention. She nodded courteously as she passed him; her conscious mind never even noticed him.

Trevayne studied the big visual display unhappily. Zapata's G2 sun was a distant, unwinking flame, and the flotillas of Fourth Fleet glittered with its feeble reflected glow. Why did the sight fill him with foreboding? Was it the unexpected lack of resistance?

His recon drones had reported two dozen type four OWPs and extensive minefields covering the Sagebrush-Zapata warp nexus. That had been enough to draw the fire of almost all of his remaining SBMHAWKs, but there had been no shock of battle when the battle-line made transit, for the "fortresses" proved to be unmanned satellites armed only with sophisticated ECM gear to masquerade as forts in the eyes of his RDs.

He brooded over the display, pondering the system spread out before him in miniature. This warp point lay nearly in the system's plane of the ecliptic, as did his destination—the Iphigena warp point. But they were almost diametrically opposite one another, and between them was the inner system: the local sun, the two small, airless innermost planets, the Earth-like third planet, and an extensive asteroid belt.

Having the sun directly between him and his destination was annoying. That colossal gravity well made any sort of straight line route impossible, even in this day and age. He'd chosen his course long since: a hyperbola at right angles to the plane of the ecliptic, passing "over" the sun and its innermost children. He wanted to avoid the ecliptic anyway; it would distance him from any traps the opposition might consider springing.

But where *was* the opposition?

He knew he would encounter some fortresses, at least, at the Iphigena warp point; there'd been a couple there even before the rebellion, and the rebels must have reinforced them. After all, that warp point was far closer to the sun than most—less than ten light-minutes beyond the asteroid belt, in fact. The rebels couldn't have failed to construct some asteroid fortresses, the cheapest and in many ways best kind. But there *had* to be heavy mobile forces lurking beyond scanner range. He couldn't be that far wrong about rebel strategy. The increasing ferocity of their commerce raiders had managed to suck off a dismayingly high proportion of his light carriers—which had to be what they'd intended, assuming they meant to engage him here. Unless, of course, they'd followed the same line of reasoning and decided to do something else, just to be difficult. . . .

He shook free of his useless speculations and walked a few paces to join Yoshinaka and Mujabi, who were huddled in consultation.

"Problems, gentlemen?"

"No, sir," Yoshinaka replied. "Admiral Remko reports the screen's deployment complete."

Trevayne nodded. Remko's screen massed twelve battlecruisers and attendant half-dozen escort cruisers—light cruisers configured for the anti-missile and anti-fighter role. With Admiral Steinmeuller's fifteen heavy cruisers attached, he would precede the battle-line by fifteen minutes, sweeping the space before the ten supermonitors, ten monitors, eight superdreadnoughts, and twelve battleships. The battlegroups were flanked by more of the new escort cruisers designed and built in the Rim, not the destroyer escorts which had been the prewar standard, and Trevayne had held back three destroyer battlegroups, built around *Goeben*-class command cruisers.

The battle-line was also accompanied by Carl Stoner's six fleet carriers and three remaining light carriers, with over two hundred fighters. The rebels could put far more fighters into space whenever they finally offered battle, but at least they could no longer count on the edge their pilots' experience normally gave them—Stoner's people had been blooded repeatedly against both rebels and Tangri.

"The fleet is ready to proceed," Yoshinaka continued. "No, we were discussing the lack of opposition. It's almost eerie."

"Yes. I suppose it's possible I've been wrong all along about where the rebels will make a stand, but I still don't think so. And yet . . . if they do plan to put up a serious defense, letting us make transit unscathed shows a high degree of *chutzpah*." Mujabi's eyebrows arched in puzzlement, and Trevayne translated. "Outrageous self-confidence."

"Oh." Mujabi nodded. "New one on me, sir." He considered for a moment. "Rigelian word?"

Li Han folded her hands in her lap and watched her display.

The data codes were more tentative than usual because the single scout cruiser hidden outside the asteroid belt was at extreme range. Still, the essentials were clear. A powerful screen had moved away from Trevayne's main force, opening the gap between itself and the battle-line to a full ninety light-seconds, and she sat expressionlessly, watching her enemy advance into what—hopefully—would prove an unsuspected trap. She glanced at Reznick.

"Time to asteroid belt?"

"Their screen will cross it headed in-system in about six hours, sir. Their battle-line will be approximately fifteen minutes behind them."

"Thank you."

She turned back to the display, wishing Trevayne hadn't jumped the gun on them. He'd begun his breakout over a month earlier than predicted, and half her carriers had yet to reach her, nor did she have any idea how the defense against the Rump pincer was proceeding. Her ignorance gnawed at her, and she wished she dared communicate with Magda or Jason, but they needed com silence to do their jobs. She felt herself relaxing as she thought of her friends. If anyone could pull it off, they could.

Sean Remko sat in his command chair like a bear. His combat vac suit and grooming were impeccable, but somehow he always struck Cyrus Waldeck as unwashed and slovenly. The flag captain shook his head distastefully and glanced back at his own display as his ship crossed the asteroid belt, moving at a—to them—leisurely pace to allow the battle-line to keep up. He stiffened as a sudden flicker of light abruptly resolved itself into the data codes of enemy vessels.

"Admiral Remko! We've got—"

"I see them, Captain," Remko interrupted. "Brian—" he turned to his chief of staff "—come to a heading of one-one-six. Increase to flank speed. Prepare for missile engagement: carriers are primary targets."

"Aye, aye, sir!"

"Captain Waldeck, stand by to engage the enemy."

"Aye, aye, sir!"

Remko glanced at his elegant flag captain from the corner of one eye, then turned to his com officer. "Get me the flagship."

"Aye, aye, sir."

Remko watched the drifting data codes as he waited for the com link to be established. With transmissions limited to light speed, there was a time lag of just over ninety seconds either way, so he wasted no time trying for an integrated conversation when Trevayne's image appeared on his screen.

"Admiral, we've detected seven fleet carriers, seven battleships, and eight battlecruisers, with nine light cruisers maneuvering as regular three-ship squadrons—almost dead ahead at max scanner range. We should be able to engage them on our own terms—the battlewagons will slow them up for us. But we'll need carrier support . . ."

Trevayne nodded as Remko paused to acknowledge a report. He waved a hand at Yoshinaka and pointed at his chief of staff's communications panel.

"Launch them," he said.

"Sir," Remko looked back out of the screen, "the rebel carriers have launched what appears to be their entire fighter complement. ETA twenty-one minutes. Let me repeat my request for carrier support . . . urgently."

"Already granted, Sean," Trevayne replied. He glanced at Yoshinaka once more and received a nod of confirmation. "Admiral Stoner is proceeding to join you, and he'll be launching directly." And he could fight this lot on slightly better than even terms, he thought. "Good luck. Out."

He watched Remko's face as the seconds ticked past. Three minutes after his last word, his burly subordinate nodded with a grin.

"Thank you, sir. One trashed rebel task force coming up. Remko out."

"Well, you were right about the rebels offering battle here." Yoshinaka spoke as the screen blanked, then paused at Trevayne's unaccustomed scowl.

"Bloody hell, Genji, that can't be their entire force! Where're their battle-line and assault carriers? And look." He pointed to his battle plot. "They're backing away now that they've launched their fighters. Why? They can't outrun Sean with battleships to slow them down. Besides, battleships don't run away from battlecruisers, they try to *close* before a force like ours can come to their opposition's support." He scowled at the plot, as if by sheer concentration he could know the minds commanding those drifting bits of light. "I don't like it at all, Genji." But the blips told him nothing, and his eyes strayed back to the big visual display as *Nelson* neared the asteroid belt. Planet Three was the second brightest object in the heavens.

"Admiral Petrovna's launching, sir."

"Thank you. Time, Bob?"

"Oh-seven-forty Zulu, Admiral."

"Log it."

Han leaned back in her chair. The Book said a commander never committed her forces to combat when she couldn't exercise tactical control, but The Book didn't cover this situation. She'd agonized over her command structure before she finally made her call. Magda had proven her mettle too often to question her ability to handle the role thrust upon her, but Han had really wanted her for the other detached force, even if it was smaller. Timing, she told herself. Timing was everything. She could entrust her own force to no one else—it *had* to be under her direct control, with no com lag—and she needed Magda for the job she had, which left Jason for what was actually the most ticklish aspect of Operation Actium. Han didn't question his ability—only his experience.

"Enemy carriers advancing, sir. They're launching. Plotting estimates two hundred plus fighters. Estimated time to our fighters is twelve minutes."

"Thank you, David. Commander Jorgensen?"

"Full decks, sir, or right next to them. They should have two-forty, plus or minus twenty."

"It sounds like they're biting, sir," Tomanaga observed cautiously.

"Perhaps. But don't underestimate Ian Trevayne, Bob." Han tapped her fingertips gently together, then glanced at Tsing Chang. "Admiral, prepare to move out. Bob, same message to the other battlegroups on whiskers."

"Aye, aye, sir."

The needle-thin com lasers woke, murmuring across the emptiness to the tightly grouped capital ships of the Terran Republic. Han looked back at her display, watching as Magda's fighters plunged into the oncoming Rim ships.

Running battle snarled viciously across the Zapata System, and space became leprous with the ugly pockmarks of nuclear warheads and dying humans. Trevayne felt *Nelson* tremble under full drive, but even at her maximum speed, the ponderous supermonitor fell further and further behind as Stoner's carriers raced ahead to cover Remko's cruisers. His pilots had moved in with the wary skill of professionals, but they'd been disconcerted to find that the rebel fighters mounted a new weapon—a kind of flechette missile, short-ranged and useless against starships but dismayingly effective against fighters. They faced a daunting exchange rate, yet they hurtled into action.

Trevayne sat motionless but for the slow drumming of his fingers. The whole unorthodox course of the battle disturbed him. Simple attrition made sense against the flanks of an extending corridor, but not in a set-piece battle to defend a vital system. And the presence of battleships this far from their retreat warp point did not offer advantages commensurate with the risk. To be sure, they were heavy metal for battlecruisers, but they weren't fast enough to crush Sean before he could fall back on the battle-line, however far ahead he got. Damn it, what *were* the rebels up to?

His battle-line had drawn almost level with Planet Three when Trevayne thought his questions had been answered.

"Admiral," Yoshinaka announced, "scanners report nine battle-cruisers leaving Zapata III. Evidently they've been hiding behind the planet—now they're on course to intercept our screen from behind." Even as he spoke, the computers dispassionately added the newcomers to the display.

Things clicked in Trevayne's mind. Of course! The rebels had known he was as likely as themselves to deduce that Zapata was the logical place for them to make a stand—so they'd decided to make it elsewhere! Iphigena? Probably. It didn't matter. What mattered was that their objective for *this* battle was to strip him of his screen for the decisive clash . . . just as their false "fortresses" had already stripped him of most of his SBMHAWKs. And, he thought grimly, they were going about it in an all-too-rational fashion. Caught between these new battlecruisers and the force with which he was already engaged, Remko would be overwhelmed before he could disengage.

But . . . the rebel's timing, while excellent, wasn't perfect. The geometry of the engagement had forced them to jump as soon as Stoner's carriers came to them . . . while the onward-lumbering battle-line was still close enough, still had the range, to reach them with its heavy external ordnance load of SBMs. Yet there was no time to lose, or the battlecruisers would soon draw out of range. He gave the command, and the capital ships' external ordnance lashed outward, the salvos of SBMs thickened by the supermonitors' internally launched HBMs.

Trevayne sat back, awaiting further reports as the missiles speckled his display. Those battlecruisers were doomed. Nothing that size could stand up to that hurricane of missiles. Nothing. Yet there remained the unidentified worry nagging at the back of his mind, the sense of something overlooked. He was still scratching at the mental itch when Yoshinaka turned a carefully controlled face to him.

"Admiral, we've lost missile lock. Those 'battlecruisers' . . . it seems they were scout cruisers with their ECM in deception mode. They've dropped it and gone to evasive action."

Their eyes met, and neither needed to speak. The rebels had just stripped the battle-line of its external ordnance.

Somewhere in the back of Trevayne's mind a part of him reflected that perhaps he'd been too worried about his subordinate's cockiness to recognize it in himself. Or had he simply fallen into a belief in the infallibility of his own judgment? It was easy to do, when Miriam wasn't around. . . .

It only remained to learn why the rebels had mousetrapped him into firing off his missiles.

⬦    ⬦    ⬦

"They've taken the bait, sir!" Tomanaga's voice was exultant. "They just flushed their XO racks at the decoys!"

"Tracking reports at least ninety percent of their external ordnance fired, sir," David Reznick confirmed.

"Sir, their battle-line's flank scouts will clear the planet in eleven minutes," Stravos Kollentai reported.

"Very well." Han drew a deep, unobtrusive breath, remembering another battle aboard another ship. She glanced at Tsing Chang and saw what might have been a shadowy smile of memory on his imperturbable face.

"Commander Reznick, send to all commands: 'Execute Actium Alpha.' "

"Aye, aye, sir."

"Admiral Tsing."

"Yes, Admiral?" There *was* an edge of memory in that voice, Han decided. She felt a surge of warmth for the bulky admiral, and her face lit with one of her rare, serene smiles.

"Yours is the honor, Admiral," she said simply. "Prepare to move out."

"Aye, aye, sir. Immediately."

"Admiral Windrider is launching!" Reznick reported.

"Very well. Admiral Tsing, engage the enemy."

"Aye, aye, sir."

The superdreadnought TRNS *Arrarat* rumbled to life, drive field bellowing muted thunder through her iron bones as Battle Group Nine, Terran Republican Navy, moved out to battle.

"Sir! Admiral Trevayne! The scanners—!"

Trevayne's head snapped around, his eyes flashing angrily at the hapless scanner rating whose incoherent report had shattered the silence. But his scathing retort died aborning as his plot altered silently. The disinterested computers updated the data quietly, and the menace of the new data codes flashed starkly on the screen.

A chain of lights crept around the disk of Zapata III in a sullen, crimson line of hostile capital ships. He sat quietly, his brain racing to assimilate the new data, as eight monitors and twenty-four battleships and superdreadnoughts abandoned their hiding place in the planet's shadow. They were too close and fast for his battle-line to avoid.

And even as they emerged from the shadows there came more

reports—reports of swarms of strikefighters spewing out of the asteroid belt behind Fourth Fleet. Of course, he thought coldly, filled with an ungrudging respect for his opponent's tactics. Escort carriers. They had one advantage over larger carriers—with their power down and a little luck, they could be mistaken for asteroids by even the best scanner teams.

Not that they'd needed much luck, he thought grimly, remembering the cloaking ECM on the escort carriers raiding his communications. He'd thought it a financially extravagant way to build such cheap carriers—now he understood why it had been done.

He was back on stride by the time the final report came in. He knew what was happening, understood the deadly ambush into which he and his ships had strayed. This was no mere attempt to stop Fourth Fleet; it was a full-blooded bid to destroy it. *That* was why they'd let him into the system unopposed—to catch his slower battle-line between warp points, unable to retreat, while they hit him from all sides. And with Fourth Fleet gone, the rebels could sweep into Zephrain at last. Oh, yes, he understood—and perhaps alone among all the personnel of the Rim's ships, he was unsurprised as the "battleships" Remko had been pursuing cut their ECM and appeared in their true guise: assault carriers, already launching the massive fighter groups they had held back from the original clash against Stoner's isolated ships.

Trevayne watched the ruby chips of the outgoing rebel fighters with bitter satisfaction. He'd been right all along . . . the decisive battle would come at Zapata, but it would be such an engagement as none of them had dreamed of in their worst nightmares. On either side, he thought grimly.

"Admiral," Yoshinaka was saying, "should I recall Commander Sandoval?"

The ops officer was on his way to *Togo* to confer with his opposite number on Desai's staff. Trevayne shook his head.

"No, Genji. His cutter has time to reach *Togo* before we engage, but not to get back here." He managed a grim smile. "I'm afraid he and Sonja are stuck with each other for the duration—just as you and I are stuck with another young lady."

"Sir?"

"That," Trevayne jutted his jaw at the oncoming rebel battle-line, "can be only one person, Genji. Admiral Li is back for a return engagement, and she's caught me with my trousers well and truly down about my ankles."

He allowed himself a brief chuckle. The sound was harsh, but it seemed to banish his last doubts. He began rapping out orders, and the battle-line wheeled ponderously, abandoning its original course to face its foes.

Trevayne remained confident. The rebel battle-line was powerful, but clearly no match for his own. The incoming fighters from the belt were a threat, but not enough to even the balance *if* Remko and Stoner could fend off the rebel carriers long enough. They were in for a nasty series of external ordnance salvos from the rebel's capital ships, but when they closed to energy weapon range his superior weight of metal would tell. And he could still draw first blood with his HBMs before they entered SBM range.

But it wasn't that simple, as his first HBM salvo revealed. The Republic's R&D teams hadn't produced such spectacular results, perhaps, but they had not been idle. For the first time, the Rim encountered a Republican weapon that was as much a breakthrough as the grav driver. The rebels mounted shields which were outwardly identical to those which had been in use for over two hundred years, and so they were, to a point. But conventional shields collapsed as they took damage and their massive fuses blew; *these* reset automatically and virtually instantaneously. They didn't "collapse"—they simply flashed out of existence, then bounced back . . . as good as new!

On the heels of that discovery came more bad news. While the survivors of the rebels' opening fighter strike returned to their hangars to rearm, the equally strong second strike ignored Remko to converge on Stoner and his decimated fighters. A tidal wave of fighter missiles overpowered the point defense of Stoner's flagship, and a Code Omega message flashed on the plot with sickening suddenness. Trevayne hid a pang of dismay as TFNS *Hellhound* vanished in a brilliant ball of flame. If the rebel's first strike rearmed and joined the clash of battle-lines . . .

Trevayne's communications section raised *Arquebus* quickly as *Nelson* and *Arrarat* lumbered towards one another. Capital ships were slow; even with the time lag, Trevayne had time to speak to Remko once more.

He outlined the situation in a few brief sentences, then looked squarely at the face of his embattled screen commander.

"It's vital that you hit those carriers hard—preferably while their first wave is aboard rearming. That means close engagement. I repeat, *close*." He paused, then leaned closer to the pickup. "Sean, you're in command of the screen because I happen to think you're the most aggressive combat commander in the Fleet. Now prove it!"

Remko stared back at him unmovingly for long, long seconds as the transmission winged through space. His face reminded Trevayne of one of Kevin's quotes from the American Civil War—a description of General U. S. Grant: "He habitually wears an expression as if he had determined to drive his head through a brick wall and was about to do it." Remko wore that kind of expression as he rumbled "Aye, aye, sir." Then he blurted out, "Admiral, I'm gonna personally shove a force beam projector up the ass of whoever's in command of those carriers and then cut loose!" He stopped, face redder than usual, and broke the connection.

"Well." Trevayne turned to Yoshinaka and smiled. "Whoever said Sean isn't eloquent?" Then he shook himself as the rebels approached SBM range.

"Genji," he said, "run down to the intelligence center and personally impress on Lavrenti the urgency of analyzing this resetting shield the rebels have."

Yoshinaka nodded and moved towards the intraship car. As an afterthought, Trevayne rose from the admiral's chair and walked with him.

"See if you can pick Kevin's brains while you're there." The intelligence center was Sanders' battle station. "And hurry back. Things could get a bit tight in the next few minutes."

Yoshinaka nodded again and stepped into the car. The doors closed, and Trevayne turned back toward his command chair and the battle as the first rebel SBM salvos began to launch. Most seemed targeted on *Nelson*. Yes, he thought, they'll try to begin by destroying one supermonitor, to show their people it can be done.

"Message from Admiral Petrovna, sir. The Rim screen isn't breaking off. She's taking heavy missile fire."

"Thank you, Bob." Han said calmly, watching the plot.

She'd hoped the screen would fall back, for her ruse had been intended to destroy Trevayne's fighters and get her own battle-line in range of his without being devastated by long-range missile fire—not to match Magda against the screen in a ship-to-ship action. But it wasn't working out that way. The bickering fight had turned suddenly even more vicious, and that screen commander had kept his wits about him. The worst thing he could possibly do, from her viewpoint, was get in among her carriers and wreck those launch bays. Well, it had always been a possibility. That was why Magda held that command. Anyone who went after *her* in close action was reaching into a buzz saw. Han only hoped that Magda wouldn't be among the chips chewed off by the blade.

"Signal to Admiral Windrider," she said suddenly. "Launch reserve strike immediately."

The escort carriers and hangar "barges" hidden among the asteroids were supposed to be the final reserve as well as the rear jaw of the trap, but the Rim screen was doing too good a job of closing with Magda; she would need to retain most of her fighter strength to fend off those cruisers, and the diversion had to be made up from Jason's units.

"Aye, aye, sir."

"Coming into SBM range, Admiral," Tsing Chang said calmly. "Captain Parbleu has a good setup."

"Then you may open fire, Admiral."

"Aye, aye, sir. Opening fire now."

And *Arrarat* bucked as BG 9's XO racks emptied in a single massive volley.

The vast majority of the SBMs targeting *Nelson* were stopped by BG 1's awesome array of datalinked point defense stations—but the laws of chance dictated that some would always get through, and the incoming salvos were massive. *Nelson*'s dying shields were centered in a vortex of nuclear flame, and under those torrents of energy, the supermonitor's massive armor boiled.

Her shields went down, and more salvos scorched in, seeking to exploit her weakening defenses. Again, most were stopped. But dozens slid through the latticelike intricacies of her point defense lasers and immolated themselves against her drive field in fireballs which gouged at her gargantuan hull. Glowing craters pitted her armor, snapped structural members, wiped away weapons . . . and personnel. And one of those craters, guided by the freakish improbability which rules the tides of war, ripped deep into the heavily armored compartments surrounding *Nelson*'s flag bridge.

"Many hits on primary target," Tsing Chang's chief of staff reported jubilantly. "Her shields are down and she's streaming air!"

"She won't have much internal damage yet," Tomanaga commented softly, "but every little bit helps."

✧       ✧       ✧

Concussion, shockwaves, and the terrible sound of buckling, tearing metal were all the universe there was. In an instant of havoc unacceptable to human senses, almost everyone on *Nelson*'s flag bridge died, except those in chairs with shock frames. Chairs like the one Trevayne was not in. The force of the explosion whipsawed the bridge, hurling him down and smashing him into the pedestal of the admiral's chair. His spinal column fractured and a shard of steel ripped his vac suit. Air hissed from the compartment, and his damaged suit began a deadly collapse. And yet he was, all things considered, unreasonably lucky.

Profiting from the confusion caused by the hit, a second missile from the same salvo drew dangerously close before it detonated—not a hit, but a near miss which flooded adjacent space with lethal radiation. The rent armor of the stricken flag bridge couldn't shield the survivors from death, but again, Trevayne was lucky. The chair behind which he lay gave him some protection. The radiation poisoning he received was not fatal . . . instantly.

Genji Yoshinaka gasped as his suit pressurized. He'd been thrown against the wall of the intraship car by the concussion, but he was dazed only briefly and he heaved himself upright and slammed his fist on the override button. The buckled doors were jammed, and his hand went to the laser pistol by his side. He blasted the doors aside, cutting his way back onto the flag bridge the car had only just begun to leave . . . and into a scene from Hell.

Bodies sprawled amid the twisted, blackened metal. Acrid smoke streamed toward the hungry rents through which atmosphere screamed into space, and severed cables lashed the escaping air like bullwhips, crackling and spitting and fountaining fire.

Yoshinaka's body responded before his numbed mind could understand. He snatched the nearest emergency kit and flung himself at the crumpled figure beside the admiral's chair. His hands moved with machinelike efficiency, slapping seals on the partially collapsing vac suit, and even as he worked he spoke calmly to the battlephone microphone in his helmet.

"Doctor Yuan to the flag bridge! Damage control to the flag bridge! Use the emergency bypass route. Captain Mujabi, have com raise Admiral Desai. Inform her she's in command . . . details to follow."

And then there was nothing he could do but wait, kneeling

at the side of the semi-conscious figure in the fleet admiral's vac suit with the blood-misted faceplate.

He was still there when Doctor Yuan arrived.

"More hits on the primary target, sir," Tomanaga reported. "Her drive field is weakening and her fire's almost ceased. Permission to shift target?"

"Granted."

"*Parnassus* reports critical HBM damage, sir. She's withdrawing."

"Acknowledged." Han glanced at the blinking data codes under the crippled superdreadnought's blip. *Parnassus* was done for—if she had time to withdraw before she went Code Omega it would be a miracle.

"BG 14 reports loss of both escort destroyers, sir. Admiral Iskan requests additional fighter support."

"Denied. We don't have it to spare. Tell him to tail in behind BG 16 and use them for cover."

"Aye, aye, sir."

"External ordnance exhausted, sir. Closing to energy range. Force beams and primaries in range in two minutes."

"Very well. Signal Admiral Kanohe: 'Destroyers attack enemy line of battle.' Signal all battle-lines units: 'Stand by to engage with beams.'"

"Standing by, sir."

"Admiral Tsing, your group will engage the enemy's lead battle-group."

"Aye, aye, sir."

Sonja Desai was speaking to her chief of staff when Joaquin Sandoval almost ran onto *Togo*'s bridge.

"...yes. Get her inside the globe. Their fighters aren't going to be busy with our escorts forever, and their capital ships are coming to us. They'll want to stay close—inside HBM range...."

Sandoval waited impatiently. His cutter had come through the beginning of the battle on its final approach to *Togo*, and he was still oversupplied with adrenaline. But he had no intention of giving Desai an excuse for dressing him down by violating any aspect of military courtesy. Finally she turned back to him.

"Commander Sandoval," she began without greeting or preliminary, "I'd better bring you up to speed. Admiral Trevayne is seriously injured and out of action. I've assumed command. *Nelson's* shields are down and there's not much left of her armor. She's taken significant internal damage, including the virtual destruction of her flag deck; she can still maneuver, but we'll have to get her inside our globe. Captain Mujabi has taken command of BG 1. We've lost *Olympus*, and *Drake* and two more superdreadnoughts have taken heavy damage. At the same time, the rebels have taken considerable HBM damage, but they're still closing. They'll be in beam range shortly."

Sandoval gaped at her. Mother of God, what did the woman use for blood? Formaldehyde? Aloud, he asked, "And Commodore Yoshinaka, sir?"

"Alive and well."

"I'd better get back, rejoin him. . . ."

"Out of the question, Commander. You can't fly a cutter through what's happening out there." Was it possible that there was a very slight ironic twinkle in her eyes? "Welcome aboard, Commander . . . and strap in tight. Things are going to get bumpy."

"Sir, we can't *stop* them! They just keep coming!"

Magda Petrovna regarded her fighter commander levelly. Commodore Huyler was a good man under normal conditions, but these weren't normal. His pilots were doing everything perfectly—but what could you do when your enemy suddenly began to ignore everything your fighters handed out while he concentrated on mauling your flight decks? And those damned improved force beams were just the weapon to do it with, she thought grimly.

"Admiral." It was the rating monitoring Han's com traffic. "*Parnassus* is Code Omega—so is *Copperhead*. *Shiriken* reports total loss of energy armament."

"Do your best, Commodore," she told Huyler. "If you can't stop them all, try to cripple as many as possible. Go for the heavy cruisers—you've got better odds there. The screen will just have to handle the battlecruisers."

"Aye, aye, sir."

The screen blanked, and Magda glanced at her battle plot. She hid her fears well, she thought, for that was part of the game. Yet her carriers *had* to remain in support range of the capital ships. If she let herself be driven away, those mammoth monitors and supermonitors would overwhelm Han no matter what. She leaned over and touched a com stud, opening an all-ships channel.

"This is Admiral Petrovna," she said calmly, watching the Rim ships close on her flagship with magnificent courage. "We're done retreating, people. We stop them here, or we don't go home."

She looked back at the plot. In one corner the opposing battle-lines were merging into a single sea of light dots.

"Admiral Li is depending on us," she said quietly. "We're not going to let her down."

She heard the cheers ripple through her flagship and closed her eyes in pain.

"Well?"

Captain Joseph Yuan, M.D., rose and looked into Genji Yoshi-naka's anxious face. Repair parties labored furiously about them, repressurizing the charnel house that had been a flag bridge. Since they and the medics had arrived, Yoshinaka had finally had time to worry. For the first time since Yuan had known him, his control was perceptibly frayed.

"The admiral is suffering from acute anoxia, shock, and con-cussion," Yuan said in a voice of dispassionate professionalism. "His spinal cord is severed just below the fifth vertebra, and he has severe radiation poisoning. It's a miracle he's alive—and he won't be for very long. I doubt a fully equipped dirtside hospital could deal with this. I can't."

Yoshinaka fumbled to grasp what he had heard. Yuan had warned him he might have gotten a bit of concussion himself, but that could not fully explain his pain and confusion.

"You're telling me you can't save him?!"

"Not necessarily. . . ."

Two of Yuan's technicians entered, wheeling in a strangely repellent object. Its attached instrumentation and tankage couldn't hide its basic shape; it was a coffin. Yuan pointed at it.

"There's one chance—not a good one, but beggars can't be choosers. If we act fast, we can get him into this cryogenic bath. 'Freeze' him, to use the vulgar term. Now, you realize that this procedure normally involves an extensive workup, but we haven't time for any of that. We won't be able to 'unfreeze' him."

Yoshinaka stared at Yuan as he would have stared at a hor-rifyingly calm, reasonable lunatic. "What . . . what's the use, then, if . . . ?"

The doctor raised a hand. "We can't unfreeze him *now*. But we can suspend his vital functions indefinitely. And maybe at some time in the future we'll be able to undo the effects of this quickie job *and* repair the other damage. I can't promise that, but . . ." His temper flared, and Yoshinaka realized that this man might feel as strongly about Ian Trevayne as he did. "Damn it, this is our only chance to save him!"

The technicians had been making hurried preparations as he talked. Now one of his medics looked up suddenly.

"Doctor, his vital signs are weakening fast."

"*Goddamn* it!" Yuan's face twisted in angry grief. "We may be too late already! Get him in there! Move, man! Move!"

On a sunlit beach in Old Terra's Midworld Sea, a little girl with chestnut hair smiled and beckoned, and Lieutenant Commander Ian Trevayne ran to join her.

Sean Remko's eyes swept the officers facing him—his flag captain and staff—and his New Detroit Accent, always harsh, was a saw.

"Ladies and gentlemen, I don't give a flying fuck about damage reports." His hand slapped his plot like a gunshot. "It's our job to keep those rebel fighters off the admiral, and that means forcing close engagement with their carriers. Those are my orders from the Admiral. So I don't want to hear about fighters or missiles or any other goddamned thing. All that matters is that *they've* stopped backing away and we can get at them. Admiral Trevayne's orders apply to every ship—including this one. If anybody hangs back, I'm going to tear him a new asshole! Is that understood?"

The staff types shrank before his fury, and it was the flag captain who spoke a heartfelt "Yes, sir!" Remko looked at him sharply and motioned him closer as the others returned hastily to their consoles. When everyone else was out of earshot, he spoke softly.

"You've never liked me much, have you, Captain?"

Cyrus Waldeck looked him straight in the eye and spoke just as quietly. "I hate your guts, sir. But for now, let's go kill those rebel bastards!"

Remko extended his hand. Waldeck took it.

"Sir, the enemy screen has forced a close engagement with Admiral Petrovna. She'll need every fighter she's got just to hold them off—she can't send her first strike back into the main engagement."

Rear Admiral Jason Windrider eyed his chief of staff coldly. He didn't know Magda, Jason thought—not if he thought she'd hold back fighters Han needed. He watched her flagship's light flicker as it took hits, and his teeth ground together. Never before had they been in the same battle aboard different ships, and only now did he truly realize how much it could cost two warriors to love.

He stared at his plot bitterly. He had nothing heavier than a destroyer under his own command—just a lot of immobile barges and tiny escort carriers without a single offensive weapon of their own. There was no way he could come to Magda's aid, even if his orders had allowed it.

"Sir! We've intercepted a signal from Admiral Petrovna." Jason's com officer faltered under his bitter eyes. "She . . . she's sending her first strike back to support Admiral Li, sir. . . ."

Jason closed his eyes briefly, staring deep into his soul. Then he nodded once, sharply. When he spoke, his voice was calm.

"Signal to Admiral Petrovna: 'Suggest you recall fighters. Am moving to support battle-line and rearm fighters engaged against enemy main body. Windrider, out.'" He turned to his chief of staff. "Leave the barges and get these buckets moving, Ivan."

"But, sir," his chief of staff said quietly, "the enemy's between us and Admiral Li." There was no fear in his voice, only logic. "If we come close enough to support her, we'll be in missile range of the Rim battle-line. The ships will never stand it, sir."

"They only have to stand it long enough for Admiral Petrovna to deal with that screen," Jason said bleakly. "Now get us moving."

"Aye, aye, sir."

Drive fields woke in twenty-four escort carriers scattered among the asteroids, stripping away the anonymity which had shielded them. Two dozen carriers—small and frail—abandoned concealment and darted towards the battling Titans while missile-hungry fighters swerved to meet them.

Jason Windrider watched his plot. Was he doing it because it was the logical move? Or in a desperate attempt to save the woman he loved? If logic dictated, his actions were correct; if he'd allowed love to rule him, they were contemptible. He closed his eyes once more and forced himself to reconsider his decision.

No, it was right, he decided finally. If Magda retained her fighters, she could beat off Trevayne's screen. She'd take losses, but she could do it. And only if her big carriers survived could Han win the battle. So he was right . . . even though so many people would die.

"Incoming missiles, sir," his chief of staff said tensely.

"Stand by point defense," Rear Admiral Windrider said.

✧ ✧ ✧

The battle-lines crunched together, and the space between them became trellised with beamed energy: the tearing x-ray fury of hetlasers and the space-distorting Erlicher-effect weapons—the metal-wrenching force beams and the stiletto-thin, unstoppable primaries. Under those intolerable hammers of energy, shields flashed and overloaded, dying in bursts of deadly radiation.

The Republic's new screens made a superdreadnought effectively equal to a monitor, at least in its ability to absorb punishment. But the battle-line Ian Trevayne had forged still held the advantage—or would have, but for the rebel fighters and formations of hetlaser-armed destroyers that swept through the carnage. The fighters came slashing in, corkscrewing and weaving to penetrate the defenses. Many died, but others survived, pouring their fire into the Rim ships, breaking off and streaming back to the fragile escort carriers to rearm. The destroyer squadrons were less maneuverable and bigger targets, but there were many of them, and they could take far more damage. They rammed their attacks down the Rim's throat, closing until their shields jarred and flashed against their opponents'. At such range, the hetlaser was a deadly weapon, and Sonja Desai was forced to divert more and more of her killer whales' firepower against those lethal minnows.

She watched the devastation mount about her furiously fighting ships. Omega reports began coming in from the lighter superdreadnoughts and battleships—only a trickle, yet, but a flood would soon follow. No one had seen such extravagant slaughter since the worst engagements of the Fourth Interstellar War—and *still* it grew. It was inconceivable.

Almost half the rebels' energy weapons were a new kind of primary, she noted almost absently. Apparently they hadn't cracked the secret of the variable-focus beam, but they seemed to have come up with something almost as good. Desai was a weapons specialist; she didn't need experts to tell her the rebels had stumbled onto a different application of the forcefield lens principle—one which allowed a "burst" longer than that of the standard primary. Long enough for the beam to "swing" slightly. Its slicing action did less damage than a force beam, simply slashing a five-centimeter-wide gash through whatever it hit. But that was more than enough to cripple any installation—and it passed effortlessly through any material object or energy shield in its path. That was what made it so deadly despite its slow rate of fire;

it could damage supermonitors without first pounding through their nearly indestructible shields and armor.

The primary has always held an especially nerve-wracking fear for spacers. One can be standing in an undamaged ship and suddenly find a five-centimeter hole through one's stomach. It happens rarely, of course—human bodies are small objects, placed aboard starships in limited numbers. But even improbable things happen occasionally.

Like the primary which suddenly sliced through *Togo*'s flag bridge. Air began howling into space. Two scanner ratings got in the beam's way, and it cut them in two in an explosion of gore. It swung towards Sonja Desai's command chair, but it did not quite reach it . . . it terminated at the midthigh level of Joaquin Sandoval's right leg. He crashed to the deck, the leg suddenly attached only by a thin strip of muscle and skin.

The primary is not a heat weapon; it does not cauterize. The stump spurted blood.

Sandoval began screaming.

Desai's reflexes thought for her as one hand slammed the release on her shock frame and she flung herself free. No one else on the shocked bridge could move as she ripped a severed cable from a shattered panel. She whipped it around his leg, jerking the crude tourniquet tight even as she summoned the medics via battlephone.

"Sir, *Adder, Coral Snake, Ortler, Thera*, and *Anderson* are Code Omega," Tomanaga reported, his voice hoarse as the nightmare tally rose, his face afire with battle and awe at the sheer scale of destruction.

Han sat in her command chair, stroking the helmet in her lap as she absorbed the litany of death. Death inflicted by humans upon humans. Death dealt out in the name of duty and honor. Her shoulders were relaxed, her face calm, but a trickle of sweat ran down one cheekbone.

*Arrarat* shuddered as another missile exploded against her drive field, and Han looked at Tsing's ops officer; he sat motionless before his panel. His datalink was gone. It was very quiet on the flag bridge, despite the dreadful butchery raging within and beyond the hull. She looked up as a shadow fell on the side of her face, and Tsing Chang looked down at her.

"Sir, you must transfer. *Arrarat* can no longer serve as your flagship."

"No," she said softly.

"Admiral," Tsing tried again, "Captain Parbleu is dead. Commander Tomas tells me we have two hetlasers and one primary left—the armament of a light cruiser, sir. Right now, they're not even shooting at us very much, but it's only a matter of time till they finish us off. You *must* transfer."

"No," she said once more. "I've had three flagships, Chang. I've lost two of them." She looked away from the plot where *Bernardo da Silva* had just died at the hands of her own ships. "I won't leave this one."

"It's your duty, Admiral," he said softly. "This task force is your responsibility—not a single ship."

"Oh? And what of you, *Admiral?*"

"I've only got two ships left," he said simply, "and they're both out of the net."

"But you still have your com." *Arrarat* was doomed, but it seemed to her hypersensitive mind that only her presence had deferred that doom this long. She knew it was irrational, yet she couldn't leave. She shook her head doggedly. "And you've still got your drive, Admiral. Instruct *Arrarat* to withdraw. I can still command from here."

"Yes, sir. You're right, of course." Tsing paused, looking down at her, and his lips curved suddenly in a warm smile. "It's been an honor to serve with you, sir."

She looked up, troubled by his gentle voice even through the mental haze of battle. It no longer sounded like the imperturbable Tsing she knew.

"I'm sorry, sir," he said softly—and his fist exploded against her jaw.

Han's head snapped back, her eyes rolling up. She lolled in her shock frame, and Tsing caught up her helmet and jammed it over her head, sealing it while the bridge crew stared in frozen disbelief. He turned to Tomanaga.

"You've got four minutes to clear this ship, Commodore," he said crisply. He punched the release of Han's shock frame, his face fierce, and snatched her up. He threw her limp body at Tomanaga, and the chief of staff caught her numbly. "Get her out of here. *Now*, goddamn it!"

Tomanaga hesitated one instant, then nodded sharply and raced for the intraship car.

"She'll need her staff," Tsing snapped. "The rest of you—out!"

Li Han's staff never hesitated. Something in his voice compelled obedience, and they were halfway to the boatbay before they even realized they'd moved.

Tsing punched a button on the arm of Han's empty chair, and his voice echoed through every battlephone aboard his savagely wounded flagship.

"This is Admiral Tsing. Our weapons are destroyed. I intend to close the enemy and ram while I still have drive power. You have three minutes to abandon ship."

He turned to his staff.

"Commander Howell, message to Admiral Windrider: 'Vice Admiral Li transferring to TRNS *Saburo Yato* via cutter. Urgently request fighter cover.' Send it and get out."

He bent and pressed buttons, slaving drive and helm to the flag bridge. He looked up a moment later—his staff remained at their stations.

"Ladies and gentlemen, perhaps you misunderstood me," he said calmly.

"No, sir," Frances Howell said softly. "We understood."

Tsing started to speak again, then closed his mouth. He nodded and dropped back into his command chair, glancing at the chronometer.

"Two minutes, Commander Howell," he said. "Then I want maximum power." He touched a brilliant dot on his plot. "That looks like a nice target."

"It does, indeed, sir."

"She's *what*?" Jason Windrider demanded. Only nine of his small carriers remained, but a destroyer flotilla and two light cruiser squadrons had broken through to protect the survivors while their hangar crews broke all speed records rearming fighters.

"The Flag is transferring, sir," his com officer repeated. "Admiral Tsing requests fighter cover for the admiral's cutter."

"What the *hell* is she playing at now?" Jason fumed, fear fraying his voice with anger. He stared at the maelstrom of capital ships and sighed. "All right, Ivan. See if you can sort anyone out of that mess!"

"Yes, sir."

Only a handful of Carl Stoner's fighters survived, and they'd been driven back by Magda's fighters once she was free to retain them for her own defense. Even Sean Remko's ships had been unable to close on her flagship as her fighters slashed away at their drive pods, slowing them, battering them. She'd lost heavily—five of her own battlecruisers were gone, and two assault carriers and three fleet carriers had been gutted or destroyed—but her remaining hangar bays supported enough fighters to make it suicide for Stoner's survivors to engage her.

Remko had realized that. In desperation, he had ordered them into the butchery of the battle-lines, hoping they might make a difference, that they and the capital ships might offer one another some mutual protection. Now three of Stoner's waifs saw an unbelievable sight: a cutter spat out of the boatbay of a rebel superdreadnought and dashed towards an embattled monitor.

"Zulu Leader to Zulu Squadron," their leader said, his voice ugly with hate and despair. "Must be someone pretty important—let's go get him!"

"Zulu Three, roger."

"Zulu Six, roger."

His two remaining wingmen dropped back to cover him, and the Rim squadron leader stooped on the cutter like a hawk.

Lieutenant Anna Holbeck shook her head in disbelief. Find a cutter and escort it through *this*?! Someone had obviously had a shock or two too many, she thought. But hers was not to reason why.

"Basilisk Leader to Basilisk Squadron," she said resignedly. "Let's go find the admiral, boys and girls."

Five agile little strikefighters slashed through vacuum, closing on Han's cutter. Death crashed about them, but so vast are the battlefields of space that even in that cauldron of beams and missiles, no weapon came close to the deadly little quintet.

"Basilisk Leader, Basilisk Two. I've got her on instruments, Skip—but she's got trouble."

"I see it. Green Section, close on the cutter. Red Section, follow me."

The three Rim pilots were so intent on their prey they never even saw the Republican ships that killed them.

"Sir! One of the rebel superdreadnoughts is closing rapidly!"

"What about it?" Vice Admiral Frederick Shespar grunted, tightening his shock frame as TFNS *Suffren*'s evasive action grew more violent.

"Sir, she's on a collision course—at maximum speed!"

"What?" Shespar stabbed one glance at his flag plot and blanched in horror. The ship coming at him could hardly be called a ship. She was a battered, broken wreck, streaming atmosphere and shedding bits of plating and escape pods as she came, but there was clearly nothing wrong with her drive. It took him barely a second to realize her grim purpose—but a second is a long, long time at such speeds.

"Gunnery! New battlegroup target! Burn that ship d—" He never finished the sentence. Tsing Chang's flagship hurled herself headlong at *Suffren*. Neither supermonitors nor superdreadnoughts are very fast, by Fleet standards—but these were on virtually reciprocal courses. Two-thirds of a million tonnes of mass collided at a closing speed of just under fifty thousand kilometers per second.

It was too intense to call an explosion.

Some events are so cataclysmic the mind cannot comprehend them. The weapons in play in the Zapata System had killed far more people than died with *Arrarat* and *Suffren*—but not so spectacularly, so . . . deliberately. The devastating boil of light and vaporized alloy and flesh hung before the eyes of the survivors like the mouth of hell, and they shrank from it.

As two fighting animals will separate momentarily to draw breath, the battle fleets pulled slightly apart. It wasn't really a lull, for weapons still fired, but a reduction of the unprecedented, unendurable intensity of close combat. As a conscious, ashen-faced Li Han turned from the cutter's viewport, something very like a respite closed in on the warring ships.

The Republic needed it. Scores of fighters were rearming aboard Windrider's and Magda's surviving carriers as Han stepped from her cutter aboard *Saburo Yato* and raced for the intraship car. Her brain was like ice over a furnace. The anguish of Tsing's death warred with a sort of horrified pride in the manner of his dying, but she couldn't let herself think of that. Not yet. There were things to do, a battle to win. She would allow herself grief and pride later. Later, when she had time to mourn as Chang deserved.

She stepped onto *Yato's* flag bridge, and Admiral Stephen Butesky leapt aside to offer her his command chair. She nodded briefly and dropped into it while a shaken Tomanaga quietly displaced Butesky's chief of staff.

"Status report!" she snapped.

She didn't really want to know. She didn't want to consider her hideous losses, or even those of her enemies. But she had a job to do. Thank God for this lull! Perhaps she could—

"Admiral Li?" A strange com rating looked up at her, eyes puzzled, and Han choked back a sob of grief for the people aboard *Arrarat*.

"Yes?" Her voice showed no sign of her sorrow.

"I've just picked up a parley signal—from Vice Admiral Sonja Desai."

Han blinked, then smoothed an incipient scowl from her face and gestured acceptance, her mind racing. Who the devil was Vice Admiral Desai? It was unheard of! An officer didn't simply send a signal to her opponent while missiles and beams were still flying! Why—

She didn't recognize the dark, sharp-featured woman who appeared on the screen. Her vac suit was drenched with blood—not her own, obviously, for she sat upright in a command chair, clearly in complete command of herself.

"Where is Admiral Trevayne?" Han demanded without preamble.

"Admiral Trevayne is in sickbay. I have assumed command." Desai's habitual expressionlessness did not alter, and she resumed after the briefest of pauses. "The position is this, Admiral Li: we can continue this battle and fight it out to a conclusion, and I believe I can win. Quite probably you disagree. But whichever of us is right, 'winning' in this context means being left with the last one or two ships, or at least with a surviving force too weak to follow up its 'victory.' As an alternative to this profitless slaughter, I propose a cease-fire in place, of indefinite duration, while we apprise our respective governments of the situation." The immobile face took on a slightly rueful expression. "We may have to ask you to transport our messenger to the Innerworlds, but we have with us a high-ranking Federation official who will be able to represent our status to the Prime Minister."

Han's face was like a sculpture as she thought furiously. Could she win if the battle resumed? Yes. With her fighters rearmed and the range too short for the Rim's HBMs to be decisive . . . yes, she could win. She felt certain of it—and she suspected this Desai knew it, too. Yet Desai was also right. Her own battle-line had been savaged, the relentless attacks of the Rim screen had hurt Magda far worse than had been allowed for, and Jason's force was devastated. And she had little idea just how much fight those looming supermonitors still had in them—three were gone, others badly damaged. One hadn't fired in minutes. Was it any more than a hulk? She *knew* she could take them, avenge Second Zephrain's blot on the Fleet's honor . . . and yet . . . and yet there was that edge of uncertainty and her ignorance of how matters stood with the Rump pincer. And there was the terrible knowledge that even victory would leave her on her knees, without the strength to follow through against Zephrain. . . .

But still . . .

Damn it, where was Trevayne? Was he really dead? They'd hardly admit it, would they? And, her dogged honesty demanded, why did she care?

Aloud she temporized. "Such an agreement might exceed my authority. At the least, you're asking me to assume a heavy responsibility."

"No heavier than I'm assuming myself."

"On the contrary; you're occupying four planetary systems of the Terran Republic which I'm under orders to recover—"

"And I am under orders to reopen contact between the Innerworlds and the Rim Feder . . . the loyalist systems of the Rim." Desai's stiffness relaxed just a trifle. "Now that we've each recited our position papers, let's turn to reality. You and I are in command on the scene. We both know our orders can't be carried out—not without a degree of slaughter which passes the limits of sanity and decency. Shall we make our governments aware of that reality? Or shall we continue to carry out our orders in spite of it?" Her eyes bored into Han's. "In the end, I suppose it comes down to a question of where our duty really lies. That's a question many of us have had to face over the last few years, isn't it?"

Two pairs of dark eyes locked. *I can win,* Han told herself. *I can win the decisive battle of this entire civil war! Or do I think that because I want to win so badly? And if I do, why? Out of duty . . . or hatred? Shame that a man who may not even be alive over there once beat me? Or for the glory? And what "glory" is there in being the woman responsible for such slaughter?*

*And could I kill them all?* Her thoughts turned ever inward. *Could I wipe them out—because that's what it comes down to; this Desai will no more surrender if I reject her offer than I would. Even after all that's passed, even if I have the capability to treat them like Arthur Ruyard, could I do it? After Ian Trevayne didn't do that to me?*

And almost before she realized she was speaking, the quiet words came.

"Very well, Admiral Desai. I agree."

Vice Admiral Li Han stood in a strange cabin, hands by her sides. Her eyes were dry, but her face was strained and drawn. She sank into a chair, her lips trembling briefly in a tired smile. She'd lost three sets of quarters now. She was once more down to a single battle-stained vac suit . . . her painfully reassembled possessions drifting atoms.

Her face crumpled as realization hit. *Arrarat* was gone. All those people. Twenty-five hundred friends. Chang.

She buried her face in her hands, feeling her nails press into her temples as she fought the tears. She wouldn't weep. She wouldn't! Chang had chosen the way he died. . . .

But he *had* died, she told herself sadly. Died under her command—with thousands of others aboard the ships she'd commanded. And she hadn't even won! She'd renounced victory, held her hand in the name of 'humanity.' But what of her debt to those who had died, trusting in her to win the battle?

She straightened her spine and stared into a mirror, her cheeks dry, and scarcely recognized the wan face that looked back at her from those brilliant black eyes. No tears, she told herself. No tears for Chang, for the dead, for the lost victory. The past was past, and the future pressed upon her.

She reached for the com panel and began to punch Magda's code, then stopped. Her hand fell into her lap, and she leaned back in the chair, closing her eyes.

Not yet. She must speak to Magda, must plan and confer. But not yet. Please, God, not just yet. . . .

An odd numbness gripped the officers in *Togo*'s briefing room. It went beyond the inevitable aftershock of battle—even of one such as this.

Sonja Desai looked at the faces of the people who had come so far and given so much for the victory which had been denied them. It wasn't defeat. Not really. But it wasn't victory, either, and the price they'd paid was terrible enough to demand victory.

Sean Remko sat staring dully at the deck, his face working with emotion. He'd learned what had happened to Trevayne, and no assurance that he'd done far more than his "duty" could reach him in the darkened chamber to which he had withdrawn and which held but one thought: he had failed the admiral.

Yoshinaka and Kirilenko sat side by side. They'd come from *Nelson* (along with Sanders, who was even now preparing for his departure) and had arrived a few minutes late, after receiving assurances that Sandoval's condition was stable. Mujabi was present in his new capacity as CO of BG 1—what remained of it. So were the other ranking survivors, including Khalid Khan, who was the first to react.

"What you're saying, Admiral, is that we're simply to keep station here in Zapata until we get orders to the contrary?"

"Correct," Desai nodded. "So are the rebels. This is the precondition to the cease-fire. All major Fleet units must remain in place. Of course, noncombatant supply vessels aren't included, nor are light combatants . . . like the rebel destroyer which will take Mister Sanders to the Innerworlds."

They all stared at her as if she had, inexplicably, left out the most obvious point. It was Kirilenko who blurted it out.

"But, sir, what about the admiral . . . er, Admiral Trevayne?"

Desai's face was at its most flinty. "*Nelson* is, of course, covered by the cease-fire terms and must remain here. But I am advised by Doctor Yuan that Admiral Trevayne can be maintained aboard *Nelson* indefinitely in his present condition. So there's really no problem. Any other questions?"

The stares changed subtly, as if these people were looking at a thing they couldn't comprehend, and were fairly sure they did not want to.

Kirilenko stiffened, and his mouth began to open. Under the edge of the table, Yoshinaka gripped his forearm, very tightly. Kirilenko's mouth closed again, and he subsided.

Desai stood. "If there are no further questions, ladies and gentlemen, please carry on."

She walked to the door, then paused and looked back. Everyone was still seated.

Desai looked straight into the eyes of Sean Remko, the senior man in the room. For a bare instant, he stared back with an unreadable expression. Then he lumbered to his feet and said, in a voice like a rockslide, "Attention on deck."

They rose slowly to attention. Desai nodded very slightly and stalked through the door.

Her expression and posture remained equally stiff in the intraship car and through the passageway to her quarters. The sentry snapped to attention, and she nodded crisply to him as she pressed the door stud and entered.

The door closed silently behind her. She stood a moment, her face wearing a vague look which slowly turned into one of pained bewilderment. Something happened inside her, something whose possibility would have been flatly denied by those who knew her. Her features collapsed into a mask of inconsolable grief, and a harsh, low cry welled out of her like the plaintive wail of a maimed animal unable to understand its pain. She hurled herself onto her bunk, burying her face in the pillow as she wept convulsively, and the sound of her empty, tearing sorrow filled her cabin.

A moment later, the door slid open with its usual soundlessness to admit Remko and Yoshinaka. They stopped, frozen with amazement, at the sight of the sobbing woman on the bunk. The woman neither of them had ever thought of as a woman at all. Remko turned to Yoshinaka and opened his mouth, but the commodore put a finger to his lips and slowly shook his head.

They departed as silently as they'd come, leaving Sonja Desai alone with her grief for the man she had loved silently and hopelessly for years.

# CONFERENCE

*"Thank God I have done my duty."*
Vice Admiral Horatio Nelson, Orlop Deck, HMS
*Victory*, Battle of Trafalgar

Oskar Dieter studied the strained faces of his Cabinet, remembering the day the first mutiny had been reported, and shuddered. This was almost worse. There'd been no treason this time, yet Fourth Fleet had lost more tonnage in two hours of close action than had been taken from Admiral Forsythe, and the shock cut deep. Even Amanda Sydon was gray-faced and stunned.

He sighed and tapped the crystal table with his knuckles.

"Ladies and gentlemen, for the record—" he looked at Sky Marshal Witcinski "—I should like to say that I concur entirely with Admiral Desai's actions." A rustling sigh ran around the table. "Even if she'd continued the action and won, it would have cost more than we can stand. Admiral Trevayne's—" his voice faltered briefly on the name "—ships are both our most powerful single striking force and our sole technical advantage. Had Admiral Desai won at the expense of crippling damage to Fourth Fleet, we would have been unable to follow up her 'victory.' Had she lost, the Terran Republic must inevitably have captured sufficient examples of the Rim's weaponry to duplicate it."

He felt his listeners' stab of surprise as he deliberately used the term "Terran Republic" instead of "rebels"—and their horror as they considered the consequences of the Republic's acquiring weapons in advance of anything they could produce.

"I would like to ask Sky Marshal Witcinski and Vice Admiral Krupskaya a few questions," Dieter went on quietly. "First the Sky Marshal. With Fourth Fleet halted, whether by a cease-fire or the destruction of its units, what are the chances for Operation Yellowbrick?"

"Nil," Witcinski said. His voice was like a gravel-crusher. "Whoever planned the *rebels'*—" he stressed the word deliberately— "tactics knew what he was doing. I still don't know how they guessed our plans, but they've put up a web of fortresses and fighters that's stopped us cold. I've suspended operations after taking only two of our target systems, Mister Prime Minister. We could still take the other three our ops plan calls for, but not and have anything left at the end.

"As for Fourth Fleet"—he shrugged—"I can only endorse your own estimate. Trevayne's ships are unique. Now that I've examined Vice Admiral Desai's report, I am even more convinced that they represent a qualitative breakthrough of the first magnitude. Trevayne and Admiral Desai managed to destroy almost fifty percent of the force engaged against them, but the rebel admiral knew the sort of action she had to fight. Trevayne's force lost at least as much as she did. As nearly as we can estimate, almost twelve million tonnes of shipping were destroyed—not damaged, *destroyed*. We don't know about the rebels, but Fourth Fleet lost over forty-one thousand dead. I think that's an effective answer as to whether it can carry out its part of the plan. Without the Rim to meet us more than halfway—"

He shrugged again.

"I see." Dieter turned to Susan Krupskaya. "Admiral Krupskaya, what are the odds of the Republic recognizing the futility of further operations on our part?"

"Excellent, sir," she said after a very brief glance at Sanders. "Analysis of our losses must tell them Operation Yellowbrick bled us white. They've been hurt, too—badly—but not as badly as we have."

"I see," Dieter repeated. "And how quickly can they duplicate Admiral Trevayne's weapons without actual samples?"

"It's hard to be precise, sir, but my analysts estimate eight months, maximum, before they have working models." Someone gasped, but Krupskaya plowed on. "We've been looking at the data Mister Sanders brought back, and they're very, very close to the variable focus beams, judging from their new primary. With that head start and the data they must have recorded during the Zapata engagement, they can have that weapon in three to five months. The HBM should take considerably longer—we've no evidence that they've begun experimenting with grav drivers—but their new shields offset that. And we," she smiled thinly, "have no way of obtaining hard data on *their* new systems, since they've carefully used them only against the Rim. It will take us much longer to duplicate them. And, Mister Prime Minister—" she paused and drew a breath "—it is my duty to point out that, judging from their order of battle at Zapata, our previous estimates of their construction rates may be as much as fifteen percent low, so even our numerical advantage is in question."

"Thank you, Admiral," Dieter said gravely, and looked back at his shaken colleagues. "Ladies and gentlemen, I already knew what Sky Marshal Witcinski and Admiral Krupskaya were going to say, and I had them plug that data into our computers. According to the new projections, we stand a sixty-five percent chance of losing the war within one year." The room was deathly silent. "If we hold out for another year, we have a seventy percent chance of final victory—but the computers project a war which will continue for another twelve to fifteen years. With losses," he finished quietly, "which will make the Battle of Zapata look like a children's picnic."

The political leaders stared at him in shock. The military leaders weren't surprised, but their expressions were those of people who'd just bitten into something spoiled. No one questioned his statements.

"I think, my friends," he said very, very softly, looking straight at Amanda Sydon and her "war party" adherents, "that under those circumstances, we cannot justify continuing this war if there is the least possibility of any other acceptable resolution. Even victory can cost too much at times."

Sydon glanced at her supporters, but they refused to meet her eyes. The glare she turned on Dieter was fulminating, yet she said nothing. There was nothing she *could* say, and the voice of protest came from another source.

"But, Mister Prime Minister!" Witcinski protested. "Victory *is* the only 'acceptable resolution!' Yellowback should have succeeded—*would* have succeeded if the rebels hadn't figured out what was coming and managed to ambush Admiral Trevayne. I'm not faulting him, sir—it was a brilliant ploy, obviously something they spent months arranging. But now that they've stopped us, they'll exploit. No strategist worth his salt would stop now!"

"Indeed, Sky Marshal? What do you think they'll do, then?"

"They'll leave their forces in the Zapata System exactly as they are," Witcinski predicted. "As far as we can tell, they committed less than ten percent of their assault carriers there—the others are still available for offensive strikes, backed up by their surviving Frontier Fleet fleet and light carriers, while we cut our defenses to the bone for Yellowbrick. They can achieve crushing local superiority wherever they choose, and they know it. They'll go on the offensive and chew us up, hoping for a knockout."

"That would certainly be their most logical course," Dieter said softly, "but they're not going to do it."

"Why not?" Witcinski demanded hotly, feeling his professional judgment called in question.

"I think because they don't want to destroy the Federation," Dieter said slowly.

"No?" Amanda Sydon laughed harshly. "They only went to war against it!"

"Agreed—but I think they just wish to be left alone," Dieter replied. Sydon stiffened angrily, and some of the others joined her, but he raised a hand and his voice was stern with hard-earned authority. "No, hear me out—all of you! From the beginning, the Fringers have been reacting to what they considered an intolerable situation. They reacted militarily because all political avenues seemed closed. They—" He shook his head firmly. "Enough. The point is that they never sought to conquer the Innerworlds. Arguably, they lacked the ability to do so, but it would seem that's no longer true—they have the ability to conquer us if they act promptly. The Sky Marshal's arguments are most cogent, but to succeed, they must act at once. Surely none of us is so foolish as to believe that their strategists are less competent than our own? They *must* know their advantage is fleeting—that they must act before we make good our losses. Yet they aren't going to do so.

"Ladies and gentlemen, I have received a communication from Ladislaus Skjorning." The atmosphere in the conference room was so brittle it could have been chipped with a knife. "He offers"—his eyes bored into Sydon's—"an immediate armistice for the purpose of concluding a general peace." Some of the people at the table looked as if he'd just punched them; others suddenly sat straighter, their eyes bright with hope. He didn't try to estimate the numbers which felt either way. "His message is accompanied by an analysis almost identical to that we have just heard. But in pursuit of his armistice, he has ordered a two-month unilateral suspension of all offensive operations, pending our reply. In short, my friends, he has voluntarily given up his best chance for outright victory to prove he desires peace!"

Ladislaus Skjorning sat in the first-class lounge of TRS *Prometheus* and watched the blue and white planet grow. It had been six years since last he saw that world, and the sight stirred something within him.

It had been hard to induce the Republic to send most of its executive branch into Federation space aboard an unarmed passenger liner, but he'd done it. His Cabinet had been relatively easy to convince, but not Congress. Only the fact that the Federation had voluntarily offered a quarter of Battle Fleet as hostages for the safe conduct of their guests had outweighed congressional memories of Fionna's assassination.

Now *Prometheus* slipped into orbit around the motherworld, and Ladislaus hid a grin. One of the more ticklish decisions during the past several months had been choosing the site of the conference. But then he'd remembered that one spot on Old Terra herself was neutral; the tiny country of Switzerland, which had maintained its traditional independence for eleven centuries.

Some of the Federation representatives seemed to regard his suggestion as a subtle compliment, but others—like Dieter—recognized the second half of the message. It was possible to be good Terrans without belonging to the Federation.

A muted bell chimed, and Ladislaus rose, offering his arm to Tatiana Illyushina. The shuttle was waiting to carry them to the city of Geneva for the meeting which might end the dying.

A crowd waited beyond the hatch as Ladislaus stepped past the Marine honor guard. The major in command of that honor guard had insisted that his troopers be fully armed, and despite some personal misgivings, Ladislaus had chosen not to argue. He would have lost anyway, he suspected, even if the MacTaggart assasination hadn't remained so fresh in so many Republican minds. He usually *did* lose arguments with Stanislaus, after all. And this time, his brother's concern wasn't solely for the safety of the *President* of the Republic.

Ladislaus gazed out of the hatch and smiled, despite his tension, as he felt Tatiana craning her neck beside him. Before the war, she'd never before been off Novaya Rodina with its vast, endless plains, and the mountainous horizon must seem as strange to her as had her first sight of his own Beaufort. She stared out at them, then turned and flashed a slightly nervous, slightly appealing smile of her own at the expressionless Stanislaus, and Ladislaus chuckled in mental satisfaction. He knew they were under close scrutiny as his vice president gawked at the peaks, and he hoped wistfully that some might mistake her youthful fascination and natural nervousness for callow inexperience. He doubted they'd be so stupid, but . . .

A band struck up, but the music was neither the Republic's "Ad Astra" nor the Federation's "Suns of Splendor." It took a moment of frowning effort to place it, then he smiled and nodded. It was indeed ancient, he thought, but the venerable "Battle Hymn of the Republic" was a fitting selection for both sides.

He recognized Oskar Dieter and David Haley among the waiting officials. The big, solid-looking fellow in all the braid must be Sky Marshal Witcinski, and the fox-faced man beside him looked suspiciously like the briefing holos of Kevin Sanders.

Ladislaus squeezed Tatiana's elbow.

"Tatiana, my love, I'm thinking it's best you deal with yon Sky Marshal and leave the sharp-faced fellow to me."

"Yes, Lad," she agreed demurely, "and I promise not to sign away our claim to Novaya Rodina, either."

"Lass, I'm only worried about your inexperience," Ladislaus teased.

The Federation dignitaries halted at the foot of the pad, and Ladislaus started down through the Marine honor guard, with Stanislaus' comforting presence towering at his shoulder. He rather wished he'd brought Li Han or Magda Petrovna for the military discussions. Fleet Admiral Holbein was a good man, but he lacked their quick wits. Yet there could be no question of recalling either of them from Zapata until these discussions were concluded. He sighed and stepped off the last step.

"Mister Skjorning." Dieter bowed, carefully observing the agreed upon protocols and avoiding official titles. "Welcome to Old Terra."

"Thank you, Mister Dieter." Ladislaus gripped the Prime Minister's hand firmly and looked into the slender New Zuricher's face. "I'm glad to see you again, sir, and only sorry that it must be under such circumstances. I've said some hard things of you in the past. I would like to retract them now."

"Thank you." Dieter looked away for a moment. "That means a great deal to me in a very personal sense." He looked as if he meant to say more, then shook his head. "Allow me to introduce you to my colleagues, sir."

"It would be an honor," Ladislaus agreed, and the long round of introductions and reintroductions began. He watched their faces carefully as they shook hands or bowed to one another, comparing their responses to those predicted in his painstaking briefings. By the time he reached the end of the line, he knew the intelligence people had been right; Dieter's colleagues were almost evenly divided on the question of peace or war.

It remained to be seen whether he could bring them to decide for peace.

"... quite impossible." Foreign Minister Roger Hadad shook his head firmly. "Even if we were prepared to stipulate that any planet which seceded—*attempted* to secede, rather—" he corrected hastily, remembering that the Federation had steadfastly denied the legality of secession "—is *prima facie* a member of your Terran Republic, we can't possibly concede that any world taken from the Federation by force of arms is a 'natural' member of your confederation. The simple fact that a planet was considered a 'Fringe World' before the rebelli—before the war, that is, is insufficient reason for us to resign all claim and abandon its citizens."

"Mister Hadad," Ladislaus rumbled semi-patiently, "that may be true. At the same time, it's to be plain there's no cause to be saying a world *isn't* a natural part of the Republic simply because it dared not secede because it was having a garrison dispatched to stop it." He fixed the dapper minister with a gimlet eye. "I'm not to have been getting off the produce shuttle yesterday, Mister Hadad. I'll not be accepting any argument which sets the ground for denying the legitimacy of *any* secession."

"But we can't simply tell the citizens of a system like Cimmaron that we've abandoned them!" Hadad protested sharply.

"Cimmaron's folk," Ladislaus said implacably, "welcomed us with open arms, sir. In point of fact, they'll have the pitching of three kinds of fits if we offer to be handing them back to you."

"But—"

"Mister Dieter," Ladislaus turned to the Prime Minister, "this point must be settled. We'll not insist that anyone leave the Federation for the Republic—but it's to be plain we must insist that the Republic is a legitimate government. And if we're to be a government, we're after having the same responsibility to *our* citizens as the Federation to its."

"I agree, Mister Skjorning." Dieter nodded, and Ladislaus could have sworn he saw a half-wink from the eye away from Hadad. "Roger, we must accept that the Terran Republic exists, whether we like it or not. It follows that its Congress has a responsibility to its citizens. Now, we've already accepted in principle that the worlds which seceded are part of the Republic. The question is what to do with those which were added to the originally seceding worlds by force of arms, correct?"

"Well, yes," Hadad said in a tone of barely suppressed anguish. "But it's not that simple. There are matters of precedent, of—"

"There *are* no precedents," Dieter said, and Hadad stared at him as if he'd tried to sell him a skimmer of questionable pedigree. "Under Federation law as presently interpreted, secession is treason, but we're plainly contemplating turning a *de facto* situation into a *de jure* one. Mister Skjorning," he turned to Ladislaus, "I would suggest plebiscites for all non-seceding planets forcibly occupied by the Republic. Any which wish to remain with the Republic, however they came to be included therein, will be free to do so, but any planet which wishes to return to the Federation must be free to do that, as well. You will appreciate, I trust, that we aren't in a position to reciprocate on every planet currently occupied by Federation forces? With, of course, the exception of systems captured during the recent offensive?"

"I do, Mister Dieter," Ladislaus agreed gravely, not mentioning that aside from the systems Trevayne had taken, the Federation did not currently control any world which had shown an interest in joining the Republic.

"Thank you, sir. Roger?" Dieter leaned back in his chair beside Sanders, returning the session to Hadad's control. The Foreign Minister didn't seem particularly grateful, but strove to conceal his disgruntlement.

"Very well, Mister Skjorning," he said, scribbling on an old-fashioned pad. "We'll agree—tentatively, of course—to a plebiscite to determine the fates of the planets captured by the Republic. But that brings up another rather delicate point. You see—"

"You're to be worrying over access between the Rump and the Rim—excuse me, between the Innerworlds and the Rim Systems—across Republican space," Ladislaus said genially, and Hadad nodded. "Well, Mister Hadad, we're prepared to be offering free passage to unarmed vessels, with armed merchant vessels to be passing under bond and with our right of examination. Mail packets and courier drones will be having freedom of passage without censorship or examination. Warships are to be another matter, but we're to be being reasonable so long as you're to be consulting us beforehand. I'm hoping that's to be satisfactory?"

"Er . . . yes," Hadad nodded. In fact, it was rather more than he'd been prepared to settle for, and he felt a sudden, unexpected liking for the big Fringer before him. He smiled.

"Well, Mister Skjorning, I must say you're being reasonable." He seemed to regret the admission as soon as he made it and set his face more sternly. "But there remains the matter of repatriation and property losses."

"Yes and no, Mister Hadad," Ladislaus said, and turned to Tatiana, who looked for all the world like an adolescent observer as she sat next to him. She nodded and opened a memo touchpad, bringing the small screen alive.

"Mister Hadad," she began crisply, "you must be aware that there will be considerable dispute over how much is owed or, indeed, whether *anything* is owed, to compensate private citizens for wartime property losses."

Hadad glanced at Dieter, who returned his look expressionlessly, and then back to Tatiana.

"That goes without saying, Ms. Illyushina. However, we must insist that some clear understanding be reached."

"Naturally. We propose a joint offer of repatriation for any who desire it, this offer to include relocation of families and personal property only. The Republic is prepared to guarantee equitable liquidation of investments and real estate if the Federation will do likewise. Repatriation and relocation costs will be shared evenly by the two governments. Is that acceptable?"

"It will certainly do for a first presentation to the Assembly, ma'am. However, there remain the matters of sequestered property and war losses."

"War losses," Tatiana retorted, "are just that: war losses. If not covered by insurance, the injured party will, unfortunately, be unable to recover. On sequestered property—" she allowed herself a sharklike grin that turned Hadad's blood suddenly cold "—the Republic is willing to be reasonable. We're prepared to stipulate that the respective governments shall compensate their own nationals for their losses."

She leaned back cheerfully as a strangled sound came from Dieter's Minister of Finance, and Ladislaus hid a smile as Hadad's face fell, though it was difficult when he saw the toothy grin Sanders directed at Tatiana.

"B-b-b-but you've seized property worth well over *nine trillion credits!*" Amanda Sydon half-screamed. "The property sequestered by the Federation amounts to less than one percent of that figure!"

"In fact," Tatiana agreed sweetly, "the value of property seized by the Federation is approximately sixty-seven billion credits, while that expropriated by the Republic had a prewar tax value—" Dieter winced; given the sleight-of-hand Corporate World accountants had routinely perpetrated against Fringe World tax assessors, the tax value could be multiplied by at least two "—of nine trillion three hundred and seventy-two billion. The Republic, however, stated at its Constitutional Convention that no Federation citizen's property would be expropriated *unless* our nationals' property was seized." She shrugged pleasantly. "Since the Assembly was in possession of that declaration before passing the Sydon-Waldeck Expropriation Act, we can only assume that the Federation wished to embark on a policy of mutual expropriation. Therefore—"

Ladislaus and Sanders leaned back and smiled at one another as Tatiana and Sydon went after each other hammer and tongs, and Dieter sighed. Amanda was outmatched, he thought, watching Tatiana's cheerful face. Odd how capable the distaff half of the Fringe had proven . . . and how fitting for that capability to cost the Corporate Worlds a bundle.

"Well, Lad," Tatiana sighed and leaned back in her lounger, "I think we've done it." She chuckled. "The Corporate Worlds shrieked like a gelded *megaovis* over the economic clauses—they think its immoral to end a war without showing a profit—but they can't carry a majority on them. Dieter's really cut them down to size since the war began."

"Aye." Ladislaus nodded slowly from his own recliner. "It's a mortal long voyage we've had, but it's to seem we've reached port at last."

"Yes." Tatiana rose on an elbow. "Will you go to the vote?"

"No, lass. I swore to myself I'd never stand in that chamber again, and no more will I be doing it. You go; I'll have the watching of it on HV."

"But you're our President! If you don't go, none of us should."

"Tatiana," Ladislaus never opened his eyes, "it's an impertinent young thing you're after being. It's no matter of policy but a personal thing—one I can't have the changing of even for Oskar Dieter, who's to be deserving better of us. Go, lass."

His obvious exhaustion silenced her, and she studied his face, seeing the lines worn there by the past six years, the almost invisible gray creeping into his blond beard and hair. She felt a sudden tenderness for the huge man who'd carried the personal burden of the Fringe World's fight for so long.

"All right, Lad," she said after a moment. "But I wish—" She broke off. "Lad?"

He didn't respond. His massive chest rose and fell slowly, and Tatiana smiled gently as she rose and left silently.

They'd matured, David Haley thought, looking out over the quietly restive Chamber of Worlds with almost paternal pride. The delegates who'd stampeded this way and that in the early days of the crisis they'd created had won their adulthood the hard way, but they'd won it. Now they sat almost silently, waiting as the computers tabulated the vote.

The peace terms represented major concessions on almost every point, he reflected. The Republic had been careful not to humble the Federation's pride, except, perhaps—his lips quirked—on that matter of expropriations, but it had been firm, as well. The Fringers had come through fire and worse to reach this moment. They were no longer suppliants, and they would not retreat a centimeter. It only remained to see if the Assembly had been sufficiently tempered to recognize the essential fairness of the settlement before it.

A light flashed on his panel, and a small screen lit with the results of the vote. He studied them briefly, then rapped his ceremonial gavel sharply, and an electric tension filled the chamber.

"Ladies and Gentlemen of the Assembly," Haley said clearly, "it is my duty to announce the result of your vote on the motion to ratify the peace terms presented by the foreign minister." He drew a deep breath. "The vote is 978 in favor; 453 opposed. The motion—" he paused for just an instant, quivering with relief "—is carried."

There was utter silence for a moment, then a soft stir of mounting conversation. There were no cheers, no shouts of victory. Reaching this moment had cost too many too much for that, but the relief was there. Haley felt it in the air about him as he turned to the Vice President of the Republic of Free Terrans and bent over her hand with a gallant flourish.

Only then did the applause begin.

# L'ENVOI

Oskar Dieter stretched out on the recliner under the night sky and pondered the vagaries of fate. He, who had never expected to be more than Simon Taliaferro's shadow, was Prime Minister—of a diminished Federation, perhaps, but one once more at peace—and Simon was gone.

Now he studied the cold stars, trying to find Fionna MacTaggart, but she had left him. Search as he might, she was gone, and it worried him.

A throat cleared itself, and he looked up to see Kevin Sanders.

"Good evening, Mister Sanders."

"Good evening, Mister Prime Minister." Sanders' voice was gently mocking, but his smile was friendly.

"To what do I owe the honor?"

"Curiosity." Sanders' eyes narrowed slightly. "Tell me, Mister Dieter, did you realize I was tapping your conduit to the rebels?"

"Please, Mister Sanders! To the Republic, if you please."

"To be sure. The Republic." Sanders paused. "Did you?"

"Well . . ." Dieter cocked an eyebrow at his guest, and then, for the first time in Sanders' memory, he laughed out loud. He nodded slowly. "I did. I realized it before I asked you to leave ONI to join my government."

"You did?" Sanders looked briefly crestfallen, but he rallied gamely.

"Of course. Your silence convinced me you were a man of initiative and discretion. I needed you."

"You needed me because your foresaw this outcome from the

beginning, didn't you?" Sanders made it a question, but both knew it was a statement.

"More or less."

"I hope you'll pardon my pointing this out, sir," Sanders said dryly, "but that's rather an odd thing for a wartime leader to admit."

"Is it?" Dieter chuckled again, softly. "I suppose so. But if you disagreed, you should have said so at the time, shouldn't you?"

"Agreed. Still, I wish you'd satisfy my curiosity in one more regard. As a return favor, as it were."

"Of course, if I can."

"Why?" Sanders asked, his humor suddenly gone.

"Because someone had to do it," Dieter said slowly. "And because I owed a debt."

"To Fionna MacTaggart?" Sanders' voice was soft.

"You are indeed a perceptive man, Mister Sanders," Dieter said quietly. "Yes, to Fionna. To all those people trapped in a war they didn't want but didn't know how to end, but especially to Fionna. I wonder if she approves?"

"Mister Dieter," Sanders looked down at the reclining prime minister, and a smile played around the corners of his mouth, "I'm sure she does. Fionna MacTaggart was a remarkable woman: understanding, intelligent, insightful . . . but that's not the reason I'm sure she approves."

"No, Mister Sanders? Then what is?"

"She also," Sanders said simply, "had a very lively sense of humor."

"Well, Lad," Tatiana raised her glass to Ladislaus as *Prometheus'* drives hurled the liner outward, "God knows how, but you did it. Even when I thought we'd never make it, you always hung on and kicked us in the backside till we made it work."

"Aye," Stanislaus agreed, raising his own glass. "Still and all, it's not to be that surprising Tatiana," he pointed out. "Lad's to be a Skjorning, when all's said. We've a way of getting whatever it is we're to be setting our minds to."

"Oh, you do, do you?" she demanded pertly. Stanislaus only grinned complacently and slipped his arm around her slim shoulders. "I'm tempted to kick you someplace strategic," she told him.

"Ah, but to be thinking what a sad waste that would be being later, love," he replied with a deep chuckle.

Tatiana laughed and shook her head wryly at him, and Ladislaus smiled gently at them both. After so much loss, so much devastation and death, watching the two of them together was like a promise for the future, and he treasured it deeply as he leaned back in his chair and savored the sensation of completion. It was not an unalloyed pleasure, but it was a vast relief.

"They're throwing a party in the Captain's Ballroom, Lad," Tatiana said, turning back to him with a winning smile made still warmer by the arm about her. "Sort of a rehearsal for the victory ball. Why don't you come?"

"No, lass." Ladislaus shook his head. "It's tired I am. I'll be staying here, I'm thinking. Here with my thoughts. You and Stanislaus go."

"All right, Lad." She accepted defeat and pecked him lightly on the cheek.

Stanislaus gazed at him for a moment, as if tempted to argue. But something in Ladislaus' eyes stopped him, and he only nodded and squeezed his older brother's shoulder firmly with his free hand.

"Get some rest," Tatiana told Laiduslaus. "You've earned it."

She and Stanislaus started for the cabin hatch, but she paused in the opening for a moment, looking back.

"Fionna would have been very proud of you, Lad," she said softly, then started to say something more, only to cut herself off with a tiny headshake. She and Stanislaus stepped through the hatch, and it sighed shut behind them.

Ladislaus waved his hand above the lighting control, dimming the cabin to comfortable twilight, and pulled a battered tri-di from his pocket. The flat representation was less perfect than a holo cube, but there was no mistaking the very young red-haired woman who stood laughing on the deck of a sloop with an equally young Ladislaus. He studied the print for long, silent moments, his smile bittersweet, then shook his head.

"Aye, Tatiana, I did it," he whispered, and lifted the tri-di until the faint light fell on Fionna's smiling face. "I'm sorry, love," he said softly, and a single tear trickled down his bearded cheek. "I know it wasn't what you wanted—but it was all that I could do."

Magda Petrovna adjusted a lustily crying infant on her hip and poured more vodka. Jason sat beside her, beaming at their guest with a smile Magda knew was far more inebriated than he was as the tiny, immaculately uniformed woman raised the glass in shaky fingers and studied it owlishly.

"I," Fleet Admiral Li Han, Second Space Lord of the Terran Republic's Admiralty, said with great precision, "am drunk. I have never been drunk before."

"I know." Magda watched her drain the glass. As soon as Han set it down, she filled it again.

"I think you planned for me to get drunk," Han said plaintively.

"Hush, Han." Magda said. "Why would I do a thing like that?"

"Because," Han said carefully, "you think it's a good idea." She hiccuped solemnly. "You think I've been holding things inside too long, don't you—" she paused and gripped the edge of the table, eyes widening as her chair moved beneath her "—my round-eyed friend?"

"Maybe, Han."

"Well, it happens," Han said very slowly, "that you're quite perceptive for a round-eye." Her expression remained relaxed, but a large tear welled in each eye, sparkling on her lashes. "Have been holding it in," she went on vaguely. "Been holding it in ever since Cimmaron, I think." She blinked at her friends through her tears, and her face began to crumple at last.

She drew a deep breath. "All those people—dead. But not me. Funny, isn't it?" She laughed, an ugly sound, and pressed her face into her hands. "They're all dead, but *I'm* alive. Me, the silly bitch who got them all killed. All . . . those . . . people . . ." Her voice broke in a sob of pain. "Chang. Chung-hui. All of them . . . because I couldn't do my job . . ."

"Han, Han!" Magda hurried around the table and put her free arm around the slim shoulders, cradling the weeping woman against her. "That's not true! You know it isn't!"

"It *is*!" Han wailed, her voice desolate as the deeps between the stars.

"It isn't," Magda repeated gently, "but you had to say it. You had to let it out and face it so you can go on with your life. Remember them, Han, but don't let the past keep you from reaching out to the future."

"What future?" Han demanded bitterly. "There isn't any future!"

"Of course there is!" Magda laughed softly and pushed her daughter into her friend's arms. Han's grip tightened instinctively, and she blinked down into the small face. Dark eyes stared back up at her, and she smiled tremulously.

"You see, Han?" Magda asked gently. "There's always a future, isn't there?"

"Yes," Han whispered, hugging her goddaughter tightly. "Yes, there is, Magda. There really is!"

"I'm glad you agree," Jason said dryly, sitting on the other side and hugging her roughly. "And since you do," he went on in the voice of one bestowing a great gift, "this time *you* can change her!"

"I could make faster progress with this prosthetic leg," Joaquin Sandoval told his three visitors, "if the damned doctors would only let me! I'm strong enough by now to spend more time on my feet. . . . Yes, *feet*, plural!"

"Don't rush it," Sean Remko growled. For him and Yoshinaka, this was simply one of the calls they'd paid regularly since returning to Xanadu. For Sonja Desai it was something more—a farewell visit to the only three men in the Rim who knew she had a heart. She was returning to the Federation.

"Yes," she'd confirmed, seeing their thunderstruck faces. "The Federation—and this Terran-Orion 'Pan-Sentient Union'—recognizes all the field promotions conferred out here, and they say they want me." Her expression had turned uncharacteristically gentle. She'd actually smiled slightly. "And I've gotten homesick for Nova Terra. Besides—" she'd broken off and waved one hand in a curiously vulnerable little gesture.

Now her eyes met Sandoval's, and he, for once, knew when no words were needed.

The air in the chamber deep below the Prescott City Medical Center was so cold it seemed brittle. A thin film of frost covered the enclosed, coffinlike tank in the center of the room with its attendant machinery.

The door slid open, and Miriam Ortega entered, heavily cloaked against the chill she did not feel. She walked to the tank, and for a long, long time stood motionless and unspeaking, her breath white puffs of condensation in the air. After a moment, the tears no one had been allowed to see began finding their way down her cheeks, very slowly in the cold. But the silent communion was unbroken.

Finally, she extended a slightly trembling right hand and gently touched the cover of the tank with her fingertips. Only then did she draw a shaken breath and speak in a very quiet, steady voice.

"Ian, this morning I gaveled to order the constitutional convention of the Rim Federation. Forgive me."

She withdrew her hand slowly, leaving five streaks in the rime. Tiny drops trickled slowly down them, glittering like tears in the cold, still air. After a moment, she took another deep breath, squared her shoulders, turned, and left the chamber.

By the time the door closed, silently condensing moisture had already begun to cover the tiny streaks.

– THE END –

# GLOSSARY

**AAM**—advanced antimatter warhead.

**AFHAWK**—Anti-Fighter Homing All the Way Killer Missile; the standard ship-launched anti-fighter missile.

**AFHAWK2**—a second-generation, much larger, extended-range version of the AFHAWK.

**AM**—antimatter warhead.

**AMBAM**—Anti-Mine Ballistic Antimatter Missile; a large missile, equipped with multiple ballistically deployed antimatter warheads, which is used to clear paths through minefields.

**AMBAMP**—Anti-Mine Ballistic Antimatter Missile Pod; a warp-capable pod designed to transport AMBAMs through warp points.

**antigerone treatments**—human age-slowing therapies.

**battlegroup**—the starships (usually six) linked together by command datalink. Also called a "command datagroup" or "command datalink datagroup."

**BB**—battleship.

**BC**—battlecruiser.

**BCR**—a capital missile-armed battlecruiser optimized for long-range engagement.

**CA**—heavy cruiser.

**CAM**—Close Assault Missile; a capital missile-sized weapon capable of "sprint mode" attacks at close range.

**caraasthyuu**—a particularly irritating biting, stinging insect from Old Valkha, the original Orion homeworld.

**chegnatyu**—semi-mythical Orion warrior heroes; paladins.

**chofak** (plural: chofaki)—literally "eater of midden scrapings," though generally translated as "dirt eater." An Orion term to describe a being so lost to all sense of honor as to be unable even to recognize it as a concept.

**CIC**—Combat Information Center.

**CL**—light cruiser.

**CM**—Capital Missile. A large, long-ranged missile with a very heavy warhead. Too large to fire from a "standard" sized launcher. It carries sophisticated ECM and is very difficult for point defense to intercept.

**command datalink**—an advanced datalink system capable of linking up to six warships simultaneously.

**Corthohardaa**—"Space Brothers," the native Ophiuchi who crew the Ophiuchi Association navy's strikefighters.

**CSG**—Commander Strikegroup, the CO of the strikegroup embarked aboard a single carrier.

**CSP**—Combat Space Patrol; a force of strikefighters and/or gunboats detailed to fly defensive missions covering a specific region of space or a specific target.

**CV**—fleet carrier.

**CVA**—assault carrier.

**CVL**—light carrier.

**Dahanaak**—"Talon Strike," the Ophiuchi equivalent of the Terran Marines Raider forces.

**datagroup**—the ships (usually three in number) linked together by standard datalink.

**datalink**—a system of computers and communication systems which effectively link the offensive and defensive capabilities of up to three starships, allowing them to operate as a single unit for combat purposes.

**DD**—destroyer.

**defargo**—the honor dirk of the Orion officer corps.

**Demons**—the Crucian term for the Arachnids.

**dirguasha**—"the beast not dead," an Orion who, for his offenses against honor, has been rejected and expelled from his family and clan and who may be killed by any other Orion in any way.

**droshkhoul** (plural: droshkhouli)—"shadow seeker," Orion term of disapprobation for someone who always finds a way to avoid combat without quite acting openly dishonorably.

**DSB**—Deep Space Buoy.

**DSBL**—Deep Space Buoy (Laser), also known as Laser Buoy. An orbital platform mounting a bomb-pumped laser to defend point targets.

**ECM**—Electronic Countermeasures. ECM1, the earliest and crudest version, simply makes the mounting ship more difficult to hit. ECM2, or "jamming ECM," serves to jam or break up enemy datalinks within relatively short range of the system. ECM3, (also known as "deception mode ECM") is a more advanced generation which can perform as ECM1 or 2 be used to project false sensor readings to make a ship appear to belong to a different class. ECM4 ("cloaking ECM") is an even more advanced system, capable within limits of making a ship invisible to enemy sensors.

**Farshalah'kiah**—"the Warrior's Way"—the ancient teachings of Shaasaal'hirtalkin, the Orion equivalent of Lancelot/Musashi, who formalized the honor code of the Orion warrior caste.

**farshathkhanaak**—"lord of the fist," Orion term for the senior strikefighter pilot assigned to a task force or fleet.

**farshatok**—"warriors of the fist," Orion term for warriors so well trained and so motivated that they fight as the individual fingers of a single fist.

**FM, FM2, FM3**—progressively more advanced and capable strikefighter missiles.

**FRAM**—a short-range, sprint mode, antimatter-armed strikefighter munition.

**GFGHQ**—Grand Fleet General Headquarters.

**ghornaku**—"sharers of union," the term for citizens of the Star Union of Crucis, regardless of their species.

**graaznaak**—an exceptionally stupid, carrion-eating lizard from New Valkha.

**Hiarnow'kharnak**—the chief deity of the ancient Orion pantheon, God of War and ruler and creator of all the other gods.

**hanaakaat**—Ophiuchi talon-based martial art.

**HARM**—Homing Anti-Radiation Missile.

**hasfrazi**—the most deadly raptor of the Ophiuchi home world, whose head is the emblem of the Corthohardaa.

**hercheqha**—an Orion marsupial, equivalent to a small deer.

**hiri'k'now**—the violation of hirikolus, the most unspeakable crime any Orion warrior can commit.

**hirikolus**—the liege-vassal relationship between an Orion warrior and his khanhaku or the Khan'a'khanaaeee himself.

**HUD**—Heads Up Display; a display projected in front of someone's eyes so that it can be read without looking down.

**ICN**—Interstellar Communications Network; the long chains of deep space buoys between warp points used to relay messages at light-speed across the intervening space.

**IDEW**—Independently Deployed Energy Weapons; individual, unprotected, remotely targeted energy weapons, usually force beams or primary beams, mounted in deep space buoys.

**Iierschtga**—anti-god of Crucian theology.

**Ithyrra'doi'khanhaku**—literally "honor-named of all clan lords," the highest Orion award for valor, equivalent of the Terran Federation's Lion of Terra.

**Khan'a'khanaaeee**—literally, "lord of the high lords," the near-deified, absolute ruler of all Orions.

**khanhaku**—"clan lord"; title of the head of one of the great Orion warrior clans.

**Khanhath'vilkshathaaeee**—literally "the high lords' blood slayers," also translated (inaccurately) as the Caste of Assassins. The highly venerated order of supreme Orion duelists charged with removing an ineffectual or corrupt Khan by challenging and killing him.

**Kkrullott**—the Crucian deity.

**Iomus**—"household"; the extended family of a Gorm, joined by complex mutual honor obligations.

**minisorchi**—a Gorm empathic sense.

**MT**—monitor.

**MTE**—escort monitor.

**MT(V)**—a carrier built on a monitor hull.

**naraham**—"detachment," the Ophiuchi concept of the ability to maintain a sense of poise, calm, and balance under any circumstances.

**Niistka Glorkhus**—"Speaking Chamber"; the supreme legislature of the Star Union of Crucis.

**PDC**—planetary defense center.

**queemharda**—"self-brotherhood," the Ophiuchi ideal of self-knowledge and acceptance.

**querhomaz**—"self-determination," the Ophiuchi ideal of an individual's absolute determination to fully fulfill his role in life.

**quurohok**—"place knowing," the Ophiuchi ideal of an individual's ability to recognize and make the life choices required to allow him to attain his maximum potential.

**RD**—Recon Drone; a remote, powered sensor platform.

**RD2**—Second Generation Recon Drone; an advanced recon drone capable of making unassisted warp transit.

**Rhustus Idk**—Prime Minister of the Star Union of Crucis.

**SBM**—Strategic Bombardment Missile; an even longer-ranged version of the Capital Missile. It sacrifices ECM capability for extended range.

**SBMHAWK**—Strategic Bombardment Missile, Homing All the Way Killer; a combination of several SBMs in a pod capable of transporting them through a warp point to attack targets on the far side.

**SD**—superdreadnought.

**sprint mode**—an extremely high-velocity attack mode, reachable by some missiles. "Sprint mode" missiles move so quickly that they are effectively impossible for point defense to track and intercept.

**SRHAWK**—Suicide Rider Homing All the Way Killer. A warp-capable pod designed to look like an SBMHAWK in order to lure attacking gunboats to short range, where they can be destroyed by the blast effect of its single massive antimatter warhead.

**shirnask**—absolute fidelity to one's sworn word. One of the two fundamental honor obligations of an Orion warrior.

**shirnow**—"oath breaking."

**shirnowmak**—"oath breaker," second worst insult in the Orion language.

**synklomchuk**—the duty owed by any Gorm to the house-kin members of his lomus under synklomus. In simplest terms, the responsibility to die before allowing any preventable harm to befall any member of the household.

**synklomus**—"House Honor." See above.

**Taainohk**—the "Four Virtues" (queemharda, naraham, quurhok, and querhomaz), the combined philosophical concepts at the core of the Ophiuchi honor code.

**talnikah**—"battle mother," the CO of any Telikan field force. Originally translated by Survey Command personnel as "combat mama."

**theernowlus**—"risk sharing," the Orion honor concept which requires a warrior to expose himself to risk before asking anyone else to share it.

**theermish**—"risk shirking," the violation of theernowlus (see above).

**Valkha'kharnak**—the second most important member of the ancient Orion pantheon, the Death Messenger of Hiarnow'kharnak and the chooser of the honorable dead.

**vilka'farshatok**—"war fist of the blood," a fusion of Orion warriors so well trained and motivated as to fight as members of a single clan, regardless of their origins.

**vilknarma**—"blood balance," the Orion concept of seeking redress for treachery or murder through the death of the offender.

**vilkshatha**—"blood sworn," the symbolic mixing of the blood of two Orion warriors who have sworn brotherhood and become members of one another's clans.

**Waldeck Weave**—Terran term for fighter evasive maneuver patterns first devised by Admiral Minerva Waldeck during ISW 3.

**zeget**—a huge and powerful predator, somewhat larger than a Kodiak bear. Top of the food chain on the original Orion homeworld.